THE WORLD'S CLASSICS

DON QUIXOTE

MIGUEL DE CERVANTES, who was born in 1547 and died in 1616, a few days after Shakespeare, had lived most of his life before he published the First Part of *Don Quixote* in 1605. He had served as a soldier in Philip II's forces in the Mediterranean area, and been held captive for five years in North Africa. After his ransom and return to Spain, he was a minor government functionary, tax-collector and aspiring dramatist. *Don Quixote* was an immediate success, and writing the sequel, composing, assembling and publishing his other works, notably the *Exemplary Novels* (1613), kept him busy for the last decade of his life. His masterpiece combines powerful character-creation with pioneering narrative techniques. It remains the work to which the Western novel from the eighteenth to the twentieth century is most indebted.

The translation by Charles Jarvis, first published in 1742, has deservedly been one of the most successful and has often been reprinted.

E. C. RILEY is Emeritus Professor of Hispanic Studies at the University of Edinburgh.

THE WORLD'S CLASSICS

MIGUEL DE CERVANTES SAAVEDRA

Don Quixote
de la Mancha

Translated by
CHARLES JARVIS

Edited with an Introduction by
E. C. RILEY

Oxford   New York

OXFORD UNIVERSITY PRESS

Oxford University Press, Walton Street, Oxford OX2 6DP

Oxford New York Toronto
Delhi Bombay Calcutta Madras Karachi
Kuala Lumpur Singapore Hong Kong Tokyo
Nairobi Dar es Salaam Cape Town
Melbourne Auckland Madrid

and associated companies in
Berlin Ibadan

Oxford is a trade mark of Oxford University Press

Published in the United States by
Oxford University Press Inc., New York

Editorial material © E. C. Riley 1992
First published as a World's Classics paperback 1992

British Library Cataloguing in Publication Data

Data available

Library of Congress Cataloging in Publication Data

Cervantes Saavedra, Miguel de, 1547 1616
[Don Quixote. English]
Don Quixote de la Mancha / Miguel de Cervantes Saavedra;
translated by Charles Jarvis; edited with an introduction by E. C. Riley.
p. cm. (The World's classics)
Includes bibliographical references.
I. Jarvis, Charles, 1675? 1739. II. Riley, E. C. III. Title. IV. Series.
PQ6323. A1 1992 863'.3--dc20 91 42957

ISBN 0 19 282726 X

3 5 7 9 10 8 6 4 2

Printed in Great Britain by
BPCC Hazells Ltd
Aylesbury, Buckss

CONTENTS

CONTENTS

INTRODUCTION

MIGUEL DE CERVANTES was 57 years old when the First Part of *Don Quixote* appeared in January, 1605. A rather marginal figure in literary circles, he was known at the time as the author of a number of plays, some occasional poems, and *La Galatea*, a pastoral romance. This last had been published twenty years before, was incomplete, and had only two editions to its name. *Don Quixote*, his belated first major success, was the product of most of a lifetime of experience and wide reading. His career as a young man—soldier, veteran of the Battle of Lepanto, captive for five years in North Africa—had been adventurous and even heroic. The next twenty-five years, spent mostly as a minor government functionary and tax collector, were humdrum and unrewarding. His work took him travelling widely about Spain, however, and thus at least helped to lay some of the groundwork for *Don Quixote*.

It is not certain when he began to write the book, but he was busy with it by 1602. A remark in the first prologue suggests that he conceived the idea of it in prison (probably in Seville in 1597), although we cannot be altogether sure of this. In the summer of 1604 he negotiated the sale of the rights with the publisher and bookseller Francisco de Robles, and it went to the press of Juan de la Cuesta in Madrid. Success was immediate. There were five or six editions (two of them unauthorized) by the end of the year. As early as June 1605, the figure of Don Quixote was well-enough known to appear in a festival masquerade in Valladolid (where Cervantes was living at the time). In 1607 this happened again in Cuzco, Peru, in 1613 in Heidelberg, and at least ten times in all by 1621.

Cervantes's new-found fame prompted a surge of writing, revising, and publishing, which continued for more than a decade until his death in 1616. Part Two appeared late in 1615—too late to forestall a sequel written by someone who called himself the Licentiate Alonso Fernández de Avellaneda.

It is a crude work by comparison. The author, despite paying Cervantes the supreme compliment of imitating him, was hostile and even insulted him in the prologue. Cervantes, who was obviously offended, replied with acid restraint in his own prologue to Part Two, and incorporated his revenge in his narrative (chapters 59, 70, 72, and passim).

There had been nothing quite like *Don Quixote* before, although it had multiple points of contact with existing literature. The Spanish public took to it at once, for in the realm of prose fiction there was a ready reception for novelty and experiment. Viewed on a broad time-scale, *Don Quixote*, for all its originality, may be regarded as the culmination of a century of experimenting with prose-fiction forms. The courtly sentimental romance *Cárcel de amor* (*Prison of Love*) by Diego de San Pedro (1492), *La Celestina*, dialogue fiction of courtly amours and back-street life, by Fernando de Rojas (1499, 1502), Antonio de Guevara's pseudo-historical compilation, the *Libro áureo de Marco Aurelio* (1528, 1535—known in contemporary England as *The Dial of Princes*), the picaresque *Lazarillo de Tormes* (1554), Jorge de Montemayor's pastoral *Diana* (1559), Ginés Pérez de Hita's historical Moorish romance, the *Guerras civiles de Granada* Part I (1595) and Mateo Alemán's picaresque novel *Guzmán de Alfarache* (1599, 1604) constitute a succession of European bestsellers as remarkable for innovation as for variety.

The most 'avant-garde' fiction when Cervantes was writing *Don Quixote* was the picaresque novel which, following the unparalleled success of *Guzmán de Alfarache*, was enjoying something like a boom. Cervantes had contributed to this new wave with his story 'Rinconete y Cortadillo', written by 1604, later revised and published as one of the *Exemplary Novels* (1613). Anti-heroic, materialistic, plebeian, the picaresque was in effect, if not in intention, a reaction against heroic, idealistic, aristocratic romance, particularly the romance of chivalry which, numerically at least, had dominated the field in the sixteenth century. Now the romance of chivalry was in deep decline, although in its pastoral and other forms romance was still flourishing. The last new book of chivalry in Spain was published in 1602. Like the picar-

esque novels, *Don Quixote* reacted against these works, but in
a profoundly different and deliberate manner. The relationship is parodic, though parodic in a very special way, as we
shall see presently.

The literature of chivalry had long outlived the medieval
practice of it. The vogue for romances in this vein had been
rekindled in Renaissance Europe following the great success
of Matteo Boiardo's *Orlando innamorato* (1486), Ludovico
Ariosto's *Orlando furioso* (1532), and Rodríguez de Montalvo's
Amadís de Gaula (1508). Cervantes followed the Italians, particularly Ariosto, rather than Montalvo, however, inasmuch
as he made fun of chivalric romance in a way that did not
rule out affection for it. His attitude to these books is
ambivalent but perfectly clear. He saw in them frequent faults
of bad construction, inflated style, and impossible subject
matter, but he could still enjoy their soaring imagination and
superhuman heroics. He relished them rather as a sophisti-
cated reader today might enjoy the novels of Ian Fleming.
He did not regard them all indiscriminately as bad either. He
evidently thought well of *Amadis of Gaul* and *Palmerin of
England*. So it is unwise to take at full face-value the protes-
tations in the first prologue and elsewhere about the urgent
need to rid the world of the plague of books of chivalry.
One need only read the *pro* and *contra* arguments of the Canon
of Toledo in Part One, Chapter 47 to see the two sides of
the question set out. For Cervantes there were good and
bad ways of writing romances as there were for writing
plays and poems. The great novelty here was that nobody
had paid them more than passing attention in a critical
context before.

The ideal mode for this state of mind is of course parody.
But rather than write a straight parody, in the manner of
Ariosto for instance, Cervantes displaces it, sets it at one
remove. Don Quixote himself is the parodist, inadvertently.
The result is a basically realistic novel about a man who tries
to turn his life into a romance of chivalry. Naturally, his
material conditions—age, physique, social and economic circumstances—are thoroughly unsuitable for such a design—so
much so that the idea could only be seriously entertained by

someone whose mind was unbalanced. At the heart of *Don Quixote*, therefore, there is a confrontation between romantic literature and 'real life'. Only it is not really real life, because Cervantes has made the whole thing up. The confrontation is between two kinds of fiction, one highly romantic and the other relatively realistic. As such, the latter is certainly not authentic biography or history such as is accepted as recording life. But this is just what Cervantes's fiction pretends to do, and in a fairly elaborate way. There is talk of historians, annals, and archives.

Yet this pretence aims to take no one in. That would be for Cervantes to treat his readers as gullible don-quixotes. On the contrary, it is a pretence which they are intended to see through; they are to recognize the illusion created by literary art for what it is. This does not spoil the enjoyment. One kind of pleasure to be had from fiction comes from surrendering to it, childlike, and letting the magic carry us away. Another comes from accepting the illusion as we do the tricks of a conjuror, which we know very well are not what they seem to be, but which we enjoy none the less for that.

An important part of the ambivalence is anchored in the fictitious author figure, Cid Hamet Benengeli. Although not mentioned until Chapter 9 of Part One, he is prefigured in Chapter 2 as the brain-child of Don Quixote. Visualizing himself as the hero of a book of chivalry, the Hidalgo is obliged to dream up an author for it. He supposes him to be a 'sage' of the type often represented in those books as being responsible for chronicling, translating, or editing the narrative. Cid Hamet turns out to be much like they are: a learned historian, with magical powers which enable him to look into the minds and read the thoughts of his personages. Like a novelist in fact. He is a contradictory figure, referred to on the one hand as a meticulously reliable chronicler, but on the other, we are warned that he is not to be believed because he is a Moor. In other words, dear reader—Cervantes is saying in his oblique way—this story pretends to be historical, but you will know better than to believe it literally. No less than the books of chivalry our hero believed in, it is all made up.

Once incorporated into the structure of the novel, the seminal motif of fiction/fact was open to further development which Cervantes was quick to exploit. The most important novelty of this kind was to bring the actual publication and success of Part One into the rest of the story told in Part Two. And when the author Avellaneda anticipated Cervantes with a rival sequel, that event too was brought in. All this inter-textual reference, this folding in of fact and fiction, this idea of the novel as record, artefact, and illusion, have combined to show up a side of *Don Quixote* very congenial to the age of Borges and Eco, Barthes and Derrida.

So an event external to the text is absorbed into the narrative. When Don Quixote's fanciful belief that his adventures were being recorded turns out to have been perfectly correct—though not quite in the way he imagined—this has some effect on his and Sancho Panza's conduct and adventures in Part Two. For example, they meet people who have heard about them in advance through reading the earlier part of the story, and the Knight and Squire are more than once received as celebrities of whom plenty of amusement may be expected. This largely accounts also for the contrived appearance of many of the adventures in the sequel, especially in the long section devoted to events centred on the ducal palace or castle (chapters 30 to 57).

However, these developments come late in the day. The first part of the book is more straightforward and less subtle. It is the part which is most remembered and referred to, and the part by which Don Quixote, a little misleadingly, is most often judged. The comedy there is more basic and uncomplicated and the encounters more apt to end in knockabout farce. At the same time, the spontaneous pleasure which, despite the knocks and bruises, Don Quixote takes in his fabricated adventures is such that it is hard not to share in it, rather as we do in those of Huckleberry Finn and Tom Sawyer. So, indeed, do the Priest, the Barber, Dorothea, Don Fernando, and others who fall in with the Knight and Squire.

Early adventures, such as the battle with the sheep, the release of the galley slaves, and above all, the attack on the

windmills have a graphic immediacy which has proved pecu-
liarly memorable. Better than most, they seem to capture the
essence of what has come to be known as 'quixotic'—mis-
directed chivalry or heroism, the admirable and the futile
combined. The readers of Cervantes have responded to this
in different ways across the centuries. In the seventeenth and
eighteenth centuries they reacted mainly with laughter. Ro-
mantics in the nineteenth and twentieth centuries have seen
quixotism rather as pathetic, or even tragic. The ironically
inclined have seen it both ways at once. This quixotism is a
powerful simplification of the densely textured content of the
novel, and contributes significantly to the fact that the figures
of Don Quixote and Sancho Panza have attained a life of
their own quite independent of the book they first appeared
in. They are visually known to countless people who have
never read the novel. In other words, they have attained
mythic status, such as is only now and then achieved by the
creations of literary art (and not always the most prestigious
of them). Were it not for this mythic, simplified, and easily
visualized quixotism, it is unlikely that Cervantes's invention
would have come to inspire the extraordinary number of
adaptations and refashionings it has in almost every known
genre and medium—from opera to animated cartoon, from
sculpture to computer game.

It is widely supposed that Cervantes began Part One as a
novella or short story, but seeing the possibilities of his
subject, changed his mind and wrote on. There is no special
evidence for this other than the brevity of Don Quixote's
first expedition (chapters 1 to 5). The second expedition, with
Sancho, occupies the bulk of Part One (chapters 7 to 52),
and the third fills nearly all of Part Two. Each is structured
broadly on the basis of outward journey, one principal stay
at an inn or castle (they are all castles to the Hidalgo), and
return home. There are, of course, numerous encounters and
short stopovers on the way.

It is predominantly Don Quixote's story. Since he goes
mad in the second paragraph, we have very little sight of his
'prehistory' before he went off his head and became 'Don

Quixote'. In this lack of early life-history he is unlike most heroes of chivalric romance and unlike the *picaros* (the anti-heroes of the picaresque novels). The basic fact or motor of his madness, from which almost everything stems, is his belief—engendered by excessive reading—that everything he has read in chivalric fiction is literally true. From this follows his sense of personal mission: the decision to become a knight errant himself and go out, seek adventures, and put the world to rights. Another, the most obvious, symptom of his madness is his falling a frequent prey to delusions whereby things and people he meets take on outward forms in line with his obsession (windmills and wineskins become giants, a barber's basin becomes Mambrino's golden helmet, and so on). The basic confusion of fiction and fact remains intact until his return to sanity at the end (Part Two, chapter 74). The sense of mission also survives, but is badly damaged. The spontaneous deception of his senses almost disappears in Part Two. But his credulity does not.

Don Quixote's confrontation with the intractable materiality of the world around him is deflected a good deal inwards in the sequel. A measure of self-doubt creeps in and he devotes time and effort to proving himself. His frustration is increased when the great deed of 'disenchanting' Dulcinea is removed from his grasp and becomes the responsibility of Sancho. Quixote's star declines, while Sancho's ascends to the point where he gets his 'island' to govern. Don Quixote, the would-be hero, is now often received in mockery as a celebrity, yet he somehow manages to transcend the absurdity of his circumstances by preserving an essential dignity which raises him above the level of the jokers and hoaxers who go to such lengths to get a laugh out of him. Ultimately the extravagance of the efforts to confirm his delusions seems to have the opposite effect. Others have taken charge of his game and he is no longer in control. Even Sancho has blundered into his dream-world, taken over the image of Dulcinea, and made his master believe that she has been transformed into an unlovely country wench. But disillusionment is coterminous with progress towards sanity. Defeat in combat (Part Two, chapter 64) consolidates this gradual process, which is no more than an undercurrent surfacing but rarely. The crisis only comes at the very end, with a fever, sleep, sanity, and death.

One of the great features of the novel is the dialogue, especially between the Knight and Squire but also involving many others. On this scale, the conversations are unprecedented in previous prose fiction for their realism, as vehicles of characterization, and for the way they are used to gloss, enlarge upon, distort, and substitute for 'straight' narration. Never in literature had verbal discourse been shown as so integral to experience before.

Two forms of discourse within the overall narrative are particularly prominent and look like digressions. One is the literary discussions (mostly in Part One). These can be justified—if justification is needed—as arising as a natural consequence of Don Quixote's peculiar, literature-based madness. The other is the 'interpolated' or 'extraneous' stories. These have proved more contentious to modern readers, though probably not to Cervantes's contemporaries, who were used to such insertions, which they would have found in *Guzmán de Alfarache*, for instance, or the second edition of Montemayor's *Diana*. The pleasures of variety had been accepted as a sufficient artistic principle. But neo-Aristotelian critical theory, with which Cervantes was very familiar, was now changing that. The classical principle of unity seems to have come to matter more to him. In Part Two (chapters 3 and 44) he introduces some discussion of the interpolated stories in Part One and in the sequel he was writing. The upshot is undoubtedly a more tightly structured second part. The interpolations are better integrated and none is so long as the longest in the first part. Typically of Cervantes, though, and perhaps mischievously, they are just as many in number (six in each part).

A large central block of Part One, from about Chapter 23 to Chapter 46, is composed in a manner resembling that of the author's full-blown romances, the *Galatea* and *Persiles y Sigismunda*, where separate stories start, stop, intertwine, and run in parallel. There are indications that Cervantes may have come to think that he had overdone them somewhat, and at some stage had a change of plan. The pastoral story of Chrysostom and Marcela (chapter 11 to 14) appears to have been lifted from the Sierra Morena section (chapter 23 to 31). The intention would no doubt have been to thin out the big cluster of stories at the centre of Part One. Unluckily, it brought one or two confusions in its train, especially the notorious muddle over the loss and recovery of Sancho's donkey (chapters 23 and 30).

What has really bothered modern readers—though, again, not the author's contemporaries—is the fact that most of the extraneous stories are in a different mode from that of the central narrative. They are, in varying degrees, romance-oriented. This does not mean at all that they are devoid of novelistic interest. Marcela, Cardenio, Dorothea, and the three main characters perversely trapped in the tragic toils of 'The Curious Impertinent' have inner lives of some depth. However, these stories do start from another generic base: they are told in a more rhetorical style for the most part; the characters are more or less idealized, in the sense of tending to have more than their fair share of blessings; and Providence likes to help out in troubled times by supplying them with happy coincidences.

What are these individuals, mostly lovelorn, doing on the roads travelled by Don Quixote and Sancho, in the woods, the mountains, and the inns? Before the nineteenth century, when the difference of literary genre became acute, not many readers would have asked this—as Thomas Mann and many others have asked since. The 'taste of the time', of course, has a lot to do with it, but this is not a satisfactory explanation in so far as it suggests that Cervantes was simply writing to please, oblivious of any discrepancy. Indeed, without a keen sense of the difference between romance and realistic novel, he could never have begun to write *Don Quixote* in the first place. Parody has been suspected, but to what degree in which story is indeterminable. It is, however, likely enough that he was seeking some kind of accommodation between romance and realism (making all due allowance for the relativism of those terms) in and through the interpolated episodes. He did the same thing repeatedly, in different ways, in the *Exemplary Novels*.

Times and tastes are changing again. Readers today are less steeped in nineteenth-century realism than their parents and grandparents were. There are some signs that, like earlier generations, they are more sensitized to the superb narrative craft of most of these stories, to their *gala y artificio*, to which the author drew attention (Part One, chapter 44). *Don Quixote* makes no more demands on the twentieth-century reader than, in their different ways, do Sterne, or Dostoevsky, or Proust for that matter. The fact that the target of Cervantes's parodic humour was chivalric romance, the popular fiction of a bygone age, is no obstacle. The descendants of that literature are still very much with us in works by J. R. R. Tolkien or Ian Fleming, for example, and other purveyors of romance and fantasy in various genres and media. Anyone who is easily able to lose him/herself in any sort of fiction is in some degree a Quixote.

Whether or not *Don Quixote* was 'the first modern novel' is not a question worth arguing about. It certainly comes very early in the history of the genre. Ortega y Gasset metaphorically described *Don Quixote* as ingrained in every subsequent novel, like the *Iliad* in every epic poem, like the stone in a fruit. Lionel Trilling, with more precise phrasing, indicated that it contained within itself 'the whole potentiality of the genre'. This accounts for the fact that, while it has been read and reread differently in every century since its first appearance, Cervantes's book remains as relevant to works by novelists of our own day as to those of previous centuries. As relevant, that is, to Joyce, Kafka, Borges, Nabokov, or Orwell as, in other ways, to Fielding, Sterne, Austen, Balzac, Stendhal, Dickens, Flaubert, Twain, Melville, Dostoevsky, and others. Not the least relevant aspect of the modern novel's debt to Cervantes, perhaps, is that which has been noted by Milan Kundera. The legacy of *Don Quixote*, he remarks, is that 'the novelist teaches the reader to comprehend the world as a question'.

NOTE ON THE TEXT

TRANSLATIONS, naturally, have played an indispensable part in the diffusion of *Don Quixote*. The first complete one in any language was Thomas Shelton's version of Part One in English, which appeared in 1612; Part Two followed in 1620. The first of the great English translations of the eighteenth century was Peter Motteux's of 1700–3, which was followed by that of Charles Jarvis (1742) and that of Tobias Smollett (1755), which owed a lot to Jarvis.

Charles Jarvis (sometimes spelt Jervas, 1675–1739) was a fashionable painter of the day, whose well-known portrait of Swift hangs in the National Portrait Gallery. He was a friend of Alexander Pope, who refers to him kindly several times in surviving writings. There were a few persons, less kind, who cast doubt on Jarvis's command of Spanish, but the slur has no justification. More than most, his translation is sensitive, careful, and full of life. It is closer in spirit and style to the original than are most more recent versions. In a letter to Swift, dated 14 December 1725, Pope speaks of the work as finished. Whether or not that is exact, the translation was first published, posthumously, in 1742. It has been deservedly popular and has often been republished since.

The present edition is based on that edited by James Fitzmaurice-Kelly for Oxford University Press (two volumes, 1907). It does not include Cervantes's dedications of Parts One and Two or the prefatory verses to Part One, which are absent from Jarvis's edition. The Introduction, Chronology, and Select Bibliography are entirely new, as are most of the explanatory notes. The text has been updated with modern paragraphing and dialogue markers for the sake of easier reading. The occasional mistranslation or really inadequate rendering—there are not many, given the size of the novel—has been amended.

SELECT BIBLIOGRAPHY

The most useful annotated modern editions of the Spanish text of *Don Quijote de la Mancha* are: that edited by Luis A. Murillo (Madrid, 1978), 3 vols., including one of bibliography; and the one edited by J. B. Avalle-Arce (Madrid, 1979), 2 vols. For readers who want to sample more of Cervantes in English, the translation by C. A. Jones of six *Exemplary Stories* (Harmondsworth, 1987) is recommended.

The most up-to-date biography of Cervantes is the English translation of Jean Canavaggio's prize-winning work in French: *Cervantes*, translated by J. R. Jones (New York, 1990). Also recommended is Melveena McKendrick, *Cervantes* (Boston, 1980).

From the huge critical bibliography I select a handful of, for the most part, recent works either written originally in English or translated. In chronological order:

On Don Quixote

José Ortega y Gasset, *Meditations on Don Quixote* [1914], ed. J. Marías (New York, 1961).

Richard L. Predmore, *The World of Don Quixote* (Cambridge, Mass., 1967).

J. J. Allen, *Don Quixote: Hero or Fool?* (Gainesville, Fla., Pt. One, 1969; Pt. Two, 1979).

Edwin Williamson, *The Halfway House of Fiction: 'Don Quixote' and the Arthurian Romance* (Oxford, 1984).

P. E. Russell, *Cervantes* (Oxford, 1985).

E. C. Riley, *Don Quixote* (London, 1986).

James A. Parr, *Don Quixote: An Anatomy of Subversive Discourse* (Newark, Del., 1988).

Carroll B. Johnson, *Don Quixote—The Quest for Modern Fiction* (Boston, 1990).

A. J. Close, *Cervantes, 'Don Quixote'* (Cambridge, 1990).

General

E. C. Riley, *Cervantes's Theory of the Novel* (Oxford, 1962).

Alban K. Forcione, *Cervantes, Aristotle and the 'Persiles'* (Princeton, 1970).

Lowry Nelson Jr. (ed.), *Cervantes: A Collection of Critical Essays*

(Englewood Cliffs, NJ, 1969): includes essays by Thomas Mann, Auerbach, Levin, Spitzer, and others.

Anthony Close, *The Romantic Approach to Don Quixote* (Cambridge, 1978).

Alexander Welsh, *Reflections on the Hero as Quixote* (Princeton, 1981).

Walter L. Reed, *An Exemplary History of the Novel: The Quixotic versus the Picaresque* (Chicago, 1981).

Ruth El Saffar, *Beyond Fiction: The Recovery of the Feminine in the Novels Of Cervantes* (Berkeley, 1984).

—— (ed.), *Critical Essays on Cervantes* (Boston, 1986). Includes excerpts from Michel Foucault, Marthe Robert, and others.

CHRONOLOGY OF CERVANTES
AND HIS TIMES

1547   Miguel de Cervantes born in Alcalá de Henares, probably on 29 September, third child of Rodrigo de Cervantes, a surgeon, and Leonor de Cortinas; baptized on 9 October.

1554   *Lazarillo de Tormes.*

1556   Abdication of Charles V and accession of Philip II.

1558   Accession of Elizabeth I of England.

1561   Madrid becomes the seat of the court and capital of Spain.

1562   Birth of Lope de Vega.

1563   End of the Council of Trent.

1564   Birth of Shakespeare.

1565   Revolt of the Low Countries.

1566   Rodrigo de Cervantes moves to Madrid, after living in different Spanish cities over the years.

1567   First poems of Miguel de Cervantes.

1568   Cervantes studying at the Estudio de la Villa, Madrid, directed by the Erasmian humanist scholar Juan López de Hoyos.

1569   A warrant issued for the arrest of one Miguel de Cervantes (identification uncertain) for wounding an opponent in a duel; December, Cervantes in Rome.

1570   In the service of Cardinal Acquaviva, Rome.

1571   Combined fleets of Venice, the Papacy, and Spain under Don Juan of Austria defeat the Turkish fleet at the Battle of Lepanto; Cervantes, serving as a soldier, is wounded and loses the use of his left hand.

1572–3 Present on expeditions to Navarino and Tunis.

1575   On route to Spain, the galley in which he is travelling is seized by the Corsair Arnaut Mami; taken captive to Algiers.

1576–9 Makes four unsuccessful attempts to escape, for which he goes unpunished.

1580   When about to be transported to Constantinople, he is ransomed by the Trinitarian friars; December, back in Madrid; Philip II annexes Portugal.

1581   Sent on official mission to Oran and returns via Lisbon.

1582–3 In Madrid; his first plays performed.

1584   Birth of a daughter, Isabel, to Ana Franca de Rojas with whom Cervantes had an affair; marries Catalina de Salazar (eighteen years his junior) from Esquivias.

1585   Publication of *La Galatea*, Part One.

1587–8 Commissary for requisitioning provisions for the Armada; working in Andalusia; defeat of the Armada; Montaigne, *Essais*.

1590   Applies unsuccessfully for a government posting in America.

1592   Imprisoned briefly in Castro del Río, charged with irregularities in his accounts; contracts with impresario Rodrigo de Osorio to supply six plays.

1594   Tax collecting in Granada.

1596   Travelling in Andalusia and Castile on tax business; sack of Cadiz by English fleet; Lopez Pinciano, *Philosophía antigua poética*.

1597   September, gaoled in Seville because of a confusion over the administration of public finances.

1598   Released by April; death of Philip II; accession of Philip III.

1599   Mateo Alemán, *Guzmán de Alfarache*, Part One; plague in Spain.

1600   Probably returns to Castile from Seville; birth of Calderon.

1601   The court moves to Valladolid; Duke of Lerma in power.

1603   Shakespeare, *Hamlet*, first quarto; death of Elizabeth I; accession of James I.

1604   Cervantes joins his wife and sisters in Valladolid.

1605   January, publication of *Don Quixote*, Part One; June, one Gaspar de Ezpeleta killed in a duel outside Cervantes's house—Cervantes and his household arrested and charged with immoral and disorderly conduct, but are quickly released.

1606   Isabel recognized by Cervantes and takes the name of Saavedra; The court returns to Madrid.

1607   Cervantes and his family move to Madrid.

1609   He joins a fashionable religious brotherhood, the Slaves of the Most Holy Sacrament, with literary affiliations; Lope de Vega, *New Art of Writing Comedies*; expulsion of the Moriscos from Spain begins.

1610   He fails to be chosen for the entourage of the Count of Lemos on his appointment as Viceroy of Naples.

1612   Participates in meetings of literary academies and salons in Madrid.

1613   Moves to Alcalá de Henares; Becomes a tertiary of the
        Franciscan Order; Publication of the *Novelas ejemplares*
        (*Exemplary Novels*).

1614   The long poem *Viaje del Parnaso* (*Journey to Parnassus*)
        published; Alonso Fernández de Avellaneda publishes se-
        quel to *Don Quixote*; French translation of *Don Quixote*,
        Part One, by César Oudin.

1615   Publication of *Ocho comedias y entremeses* (*Eight Plays and
        Interludes*); also *Don Quixote*, Part Two.

1616   On 19 April dictates the dedication of *Persiles y Sigismunda*;
        dies on 22 April; death of Shakespeare.

1617   January, *Persiles y Sigismunda* published.

Don Quixote

PART I

PART II

PART ONE

THE AUTHOR'S PREFACE

YOU may believe me without an oath, gentle reader, that I wish this book, as the child of my brain, were the most beautiful, the most sprightly, and the most ingenious, that can be imagined. But I could not control the order of nature, whereby each thing engenders its like: and therefore what could my sterile and uncultivated genius produce, but the history of a child, meagre, adust, and whimsical, full of various wild imaginations, never thought of before; like one you may suppose born in a prison,* where every inconvenience keeps its residence, and every dismal sound its habitation? Whereas repose of body, a desirable situation, unclouded skies, and above all, a mind at ease, can make the most barren Muses fruitful, and produce such offsprings to the world, as fill it with wonder and content. It often falls out, that a parent has an ugly child, without any good quality; and yet fatherly fondness claps such a bandage over his eyes, that he cannot see its defects: on the contrary, he takes them for wit and pleasantry, and recounts them to his friends for smartness and humour. But I, though I seem to be the father, being really but the step-father of *Don Quixote*, will not go down with the stream of custom, nor beseech you, almost as it were with tears in my eyes, as others do, dearest reader, to pardon or dissemble the faults you shall discover in this my child. You are neither his kinsman nor friend; you have your soul in your body, and your will as free as the bravest of them all, and are as much lord and master of your own house, as the king of his subsidies, and know the common saying, 'Under my cloak, a fig for the king'. All which exempts and frees you from every regard and obligation: and therefore you may say of this history whatever you think fit, without fear of being calumniated for the evil, or rewarded for the good you shall say of it.

Only I would give it you neat and naked, without the ornament of a preface, or the rabble and catalogue of the accustomed sonnets, epigrams, and encomiums, that are wont to be placed at the beginning of books. For, let me tell you, though it cost me some pains to write it, I reckoned none greater than the writing of this preface you are now reading. I often took pen in hand, and as often laid it down, not knowing what to say: and once upon a time, being in deep suspense, with the paper before me, the pen behind my ear, my elbow on the table, and my cheek on my hand, thinking what I should say, unexpectedly in came a friend of mine, a pleasant gentleman, and of a very good understanding; who, seeing me so pensive, asked me the cause of my musing. Not willing to conceal it from him, I answered, that I was musing on what preface I should make to *Don Quixote*, and that I was so much at a stand about it, that I intended to make none at all, nor publish the achievements of that noble knight. 'For would you have me not be concerned at what that ancient lawgiver, the vulgar, will say, when they see me, at the end of so many years, slept away in the silence of oblivion, appear, with all my years upon my back,* with a legend as dry as a kex, empty of invention, the style flat, the conceits poor, and void of all learning and erudition; without quotations in the margin, or annotations at the end of the book; seeing that other books, though fabulous and profane, are so full of sentences of Aristotle, of Plato, and of all the tribe of philosophers, that the readers are in admiration, and take the authors of them for men of great reading, learning, and eloquence? for, when they cite the Holy Scriptures, they pass for so many St. Thomases, and doctors of the church; observing herein a decorum so ingenious, that, in one line, they describe a raving lover, and, in another give you a little scrap of a Christian homily, that it is a delight, and a perfect treat, to hear or read it. All this my book is likely to want; for I have nothing to quote in the margin, nor to make notes on at the end; nor do I know what authors I have followed in it, to put them at the beginning, as all others do, by the letters A, B, C, beginning with Aristotle, and ending at Xenophon, Zoilus, or Zeuxis: though the one was a railer, and the other a painter. My book will also want sonnets at the beginning, at least such sonnets whose authors are dukes, marquesses, earls, bishops, ladies, or celebrated poets: though, should I desire them of two or three obliging friends, I know they would furnish me, and with such, as those of greater reputation in our Spain could not equal.* In short, my dear friend,' continued I, 'it is resolved, that Señor Don Quixote remain buried in the records of La Mancha, until heaven sends somebody to supply him with such ornaments as he wants; for I find myself incapable of helping him, through my own insufficiency and want of learning; and because I am naturally too idle and lazy to hunt after authors, to say what I can say as well without them. Hence proceeds the suspense and thoughtfulness you found me in, sufficiently occasioned by what I have told you.'

My friend, at hearing this, striking his forehead with the palm of his hand, and setting up a loud laugh, said: 'Before God, brother, I am now perfectly undeceived of a mistake I have been in ever since I knew you, still taking you for a discreet and prudent person in all your actions: but now I see you are as far from being so, as heaven is from earth. For how is it possible, that things of such little moment, and so easy to be remedied, can have the power to puzzle and confound a genius so ripe as yours, and so made to break through and trample upon greater difficulties? In faith, this does not spring from want of ability, but from an excessive laziness, and penury of right reasoning. Will you see whether what I say be true? then listen attentively, and you shall perceive, that, in the twinkling of an eye, I will confound all your difficulties, and remedy all the defects that, you say, suspend and deter you from introducing into the world the history of this your famous Don Quixote, the light and mirror of all knight-errantry.'

'Say on,' replied I, hearing what he said to me: 'after what manner do you think to fill up the vacuity made by my fear, and reduce the chaos of my confusion to clearness?'

To which he answered:

'The first thing you seem to stick at, concerning the sonnets, epigrams, and eulogies, that are wanting for the beginning, and should be the work of grave personages, and people of quality, may be remedied by taking some pains yourself to make them, and then baptizing them, giving them what names you please, fathering them on Prester John of the Indies, or on the Emperor of Trapisonda; of whom I have certain intelligence that they are both famous poets: and though they were not such, and though some pedants and bachelors should backbite you, and murmur at this truth, value them not two farthings; for, though they should convict you of a lie, they cannot cut off the hand that wrote it.

'As to citing in the margin the books and authors from whom you collected the sentences and sayings you have interspersed in your history, there is no more to do but to contrive it so, that some sentences and phrases may fall in pat, which you have by heart, or at least which will cost you very little trouble to find.* As for example, treating of liberty and slavery:

> Non bene pro toto libertas venditur auro.

And then in the margin cite Horace, or whoever said it.* If you are treating of the power of death presently you have:

> Pallida Mors aequo pulsat pede pauperum tabernas
> Regumque turres.*

If of friendship and loving our enemies, as God enjoins, go to the Holy Scripture, if you have never so little curiosity, and set down God's own words: *Ego autem dico vobis, diligite inimicos vestros.** If you are speaking of evil thoughts, bring in the gospel again: *De corde exeunt cogitationes malae.** On the instability of friends, Cato will lend you his distich:

> Donec eris felix, multos numerabis amicos,
> Tempora si fuerint nubila, solus eris.*

And so with these scraps of Latin and the like, it is odds but people will take you for a great grammarian, which is a matter of no small honour and advantage in these days. As to clapping annotations at the end of the book, you may do it safely in this manner. If you name any giant in your book, see that it be the giant Goliath; and with this alone (which will cost almost nothing) you have a grand annotation; for you may put: "The giant Golias, or Goliat, was a Philistine, whom the shepherd David slew with a great blow of a stone from a sling, in the valley of Terebinthus, as it is related in the book of Kings, in the chapter wherein you shall find it".

'Then, to show yourself a great humanist, and skilful in cosmography, let the river Tagus be introduced into the history, and you will gain another notable annotation, thus: "The river Tagus was so called from a certain king of Spain: it has its source in such a place, and is swallowed up in the ocean, first kissing the walls of the famous city of Lisbon; and some are of opinion its sands are of gold", &c. If you have occasion to treat of robbers, I will tell you the story of Cacus, for I have it by heart. If you write of courtesans, there is the bishop of Mondoñedo* will lend you a Lamia, Lais, and Flora, and this annotation must needs be very much to your credit. If you would tell of cruel women, Ovid will bring you acquainted with Medea. If enchanters and witches are your subject, Homer has a Calypso, and Virgil a Circe. If you would give us a history of valiant commanders, Julius Caesar gives you himself in his *Commentaries*, and Plutarch will furnish you with a thousand Alexanders. If you treat of love, and have but two drams of the Tuscan tongue, you will light on Leon Hebreo,* who will give you enough of it. And if you care not to visit foreign parts, you have at home Fonseca, "On the love of God",* where he describes all that you, or the most ingenious persons can imagine upon that fruitful subject. In fine, there is no more to be done but naming these names, or hinting these stories in your book, and let me alone to settle the annotations and quotations; for I will warrant to fill the margins for you, and enrich the end of your book with half a dozen leaves into the bargain.

'We come now to the catalogue of authors, set down in other books, that is wanting in yours. The remedy whereof is very easy; for you have nothing to do but to find a book that has them all, from A down to Z, as you say, and then transcribe that very alphabet into your work; and suppose the falsehood be ever so apparent, from the little need you have to make use of them, it signifies nothing; and perhaps some will be so foolish as to believe you had occasion for them all in your simple and sincere history. But though it served for nothing else, that long catalogue of authors will, however, at the first blush, give some authority to the book. And who will go about to disprove, whether you followed them or no, seeing they can get nothing by it?

'After all, if I take the thing right, this book of yours has no need of these ornaments you say it wants; for it is only an invective against the books of chivalry, which sort of books Aristotle never dreamed of, Saint Basil never mentioned, nor Cicero once heard of. Nor does the relation of its fabulous extravagances fall under the punctuality and preciseness of truth; nor do the observations of astronomy come within its sphere: nor have the dimensions of geometry, or the rhetorical arguments of logic, any thing to do with it; nor has it any concern with preaching, mixing the human with the divine, a kind of mixture which no Christian judgement should meddle with. All it has to do is, to copy nature: imitation is the business, and how much the more perfect that is, so much the better what is written will be. And since this writing of yours aims at no more than to destroy the authority and acceptance the books of chivalry have had in the world, and among the vulgar, you have no business to go begging sentences of philosophers, passages of holy writ, poetical fables, rhetorical orations, or miracles of saints; but only to endeavour, with plainness, and significant, decent, and well-ordered words, to give your periods a pleasing and harmonious turn, expressing the design in all you advance, and as much as possible making your conceptions clearly understood, without being intricate or obscure. Endeavour also, that, by reading your history, the melancholy may be provoked to laugh, the gay humour be heightened, and the simple not tired; that the judicious may admire the invention, the grave not undervalue it, nor the wise forbear commending it. In conclusion, carry your aim steady to overthrow that ill-compiled machine of books of chivalry, abhorred by many, but applauded by more: and, if you carry this point, you gain a considerable one.'

I listened with great silence to what my friend said to me, and his words made so strong an impression upon me, that I approved them without disputing, and out of them chose to compose this Preface, wherein, sweet reader, you will discern the judgement of my friend, my own good hap in finding such a counsellor at such a pinch, and your own ease in receiving, in so sincere and unostentatious a manner, the history of the famous Don Quixote de la Mancha; of whom it is clearly the opinion of all the inhabitants of the district of the field of Montiel, that he was the chastest lover, and the most valiant knight, that has been seen in those parts for many years. I will not enhance the service I do you in bringing you acquainted with so notable and so worthy a knight; but I beg the favour of some small acknowledgement for the acquaintance of the famous Sancho Panza, his squire, in whom I think I have deciphered all the squire-like graces that are scattered up and down in the whole rabble of books of chivalry. And so, God give you health, not forgetting me. Farewell.*

THE INGENIOUS GENTLEMAN

Don Quixote
de la Mancha

FIRST PART

CHAPTER 1

*Which treats of the quality and manner of life of the
renowned gentleman Don Quixote de la Mancha.*

IN a village of La Mancha,* the name of which I purposely
omit, there lived not long ago, one of those gentlemen, who
usually keep a lance upon a rack, an old target, a lean horse,
and a greyhound for coursing. A dish of boiled meat, consisting
of somewhat more beef than mutton, the fragments served up
cold on most nights, an omelet* on Saturdays, lentils on Fridays,
and a small pigeon by way of addition on Sundays, consumed
three-fourths of his income. The rest was laid out in a surtout
of fine black cloth, a pair of velvet breeches for holidays, with
slippers of the same; and on week-days he prided himself in
the very best of his own homespun cloth. His family consisted
of a housekeeper somewhat above forty, a niece not quite
twenty, and a lad for the field and the market, who both saddled
the horse and handled the pruning-hook. The age of our
gentleman bordered upon fifty years. He was of a robust
constitution, spare-bodied, of a meagre visage; a very early riser,
and a keen sportsman. It is said his surname was Quixada, or
Quesada (for in this there is some difference among the authors
who have written upon this subject), though by probable
conjectures it may be gathered that he was called Quixana.* But
this is of little importance to our story; let it suffice that in
relating we do not swerve a jot from the truth.

You must know then, that this gentleman aforesaid, at
times when he was idle, which was most part of the year,

gave himself up to the reading of books of chivalry, with so much attachment and relish, that he almost forgot all the sports of the field, and even the management of his domestic affairs; and his curiosity and extravagant fondness herein arrived to that pitch, that he sold many acres of arable land to purchase books of knight-errantry, and carried home all he could lay hands on of that kind. But, among them all, none pleased him so much as those composed by the famous Feliciano de Silva: for the glaringness of his prose, and the intricacy of his style, seemed to him so many pearls; and especially when he came to peruse those love-speeches and challenges, wherein in several places he found written: 'The reason of the unreasonable treatment of my reason enfeebles my reason in such wise, that with reason I complain of your beauty':* and also when he read—'The high heavens that with your divinity divinely fortify you with the stars, making you meritorious of the merit merited by your greatness'.

With this kind of language the poor gentleman lost his wits, and distracted himself to comprehend and unravel their meaning; which was more than Aristotle himself could do, were he to rise again from the dead for that purpose alone. He had some doubt as to the dreadful wounds which Don Belianis* gave and received; for he imagined, that notwithstanding the most expert surgeons had cured him, his face and whole body must still be full of seams and scars. Nevertheless he commended in his author the concluding his book with a promise of that unfinishable adventure: and he often had it in his thoughts to take pen in hand, and finish it himself, precisely as it is there promised: which he had certainly performed, and successfully too, if other greater and continual cogitations had not diverted him.

He had frequent disputes with the priest of his village (who was a learned person, and had taken his degrees in Sigüenza*) which of the two was the better knight, Palmerin of England,* or Amadis de Gaul.* But master Nicholas, barber-surgeon of the same town, affirmed, that none ever came up to the Knight of the Sun,* and that if any one could be compared to him, it was Don Galaor, brother of Amadis de Gaul; for he was of a disposition fit for everything, no finical gentleman, nor such a whimperer as his brother; and as to courage, he was by no means inferior to him. In short, he so bewildered himself in this kind of study, that he passed the nights in reading from sunset to sunrise, and the days from sunrise to sunset: and thus, through little sleep and much reading, his brain was dried up in such a manner, that he came at last to lose his wits. His imagination was full of all that he read in his books, to wit, enchantments, battles, single combats, challenges, wounds, courtships, amours, tempests, and impossible absurdities. And so firmly was he persuaded that the whole system of chimeras he read of was true, that he thought no history in the world was more to be depended upon. The Cid Ruy Diaz,* he was wont to say, was a very good knight, but not comparable to the Knight of the Burning Sword,* who with a single back-stroke cleft asunder two fierce and monstrous giants. He was better pleased with Bernardo del Carpio for putting Orlando the Enchanted to death in Roncesvalles, by means of the same stratagem which Hercules used, when he suffocated Anteus, son of the Earth, by squeezing him between his arms.* He spoke mighty well of the giant Morgante;* for, though he was of that monstrous brood who are always proud and insolent, he alone was affable and well-bred: but, above all, he was charmed with Reynaldos de Montalvan,* especially when he saw him sallying out of his castle and plundering all he met; and when abroad he seized that image of Mahomet, which was all of massive gold, as his history records. He would have given his housekeeper, and niece to boot, for a fair opportunity of handsomely kicking the traitor Galalon.*

In fine, having quite lost his wits, he fell into one of the strangest conceits that ever entered the head of any madman; which was, that he thought it expedient and necessary, as well for the advancement of his own reputation, as for the public good, that he should commence knight-errant, and wander through the world, with his horse and arms, in quest of adventures, and to put in practice whatever he had read to have been practised by knights-errant; redressing all kind of grievances, and exposing himself to danger on all occasions; that by accomplishing such enterprises he might

acquire eternal fame and renown. The poor gentleman already
imagined himself at least crowned Emperor of Trapisonda*
by the valour of his arm; and thus wrapped up in these
agreeable delusions, and hurried on by the strange pleasure
he took in them, he hastened to put in execution what he
so much desired.

And the first thing he did was, to scour up a suit of armour,
which had been his great-great-grandfather's, and, being
mouldy and rust-eaten, had lain by, many long years, forgotten in a corner. These he cleaned and furbished up the best
he could; but he perceived they had one grand defect, which
was, that, instead of a helmet, they had only a simple morion,
or steel cap; but he dexterously supplied this want by contriving a sort of visor of pasteboard, which, being fixed to
the head-piece, gave it the appearance of a complete helmet.
It is true, indeed, that, to try its strength, and whether it was
proof against a cut, he drew his sword, and giving it two
strokes, undid in an instant what he had been a week in
doing. But not altogether approving of his having broken it
to pieces with so much ease, to secure himself from the like
danger for the future, he made it over again, fencing it with
small bars of iron within, in such a manner, that he rested
satisfied of its strength; and without caring to make a fresh
experiment on it, he approved and looked upon it as a most
excellent helmet.

The next thing he did was to visit his steed; and though
his bones stuck out like the corners of a real, and he had
more faults than Gonela's horse,* which *tantum pellis et ossa
fuit** he fancied that neither Alexander's Bucephalus, nor [the]
Cid's Babieca, was equal to him. Four days was he considering
what name to give him; for (as he said within himself) it was
not fit that a horse so good, and appertaining to a knight so
famous, should be without some name of eminence; and
therefore he studied to accommodate him with one, which
should express what he had been before he belonged to a
knight-errant, and what he actually now was; for it seemed
highly reasonable, if his master changed his state, he likewise
should change his name, and acquire one famous and high
sounding, as became the new order, and the new way of life

he now professed. And so, after sundry names devised and rejected, liked and disliked again, he concluded at last to call him Rosinante;* a name, in his opinion, lofty and sonorous, and at the same time expressive of what he had been when he was but a common steed, and before he had acquired his present superiority over all the steeds in the world.

Having given his horse a name so much to his satisfaction, he resolved to give himself one. This consideration took him up eight days more, and at length he determined to call himself Don Quixote; from whence, as is said, the authors of this most true history conclude, that his name was certainly Quixada, and not Quesada, as others would have it. But recollecting that the valorous Amadis, not content with the simple appellation of Amadis, added thereto the name of his kingdom and native country, in order to render it famous, and styled himself Amadis de Gaul; so he, like a good knight did in like manner call himself Don Quixote de la Mancha; whereby, in his opinion, he set forth in a very lively manner his lineage and country, and did it due honour by taking his surname from thence.

And now, his armour being furbished up, the morion converted into a perfect helmet, and both his steed and himself new-named, he persuaded himself that he wanted nothing but to make choice of some lady to be in love with; for a knight-errant without a mistress, was a tree without leaves or fruit, and a body without a soul.

'If,' said he, 'for the punishment of my sins, or through my good fortune, I should chance to meet some giant, as is usual with knights-errant, and should overthrow him in fight, or cleave him asunder, or in fine vanquish and force him to yield, will it not be proper to have some lady to send him to as a present; that, when he comes before her, he may kneel to her sweet ladyship, and with humble and submissive tone, accost her thus: "Madam, I am the Giant Caraculiambro, lord of the island [of] Malindrania, whom the never-enough-to-be-praised Don Quixote de la Mancha has overcome in single combat, and has commanded to present myself before your ladyship, that your grandeur may dispose of me as you think proper"?'

Oh! how did our good gentleman exult when he had made this harangue, and especially when he had found out a person on whom to confer the title of his mistress; which, it is believed, happened thus. Near the place where he lived, there dwelt a very comely country lass, with whom he had formerly been in love; though, as it is supposed, she never knew it, nor troubled herself about it. Her name was Aldonza Lorenzo, and her he pitched upon to be the lady of his thoughts; then, casting about for a name, which should have some affinity with her own, and yet incline towards that of a great lady or princess, he resolved to call her Dulcinea del Toboso (for she was born at that place), a name, to his thinking, harmonious, uncommon, and significant, like the rest he had devised for himself, and for all that belonged to him.

CHAPTER 2

Which treats of the first sally the ingenious Don Quixote made from his Village.

Now, these dispositions being made, he would no longer defer putting his design in execution, being the more strongly excited thereto by the mischief he thought his delay occasioned in the world; such and so many were the grievances he proposed to redress, the wrongs he intended to rectify, the exorbitances to correct, the abuses to reform, and the debts to discharge. And therefore, without making any one privy to his design, or being seen by anybody, one morning before day (which was one of the hottest of the month of July) he armed himself cap-à-pie, mounted Rosinante, adjusted his ill-composed beaver, braced on his target, grasped his lance, and issued forth into the fields at a private door of his backyard, with the greatest satisfaction and joy, to find with how much ease he had given a beginning to his honourable enterprise. But scarcely was he got into the plain, when a terrible thought assaulted him and such as had well nigh made him abandon his new undertaking; for it came into his remembrance, that he was not dubbed a knight, and that according to the laws of chivalry, he neither could nor ought to enter the lists against any knight: and though he had been dubbed, still he must wear white armour, as a new knight, without any device on his shield, until he had acquired one by his prowess. These reflections staggered his resolution; but his frenzy prevailing above any reason whatever, he purposed to get himself knighted by the first person he should meet, in imitation of many others who had done the like, as he had read in the books which had occasioned his madness. As to the white armour, he proposed to scour his own, the first opportunity, in such sort that it should be whiter than ermine: and herewith quieting his mind, he went on his way, following no other road than what his horse pleased to take; believing that therein consisted the life and spirit of adventures.

Thus our flaming adventurer jogged on, talking to himself, and saying:

'Who doubts, but that, in future times, when the faithful history of my famous exploits shall come to light, the sage who writes them, when he gives a relation of this my first sally, so early in the morning, will do it in words like these: "Scarcely had the ruddy Phoebus spread the golden tresses of his beauteous hair over the face of the wide and spacious earth; and scarcely had the painted birds, with the sweet and mellifluous harmony of their forked tongues, saluted the approach of rosy Aurora, who, quitting the soft couch of her jealous husband, disclosed herself to mortals through the gate and balconies of the Manchegan horizon; when the renowned Don Quixote de la Mancha, abandoning the lazy down, mounted his famous courser Rosinante, and began to travel through the ancient and noted field of Montiel"'' (and true it is, that was the very field); and passing along it, he continued saying:

'Happy times, and happy age, in which my famous exploits shall come to light, worthy to be engraved in brass, carved in marble, and drawn in picture, for a monument to all posterity! O thou sage enchanter! whoever thou art, to whose lot it shall fall to be the chronicler of this wonderful history, I beseech thee not to forget my good Rosinante, the inseparable companion of all my travels and excursions.'

Then on a sudden, as one really enamoured, he went on saying.

'O princess Dulcinea! mistress of this captive heart, great injury hast thou done me in discarding and disgracing me by thy rigorous decree, forbidding me to appear in the presence of thy beauty. Vouchsafe, lady, to remember this thine enthralled heart, that endures so many afflictions for love of thee.'

Thus he went on, stringing one extravagance upon another, in the style his books had taught him, and imitating as near as he could, their very phrase. He travelled on so leisurely, and the sun advanced so fast, and with such intense heat, that it was sufficient to have melted his brains, if he had had any. He travelled almost that whole day without meeting with anything worth relating, which disheartened him much; for he wanted immediately to have encountered somebody, to make trial of the force of his valiant arm.

Some authors say, his first adventure was that of [Puerto] Lápice; others pretend, it was that of the windmills. But what I have been able to discover of this matter, and what I have found written in the annals of La Mancha is, that he travelled all that day, and, toward the fall of night, his horse and he found themselves tired, and almost dead with hunger; and looking round about to see if he could discover some castle, or sheepfold, to which he might retire, and relieve his extreme necessity, he perceived not far from the road an inn; which was as if he had seen a star directing him to the porticoes, or palace of his redemption. He made all the haste he could, and came up to it just as the day shut in.

There chanced to stand at the door two young women, ladies of pleasure as they are called, who were going to Seville with certain carriers who happened to take up their lodging at the inn that night. And as whatever our adventurer thought, saw, or imagined, seemed to him to be done and transacted in the manner he had read of, immediately, at sight of the inn, he fancied it to be a castle, with four turrets and battlements of refulgent silver, together with its drawbridge, deep moat, and all the appurtenances with which such castles are usually described. As he was making up to the inn, which he took for a castle, at some little distance from it, he checked Rosinante by the bridle, expecting some dwarf to appear on the battlements, and give notice, by sound of trumpet, of the arrival of a knight at the castle. But finding they delayed, and that Rosinante pressed to get to the stable, he drew near to the inn door, and saw there the two strolling wenches, who seemed to him to be two beautiful damsels, or graceful ladies, who were taking their pleasure at the castle-gate.

It happened that a swineherd, getting together his hogs (for, without begging pardon, so they are called) from the stubble field, winding his horn, at which signal they are wont to assemble; and at that instant Don Quixote's imagination represented to him what he wished, namely that some dwarf gave the signal of his arrival; and therefore, with wondrous content, he came up to the inn, and to the ladies, who perceiving a man armed in that manner with lance and buckler, were frightened, and began to run into the house. But Don Quixote, guessing at their fear by their flight, lifted up his pasteboard visor, and discovering his withered and dusty visage, with courteous demeanour and grave voice thus accosted them:

'Fly not, ladies, nor fear any discourtesy; for the order of knighthood, which I profess, permits me not to offer injury to any one, much less to virgins of such high rank as your presence denotes.'

The wenches stared at him, and with all the eyes they had, were looking to find his face, which the scurvy beaver almost covered. But when they heard themselves styled virgins, a thing so out of the way of their profession, they could not contain their laughter, and that in so violent a manner, that Don Quixote began to grow angry, and said to them:

'Modesty well becomes the fair, and nothing is so foolish as excessive laughter proceeding from a slight occasion: but I do not say this to disoblige you, or to cause you to discover any ill disposition towards me; for mine is no other than to do you service.'

This language, which they did not understand, and the uncouth mien of our knight, increased their laughter, and his

wrath; and things would have gone much further, had not
the innkeeper come out at that instant (a man, who, by being
very bulky, was inclined to be very peaceable), who, beholding such an odd figure all in armour, the pieces of which
were so ill sorted, as were the bridle, lance, buckler, and
corselet, could scarcely forbear keeping the damsels company
in the demonstrations of their mirth. But, being in some fear
of a pageant equipped in so warlike a manner, he resolved
to speak him fair, and therefore accosted him thus:

'If your worship, Señor Cavalier, is in quest of a lodging,
bating a bed (for in this inn there is none to be had),
everything else will be found here in great abundance.'

Don Quixote, perceiving the humility of the governor of
the fortress (for such to him appeared the innkeeper and the
inn) answered:

'Anything will serve me, Señor Castellano, for "arms are
my ornaments, and fighting my repose".' The host thought
he called him Castellano because he took him for an honest
Castilian,* whereas he was an Andalusian, and of the coast
of San Lúcar, as arrant a thief as Cacus, and as sharp and
unlucky as a collegian or a court-page; and therefore he
replied:

'If it be so, your worship's beds are hard rocks, and your
sleep the being always awake;* and since it is so, you may
venture to alight, being sure of finding in this poor hut
sufficient cause for not sleeping a whole twelvemonth, much
more one single night.'

And so saying, he went and held Don Quixote's stirrup,
who alighted with much difficulty and pains; for he had not
broke his fast all that day. He presently requested of the host
to take especial care of his steed, for he was the best piece
of horseflesh that ever ate bread in the world. The innkeeper
viewed him, but did not think him so good as Don Quixote
represented him to be, no, not by half; and having set him
up in the stable, he returned to see what his guest would be
pleased to order; whom the damsels were unarming (for they
were already reconciled to him), and though they had taken
off the back and breast-pieces, they could not find out how
to unlace his gorget, or take off the counterfeit beaver, which

he had fastened in such a manner with green ribbons, that, there being no possibility of untying them, they must of necessity be cut, which he would by no means consent to, and so he remained all that night with his helmet on, and was the strangest and most ridiculous figure imaginable. Whilst the girls were taking off his armour, imagining them to be persons of the first quality, and ladies of that castle, he said to them with great gaiety:

'"Never sure was knight so nobly served by ladies as was Don Quixote after his departure from his village: damsels waited on his person, and princesses on his steed".* O Rosinante! for that, dear ladies, is my horse's name, and Don Quixote de la Mancha is my own; for though I was not willing to discover myself, until the exploits done for your service and benefit should discover me, the necessity of accommodating the old romance of Sir Lancelot to our present purpose has been the occasion of your knowing my name before the proper season: but the time will come, when your ladyships may command and I obey; and the valour of my arm shall manifest the desire I have to serve you.'

The lasses, who were not accustomed to such rhetorical flourishes, answered not a word, but only asked whether he would be pleased to eat anything.

'With all my heart,' answered Don Quixote; 'anything eatable would, I apprehend, come very seasonably.'

That day happened to be Friday, and there was nothing to be had in the inn, excepting a parcel of dried fish, which in Castile they call 'abadexo', in Andalusia 'baccalao', in some parts 'curadillo', and in others 'truchuela'. They asked him, whether he would be pleased to eat some 'truchuelas', for they had no other fish to offer him.

'So there be many troutlings,' answered Don Quixote, 'they may serve me instead of one trout; for I would as willingly be paid eight single reals as one real of eight; and the rather, because, perhaps, these troutlings are like veal, which is preferable to beef, or like kid, which is better than the goat. But, be that as it will, let it come quickly; for the toil and weight of arms cannot be supported without supplying the belly well.'

They laid the cloth at the door of the inn, for the sake of the fresh breeze; and the landlord brought him some of the ill-watered and worse-boiled 'baccalao', and a loaf of bread as black and mouldy as his armour: but it was a matter of great laughter to see him eat; for, having his helmet on, and the beaver up, he could not put anything into his mouth with his own hands, but somebody must do it for him; and so one of the aforesaid ladies performed this office. But to give him to drink was utterly impossible, if the host had not bored a reed, and, putting one end into his mouth, poured in the wine leisurely at the other: and all this he suffered patiently rather than cut the lacings of his helmet.

In the meantime there came to the inn a sowgelder, who, as soon as he arrived, sounded his whistle of reeds four or five times; which entirely confirmed Don Quixote in the thought, that he was in some famous castle, that they served him with music, and that the poor-jacks were trouts, the coarse loaf the finest white bread, the wenches ladies, and the host governor of the castle; and so he concluded his resolution to be well taken, and his sally attended with success. But what gave him the most disturbance was, that he was not yet dubbed a knight; thinking he could not lawfully undertake any adventure until he had first received the order of knighthood.

CHAPTER 3

In which is related the pleasant method Don Quixote took to be dubbed a knight.

AND now, being disturbed with this thought, he made an abrupt end of his short supper; which done, he called the landlord, and, shutting himself up with him in the stable, he fell upon his knees before him, and said:

'I will never rise from this place, valorous knight, until your courtesy vouchsafes me a boon I mean to beg of you; which will redound to your own honour, and to the benefit of human kind.'

The host, seeing his guest at his feet, and hearing such expressions, stood confounded, gazing at him, and not knowing what to do or say: he then strove to raise him from the ground, but in vain, until he had promised to grant him the boon he requested.

'I expected no less, Sir, from your great magnificence,' answered Don Quixote; 'and therefore know, that the boon I would request, and has been vouchsafed me by your liberality, is, that you shall to-morrow dub me a knight; and this night in the chapel of your castle I will watch my armour: and to-morrow, as I have said, what I so earnestly desire shall be accomplished; that I may be duly qualified to wander through the four quarters of the world, in quest of adventures, for the relief of the distressed, as is the duty of chivalry, and of knights-errant, whose hearts, like mine, are strongly bent on such achievements.'

The host who (as we have said) was an arch fellow, and had already entertained some suspicions of the madness of his guest, was now, at hearing such expressions, thoroughly convinced of it; and that he might have something to make sport with that night, he resolved to keep up the humour; and said to him, that he was certainly very much in the right in what he desired and requested; and that such achievements were peculiar and natural to cavaliers of such prime quality as he seemed to be of, and as his gallant deportment did demonstrate: that he himself, in the days of his youth, had betaken himself to that honourable employ, wandering through divers parts of the world in search of adventures, not omitting to visit the suburbs of Málaga, the isle of Riarán, the compass of Seville, the aqueduct-market of Segovia, the olive-yard of Valencia, the rondilla of Granada, the coast of San Lúcar, the fountain of Córdova, the hedge taverns of Toledo,* and sundry other parts, where he had exercised the agility of his feet and the dexterity of his hands; doing sundry wrongs, soliciting sundry widows, undoing some damsels, and bubbling several young heirs;* in fine, making himself known to most of the tribunals and courts of judicature in Spain: and that at last he had retired to this castle, where he lived upon his own means and other people's, entertaining all knights-errant, of whatever quality or condition they were, merely for the great love he bore them, and that they might share their gettings with him in requital for his good-will.

He further told him there was no chapel in his castle, in which to watch his armour (for it had been pulled down in order to be rebuilt): however, in cases of necessity, he knew it might be watched wherever he pleased, and that he might do it that night in a court of the castle; and the next day, if it pleased God, the requisite ceremonies should be performed, in such a manner that he should be dubbed a knight and so effectually knighted, that no one in the world could be more so. He asked him also, whether he had any money about him. Don Quixote replied, he had not a farthing, having never read in the histories of knights-errant, that they carried any. To this the host replied, he was under a mistake; for, supposing it was not mentioned in the story, the authors thinking it superfluous to specify a thing so plain, and so indispensably necessary to be carried, as money and clean shirts, it was not therefore to be inferred, that they had none: and therefore he might be assured, that all the knights-errant (of whose actions there are such authentic histories) did carry their purses well lined for whatever might befall them; and they also carried shirts, and a little box of ointment to heal the wounds they might receive, because there was not always one at hand to cure them in the fields and deserts where they fought, unless they had some sage enchanter for their friend, to assist them immediately, bringing some damsel or dwarf in a cloud through the air, with a vial of water of such virtue, that, in tasting a drop of it, they should instantly become as sound and whole of their bruises and wounds as if they had never been hurt: but that so long as they wanted this advantage, the knights-errant of times past never failed to have their squires provided with money, and other neces-sary things, such as lint and salves, to cure themselves with; and when it happened that the said knights had no squires (which fell out very rarely), they carried all these things behind them upon their horses, in a very small wallet, hardly visible, as if it were something of greater importance; for were it not upon such an account, this carrying of wallets was not currently admitted among knights-errant: therefore he advised him, though he might command him as his godson (which he was to be very soon) that from henceforward he should not travel without money, and without the aforesaid precautions; and he would find how useful they would be to him when he least expected it.

Don Quixote promised to follow his advice with all punctuality; and now order was presently given for performing the watch of the armour in a large yard adjoining to the inn; and Don Quixote gathering all the pieces of it together, laid them upon a cistern* that stood close to a well: and bracing on his buckler, and grasping his lance, with a solemn pace he began to walk backward and forward before the cistern, beginning his parade just as the day shut in.

The host acquainted all that were in the inn with the frenzy of his guest, the watching of his armour, and the knighting he expected. They all wondered at so odd a kind of madness, and went out to observe him at a distance; and they perceived, that with a composed air he sometimes continued his walk: at other times, leaning upon his lance, he looked wistfully at his armour, without taking off his eyes for a long time together. It was now quite night; but the moon shone with such a lustre as might almost vie with his who lent it; so that whatever our new knight did was distinctly seen by all the spectators.

While he was thus employed, one of the carriers, who inned there, had a mind to water his mules, and it was necessary first to remove Don Quixote's armour from off the cistern; who, seeing him approach, called to him with a loud voice:

'Ho, there, whoever thou art, rash knight, that approachest to touch the arms of the most valorous adventurer that ever girded sword, take heed what thou doest, and touch them not, unless thou wouldst leave thy life a forfeit for thy temerity.'

The carrier troubled not his head with these speeches (but it had been better for him if he had, for he might have saved his carcass) but, instead of that, taking hold of the straps, he tossed the armour a good distance from him; which Don

Quixote perceiving, he lifted up his eyes to heaven, and fixing his thoughts (as it seemed) on his mistress Dulcinea, he said:

'Assist, me, dear lady, in this first affront offered to this breast enthralled to thee; let not thy favour and protection fail me in this first moment of danger.'

And uttering these and the like ejaculations, he let slip his target, and lifting up his lance with both hands, gave the carrier such a blow on the head, that he laid him flat on the ground in such piteous plight, that, had he seconded his blow, there would have been no need of a surgeon. This done, he gathered up his armour and walked backward and forward with the same gravity as at first. Soon after, another carrier, not knowing what had happened (for still the first lay stunned) came out with the same intention of watering his mules; and as he was going to clear the cistern by removing the armour, Don Quixote, without speaking a word, or imploring anybody's protection, again let slip his target, and lifting up his lance, broke the second carrier's head in three or four places. All the people of the inn ran together at the noise, and the innkeeper among the rest: which Don Quixote perceiving, he braced on his target, and laying his hand on his sword, he said:

'O queen of beauty, the strength and vigour of my enfeebled heart, now is the time to turn the eyes of thy greatness toward this thy captived knight, whom so prodigious an adventure at this instant awaits.'

Hereby in his opinion, he recovered so much courage, that, if all the carriers in the world had attacked him, he would not have retreated an inch. The comrades of those that were wounded (for they perceived them in that condition) began to let fly a shower of stones at Don Quixote; who sheltered himself the best he could under his shield, and durst not stir from the cistern, lest he should seem to abandon his armour. The host cried out to them to let him alone, for he had already told them he was mad, and that he would be acquitted as a madman though he should kill them all. Don Quixote also cried out louder, calling them cowards and traitors, and the lord of the castle a poltroon and a base-born knight, for suffering knights-errant to be treated in that manner; and that, if he had received the order of knighthood, he would make him smart for his treachery.

'But for you, rascally and base scoundrels' (said he) 'I do not value you a straw: draw near, come on, and do your worst; you shall quickly see the reward you are likely to receive of your folly and insolence.'

This he uttered with so much vehemence and resolution, that he struck a terrible dread into the hearts of the assailants; and for this reason, together with the landlord's persuasions, they forbore throwing any more stones; and he permitted the wounded to be carried off, and returned to the watch of his armour with the same tranquillity and sedateness as before.

The host did not relish these pranks of his guest, and therefore determined to put an end to them by giving him the unlucky order of knighthood out of hand before any further mischief should ensue; and so coming up to him, he begged pardon for the rudeness those vulgar people had been guilty of, without his knowing anything of the matter; however, he said, they had been sufficiently chastised for their rashness. He repeated to him, that there was no chapel in that castle, neither was it necessary for what remained to be done; for the whole stress of being dubbed a knight, lay in the blows on the neck and shoulders, as he had learned from the ceremonial of the order; and that it might be effectually performed in the middle of a field: that he had already discharged all that belonged to the watching of the armour, which was sufficiently performed in two hours; and much more, since he had been above four about it. All which Don Quixote believed, and said he was there ready to obey him; and desired him to finish the business with the utmost dispatch, because, if he should be assaulted again, and found himself dubbed a knight, he was resolved not to leave a soul alive in the castle, except those he should command him to spare for his sake.

The constable,* thus warned, and apprehensive of what might be the event of this resolution, presently brought the book, in which he entered the account of the straw and barley he furnished to the carriers; and with the two abovesaid damsels (a boy carrying an end of candle before them) he came where Don Quixote was, whom he commanded to kneel; and reading in his manual (as if he had been saying some devout prayer), in the midst of the reading he lifted up his hand, and gave him a good blow on the nape of the neck, and after that with his own sword a handsome thwack on the shoulder, still muttering between his teeth as if he was praying. This done, he ordered one of the ladies to gird on his sword, which she did with the most obliging freedom, and discretion too, of which not a little was needful to keep them from bursting with laughter at every period of the ceremonies; but indeed the exploits they had already seen our new knight perform, kept their mirth within bounds. At girding on the sword, the good lady said:

'God make you a fortunate knight, and give you success in battle.'

Don Quixote asked her name that he might know from thenceforward to whom he was indebted for the favour received: for he intended her a share of the honour he should acquire by the valour of his arm. She replied with much humility, that she was called La Tolosa, and was a cobbler's daughter of Toledo, who lived at the little shops of Sancho-bienaya;* and wherever she was, she would serve and honour him as her lord. Don Quixote then desired her, for his sake, thenceforward to add to her name the Don, and to call herself Doña Tolosa; which she promised to do. The other buckled on his spurs; with whom he held almost the same kind of dialogue as he had done with her companion: he asked her name also, and she said she was called La Molinera, and was the daughter of an honest miller of Antequera. Don Quixote entreated her also to add the Don, and call herself Doña Molinera, making her fresh offers of service and thanks.

Thus the never-till-then-seen ceremonies being hastily dispatched, Don Quixote, who was impatient to see himself on horseback, and sallying out in quest of adventures, immediately saddled Rosinante, and embracing his host, mounted; and at parting said such strange things to him, acknowledging the favour of dubbing him a knight, that it is impossible to express them. The host, to get him sooner out of the inn, returned his compliments with no less flourishes, though in fewer words, and, without demanding anything for his lodging, wished him a good journey.

CHAPTER 4

Of what befell our knight after he had sallied out from the inn.

It was about break of day, when Don Quixote issued forth from the inn, so satisfied, so gay, so blithe, to see himself knighted, that the joy thereof almost burst his horse's girths. But recollecting the advice of his host concerning the necessary provisions for his undertaking, especially the articles of money and clean shirts, he resolved to return home, and furnish himself accordingly, and also provide himself with a squire; purposing to take into his service a certain country-fellow of the neighbourhood, who was poor, and had children, yet was very fit for the squirely office of chivalry. With this thought, he turned Rosinante towards his village; who, as it were, knowing what his master would be at, began to put on with so much alacrity, that he hardly seemed to set his feet to the ground. He had not gone far, when, on his right hand, from a thicket hard by, he fancied he heard a weak voice, as of a person complaining. And scarcely had he heard it, when he said:

'I thank heaven for the favour it does me, in laying before me so early an opportunity of complying with the duty of my profession, and of reaping the fruit of my honourable desires. These are doubtless the cries of some distressed person, who stands in need of my protection and assistance.'

And turning the reins, he put Rosinante forward toward the place from whence he thought the voice proceeded. And he had entered but a few paces into the wood, when he saw a mare tied to an oak, and a lad to another, naked from the waist upwards, about fifteen years of age, who was that person that cried out; and not without cause, for a lusty country-fellow was laying him on very severely with a belt, and accompanied every lash with a reprimand and a word of advice; for, said he,

'The tongue slow, and the eyes quick.'

The boy answered,

'I will do so no more, dear Sir; by the passion of God, I will never do so again; and I promise for the future to take more care of the flock.'

Now Don Quixote, seeing what passed, said in an angry tone:

'Discourteous knight, it ill becomes thee to meddle with one who is not able to defend himself; get upon thy horse, and take thy lance' (for he had also a lance leaning against the oak to which the mare was fastened), 'for I'll make thee to know that it is cowardly to do what thou art doing.'

The countryman, seeing such a figure coming towards him, armed from head to foot, and brandishing his lance at his face, gave himself up for a dead man, and with good words answered:

'Señor Cavalier, this lad whom I am chastising, is a servant of mine; I employ him to tend a flock of sheep which I have hereabouts, and he is so careless, that I lose one every day; and because I correct him for his negligence, or roguery, he says I do it out of covetousness, and for an excuse not to pay him his wages; but, before God, and on my conscience he lies.'

'"Lies" in my presence! pitiful rascal,' said Don Quixote; 'by the sun that shines upon us, I have a good mind to run thee through and through with this lance: pay him immediately without further reply; if not, by that God that rules us, I will dispatch and annihilate thee in a moment; untie him presently.'

The countryman hung down his head, and, without replying a word, untied the boy. Don Quixote asked the lad, how much his master owed him; who answered, nine months' wages, at seven reals a month. Don Quixote computed it, and found that it amounted to sixty-three reals;* and he bade the countryman instantly disburse them, otherwise he must expect to die for it. The fellow in a fright answered, that on the word of a dying man, and upon the oath he had taken (though, by the way, he had taken no oath) it was not so much; for he must deduct the price of three pair of shoes he had given him upon account, and a real for two blood-lettings when he was not well.

'All this is very right,' said Don Quixote; 'but set the shoes and the blood-lettings against the stripes you have given him undeservedly: for if he tore the leather of the shoes you paid for, you have torn his skin; and if the barber-surgeon drew blood from him when he was sick, you have drawn blood from him when he is well; so that upon these accounts he owes you nothing.'

'The mischief is, Señor Cavalier,' quoth the countryman, 'that I have no money about me; but let Andres go home with me, and I will pay him all, real by real.'

'I go with him,' said the lad; 'the devil a bit: no, Sir, I design no such thing; for when he has me alone, he will flay me like any Saint Bartholomew.'

'He will not do so,' replied Don Quixote; 'it is sufficient to keep him in awe, that I lay my commands upon him; and upon condition he swears to me, by the order of knighthood which he has received, I will let him go free, and will be bound for the payment.'

'Take heed, good Sir, what you say,' quoth the boy, 'for my master is no knight, nor ever received any order of knighthood: he is John Haldudo the Rich, of the neighbourhood of Quintanar.'

'That is little to the purpose,' answered Don Quixote; 'there may be knights of the family of the Haldudos, and the rather since every man is the son of his own works.'

'That's true,' quoth Andres; 'but what works is my master the son of, who refuses me the wages of my sweat and labour?'

'I do not refuse thee, friend Andres,' replied the countryman; 'and be so kind to go with me; for I swear, by all the orders of knighthood that are in the world, to pay thee, as I have said, every penny down, and perfumed into the bargain.'

'As to the perfuming, I thank you for that,' said Don Quixote, 'give it him in reals, and I shall be satisfied: and see that you perform what you have sworn, else I swear to you by the same oath, to return to find you out, and chastise you; for I shall find you out, though you should hide yourself closer than a lizard. And if you would know, who it is that commands you this, that you may be the more strictly obliged to perform your promise know that I am the valorous Don Quixote de la Mancha, the redresser of wrongs and abuses; and so farewell, and do not forget what you have promised and sworn, on pain of the penalties aforesaid.'

And so saying, he clapped spurs to Rosinante, and was soon got a good way off.

The countryman followed him with all the eyes he had, and, when he found he was quite past the wood, and out of sight, he turned to his man Andres, and said:

'Come hither, child, I am resolved to pay thee what I owe thee, as that redresser of wrongs commanded me.'

'And I swear so you shall,' quoth Andres; 'and you will do well to perform what that honest gentleman has commanded, whom God grant to live a thousand years, and who is so brave a man, and so just a judge, that truly, if you do not pay me, he will come back and execute what he had threatened.'

'And I swear so too,' quoth the countryman; 'but to show thee how much I love thee, I am resolved to augment the debt, to increase the payment.'

And taking him by the arm, he tied him again to the tree, where he gave him so many stripes, that he left him for dead.

'Now, master Andres, call upon that redresser of wrongs; thou wilt find he will hardly redress this, though I believe I have not quite done with thee yet; for I have a good mind to flay thee alive, as thou fearedst but now.'

But at length he untied him, and gave him leave to go in quest of his judge, to execute the sentence he had pronounced. Andres went away in dudgeon, swearing he would find out the valorous Don Quixote de la Mancha, and tell him all that had passed, and that he should pay for it sevenfold. Notwithstanding all this, away he went weeping, and his master stayed behind laughing.

In this manner the valorous Don Quixote redressed this

wrong; and overjoyed at his success, as thinking he had given a most fortunate and glorious beginning to his knight-errantry, he went on toward his village, entirely satisfied with himself, and saying in a low voice:

'Well mayest thou deem thyself happy above all women living on the earth, O Dulcinea del Toboso, beauteous above the most beautiful, since it has been thy lot to have subject and obedient to thy whole will and pleasure so valiant and renowned a knight as is, and ever shall be, Don Quixote de la Mancha; who (as all the world knows) received but yesterday the order of knighthood, and to-day has redressed the greatest injury and grievance that injustice could invent and cruelty commit: to-day hath he wrested the scourge out of the hand of that pitiless enemy, who so undeservedly lashed that tender stripling.'

Just as he had done speaking, he came to the centre of four roads, and presently it came into his imagination, that the knights-errant, when they came to these crossways, set themselves to consider which of the roads they should take: and, to imitate them, he stood still awhile, and at last, after mature consideration, he let go the reins, submitting his own will to be guided by that of his horse, who following his first motion, took the direct road toward his stable. And having gone about two miles, Don Quixote discovered a company of people, who, as it afterwards appeared, were certain merchants of Toledo, going to buy silks in Murcia. There were six of them, and they came with their umbrellas, and four servants on horseback, and three muleteers on foot. Scarcely had Don Quixote espied them, when he imagined it must be some new adventure; and, to imitate, as near as possibly he could, the passages* he had read [of] in his books, he fancied this to be cut out on purpose for him to achieve. And so, with a graceful deportment and intrepidity, he settled himself firm in his stirrups, grasped his lance, covered his breast with his target, and posting himself in the midst of the highway, stood waiting the coming up of those knights-errant; for such he already judged them to be: and when they were come so near as to be seen and heard, Don Quixote raised his voice, and with an arrogant air, cried out:

'Let the whole world stand, if the whole world does not confess, that there is not in the whole world a damsel more beautiful than the empress of la Mancha, the peerless Dulcinea del Toboso.'

The merchants stopped at the sound of these words, and to behold the strange figure of him who pronounced them; and by one and the other they soon perceived the madness of the speaker: but they had a mind to stay and see what that confession meant, which he required of them; and one of them, who was somewhat of a wag, but withal very discreet, said to him:

'Señor Cavalier, we do not know who this good lady you mention may be: let us but see her, and, if she is of so great beauty as you intimate, we will, with all our hearts, and without any constraint, confess that truth you demand from us.'

'Should I show her to you,' replied Don Quixote, 'where would be the merit in confessing a truth so notorious? The business is, that, without seeing her, you believe, confess, affirm, swear, and maintain it; and if not, I challenge you all to battle, proud and monstrous as you are: and whether you come on one by one (as the laws of chivalry require) or altogether, as is the custom and wicked practice of those of your stamp, here I wait for you, confiding in the justness of my cause.'

'Señor Cavalier,' replied the merchant, 'I beseech your worship, in the name of all the princes here present, that we may not lay a burden upon our consciences, by confessing a thing we never saw nor heard, and especially what is so much to the prejudice of the Empresses and Queens of Alcarria and Estremadura, that your worship would be pleased to show us some picture of this lady, though no bigger than a barley-corn; for we shall guess at the clue by the thread: and herewith we shall rest satisfied and safe, and your worship remain contented and pleased: nay, I verily believe we are already so far inclined to your side, that, though her picture should represent her squinting with one eye, and distilling vermilion and brimstone from the other, notwithstanding all this, to oblige you, we will say whatever you please in her favour.'

'There distils not, base scoundrels,' answered Don Quixote, burning with rage, 'there distils not from her what you say, but rather ambergris and civet among cotton; neither is she crooked, nor humpbacked, but as straight as a spindle of Guadarrama: but you shall pay for the horrid blasphemy you have uttered against so transcendent a beauty as my mistress.'

And so saying, with his lance couched, he ran at him who had spoken, with so much fury and rage, that, if good fortune had not ordered it that Rosinante stumbled and fell in the midst of his career, it had gone hard with the daring merchant. Rosinante fell, and his master lay rolling about the field a good while, and endeavouring to rise; but in vain, so encumbered was he with his lance, target, spurs, and helmet, and with the weight of his antique armour. And while he was thus struggling to get up, and could not, he continued calling out:

'Fly not, ye dastardly rabble; stay, ye race of slaves; for it is through my horse's fault, and not my own, that I lie here extended.'

A muleteer of the company, not over good-natured, hearing the poor fallen gentleman vent such arrogancies, could not bear it without returning him an answer on his ribs; and, coming to him, he took the lance, and, after he had broken it to pieces, with one of the splinters he so belaboured Don Quixote, that in spite of his armour, he threshed him to chaff. His masters cried out, not to beat him so much, and to leave him; but the muleteer was provoked, and would not quit the game until he had quite spent the remainder of his choler; and running for the other pieces of the lance, he finished the breaking of them upon the poor fallen knight, who, notwithstanding the tempest of blows that rained upon him, never shut his mouth, threatening heaven and earth, and those assassins, for such they seemed to him. At length the fellow was tired, and the merchants went on their way, sufficiently furnished with matter of discourse concerning the poor belaboured knight; who, when he found himself alone, tried again to raise himself; but if he could not do it when whole and well, how should he when bruised and almost battered to pieces? Yet still he thought himself a happy man, looking upon this as a misfortune peculiar to knights-errant, and imputing the whole to his horse's fault; nor was it possible for him to raise himself up, his whole body was so horrible bruised.

CHAPTER 5

Wherein is continued the narration of our knight's misfortune.

BUT finding that he was really not able to stir, he bethought himself of having recourse to his usual remedy, which was to recollect some passage of his books; and his frenzy instantly presented to his remembrance that of Valdovinos and the Marquess of Mantua,* when Carloto left him wounded on the mountain; a story known to children, not unknown to youth, commended and credited by old men, and for all that no truer than the miracles of Mahomet. Now this example seemed to him as if it had been cast in a mould to fit the distress he was in: and so, with signs of great bodily pain, he began to roll himself on the ground, and said with a faint tone, what was said by the wounded knight of the wood:

> 'Where art thou, mistress of my heart,
> Unconscious of thy lover's smart?
> Ah me! thou know'st not my distress;
> Or thou art false and pitiless.'

And in this manner he went on with the romance until he came to those verses where it is said; 'O noble Marquess of Mantua, my uncle and lord by blood'. And it so fortuned that, just as he came to that verse, there passed by a countryman of his own village, and his near neighbour, who had been carrying a load of wheat to the mill; who seeing a man lying stretched on the earth, came up and asked him who he was, and what ailed him, that he made such a doleful lamentation? Don Quixote believed he must certainly be the Marquess of Mantua his uncle, and so returned him no answer, but went on with his romance, giving an account of his misfortune, and of the amours of the emperor's son with his spouse, just in the same manner as it is there recounted. The peasant stood confounded at hearing such extravagances; and taking off his vizor which was beaten all to pieces, he wiped his face which was covered with dust; and the moment he had done wiping it he knew him, and said.

'Ah! Señor Quixana' (for so he was called* before he had lost his senses, and was transformed from a sober gentleman to a knight-errant) 'how came your worship in this condition?'

But he answered out of his romance to whatever question he asked him. The good man seeing this, made a shift to take off his back and breast-piece, to see if he had received any wound; but he saw no blood, nor sign of any hurt. Then he endeavoured to raise him from the ground, and with much ado set him upon his ass, as being the beast of easiest carriage. He gathered together all the arms, not excepting the broken pieces of the lance, and tied them upon Rosinante; and so taking him by the bridle, and his ass by the halter, he went on toward his village, full of reflection at hearing the extravagances which Don Quixote uttered; and no less thoughtful was the knight who, through the mere force of bruises and bangs, could scarcely keep himself upon the ass, and ever and anon sent forth such groans as seemed to pierce the skies; insomuch that the peasant was again forced to ask him what ailed him. And sure nothing but the devil himself could furnish his memory with stories so suited to what had befallen him; for at that instant, forgetting Valdovinos, he bethought himself of the Moor Abindarraez, at the time when the governor of Antequera, Rodrigo de Narvaez, had taken him prisoner, and conveyed him to his castle.* So that when the peasant asked him again how he did, he answered him in the very same words and expressions in which the prisoner Abindarraez answered Rodrigo de Narvaez, according as he had read the story in the *Diana* of George of Montemayor, applying it so patly to his own case, that the peasant went on cursing himself to the devil to hear such a monstrous heap of nonsense; from whence he collected that his neighbour was run mad, and therefore made what haste he could to reach the village, to free himself from the vexation of Don

Quixote's tiresome and impertinent speeches, who in conclusion said:

'Be it known to your worship, Señor Don Rodrigo de Narvaez, that this beauteous Xarifa, whom I mentioned, is now the fair Dulcinea del Toboso, for whom I have done, do, and will do, the most famous exploits of chivalry that have been, are, or shall be seen in the world.'

To this the peasant answered:

'Look you, Sir, as I am a sinner, I am not Don Rodrigo de Narvaez, nor the Marquess of Mantua, but Pedro Alonso your neighbour: neither is your worship Valdovinos, nor Abindarraez, but the worthy gentleman Señor Quixana.'

'I know who I am,' answered Don Quixote; 'and I know too that I am not only capable of being those I have mentioned, but all the Twelve Peers of France, yea, and the Nine Worthies,* since my exploits will far exceed all that they have jointly or separately achieved.'

With these and the like discourses, they reached the village about sunset: but the peasant stayed until the night was a little advanced, that the people might not see the poor battered gentleman so scurvily mounted. When the hour he thought convenient was come, he entered the village, and arrived at Don Quixote's house, which he found all in an uproar. The priest and the barber of the place, who were Don Quixote's great friends, happened to be there; and the housekeeper was saying to them aloud:

'What is your opinion, Señor Licentiate Pero Perez' (for that was the priest's name) 'of my master's misfortune? for neither he, nor his horse, nor the target, nor the lance, nor the armour have been seen these six days past.'*

'Woe is me! I am verily persuaded, and it is as certainly true as I was born to die, that these cursed books of knight-errantry which he keeps, and is so often reading, have turned his brain; and now I think of it, I have often heard him say, talking to himself, that he would turn knight-errant, and go about the world in quest of adventures. The devil and Barabbas take all such books, that have thus spoiled the finest understanding in all La Mancha.'

The niece joined with her, and said moreover:

'Know, master Nicholas' (for that was the barber's name), 'that it has often happened, that my honoured uncle has continued poring on these confounded books of disadventures two whole days and nights; and then throwing the book out of his hand, he would draw his sword, and fence back-stroke and fore-stroke, with the walls; and when he was heartily tired, would say, he had killed four giants as tall as so many steeples, and that the sweat, which ran from him, when weary, was the blood of the wounds he had received in the fight; and then he would presently drink off a large jug of cold water, and be as quiet and as well as ever, telling us that water was a most precious liquor brought him by the sage Esquife,* a great enchanter, and his friend. But I take the blame of all this to myself, that I did not advertise you, gentlemen, of my dear uncle's extravagances, before they were come to the height they now are, that you might have prevented them by burning all those cursed books, of which he has so great a store, and which as justly deserve to be committed to the flames, as if they were heretical.'

'I say the same,' quoth the priest, 'and in faith to-morrow shall not pass without holding a public inquisition against them, and condemning them to the fire, that they may no more minister occasion to those who read them, to do what I fear my good friend has done.'

All this the peasant and Don Quixote overheard, and it confirmed the countryman in the belief of his neighbour's infirmity; and so he began to cry aloud:

'Open the doors, gentlemen, to Señor Valdovinos and the Marquess of Mantua, who comes dangerously wounded, and to Señor Abindarraez the Moor, whom the valorous Rodrigo de Narvaez, governor of Antequera, brings as his prisoner.'

At hearing this they all came out; and as some knew their friend, and others their master and uncle, they all ran to embrace him, who was not yet alighted from the ass, for indeed he could not.

'Forbear all of you,' he cried, 'for I am sorely wounded through my horse's fault: carry me to my bed, and if it be possible, send for the sage Urganda, to search and heal my wounds.'

'Look ye, in the devil's name,' said the housekeeper immediately, 'if my heart did not tell me right, on which leg my
master halted. Get up stairs, in God's name; for, without the
help of that same Urgada,* we shall find a way to cure you
ourselves. Cursed, say I again, and a hundred times cursed,
be those books of knight-errantry that have brought your
worship to this pass.'

They carried him presently to his chamber, and searching
for his wounds, they found none at all: and he told them he
was only bruised by a great fall he got with his horse
Rosinante, as he was fighting with ten of the most prodigious
and audacious giants that were to be found on the earth.

'Ho, ho,' says the priest, 'what! there are giants too in the
dance? By my faith, I shall set fire to them all before
to-morrow night.'

They asked Don Quixote a thousand questions, and he
would answer nothing, but only desired something to eat,
and that they would let him sleep, which was what he stood
most in need of. They did so, and the priest inquired
particularly of the countryman in what condition he had
found Don Quixote; who gave him an account of the whole,
with the extravagances he had uttered, both at the time of
finding him and all the way home; which increased the
Licentiate's desire to do what he did the next day, which was
to call on his friend, master Nicholas the barber, with whom
he came to Don Quixote's house.

CHAPTER 6

*Of the pleasant and grand scrutiny made by the priest and
the barber in our ingenious gentleman's library.*

WHILST Don Quixote still slept on, the priest asked the
niece for the keys of the chamber where the books were,
those authors of the mischief; and she delivered them with
a very good will. They all went in, and the housekeeper with
them. They found above a hundred volumes in folio, very
well bound, besides a great many small ones. And no sooner

did the housekeeper see them, than she ran out of the room in great haste, and immediately returned with a pot of holy water and a bunch of hyssop, and said:

'Señor Licentiate, take this and sprinkle the room, lest some enchanter, of the many these books abound with, should enchant us in revenge for what we intend to do, in banishing them out of the world.'

The priest smiled at the housekeeper's simplicity, and ordered the barber to reach him the books one by one, that they might see what they treated of; for, perhaps, they might find some that might not deserve to be chastised by fire.

'No,' said the niece, 'there is no reason why any of them should be spared; for they have all been mischief-makers: it will be best to fling them out of the window into the court-yard, and make a pile of them, and set fire to it, or else carry them into the back-yard, and there make a bonfire of them, and the smoke will offend nobody.'

The housekeeper said the same; so eagerly did they both thirst for the death of those innocents. But the priest would not agree to that, without first reading the titles at least.

The first that master Nicholas put into his hands, was *Amadis de Gaul*, in four parts;* and the priest said:

'There seems to be some mystery in this; for, as I have heard say, this was the first book of chivalry printed in Spain, and all the rest have had their foundation and rise from it; and therefore I think, as head of so pernicious a sect, we ought to condemn him to the fire without mercy.'

'Not so, Sir,' said the barber; 'for I have heard also, that it is the best of all books of this kind; and therefore, as being singular in his art, he ought to be spared.'

'It is true,' said the priest, 'and for that reason his life is granted him for the present. Let us see that other that stands next him.'

'It is,' said the barber, 'the *Adventures of Esplandian*,* the legitimate son of Amadis de Gaul.'

'Verily,' said the priest, 'the goodness of the father shall avail the son nothing; take him, mistress housekeeper, open yon casement, and throw him into the yard, and let him give a beginning to the pile for the intended bonfire.'

The housekeeper did so with much satisfaction, and honest *Esplandian* was sent flying into the yard, there to wait with patience for the fire with which he was threatened.

'Proceed,' said the priest.

'The next,' said the barber, 'is *Amadis of Greece*;* yea, and all these on this side, I believe, are of the lineage of Amadis.'

'Then into the yard with them all,' quoth the priest; 'for rather than not burn queen Pintiquiniestra, and the shepherd Darinel with his eclogues, and the devilish intricate discourses of its author, I would burn the father who begot me, did I meet him in the garb of a knight-errant.'

'Of the same opinion am I,' said the barber.

'And I too,' added the niece.

'Since it is so,' said the housekeeper, 'away with them all into the yard.'

They handed them to her; and, there being great numbers of them, to save herself the trouble of the stairs, she threw them all, the shortest way, out of the window.

'What tun of an author is that?' said the priest.

'That is,' answered the barber, '*Don Olivante de Laura*.'*

'The author of that book,' said the priest, 'was the same who composed *The Garden of Flowers*;* and in good truth I know not which of the two books is the truest, or rather the least lying; I can only say that this goes to the yard for its arrogance and absurdity.'

'This that follows is *Florismarte of Hyrcania*,'* said the barber.

'What! is Señor Florismarte there?' replied the priest: 'now, in good faith, he shall soon make his appearance in the yard, notwithstanding his strange birth and chimerical adventures; for the harshness and dryness of his style will admit of no excuse. To the yard with him, and this other, mistress housekeeper.'

'With all my heart, dear Sir,' answered she, and with much joy executed what she was commanded.

'This is *The Knight Platir*,'* said the barber.

'That,' said the priest, 'is an ancient book, and I find nothing in him deserving pardon; let him keep the rest company without more words.' Which was accordingly done. They opened another book, and found it entitled, *The Knight of the Cross*.*

'So religious a title,' quoth the priest, 'might, one would think, atone for the ignorance of the author; but it is a common saying, The devil lurks behind the cross: so to the fire with him.'

The barber, taking down another book, said:

'This is *The Mirror of Chivalry*.'*

'Oh! I know his worship very well,' quoth the priest.

'Here comes Señor Reynaldos de Montalvan, with his friends and companions, greater thieves than Cacus; and the twelve peers, with the faithful historiographer Turpin. However, I am only for condemning them to perpetual banishment, because they contain some things of the famous Mateo Boiardo's invention; from whom also the Christian poet Ludovico Ariosto spun his web:* but if I find even him here, and speaking any other language than his own, I will show him no respect; but, if he speaks in his own tongue, I will put him upon my head.'*

'I have him in Italian,' said the barber, 'but I do not understand him.'

'Neither is it any great matter whether you understand him or not,' answered the priest; 'and we would willingly have excused the good captain* from bringing him into Spain, and making him a Castilian; for he has deprived him of a great deal of his native value: and this is the misfortune of all those who undertake to translate books of verse into other languages; for, with all their care and skill, they can never raise them to the pitch they were at in their first production. I pronounce, in short, that this, and all other books that shall be found treating of French matters, be thrown aside, and deposited in some dry vault, until we can determine with more deliberation what is to be done with them, excepting *Bernardo del Carpio*,* and another called *Roncesvalles*,* who, if they fall into my hands, shall pass into the housekeeper's, and thence into the fire, without any remission.'

The barber confirmed the sentence, and held it for good, and a matter well determined, knowing that the priest was so good a Christian, and so much a friend to truth, that he would not utter a falsehood for all the world. And so opening another book, he saw it was *Palmerin de Oliva*,* and next it

another called *Palmerin of England*, which the licentiate espying, said:

'Let this *Oliva* be torn to pieces and burnt, that not so much
as the ashes remain; but let *Palmerin of England* be preserved,
and kept, as a singular piece; and let such another case be made
for it, as that which Alexander found among the spoils of
Darius, and appropriated to preserve the works of the poet
Homer. This book, gossip, is considerable upon two accounts;
the one, that it is very good in itself; and the other, because
there is a tradition that it was written by an ingenious king of
Portugal. All the adventures of the Castle of Miraguarda are
most excellent, and artificial; the dialogue courtly and clear; and
the decorum preserved in all the characters with great judgement
and propriety. Therefore, master Nicholas, saving your better
judgement, let this and *Amadis de Gaul* be exempted from the
fire, and let all the rest perish without any further inquiry.'

'Not so, gossip,' replied the barber; 'for this that I have
here is the renowned *Don Belianis*.'

The priest replied:

'This, with the second, third, and fourth parts, wants a
little rhubarb to purge away its excessive choler; besides, we
must remove all that relates to the Castle of Fame, and other
impertinences of greater consequence; wherefore let them
have the benefit of transportation, and as they show signs of
amendment, they shall be treated with mercy or justice; in
the meantime, neighbour, give them room in your house; but
let nobody read them.'

'With all my heart,' quoth the barber, and without tiring
himself any further in turning over books of chivalry, he bid
the housekeeper take all the great ones, and throw them into
the yard. This was not spoken to one stupid or deaf, but to
one who had a greater mind to be burning them than weaving the finest and largest web. And therefore, laying hold of
seven or eight at once, she tossed them out at the window.
By her taking so much together, there fell one at the barber's
feet, who had a mind to see what it was, and found it to
be *The History of the renowned knight Tirante the White*.*

'God save me!' quoth the priest, with a loud voice, 'is
Tirante the White there? Give me him here, neighbour; for I

make account I have found in him a treasure of delight, and a mine of entertainment. Here we have Don Kyrieleison of Montalvan, a valorous knight, and his brother Thomas of Montalvan, and the knight Fonseca, and the combat which the valiant Tirante fought with [the mastiff], and the smart conceits of the damsel Plazerdemivida, with the amours and artifices of the widow Reposada; and madam the empress in love with her squire Hypolito. Verily, gossip, in its way, it is the best book in the world: here the knights eat and sleep, and die in their beds, and make their wills before their deaths; with several things which are wanting in other books of this kind. Notwithstanding all this, I tell you, the author deserved, for writing so many foolish things seriously, to be sent to the galleys for all the days of his life: carry it home, and read it, and you will find all I say of him to be true.'

'I will do so,' answered the barber; 'but what shall we do with these little books that remain?'

'These,' said the priest, 'are probably not books of chivalry, but of poetry:' and opening one he found it was the *Diana* of George of Montemayor,* and said (believing all the rest to be of the same kind):

'These do not deserve to be burnt like the rest; for they cannot do the mischief that those of chivalry have done; they are works of genius and fancy, and do nobody any hurt.'

'O Sir,' said the niece, 'pray order these to be burnt with the rest; for should my uncle be cured of this distemper of chivalry, he may possibly, by reading these books, take it into his head to turn shepherd, and wander through the woods and fields singing and playing on a pipe; and, what would be still worse, to turn poet, which they say is an incurable and contagious disease.'

'The damsel says true,' quoth the priest; 'and it will not be amiss to remove this stumbling-block and occasion out of our friend's way. And since we begin with the *Diana* of Montemayor, I am of opinion not to burn it, but to take away all that treats of the sage Felicia, and of the enchanted fountain, and almost all the longer poems; and leave him the prose in God's name, and the honour of being the first in that kind of writing.'

'This that follows,' said the barber, 'is *Diana*, called the Second, by [the] Salmantino;* and another of the same name, whose author is Gil Polo.'*

'The Salmantinian,' answered the priest, 'may accompany and increase the number of the condemned; to the yard with him; but let that of Gil Polo be preserved, as if it were written by Apollo himself. Proceed, gossip, and let us dispatch, for it grows late.'

'This,' said the barber, opening another, 'is the *Ten Books of the Fortune of Love*,* composed by Antonio de Lofrasso, a Sardinian poet.'

'By the holy orders I have received,' said the priest, 'since Apollo was Apollo, the muses muses, and the poets poets, so humorous and so whimsical a book as this was never written; it is the best and most singular of the kind that ever appeared in the world; and he who has not read it, may reckon that he never read anything of taste: give it me here, gossip, for I value the finding it more than if I had been presented with a cassock of Florence satin.'

He laid it aside with exceeding pleasure, and the barber proceeded, saying:

'These that follow are *The Shepherd of Iberia,** The Nymphs of Henares,** and *The Cures of Jealousy.'**

'There is no more to be done,' said the priest, 'but to deliver them up to the secular arm of the housekeeper; and ask me not why, for then we should never have done.'

'This that comes next is *The Shepherd of Filida.'**

'He is no shepherd,' said the priest, 'but an ingenious courtier; let him be preserved and laid up as a precious jewel.'

'This bulky volume here,' said the barber, 'is entitled *The Treasure of Divers Poems.'**

'Had they been fewer,' replied the priest, 'they would have been more esteemed; it is necessary this book should be weeded and cleared of all the low things interspersed amongst its sublimities; let it be preserved, both as the author is my friend, and out of regard to other more heroic and exalted pieces of his writing.'

'This,' pursued the barber, 'is a *Book of Songs** by Lopez Maldonado.'

'The author of this book, also,' replied the priest, 'is a great friend of mine: his verses, sung by himself, raise admiration in the hearers; and such is the sweetness of his voice in singing them that they perfectly enchant. He is a little too prolix in his eclogues; but there can never be too much of what is really good; let it be kept with the select. But what book is that next to it?'

'The *Galatea* of Michael de Cervantes,' said the barber.

'That Cervantes has been a great friend of mine these many years, and I know that he is better acquainted with misfortunes than with poetry. His book has somewhat of good invention in it; he proposes something, but concludes nothing: we must wait for the second part, which he promises;* perhaps, on his amendment, he may obtain that entire pardon which is now denied him: in the meantime, gossip, keep him a recluse in your chamber.'

'With all my heart,' answered the barber; 'and here come three together; *The Araucana** of Don Alonso de Ercilla; *The Austríada** of John Rufo, a magistrate of Córdova; and *The Monserrate** of Christoval de Virues, a poet of Valencia.'

'These three books,' said the priest, 'are the best that are written in heroic verse in the Castilian tongue, and may stand in competition with the most famous of Italy; let them be preserved as the best performances in poetry Spain can boast of.'

The priest grew tired of looking over so many books, and so, inside and contents unknown, he would have all the rest burnt. But the barber had already opened one called the *Tears of Angelica*.*

'I should have shed tears myself' (said the priest, hearing the name), 'had I ordered that book to be burnt; for its author was one of the most famous poets, not of Spain only, but of the whole world, and translated some fables of Ovid with great success.'

CHAPTER 7

Of the second sally of our good knight Don Quixote de la Mancha.

WHILE they were thus employed, Don Quixote began to call out aloud, saying:

'Here, here, valorous knights, here ye must exert the force of your valiant arms; for the courtiers begin to get the better of the tournament.'

This noise and outcry, to which they all ran, put a stop to all further scrutiny of the books that remained; and therefore it is believed, that to the fire, without being seen or heard, went *The Carolea,** and *Lion of Spain,** with *The Acts of the Emperor*, composed by Don Louis de Avila,* which, without doubt, must have been among those that were left; and perhaps had the priest seen them, they had not undergone so rigorous a sentence. When they came to Don Quixote, he was already got out of bed, and continued his outcries and ravings with his drawn sword, laying furiously about him, back-stroke, and fore-stroke, being as broad awake as if he had never been asleep. They closed in with him, and laid him upon his bed by main force; and after he was a little composed, turning himself to talk to the priest, he said:

'Certainly, my lord archbishop Turpin, it is a great disgrace to us, who call ourselves the twelve peers, to let the knights-courtiers carry off the victory without more opposition, after we, the adventurers, had gained the prize in the three preceding days.'

'Say no more, good gossip,' said the priest; 'it may be God's will to change our fortune, and what is lost to-day may be won to-morrow; mind your health for the present; for I think you must needs be extremely fatigued, if not sorely wounded.'

'Wounded! no,' said Don Quixote; 'but bruised and battered I am for certain; for that bastard, Don Roldan, has pounded me to mash with the trunk of an oak, and all out of mere envy, because he sees that I am the sole rival of his prowess. But let me never more be called Reynaldos de

Montalvan, if, as soon as I am able to rise from this bed, I do not make him pay dear for it, in spite of all his enchantments; but at present bring me some breakfast, for I know nothing will do me so much good, and let me alone to revenge myself.'

They did so; they gave him some victuals, and he fell fast asleep again, and left them in fresh admiration at his madness.

That night the housekeeper set fire to, and burnt, all the books that were in the yard, and in the house too; and some must have perished, that deserved to be treasured up in perpetual archives; but their fate, and the laziness of the scrutineer, would not permit it; and in them was fulfilled the saying, that 'the just sometimes suffer for the unjust'. One of the remedies which the priest and barber prescribed at that time for their friend's malady, was to alter his apartment, and wall up the room where the books had been, that when he got up he might not find them; in hopes that the cause being removed, the effect might cease, and that they should pretend that an enchanter had carried them away, room and all, which was presently done accordingly. Within two days after Don Quixote got up, and the first thing he did was to visit his books; and, not finding the room where he left it, he went up and down looking for it: he came to the place where the door used to be, and he felt with his hands, and stared about every way without speaking a word; but after some time he asked the housekeeper whereabouts the room stood where his books were. She, who was already well tutored what to answer, said to him:

'What room or what nothing, does your worship look for? there is neither room nor books in this house; for the devil himself has carried all away.'

'It was not the devil,' said the niece, 'but an enchanter, who came one night upon a cloud, after the day of your departure hence, and alighting from a serpent on which he rode, entered into the room; and I know not what he did there, but after some little time, out he came, flying through the roof, and left the house full of smoke; and when we went to see what he had been doing, we saw neither books nor room; only we very well remember, both I and mistress housekeeper here, that when the old thief went away, he said, with a loud voice, that, for a secret enmity he bore to the owner of those books and of the room, he had done a mischief in this house, which should soon be manifest: he told us also, that he was called the sage Muñaton.'

'Friston* he meant to say,' quoth Don Quixote.

'I know not,' answered the housekeeper, 'whether his name be Friston, or Friton: all I know is, that it ended in ton.'

'It doth so,' replied Don Quixote: 'he is a wise enchanter, a great enemy of mine, and bears me a grudge, because by his skill and learning he knows that, in process of time, I shall engage in single combat with a knight whom he favours, and shall vanquish him, without his being able to prevent it; and for this cause he endeavours to do me all the unkindness he can: but let him know from me, it will be difficult for him to withstand or avoid what is decreed by heaven.'

'Who doubts of that?' said the niece; 'but, dear uncle, who puts you upon these squabbles? Would it not be better to stay quietly at home, and not ramble about the world, seeking for better bread than wheaten, and not considering that many go for wool, and return shorn themselves.'

'Oh! dear niece,' answered Don Quixote, 'how little do you know of the matter: before they shall shear me I will pluck and tear off the beards of all those who dare think of touching the tip of a single hair of mine.'

Neither of them would make any further reply, for they saw his choler begin to take fire.

He stayed after this fifteen days at home, very quiet, without discovering any symptom of an inclination to repeat his late frolics; in which time there passed very pleasant discourses between him and his two gossips, the priest and the barber; he affirming that the world stood in need of nothing so much as knights-errant and the revival of chivalry. The priest sometimes contradicted him, and at other times acquiesced; for had he not made use of this artifice, there would have been no means left to bring him to reason.

In the meantime Don Quixote tampered with* a labourer, a neighbour of his, and an honest man (if such an epithet

may be given to one that is poor), but very shallow-brained.
In short, he said so much, used so many arguments, and
promised him such great matters, that the poor fellow resolved to sally out with him, and serve him as his squire.
Among other things, Don Quixote told him he should
dispose himself to go with him willingly; for some time or
other such an adventure might present, that an island might
be won in the turn of a hand, and he be left governor thereof.
With these and the like promises, Sancho Panza (for that was
the labourer's name) left his wife and children, and hired
himself for a squire to his neighbour. Don Quixote presently
cast about how to raise money, and by selling one thing, and
pawning another, and losing by all, he scraped together a
tolerable sum. He fitted himself likewise with a buckler, which
he borrowed of a friend, and patching up his broken helmet
the best he could, he acquainted his squire Sancho of the
day and hour he intended to set out, that he might provide
himself with what he should find to be most needful. Above
all, he charged him not to forget a wallet; and Sancho said
he would be sure to carry one, and that he intended also to
take with him an ass he had, being a very good one, because
he was not used to travel much on foot. As to the ass, Don
Quixote paused a little, endeavouring to recollect whether
any knight-errant had ever carried a squire mounted ass-wise:
but no instance of the kind occurred to his memory. However, he consented that he should take his ass with him,
purposing to accommodate him more honourably, the first
opportunity, by dismounting the first discourteous knight he
should meet. He provided himself also with shirts, and what
other things he could, conformably to the advice given him
by the innkeeper.

All which being done and accomplished, Don Quixote and
Sancho Panza, without taking leave, the one of his wife and
children, and the other of his housekeeper and niece, one
night sallied out of the village, unperceived by any one; and
they travelled so hard, that by break of day, they believed
themselves secure of not being found, though search were
made after them. Sancho Panza went riding upon his ass like
any patriarch, with his wallet and leathern bottle, and with a

vehement desire to find himself governor of the island which his master had promised him. Don Quixote happened to take the same route he had done in his first expedition, through the plain of Montiel, which he passed over with less uneasiness than the time before; for it was early in the morning, and the rays of the sun darting on them aslant gave them no disturbance. Now Sancho Panza said to his master:

'I beseech your worship, good Sir knight-errant, that you forget not your promise concerning that same island; for I shall know how to govern it, be it never so big.'

To which Don Quixote answered:

'You must know, friend Sancho Panza, that it was a custom much in use among the knights-errant of old, to make their squires governors of the islands or kingdoms they conquered; and I am determined that so laudable a custom shall not be lost for me: on the contrary, I resolve to outdo them in it; for they sometimes, and perhaps most times, stayed till their squires were grown old; and when they were worn out in their service, and had undergone many bad days and worse nights, they gave them some title, as that of Count, or at least Marquess, of some valley or province, be it greater or less: but if you live and I live, before six days are ended, I may probably win such a kingdom, as may have others depending on it, as fit as if they were cast in a mould, for thee to be crowned king of one of them. And do not think this any extraordinary matter; for things fall out to such knights by such unforeseen and unexpected ways, that I may easily give thee more than I promise.'

'So then,' answered Sancho Panza, 'if I were a king by some of those miracles you are pleased to mention, Mari Gutierrez* my crooked rib, would at least come to be a queen, and my children infantes.'

'Who doubts it?' answered Don Quixote.

'I doubt it,' replied Sancho Panza; 'for I am verily persuaded, that if God were to rain down kingdoms upon the earth, none of them would sit well upon the head of Mari Gutierrez; for you must know, Sir, she is not worth two farthings for a queen. The title of countess would sit better upon her, and that too with the help of God, and good friends.'

'Recommend her to God, Sancho,' answered Don Quixote, 'and he will do what is best for her: but do thou have a care not to debase thy mind so low, as to content thyself with being less than a lord-lieutenant.'

'Sir, I will not,' answered Sancho, 'especially having so great a man for my master as your worship, who will know how to give me whatever is most fitting for me, and what you find me best able to bear.'

CHAPTER 8

Of the good success which the valorous Don Quixote had in the dreadful and never-before-imagined adventure of the windmills, with other events worthy to be recorded.

As they were thus discoursing, they perceived some thirty or forty windmills that are in that plain; and as soon as Don Quixote espied them, he said to his squire:

'Fortune disposes our affairs better than we ourselves could have desired; look yonder, friend Sancho Panza, where you may discover somewhat more than thirty monstrous giants, with whom I intend to fight, and take away all their lives: with whose spoils we will begin to enrich ourselves; for it is lawful war, and doing God good service to take away so wicked a generation from off the face of the earth.'

'What giants?' said Sancho Panza.

'Those you see yonder,' answered his master, 'with those long arms; for some of them are wont to have them almost of the length of two leagues.'

'Consider, Sir,' answered Sancho, 'that those which appear yonder, are not giants, but windmills; and what seem to be arms are the sails, which, whirled about by the wind, make the millstone go.'

'One may easily see,' answered Don Quixote, 'that you are not versed in the business of adventures: they are giants; and,

if you are afraid, get aside and pray, whilst I engage with
them in a fierce and unequal combat.'

And so saying, he clapped spurs to Rosinante, without
minding the cries his squire sent after him, assuring him
that those he went to assault were without all doubt,
windmills, and not giants. But he was so fully possessed
that they were giants, that he neither heard the outcries of
his squire Sancho, nor yet discerned what they were,
though he was very near them, but went on, crying out
aloud:

'Fly not, ye cowards and vile caitiffs; for it is a single knight
who assaults you.'

Now the wind rose a little, and the great sails began to
move: which Don Quixote perceiving, he said:

'Well, though you should move more arms than the giant
Briareus,* you shall pay for it.'

And so saying, and recommending himself devoutly to
his lady Dulcinea, beseeching her to succour him in the
present danger, being well covered with his buckler, and
setting his lance in the rest, he rushed on as fast as
Rosinante could gallop, and attacked the first mill before
him; and running his lance into the sail, the wind whirled
it about with so much violence that it broke the lance to
shivers, dragging horse and rider after it, and tumbling
them over and over on the plain, in very evil plight. Sancho
Panza hastened to his assistance, as fast as his ass could
carry him; and when he came up to him, he found him
not able to stir; so violent was the blow he and Rosinante
had received in falling.

'God save me,' quoth Sancho, 'did not I warn you to have
a care of what you did, for that they were nothing but
windmills; and nobody could mistake them, but one that had
the like in his head.'

'Peace, friend Sancho,' answered Don Quixote; 'for matters
of war are, of all others, most subject to continual mutations.
Now I verily believe, and it is most certainly so, that the sage
Friston who stole away my chamber and books, has metamorphosed these giants into windmills, on purpose to deprive
me of the glory of vanquishing them, so great is the enmity

he bears me; but when he has done his worst, his wicked arts will avail but little against the goodness of my sword.'

'God grant it, as he can,' answered Sancho Panza; and, helping him to rise, he mounted him again upon Rosinante, who was half shoulder-slipped.

And discoursing of the late adventure, they followed the road that led to the pass of Lapice; for there, Don Quixote said, they could not fail to meet with many and various adventures, it being a great thoroughfare; and yet he went on very melancholy for want of his lance; and, speaking of it to his squire, he said:

'I remember to have read that a certain Spanish knight, called Diego Perez de Vargas,* having broken his sword in fight, tore off a huge branch or limb from an oak, and performed such wonders with it that day, and dashed out the brains of so many Moors, that he was surnamed Machuca;* and from that day forward, he and his descendants bore the names of Vargas and Machuca. I tell you this because from the first oak or crabtree we meet, I mean to tear such another limb, at least as good as that; and I purpose and resolve to do such feats with it, that you shall deem yourself most fortunate in meriting to behold them; and to be an eye-witness of things which can scarcely be believed.'

'God's will be done,' quoth Sancho: 'I believe all just as you say, Sir: but, pray, set yourself upright in your saddle; for you seem to me to ride sideling, occasioned, doubtless, by your being so sorely bruised by the fall.'

'It is certainly so,' answered Don Quixote; 'and if I do not complain of pain, it is because knights-errant are not allowed to complain of any wound whatever, though their entrails came out at it.'

'If it be so, I have nothing to reply,' answered Sancho; 'but God knows I should be glad to hear your worship complain, when anything ails you. As for myself, I must complain of the least pain I feel, unless this business of not complaining be understood to extend to the squires of knights-errant.'

Don Quixote could not forbear smiling at the simplicity of his squire, and told him he might complain whenever, and as much as he pleased, with or without cause, having never yet read anything to the contrary in the laws of chivalry.

Sancho put him in mind that it was time to dine. His master answered, that at present he had no need; but that he might eat whenever he thought fit. With this licence, Sancho adjusted himself the best he could upon his beast; and taking out what he carried in his wallet, he jogged on eating, behind his master, very leisurely, and now and then lifted the bottle to his mouth with so much relish, that the best-fed victualler of Malaga might have envied him. And whilst he went on in this manner, repeating his draughts, he thought no more of the promises his master had made him; nor did he think it any toil, but rather a recreation to go in quest of adventures, though never so perilous. In fine, they passed that night among some trees, and from one of them Don Quixote tore a withered branch, that might serve him in some sort for a lance, and fixed it to the iron head or spear of that which was broken. All that night Don Quixote slept not a wink, ruminating on his lady Dulcinea, in conformity to what he had read in his books where the knights are wont to pass many nights together, without closing their eyes, in forests and deserts, entertaining themselves with the remembrance of their mistresses. Not so did Sancho pass the night; whose stomach being full (and not of dandelion-water) he made but one sleep of it: and if his master had not roused him, neither the beams of the sun that darted full in his face, nor the melody of the birds, which in great numbers most cheerfully saluted the approach of the new day, could have awaked him. At this uprising he took a swig at his bottle, and found it much lighter than the evening before; which grieved his very heart, for he did not think they were in the way to remedy that defect very soon. Don Quixote would not break his fast; for, as it is said, he resolved to subsist upon savoury remembrances. They returned to the way they had entered upon the day before, toward [Puerto] Lápice, which they discovered about three in the afternoon.

'Here' (said Don Quixote, espying it) 'brother Sancho Panza, we may thrust our hands up to the elbows in what they call adventures. But take this caution with you, that, though you should see me in the greatest peril in the world, you must not lay your hand to your sword to defend me, unless you see that they who assault me are a vile mob and mean scoundrels; in that case you may assist me: but if they should be knights, it is in nowise lawful nor allowed by the laws of chivalry, that you should intermeddle, until you are dubbed a knight.'

'I assure you, sir,' answered Sancho, 'your worship shall be obeyed most punctually herein, and the rather, because I am naturally very peaceable, and an enemy to thrusting myself into brangles and squabbles: but for all that, as to what regards the defence of my own person, I shall make no great account of those same laws, since both divine and human allow every one to defend himself against whoever would annoy him.'

'I say no less,' answered Don Quixote; 'but in the business of assisting me against knights, you must restrain and keep in your natural impetuosity.'

'I say I will do so,' answered Sancho; 'and I will observe this precept as religiously as the Lord's day.'

As they were thus discoursing, there appeared in the road two monks of the order of St. Benedict, mounted upon two dromedaries; for the mules whereon they rode were not much less. They wore travelling masks, and carried umbrellas. Behind them came a coach, and four or five men on horseback, who accompanied it, with two muleteers on foot. There was in the coach, as it was afterwards known, a certain Biscaine lady, going to Seville to her husband, who was there ready to embark for the Indies in a very honourable post. The monks came not in her company, though they were travelling the same road. But scarcely had Don Quixote espied them, when he said to his squire:

'Either I am deceived, or this is like to prove the most famous adventure that ever was seen; for those black bulks that appear yonder must be, and without doubt are enchanters, who are carrying away some princess, whom they have stolen, in that coach; and I am obliged to redress this wrong to the utmost of my power.'

'This may prove a worse job than the windmills,' said Sancho: 'pray, Sir, take notice that those are Benedictine monks, and the coach must belong to some travellers. Pray, hearken to my advice, and have a care what you do, and let not the devil deceive you.'

'I have already told you, Sancho,' answered Don Quixote, 'that you know little of the business of adventures: what I say is true, and you will see it presently.'

And so saying, he advanced forward and planted himself in the midst of the highway, by which the monks were to pass; and when they were so near, that he supposed they could hear what he said, he cried out with a loud voice:

'Diabolical and monstrous race, either instantly release the high-born princesses, whom you are carrying away in that coach against their wills, or prepare for instant death, as the just chastisement of your wicked deeds.'

The monks stopped their mules, and stood admiring* as well at the figure of Don Quixote, as at his expressions; to which they answered:

'Señor Cavalier, we are neither diabolical nor monstrous, but a couple of monks of the Benedictine order, who are travelling on our own business, and are entirely ignorant whether any princesses are carried away by force in that coach, or not.'

'Soft words do nothing with me; for I know ye, treacherous scoundrels,' said Don Quixote: and without staying for any other reply, he clapped spurs to Rosinante, and with his lance couched, ran at the foremost monk with such fury and resolution, that, if he had not slid down from his mule, he would have brought him to the ground, in spite of his teeth,* and wounded to boot, if not killed outright.

The second monk seeing his comrade treated in this manner, clapped spurs to his mule's sides, and began to scour along the plain, lighter than the wind itself. Sancho Panza, seeing the monk on the ground, leaped nimbly from his ass, and running to him, began to take off his habit. In the meanwhile the monk's two lackeys coming up, asked him why he was stripping their master of his clothes. Sancho answered, that they were his lawful perquisites, as being the spoils of the battle which his lord Don Quixote had just won. The lackeys, who did not understand raillery, nor what was meant by spoils or battles, seeing Don Quixote at a distance, talking with those in the coach, fell upon Sancho, and threw him down, and, leaving him not a hair in his beard,* gave him a hearty kicking and left him stretched on the ground, breathless and senseless. And without losing a minute, the monk got upon his mule again, trembling, and terribly frighted, and as pale as death; and no sooner was he mounted, but he spurred after his companion, who stood waiting at a good distance, to see what would be the issue of that strange encounter; but being unwilling to wait the event, they went on their way, crossing themselves oftener than if the devil had been close at their heels.

Don Quixote, as was said, stood talking to the lady in the coach, saying:

'Your beauty, dear lady, may dispose of your person as pleaseth you best, for your haughty ravishers lie prostrate on the ground, overthrown by my invincible arm; and that you may not be at any pains to learn the name of your deliverer, know that I am called Don Quixote de la Mancha, knight-errant and adventurer, and captive to the peerless and beauteous Dulcinea del Toboso; and in requital of the benefit you have received at my hands, all I desire is, that you would return to Toboso, and in my name, present yourselves before that lady, and tell her what I have done to obtain your liberty.'

All that Don Quixote said was overhead by a certain squire who accompanied the coach, a Biscainer, who finding he would not let the coach go forward, but insisted upon its immediately returning to Toboso, flew at Don Quixote, and taking hold of his lance, addressed him in bad Castilian, and worse Biscaine, after this manner:

'Begone, cavalier, and the devil go with thee: I swear by that God that made me, if thou dost not quit the coach, thou forfeitest thy life, as I am a Biscainer.'

Don Quixote understood him very well, and with great calmness answered:

'Wert thou a gentleman, as thou art not, I would before now have chastised thy folly and presumption, thou pitiful slave.'

To which the Biscainer replied:

'I no gentleman! I swear by the great God thou liest, as I am a Christian; if thou wilt throw away thy lance, and draw thy sword, thou shalt see I will make no more of thee than a cat does of a mouse: Biscainer by land, gentleman by sea, gentleman for the devil, and thou liest: look then if thou hast anything else to say.'

'Thou shalt see that presently, as said Agrages,'* answered Don Quixote; and throwing down his lance, he drew his sword, and grasping his buckler, set upon the Biscainer, with a resolution to kill him. The Biscainer, seeing him come on in that manner, though he would fain have alighted from his mule, which, being of the worst kind of hackneys, was not to be depended upon, had yet only time to draw his sword; but it happened well for him that he was close to the coachside, out of which he snatched a cushion, which served him for a shield; and immediately to it they went, as if they had been mortal enemies. The rest of the company would have made peace between them, but they could not; for the Biscainer swore in his gibberish, that, if they would not let him finish the combat, he would kill his mistress, and everybody that offered to hinder him. The lady of the coach, amazed and affrighted at what she saw, bid the coachman put a little out of the way, and so sat at a distance, beholding the rigorous conflict; in the progress of which, the Biscainer gave Don Quixote such a huge stroke on one of his shoulders, and above his buckler, that, had it not been for his coat of mail, he had cleft him down to the girdle. Don Quixote feeling the weight of that unmeasurable blow, cried out aloud, saying:

'O lady of my soul, Dulcinea, flower of all beauty, succour this thy knight, who, to satisfy thy great goodness, exposes himself to this rigorous extremity.'

The saying this, the drawing his sword, the covering himself well with his buckler, and falling furiously on the Biscainer, was all done in one moment, he resolving to venture all on the fortune of one single blow. The Biscainer who saw him coming thus upon him, and perceived his bravery by his resolution, resolved to do the same thing that Don Quixote had done; and so he waited for him, covering himself well with his cushion, but was not able to turn his mule about to the right, or the left, she being already so jaded, and so little used to such sport, that she would not stir a step.

Now Don Quixote, as has been said, advanced against the wary Biscainer, with his lifted sword, fully determined to cleave him asunder; and the Biscainer expected him, with his sword also lifted up, and guarded by his cushion. All the bystanders were trembling, and in suspense what might be the event of those prodigious blows with which they threatened each other; and the lady of the coach, and her waiting-women, were making a thousand vows and promises of offerings, to all the images and places of devotion in Spain, that God would deliver them and their squire from the great peril they were in.

But the misfortune is that the author of this history, in this very crisis, leaves the combat unfinished, excusing himself, that he could find no more written of these exploits of Don Quixote than what he has already related. It is true indeed, that the second undertaker of this work could not believe, that so curious an history could be lost in oblivion, or that the wits of La Mancha should have so little curiosity, as not to preserve in their archives or their cabinets, some papers that treated of this famous knight; and upon that presumption he did not despair to find the conclusion of this delectable history: which, heaven favouring him, he has at last done, in the manner as shall be recounted in the second part.

CHAPTER 9

Wherein is concluded, and an end put to the stupendous battle between the vigorous Biscainer and the valiant Manchegan.

IN the first part of this history* we left the valiant Biscainer and the renowned Don Quixote with their swords lifted up and naked, ready to discharge two such furious and cleaving strokes, as must, if they had lighted full, at least have divided

the combatants from head to heel, and split them asunder
like a pomegranate: but in that critical instant this relishing
history stopped short, and was left imperfect, without the
author's giving us any notice where what remained of it might
be found.

This grieved me extremely: and the pleasure of having read
so little was turned into disgust to think what small probability there was of finding the much that, in my opinion,
was yet wanting of so savoury a story. It seemed to me
impossible, and quite beside all laudable custom, that so
accomplished a knight should want a sage, to undertake the
penning his unparalleled exploits, a circumstance that never
before failed any of those knights-errant, who travelled in
quest of adventures;* every one of whom had one or two
sages, made, as it were on purpose, who not only recorded
their actions, but described likewise their most minute and
trifling thoughts, though never so secret. Surely then so
worthy a knight could not be so unfortunate, as to want what
Platir and others like him, abounded with. For this reason I
could not be induced to believe that so gallant a history could
be left maimed and imperfect; and I laid the blame upon the
malignity of time, the devourer and consumer of all things,
which either kept it concealed or had destroyed it.

On the other side, I considered that, since among his books
there were found some so modern as the *Cure of Jealousy*, and
the *Nymphs and Shepherds of Henares*, his history also must be
modern; and if it was not as yet written, might, at least, still
remain in the memories of the people of his village, and
those of the neighbouring places. This thought held me in
suspense, and made me desirous to learn, really and truly,
the whole life and wonderful actions of our renowned Spaniard, Don Quixote de la Mancha, the light and mirror of
Manchegan chivalry, and the first, who, in our age, and in
these calamitous times, took upon him the toil and exercise
of arms-errant; to redress wrongs, succour widows, and
relieve that sort of damsels, who, with whip and palfrey, and
with all their virginity about them, rambled up and down
from mountain to mountain, and from valley to valley: (unless
some miscreant or some lewd clown, with hatchet and steel

cap, or some prodigious giant, ravished them) damsels there were, in days of yore, who, at the expiration of fourscore years, and never sleeping all that time under a roof, went as spotless virgins to the grave, as the mothers that bore them. Now, I say, upon these and many other accounts, our gallant Don Quixote is worthy of immortal memory and praise; nor ought some share to be denied even to me, for the labour and pains I have taken to discover the end of this delectable history; though I am very sensible, that, if heaven and fortune had not befriended me, the world would have still been without that pastime and pleasure, which an attentive reader of it may enjoy for near two hours. Now the manner of finding it was this.

As I was walking one day on the exchange of Toledo, a boy came to sell some bundles of old papers to a mercer; and, as I am fond of reading, though it be torn papers thrown about the streets, carried by this my natural inclination, I took a parcel of those the boy was selling, and perceived therein characters which I knew to be Arabic. And whereas, though I knew the letters, I could not read them, I looked about for some Moorish rabbi,* to read them for me: and it was not very difficult to find such an interpreter; for had I sought one for some better and more ancient language,* I should have found him there. In fine, my good fortune presented one to me; and acquainting him with my desire, and putting the book into his hands, he opened it towards the middle, and reading a little in it, began to laugh. I asked him what he smiled at, and he answered me, at something which he found written in the margin, by way of annotation. I desired him to tell me what it was; and he, laughing on, said; there is written on the margin, as follows: 'This Dulcinea del Toboso, so often mentioned in this history, had, they say, the best hand at salting pork of any woman in all La Mancha'. When I heard the name of Dulcinea del Toboso, I stood amazed and confounded; for I presently fancied to myself that those bundles of paper contained the history of Don Quixote.

With this thought I pressed him to read the beginning; which he did, and rendering extempore the Arabic into

Castilian, said that it began thus: 'The history of Don Quixote de la Mancha, written by Cid Hamet Ben Engeli, Arabian historiographer'. Much discretion was necessary to dissemble the joy I felt at hearing the title of the book, and snatching it out of the mercer's hands, I bought the whole bundle of papers from the boy for half a real; who, if he had been cunning, and had perceived how eager I was to have them, might very well have promised himself, and have really had, more than six for the bargain. I went off immediately with the Morisco, through the cloister of the great church, and desired him to translate for me those papers (all those that treated of Don Quixote) into the Castilian tongue, without taking away or adding anything to them, offering to pay him whatever he should demand. He was satisfied with fifty pounds of raisins, and two bushels of wheat; and promised to translate them faithfully and expeditiously. But I, to make the business more sure, and not let so valuable a prize slip through my fingers, took him home to my own house, where in a little more than six weeks he translated the whole in the manner you have it here related.

In the first sheet was drawn in a most lively manner, Don Quixote's combat with the Biscainer, in the same attitude in which the history sets it forth; the swords lifted up; the one covered with his buckler, the other with his cushion; and the Biscainer's mule so to the life that you might discover it to be a hackney-jade a bow-shot off. The Biscainer had a label at his feet, on which was written, 'Don Sancho de Azpeitia'; which, without doubt, must have been his name: and at the feet of Rosinante was another, on which was written, 'Don Quixote'. Rosinante was wonderfully well delineated; so long and lank, so lean and feeble, with so sharp a back-bone, and so like one in a galloping consumption, that you might see plainly with what exactness and propriety the name of Rosinante had been given him. Close by him stood Sancho Panza, holding his ass by the halter; at whose feet was another scroll, whereon was written 'Sancho Zancas': and not without reason, if he was, as the painting expressed, paunch-bellied, short of stature, and spindle shanked: which doubtless gave him the names of Panza and Zancas; for the history sometimes calls him by the one, and sometimes by the other of these surnames. There were some other minuter particulars observable; but they are all of little importance, and contribute nothing to the faithful narration of the history; though none are to be· despised, if true.

But if any objection lies against the truth of this history, it can only be, that the author was an Arab, those of that nation being not a little addicted to lying; though they being so much our enemies, one should rather think he fell short of, than exceeded, the bounds of truth. And so in fact, he seems to have done: for when he might, and ought to have launched out, in celebrating the praises of so excellent a knight, it looks as if he industriously passed them over in silence: a thing ill done and worse designed; for historians ought to be precise, faithful, and unprejudiced; and neither interest nor fear, hatred nor affection, should make them swerve from the way of truth, whose mother is history, the rival of time, the depository of great actions, the witness of what is past, the example and instruction to the present, and monitor to the future. In this* you will certainly find whatever you can desire in the most agreeable; and if any perfection is wanting to it, it must, without all question, be the fault of the infidel its author,* and not owing to any defect in the subject. In short, its second part, according to the translation, began in this manner.

The trenchant blades of the two valorous and enraged combatants being brandished aloft, seemed to stand threatening heaven and earth, and the deep abyss; such was the courage and gallantry of their deportment. And the first who discharged his blow was the choleric Biscainer; which fell with such force and fury, that, if the edge of the sword had not turned aslant by the way, that single blow had been enough to put an end to this cruel conflict, and to all the adventures of our knight: but good fortune, that preserved him for greater things, so twisted his adversary's sword, that though it alighted on the left shoulder, it did him no other hurt than to disarm that side, carrying off by the way a great part of his helmet, with half an ear; all which with hideous ruin fell to the ground, leaving him in a piteous plight.

Good God! who is he that can worthily recount the rage that entered into the breast of our Manchegan, at seeing himself so roughly handled? Let it suffice that it was such, that he raised himself afresh in his stirrups, and, grasping his sword faster in both hands, discharged it with such fury upon the Biscainer, taking him full upon the cushion, and upon the head (which he could not defend), that, as if a mountain had fallen upon him, the blood began to gush out at his nostrils, his mouth, and his ears; and he seemed as if he was just falling down from his mule, which doubtless he must have done, if he had not laid fast hold of her neck: but, notwithstanding that, he lost his stirrups, and let go his hold; and the mule, frightened by the terrible stroke, began to run about the field, and at two or three plunges laid her master flat upon the ground. Don Quixote stood looking on with great calmness, and when he saw him fall, leaped from his horse, and with much agility ran up to him, and clapping the point of his sword to his eyes, bid him yield or he would cut off his head. The Biscainer was so stunned that he could not answer a word; and it had gone hard with him (so blinded with rage was Don Quixote) if the ladies of the coach, who hitherto in great dismay beheld the conflict, had not approached him, and earnestly besought him, that he would do them the great kindness and favour to spare the life of their squire. Don Quixote answered with much solemnity and gravity:

'Assuredly, fair ladies, I am very willing to grant your request, but it is upon a certain condition and compact; which is, that this knight shall promise me to repair to the town of Toboso, and present himself as from me, before the peerless Dulcinea, that she may dispose of him as she shall think fit.'

The terrified and disconsolate lady, without considering what Don Quixote required, and without inquiring who Dulcinea was, promised him her squire should perform whatever he enjoined him.

'In reliance upon this promise,' said Don Quixote, 'I will do him no further hurt, though he has well deserved it at my hands.'

CHAPTER 10

Of the discourse Don Quixote had* with his good squire
Sancho Panza.

BY this time Sancho Panza had got upon his legs, somewhat
roughly handled by the monk's lackeys, and stood beholding
very attentively the combat of his master Don Quixote, and
besought God in his heart that he would be pleased to give
him the victory, and that he might thereby win some island,
of which to make him governor, as he had promised him.
Now, seeing the conflict at an end, and that his master was
ready to mount again upon Rosinante, he came and held his
stirrup; and before he got up, he fell upon his knees before
him, and, taking hold of his hand, kissed it, and said to him:

'Be pleased, my lord Don Quixote, to bestow upon me the
government of that island, which you have won in this
rigorous combat; for, be it never so big, I find in myself
ability sufficient to govern it, as well as the best that ever
governed an island in the world.'

To which Don Quixote answered:

'Consider, brother Sancho, that this adventure, and others
of this nature, are not adventures of islands, but of cross-
ways, in which nothing is to be gotten but a broken head,
or the loss of an ear. Have patience; for adventures will offer,
whereby I may not only make thee a governor, but something
better.'

Sancho returned him abundance of thanks, and kissing his
hand again, and the skirt of his coat of mail, he helped him
to get upon Rosinante, and himself mounting his ass, began
to follow his master; who going off at a round rate, without
taking his leave, or speaking to those of the coach, entered
into a wood that was hard by. Sancho followed him as fast
as his beast could trot; but Rosinante made such way, that,
seeing himself like to be left behind, he was forced to call
aloud to his master to stay for him. Don Quixote did so,
checking Rosinante by the bridle, until his weary squire
overtook him; who, as soon as he came near, said to him:

'Methinks, Sir, it would not be amiss to retire to some
church; for considering in what condition you have left your

adversary, it is not improbable they may give notice of the fact to the Holy Brotherhood,* and they may apprehend us: and in faith, if they do, before we get out of their clutches, we may chance to sweat for it.'

'Peace,' quoth Don Quixote; 'for where have you ever seen or read of a knight-errant's being brought before a court of justice, let him have committed never so many homicides?'

'I know nothing of your omecils,' answered Sancho, 'nor in my life have I ever concerned myself about them; only this I know, that the Holy Brotherhood have something to say to those who fight in the fields; and as to this other matter, I intermeddle not in it.'

'Set your heart at rest, friend,' answered Don Quixote; 'for I should deliver you out of the hands of the Chaldeans: how much more out of those of the Holy Brotherhood! but tell me, on your life, have you ever seen a more valorous knight than I, upon the whole face of the known earth? Have you read in story of any other, who has, or ever had, more bravery in assailing, more breath in holding out, more dexterity in wounding, or more address in giving a fall?'

'The truth is,' answered Sancho, 'that I never read any history at all; for I can neither read nor write: but what I dare affirm is, that I never served a bolder master than your worship, in all the days of my life; and pray God we be not called to an account for these darings, where I just now said. What I beg of your worship is, that you would let your wound be dressed, for there comes a great deal of blood from that ear; and I have here some lint and a little white ointment in my wallet.'

'All this would have been needless,' answered Don Quixote, 'if I had bethought myself of making a phial of the balsam of Fierabras;* for, with one single drop of that, we might have saved both time and medicines.'

'What phial, and what balsam is that?' said Sancho Panza.

'It is a balsam,' answered Don Quixote, 'of which I have the receipt by heart; and he that has it need not fear death, nor so much as think of dying by any wound. And therefore, when I shall have made it, and given it you, all you will have to do is, when you see me in some battle cleft asunder (as it frequently happens), to take up fair and softly that part of my body which shall fall to the ground, and with the greatest nicety, before the blood is congealed, place it upon the other half that shall remain in the saddle, taking especial care to make them tally exactly. Then must you immediately give me to drink only two draughts of the balsam aforesaid, and then you will see me become sounder than any apple.'

'If this be so,' said Sancho, 'I renounce from henceforward the government of the promised island, and desire no other thing, in payment, of my many and good services, but only that your worship will give me the receipt of this extraordinary liquor; for I dare say it will anywhere fetch more than two reals an ounce, and I want no more to pass this life creditably and comfortably. But I should be glad to know whether it would cost much the making?'

'For less than three reals one may make nine pints,' answered Don Quixote.

'Sinner that I am,' replied Sancho, 'why then does your worship delay to make it, and to teach it me?'

'Peace, friend,' answered Don Quixote, 'for I intend to teach thee greater secrets, and to do thee greater kindnesses; and for the present, let us set about the cure; for my ear pains me more than I could wish.'

Sancho took some lint and ointment out of his wallet; but when Don Quixote perceived that his helmet was broken, he was ready to run stark mad; and laying his hand on his sword, and lifting up his eyes to heaven, he said:

'I swear by the Creator of all things, and by all that is contained in the four holy evangelists, to lead the life that the great Marquess of Mantua led, when he vowed to revenge the death of his nephew Valdovinos (which was, not to eat bread on a tablecloth, nor solace himself with his wife, and other things, which, though I do not now remember, I allow here for expressed), until I am fully revenged on him who hath done me this outrage.'

Sancho hearing this, said to him:

'Pray consider, Señor Don Quixote, that, if the knight has performed what was enjoined him, namely, to go and present himself before my lady Dulcinea del Toboso, he will then have done his duty, and deserves no new punishment, unless he commit a new crime.'

'You have spoken and remarked very justly,' answered Don Quixote, 'and I annul the oath, so far as concerns the taking a fresh revenge; but I make it, and confirm it anew, as to leading the life I have mentioned, until I shall take by force such another helmet, or one as good, from some other knight. And think not, Sancho, I undertake this lightly, or make a smoke of straw: I know what example I follow therein; for the same thing happened exactly with regard to Mambrino's helmet, which cost Sacripante* so dear.'

'Good Sir,' replied Sancho, 'give such oaths to the devil; for they are very detrimental to health, and prejudicial to the conscience. Besides, pray tell me, if perchance in many days we should not light upon a man armed with a helmet, what must we do then? must the oath be kept, in spite of so many difficulties and inconveniences; such as sleeping in your clothes, and not sleeping in any inhabited place, and a thousand other penances, contained in the oath of that mad old fellow the Marquess of Mantua, which you, Sir, would now revive? Consider well that none of these roads are frequented by armed men, and that here are only carriers and carters, who are so far from wearing helmets, that, perhaps, they never heard them so much as named, in all the days of their lives.'

'You are mistaken in this,' said Don Quixote; 'for we shall not be two hours in these cross-ways, before we shall see more armed men than came to the siege of Albracca,* to carry off Angelica the fair.'

'Well, then, be it so,' quoth Sancho, 'and God grant us good success, and that we may speedily win this island, which costs me so dear; and then no matter how soon I die.'

'I have already told you, Sancho, to be in no pain upon that account; for, if an island cannot be had, there is the kingdom of Denmark, or that of Sobradisa,* which will fit you like a ring to your finger; and, moreover, being upon *terra firma*, you should rejoice the more. But let us leave this to its own time, and see if you have anything for us to eat in your wallet; and we will go presently in quest of some castle, where we may lodge this night, and make the balsam that I told you of; for I vow to God my ear pains me very much.'

'I have here an onion, and a piece of cheese, and I know not how many crusts of bread,' said Sancho, 'but they are not eatables fit for so valiant a knight as your worship.'

'How ill you understand this matter!' answered Don Quix-ote. 'You must know, Sancho, that it is an honour to knights-errant not to eat once in a month; and if they do eat, it must be of what comes next to hand; and if you had read as many histories as I have done you would have known this; for though I have perused a great many, I never yet found any account given in them, that ever knights-errant did eat, unless it were by chance, and at certain sumptuous banquets made on purpose for them; and the rest of their days they lived, as it were, upon their smelling.* And though it is to be presumed, they could not subsist without eating, and without satisfying all other natural wants, it must likewise be supposed that, as they passed most part of their lives in wandering through forests and deserts, and without a cook, their most usual diet must consist of rustic viands, such as those you now offer me. So that, friend Sancho, let not that trouble you, which gives me pleasure; nor endeavour to make a new world, or to throw knight-errantry off its hinges.'

'Pardon me, Sir,' said Sancho; 'for, as I can neither read nor write, as I told you before, I am entirely unacquainted with the rules of the knightly profession; and from hence-forward I will furnish my wallet with all sorts of dried fruits for your worship, who are a knight; and for myself, who am none, I will supply it with poultry, and other things of more substance.'

'I do not say, Sancho,' replied Don Quixote, 'that knights-errant are obliged to eat nothing but dried fruit, as you say; but that their most usual sustenance was of that kind, and of certain herbs they found up and down in the fields, which they very well knew; and so do I'.

'It is a happiness to know these same herbs,' answered Sancho; 'for I am inclined to think we shall one day have occasion to make use of that knowledge.'

And so saying, he took out what he had provided, and they ate together in a very peaceable and friendly manner. But, being desirous to seek out some place to lodge in that night, they soon finished their poor and dry repast. They presently mounted, and made what haste they could to get to some inhabited place before night; but both the sun, and their hopes failed them near the huts of certain goatherds; and so they determined to take up their lodging there: but, if Sancho was grieved that they could not reach some habitation, his master was so much rejoiced to lie in the open air, making account that every time this befell him, he was doing an act possessive, or such an act as gave a fresh evidence of his title to chivalry.

CHAPTER 11

Of what befell Don Quixote with certain goatherds.

HE was kindly received by the goatherds; and Sancho, having accommodated Rosinante and his ass the best he could, followed the scent of certain pieces of goat's flesh, that were boiling in a kettle on the fire; and though he would willingly, at that instant, have tried whether they were fit to be translated from the kettle to the stomach, he forbore doing it; for the goatherds themselves took them off the fire, and, spreading some sheep-skins on the ground, very speedily served up their rural mess, and invited them both, with show of much good will, to take share of what they had. Six of them, that belonged to the fold, sat down round about the skins, having first with rustic compliments, desired Don Quixote that he would seat himself upon a trough, with the bottom upwards, placed on purpose for him. Don Quixote sat down, and Sancho remained standing to serve the cup, which was made of horn. His master, seeing him standing, said to him:

'That you may see, Sancho, the intrinsic worth of knight-errantry, and how fair a prospect its meanest retainers have of speedily gaining the respect and esteem of the world, I will, that you sit here by my side, and in company with these good folks, and that you be one and the same thing with me, who am your master and natural lord; that you eat from off my plate, and drink of the same cup in which I drink: for the same may be said of knight-errantry which is said of love, that it makes all things equal.'

'I give you a great many thanks, Sir,' said Sancho; 'but let me tell your worship, that, provided I have victuals enough, I can eat as well, or better standing, and alone by myself, than if I were seated close by an emperor. And further, to tell you the truth, what I eat in my corner, without compliments or ceremonies, though it were nothing but bread and an onion, relishes better than turkeys at other folks' tables, where I am forced to chew leisurely, drink little, wipe my mouth often, neither sneeze nor cough when I have a mind, nor do other things, which follow the being alone and at liberty. So that, good Sir, as to these honours your worship is pleased to confer upon me, as a menial servant, and hanger-on of knight-errantry (being squire to your worship) be pleased to convert them into something of more use and profit to me: for though I place them to account as received in full, I renounce them from this time forward to the end of the world.'

'Notwithstanding all this,' said Don Quixote, 'you shall sit down; for whosoever humbleth himself God doth exalt.'

And, pulling him by the arm, he forced him to sit down next him. The goatherds did not understand this jargon of squires and knights-errant and did nothing but eat and listen, and stare at their guests who, with much cheerfulness and appetite, swallowed down pieces as big as one's fist. The service of flesh being finished, they spread upon the skins a great quantity of acorns, together with half a cheese, harder than if it had been made of plaster of Paris. The horn stood not idle all this while; for it went round so often, now full, now empty, like the bucket of a well, that they presently emptied one of the two wine-bags that hung in view. After Don Quixote had satisfied his hunger, he took up a handful of acorns, and looking on them attentively, gave utterance to expressions like these:

'Happy times, and happy ages!* those, to which the
ancients gave the name of golden, not because gold (which
in this our iron age, is so much esteemed) was to be had in
that fortunate period without toil and labour; but because
they who then lived were ignorant of these two words, *meum*
and *tuum*. In that age of innocence all things were in common:
no one needed to take any other pains for his ordinary
sustenance, than to lift up his hand and take it from the
sturdy oaks, which stood inviting him liberally to taste of
their sweet and relishing fruit. The limpid fountains, and
running streams, offered them in magnificent abundance their
delicious and transparent waters. In the clefts of rocks, and
in the hollow of trees, did the industrious and provident bees
form their commonwealths, offering to every hand, without
usury, the fertile produce of their most delicious toil. The
stout cork-trees, without any other inducement than that of
their own courtesy, divested themselves of their light and
expanded bark; with which men began to cover their houses,
supported by rough poles, only for a defence against the
inclemency of the seasons. All then was peace, all amity, all
concord. As yet the heavy coulter of the crooked plough had
not dared to force open, and search into the tender bowels
of our first mother who, unconstrained, offered from every
part of her fertile and spacious bosom whatever might feed,
sustain, and delight those her children, who then had her in
possession. Then did the simple and beauteous young shepherdesses trip it from dale to dale, and from hill to hill, their
tresses sometimes plaited, sometimes loosely flowing, with no
more clothing than was necessary modestly to cover what
modesty has always required to be concealed: nor were their
ornaments like those nowadays in fashion, to which the
Tyrian purple and the so-many-ways martyred silk give a
value; but composed of green dock-leaves and ivy interwoven;
with which, perhaps, they went as splendidly and elegantly
decked, as our court-ladies do now, with all those rare and
foreign inventions which idle curiosity hath taught them.
Then were the amorous conceptions of the soul clothed in
simple and sincere expressions, in the same way and manner
they were conceived without seeking artificial phrases to set

them off. Nor as yet were fraud, deceit, and malice, inter-mixed with truth and plain-dealing. Justice kept within her proper bounds; favour and interest, which now so much depreciate, confound, and persecute her, not daring then to disturb or offend her. As yet the judge did not make his own will the measure of justice; for then there was neither cause nor person to be judged. Maidens and modesty, as I said before, went about alone, and mistress of themselves, without fear of any danger from the unbridled freedom and lewd designs of others; and if they were undone, it was entirely owing to their own natural inclination and will. But now, in these detestable ages of ours, no damsel is secure, though she were hidden and locked up in another labyrinth like that of Crete; for even there, through some cranny or through the air, by the zeal of cursed importunity, the amorous pestilence finds entrance, and they miscarry in spite of their closest retreat. For the security of whom, as times grew worse and wickedness increased, the order of knight-errantry was instituted to defend maidens, to protect widows, and to relieve orphans and persons distressed. Of this order am I, brother goatherds, from whom I take kindly the good cheer and civil reception you have given me and my squire; for though, by the law of nature, every one living is obliged to favour knights-errant, yet knowing that without your being acquainted with this obligation, you have entertained and regaled me, it is but reason that with all possible goodwill towards you, I should acknowledge yours to me.'

Our knight made this tedious discourse (which might very well have been spared), because the acorns they had given him put him in mind of the golden age, and inspired him with an eager desire to make that impertinent harangue to the goatherds; who stood in amaze, gaping and listening, without answering him a word. Sancho himself was silent, stuffing himself with the acorns, and often visiting the second wine-bag, which, that the wine might be cool, was kept hung upon a cork-tree.

Don Quixote spent more time in talking than in eating; and supper being over, one of the goatherds said:

'That your worship, Señor knight-errant, may the more

truly say, that we entertain you with a ready goodwill, we will give you some diversion and amusement, by making one of our comrades sing, who will soon be here: he is a very intelligent lad, and deeply enamoured; and above all, can read and write, and plays upon the rebeck to heart's content.'

The goatherd had scarcely said this, when the sound of the rebeck reached their ears, and presently after, came he that played on it, who was a youth of about two and twenty, and of a very good mien. His comrades asked him if he had supped, and he answering, yes,—he who had made the offer, said:

'Then, Antonio, you may afford us the pleasure of hearing you sing a little, that this gentleman, our guest, may see we have here among the mountains and woods some that understand music. We have told him your good qualities, and would have you show them, and make good what we have said; and therefore I entreat you to sit down and sing the ditty of your loves, which your uncle the prebendary composed for you, and which was so well liked in our village.'

'With all my heart,' replied the youth; and without further entreaty he sat down upon the trunk of an old oak, and tuning his rebeck, after a while, with a singular good grace, he began to sing as follows:

ANTONIO

'Yes, lovely nymph, thou art my prize;
    I boast the conquest of thy heart,
Though nor thy tongue, nor speaking eyes,
    Have yet reveal'd the latent smart.

'Thy wit and sense assure my fate,
    In them my love's success I see,
Nor can he be unfortunate,
    Who dares avow his flame for thee.

'Yet sometimes hast thou frown'd, alas!
    And given my hopes a cruel shock;
Then did thy soul seem form'd of brass,
    Thy snowy bosom of the rock.

'But in the midst of thy disdain,
 Thy sharp reproaches, cold delays,
Hope from behind, to ease my pain,
 The border of her robe displays.

'Ah! lovely maid! in equal scale
 Weigh well thy shepherd's truth and love,
Which ne'er, but with his breath, can fail,
 Which neither frowns nor smiles can move.

'If love, as shepherds wont to say,
 Be gentleness and courtesy,
So courteous is Olalia,
 My passion will rewarded be:

'And if obsequious duty paid
 The grateful heart can ever move,
Mine sure, my fair, may well persuade
 A due return, and claim thy love.

'For, to seem pleasing in thy sight,
 I dress myself with studious care,
And, in my best apparel dight,
 My Sunday clothes on Monday wear.

'And shepherds say, I'm not to blame;
 For cleanly dress and spruce attire
Preserve alive love's wanton flame,
 And gently fan the dying fire.

'To please my fair, in mazy ring
 I join the dance, and sportive play,
And oft beneath thy window sing,
 When first the cock proclaims the day.

'With rapture on each charm I dwell,
 And daily spread thy beauty's fame;
And still my tongue thy praise shall tell,
 Though envy swell, or malice blame.

'Teresa of the Berrocal,
 When once I praised you, said in spite,
Your mistress you an angel call,
 But a mere ape is your delight:

'Thanks to the bugle's artful glare,
 And all the graces counterfeit;

Thanks to the false and curled hair,
   Which wary love himself might cheat.

'I swore, 'twas false; and said, she lied;
   At that, her anger fiercely rose:
I box'd the clown that took her side,
   And how I box'd my fairest knows.

'I court thee not, Olalia,
   To gratify a loose desire;
My love is chaste, without allay
   Of wanton wish, or lustful fire.

'The church hath silken cords that tie
   Consenting hearts in mutual bands:
If thou, my fair, its yoke wilt try,
   Thy swain its ready captive stands.

'If not, by all the saints I swear,
   On these bleak mountains still to dwell,
Nor ever quit my toilsome care,
   But for the cloister and the cell.'

Here ended the goatherd's song, and though Don Quixote
desired him to sing something else, Sancho Panza was of
another mind, being more disposed to sleep, than to hear
ballads; and therefore he said to his master:

'Sir, you had better consider where you are to lie to-night;
for the pains these honest men take all day will not suffer
them to pass the nights in singing.'

'I understand you, Sancho,' answered Don Quixote; 'for I
see plainly, that the visits to the wine-bag require to be paid
rather with sleep than music.'

'It relished well with us all, blessed be God,' answered
Sancho.

'I do not deny it,' replied Don Quixote; 'but lay yourself
down where you will, for it better becomes those of my
profession to watch than to sleep. However, it would not be
amiss, Sancho, if you would dress this ear again; for it pains
me more than it should.'

Sancho did what he was commanded; and one of the
goatherds, seeing the hurt, bid him not be uneasy; for he

would apply such a remedy as should quickly heal it. And
taking some rosemary leaves, of which there was plenty
thereabouts, he chewed them, and mixed them with a little
salt, and laying them to the ear, bound them on very fast,
assuring him he would want no other salve, as it proved in
effect.

CHAPTER 12

*What a certain goatherd related to those who were with Don
Quixote.*

WHILE this passed, there came another of those young lads,
who brought them their provisions from the village, and said:
'Comrades, do you know what passes in the village?'*
'How should we know?' answered one of them.
'Know then,' continued the youth, 'that this morning died
that famous shepherd and scholar, Chrysostom; and it is
whispered that he died for love of that devilish untoward
lass Marcela, daughter of William the Rich; she, who rambles
about these woods and fields in the dress of a shepherdess.'
'For Marcela! say you?' quoth one.
'For her, I say,' answered the goatherd: 'and the best of it
is, he has ordered in his will that they should bury him in
the fields as if he had been a Moor,* and that it should be
at the foot of the rock by the cork-tree fountain; for,
according to report and what they say he himself declared,
that was the very place he himself saw her. He ordered also
other things so extravagant that the clergy say they must not
be performed; nor is it fit they should, for they seem to be
heathenish. To all which that great friend of his, Ambrosio
the student, who accompanied him likewise in the dress of
a shepherd, answers, that the whole must be fulfilled without
omitting anything, as Chrysostom enjoined; and upon this the
village is all in an uproar: but, by what I can learn, they will
at last do what Ambrosio and all the shepherd's friends
require; and to-morrow they come to inter him with great
solemnity, in the place I have already told you of. And I am

of opinion it will be very well worth seeing; at least, I will not fail to go, though I knew I should not return to-morrow to the village.'

'We will do so too,' answered the goatherds, 'and let us cast lots who shall stay behind to look after all our goats.'

'You say well, Pedro,' quoth another: 'but it will be needless to make use of this expedient, for I will stay for you all; and do not attribute this to virtue or want of curiosity in me, but to the thorn which stuck into my foot the other day, and hinders me from walking.'

'We are obliged to you, however,' answered Pedro.

Don Quixote desired Pedro to tell him who the deceased was, and who that shepherdess. To which Pedro answered, that all he knew was, that the deceased was a wealthy gentleman of a neighbouring village among the hills thereabout, who had studied many years in Salamanca; at the end of which time he returned home, with the character of a very knowing and well-read person.

Particularly, it is said, he understood the science of the stars, and what the sun and moon are doing in the sky: for he told us punctually the clipse of the sun and moon.

'Friend,' quoth Don Quixote, 'the obscuration of those two greater luminaries is called an eclipse, and not a clipse.'

But Pedro, not regarding niceties, went on with his story, saying he also foretold when the year would be plentiful, or estril.

'Sterile, you would say, friend,' quoth Don Quixote.

'Sterile or estril,' answered Pedro, 'comes all to the same thing. And as I was saying, his father and friends who gave credit to his words, became very rich thereby; for they followed his advice in everything. This year, he would say, sow barley, and not wheat; in this you sow vetches, and not barley may: the next year there will be plenty of oil: the three following there will not be a drop.'

'This science they call astrology,' said Don Quixote.

'I know not how it is called,' replied Pedro; 'but I know that he knew all this, and more too. In short, not many months after he came from Salamanca, on a certain day he appeared dressed like a shepherd, with his crook and sheepskin jacket, having thrown aside his scholar's gown; and with him another, a great friend of his, called Ambrosio, who had been his fellow student, and now put himself into the same dress of a shepherd. I forgot to tell you how the deceased Chrysostom was a great man at making verses; insomuch that he made the carols for Christmas Eve, and the religious plays for Corpus Christi, which the boys of our village represented; and everybody said they were most excellent. When the people of the village saw the two scholars so suddenly habited like shepherds, they were amazed, and could not guess at the cause that induced them to make that strange alteration in their dress. About this time the father of Chrysostom died, and he inherited a large estate in lands and goods, flocks, herds, and money, of all which the youth remained dissolute master;* and indeed he deserved it all, for he was a very good companion, a charitable man, and a friend to those that were good, and had a face like any blessing. Afterwards it came to be known that he changed his habit for no other purpose, but that he might wander about these desert places after that shepherdess Marcela, whom our lad told you of before, and with whom the poor deceased Chrysostom was in love. And I will now tell you (for it is fit you should know) who this young slut is; for perhaps, and even without a perhaps, you may never have heard the like in all the days of your life, though you were as old as the itch.'*

'Say, "as old as Sarah",' replied Don Quixote, not being able to endure the goatherd's mistaking words.

'The itch is old enough,' answered Pedro; 'and Sir, if you must at every turn be correcting my words, we shall not have done this twelvemonth.'

'Pardon me, friend,' said Don Quixote, 'I told you of it because there is a wide difference between the itch and Sarah: and so go on with your story; for I will interrupt you no more.'

'I say then, dear sir of my soul,' quoth the goatherd, 'that in our village there was a farmer richer than the father of Chrysostom, called William; on whom God bestowed, besides much and great wealth, a daughter, of whom her mother died in childbed, and she was the most respected woman of all our country. I cannot help thinking I see her now, with that presence, looking as if she had the sun on one side of her, and the moon on the other: and above all, she was a notable housewife, and a friend to the poor; for which I believe her soul is at this very moment enjoying God in the other world. Her husband William died for grief at the death of so good a woman, leaving his daughter Marcela, young and rich, under the care of an uncle, a priest, and beneficed in our village. The girl grew up with so much beauty, that it put us in mind of her mother, who had a great share; and for all that it was judged that her daughter would surpass her. And so it fell out; for when she came to be fourteen or fifteen years of age, nobody beheld her without blessing God for making her so handsome, and most men were in love with, and undone for her. Her uncle kept her very carefully and very close: notwithstanding which, the fame of her extraordinary beauty spread itself so, that, partly for her person, partly for her great riches, her uncle was applied to, solicited, and importuned, not only by those of our own village, but by many others, and those the better sort too, for several leagues round, to dispose of her in marriage. But he (who, to do him justice, is a good Christian), though he was desirous to dispose of her as soon as she was marriageable, yet would not do it without her consent, having no eye to the benefit and advantage he might have made of the girl's estate by deferring her marriage. And in good truth, this has been told in praise of the good priest in more companies than one in our village. For I would have you to know, Sir-errant, that, in these little places, everything is talked of, and everything censured. And, my life for yours, that clergyman must be over and above good, who obliges his parishioners to speak well of him, especially in country towns.'

'It is true,' said Don Quixote, 'and proceed: for the story is excellent, and, honest Pedro, you tell it with a good grace.'

'May the grace of the Lord never fail me, which is most to the purpose! And further know,' quoth Pedro, 'that, though the uncle proposed to his niece, and acquainted her with the qualities of every one in particular, of the many who sought her in marriage, advising her to marry, and choose to her

liking, she never returned any other answer, but that she was
not disposed to marry at present, and that, being so young,
she did not find herself able to bear the burden of matrimony.
Her uncle, satisfied with these seemingly just excuses, ceased
to importune her, and waited till she was grown a little older,
and knew how to choose a companion to her taste. For, said
he, and he said very well, parents ought not to settle their
children against their will.

'But, behold! when we least imagined it, on a certain day
the coy Marcela appears a shepherdess, and without the
consent of her uncle, and against the persuasions of all the
neighbours, would needs go into the fields with the other
country lasses, and tend her own flock. And now that she
appeared in public, and her beauty was exposed to all beholders, it is impossible to tell you how many wealthy youths,
gentlemen, and farmers, have taken Chrysostom's dress, and
go up and down these plains, making their suit to her; one
of whom, as is said already, was the deceased, of whom it
is said that he rather adored, than loved her. But think not,
that because Marcela has given herself up to this free and
unconfined way of life, and that with so little, or rather no
reserve, she has given any the least colour of suspicion to
the prejudice of her modesty and discretion: no, rather so
great and strict is the watch she keeps over her honour, that
of all those who serve and solicit her, no one has boasted,
or can boast with truth, that she has given him the least hope
of obtaining his desire. For though she does not fly nor shun
the company and conversation of the shepherds, but treats
them with courtesy, and in a friendly manner; yet upon any
one's beginning to discover his intention, though it be as just
and holy as that of marriage, she casts him from her as out
of a stonebow. And by this sort of behaviour, she does more
mischief in this country, than if she carried the plague about
with her; for her affability and beauty attract the hearts of
those who converse with her, to serve and love her; but her
disdain and frank dealing drive them to terms of despair: and
so they know not what to say to her, and can only exclaim
against her, calling her cruel and ungrateful, with such other
titles as plainly denote her character. And were you to abide

here, sir, awhile, you would hear these mountains and valleys resound with the complaints of those undeceived wretches that yet follow her. There is a place not far from hence, where there are about two dozen of tall beeches, and not one of them but has the name of Marcela written and engraved on its smooth bark; and over some of them is a crown carved in the same tree, as if the lover would more clearly express, that Marcela bears away the crown, and deserves it above all human beauty. Here sighs one shepherd; there complains another: here are heard amorous sonnets, there despairing ditties. You shall have one pass all the hours of the night, seated at the foot of some oak or rock; and there, without closing his weeping eyes, wrapped up and transported in his thoughts, the sun finds him in the morning. You shall have another, without cessation or truce to his sighs, in the midst of the most irksome noonday heat of the summer, extended on the burning sand, and sending up his complaints to all-pitying heaven. In the meantime, the beautiful Marcela, free and unconcerned, triumphs over them all.

'We who know her, wait with impatience to see what her haughtiness will come to, and who is to be the happy man that shall subdue so intractable a disposition, and enjoy so incomparable a beauty. All that I have recounted being so assured a truth, I the more easily believe what our companion told us concerning the cause of Chrysostom's death. And therefore I advise you, sir, that you do not fail to-morrow to be at his funeral, which will be very well worth seeing: for Chrysostom has a great many friends; and it is not half a league from this place to that where he ordered himself to be buried.'

'I will certainly be there,' said Don Quixote, 'and I thank you for the pleasure you have given me by the recital of so entertaining a story.'

'Oh!' replied the goatherd, 'I do not yet know half the adventures that have happened to Marcela's lovers; but to-morrow, perhaps, we shall meet by the way with some shepherd, who may tell us more: at present it will not be amiss, that you get you to sleep under some roof; for the cold dew of the night may do your wound harm, though the salve I have put to it is such, that you need not fear any cross accident.'

Sancho Panza, who, for his part, gave this long-winded tale of the goatherd's to the devil, pressed his master to lay himself down to sleep in Pedro's hut. He did so, and passed the rest of the night in remembrances of his lady Dulcinea, in imitation of Marcela's lovers. Sancho Panza took up his lodging between Rosinante and his ass, and slept it out, not like a discarded lover, but like a person well rib-roasted.

CHAPTER 13

The conclusion of the story of the shepherdess Marcela, with other incidents.

BUT scarcely had the day began to discover itself through the balconies of the east, when five of the six goatherds got up, and went to awake Don Quixote, and asked him, whether he continued in his resolution of going to see the famous funeral of Chrysostom, for they would bear him company. Don Quixote, who desired nothing more, got up, and bid Sancho saddle and pannel immediately; which he did with great expedition: and with the same dispatch they all presently set out on their way.

They had not gone a quarter of a league, when, upon crossing a pathway, they saw six shepherds making towards them, clad in black sheepskin jerkins, and their heads crowned with garlands of cypress and bitter rosemary. Each of them had a thick holly-club in his hand. There came also with them two cavaliers on horseback in very handsome riding habits, attended by three lackeys on foot. When they had joined companies, they saluted each other courteously; and asking one another whither they were going, they found they were all going to the place of burial; and so they began to travel in company.

One of those on horseback, speaking to his companion, said: 'I fancy, Señor Vivaldo, we shall not think the time mis-spent in staying to see this famous funeral; for it cannot but

be extraordinary, considering the strange things these shepherds have recounted, as well of the deceased shepherd, as
of the murdering shepherdess.'

'I think so too,' answered Vivaldo; 'and I do not only not
think much of spending one day, but I would even stay four
to see it.'

Don Quixote asked them, what it was they had heard of
Marcela and Chrysostom. The traveller said they had met
those shepherds early that morning, and that, seeing them in
that mournful dress, they had asked the occasion of their
going clad in that manner; and that one of them had related
the story, telling them of the beauty, and unaccountable
humour, of a certain shepherdess called Marcela, and the
loves of many that wooed her; with the death of Chrysostom,
to whose burial they were going. In fine, he related all that
Pedro had told to Don Quixote.

This discourse ceased, and another began; he who was
called Vivaldo, asking Don Quixote what might be the reason
that induced him to go armed in that manner through a
country so peaceable. To which Don Quixote answered:

'The profession I follow will not allow or suffer me to go
in any other manner. The dance, the banquet, and the bed
of down, were invented for soft and effeminate courtiers; but
toil, disquietude, and arms, were designed for those whom
the world calls knights-errant, of which number I, though
unworthy, am the least.'

Scarcely had they heard this, when they all concluded he
was a madman. And for the more certainty, and to try what
kind of madness his was, Vivaldo asked him, what he meant
by knights-errant.

'Have you not read, Sir,' answered Don Quixote, 'the
annals and histories of England, wherein are recorded the
famous exploits of King Arthur, whom, in our Castilian
tongue, we perpetually call King Artús; of whom there goes
an old tradition, and a common one all over that kingdom
of Great Britain, that this king did not die, but that by magic
art, he was turned into a raven; and that, in process of time,
he shall reign again, and recover his kingdom and sceptre;
for which reason it cannot be proved that, from that time

to this, any Englishman hath killed a raven? Now, in this good king's time was instituted that famous order of the Knights of the Round Table; and the amours therein related, of Sir Lancelot of the Lake with the queen Guinevere,* passed exactly as they are recorded; that honourable duenna Quintañona being their go-between and confidante: which gave birth to that well-known ballad, so cried up here in Spain, of "Never was knight by ladies so well served, as was Sir Lancelot when he came from Britain":* with the rest of that sweet and charming recital of his amours and exploits. Now, from that time, the order of chivalry has been extending and spreading itself through many and divers parts of the world: and in this profession many have been distinguished and renowned for their heroic deeds; as the valiant Amadis de Gaul, with all his sons and nephews, to the fifth generation;* the valorous Felixmarte of Hyrcania; and the never-enough-to-be-praised Tirante the White: and we, in our days, have in a manner seen, heard, and conversed with the invincible and valorous knight Don Belianis of Greece. This, gentlemen, it is to be a knight-errant, and what I have told you of is the order of chivalry: of which, as I said before, I, though a sinner, have made profession; and the very same thing that the aforesaid knights professed, I profess: and so I travel through these solitudes and deserts, seeking adventures, with a determined resolution to oppose my arm and my person to the most perilous that fortune shall present, in aid of the weak and the needy.'

By these discourses the travellers were fully convinced that Don Quixote was out of his wits, and what kind of madness it was that influenced him; which struck them with the same admiration that it did all others at the first hearing. And Vivaldo, who was a very discerning person, and withal of a mirthful disposition, that they might pass without irksomeness the little of the way that remained before they came to the funeral mountain, resolved to give him an opportunity of going on in his extravagances. And therefore he said to him:

'Methinks, Sir Knight-errant, you have taken upon you one of the strictest professions upon earth; and I verily believe, that of the Carthusian monks themselves is not so rigid.'

'It may be as strict for aught I know,' answered our Don Quixote; 'but that it is so necessary to the world I am within two fingers' breadth of doubting; for to speak the truth, the soldier, who executes his captain's orders, does no less than the captain himself, who gives him the orders. I would say, that the religious with all peace and quietness, implore heaven for the good of the world; but we soldiers and knights really execute what they pray for, defending it with the strength of our arms and the edge of our swords; and that, not under covert, but in open field, exposed to the unsufferable beams of summer's sun and winter's horrid ice. So that we are God's ministers upon earth, and the arms by which he executes his justice in it. And considering that matters of war, and those relating thereto, cannot be put in execution without sweat, toil, and labour, it follows that they who profess it do unquestionably take more pains than they who, in perfect peace and repose, are employed in praying to heaven to assist those who can do but little for themselves. I mean not to say, nor do I so much as imagine, that the state of the knight-errant is as good as that of the recluse religious: I would only infer from what I suffer, that it is doubtless more laborious, more bastinadoed, more hungry and thirsty, more wretched, more ragged, and more lousy. For there is no doubt but that the knights-errant of old underwent many misfortunes in the course of their lives; and if some of them rose to be emperors by the valour of their arm, in good truth they paid dearly for it in blood and sweat; and if those who arrived to such honour, had wanted enchanters and sages to assist them, they would have been mightily deceived in their hopes, and much disappointed in their expectations.'

'I am of the same opinion,' replied the traveller; 'but there is one thing in particular, among many others, which I dislike in knights-errant, and it is this: when they are prepared to engage in some great and perilous adventure, in which they are in manifest danger of losing their lives, in the very instant of the encounter, they never once remember to commend themselves to God, as every Christian is bound to do in the like perils; but rather commend themselves to their mistresses, and that with as much fervour and devotion as if they were their God, a thing which to me savours strongly of paganism.'

'Señor,' answered Don Quixote, 'this can by no means be otherwise; and the knight-errant who should act in any other manner, would digress much from his duty; for it is a received maxim and custom in chivalry, that the knight-errant, who, being about to attempt some great feat of arms, has his lady before him, must turn his eyes fondly and amorously towards her, as if by them he implored her favour and protection in the doubtful moment of distress he is just entering upon. And though nobody hears him, he is obliged to mutter some words between his teeth, by which he commends himself to her with his whole heart; and of this we have innumerable examples in the histories. And you must not suppose by this that they are to neglect commending themselves to God; for there is time and leisure enough to do it in the progress of the work.'

'But, for all that,' replied the traveller, 'I have one scruple still remaining; which is, that I have often read, that words arising between two knights-errant, and choler beginning to kindle in them both, they turn their horses round, and fetching a large compass about the field, immediately, without more ado, encounter at full speed; and in the midst of their career, they commend themselves to their mistresses; and what commonly happens in the encounter is, that one of them tumbles back over his horse's crupper, pierced through and through by his adversary's lance; and, if the other had not laid hold of his horse's mane, he could not have avoided coming to the ground. Now I cannot imagine what leisure the deceased had to commend himself to God in the course of this so hasty a work. Better it had been, if the words he spent in commending himself to his lady in the midst of the career had been employed about that, to which, as a Christian, he was obliged. And besides, it is certain all knights-errant have not ladies to commend themselves to, because they are not all in love.'

'That cannot be,' answered Don Quixote: 'I say there cannot be a knight-errant without a mistress; for it is as proper and as natural to them to be in love, as to the sky to be full of stars. And I affirm, you cannot show me a history in which a knight-errant is to be found without an amour; and for the very reason of his being without one, he would not be reckoned a legitimate knight, but a bastard and one that got into the fortress of chivalry, not by the door, but over the pales, like a thief and a robber.'

'Yet, for all that,' said the traveller, 'I think (if I am not much mistaken) I have read, that Don Galaor, brother to the valorous Amadis de Gaul, never had a particular mistress to whom he might commend himself; notwithstanding which, he was not the less esteemed, and was a very valiant and famous knight.'

To which our Don Quixote answered:

'Señor, one swallow makes no summer. Besides, I very well know, that this knight was in secret very deeply enamoured: he was a general lover, and could not resist his natural inclination towards all ladies whom he thought handsome. But, in short, it is very well attested that he had one whom he had made mistress of his will, and to whom he often commended himself, but very secretly; for it was upon this quality of secrecy that he especially valued himself.'

'If it be essential that every knight-errant must be a lover,' said the traveller, 'it is to be presumed that your worship is one, as you are of the profession; and if you do not pique yourself upon the same secrecy as Don Galaor, I earnestly entreat you, in the name of all this good company, and in my own, to tell us the name, country, quality, and beauty, of your mistress, who cannot but account herself happy if all the world knew that she is loved and served by so worthy a knight as your worship appears to be.'

Here Don Quixote fetched a deep sigh, and said:

'I cannot positively affirm, whether this sweet enemy of mine is pleased or not that the world should know I am her servant: I can only say, in answer to what you so very courteously inquire of me, that her name is Dulcinea; her country Toboso, a town of La Mancha; her quality at least that of a princess, since she is my queen and sovereign lady; her beauty more than human, since in her all the impossible and chimerical attributes of beauty, which the poets ascribe to their mistresses, are realized; for her hairs are of gold, her forehead the Elysian fields, her eyebrows rainbows, her eyes suns, her cheeks roses, her lips coral, her teeth pearls, her neck alabaster, her bosom marble, her hands ivory, her whiteness snow; and the parts which modesty veils from human sight, such as (to my thinking) the most exalted imagination can only conceive, but not find a comparison for.'

'We would know,' replied Vivaldo, 'her lineage, race, and family.'

To which Don Quixote answered:

'She is not of the ancient Roman Curtii, Caii, and Scipios, nor of the modern Colonnas and Orsinis; nor of the Moncadas and Requesenes of Catalonia; neither is she of the Rebellas and Villanovas of Valencia; the Palafoxes, Nuças, Rocabertis, Corellas, Lunas, Alagones, Urreas, Foçes, and Gurreas of Aragon; the Cerdas, Manriques, Mendoças, and Guzmans of Castile; the Alencastros, Pallas, and Meneses of Portugal: but she is of those of Toboso de la Mancha; a lineage, though modern, yet such as may give a noble beginning to the most illustrious families of the ages to come: and in this let no one contradict me, unless it be on the conditions that Zerbino fixed under Orlando's arms, where it was said: "Let no one remove these, who cannot stand a trial with Orlando".'*

'Although mine be of the Cachopines of Laredo,'* replied the traveller, 'I dare not compare it with that of Toboso de la Mancha; though, to say the truth, no such appellation hath ever reached my ears until now.'

'Is it possible you should never have heard of it?' replied Don Quixote.

All the rest went on listening with great attention to the dialogue between these two: and even the goatherds and shepherds perceived the notorious distraction of our Don Quixote. Sancho Panza alone believed all that his master said to be true, knowing who he was, and having been acquainted with him from his birth. But what he somewhat doubted of was, what concerned the fair Dulcinea del Toboso: for no such a name or princess had ever come to his hearing, though he lived so near Toboso.

In these discourses they went on, when they discovered through an opening made by two high mountains, about twenty shepherds coming down, all in jerkins of black wool, and crowned with garlands, which (as appeared afterwards) were some of yew, and some of cypress. Six of them carried a bier, covered with a great variety of flowers and boughs; which one of the goatherds espying, he said:

'They who come yonder, are those who bring the corpse of Chrysostom; and the foot of yonder mountain is the place where he ordered them to bury him.'

They made haste, therefore, to arrive; which they did just as the bier was set down on the ground: and four of them, with sharp pickaxes, were making the grave by the side of a hard rock. They saluted one another courteously: and presently Don Quixote and his company went to take a view of the bier; upon which they saw a dead body, strewed with flowers, in the dress of a shepherd, seemingly about thirty years of age; and, though dead, you might perceive that he had been, when alive, of a beautiful countenance, and hale constitution. Several books, and a great number of papers, some open and others folded up, lay round about him on the bier. All that were present, as well those who looked on, as those who were opening the grave, kept a marvellous silence; until one of those, who brought the deceased, said to another:

'Observe carefully, Ambrosio, whether this be the place which Chrysostom mentioned, since you are so punctual in performing what he commanded in his will.'

'This is it,' answered Ambrosio; 'for in this very place, he often recounted to me the story of his misfortune. Here it was, he told me, that he first saw that mortal enemy of the human race: here it was that he declared to her his no less honourable than ardent passion: here it was that Marcela finally undeceived, and treated him with such disdain, that she put an end to the tragedy of his miserable life; and here, in memory of so many misfortunes, he desired to be deposited in the bowels of eternal oblivion.'

Then turning himself to Don Quixote and the travellers, he went on, saying:

'This body, sirs, which you are beholding with compassionate eyes, was the receptacle of a soul in which heaven had
placed a great part of its treasure: this is the body of
Chrysostom, who was singular for wit, matchless in courtesy,
perfect in politeness, a phoenix in friendship, magnificent
without ostentation, grave without arrogance, cheerful without meanness; in fine, the first in everything that was good,
and second to none in everything that was unfortunate. He
loved, he was abhorred: he adored, he was scorned; he
courted a savage; he solicited marble; he pursued the wind;
he called aloud to solitude; he served ingratitude; and the
recompense he obtained was, to become a prey to death, in
the midst of the career of his life, to which an end was put
by a certain shepherdess, whom he endeavoured to render
immortal in the memories of men, as these papers you are
looking at would sufficiently demonstrate, had he not ordered
me to commit them to the flames, at the same time that his
body was deposited in the earth.'

'You would then be more rigorous and cruel to them,' said
Vivaldo, 'than their master himself; for it is neither just nor
right to fulfil the will of him, who commands something
utterly unreasonable. Augustus Caesar would not consent to
the execution of what the divine Mantuan* had commanded
in his will. So that, Señor Ambrosio, though you commit
your friend's body to the earth, do not, therefore, commit
his writings to oblivion; and if he ordered it as a person
injured, do not you fulfil it as one indiscreet; rather act so,
that, by giving life to these papers, the cruelty of Marcela
may never be forgotten, but may serve for an example to
those, who shall live in times to come, that they may avoid
falling down the like precipices; for I, and all here present,
already know the story of this your enamoured and despairing
friend; we know also your friendship, and the occasion of
his death, and what he ordered on his deathbed; from which
lamentable history may be gathered, how great has been the
cruelty of Marcela, the love of Chrysostom, and the sincerity
of your friendship; as also the end of those, who run
headlong in the path that inconsiderate and ungoverned love
sets before them. Last night we heard of Chrysostom's death,

and that he was to be interred in this place: and so out of curiosity and compassion, we turned out of our way, and agreed to come, and behold with our eyes, what had moved us so much in the recital: and in return for our pity, and our desire to remedy it, if we could, we beseech you, O discreet Ambrosio, at least I request it on my own behalf, that you will not burn the papers, but let me carry away some of them.'

And, without staying for the shepherd's reply, he stretched out his hand, and took some of those that were nearest. Which Ambrosio perceiving, he said:

'Out of civility, Señor, I will consent to your keeping those you have taken; but to imagine that I shall forbear burning those that remain, is a vain thought.'

Vivaldo, who desired to see what the papers contained, presently opened one of them, which had for its title *The Song of Despair*. Ambrosio, hearing it, said:

'This is the last paper this unhappy man wrote: and that you may see, Señor, to what state he was reduced by his misfortunes, read it so as to be heard; for you will have leisure enough, while they are digging the grave.'

'That I will with all my heart,' said Vivaldo.

And as all the bystanders had the same desire, they drew round about him, and he read, in an audible voice, as follows:

CHAPTER 14

Wherein are rehearsed the despairing verses of the deceased shepherd, with other unexpected events.

CHRYSOSTOM'S SONG

I

'Since, cruel maid, you force me to proclaim
From clime to clime the triumphs of your scorn,
Let hell itself inspire my tortur'd breast
With mournful numbers, and untune my voice;

Whilst the sad pieces of my broken heart
Mix with the doleful accents of my tongue,
At once to tell my griefs and thy exploits.
Hear then, and listen with attentive ear,
Not to harmonious sounds, but echoing groans,
Fetch'd from the bottom of my lab'ring breast,
To ease, in spite of thee, my raging smart.

2

'The lion's roar, the howl of midnight wolves,
The scaly serpent's hiss, the raven's croak,
The burst of fighting winds that vex the main,
The widow'd owl and turtle's plaintive moan,
With all the din of hell's infernal crew,
From my griev'd soul forth issue in one sound,
Leaving my senses all confus'd and lost.
For ah! no common language can express
The cruel pains that torture my sad heart.

3

' Yet let not echo bear the mournful sounds
To where old Tagus rolls his yellow sands,
Or Betis crown'd with olives, pours his flood.
But here midst rocks and precipices deep,
Or to obscure and silent vales remov'd,
On shores by human footsteps never trod,
Where the gay sun ne'er lifts his radiant orb,
Or with th' envenom'd race of savage beasts
That range the howling wilderness for food,
Will I proclaim the story of my woes;
Poor privilege of grief! whilst echoes hoarse
Catch the sad tale, and spread it round the world.

4

' Disdain gives death; suspicions, true or false,
O'erturn th' impatient mind; with surer stroke
Fell jealousy destroys; the pangs of absence
No lover can support; nor firmest hope
Can dissipate the dread of cold neglect:
Yet I, strange fate! though jealous, though disdain'd,
Absent and sure of cold neglect, still live.
And midst the various torments I endure,
No ray of hope e'er darted on my soul:

Nor would I hope; rather in deep despair
Will I sit down, and brooding o'er my griefs,
Vow everlasting absence from her sight.

5

'Can hope and fear at once the soul possess,
Or hope subsist with surer cause of fear?
Shall I, to shut out frightful jealousy,
Close my sad eyes, when ev'ry pang I feel
Presents the hideous phantom to my view?
What wretch so credulous, but must embrace
Distrust with open arms, when he beholds
Disdain avow'd, suspicions realiz'd,
And truth itself converted to a lie?
O cruel tyrant to the realm of love,
Fierce jealousy, arm with a sword this hand,
Or thou, disdain, a twisted cord bestow.

6

'Let me not blame my fate, but dying think
The man most blest who loves, the soul most free
That love has most enthralled: still to my thoughts
Let fancy paint the tyrant of my heart
Beauteous in mind as face, and in myself
Still let me find the source of her disdain;
Content to suffer, since imperial love
By lover's woes maintains his sovereign state.
With this persuasion and the fatal noose,
I hasten to the doom her scorn demands,
And dying offer up my breathless corse,
Uncrown'd with garlands, to the whistling winds.

7

'O thou, whose unrelenting rigour's force
First drove me to despair, and now to death,
When the sad tale of my untimely fall
Shall reach thy ear, though it deserve a sigh,
Veil not the heav'n of those bright eyes in grief,
Nor drop one pitying tear, to tell the world,
At length my death has triumph'd o'er thy scorn;
But dress thy face in smiles, and celebrate
With laughter and each circumstance of joy,
The festival of thy disastrous end.

Ah! need I bid thee smile? too well I know
My death's thy utmost glory and thy pride.

8

'Come, all ye phantoms of the dark abyss;
Bring, Tantalus, thy unextinguish'd thirst,
And, Sisyphus, thy still-returning stone;
Come, Tityus, with the vulture at thy heart,
And thou, Ixion, bring thy giddy wheel;
Nor let the toiling sisters stay behind.
Pour your united griefs into this breast,
And in low murmurs sing sad obsequies
(If a despairing wretch such rights may claim)
O'er my cold limbs, denied a winding-sheet.
And let the triple porter of the shades
The sister furies, and chimeras dire,
With notes of woe the mournful chorus join.
Such funeral pomp alone befits the wretch
By Beauty sent untimely to the grave.

9

'And thou, my song, sad child of my despair,
Complain no more; but since my wretched fate
Improves her happier lot, who gave thee birth,
Be all thy sorrows buried in my tomb.'

Chrysostom's song was very much approved by those who heard it: but he who read it said it did not seem to agree with the account he had heard of the reserve and goodness of Marcela; for Chrysostom complains in it of jealousies, suspicions, and absence, all in prejudice of the credit and good name of Marcela. To which Ambrosio answered, as one well acquainted with the most hidden thoughts of his friend:

'To satisfy you, Señor, as to this doubt, you must know, that when this unhappy person wrote this song he was absent from Marcela,* from whom he had voluntarily banished himself, to try whether absence would have its ordinary effect upon him. And as an absent lover is disturbed by everything, and seized by every fear, so was Chrysostom perplexed with imaginary jealousies and suspicious apprehensions, as much as if they had been real. And thus the truth, which fame proclaims of Marcela's goodness, remains unimpeached; and, excepting that she is cruel, somewhat arrogant, and disdainful, envy itself neither ought nor can lay any defect to her charge.'

'It is true,' answered Vivaldo.

And going to read another paper of those he had saved from the fire, he was interrupted by a wonderful vision, for such it seemed to be, which on a sudden presented itself to their sight: for on the top of a rock, under which they were digging the grave, appeared the shepherdess Marcela, so handsome that her beauty surpassed the very fame of it. Those who had never seen her until that time, beheld her with silence and admiration, and they who had been used to the sight of her were no less surprised than those who had never seen this fair shepherdess before. But Ambrosio had scarcely espied her, when, with signs of indignation, he said to her.

'Comest thou, O fierce basilisk of these mountains, to discover whether the wounds of this wretch, whom thy cruelty has deprived of life, will bleed afresh at thy appearance? or comest thou to triumph in the cruel exploits of thy inhuman disposition? or to behold from that eminence, like another pitiless Nero. the flames of burning Rome? or insolently to trample on this unhappy corpse, as did the impious daughter on that of her father Tarquin?* tell us quickly, what you come for, or what it is you would have: for since I know that Chrysostom, while living, never disobeyed you, so much as in thought, I will take care that all those who called themselves his friends, shall obey you, though he be dead.'

'I come not, O Ambrosio, for any of those purposes you have mentioned,' answered Marcela; 'but to vindicate myself, and to let the world know, how unreasonable those are who blame me for their own sufferings, or for the death of Chrysostom: and therefore I beg of all here present, that they would hear me with attention; for I need not spend much time, nor use many words to convince persons of sense of the truth.

'Heaven, as you say, made me handsome, and to such a degree that my beauty influences you to love me, whether you will or no. And in return for the love you bear me, you pretend and insist that I am bound to love you. I know by the natural sense God has given me, that whatever is beautiful is amiable: but I do not comprehend, that merely for being loved, the person that is loved for being handsome is obliged to return love for love. Besides, it may chance that the lover of the beautiful person may be ugly; and what is ugly deserving to be loathed, it would sound oddly to say, I love you for being handsome: you must love me, though I am ugly. But, supposing the beauty on both sides to be equal, it doth not therefore follow that the inclinations should be so too: for all beauty doth not inspire love; and there is a kind of it, which only pleases the sight, but does not captivate the affections. If all beauties were to enamour and captivate, the wills of men would be eternally confounded and perplexed, without knowing where to fix: for the beautiful objects being infinite, the desires must be infinite too. And, as I have heard say, true love cannot be divided, and must be voluntary and unforced:—this being so, as I believe it is, why would you have me subject my will by force, being not otherwise obliged thereto, than only because you say you love me? For, pray tell me, if, as heaven has made me handsome, it had made me ugly, would it have been just that I should have complained of you because you did not love me? Besides, you must consider that my beauty is not my own choice; but such as it is, heaven bestowed it on me freely without my asking or desiring it. And, as the viper does not deserve blame for her sting, though she kills with it, because it is given her by nature, as little do I deserve reprehension for being handsome. Beauty in a modest woman is like fire at a distance, or like a sharp sword: neither doth the one burn, nor the other wound those that come not too near them. Honour and virtue are ornaments of the soul, without which the body, though it be really beautiful, ought not to be thought so. Now if modesty be one of the virtues which most adorns and beautifies both body and mind, why should she, who is loved for being beautiful, part with it to gratify the desires of him who, merely for his own pleasure, uses his utmost endeavours to destroy it?

'I was born free, and that I might live free, I choose the solitude of these fields: the trees on these mountains are my companions; the transparent waters of these brooks my looking-glass: to the trees and the waters I communicate my thoughts and my beauty. I am a fire at a distance, and a sword afar off. Those whom the sight of me has enamoured, my words have undeceived. And if desires are kept alive by hopes, as I gave none to Chrysostom, nor to any one else, all hope being at an end, sure it may well be said, that his own obstinacy, rather than my cruelty, killed him. If it be objected to me, that his intentions were honourable, and that therefore I ought to have complied with them; I answer, that, when in this very place, where they are now digging his grave, he discovered to me the goodness of his intention, I told him that mine was to live in perpetual solitude, and that the earth alone should enjoy the fruit of my reservedness and the spoils of my beauty: and if he, notwithstanding all this plain-dealing, would obstinately persevere against hope, and sail against the wind, what wonder if he drowned himself in the midst of the gulf of his own indiscretion? If I had held him in suspense, I had been false: if I had complied with him, I acted contrary to my better intention and resolution. He persisted, though undeceived; he despaired, without being hated. Consider now, whether it be reasonable to lay the blame of his sufferings upon me. Let him who is deceived, complain; let him to whom I have broken my promise, despair; let him whom I shall encourage, presume; and let him pride himself, whom I shall admit: but let not him call me cruel, or murderous, whom I neither promise, deceive, encourage, nor admit. Heaven has not yet ordained that I should love by destiny; and from loving by choice, I desire to be excused.

'Let every one of those who solicit me, make their own particular use of this declaration; and be it understood from henceforward, that if any one dies for me, he does not die through jealousy or disdain; for she, who loves nobody, should make nobody jealous; and plain-dealing ought not to pass for disdain. Let him who calls me a savage and a basilisk, shun me as a mischievous and evil thing: let him who calls me ungrateful, not serve me; him, who thinks me shy, not know me; who cruel, not follow me; for this savage, this basilisk, this ungrateful, this cruel, this shy thing, will in nowise either seek, serve, know, or follow them. If Chrysostom's impatience and precipitate desires killed him, why should he blame my modest procedure and reserve? If I preserve my purity unspotted among these trees, why should he desire me to lose it among men? You all know that I have riches enough of my own, and do not covet other people's. My condition is free, and I have no mind to subject myself: I neither love nor hate anybody; I neither deceive this man, nor lay snares for that; I neither toy with one, nor divert myself with another. The modest conversation of the shepherdesses of these villages, and the care of my goats, are my entertainment. My desires are bounded within these mountains, and if they venture out hence, it is to contemplate the beauty of heaven, those steps by which the soul advances to its original dwelling.'

And in saying this, without staying for an answer, she turned her back, and entered into the most inaccessible part of the neighbouring mountain, leaving all those present in admiration as well of her sense as of her beauty.

Some of those who had been wounded by the powerful darts of her bright eyes, discovered an inclination to follow her, without profiting by so express a declaration as they had heard her make. Which Don Quixote perceiving, and thinking this a proper occasion to employ his chivalry in the relief of distressed damsels, he laid his hand on the hilt of his sword, and with a loud and intelligible voice, said.

'Let no person, of what state or condition soever he be, presume to follow the beautiful Marcela, on pain of incurring my furious indignation. She has demonstrated by clear and sufficient reasons, the little or no fault she ought to be charged with on account of Chrysostom's death, and how far she is from countenancing the desires of any of her lovers; for which reason, instead of being followed and persecuted, she ought to be honoured and esteemed by all good men in the world, for being the only woman in it whose intentions are so virtuous.'

Now, whether it were through Don Quixote's menaces, or because Ambrosio desired them to finish that last office to his friend, none of the shepherds stirred from thence, until, the grave being made, and Chrysostom's papers burnt, they laid his body in it, not without many tears of the bystanders. They closed the sepulchre with a large fragment of a rock, until a tombstone could be finished, which, Ambrosio said, he intended to have made, with an epitaph after this manner:

> Here lies a gentle shepherd swain,
> Through cold neglect untimely slain.
> By rigour's cruel hand he died,
> A victim to the scorn and pride
> Of a coy, beautiful ingrate,
> Whose eyes enlarge love's tyrant state.

Then they strewed abundance of flowers and boughs on the grave, and condoling with his friend Ambrosio, took leave and departed. Vivaldo and his companion did the same; and Don Quixote bade adieu to his hosts and the travellers, who entreated him to accompany them to Seville, that being a place the most likely to furnish him with adventures, since, in every street, and at every turning, more were to be met with there, than in any other place whatever. Don Quixote thanked them for the notice they gave him, and the disposition they showed to do him a courtesy, and said, that for the present he could not, and ought not to go to Seville, until he had cleared all those mountains of robbers and assassins of which, it was reported, they were full. The travellers seeing his good intention, would not importune him farther; but taking leave again, left him, and pursued their journey: in which they wanted not a subject for discourse, as well of the story of Marcela and Chrysostom, as of the madness of Don Quixote, who resolved to go in quest of the shepherdess Marcela, and offer her all that was in his power for her service. But it fell not out as he intended, as is related in the progress of this true history, the second part ending here.*

CHAPTER 15

Wherein is related the unfortunate adventure which befell Don Quixote in meeting with certain bloody-minded Yangüeses.

THE sage Cid Hamet Ben Engeli relates, that when Don Quixote had taken leave of his hosts, and of all those who were present at Chrysostom's funeral, he and his squire entered the same wood into which they had seen the shepherdess Marcela enter before. And having ranged through it for above two hours, looking for her everywhere, without being able to find her, they stopped in a meadow full of fresh grass, near which ran a pleasant and refreshing brook; insomuch that it invited and compelled them to pass there the sultry hours of the noonday heat, which already began to come on with great violence. Don Quixote and Sancho alighted, and leaving the ass and Rosinante at large, to feed upon the abundance of grass that sprung in the place, they ransacked the wallet; and without any ceremony, in friendly and social wise, master and man ate what they found in it. Sancho had taken no care to fetter Rosinante, being well assured he was so tame and so little gamesome, that all the mares of the pastures of Cordova would not provoke him to any unlucky pranks. But fortune, or the devil, who is not always asleep, so ordered it, that there were grazing in that valley a parcel of Galician mares, belonging to certain Yangüesian carriers,* whose custom it is to pass the mid-day with their drove, in places where there is grass and water: and that, where Don Quixote chanced to be, was very fit for the purpose of the Yangüeses. Now it fell out, that Rosinante had a mind to solace himself with the fillies and, having them in the wind, broke out of his natural and accustomed pace, and without asking his master's leave, betook himself to a smart trot, and went to communicate his need to them. But they, as it seemed, having more inclination to feed than anything else, received him with their heels and their teeth, in such a manner, that in a little time his girths broke, and he lost his saddle. But what must have more sensibly affected him, was that the carriers, seeing the violence offered to their mares, ran to him with their pack-staves, and so belaboured him, that they laid him along on the ground in wretched plight.

By this time Don Quixote and Sancho, who had seen the drubbing of Rosinante, came up out of breath; and Don Quixote said to Sancho:

'By what I see, friend Sancho, these are no knights, but rascally people, of a scoundrel race. I tell you this, because you may very well help me to take ample revenge for the outrage they have done to Rosinante before our eyes.'

'What the devil of revenge can we take,' answered Sancho, 'they being above twenty, and we no more than two, and perhaps but one and a half?'

'I am as good as a hundred,' replied Don Quixote: and without saying more, he laid his hand on his sword, and flew at the Yangüeses; and Sancho did the same, incited and moved thereto by the example of his master. At the first blow, Don Quixote gave one of them a terrible wound, through a leathern doublet which he wore, on the shoulder. The Yangüeses, seeing themselves assaulted in this manner by two men only, they being so many, betook themselves to their clubs, and hemming them in, began to belabour them with great vehemence and animosity. It is true, that at the second pale they brought Sancho to the ground; and the same befell Don Quixote, neither his dexterity nor courage standing him in any stead; and as fate would have it, he fell just at Rosinante's feet, who had not yet got up: whence we may learn how unmercifully pack-staves will bruise, when put into rustic and wrathful hands. The Yangüeses, perceiving the mischief they had done, loaded their beasts with all speed, and pursued their journey, leaving the two adventurers in evil plight.

The first who came to himself was Sancho Panza: who finding himself close to his master, with a feeble and plaintive voice, cried:

'Señor Don Quixote! ah! Señor Don Quixote!'

'What would you have, brother Sancho!' answered Don Quixote, in the same feeble and lamentable tone.

'I could wish, if it were possible,' answered Sancho Panza, 'your worship would give me two draughts of that drink of

Feo Blas,* if you have it here at hand; perhaps it may do as well for broken bones, as it does for wounds.'

'Unhappy I, that we have it not!' answered Don Quixote. 'But I swear to you, Sancho Panza, on the faith of a knight-errant, that before two days pass (if fortune does not order it otherwise) I will have it in my power, or my hand shall be very much out.'

'But in how many days, do you think, Sir, we shall recover the use of our feet?' replied Sancho Panza.

'For my part,' said the battered knight Don Quixote, 'I cannot limit the number; but it is all my own fault; for I ought not to have laid hand on my sword against men, who were not dubbed knights like myself. And therefore, I believe the God of battles has permitted this chastisement to fall upon me as a punishment for having transgressed the laws of chivalry. Wherefore, brother Sancho, it is requisite you be forewarned of what I shall now tell you; for it highly concerns the good of us both: and it is this; that when you see we are insulted by such rascally rabble, do not stay till I lay hand on my sword against them, for I will in nowise do it; but do you draw your sword, and chastise them to your own heart's content: but if any knights shall come up to their assistance, I shall then know how to defend you, and offend them with all my might: for you have already seen by a thousand tokens and experiments, how far the valour of this strong arm of mine extends: so arrogant was the poor gentleman become by the victory over the valiant Biscainer.'

But Sancho Panza did not so thoroughly like his master's instructions, as to forbear answering, and saying:

'Sir, I am a peaceable, tame, quiet man, and can dissemble any injury whatsoever; for I have a wife and children to maintain and bring up: so that give me leave, Sir, to tell you, by way of hint, since it is not my part to command, that I will upon no account draw my sword, neither against peasant nor against knight; and that, from this time forward, in the presence of God, I forgive all injuries any one has done or shall do me, or that any person is now doing or may hereafter do me, whether he be high or low, rich or poor, gentle or simple, without excepting any state or condition whatever.'

Which his master hearing, he answered:

'I wish I had breath to talk a little at my ease, and that the pain I feel in this rib would cease ever so short a while, that I might convince you, Panza, of the error you are in. Harkye, sinner, should the gale of fortune, hitherto so contrary, come about in our favour, filling the sails of our desires, so that we may safely and without any hindrance, make the port of some one of those islands I have promised you, what would become of you, if, when I had gained it, and made you lord thereof, you should render all ineffectual by not being a knight, nor desiring to be one, and by having neither valour nor intention to revenge the injuries done you, or to defend your dominions? For you must know, that in kingdoms and provinces newly conquered, the minds of the natives are never so quiet, nor so much in the interest of their new master, but there is still ground to fear that they will endeavour to bring about a change of things, and once more, as they call it, try their fortune: and therefore the new possessor ought to have understanding to know how to conduct himself, and courage to act offensively and defensively, whatever shall happen.'

'In this that hath now befallen us,' answered Sancho, 'I wish I had been furnished with that understanding and valour your worship speaks of; but I swear on the faith of a poor man, I am at this time fitter for plasters than discourses. Try, Sir, whether you are able to rise, and we will help up Rosinante, though he does not deserve it; for he was the principal cause of all this mauling. I never believed the like of Rosinante, whom I took to be chaste, and as peaceable as myself. But it is a true saying, that "much time is necessary to come to a thorough knowledge of persons"; and that "we are sure of nothing in this life". Who could have thought that, after such swinging slashes as you gave that unfortunate adventurer, there should come post, as it were, in pursuit of you, this vast tempest of pack-staves, which has discharged itself upon our shoulders?'

'Thine, Sancho,' replied Don Quixote, 'should, one would think, be used to such storms; but mine, that were brought up between muslins and cambrics, must needs be more sensible of the grief of this mishap. And were it not that I imagine; (do I say imagine?) did I not know for certain, that all these inconveniences are inseparably annexed to the profession of arms, I would suffer myself to die here out of pure vexation.'

To this replied the squire:

'Sir, since these mishaps are the genuine fruits and harvests of chivalry, pray tell me whether they fall out often, or whether they have their set times in which they happen; for, to my thinking, two more such harvests will disable us from ever reaping a third, if God of his infinite mercy does not succour us.'

'Learn, friend Sancho,' answered Don Quixote, 'that the life of knights-errant is subject to a thousand perils and mishaps: but then they are every whit as near becoming kings and emperors; and this experience hath shown us in many and divers knights, whose histories I am perfectly acquainted with. I could tell you now, if the pain would give me leave, of some, who, by the strength of their arm alone, have mounted to the high degrees I have mentioned; and these very men were, before and after, involved in sundry calamities and misfortunes. For the valorous Amadis de Gaul saw himself in the power of his mortal enemy, Archelaus the enchanter, of whom it is positively affirmed, that when he had him prisoner, he gave him above two hundred lashes with his horse's bridle, after he had tied him to a pillar in his court-yard. And moreover there is a private author, of no small credit, who tells us that the Knight of the Sun, being caught by a trap-door, which sunk under his feet, in a certain castle, found himself at the bottom in a deep dungeon underground, bound hand and foot; where they administered to him one of those things they call a clyster, of snow-water and sand, that almost did his business; and if he had not been succoured in that great distress by a certain sage, his special friend, it had gone very hard with the poor knight. So that I may very well suffer among so many worthy persons, who underwent much greater affronts than those we now undergo: for I would have you know, Sancho, that wounds, which are given with instruments that are accidentally in one's hand, are no affront. And thus it is expressly written in the law of combat, that if a shoemaker strikes a person with the last he has in his hand, though it be really of wood, it will not therefore be said, that the person thus beaten with it was cudgelled. I say this, that you may not think, though we are mauled in this scuffle, we are disgraced; for the arms those men carried, wherewith they pounded us, were no other than their pack-staves; and none of them as I remember, had either tuck, sword, or dagger.'*

'They gave me no leisure,' answered Sancho, 'to observe so narrowly; for scarcely had I laid hand on my whinyard,* when they crossed my shoulders with their saplings, in such a manner, that they deprived my eyes of sight, and my feet of strength, laying me where I now lie, and where I am not so much concerned to think whether the business of the threshing be an affront or no, as I am troubled at the pain of the blows, which will leave as deep an impression on my memory, as on my shoulders.'

'All this, notwithstanding, I tell you, brother Panza,' replied Don Quixote, 'there is no remembrance which time does not obliterate, nor pain which death does not put an end to.'

'What greater misfortune can there be,' replied Panza, 'than that which remains till time effaces it, and till death puts an end to it? If this mischance of ours were of that sort, which people cure with a couple of plasters, it would not be altogether so bad: but for aught I see, all the plasters of an hospital will not be sufficient to set us to rights again.'

'Have done with this, and gather strength out of weakness, Sancho,' answered Don Quixote; 'for so I purpose to do: and let us see how Rosinante does; for, by what I perceive, not the least part of this misfortune has fallen to the poor beast's share.'

'That is not at all strange,' answered Sancho, 'since he also appertains to a knight-errant. But what I wonder at is, that my ass should come off scot-free, where we have paid so dear.'

'Fortune always leaves some door open in disasters, whereby to come at a remedy,' said Don Quixote. 'I say this, because this poor beast may now supply the want of Rosinante, by carrying me hence to some castle, where I may be cured of my wounds. Nor do I take the being mounted in this fashion to be dishonourable; for I remember to have read that the good Silenus, governor and tutor of the merry god of laughter, when he made his entry into the city of the hundred gates,* went riding, much to his satisfaction, on a most beautiful ass.'

'It is like he rode as your worship says,' answered Sancho: 'but there is a main difference between riding and lying athwart, like a sack of rubbish.'

To which Don Quixote answered:

'The wounds received in battle rather give honour than take it away; so that, friend Panza, answer me no more, but as I have already said to you, raise me up as well as you can, and place me in whatever manner you please, upon your ass, that we may get hence, before night comes on, and overtakes us in this uninhabited place.'

'Yet I have heard your worship say,' quoth Panza, 'that it is usual for knights-errant, to sleep on heaths and deserts most part of the year, and that they look upon it to be very fortunate.'

'That is,' said Don Quixote, 'when they cannot help it, or are in love: and this is so true, that there have been knights, who, unknown to their mistresses, have exposed themselves, for two years together, upon rocks, to the sun and the shade, and to the inclemencies of heaven. One of these was Amadis, when calling himself Beltenebros, he took up his lodging on the Peña Pobre* whether for eight years or eight months I know not, for I am not perfect in his history. It is sufficient that there he was, doing penance for I know not what distaste shown to him by the lady Oriana. But let us have done with this, Sancho, and dispatch, before such another misfortune happens to the ass as hath befallen Rosinante.'

'That would be the devil, indeed,' quoth Sancho.

And sending forth thirty alas's, and sixty sighs, and a hundred and twenty curses on whosoever had brought him hither, he raised himself up, but stayed bent by the way, like a Turkish bow, entirely unable to stand upright: and with all this fatigue he made a shift to saddle his ass, who had also taken advantage of that day's excessive liberty, to go a little astray. He then heaved up Rosinante, who, had he had a tongue to complain with, most certainly would not have been outdone either by Sancho or his master. In fine, Sancho settled Don Quixote upon the ass, and tying Rosinante by the head to his tail, led them both by the halter, proceeding now faster, now slower, towards the place where he thought the road might lie. And he had scarce gone a short league, when fortune (which was conducting his affairs from good to better) discovered to him the road, in which he espied an inn; which, to his sorrow and Don Quixote's joy, must needs be a castle. Sancho positively maintained it was an inn, and his master that it was a castle; and the obstinate dispute lasted so long, that they had time to arrive there before it ended; and without more ado Sancho entered into it with his string of cattle.

CHAPTER 16

Of what happened to the ingenious gentleman in the inn, which he imagined to be a castle.

THE innkeeper, seeing Don Quixote laid across the ass, inquired of Sancho, what ailed him? Sancho answered him, that it was nothing but a fall from a rock, whereby his ribs were somewhat bruised. The innkeeper had a wife of a different disposition from those of the like occupation; for she was naturally charitable, and touched with the misfortunes of her neighbours: so that she presently set herself to cure Don Quixote, and made her daughter, a very comely young maiden, assist her in the cure of her guest. There was also a servant in the inn, an Asturian wench, broad-faced, flat-headed, and saddle-nosed, with one eye squinting, and the other not much better. It is true, the activity of her body* made amends for her other defects. She was not seven hands high from her feet to her head; and her shoulders, which burdened her a little too much, made her look down to the ground more than she cared to do. Now this agreeable lass helped the damsel; and they two made Don Quixote a very sorry bed in a garret, which gave evident tokens of having formerly served many years as a horse-loft. In which room lodged also a carrier, whose bed lay a little beyond that of our Don Quixote. And though it was composed of pannels, and other trappings of his mules, it had much the advantage of Don Quixote's, which consisted of four not very smooth boards, upon two not very equal tressels, and a flock bed no thicker than a quilt, and full of knobs, which if one had not seen through the breaches that they were wool, by the hardness might have been taken for pebble-stones; with two sheets like the leather of an old target, and a rug, the threads of which, if you had a mind, you might number without losing a single one of the account.

In this wretched bed was Don Quixote laid; and immediately the hostess and her daughter plastered him from head to foot, Maritornes (for so the Asturian was called) holding the light. And as the hostess laid on the plasters, perceiving Don Quixote to be so full of bruises in all parts, she said, that they seemed to be rather marks of blows than of a fall.

'They were not blows,' said Sancho; 'but the rock had many sharp points and knobs, and every one has left its mark.'

He said also:

'Pray, forsooth, order it so, that some tow may be left; somebody else may have occasion for it, for my sides also ache a little.'

'So then,' said the hostess, 'you have had a fall too.'

'No fall,' said Sancho Panza; 'but the fright I took at seeing my master fall has made my body so sore, that methinks I have received a thousand drubs.'

'That may very well be,' said the girl; 'for I have often dreamed that I was falling down from some high tower, and could never come to the ground; and when I have awakened, I have found myself as bruised and battered, as if I had really fallen.'

'But here is the point, mistress,' answered Sancho Panza, 'that I, without dreaming at all, and more awake than I am now, find myself with almost as many bruises as my master Don Quixote.'

'How is this cavalier called?' quoth the Asturian Maritornes.

'Don Quixote de la Mancha,' answered Sancho Panza: 'he is a knight-errant, and one of the best and most valiant that has been seen this long time in the world.'

'What is a knight-errant?' replied the wench.

'Are you such a novice, that you do not know?' answered Sancho Panza. 'Then learn, sister of mine, that a knight-errant is a thing, that, in two words, is seen cudgelled and an emperor; to-day is the most unfortunate creature in the world, and the most necessitous, and to-morrow will have two or three crowns of kingdoms to give to his squire.'

'How comes it then to pass, that you, being squire to this so worthy a gentleman,' said the hostess, 'have not yet, as it seems, got so much as an earldom?'

'It is early days yet,' answered Sancho; 'for it is but a month* since we set out in quest of adventures, and hitherto we have met with none that deserve the name. And sometimes one looks for one thing, and finds another. True it is, if my master, Don Quixote, recovers of this wound or fall, and I am not disabled, thereby, I would not truck my hopes for the best title in Spain.'

All this discourse Don Quixote listened to very attentively; and, setting himself up in his bed as well as he could, and taking the hostess by the hand, he said to her:

'Believe me, beauteous lady, you may reckon yourself happy in having lodged my person in this your castle, and such a person, that, if I do not praise myself, it is because, as is commonly said, self-praise depreciates: but my squire will inform you who I am. I only say, that I shall retain the service you have done me, eternally engraved in my memory, and be grateful to you whilst my life shall remain. And had it pleased the high heavens that love had not held me so enthralled, and subjected to his laws, and to the eyes of that beautiful ingrate, whose name I mutter between my teeth, the eyes of this lovely virgin had been mistresses of my liberty.'

The hostess, her daughter, and the good Maritornes, stood confounded at hearing our knight-errant's discourse, which they understood just as much as if he had spoken Greek;

though they guessed that it all tended to compliments and offers of service. And, not being accustomed to such kind of language, they stared at him with admiration, and thought him another sort of man than those now in fashion; and so, thanking him with innlike phrase for his offers, they left him. The Asturian Maritornes doctored Sancho, who stood in no less need of it than his master.

The carrier and she had agreed to solace themselves together that night; and she had given him her word, that, when the guests were a-bed, and her master and mistress asleep, she would repair to him, and satisfy his desire as much as he pleased. And it is said of this honest wench, that she never made the like promise, but she performed it, though she had made it on the mountain, without any witness: for she stood much upon her gentility, and yet thought it no disgrace to be employed in that calling of serving in an inn; often saying, that misfortunes and unhappy accidents had brought her to that state.

Don Quixote's hard, scanty, beggarly, feeble bed stood first in the middle of that illustrious cock-loft;* and close by it stood Sancho's, which consisted only of a flag-mat, and a rug that seemed to be rather of beaten hemp than of wool. Next these two, stood the carrier's, made up, as has been said, of pannels, and the whole furniture of two of the best mules he had; which were twelve in number, fat and stately: for he was one of the richest carriers of Arévalo, as the author of this history relates, who makes particular mention of this carrier, whom he knew very well; nay, some go so far as to say, he was somewhat of kin to him. Besides, Cid Hamet Ben Engeli was a very curious and very punctual historian in all things: and this appears plainly from the circumstances already related; which, however seemingly minute and trivial, he would not pass over in silence. Which may serve as an example to the grave historians, who relate facts so very briefly and succinctly, that we have scarcely a taste of them, leaving behind, either through neglect, malice, or ignorance, the most substantial part of the work. The blessing of God a thousand times on the author of *Tablante of Ricamonte*, and on him who wrote the exploits of the Count

de Tomillas, with what punctuality do they describe everything!*

I say then, that, after the carrier had visited his mules, and
given them their second course, he laid himself down upon
his pannels, in expectation of his most punctual Maritornes.
Sancho was already plastered and laid down; and though he
endeavoured to sleep, the pain of his ribs would not consent;
and Don Quixote, through the anguish of his, kept his eyes
as wide open as a hare. The whole inn was in profound
silence, and no other light in it than what proceeded from a
lamp, which hung burning in the middle of the entry. This
marvellous stillness, and the thoughts which our knight always carried about him, from the accidents recounted in every
page of the books, the authors of his misfortune, brought to
his imagination one of the strangest whimsies that can well
be conceived; which was, that he fancied he was arrived at
a certain famous castle (for, as has been said, all the inns
where he lodged were, in his opinion, castles), and that the
innkeeper's daughter was daughter to the lord of the castle;
who, captivated by his fine appearance, was fallen in love
with him, and had promised him that night, unknown to her
parents, to steal privately to him, and pass a good part of it
with him. And taking all this chimera (which he had formed
to himself) for reality and truth, he began to be uneasy, and
to reflect on the dangerous crisis to which his fidelity was
going to be exposed; and he resolved in his heart not to
commit disloyalty against his lady Dulcinea del Toboso,
though queen Guinevere herself with the lady Quintañona
should present themselves before him.

Whilst his thoughts were taken up with these extravagances,
the time and the hour (which to him proved an unlucky one)
of the Asturian's coming drew near; who, in her smock, and
bare-footed, her hair tucked up under a fustian coif, came
with silent and cautious steps into the room where the three
were lodged, to find her carrier. But scarcely was she come
to the door, when Don Quixote perceived her, and, sitting
up in his bed, in spite of his plasters, and the pain of his
ribs, stretched out his arms to receive his beauteous damsel
the Asturian, who, crouching and holding her breath, went

with hands extended feeling for her lover. Thus she encountered Don Quixote's arms, who caught fast hold of her
by the wrist, and pulling her towards him, she not daring to
speak a word, made her sit down on the bed by him.
Presently he fell to feeling her smock, which, though it was
of canvas, seemed to him to be of the finest and softest
lawn. She had on her wrist a string of glass beads; but to
his fancy they were precious oriental pearls. Her hairs, not
unlike those of a horse's mane, he took for threads of the
brightest gold of Arabia, whose splendour obscures that of
the sun itself. And though her breath, doubtless, smelled of
last night's stale salt fish, he fancied himself sucking from
her lips a delicious and aromatic odour. In short, he painted
her in his imagination in the very form and manner he had
read described in his books, of some princess, who comes,
adorned in the manner here mentioned, to visit the danger-
ously-wounded knight with whom she is in love. And so great
was the poor gentleman's infatuation, that neither the touch,
nor the breath, nor other things the good wench had about
her, could undeceive him, though enough to make any one
but a carrier vomit. Yet he imagined he held the goddess of
beauty between his arms; and clasping her fast, with an
amorous and low voice, he began to say to her:

'O that I were in a condition, beautiful and high lady, to
be able to return so vast a favour as this you have done me
by the presence of your great beauty! But fortune, who is
never weary of persecuting the good, is pleased to lay me on
this bed, where I lie so bruised and disabled, that, though I
were ever so much inclined to gratify your desires, it would
be impossible. And to this is added another still greater
impossibility, which is the plighted faith I have given to the
peerless Dulcinea del Toboso, the sole mistress of my most
hidden thoughts. Had it not been for these obstacles, I should
not have been so dull a knight as to let slip the happy
opportunity your great goodness has put into my hands.'

Maritornes was in the utmost pain, and in a violent sweat,
to find herself held so fast by Don Quixote; and not hearing
or minding what he said to her, she struggled, without
speaking a word, to get loose from him. The honest carrier,

whose loose desires kept him awake, heard his sweetheart from the first moment she entered the door, and listened attentively to all that Don Quixote said; and, jealous that the Asturian had broken her word with him for another, he drew nearer and nearer to Don Quixote's bed, and stood still, to see what would come of those speeches, which he did not understand. But, seeing that the wench strove to get from him, and that Don Quixote laboured to hold her, not liking the jest, he lifted up his arm, and discharged so terrible a blow on the lantern jaws of the enamoured knight, that he bathed his mouth in blood; and, not content with this, he mounted upon his ribs, and paced them over, somewhat above a trot, from end to end.

The bed, which was a little crazy, and its foundations none of the strongest, being unable to bear the additional weight of the carrier, came down with them to the ground; at which great noise the host awaked, and presently imagined it must be some prank of Maritornes; for, having called to her aloud, she made no answer. With this suspicion he got up, and lighting a candle, went towards the place where he had heard the bustle. The wench, perceiving her master coming, and knowing him to be terribly passionate, all trembling and confounded, betook herself to Sancho Panza's bed, who was now asleep; and creeping in, she lay close to him, and as round as an egg. The innkeeper entering, said:

'Where are you, strumpet? these are most certainly some of your doings.'

Now Sancho awaked, and perceiving that bulk lying as it were a-top of him, fancied he had got the nightmare, and began to lay about him on every side; and not a few of his fisticuffs reached Maritornes, who, provoked by the smart, and laying all modesty aside, made Sancho such a return in kind, that she quite roused him from sleep in spite of his drowsiness; who, finding himself handled in that manner, without knowing by whom, raised himself up as well as he could and grappled with Maritornes; and there began between these two the toughest and pleasantest skirmish in the world. The carrier, perceiving by the light of the host's candle, how it fared with his mistress, quitted Don Quixote, and ran to give her the necessary assistance. The landlord did the same, but with a different intention; for his was to chastise the wench, concluding without doubt that she was the sole occasion of all this harmony. And so, as the proverb goes, the cat to the rat, the rat to the rope, and the rope to the stick: the carrier belaboured Sancho, Sancho the wench, the wench him, the innkeeper the wench: and all laid about them so thick, that they gave themselves not a minute's rest: and the best of it was, that the landlord's candle went out; and they, being left in the dark, threshed one another so unmercifully, that, let the hand light where it would, it left nothing sound.

There lodged by chance that night in the inn an officer of those they call the Holy Brotherhood of Toledo; who likewise hearing the strange noise of the scuffle, catched up his wand, and the tin box which held his commission, and entered the room in the dark, crying out:

'Forbear in the name of justice; forbear in the name of the Holy Brotherhood.'

And the first he lighted on was the battered Don Quixote who lay on his demolished bed, stretched upon his back, and quite senseless; and laying hold of his beard, as he was groping about, he cried out incessantly:

'I charge you to aid and assist me.'

But, finding that the person he had laid hold of neither stirred nor moved, he concluded that he must be dead, and that the people within the room were his murderers: and with this suspicion he raised his voice still louder, crying:

'Shut the inn door, see that nobody gets out; for they have killed a man here.'

This voice astonished them all, and each of them left the conflict the very moment the voice reached them. The landlord withdrew to his chamber, the carrier to his pannels, and the wench to her straw: only the unfortunate Don Quixote and Sancho could not stir from the place they were in. Now the officer let go Don Quixote's beard, and went out to get a light, to search after and apprehend the delinquents: but he found none; for the innkeeper had purposely extinguished the lamp, when he retired to his chamber; and the officer was forced to have recourse to the chimney, where, after much pains and time, he lighted another lamp.

CHAPTER 17

Wherein are continued the numberless hardships which the brave Don Quixote and his good squire Sancho Panza underwent in the inn, which he unhappily took for a castle.

By this time Don Quixote was come to himself, and with the very same tone of voice with which, the day before, he had called to his squire, when he lay stretched along 'in the Valley of Pack-staves',* he began to call to him, saying:

'Sancho, friend, sleepest thou? sleepest thou, friend Sancho?'

'How should I sleep? woe is me?' answered Sancho, full of trouble and vexation; 'I cannot but think all the devils in hell have been in my company to-night.'

'You may very well believe so,' answered Don Quixote; 'and either I know little, or this castle is enchanted. For you must know—but what I am now going to tell you, you must swear to keep secret until after my death.'

'Yes, I swear', answered Sancho.

'I say it,' replied Don Quixote, 'because I am an enemy to the taking away anybody's reputation.'

'I do swear,' said Sancho again, 'I will keep it secret until after your decease, and God grant I may discover it to-morrow.'

'Have I done you so many ill turns, Sancho,' answered Don Quixote, 'that you would willingly see me dead so very soon?'

'It is not for that,' answered Sancho; 'but I am an enemy to keeping things long, and I would not have them rot with keeping.'

'Be it for what it will,' said Don Quixote; 'I trust for greater matters than that to your love and kindness; and therefore you must know, that this night there has befallen on me one of the strangest adventures imaginable; and to tell it you in few words, know, that a little while ago, there came to me the daughter of the lord of this castle, who is the most accomplished and beautiful damsel that is to be found in a great part of the inhabitable earth. What could I not tell you of the gracefulness of her person? what of the sprightliness of her wit? what of other hidden charms, which to preserve the fidelity I owe to my lady Dulcinea del Toboso, I will pass over untouched and in silence? Only I must tell you, that heaven, envying so great happiness as fortune had put into my hands, or perhaps (which is more probable) this castle, as I said before, being enchanted, at the time that she and I were engaged in the sweetest and most amorous conversation, without my seeing it, or knowing whence it came, comes a hand, fastened to the arm of some monstrous giant, and gave me such a douse on the chops, that they were all bathed in blood; and it afterwards pounded me in such sort, that I am in a worse case than yesterday, when the carriers, for Rosinante's frolic, did us the mischief you know. Whence I conjecture that the treasure of this damsel's beauty is guarded by some enchanted Moor, and is not reserved for me.'

'Nor for me neither,' answered Sancho; 'for more than four hundred Moors have cudgelled me in such a manner, that the basting of the pack-staves was tarts and cheesecakes to it. But tell me, pray Sir, call you this an excellent and rare adventure, which has left us in such a pickle? though it was not quite so bad with your worship, who had between your arms that incomparable beauty aforesaid. But I, what had I, besides the heaviest blows that, I hope, I shall ever feel as long as I live? Woe is me, and the mother that bore me! for I am no knight-errant, nor ever mean to be one; and yet, of all the misadventures, the greater part still falls to my share.'

'What! have you been pounded too?' answered Don Quixote.

'Have I not told you, yes? Evil befall my lineage!' quoth Sancho.

'Be in no pain, friend,' said Don Quixote; 'for I will now make the precious balsam, with which we will cure ourselves in the twinkling of an eye.'

By this time the officer had lighted his lamp, and entered to see the person he thought was killed; and Sancho seeing

him come in, and perceiving him to be in his shirt, with a
night-cap on his head, a lamp in his hand, and a very
ill-favoured countenance, he demanded of his master;

'Pray, Sir, is this the enchanted Moor, coming to finish the
correction he has bestowed upon us?'

'It cannot be the Moor,' answered Don Quixote; 'for the
enchanted suffer not themselves to be seen by anybody.'

'If they will not be seen, they will be felt,' said Sancho;
'witness my shoulders.'

'Mine might speak too,' answered Don Quixote: 'but this
is not sufficient evidence to convince us that what we see is
the enchanted Moor.'

The officer entered, and, finding them communing in so
calm a manner, stood in suspense. It is true, indeed, Don
Quixote still lay flat on his back without being able to stir
through mere pounding and plastering. The officer approached him, and said:

'How fares it, honest friend?'*

'I would speak more respectfully,' answered Don Quixote,
'were I in your place. Is it the fashion of this country to talk
in this manner to knights-errant, blockhead?'

The officer, seeing himself so ill-treated by one of so scurvy
an appearance, could not bear it, and lifting up the brass
lamp with all its oil, gave it Don Quixote over the pate, in
such sort that he broke his head; and all being in the dark,
he ran instantly out of the room.

'Doubtless, Sir,' quoth Sancho Panza, 'this is the enchanted
Moor; and he reserves the treasure for others, and for us
only blows and lamp-knocks.'

'It is even so,' answered Don Quixote: 'and it is to no
purpose to regard this business of enchantments, or to be
out of humour or angry with them: for as they are invisible
and fantastical only, we shall find nothing to be revenged on,
though we endeavour it never so much. Get you up, Sancho,
if you can, and call the governor of this fortress; and take
care to get me some oil, wine, salt, and rosemary, to make
the healing balsam: for in truth, I believe I want it very much
at this time; for the wounds this phantom has given me bleed
very fast.'

Sancho got up, with pain enough of his bones, and went in the dark towards the landlord's chamber, and meeting with the officer who was listening to discover what his enemy would be at, said to him:

'Sir, whoever you are, do us the favour and kindness to help us to a little rosemary, oil, salt, and wine; for they are wanted to cure one of the best knights-errant in the world, who lies in yon bed, sorely wounded by the hands of the enchanted Moor that is in this inn.'

The officer, hearing him talk at this rate, took him for one out of his senses. And the day beginning to dawn, he opened the inn door, and calling the host, told him what that honest man wanted. The innkeeper furnished him with what he desired, and Sancho carried them to Don Quixote, who lay with his hands on his head, complaining of the pain of the lamp-knock, which had done him no other hurt than the raising a couple of bumps pretty much swelled: and what he took for blood was nothing but sweat, occasioned by the anguish of the past storm. In fine, he took his simples, and made a compound of them, mixing them together, and boiling them a good while, until he thought they were enough. Then he asked for a phial to put it in: and there being no such thing in the inn, he resolved to put it in a cruse, or oil-flask of tin, which the host made him a present of. And immediately he said over the cruse above four-score Paternosters, and as many Ave-Marias, Salves and Credos, and every word was accompanied with a cross, by way of benediction: at all which were present Sancho, the innkeeper, and the officer: as for the carrier, he was gone soberly about the business of tending his mules.

This done, he resolved immediately to make trial of the virtue of that precious balsam, as he imagined it to be; and so he drank about a pint and a half of what the cruse could not contain, and which remained in the pot it was infused and boiled in: and scarcely had he done drinking, when he began to vomit so violently, that nothing was left in his stomach; and, through the convulsive reachings and agitation of the vomit, he fell into a most copious sweat: wherefore he ordered them to cover him up warm, and to leave him alone. They did so, and he continued fast asleep above three hours, when he awoke and found himself greatly relieved in his body, and so much recovered of his bruising, that he thought himself as good as cured. And he was thoroughly persuaded that he had hit on the true balsam of Fierabras; and that with this remedy, he might thenceforward encounter without fear any dangers, battles, and conflicts whatever, though never so perilous.

Sancho Panza, who likewise took his master's amendment for a miracle, desired he would give him what remained in the pipkin, which was no small quantity. Don Quixote granting his request, he took it in both hands, and with a good faith and better will, tossed it down into his stomach, swallowing very little less than his master had done. Now the case was, that poor Sancho's stomach was not so nice and squeamish as his master's: and therefore, before he could throw it up, it gave him such pangs and loathings, with such cold sweats and faintings, that he verily thought his last hour was come: and finding himself so afflicted and tormented, he cursed the balsam, and the thief that had given it him. Don Quixote seeing him in that condition, said to him:

'I believe, Sancho, that all this mischief has befallen you because you are not dubbed a knight; for I am of opinion, this liquor can do no good to those who are not.'

'If your worship knew that,' replied Sancho '(evil betide me and all my generation!), why did you suffer me to drink it?'

By this time the drench operated effectually, and the poor squire began to discharge at both ends with so much precipitation, that the flag-mat upon which he lay, and the blanket in which he wrapped himself were never after fit for use. He sweated and sweated again, with such faintings and fits, that not only himself, but everybody else thought he was expiring. This hurricane and evacuation lasted him near two hours; at the end of which he did not remain as his master did, but so shattered and broken that he was not able to stand. But Don Quixote, who, as is said, found himself at ease and whole, would needs depart immediately in quest of adventures, believing that all the time he loitered away there was depriving the world, and the distressed in it, of his aid and protection; and the rather through the security and confidence he placed in the balsam and thus, hurried away by this strong desire, he saddled Rosinante with his own hands, and pannelled his squire's beast, whom he also helped to dress, and to mount him upon the ass. He presently got on horseback, and coming to a corner of the inn, he laid hold of a pike that stood there, to serve him for a lance.

All the folks in the inn stood gazing at him, being somewhat about twenty persons: among the rest the host's daughter stared at him, and he on his part removed not his eyes from her, and ever and anon sent forth a sigh, which he seemed to tear up from the bottom of his bowels; all imagining it to proceed from the pain he felt in his ribs, at least those who the night before had seen how he was plastered.

They being now both mounted, and standing at the door of the inn, he called to the host, and, with a very solemn and grave voice, said to him:

'Many and great are the favours, Señor governor, which in this your castle I have received, and I remain under infinite obligations to acknowledge them all the days of my life. If I could make you a return by revenging you on any insolent who has done you outrage, know that the duty of my profession is no other than to strengthen the weak, to revenge the injured, and to chastise the perfidious. Run over your memory, and if you find anything of this nature to recommend to me, you need only declare it; for I promise you, by the order of knighthood I have received, to procure you satisfaction and amends to your heart's desire.'

The host answered with the same gravity:

'Sir knight, I have no need of your worship's avenging any wrong for me; I know how to take the proper revenge when any injury is done me; I only desire your worship to pay me for what you have had in the inn, as well for the straw and barley for your two beasts, as for your supper and lodging.'

'What, then, is this an inn?' replied Don Quixote.

'And a very creditable one,' answered the host.

'Hitherto, then, I have been in an error,' answered Don Quixote; 'for, in truth, I took it for a castle, and no bad one either: but since it is so, that it is no castle, but an inn, all that can now be done is, that you excuse the payment; for I cannot act contrary to the law of knights-errant, of whom I certainly know (having hitherto read nothing to the contrary) that they never paid for lodging, or anything else, in any inn where they have lain; and that because of right and good reason, all possible good accommodation is due to them, in recompense of the insufferable hardships they endure in quest of adventures, by night and by day, in winter and in summer, on foot and on horseback, with thirst and with hunger, with heat and with cold, subject to all the inclemencies of heaven, and to all the inconveniences upon earth.'

'I see little to my purpose in all this,' answered the host: 'pay me what is my due, and let us have none of your stories and knight-errantries; for I make no account of anything, but how to come by my own.'

'Thou art a blockhead, and a pitiful innkeeper,' answered Don Quixote; so clapping spurs to Rosinante, and brandishing his lance, he sallied out of the inn, without anybody's opposing him, and without looking to see whether his squire followed him or not, got a good way off.

The host seeing him go off without paying him, ran to seize on Sancho Panza, who said that since his master would not pay, he would not pay either; for being squire to a knight-errant, as he was, the same rule and reason held as good for him as for his master, not to pay anything in public-houses and inns. The innkeeper grew very testy at this, and threatened him, if he did not pay him, he would get it in a way he should be sorry for. Sancho swore by the order of chivalry, which his master had received, that he would not pay a single farthing, though it should cost him his life; for the laudable and ancient usage of knights-errant should not be lost for him, nor should the squires of future knights have reason to complain of, or reproach him for the breach of so just a right.

Poor Sancho's ill luck would have it, that among those who were in the inn, there were four cloth-workers of Segovia, three needle-makers of the horse fountain of Córdova,* and two butchers of Seville, all arch, merry, unlucky, and frolic-

some fellows; who, as it were, instigated and moved by the
selfsame spirit, came up to Sancho, and dismounting him
from the ass, one of them went in for the landlord's bed-
blanket; and putting him therein, they looked up and saw
that the ceiling was somewhat too low for their work, and
determined to go out into the yard, which was bounded only
by the sky. There Sancho being placed in the midst of the
blanket, they began to toss him aloft, and to divert themselves
with him, as with a dog at Shrovetide. The cries which the
poor blanketed squire sent forth were so many and so loud,
that they reached his master's ears; who, stopping to listen
attentively, believed that some new adventure was at hand,
until he found plainly that he who cried was his squire; and
turning the reins, with a constrained gallop he came up to
the inn; and finding it shut, he rode round it to discover, if
he could, an entrance. But he was scarcely got to the wall
of the yard, which was not very high, when he perceived the
wicked sport they were making with his squire. He saw him
ascend and descend through the air with so much grace and
agility, that if his choler would have suffered him, I am of
opinion he would have laughed. He tried to get from his
horse upon the pales; but he was so bruised and battered,
that he could not so much as alight, and so from on
horseback he began to utter so many reproaches and revilings
against those who were tossing Sancho, that it is impossible
to put them down in writing; but that they did not therefore
desist from their laughter, nor their labour; nor did the flying
Sancho forbear his complaints, mixed sometimes with menaces, sometimes with entreaties; yet all availed little, nor
would have availed; but at last they left off from pure
weariness. They then brought him his ass, and wrapping him
in his loose coat, mounted him thereon. The compassionate
Maritornes, seeing him so harassed, thought good to help
him to a jug of water, which she fetched from the well, that
it might be the cooler. Sancho took it, and as he was lifting
it to his mouth, stopped at his master's calling to him aloud,
saying:

'Son Sancho, drink not water: child, do not drink it; it will
kill thee: see here, I hold the most holy balsam' (showing

him the cruse of the potion) 'by drinking but two drops of which, you will doubtless be whole and sound again.'

At these words Sancho turned his eyes as it were askew, and said with a loud voice:

'Perhaps you have forgot, Sir, that I am no knight, or you would have me vomit up what remains of my guts, after last night's work. Keep you liquor in the devil's name, and let me alone.'

His ceasing to speak, and beginning to drink, was all in a moment: but at the first sip finding it was water, he would proceed no further, and prayed Maritornes to bring him some wine: which she did with a very good will, and paid for it with her own money; for they say of her, that though she was in that station, she had some shadows and faint outlines of a Christian. As soon as Sancho had done drinking, he fell a-kicking his ass; and the inn gate being thrown wide open, out he went, mightily satisfied that he had paid nothing, and had carried his point, though at the expense of his accustomed surety, his carcase. The landlord, indeed, was in possession of his wallets for payment of what was due to him; but Sancho never missed them, so confused was he at going off. The innkeeper would have fastened the door well after him, as soon as he saw him out; but the blanketeers would not consent, being persons of that sort, that though Don Quixote had really been one of the Knights of the Round Table, they would not have cared two farthings for him.

CHAPTER 18

In which is rehearsed the discourse which Sancho Panza held with his master Don Quixote, with other adventures worth relating.

SANCHO came up to his master, pale, and dispirited to that degree, that he was not able to spur on his ass. Don Quixote, perceiving him in that condition, said:

'Now am I convinced, honest Sancho, that that castle, or inn, is doubtless enchanted, for they who so cruelly sported themselves with you, what could they be but hobgoblins, and people of the other world? And I am confirmed in this by having found, that when I stood at the pales of the yard, beholding the acts of your sad tragedy, I could not possibly get over them, nor so much as alight from Rosinante; so that they must certainly have held me enchanted: for I swear to you, by the faith of what I am, that if I could have got over, or alighted, I would have avenged you in such a manner, as would have made those poltroons and assassins remember the jest as long as they lived, though I knew I had transgressed the laws of chivalry thereby: for, as I have often told you, they do not allow a knight to lay hand on his sword against any one who is not so, unless it be in defence of his own life and person, and in case of urgent and extreme necessity.'

'And I too,' quoth Sancho, 'would have revenged myself if I could, dubbed or not dubbed; but I could not: though I am of opinion, that they who diverted themselves at my expense, were no hobgoblins, but men of flesh and bones, as we are; and each of them, as I heard while they were tossing me, had his proper name: one was called Pedro Martinez, another Tenorio Hernandez; and the landlord's name is John Palomeque the Left-handed: so that, Sir, as to your not being able to leap over the pales, nor to alight from your horse, the fault lay in something else, and not in enchantment. And what I gather clearly from all this is, that these adventures we are in quest of, will at the long run bring us into so many disadventures, that we shall not know which is our right foot. So that, in my poor opinion, the better and surer way would be to return to our village, now that it is reaping-time, and look after our business, and not run rambling from Ceca to Mecca,* leaping out of the frying pan into the fire.'

'How little do you know, Sancho,' answered Don Quixote, 'what belongs to chivalry! peace, and have patience; the day will come when you will see with your eyes how honourable a thing it is to follow this profession: for tell me, what greater satisfaction can there be in the world, or what pleasure can be compared with that of winning a battle, and triumphing over one's enemy? none without doubt.'

'It may be so,' answered Sancho, 'though I do not know it. I only know that since we have been knights-errant, or you have been, Sir (for there is no reason I should reckon myself in that honourable number), we have never won any battle, except that of the Biscainer; and even there you came off with the loss of half an ear, and half a helmet; and from that day to this, we have had nothing but drubbings upon drubbings, cuffs upon cuffs, beside my blanket-tossing into the bargain, and that by persons enchanted, on whom I cannot revenge myself, to know how far the pleasure reaches of overcoming an enemy, as your worship is pleased to say.'

'That is what troubles me, and ought to trouble you, Sancho,' answered Don Quixote; 'but henceforward I will endeavour to have ready at hand a sword made by such art, that no kind of enchantment can touch him that wears it. And perhaps fortune may procure me that of Amadis,* when he called himself "Knight of the Burning Sword", which was one of the best weapons that ever knight had in the world; for beside the virtue aforesaid, it cut like a razor, and no armour, though never so strong, or ever so much enchanted, could stand against it.'

'I am so fortunate,' quoth Sancho, 'that, though this were so, and you should find such a sword, it would be of service and use only to those who are dubbed knights, like the balsam: as for the poor squires, they may sing sorrow.'

'Fear not that, Sancho,' said Don Quixote; 'heaven will deal more kindly by thee.'

Don Quixote and his squire went on thus conferring together, when Don Quixote perceived on the road they were in, a great and thick cloud of dust coming towards them; and seeing it, he turned to Sancho, and said:

'This is the day, O Sancho, wherein will be seen the good that fortune has in store for me. This is the day, I say, wherein will appear, as much as in any, the strength of my arm; and in which I shall perform such exploits as shall remain written in the book of fame to all succeeding ages. Seest thou you cloud of dust, Sancho? it is raised by a prodigious army of divers and innumerable nations, who are on the march this way.'

'By this account there must be two armies,' said Sancho; 'for on this opposite side there rises such another cloud of dust.'

Don Quixote turned to view it, and seeing it was so, rejoiced exceedingly, taking it for granted they were two armies coming to engage in the midst of that spacious plain: for at all hours and moments his imagination was full of the battles, enchantments, adventures, extravagances, amours, and challenges, which he found in the books of chivalry, and whatever he said, thought, or did, had a tendency that way. Now, the cloud of dust he saw was raised by two great flocks of sheep, going the same road from different parts, and the dust hindered them from being seen until they came near. But Don Quixote affirmed with so much positiveness, that they were armies, that Sancho began to believe it, and said:

'Sir, what then must we do?'

'What,' replied Don Quixote, 'but favour and assist the weaker side? Now you must know, Sancho, that the army which marches towards us in front, is led and commanded by the great emperor Alifanfaron, lord of the great island of Tra-pobana:* this other, which marches behind us, is that of his enemy, the king of the Garamantes,* Pentapolin of the Naked Arm; for he always enters into battle with his right arm bare.'

'But why do these two princes hate one another so?' demanded Sancho.

'They hate one another,' answered Don Quixote, 'because this Alifanfaron is a furious pagan, and is in love with the daughter of Pentapolin, who is a most beautiful and super-latively graceful lady, and a Christian; and her father will not give her in marriage to the pagan king, unless he will first renounce the religion of his false prophet Mahomet, and turn Christian.'

'By my beard,' said Sancho, 'Pentapolin is in the right, and I am resolved to assist him to the utmost of my power.'

'In so doing, you will do your duty, Sancho,' said Don Quixote; 'for, in order to engage in such fights, it is not necessary to be dubbed a knight.'

'I easily comprehend that,' answered Sancho; 'but where shall we dispose of this ass, that we may be sure to find him

when the fray is over? for I believe it was never yet the
fashion to go to battle upon such a kind of beast.'

'You are in the right,' said Don Quixote; 'and what you
may do with him is, to let him take his chance, whether he
be lost or not; for we shall have such choice of horses after
the victory, that Rosinante himself will run a risk of being
trucked for another. But listen with attention, whilst I give
you an account of the principal knights of both the armies.
And, that you may see and observe them the better, let us
retire to yon rising ground, from whence both the armies
may be distinctly seen.'

They did so, and got upon a hillock, from whence the two
flocks which Don Quixote took for two armies, might easily
have been discerned, had not the clouds of dust they raised
obstructed and blinded the sight: but for all that, seeing in
his imagination what he neither did, nor could see, he began
with a loud voice to say:

'The knight you see yonder with the gilded armour, who
bears in his shield a lion crowned, couchant at a damsel's
feet, is the valorous Laurcalco, Lord of the Silver Bridge: the
other with the armour flowered with gold, who bears three
crowns argent in a field azure, is the formidable Micocolem-
bo, Grand Duke of Quirocia: the third, with gigantic limbs,
who marches on his right, is the undaunted Brandabarbaran
of Boliche, Lord of the three Arabias; he is armed with a
serpent's skin, and bears, instead of a shield, a gate, which
fame says, is one of those belonging to the temple which
Sampson pulled down, when with his death he avenged
himself upon his enemies. But turn your eyes to this other
side, and you will see in the front of this other army, the
ever-victorious and never-vanquished Timonel de Carcajona,
Prince of the New Biscay, who comes armed with armour
quartered, azure, vert, argent, and or, bearing on his shield a
cat, or, on a field gules, with a scroll inscribed *Miau*, being
the beginning of his mistress's name, who, it is reported, is
the peerless Miaulina, daughter to Alfeñiquen, Duke of Al-
garve. That other, who burdens and oppresses the back of
yon sprightly steed, whose armour is as white as snow, and
his shield white, without any device, is a new knight, by birth

a Frenchman, called Peter Papin, Lord of the baronies of Utrique. The other whom you see, with his armed heels, pricking the flanks of that pied fleet courser, and his armour of pure azure, is the powerful Duke of Nerbia, Espartafilardo of the Wood, whose device is an asparagus-bed with this motto in Castilian—*Rastrea mi suerte*—"Thus drags my fortune."'

In this manner he went on, naming sundry knights of each squadron, as his fancy dictated, and giving to each their arms, colours, devices, and mottoes, extempore, carried on by the strength of his imagination and unaccountable madness: and so, without hesitation, he went on thus:

'That body fronting us is formed and composed of people of different nations: here stand those who drink the sweet waters of the famous Xanthus;* the mountaineers, who tread the Massilian fields;* those who sift the pure and fine gold-dust of Arabia Felix; those who dwell along the famous and refreshing banks of the clear Thermodon;* those who drain, by sundry and divers ways, the golden veins of Pactolus;* the Numidians, unfaithful in their promises; the Persians, famous for bows and arrows; the Parthians and Medes, who fight flying; the Arabians, perpetually shifting their habitations; the Scythians, as cruel as fair; the broad-lipped Ethiopians: and an infinity of other nations, whose countenances I see and know, though I cannot recollect their names. In that other squadron come those who drink the crystal streams of olive-bearing Betis;* those who brighten and polish their faces with the liquor of the ever-rich and golden Tagus; those who enjoy the profitable waters of the divine Genil;* those who tread the Tartesian fields,* abounding in pasture; those who recreate themselves in the Elysian meads of Xerez; the rich Manchegans, crowned with yellow ears of corn; those clad in iron, the antique remains of the Gothic race; those who bathe themselves in the Pisuerga, famous for the gentleness of its current; those who feed their flocks on the spacious pastures of the winding Guadiana, celebrated for its hidden source; those who shiver on the cold brow of shady Pyreneus, and the snowy tops of lofty Apenninus; in a word, all that Europe contains and includes.'

Good God! how many provinces did he name! how many nations did he enumerate! giving to each with wonderful readiness, its peculiar attributes, wholly absorbed and wrapped up in what he had read in his lying books. Sancho Panza stood confounded at his discourse, without speaking a word; and now and then he turned his head about, to see whether he could discover the knights and giants his master named. But seeing none, he said:

'Sir, the devil a man, or giant, or knight, of all you have named, appears anywhere; at least I do not see them: perhaps all may be enchantment, like last night's goblins.'

'How say you, Sancho?' answered Don Quixote: 'do you not hear the neighing of the steeds, the sound of the trumpets, and rattling of the drums?'

'I hear nothing,' answered Sancho, 'but the bleating of sheep and lambs.'

And so it was; for now the two flocks were come very near them.

'The fear you are in, Sancho,' said Don Quixote, 'makes you that you can neither see nor hear aright; for one effect of fear is to disturb the senses, and make things not to appear what they are; and if you are so much afraid, get you aside, and leave me alone; for I am able, with my single arm, to give the victory to that side I shall favour with my assistance.'

And saying this, he clapped spurs to Rosinante, setting his lance in its rest, and darted down the hillock like lightning. Sancho cried out to him:

'Hold, Señor Don Quixote, come back: as God shall save me, they are lambs and sheep you are going to encounter: pray come back; woe to the father that begot me! what madness is this? Look! there is neither giant, nor knight, nor cats, nor arms, nor shields quartered nor entire, nor true azures nor be-devilled; sinner that I am! what is it you do?'

For all this Don Quixote turned not again, but still went on, crying aloud:

'Ho, knights, you that follow and fight under the banner of the valiant emperor Pentapolin of the Naked Arm, follow me all, and you shall see with how much ease I revenge him on his enemy Alifanfaron of Trapobana.'

And saying thus he rushed into the midst of the squadron of sheep, and began to attack them with his lance, as courageously and intrepidly as if in good earnest he was engaging his mortal enemies. The shepherds and herdsmen, who came with the flocks, called out to him to desist; but seeing it was to no purpose, they unbuckled their slings, and began to let drive about his ears with stones as big as one's fist. Don Quixote did not mind the stones, but, running about on all sides, cried out:

'Where art thou, proud Alifanfaron? present thyself before me: I am a single knight, desirous to prove thy valour hand to hand, and to punish thee with the loss of life for the wrong thou dost to the valiant Pentapolin Garamanta.'

At that instant came a large pebble-stone, and struck him such a blow on the side that it buried a couple of his ribs in his body. Finding himself thus ill-treated, he believed for certain he was slain, or sorely wounded; and remembering his liquor, he pulled out his cruse, and set it to his mouth, and began to let some go down: but, before he could swallow what he thought sufficient, comes another of those almonds, and hit him so full on the hand, and on the cruse, that it dashed it to pieces, carrying off three or four of his teeth by the way, and grievously bruising two of his fingers. Such was the first blow, and such the second, that the poor knight tumbled from his horse to the ground. The shepherds ran to him, and verily believed they had killed him: whereupon in all haste they got their flock together, took up their dead, which were about seven, and marched off without further inquiry.

All this while Sancho stood upon the hillock, beholding his master's extravagances, tearing his beard, and cursing the unfortunate hour and moment that ever he knew him. But, seeing him fallen to the ground, and the shepherds already gone off, he descended from the hillock, and running to him, found him in a very ill plight, though he had not quite lost the use of his senses; and said to him:

'Did I not desire you, Señor Don Quixote, to come back, for those you went to attack were a flock of sheep, and not an army of men?'

'How easily,' replied Don Quixote, 'can that thief of an enchanter, my enemy, make things appear or disappear! You must know, Sancho, that it is a very easy matter for such to make us seem what they please; and this malignant, who persecutes me, envious of the glory he saw I was likely to acquire in this battle, has transformed the hostile squadrons into flocks of sheep. However, do one thing, Sancho, for my sake, to undeceive yourself, and see the truth of what I tell you: get upon your ass, and follow them fair and softly, and you will find that, when they are got a little farther off, they will return to their first form, and, ceasing to be sheep, will become men, proper and tall, as I described them at first. But do not go now; for I want your help and assistance; come hither to me, and see how many grinders I want; for it seems to me that I have not one left in my head.'

Sancho came so close to him, that he almost thrust his eyes into his mouth: and it being precisely at the time the balsam began to work in Don Quixote's stomach, at the instant Sancho was looking into his mouth, he discharged the contents with as much violence as if it had been shot out of a demi-culverin, directly in the face and beard of the compassionate squire.

'Blessed Virgin!' quoth Sancho, 'what is this has befallen me? without doubt this poor sinner is mortally wounded, since he vomits blood at the mouth.' But reflecting a little, he found by the colour, savour, and smell, that it was not blood, but the balsam of the cruse he saw him drink; and so great was the loathing he felt thereat, that his stomach turned, and he vomited up his very guts upon his master; so that they both remained in the same pickle. Sancho ran to his ass to take something out of his wallets to cleanse himself, and cure his master; but not finding them, he was very near running distracted. He cursed himself afresh, and proposed in his mind to leave his master, and return home, though he should lose his wages for the time past, and his hopes of the government of the promised island.

Hereupon Don Quixote got up, and laying his left hand on his mouth, to prevent the remainder of his teeth from falling out, with the other he laid hold on Rosinante's bridle, who had not stirred from his master's side (so trusty was he and good-conditioned), and went where his squire stood leaning his breast on his ass, and his cheek on his hand, in the posture of a man overwhelmed with thought. Don Quixote, seeing him in that guise, with the appearance of so much sadness, said:

'Know, Sancho, that one man is no more than another, unless he does more than another. All these storms, that fall upon us, are signs that the weather will clear up, and things will go smoothly; for it is impossible that either evil or good should be durable; and hence it follows, that, the evil having lasted long, the good cannot be far off. So that you ought not to afflict yourself for the mischances that befall me, since you have no share in them.'

'How no share in them?' answered Sancho: 'peradventure he they tossed in a blanket yesterday was not my father's son; and the wallets I miss to-day, with all my moveables, are somebody's else?'

'What! are the wallets missing, Sancho?' quoth Don Quixote.

'Yes, they are,' answered Sancho.

'Then we have nothing to eat to-day,' replied Don Quixote.

'It would be so,' answered Sancho, 'if these fields did not produce those herbs you say you know, with which such unlucky knights-errant as your worship are wont to supply the like necessities.'

'For all that,' answered Don Quixote, 'at this time I would rather have a slice of bread, and a couple of heads of salt pilchards, than all the herbs described by Dioscorides, though commented upon by Doctor Laguna himself.* But, good Sancho, get upon your ass, and follow me; for God, who is the provider of all things, will not fail us, and the rather seeing we are so employed in His service as we are, since He does not fail the gnats of the air, the wormlings of the earth, nor the froglings of the water; and so merciful is He, that He makes his sun to shine upon the good and the bad, and causes rain to fall upon the just and unjust.'

'Your worship,' said Sancho, 'would make a better preacher than a knight-errant.'

'Sancho,' said Don Quixote, 'the knights-errant ever did and must know something of everything; and there have been knights-errant in times past, who would make sermons or harangues on the king's highway, with as good a grace, as if they had taken their degrees in the university of Paris; whence we may infer, that the lance never blunted the pen, nor the pen the lance.'

'Well, let it be as your worship says,' answered Sancho; 'but let us be gone hence, and endeavour to get a lodging to-night; and pray God it be where there are neither blankets nor blanket-heavers, nor hobgoblins, nor enchanted Moors; for, if there be, the devil take both the flock and the fold.'

'Child,' said Don Quixote, 'do thou pray to God, and conduct me whither thou wilt; for this time, I leave it to your choice where to lodge us; but reach hither your hand, and feel with your finger how many grinders I want on the right side of my upper jaw; for there I feel the pain.'

Sancho put in his fingers, and, feeling about, said:

'How many did your worship use to have on this side?'

'Four,' answered Don Quixote, 'beside the eye-tooth, all whole, and very sound.'

'Take care what you say, Sir,' answered Sancho.

'I say four, if not five,' replied Don Quixote; 'for in my whole life I never drew tooth nor grinder, nor have I lost one by rheum or decay.'

'Well then,' said Sancho, 'on this lower side, your worship has but two grinders and a half; and in the upper, neither half nor whole; all is as smooth and even as the palm of my hand.'

'Unfortunate that I am!' said Don Quixote, hearing the sad news his squire told him; 'I had rather they had torn off an arm, provided it were not the sword arm; for, Sancho, you must know, that a mouth without grinders, is like a mill without a stone; and a diamond is not so precious as a tooth. But all this we are subject to who profess the strict order of chivalry. Mount, friend Sancho, and lead on; for I will follow thee what pace thou wilt.'

Sancho did so, and went toward the place where he thought to find a lodging, without going out of the high road, which was thereabouts very much frequented. As they thus went on, fair and softly (for the pain of Don Quixote's jaws gave him no ease, nor inclination to make haste), Sancho had a mind to amuse and divert him by talking to him, and said, among other things, what you will find written in the following chapter.

CHAPTER 19

Of the sage discourse that passed between Sancho and his master, and the succeeding adventure of the dead body; with other famous occurrences.

'IT is my opinion, master of mine, that all the disadventures which have befallen us of late, are doubtless in punishment of the sin committed by your worship against your own order of knighthood, in not performing the oath you took, not to eat bread on a table-cloth, nor solace yourself with the queen, with all the rest that you swore to accomplish, until your taking away that helmet of Malandrino,* or how do you call the Moor? for I do not well remember.'

'Sancho, you are in the right,' said Don Quixote; 'but, to tell you the truth, it had quite slipped out of my memory; and you may depend upon it, the affair of the blanket happened to you for your fault in not putting me in mind of it in time: but I will make amends; for, in the order of chivalry, there are ways of compounding for everything.'

'Why, did I swear anything?' answered Sancho.

'It matters not that you have not sworn,' said Don Quixote; 'it is enough that I know you are not free from the guilt of an accessory; and, at all adventures, it will not be amiss to provide ourselves a remedy.'

'If it be so,' said Sancho, 'see, Sir, you do not forget this too, as you did the oath; perhaps the goblins may again take a fancy to divert themselves with me, and perhaps with your worship, if they find you so obstinate.'

While they were thus discoursing, night overtook them in the middle of the highway, without their lighting on, or discovering, any place of reception; and the worst of it was, they were perishing with hunger; for, with the loss of their wallets, they had lost their whole larder of provisions. And, as an additional misfortune, there befell them an adventure, which, without any forced construction, had really the face of one. It happened thus. The night fell pretty dark; notwithstanding which, they went on, Sancho believing, that, since it was the king's highway, they might very probably find an inn within a league or two.

Thus travelling on, the night dark, the squire hungry, and the master with a good appetite, they saw advancing towards them on the same road, a great number of lights, resembling so many moving stars. Sancho stood aghast at the sight of them, and Don Quixote could not well tell what to make of them. The one checked his ass by the halter, and the other his horse by the bridle, and stood still, viewing attentively what it might be. They perceived the lights were drawing toward them, and the nearer they came, the bigger they appeared. Sancho trembled at the sight, as if he had been quicksilver; and Don Quixote's hair bristled upon his head; who, recovering a little courage, cried out:

'Sancho, this must be a most prodigious and most perilous adventure, wherein it will be necessary for me to exert my whole might and valour.'

'Woe is me!' answered Sancho; 'should this prove to be an adventure of goblins, as to me it seems to be, where shall I find ribs to endure?'

'Let them be never such goblins,' said Don Quixote, 'I will not suffer them to touch a thread of your garment: for, if they sported with you last time, it was because I could not get over the pales: but we are now upon even ground, where I can brandish my sword at pleasure.'

'But, if they should enchant and benumb you, as they did the other time,' quoth Sancho, 'what matters it whether we are in the open field, or no?'

'For all that,' replied Don Quixote, 'I beseech you, Sancho, be of good courage; for experience will show you how much of it I am master of.'

'I will, an't please God,' answered Sancho.

And, leaving the highway a little on one side, they looked again attentively to discover what those walking lights might be; and soon after they perceived a great many persons in white;* which dreadful apparition entirely sunk Sancho Panza's courage, whose teeth began to chatter, as if he were in a quartan ague; and his trembling and chattering increased, when he saw distinctly what it was: for now they discovered about twenty persons in white robes, all on horseback, with lighted torches in their hands; behind whom came a litter, covered with black; which was followed by six persons in deep mourning; and the mules they rode on were covered likewise with black down to their heels; and it was easily seen they were not horses by the slowness of their pace. Those in white came muttering to themselves in a low and plaintive tone.

This strange vision, at such an hour, and in a place so uninhabited, might very well strike terror into Sancho's heart, and even into that of his master; and so it would have done had he been any other than Don Quixote. As for Sancho, his whole stock of courage was already exhausted. But it was quite otherwise with his master, whose lively imagination at that instant represented to him, that this must be one of the adventures of his books. He figured to himself, that the litter was a bier, whereon was carried some knight sorely wounded or slain, whose revenge was reserved for him: and without more ado he couched his spear, settled himself firm in his saddle, and with a sprightly vigour and mien, posted himself in the middle of the road, by which the men in white must of necessity pass; and when he saw them come near he raised his voice, and said:

'Hold, knights, whoever you are, give me an account, to whom you belong, from whence you come, whither you are going, and what it is you carry upon that bier? for, in all appearance, either you have done some injury to others, or others to you; and it is expedient and necessary that I be informed of it, either to chastise you for the evil you have done, or to revenge you of the wrong done you.'

'We are going in haste,' answered one of those in white; 'the inn is a great way off, and we cannot stay to give so long an account as you require.'

And so, spurring his mule, he passed forward. Don Quixote, highly resenting this answer, laid hold of his bridle, and said:

'Stand and be more civil, and give me an account of what I have asked you; otherwise I challenge you all to battle.'

The mule was skittish, and started at his laying his hand on the bridle; so that rising upright on her hind legs, she fell backward to the ground with her rider under her. A lackey that came on foot, seeing him in white fall, began to revile Don Quixote, whose choler being already stirred, he couched his spear, and, without staying any longer, assaulted one of the mourners, and laid him on the ground grievously wounded; and turning him about to the rest, it was worth seeing with what agility he attacked and defeated them, insomuch that you would have thought Rosinante had wings grown on him in that instant, so nimbly and proudly did he bestir himself. All those in white were timorous and unarmed people, and of course presently quitted the skirmish, and ran away over the field, with the lighted torches in their hands, looking like so many masqueraders on a carnival or a festival night. The mourners likewise were so wrapped up and muffled in their long robes, that they could not stir: so that Don Quixote, with entire safety to himself, demolished them all, and obliged them to quit the field sorely against their wills: for they thought him no man, but the devil from hell broke loose upon them, to carry away the dead body they bore in the litter.

All this Sancho beheld, with admiration at his master's intrepidity, and said to himself:

'Without doubt this master of mine is as valiant and magnanimous as he pretends to be.'

There lay a burning torch on the ground, just by the first whom the mule had overthrown; by the light of which Don Quixote espied him, and coming to him set the point of his spear to his throat, commanding him to surrender, or he would kill him. To which the fallen man answered:

'I am more than enough surrendered already; for I cannot stir, having one of my legs broken. I beseech you, Sir, if you are a Christian gentleman, do not kill me; you would commit a great sacrilege; for I am a licentiate, and have taken the lesser orders.'

'Who the devil then,' said Don Quixote, 'brought you hither, being an ecclesiastic?'

'Who, Sir?' replied he that was overthrown: 'my misfortune.'

'A greater yet threatens you,' said Don Quixote, 'if you do not satisfy me in all I first asked of you.'

'Your worship shall soon be satisfied,' answered the licentiate; 'and therefore you must know, Sir, that, though I told you before I was a licentiate, I am indeed only a bachelor of arts, and my name is Alonso Lopez. I am a native of Alcovendas: I come from the city of Baeça, with eleven more ecclesiastics, the same who fled with the torches; we are accompanying a corpse in that litter to the city of Segovia: it is that of a gentleman, who died in Baeça, where he was deposited; and now, as I say, we are carrying his bones to his burying place in Segovia, where he was born.'

'And who killed him?' demanded Don Quixote.

'God,' replied the bachelor, 'by means of a pestilential fever he sent him.'

'Then,' said Don Quixote, 'our Lord has saved me the labour of revenging his death in case anybody else had slain him; but since he fell by the hand of heaven, there is no more to be done, but to be silent and shrug up our shoulders: for just the same must I have done had it been pleased to have slain me. And I would have your reverence know, that I am a knight of La Mancha, Don Quixote by name, and that it is my office and exercise to go through the world, righting wrongs, and redressing grievances.'

'I do not understand your way of righting wrongs,' said the bachelor: 'for from right you have set me wrong, having broken my leg, which will never be right again whilst I live; and the grievance you have redressed in me is, to leave me so aggrieved, that I shall never be otherwise; and it was a very unlucky adventure to me, to meet you who are seeking adventures.'

'All things,' answered Don Quixote, 'do not fall out the same way: the mischief, master bachelor Alonso Lopez, was occasioned by your coming, as you did, by night, arrayed in those surplices, with lighted torches, chanting, and clad in doleful weeds, so that you really resembled something wicked, and of the other world; which laid me under the necessity of complying with my duty, and of attacking you; and I would have attacked you, though I had certainly known you to be so many devils of hell; for until now I took you to be no less.'

'Since my fate would have it so,' said the bachelor, 'I beseech you, Señor knight-errant, who have done me such arrant mischief, help me to get from under this mule, for my leg is held fast between the stirrup and the saddle.'

'I might have talked on until to-morrow morning,' said Don Quixote: 'why did you delay acquainting me with your uneasiness?'

Then he called out to Sancho Panza to come to him; but he did not care to stir, being employed in ransacking a sumpter-mule, which those good men had brought with them, well stored with eatables. Sancho made a bag of his cloak, and cramming into it as much as it would hold, he loaded his beast; and then running to his master's call, he helped to disengage the bachelor from under the oppression of his mule, and setting him thereon, gave him the torch; and Don Quixote bid him follow the track of his comrades, and beg their pardon in his name for the injury which he could not avoid doing them. Sancho likewise said:

'If perchance those gentlemen would know who the champion is that routed them, tell them it is the famous Don Quixote de la Mancha, otherwise called "the Knight of the Sorrowful Figure".'*

The bachelor being gone, Don Quixote asked Sancho what induced him to call him the "Knight of the Sorrowful Figure", at that time more than any other?

'I will tell you,' answered Sancho; 'it is because I have been viewing you by the light of the torch which that unfortunate man carried; and in truth, your worship makes, at present, very near the most woeful figure I have ever seen; which must be occasioned either by the fatigue of this combat, or by the want of your teeth.'

'It is owing to neither,' replied Don Quixote; 'but the sage, who has the charge of writing the history of my achievements, has thought fit I should assume a surname, as all the knights of old were wont to do: one called himself "the Knight of the Burning Sword"; another, that "of the Unicorn"; this "of the Damsels"; that "of the Phoenix"; another "the Knight of the Griffin"; and another that "of Death"; and were known by these names and ensigns over the whole surface of the earth. And therefore I say, that the aforesaid sage has now put it into your head, and into my mouth, to call me "the Knight of the Sorrowful Figure", as I purpose to call myself from this day forward: and that this name may fit me the better, I determine, when there is an opportunity, to have a most sorrowful figure painted on my shield.'

'You need not spend time and money in getting this figure made,' said Sancho; 'your worship need only show your own, and present yourself to be looked at; and, without other image or shield, they will immediately call you "Him of the Sorrowful Figure"; and be assured I tell you the truth; for I promise you, Sir (and let this be said in jest), that hunger, and the loss of your grinders, make you look so ruefully, that, as I have said, the sorrowful picture may very well be spared.'

Don Quixote smiled at Sancho's conceit, yet resolved to call himself by that name, and to paint his shield or buckler as he had imagined;* and he said:

'I conceive, Sancho, that I am liable to excommunication, for having laid violent hands on holy things, *Juxta illud, si quis suadente diabolo*, &c.; though I know I did not lay my hands, but my spear, upon them: besides, I did not think I had to do with priests, or things belonging to the church, which I respect and reverence like a good Catholic and faithful Christian as I am, but with ghosts and goblins of the other world. And though it were so, I perfectly remember what befell the Cid Ruy Diaz, when he broke the chair of that king's ambassador in the presence of his Holiness the Pope, for which he was excommunicated;* yet honest Rodrigo de Vivar passed that day for an honourable and courageous knight.'

The bachelor being gone off, as has been said, without replying a word, Don Quixote had a mind to see whether the corpse in the hearse were only bones or not; but Sancho would not consent, saying,

'Sir, your worship has finished this perilous adventure at the least expense of any I have seen; and, though these folks are conquered and defeated, they may chance to reflect, that they were beaten by one man, and being confounded and ashamed thereat, may recover themselves, and return in quest of us, and then we may have enough to do. The ass is properly furnished; the mountain is near; hunger presses; and we have no more to do but decently to march off; and, as the saying is, "To the grave with the dead, and the living to the bread"'; and driving on his ass before him, he desired his master to follow; who, thinking Sancho in the right, followed without replying. They had not gone far between two little hills, when they found themselves in a spacious and retired valley, where they alighted. Sancho disburdened the ass; and lying along on the green grass, with hunger for sauce, they dispatched their breakfast, dinner, afternoon's luncheon, and supper all at once, regaling their palates with more than one cold mess, which the ecclesiastics, that attended the deceased (such gentlemen seldom failing to make much of themselves), had brought with them on the sumpter-mule. But another mishap befell them, which Sancho took for the worst of all; which was, that they had no wine, nor so much as water to drink; and they being very thirsty, Sancho, who perceived the meadow they were in covered with green and fine grass, said what will be related in the following chapter.

CHAPTER 20

Of the adventure (the like never before seen or heard of) achieved by the renowned Don Quixote de la Mancha, with less hazard, than ever any was achieved by the most famous knight in the world.*

'IT is impossible, Sir, but there must be some fountain or brook hereabouts, to water these herbs; and therefore we should go a little farther on; for we shall meet with something to quench this terrible thirst that afflicts us, and is doubtless more painful than hunger itself.'

Don Quixote approved the advice; and he taking Rosinante by the bridle, and Sancho his ass by the halter, after he had placed upon him the relics of the supper, they began to march forward through the meadow, feeling their way; for the night was so dark they could see nothing. But they had not gone two hundred paces, when a great noise of water reached their ears, like that of some mighty cascade pouring down from a vast and steep rock. The sound rejoiced them exceedingly, and stopping to listen from whence it came, they heard on a sudden another dreadful noise, which abated the pleasure occasioned by that of the water, especially in Sancho, who was naturally fearful and pusillanimous. I say, they heard a dreadful din of irons and chains rattling across one another, and giving mighty strokes in time and measure; which, together with the furious noise of the water, would have struck terror into any other heart but that of Don Quixote.

The night, as is said, was dark; and they chanced to enter among certain tall trees, whose leaves, agitated by a gentle breeze, caused a kind of fearful and still noise: so that the solitude, the situation, the darkness, and the noise of the water, with the whispering of the leaves, all occasioned horror and astonishment; especially when they found, neither the blows ceased, nor the wind slept, nor the morning approached; and, as an addition to all this, a total ignorance where they were. But Don Quixote, accompanied by his intrepid heart, leaped upon Rosinante, and, bracing on his buckler, brandished his spear, and said:

'Friend Sancho, you must know, that, by the will of heaven, I was born in this age of iron, to revive in it that of gold, or, as people usually express it, "the golden age". I am he, for whom are reserved dangers, great exploits, and valorous achievements. I am he, I say again, who am destined to revive the order of the round table, that of the twelve peers of France, and the nine worthies, and to obliterate the memory of the Platirs, the Tablantes, Olivantes, and Tirantes, the "Knights of the Sun", and the Belianises, with the whole tribe of the famous knights-errant, of times past, performing, in this age, in which I live, such stupendous deeds and feats of arms, as are sufficient to obscure the brightest they ever achieved. Trusty and loyal squire, you observe the darkness of this night, its strange silence, the confused and [deadened] sound of these trees, the fearful noise of that water we come to seek, which, one would think, precipitated itself headlong from the high mountains of the moon; that incessant striking and clashing that wounds our ears: all which together, and each by itself, are sufficient to infuse terror, fear, and amazement into the breast of Mars himself; how much more into that, which is not accustomed to the like adventures and accidents. Now all I have described to you serves to rouse and awaken my courage, and my heart already beats in my breast with eager desire of encountering this adventure, however difficult it may appear. Wherefore straiten Rosinante's girths a little, and God be with you; and stay for me here three days, and no more: if I do not return in that time, you may go back to our town; and thence, to do me a favour and good service, you shall go to Toboso, where you shall say to my incomparable lady Dulcinea, that her enthralled knight died in the attempting things that might have made him worthy to be styled hers.'

When Sancho heard these words of his master, he began to weep with the greatest tenderness in the world, and to say:

'Sir, I do not understand why your worship should encounter this so fearful an adventure: it is now night, and nobody sees us; we may easily turn aside, and get out of harm's way, though we should not drink these three days: and, as nobody sees us, much less will there be anybody to tax us with cowardice. Besides I have heard the priest of our village, whom your worship knows very well, preach, that, "he who seeketh danger perisheth, therein": so that it is not good to tempt God, by undertaking so extravagant an exploit, whence there is no escaping but by a miracle. Let it suffice, that heaven has delivered you from being tossed in a blanket, as I was, and brought you off victorious, safe, and sound, from among so many enemies as accompanied the dead man. And though all this be not sufficient to move you, nor soften your stony heart, let this thought and belief prevail, that, scarcely shall your worship be departed hence, when I, for very fear, shall give up my soul to whosoever shall be pleased to take it. I left my country, and forsook my wife and children, to follow and serve your worship, believing I should be the better, and not the worse, for it: but, as covetousness bursts the bag, so hath it rent from me my hopes: for, when they were most lively, and I just expecting to obtain that cursed and unlucky island, which you have so often promised me, I find myself, in exchange thereof, ready to be abandoned by your worship in a place remote from all human society. For God's sake, dear Sir, do me not such a diskindness;* and, since your worship will not wholly desist from this enterprise, at least adjourn it until daybreak, to which according to the little skill I learned when a shepherd, it cannot be above three hours; for the muzzle of the north-bear* is at the top of the heads, and makes midnight in the line of the left arm.

'How can you, Sancho,' said Don Quixote, 'see where this line is made, or where this muzzle or top of the head you talk of, is, since the night is so dark that not a star appears in the whole sky?'

'True,' said Sancho; 'but fear has many eyes, and sees things beneath the earth, how much more above in the sky: besides, it is reasonable to think it does not want much of daybreak.'

'Want what it will,' answered Don Quixote, 'it shall never be said of me, neither now nor at any other time, that tears or entreaties could dissuade me from doing the duty of a knight: therefore, pray thee, Sancho, hold thy tongue; for God, who has put it in my heart to attempt this unparalleled and fearful adventure, will take care to watch over my safety, and to comfort thee in thy sadness. What you have to do, is, to girt Rosinante well, and to stay here; for I will quickly return, alive or dead.'

Sancho, then, seeing his master's final resolution, and how little his tears, prayers and counsels prevailed with him, determined to have recourse to a stratagem, and oblige him to wait until day, if he could: and so while he was straightening the horse's girths, softly, and without being perceived, he tied Rosinante's two hinder feet together with his ass's halter, so that, when Don Quixote would have departed he was not able; for the horse could not move but by jumps. Sancho, seeing the good success of his contrivance, said:

'Ah, Sir! behold how heaven, moved by my tears and prayers, has ordained that Rosinante cannot go: and, if you will obstinately persist to spur him, you will but provoke fortune and, as they say, "kick against the pricks".'

This made Don Quixote quite desperate, and the more he spurred his horse, the less he could move him: and, without suspecting the ligature, he thought it best to be quiet, and either stay until day appeared, or until Rosinante could stir, believing certainly that it proceeded from some other cause, and not from Sancho's cunning; to whom he thus spoke:

'Since it is so, Sancho, that Rosinante cannot stir, I am contented to stay until the dawn smiles, though I weep all the time she delays her coming.'

'You need not weep,' answered Sancho; 'for I will entertain you until dawn with telling you stories, if you had not rather alight and compose yourself to sleep a little upon the green grass, as knights-errant are wont to do, and so be the less weary, when the day and hour comes for attempting that unparalleled adventure you wait for.'

'What call you alighting, or sleeping?' said Don Quixote: 'Am I one of those knights, who take repose in time of danger? Sleep thou, who wert born to sleep, or do what thou wilt: I will do what I see best befits my profession.'

'Pray, good Sir, be not angry,' answered Sancho: 'I do not say it with that design; and coming close to him, he put one hand on the pommel of the saddle before, and the other on the pique behind, and there he stood embracing his master's left thigh, without daring to stir from him a finger's breadth, so much was he afraid of the blows which still sounded alternately in his ears. Don Quixote bade him tell some story to entertain him, as he promised: to which Sancho replied he would if the dread of what he heard would permit him;

'Notwithstanding,' said he, 'I will force myself to tell a story, which, if I can hit upon it, and it slips not through my fingers, is the best of all stories; and pray be attentive, for now I begin.'

'What hath been, hath been: the good that shall befall, be for us all, and evil to him that evil seeks. And pray, Sir, take notice, that the beginning which the ancients gave to their tales, was not just what they pleased, but rather some sentence of Cato Zonzorino* the Roman, who says, "And evil to him that evil seeks"; which is as apt to the present purpose as a ring to your finger, signifying, that your worship should be quiet, and not go about searching after evil, but rather that we turn aside into some other road; for we are under no obligation to continue in this, wherein so many fears overwhelm us.'

'Go on with your story, Sancho,' said Don Quixote, 'and leave me to take care of the road we are to follow.'

'I say then,' continued Sancho, 'that, in a place of Estremadura, there was a shepherd, I mean a goatherd; which shepherd or goatherd, as my story says, was called Lope Ruiz; and this Lope Ruiz was in love with a shepherdess called Torralva; which shepherdess called Torralva was a daughter to a rich herdsman, and this rich herdsman——'

'If you tell your story after this fashion, Sancho,' said Don Quixote, 'repeating every thing you say twice, you will not have done these two days: tell it concisely, and like a man of sense, or else say no more.'

'In the very same manner that I tell it,' answered Sancho, 'they tell all stories in my country; and I can tell it no otherwise, nor is it fit your worship should require me to make new customs.'

'Tell it as you will then,' answered Don Quixote; 'since fate will have it that I must hear thee, go on.'

'And so, dear Sir of my soul,' continued Sancho, 'as I said before, this shepherd was in love with the shepherdess Torralva, who was a jolly strapping wench, a little scornful, and somewhat masculine; for she had certain small whiskers; and methinks I see her just now.'

'What, did you know her?' said Don Quixote.

'I did not know her,' answered Sancho; 'but he who told me this story said it was so certain and true, that I might, when I told it to another, affirm and swear I had seen it all. And so, in process of time, the devil, who sleeps not, and troubles all things, brought it about, that the love which the shepherd bore to the shepherdess, was converted into mortal hatred; and the cause, according to evil tongues, was a certain quantity of little jealousies she gave him, beyond measure: and so much did he hate her from thenceforward, that, to avoid the sight of her, he chose to absent himself from that country, and go where his eyes should never behold her more. Torralva, who found herself disdained by Lope, presently began to love him better than ever she had loved him before.'

'It is a natural quality of women,' said Don Quixote, 'to slight those who love them, and love those who slight them. Go on, Sancho.'

'It fell out,' proceeded Sancho, 'that the shepherd put his design into execution, and collecting together his goats, went on towards the plains of Estremadura, in order to pass over into the kingdom of Portugal. Torralva, knowing it, went after him, following him on foot and bare-legged, at a distance, with a pilgrim's staff in her hand, and a wallet about her neck, in which she carried, as is reported, a piece of looking-glass, a piece of a comb, and a sort of a small gallipot of pomatum for the face. But, whatever she carried (for I shall not now set myself to vouch what it was), I only tell you, that, as they say, the shepherd came with his flock to pass the river Guadiana, which at that time was swollen, and had almost overflowed its banks: and, on the side he came to, there was neither boat nor anybody to ferry him or his flock over to the other side, which grieved him mightily, for he saw that Torralva was at his heels, and would give him much disturbance by her entreaties and tears. He therefore looked about until he espied a fisherman with a boat near him, but so small that it could hold only one person and one goat: however, he spoke to him, and agreed with him to carry him over, and his three hundred goats. The fisherman got into the boat and carried over a goat; he returned, and carried over another; he came back again, and again carried over another. Pray, Sir, keep an account of the goats that the fisherman is carrying over; for if one slips out of your memory, the story will be at an end, and it will be impossible to tell a word more of it. I go on then, and say, that the landing place on the opposite side was covered with mud, and slippery, and the fisherman was a great while in coming and going. However, he returned for another goat, and for others, and for another.'

'Make account he carried them all over,' said Don Quixote, 'and do not be going and coming in this manner; for, at this rate, you will not have done carrying them over in a twelve-month.'

'How many are passed already?' said Sancho.

'How the devil should I know?' answered Don Quixote.

'See there now; did I not tell you to keep an exact account? Before God, there is an end of the story; I can go no further.'

'How can this be?' answered Don Quixote. 'Is it so essential to the story to know the exact number of goats that passed over, that, if one be mistaken, the story can proceed no further?'

'No, Sir, in nowise,' answered Sancho: 'for when I desired your worship to tell me how many goats had passed, and you answered you did not know, in that very instant all that I had left to say fled out of my memory; and in faith it was very edifying and satisfactory.'

'So then,' said Don Quixote, 'the story is at an end.'

'As sure as my mother is,' quoth Sancho.

'Verily,' answered Don Quixote 'you have told one of the rarest tales, fables, or histories imaginable; and your way of telling and concluding it is such as never was, nor will be seen in one's whole life; though I expected nothing less from your good sense: but I do not wonder at it; for perhaps this incessant din may have disturbed your understanding.'

'All that may be,' answered Sancho; 'but as to my story, I know there's no more to be said; for it ends just where the error in the account of carrying over the goats begins.'*

'Let it end where it will, in God's name,' said Don Quixote, 'and let us see whether Rosinante can stir himself.'

Again he clapped spurs to him, and again he jumped, and then stood stock still, so effectually was he fettered.

Now, whether the cold of the morning, which was at hand, or whether some lenitive food on which he had supped, or whether the motion was purely natural (which is rather to be believed), it so befell that Sancho had a desire to do what nobody could do for him. But so great was the fear that had possessed his heart, that he durst not stir the breadth of a finger from his master; and, to think to leave that business

undone, was also impossible: and so what he did for peace
sake was, to let go his right hand, which held the hinder part
of the saddle, with which, softly, and without any noise, he
loosed the running point that kept up his breeches; whereupon down they fell, and hung about his legs like shackles:
then he lifted up his shirt the best he could, and exposed to
the open air those buttocks which were none of the smallest.
This being done, which he thought the best expedient towards getting out of that terrible anguish and distress, another
and a greater difficulty attended him, which was, that he
thought he could not ease himself without making some
noise: so he set his teeth close, and squeezed up his shoulders, and held his breath as much as possibly he could. But,
notwithstanding all these precautions, he was so unlucky after
all as to make a little noise, very different from that which
had put him into so great a fright. Don Quixote heard it and
said:

'What noise is this, Sancho?'

'I do not know Sir,' answered he, 'it must be some new
business; for adventures and misadventures never begin with
a little matter.'

He tried his fortune a second time, and it succeeded so
well with him, that, without the least noise or rumbling more,
he found himself discharged of the burden that had given
him so much uneasiness. But, as Don Quixote had the sense
of smelling no less perfect than that of hearing, and Sancho
stood so close, and as it were sewed to him, some of the
vapours, ascending in a direct line, could not fail to reach
his nostrils; which they had no sooner done, but he relieved
his nose by taking it between his fingers, and, with a kind
of snuffling tone, said:

'Methinks, Sancho, you are in great bodily fear.'

'I am so,' said Sancho; 'but wherein does your worship
perceive it now more than ever?'

'In that you smell stronger than ever, and not of ambergris,'
answered Don Quixote.

'That may very well be,' said Sancho, 'but your worship
alone is in fault, for carrying me about at these unseasonable
hours, and into these unfrequented places.'

'Get three or four steps off, friend,' said Don Quixote (all this without taking his fingers from his nostrils), 'and henceforward be more careful of your own person, and of what you owe to mine; my overmuch familiarity with you has bred contempt.'

'I will lay a wager,' replied Sancho, 'you think I have been doing something with my person that I ought not.'

'The more you stir it, friend Sancho, the worse it will savour,' answered Don Quixote.

In these and the like dialogues the master and man passed the night. But Sancho, perceiving that at length the morning was coming on, with much caution untied Rosinante, and tied up his breeches. Rosinante, finding himself at liberty, though naturally he was not over-mettlesome, seemed to feel himself alive, and began to paw the ground; but as for curvetting (begging his pardon) he knew not what it was. Don Quixote, perceiving that Rosinante began to bestir himself, took it for a good omen, and believed it signified he should forthwith attempt that fearful adventure. By this time the dawn appeared, and everything being distinctly seen, Don Quixote perceived he was got among some tall chestnut-trees, which afforded a gloomy shade: he perceived also that the striking did not cease; but he could not see what caused it. So without further delay, he made Rosinante feel the spur, and, turning again to take leave of Sancho, commanded him to wait there for him three days at the farthest, as he had said before, and that, if he did not return by that time, he might conclude for certain it was God's will he should end his days in that perilous adventure. He again repeated the embassy and message he was to carry to his lady Dulcinea; and as to what concerned the reward of his service, he need be in no pain, for he had made his will before he left his village, wherein he would find himself gratified as to his wages, in proportion to the time he had served; but, if God should bring him off safe and sound from that danger, he might reckon himself infallibly secure of the promised island. Sancho wept afresh at hearing again the moving expressions of his good master, and resolved not to leave him till the last moment and end of this business.

The author of this history gathers from the tears, and this so honourable a resolution of Sancho Panza's, that he must have been well born, and at least an Old Christian.* This tender concern somewhat softened his master, but not so much as to make him discover any weakness: on the contrary, dissembling the best he could, he began to put on towards the place, from whence, the noise of the water and of the strokes seemed to proceed. Sancho followed him on foot, leading as usual his ass—that constant companion of his prosperous and adverse fortunes, by the halter. And having gone a good way among those shady chestnut-trees, they came to a little green spot at the foot of some steep rocks, from which a mighty gush of water precipitated itself. At the foot of the rocks were certain miserable huts, which seemed rather the ruins of buildings than houses; from amidst which proceeded, as they perceived, the sound and din of the strokes, which did not yet cease. Rosinante started, and was in disorder, at the noise of the water and of the strokes; and Don Quixote, quieting him, went on fair and softly towards the huts, recommending himself devoutly to his lady, and beseeching her to favour him in that fearful expedition and enterprise; and, by the by, besought God also not to forget him. Sancho stirred not from his side, stretching out his neck, and looking between Rosinante's legs, to see if he could perceive what held him in such dread and suspense.

They had gone about a hundred yards further, when, at doubling a point, the very cause (for it could be no other) of that horrible and dreadful noise, which had held them all night in such suspense and fear, appeared plain, and exposed to view. It was (kind reader, take it not in dudgeon) six fulling-hammers,* whose alternative strokes formed that hideous sound.

Don Quixote, seeing what it was, was struck dumb, and in the utmost confusion. Sancho looked at him, and saw he hung down his head upon his breast, with manifest indications of being quite abashed. Don Quixote looked also at Sancho, and saw his cheeks swollen, and his mouth full of laughter, with evident signs of being ready to burst with it; and, notwithstanding his vexation, he could not forbear laughing himself at sight of Sancho; who, seeing his master had led the way, burst out in so violent a manner, that he was forced to hold his sides with his hands, to save himself from splitting with laughter. Four times he ceased, and four times he returned to his laughter with the same impetuosity as at first. Whereat Don Quixote gave himself to the devil, especially when he heard him say, by way of irony:

'"You must know, friend Sancho, that I was born by the will of heaven, in this our age of iron, to revive in it the golden, or that of gold. I am he for whom are reserved dangers, great exploits, and valorous achievements".'

And so he went on, repeating most or all of the expressions which Don Quixote had used at the first hearing those dreadful strokes. Don Quixote, perceiving that Sancho played upon him, grew so ashamed, and enraged to that degree, that he lifted up his lance, and discharged two such blows on him, that, had he received them on his head as he did on his shoulders, the knight had acquitted himself of the payment of his wages, unless it were to his heirs. Sancho, finding he paid so dearly for his jokes, and fearing lest his master should proceed further, cried out with much humility:

'Pray, Sir, be pacified; by the living God, I did but jest.'

'Though you jest, I do not,' answered Don Quixote. 'Come hither, merry Sir, what think you? suppose these mill-hammers had been some perilous adventure, have I not showed the courage requisite to undertake and achieve it? Am I, think you, obliged, being a knight as I am, to distinguish sounds, and know which are, or are not, of a fulling-mill? Besides, it may be (as it really is), that I never saw any fulling-mills in my life, as thou hast, like a pitiful rustic as thou art, having been born and bred amongst them. But let these six fulling-hammers be transformed into six giants, and let them beard me one by one, or all together, and if I do not set them all on their heads, then make what jest you will of me.'

'It is enough, good Sir,' replied Sancho; 'I confess I have been a little too jocose: but pray, tell me, now that it is peace between us, as God shall bring you out of all the adventures that shall happen to you, safe and sound, as he has brought you out of this, was it not a thing to be laughed at, and worth telling, what great fear we were in, at least what I was in? for, as to your worship, I know you are unacquainted with it, nor do you know what fear or terror are.'

'I do not deny,' answered Don Quixote, 'but that what has befallen to us is fit to be laughed at, but not fit to be told; for all persons are not discreet enough to know how to take things by the right handle.'

'But,' answered Sancho, 'your worship knew not how to handle your lance aright, when you pointed it at my head, and hit me on my shoulders; thanks be to God and to my own agility in slipping aside. But let that pass, it will out in the bucking; for I have heard say, "he loves thee well, who makes thee weep"; and besides, your people of condition, when they have given a servant a hard word, presently give him some old hose and breeches; though what is usually given after a beating I cannot tell, unless it be that your knights-errant, after bastinados, bestow islands or kingdoms on the continent.'

'The die may run so,' quoth Don Quixote, 'that all you have said may come to pass; and forgive what is past, since you are considerate; and know, that the first motions are not in a man's power; and henceforward be apprised of one thing (that you may abstain and forbear talking too much with me), that, in all the books of chivalry I ever read, infinite as they are, I never found that any squire conversed so much with his master as you do with yours. And really I account it a great fault both in you and me; in you, because you respect me so little; in me, that I do not make myself respected more. Was not Gandalin, squire to Amadis de Gaul, earl of the Firm Island? and we read of him, that he always spoke to his master cap in hand, his head inclined, and his body bent after the Turkish fashion. What shall we say of Gasabal, squire to Don Galaor, who was so silent that, to illustrate the excellency of his marvellous taciturnity, his name is mentioned but once in all that great and faithful history? From what I have said, you may infer, Sancho, that there ought to be a difference between master and man, between lord and lackey, and between knight and squire. So that, from this day forward, we must be treated with more respect; for which way soever I am angry with you, it will go ill with the pitcher. The favours and benefits I promised you, will come in due time; and if they do not come, the wages at least, as I have told you, will not be lost.'

'Your worship says very well,' quoth Sancho; 'but I would fain know (if perchance the time of the favours should not come, and it should be expedient to have recourse to the article of the wages), how much might the squire of a knight-errant get in those times? and whether they agreed by the month, or by the day, like labourers?'

'I do not believe,' answered Don Quixote, 'that those squires were at stated wages, but relied on courtesy. And if I have appointed you any in the will I left sealed at home, it was for fear of what might happen; for I cannot yet tell how chivalry may succeed in these calamitous times of ours, and I would not have my soul suffer in the other world for a trifle; for I would have you to know, Sancho, that there is no state more perilous than that of adventures.'

'It is so in truth,' said Sancho, 'since the noise of the hammers of a fulling-mill were sufficient to disturb and discompose the heart of so valorous a knight as your worship. But you may depend upon it, that from henceforward I shall not open my lips to make merry with your worship's matters, but shall honour you as my master and natural lord.'

'By so doing,' replied Don Quixote, 'your days shall be long in the land; for, next to our parents, we are bound to respect our masters as if they were our fathers.'

CHAPTER 21

Which treats of the high adventure and rich prize of Mambrino's helmet, with other things which befell our invincible knight.

ABOUT this time it began to rain a little, and Sancho had a mind they should betake themselves to the fulling-mills. But Don Quixote had conceived such an abhorrence of them for the late jest, that he would by no means go in: and so, turning to the right-hand, they struck into another road like that they had lighted upon the day before. Soon after, Don Quixote discovered a man on horseback, who had on his head something which glittered, as if it had been of gold; and scarcely had he seen it, but, turning to Sancho, he said:

'I am of opinion, Sancho, there is no proverb but what is true, because they are all sentences drawn from experience itself, the mother of all the sciences; especially that which says; "Where one door is shut another is opened". I say this, because, if fortune last night shut the door against what we looked for, deceiving us with the fulling-mills, it now sets another wide open for a better and more certain adventure, which if I fail to enter right into, the fault will be mine, without imputing it to my little knowledge of fulling-mills, or to the darkness of the night. This I say, because, if I mistake not, there comes one towards us, who carries on his head Mambrino's helmet,* about which I swore the oath you know.'

'Take care, Sir, what you say, and more what you do,' said Sancho; 'for I would not wish for other fulling-mills to finish the milling and mashing our senses.'

'The devil take you!' replied Don Quixote: 'what has a helmet to do with fulling-mills?'

'I know not,' answered Sancho; 'but, in faith, if I might talk as much as I used to do, perhaps I could give such reasons that your worship would see you are mistaken in what you say.'

'How can I be mistaken in what I say, scrupulous traitor?' said Don Quixote. 'Tell me, seest thou not yon knight coming towards us on a dapple-grey steed, with a helmet of gold on his head?'

'What I see and perceive,' answered Sancho, 'is only a man on a grey ass like mine, with something on his head that glitters.'

'Why, that is Mambrino's helmet,' said Don Quixote: 'get aside, and leave me alone to deal with him; you shall see me conclude this adventure (to save time) without speaking a word; and the helmet I have so much longed for, shall be my own.'

'I shall take care to get out of the way,' replied Sancho: 'but, I pray God, I say again, it may not prove another fulling-mill adventure.'

'I have already told you, brother, not to mention those fulling-mills, nor so much as to think of them any more,' said Don Quixote: 'if you do, I say no more, but I vow to mill your soul for you.'

Sancho held his peace, fearing lest his master should perform his vow, which had struck him all of a heap.

Now the truth of the matter concerning the helmet, the steed, and the knight, which Don Quixote saw, was this. There were two villages in that neighbourhood, one of them so small, that it had neither shop nor barber, but the other adjoining to it had both; and the barber of the bigger served also the lesser; in which a person indisposed wanted to be let blood, and another to be trimmed; and for this purpose was the barber coming, and brought with him his brass basin. And fortune so ordered it, that as he was upon the road, it began to rain, and, that his hat might not be spoiled (for it was a new one) he clapped the basin on his head, and being new scoured, it glittered half a league off. He rode on a grey ass, as Sancho said; and this was the reason why Don Quixote took the barber for a knight, his ass for a dappled-grey steed, and his basin for a golden helmet: for he very readily adapted whatever he saw to his knightly extravagances and wild conceits. And when he saw the poor cavalier approach, without staying to reason the case with him, he advanced at Rosinante's best speed, and couched his lance low, designing to run him through and through. But when he came up to him, without checking the fury of his career, he cried out:

'Defend yourself, caitiff, or surrender willingly what is so justly my due.'

The barber, who, not suspecting or apprehending any such thing, saw this phantom coming upon him, had no other way to avoid the thrust of the lance, but to let himself fall down from his ass: and no sooner had he touched the ground, when, leaping up nimbler than a roebuck, he began to scour over the plain, with such speed that the wind could not overtake him. He left the basin on the ground; with which

Don Quixote was satisfied, and said, the miscreant had acted discreetly in imitating the beaver, who, finding itself closely pursued by the hunters, tears off, with its teeth, that for which it knows, by natural instinct, it is hunted. He ordered Sancho to take up the helmet, who holding it in his hand, said:

'Before God, the basin is a special one, and is as well worth a piece of eight as a farthing.'

Then he gave it to his master, who immediately clapped it on his head, twirling it about to find the visor; and not finding it, he said:

'Doubtless the pagan for whom this famous helmet was first forged, must have had a prodigious large head; and the worst of it is, that one half is wanting.'

When Sancho heard the basin called an helmet, he could not forbear laughing; but, recollecting his master's late choler, he checked it in the middle.

'What dost thou laugh at, Sancho?' said Don Quixote.

He answered,

'I laugh to think what a huge head the pagan had, who owned this helmet, which is, for all the world, just like a barber's basin.'

'Knowest thou, Sancho, what I take to be the case? This famous piece, this enchanted helmet, by some strange accident, must have fallen into the hands of some one, who, being ignorant of its true value, and not considering what he did, seeing it to be the purest gold, has melted down the one half for lucre's sake, and of the other half made this, which, as you say, does look like a barber's basin: but, be it what it will, to me, who knows it, its transformation signifies nothing; for I will get it put to rights in the first town where there is a smith, and in such sort, that even that, which the god of smiths made and forged for the god of battles,* shall not surpass, nor equal it; in the meantime, I will wear it as I can; for something is better than nothing; and the rather, since it will be more than sufficient to defend me from stones.'

'It will so,' said Sancho, 'if they do not throw them with slings, as they did in the battle of the two armies, when they crossed your worship's chops, and broke the cruse, in which was contained that most blessed drench which made me vomit up my guts.'

'I am in no great pain for having lost it, for you know, Sancho,' said Don Quixote, 'I have the receipt by heart.'

'So have I too,' answered Sancho; 'but if ever I make or try it again while I live, may I never stir from this place. Besides, I do not intend to expose myself to the hazard of standing in need of it; for I intend to keep myself, with all my five senses, from being wounded, or from wounding anybody. As to being tossed again in a blanket, I say nothing; for it is difficult to prevent such mishaps: and if they do come, there is nothing to be done, but to shrug up one's shoulders, hold one's breath, shut one's eyes, and let one's self go whither fortune and the blanket please to toss one.'

'You are no Christian, good Sancho,' said Don Quixote, at hearing this; 'for you never forget an injury once done you: but know, it is inherent in generous and noble breasts to lay no stress upon trifles. What leg have you lamed, what rib, or what head have you broken, that you cannot yet forget that jest? for, to take the thing right, it was mere jest and pastime; and, had I not understood it so, I had long ago returned thither, and done more mischief in revenging your quarrel, than the Greeks did for the rape of Helen: who, if she had lived in these times, or my Dulcinea in those, would never, you may be sure, have been so famous for beauty as she is.'

And here he uttered a sigh, and sent it to the clouds.

'Let it then pass for a jest,' said Sancho, 'since it is not likely to be revenged in earnest: but I know of what kind the jests and the earnests were, and I know also, they will no more slip out of my memory than off my shoulders. But setting this aside, tell me, Sir, what we shall do with this dapple-grey steed, which looks so like a grey ass, and which that caitiff, whom your worship overthrew, has left behind here to shift for itself: for, to judge by his scouring off so hastily, and flying for it, he does not think of ever returning for him; and, by my beard, Dapple is a special one.'

'It is not my custom,' said Don Quixote, 'to plunder those I overcome, nor is it the usage of chivalry to take from them their horses, and leave them on foot, unless the victor hath lost his own in the conflict; for, in such a case, it is lawful to take that of the vanquished, as fairly won in the battle. Therefore, Sancho, leave this horse, or ass, or what you will have it to be; for when his owner sees us gone a pretty way off, he will come again for him.'

'God knows whether it were best for me to take him,' replied Sancho, 'or at least to truck mine for him, which methinks is not so good; verily the laws of chivalry are very strict, since they do not extend to the swapping of one ass for another; and I would fain know whether I might exchange furniture, if I had a mind.'

'I am not very clear as to that point,' answered Don Quixote; 'and in case of doubt, until better information can be had, I say, you may truck, if you are in extreme want of them.'

'So extreme,' replied Sancho, 'that I could not want them more, if they were for my own proper person.'

And so saying, he proceeded, with that licence, to an exchange of caparisons,* and made his own beast three parts in four* the better for his new furniture. This done, they breakfasted on the remains of the plunder of the sumpter-mule, and drank of the water of the fulling-mills, without turning their faces to look at them, such was their abhorrence of them for the fright they had put them in. Their choler and hunger being thus allayed, they mounted, and without resolving to follow any particular road (as is the custom of knights-errant) they put on whithersoever Rosinante's will led him, which drew after it that of his master, and also that of the ass, which followed, in love and good fellowship, wherever he led the way. Notwithstanding which, they soon turned again into the great road, which they followed at a venture, without any other design.

As they thus sauntered on, Sancho said to his master:

'Sir, will your worship be pleased to indulge me the liberty of a word or two; for, since you imposed on me that harsh command of silence, sundry things have rotted in my breast, and I have one jest now at my tongue's end, that I would not for any thing should miscarry.'

'Out with it,' said Don Quixote, 'and be brief in thy discourse; for none that is long can be pleasing.'

'I say then, Sir,' answered Sancho, 'that for some days past, I have been considering how little is gained by wandering up and down in quest of those adventures your worship is seeking through these deserts and cross-ways, where, though you overcome and achieve the most perilous, there is nobody to see or know anything of them; so that they must remain in perpetual oblivion, to the prejudice of your worship's intention, and their deserts. And therefore I think it would be more advisable, with submission to your better judgement, that we went to serve some emperor or other great prince, who is engaged in war; in whose service your worship may display the worth of your person, your great courage, and greater understanding: which being perceived by the lord we serve, he must of necessity reward each of us according to his merits; nor can you there fail of meeting with somebody to put your worship's exploits in writing, for a perpetual remembrance of them. I say nothing of my own, because they must not exceed the squirely limits; though I dare say, if it be the custom in chivalry to pen the deeds of squires, mine will not be forgotten.'

'You are not much out, Sancho,' answered Don Quixote: 'but before it comes to that, it is necessary for a knight-errant to wander about the world, seeking adventures, by way of probation; that by achieving some he may acquire such fame and renown, that, when he comes to the court of some great monarch, he shall be known by his works beforehand; and scarcely shall the boys see him enter the gates of the city, but they shall all follow and surround him, crying aloud, this is the "Knight of the Sun", or of the "Serpent", or of any other device, under which he may have achieved great exploits. This is he, will they say, who overthrew the huge giant Brocabruno of the mighty force, in single combat; he who disenchanted the great Mameluke of Persia from the long enchantment, which held him confined almost nine hundred years. Thus from hand to hand, they shall go on blazoning his deeds; and presently at the bustle of the boys, and of the rest of the people, the king of that country shall appear at

the windows of his royal palace; and, as soon as he espies
the knight, knowing him by his armour, or by the device on
his shield, he must necessarily say: "Ho there, go forth, my
knights, all that are at court, to receive the flower of chivalry,
who is coming yonder." At which command they all shall go
forth, and the king himself, descending half-way down the
stairs, shall receive him with a close embrace, saluting and
kissing him; and then, taking him by the hand, shall conduct
him to the apartment of the queen, where the knight shall
find her accompanied by her daughter the infanta, who is so
beautiful and accomplished a damsel that her equal cannot
easily be found in any part of the known world. After this,
it must immediately fall out, that she fixes her eyes on the
knight, and he his eyes upon hers, and each shall appear to
the other something rather divine than human; and without
knowing how, or which way, they shall be taken and entangled in the inextricable net of love, and be in great perplexity
of mind through not knowing how to converse, and discover
their amorous anguish to each other.

'From thence, without doubt, they will conduct him to some
quarter of the palace richly furnished, where having taken off
his armour, they will bring him a rich scarlet mantle to put
on; and if he looked well in armour, he must needs make a
much more graceful figure in ermines. The knight being
come, he shall sup with the king, queen, and infanta, where
he shall never take his eyes off the princess, viewing her by
stealth, and she doing the same by him with the same
wariness: for, as I have said, she is a very discreet damsel.
The tables being removed, there shall enter, unexpectedly, at
the hall-door, a little ill-favoured dwarf, followed by a beautiful matron between two giants, with the offer of a certain
adventure, so contrived by a most ancient sage, that he who
shall accomplish it, shall be esteemed the best knight in the
world. The king shall immediately command all who are
present to try it, and none shall be able to finish it but the
stranger knight, to the great advantage of his fame; at which
the infanta will be highly delighted, and reckon herself over-
paid for having placed her thoughts on so exalted an object.
And the best of it is, that this king, or prince, or whatever

he be, is carrying on a bloody war with another monarch as powerful as himself; and the stranger knight, after having been a few days at his court, asks leave to serve his majesty in the aforesaid war. The king shall readily grant his request, and the knight shall most courteously kiss his royal hands for the favour he does him.

'And that night he shall take his leave of his lady the infanta at the iron rails of a garden adjoining to her apartment, through which he had already conversed with her several times, by the mediation of a certain female confidante, in whom the infanta greatly trusted. He sighs, she swoons; the damsel runs for cold water, he is very uneasy at the approach of the morning light, and would by no means they should be discovered, for the sake of his lady's honour. The infanta at length comes to herself, and gives her snowy hands to the knight to kiss through the rails, who kisses them a thousand and a thousand times over, and bedews them with his tears. They agree how to let one another know their good or ill fortune: and the princess desires him to be absent as little a while as possible; which he promises with many oaths: he kisses her hands again, and takes leave with so much concern, that it almost puts an end to his life. From thence he repairs to his chamber, throws himself on his bed, and cannot sleep for grief at the parting: he rises early in the morning, and goes to take leave of the king, the queen, and the infanta: having taken his leave of the two former, he is told that the princess is indisposed, and cannot admit of a visit; the knight thinks it is for grief at his departure: his heart is pierced, and he is very near giving manifest indications of his passion: the damsel confidante is all this time present, and observes what passes: she goes and tells it her lady, who receives the account with tears, and tells her that her chief concern is, that she does not know who her knight is, and whether he be of royal descent or not: the damsel assures her he is, since so much courtesy, politeness, and valour, as her knight is endowed with, cannot exist but in a royal and grave subject. The afflicted princess is comforted hereby, and endeavours to compose herself, that she may not give her parents cause to suspect anything amiss, and two days after she appears in public.

'The knight is now gone to the war; he fights, and over-comes the king's enemy; takes many towns; wins several battles; returns to court; sees his lady at the usual place of interview; it is agreed he shall demand her in marriage of her father, in recompense for his services: the king does not consent to give her to him, not knowing who he is. Notwith-standing which, either by carrying her off, or by some other means, the infanta becomes his spouse, and her father comes to take it for a piece of the greatest good fortune, being assured that the knight is son of a valorous king of I know not what kingdom, for I believe it is not in the map. The father dies; the infanta inherits; and in two words, the knight becomes a king. Here presently comes in the rewarding his squire, and all those who assisted him in mounting to so exalted a state. He marries his squire to one of the infanta's maids of honour, who is, doubtless, the very confidante of his amour and daughter to one of the chief dukes.'

'This is what I would be at, and a clear stage,' quoth Sancho: 'this I stick to; for every tittle of this must happen precisely to your worship, being called "the Knight of the Sorrowful Figure".'

'Doubt it not Sancho,' replied Don Quixote; 'for by those very means, and those very steps, I have recounted, the knights-errant do rise, and have risen to be kings and em-perors. All that remains to be done is, to look out, and find what king of the Christians, or of the pagans, is at war, and has a beautiful daughter: but there is time enough to think of this; for, as I have told you, we must procure renown elsewhere, before we repair to court. Besides, there is still another thing wanting; for supposing a king were found, who is at war, and has a handsome daughter, and that I have gotten incredible fame throughout the whole universe, I do not see how it can be made appear, that I am of the lineage of kings, or even second cousin to an emperor: for the king will not give me his daughter to wife, until he is first very well assured that I am such, though my renowned actions should deserve it ever so well. So that, through this defect, I am afraid I shall lose that which my arm has richly deserved. It is true, indeed, I am a gentleman of an ancient family, possessed of a real estate of one hundred and twenty crowns a year,* and perhaps the sage, who writes my history, may so brighten up my kindred and genealogy, that I may be found the fifth or sixth in descent from a king.

'For you must know, Sancho, that there are two sorts of lineages in the world. Some there are, who derive their pedigree from princes and monarchs, whom time has reduced, by little and little, until they have ended in a point, like a pyramid reversed: others have had poor and low beginnings, and have risen by degrees, until at last they have become great lords. So that the difference lies in this, that some have been what now they are not, and others are now what they were not before; and who knows but I may be one of the former, and that upon examination, my origin may be found to have been great and glorious; with which the king, my father-in-law, that is to be, ought to be satisfied: and though he should not be satisfied, the infanta is to be so in love with me, that, in spite of her father, she is to receive me for her lord and husband, though she certainly knew I was the son of a water-carrier; and in case she should not, then is the time to take her away by force, and convey her whither I please; and time or death will put a period to the displeasure of her parents.'

'Here,' said Sancho, 'comes in properly what some naughty people say, "never stand begging for that which you may take by force", though this other is nearer to the purpose; "a leap from a hedge is better than the prayer of a good man". I say this, because, if my lord the king, your worship's father-in-law, should not vouchsafe to yield unto you my lady the infanta, there is no more to be done, as your worship says, but to steal and carry her off. But the mischief is, that while peace is making, and before you can enjoy the kingdom quietly, the poor squire may go whistle for his reward; unless the damsel go-between, who is to be his wife, goes off with the infanta, and he share his misfortune with her, until it shall please heaven to ordain otherwise; for I believe his master may immediately give her to him for his lawful spouse.'

'That you may depend upon,' said Don Quixote.

'Since it is so,' answered Sancho, 'there is no more to be done but to commend ourselves to God and let things take their course.'

'God grant it,' answered Don Quixote, 'as I desire and you need, and let him be wretched who thinks himself so.'

'Let him, in God's name,' said Sancho; 'for I am an Old Christian, and that is enough to qualify me to be an earl.'

'Aye, and more than enough,' said Don Quixote: 'but it matters not whether you are or no; for I being a king, can easily bestow nobility on you, without your buying it, or doing me the least service; and in creating you an earl, I make you a gentleman of course; and say what they will, in good faith, they must style you "you lordship", though it grieved them never so much.'

'Do you think,' quoth Sancho, 'I should not know how to give authority to the indignity?'

'Dignity, you should say, and not indignity,' said his master.

'So let it be,' answered Sancho Panza: 'I say, I should do well enough with it; for I assure you I was once beadle of a company, and the beadle's gown became me so well, that everybody said I had a presence fit to be warden of the said company. Then what will it be when I am arrayed in a duke's robe, all shining in gold and pearls, like a foreign count? I am of opinion folks will come a hundred leagues to see me.'

'You will make a goodly appearance, indeed,' said Don Quixote: 'but it will be necessary to trim your beard a little oftener; for it is so rough and frowzy, that, if you do not shave with a razor every other day at least, they will discover what you are a musket shot off.'

'Why,' said Sancho, 'it is but taking a barber into the house, and giving him wages; and if there be occasion, I will make him follow me like a gentleman of the horse to a grandee.'

'How came you to know,' demanded Don Quixote, 'that grandees have their gentlemen of the horse to follow them?'

'I will tell you,' said Sancho: 'some years ago I was about the court for a month, and there I saw a very little gentleman riding backward and forward, who, they said, was a very great lord: a man followed him on horseback, turning about as he turned, that one would have thought he had been his tail. I asked why that man did not ride by the other's side, but kept always behind him? they answered me, that it was his gentle-man of the horse, and that noblemen commonly have such to follow them; and from that day to this I have never forgotten it.'

'You are in the right,' said Don Quixote, 'and in the same manner you may carry about your barber; for all customs do not arise together, nor were they invented at once; and you may be the first earl, who carried about his barber after him, and indeed it is a greater trust to shave the beard than to saddle a horse.'

'Leave the business of the barber to my care,' said Sancho; 'and let it be your worship's to procure yourself to be a king, and to make me an earl.'

'So it shall be,' answered Don Quixote, and lifting up his eyes, he saw what will be told in the following chapter.

CHAPTER 22

How Don Quixote set at liberty several unfortunate persons, who were being taken, much against their wills, to a place they did not like.

CID HAMET BEN ENGELI, the Arabian and Manchegan author, relates, in this most grave, lofty, accurate, delightful, and ingenious history, that, presently after those discourses which passed between the famous Don Quixote de la Mancha and Sancho Panza his squire, as they are related at the end of the foregoing chapter. Don Quixote lifted up his eyes, and saw coming on, in the same road, about a dozen men on foot, strung like beads in a row, by the necks, in a great iron chain, and all handcuffed. There came also with them two men on horseback and two on foot; those on horseback armed with firelocks, and those on foot with pikes and swords, and Sancho Panza, espying them, said:

'This is a chain of galley-slaves, persons forced by the king to the galleys.'

'How! persons forced!' quoth Don Quixote; 'is it possible the king should force anybody?'

'I say not so,' answered Sancho, 'but that they are persons condemned by the law for their crimes to serve the king in the galleys per force.'

'In short,' replied Don Quixote, 'however it be, still they are going by force, and not with their own liking.'

'It is so,' said Sancho.

'Then,' said his master, 'here the execution of my office takes place, to defeat violence, and to succour and relieve the miserable.'

'Consider, Sir,' quoth Sancho, 'that justice, that is, the king himself, does no violence nor injury to such persons, but only punishes them for their crimes.'

By this the chain of galley-slaves were come up, and Don Quixote, in most courteous terms, desired of the guard that they would be pleased to inform and tell him the cause or causes why they conducted those persons in that manner. One of the guards on horseback answered, that they were slaves belonging to his majesty, and going to the galleys, which was all he could say, or the other need know of the matter.

'For all that,' replied Don Quixote, 'I should be glad to know from each of them in particular the cause of his misfortune.'

To these he added such other courteous expressions to induce them to tell him what he desired, that the other horseman said:

'Though we have here the record and certificate of the sentence of each of these wretches, this is no time to produce and read them: draw near, Sir, and ask it of themselves; they may inform you if they please; and inform you they will, for they are such as take a pleasure both in acting and relating rogueries.'

With this leave (which Don Quixote would have taken though they had not given it) he drew near to the chain, and demanded of the first for what offence he marched in such evil plight. He answered, that he went in that manner for being in love.

'For that alone?' replied Don Quixote: 'if they send folks to the galleys for being in love, I might long since have been rowing in them.'

'It was not such love as your worship imagines,' said the galley-slave: 'mine was the being so deeply enamoured of a basket of fine linen, and embracing it so close, that, if justice had not taken it from me by force, I should not have parted with it by my goodwill to this very day. I was taken in the fact, so there was no place for the torture; the process was short; they accommodated my shoulders with a hundred lashes, and have sent me, by way of supplement, for three years to the *gurapas*, and there is an end of it.'

'What are the *gurapas*?' quoth Don Quixote.

'The *gurapas* are galleys' answered the slave, who was a young man about twenty-four years of age, and said he was born at Piedrahita.

Don Quixote put the same question to the second, who returned no answer, he was so melancholy and dejected: but the first answered for him, and said:

'This gentleman goes for being a canary bird, I mean, for being a musician and a singer.'

'How so,' replied Don Quixote, 'are men sent to the galleys for being musicians and singers?'

'Yes, Sir,' replied the slave; 'for there is nothing worse than to sing in an agony.'

'Nay,' said Don Quixote, 'I have heard say, "Who sings in grief, procures relief".'

'This is the very reverse,' said the slave; 'for here, he who sings once, weeps all his life after.'

'I do not understand that,' said Don Quixote.

One of the guards said to him:

'Señor cavalier, to sing in an agony, means, in the cant of these rogues, to confess upon the rack. This offender was put to the torture, and confessed his crime, which was that of being a *quatrero*, that is, a stealer of cattle; and, because he confessed, he is sentenced for six years to the galleys, besides two hundred lashes he has already received on the shoulders. And he is always so pensive and sad, because the rest of the rogues, both those behind, and those before,

abuse, vilify, flout, and despise him for confessing, and not
having the courage to say No: for, say they, No contains the
same number of letters as Ay; and it is lucky for a delinquent,
when his life or death depends upon his own tongue, and
not upon proofs and witnesses; and, for my part, I think they
are in the right of it.'

'And I think so too,' answered Don Quixote; who, passing
on to the third, interrogated him as he had done the others:
who answered very readily, and with very little concern;

'I am going to Mesdames the *gurapas* for five years, for
wanting ten ducats.'

'I will give twenty with all my heart,' said Don Quixote,
'to redeem you from this misery.'

'That,' said the slave, 'is like having money at sea, and
dying for hunger, where there is nothing to be bought with
it. I say this, because, if I had been possessed in time of
those twenty ducats you now offer me, I would have so
greased the clerk's pen, and sharpened my advocate's wit,
that I should have been this day upon the market-place of
Zocodóver in Toledo, and not upon this road, coupled and
dragged like a hound: but God is great; patience; I say no
more.'

Don Quixote passed on to the fourth, who was a man of
a venerable aspect, with a white beard reaching below his
breast; who, hearing himself asked the cause of his coming
thither, began to weep, and answered not a word: but the
fifth lent him a tongue, and said:

'This honest gentleman goes for four years to the galleys,
after having gone in the usual procession, pompously apparelled and mounted.'

'That is, I suppose,' said Sancho, 'put to public shame.'

'Right,' replied the slave; 'and the offence, for which he
underwent this punishment, was his having been a broker of
the ear, yea, and of the whole body: in effect, I would say
that this cavalier goes for pimping, and exercising the trade
of a conjurer.'

'Had it been merely for pimping,' said Don Quixote, 'he
had not deserved to row in, but to command, and be a
general of the galleys; for the office of a pimp is not a slight

business, but an employment fit only for discreet persons, and a most necessary one in a well-regulated commonwealth; and none but persons well-born ought to exercise it; and in truth there should be inspectors and controllers of it, as there are of other offices, with a certain number of them deputed, like exchange-brokers; by which means many mischiefs would be prevented, which now happen, because this office and profession is in the hands of foolish and ignorant persons, such as silly waiting-women, pages, and buffoons of a few years standing, and of small experience, who, in the greatest exigency, and when there is occasion for the most dexterous management and address, suffer the morsel to freeze between the fingers and the mouth, and scarcely know which is their right hand. I could go on, and assign the reasons, why it would be expedient to make choice of proper persons, to exercise an office so necessary in the commonwealth: but this is no proper place for it; and I may one day or other lay this matter before those, who can provide a remedy. At present I only say, that the concern I felt at seeing those gray hairs, and that venerable countenance in so much distress for pimping, is entirely removed by the additional character of his being a wizard: though I very well know, there are no sorceries in the world, which can affect and force the will, as some foolish people imagine; for our will is free, and no herb nor charm can compel it. What some silly women and crafty knaves are wont to do is, with certain mixtures and poisons, to turn people's brains, under pretence that they have power to make one fall in love: it being, as I say, a thing impossible to force the will.'

'It is so,' said the honest old fellow: 'and truly, Sir, as to being a wizard, I am not guilty; but as for being a pimp, I cannot deny it, but I never thought there was any harm in it; for the whole of my intention was, that all the world should divert themselves, and live in peace and quiet, without quarrels or troubles: but this good design could not save me from going whence I shall have no hope of returning, considering I am so laden with years, and so troubled with the stranguary,* which leaves me not a moment's repose.'

And here he began to weep, as at first; and Sancho was so moved with compassion, that he drew out from his bosom a real, and gave it him as an alms.

Don Quixote went on, and demanded of another what his offence was; who answered, not with less, but much more alacrity than the former:

'I am going for making a little too free with two she-cousins-german of mine, and with two other cousins-german not mine: in short, I carried the jest so far with them all, that the result of it was the increasing of kindred so intricately, that no casuist can make it out. The whole was proved upon me; I had neither friends nor money; my windpipe was in the utmost danger; I was sentenced to the galleys for six years. I submit—it is the punishment of my fault; I am young; and life may last, and time brings everything about: if your worship señor cavalier, has anything about you to relieve us poor wretches, God will repay you in heaven, and we will make it the business of our prayers to beseech him, that your worship's life and health may be as long and prosperous, as your goodly presence deserves.'

This slave was in the habit of a student; and one of the guards said he was a great talker, and a very pretty Latinist.

Behind all these came a man some thirty years of age, of a goodly aspect; only he seemed to thrust one eye into the other: he was bound somewhat differently from the rest; for he had a chain to his leg, so long, that it was fastened round his middle, and two collars about his neck, one of which was fastened to the chain, and the other, called a keep-friend, or friend's-foot, had two straight irons, which came down from it to his waist, at the ends of which were fixed two manacles, wherein his hands were secured with a huge padlock; insomuch that he could neither lift his hands to his mouth, nor bend down to his hands. Don Quixote asked why this man went fettered and shackled so much more than the rest. The guard answered, because he alone had committed more villainies than all the rest put together; and that he was so bold and desperate a villain, that, though they carried him in that manner, they were not secure of him, but were still afraid he would make his escape.

'What kind of villainies has he committed,' said Don Quixote, 'that they have deserved no greater punishment than being sent to the galleys?'

'He goes for ten years,' said the guard, 'which is a kind of civil death: you need only be told, that this honest gentleman is the famous Gines de Pasamonte, alias Ginesillo de Parapilla.'

'Fair and softly, Señor commissary,' said then the slave; 'let us not now be lengthening our names and surnames. Gines is my name, and not Ginesillo; and Pasamonte is the name of my family, and not Parapilla, as you say; and let every one turn himself round, and look at home, and he will find enough to do.'

'Speak with more respect, Sir Thief-above-measure,' replied the commissary, 'unless you will oblige me to silence you to your sorrow.'

'You may see,' answered the slave, 'that man goeth as God pleaseth; but somebody may learn one day, whether my name is Ginesillo de Parapilla, or no.'

'Are you not called so, lying rascal?' said the guard.

'They do call me so,' answered Gines; 'but I will oblige them not to call me so, or I will flay them where I care not at present to say. Señor cavalier,' continued he, 'if you have anything to give us, give it us now, and God be with you; for you tire us with inquiring so much after other men's lives: if you would know mine, know that I am Gines de Pasamonte, whose life is written by these very fingers.'

'He says true,' said the commissary; 'for he himself has written his own history, as well as heart could wish, and has left the book in prison, in pawn for two hundred reals.'

'Aye, and I intend to redeem it,' said Gines, 'if it lay for two hundred ducats.'

'What! is it so good?' said Don Quixote.

'So good,' answered Gines, 'that woe be to *Lazarillo de Tormes*,* and to all that have written or shall write in that way.* What I can affirm is, that it relates truths, and truth so ingenious and entertaining, that no fictions can come up to them.'

'How is the book intituled?' demanded Don Quixote.

'*The Life of Gines de Pasamonte*,' replied Gines himself.

'And is it finished?' quoth Don Quixote.

'How can it be finished?' answered he, 'since my life is not yet finished? what is written, is from my cradle to the moment of my being sent this last time to the galleys.'

'Then you have been there before,' said Don Quixote.

'Four years the other time,' replied Gines, 'to serve God and the king; and I know already the relish of the biscuit and bull's-pizzle: nor does it grieve me much to go to them again, since I shall there have the opportunity of finishing my book: for I have a great many things to say, and in the galleys of Spain there is leisure more than enough, though I shall not want much for what I have to write, because I have it by heart.'

'You seem to be a witty fellow,' said Don Quixote.

'And an unfortunate one,' answered Gines: 'but misfortunes always pursue the ingenious.'

'Pursue the villainous,' said the commissary.

'I have already desired you, Señor commissary,' answered Pasamonte, 'to go on fair and softly; for your superiors did not give you that staff to misuse us poor wretches here, but to conduct and carry us whither his majesty commands: now by the life of—I say no more; but the spots which were contracted in the inn, may perhaps one day come out in the bucking;* and let every one hold his tongue, and live well, and speak better; and let us march on, for this has held us long enough.'

The commissary lifted up his staff to strike Pasamonte in return for his threats; but Don Quixote interposed, and desired he would not abuse him, since it was but fair, that he who had his hands so tied up, should have his tongue a little at liberty. Then turning about to the whole string he said:

'From all you have told me, dearest brethren, I clearly gather, that though it be only to punish you for your crimes, you do not much relish the punishment you are going to suffer, and that you go to it much against the grain and against your good liking: and, perhaps, the pusillanimity of him who was put to the torture, this man's want of money, and the other's want of friends, and in short the judge's wresting of the law, may have been the cause of your ruin, and that you did not come off, as in justice you ought to have done. And I have so strong a persuasion that this is the truth of the case, that my mind prompts, and even forces me, to show in you the effect, for which heaven threw me into the world and ordained me to profess the order of chivalry, which I do profess, and the vow I made in it to succour the needy, and those oppressed by the mighty. But knowing that it is one part of prudence, not to do that by foul means, which may be done by fair, I will entreat these gentlemen your guard, and the commissary, that they will be pleased to loose, and let you go in peace, there being people enough to serve the king for better reasons; for it seems to me a hard case to make slaves of those whom God and nature made free. Besides, gentlemen guards,' (added Don Quixote) 'these poor men have committed no offence against you: let every one answer for his sins in the other world: there is a God in heaven, who does not neglect to chastise the wicked, nor to reward the good; neither is it fitting that honest men should be the executioners of others, they having no interest in the matter. I request this of you in this calm and gentle manner, that I may have some ground to thank you for your compliance: but if you do it not willingly, this lance, and this sword, with the vigour of my arm, shall compel you to do it.'

'This is pleasant fooling,' answered the commissary; 'an admirable conceit he has hit upon at last: he would have us let the king's prisoners go, as if we had authority to set them free, or he to command us to do it. Go on your way, Señor, and adjust that basin on your noddle, and do not go feeling for three legs in a cat.'

'You are a cat, and a rat, and a rascal to boot,' answered Don Quixote; and so, with a word and a blow, he attacked him so suddenly, that before he could stand upon his defence, he threw him to the ground, much wounded with a thrust of the lance. And it happened luckily for Don Quixote, that this was one of the two who carried firelocks. The rest of the guards were astonished and confounded at the unexpected encounter; but recovering themselves, those on horseback drew their swords, and those on foot laid hold on their

javelins, and fell upon Don Quixote, who waited for them
with much calmness; and doubtless it had gone ill with him,
if the galley-slaves, perceiving the opportunity which offered
itself to them of recovering their liberty, had not procured
it, by breaking the chain with which they were linked
together. The hurry was such, that the guards now endeavouring to prevent the slaves from getting loose, and now
engaging with Don Quixote, who attacked them, did nothing
to any purpose.

Sancho, for his part, assisted in loosing Gines de Pasamonte, who was the first that leaped free and disembarrassed
upon the plain; and setting upon the fallen commissary, he
took away his sword and his gun, with which, levelling it,
first at one, and then at another, without discharging it, he
cleared the field of all the guard, who fled no less from
Pasamonte's gun than from the shower of stones which the
slaves, now at liberty, poured upon them.

Sancho was much grieved at what had happened; for he
imagined that the fugitives would give notice of the fact to
the Holy Brotherhood, which, upon ringing a bell, would
sally out in quest of the delinquents; and so he told his
master, and begged of him to be gone from thence immediately, and take shelter among the trees and rocks of the
neighbouring mountain.

'It is well,' said Don Quixote; 'but I know what is now
expedient to be done.'

Then having called all the slaves together, who were in a
fright, and had stripped the commissary to his buff, they
gathered in a ring about him to know his pleasure; when he
thus addressed them.

'To be thankful for benefits received is the property of
persons well-born; and one of the sins, at which God is most
offended, is ingratitude. This I say, gentlemen, because you
have already found by manifest experience, the benefit you
have received at my hands; in recompense whereof my will
and pleasure is, that, laden with this chain, which I have
taken from your necks, you immediately set out, and go to
the city of Toboso, and there present yourselves before the
lady Dulcinea del Toboso, and tell her, that her Knight of

the Sorrowful Figure sends you to present his service to her: and recount to her every tittle and circumstance of this memorable adventure, to the point of setting you at your wished-for liberty: this done, you may go, in God's name, whither you list.'

Gines de Pasamonte answered for them all, and said:

'What your worship command us, noble Sir, and our deliverer, is of all impossibilities the most impossible to be complied with: for we dare not be seen together on the road, but must go separate and alone, each man by himself, and endeavour to hide ourselves in the very bowels of the earth from the Holy Brotherhood, who doubtless will be out in quest of us. What your worship may, and ought to do, is to change this service and duty to the lady Dulcinea del Toboso into a certain number of Ave-Marias and Credos, which we will say for the success of your design; and this is what we may do, by day or by night, flying or reposing, in peace or in war: but to think that we will now return to the brick-kilns of Egypt, I say, to take our chains, and put ourselves on the way to Toboso, is to think it is now night already, whereas it is not yet ten o'clock in the morning; and to expect this from us is to expect pears from an elm-tree.'

'I vow then,' quoth Don Quixote, already enraged, 'Don son of a whore, Don Ginesillo de Parapilla, or however you call yourself, you alone shall go with your tail between your legs, and the whole chain upon your back.'

Pasamonte, who was not over passive, and had already perceived that Don Quixote was not wiser than he should be, since he committed such an extravagance as the setting them at liberty, seeing himself treated in this manner, winked upon his comrades; and they all, stepping aside, began to rain such a shower of stones upon Don Quixote, that he could not contrive to cover himself with his buckler; and poor Rosinante made no more of the spur than if he had been made of brass. Sancho got behind his ass, and thereby sheltered himself from the storm and hail that poured upon them both. Don Quixote could not screen himself so well but that he received I know not how many thumps on the body, with such force that they brought him to the ground;

and scarcely was he fallen, when the student set upon him, and, taking the basin from off his head, gave him three or four blows with it on the shoulders, and then struck it as often against the ground, whereby he almost broke it to pieces. They stripped him of a jacket he wore over his armour, and would have stripped him of his trousers too, if the greaves had not hindered him. They took from Sancho his cloak, leaving him in his doublet; and sharing among themselves the spoils of the battle, they made the best of their way off, each a several way, with more care how to escape the Holy Brotherhood they were in fear of, than to load themselves with the chain, and to go and present themselves before the lady Dulcinea del Toboso.

The ass and Rosinante, Sancho and Don Quixote, remained by themselves; the ass hanging his head and pensive, and now and then shaking his ears, thinking that the storm of stones was not yet over, but still whizzing about his head; Rosinante stretched along close by his master, he also being knocked down with another stone; Sancho in his doublet, and afraid of the Holy Brotherhood: and Don Quixote very much out of humour to find himself so ill treated by those very persons to whom he had done so much good.

CHAPTER 23

Of what befell the renowned Don Quixote in the Sierra Morena* being one of the most curious and uncommon adventures of any related in this faithful history.

Don Quixote, finding himself so ill treated, said to his squire:

'Sancho, I have always heard it said, that to do good to low fellows is to throw water into the sea. Had I believed what you said to me, I might have prevented this trouble; but it is done, I must have patience, and take warning from henceforward.'

'Your worship will as much take warning,' answered Sancho, 'as I am a Turk: but since you say, that, if you had believed me, you had avoided this mischief, believe me now, and you will avoid a greater; for, let me tell you, there is no putting off the Holy Brotherhood with chivalries: they do not care two farthings for all the knights-errant in the world; and know, that I fancy already I hear their arrows whizzing about my ears.'

'Thou art naturally a coward, Sancho,' said Don Quixote; 'but that you may not say I am obstinate, and that I never do what you advise, I will for once take your counsel, and get out of the reach of that fury you fear so much; but upon this one condition, that neither living nor dying, you shall ever tell anybody that I retired and withdrew myself from this peril out of fear, but that I did it out of mere compliance with your entreaties: for if you say otherwise, you will lie in so doing; and from this time to that, and from that time to this, I tell you, you lie, and will lie, every time you say or think it: and reply no more; for the bare thought of withdrawing and retreating from any danger, and especially from this, which seems to carry some or no appearance of fear with it, makes me, that I now stand prepared to abide here, and expect alone, not only that Holy Brotherhood you talk of and fear, but the brothers of the twelve tribes of Israel, and the seven Maccabees and Castor and Pollux, and even all the brothers and brotherhoods that are in the world.'

'Sir,' answered Sancho, 'retreating is not running away, nor is staying wisdom, when the danger overbalances the hope: and it is the part of wise men to secure themselves to-day for to-morrow, and not to venture all upon one throw. And know, though I am but a clown and a peasant, I have yet some smattering of what is called good conduct: therefore, repent not of having taken my advice, but get upon Rosinante, if you can, and if not, I will assist you; and follow me; for my noddle tells me, that for the present we have more need of heels than hands.'

Don Quixote mounted, without replying a word more; and Sancho leading the way upon his ass, they entered on one side of the Sierra Morena, which was close by, it being Sancho's intention to pass quite across it, and to get out at Viso or Almodóvar del Campo, and to hide themselves for some days among those craggy rocks, that they might not be found, if the Holy Brotherhood should come in quest of them. He was encouraged to this by seeing that the provisions carried by his ass had escaped safe from the skirmish with the galley-slaves, which he looked upon as a miracle, considering what the slaves took away, and how narrowly they searched.*

That night they got into the heart of the Sierra Morena, where Sancho thought it convenient to pass that night, and also some days, at least as long as the provisions he had with him lasted: so they took up their lodging between two great rocks, and amidst abundance of cork-trees. But destiny, which, according to the opinion of those who have not the light of the true faith, guides, fashions, and disposes all things its own way, so ordered it, that Gines de Pasamonte, the famous cheat and robber, whom the valour and madness of Don Quixote had delivered from the chain, being justly afraid of the Holy Brotherhood, took it into his head to hide himself in those very mountains; and his fortune and his fear carried him to the same place where Don Quixote's and Sancho Panza's had carried them, just at the time he could distinguish who they were, and at the instant they were fallen asleep. And as the wicked are always ungrateful, and necessity puts people upon applying to shifts, and the present conveniency overcomes the consideration of the future, Gines, who had neither gratitude nor good-nature, resolved to steal Sancho Panza's ass, making no account of Rosinante, as a thing neither pawnable nor saleable. Sancho Panza slept; the varlet stole his ass, and before it was day he was too far off to be found.

Aurora issued forth, rejoicing the earth, and saddening Sancho Panza, who missed his Dapple, and finding himself deprived of him, began the dolefullest lamentation in the world; and so loud it was, that Don Quixote awaked at his cries, and heard him say:

'O child of my bowels, born in my own house, the joy of my children, the entertainment of my wife, the envy of my neighbours, the relief of my burdens, and lastly, the half of my maintenance! for, with six and twenty maravedis I earned every day by thy means, I half supported my family.'

Don Quixote hearing the lamentation, and learning the cause, comforted Sancho with the best reasons he could, and desired him to have patience, promising to give him a bill of exchange for three young asses out of five he had left at home. Sancho was comforted herewith, wiped away his tears, moderated his sighs, and thanked his master for the kindness he showed him. Don Quixote's heart leaped for joy at entering into the mountains, such kind of places seeming to him the most likely to furnish him with those adventures he was in quest of. They recalled to his memory the marvellous events which had befallen knights-errant in such solitudes and deserts. He went on meditating on these things, and so wrapped and transported in them that he remembered nothing else. Nor had Sancho any other concern (now that he thought he was out of danger) than to appease his hunger with what remained of the clerical spoils: and thus, sitting sideling, as women do, upon his beast, he jogged after his master, emptying the bag, and stuffing his paunch: and while he was thus employed, he would not have given a farthing to have met with any new adventure whatever.

Being thus busied, he lifted up his eyes, and saw his master had stopped, and was endeavouring, with the point of his lance, to raise up some heavy bundle that lay upon the ground: wherefore he made haste to assist him, if need were, and came up to him just as he had turned over with his lance a saddle-cushion and a portmanteau fastened to it, half, or rather quite rotten and torn; but so heavy that Sancho was forced to alight and help to take it up; and his master ordered him to see what was in it.* Sancho very readily obeyed; and though the portmanteau was secured with its chain and padlock, you might see through the breaches what it contained; which was, four fine holland shirts, and other linen, no less curious than clean; and, in a handkerchief, he found a good heap of gold crowns; and as soon as he espied them, he cried:

'Blessed be heaven, which has presented us with one profitable adventure.'

And searching further, he found a little pocket-book, richly bound. Don Quixote desired to have it, and bid him take the money and keep it for himself. Sancho kissed his hands for the favour; and emptying the portmanteau of the linen, he put it in the provender-bag. All which Don Quixote perceiving, he said:

'I am of opinion, Sancho (nor can it possibly be otherwise), that some traveller must have lost his way in these mountains, and have fallen into the hands of robbers, who have killed him, and brought him to this remote and secret part to bury him.'

'It cannot be so,' answered Sancho; 'for, had they been robbers, they would not have left this money here.'

'You say right,' said Don Quixote; 'and I cannot guess nor think what it should be; but stay, let us see whether this pocket-book has anything written in it, whereby we may trace and discover what we want to know.' He opened it, and the first thing he found was a kind of rough draught, but very legible, of a sonnet, which he read aloud that Sancho might hear it, to this purpose:—

> Or love doth nothing know, or cruel is,
> Or my affliction equals not the cause
> That doth condemn me to severest pains.
> But if love be a god, we must suppose
> His knowledge boundless, nor can cruelty
> With reason be imputed to a god.
> Whence then the grief, the cruel pains I feel?
> Chloë, art thou the cause? impossible!
> Such ill can ne'er subsist with so much good;
> Nor does high heaven's behest ordain my fall.
> I soon shall die; my fate's inevitable;
> For where we know not the disease's cause,
> A miracle alone can hit the cure.

'From this parcel of verses,' quoth Sancho, 'nothing can be collected, unless by the clue here given, you can come at the whole bottom.'

'What clue is here?' said Don Quixote.

'I thought,' said Sancho, 'your worship named a clue.'

'No, I said Chloë,'* answered Don Quixote; 'and doubtless that is the name of the lady whom the author of this sonnet complains of; and, in faith, either he is a tolerable poet, or I know but little of the art.'

'So, then,' said Sancho, 'your worship understands making verses too!'

'Yes, and better than you think,' answered Don Quixote; 'and you shall see I do, when you carry a letter to my lady Dulcinea del Toboso, written in verse from top to bottom: for know, Sancho, that all, or most of the knights-errant of time past, were great poets, and great musicians; these two accomplishments, or rather graces, being annexed to lovers-errant. True it is, that the couplets of former knights have more of passion than elegance in them.'

'Pray, Sir, read on further,' said Sancho; 'perhaps you may find something to satisfy us.'

Don Quixote turned over the leaf, and said:

'This is in prose, and seems to be a letter.'

'A letter of business, Sir?' demanded Sancho.

'By the beginning, it seems rather one of love,' answered Don Quixote.

'Then pray, Sir, read it aloud,' said Sancho; 'for I mightily relish these love matters.'

'With all my heart,' said Don Quixote; and reading aloud, as Sancho desired, he found it to this effect:—

'Your promise, and my certain hard fate, hurry me to a place, from whence you will sooner hear the news of my death, than the cause of my complaint. You have undone me, ungrateful maid, for the sake of one who has larger possessions, but not more merit, than I. But, if virtue were a treasure now in esteem, I should have had no reason to envy any man's good fortune, not to bewail my own wretchedness; what your beauty built up, your behaviour has thrown down: by that I took you for an angel, and by this I find you are a woman. Farewell, O causer of my disquiet; and may heaven grant that your husband's perfidy may never come to your knowledge, to make you repent of what you have done, and afford me that revenge which I do not desire.'

The letter being read, Don Quixote said:

'We can gather little more from this, than from the verses; only that he who wrote it is some slighted lover.'

And, turning over most of the book, he found other verses and letters, some of which were legible, and some not; but the purport of them all was complaints, lamentations, suspicions, desires, dislikings, favours, and slights, some extolled with rapture, and others as mournfully deplored.

While Don Quixote was examining the book, Sancho examined the portmanteau, without leaving a corner in it, or in the saddle-cushion, which he did not search, scrutinize, and look into; nor seam which he did not rip; nor lock of wool, which he did not carefully pick; that nothing might be lost for want of diligence, or through carelessness; such a greediness the finding the gold crowns, which were more than a hundred, had excited in him. And though he found no more of them, he thought himself abundantly rewarded, by the leave given him to keep what he had found, for the tossings in the blanket, the vomitings of the balsam, the benedictions of the pack-staves, the cuffs of the carrier, the loss of the wallet, and the theft of his cloak; together with all the hunger, thirst, and weariness, he had undergone in his good master's service.

The Knight of the Sorrowful Figure was extremely desirous to know who was the owner of the portmanteau, conjecturing by the sonnet and the letter, by the money in gold, and by the fineness of the shirts, that it must doubtless belong to some lover of condition, whom the slights and ill treatment of his mistress had reduced to terms of despair. But there being no one, in that uninhabitable and craggy place, to give him any information, he thought of nothing but going forward, which way soever Rosinante pleased, and that was wherever he found the way easiest; still possessed with the imagination that he could not fail of meeting with some strange adventure among those briars and rocks.

As he thus went on musing, he espied, on the top of a hillock, just before him, a man skipping from crag to crag, and from bush to bush, with extraordinary agility. He seemed to be naked, his beard black and bushy, his hair long and tangled, his legs and feet bare: on his thighs he wore a pair of breeches of sad-coloured velvet, but so ragged, that his skin appeared through several parts. His head was bare; and, though he passed with the swiftness already mentioned, the Knight of the Sorrowful Figure saw and observed all these particulars; but though he endeavoured to follow him, he could not; for it was not given to Rosinante's feebleness to make way through those craggy places; and besides, he was naturally slow-footed and phlegmatic. Don Quixote immediately fancied this must be the owner of the saddle-cushion and portmanteau, and so resolved to go in search of him, though he were sure to wander a whole year among those mountains before he should find him: wherefore he commanded Sancho to cut short over one side of the mountain, while he coasted on the other, in hopes that by this diligence they might light on the man who had so suddenly vanished out of their sight.

'I cannot do it,' answered Sancho; 'for the moment I offer to stir from your worship, fear is upon me, assaulting me with a thousand kinds of terrors and apparitions: and let this serve to advertise you, that, from henceforward, I have not the power to stir a finger's breadth from your presence.'

'Be it so,' said he of the Sorrowful Figure, 'and I am very well pleased that you rely upon my courage, which shall never be wanting to you, though your very soul in your body should fail you: and now follow me step by step, or as you can, and make spying-glasses of your eyes: we will go round this craggy hill, and perhaps we may meet with the man we saw, who, doubtless, is the owner of what we have found.'

To which Sancho replied:

'It would be much more prudent not to look after him; for, if we should find him, and he perchance proves to be the owner of the money, it is plain I must restore it; and therefore it would be better, without this unnecessary diligence, to keep possession of it, *bona fide*, until by some way less curious and officious, its true owner shall be found; and perhaps that may be at a time when I shall have spent it all, and then I am truly free by the law.'

'You deceive yourself in this, Sancho,' answered Don Quixote: 'for, since we have a suspicion who is the right owner, we are obliged to seek him, and return it; and if we should not look for him, the vehement suspicion we have that this may be him, makes us already as guilty as if he really were. So that, friend Sancho, you should be in no pain at searching after him, considering the uneasiness I shall be freed from in finding him.'

Then he pricked Rosinante on, and Sancho followed at the usual rate; and, having gone round part of the mountain, they found a dead mule lying in a brook, saddled and bridled, and half devoured by dogs and crows. All which confirmed them the more in the suspicion that he who fled from them, was owner of the mule and of the bundle.

While they stood looking at the mule, they heard a whistle, like that of a shepherd tending his flock; and presently, on their left hand, appeared a good number of goats, and behind them, on the top of the mountain, the goatherd that kept them, who was an old man. Don Quixote called aloud to him, and desired him to come down to them. He answered as loudly, and demanded who had brought them to that desolate place, seldom or never trodden, unless by the feet of goats, wolves, or other wild beasts, which frequented those mountains. Sancho replied, if he could come down, they would satisfy his curiosity in everything. The goatherd descended, and coming to the place where Don Quixote was, he said:

'I will lay a wager you are viewing the hackney mule which lies dead in this bottom: in good faith it has lain there these six months already. Pray tell me, have you lighted on his master hereabouts?'

'We have lighted on nothing,' answered Don Quixote, 'but a saddle-cushion and a small portmanteau, which we found not far from hence.'

'I found it too,' answered the goatherd, 'but would by no means take it up, nor come near it, for fear of some mischief, and lest I should be charged with having stolen it; for the devil is subtle, and lays stumbling-blocks and occasions of falling in our way, without our knowing how or how not.'

'I say so too,' answered Sancho; 'for I also found it, and would not go within a stone's throw of it; there I left it, and there it lies as it was for me; for I will not have a dog with a bell.'

'Tell me, honest man,' said Don Quixote, 'do you know who is the owner of these goods?'

'What I know,' said the goatherd, 'is, that six months ago, more or less, there arrived at the huts of certain shepherds, about three leagues from this place, a genteel and comely youth mounted on this very mule, which lies dead here, and with the same saddle-cushion and portmanteau, you say you found, and touched not. He inquired of us, which part of this hill was the most craggy, and least accessible. We told him it was this where we now are: and so it is, truly; for if you were to go on about half a league further, perhaps you would not easily find the way out: and I admire how you could get even hither, since there is no road nor path that leads to this place. The youth then, I say, hearing our answer, turned about his mule, and made towards the place we showed him, leaving us all pleased with his goodly appearance, and in admiration at his question, and the haste he made to reach the mountain; and, from that time, we saw him not again, until, some days after, he issued out upon one of our shepherds, and, without saying a word, came up to him, and gave him several cuffs and kicks, and immediately went to our sumpter-ass, which he plundered of all the bread and cheese she carried; and, this done, he fled again to the rocks with wonderful swiftness.

'Some of us goatherds knowing this, went almost two days in quest of him, through the most intricate part of this craggy hill; and at last we found him lying in the hollow of a large cork-tree. He came out to us with much gentleness, his garment torn, and his face so disfigured and scorched by the sun, that we should scarcely have known him, but that his clothes, ragged as they were, with the description given us of them, assured us he was the person we were in search after. He saluted us courteously, and in few, but complaisant terms, bade us not wonder to see him in that condition, to which he was necessitated, in order to perform a certain penance enjoined him for his manifold sins. We entreated him to tell us who he was, but we could get no more out of him. We desired him likewise, that, when he stood in need of food, without which he could not subsist, he would let us know where we might find him, and we would very freely and willingly bring him some; and if this was not to his liking, that, at least, he would come out and ask for it, and not take it away from the shepherds by force. He thanked us for our offers, begged pardon for the violences passed, and promised from thenceforth to ask it for God's sake, without giving disturbance to anybody. As to the place of his abode, he said, he had no other than what chance presented him, wherever the night overtook him; and he ended his discourse with such melting tears, that we who heard him, must have been very stones not to have borne him company in them, considering what he was the first time we saw him, and what we saw him now to be; for, as I before said, he was a very comely and graceful youth, and by his courteous behaviour and civil discourse, showed himself to be well-born, and a court-like person; for though we who heard him were country-people, his genteel carriage was sufficient to discover itself, even to rusticity.

'In the height of his discourse he stopped short, and stood silent, riveting his eyes to the ground for a considerable time, whilst we all stood still in suspense, waiting to see what that fit of distraction would end in, with no small compassion at the sight: for by his demeanour, his staring, and fixing his eyes unmoved for a long while on the ground, and then shutting them again; by his biting his lips, and arching his brows, we easily judged that some fit of madness was come upon him; and he quickly confirmed us in our suspicions; for he started up with great fury from the ground on which he had just before thrown himself, and fell upon the first that stood next him, with such resolution and rage, that, if we had not taken him off, he would have bit and cuffed him to death. And all this while he cried out: "Ah traitor Fernando! here, here you shall pay for the wrong you have done me; these hands shall tear out that heart, in which all kinds of wickedness, and especially deceit and treachery, do lurk and are harboured" and to these he added other expressions, all tending to revile the said Fernando, and charging him with falsehood and treachery. We disengaged him from our companion at last, with no small difficulty; and he, without saying

a word, left us, and plunged amidst the thickest of the bushes
and briars; so that we could not possibly follow him.

'By this we guessed that his madness returned by fits, and
that some person, whose name is Fernando, must have done
him some injury of as grievous a nature as the condition to
which it has reduced him sufficiently declares. And this has
been often confirmed to us, since that time, by his issuing
out one while to beg of the shepherds part of what they had
to eat, and at other times to take it from them by force; for,
when the mad fit is upon him, though the shepherds freely
offer it him, he will not take it without coming to blows for
it; but when he is in his senses, he asks it for God's sake,
with courtesy and civility, and is very thankful for it, not
without shedding tears. And truly, gentlemen, I must tell you'
(pursued the goatherd) 'that yesterday I, and four young
swains, two of them my servants, and two my friends,
resolved to go in search of him, and having found him, either
by force, or by fair means, to carry him to the town of
Almodóvar, which is eight leagues off, and there to get him
cured, if his distemper be curable; or at least inform ourselves
who he is, when he is in his senses, and whether he has any
relations, to whom we may give notice of his misfortune.
This, gentlemen, is all I can tell you in answer to your inquiry,
by which you may understand, that the owner of the goods
you found, is the same whom you saw pass by you so swiftly
and so nakedly.'

For Don Quixote had already told him, how he had seen
that man pass skipping over the craggy rocks.

Don Quixote was in admiration at what he heard from the
goatherd; and having now a greater desire to learn who the
unfortunate madman was, he resolved, as he had before
purposed, to seek him all over the mountain, without leaving
a corner or cave in it unsearched, until he should find him.
But fortune managed better for him than he thought or
expected, for in that very instant the youth they sought
appeared from between some clefts of a rock, coming toward
the place where they stood, and muttering to himself something, which could not be understood, though one were near
him, much less at a distance. His dress was such as has been

described; but, as he drew near, Don Quixote perceived, that a buff doublet he had on, though torn to pieces, still retained the perfume of amber; whence he positively concluded that the person who wore such apparel could not be of the lowest quality.

When the youth came up to them, he saluted them with a harsh unmusical accent, but with much civility. Don Quixote returned him the salute with no less complaisance, and alighting from Rosinante with a genteel air and address, advanced to embrace him, and held him a good space very close between his arms, as if he had been acquainted with him a long time. The other, whom we may call 'the Ragged Knight of the Sorry Figure' (as Don Quixote of the Sorrowful), after he had suffered himself to be embraced, drew back a little, and laying both his hands on Don Quixote's shoulders, stood beholding him, as if to see whether he knew him; in no less admiration, perhaps, at the figure, mien, and armour, of Don Quixote, than Don Quixote was at the sight of him. In short, the first who spoke after the embracing was the Ragged Knight, and he said what shall be told in the next chapter.

CHAPTER 24

A continuation of the adventure of the Sierra Morena.

THE history relates, that great was the attention wherewith Don Quixote listened to the Ragged Knight of the mountain, who began his discourse thus:

'Assuredly, señor, whoever you are (for I do not know you), I am obliged to you for your expressions of civility to me; and I wish it were in my power to serve you with more than my bare goodwill, for the kind reception you have given me; but my fortune allows me nothing but good wishes to return you, for your kind intentions towards me.'

'Mine,' answered Don Quixote, 'are to serve you, inasmuch that I determined not to quit these mountains until I had found you, and learned from your own mouth, whether the affliction, which, by your leading this strange life, seems to possess you, may admit of any remedy, and, if need were, to use all possible diligence to compass it; and though your misfortune were of that sort which keeps the door locked against all kind of comfort, I intended to assist you in bewailing and bemoaning it the best I could; for it is some relief in misfortunes to find those who pity them. And if you think my intention deserves to be taken kindly, and with any degree of acknowledgement, I beseech you, Sir, by the abundance of civility I see you are possessed of; I conjure you also by whatever in this life you have loved, or do love most, to tell me who you are, and what has brought you hither, to live and die like a brute beast, amidst these solitudes; as you seem to intend, by frequenting them in a manner so unbecoming of yourself, if I may judge by your person, and what remains of your attire. And I swear' (added Don Quixote) 'by the order of knighthood I have received, though unworthy and a sinner, and by the profession of a knight-errant, if you gratify me in this, to serve you to the utmost of what my profession obliges me to, either in remedying your misfortune, if a remedy may be found, or in assisting you to bewail it, as I have already promised.'

The Knight of the Wood, hearing him of the Sorrowful Figure, talk in this manner, did nothing but view him and review him, and view him again from head to foot; and when he had surveyed him thoroughly, he said to him:

'If you have anything to give me to eat, give it me, for God's sake, and when I have eaten, I will do all you command me, in requital for the good wishes you have expressed toward me.'

Sancho immediately drew out of his wallet, and the goatherd out of his scrip, some meat, wherewith the Ragged Knight satisfied his hunger, eating what they gave him like a distracted person, so fast, that he took no time between one mouthful and another; for he rather devoured than ate; and while he was eating, neither he nor the bystanders spoke a word. When he had done, he made signs to them to follow him, which they did; and he led them to a little green meadow not far off, at the turning of a rock, a little out of the way.

Where being arrived, he stretched himself along upon the grass, and the rest did the same; and all this without a word spoken, until the Ragged Knight, having settled himself in his place, said:

'If you desire, gentlemen, that I should tell you in few words the immensity of my misfortunes, you must promise me not to interrupt, by asking questions, or otherwise, the thread of my doleful history; for, in the instant you do so, I shall break off, and tell no more.'

These words brought to Don Quixote's memory the tale his squire had told him, which, by his mistaking the number of the goats that had passed the river, remained still unfinished. But to return to our Ragged Knight: he went on, saying:

'I give this caution, because I would pass briefly over the account of my misfortunes; for the bringing them back to my remembrance, serves only to add new ones; and though the fewer questions I am asked the sooner I shall have finished my story, yet will I not omit any material circumstance, designing entirely to satisfy your desire.'

Don Quixote promised, in the name of all the rest, it should be so; and, upon this assurance, he began in the following manner.

'My name is Cardenio; the place of my birth one of the best cities of all Andalusia; my family noble; my parents rich; my wretchedness so great that my parents must have lamented it, and my relations felt it without being able to remedy it by all their wealth; for the goods of fortune seldom avail anything towards the relief of misfortunes sent from heaven. In this country there lived a heaven, wherein love had placed all the glory I could wish for. Such is the beauty of Lucinda, a damsel of as good a family, and as rich as myself, but of more good fortune, and less constancy than was due to my honourable intentions. This Lucinda I loved, courted, and adored, from my childhood and tender years; and she on her part loved me with that innocent affection proper to her age. Our parents were not unacquainted with our inclinations, and were not displeased at them; foreseeing, that if they went on, they could end in nothing but our marriage; a thing pointed out as it were by the equality of our birth and circumstances. Our love increased with our years, insomuch that Lucinda's father thought proper, for reasons of decency, to deny me access to his house; imitating, as it were, the parents of that Thisbe, so celebrated by the poets. This restraint was only adding flame to flame, and desire to desire; for, though it was in their power to impose silence on our tongues, they could not on our pens, which discover to the person beloved the most hidden secrets of the soul, and that with more freedom than the tongue; for oftentimes the presence of the beloved object disturbs and strikes mute the most determined intention, and the most resolute tongue. O heavens! how many billets-doux did I write to her! what charming, what modest answers did I receive! how many sonnets did I pen! how many love-verses indite! in which my soul unfolded all its passion, described its inflamed desires, cherished its remembrances, and gave a loose to its wishes.

'In short, finding myself at my wit's end, and my soul languishing with desire of seeing her, I resolved at once to put in execution what seemed to me the most likely means to obtain my desired and deserved reward; and that was, to demand of her father, her for my lawful wife; which I accordingly did. He answered me, that he thanked me for the inclination I showed to do him honour in my proposed alliance with his family; but that, my father being alive, it belonged more properly to him to make this demand; for, without his full consent and approbation, Lucinda was not a woman to be taken or given by stealth. I returned him thanks for his kind intention, thinking there was reason in what he said, and that my father would come into it as soon as I should break it to him. In that very instant I went to acquaint my father with my desires; and upon entering the room where he was, I found him with a letter open in his hand, which he gave me before I spoke a word, saying to me: "By this letter you will see, Cardenio, the inclination Duke Ricardo has to do you service."

'This Duke Ricardo, gentlemen, as you cannot but know, is a grandee of Spain, whose estate lies in the best part of

Andalusia. I took and read the letter, which was so extremely kind, that I myself judged it would be wrong in my father not to comply with what he requested in it; which was, that he would send me presently to him, being desirous to place me not as a servant, but as a companion to his eldest son; and that he engaged to put me into a post answerable to the opinion he had of me. I was confounded at reading the letter, and especially when I heard my father say: "Two days hence, Cardenio, you shall depart, to fulfil the Duke's pleasure; and give thanks to God, who is opening you a way to that preferment I know you deserve." To these he added several other expressions, by way of fatherly admonition.

'The time fixed for my departure came: I talked the night before to Lucinda, and told her all that had passed; and I did the same to her father, begging of him to wait a few days, and not to dispose of her, until I knew what Duke Ricardo's pleasure was with me. He promised me all I desired; and she, on her part, confirmed it with a thousand vows, and a thousand faintings. I arrived at length where Duke Ricardo resided; who received and treated me with so much kindness, that envy presently began to do her office, by possessing his old servants with an opinion, that every favour the Duke conferred upon me, was prejudicial to their interest.

'But the person the most pleased with my being there, was a second son of the Duke's called Fernando, a sprightly young gentleman of a genteel, generous, and amorous disposition, who in a short time, contracted so intimate a friendship with me, that it became the subject of everybody's discourse; and though I had a great share likewise in the favour and affection of the elder brother, yet they did not come up to that distinguishing manner in which Don Fernando loved and treated me. Now, as there is no secret which is not communicated between friends, and as the intimacy I held with Don Fernando ceased to be barely such by being converted into friendship, he revealed to me all his thoughts and especially one relating to his being in love, which gave him no small disquiet.

'He loved a country girl, a vassal of his father's: her parents were very rich, and she herself was so beautiful, reserved, discreet, and modest, that no one who knew her could determine in which of these qualifications she most excelled, or was most accomplished. These perfections of the country-maid raised Don Fernando's desires to such a pitch, that he resolved, in order to carry his point, and subdue the chastity of the maiden, to give her his promise to marry her; for, otherwise, it would have been to attempt an impossibility. The obligation I was under to his friendship put me upon using the best reasons, and the most lively examples, I could think of, to divert and dissuade him from such a purpose. But, finding it was all in vain, I resolved to acquaint his father, Duke Ricardo, with the affair. Don Fernando, being sharp-sighted and artful, suspected and feared no less, knowing that I was obliged, as a faithful servant, not to conceal from my lord and master the Duke, a matter so prejudicial to his honour: and therefore, to amuse and deceive me, he said, that he knew no better remedy for effacing the remembrance of the beauty that had so captivated him, than to absent himself for some months; and this absence, he said, should be effected by our going together to my father's house, under pretence, as he would tell the Duke, of seeing and cheapening some very fine horses in our town, which produces the best in the world. Scarcely had I heard him say this, when, prompted by my own love, I approved of his proposal, as one of the best concerted imaginable, and should have done so, had it not been so plausible a one, since it afforded me so good an opportunity of returning to see my dear Lucinda. Upon this motive: I came into his opinion, and seconded his design, desiring him to put it in execution as soon as possible; since, probably, absence might have its effect in spite of the strongest inclinations.

'At the very time he made this proposal to me, he had already, as appeared afterwards, enjoyed the maiden, under the title of a husband, and only waited for a convenient season to divulge it with safety to himself, being afraid of what the Duke his father might do, when he should hear of his folly. Now as love in young men is, for the most part, nothing but appetite, and as pleasure is its ultimate end, it is terminated by enjoyment; and what seemed to be love vanishes, because it cannot pass the bounds assigned by nature; whereas true love admits of no limits. I would say, that, when Don Fernando had enjoyed the country girl, his desires grew faint, and his fondness abated; so that, in reality, that absence, which he proposed as a remedy for his passion, he only chose, in order to avoid, what was now no longer agreeable to him. The Duke gave him his leave, and ordered me to bear him company.

'We came to our town: my father received him according to his quality; I immediately visited Lucinda; my passion revived, though, in truth, it had been neither dead nor asleep: unfortunately for me, I revealed it to Don Fernando, thinking that, by the laws of friendship, I ought to conceal nothing from him. I expatiated to him, in so lively a manner, on the beauty, good humour, and discretion of Lucinda, that my praises excited in him a desire of seeing a damsel endowed with such fine accomplishments. I complied with it, to my misfortune, and showed her to him one night by the light of a taper at a window, where we two used to converse together. She appeared to him, though in an undress, so charming, as to blot out of his memory all the beauties he had ever seen before. He was struck dumb; he lost all sense; he was transported: in short, he fell in love to such a degree, as will appear by the sequel of the story of my misfortunes. And, the more to inflame his desire, which he concealed from me, and disclosed to heaven alone, fortune so ordered it, that he one day found a letter of hers to me, desiring me to demand her of her father in marriage, so ingenious, so modest, and so full of tenderness, that, when he had read it, he declared to me, that he thought in Lucinda alone, were united all the graces of beauty and good sense, which are dispersed and divided among the rest of her sex.

'True it is (I confess it now) that though I knew what just grounds Don Fernando had to commend Lucinda, I was grieved to hear those commendations from his mouth: I began to fear and suspect him: for he was every moment putting me upon talking of Lucinda, and would begin the discourse himself, though he brought it in never so abruptly: which awakened in me I know not what jealousy: and though

I did not fear any change in the goodness and fidelity of Lucinda, yet I could not but dread the very thing they secured me against. Don Fernando procured a sight of the letters I wrote to Lucinda, and her answers, under pretence that he was mightily pleased with the wit of both.

'Now it fell out, that Lucinda, who was very fond of books of chivalry, having desired me to lend her that of *Amadis de Gaul*—'

Scarce had Don Quixote heard him mention books of chivalry, when he said:

'Had you told me, Sir, at the beginning of your story, that the lady Lucinda was fond of reading books of chivalry, there would have needed no other exaggeration to convince me of the sublimity of her understanding; for it could never have been so excellent as you have described it, had she wanted a relish for such savory reading; so that, with respect to me it is needless to waste more words in displaying her beauty, worth, and understanding; for, from only knowing her taste, I pronounce her to be the most beautiful and the most ingenious woman in the world. And I wish, Sir, that, together with *Amadis de Gaul*, you had sent her the good *Don Rugel of Greece*;* for I know that the lady Lucinda will be highly delighted with Daraida and Garaya, and the witty conceits of the shepherd Darinel; also with those admirable verses of his Bucolics, which he sung and repeated with so much good humour, wit, and freedom; but the time may come when this fault may be amended, and the reparation may be made, as soon as ever you will be pleased, Sir, to come with me to our town; where I can furnish you with more than three hundred books, that are the delight of my soul, and the entertainment of my life: though, upon second thoughts, I have not one of them left, thanks to the malice of wicked and envious enchanters. Pardon me, Sir, the having given you this interruption, contrary to what I promised; but, when I hear of matters of chivalry and knights-errant, I can as well forbear talking of them, as the beams of the sun can cease to give heat, or those of the moon to moisten. So that, pray excuse me, and go on; for that is of most importance to us at present.'

While Don Quixote was saying all this, Cardenio hung down his head upon his breast, with all the signs of being profoundly thoughtful; and though Don Quixote twice desired him to continue his story, he neither lifted up his head, nor answered a word. But after some time, he raised it, and said:

'I cannot get it out of my mind, nor can any one persuade me to the contrary, and he must be a blockhead who understands or believes otherwise, but that that great villain master Elisabat lay with Queen Madásima.'*

'It is false, I swear,' answered Don Quixote, in great wrath; 'it is extreme malice, or rather villany, and it is not to be presumed, that so high a princess should lie with a quack; and whoever pretends she did, lies like a very great rascal; and I will make him know it on foot or on horseback, armed or unarmed, by night or by day, or how he pleases.'

Cardenio sat looking at him very attentively, and, the mad fit being already come upon him, he was in no condition to prosecute his story; neither would Don Quixote have heard him, so disgusted was he at what he had heard of Madásima: and strange it was to see him take her part with as much earnestness, as if she had really been his true and natural princess; so far had his cursed books turned his head.

I say, then, that Cardenio, being now mad, and hearing himself called liar and villain, with other such opprobrious words, did not like the jest; and, catching up a stone that lay close by him, he gave Don Quixote such a thump with it on the breast, that it tumbled him down backwards. Sancho Panza, seeing his master handled in this manner, attacked the madman with his clenched fist; and the Ragged Knight received him in such sort, that with one blow he laid him along at his feet; and presently, getting upon him, he pounded his ribs, much to his own heart's content. The goatherd, who endeavoured to defend him, fared little better; and when he had beaten and thrashed them all, he left them, and very quietly marched off to his haunts amidst the rocks. Sancho got up in a rage, to find himself so roughly handled, and so undeservedly withal, and was for taking his revenge on the goatherd, telling him he was in fault for not having given them warning, that this man had his mad fits; for had they known as much, they should have been aware, and upon their guard. The goatherd answered, that he had already given them notice of it, and that, if he had not heard it, the fault was none of his. Sancho Panza replied, and the goatherd rejoined; and the replies and rejoinders ended in taking one another by the beard, and cuffing one another so, that, if Don Quixote had not made peace between them, they would have beat one another to pieces. Sancho, still keeping fast hold of the goatherd, said:

'Let me alone, Sir Knight of the Sorrowful Figure; for, this fellow being a bumpkin, like myself, and not dubbed a knight, I may very safely revenge myself on him for the injury he has done me, by fighting with him hand to hand, like a man of honour.'

'True,' said Don Quixote; 'but I know that he is not to blame for what has happened.'

Herewith he pacified them; and Don Quixote inquired again of the goatherd, whether it were possible to find out Cardenio; for he had a mighty desire to learn the end of his story. The goatherd told him, as at first, that he did not certainly know his haunts; but that, if he walked thereabouts pretty much, he would not fail to meet him, either in or out of his senses.

CHAPTER 25

Which treats of the strange things that befell the valiant knight of La Mancha in the Sierra Morena; and how he imitated the penance of Beltenebros.

DON QUIXOTE took his leave of the goatherd, and mounting again on Rosinante, commanded Sancho to follow him; which he did, with a very ill will. They jogged on softly, entering into the most craggy part of the mountain; and Sancho was ready to burst, for want of some talk with his master, but would fain have had him begin the discourse, that he might not break through what he had enjoined him; but, not being able to endure so long a silence, he said to him:

'Señor Don Quixote, be pleased to give me your worship's blessing, and my dismission; for I will get me home to my wife and children, with whom I shall, at least, have the privilege of talking, and speaking my mind; for, to desire me to bear your worship company through these solitudes, night and day, without suffering me to talk when I list, is to bury me alive. If fate had ordered it, that beasts should talk now, as they did in the days of Guisopete,* it had not been quite so bad; since I might then have communed with my ass as I pleased, and thus have forgotten my ill fortune; for it is very hard, and not to be borne with patience, for a man to ramble about all his life in quest of adventures, and to meet with nothing but kicks and cuffs, tossings in a blanket, and brickbat bangs, and, with all this, to sew up his mouth, and not dare to utter what he has in his heart, as if he were dumb.'

'I understand you, Sancho,' answered Don Quixote; 'you are impatient until I take off the embargo I have laid on your tongue: suppose it taken off, and say what you will, upon condition that this revocation is to last no longer than whilst we are wandering among these craggy rocks.'

'Be it so,' said Sancho: 'let me talk now, for God knows what will be hereafter. And so beginning to enjoy the benefit of this licence, I say: What had your worship to do to stand up so warmly for that same Queen Magimasa, or what's her name? or, what was it to the purpose, whether that abbot* was her gallant, or no? for, had you let that pass, seeing you were not his judge, I verily believe the madman would have gone on with his story, and you would have escaped the thump with the stone, the kicks, and above half a dozen buffets.'

'In faith Sancho,' answered Don Quixote, 'if you did but know, as I do, how honourable and how excellent a lady Queen Madásima was, I am certain you would own I had a great deal of patience, that I did not dash to pieces that mouth, out of which such blasphemies issued. For it is a very great blasphemy to say, or even to think, that a queen should be punk to a barber-surgeon. The truth of the story is, that

that same master Elisabat, whom the madman spoke of, was a very prudent man, and of a very sound judgement, and served as tutor and physician to the queen: but, to think she was his paramour, is an impertinence that deserves to be severely chastised. And to show you that Cardenio did not know what he said, you may remember, that when he said it, he was out of his wits.'

'So say I,' quoth Sancho; 'and therefore no account should have been made of his words; for if good fortune had not been your friend; and the flint-stone had been directed at your head as it was at your breast, we had been in a fine condition for standing up in defence of that dear lady, whom God confound. Besides, do you think Cardenio, if he had killed you, would not have come off as being a madman?'

'A knight-errant,' answered Don Quixote, 'is obliged to defend the honour of women, be they what they will, both against men in their senses and those out of them; how much more then should he stand up in defence of queens of such high degree and worth, as was Queen Madásima, for whom I have a particular affection on account of her good parts: for, besides her being extremely beautiful, she was very prudent, and very patient in her afflictions, of which she had many. And the counsels and company of master Elisabat were of great use and comfort to her, in helping her to bear her sufferings with prudence and patience. Hence the ignorant and evil-minded vulgar took occasion to think and talk that she was his paramour; and I say again they lie, and will lie two hundred times more, all who say or think her so—'

'I neither say or think so,' answered Sancho; 'let those who say it eat the lie, and swallow it with their bread: whether they were guilty or no they have given an account to God before now: I come from my vineyard; I know nothing; I am no friend to inquiring into other men's lives; for he that buys and lies shall find the lie left in his purse behind; besides, naked was I born, and naked I remain. I neither win nor lose; if they were guilty what is that to me? Many think to find bacon where there is not so much as a pin to hang it on: but who can hedge in the cuckoo? Especially, do they spare God himself?'

'God be my aid,' quoth Don Quixote, 'what a parcel of impertinences are you stringing! what has the subject you are upon to do with the proverbs you are threading like beads! Prithee, Sancho, hold your tongue, and henceforward mind spurring your ass, and forbear meddling with what does not concern you. And understand, with all your five senses, that whatever I have done, do, or shall do, is highly reasonable, and exactly conformable to the rules of chivalry, which I am better acquainted with than all the knights who have professed it in the world.'

'Sir,' replied Sancho, 'is it a good rule of chivalry, that we go wandering through these mountains, without path or road, in quest of a madman, who, perhaps, when he is found, will have a mind to finish what he began, not his story—but the breaking of your head, and my ribs?'

'Peace, I say, Sancho, once again,' said Don Quixote: 'for know, that it is not barely the desire of finding the madman that brings me to these parts, but the intention I have to perform an exploit in them, whereby I shall acquire a perpetual name and renown over the face of the whole earth: and it shall be such an one as shall set the seal to all that can render a knight-errant complete and famous.'

'And is this same exploit a very dangerous one?' quoth Sancho Panza.

'No,' answered he of the Sorrowful Figure; 'though the die may chance to run so, that we may have an unlucky throw: but the whole will depend on your diligence.'

'Upon my diligence?' quoth Sancho.

'Yes,' said Don Quixote; 'for if you return speedily from the place whither I intend to send you, my pain will soon be over, and my glory will presently commence: and, because it is not expedient to keep you any longer in suspense, waiting to know what my discourse drives at, understand Sancho, that the famous Amadis de Gaul was one of the most complete knights-errant: I should not have said one of—he was the sole, the principal, the only one, in short the prince of all that were in his time in the world. A fig for Don Belianis, and for all those who say he equalled him in anything! for I swear they are mistaken.

'I say also, that, if a painter would be famous in his art, he must endeavour to copy after the originals of the most excellent masters he knows. And the same rule holds good for all other arts and sciences that serve as ornaments of the commonwealth. In like manner, whoever aspires to the character of prudent and patient, must imitate Ulysses, in whose person and toils Homer draws a lively picture of prudence and patience; as Virgil also does of a pious son, and a valiant and expert captain, in the person of Aeneas; not delineating or describing them as they really were, but as they ought to be, in order to serve as patterns of virtue to succeeding generations. In this very manner was Amadis the polar, the morning star, and the sun of all valiant and enamoured knights, and he whom all we, who militate under the banners of love and chivalry, ought to follow.

'This being so, friend Sancho, the knight-errant who imitates him the most nearly, will, I take it, stand the fairest to arrive at the perfection of chivalry. And one circumstance in which this knight most eminently discovered his prudence, worth, courage, patience, constancy, and love, was his retiring, when disdained by the lady Oriana, to do penance on Peña Pobre, changing his name to that of Beltenebros; a name most certainly significant, and proper for the life he had voluntarily chosen. Now, it is easier for me to copy after him in this than in cleaving giants, beheading serpents, slaying dragons, routing armies, shattering fleets, and dissolving enchantments. And, since this place is so well adapted for the purpose, there is no reason why I should let slip the opportunity which now so commodiously offers me its forelock.'

'In effect,' quoth Sancho, 'what is it your worship intends to do in so remote a place as this?'

'Have I not told you,' answered Don Quixote, 'that I design to imitate Amadis, acting here the desperado, the senseless, and the madman; at the same time copying the valiant Don Orlando, when he found, by the side of a fountain, some indications that Angelica the Fair had dishonoured herself with Medoro: at grief whereof he ran mad, tore up trees by the roots, disturbed the waters of the crystal springs, slew shepherds, destroyed flocks, fired cottages, demolished houses, dragged mares on the ground, and did an hundred thousand other extravagances, worthy to be recorded, and had in eternal remembrance. And, supposing that I do not intend to imitate Roldan, or Orlando, or Rotolando (for he had all these three names) in every point, and in all the mad things he acted, said, and thought, I will make a sketch of them the best I can, in what I judge the most essential. And, perhaps, I may satisfy myself with only copying Amadis, who, without playing any mischievous pranks, by weepings and tendernesses, arrived to as great fame as the best of them all.'

'It seems to me,' quoth Sancho, 'that the knights, who acted in such manner, were provoked to it, and had a reason for doing these follies and penances: but, pray, what cause has your worship to run mad? What lady has disdained you? or what tokens have you discovered to convince you that the lady Dulcinea del Toboso has committed folly either with Moor or Christian?'

'There lies the point,' answered Don Quixote, 'and in this consists the finesse of my affair: a knight-errant who runs mad upon a just occasion deserves no thanks; but to do so without reason is the business, giving my lady to understand what I should perform in the wet, if I do this in the dry. How much rather, since I have cause enough given me, by being so long absent from my ever-honoured lady Dulcinea del Toboso; for, as you may have heard from that whilom shepherd Ambrosio, "The absent feel and fear every ill". So that, friend Sancho, do not waste time in counselling me to quit so rare, so happy, and so unheard-of an imitation. Mad I am, and mad I must be, until your return with an answer to a letter I intend to send by you to my lady Dulcinea; and, if it proves such as my fidelity deserves, my madness and my penance will be at an end: but, if it proves the contrary, I shall be mad in earnest, and, being so, shall feel nothing: so that what answer soever she returns, I shall get out of the conflict and pain, wherein you leave me, either enjoying the good you shall bring, if in my senses; or not feeling the ill you bring, if out of them.

'But tell me, Sancho, have you taken care of Mambrino's helmet, which I saw you take off the ground, when that graceless fellow would have broken it to pieces, but could not? whence you may perceive the excellence of its temper.'

To which Sancho answered:

'As God liveth, Sir Knight of the Sorrowful Figure, I cannot endure nor bear with patience some things your worship says: they are enough to make me think, that all you tell me of chivalry, and of winning kingdoms and empires, of bestowing islands, and doing other favours and mighty things, according to the custom of knights-errant, must be mere vapour, and a lie, and all friction, or fiction, or how do you call it? for, to hear you say, that a barber's basin is Mambrino's helmet, and that you cannot be beaten out of this error in several days, what can one think, but that he, who says and affirms such a thing, must be crack-brained? I have the basin in my wallet, all battered, and I carry it to get it mended at home, for the use of my beard, if God be so gracious to me, as to restore me one time or other to my wife and children.'

'Behold, Sancho,' said Don Quixote, 'I swear likewise, that thou hast the shallowest brain that any squire has, or ever had, in the world. Is it possible, that, in all the time you have gone about with me, you do not perceive that all matters relating to knights-errant appear chimeras, follies, and extravagances, and seem all done by the rule of contraries? not that they are in reality so, but because there is a crew of enchanters always about us, who alter and disguise all our matters, and turn them according to their own pleasure, and as they are inclined to favour or distress us: hence it is that this, which appears to you a barber's basin, appears to me Mambrino's helmet, and to another will perhaps appear something else: And it was a singular foresight of the sage my friend, to make that appear to everybody to be a basin, which, really and truly, is Mambrino's helmet: because, being of so great value, all the world would persecute me, in order to take it from me: but now that they take it for nothing but a barber's basin, they do not trouble themselves to get it; as was evident in him who endeavoured to break it, and left it on the ground without carrying it off; for, in faith, had he known what it was he would never have left it. Take care of it, friend; for I have no need of it at present; I rather think of putting off all my armour, and being naked as I was born, in case I should have more mind to copy Orlando, in my penance, than Amadis.'*

While they were thus discoursing, they arrived at the foot of a steep rock, which stood alone among several others that surrounded it, as if it had been hewn out from the rest. By its skirts ran a gentle stream, and it was encircled by a meadow so verdant and fertile, that it delighted the eyes of all who beheld it. There grew about it several forest trees, and some plants and flowers, which added greatly to the pleasantness of the place. This was the scene in which the Knight of the Sorrowful Figure chose to perform his penance, and upon viewing it he thus broke out in a loud voice, as if he had been beside himself:

'This is the place, O ye heavens, which I select and appoint for bewailing the misfortune in which yourselves have involved me. This is the spot where my flowing tears shall increase the waters of this crystal rivulet, and my continual and profound sighs shall incessantly move the leaves of those lofty trees, in testimony and token of the pain my persecuted heart endures. O ye rural deities, whoever ye be that inhabit these remote deserts, give ear to the complaints of an unhappy lover, whom long absence and some pangs of jealousy have driven to bewail himself among these craggy rocks, and to complain of the cruelty of that ungrateful fair, the utmost extent and ultimate perfection of all human beauty! O ye wood-nymphs and dryads, who are accustomed to inhabit the closest recesses of the mountains (so may the nimble and lascivious satyrs, by whom you are beloved in vain, never disturb your sweet repose), assist me to lament my hard fate, or at least be not weary of hearing my moan! O Dulcinea del Toboso, light of my darkness, glory of my pain, the north-star of my travels, and overruling planet of my fortune (so may heaven prosper you in whatever you pray for) consider, I beseech you, the place and state to which your absence has reduced me, and how well you return what is due to my fidelity! O ye solitary trees, who from henceforth are to be the companions of my retirement, wave gently your branches, in token of your kind acceptance of my person! And, O thou my squire, agreeable companion in my most prosperous and adverse fortune, carefully imprint in thy memory what thou shalt see me here perform, that thou mayest recount and recite it to her, who is the sole cause of it all!'

And, saying this, he alighted from Rosinante, and, in an instant, took off his bridle and saddle, and giving him a slap on the buttocks, said to him:

'O steed, as excellent for thy performances, as unfortunate by thy fate, he gives thee liberty who wants it himself! Go whither thou wilt; for thou hast it written in thy forehead, that neither Astolfo's Hippogriff,* nor the famous Frontino,* which cost Bradamante so dear, could match thee in speed.'

Sancho, observing all this, said:

'God's peace be with him, who saved us the trouble of unpannelling Dapple; for, in faith, he should not have wanted a slap on the buttocks, nor a speech in his praise: but, if he were here, I would not consent to his being unpannelled, there being no occasion for it; for he had nothing to do with love or despair, any more than I, who was once his master when it so pleased God. And truly, Sir Knight of the Sorrowful Figure, if it be so, that my departure and your madness go on in earnest, it will be needful to saddle Rosinante again, that he may supply the loss of my Dapple, and save me time in going and coming; for, if I go on foot, I know not when I shall get thither, nor when return, being in truth a sorry footman.'

'Be it as you will,' answered Don Quixote; 'for I do not disapprove your project; and I say, you shall depart within three days; for I intend in that time to show you what I can do and say for her, that you may tell it her.'

'What have I more to see,' quoth Sancho, 'than what I have already seen?'

'You are very far from being perfect in the story,' answered Don Quixote; 'for I have not yet torn my garments, scattered my arms about, and dashed my head against these rocks, with other things of the like sort, that will strike you with admiration.'

'For the love of God,' said Sancho, 'have a care how you give yourself those knocks; for you may chance to light upon such an unlucky point of a rock, that, at the first dash, you may dissolve the whole machine of this penance: and I should think, since your worship is of opinion that knocks of the head are necessary, and that this work cannot be done without them, you might content yourself (since it is a fiction, a counterfeit, and a sham), I say, you might content yourself with running your head against water, or some soft thing, such as cotton; and leave it to me to tell my lady that you dashed your head against the point of a rock harder than that of a diamond.'

'I thank you for your goodwill, friend Sancho,' answered Don Quixote; 'but I would have you to know, that all these things that I do are not in jest, but very good earnest: for, otherwise, it would be to transgress the rules of chivalry, which enjoins us to tell no lie at all, on pain of being punished as apostates; and the doing one thing for another is the same as lying. And therefore my knocks on the head must be real, substantial, and sound ones, without equivocation, or mental reservation. However, it will be necessary to leave me some lint to heal me, since fortune will have it that we have lost the balsam.'

'It was worse to lose the ass,' answered Sancho; 'for in losing him, we lost lint and everything else; and I beseech your worship not to put me in mind of that cursed drench; for in barely hearing it mentioned my very soul is turned upside-down, not to say my stomach. As for the three days allowed me for seeing the mad pranks you are to perform, make account, I beseech you, that they are already passed; for I take them all for granted, and will tell wonders to my lady: and write you the letter, and dispatch me quickly: for I long to come back, and release your worship from this purgatory wherein I leave you.'

'Purgatory, do you call it, Sancho?' said Don Quixote. 'Call it rather hell, or worse, if anything can be worse.'

'I have heard say,' quoth Sancho, 'that "out of hell there is no retention".'

'I know not,' said Don Quixote, 'what retention means.'

'Retention,' answered Sancho, 'means, that he who is once in hell, never does, nor ever can, get out. But it will be quite the reverse with your worship, or it shall go hard with my heels if I have but spurs to enliven Rosinante: and let me but once get to Toboso, and into the presence of my lady Dulcinea, and I warrant you I will tell her such a story of the foolish and mad things (for they are all no better) which your worship has done, and is doing, that I shall bring her to be as supple as a glove, though I find her harder than a cork-tree: with whose sweet and honeyed answer I will return through the air like a witch, and fetch your worship out of this purgatory, which seems a hell, and is not, because there is hope to get out of it; which, as I have said, none can have that are in hell; nor do I believe you will say otherwise.'

'That is true,' answered he of the Sorrowful Figure; 'but how shall we contrive to write the letter?'

'And the ass-colt bill?' added Sancho.

'Nothing shall be omitted,' said Don Quixote; 'and, since we have no paper, we shall do well to write it, as the ancients did, on the leaves of trees, or on tablets of wax; though it will be as difficult to meet with these at present as with paper. But, now I recollect, it may be as well, or rather better, to write it in Cardenio's pocket-book, and you shall take care to get it fairly transcribed upon paper, in the first town you come to where there is a schoolmaster; or, if there be none, any parish-clerk will transcribe it for you: but be sure you give it to no hackney-writer of the law; for the devil himself will never be able to read their confounded court-hand.'

'But what must we do about the signing it with your own hand?' said Sancho.

'Billets-doux are never subscribed,' answered Don Quixote.

'Very well,' replied Sancho; 'but the warrant for the colts must of necessity be signed by yourself; for, if that be copied, people will say the signing is counterfeited, and I shall be forced to go without the colts.'

'The warrant shall be signed in the same pocket-book; and at sight of it my niece will make no difficulty to comply with it. As to what concerns the love-letter, let it be subscribed thus: "Yours, until death, the Knight of the Sorrowful Figure". And it is no great matter if it be in another hand; for, by what I remember, Dulcinea can neither write nor read, nor has she ever seen a letter or writing of mine in her whole life; for our loves have always been of the Platonic kind, extending no farther than to modest looks at one another; and even those so very rarely, that I dare truly swear, in twelve years that I have loved her more than the sight of these eyes, which the earth must one day devour, I have not seen her four times; and perhaps of these four times she may not have once perceived that I looked at her. Such is the reserve and strictness with which her father Lorenzo Cor- chuelo and her mother Aldonza Nogales have brought her up.'

'Hey day!' quoth Sancho; 'what, the daughter of Lorenzo Corchuelo! is she the lady Dulcinea del Toboso, alias Aldonza Lorenzo?'

'It is even she,' said Don Quixote; 'and she who deserves to be mistress of the universe.'

'I know her well,' quoth Sancho; 'and I can assure you she will pitch the bar with the lustiest swain in the parish: Long live the giver; why, she is a mettled lass, tall, straight, and vigorous, and can make her part good with any knight-errant that shall have her for a mistress. O the jade! what a pair of lungs and a voice she has! I remember she got one day upon the church steeple to call some young ploughmen, who were in the field of her father's; and though they were half a league off they heard her as plainly as if they had stood at the foot of the tower; and the best of her is, that she is not at all coy; for she has much of the courtier in her, and makes a jest and a may-game of everybody. I say, then, Sir Knight of the Sorrowful Figure, that you not only may, and ought to run mad for her, but also you may justly despair and hang yourself, and nobody that hears it but will say you did extremely well, though the devil should carry you away. I would fain be gone, if it were only to see her; for I have not seen her this many a day, and by this time she must needs be altered; for it mightily spoils women's faces to be always abroad in the field, exposed to the sun and weather. And I confess to your worship, Señor Don Quixote, that hitherto I have been in a great error; for I thought, for certain, that the lady Dulcinea was some great princess, with whom you was in love, or at least some person of such great quality, as to deserve the rich presents you have sent her, as well that of the Biscainer as that of the galley-slaves, and many others there must have been, considering the many victories you must have gained before I came to be your squire. But, all things considered, what good can it do the lady Aldonza Lorenzo (I mean the lady Dulcinea del Toboso) to have the vanquished, whom your worship sends, or may send, fall upon their knees before her? for who knows, but at the time they arrive, she may be carding flax, or thrashing in the barn, and they may be ashamed to see her, and she may laugh, or be disgusted at the present?'

'I have often told thee, Sancho,' said Don Quixote, 'that thou art an eternal babbler; and, though void of wit, your bluntness often occasions smarting: but to convince you at once of your folly and my discretion, I will tell you a short story.

'Know, then, that a certain widow, handsome, young, gay, and rich, and withal no prude, fell in love with a young, strapping, well-set lay brother. His superior heard of it, and one day took occasion to say to the good widow, by way of brotherly reprehension, "I wonder, madam, and not without great reason, that a woman of such quality, so beautiful, and so rich, should fall in love with such a despicable, mean, silly fellow, when there are in this house so many graduates, dignitaries, and divines, among whom you might pick and choose as you would among pears, and say, this I like, that I do not like." But she answered him with great frankness and good humour: "You are much mistaken, worthy Sir, and think altogether in the old-fashioned way, if you imagine that I have made an ill choice in that fellow, how silly soever he may appear, since, for the purpose I intend him, he knows as much or more philosophy than Aristotle himself." In like manner, Sancho, Dulcinea del Toboso for the purpose I intend her, deserves as highly as the greatest princess on earth.

'The poets, who have celebrated the praises of ladies under fictitious names imposed at pleasure, had not all of them real mistresses. Thinkest thou that the Amaryllises, the Phyllises, the Silvias, the Dianas, the Galateas, the Alidas, and the like, of whom books, ballads, barber-shops, and stage-plays, are full, were really mistresses of flesh and blood, and to those who do, and have celebrated them? No, certainly; but they are for the most part feigned, on purpose to be subjects of their verse, and to make the authors pass for men of gallant and amorous dispositions. And therefore it is sufficient that I think and believe that the good Aldonza Lorenzo is beautiful and chaste; and as to her lineage, it matters not; for there needs no inquiry about it, as if she were to receive some order of knighthood; and, for my part, I make account that she is the greatest princess in the world.

'For you must know, Sancho, if you do not know it already, that two things, above all others, incite to love; namely, great beauty, and a good name: now both of these are to be found in perfection in Dulcinea; for in beauty none can be compared to her, and for a good name few can come near her. To conclude, I imagine that everything is exactly as I say, without addition or diminution; and I represent her to my thoughts just as I wish her to be both in beauty and quality. Helen is not comparable to her, nor is she excelled by Lucretia, or any other of the famous women of antiquity, whether Grecian, Latin, or Barbarian. And let every one say what he pleases; for if, upon this account, I am blamed by the ignorant, I shall not be censured by the most severe judges.'

'Your worship,' replied Sancho, 'is always in the right, and I am an ass: but why do I mention an ass, when one ought not to talk of an halter in his house who was hanged? but give me the letter, and God be with you; for I am upon the wing.'

Don Quixote pulled out the pocket-book, and, stepping aside, began very gravely to write the letter; and when he had done, he called Sancho, and said he would read it to him, that he might have it by heart if he should chance to lose it by the way; for everything was to be feared from his ill fortune. To which Sancho answered:

'Write it, Sir, two or three times in the book, and give it me, and I will carry it carefully; but to think that I can carry it in my memory is a folly; for mine is so bad, that I often forget my own name. Nevertheless, read it to me; I shall be glad to hear it, for it must needs be a clever one.'

'Listen, then,' said Don Quixote, 'for it runs thus:—

DON QUIXOTE'S LETTER TO DULCINEA DEL TOBOSO.

"Sovereign and high lady,

"The stabbed by the point of absence, and the pierced to the heart, O sweetest Dulcinea del Toboso, sends that health to you which he wants himself. If your beauty despises me, if your worth profits me nothing, and if your disdain still pursues me, though I am inured to suffering, I shall ill support an affliction, which is not only violent, but the more durable for being so. My good squire Sancho will give you a full account, O ungrateful fair, and my beloved enemy, of the condition I am in for your sake. If it pleases you to relieve me, I am yours; and if not, do what seems good to you; for, by my death, I shall at once satisfy your cruelty and my own passion.

"Yours until death,

"The Knight of the Sorrowful Figure."'

'By the life of my father,' quoth Sancho, hearing the letter, 'it is the toppingest thing I ever heard. Odds my life, how curiously your worship expresses in it whatever you please! and how excellently do you close all with "the Knight of the Sorrowful Figure"! Verily your worship is the devil himself: and there is nothing but what you know.'

'The profession I am of,' answered Don Quixote, 'requires me to understand everything.'

'Well then,' said Sancho, 'pray clap, on the other side of the leaf, the bill for the three ass-colts, and sign it very plain, that people may know your hand at first sight.'

'With all my heart,' said Don Quixote; 'and, having written it, he read as follows:—

'"Dear niece, at sight of this my first bill of ass-colts, give order that three of the five I left at home in your custody be delivered to Sancho Panza, my squire; which three colts I order to be delivered and paid for the like number received of him here in tale; and this, with his acquaintance, shall be your discharge. Done in the heart of the Sierra Morena, the twenty-second of August, this present year.'"

'It is mighty well,' said Sancho; 'pray sign it.'

'It wants no signing,' said Don Quixote; 'I need only put my cipher to it,* which is the same thing, and is sufficient, not only for three asses, but for three hundred.'

'I rely upon your worship,' answered Sancho: 'let me go and saddle Rosinante, and prepare to give me your blessing; for I intend to depart immediately, without staying to see the follies you are about to commit; and I will relate that I saw you act so many, that she can desire no more.'

'At least, Sancho,' said Don Quixote, 'I would have you see (nay, it is necessary you should see), I say, I will have you see me naked, and do a dozen or two of mad pranks; for I shall dispatch them in less than half an hour: and having seen these with your own eyes, you may safely swear to those you intend to add; for assure yourself, you will not relate so many as I intend to perform.'

'For the love of God, dear Sir,' quoth Sancho, 'let me not see your worship naked; for it will move my compassion much, and I shall not be able to forbear weeping: and my head is so disordered with last night's grief for the loss of poor Dapple, that I am in no condition at present to begin new lamentations. If your worship has a mind I should be an eye-witness of some mad pranks, pray do them clothed, and with brevity, and let them be such as will stand you in most stead: and the rather, because for me there needed nothing of all this; and, as I said before, it is but delaying my return with the news your worship so much desires and deserves. If otherwise, let the lady Dulcinea prepare herself; for if she does not answer as she should do, I protest solemnly I will fetch it out of her stomach by dint of kicks and buffets; for it is not to be endured, that so famous a knight-errant as your worship should run mad, without why or wherefore, for a—Let not madam provoke me to speak out; before God, I shall blab, and out with all by wholesale, though it spoil the market. I am pretty good at this sport: she does not know me; if she did, in faith she would agree with me.'

'In troth, Sancho,' said Don Quixote, 'to all appearance you are as mad as myself.'

'Not quite so mad,' answered Sancho, 'but a little more choleric. But, setting aside all this, what is it your worship is to eat until my return? Are you to go upon the highway, to rob the shepherds like Cardenio?'

'Trouble not yourself about that,' answered Don Quixote: 'though I were provided I would eat nothing but herbs and fruits, which this meadow and these trees will afford me; for the finesse of my affair consists in not eating, and other austerities.'

Then Sancho said:

'Do you know, Sir, what I fear? that I shall not be able to find the way again to this place, where I leave you, it is so concealed.'

'Observe well the marks; for I will endeavour to be hereabouts,' said Don Quixote, 'and will moreover take care to get to the top of some of the highest cliffs, to see if I can discover you when you return. But the surest way not to miss me, nor lose yourself, will be to cut down some boughs off the many trees that are here, and strew them, as you go on, from space to space, until you have got down into the plain; and they will serve as landmarks and tokens to find me by at your return, in imitation of Theseus's clue to the labyrinth.'

'I will do so,' answered Sancho Panza; and having cut down several, he begged his master's blessing, and, not without many tears on both sides, took his leave of him. And mounting upon Rosinante, of whom Don Quixote gave him an especial charge, desiring him to be careful of him as of his own proper person, he rode towards the plain, strewing broom-boughs here and there, as his master had directed him; and so away he went, though Don Quixote still importuned him to stay, and see him perform, though it were but a couple of mad pranks. But he had not gone above a hundred paces, when he turned back, and said:

'Your worship, Sir, said very well, that in order to my being able to swear with a safe conscience that I have seen you do mad tricks, it would be proper I should at least see you do one; though in truth I have seen a very great one already in your staying here.'

'Did I not tell you so?' quoth Don Quixote: 'stay but a moment, Sancho, I will dispatch them in the repeating of a Credo.'

Then stripping off his breeches in all haste he remained naked from the waist downwards, and covered only with the tail of his shirt: and presently, without more ado, he cut a couple of capers in the air, and a brace of tumbles, head down and heels up, exposing things that made Sancho turn Rosinante about, that he might not see them a second time; and fully satisfied him that he might safely swear his master was stark mad; and so we will leave him going on his way until his return, which was speedy.

CHAPTER 26

A continuation of the refinements practised by Don Quixote, as a lover, in the Sierra Morena.

THE history, turning to recount what the Knight of the Sorrowful Figure did, when he found himself alone, informs us, that Don Quixote, having finished his tumbles and gambols, naked from the middle downward, and clothed from the middle upward, and perceiving that Sancho was going without caring to see any more of his foolish pranks, got upon the top of a high rock, and there began to think again of what he had often thought before, without ever coming to any resolution: and that was, which of the two was best, and would stand him in most stead, to imitate Orlando in his extravagant madness, or Amadis in his melancholic moods. And, talking to himself, he said:

'If Orlando was so good and valiant a knight, as everybody allows he was, what wonder is it since, in short, he was enchanted, and nobody could kill him, but by thrusting a needle into the sole of his foot; and therefore he always wore shoes with seven soles of iron? These contrivances, however, stood him in no stead against Bernando del Carpio, who knew the secret, and pressed him to death, between his arms, in Roncesvalles. But setting aside his valour, let us come to his losing his wits, which it is certain he did, occasioned by some tokens he found in the forest, and by the news brought him by the shepherd, that Angelica had slept more than two afternoons with Medoro, a little Moor with curled locks, and page to Agramante. And if he knew this to be true, and that his lady played him false, he did no great matter in running mad. But how can I imitate him in his madnesses, if I do not imitate him in the occasion of them? for I dare swear my Dulcinea del Toboso never saw a Moor, in his own dress, in all her life, and that she is this day as the mother that bore her: and I should do her a manifest wrong, if, suspecting her, I should run mad of the same kind of madness with that of Orlando Furioso.

'On the other side, I see that Amadis de Gaul, without losing his wits, and without acting the madman, acquired the reputation of a lover, as much as the best of them. For, as the history has it, finding himself disdained by his lady Oriana, who commanded him not to appear in her presence, until it was her pleasure, he only retired to the Peña Pobre, accompanied by a hermit, and there wept his bellyful, until heaven came to his relief, in the midst of his trouble and greatest anguish. And, if this be true, as it really is, why should I take pains to strip myself stark naked, or grieve these trees that never did me any harm? neither have I any reason to disturb the water of these crystal streams, which are to furnish me with drink when I want it. Live the memory of Amadis, and let him be imitated, as far as may be, by Don Quixote de la Mancha, of whom shall be said what was said of another, that, if he did not achieve great things, he died in attempting them. And if I am not rejected, nor disdained, by my Dulcinea, it is sufficient, as I have already said, that I am absent from her. Well, then; hands to your work: come to my memory, ye deeds of Amadis, and teach me where I am to begin to imitate you: but I know that the most he did was to pray; and so will I do.'

Whereupon he strung some large galls of a cork-tree, which served him for a rosary.* But what troubled him very much, was, his not having a hermit to hear his confession, and to comfort him; and so he passed the time in walking up and down the meadow, writing and graving on the barks of trees, and in the fine sand, a great many verses, all accommodated to his melancholy, and some in praise of Dulcinea. But those that were found entire and legible, after he was found in that place, were only these following:—

I

Ye trees, ye plants, ye herbs that grow
    So tall, so green, around this place,
If ye rejoice not at my woe,
    Hear me lament my piteous case.
Nor let my loud-resounding grief
    Your tender trembling leaves dismay,
Whilst from my tears I seek relief,
    In absence from Dulcinea
                Del Toboso.

2

Here the sad lover shuns the light,
    By sorrow to this desert led;
Here exiled from his lady's sight,
    He seeks to hide his wretched head.
Here, bandied betwixt hopes and fears,
    By cruel love in wanton play,
He weeps a pipkin full of tears,
    In absence from Dulcinea
                Del Toboso.

3

O'er craggy rocks he roves forlorn,
    And seeks mishaps from place to place,
Cursing the proud relentless scorn
    That banish'd him from human race.
To wound his tender bleeding heart,
    Love's hands the cruel lash display;

> He weeps, and feels the raging smart,
> In absence from Dulcinea
>   Del Toboso.

The addition of Del Toboso to the name of Dulcinea, occasioned no small laughter in those who found the above recited verses, for they concluded that Don Quixote imagined, that if, in naming Dulcinea, he did not add Del Toboso, the couplet could not be understood; and it was really so, as he afterwards confessed.

He wrote many others: but, as is said, they could transcribe no more than those three stanzas fair and entire. In this amusement, and in sighing, and invoking the fauns and sylvan deities of those woods, the nymphs of the brooks, and the mournful and humid echo, to answer, to condole, and listen to his moan, he passed the time, and in gathering herbs to sustain himself until Sancho's return; who, if he had tarried three weeks, as he did three days, the Knight of the Sorrowful Figure would have been so disfigured, that the very mother who bore him could not have known him. And here it will be proper to leave him, wrapped up in his sighs and verses, to relate what befell Sancho in his embassy.

Which was, that when he got into the high road he steered towards Toboso; and the next day he came within sight of the inn where the mishap of the blanket had befallen him; and scarcely had he discovered it at a distance, when he fancied himself again flying in the air, and therefore would not go in, though it was the hour that he might and ought to have stopped, that is, about noon: besides he had a mind to eat something warm, all having been cold treat with him for many days past. This necessity forced him to draw nigh to the inn, still doubting whether he should go in or not. And, while he was in suspense, there came out of the inn two persons, who presently knew him; and one said to the other:

'Pray, Señor licentiate, is not that Sancho Panza yonder on horseback, who, as our adventurer's housekeeper told us, was gone with her master as his squire?'

'Yes it is,' said the licentiate, 'and that is our Don Quixote's horse.'

And no wonder they knew him so well, they being the
priest and the barber of his village, and the persons who had
made the scrutiny and gaol-delivery of the books; and being
now certain it was Sancho Panza and Rosinante, and being
desirous withal to learn some tidings of Don Quixote, they
went up to him, and the priest, calling him by his name, said:

'Friend Sancho Panza, where have you left your master?'

Sancho Panza immediately knew them, and resolved to
conceal the place and circumstances in which he had left his
master: so he answered, that his master was very busy in a
certain place, and about a certain affair of the greatest
importance to him, which he durst not discover for the eyes
he had in his head.

'No, no,' quoth the barber, 'Sancho Panza, if you do not
tell us where he is, we shall conclude, as we do already, that
you have murdered and robbed him, since you come thus
upon his horse; and see that you produce the horse's owner,
or woe be to you.'

'There is no reason why you should threaten me,' quoth
Sancho; 'for I am not a man to rob or murder anybody: let
every man's fate kill him, or God that made him. My master
is doing a certain penance, much to his liking, in the midst
of yon mountain.'

And thereupon, very glibly, and without hesitation, he
related to them in what manner he had left him, the adventures that had befallen him, and how he was carrying a letter
to the lady Dulcinea del Toboso, who was the daughter of
Lorenzo Corchuelo, with whom his master was up to the
ears in love.

They both stood in admiration at what Sancho told them;
and, though they already knew Don Quixote's madness, and
of what kind it was, they were always struck with fresh
wonder at hearing it. They desired Sancho Panza to show
them the letter he was carrying to the lady Dulcinea del
Toboso. He said it was written in a pocket-book, and that it
was his master's orders he should get it copied out upon
paper, at the first town he came at. The priest said, if he
would show it him, he would transcribe it in a very fair
character. Sancho Panza put his hand into his bosom, to take

out the book, but found it not; nor could he have found it, had he searched for it until now; for it remained with Don Quixote, who had forgotten to give it him, and he to ask for it. When Sancho perceived he had not the book, he turned as pale as death; and feeling again all over his body, in a great hurry, and seeing it was not to be found, without more ado, he laid hold of his beard with both hands, and tore away half of it; and presently after he gave himself half a dozen cuffs on the nose and mouth, and bathed them all in blood. Which the priest and barber seeing, they asked him what had happened to him, that he handled himself so roughly?

'What should happen to me,' answered Sancho, 'but that I have lost, and let slip through my fingers, three ass-colts each of them as stately as a castle?'

'How so?' replied the barber.

'I have lost the pocket-book,' answered Sancho, 'in which was the letter to Dulcinea, and a bill signed by my master, by which he ordered his niece to deliver to me three colts out of four or five he had at home.'

And, at the same time, he recounted to them the loss of Dapple. The priest bid him be of good cheer, telling him, that, when he saw his master, he would engage him to renew the order, and draw the bill over again upon paper, according to usage and custom, since those that were written in pocket-books were never accepted, nor complied with. Sancho was comforted by this, and said, that, since it was so, he was in no great pain for the loss of the letter to Dulcinea, for he could almost say it by heart; so that they might write it down from his mouth, where and when they pleased.

'Repeat it, then, Sancho,' quoth the barber, 'and we will write it down afterwards.'

Then Sancho began to scratch his head, to bring the letter to his remembrance; and now stood upon one foot, and then upon another: one time he looked down upon the ground, another up to the sky: and after he had bit off half a nail of one of his fingers, keeping them in suspense and expectation of hearing him repeat it, he said, after a very long pause:

'Before God, master licentiate, let the devil take all I remember of the letter; though at the beginning it said, "High and subterrane lady."'

'No,' said the barber, 'not subterrane, but super-humane, or sovereign lady.'

'It was so,' said Sancho. 'Then, if I do not mistake, it went on: "the wounded, and the waking, and the smitten, kisses your honour's hands, ungrateful and regardless fair"; and then it said I know not what of "health and sickness that he sent"; and so he went on, until at last he ended with "thine till death, the Knight of the Sorrowful Figure."'

They were both not a little pleased to see how good a memory Sancho had, and commended it much, and desired him to repeat the letter twice more, that they also might get it by heart, in order to write it down in due time. Thrice Sancho repeated it again, and thrice he added three thousand other extravagances. After this, he recounted also many other things concerning his master, but said not a word of the tossing in the blanket, which had happened to himself in that inn, into which he refused to enter. He said likewise, how his lord, upon his carrying him back a kind dispatch from his lady Dulcinea del Toboso, was to set forward, to endeavour to become an emperor, or at least a king; for so it was concerted between them two; and it would be a very easy matter to bring it about, considering the worth of his person and the strength of his arm; and when this was accomplished, his master was to marry him (for by that time he should, without doubt, be a widower) and to give him to wife one of the empress's maids of honour, heiress to a large and rich territory on the mainland; for, as to islands, he was quite out of conceit with them.

Sancho said all this with so much gravity, ever and anon blowing his nose, and so much in his senses, that they were struck with fresh admiration at the powerful influence of Don Quixote's madness, which had carried away with it this poor fellow's understanding also. They would not give themselves the trouble to convince him of his error, thinking it better, since it did not at all hurt his conscience, to let him continue in it; besides that it would afford them the more pleasure in hearing his follies; and therefore they told him, he should pray to God for his lord's health, since it was very possible, and very feasible, for him, in process of time, to become an emperor, as he said, or at least an archbishop, or something else of equal dignity. To which Sancho answered:

'Gentlemen, if fortune should so order it, that my master should take it into his head not to be an emperor, but an archbishop, I would fain know what archbishops-errant usually give to their squires?'

'They usually give them,' answered the priest, 'some benefice, or cure, or vergership, which brings them in a good penny-rent, besides the perquisites of the altar, usually valued at as much more.'

'For this, it will be necessary,' replied Sancho, 'that the squire be not married, and that he knows, at least, the responses to the mass: and if so, woe is me; for I am married, and do not know the first letter of A, B, C. What will become of me if my master should have a mind to be an archbishop, and not an emperor, as is the fashion and custom of knights-errant?'

'Be not uneasy, friend Sancho,' said the barber; 'for we will entreat your master, and advise him, and even make it a case of conscience, that he be an emperor, and not an archbishop; for it will be better for him also, by reason he is more a soldier than a scholar.'

'I have thought the same,' answered Sancho, 'though I can affirm that he has ability for everything. What I intend to do, on my part, is, to pray to our Lord, that he will direct him to that which is best for him, and will enable him to bestow most favours upon me.'

'You talk like a wise man,' said the priest, 'and will act therein like a good Christian. But the next thing now to be done, is, to contrive how we may bring your master off from the performance of that unprofitable penance; and, that we may concert the proper measures, and get something to eat likewise (for it is high time), let us go into the inn.'

Sancho desired them to go in, and said he would stay there without, and afterwards he would tell them the reason why he did not, nor was it convenient for him to go in; but he prayed them to bring him out something to eat that was warm, and also some barley for Rosinante. They went in, and left him, and soon after the barber brought him out some meat.

Then they two having laid their heads together how to bring about their design, the priest bethought him of a device exactly fitted to Don Quixote's humour, and likely to effect what they desired. Which was, as he told the barber, that he designed to put himself into the habit of a damsel-errant, and would have him to equip himself, the best he could, so as to pass for his squire; and that in this disguise they should go to the place where Don Quixote was; and himself, pretending to be an afflicted damsel, and in distress, would beg a boon of him, which he, as a valorous knight-errant, could not choose but vouchsafe; and that the boon he intended to beg, was, that he would go with her whither she should carry him, to redress an injury done her by a discourteous knight, entreating him, at the same time, that he would not desire her to take off her mask, nor inquire anything further concerning her, until he had done her justice on that wicked knight; and he made no doubt but that Don Quixote would, by these means, be brought to do whatever they desired of him, and so they should bring him away from that place, and carry him to his village, where they would endeavour to find some remedy for his unaccountable madness.

CHAPTER 27

How the priest and the barber put their design in execution with other matters worthy to be recited in this history.

THE barber liked the priest's contrivance so well, that it was immediately put in execution. They borrowed of the landlady a petticoat and head-dress, leaving a new cassock of the priest's in pawn for them. The barber made himself a huge beard of the sorrel tail of a pied ox, in which the innkeeper used to hang his comb. The hostess asked them, why they desired those things? The priest gave them a brief account of Don Quixote's madness, and how necessary that disguise was, in order to get him from the mountain where he then was. The host and hostess presently conjectured that this madman was he who had been their guest, the maker of the balsam, and master of the blanketed squire; and they related to the priest what had passed between him and them, without concealing what Sancho so industriously concealed. In fine, the landlady equipped the priest so nicely, that nothing could be better. She put him on a cloth petticoat, laid thick with stripes of black velvet, each the breadth of a span, all pinked and slashed; and a tight waistcoat of green velvet, trimmed with a border of white satin; which, together with the petticoat, must have been made in the days of King Wamba.* The priest would not consent to wear a woman's head-dress, but put on a little white quilted cap, which he wore at nights, and bound one of his garters of black taffeta about his forehead, and with the other made a kind of vizard, which covered his face and beard very neatly. Then he sunk his head into his beaver, which was so broad-brimmed, that it might serve him for an umbrella; and, lapping himself up in his cloak, he got upon his mule sideways, like a woman: the barber got also upon his, with his beard, that reached to his girdle, between sorrel and white, being, as has been said, made of the sorrel tail of a pied ox. They took leave of all, and of good Maritornes, who promised, though a sinner, to pray over an entire rosary, that God might give them good success in so arduous and Christian a business as that they had undertaken.

But scarcely had they got out of the inn, when the priest began to think he had done amiss in equipping himself after that manner, it being an indecent thing for a priest to be so accoutred, though much depended upon it; and acquainting the barber with his scruple, he desired that they might change dresses, it being fitter that he should personate the distressed damsel, and himself act the squire, as being a less profanation of his dignity; and if he would not consent to do so, he was determined to proceed no further, though the devil should run away with Don Quixote. Upon this Sancho came up to them, and, seeing them both tricked up in that manner, could not forbear laughing. The barber, in short, consented to what the priest desired, and the scheme being thus altered, the priest began to instruct the barber how to act his part, and what expressions to use to Don Quixote, to prevail upon him to go with them, and to make him out of conceit with the place he had chosen for his fruitless penance. The barber answered, that, without his instructions, he would undertake to manage that point to a tittle. He would not put on the dress until they came near to the place where Don Quixote was; and so he folded up his habit, and the priest adjusted his beard, and on they went, Sancho Panza being their guide; who, on the way, recounted to them what had happened in relation to the madman they met in the mountain; but said not a word of finding the portmanteau, and what was in it; for, with all his folly and simplicity, the spark was somewhat covetous.

The next day they arrived at the place where Sancho had strewed the broom-boughs, as tokens to ascertain the place where he had left his master; and knowing it again, he told them, that was the entrance into it, and therefore they would do well to put on their disguise, if that was of any significancy toward delivering his master; for they had before told him, that their going dressed in that manner, was of the utmost importance towards disengaging his master from that evil life he had chosen; and that he must by no means let his master know who they were, nor that he knew them; and if he should ask him, as no doubt he would, whether he had delivered the letter to Dulcinea, he should say he had, and that she, not being able to read or write, had answered by word of mouth, that she commanded him, on pain of her displeasure, to repair to her immediately, it being a matter of great consequence to him; for with this, and what they intended to say to him themselves, they made sure account of reducing him to a better life, and managing him so, that he should presently set out in order to become an emperor, or a king; for as to his being an archbishop, there was no need to fear that.

Sancho listened attentively to all this, and imprinted it well in his memory, and thanked them mightily for their design of advising his lord to be an emperor, and not an archbishop;

for he was of opinion, that, as to rewarding their squires, emperors could do more than archbishops-errant. He told them also, it would be proper he should go before, to find him, and deliver him his lady's answer; for, perhaps, that alone would be sufficient to bring him out of that place, without their putting themselves to so much trouble. They approved of what Sancho said, and so they resolved to wait for his return with the news of finding his master. Sancho entered the openings of the mountain, leaving them in a place through which there ran a little smooth stream, cool, and pleasantly shaded by some rocks and neighbouring trees.

It was in the month of August, when the heats in those parts are very violent: the hour was three in the afternoon: all which made the situation the more agreeable, and invited them to wait there for Sancho's return, which accordingly they did. While they reposed themselves in the shade, a voice reached their ears, which, though unaccompanied by any instrument, sounded sweetly and delightfully: at which they were not a little surprised, that being no place where they might expect to find a person who could sing so well; for, though it is usually said, there are in the woods and fields shepherds with excellent voices, it is rather an exaggeration of the poets, than what is really true; and especially when they observed, that the verses they heard sung, were not like the compositions of rustic shepherds, but like those of witty and courtly persons. And the verses, which confirmed them in their opinion, were these following:—

I

What causes all my grief and pain?
   Cruel disdain.
What aggravates my misery?
   Accursed jealousy.
How has my soul its patience lost?
   By tedious absence cross'd.
Alas! no balsam can be found
To heal the grief of such a wound,
When absence, jealousy, and scorn,
Have left me helpless and forlorn.

2

What in my breast this grief could move?
   Neglected love.
What doth my fond desires withstand?
   Fate's cruel hand.
And what confirms my misery?
   Heaven's fix'd decree.
Ah me! my boding fears portend
This strange disease my life will end:
For, die I must, when three such foes,
Heav'n, fate, and love, my bliss oppose.

3

My peace of mind what can restore?
   Death's welcome hour.
What gains love's joys most readily?
   Fickle inconstancy.
Its pains what med'cine can assuage?
   Wild frenzy's rage.
'Tis therefore little wisdom, sure,
For such a grief to seek a cure,
As knows no better remedy,
Than frenzy, death, inconstancy.

The hour, the season, the solitude, the voice, and the skill of the person who sung, raised both wonder and delight in the two hearers, who lay still, expecting if perchance they might hear something more: but, perceiving the silence continued a good while, they resolved to issue forth in search of the musician, who had sung so agreeably. And, just as they were about to do so, the same voice hindered them from stirring, and again reached their ears with this sonnet.

Friendship, thou hast with nimble flight
Exulting gain'd th' empyreal height,
In heav'n to dwell, whilst here below
Thy semblance reigns in mimic show!
From thence to earth, at thy behest,
Descends fair peace, celestial guest;
Beneath whose veil of shining hue
Deceit oft lurks, concealed from view.
Leave, friendship, leave thy heav'nly seat;

> Or strip the livery off the cheat.
> If still he wears thy borrowed smiles,
> And still unwary truth beguiles,
> Soon must this dark terrestrial ball
> Into its first confusion fall.

The song ended with a deep sigh, and they again listened very attentively in hopes of more; but finding that the music was changed into groans and laments, they agreed to go and find out the unhappy person whose voice was as excellent as his complaints were mournful. They had not gone far, when at doubling the point of a rock, they perceived a man of the same stature and figure that Sancho had described to them, when he told them the story of Cardenio. The man expressed no surprise at the sight of them, but stood still, inclining his head upon his breast, in a pensive posture, without lifting up his eyes to look at them; until just at the instant when they came unexpectedly upon him. The priest, who was a well-spoken man, being already acquainted with his misfortune, and knowing him by the description, went up to him, and in few, but very significant words, entreated and pressed him to forsake that miserable kind of life, lest he should lose it in that place; which, of all misfortunes, would be the greatest. Cardenio was then in his perfect senses, free from those outrageous fits that so often drove him beside himself: and seeing them both in a dress not worn by any that frequented those solitudes, he could not forbear wondering at them for some time; and especially when he heard them speak of his affair as of a thing known to them; for, by what the priest had said to him, he understood as much: wherefore he answered in this manner:

'I am sensible, gentlemen, whoever you be, that heaven, which takes care to relieve the good, and very often even the bad, sometimes, without any desert of mine, sends into these places, so remote and distant from the commerce of human kind, persons, who, setting before my eyes, with variety of lively arguments, how far the life I lead is from being reasonable, have endeavoured to draw me from hence to some better place: but, not knowing, as I do, that I shall no sooner get out of this mischief, but I shall fall into a greater, they, doubtless, take me for a very weak man, and, perhaps, what is worse, a fool, or a madman. And no wonder; for I have some apprehension, that the sense of my misfortunes is so forcible and intense, and so prevalent to my destruction, that, without my being able to prevent it, I sometimes become like a stone, void of all knowledge and sensation: and I find this to be true, by people's telling and showing me the marks of what I have done, while the terrible fit has had the mastery of me: and all I can do, is, to bewail myself in vain, to load my fortune with unavailing curses, and to excuse my follies, by telling the occasion of them to as many as will hear me; for men of sense, seeing the cause, will not wonder at the effects, and, if they administer no remedy, at least they will not throw the blame upon me, but convert their displeasure at my behaviour into compassion for my misfortune. And, gentlemen, if you come with the same intention that others have done, before you proceed any further in your prudent persuasions, I beseech you to hear the account of my numberless misfortunes: for, perhaps, when you have heard it, you may save yourselves the trouble of endeavouring to cure a malady that admits of no consolation.'

The two, who desired nothing more than to learn, from his own mouth, the cause of his misery, entreated him to relate it, assuring him they would do nothing but what he desired, either by way of remedy or advice: and, upon this, the poor gentleman began his melancholy story, almost in the same words and method he had used, in relating it to Don Quixote and the goatherd, some few days before, when, on the mention of master Elisabat, and Don Quixote's punctuality in observing the decorum of knight-errantry, the tale was cut short, as the history left it above. But now, as good fortune would have it, Cardenio's mad fit was suspended, and afforded him leisure to rehearse it to the end: and so, coming to the passage of the love-letter which Don Fernando found between the leaves of the book of *Amadis de Gaul*, he said he remembered it perfectly well, and that it was as follows.

LUCINDA TO CARDENIO.

'"I every day discover such worth in you, as obliges and forces me to esteem you more and more; and therefore, if you would put it in my power to discharge my obligations to you, without prejudice to my honour, you may easily do it. I have a father, who knows you, and has an affection for me; who will never force my inclinations, and will comply with whatever you can justly desire, if you really have that value for me, which you profess, and I believe you to have."

'This letter made me resolve to demand Lucinda in marriage, as I have already related, and was one of those which gave Don Fernando such an opinion of Lucinda, that he looked upon her as one of the most sensible and prudent women of her time. And it was this letter which put him upon the design of undoing me, before mine could be effected. I told Don Fernando what Lucinda's father expected; which was, that my father should propose the match; but that I durst not mention it to him, lest he should not come into it: not because he was unacquainted with the circumstances, goodness, virtue, and beauty of Lucinda, and that she had qualities sufficient to adorn any other family of Spain whatever; but because I understood by him, that he was desirous I should not marry soon, but wait until we should see what Duke Ricardo would do for me. In a word, I told him, that I durst not venture to speak to my father about it, as well for that reason, as for many others, which disheartened me, I knew not why; only I presaged, that my desires were never to take effect. To all this Don Fernando answered, that he took it upon himself to speak to my father, and to prevail upon him to speak to Lucinda's. O ambitious Marius! O cruel Catiline! O wicked Sulla! O crafty Galalon! O perfidious Vellido!* O vindictive Julian!* O covetous Judas! traitor! cruel, vindictive, and crafty! what disservice had this poor wretch done you, who so frankly discovered to you the secrets and the joys of his heart? wherein had I offended you? what word did I ever utter, or advice did I ever give, that were not all directed to the increase of your honour and your interest? But why do I complain? miserable wretch that

I am! since it is certain, that, when the strong influences of the stars pour down misfortunes upon us, they fall from on high with such violence and fury, that no human force can stop them, nor human address prevent them. Who could have thought that Don Fernando, an illustrious cavalier, of good sense, obliged by my services, and secure of success wherever his amorous inclinations led him, should take cruel pains to deprive me of my single ewe-lamb, which was not yet in my possession? But, setting aside these reflections as vain and unprofitable, let us resume the broken thread of my unhappy story.

'I say then, that Don Fernando, thinking my presence an obstacle to the putting his treacherous and wicked design in execution, resolved to send me to his elder brother for money to pay for six horses, which merely for the purpose of getting me out of the way, that he might the better succeed in his hellish intent, he had bought that very day on which he offered to speak to my father, and on which he dispatched me for the money. Could I prevent this treachery? could I so much as suspect it? No, certainly; on the contrary, with great pleasure I offered to depart instantly, well satisfied with the good bargain he had made. That night I spoke with Lucinda, and told her what had been agreed upon between Don Fernando and me, bidding her not doubt the success of our just and honourable desires. She, as little suspecting Don Fernando's treachery as I did, desired me to make haste back, since she believed the completion of our wishes would be no longer deferred than until my father had spoken to hers. I know not whence it was, but she had no sooner said this than her eyes stood full of tears, and some sudden obstruction in her throat would not suffer her to utter one word of a great many she seemed endeavouring to say to me. I was astonished at this strange accident, having never seen the like in her before; for, whenever good fortune, or my assiduity, gave us an opportunity, we always conversed with the greatest pleasure and satisfaction, nor ever intermixed with our discourse tears, sighs, jealousies, suspicions, or fears. I did nothing but applaud my good fortune in having her given me by heaven for a mistress. I magnified her beauty, and admired her merit and understanding. She returned the compliment, by commending in me what, as a lover, she thought worthy of commendation. We told one another a hundred thousand little childish stories concerning our neighbours and acquaintance; and the greatest length my presumption ran was to seize, as it were, by force, one of her fair and snowy hands, and press it to my lips, as well as the narrowness of the iron grate which was between us would permit. But the night that preceded the doleful day of my departure she wept and sighed, and withdrew abruptly, leaving me full of confusion and trepidation, and astonished at seeing such new and sad tokens of grief and tender concern in Lucinda. But, not to destroy my hopes, I ascribed it all to the violence of the love she bore me, and to the sorrow which parting occasions in those who love one another tenderly. In short, I went away sad and pensive, my soul filled with imaginations and suspicions, without knowing what I imagined or suspected; all manifest presages of the dismal event reserved in store for me.

'I arrived at the place whither I was sent: I gave the letters to Don Fernando's brother: I was well received; but my business was not soon dispatched; for he ordered me to wait (much to my sorrow) for eight days, and to keep out of his father's sight; for his brother, he said, had written to him to send him a certain sum of money without the duke's knowledge. All this was a contrivance of the false Don Fernando; for his brother did not want money to have dispatched me immediately. This injunction put me into such a condition, that I could not presently think of obeying it, it seeming to me to be impossible to support life under an absence of so many days from Lucinda, especially considering I had left her in so much sorrow, as I have already told you. Nevertheless I did obey, like a good servant, though I found it was likely to be at the expense of my health. But, four days after my arrival, there came a man in quest of me, with the letter which he gave me, and which by the superscription I knew to be Lucinda's; for it was her own hand. I opened it with fear and trembling, believing it must be some very extraordinary matter, that put her to writing to me at a distance, a thing she very seldom did when I was near her. Before I read it, I inquired of the messenger who gave it him, and how long he had been coming. He told me, that, passing accidentally through a street of the town about noon, a very beautiful lady, with tears in her eyes, called to him from a window, and said to him in a great hurry. "Friend, if you are a Christian, as you seem to be, I beg of you, for the love of God, to carry this letter, with all expedition, to the place and person it is directed to; for both are well known; and in so doing you will do a charity acceptable to our Lord. And that you may not want wherewithal to do it, take what is tied up in this handkerchief," and, so saying, she threw the handkerchief out at the window; in which were tied up a hundred reals, and this good ring I have here, with the letter I have given you: and presently, without staying for my answer, she quitted the window; but first she saw me take up the letter and the handkerchief; and I assured her by signs, that I would do what she commanded. And now, seeing myself so well paid for the pains I was to take in bringing the letter, and knowing by the superscription it was for you (for, sir, I know you very well), and obliged besides by the tears of that beautiful lady, I resolved not to trust any other person, but to deliver it to you with my own hands. And, in sixteen hours (for so long it is since it was given me) I have performed the journey, which you know is eighteen leagues. While the kind messenger was speaking thus to me, I hung upon his words, my legs trembling so that I could scarcely stand. At length I opened the letter, and saw it contained these words:

'"The promise Don Fernando gave you, that he would desire your father to speak to mine, he has fulfilled, more for his own gratification than your interest. Know, sir, he has demanded me to wife; and my father, allured by the advantage he thinks Don Fernando has over you, has accepted this proposal with so much earnestness, that the marriage is to be solemnized two days hence, and that with so much secrecy and privacy, that the heavens alone, and a few of our own family, are to be witnesses of it. Imagine what a condition I am in, and consider whether it be convenient for you to return home. Whether I love you or not, the event of this business will show you. God grant this may come to your hand, before mine be reduced to the extremity of being joined with his, who keeps his promised faith so ill."

'These, in fine, were the contents of the letter, and such as made me set out immediately, without waiting for any other answer, or the money: for now I plainly saw it was not the buying of the horses, but the indulging his own pleasure, that had moved Don Fernando to send me to his brother. The rage I conceived against Don Fernando, joined with the fear of losing the prize I had acquired by the services and wishes of so many years, added wings to my speed; so that the next day I reached our town, at the hour and moment most convenient for me to go and talk with Lucinda. I went privately, having left the mule I rode on at the house of the honest man who brought me the letter. And fortune, which I then found propitious, so ordered it that Lucinda was standing at the grate,* the witness of our loves. She presently knew me and I her; but not as she ought to have known me and I her. But who is there in the world that can boast of having fathomed, and thoroughly seen into the intricate and variable nature of a woman? Nobody, certainly. I say then, that, as soon as Lucinda saw me, she said: "Cardenio, I am in my bridal habit: there are now staying for me in the hall the treacherous Don Fernando and my covetous father, with some others, who shall sooner be witnesses of my death than of my nuptials. Be not troubled, my friend; but procure the means to be present at this sacrifice, which, if my arguments cannot avert, I carry a dagger about me, which can prevent a more determined force, by putting an end to my life, and giving you a convincing proof of the affection I have borne, and still do bear you."

'I replied to her, with confusion and precipitation, fearing I should want time to answer her:

"Let your actions, madam, make good your words; if you carry a dagger to secure your honour, I carry a sword to defend you, or kill myself, if fortune proves adverse to us."

'I do not believe she heard all these words, being, as I perceived, called away hastily; for the bridegroom waited for her. Herewith the night of my sorrow was fallen! the sun of my joy was set! I remained without light in my eyes, and without judgement in my intellect! I was irresolute as to going into her house, nor did I know which way to turn me: but when I reflected on the consequences of my being present at what might happen in that case, I animated myself the best I could, and at last got into her house. And as I was perfectly acquainted with all the avenues, and the whole family was busied about the secret affair then transacting, I escaped being perceived by anybody. And so, without being seen, I had leisure to place myself in the hollow of a bow-window of the hall, behind the hangings, where two pieces of tapestry met; whence, without being seen myself, I could see all that was done in the hall. Who can describe the emotions and beatings of heart I felt while I stood there? the thoughts that occurred to me? the reflections I made? Such and so many were they, that they neither can nor ought to be told. Let it suffice to tell you, that the bridegroom came into the hall without other ornament than the clothes he usually wore. He had with him, for bridesman, a cousin-german of Lucinda's, and there was no other person in the room but the servants of the house. Soon after, from a withdrawing room, came out Lucinda, accompanied by her mother and two of her own maids, as richly dressed and adorned as her quality and beauty deserved, and as befitted the height and perfection of all that was gallant and courtlike: the agony and distraction I was in, gave me no leisure to view and observe the particulars of her dress; I could only take notice of the colours, which were carnation and white, and of the splendour of the precious stones and jewels of her head-attire, and of the rest of her habit; which yet were exceeded in lustre by the singular beauty of her fair and golden tresses, which vying with the precious stones, and the light of four flambeaux that were in the hall, struck the eyes with superior brightness.

'O memory, thou mortal enemy of my repose! why dost thou represent to me now the incomparable beauty of that my adored enemy? Were it not better, cruel memory, to put me in mind of, and represent to my imagination what she then did; that moved by so flagrant an injury, I may strive, since I do not revenge it, at least to put an end to my life? Be not weary, gentlemen, of hearing the digressions I make; for my misfortune is not of that kind that can or ought to be related succinctly and methodically, since each circumstance seems to me to deserve a long discourse.'

To this the priest replied; that they were so far from being tired with hearing it, that they took great pleasure in the minutest particulars he recounted, being such as deserved not to be passed over in silence, and merited no less attention than the principal parts of the story.

'I say then,' continued Cardenio, 'that, they being all assembled in the hall, the parish priest entered, and having taken them both by the hand, in order to perform what is necessary on such occasions, when he came to these words, "Will you, Madam Lucinda, take Señor Don Fernando, who is here present, for your lawful husband, as our holy mother the church commands?"

'I thrust out my head and neck through the partings of the tapestry, and with the utmost attention and distraction of soul, set myself to listen to what Lucinda answered; expecting from her answer the sentence of my death, or the confirmation of my life. O! that I had dared to venture out then, and to have cried aloud, "Ah! Lucinda, Lucinda! take heed what you do; consider what you owe me; behold, you are mine, and cannot be another's. Take notice, that your saying Yes, and the putting an end to my life, will both happen in the same moment. Ah, traitor Don Fernando! ravisher of my glory, death of my life! what is it you would have? what is it you pretend to? consider, you cannot, as a Christian, arrive at the end of your desires; for Lucinda is my wife, and I am her husband." Ah, fool that I am! now that I am absent, and at a distance from the danger, I am saying I ought to have done what I did not do. Now that I have suffered myself to be robbed of my soul's treasure, I am cursing the thief on whom I might have revenged myself, if I had had as much heart to do it as I have now to complain.

In short, since I was then a coward and a fool, no wonder if I die now ashamed, repentant, and mad.

'The priest stood expecting Lucinda's answer, who gave it not for a long time; and, when I thought she was pulling out the dagger in defence of her honour, or letting loose her tongue to avow some truth, which might undeceive them, and redound to my advantage, I heard her say, with a low and faint voice, "I will." The same said Don Fernando, and, the ring being put on, they remained tied in an indissoluble band. The bridegroom came to embrace his bride; and she, laying her hand on her heart, swooned away between her mother's arms.

'It remains now to tell you what condition I was in, when I saw in the "Yes" I had heard, my hopes frustrated, Lucinda's vows and promises broken, and no possibility left of my ever recovering the happiness I in that moment lost. I was totally confounded, and thought myself abandoned of heaven, and become an enemy to the earth that sustained me, the air denying me breath for my sighs, and the water moisture for my tears: the fire alone was so increased in me, that I was all inflamed with rage and jealousy. They were all affrighted at Lucinda's swooning; and her mother, unlacing her bosom to give her air, she discovered in it a paper folded up, which Don Fernando presently seized, and read it by the light of one of the flambeaux; and, having done reading it, he sat himself down in a chair, leaning his cheek on his hand, with all the signs of a man full of thought, and without attending to the means that they were using to recover his bride from her fainting fit.

'Perceiving the whole house in a consternation, I ventured out, not caring whether I was seen or not; and with a determined resolution, if seen, to act so desperate a part, that all the world should have known the just indignation of my breast, by the chastisement of the false Don Fernando, and of the fickle, though swooning traitress. But my fate, which has doubtless reserved me for greater evils, if greater can possibly be, ordained, that, at that juncture I had the use of my understanding, which has since failed me; and so, without thinking to take revenge on my greatest enemies (which might very easily have been done, when they thought so little of me), I resolved to take it on myself, and to execute on my own person that punishment which they deserved; and perhaps with greater rigour than I should have done on them, even in taking away their lives; for a sudden death soon puts one out of pain; but that which is prolonged by tortures, is always killing, without putting an end to life.

'In a word, I got out of the house, and went to the place where I had left the mule: I got it saddled and without taking any leave, I mounted, and rode out of the town, not daring, like another Lot, to look behind me; and, when I found myself in the field alone, and covered by the darkness of the night, and the silence thereof inviting me to complain, without regard or fear of being heard or known, I gave a loose to my voice, and untied my tongue, in a thousand exclamations on Lucinda and Don Fernando, as if that had been satisfaction for the wrong they had done me. I called her cruel, false, and ungrateful; but, above all, covetous, since the wealth of my enemy had shut the eyes of her affection, and withdrawn it from me to engage it to another, to whom fortune had shown herself more bountiful and liberal. But in the height of these curses and reproaches, I excused her, saying: It was no wonder that a maiden, kept up close in her father's house, and always accustomed to obey her parents, should comply with their inclination, especially since they gave her for a husband so considerable, so rich, and so accomplished a cavalier; and that to have refused him, would have made people think she had no judgement, or that her affections were engaged elsewhere; either of which would have redounded to the prejudice of her honour and good name. But, on the other hand, supposing she had owned her engagement to me, it would have appeared, that she had not made so ill a choice, but she might have been excused, since, before Don Fernando offered himself, they themselves could not, consistently with reason, have desired a better match for their daughter: and how easily might she, before she came to the last extremity of giving her hand, have said, that I had already given her mine; for I would have appeared, and have confirmed whatever she had invented on this occasion. In fine, I concluded, that little love, little judgement, much ambition, and a desire of greatness, had made her forget those words, by which she had deluded, kept up, and nourished my firm hopes, and honest desires.

'With these soliloquies, and with this disquietude, I journeyed on the rest of the night, and at daybreak arrived at an opening into these mountainous parts, through which I went on three days more, without any road or path, until at last I came to a certain meadow, that lies somewhere hereabouts; and there I inquired of some shepherds, which was the most solitary part of these craggy rocks. They directed me towards this place. I presently came hither, with design to end my life here; and, at the entering among these brakes, my mule fell down dead through weariness and hunger; or, as I rather believe, to be rid of so useless a burden. Thus I was left on foot, quite spent and famished, without having or desiring any relief. In this manner I continued, I know not how long, extended on the ground; at length I got up, somewhat refreshed, and found near me some goatherds, who must needs be the persons that relieved my necessity; for they told me in what condition they found me, and that I said so many senseless and extravagant things, that they wanted no further proof of my having lost my understanding; and I am sensible I have not been perfectly right ever since, but so shattered and crazy, that I commit a thousand extravagances, tearing my garments, howling aloud through these solitudes, cursing my fortune, and in vain repeating the beloved name of my enemy, without any other design or intent, at the time, than to end my life with outcries and exclamations. And when I come to myself, I find I am so weary, and so sore, that I can hardly stir.

'My usual abode is in the hollow of a cork-tree, large enough to be a habitation for this miserable carcass. The goatherds, who feed their cattle hereabouts, provide me sustenance out of charity, laying victuals on the rocks, and in places where they think I may chance to pass and find it; and though, at such times, I happen to be out of my senses, natural necessity makes me know my nourishment, and awakes in me an appetite to desire it, and the will to take it.

At other times, as they tell me when they meet me in my senses, I come into the road, and though the shepherds, who are bringing food from the village to their huts, willingly offer me a part of it, I rather choose to take it from them by force. Thus I pass my sad and miserable life, waiting until it shall please heaven to bring it to a final period, or by fixing the thoughts of that day in my mind, to erase out of it all memory of the beauty and treachery of Lucinda, and the wrongs done me by Don Fernando; for if it vouchsafes me this mercy before I die, my thoughts will take a more rational turn; if not, it remains only to beseech God to have mercy on my soul; for I feel no ability nor strength in myself to raise my body out of this strait, into which I have voluntarily brought it.

'This, gentlemen, is the bitter story of my misfortune: tell me now, could it be borne with less concern than what you have perceived in me? And, pray, give yourselves no trouble to persuade or advise me to follow what you may think reasonable and proper for my cure, for it will do me just as much good as a medicine prescribed by a skilful physician will do a sick man who refuses to take it. I will have no health without Lucinda; and, since she was pleased to give herself to another, when she was, or ought to have been, mine, let me have the pleasure of indulging myself in unhappiness, since I might have been happy if I had pleased. She, by her mutability, would have me irretrievably undone; I, by endeavouring to destroy myself, would satisfy her will; and I shall stand as an example to posterity, of having been the only unfortunate person whom the impossibility of receiving consolation could not comfort, but plunged in still greater afflictions and misfortunes; for I verily believe they will not have an end even in death itself.'

Here Cardenio ended his long discourse, and his story, no less full of misfortunes than of love; and, just as the priest was preparing to say something to him, by way of consolation, he was prevented by a voice, which, in mournful accents, said what will be related in the fourth book of this history; for, at this point the wise and judicious historian Cid Hamet Ben Engeli put an end to the third.

CHAPTER 28

*Which treats of the new and agreeable adventure that befell
the priest and the barber in the Sierra Morena.*

MOST happy and fortunate were the times in which the most
daring knight Don Quixote de la Mancha was ushered into
the world; since, through the so honourable resolution he
took of reviving and restoring to the world the long since
lost, and as it were buried, order of knight-errantry, we, in
these our times, barren and unfruitful of amusing entertainments, enjoy not only the sweets of his true history, but also
the stories and episodes of it, which are, in some sort, no
less pleasing, artificial, and true, than the history itself: which
resuming the broken thread of the narration, relates, that, as
the priest was preparing himself to comfort Cardenio, he was
hindered by a voice, which, with mournful accents, spoke in
this manner:

'O heavens! is it possible I have at last found a place that
can afford a secret grave for the irksome burden of this body,
which I bear about so much against my will? yes, it is, if the
solitude, which these rocks promise, do not deceive me. Ah,
woe is me! how much more agreeable society shall I find in
these crags and brakes, which will at least afford me leisure
to communicate my miseries to heaven by complaints, than
in the conversation of men, since there is no one living from
whom I can expect counsel in doubts, ease in complaints, or
remedy in misfortunes.'

The priest, and they that were with him, heard all this very
distinctly; and perceiving, as indeed it was, that the voice was
near them, they rose up in quest of the speaker; and they
had not gone twenty paces, when, behind a rock, they espied
a youth, dressed like a peasant, sitting at the foot of an
ash-tree; whose face they could not then discern, because he
hung down his head, on account that he was washing his
feet in a rivulet which ran by. They drew near so silently that
he did not hear them; nor was he intent upon anything but
washing his feet, which were such, that they seemed to be
two pieces of pure crystal growing among the other pebbles
of the brook. They stood in admiration at the whiteness and

beauty of the feet, which did not seem to them to be made for breaking of clods, or following the plough, as their owner's dress might have persuaded them they were: and finding they were not perceived, the priest, who went foremost, made signs to the other two, to crouch low, or hide themselves behind some of the rocks thereabouts: which they accordingly did, and stood observing attentively what the youth was doing.

He had on a grey double-skirted jerkin, girt tight about his body with a linen towel. He wore also a pair of breeches and gamashes* of grey cloth, and a grey huntsman's cap on his head. His gamashes were now pulled up to the middle of his leg, which really seemed to be of snowy alabaster. Having made an end of washing his beauteous feet, he immediately wiped them with a handkerchief, which he pulled out from under his cap; and, at the taking it from thence, he lifted up his face, and the lookers-on had an opportunity of beholding an incomparable beauty, and such a beauty, that Cardenio said to the priest, in a low voice;

'Since this is not Lucinda, it can be no human, but must be a divine creature.'

The youth took off his cap, and shaking his head, there began to flow down, and spread over his shoulders, a quantity of lovely hair, that Apollo himself might envy. By this they found that the person who seemed to be a peasant was, in reality, a woman, and a delicate one; nay, the handsomest that two of the three had ever beheld with their eyes, or even Cardenio himself, if he had never seen and known Lucinda; for, as he afterwards affirmed, the beauty of Lucinda alone could come in competition with hers. Her long and golden tresses not only fell on her shoulders, but covered her whole body, excepting her feet. Her fingers served instead of a comb; and if her feet in the water seemed to be of crystal, her hands in her hair were like driven snow. All which excited a still greater admiration and desire in the three spectators to learn who she was. For this purpose they resolved to show themselves; and, at the rustling they made in getting upon their feet, the beautiful maiden raised her head, and, with both her hands, parting her hair from before

her eyes, saw those who had made the noise: and scarcely
had she seen them, when she rose up, and, without staying
to put on her shoes, or replace her hair, she hastily snatched
up something like a bundle of clothes which lay close by her,
and betook herself to flight, all in confusion and surprise:
but she had not gone six steps, when, her tender feet not
being able to endure the sharpness of the stones, she fell
down; which the three perceiving, they went up to her, and
the priest was the first, who said:

'Stay, madam, whoever you are; for those you see here
have no other intention but that of serving you; there is no
reason why you should endeavour to make so needless an
escape, which neither your feet can bear, nor ours permit.'

To all this she answered not a word, being astonished and
confounded. Then the priest, taking hold of her hand, went
on, saying:

'What your dress, madam, would conceal from us, your
hair discovers; a manifest indication, that no slight cause has
disguised your beauty in so unworthy a habit, and brought
you to such a solitude as this, in which it has been our good
luck to find you, if not to administer a remedy to your
misfortunes, at least to assist you with our advice, since no
evil, which does not destroy life itself, can afflict so much,
or arrive to that extremity, as to make the sufferer refuse to
hearken to advice, when given with a sincere intention; and
therefore, dear madam, or dear sir, or whatever you please
to be, shake off the surprise which the sight of us has
occasioned, and relate to us your good or ill fortune; for you
will find us jointly, or severally disposed to sympathize with
you in your misfortunes.'

While the priest was saying this, the disguised maiden
stood like one stupefied, her eyes fixed on them all, without
moving her lips, or speaking a word: just like a country clown,
when he is shown of a sudden something curious, or never
seen before. But the priest adding more to the same purpose
she fetched a deep sigh, and, breaking silence, said:

'Since neither the solitude of these rocks has been sufficient
to conceal me, nor the discomposure of my hair has suffered
my tongue to belie my sex, it would be in vain for me now

to dress up a fiction, which, if you seemed to give credit to, it would be rather out of complaisance, than for any other reason. This being the case, I say, gentlemen, that I take kindly the offers you have made me, which have laid me under an obligation to satisfy you in whatever you have desired of me; though I fear the relation I shall make of my misfortunes will raise in you a concern equal to your compassion; since it will not be in your power, either to remedy or alleviate them. Nevertheless, that my honour may not suffer in your opinions, from your having already discovered me to be a woman, and your seeing me young, and alone, and in this garb, any one of which circumstances is sufficient to bring discredit on the best reputation, I must tell you what I would gladly have concealed, if it was in my power.'

All this she, who appeared so beautiful a woman, spoke without hesitating, so readily, and with so much ease, and sweetness both of tongue and voice, that her good sense surprised them no less than her beauty. And they again repeating their kind offers, and entreaties to her, that she would perform her promise; she, without more asking, having first modestly put on her shoes and stockings, and gathered up her hair, seated herself upon a flat stone; and the three being placed round her, after she had done some violence to herself in restraining the tears that came into her eyes, she began the history of her life, with a clear and sedate voice, in this manner:

'There is a place in this country of Andalusia, from which a duke takes a title, which makes him one of those they call Grandees of Spain. This duke has two sons; the elder, heir to his estate, and in appearance, to his virtues; and the younger, heir to I know not what, unless it be to the treachery of Vellido, and the deceitfulness of Galalon. My parents are vassals to this nobleman; it is true, they are of low extraction, but so rich, that, if the advantages of their birth had equalled those of their fortune, neither would they have had anything more to wish for, nor should I have had any reason to fear being exposed to the misfortunes I am now involved in; for it is probable, my misfortunes arise from their not being nobly born. It is true, indeed, they are not so low, that they need to be ashamed of their condition, nor so high, as to hinder me from thinking, that their meanness is the cause of my unhappiness. In a word, they are farmers, plain people, without mixture of bad blood, and, as they usually say, rusty Old Christians; but so rusty, that their wealth, and handsome way of living, is, by degrees, acquiring them the name of gentlemen, and even of cavaliers; though the riches and nobility they valued themselves most upon, was, their having me for their daughter: and, as they had no other child to inherit what they possessed, and were besides very affectionate parents, I was one of the most indulged girls that ever father or mother fondled. I was the mirror, in which they beheld themselves, the staff of their old age, and she whose happiness was the sole object of all their wishes, under the guidance of heaven; to which, being so good, mine were always entirely conformable. And, as I was mistress of their affections, so was I of all they possessed. As I pleased, servants were hired and discharged; through my hands passed the account and management of what was sowed and reaped. The oil-mills, the wine-presses, the number of herds, flocks, bee-hives; in a word, all that so rich a farmer as my father has, or can be supposed to have, was entrusted to my care: I was both steward and mistress, with so much diligence on my part, and satisfaction on theirs, that I cannot easily enhance it to you. The hours of the day that remained after giving directions, and assigning proper tasks to the head servants, overseers, and day-labourers, I employed in such exercises as are not only allowable, but necessary to young maidens, to wit, in handling the needle, making lace, and sometimes spinning: and if now and then, to recreate my mind, I quitted those exercises, I entertained myself with reading some book of devotion, or touching the harp; for experience showed me that music composes the mind when it is disordered, and relieves the spirits after labour. Such was the life I led in my father's house; and if I have been so particular in recounting it, it was not out of ostentation, nor to give you to understand that I am rich, but that you may be apprised how little I deserved to fall from that state into the unhappy one I am now in.

'While I passed my time in so many occupations, and in a retirement that might be compared to that of a nunnery, without being seen, as I imagined, by any one besides our own servants, because, when I went to Mass, it was very early in the morning, and always in company with my mother, and some of the maidservants, and I was so closely veiled and reserved, that my eyes scarce saw more ground than the space I set my foot upon; it fell out, I say, notwithstanding all this, that the eyes of love, or rather of idleness to which those of a lynx are not to be compared, discovered me through the industrious curiosity of Don Fernando; for that is the name of the duke's younger son, whom I told you of.'

She had no sooner named Don Fernando, than Cardenio's colour changed, and he began to sweat with such violent perturbation, that the priest and the barber, who perceived it, were afraid he was falling into one of the mad fits, to which they had heard he was now and then subject. But Cardenio did nothing but sweat, and sat still, fixing his eyes most attentively on the country-maid, imagining who she must be; who, taking no notice of the emotions of Cardenio, continued her story, saying:

'Scarcely had he seen me, when (as he afterwards declared) he fell desperately in love with me, as the proofs he then gave of it sufficiently evinced. But to shorten the account of my misfortunes, which are endless, I pass over in silence the diligence Don Fernando used in getting an opportunity to declare his passion to me. He bribed our whole family; he gave and offered presents, and did favours to several of my relations. Every day was a festival and day of rejoicing in our street: nobody could sleep of nights for the serenades. Infinite were the billets-doux that came, I knew not how, to my hands, filled with amorous expressions, and offers of kindness, with more promises and oaths in them than letters. All which was so far from softening me, that I grew the more obdurate, as if he had been my mortal enemy, and all the measures he took to bring me to his lure had been designed for quite a contrary purpose; not that I disliked the gallantry of Don Fernando, or thought him too importunate; for it gave me I know not what secret satisfaction to see myself thus courted and respected by so considerable a cavalier, and it was not disagreeable to me to find my own praises in his letters: for let us women be never so ill-favoured, I take it, we are always pleased to hear ourselves called handsome.

'But all this was opposed by my own virtue, together with the repeated good advice of my parents, who plainly saw through Don Fernando's design; for, indeed, he took no pains to hide it from the world. My parents told me, that they reposed their credit and reputation in my virtue and integrity alone; they bade me consider the disproportion between me and Don Fernando, from whence I ought to conclude that his thoughts, whatever he might say to the contrary, were more intent upon his own pleasure, than upon my good: and if I had a mind to throw an obstacle in the way of his designs in order to make him desist from his unjust pretensions, they would marry me, they said, out of hand, to whomsoever I pleased, either of the chief of our town, or of the whole neighbourhood around us; since their considerable wealth, and my good character, put it in their power easily to provide a suitable match for me. With this promise, and the truth of what they said, I fortified my virtue, and would never answer Don Fernando the least word that might afford him the most distant hope of succeeding in his design. All this reservedness of mine which he ought to have taken for disdain, served rather to quicken his lascivious appetite; for I can give no better name to the passion he showed for me, which, had it been such as it ought, you would not now have known it, since there would have been no occasion for my giving you this account of it.

'At length Don Fernando discovered, that my parents were looking out for a match for me, in order to deprive him of all hope of gaining me, or at least were resolved to have me more narrowly watched. And this news, or suspicion, put him upon doing what you shall presently hear; which was, that, one night as I was in my chamber, attended only by a maid that waited upon me, the doors being fast locked, lest by any neglect my virtue might be endangered, without my knowing or imagining how, in the midst of all this care and precaution, and the solitude of this silence and recluseness, he stood before me; at whose sight I was struck blind and dumb, and had not power to cry out; nor do I believe he would have suffered me to have done it: for he instantly ran to me, and, taking me in his arms (for, as I said, I had no power to struggle, being in such confusion) he began to say such things that one would think it impossible falsehood should be able to frame them with such an appearance of truth. The traitor made his tears gain credit to his words, and his sighs to his designs. I, an innocent girl, bred always at home, and not at all versed in affairs of this nature, began, I know not how, to deem for true so many and so great falsities; not that his tears or sighs could move me to any criminal compassion.

'And so my first surprise being over, I began a little to recover my lost spirits; and with more courage than I thought I could have had, said:

'"If, sir, as I am between your arms, I were between the paws of a fierce lion, and my deliverance depended upon my doing or saying anything to the prejudice of my virtue, it would be as impossible for me to do or say it, as it is impossible for that which has been not to have been: so that, though you hold my body confined between your arms, I hold my mind restrained within the bounds of virtuous inclinations, very different from yours, as you will see, if you proceed to use violence. I am your vassal, but not your slave: the nobility of your blood neither has, nor ought to have, the privilege to dishonour and insult the meanness of mine; and though a country girl, and a farmer's daughter, my reputation is as dear to me, as yours can be to you, who are a noble cavalier. Your employing force, will do little with me; I set no value upon your riches; your words cannot deceive me, nor can your sighs and tears mollify me. If I saw any of these things in a person whom my parents should assign me for a husband, my will should conform itself to theirs, and not transgress the bounds which they prescribed it. And therefore, sir, with the safety of my honour, though I sacrificed my private satisfaction, I might freely bestow on you what you are now endeavouring to obtain by force. I have said all this, because I would not have you think, that any one who is not my lawful husband shall ever prevail on me."

'"If that be all you stick at, most beautiful Dorothea (for that is the name of this unhappy woman)," said the treacherous cavalier, "lo! here I give you my hand to be yours, and let the heavens, from which nothing is hid, and this image of Our Lady you have here, be witnesses to this truth."'

When Cardenio heard her call herself Dorothea, he fell again into his disorder, and was thoroughly confirmed in his first opinion: but he would not interrupt the story, being desirous to hear the event of what he partly knew already; only he said:

'What! Madam, is your name Dorothea? I have heard of one of the same name, whose misfortunes very much resemble yours. But proceed; for some time or other I may tell you things that will equally move your wonder and compassion.'

Dorothea took notice of Cardenio's words, and of his strange and tattered dress; and desired him, if he knew anything of her affairs, to tell it presently; for, if fortune had left her anything that was good, it was the courage she had to bear any disaster whatever that might befall her, secure in this, that none could possibly happen, that could in the least add to those she already endured.

'Madam,' replied Cardenio, 'I would not be the means of destroying that courage in you, by telling you what I think, if what I imagine should be true; and hitherto there is no opportunity lost, nor is it of any importance that you should know it as yet.'

'Be that as it will,' answered Dorothea; 'I go on with my story. Don Fernando, taking the image that stood in the room, and placing it for a witness of our espousals, with all the solemnity of vows and oaths, gave me his word to be my husband; although I warned him, before he had done, to consider well what he was about, and the uneasiness it must needs give his father, to see him married to a farmer's daughter, and his own vassal; and therefore he ought to beware, lest my beauty, such as it was, should blind him, since that would not be a sufficient excuse for his fault; and if he intended me any good, I conjured him, by the love he bore me, that he would suffer my lot to fall equal to what my rank could pretend to; for such disproportionate matches are seldom happy, or continue long in that state of pleasure, with which they set out.

'All these reasons here recited, and many more which I do not remember, I then urged to him; but they availed nothing towards making him desist from prosecuting his design; just as he who never intends to pay sticks at nothing in making a bargain. Upon that occasion I briefly reasoned thus with myself: "Well: I shall not be the first, who, by the way of marriage, has risen from a low to a high condition, nor will Don Fernando be the first, whom beauty, [or] rather blind affection, has induced to take a wife beneath his quality. Since then I neither make a new world, nor a new custom, sure I may be allowed to accept this honour, which fortune throws in my way, even though the inclination he shows for me, should last no longer than the accomplishment of his will; for in short, in the sight of God, I shall be his wife. Besides, should I reject him with disdain, I see him prepared to set aside all sense of duty, and to have recourse to violence: and so I shall remain dishonoured, and without excuse, when I am censured by those, who do not know how innocently I came into this strait. For what reasons can be sufficient to persuade my parents, and others, that this cavalier got into my apartment without my consent?"

'All these questions and answers I revolved in my imagination in an instant. But what principally inclined and drew me, thoughtless as I was, to my ruin, was Don Fernando's oaths, the witnesses by which he swore, the tears he shed, and, in fine, his genteel carriage and address, which, together with the many tokens he gave me of unfeigned love, might have captivated any heart, though before as much disengaged, and as reserved as mine. I called in my waiting-maid, to be a joint witness on earth with those in heaven. Don Fernando repeated and confirmed his oaths. He attested new saints, and imprecated a thousand curses on himself, if he failed in the performance of his promise. The tears came again into his eyes; he redoubled his sighs, and pressed me closer between his arms, from which he had never once loosed me. And with this, and my maid's going again out of the room, I ceased to be one, and he became a traitor and perjured.

'The day that succeeded the night of my misfortune came on, but not so fast as I believe Don Fernando wished. For, after the accomplishment of our desires, the greatest pleasure is to get away from the place of enjoyment. I say this, because Don Fernando made haste to leave me; and by the diligence of the same maid who had betrayed me, was got in the street before break of day. And, at parting, he said, though not with the same warmth and vehemency as at his coming, I might entirely depend upon his honour, and the truth and sincerity of his oaths; and as a confirmation of his promise, he drew a ring of great value from his finger, and put it on mine. In short, he went away, and I remained I know not whether sad or joyful; this I can truly say, that I remained confused and thoughtful, and almost distracted at what had passed; and either I had no heart, or I forgot to chide my maid for the treachery she had been guilty of in conveying Don Fernando into my chamber: for, indeed, I had not yet determined with myself, whether what had befallen me was to my good or harm. I told Don Fernando, at parting, he might, if he pleased, since I was now his own, see me on other nights by the same method he had now taken, until he should be pleased to publish what was done to the world. But he came no more after the following night, nor could I get a sight of him in the street, or at church, in above a month, though I tired myself with looking after him in vain; and though I knew he was in the town, and that he went almost every day to hunt, an exercise he was very fond of.

'Those days, and those hours, I too well remember, were sad and dismal ones to me; for in them I began to doubt, and at last to disbelieve, the fidelity of Don Fernando. I remember too, that I then made my damsel hear those reproofs for her presumption, which she had escaped before. I was forced to set a watch over my tears, and the air of my countenance, that I might avoid giving my parents occasion to inquire into the cause of my discontent, and laying myself under the necessity of inventing lies to deceive them.

'But all this was soon put an end to by an accident which bore down all respect and regard to my reputation, which deprived me of all patience, and exposed my most secret thoughts on the public stage of the world; which was this. Some few days after, a report was spread in the town, that Don Fernando was married in a neighbouring city to a young lady of extreme beauty, and whose parents were of considerable quality, but not so rich, that her dowry might make her aspire to so noble an alliance. Her name, it was said, was Lucinda, and many strange things were reported to have happened at their wedding.'

Cardenio heard the name of Lucinda, but did nothing more than shrug up his shoulders, bite his lips, arch his brows, and soon after let fall two streams of tears from his eyes. Dorothea did not, however, discontinue her story, but went on saying:

'This sad news soon reached my ears; and my heart, instead of being chilled at hearing it, was so incensed and inflamed with rage and anger, that I could scarce forbear running out into the streets, crying out and publishing aloud, how basely and treacherously I had been used. But this fury was moderated for the present by a resolution I took, and executed that very night; which was, to put myself into this garb, which was given me by one of those, who, in farmer's houses, are called swains, to whom I discovered my whole misfortune, and begged of him to accompany me to the city, where I was informed my enemy then was. He, finding me bent upon my design, after he had condemned the rashness of my undertaking, and blamed my resolution, offered himself to bear me company, as he expressed it, to the end of the world. I immediately put up, in a pillow-case, a woman's dress, with some jewels and money, to provide against whatever might happen: and in the dead of that very night, without letting my treacherous maid into the secret, I left our house, accompanied only by my servant, and a thousand anxious thoughts, and took the way that led to the town on foot, the desire of getting thither adding wings to my flight, that, if I could not prevent what I concluded was already done, I might at least demand of Don Fernando, with what conscience he had done it.

'In two days and a half I arrived at the place, and, going into the town, I inquired where Lucinda's father lived; and the first person I addressed myself to answered me more than I desired to hear. He told me where I might find the house, and related to me the whole story of what had happened at the young lady's wedding; all which was so public in the town, that the people assembled in every street to talk of it. He told me that, on the night Don Fernando was married to Lucinda, after she had pronounced the "Yes," by which she became his wedded wife, she fell into a swoon; and the bridegroom, in unclasping her bosom to give her air, found a paper written with Lucinda's own hand, in which she affirmed and declared, that she could not be wife to Don Fernando, because she was already Cardenio's (who, as the man told me, was a very considerable cavalier of the same town) and that she had given her consent to Don Fernando, merely in obedience to her parents. In short, the paper gave them to understand, that she designed killing herself as soon as the ceremony was over, and contained likewise her reasons for so doing: all which they say, was confirmed by a poniard they found about her, in some part of her clothes. Don Fernando, seeing all this, and concluding himself deluded, mocked, and despised by Lucinda, made at her, before she recovered from her fainting fit, and, with the same poniard that was found, endeavoured to stab her; and had certainly done it, if her parents and the rest of the company, had not prevented him. They said further, that Don Fernando immediately absented himself, and that Lucinda did not come to herself until the next day, when she confessed to her parents, that she was really wife to the cavalier aforesaid. I learned moreover, it was rumoured that Cardenio was present at the ceremony, and that, seeing her married, which he could never have thought, he went out of the town in despair, leaving behind him a written paper, in which he set forth at large the wrong Lucinda had done him, and his resolution of going where human eyes should never more behold him.

'All this was public and notorious over the town, and in everybody's mouth; but the talk increased, when it was known that Lucinda also was missing from her father's house; at which her parents were almost distracted, not knowing what means to use, in order to find her. This news rallied my scattered hopes, and I was better pleased not to find Don Fernando, than to have found him married, flattering myself, that the door of my relief was not quite shut; and hoping that, possibly, heaven might have laid this impediment in the way of his second marriage, to reduce him to a sense of what he owed to the first, and to make him reflect, that he was a Christian, and obliged to have more regard to his soul than to any worldly considerations. All these things I revolved in my imagination, and having no real consolation, comforted myself with framing some faint and distant hopes in order to support a life I now abhor.

'Being, then, in the town, without knowing what to do with myself, since I did not find Don Fernando, I heard a public crier promising a great reward to any one who should find me, describing my age, and the very dress I wore. And, as I heard, it was reported that I was run away from my father's house with the young fellow that attended me; a thing which struck me to the very soul, to see how low my credit was sunk; as if it was not enough to say that I was gone off, but it must be added with whom, and he too a person so much below me, and so unworthy of my better inclinations. At the instant I heard the crier, I went out of the town with my servant, who already began to discover some signs of staggering in his promised fidelity; and that night we got into the thickest of this mountain, for fear of being found.

'But, as it is commonly said, that one evil calls upon another, and that the end of one disaster is the beginning of a greater, so it befell me; for my good servant, until then faithful and trusty, seeing me in this desert place, and incited by his own baseness rather than by any beauty of mine, resolved to lay hold of the opportunity this solitude seemed to afford him; and, with little shame, and less fear of God, or respect to his mistress, began to make love to me; but, finding that I answered him with such language as the impudence of his attempt deserved, he laid aside entreaties, by which, at first, he hoped to succeed, and began to use force. But just heaven, that seldom or never fails to regard and favour righteous intentions, favoured mine in such a manner, that, with the little strength I had, and without much difficulty, I pushed him down a precipice, where I left him, I know not whether alive or dead. And then, with more nimbleness than could be expected from my surprise and weariness, I entered into this desert mountain, without any other thought or design than to hide myself here from my father, and others, who, by his order, were in search after me.

'It is I know not how many months since, with this design, I came hither, where I met with a shepherd who took me for his servant to a place in the very midst of these rocks. I served him, all this time, as a shepherd's boy, endeavouring to be always abroad in the field, the better to conceal my hair, which has now so unexpectedly discovered me. But all my care and solicitude were to no purpose; for my master came to discover I was not a man, and the same wicked thoughts sprung up in his breast that had possessed my servant. But, as fortune does not always with the difficulty present the remedy, and as I had now no rock nor precipice to rid me of the master, as before of the servant, I thought it more advisable to leave him, and hide myself once more among these brakes and cliffs, than to venture a trial of my strength or dissuasions with him. I say, then, I again betook myself to these deserts, where, without molestation, I might beseech heaven with sighs and tears to have pity on my disconsolate state, and either to assist me with ability to struggle through it, or to put an end to my life among these solitudes, where no memory might remain of this wretched creature, who, without any fault of hers, has ministered matter to be talked of, and censured, in her own and in other countries.'

CHAPTER 29

Which treats of the beautiful Dorothea's discretion, with other very ingenious and entertaining particulars.

'THIS, gentlemen, is the true history of my tragedy; see now, and judge, whether you might not reasonably have expected more sighs than those you have listened to, more words than those you have heard, and more tears than have yet flowed from my eyes; and, the quality of my misfortune considered, you will perceive that all counsel is in vain, since a remedy is nowhere to be found. All I desire of you is (what with ease you can and ought to do) that you would advise me where I may pass my life, without the continual dread and apprehension of being discovered by those who are searching after me; for, though I know I may depend upon the great love of my parents towards me for a kind reception, yet so great is the shame that overwhelms me at the bare thought of appearing before them not such as they expected, that I choose rather to banish myself for ever from their sight, than to behold their face under the thought that they see mine estranged from that integrity, they had good reason to promise themselves from me.'

Here she held her peace, and her face was overspread with such a colour, as plainly discovered the concern and shame of her soul. The hearers felt in theirs no less pity than admiration at her misfortune. The priest was just going to administer to her some present comfort and counsel; but Cardenio prevented him, saying:

'It seems then, madam, you are the beautiful Dorothea, only daughter of the rich Clenardo.'

Dorothea was surprised at hearing her father's name, and to see what a sorry figure he made who named him; for we have already taken notice how poorly Cardenio was apparelled: and she said to him:

'Pray, sir, who are you that are so well acquainted with my father's name? for, to this minute, if I remember right, I have not mentioned his name in the whole series of the account of my misfortune.'

'I am,' answered Cardenio, 'that unfortunate person, whom, according to your relation, Lucinda owned to be her husband. I am the unhappy Cardenio, whom the base actions of him who has reduced you to the state you are in, have brought to the pass you see, to be thus ragged, naked, destitute of all human comfort, and what is worst of all, deprived of reason; for I enjoy it only when heaven is pleased to bestow it on me for some short interval. I, Dorothea, am he, who was an eye-witness of the wrong Don Fernando did me; he,

who waited to hear the fatal Yes, by which Lucinda confirmed herself his wife. I am he, who had not the courage
to stay, and see what would be the consequence of her
swooning, nor what followed the discovery of the paper in
her bosom: for my soul could not bear such accumulated
misfortunes: and therefore I abandoned the house and my
patience together; and, leaving a letter with my host, whom
I entreated to deliver it into Lucinda's own hands, I betook
myself to these solitudes, with a resolution of ending my life,
which, from that moment, I abhorred as my mortal enemy.
But fate would not deprive me of it, contenting itself with
depriving me of my senses, perhaps to preserve me for the
good fortune I have had in meeting with you; and, as I have
no reason to doubt of the truth of what you have related,
heaven, peradventure, may have reserved us both for a better
issue out of our misfortunes than we think. For since Lucinda
cannot marry Don Fernando, because she is mine, as she has
publicly declared, nor Don Fernando Lucinda, because he is
yours, there is still room for us to hope that heaven will
restore to each of us our own, since it is not yet alienated,
nor past recovery. And, since we have this consolation, not
arising from very distant hopes, nor founded in extravagant
conceits, I entreat you, madam, to entertain other resolutions
in your honourable thoughts, as I intend to do in mine,
preparing yourself to expect better fortune. For I swear to
you upon the faith of a cavalier and a Christian, not to
forsake you, until I see you in possession of Don Fernando,
and, if I cannot by fair means persuade him to acknowledge
what he owes to you, then to take the liberty, allowed me
as a gentleman, of calling him to an account with my sword
for the wrong he has done you; without reflecting on the
injuries done to myself, the revenge of which I leave to
heaven, that I may the sooner redress yours on earth.'

Dorothea was quite amazed at what Cardenio said; and,
not knowing what thanks to return him for such great and
generous offers, she would have thrown herself at his feet,
to have kissed them; but Cardenio would by no means suffer
her. The licentiate answered for them both, and approved of
Cardenio's generous resolution, and, above all things, be-

sought and advised them to go with him to his village, where they might furnish themselves with whatever they wanted, and there consult how to find Don Fernando, or to carry back Dorothea to her parents, or do whatever they thought most expedient. Cardenio and Dorothea thanked him, and accepted of the favour he offered them.

The barber, who all this time had stood silent and in suspense, paid also his compliment, and, with no less good-will than the priest, made them an offer of whatever was in his power for their service. He told them also, briefly, the cause that brought them thither, with the strange madness of Don Quixote, and that they were then waiting for his squire, who was gone to seek him. Cardenio hereupon remembered, as if it had been a dream, the quarrel he had with Don Quixote, which he related to the company, but could not recollect whence it arose.

And this instant they heard a voice, and, knowing it to be Sancho Panza's, who, not finding them where he had left them, was calling as loud as he could to them, they went forward to meet him; and asking him after Don Quixote, he told them, that he had found him, naked to his shirt, feeble, wan, and half dead with hunger, and sighing for his lady Dulcinea; and though he had told him, that she laid her commands on him to come out from that place, and repair to Toboso, where she expected him, his answer was, that he was determined not to appear before her beauty, until he had performed exploits that might render him worthy of her favour: and, if his master persisted in that humour, he would run a risk of never becoming an emperor, as he was in honour bound to be, nor even an archbishop, which was the least he could be: therefore they should consider what was to be done to get him from that place. The licentiate bid him be in no pain about that matter; for they would get him away, whether he would or no.

He then recounted to Cardenio and Dorothea what they had contrived for Don Quixote's cure, or at least for decoying him to his own house. Upon which Dorothea said, she would undertake to act the distressed damsel better than the barber, especially since she had a woman's apparel, with which she could do it to the life; and they might leave it to her to perform what was necessary for carrying on their design, she having read many books of chivalry, and being well acquainted with the style the distressed damsels were wont to use, when they begged their boons of the knights-errant.

'Then there needs no more,' quoth the priest, 'to put the design immediately in execution; for, doubtless, fortune declares in our favour, since she has begun so unexpectedly to open a door for your relief, and furnished us so easily with what we stood in need of.'

Dorothea presently took out of her bundle a petticoat of very rich stuff, and a mantle of fine green silk; and, out of a casket, a necklace, and other jewels; with which, in an instant, she adorned herself in such a manner, that she had all the appearance of a rich and great lady. All these, and more, she said, she had brought from home, to provide against what might happen; but until then she had had no occasion to make use of them. They were all highly delighted with the gracefulness of her person, the gaiety of her disposition, and her beauty; and they agreed, that Don Fernando must be a man of little judgement or taste, who could slight so much excellence. But he, who admired most, was Sancho Panza, who thought (and it was really so) that, in all the days of his life, he had never seen so beautiful a creature; and therefore he earnestly desired the priest to tell him, who that extraordinary beautiful lady was, and what she was looking for in those parts.

'This beautiful lady, friend Sancho,' answered the priest, 'is, to say the least of her, heiress in the direct male line of the great kingdom of Micomicon; and she comes in quest of your master, to beg a boon of him, which is, to redress her a wrong of injury done her by a wicked giant: for it is the fame of your master's prowess, which is spread over all Guinea, that has brought this princess to seek him.'

'Now, a happy seeking, and a happy finding,' quoth Sancho Panza; 'and especially if my master prove so fortunate as to redress that injury, and right that wrong, by killing that whoreson giant you mention; and kill him he certainly will, if he encounters him, unless he be a goblin; for my master has no power at all over goblins. But one thing, among others, I would beg of your worship, señor licentiate, which is, that you would not let my master take it into his head to be an archbishop, which is what I fear, but that you would advise him to marry this princess out of hand, and then he will be disqualified to receive archi-episcopal orders; and so he will come with ease to his kingdom, and I to the end of my wishes; for I have considered the matter well, and find, by my account, it will not be convenient for me, that my master should be an archbishop; for I am unfit for the church, as being a married man; and for me to be now going about to procure dispensations for holding church-livings, having, as I have, a wife and children, would be an endless piece of work. So that, sir, the whole business rests upon my master's marrying this lady out of hand. I do not yet know her grace, and therefore do not call her by her name.'

'She is called,' replied the priest, 'the Princess Micomicona; for her kingdom being called Micomicon, it is clear she must be called so.'

'There is no doubt of that,' answered Sancho; 'for I have known many take their title and surname from the place of their birth, as, Pedro de Alcalá, John de Úbeda, Diego de Valladolid; and, for aught I know, it may be the custom, yonder in Guinea, for queens to take the names of their kingdoms.'

'It is certainly so,' said the priest; 'and, as to your master's marrying, I will promote it to the utmost of my power.'

With which assurance Sancho rested as well satisfied, as the priest was amazed at his simplicity, and to see how strongly the same absurdities were rivetted in his fancy as in his master's, since he could so firmly persuade himself, that Don Quixote would, one time or other, come to be an emperor.

By this time Dorothea had got upon the priest's mule, and the barber had fitted on the ox-tail beard and they bid Sancho conduct them to the place where Don Quixote was, cautioning him not to say he knew the licentiate or the barber, for that the whole stress of his master's coming to be an emperor depended upon his not seeming to know them. Neither the priest, nor Cardenio, would go with them; the latter, that he might not put Don Quixote in mind of the quarrel he had with him; and the priest, because his presence was not then necessary: and therefore they let the others go on before, and followed them fair and softly on foot. The priest would have instructed Dorothea in her part; who said, they need give themselves no trouble about that, for she would perform all to a tittle, according to the rules and precepts of the books of chivalry.

They had gone about three quarters of a league, when, among some intricate rocks, they discovered Don Quixote, by this time clothed, but not armed; and as soon as Dorothea espied him, and was informed by Sancho, that was his master, she whipped on her palfrey, being attended by the well-bearded barber; and, when she was come up to Don Quixote, the squire threw himself off his mule, and went to take down Dorothea in his arms, who, alighting briskly, went and kneeled at Don Quixote's feet: and though he strove to raise her up, she, without getting up, addressed him in this manner:

'I will never arise from this place, O valorous and redoubted knight, until your goodness and courtesy vouchsafe me a boon, which will redound to the honour and glory of your person, and to the weal of the most disconsolate and aggrieved damsel the sun has ever beheld. And if it be so, that the valour of your puissant arm be correspondent to the voice of your immortal fame, you are obliged to protect an unhappy wight, who is come from regions so remote, led by the odour of your renowned name, to seek at your hands a remedy for her misfortunes.'

'I will not answer you a word, fair lady,' replied Don Quixote, 'nor will I hear a jot more of your business, until you arise from the ground.'

'I will not arise, Señor,' answered the afflicted damsel, 'if, by your courtesy, the boon I beg be not first vouchsafed me.'

'I do vouchsafe, and grant it you,' answered Don Quixote, 'provided my compliance therewith be of no detriment or disservice to my king, my country, or her who keeps the key of my heart and liberty.'

'It will not be to the prejudice or disservice of any of these, dear sir,' replied the doleful damsel.

And as she was saying this, Sancho Panza approached his master's ear, and said to him softly:

'Your worship, sir, may very safely grant the boon she asks; for it is a mere trifle; only to kill a great lubberly giant: and she, who begs it, is the mighty Princess Micomicona, queen of the great kingdom of Micomicon in Ethiopia.'

'Let her be who she will,' answered Don Quixote, 'I shall do what is my duty, and what my conscience dictates, in conformity to the rules of my profession.'

And, turning himself to the damsel, he said:

'Fairest lady, rise; for I vouchsafe you whatever boon you ask.'

'Then, what I ask,' said the damsel, 'is, that your magnanimous person will go with me, whither I will conduct you; and that you will promise me not to engage in any other adventure, or comply with any other demand whatever, until you have avenged me on a traitor who, against all right, human and divine, has usurped my kingdom.'

'I repeat it, that I grant your request,' answered Don Quixote; 'and therefore, lady, from this day forward shake off the melancholy that disturbs you, and let your fainting hopes recover fresh force and spirits: for by the help of God, and of my arm, you shall soon see yourself restored to your kingdom, and seated on the throne of your ancient and high estate, in despite of all the miscreants that shall oppose it: and therefore all hands to the work; for the danger, they say, lies in the delay.'

The distressed damsel would fain have kissed his hands; but Don Quixote, who was in everything a most gallant and courteous knight, would by no means consent to it, but, making her arise, embraced her with much politeness and respect, and ordered Sancho to get Rosinante ready, and to help him on with his armour instantly. Sancho took down the arms, which were hung, like a trophy, on a tree, and having got Rosinante ready, helped his master on with his armour in an instant; who, finding himself armed, said:

'Let us go hence, in God's name, to succour this great lady.'

The barber was still kneeling, and had enough to do to forbear laughing, and to keep his beard from falling, which had it happened, would probably have occasioned the miscarriage of their ingenious device: and seeing that the boon was already granted, and with what alacrity Don Quixote prepared himself to accomplish it, he got up, and took his lady by the other hand: and thus, between them both, they set her upon the mule. Immediately Don Quixote mounted Rosinante, and the barber settled himself upon his beast, Sancho remaining on foot; which renewed his grief for the loss of his Dapple: but he bore it cheerfully, with the thought that his master was now in the ready road, and just upon the point of being an emperor: for he made no doubt that he was to marry that princess, and be at least king of Micomicon; only he was troubled to think, that that kingdom was in the land of the negroes, and that the people who were to be his subjects, were all blacks: but he presently bethought himself of a special remedy, and said to himself:

'What care I, if my subjects be blacks? what have I to do, but to ship them off, and bring them over to Spain, where I may sell them for ready money; with which money I may buy some title or employment, on which I may live at my ease all the days of my life? no! sleep on, and have neither sense nor capacity to manage matters, nor to sell thirty or ten thousand slaves in the turn of a hand. Before God, I will make them fly, little and big, or as I can: and let them be never so black, I will transform them into white and yellow:* let me alone to lick my own fingers.'

With these conceits he went on, so busied, and so satisfied, that he forgot the pain of travelling on foot.

All this Cardenio and the priest beheld from behind the bushes, and did not know how to contrive to join companies: but the priest, who was a grand schemist, soon hit upon an expedient; which was, that with a pair of scissors, which he carried in a case, he whipped off Cardenio's beard in an instant; then put him on a grey capouch, and gave him his own black cloak, himself remaining in his breeches and doublet: and now Cardenio made so different a figure from what he did before that he would not have known himself, though he had looked in a glass. This being done, though the others were got a good way before them, while they were thus disguising themselves, they easily got first into the high road; for the rockiness and narrowness of the way would not permit those on horseback to go on so fast as those on foot. In short, they got into the plain at the foot of the mountain; and, when Don Quixote and his company came out, the priest set himself to gaze at him very earnestly for some time, giving signs as if he began to know him: and, after he had stood a pretty while viewing him, he ran to him with open arms, crying aloud:

'In an happy hour are you met, mirror of chivalry, my noble countryman Don Quixote de la Mancha, the flower and cream of gentility, the shelter and relief of the needy, the quintessence of knights-errant!'

And, in saying this he embraced Don Quixote by the knee of his left leg; who being amazed at what he saw and heard, set himself to consider him attentively: at length he knew him, and was surprised to see him, and made no small effort to alight. But the priest would not suffer it: whereupon Don Quixote said:

'Permit me, señor licentiate, to alight; for it is not fit I should be on horseback, and so reverend a person as your worship on foot.'

'I will by no means consent to it,' said the priest: 'let your greatness continue on horseback; for on horseback you achieve the greatest exploits and adventures that our age hath beheld: as for me, who am a priest, though unworthy, it will suffice me to get up behind some one of these gentlemen, who travel with you, if it be not too troublesome to them; and I shall fancy myself mounted on Pegasus, or on a zebra, or the sprightly courser bestrode by the famous Moor Muzaraque, who lies to this day enchanted in the great mountain Zulema, not far distant from the grand Compluto.'*

'I did not think of that, dear Señor Licentiate,' said Don Quixote; 'and I know my lady the princess will, for my sake, order her squire to accommodate you with the saddle of his mule; and he may ride behind, if the beast will carry double.'

'I believe she will,' answered the princess; 'and I know it will be needless to lay my commands upon my squire; for he is so courteous and well-bred, that he will not suffer any ecclesiastic to go on foot, when he may ride.'

'Very true,' answered the barber; and, alighting in an instant, he complimented the priest with the saddle, which he accepted of without much entreaty. But it unluckily happened, that, as the barber was getting up behind, the mule, which was no other than a hackney, and consequently a vicious jade, flung up her hind legs twice or thrice into the air; and, had they met with master Nicholas's breast or head, he would have given his coming for Don Quixote to the devil. However, he was so frighted, that he tumbled to the ground, with so little heed of his beard, that it fell off: and perceiving himself without it, he had no other shift but to cover his face with both hands, and to cry out that his jaw-bone was broke. Don Quixote, seeing that bundle of a beard, without jaws, and without blood, lying at a distance from the face of the fallen squire, said:

'Odds life! this is very wonderful! no barber could have shaved off his beard more clean and smooth.'

The priest, who saw the danger their project was in of being discovered, immediately picked up the beard, and ran with it to master Nicholas, who still lay bemoaning himself; and, holding his head close to his breast, at one jerk he fixed it on again, muttering over him some words, which he said were a specific charm for fastening on beards, as they should soon see: and, when all was adjusted, he left him, and the squire remained as well-bearded, and as whole, as before: at which Don Quixote marvelled greatly, and desired the priest, when he had leisure, to teach him that charm; for he was of opinion, that its virtue must extend further than to the fastening on of beards, since it was clear, that, where the beard was torn off, the flesh must be left wounded and bloody, and since it wrought a perfect cure, it must be good for other things besides beards.

'It is so,' said the priest, and promised to teach it him the very first opportunity.

They now agreed, that the priest should get up first, and that they should all three ride by turns, until they came to the inn, which was about two leagues off. The three being mounted, that is to say, Don Quixote, the princess, and the priest; and the other three on foot, to wit, Cardenio, the barber, and Sancho Panza; Don Quixote said to the damsel:

'Your grandeur, madam, will be pleased to lead on which way you like best.'

And, before she could reply, the licentiate said:

'Towards what kingdom would your ladyship go? towards that of Micomicon, I presume, for it must be thither, or I know little of kingdoms.'

She, being perfect in her lessons, knew very well she was to answer Yes, and therefore said:

'Yes, señor, my way lies towards that kingdom.'

'If it be so,' said the priest, 'we must pass through our village, and from thence you must go straight to Carthagena, where you may take shipping in God's name; and, if you have a fair wind, a smooth sea, and no storms, in little less than nine years, you may get sight of the great lake Meona, I mean Meotis,* which is little more than a hundred days' journey on this side of your highness's kingdom.'

'You are mistaken, good sir,' said she; 'for it is not two years since I left it; and though, in truth, I had very bad weather during the whole passage, I am already got hither, and behold with my eyes, what I so much longed for, namely, Señor Don Quixote de la Mancha, the fame of whose valour reached my ears the moment I set foot in Spain, and put me upon finding him out, that I might recommend myself to his courtesy, and commit the justice of my cause to the valour of his invincible arm.'

'No more; cease your compliments,' said Don Quixote, 'for I am an enemy to all sort of flattery, and though this be not such, still my chaste ears are offended at this kind of discourse. What I can say, dear madam, is, that, whether I have valour or not, what I have or have not, shall be employed in your service, even to the loss of my life: and so, leaving these things to a proper time, I desire, that the señor licentiate would tell me, what has brought him into these parts, so alone, so unattended, and so lightly clad, that I am surprised at it.'

'To this I shall answer briefly,' replied the priest. 'Your worship, then, is to know, Señor Don Quixote, that I, and Master Nicholas, our friend and barber, were going to Seville, to receive some moneys, which a relation of mine, who went many years ago to the Indies, had sent me: and it was no inconsiderable sum; for it was about sixty thousand pieces of eight, all of due weight, which is no trivial matter; and passing yesterday through these parts, we were set upon by four highway robbers, who stripped us of all we had to our very beards, and in such a manner, that the barber thought it expedient to put on a counterfeit one: and, as for this youth here (pointing to Cardenio), you see how they have transformed his. And the best of the story is, that it is publicly reported hereabouts, that the persons who robbed us, were certain galley-slaves, who, they say, were set at liberty near this very place, by a man so valiant, that in spite of the commissary and all his guards, he let them all loose: and, without all doubt, he must needs have been out of his senses, or as great a rogue as they, or one void of all conscience and humanity, that could let loose the wolf among the sheep, the fox among the hens, and the wasps among the honey. He has defrauded justice of her due, and has set himself up against his king and natural lord, by acting against his lawful authority: he has, I say, disabled the galleys of their feet,* and disturbed the many years' repose of the Holy Brotherhood: in a word, he has done a deed whereby he may lose his soul, and not gain his body.'

Sancho had related to the priest and the barber the adventure of the galley-slaves, achieved with so much glory by his master; and therefore the priest laid it on thick in the relation, to see what Don Quixote would do, or say: whose colour changed at every word, and yet he durst not own, that he had been the deliverer of those worthy gentlemen.

'These,' said the priest, 'were the persons who robbed us; and God of his mercy pardon him, who prevented their being carried to the punishment they so richly deserved.'

CHAPTER 30

Which treats of the pleasant and ingenious method of drawing our enamoured knight from the very rigorous penance he had imposed on himself.

SCARCE had the priest done speaking, when Sancho said:

'By my troth, señor licentiate, it was my master who did this feat; not but that I gave him fair warning and advised him to beware what he did, and that it was a sin to set them at liberty, for that they were all going to the galleys for being most notorious villains.'

'Blockhead,' said Don Quixote, 'knights-errant have nothing to do, nor does it concern them, to inquire whether the afflicted, enchained, and oppressed, whom they meet upon the road, are reduced to those circumstances, or that distress, by their faults or their misfortunes: they are bound to assist them merely as being in distress, and to regard their sufferings alone, and not their crimes. I lighted on a bead-roll and string of miserable wretches, and did by them what my profession requires of me;* and for the rest I care not: and whoever takes it amiss, saving the holy dignity of Señor the Licentiate, and his honourable person, I say, he knows little of the principles of chivalry, and lies like the base-born son of a whore: and this I will make good with my sword in the most ample manner.'

This he said, setting himself in his stirrups, and clapping down the visor of his helmet; for the barber's basin, which, in his account, was Mambrino's helmet, hung at his saddle-bow, until it could be repaired of the damages it had received from the galley-slaves.

Dorothea, who was witty, and of a pleasant disposition, already perceiving Don Quixote's frenzy, and that everybody, excepting Sancho Panza, made a jest of him, resolved not to be behind-hand with the rest; and seeing him in such a heat, said to him:

'Sir knight, be pleased to remember the boon you have promised me, and that you are thereby engaged not to intermeddle in any other adventure, be it ever so urgent: therefore assuage your wrath; for, if Señor the Licentiate had

known that the galley-slaves were freed by that invincible
arm, he would sooner have sewed up his mouth with three
stitches, and thrice have bit his tongue, than he would have
said a word that might redound to the disparagement of your
worship.'

'I would so, I swear,' quoth the priest, 'and even sooner
have pulled off a moustache.'

'I will say no more, madam,' said Don Quixote; 'and I will
repress that just indignation raised in my breast, and will go
on peaceably and quietly, until I have accomplished for you
the promised boon. But in requital of this good intention, I
beseech you to tell me, if it be not too much trouble, what
is your grievance, and who, how many, and of what sort, are
the persons, on whom I must take, due, satisfactory, and
complete revenge.'

'That I will do, with all my heart,' answered Dorothea, 'if
it will not prove tedious and irksome to you to hear nothing
but afflictions and misfortunes.'

'Not at all, dear madam,' answered Don Quixote.

To which Dorothea replied:

'Since it is so, pray favour me with your attention.'

She had no sooner said this, but Cardenio and the barber
placed themselves on each side of her, to hear what kind of
a story the ingenious Dorothea would invent. The same did
Sancho, who was as much deceived about her as his master.
And she, after settling herself well in her saddle, with a hem
or two, and the like preparatory airs, began, with much good
humour, in the manner following:

'In the first place, you must know, gentlemen, that my
name is—' Here she stopped short, having forgot the name
the priest had given her: but he presently helped her out; for
he knew what she stopped at, and said:

'It is no wonder, madam, that your grandeur should be
disturbed, and in some confusion, at recounting your misfortunes; for they are often of such a nature, as to deprive us
of our memory, and make us forget our very names; as they
have now done by your high ladyship, who have forgotten
that you are called the Princess Micomicona, rightful heiress
of the great kingdom of Micomicon: and with this intimation

your grandeur may easily bring back to your doleful remembrance whatever you have a mind to relate.'

'You are in the right,' answered Dorothea, 'and henceforward I believe it will be needless to give me any more hints; for I shall be able to conduct my true history to a conclusion without them.

'My father, who was called Tinacrio the Wise, was very learned in what they call the magic art, and knew, by his science, that my mother, who was called Queen Xaramilla, would die before him, and that he himself must, soon after, depart this life, and I be left an orphan, deprived both of father and mother. But this, he used to say, did not trouble him so much, as the certain fore-knowledge he had, that a monstrous giant, lord of a great island, almost bordering upon our kingdom, called Pandafilando of the Gloomy Aspect* (for it is averred, that though his eyes stand right, and in their proper place, he always looks askew as if he squinted; and this he does out of pure malignity, to scare and frighten those he looks at): I say, he knew that this giant would take the advantage of my being an orphan, and invade my kingdom with a mighty force, and take it all from me, without leaving me the smallest village to hide my head in: but that it was in my power to avoid all this ruin and misfortune, by marrying him; though, as far as he could understand, he never believed I would hearken to so unequal a match; and in this he said the truth, for it never entered into my head to marry this giant, nor any other, though never so huge and unmeasureable. My father said also, that, after his death, when I should find Pandafilando begin to invade my kingdom, he advised me not to stay to make any defence, for that would be my ruin; but, if I would avoid death, and prevent the total destruction of my faithful and loyal subjects, my best way was, freely to quit the kingdom to him without opposition, since it would not be possible for me to defend myself against the hellish power of the giant; and immediately to set out with a few attendants for Spain, where I should find a remedy for my distress, by meeting with a knight-errant, whose fame, about that time, should extend itself all over this kingdom, and whose name, if I remember right, was to be Don Açote, or Don Gigote.'

'Don Quixote, you would say, madam,' quoth Sancho Panza, 'or as others call him, the Knight of the Sorrowful Figure.'

'You are in the right,' said Dorothea. 'He said further, that he was to be tall and thin-visaged, and that on his right side under the left shoulder, or thereabouts, he was to have a grey mole with hairs like bristles.'

Don Quixote, hearing this, said to his squire; 'Here, son Sancho, help me to strip: I would know whether, I am the knight prophesied of by that wise king.'

'Why would you pull off your clothes, sir?' said Dorothea.

'To see whether I have the mole your father spoke of,' answered Don Quixote.

'You need not strip,' said Sancho; 'I know you have a mole with those same marks on the ridge of your back, which is a sign of being a strong man.'

'It is enough,' said Dorothea; 'for, among friends, we must not stand upon trifles; and whether it be on the shoulder, or on the back-bone, imports little: it is sufficient that there is a mole, let it be where it will, since it is all the same flesh: and doubtless my good father hit right in everything, and I have not aimed amiss in recommending myself to Señor Don Quixote; for he must be the knight, of whom my father spoke, since the features of his face correspond exactly with the great fame he has acquired, not only in Spain, but in all La Mancha: for I was hardly landed in Osuna, before I heard so many exploits of his recounted, that my mind immediately gave me, that he must be the very person I came to seek.'

'But, dear madam, how came you to land at Osuna?' answered Don Quixote, 'since it is no seaport town.'

But, before Dorothea could reply, the priest interposing, said:

'Doubtless the princess meant to say, that, after she had landed at Málaga, the first place where she heard news of your worship, was Osuna.'

'That was my meaning,' said Dorothea.

'It is very likely,' quoth the priest; 'please your majesty to proceed.'

'I have little more to add,' replied Dorothea, 'but that, having at last had the good fortune to meet with Señor Don

Quixote, I already look upon myself as queen and mistress of my whole kingdom, since he, out of his courtesy and generosity, has promised, in compliance with my request, to go with me wherever I please to carry him; which shall be only where he may have a sight of Pandafilando of the Gloomy Aspect, that he may slay him, and restore to me what is so unjustly usurped from me: for all this is to come about with the greatest ease, according to the prophecy of the wise Tinacrio, my good father; who, moreover, left it written in letters Chaldean or Greek (for I cannot read them) that, if this knight of the prophecy, after he has cut off the giant's head, should have a mind to marry me, I should immediately submit to be his lawful wife, without any reply, and give him possession of my kingdom, together with my person.'

'What think you now, friend Sancho?' quoth Don Quixote; 'do you not hear what passes; did not I tell you so? see whether we have not now a kingdom to command, and a queen to marry?'

'I swear it is so,' quoth Sancho; 'and pox take him for a son of a whore, who will not marry as soon as Señor Pandafilando's weasand* is cut. About it then; her majesty's a dainty bit; I wish all the fleas in my bed were no worse.'

And so saying he cut a couple of capers, with signs of very great joy; and presently laying hold of the reins of Dorothea's mule, and making her stop, he fell down upon his knees before her, beseeching her to give him her hand to kiss, in token that he acknowledged her for his queen and mistress. Which of the bystanders could forbear laughing, to see the madness of the master, and the simplicity of the man? In short, Dorothea held out her hand to him, and promised to make him a great lord in her kingdom, when heaven should be so propitious, as to put her again in possession of it. Sancho returned her thanks in such expressions, as to set the company again a-laughing.

'This, gentlemen,' continued Dorothea, 'is my history: it remains only to tell you, that, of all the attendants I brought with me out of my kingdom, I have none left but this honest squire with the long beard; for the rest were all drowned in a violent storm, which overtook us in sight of the port. He

and I got ashore on a couple of planks as it were by miracle;
and indeed the whole progress of my life is miracle and
mystery, as you may have observed. And if I have exceeded
in anything, or not been so exact as I ought to have been,
let it be imputed to what Señor the Licentiate said, at the
beginning of my story, that continual and extraordinary troubles deprive the sufferers of their very memory.'

'I will preserve mine, O high and worthy lady,' said Don
Quixote, 'under the greatest that can befall me in your service:
and so I again confirm the promise I have made you, and I
swear to bear you company to the end of the world, until I
come to grapple with that fierce enemy of yours, whose proud
head I intend, by the help of God, and of this my arm, to
cut off, with the edge of this (I will not say good) sword;
thanks to Gines de Pasamonte, who carried off my own.'*

This he muttered between his teeth, and went on saying:

'And after having cut it off, and put you into peaceable
possession of your dominions, it shall be left to your own
will to dispose of your person as you shall think proper;
since, while my memory is taken up, my will enthralled, and
my understanding subjected to her—I say no more, it is
impossible I should prevail upon myself so much as to think
of marrying, though it were a phoenix.'

What Don Quixote said last, about not marrying, was so
displeasing to Sancho, that, in a great fury, he said, raising
his voice:

'I vow and swear, Señor Don Quixote, your worship cannot
be in your right senses; how else is it possible you should
scruple to marry so high a princess as this lady is? think you,
fortune is to offer you at every turn such good luck as she
now offers? is my lady Dulcinea more beautiful? no indeed,
not by half? nay, I could almost say, she is not worthy to
tie this lady's shoe-string. I am like, indeed, to get the earldom
I expect, if your worship stands fishing for mushrooms in
the bottom of the sea. Marry, marry out of hand, in the
devil's name, and take this kingdom that is ready to drop
into your mouth; and, when you are a king, make me a
marquess, or a lord-lieutenant, and then the devil take all the
rest if he will.'

Don Quixote, hearing such blasphemies against his lady Dulcinea, could not bear it, and, lifting up his lance, without speaking a word to Sancho, or giving him the least warning, gave him two such blows, that he laid him flat on the ground; and, had not Dorothea called out to him to hold his hand, doubtless he had killed him there upon the spot.

'Thinkest thou,' said he to him, after some pause, 'pitiful scoundrel, that I am always to stand with my hands in my pockets, and that there is, nothing to be done but transgressing on thy side, and pardoning on mine? Never think it, excommunicated varlet; for so doubtless thou art, since thou hast dared to speak ill of the peerless Dulcinea. Knowest thou not, rustic, slave, beggar, that, were it not for the force she infuses into my arm, I should not have enough to kill a flea? Tell me, envenomed scoffer, who thinkest thou has gained this kingdom, and cut off the head of this giant, and made thee a marquess (for all this I look upon as already done) but the valour of Dulcinea, employing my arms as the instrument of her exploits? She fights in me, and overcomes in me: and in her I live and breathe, and of her I hold my life and being. O whoreson villain! what ingratitude, when thou seest thyself exalted from the dust of the earth to the title of a lord, to make so base a return for so great a benefit, as to speak contemptuously of the hand that raised thee!'

Sancho was not so much hurt, but he heard all his master said to him; and, getting up pretty nimbly, he ran behind Dorothea's palfrey, and from thence said to his master:

'Pray, sir, tell me; if you are resolved not to marry this princess, it is plain the kingdom will not be yours, and then what favours will you be able to bestow on me? this is what I complain of. Marry her, Sir, once for all, now we have her, as it were, rained down upon us from heaven, and afterwards you may converse with my lady Dulcinea; for, I think it is no new thing for kings to keep mistresses. As to the matter of beauty, I have nothing to say to that; for, if I must speak the truth, I really think them both very well to pass, though I never saw the lady Dulcinea.'

'How! never saw her, blasphemous traitor!' said Don Quixote: 'have you not just brought me a message from her?'

'I say, I did not see her so leisurely,' said Sancho, 'as to take particular notice of her beauty, and her features, piece by piece; but take her altogether, she looks well enough.'

'Now I excuse you,' said Don Quixote, 'and pardon me the displeasure I have given you; for the first motions are not in our own power.'

'I have found it so,' answered Sancho; 'and so, in me, the desire of talking is always a first motion, and I cannot forbear uttering, for once at least, whatever comes to my tongue's end.'

'For all that,' quoth Don Quixote, 'take heed, Sancho, what it is you utter; for the pitcher goes so often to the well—I say no more.'

'Well, then,' answered Sancho, 'God is in heaven, who sees all guiles, and shall be a judge who does most harm, I, in not speaking well, or your worship in not doing so.'

'Let there be no more of this,' said Dorothea; 'run Sancho and kiss your master's hand, and ask him forgiveness; and henceforward go more warily to work with your praises and dispraises; and speak no ill of that lady Toboso, whom I do not know any otherwise than as I am her humble servant; and put your trust in God, for there will not be wanting an estate for you to live upon like a prince.'

Sancho went, hanging his head, and begged his master's hand, which he gave him with great gravity; and, when he had kissed it, Don Quixote gave Sancho his blessing, and told him he would have him get on a little before, for he had some questions to put to him, and wanted to talk with him about some matters of great consequence. Sancho did so: and, when they two were got a little before the rest, Don Quixote said:

'Since your return, I have had neither opportunity nor leisure to inquire after many particulars concerning the message you carried, and the answer you brought back; and now, that fortune affords us time and leisure, do not deny me the satisfaction you may give me by such good news.'

'Ask me what questions you please, sir,' answered Sancho: 'I warrant I shall get out as well as I got in. But I beseech your worship, dear sir, not to be so very revengeful for the future.'

'Why do you press that, Sancho?' quoth Don Quixote.

'Because,' replied Sancho, 'the blows you were pleased to bestow on me, even now, were rather on account of the quarrel the devil raised between us the other night,* than for what I said against my lady Dulcinea, whom I love and reverence, like any relic (though she be not one), only as she belongs to your worship.'

'No more of these discourses, Sancho, on your life,' said Don Quixote; 'for they offend me: I forgave you before, and you know the common saying, "For a new sin a new penance."'*

While they were thus talking, they saw coming along the same road, in which they were going, a man riding upon an ass; and when he came near, he seemed to be a gipsy: but Sancho Panza, who, wherever he saw an ass, had his eyes and his soul fixed there, had scarce seen the man, when he knew him to be Gines de Pasamonte, and, by the clue of the gipsy, found the bottom of his ass: for it was really Dapple, upon which Pasamonte rode; who, that he might not be known, and that he might sell the ass the better, had put himself into the garb of a gipsy, whose language, as well as several others, he could speak as readily, as if they were his own native tongues. Sancho saw and knew him; and scarce had he seen and known him, when he cried out to him aloud:

'Ah, rogue Ginesillo, leave my darling, let go my life, rob me not of my repose, quit my ass, leave my delight; fly, whoreson; get you gone, thief, and relinquish what is not your own.'

There needed not so many words, nor so much railing: for, at the first word, Gines nimbly dismounted, and, taking to his heels, as if it had been a race, was gone in an instant, and out of reach of them all. Sancho ran to his Dapple, and, embracing him, said:

'How hast thou done, my dearest Dapple, delight of my eyes, my sweet companion'?

And then he kissed and caressed him as if he had been a human creature. The ass held his peace, and suffered himself to be kissed and caressed by Sancho, without answering him one word. They all came up, and wished him joy of the finding his Dapple; especially Don Quixote, who assured him that he did not, for all this, revoke the order for the three colts. Sancho thanked him heartily.

While this passed, the priest said to Dorothea, that she had performed her part very ingeniously, as well in the contrivance of the story, as in its brevity, and the resemblance it bore to the narrations in books of chivalry. She said, she had often amused herself with reading such kind of books, but that she did not know the situation of provinces or of seaports, and therefore had said at a venture, that she landed at Osuna.

'I found it was so,' said the priest, 'and therefore I immediately said what you heard, which set all to rights. But is it not strange to see how readily this unhappy gentleman believes all these inventions and lies, only because they resemble the style and manner of his foolish books?'

'It is indeed,' said Cardenio, 'and something so rare, and unseen before, that I much question, whether, if one had a mind to dress up a fiction like it, any genius could be found capable of succeeding in it.'

'There is another thing remarkable in it,' said the priest, 'which is, that, setting aside the follies this honest gentleman utters in everything relating to his madness, he can discourse very sensibly upon other points, and seems to have a clear and settled judgement in all things; insomuch that, if you do not touch him upon the subject of chivalries you would never suspect but that he had a sound understanding.'

While the rest went on in this conversation, Don Quixote proceeded in his, and said to Sancho:

'Friend Panza, let us forget what is past; and tell me now, all rancour and animosity apart, where, how, and when, did you find Dulcinea? what was she doing? what did you say to her? what answer did she return? how did she look when she read my letter? who transcribed it for you? and whatever else in this case is worth knowing, inquiring after, or being satisfied in, inform me of all, without adding or diminishing, to give me pleasure, or curtailing aught to deprive me of any satisfaction.'

'Sir,' answered Sancho, 'if I must tell you the truth, nobody transcribed the letter for me; for I carried no letter at all.'

'It is as you say,' quoth Don Quixote; 'for I found the pocket-book I had written it in, two days after your departure; which troubled me exceedingly, not knowing what you would do, when you should find you had no letter; and I still believed you would come back, as soon as you should miss it.'

'So I should have done,' answered Sancho, 'had I not got it by heart, when your worship read it me, and so perfectly, that I repeated it to a parish clerk, who wrote it down, as I dictated it, so exactly, that he said, though he had read many letters of excommunication, he had never seen or read so pretty a letter as that in all the days of his life.'

'And have you it still by heart, Sancho?' said Don Quixote.

'No, sir,' answered Sancho: 'for after I had delivered it, seeing it was to be of no further use, I forgot it on purpose; and if I remember aught of it, it is that of "the high and subterrane (I mean sovereign) lady", and the conclusion, "thine until death, the Knight of the Sorrowful Figure"; and between these two things, I put above three hundred souls and lives, and dear eyes.'*

CHAPTER 31

Of the relishing conversation which passed between Don Quixote and his squire Sancho Panza, with other incidents.

'ALL this does not displease me; go on,' said Don Quixote. 'You arrived; and what was that queen of beauty doing? Without doubt, you found her stringing pearls, or embroidering some device with threads of gold for this her captive knight.'

'No, I did not,' answered Sancho; 'but I found her winnowing two bushels of wheat in a backyard of her house.'

'Then make account,' said Don Quixote, 'that the grains of that wheat were so many grains of pearl, when touched by her hands. And did you take notice, friend, whether the wheat was fine, or the ordinary sort?'

'It was neither,' answered Sancho, 'but of the reddish kind.'

'Be assured, however,' quoth Don Quixote, 'that, when winnowed by her hands, it certainly made the finest manchet bread—but go on. When you gave her my letter, did she kiss it? Did she put it upon her head? Did she use any ceremony worthy of such a letter? or what did she do?'

'When I was going to give it her,' answered Sancho, 'she was very busy in winnowing a good sieve full of the wheat; and she said to me: "Lay the letter, friend, upon the sack, for I cannot read it until I have done winnowing all that is here."'

'Discreet lady!' said Don Quixote; 'this was, to be sure, that she might read it, and entertain herself with it, at leisure. Proceed, Sancho: while she was thus employed, what discourse had she with you? what did she inquire of you concerning me? and what did you answer? Make an end, tell it me all; leave nothing at the bottom of the inkhorn.'

'She asked me nothing,' said Sancho; 'but I told her how your worship was doing penance, for her service, among these rocks, naked from the waist upwards, as if you were a savage, sleeping on the ground, not eating bread on a napkin, nor combing your beard, weeping and cursing your fortune.'

'In saying that I cursed my fortune, you said amiss,' quoth Don Quixote: 'I rather bless it, and shall bless it all the days of my life, for having made me worthy to love so high a lady as Dulcinea del Toboso.'

'So high indeed,' answered Sancho, 'that in good faith, she is a handful taller than I am.'

'Why, how, Sancho,' said Don Quixote, 'have you measured with her?'

'I measured thus,' answered Sancho: 'as I was helping her to put a sack of wheat upon an ass, we stood so close, that I perceived she was taller than I by more than a full span.'

'If it be so,' replied Don Quixote, 'does she not accompany and set off this stature of her body with a thousand millions of graces of the mind? But Sancho, conceal not one thing from me: when you stood so near her, did you not perceive a Sabaean odour, an aromatic fragrancy, and something so sweet, that I know not what name to give it? I say, a scent, a smell, as if you were in some curious glover's shop?'

'All I can say is,' quoth Sancho, 'that I perceived somewhat of a mannish smell, which must have proceeded from her being in a dripping sweat with overmuch painstaking.'

'It could not be so,' answered Don Quixote: 'you must either have had a cold in your head, or have smelt your own self: for I very well know the scent of that rose among thorns, that lily of the valley, that liquid amber.'

'All that may be,' answered Sancho; 'for the same smell often comes from me, as, methought, then came from my lady Dulcinea; but where's the wonder, that one devil should be like another?'

'Well then,' continued Don Quixote, 'she has now done winnowing, and the corn is sent to the mill. What did she do, when she had read the letter?'

'The letter,' quoth Sancho, 'she did not read; for she told me she could neither read nor write: on the contrary, she tore it to pieces, saying, she would not give it to anybody to read, that her secrets might not be known in the village: and that what I had told her by word of mouth, concerning the love your worship bore her, and the extraordinary penance you were doing for her sake, was enough: lastly, she bid me tell your worship that she kissed your hands, and that she remained with greater desire to see you than to write to you; and therefore she humbly entreated, and commanded you, at sight hereof, to quit those brakes and bushes, and leave off those foolish extravagances, and set out immediately for Toboso, if some other business of greater importance did not intervene; for she had a mighty mind to see your worship. She laughed heartily when I told her how you called yourself the Knight of the Sorrowful Figure. I asked her whether the Biscainer of t'other day had been there with her: she told me he had, and that he was a very honest fellow: I asked her also after the galley-slaves; but she told me she had not yet seen any of them.'

'All goes well, as yet,' said Don Quixote. 'But, tell me, what jewel did she give you at your departure for the news you had brought her of me? For it is an usual and ancient custom among knights- and ladies-errant to bestow some rich jewel on the squires, damsels, or dwarfs, who bring them news of their mistresses or servants, as a reward or acknowledgement for their welcome news.'

'Very likely,' quoth Sancho, 'and a very good custom it was; but it must have been in days of yore, for nowadays the custom is to give only a piece of bread and cheese: for that was what my lady Dulcinea gave me, over the pales of the yard, when she dismissed me; by the same token that the cheese was made of sheep's milk.'

'She is extremely generous,' said Don Quixote; 'and if she did not give you a jewel of gold, it must be because she had not one about her: but sleeves are good after Easter.* I shall see her, and all shall be set to rights.

'But, do you know, Sancho, what I am surprised at? it is, that you must have gone and come through the air; for you have been little more than three days in going and coming, between this and Toboso, though it is more than thirty leagues from hence thither; from whence I conclude that the sage enchanter, who has the superintendence of my affairs, and is my friend (for such a one there is, and must of necessity be, otherwise I should be no true knight-errant), I say, this same enchanter must have assisted you in travelling, without your perceiving it: for there are sages, who will take you up a knight-errant sleeping in his bed; and, without his knowing how, or in what manner, he awakes the next day above a thousand leagues from the place where he fell asleep. And, were it not for this, the knights-errant could not succour one another in their dangers, as they now do at every turn. For a knight happens to be fighting, in the mountains of Armenia, with some dreadful monster, or fierce goblin, or some other knight, and has the worst of the combat, and is just upon the point of being killed; and, when he least expects it, there appears upon a cloud, or in a chariot of fire, another knight, his friend, who just before was in England, who succours him, and delivers him from death; and that night he finds himself in his own chamber, supping with a very good appetite, though there be the distance of two or three thousand leagues between the two countries. And all this is brought about by the industry and skill of those sage enchanters, who undertake the care of those valorous knights. So that, friend Sancho, I make no difficulty in believing that you went and came in so short a time, between this place and Toboso, since, as I have already said, some sage, our friend, must have expedited your journey without your being sensible of it.'

'It may be so,' quoth Sancho; 'for, in good faith, Rosinante went like any gipsy's ass with quicksilver in his ears.'

'With quicksilver!' said Don Quixote, 'aye, and with a legion of devils to boot; a sort of cattle that travel, and make others travel, as fast as they please without being tired.

'But, setting this aside, what would you advise me to do now, as to what my lady commands me, about going to see her? for, though I know I am bound to obey her commands, I find myself at present under an impossibility of doing it, on account of the boon I have promised to grant the princess, who is now with us; and the laws of chivalry oblige me to comply with my word, rather than indulge my pleasure. On the one hand, the desire of seeing my lady persecutes and perplexes me: on the other, I am incited and called by my promised faith, and the glory I shall acquire in this enterprise. But what I propose to do, is to travel fast, and get quickly to the place where this giant is, and, presently after my arrival, to cut off his head, and settle the princess peaceably in her kingdom, and that instant to return and see that sun that enlightens my senses; to whom I will make such an excuse, that she shall allow my delay was necessary; for she will perceive that all redounds to the increase of her glory and fame, since what I have won, do win, or shall win, by force of arms, in this life, proceeds wholly from the succour she affords me, and from my being hers.'

'Ah!' quoth Sancho, 'how is your worship disordered in your head! Pray, tell me, sir, do you intend to take this journey for nothing? and will you let slip so considerable a match as this, when the dowry is a kingdom, which, as I have heard say, is above twenty thousand leagues in circumference, and abounding in all things necessary for the support of human life, and bigger than Portugal and Castile together?

For the love of God, say no more, and take shame to yourself
for what you have said already; and follow my advice, and
pardon me, and be married out of hand at the first place
where there is a priest; and, if there be none, here is our
licentiate, who will do it cleverly. And pray take notice, I am
of age to give advice, and what I now give is as fit as if it
were cast in a mould for you; for a sparrow in the hand is
worth more than a bustard on the wing; and he that may
have good if he will, it is his own fault if he chooses ill.'

'Look you, Sancho,' replied Don Quixote, 'if you advise
me to marry, that, by killing the giant, I may immediately
become a king, and have it in my power to reward you by
giving you what I promised you, I would have you to know,
that, without marrying, I can easily gratify your desire: for I
will convenant before I enter into the battle, that, upon my
coming off victorious, without marrying the princess, I shall
be entitled to a part of the kingdom to bestow it on whom
I please; and when I have it, to whom do you think I should
give it, but to yourself?'

'That is clear,' answered Sancho: 'but pray, sir, take care
to choose it toward the sea, that, if I should not like living
there, I may ship off my black subjects, and dispose of them
as I said before. And trouble not yourself now to go and see
my lady Dulcinea, but go and kill the giant, and let us make
an end of this business; for, before God, I verily believe it
will bring us much honour and profit.'

'You are in the right, Sancho,' said Don Quixote, 'and I
take your advice as to going first with the princess, before I
go to see Dulcinea. And be sure you say nothing to anybody,
no, not to those who are in our company, of what we have
been discoursing and conferring upon: for since Dulcinea is
so reserved that she would not have her thoughts known, it
is not fit that I, or any one else for me, should discover
them.'

'If it be so,' quoth Sancho, 'why does your worship send
all those you conquer by the might of your arm, to present
themselves before my lady Dulcinea, this being to give it
under your hand that you are in love with her? If these
persons must fall on their knees before her, and declare they

come from you to pay their obeisance to her, how can your mutual inclinations be a secret?'

'How dull and foolish you are!' said Don Quixote. 'You perceive not, Sancho, that all this redounds the more to her exaltation. For you must know, that in this is our style of chivalry, it is a great honour for a lady to have many knights-errant, who serve her merely for her own sake, without expectation of any other reward of their manifold and good desires, than the honour of being admitted into the number of her knights.'

'I have heard it preached,' quoth Sancho, 'that God is to be loved with this kind of love, for Himself alone, without our being moved to it by the hope of reward, or the fear of punishment: though for my part, I am inclined to love and serve Him for what He is able to do for me.'

'The devil take you for a bumpkin,' said Don Quixote; 'you are ever and anon saying such smart things, that one would almost think you had studied.'

'And yet, by my faith,' quoth Sancho, 'I cannot so much as read.'

While they were thus talking, Master Nicholas called aloud to them to halt a little; for they had a mind to stop and drink at a small spring hard by. Don Quixote stopped, much to the satisfaction of Sancho, who began to be tired of telling so many lies, and was afraid his master should at last catch him tripping: for, though he knew Dulcinea was a farmer's daughter of Toboso, he had never seen her in all his life. In the meanwhile Cardenio had put on the clothes which Dorothea wore when they found her; and, though they were none of the best, they were far beyond those he had put off. They all alighted near the fountain, and, with what the priest had furnished himself with at the inn, they somewhat appeased the violence of their hunger.

While they were thus employed a young lad happened to pass by, travelling along the road; who, looking very earnestly at those who were at the fountain, presently ran to Don Quixote, and embracing his legs, fell a-weeping in good earnest, and said:

'Ah! dear sir, does not your worship know me? Consider me well: I am Andres, the lad whom you delivered from the oak to which I was tied.'

Don Quixote knew him again, and, taking him by the hand, he turned to the company and said,

'To convince you of what importance it is that there should be knights-errant in the world to redress the wrongs and injuries committed in it by insolent and wicked men; you must know, good people, that a few days ago, as I was passing by a wood, I heard certain outcries, and a very lamentable voice, as of some person in affliction and distress. I hasted immediately, prompted by my duty, toward the place from which the voice seemed to come; and I found, tied to an oak, this lad, whom you see here (I am glad, in my soul, he is present! for he will attest the truth of what I say): I say, he was tied to the oak, naked from the waist upward; and a country-fellow, whom I afterward found to be his master, was cruelly lashing him with the reins of a bridle: and, as soon as I saw it, I asked him the reason of so severe a whipping. The clown answered, that he was his servant, and that he whipped him for some instances of neglect, which proceeded rather from knavery than simplicity. On which this boy said: "Sir, he whips me only because I ask him for my wages." The master replied, with I know not what speeches and excuses, which I heard indeed, but did not admit. In short, I made him untie the boy, and swear to take him home, and pay him every real down upon the nail, and perfumed into the bargain. Is not all this true, son Andres? and did you not observe, with what authority I commanded, and how submissively he promised to do whatever I enjoined, notified and required of him? Answer, be under no concern, but tell these gentlefolks what passed, that they may see and consider how useful it is, as I said, that there should be knights-errant upon the road.'

'All that your worship has said is very true,' answered the lad; 'but the business ended quite otherwise than you imagine.'

'How otherwise?' replied Don Quixote: 'did not the rustic instantly pay you?'

'He not only did not pay me,' answered the boy, 'but as soon as your worship was got out of the wood, and we were left alone, he tied me again to the same tree, and gave me so many fresh strokes, that I was flayed like any Saint Bartholomew; and, at every lash he gave me, he said something by way of scoff or jest upon your worship; at which, if I had not felt so much pain, I could not have forborne laughing. In short, he laid on me in such manner, that I have been ever since in an hospital, under cure of the bruises the barbarous countryman then gave me. And your worship is in the fault of all this; for had you gone on your way, and not come where you was not called, nor meddled with other folks' business, my master would have been satisfied with giving me a dozen or two lashes, and then would have loosed me, and paid me what he owed me. But, by your worship's abusing him so unmercifully, and calling him so many hard names, his wrath was kindled; and, not having it in his power to be revenged on you, no sooner had you left him, but he discharged the tempest upon me, in such sort, that I shall never be a man again while I live.'

'The mischief,' said Don Quixote, 'was in my going away: I should not have stirred until I had seen you paid; for I might have known, by long experience, that no rustic will keep his word, if he finds it inconvenient for him so to do. But you may remember, Andres, that I swore, if he did not pay you, I would seek him out, and find him, though he hid himself in a whale's belly.'

'That is true,' quoth Andres; 'but it signified nothing.'

'You shall see now whether it signifies,' said Don Quixote: and so saying, he arose up very hastily, and ordered Sancho to bridle Rosinante, who was grazing while they were eating. Dorothea asked him what it was he meant to do. He answered, that he would go and find out the rustic, and chastise him for so base a proceeding, and make him pay Andres to the last farthing, in spite and defiance of all the rustics in the world. She desired he would consider what he did, since, according to the promised boon, he could not engage in any other adventure, until he had accomplished hers; and, since he could not but know this better than

anybody else, she entreated him to moderate his resentment
until his return from her kingdom.

'You are in the right,' answered Don Quixote; 'and Andres
must have patience until my return, as you say, madam; and
I again swear and promise not to rest until he is revenged
and paid.'

'I do not depend upon these oaths,' said Andres: 'I
would rather have wherewithal to carry me to Seville, than
all the revenges in the world. If you have anything to give
me to eat, and to carry with me, let me have it; and God
be with your worship, and with all knights-errant, and may
they prove as luckily errant to themselves, as they have
been to me.'

Sancho pulled a piece of bread, and another of cheese, out
of his knapsack, and, giving it to the lad, said to him:

'Here, brother Andres, we all have a share in your misfortune.'

'Why, what share have you in it?' said Andres.

'This piece of bread and cheese which I give you,' answered
Sancho: 'God knows whether I may not want it myself; for
I would have you to know, friend, that we squires to knights-
errant are subject to much hunger, and to ill luck, and to
other things too, which are more easily, conceived than told.'

Andres laid hold on the bread and cheese, and, seeing that
nobody else gave him anything, he made his bow, and
marched off.

'It is true,' he said, at parting, to Don Quixote: 'For the
love of God, Señor Knight-errant, if ever you meet me again,
though you see they are beating me to pieces, do not succour
nor assist me, but leave me to my misfortune, which cannot
be so great, but a greater will follow from your worship's
aid, whom may the curse of God light upon, and upon all
the knights-errant that ever were born in the world.'

Don Quixote was getting up to chastise him; but he fell
a-running so fast, that nobody offered to pursue him. Don
Quixote was mightily abashed at Andres's story: and the rest
were forced to refrain, though with some difficulty, from
laughing, that they might not put him quite out of countenance.

CHAPTER 32

*Which treats of what befell Don Quixote's whole company
in the inn.*

THE notable repast being ended, they saddled immediately,
and, without anything happening to them worthy to be
related, they arrived the next day at the inn, that dread and
terror of Sancho Panza, who, though he would fain have
declined going in, could not avoid it. The hostess, the host,
their daughter, and Maritornes, seeing Don Quixote and
Sancho coming, went out to meet them, with signs of much
joy; and he received them with a grave deportment, and a
nod of approbation, bidding them prepare him a better bed
than they had done the time before: to which the hostess
answered, that, provided he would pay better than the time
before, she would get him a bed for a prince. Don Quixote
said he would; and so they made him a tolerable one in the
same large room where he had lain before: and he immediately threw himself down upon it; for he arrived very much
shattered both in body and brains. He was no sooner shut
into his chamber, but the hostess fell upon the barber, and
taking him by the beard, said:

'By my faith, you shall use my tail no longer for a beard:
give me my tail again; for my husband's thing is tossed up
and down, that it is a shame; I mean the comb I used to
stick in my good tail.'

The barber would not part with it, for all her tugging, until
the licentiate bade him give it her; for there was no farther
need of that artifice, but he might now discover himself, and
appear in his own shape, and tell Don Quixote, that being
robbed by those thieves the galley-slaves, he had fled to this
inn; and, if he should ask for the princess's squire, they
should tell him, she had dispatched him before with advice to
her subjects, that she was coming, and bringing with her their
common deliverer. With this the barber willingly surrendered
to the hostess the tail, together with all the other appurtenances she had lent them, for Don Quixote's deliverance.

All the folks of the inn were surprised, both at the beauty
of Dorothea, and the comely personage of the shepherd

Cardenio. The priest ordered them to get ready what the house afforded, and the host, in hopes of being better paid, soon served a pretty tolerable supper. All this while Don Quixote was asleep, and they agreed not to awake him: for at that time he had more occasion for sleep than victuals.

The discourse at supper, at which were present the inn-keeper, his wife, his daughter, and Maritornes, and all the passengers, turned upon the strange madness of Don Quixote, and the condition in which they had found him. The hostess related to them what befell him with the carrier; and looking about to see whether Sancho was by, and not seeing him, she gave them a full account of his being tossed in a blanket, at which they were not a little diverted. And the priest happened to say, that the books of chivalry, which Don Quixote had read, had turned his brain, the innkeeper said:

'I cannot conceive how that can be; for really, as far as I can understand, there is no choicer reading in the world; and I have by me three or four of them, with some manuscripts, which, in good truth, have kept me alive, and not me only, but many others beside. For, in the harvest time, many of the reapers come hither every day for shelter, during the noonday heat; and there is always one or other among them that can read, who takes one of these books in hand, and about thirty of us place ourselves round him, and listen to him with so much pleasure that it prevents a thousand hoary hairs: at least I can say for myself, that, when I hear of those furious and terrible blows, which the knights-errant lay on, I have a month's mind to be doing as much, and could sit and hear them day and night.'

'I wish you did,' quoth the hostess; 'for I never have a quiet moment in my house but when you are listening to the reading; for then you are so besotted, that you forget to scold for that time.'

'It is true,' said Maritornes, 'and, in good faith, I too am very much delighted at hearing those things; for they are very fine, especially when they tell us how such a lady, and her knight, lie embracing each other under an orange tree, and how a duenna stands upon the watch, dying with envy, and her heart going pit-a-pat. I say, all this is pure honey.'

'And pray, miss, what is your opinion of these matters?' said the priest, addressing himself to the innkeeper's daughter.

'I do not know indeed, sir,' answered the girl: 'I listen too; and truly, though I do not understand it, I take some pleasure in hearing it: but I have no relish for those blows and slashes, which please my father so much; what I chiefly like is the complaints the knights make when they are absent from their mistresses; and really, sometimes, they make me weep, out of the pity I have for them.'

'You would soon afford them relief, young gentlewoman,' said Dorothea, 'if they wept for you?'

'I do not know what I should do,' answered the girl; 'only I know, that several of those ladies are so cruel, that their knights call them tigers and lions, and a thousand other ugly names. And, Jesu! I cannot imagine what kind of folks they be, who are so hard-hearted and unconscionable, that, rather than bestow a kind look on an honest gentleman, they will let him die, or run mad. And, for my part, I cannot see why all this coyness: if it is out of honesty, let them marry them; for that is what the gentlemen would be at.'

'Hold your tongue, hussy,' said the hostess; 'methinks you know a great deal of these matters; and it does not become young maidens to know, or talk, so much.'

'When this gentleman asked me a civil question,' replied the girl, 'I could do no less, sure, than answer him.'

'It is mighty well,' said the priest; 'pray, landlord, bring me those books, for I have a mind to see them.'

'With all my heart,' answered the host; and, going into his chamber, he brought out a little old cloak-bag, with a padlock and chain to it, and opening it, he took out three large volumes, and some manuscript papers written in a very fair character. The first book he opened, he found to be *Don Cirongilio of Thrace*,* the next *Felixmarte of Hyrcania*,* and the third the *History of the Grand Captain Gonçalo Hernandez of Córdova*, with the *Life of Diego Garcia de Paredes*.* When the priest had read the titles of the two first, he turned about to the barber, and said:

'We want here our friend's housekeeper and niece.'

'Not at all,' answered the barber; 'for I myself can carry them to the yard, or to the chimney, where there is a very good fire.'

'What, sir, would you burn my books?' said the innkeeper.

'Only these two,' said the priest, 'that of Don Cirongilio, and that of Felixmarte.'

'What, then, are my books heretical, or phlegmetical, that you have a mind to burn them?'

'Schismatical, you would say, friend,' said the barber, 'and not phlegmetical.'

'It is true,' replied the innkeeper; 'but if you intend to burn any, let it be this of the Grand Captain, and this of Diego de Garcia; for I will sooner let you burn one of my children, than either of the others.'

'Dear brother,' said the priest, 'these two books are great liars, and full of extravagant and foolish conceits; and this of the Grand Captain is a true history, and contains the exploits of Gonçalo Hernandez of Córdova, who, for his many and brave actions, deserved to be called by all the world the Grand Captain; a name renowned and illustrious, and merited by him alone. As for Diego Garcia de Paredes, he was a gentleman of note, born in the town of Truxillo in Estremadura, a very brave soldier, and of such great natural strength, that he could stop a millwheel, in its greatest rapidity, with a single finger; and, being once posted with a two-handed sword at the entrance upon a bridge, he repelled a prodigious army, and prevented their passage over it. And he performed other such things, that if, instead of being related by himself, with the modesty of a cavalier who is his own historian, they had been written by some other dispassionate and unprejudiced author, they would have eclipsed the actions of the Hectors, Achilleses, and Orlandos.'

'Persuade my grandmother to that,' quoth the innkeeper; 'do but see what it is he wonders at—the stopping of a millwheel! Before God, your worship should have read what I have read, concerning Felixmarte of Hyrcania, who with one back-stroke cut asunder five giants in the middle, as if they had been so many bean-cods, of which the children make little puppet-friars. At another time he encountered a very great and powerful army, consisting of above a million and six hundred thousand soldiers, all armed from head to foot, and defeated them all, as if they had been a flock of sheep. But what will you say of the good Don Cirongilio of Thrace, who was so stout and valiant, as you may see in the book, wherein is related that, as he was sailing on a river, a fiery serpent appeared above water; and he, as soon as he saw it, threw himself upon it, and getting astride upon its scaly shoulders, squeezed its throat with both his hands, with so much force, that the serpent, finding itself in danger of being choked, had no other remedy but to let itself sink to the bottom of the river, carrying along with him the knight, who would not quit his hold: and, when they were got to the bottom, he found himself in a fine palace, and in so pretty a garden that it was wonderful; and presently the serpent turned to a venerable old man, who said so many things to him, that the like was never heard. Therefore, pray say no more, sir; for, if you were but to hear all this, you would run mad with pleasure. A fig for the Grand Captain, and for that Diego Garcia you speak of.'

Dorothea, hearing this, said softly to Cardenio:

'Our landlord wants but little to make the second part of Don Quixote.'

'I think so too,' answered Cardenio; 'for, according to the indications he gives, he takes all that is related in these books for gospel, and neither more nor less than matters of fact; and the barefooted friars themselves could not make him believe otherwise.'

'Look you, brother,' said the priest, 'there never was in the world such a man as Felixmarte of Hyrcania, nor Don Cirongilio of Thrace, nor any other knights, such as the books of chivalry mention: for all is but the contrivance and invention of idle wits, who composed them for the purpose of whiling away time, as you see your reapers do in reading them; for I vow and swear to you, there never were any such knights in the world, nor did such feats, or extravagant things, ever happen in it.'

'To another dog with this bone,' answered the host; 'as if I did not know how many make five, or where my own shoe pinches: do not think, sir, to feed me with pap; for, before God I am no suckling. A good jest indeed, that your worship should endeavour to make me believe, that all the contents of these good books are lies and extravagances, being printed with the licence of the king's privy council; as if they were people that would allow the impression of such a pack of lies, battles, and enchantments, as are enough to make one distracted.'

'I have already told you, friend,' replied the priest, 'that it is done for the amusement of our idle thoughts: and as, in all well-instituted commonwealths, the games of chess, tennis, and billiards are permitted for the entertainment of those who have nothing to do, and who ought not, or cannot work; for the same reason they permit such books to be written and printed, presuming, as they well may, that nobody can be so ignorant as to take them for true histories. And, if it were proper at this time, and my hearers required it, I could lay down such rules for composing books of chivalry, as should, perhaps, make them agreeable, and even useful to many persons: but I hope the time will come that I may communicate this design to those who can remedy it; and, in the meanwhile, Señor Innkeeper, believe what I have told you, and here take your books, and settle the point, whether they contain truths or lies, as you please; and much good may you do with them, and God grant you do not halt on the same foot your guest Don Quixote does.'

'Not so,' answered the innkeeper, 'I shall not be so mad as to turn knight-errant; for I know very well that times are altered since those famous knights-errant wandered about the world.'

Sancho came in about the middle of this conversation, and was much confounded, and very pensive at what he heard said, that knights-errant were not now in fashion, and that all books of chivalry were mere lies and fooleries; and he resolved with himself to wait the event of this expedition of his master's; and if it did not succeed as happily as he expected, he determined to leave him, and return home to his wife and children, and to his accustomed labour.

The innkeeper was carrying away the cloak-bag and the books; but the priest said to him:

'Pray stay, for I would see what papers those are that are written in so fair a character.'

The host took them out, and having given them to him to read, he found about eight sheets in manuscript, and at the beginning a large title, which was, *The Novel of the Curious Impertinent.* The priest read three or four lines to himself, and said:

'In truth I do not dislike the title of this novel, and I have a mind to read it all.'

To which the innkeeper answered:

'Your reverence may well venture to read it; for I assure you that some of my guests, who have read it, liked it mightily, and begged it of me with great earnestness; but I would not give it them, designing to restore it to the person who forgot and left behind him this cloak-bag, with these books and papers; for perhaps their owner may come this way again some time or other; and though I know I shall have a great want of the books, in faith I will restore them; for though I am an innkeeper, thank God I am a Christian.'

'You are much in the right, friend,' said the priest; 'nevertheless, if the novel please me, you must give me leave to take a copy of it.'

'With all my heart,' answered the innkeeper.

While they two were thus talking, Cardenio had taken up the novel, and began to read it; and, being likewise pleased with it, he desired the priest to read it so as that they might all hear it.

'I will,' said the priest, 'if it be not better to spend our time in sleeping than in reading.'

'It will be as well for me,' said Dorothea, 'to pass the time in listening to some story; for my spirits are not yet so composed as to give me leave to sleep, though it were needful.'

'Well then,' said the priest, 'I will read it, if it were but for curiosity; perhaps it may contain something that is entertaining.'

Master Nicholas and Sancho joined in the same request: on which the priest, perceiving that he should give them all pleasure, and receive some himself, said:

'Be all attentive then, for the novel begins in the following manner:'

CHAPTER 33

*In which is recited 'The Novel of the Curious Impertinent'.**

IN Florence, a rich and famous city of Italy, in the province called Tuscany, lived Anselmo and Lothario, two gentlemen of fortune and quality, and such great friends that all who knew them styled them, by way of eminence and distinction, 'the Two Friends'. They were both bachelors, young, of the same age, and of the same manners: all which was a sufficient foundation for their reciprocal friendship. It is true indeed that Anselmo was somewhat more inclined to amorous dalliance than Lothario, who was fonder of country sports; but, upon occasion, Anselmo neglected his own pleasures, to pursue those of Lothario; and Lothario quitted his, to follow those of Anselmo: and thus their inclinations went hand in hand with such harmony, that no clock kept such exact time.

Anselmo fell desperately in love with a beautiful young lady of condition in the same city, called Camilla, daughter of such good parents, and herself so good, that he resolved (with the approbation of his friend Lothario, without whom he did nothing) to demand her of her father in marriage; which he accordingly did. It was Lothario who carried the message; and it was he who concluded the match, so much to the good liking of his friend, that, in a little time, he found himself in the possession of what he desired, and Camilla so satisfied with having obtained Anselmo for her husband, that she ceased not to give thanks to heaven, and to Lothario, by whose means such good fortune had befallen her. For some days after the wedding, days usually dedicated to mirth, Lothario frequented his friend Anselmo's house as he was wont to do, striving to honour, please, and entertain him to the utmost of his power: but the nuptial season being over, and compliments of congratulation at an end, Lothario began to remit the frequency of his visits to Anselmo, thinking, as all discreet men should, that one ought not to visit and frequent the houses of one's friends, when married, in the same manner as when they were bachelors. For, though true and real friendship neither can nor ought to be suspicious in anything, yet so nice is the honour of a married man, that it is thought it may suffer even by a brother, and [how] much more by a friend?

Anselmo took notice of Lothario's remissness, and complained greatly of it, telling him, that, had he suspected that his being married would have been the occasion of their not conversing together as formerly, he would never have done it; and since, by the entire harmony between them, while both bachelors, they had acquired so sweet a name as that of the Two Friends, he desired he would not suffer so honourable and so pleasing a title to be lost, by over-acting the cautious part; and therefore he besought him (if such a term might be used between them) to return, and be master of his house, and come and go as heretofore; assuring him, that his wife Camilla had no other pleasure, or will, than what he desired she should have; and that knowing how sincerely and ardently they loved each other, she was much surprised to find him so shy.

To all these, and many other reasons, which Anselmo urged to Lothario, to persuade him to use his house as before, Lothario replied with so much prudence, discretion, and judgement, that Anselmo rested satisfied with the good intention of his friend; and they agreed, that, two days in a week, besides holidays, Lothario should come and dine with him: and, though this was concerted between them two, Lothario resolved to do what he should think most for the honour of his friend, whose reputation was dearer to him than his own. He said, and he said right, that a married man, on whom heaven has bestowed a beautiful wife, should be as careful what men he brings home to his house, as what female friends she converses with abroad; for that which cannot be done, nor concerted, in the markets, at churches, at public shows, or assemblies (things, which husbands must not always deny their wives) may be concerted and brought about at the house of a female friend or relation, of whom we are most secure. Lothario said also, that a married man stood in need of some friend to advertise him of any mistakes in his conduct; for it often happens, that the fondness a man has at first for his wife, makes him either not take notice, or not tell her, for fear of offending her, that she ought to do, or avoid doing, some things, the doing, or not doing, whereof may reflect honour or disgrace; all which might easily be remedied by the timely admonition of a friend. But where shall we find a friend so discreet, so faithful, and sincere, as Lothario here seems to require? Indeed I cannot tell, unless in Lothario himself, who, with the utmost diligence and attention, watched over the honour of his friend, and contrived to retrench, cut short, and abridge the number of visiting-days agreed upon, lest the idle vulgar, and prying malicious eyes, should censure the free access of a young and rich cavalier, so well-born, and of such accomplishments, as he could not but be conscious to himself he was master of, to the house of a lady so beautiful as Camilla; and though his integrity and worth might bridle the tongues of the censorious, yet he had no mind that his own honour, or that of his friend, should be in the least suspected; and therefore, on most of the days agreed upon, he busied and employed himself about such things as he pretended were indispensable. And thus the time passed on in complaints on the one hand, and excuses on the other.

Now it fell out one day, as they two were walking in a meadow without the city, Anselmo addressed Lothario in words to this effect:

'I know very well, friend Lothario, I can never be thankful enough to God for the blessings he has bestowed upon me, first in making me the son of such parents as mine were, and giving me with so liberal a hand what men call the goods of nature and fortune; and especially in having given me such a friend as yourself, and such a wife as Camilla; two jewels, which, if I value not as high as I ought, I value at least as high as I am able. Yet, notwithstanding all these advantages, which usually are sufficient to make men live contented, I live the most uneasy and dissatisfied man in the whole world; having been for some time past harassed and oppressed with a desire so strange, and so much out of the common tract of other men, that I wonder at myself, and blame and rebuke myself for it when I am alone, endeavouring to stifle and conceal it even from my own thoughts, and yet I have succeeded no better in my endeavours to stifle and conceal it, than if I had made it my business to publish it to all the world. And since, in short, it must one day break out, I would fain have it lodged in the archives of your breast; not doubting but that, through your secrecy, and friendly application to relieve me, I shall soon be freed from the vexation it gives me, and that, by your diligence, my joy will rise to as high a pitch as my discontent has done by my own folly.'

Lotario was in great suspense at Anselmo's discourse, and unable to guess at what he aimed by so tedious a preparation and preamble; and though he revolved in his imagination what desire it could be that gave his friend so much disturbance, he still shot wide of the mark; and, to be quickly rid of the perplexity into which this suspense threw him, he said to him, that it was doing a notorious injury to their great friendship, to seek for roundabout ways to acquaint him with his most hidden thoughts, since he might depend upon him, either for advice or assistance in what concerned them.

'It is very true,' answered Anselmo; 'and in this confidence I give you to understand, friend Lotario, that the thing which disquiets me is, a desire to know whether my wife Camilla be as good and as perfect as I imagine her to be; and I cannot be thoroughly informed of this truth, but by trying her in such a manner, that the proof may manifest the perfection of her goodness, as fire does that of gold. For it is my opinion, my friend, that a woman is honest only so far as she is, or is not, courted and solicited: and that she alone is really chaste who has not yielded to the force of promises, presents, and tears, or the continual solicitations of importunate lovers. For what thanks, said he, to a woman for being virtuous, when nobody persuades her to be otherwise? what mighty matter if she be reserved and cautious, who has no opportunity given her of going astray and knows she has a husband who, the first time he catches her transgressing, will be sure to take away her life? The woman, therefore, who is honest out of fear, or for want of opportunity, I shall not hold in the same degree of esteem with her who, after solicitation and importunity, comes off with the crown of victory. So that for these reasons, and for many more I could assign in support of my opinion, my desire is that my wife Camilla may pass through these trials, and be purified and refined in the fire of courtship and solicitation, and that by some person worthy of placing his desires on her: and if she comes off from this conflict, as I believe she will, with the palm of victory, I shall applaud my matchless fortune: I shall then have it to say, that I have attained the utmost of my wishes, and may safely boast, that the virtuous woman is fallen to my lot, of whom the wise man says, "Who can find her?"* And if the reverse of all this should happen, the satisfaction of being confirmed in my opinion will enable me to bear, without regret, the trouble so costly an experiment may reasonably give me. And as nothing you can urge against my design can be of any avail towards hindering me from putting it in execution, I would have you, my friend Lothario, dispose yourself to be the instrument of performing this work of my fancy; and I will give you opportunity to do it, and you shall want for no means that I can think necessary towards gaining upon a modest, virtuous, reserved, and disinterested woman. And, among other reasons which induce me to trust this nice affair to your management, one is, my being certain that, if Camilla should be overcome, you will not push the victory to the last extremity, but only account that for done which, for good reasons, ought not to be done; and thus I shall be wronged only in the intention, and the injury will remain hid in the virtue of your silence, which, in what concerns me, will, I am assured, be eternal as that of death. Therefore, if you would have me enjoy a life that deserves to be called such, you must immediately enter upon this amorous combat, not languidly and lazily, but with all the fervour and diligence my design requires, and with the confidence our friendship assures me of.'

This was what Anselmo said to Lothario; to all which he was so attentive, that, excepting what he is already mentioned to have said, he opened not his lips until his friend had done:

but now, perceiving that he was silent, after he had gazed at him earnestly for some time, as if he had been looking at something he had never seen before, and which occasioned in him wonder and amazement, he said to him:

'I cannot persuade myself, friend Anselmo, but that what you have been saying to me is all in jest; for, had I thought you in earnest, I would not have suffered you to proceed so far; and, by not listening to you, I should have prevented your long harangue. I cannot but think, either that you do not know me, or that I do not know you. But, no: I well know that you are Anselmo, and you know that I am Lothario: the mischief is, that I think you are not the Anselmo you used to be, and you must imagine I am not that Lothario I ought to be; for neither is what you have said to me becoming that friend of mine, Anselmo; nor is what you require of me to be asked of that Lothario whom you know. For true friends ought to prove and use their friends, as the poet expresses it,* *usque ad aras*; as much as to say, they ought not to employ their friendship in matters against the law of God. If an heathen had this notion of friendship, how much more ought a Christian to have it, who knows that the divine friendship ought not to be forfeited for any human friendship whatever. And when a friend goes so far, as to set aside his duty to heaven, in compliance with the interests of his friend, it must not be for light and trivial matters, but only when the honour and life of his friend are at stake. Tell me then, Anselmo, which of these two are in danger, that I should venture to compliment you with doing a thing in itself so detestable as that you require of me? Neither, assuredly: on the contrary, if I understand you right, you would have me take pains to deprive you of honour and life, and, at the same time, myself too of both. For, if I must do that which will deprive you of your honour, it is plain I take away your life, since a man without honour is worse than if he were dead: and I being the instrument, as you would have me to be, of doing you so much harm, shall I not bring dishonour upon myself, and, by consequence, rob myself of life? Hear me, friend Anselmo, and have patience, and forbear answering until I have done urging what I have to say, as to what your desire exacts of me; for there will be time enough for you to reply, and for me to hear you.'

'With all my heart,' said Anselmo; 'say what you please.'

Then Lothario went on, saying:

'Methinks, O Anselmo, you are at this time in the same disposition that the Moors are always in, whom you cannot convince of the error of their sect, by citations from Holy Scripture, nor by arguments drawn from reason, or founded upon articles of faith; but you must produce examples that are plain, easy, intelligible, demonstrative, and undeniable, with such mathematical demonstrations as cannot be denied; as when it is said: "If from equal parts we take equal parts, those that remain are also equal". And, when they do not comprehend this in words, as in reality they do not, you must show it to them with your hands, and set it before their very eyes; and, after all, nothing can convince them of the truths of our holy religion. In this very way and method must I deal with you; for this desire, which possesses you, is so extravagant and wide of all that has the least shadow of reason, that I look upon it as mis-spending time to endeavour to convince you of your folly; for, at present, I can give it no better name; and I am even tempted to leave you to your indiscretion, as a punishment of your preposterous desire: but the friendship I have for you will not let me deal so rigorously with you, nor will it consent that I should desert you in such manifest danger of undoing yourself. And, that you may clearly see that it is so, say, Anselmo, have you not told me, that I must solicit her that is reserved, persuade her that is virtuous, bribe her that is disinterested, and court her that is prudent? Yes, you have told me so. If then you know that you have a reserved, virtuous, disinterested, and prudent wife, what is it you would have? And, if you are of opinion she will come off victorious from all my attacks, as doubtless she will, what better titles do you think to bestow on her afterwards, than those she has already? or what will she be more then, than she is now? Either you do not take her for what you pretend, or you do not know what it is you ask. If you do not take her for what you say you do, to what purpose would you try her, and not rather suppose her guilty, and treat her as such? But, if she be as good as you believe she is, it is impertinent to try experiments upon truth itself, since, when that is done it will remain but in the same degree of esteem it had before. And, therefore, we must conclude, that to attempt things from whence mischief is more likely to ensue than any advantage to us, is the part of rash and inconsiderate men; and especially when they are such as we are no way forced nor obliged to attempt, and when it may be easily seen at a distance, that the enterprise itself is downright madness.

'Difficult things are undertaken for the sake of God, of the world, or of both together: those which are done for God's sake are such as are enterprised by the saints, while they endeavour to live a life of angels in human bodies: those which are taken in hand for love of the world are done by those who pass infinite oceans of water, various climates, and many foreign nations, to acquire what are usually called "the goods of fortune"; and those which are undertaken for the sake of God and the world together are the actions of brave soldiers, who no sooner espy in the enemy's wall so much breach as may be made by a single cannon-ball, but laying aside all fear, without deliberating, or regarding the manifest danger that threatens them, and borne upon the wings of desire to act in defence of their faith, their country, and their king, they throw themselves intrepidly into the midst of a thousand opposing deaths that await them. These are the difficulties which are commonly attempted; and it is honour, glory, and advantage, to attempt them, though so full of dangers and inconveniencies. But that, which you say you would have attempted and put in execution, will neither procure you glory from God, the goods of fortune, nor reputation among men. For, supposing the event to answer your desires, you will be neither happier, richer, nor more honoured than you are at present: and if you should miscarry, you will find yourself in the most miserable condition that can be imagined; for then it will avail you nothing to think that nobody else knows the misfortune that has befallen you: it will sufficiently afflict and undo you to know it yourself. And, as a further confirmation of this truth, I will repeat the following stanza of the famous poet, Louis Tansillo, at the end of the first part of the *Tears of Saint Peter*:

> When conscious Peter saw the blushing East,
> He felt redoubled anguish in his breast,
> And, though by privacy secured from blame,
> Saw his own guilt, and seeing, died with shame.
> For generous minds, betrayed into a fault,
> No witness want but self-condemning thought:
> To such the conscious earth alone and skies
> Supply the place of thousand prying eyes.

'And, therefore, its being a secret will not prevent your sorrow, but rather make it perpetual, and be a continual subject for weeping, if not tears from your eyes, tears of blood from your heart, such as that simple doctor wept, who, as the poet relates of him, made trial of the cup, which the prudent Rinaldo more wisely declined doing.* And though this be a poetical fiction, there is a concealed moral in it, worthy to be observed, understood, and imitated. But I have still something more to say upon this subject; which, I hope, will bring you to a full conviction of the great error you are going to commit.

'Tell me, Anselmo, if heaven or good fortune had made you master and lawful possessor of a superlative fine diamond, of whose goodness and beauty all jewellers who had seen it were fully satisfied, and should unanimously declare that, in weight, goodness, and beauty, it came up to whatever the nature of such a stone is capable of, and you yourself should believe as much, as knowing nothing to the contrary; would it be right that you should take a fancy to lay this diamond between the anvil and the hammer, and by mere dint of blows try whether it was so hard, and so fine, as it was thought to be? and further, supposing this put in execution, and that the stone resists so foolish a trial, would it acquire thereby any additional value or reputation? and, if it should break, as it might, would not all be lost? Yes, certainly, and make its owner to pass for a simple fellow in everybody's opinion. Make account then, friend Anselmo, that Camilla is an exquisitely fine diamond, both in your own opinion, and in that of other people, and that it is unreasonable to put her to the hazard of being broken, since though she should remain entire, she cannot rise in her value: and should she fail and not resist, consider in time what a condition you would be in without her, and how justly you might blame yourself for having been the cause both of her ruin and your own. There is no jewel in the world so valuable as a chaste and virtuous woman; and all the honour of women consists in the good opinion the world has of them: and since that of your wife is unquestionably good, why will you bring this truth into doubt?

'Consider, friend, that woman is an imperfect creature, and that one should not lay stumbling-blocks in her way to make her trip and fall, but rather remove them, and clear the way before her, that she may without hindrance advance towards her proper perfection, which consists in being virtuous. Naturalists inform us that the ermine is a little white creature with a fine fur, and that, when the hunters have a mind to catch it, they make use of this artifice: knowing the way it usually takes, or the places it haunts, they lay all the passes with dirt, and then frighten the creature with noise and drive it toward those places; and when the ermine comes to the dirt it stands still, suffering itself rather to be taken, than, by passing through the mire, destroy and sully its whiteness, which it values more than liberty or life. The virtuous and modest woman is an ermine, and the virtue of chastity is whiter and cleaner than snow; and he who would not have her lose, but rather guard and preserve it, must take quite a different method from that which is used with the ermine: for he must not lay in her way the mire of courtship and assiduity of importunate lovers, since perhaps, and without a perhaps, she may not have virtue and natural strength enough to enable her, of herself, to trample down and get clear over those impediments; it is necessary, therefore, to remove such things out of her way, and set before her pure and unspotted virtue, and the charms of an unblemished reputation.

'A good woman may also be compared to a mirror of crystal, shining and bright, but liable to be sullied and dimmed by every breath that comes near it. The virtuous woman is to be treated in the same manner as relics are, to be adored, but not handled. The good woman is to be looked after and prized, like a fine garden full of roses and other flowers, the owner of which suffers nobody to walk among them, or touch anything, but only at a distance, and through iron rails, to enjoy its fragrance and beauty.

'Lastly, I will repeat to you some verses, which I remember to have heard in a modern comedy,* and which seem very applicable to our present purpose. A prudent old man advises another, who is father of a young maiden, to look well after her, and lock her up; and, among other reasons, gives these following:

1

If woman's glass, why should we try
    Whether she can be broke, or no?
Great hazards in the trial lie,
    Because perchance she may be so.

2

Who that is wise, such brittle ware
    Would careless dash upon the floor,
Which, broken, nothing can repair,
    Nor solder to its form restore?

3

In this opinion all are found,
    And reason vouches what I say,
Wherever Danaës abound,
    There golden showers will make their way.

'All that I have hitherto said, O Anselmo, relates only to you: it is now fit I should say something concerning myself; and pardon me if I am prolix; for the labyrinth into which you have run yourself, and out of which you would have me extricate you, requires no less. You look upon me as your friend, and yet, against all rules of friendship, would deprive me of my honour: nor is this all; you would have me take away yours. That you will rob me of mine, is plain: for, when Camilla finds that I make love to her, as you desire I should, it is certain she will look upon me as a man void of honour, and base, since I attempt, and do a thing so contrary to what

I owe to myself, and to your friendship. That you would have me deprive you of yours, there is no doubt: for Camilla, perceiving that I make addresses to her, must think I have discovered some mark of lightness in her, which has emboldened me to declare to her my guilty passion; and her looking upon herself as dishonoured, affects you, as being her husband. And hence arises what we so commonly find, that the husband of the adulterous wife, though he does not know it, nor has given his wife any reason for transgressing her duty, and though his misfortune be not owing to his own neglect, or want of care, is nevertheless called by a vilifying and opprobrious name, and those who are not unacquainted with his wife's incontinence, are apt to look upon him with an eye rather of contempt than of pity. But I will tell you the reason why the husband of a vicious wife is justly dishonoured, though he does not know that he is, nor has been at all in fault, or connived at, or given her occasion to become such: and be not weary of hearing me, since the whole will redound to your own advantage.

'When God created our first parent in the terrestrial paradise (as the Holy Scriptures inform us) he infused a sleep into Adam; and, while he slept, he took a rib out of his left side, of which he formed our mother Eve: and, when Adam awoke, and beheld her, he said: "This is flesh of my flesh, and bone of my bone". And God said: "For this cause shall a man leave father and mother, and they two shall be one flesh". And at that time the holy sacrament of marriage was instituted, with such ties as death only can loose. And this miraculous sacrament is of such force and virtue that it makes two different persons to be but one flesh: nay, it doth more in the properly married; for though they have two souls, they have but one will. And hence it is, that, as the flesh of the wife is the very same with that of the husband, the blemishes or defects thereof are participated by the flesh of the husband, though, as is already said, he was not the occasion of them. For, as the whole body feels the pain of the foot, or of any other member, because they are all one flesh; and the head feels the smart of the ankle though it was not the cause of it: so the husband partakes of the wife's dishonour by being the selfsame thing with her. And as the honours and dishonours of the world all proceed from flesh and blood, and those of the naughty wife being of this kind, the husband must of necessity bear his part in them, and be reckoned dishonoured without his knowing it.

'Behold then, O Anselmo, the danger to which you expose yourself in seeking to disturb the quiet your virtuous consort enjoys. Consider through how vain and impertinent a curiosity you would stir up the humours that now lie dormant in the breast of your chaste spouse. Reflect that what you adventure to gain is little, and what you may lose will be so great, that I will pass over in silence what I want words to express. But if all I have said be not sufficient to dissuade you from your preposterous design, you must look out for some other instrument of your disgrace and misfortune, for I resolve not to act this part, though I should thereby lose your friendship which is the greatest loss I am able to conceive.'

Here the virtuous and discreet Lothario ceased, and Anselmo was so confounded and pensive that, for some time, he could not answer him a word; but at last he said:

'I have listened, friend Lothario, to all you have been saying to me, with the attention you may have observed; and in your arguments, examples, and comparisons, I plainly discover your great discretion, and the perfection of that friendship you have attained to; I see also and acknowledge, that in rejecting your opinion and adhering to my own, I fly the good and pursue the evil. Yet, this supposed, you must consider that I labour under the infirmity to which some women are subject, who have a longing to eat dirt, chalk, coals, and other things still worse, even such as are loathsome to the sight, and much more so to the taste. And therefore some art must be made use of to cure me: and it may be done with ease only by your beginning to court Camilla, though but coldly and feignedly, who cannot be so yielding and pliant that her modesty should fall to the ground at the first onset: and with this faint beginning I shall rest satisfied, and you will have complied with what you owe to your friendship, not only in restoring me to life, but by persuading me not to be the cause of my own dishonour. And there is one reason especially, which obliges you to undertake this business, which is, that whereas I am determined, as I am, to put this experiment in practice, it behoves you not to let me disclose my frenzy to another person, and so hazard that honour you are endeavouring to preserve: and though your own should lose ground in Camilla's opinion while you are making love to her, it is of little or no consequence; since, in a short time, when we have experienced in her the integrity we expect, you may then discover to her the pure truth of our contrivance; whereupon you will regain your former credit with her. And since you hazard so little, and may give me so much pleasure by the risk, do not decline the task, whatever inconveniences may appear to you in it, since, as I have already said, if you will but set about it, I shall give up the cause for determined.'

Lothario, perceiving Anselmo's fixed resolution, and not knowing what other examples to produce, nor what further reasons to offer to dissuade him from his purpose; and finding he threatened to impart his extravagant desire to some other person, resolved, in order to avoid a greater evil, to gratify him and undertake what he desired; but with a full purpose and intention so to order the matter that, without giving Camilla any disturbance, Anselmo should rest satisfied; and therefore he returned for answer that he desired he would not communicate his design to any other person whatever, for he would take the business upon himself, and would begin it whenever he pleased. Anselmo embraced him with great tenderness and affection, thanking him for this offer as if he had done him some great favour; and it was agreed between them, that he should set about the work the very next day, when he would give him opportunity and leisure to talk with Camilla alone, and would also furnish him with money and jewels to present her with. He advised him to give her music, and write verses in her praise, and, if he did not care to be at the pains he would make them for him. Lothario consented to everything, but with an intention very different from what Anselmo imagined. Things thus settled they returned to Anselmo's house, where they found Camilla waiting with great uneasiness and anxiety for her spouse, who had stayed abroad longer that day than usual.

Lothario after some time retired to his own house, and Anselmo remained in his, as contented as Lothario was pensive, who was at a loss what stratagem to invent to extricate himself handsomely out of this impertinent business. But that night he bethought himself of a way how to deceive Anselmo, without offending Camilla: and the next day he came to dine with his friend, and was kindly received by Camilla, who always entertained and treated him with much good will, knowing the affection her spouse had for him. Dinner being ended and the cloth taken away, Anselmo desired Lothario to stay with Camilla while he went upon an urgent affair, which he would dispatch and be back in about an hour and a half. Camilla prayed him not to go, and Lothario offered to bear him company: but it signified nothing with Anselmo; on the contrary, he importuned Lothario to stay and wait for him; for he had a matter of great importance to talk to him about. He also desired Camilla to bear Lothario company until his return. In short, he knew so well how to counterfeit a necessity for his absence, though that necessity proceeded only from his own folly, that no one could perceive it was feigned.

Anselmo went away, and Camilla and Lothario remained by themselves at table, the rest of the family being all gone to dinner. Thus Lothario found himself entered in the lists, as his friend had desired, with an enemy before him, able to conquer by her beauty alone a squadron of armed cavaliers: think then, whether Lothario had not cause to fear. But the first thing he did, was, to lay his elbow on the arm of the chair and his cheek on his hand, and, begging Camilla to pardon his ill-manners, he said he would willingly repose himself a little until Anselmo's return. Camilla answered, that he might repose himself more at ease on the couch than in the chair, and therefore desired him to walk in and lie down there. Lothario excused himself, and slept where he was until Anselmo's return: who, finding Camilla retired to her chamber, and Lothario asleep, believed that, as he had stayed so long, they had had time enough both to talk and to sleep; and he thought it long until Lothario awoke, that he might go out with him, and inquire after his success.

All fell out as he wished. Lothario awoke, and presently they went out together, and Anselmo asked him concerning what he wanted to be informed of. Lothario answered that he did not think it proper to open too far the first time, and therefore all he had done was to tell her she was very handsome, and that the whole town rang of her wit and beauty; and this he thought a good introduction, as it might insinuate him into her good will, and dispose her to listen to him the next time with pleasure: in which he employed the same artifice, which the devil uses to deceive a person who is on his guard; who, being in reality an angel of darkness, transforms himself into one of light, and setting plausible appearances before him, at length discovers himself, and carries his point, if his deceit be not found out at the beginning. Anselmo was mightily pleased with all this, and said he would give him the like opportunity every day without going abroad; for he would so employ himself at home that Camilla should never suspect his stratagem.

Now many days passed, and Lothario, though he spoke not a word to Camilla on the subject, told Anselmo that he had, and that he could never perceive in her the least sign of anything that was amiss, or even discover the least glimpse or shadow of hope for himself; on the contrary, that she threatened to tell her husband, if he did not quit his base design.

'It is very well,' said Anselmo, 'hitherto Camilla has resisted words: we must next see how she will resist deeds: to-morrow I will give you two thousand crowns in gold to present her with, and as many more to buy jewels by way of lure; for women, especially if they are handsome, though never so chaste, are fond of being well-dressed and going fine: and if she resists this temptation, I will be satisfied, and give you no further trouble.'

Lothario answered, that, since he had begun, he would go through with this affair, though he was sure he should come off wearied and repulsed. The next day he received the four thousand crowns, and with them four thousand confusions, not knowing what new lie to invent: but, in fine, he resolved to tell him, that Camilla was as inflexible to presents and promises as to words, so that he need not weary himself any further, since all the time was spent in vain.

But fortune, which directed matters otherwise, so ordered it that Anselmo, having left Lothario and Camilla alone as usual, shut himself up in an adjoining chamber, and stood looking and listening through the keyhole, how they behaved themselves, and saw that in above half an hour Lothario said not a word to Camilla; nor would he have said a word had he stood there an age. On which he concluded that all his friend had told him of Camilla's answers was mere fiction and lies. And, to try whether they were so or not, he came out of the chamber, and, calling Lothario aside, asked him what news he had for him, and in what disposition he found Camilla. Lothario replied, that he was resolved not to mention that business any more to her, for she had answered him so sharply and angrily, that he had not the courage to open his lips again to her.

'Ah!' said Anselmo, 'Lothario! Lothario! how ill do you answer your engagement to me, and the great confidence I repose in you! I am just come from looking through the keyhole of that door, and have found that you have not spoken a word to Camilla; whence I conclude, that you have never yet spoken to her at all. If it be so, as doubtless it is, why do you deceive me? or why would you industriously deprive me of those means I might otherwise find to compass my desire?'

Anselmo said no more; but what he had said was sufficient to leave Lothario abashed and confounded: who, thinking his honour touched by being caught in a lie, swore to Anselmo, that from that moment he took upon him to satisfy him, and would tell him no more lies, as he should find, if he had the curiosity to watch him: which however he might save himself the trouble of doing; for he would endeavour so earnestly to procure him satisfaction, that there should be no room left for suspicion. Anselmo believed him; and to give him an opportunity, more secure and less liable to surprise, he resolved to absent himself from home for eight days, and to visit a friend of his who lived in a village not far from the city. And, to excuse his departure to Camilla, he contrived that his friend should press earnestly for his company.

Rash and unhappy Anselmo! what is it you are doing? what is it you intend? what is it you are contriving? consider, you are acting against yourself, designing your own dishonour and contriving your own ruin. Your spouse Camilla is virtuous; you possess her peaceably and quietly; nobody disturbs your enjoyment of her; her thoughts do not stray beyond the walls of her house; you are her heaven upon earth, the aim of her desires, the accomplishment of her wishes, and the rule by which she measures her will, adjusting it wholly according to yours, and that of heaven. If, then, the mine of her honour, beauty, virtue, and modesty, yield you, without any toil, all the wealth they contain, or you can desire, why will you ransack those mines for other veins of new and unheard-of treasures, and thereby put the whole in danger of ruin, since, in truth, it is supported only by the feeble props of woman's weak nature? Consider, that he who seeks after what is impossible ought in justice to be denied what is possible; as a certain poet* has better expressed it in these verses:

> In death I life desire to see,
>   Health in disease, in tortures rest;
> In chains and prisons liberty,
>   And truth in a disloyal breast.
>
> But adverse fate, and heav'n's decree,
>   In this to baffle me are joined,
> That, since I ask what cannot be,
>   What can be I shall never find.

The next day Anselmo went to his friend's house in the country, telling Camilla that, during his absence, Lothario would come to take care of his house and dine with her, and desiring her to treat him as she would do his own person. Camilla, as a discreet and virtuous woman should, was troubled at the order her husband gave her, and represented to him, how improper it was, that anybody, in his absence, should take his place at his table; and, if he did it, as doubting her ability to manage his family, she desired he would try her for this time, and he should see by experience that she was equal to trusts of greater consequence. Anselmo replied it was his pleasure it should be so, and that she had nothing to do but to acquiesce and be obedient. Camilla said, she would, though much against her inclination.

Anselmo went away, and the next day Lothario came to his house, where he was received by Camilla with a kind and modest welcome. But she never exposed herself to be left alone with Lothario, being constantly attended by her men and maidservants, especially by her own maid called Leonela, whom, as they had been brought up together from their infancy in her father's house, she loved very much, and, upon her marriage with Anselmo, had brought with her. Lothario said nothing to her the three first days, though he had opportunities when the cloth was taken away, and the servants were gone to make a hasty dinner: for so Camilla had directed; and further, Leonela had orders to dine before her mistress and never to stir from her side; but she, having her thoughts intent upon other matters of her own pleasure, and wanting to employ those hours, and that opportunity, to her own purposes, did not always observe her mistress's orders, but often left them alone as if she had been expressly commanded so to do. Nevertheless, the modest presence of Camilla, the gravity of her countenance, and her composed behaviour, were such that they awed and bridled Lothario's tongue.

But the influence of her virtues in silencing Lothario's tongue redounded to the greater prejudice of them both. For if his tongue lay still his thoughts were in motion; and he had leisure to contemplate, one by one, all those perfections of goodness and beauty of which Camilla was mistress, and which were sufficient to inspire love into a statue of marble, and how much more into a heart of flesh. Lothario gazed at her all the while he might have talked to her, and considered how worthy she was to be beloved: and this consideration began by little and little to undermine the regards he had for Anselmo: and, a thousand times, he thought of withdrawing from the city, and going where Anselmo should never see him, nor he Camilla, more: but the pleasure he took in beholding her had already thrown an obstacle in the way of his intention. He did violence to himself, and had frequent struggles within him, to get the better of the pleasure he received in gazing on Camilla. He blamed himself, when alone, for his folly; he called himself a false friend and a bad Christian. He reasoned upon, and made comparisons between his own conduct and that of Anselmo, and still concluded that Anselmo's folly and presumption were greater than his own infidelity: and if what he had in his thoughts were but as excusable before God as it was before men, he should fear no punishment for his fault.

In fine, the beauty and goodness of Camilla, together with the opportunity which the thoughtless husband had put into his hands, quite overturned Lothario's integrity. And without regarding anything but what tended to the gratification of his passion, at the end of three days from the time of Anselmo's absence, during which he had been in perpetual struggle with his desires, he began to solicit Camilla with such earnestness and disorder, and with such amorous expressions, that Camilla was astonished, and could only rise from her seat, and retire to her chamber, without answering a word. But, notwithstanding this sudden blast, Lothario's hope was not withered: for hope, being born with love, always lives with it. On the contrary, he was the more eager in the pursuit of Camilla: who, having discovered in Lothario what she could never have imagined, was at a loss how to behave. But thinking it neither safe nor right to give him opportunity or leisure of talking to her any more, she resolved, as she accordingly did, to send that very night one of her servants to Anselmo with a letter, wherein she wrote as follows.

CHAPTER 34

In which is continued The Novel of the Curious Impertinent.

CAMILLA'S LETTER TO ANSELMO.

'AN army, it is commonly said, makes but an ill appearance without its general, and a castle without its governor; but a young married woman, I say, makes a worse without a husband, when there is no just cause for his absence. I am so uneasy without you, and so entirely unable to support this absence, that, if you do not return speedily, I must go and pass my time at my father's house, though I leave yours without a guard: for the guard you left me, if you left him with that title, is, I believe, more intent upon his own pleasure than upon anything which concerns you: and, since you are wise, I shall say no more, nor is it proper I should.'

Anselmo received this letter, and understood by it that Lothario had begun the attack, and that Camilla must have received it according to his wish: and overjoyed at this good news, he sent Camilla a verbal message, not to stir from her house upon any account, for he would return very speedily. Camilla was surprised at Anselmo's answer, which increased the perplexity she was under; for now she durst neither stay in her own house, nor retire to that of her parents; since in staying she hazarded her virtue, and in going she should act contrary to her husband's positive command. At length she resolved upon that which proved the worst for her; which was, to stay and not to shun Lothario's company, lest it might give her servants occasion to talk; and she already began to be sorry she had written what she did to her spouse, fearing lest he should think Lothario must have observed some signs of lightness in her, which had emboldened him to lay aside the respect he owed her. But, conscious of her own integrity, she trusted in God, and her own virtuous disposition, resolving to resist, by her silence, whatever Lothario should say to her, without giving her husband any further account, lest it should involve him in any quarrel or trouble. She even began to consider how she might excuse Lothario to Anselmo, when he should ask her the cause of her writing that letter.

With these thoughts, more honourable than proper or beneficial, the next day she sat still, and heard what Lothario had to say to her; who plied her so warmly, that Camilla's firmness began to totter; and her virtue had much ado to get into her eyes, and prevent some indications of an amorous compassion, which the tears and arguments of Lothario had awakened in her breast. All this Lothario observed, and all contributed to inflame him the more. In short, he thought it necessary, whilst he had the time and opportunity, which

Anselmo's absence afforded him, to shorten the siege of this fortress. And therefore he attacked her pride with the praises of her beauty; for there is nothing which sooner reduces and levels the towering castles of the vanity of the fair sex, than vanity itself, when posted upon the tongue of flattery. In effect, he undermined the rock of her integrity with such engines, that, though she had been made of brass, she must have fallen to the ground. Lothario wept, entreated, flattered, and solicited with such earnestness and demonstrations of sincerity that he quite overthrew all Camilla's reserve, and at last triumphed over what he least expected, and most desired.

She surrendered—even Camilla surrendered: and what wonder, when even Lothario's friendship could not stand its ground? A plain example, showing us, that the passion of love is to be vanquished only by flying, and that we must not pretend to grapple with so powerful an enemy, since divine succours are necessary to subdue such force, though human. Leonela alone was privy to her lady's frailty; for the two faithless friends, and new lovers, could not hide it from her. Lothario would not acquaint Camilla with Anselmo's project, nor with his having designedly given him the opportunity of arriving at that point, lest she should esteem his passion the less, or should think he had made love to her by chance, rather than out of choice.

A few days after, Anselmo returned home, and did not miss what he had lost, which was what he took least care of, and yet valued most. He presently went to make a visit to Lothario, and found him at home. They embraced each other, and the one inquired what news concerning his life or death.

'The news I have for you, O friend Anselmo,' said Lothario, 'is, that you have a wife worthy to be the pattern and crown of all good women. The words I have said to her are given to the wind; my offers have been despised, my presents refused; and, when I shed some few feigned tears, she made a mere jest of them. In short, as Camilla is the sum of all beauty, she is also the repository in which modesty, good nature, and reserve, with all the virtues which can make a good woman praiseworthy and happy, are treasured up. Therefore, friend, take back your money; here it is; I had no occasion to make use of it; for Camilla's integrity is not to be shaken by things so mean as presents and promises. Be satisfied, Anselmo, and make no further trials; and since you have safely passed the gulf of those doubts and suspicions we are apt to entertain of women, do not again expose yourself on the deep sea of new disquiets, nor make a fresh trial, with another pilot, of the goodness and strength of the vessel, which heaven has allotted you for your passage through the ocean of this world; but make account, that you are arrived safe in port; and secure yourself with the anchor of serious consideration, and lie by, until you are required to pay that duty from which no human rank is exempted.'

Anselmo was entirely satisfied with Lothario's words, and believed them as if they had been delivered by some oracle. Nevertheless, he desired him not to give over the undertaking, though he carried it on merely out of curiosity and amusement; however he need not, for the future, ply her so close as he had done: all that he now desired of him, was, that he would write some verses in her praise under the name of Chloris, and he would give Camilla to understand that he was in love with a lady, to whom he had given that name, that he might celebrate her with the regard due to her modesty: and, if Lothario did not care to be at the trouble of writing the verses himself, he would do it for him.

'There will be no need of that,' said Lothario; 'for the Muses are not so unpropitious to me, but that, now and then, they make a visit. Tell Camilla your thoughts of my counterfeit passion, and leave me to make the verses; which, if not so good as the subject deserves, shall, at least, be the best I can make.'

Thus agreed the impertinent and the treacherous friend. And Anselmo, being returned to his house, inquired of Camilla, what she wondered he had not already inquired, namely, the occasion of her writing the letter she had sent him. Camilla answered, that she then fancied Lothario looked at her a little more licentiously than when he was at home; but that now she was undeceived, and believed it to be but a mere imagination of her own; for Lothario had, of late, avoided seeing, and being alone with her. Anselmo replied, that she might be very secure from that suspicion; for, to his knowledge, Lothario was in love with a young lady of condition in the city, whom he celebrated under the name of Chloris; and, though it were not so, she had nothing to fear, considering Lothario's virtue, and the great friendship that subsisted between them. Had not Camilla been beforehand advertised by Lothario, that this story of his love for Chloris was all a fiction, and that he had told it Anselmo, that he might have an opportunity, now and then, of employing himself in the praises of Camilla herself, she had doubtless fallen into the desperate snare of jealousy: but, being prepared for it, it gave her no disturbance.

The next day, they three being together at table, Anselmo desired Lothario to recite some of the verses he had composed on his beloved Chloris; for, since Camilla did not know her, he might safely repeat what he pleased.

'Though she did know her,' answered Lothario, 'I should have no reason to conceal what I have written; for, when a lover praises his mistress's beauty, and at the same time taxes her with cruelty, he casts no reproach upon her good name. But, be that as it will, I must tell you, that yesterday I made a sonnet on the ingratitude of Chloris; and it is this:

> 'In the dead silence of the peaceful night,
>   When others' cares are hush'd in soft repose,
>   The sad account of my neglected woes
>   To conscious heaven and Chloris I recite.
> And when the sun with his returning light,
>   Forth from the east his radiant journey goes,
>   With accents such as sorrow only knows,
>   My griefs to tell, is all my poor delight.
> And when bright Phoebus, from his starry throne,
>   Sends rays direct upon the parched soil,
>   Still in the mournful tale I persevere.
> Returning night renews my sorrow's toil;
>   And though from morn to night I weep and moan,
>   Nor heaven nor Chloris my complainings hear.'*

Camilla was very well pleased with the sonnet, but Anselmo more: he commended it, and said, the lady was extremely cruel, who made no return to so much truth.

'What then!' replied Camilla, 'are we to take all that the enamoured poets tell us for truth?'

'Not all they tell us as poets,' answered Lothario, 'but as lovers; for though as poets they may exceed, as lovers they always fall short of the truth.'

'There is no doubt of that,' replied Anselmo, resolved to second and support the credit of everything Lothario said with Camilla, who was now become as indifferent to Anselmo's artifice, as she was in love with Lothario. Being therefore pleased with everything that was his, and besides taking it for granted, that all his desires and verses were addressed to her, and that she was the true Chloris, she desired him, if he could recollect any other sonnet or verses, to repeat them.

'I remember one,' answered Lothario; 'but I believe it is not so good as the former, or to speak properly, less bad; as you shall judge; for it is this:

'I die, if not believed, 'tis sure I die,
    For ere I cease to love and to adore,
    Or fly, ungrateful fair, your beauty's pow'r,
    Dead at your feet you shall behold me lie.
When to the regions of obscurity
    I hence am banish'd to enjoy no more
    Glory and life, you, in that luckless hour,
    Your image graven in my heart shall see.
That relic, with a lover's generous pride,
    I treasure in my breast, the only source
    Of comfort whilst thy rigour lets me live.
Unhappy he, who steers his dangerous course
    Through unfrequented seas, no star to guide,
    Nor port his shatter'd vessel to receive.'

Anselmo commended this second sonnet as much as he had done the first; and thus he went on, adding link after link to the chain, wherewith he bound himself, and secured his own dishonour; for when Lothario dishonoured him most, he then assured him his honour was safest. And thus, every step of the ladder Camilla descended towards the centre of her disgrace, she ascended in her husband's opinion, towards the uppermost round of virtue and her good fame.

Now it happened one day that Camilla, being alone with her maid, said to her:

'I am ashamed, dear Leonela, to think how little value I set upon myself, in not making it cost Lothario more time to gain the entire possession of my inclinations, which I gave up so soon: I fear he will look upon my easiness in surrendering as levity, without reflecting on the violence he used, which put it out of my power to resist him.'

'Dear madam,' answered Leonela, 'let not this trouble you; for there is nothing in it; the value of a gift if it be good in itself, and worthy of esteem, is not lessened by being soon given; and therefore they say, he who gives quickly, gives twice.'

'They say also,' quoth Camilla, 'that which costs little is less valued.'

'This does not affect your case,' answered Leonela; 'for love, as I have heard say, sometimes flies and sometimes walks; runs with one person and goes leisurely with another; some he warms and some he burns; some he wounds, and others he kills; in one and the same instant he begins and concludes the career of his desires. He often in the morning lays siege to a fortress, and in the evening has it surrendered to him; for no force is able to resist him. And, this being so, what are you afraid of, if this be the very case of Lothario, love having made my master's absence the instrument to oblige you to surrender to him, and it being absolutely necessary to finish, in that interval, what love had decreed, without giving Time himself any time to bring back Anselmo, and, by his presence, render the work imperfect? for love has no surer minister to execute his designs than opportunity: it is that he makes use of in all his exploits, especially in the beginnings. All this I am well acquainted with, and from experience rather than hearsay; and, one day or other, madam, I may let you see, that I also am a girl of flesh and blood. Besides, madam, you did not declare your passion, nor engage yourself so soon, but you had first seen, in his eyes, in his sighs, in his expressions, in his promises, and his presents, Lothario's whole soul; and in that, and all his accomplishments, how worthy Lothario was of your love. Then, since it is so, let not these scruples and niceties disturb you, but rest assured, that Lothario esteems you no less than you do him; and live contented and satisfied, that, since you are fallen into the snare of love, it is with a person of worth and character, and one who possesses not only the four SS,* which they say, all true lovers ought to have, but the whole alphabet. Do but hear me, and you shall see how I have it by heart. He is, if I judge right, amiable, bountiful, constant, daring, enamoured, faithful, gallant, honourable, illustrious, kind, loyal, mild, noble, obliging, prudent, quiet, rich, and the SS, as they say; lastly, true, valiant, and wise: the X suits him not, because it is a harsh letter; the Y, he is young; the Z, zealous of your honour.'

Camilla smiled at her maid's alphabet, and took her to be more conversant in love matters than she had hitherto owned; and indeed she now confessed to Camilla, that she had a love affair with a young gentleman of the same city. At which Camilla was much disturbed, fearing lest from that quarter her own honour might be in danger. And therefore she sifted her, to know whether her amour had gone further than words. She, with little shame, and much boldness, owned it had. For, it is certain, that the slips of the mistress take off all shame from the maidservants, who, when they see their mistresses trip, make nothing of downright halting, nor of its being known.

Camilla could do no more but beg of Leonela to say nothing of her affair to the person she said was her lover, and to manage her own with such secrecy, that it might not come to the knowledge of Anselmo or of Lothario. Leonela answered, she would do so; but she kept her word in such a manner as justified Camilla's fears that she might lose her reputation by her means. For the lewd and bold Leonela, when she found that her mistress's conduct was not the same it used to be, had the assurance to introduce and conceal her lover in the house, presuming that her lady durst not speak of it, though she knew it. For this inconvenience, among others, attends the failings of mistresses, that they become slaves to their very servants, and are necessitated to conceal their dishonesty and lewdness; as was the case with Camilla:

for, though she saw, not once only but several times, that Leonela was with her gallant in a room of her house, she was so far from daring to chide her, that she gave her opportunities of locking him in, and did all she could to prevent his being seen by her husband.

But all could not hinder Lothario from seeing him once go out of the house at break of day; who, not knowing who he was, thought, at first, it must be some apparition. But when he saw him steal off, muffling himself up, and concealing himself with care and caution, he changed one foolish opinion for another, which must have been the ruin of them all, if Camilla had not remedied it. Lothario was so far from thinking that the man whom he had seen coming out of Anselmo's house, at so unseasonable an hour, came thither upon Leonela's account, that he did not so much as remember there was such a person as Leonela in the world. What he thought, was, that Camilla, as she had been easy and complying to him, was so to another also: for the wickedness of a bad woman carries this additional mischief along with it, that it weakens her credit even with the man to whose entreaties and persuasions she surrendered her honour; and he is ready to believe, upon the slightest grounds, that she yields to others even with greater facility.

All Lothario's good sense and prudent reasonings seem to have failed him upon this occasion: for, without making one proper, or even rational reflection, without more ado, grown impatient, and blinded with a jealous rage that gnawed his bowels, and dying to be revenged on Camilla, who had offended him in nothing, he went to Anselmo before he was up, and said to him:

'Know, Anselmo, that for several days past I have struggled with myself to keep from you what is no longer possible nor just to conceal. Know, that Camilla's fort is surrendered, and submitted to my will and pleasure; and if I have delayed discovering to you this truth, it was to satisfy myself whether it was any wanton desire in her, or whether she had a mind to try me, and to see whether the love I made to her, with your connivance, was in earnest. And I still believed, if she was what she ought to be, and what we both thought her, she would, before now, have given you an account of my solicitations. But, since I find she has not, I conclude she intends to keep the promise she has made me of giving me a meeting the next time you are absent from home, in the wardrobe (and, indeed, that was the place where Camilla used to entertain him). And, since the fault is not yet committed, excepting in thought only, I would not have you run precipitately to take revenge; for, perhaps, between this and the time of putting it in execution, Camilla may change her mind and repent. And therefore, as you have hitherto always followed my advice, in whole or in part, follow and observe this I shall now give you, that without possibility of being mistaken, and upon maturest deliberation, you may satisfy yourself as to what is most fitting for you to do. Pretend an absence of three or four days, as you used to do at other times, and contrive to hide yourself in the wardrobe, where the tapestry and other movables may serve to conceal you; and then you will see with your own eyes, and I with mine, what Camilla intends; and if it be wickedness, as is rather to be feared than expected, you may then, with secrecy and caution, be the avenger of your own injury.'

Anselmo was amazed, confounded, and astonished at Lothario's words, which came upon him at a time when he least expected to hear them; for he already looked upon Camilla as victorious over Lothario's feigned assaults, and began to enjoy the glory of the conquest. He stood a good while with his eyes fixed motionless on the ground, and at length said:

'Lothario, you have done what I expected from your friendship; I must follow your advice in everything; do what you will, and be as secret as so unlooked-for an event requires.'

Lothario promised him he would; and scarcely had he left him when he began to repent of all he had said, and was convinced he had acted foolishly, since he might have revenged himself on Camilla by a less cruel and less dishonourable method. He cursed his want of sense, condemned his heedless resolution, and was at a loss how to undo what was done, or to get tolerably well out of the scrape. At last he resolved to discover all to Camilla; and, as he could not

long want an opportunity of doing it, that very day he found
her alone; and immediately on his coming in, she said:

'Know, dear Lothario, that I have an uneasiness at heart,
which tortures me in such a manner, that methinks it is ready
to burst it, and, indeed, it is a wonder that it does not; for
Leonela's impudence is arrived to that degree, that she every
night entertains a gallant in the house, who stays with her
until daylight, so much to the prejudice of my reputation,
that it will leave room for censure to whoever shall see him
go out at such unseasonable hours: and what gives me the
most concern is, that I cannot chastise or so much as
reprimand her; for her being in the secret of our correspondence puts a bridle into my mouth, and obliges me to conceal
hers; and I am afraid of some unlucky event from this
quarter.'

At first, when Camilla said this, Lothario believed it a piece
of cunning to deceive him, by persuading him that the man
he saw go out was Leonela's gallant, and not Camilla's; but,
perceiving that she wept, and afflicted herself, and begged
his assistance in finding a remedy, he soon came into the
belief of what she said; and so was filled with confusion and
repentance for what he had done. He desired Camilla to make
herself easy, for he would take an effectual course to restrain
Leonela's insolence. He also told her what the furious rage
of jealousy had instigated him to tell Anselmo, and how it
was agreed that Anselmo should hide himself in the wardrobe, to be an eye-witness from thence of her disloyalty to
him. He begged her to pardon this madness, and desired her
advice how to remedy what was done, and extricate them
out of so perplexed a labyrinth, as his rashness had involved
them in.

Camilla was astonished at hearing what Lothario had said,
and, with much resentment, reproached him for the ill
thoughts he had entertained of her; and with many and
discreet reasons set before him the folly and inconsiderateness of the resolution he had taken. But, as women have
naturally a more ready invention, either for good or bad
purposes, than men, though it often fails them when they set
themselves purposely to deliberate, Camilla instantly hit upon

a way to remedy an affair seemingly incapable of all remedy. She bid Lothario see that Anselmo hid himself the next day where he had proposed; for by this very hiding she proposed to secure, for the future, their mutual enjoyment without fear of surprise; and, without letting him into the whole of her design, she only desired him, after Anselmo was posted, to be ready at Leonela's call, and that he should take care to answer to whatever she should say to him, just as he would do if he did not know that Anselmo was listening. Lothario pressed her to explain to him her whole design, that he might with the more safety and caution be upon his guard in all he thought necessary.

'No other guard,' said Camilla, 'is necessary, but only to answer me directly to what I shall ask you.'

For she was not willing to let him into the secret of what she intended to do, lest he should not come into that design, which she thought so good, and should look out for some other not likely to prove so successful.

Lothario then left her; and the next day Anselmo, under pretence of going to his friend's villa, went from home, but turned presently back to hide himself, which he might conveniently enough do, for Camilla and Leonela were out of the way on purpose.

Anselmo being now hid, with all that palpitation of heart which may be imagined in one who expected to see with his own eyes the bowels of his honour ripped up, and was upon the point of losing that supreme bliss he thought himself possessed of in his beloved Camilla; she and Leonela, being well assured that Anselmo was behind the hangings, came together into the wardrobe; and Camilla had scarce set her foot in it, when, fetching a deep sigh, she said:

'Ah, dear Leonela, would it not be better before I put that in execution, which I would keep secret from you, lest you should endeavour to prevent it, that you should take Anselmo's dagger, and plunge it into this infamous breast? But do it not; for it is not reasonable I should bear the punishment of another's fault. I will first know what the bold and wanton eyes of Lothario saw in me, that could give him the assurance to imagine so wicked a design, as that he has discovered to me, in contempt of his friend and of my honour. Step to the window, Leonela, and call him, for, doubtless, he is waiting in the street in hopes of putting his wicked design in execution. But first my cruel, but honourable purpose shall be executed.'

'Ah! dear madam,' answered the cunning and well-instructed Leonela, 'what is it you intend to do with this dagger? is it to take away your own life, or Lothario's? whichever of the two you do will redound to the ruin of your credit and fame. It is better you should dissemble your wrong than to let this wicked man now into the house while we are alone. Consider, madam, we are weak women, and he a man, and resolute; and, as he comes blinded and big with his wicked purpose, he may perhaps, before you can execute yours, do what would be worse for you than taking away your life. A mischief take my master Anselmo for giving this impudent fellow such an ascendant in his house. But pray, madam, if you kill him, as I imagine you intend, what shall we do with him after he is dead?'

'What, child?' answered Camilla; 'why leave him here for Anselmo to bury him; for it is but just he should have the agreeable trouble of burying his own infamy. Call him without more ado; for all the time I lose in delaying to take due revenge for my wrong, methinks I offend against that loyalty I owe to my husband.'

All this Anselmo listened to, and at every word Camilla spoke his sentiments changed. But when he understood that she intended to kill Lothario, he was inclined to prevent it, by coming out and discovering himself; but was withheld by the strong desire he had to see what would be the end of so brave and virtuous a resolution; purposing, however, to come out in time enough to prevent mischief.

And now Camilla was taken with a strong fainting fit; and throwing herself upon a bed that was there, Leonela began to weep bitterly, and to say:

'Ah, woe is me! that I should be so unhappy as to see die here, between my arms, the flower of the world's virtue, the crown of good women, the pattern of chastity . . .'

With other such expressions, that nobody, who had heard her, but would have taken her for the most compassionate and faithful damsel in the universe, and her lady for another persecuted Penelope.

Camilla soon recovered from her swoon, and, when she was come to herself, she said:

'Why do you not go, Leonela, and call the most faithless friend of all friends that the sun ever saw, or the night covered? Be quick, run, fly; let not the fire of my rage evaporate and be spent by delay, and the just vengeance I expect pass off in empty threatenings and curses.'

'I am going to call him,' said Leonela; 'but, dear madam, you must first give me that dagger, lest, when I am gone, you should do a thing which might give those who love you cause to weep all their lives long.'

'Go, dear Leonela, and fear not,' said Camilla; 'I will not do it, for though I am resolute, and, in your opinion sincere in defending my honour, I shall not be so to the degree that Lucretia was, of whom it is said that she killed herself without having committed any fault, and without first killing him who was the cause of her misfortune. Yes, I will die, if die I must; but it shall be after I have satiated my revenge on him who is the occasion of my being now here to bewail his insolence, which proceeded from no fault of mine.'

Leonela wanted a great deal of entreaty before she would go and call Lothario; but at last she went, and, while she was away, Camilla, as if she was talking to herself, said:

'Good God! would it not have been more advisable to have dismissed Lothario, as I have done many other times, than to give him room, as I have now done, to think me dishonest and naught, though it be only for the short time I defer the undeceiving him? without doubt it would have been better: but I shall not be revenged, nor my husband's honour satisfied, if he gets off so clean, and so smoothly, from an attempt to which his wicked thoughts have led him. No! let the traitor pay with his life for what he enterprises with so lascivious a desire. Let the world know (if perchance it comes to know it) that Camilla not only preserved her loyalty to her husband, but revenged him on the person who

dared to wrong him. But, after all, it would perhaps be better
to give an account of the whole matter to Anselmo; but I
have already hinted it to him in the letter I wrote him into
the country; and I fancy his neglecting to remedy the mischief
I pointed out to him, must be owing to pure good nature,
and a confidence in Lothario which would not let him believe
that the least thought, to the prejudice of his honour, could
be lodged in the breast of so faithful a friend: nor did I
myself believe it, for many days, nor should ever have given
credit to it, if his insolence had not risen so high, and his
avowed presents, large promises, and continual tears, put it
past all dispute. But why do I talk thus? does a brave
resolution stand in need of counsel? No, certainly. Traitor,
avaunt! come vengeance! let the false one come, let him enter,
let him die, and then befall what will. Unspotted I entered
into the power of him whom heaven allotted me for my
husband, and unspotted I will leave him, though bathed all
over in my own chaste blood and the impure gore of the
falsest friend that friendship ever saw.'

And saying this she walked up and down the room with
the drawn dagger in her hand, taking such irregular and huge
strides, and with such gestures, that one would have thought
her beside herself, and have taken her, not for a soft and
delicate woman, but for some desperate ruffian.

Anselmo observed all from behind the arras, where he had
hid himself, and was amazed at all, and already thought what
he had seen and heard sufficient to balance still greater suspicions, and began to wish that Lothario might not come, for
fear of some sudden disaster. And being now upon the point
of discovering himself, and coming out to embrace and undeceive his wife, he was prevented by seeing Leonela return with
Lothario by the hand; and, as soon as Camilla saw him, she drew
with the dagger a long line between her and him, and said:

'Take notice, Lothario, of what I say to you: if you shall
dare to pass this line you see here, or but come up to it, the
moment I see you attempt it, I will pierce my breast with
this dagger I hold in my hand: but before you answer me a
word to this, hear a few more I have to say to you, and then
answer me as you please. In the first place, Lothario, I desire

you to tell me, whether you know Anselmo my husband, and in what estimation you hold him? and, in the next place, I would be informed whether you know me? Answer me to this, and be under no concern, nor study for an answer; for they are no difficult questions I ask you.'

Lothario was not so ignorant, but that from the instant Camilla bid him hide Anselmo, he guessed what she intended to do, and accordingly humoured her design so well, that they were able, between them, to make the counterfeit pass for something more than truth; and therefore he answered Camilla in this manner:

'I did not imagine, fair Camilla, that you called me to answer to things so wide of the purpose for which I came hither. If you do it to delay me the promised favour, why did you not adjourn it to a still further day? for the nearer the prospect of possession is, the more eager we are to enjoy the desired good. But, that you may not say I do not answer to your questions, I reply, that I know your husband Anselmo, and that we have known each other from our tender years: of our friendship I will say nothing, that I may not be a witness against myself of the wrong which love, that powerful excuse for greater faults, has made me do him. You too I know, and prize you as highly as he does: for, were it not so, I should not for less excellence, have acted so contrary to my duty as a gentleman, and so much against the holy laws of true friendship, which I have now broken and violated, through the tyranny of that enemy, love.'

'If you acknowledge so much,' replied Camilla, 'mortal enemy of all that justly deserves to be loved, with what face dare you appear before her, whom you know to be the mirror in which Anselmo looks, and [in] which you might have seen upon what slight grounds you injure him? But ah! unhappy me! I now begin to find what it was that made you forget yourself: it was, doubtless, some indiscretion of mine: for I will not call it immodesty, since it proceeded not from design, but from some one of those inadvertencies which women frequently fall into unawares, when there is nobody present before whom they think they need be upon the reserve. But tell me, O traitor, when did I ever answer your addresses with any word or sign, that could give you the least shadow of hope, that you should ever accomplish your infamous desires? when were not your amorous expressions repulsed and rebuked with rigour and severity? when were your many promises and greater presents believed or accepted? but knowing that no one can persevere long in an affair of love, unless it be kept alive by some hope, I take upon myself the blame of your impertinence; since without doubt, some inadvertency of mine has nourished your hope so long, and therefore I will chastise, and inflict that punishment on myself, which your offence deserves. And, to convince you, that, being so severe to myself, I could not possibly be otherwise to you, I had a mind you should come hither to be a witness to the sacrifice I intend to make to the offended honour of my worthy husband, injured by you with the greatest deliberation imaginable, and by me too through my carelessness in not shunning the occasion (if I gave you any) of countenancing and authorizing your wicked intentions. I say again that the suspicion I have, that some inadvertency of mine has occasioned such licentious thoughts in you, is what disturbs me the most, and what I most desire to punish with my own hands: for should some other executioner do it, my crime, perhaps, would be more public. Yes, I will die, but I will die killing, and carry with me one, who shall entirely satisfy the thirst of that revenge I expect, and partly enjoy already, as I shall have before my eyes, to what place soever I go, the vengeance of impartial justice strictly executed on him who has reduced me to this desperate condition.'

At these words, she flew upon Lothario, with the drawn dagger, so swiftly, and with such incredible violence, and with such seeming earnestness to stab him to the heart, that he was almost in doubt himself whether those efforts were feigned or real: and he was forced to make use of all his dexterity and strength to prevent his being wounded by Camilla, who played the counterfeit so to the life, that, to give this strange imposture a colour of truth she resolved to stain it with her own blood. For, perceiving, or pretending, that she could not wound Lothario, she said:

'Since fortune denies a complete satisfaction to my just desires, it shall not, however, be in its power to defeat that satisfaction entirely.'

And so struggling to free her dagger-hand, held by Lothario, she got it loose, and directing the point to a part where it might give but a slight wound, she stabbed herself above the breast, near the left shoulder, and presently fell to the ground as in a swoon.

Leonela and Lothario stood in suspense, and astonished at this accident, and were in doubt what to think of it, especially when they saw Camilla lying on the floor, and bathed in her own blood. Lothario ran hastily, frighted, and breathless, to draw out the dagger; but perceiving the slightness of the wound, the fear he had been in vanished, and he admired afresh the sagacity, prudence, and great ingenuity of the fair Camilla. And now, to act his part, he began to make a long and sorrowful lamentation over the body of Camilla, as if she were dead, imprecating heavy curses, not only on himself, but on him who had been the cause of bringing him to that pass, and, knowing that his friend Anselmo overheard him, he said such things, that whoever had heard them would have pitied him more than they would have done Camilla herself, though they had judged her to be really dead.

Leonela took her in her arms, and laid her on the bed, beseeching Lothario to procure somebody to dress Camilla's wound secretly. She also desired his advice and opinion what they should say to Anselmo about it, if he should chance to come home before it was healed. He answered, that they might say what they pleased; that he was not in a condition of giving any advice worth following: he bid her endeavour to staunch the blood; and, as for himself, he would go where he should never be seen more. And so, with a show of much sorrow and concern, he left the house, and when he found himself alone, and in a place where nobody saw him, he ceased not to cross himself in admiration at the cunning of Camilla, and the suitable behaviour of Leonela. He considered what a thorough assurance Anselmo must have of his wife's being a second Portia, and wanted to be with him, that they might rejoice together at the imposture and the truth, the most artfully disguised that can be imagined.

Leonela, as she was bidden, staunched her mistress's blood, which was just as much as might serve to colour her stratagem; and washing the wound with a little wine, she bound it up the best she could, saying such things while she was dressing it, as were alone sufficient to make Anselmo believe that he had in Camilla an image of chastity. To the words Leonela said, Camilla added others, calling herself coward and poor spirited, in that she wanted the resolution, at a time when she stood most in need, to deprive herself of that life she so much abhorred. She asked her maid's advice whether she should give an account of what had happened to her beloved spouse, or no. Leonela persuaded her to say nothing about it, since it would lay him under a necessity of revenging himself on Lothario, which he could not do without great danger to himself; and a good woman was obliged to avoid all occasion of involving her husband in a quarrel, and should rather prevent all such as much as she possibly could. Camilla replied she approved of her opinion, and would follow it; but that by all means they must contrive what to say to Anselmo about the wound which he must needs see. To which Leonela answered, that, for her part, she knew not how to tell a lie, though but in jest.

'Then, pray thee,' replied Camilla, 'how should I know how, who dare not invent, or stand in one, though my life were at a stake? If we cannot contrive to come well off, it will be better to tell him the whole truth, than that he should catch us in a false story.'

'Be in no pain, madam,' answered Leonela; 'for, between this and to-morrow morning, I will study what we shall tell him; and perhaps the wound being where it is, you may conceal it from his sight, and heaven may be pleased to favour our just and honourable intentions. Compose yourself, good madam; endeavour to quiet your spirits, that my master may not find you in so violent a disorder; and leave the rest to my care, and to that of heaven, which always favours honest designs.'

Anselmo stood, with the utmost attention, listening to, and beholding represented, the tragedy of the death of his honour;

which the actors performed with such strange and moving passions, that it seemed as if they were transformed into the very characters they personated. He longed for the night, and for an opportunity of slipping out of his house, that he might see his dear friend Lothario, and rejoice with him on the finding so precious a jewel, by the perfectly clearing up of his wife's virtue. They both took care to give him a convenient opportunity of going out; which he made use of, and immediately went to seek Lothario; and, having found him, it is impossible to recount the embraces he gave him, the satisfaction he expressed, and the praises he bestowed on Camilla. All which Lothario hearkened to, without being able to show any signs of joy; for he could not but reflect how much his friend was deceived, and how ungenerously he treated him. And though Anselmo perceived that Lothario did not express any joy, he believed it was because Camilla was wounded, and he had been the occasion of it. And therefore, among other things, he desired him to be in no pain about Camilla: for, without doubt, the wound must be very slight, since her maid and she had agreed to hide it from him: and as he might depend upon it there was nothing to be feared, he desired that thenceforward he would rejoice and be merry with him, since, through his diligence, and by his means, he found himself raised to the highest pitch of happiness he could wish to arrive at; and, for himself, he said, he would make it his pastime and amusement to write verses in praise of Camilla, to perpetuate her memory to all future ages. Lothario applauded his good resolution, and said, that he too would lend a helping hand towards raising so illustrious an edifice.

Anselmo now remained the man of [all] the world the most agreeably deceived. He led home by the hand the instrument, as he thought, of his glory, but in reality the ruin of his fame. Camilla received Lothario with a countenance seemingly shy, but with inward gladness of heart. This imposture lasted some time, until, a few months after, fortune turned her wheel, and the iniquity, until then so artfully concealed, came to light, and his impertinent curiosity cost poor Anselmo his life.

CHAPTER 35

*The conclusion of 'The Novel of the Curious Impertinent',
with the dreadful battle betwixt Don Quixote and
certain wine-skins.* *

THERE remained but little more of the novel to be read,
when from the room, where Don Quixote lay, Sancho Panza
came running out all in a fright, crying aloud:

'Run, sirs, quickly, and succour my master, who is over
head and ears in the toughest and closest battle my eyes have
ever beheld. As God shall save me, he has given the giant,
that enemy of the princess Micomicona, such a stroke, that
he has cut off his head close to his shoulders, as if it had
been a turnip.'

'What say you, brother?' quoth the priest (leaving off
reading the remainder of the novel), 'are you in your senses,
Sancho? How the devil can this be, seeing the giant is two
thousand leagues off?'

At that instant they heard a great noise in the room, and
Don Quixote calling aloud:

'Stay, cowardly thief, robber, rogue; for here I have you,
and your scimitar shall avail you nothing.'

And it seemed as if he gave several hacks and slashes
against the walls.

'Do not stand listening,' quoth Sancho; 'but go in and part
the fray, or aid my master: though by this time there will be
no occasion; for doubtless the giant is already dead, and
giving an account to God of his past wicked life; for I saw
the blood run about the floor, and the head cut off, and
fallen on one side, and as big as a great wine-skin.'

'I will be hanged,' quoth the innkeeper, at this juncture, 'if
Don Quixote, or Don Devil, has not given a gash to some
of the wine-skins that stand at his bed's-head, and the wine
he has let out must be what this honest fellow takes for
blood.'

And, so saying, he went into the room, and the whole
company after him; and they found Don Quixote in the
strangest situation in the world. He was in his shirt, which
was not quite long enough before to cover his thighs, and

was six inches shorter behind: his legs were very long and lean, full of hair, and not over clean: he had on his head a little red cap, somewhat greasy, which belonged to the innkeeper. About his left arm he had twisted the bed-blanket (to which Sancho owed a grudge, and he very well knew why), and in his right hand he held his drawn sword, with which he was laying about him on all sides, and uttering words as if he had really been fighting with some giant: and the best of it was, his eyes were shut; for he was asleep, and dreaming that he was engaged in battle with the giant: for his imagination was so taken up with the adventure he had undertaken, that it made him dream he was already arrived at the kingdom of Micomicon, and already engaged in fight with his enemy; and, fancying he was cleaving the giant down, he had given the skins so many cuts, that the whole room was afloat with wine. The innkeeper, perceiving it, fell into such a rage, that he set upon Don Quixote, and, with his clenched fists, began to give him so many cuffs, that if Cardenio and the priest had not taken him off, he would have put an end to the war of the giant; and yet notwithstanding all this, the poor gentleman did not awake until the barber brought a large bucket of cold water from the well, and soused it all over his body at a dash; whereat Don Quixote awoke, but not so thoroughly as to be sensible of the pickle he was in. Dorothea, perceiving how scantily and airily he was arrayed, would not go in to see the fight between her champion and her adversary. Sancho was searching all about the floor for the head of the giant; and not finding it, he said:

'Well, I see plainly, that everything about this house is enchantment: for, the time before, in this very same place where I now am, I had several punches and thumps given me, without knowing from whence they came, or seeing anybody: and now the head is vanished, which I saw cut off with my own eyes, and the blood spouting from the body like any fountain.'

'What blood, and what fountain? thou enemy to God and his saints!' said the innkeeper: 'dost thou not see, thief, that the blood and the fountain are nothing but these skins pierced and ripped open, and the red wine floating about the room? I wish I may see his soul floating in hell that pierced them!'

'I know nothing,' said Sancho; 'only that I should be so unfortunate, that, for want of finding this head, my earldom will melt away like salt in water.'

Now Sancho awake, was madder than his master asleep; so besotted was he with the promises he had made him. The innkeeper lost all patience to see the squire's phlegm, and the knight's wicked handiwork; and he swore they should not escape, as they did the time before, without paying; and that, this bout, the privileges of his chivalry should not exempt him from discharging both reckonings, even to the patches of the torn skins.

The priest held Don Quixote by the hands; who, imagining he had finished the adventure, and that he was in the presence of the princess Micomicona, fell on his knees before the priest, and said:

'High and renowned lady, well may your grandeur from this day forward live more secure, now that this ill-born creature can do you no hurt; and I also, from this day forward, am freed from the promise I gave you, since by the assistance of the most high God, and through the favour of her by whom I live and breathe, I have so happily accomplished it.'

'Did not I tell you so?' quoth Sancho, hearing this; 'so that I was not drunk; see, if my master has not already put the giant in pickle: here are the bulls; my earldom is safe.'

Who could forbear laughing at the absurdities of both master and man? they all laughed except the innkeeper, who cursed himself to the devil. But at length, the barber, Cardenio, and the priest, with much ado, threw Don Quixote on the bed, who fell fast asleep, with signs of very great fatigue. They left him to sleep on, and went out to the inn door, to comfort Sancho for not finding the giant's head, though they had most to do to pacify the innkeeper, who was out of his wits for the murder of his wine-skins. The hostess muttered, and said:

'In an unlucky minute, and in an evil hour, came this knight-errant into my house: O that my eyes had never seen

him! he has been a dear guest to me. The last time he went
away with a night's reckoning, for supper, bed, straw, and
barley, for himself, and for his squire, for a horse and an
ass, telling us, forsooth, that he was a knight-adventurer (evil
adventures befall him, and all the adventurers in the world!)
and that therefore he was not obliged to pay anything; for
so it was written in the registers of knight-errantry: and now
again, on his account too, comes this other gentleman, and
carries off my tail, and returns it me with two-pennyworth
of damage, all the hair off, so that it can serve no more for
my husband's purpose. And, after all, to rip open my skins,
and let out my wine! would I could see his blood so let out.
But let him not think to escape; for by the bones of my
father, and the soul of my mother, they shall pay me down
upon the nail every farthing, or may I never be called by my
own name, nor be my own father's daughter.'

The hostess said all this and more, in great wrath; and
honest Maritornes, her maid, seconded her. The daughter
held her peace, but now and then smiled. The priest quieted
all, promising to make them the best reparation he could for
their loss, as well in the wine-skins as the wine, and especially
for the damage done to the tail, which they valued so much.
Dorothea comforted Sancho Panza, telling him, that whenever it should really appear, that his master had cut off the
giant's head, she promised when she was peaceably seated on
her throne, to bestow on him the best earldom in her
dominions. Herewith Sancho was comforted, and assured the
princess, she might depend upon it, that he had seen the
giant's head, by the same token that it had a beard which
reached down to the girdle; and if it was not to be found,
it was because everything passed in that house by way of
enchantment, as he had experienced the last time he lodged
there. Dorothea said she believed so, and bid him be in no
pain; for all would be well, and succeed to his heart's desire.

All being now pacified, the priest had a mind to read the
remainder of the novel; for he saw it wanted but little.
Cardenio, Dorothea, and the rest entreated him so to do; and
he, willing to please all the company, and himself among the
rest, went on with the story as follows:

'Now so it was, that Anselmo, through the satisfaction he took in the supposed virtue of Camilla, lived with all the content and security in the world; and Camilla purposely looked shy on Lothario, that Anselmo might think she rather hated than loved him: and Lothario, for further security in this affair, begged Anselmo to excuse his coming any more to his house, since it was plain, the sight of him gave Camilla great uneasiness. But the deceived Anselmo would by no means comply with his request: and thus, by a thousand different ways, he became the contriver of his own dishonour, while he thought he was so of his pleasure. As for Leonela, she was so pleased to find herself thus at liberty to follow her amour, that, without minding anything else, she let loose the reins, and took her swing, being confident that her lady would conceal it, and even put her in the most commodious way of carrying it on.

'In short, one night, Anselmo perceived somebody walking in Leonela's chamber, and being desirous to go in to know who it was, he found the door was held against him, which increased his desire of getting in; and he made such an effort, that he burst open the door, and, just as he entered, he saw a man leap down from the window into the street: and running hastily to stop him, or to see who he was, he could do neither: for Leonela clung about him, crying:

"Dear sir, be calm, and be not so greatly disturbed, nor pursue the man who leaped out; he belongs to me; in short he is my husband."

'Anselmo would not believe Leonela, but, blind with rage, drew his poniard, and offered to stab her, assuring her, that, if she did not tell him the whole truth, he would kill her: she, with the fright, not knowing what she was saying, said:

"Do not kill me, sir, and I will tell you things of greater importance than any you can imagine."

"Tell me then quickly," said Anselmo, "or you are a dead woman."

"At present, it is impossible," said Leonela, "I am in such confusion: let me alone until to-morrow morning, and then you shall know from me what will amaze you: in the mean-

time be assured, that the person who jumped out at the
window is a young man of this city, who has given me a
promise of marriage."

'With this Anselmo was somewhat pacified, and was content to wait the time she desired, not dreaming he should
hear anything against Camilla, of whose virtue he was so
satisfied and secure; and so leaving the room, he locked
Leonela in, telling her she should not stir from thence, until
she had told him what she had to say to him. He went
immediately to Camilla, and related to her all that had passed
with her waiting-woman, and the promise she had given him
to acquaint him with things of the utmost importance. It is
needless to say, whether Camilla was disturbed or not: so
great was the consternation she was in, that, verily believing
(as indeed it was very likely) that Leonela would tell Anselmo
all she knew of her disloyalty, she had not the courage to
wait until she saw whether her suspicion was well or ill
grounded: and that very night, when she found Anselmo was
asleep, taking with her all her best jewels, and some money,
without being perceived by anybody, she left her house, and
went to Lothario's, to whom she recounted what had passed,
desiring him to conduct her to some place of safety, or to
go off with her, where they might live secure from Anselmo.
Camilla put Lothario into such confusion, that he knew not
how to answer her a word, much less to resolve what was
to be done.

'At length, he bethought himself of carrying Camilla to a
convent, the prioress of which was his sister. Camilla consented, and Lothario conveyed her thither with all the haste
the case required, and left her in the monastery; and he too
presently left the city, without acquainting anybody with his
absence.

'When it was daybreak, Anselmo, without missing Camilla
from his side (so impatient was he to know what Leonela
had to tell him), got up, and went to the chamber where he
had left her locked in. He opened the door, and went in, but
found no Leonela there: he only found the sheets tied to the
window, an evident sign that by them she had slid down,
and was gone off. He presently returned, full of concern, to

acquaint Camilla with it; and, not finding her in bed, nor anywhere in the house, he stood astonished. He inquired of the servants for her, but no one could give him any tidings.

'It accidentally happened, as he was searching for Camilla, that he found her cabinet open, and most of her jewels gone; and this gave him the first suspicion of his disgrace, and that Leonela was not the cause of his misfortune. And so, just as he then was but half dressed, he went sad and pensive, to give an account of his disaster to his friend Lothario; but not finding him, and his servants telling him that their master went away that night, and took all the money he had with him, he was ready to run mad. And, to complete all, when he came back to his house, he found not one of all his servants, man nor maid, but the house left alone and deserted.

'He knew not what to think, say, or do, and, by little and little, his wits began to fail him. He considered, and saw himself, in an instant, deprived of wife, friend, and servants; abandoned as he thought by the heaven that covered him, but, above all, robbed of his honour, since, in missing Camilla, he saw his own ruin.

'After some thought, he resolved to go to his friend's country house, where he had been, when he gave the opportunity for plotting this unhappy business. He locked the doors of his house, got on horseback, and set forward with great oppression of spirits: and scarcely had he gone half way, when, overwhelmed by his melancholy thoughts, he was forced to alight, and tie his horse to a tree, at the foot whereof he dropped down, breathing out bitter and mournful sighs, and stayed there until almost night; about which time, he saw a man coming on horseback from the city; and, having saluted him, he inquired what news there was in Florence.

"The strangest," replied the citizen, "that has been heard these many days; for it is publicly talked, that last night Lothario, that great friend of Anselmo the Rich, who lived at St. John's, carried off Camilla, wife to Anselmo, and that he is also missing. All this was told by a maidservant of

Camilla's, whom the governor caught in the night letting herself down by a sheet from a window of Anselmo's house. In short, I do not know the particulars; all I know is, that the whole town is in astonishment at this accident: for no one could have expected any such thing, considering the great and entire friendship between them, which, it is said, was so remarkable, that they were styled 'the Two Friends'."

"Pray, is it known," said Anselmo, "which way Lothario and Camilla have taken?"

"It is not," replied the citizen, "though the governor has ordered diligent search to be made after them."

"God be with you," said Anselmo.

"And with you also," said the citizen, and went his way.

'This dismal news reduced Anselmo almost to the losing, not only of his wits, but his life. He got up as well as he could, and arrived at his friend's house, who had not yet heard of his misfortune; but seeing him come in pale, spiritless, and faint, he concluded he was oppressed by some heavy affliction. Anselmo begged him to lead him immediately to a chamber, and to let him have pen, ink, and paper. They did so, and left him alone on the bed, locking the door, as he desired. And now, finding himself alone, he so overcharged his imagination with his misfortunes, that he plainly perceived he was drawing near his end, and therefore resolved to leave behind him some account of the cause of his strange death: and beginning to write, before he had set down all he had intended, his breath failed him, and he yielded up his life into the hands of that sorrow, which was occasioned by his impertinent curiosity.

'The master of the house, finding it grow late, and that Anselmo did not call, determined to go in to him, to know whether his indisposition increased, and found him with his face downwards, half of his body in bed, and half leaning on the table, with the paper he had written open, and his hand still holding the pen. His friend having first called to him, went and took him by the hand; and finding he did not answer him, and that he was cold, he perceived that he was dead. He was very much surprised and troubled, and called the family to be witnesses of the sad mishap that had befallen

Anselmo: afterwards he read the paper, which he knew to be written with Anselmo's own hand, wherein were these words:

ANSELMO'S PAPER.

"A foolish and impertinent desire has deprived me of life. If the news of my death reaches Camilla's ears, let her know I forgive her; for she was not obliged to do miracles, nor was I under a necessity of desiring she should: and, since I was the contriver of my own dishonour, there is no reason why—"

'Thus far Anselmo wrote; by which it appeared, that, at this point, without being able to finish the sentence, he gave up the ghost.

'The next day his friend sent his relations an account of his death; who had already heard of his misfortune, and of Camilla's retiring to the convent, where she was almost in a condition of bearing her husband company in that inevitable journey; not through the news of his death, but of her lover absenting himself. It is said, that, though she was now a widow, she would neither quit the convent, nor take the veil, until, not many days after, news being come of Lothario's being killed in a battle, fought about that time between Monsieur de Lautrec, and the Great Captain Goncalo Hernandez of Córdova, in the kingdom of Naples,* whither the too-late repenting friend had made his retreat, she then took the religious habit, and soon after gave up her life into the rigorous hands of grief and melancholy. This was the end of them all, an end sprung from an extravagant rashness at the beginning.'

'I like this novel very well,' said the priest; 'but I cannot persuade myself it is a true story: and if it be a fiction, the author has erred against probability: for it cannot be imagined, there can be any husband so senseless, as to desire to make so dangerous an experiment, as Anselmo did: had this case been supposed between a gallant and his mistress, it might pass; but, between husband and wife, there is something impossible in it: however, I am not displeased with the manner of telling it.'

CHAPTER 36

*Which treats of other uncommon accidents, that
happened at the inn.*

WHILE these things passed, the host, who stood at the inn-
door, said:

'Here comes a goodly company of guests: if they stop here,
we will sing Gaudeamus.'

'What folks are they?' said Cardenio.

'Four men,' answered the host, 'on horseback *a la gineta*,*
with lances and targets, and black masks on their faces; and
with them a woman on a side-saddle, dressed in white, and
her face likewise covered: and two lads besides on foot.'

'Are they near at hand?' demanded the priest.

'So near,' replied the innkeeper, 'that they are already at
the door.'

Dorothea, hearing this, veiled her face; and Cardenio went
into Don Quixote's chamber; and scarcely had they done so,
when the persons the host mentioned entered the yard; and
the four horsemen, who, by their appearance, seemed to be
persons of distinction, having alighted, went to help down
the lady, who came on the side-saddle: and one of them,
taking her in his arms, set her down in a chair, which stood
at the door of the room, into which Cardenio had withdrawn.
In all this time, neither she, nor they, had taken off their
masks, or spoken one word: only the lady, at sitting down
in the chair, fetched a deep sigh, and let fall her arms, like
one sick, and ready to faint away. The servants on foot took
the horses to the stable. The priest, seeing all this, and
desirous to know who they were in that odd guise, and that
kept such silence, went where the lads were, and inquired of
one of them; who answered him:

'In truth, señor, I cannot inform you who these gentlefolks
are; I can only tell you, they must be people of considerable
quality, especially he who took the lady down in his arms: I
say this, because all the rest pay him such respect, and do
nothing but what he orders and directs.'

'And the lady, pray, who is she?' demanded the priest.

'Neither can I tell that,' replied the lackey: 'for I have not once seen her face during the whole journey; I have indeed often heard her sigh, and utter such groans, that one would think any one of them enough to break her heart: and it is no wonder we know no more than what we have told you; for it is not above two days since my comrade and I came to serve them: for, having met us upon the road, they asked and persuaded us to go with them as far as Andalusia, promising to pay us very well.'

'And have you heard any of them called by their names?' said the priest.

'No, indeed,' answered the lad; 'for they all travel with so much silence that you would wonder; and you hear nothing among them but the sighs and sobs of the poor lady, which move us to pity her: and whithersoever it is she is going, we believe it must be against her will; and, by what we can gather from her habit, she must be a nun, or going to be one, which seems most probable: and, perhaps, because the being one does not proceed from her choice, she goes thus heavily.'

'Very likely,' quoth the priest.

And, leaving them, he returned to the room where he had left Dorothea: who, hearing the lady in the mask sigh, moved by a natural compassion, went to her, and said:

'What is the matter, dear madam? if it be anything that we women can assist you in, speak; for, on my part, I am ready to serve you with great goodwill.'

To all this the afflicted lady returned no answer; and, though Dorothea urged her still more, she persisted in her silence, until the cavalier in the mask, who the servant said was superior to the rest, came up, and said to Dorothea:

'Trouble not yourself, madam, to offer anything to this woman; for it is her way not to be thankful for any service done her; nor endeavour to get an answer from her, unless you would hear some lie from her mouth.'

'No,' said she, who had hitherto held her peace; 'on the contrary, it is for being so sincere, and so averse from lying and deceit, that I am now reduced to such hard fortune: and of this you may be a witness yourself, since it is my truth alone which makes you act so false and treacherous a part.'

Cardenio heard these words plainly and distinctly, being

very near to her who spoke them; for Don Quixote's chamber-door only was between, and as soon as he heard them, he cried out aloud:

'Good God! what is this I hear? what voice is this, which has reached my ears?'

The lady, all in surprise, turned her head at these exclamations; and, not seeing who uttered them, she got up, and was going into the room; which the cavalier perceiving, he stopped her, and would not suffer her to stir a step. With this perturbation, and her sudden rising, her mask fell off, and she discovered a beauty incomparable, and a countenance miraculous, though pale and full of horror: for she rolled her eyes round as far as she could see, examining every place with so much eagerness, that she seemed distracted; at which Dorothea, and the rest, without knowing why she did so, were moved to great compassion. The cavalier held her fast by the shoulders; and, his hands being thus employed, he could not keep on his mask, which was falling off, as indeed at last it did; and Dorothea, who had clasped the lady in her arms, lifting up her eyes, discovered that the person who also held her, was her husband, Don Fernando: and scarcely had she perceived it was he, when, fetching from the bottom of her heart a deep and dismal 'Oh!' she fell backwards in a swoon; and, had not the barber, who stood close by, caught her in her arms, she would have fallen to the ground.

The priest ran immediately, and took off her veil, to throw water in her face; and no sooner had he uncovered it, but Don Fernando (for it was he who held the other in his arms) knew her, and stood like one dead at the sight of her: nevertheless, he did not let go Lucinda, who was the lady that was struggling so hard to get from him; for she knew Cardenio's voice in his exclamations, and he knew hers. Cardenio heard also the groan, which Dorothea gave when she fainted away; and believing it came from his Lucinda, he ran out of the room in a fright, and the first he saw was Don Fernando holding Lucinda close in his arms. Don Fernando presently knew Cardenio; and all three, Lucinda, Cardenio, and Dorothea, were struck dumb, hardly knowing what had happened to them.

They all stood silent, and gazing on one another, Dorothea on Don Fernando,* Don Fernando on Cardenio, Cardenio on Lucinda, and Lucinda on Cardenio. But the first who broke silence was Lucinda, who addressed herself to Don Fernando in this manner:

'Suffer me, Señor Don Fernando, as you are a gentleman, since you will not do it upon any other account, suffer me to cleave to that wall, of which I am the ivy; to that prop, from which neither your importunities, your threats, your promises, nor your presents, were able to separate me. Observe how heaven, by unusual, and to us hidden ways, has brought me into the presence of my true husband; and well you know, by a thousand dear-bought experiences, that death alone can efface him out of my memory. Then (since all further attempts are vain) let this open declaration convert your love into rage, your goodwill into despite, and thereby put an end to my life; for if I lose it in the presence of my dear husband, I shall reckon it well disposed of; and, perhaps, my death may convince him of the fidelity I have preserved for him to my last moment.'

By this time Dorothea was come to herself, and had listened to all that Lucinda said, whereby she discovered who she was: but, seeing that Don Fernando did not yet let her go from between his arms, nor make any answer to what she said, she got up as well as she could, and went and kneeled down at his feet, and pouring forth an abundance of lovely and piteous tears, she began to say thus:—

'If, my dear lord, the rays of that sun you hold now eclipsed between your arms had not dazzled and obscured your eyes, you must have seen, that she who lies prostrate at your feet is the unhappy (so long as you are pleased to have it so) and unfortunate Dorothea. I am that humble country girl, whom you, through goodness or love, did deign to raise to the honour of calling herself yours. I am she, who, confined within the bounds of modesty, lived a contented life, until, to the voice of your importunities, and seemingly sincere and real passion, she opened the gates of her reserve, and delivered up to you the keys of her liberty: a gift by you so ill requited, as appears by my being driven into the circumstances in which you find me, and forced to see you in the posture you are in now. Notwithstanding all this, I would not have you imagine that I am brought hither by any dishonest motives, but only by those of grief and concern, to see myself neglected and forsaken by you. You would have me be yours, and would have it in such a manner, that though now you would not have it be so, it is not possible you should cease to be mine. Consider, my lord, that the matchless affection I have for you may balance the beauty and nobility of her, for whom I am abandoned. You cannot be the fair Lucinda's, because you are mine; nor can she be yours, because she is Cardenio's. And it is easier, if you take it right, to reduce your inclination to love her, who adores you, than to bring her to love, who abhors you. You importuned my indifference; you solicited my integrity; you were not ignorant of my condition; you know very well in what manner I gave myself up entirely to your will; you have no room to pretend any deceit; and if this be so, as it really is, and if you are as much a Christian as a gentleman, why do you, by so many evasions delay making me as happy at last as you did at first? And if you will not acknowledge me for what I am, your true and lawful wife, at least admit me for your slave; for, so I be under your power, I shall account myself happy and very fortunate. Do not, by forsaking and abandoning me, give the world occasion to censure and disgrace me. Do not so sorely afflict my aged parents, whose constant and faithful services, as good vassals to yours, do not deserve it. And if you fancy your blood is debased by mixing it with mine, consider, there is little or no nobility in the world but what has run in the same channel, and that what is derived from women is not essential in illustrious descents: besides, true nobility consists in virtue; and if you forfeit that by denying me what is so justly my due, I shall then remain with greater advantages of nobility than you.

'In short, sir, I shall only add, that, whether you will or no, I am your wife: witness your words, which, if you value yourself on that account, on which you undervalue me, ought not to be false; witness your handwriting; and witness heaven, which you invoked to bear testimony to what you promised me. And though all this should fail, your conscience will not fail to whisper [to] you in the midst of your joys, justifying this truth I have told you, and disturbing your greatest pleasures and satisfactions.'

These and other reasons did the afflicted Dorothea urge so feelingly, and with so many tears, that all who accompanied Don Fernando, and all who were present besides, sympathized with her. Don Fernando listened to her without answering a word, until she had put an end to what she had to say, and a beginning to so many sighs and sobs, that it must have been a heart of brass which the signs of so much sorrow could not soften. Lucinda gazed at her with no less pity for her affliction than admiration at her wit and beauty; and, though she had a mind to go to her, and endeavour to comfort her, she was prevented by Don Fernando's still holding her fast in his arms; who, full of confusion and astonishment, after he had attentively beheld Dorothea for a good while, opened his arms, and, leaving Lucinda free, said:

'You have conquered, fair Dorothea, you have conquered; for there is no withstanding so many united truths.'

Lucinda was so faint, when Don Fernando let her go, that she was just falling to the ground. But Cardenio, who was near her, and had placed himself behind Don Fernando, that he might not know him,* now laying aside all fear, and at all adventures, ran to support Lucinda; and, catching her between his arms, he said:

'If it pleases pitying heaven, that now at last you should have some rest, my dear, faithful, and constant mistress, I believe you can find it nowhere more secure than in these arms, which now receive you, and did receive you heretofore, when fortune was pleased to allow me to call you mine.'

At these expressions Lucinda fixed her eyes on Cardenio; and having begun first to know him by his voice, and being now assured by sight that it was him, almost beside herself, and without any regard to the forms of decency, she threw her arms about his neck, and joining her face to his, she said to him:

'You, my dear Cardenio, you are the true owner of this your slave, though fortune were yet more adverse, and though my life, which depends upon yours, were threatened yet more than it is.'

A strange sight this was to Don Fernando, and all the bystanders, who were astonished at so unexpected an event. Dorothea fancied that Don Fernando changed colour, and looked as if he had a mind to revenge himself on Cardenio; for she saw him put his hand toward his sword; and no sooner did she perceive it, but she ran immediately, and, embracing his knees, and kissing them, she held him so fast that he could not stir; and, her tears trickling down without intermission, she said to him:

'What is it you intend to do, my only refuge, in this unexpected crisis? you have your wife at your feet, and she, whom you would have to be yours, is in the arms of her own husband: consider, whether it be fit or possible for you to undo what heaven has done, or whether it will become you to raise her to an equality with yourself, who, regardless of all obstacles, and confirmed in her truth and constancy, is bathing the bosom of her true husband before your face, with the tears of love flowing from her eyes. For God's sake, and your own character's sake, I beseech you, that this public declaration may be so far from increasing your wrath, that it may appease it in such sort, that these two lovers may be permitted, without any impediment from you, to live together in peace all the time heaven shall be pleased to allot them: and by this you will show the generosity of your noble and illustrious breast, and the world will see, that reason sways more with you than appetite.'

While Dorothea was saying this, Cardenio, though he held Lucinda between his arms, kept his eyes fixed on Don Fernando, with a resolution, if he saw him make any motion towards assaulting him, to endeavour to defend himself, and also to act offensively as well as he could, against all who should take part against him, though it should cost him his life. But now Don Fernando's friends, together with the priest and the barber, who were present all the while, not omitting honest Sancho Panza, ran, and surrounded Don Fernando, entreating him to have regard to Dorothea's tears; and, as they verily believed she had said nothing but was true, they begged of him, that he would not suffer her to be disappointed in her just expectations: they desired he would consider, that, not by chance, as it seemed, but by the particular providence of heaven, they had all met in a place where one would have least imagined they should; and the priest put him in mind, that nothing but death could part Lucinda from Cardenio, and that, though they should be severed by the edge of the sword, they would account their deaths most happy: and that, in a case which could not be remedied, the highest wisdom would be, by forcing and overcoming himself, to show a greatness of mind, in suffering that couple, by his mere goodwill, to enjoy that happiness which heaven had already granted them: he desired him also to turn his eyes on the beauty of Dorothea, and see how few, if any could equal, much less exceed her: and that to her beauty he would add her humility, and the extreme love she had for him; but especially that he would remember, that, if he valued himself on being a gentleman, and a Christian, he could do no less than perform the promise he had given her, and that, in so doing, he would please God, and do what was right in the eyes of all wise men, who know and understand, that it is the prerogative of beauty, though in a mean subject, if it be accompained with modesty, to be able to raise and equal itself to any height, without any disparagement to him who raises and equals it to himself; and that in complying with the strong dictates of appetite, there is nothing blameworthy, provided there be no sin in the action.

In short, to these they all added such and so many powerful arguments, that the generous heart of Don Fernando, being nourished with noble blood, was softened, and suffered itself to be overcome by that truth, which, if he had had a mind, he could not have resisted: and the proof he gave of surrendering himself, and submitting to what was proposed, was, to stoop down, and embrace Dorothea, saying to her.

'Rise, dear madam; for it is not fit she should kneel at my feet, who is mistress of my soul: and if hitherto I have given no proof of what I say, perhaps it has been so ordered by heaven, that by finding in you the constancy of your affection to me, I may know how to esteem you as you deserve. What

I beg of you is, not to reproach me with my past unkind behaviour and great neglect of you: for the very same cause and motive that induced me to take you for mine influenced me to endeavour not to be yours: and, to show you the truth of what I say, turn and behold the eyes of the now satisfied Lucinda, and in them you will see an excuse for all my errors: and since she has found and attained to what she desired, and I have found in you all I want, let her live secure and contented many happy years with her Cardenio; and I will beseech heaven that I may do the like with my dear Dorothea.'

And saying this, he embraced her again, and joined his face to hers, with such tenderness of passion, that he had much ado to prevent his tears from giving undoubted signs of his love and repentance. It was not so with Lucinda and Cardenio, and almost all the rest of the company present; for they began to shed so many tears, some for joy on their own account, and some on the account of others, that one would have thought some heavy and dismal disaster had befallen them all. Even Sancho Panza wept, though he owned afterwards, that, for his part, he wept only to see that Dorothea was not, as he imagined, the queen Micomicona, from whom he expected so many favours.

The joint wonder and weeping lasted for some time; and then Cardenio and Lucinda went and kneeled before Don Fernando, thanking him for the favour he had done them, in such terms of respect, that Don Fernando knew not what to answer; and so he raised them up, and embraced them with much courtesy and many demonstrations of affection. Then he desired Dorothea to tell him how she came to that place so far from home. She repeated in few and discreet words all she had before related to Cardenio; with which Don Fernando and his company were so pleased, that they wished the story had lasted much longer, such was the grace with which Dorothea recounted her misfortunes.

And when she had made an end, Don Fernando related what had befallen him in the city, after his finding the paper in Lucinda's bosom, wherein she declared that she was wife to Cardenio, and could not be his. He said that he had a mind to have killed her, and should have done it, if her parents had not hindered him; upon which he left the house, enraged and ashamed, with a resolution of revenging himself at a more convenient time; that, the following day, he heard that Lucinda was missing from her father's house, without anybody's knowing whither she was gone; in fine, that, at the end of some months, he came to know that she was in a convent, purposing to remain there all her days, unless she could spend them with Cardenio; and that, as soon as he knew it, choosing those three gentlemen for his companions, he went to the place where she was, but did not speak to her, fearing, if she knew he was there, the monastery would be better guarded; and so waiting for a day, when the porter's lodge was open, he left two to secure the door, and he with the other entered into the convent in search of Lucinda, whom they found in the cloisters talking to a nun; and snatching her away, without giving her time for anything, they came with her to a place where they accommodated themselves with whatever was needful for the carrying her off; all which they could very safely do, the monastery being in the fields, a good way out of the town. He said, that, when Lucinda saw herself in his power, she swooned away, and that when she came to herself, she did nothing but weep, and sigh, without speaking one word: and that in this manner, accompanied with silence and tears, they arrived at that inn, which to him was arriving at heaven, where all earthly misfortunes have an end.

CHAPTER 37

Wherein is continued the history of the famous Infanta Micomicona, with other pleasant adventures.

SANCHO heard all this with no small grief of mind, seeing that the hope of his preferment was disappearing and vanishing into smoke; and that the fair princess Micomicona was turned into Dorothea, and the giant into Don Fernando, while his master lay in a sound sleep without troubling his head about what passed. Dorothea could not be sure whether the happiness she enjoyed was not a dream. Cardenio was in the same doubt; and Lucinda knew not what to think. Don Fernando gave thanks to heaven for the blessing bestowed on him, in bringing him out of that perplexed labyrinth, in which he was upon the brink of losing his honour and his soul. In short, all that were in the inn were pleased at the happy conclusion of such intricate and hopeless affairs. The priest, like a man of sense, placed everything in its true light, and congratulated every one upon their share of the good that had befallen them. But she who rejoiced most, and was most delighted, was the hostess, Cardenio and the priest having promised to pay her with interest for all the damages sustained upon Don Quixote's account.

Sancho, as has been said, was the only afflicted, unhappy, and sorrowful person: and so, with dismal looks, he went in to his master, who was then awake, to whom he said:

'Your worship may very well sleep your fill, Señor Sorrowful Figure, without troubling yourself about killing any giant or restoring the princess to her kingdom; for all is done and over already.'

'I verily believe it,' answered Don Quixote; 'for I have had the most monstrous and dreadful battle with the giant, that ever I believe I shall have in all the days of my life; and with one back-stroke I tumbled his head to the ground, and so great was the quantity of blood that gushed from it, that the streams ran along the ground, as if it had been water.'

'As if it had been red wine, your worship might better say,' answered Sancho: 'for I would have you to know, if you do not know it already, that the dead giant is a pierced skin: and the blood, eighteen gallons of red wine contained in its belly: and the head cut off is—the whore that bore me, and the devil take all for me.'

'What is it you say, fool?' replied Don Quixote; 'are you in your senses?'

'Pray, get up, sir,' quoth Sancho, 'and you will see what a fine spot of work you have made, and what a reckoning we have to pay; and you will see the queen converted into a private lady called Dorothea, with other accidents, which, if you take them right, will astonish you.'

'I shall wonder at nothing of all this,' replied Don Quixote; 'for, if you remember well, the last time we were here, I told you, that all things in this place went by enchantment, and it would be no wonder if it should be so now.'

'I should believe so too,' answered Sancho, 'if my being tossed in the blanket had been a matter of this nature: but it was downright real and true; and I saw, that the innkeeper, who was here this very day, held a corner of the blanket, and canted me towards heaven with notable alacrity and vigour, and with as much laughter as force; and whenever it happens that we know persons, in my opinion, though simple and a sinner, there is no enchantment at all, but much misusage and much mishap.'

'Well, God will remedy it,' quoth Don Quixote; 'give me my clothes, that I may go and see the accidents and transformations you talk of.'

Sancho reached him his apparel; and, while he was dressing, the priest gave Don Fernando and the rest an account of Don Quixote's madness, and of the artifice they had made use of to get him from the Peña Pobre, to which he imagined himself banished, through his lady's disdain. He related also to them almost all the adventures which Sancho had recounted; at which they did not a little wonder and laugh, thinking, as everybody did, that it was the strangest kind of madness that ever entered into an extravagant imagination. The priest said further, that, since Madame Dorothea's good fortune would not permit her to go on with their design, it was necessary to invent and find out some other way of getting him home to his village. Cardenio offered to assist in carrying on the project, and proposed that Lucinda should personate Dorothea.

'No,' said Don Fernando, 'it must not be so; for I will have Dorothea herself go on with her contrivance: and as it is not far from hence to this good gentleman's village, I shall be glad to contribute to his cure.'

'It is not above two days' journey,' said the priest.

'Though it were farther,' said Don Fernando, 'I would undertake it with pleasure, to accomplish so good a work.'

By this time Don Quixote sallied forth, completely armed with his whole furniture; Mambrino's helmet, though bruised and battered, on his head, his target braced on, and resting on his saplin or lance. The strange appearance he made greatly surprised Don Fernando and his company, especially when they perceived his tawny and withered lantern-jaws, his ill-matched armour, and the stiffness of his measured pace: and they stood silent to hear what he would say, when, with much gravity and solemnity, fixing his eyes on the fair Dorothea, he said:

'I am informed, fair lady, by this my squire, that your grandeur is annihilated, and your very being demolished, and that from a queen and great lady, which you were wont to be, you are metamorphosed into a private maiden. If this has been done by order of the necromantic king your father, out of fear lest I should not afford you the necessary and due aid, I say, he neither knows, nor ever did know, one half of his trade, and that he is but little versed in histories of knight-errantry: for had he read and considered them as attentively, and as much at his leisure, as I have read and considered them, he would have found at every turn, how other knights, of a great deal less fame than myself, have achieved matters much more difficult, it being no such mighty business to kill a pitiful giant, be he never so arrogant; for not many hours are past since I had a bout with one myself, and—I say no more, lest I should be thought to lie: but time, the revealer of all things, will tell it, when we least think of it.'

'It was with a couple of wine-skins, and not a giant,' quoth the innkeeper: but Don Fernando commanded him to hold his peace, and in no wise to interrupt Don Quixote's discourse, who went on, saying:

'I say, in fine, high and disinherited lady, that, if for the cause aforesaid, your father has made this metamorphosis in your person, I would have you give no heed to it at all: for there is no danger upon earth, through which my sword shall not force a way, and, by bringing down the head of your enemy to the ground, place the crown of your kingdom upon your own in a few days.'

Don Quixote said no more, but awaited the princess's answer; who, knowing Don Fernando's inclination, that she should carry on the deceit, until Don Quixote was brought home to his house, with much grace and gravity, answered him:

'Whoever told you, valorous Knight of the Sorrowful Figure, that I was changed and altered from what I was, did not tell you the truth: for I am the same to-day that I was yesterday: it is true indeed, some fortunate accidents, that have befallen me, to my heart's desire, have made some alteration in me for the better: yet, for all that, I do not cease to be what I was before, and to have the same thoughts I always had of employing the prowess of your redoubted and invincible arm. So that, dear sir, of your accustomed bounty, restore to the father who begot me his honour, and esteem him to be a wise and prudent man, since by his skill he found out so easy and certain a way to remedy my misfortune: for I verily believe, had it not been for you, sir, I should never have lighted on the happiness I now enjoy; and in this I speak the very truth, as most of these gentlemen here present can testify. What remains is, that to-morrow morning we set forward on our journey; for to-day we could not go far, and for the rest of the good success I expect, I refer it to God, and to the valour of your breast.'

Thus spoke the discreet Dorothea, and Don Quixote, having heard her, turned to Sancho, and, with an air of much indignation, said to him:

'I tell thee now, little Sancho, that thou art the greatest little rascal in all Spain: tell me, thief, vagabond; didst thou not tell me just now, that this princess was transformed into a damsel called Dorothea; and that the head, which, as I take it, I lopped off from a giant, was the whore that bore thee; with other absurdities, which put me into the greatest confusion I ever was in all the days of my life? I vow' (and here he looked up to heaven, and gnashed his teeth) 'I have a great mind to make such havoc of thee, as shall put wit into the noddles of all the lying squires of knights-errant that shall be from henceforward in the world.'

'Pray, dear sir, be pacified,' answered Sancho; 'for I may

easily be mistaken as to the transformation of madam the princess of Micomicona; but as to the giant's head, or at least the piercing of the skins, and the blood's being but red wine, I am not deceived, as God liveth: for the skins yonder at your worship's bed's-head are cut and slashed, and the red wine has turned the room into a pond; and if not, it will be seen in the frying of the eggs, I mean, you will find it, when his worship señor innkeeper here demands damages. As for the rest, I rejoice in my heart that madam the queen is as she was; for I have my share in it, as every neighbour's child has.'

'I tell thee, Sancho,' said Don Quixote, 'thou art an ass; forgive me, that's enough.'

'It is enough,' said Don Fernando, 'and let no more be said of this; and since madam the princess says we must set forward in the morning, it being too late to-day, let us do so, and let us pass this night in agreeable conversation, until to-morrow, when we will all bear Señor Don Quixote company: for we desire to be eye-witnesses of the valorous and unheard-of deeds, which he is to perform in the progress of this grand enterprise, which he has undertaken.'

'It is I that am to wait upon you, and bear you company,' answered Don Quixote; 'and I am much obliged to you for the favour you do me, and the good opinion you have of me; which it shall be my endeavour not to disappoint, or it shall cost me my life, and even more, if more it could cost me.'

Many compliments, and many offers of service, passed between Don Quixote and Don Fernando: but all was put a stop to by a traveller who just then entered the inn; who by his garb seemed to be a Christian newly come from among the Moors; for he had on a blue cloth loose coat, with short skirts, half sleeves, and no collar: his breeches also were of blue cloth, and he wore a cap of the same colour: he had on a pair of date-coloured stockings, and a Moorish scimitar hung in a shoulder-belt that came across his breast. There came in immediately after him a woman mounted on an ass, in a Moorish dress, her face veiled, a brocade turban on her head, and covered with a mantle from her shoulders to her feet. The man was of a robust and agreeable make, a little above forty years old, of a brownish complexion, large whiskers, and a well-set beard: in short, his mien, if he had been well-dressed, would have denoted him a person of quality and well-born.

At coming in, he asked for a room, and, being told there was none to spare in the inn, he seemed to be troubled, and going to the woman, who by her habit seemed to be a Moor, he took her down in his arms. Lucinda, Dorothea, the landlady, her daughter, and Maritornes, gathered about the Moorish lady, on account of the novelty of her dress, the like of which they had never seen before: and Dorothea, who was always obliging, complaisant, and discreet, imagining that both she and her conductor were uneasy for want of a room, said to her:

'Be not much concerned, madam, about proper accommodations; it is what one must not expect to meet with at inns. And since it is so, if you please to take share with us' (pointing to Lucinda) 'perhaps, in the course of your journey, you may have met with worse entertainment.'

The veiled lady returned her no answer, but only, rising from her seat, and laying her hands across on her breast, bowed her head and body in token that she thanked her. By her silence they concluded she must be a Moor, and could not speak the Christian language.

By this time her companion, who had hitherto been employed about something else, came in, and seeing that they were all standing about the woman that came with him, and that, whatever they said to her, she continued silent, he said:

'Ladies, this young woman understands scarce anything of our language, nor can she speak any other than that of her own country; and therefore it is, that she has not answered to anything you may have asked her.'

'Nothing has been asked her,' answered Lucinda, 'but only whether she would accept of our company for this night, and take part of our lodging, where she shall be accommodated, and entertained, as well as the place will afford, and with that goodwill which is due to all strangers that are in need of it, and especially from us to her, as she is of our own sex.'

'Dear madam,' answered the stranger, 'I kiss your hands for her and for myself, and highly prize, as I ought, the favour offered us, which, at such a time, and from such persons as you appear to be, must be owned to be very great.'

'Pray tell me, señor,' said Dorothea, 'is this lady a Christian or a Moor? for her habit and her silence make us think she is what we wish she were not.'

'She is a Moor,' answered the stranger, 'in her attire and in her body; but in her soul she is already very much a Christian, having a very strong desire to become one.'

'She is not yet baptized then?' answered Lucinda.

'There has been no time for that yet,' answered the stranger, 'since she left Algiers, her native country and place of abode, and she has not hitherto been in any danger of death so imminent, as to make it necessary to have her baptized, before she be instructed in all the ceremonies our holy mother the church enjoins; but I hope, if it please God, she shall soon be baptized, with the decency becoming her quality, which is above what either her habit or mine seem to denote.'

This discourse gave all who heard him a desire to know who the Moor and the stranger were; but nobody would ask them just then, seeing it was more proper, at that time, to let them take some rest, than to be inquiring into their lives. Dorothea took her by the hand, and led her to sit down by her, desiring her to uncover her face. She looked at the stranger, as if she asked him what they said, and what she should do. He told her in Arabic that they desired she would uncover her face, and that he would have her do so: accordingly she did, and discovered a face so beautiful, that Dorothea thought her handsomer than Lucinda, and Lucinda than Dorothea; and all the bystanders saw, that, if any beauty could be compared with theirs, it must be that of the Moor; nay, some of them thought she surpassed them in some things. And, as beauty has the prerogative and power to reconcile minds, and attract inclinations, they all presently fell to caressing and making much of the beautiful Moor. Don Fernando asked of the stranger the Moor's name, who answered, 'Lela Zoraida'.

And as soon as she heard this, understanding what they had inquired of the Christian, she said hastily, with a sprightly but concerned air.

'No, not Zoraida; Maria, Maria;' letting them know her name was Maria, and not Zoraida.

These words, and the great earnestness with which she pronounced them, extorted more than one tear from those who heard her, especially from the women, who are naturally tender-hearted and compassionate. Lucinda embraced her very affectionately, saying to her:

'Yes, yes, Maria, Maria.'

To whom the Moor answered:

'Yes, yes, Maria, Zoraida macange;' as much as to say, 'not Zoraida.'

By this time it was four in the afternoon*, and, by order of Don Fernando and his company, the innkeeper had taken care to provide a collation for them, the best it was possible for him to get; which being now ready, they all sat down at a long table, like those in halls, there being neither a round, nor a square one, in the house. They gave the upper-end and principal seat (though he would have declined it) to Don Quixote, who would needs have the lady Micomicona sit next him, as being her champion. Then sat down Lucinda and Zoraida, and opposite to them Don Fernando and Cardenio, and then the stranger and the rest of the gentlemen; and next to the ladies sat the priest and the barber: and thus they banqueted much to their satisfaction; and it gave them an additional pleasure to hear Don Quixote, who, moved by such another spirit, as that which had moved him to talk so much when he supped with the goatherds, instead of eating, spoke as follows:

'In truth, gentlemen, if it be well considered, great and unheard-of things do they see, who profess the order of knight-errantry.* If any one thinks otherwise, let me ask him, what man living, that should now enter at this castle gate, and see us sitting in this manner, could judge or believe us to be the persons we really are? Who could say, that this lady, sitting here by my side, is that great queen that we all know her to be, and that I am that Knight of the Sorrowful

Figure, so blazoned abroad by the mouth of fame?

'There is no doubt, but that this art and profession exceeds all that have ever been invented by men; and so much the more honourable is it, by how much it is exposed to more dangers. Away with those who say, that letters have the advantage over arms: I will tell them, be they who they will, that they know not what they say. For the reason they usually give, and which they lay the greatest stress upon, is, that the labours of the brain exceed those of the body, and that arms are exercised by the body alone; as if the use of them were the business of porters, for which nothing is necessary but downright strength; or as if in this, which we who profess it call chivalry, were not included the acts of fortitude, which require a very good understanding to execute them; or as if the mind of the warrior, who has an army, or the defence of a besieged city, committed to his charge, does not labour with his understanding as well as his body. If not, let us see how, by mere bodily strength, he will be able to penetrate into the designs of the enemy, to form stratagems, overcome difficulties, and prevent dangers which threaten: for all these things are acts of the understanding, in which the body has no share at all. It being so then, that arms employ the mind as well as letters, let us next see whose mind labours most, the scholar's or the warrior's. And this may be determined by the scope and ultimate end of each: for that intention is to be the most esteemed, which has the noblest end for its object.

'Now the end and design of letters (I do not now speak of divinity, which has for its aim the raising and conducting souls to heaven; for to an end so endless as this no other can be compared), I speak of human learning, whose end, I say, is to regulate distributive justice, and give to every man his due; to know good laws, and cause them to be strictly observed; an end most certainly generous and exalted, and worthy of high commendation; but not equal to that which is annexed to the profession of arms, whose object and end is peace, the greatest blessing men can wish for in this life. Accordingly, the first good news the world and men received, was what the angels brought, on that night which was our day, when they sung in the clouds: "Glory be to God on high, and on earth peace, and good will towards men" and the salutation, which the best master of earth or heaven taught his followers and disciples, was, that when they entered into any house, they should say, "Peace be to this house": and many other times he said: "My peace I give unto you, my peace I leave with you, peace be amongst you". A jewel and legacy worthy of coming from such a hand! a jewel, without which there can be no happiness either in earth or in heaven! This peace is the true end of war; for to say arms or war, is the same thing. Granting therefore this truth, that the end of war is peace, and that in this it has the advantage of the end proposed by letters, let us come now to the bodily labours of the scholar, and to those of the professor of arms; and let us see which are the greatest.'

Don Quixote went on with his discourse in such a manner, and in such proper expressions, that none of those who heard him at that time could take him for a madman. On the contrary, most of his hearers being gentlemen, to whom the use of arms properly belongs, they listened to him with pleasure, and he continued saying:

'I say then, that the hardships of the scholar are these: in the first place, poverty; not that they are all poor, but I would put the case in the strongest manner possible: and when I have said that he endures poverty, methinks no more need be said to show his misery; for he who is poor is destitute of every good thing: he endures poverty in all its parts, sometimes in hunger and cold, and sometimes in nakedness, and sometimes in all these together. But notwithstanding all this, it is not so great, but that still he eats, though somewhat later than usual, or of the rich man's scraps and leavings, or, which is the scholar's greatest misery, by what is called among them going a-sopping. Neither do they always want a fireside or chimney-corner of some other person, which, if it does not quite warm them, at least abates their extreme cold: and lastly, at night, they sleep somewhere under cover. I will not mention other trifles, such as want of shirts, and no plenty of shoes, the thinness and threadbareness of their clothes, nor that laying about them with so much eagerness and pleasure, when good fortune sets a plentiful table in their way. By this way that I have described, rough and difficult, here stumbling, there falling, now rising, then falling again, they arrive to the degree they desire, which being attained, we have seen many, who, having passed these Syrtes,* these Scyllas, these Charybdises, buoyed up as it were by a favourable fortune, I say, we have seen them from a chair command and govern the world; their hunger converted into satiety, their pinching cold into refreshing coolness, their nakedness into embroidery, and their sleeping on a mat to reposing in holland* and damask; a reward justly merited by their virtue. But their hardships, opposed to and compared with those of the warrior, fall far short of them, as I shall presently show.'

CHAPTER 38

The continuation of Don Quixote's curious discourse upon arms and letters.

DON QUIXOTE, continuing his discourse, said:

'Since in speaking of the scholar, we began with his poverty, and its several branches, let us see whether the soldier be richer. And we shall find that poverty itself is not poorer: for he depends on his wretched pay, which comes late, or perhaps never; or else on what he can pilfer, with great peril of his life and conscience. And sometimes his nakedness is such, that his slashed buff doublet serves him both for finery and shirt; and in the midst of winter, being in the open field, he has nothing to warm him but the breath of his mouth, which, issuing from an empty place, must needs come out cold, against all the rules of nature. But let us wait until night, and see whether his bed will make amends for these inconveniencies: and that, if it be not his own fault, will never offend in point of narrowness; for he may measure out as many feet of earth as he pleases, and roll himself thereon at pleasure, without fear of rumpling the sheets. Suppose now the day and hour come of taking the degree of his profession; I say, suppose the day of battle come; and then his doctoral cap will be of lint, to cure some wound made by a musket shot, which, perhaps, has gone through his temples, or lamed him a leg or an arm. And though this should not happen, but merciful heaven should keep and preserve him alive and unhurt, he shall remain, perhaps, in the same poverty as before; and there must happen a second and a third engagement, and battle after battle, and he must come off victor from them all, to get anything considerable by it. But these miracles are seldom seen. And tell me, gentlemen, if you have observed it, how much fewer are they, who are rewarded for their services in war, than those who have perished in it? Doubtless, you must answer, that there is no comparison between the numbers; that the dead cannot be reckoned up, whereas those who live and are rewarded, may be numbered with three figures. All this is quite otherwise with scholars, who from the gown (I am loath to say the sleeves*) are all handsomely provided for. Thus, though the hardships of the soldier are greater, his reward is less. But to this may be answered, that it is easier to reward two thousand scholars, than thirty thousand soldiers: for the former are rewarded by giving them employments, which must of course be given to men of their profession; whereas the latter cannot be rewarded but with the very property of the master whom they serve; and this impossibility serves to strengthen my assertion.

'But, setting aside this, which is a very intricate point, let us turn to the pre-eminence of arms over letters; a controversy hitherto undecided, so strong are the reasons which each party alleges on its own side: for, besides those I have already mentioned, letters say, that, without them, arms could not subsist; for war also has its laws, to which it is subject, and laws are the province of letters, and learned men. To this arms answer, that laws cannot be supported without them: for by arms republics are defended, kingdoms are preserved, cities are guarded, highways are secured, and the seas are cleared from corsairs and pirates; in short, were it not for them, republics, kingdoms, monarchies, cities, journeys by land and voyages by sea, would be subject to the cruelties and confusion, which war carries along with it, while it lasts, and is at liberty to make use of its privileges and its power. Besides, it is past dispute, that what costs most the attaining is, and ought to be, most esteemed. Now, in order to arrive at a degree of eminence in learning, it costs time, watching, hunger, nakedness, dizziness in the head, weakness of the stomach, and other such like inconveniencies, as I have already mentioned in part. But for a man to rise gradually to be a good soldier, costs him all it can cost the scholar, and that in so much a greater degree, that there is no comparison, since at every step he is in imminent danger of his life. And what dread of necessity and poverty can affect or distress a scholar, equal to that which a soldier feels, who, being besieged in some fortress, and placed as a sentinel in some ravelin or cavalier, perceives that the enemy is mining towards the place where he stands, and yet must on no account stir from his post, or shun the danger that so nearly threatens him? all that he can do in such a case, is to give notice to his officer of what passes, that he may remedy it by some countermine, and, in the meantime, he must stand his ground, fearing and expecting when of a sudden he is to mount to the clouds without wings, and then descend headlong to the deep against his will. And if this be thought but a trifling danger, let us see whether it be equalled or exceeded by the encounter of two galleys prow to prow, in the midst of the wide sea; which being locked and grappled together, there is no more room left for the soldier than the two-foot plank at the beakhead: and though he sees as many threatening ministers of death before him, as there are pieces of artillery and small arms pointed at him from the opposite side, not the length of a lance from his body; and though he knows, that the first slip of his foot will send him to visit the profound depths of Neptune's bosom; notwithstanding all this, with an undaunted heart, carried on by honour that inspires him, he exposes himself as a mark to all their fire, and endeavours, by that narrow pass, to force his way into the enemy's vessel: and what is most to be admired is, that scarce is one fallen, whence he cannot arise until the end of the world, when another takes his place; and if he also fall into the sea, which lies in wait for him like an enemy, another and another succeeds without any intermission between their deaths; an instance of bravery and intrepidity the greatest that is to be met with in all the extremities of war.

'A blessing on those happy ages, strangers to the dreadful fury of those devilish instruments of artillery, whose inventor, I verily believe, is now in hell receiving the reward of his diabolical invention; by means of which it is in the power of a cowardly and base hand to take away the life of the bravest cavalier, and to which is owing, that without knowing how, or from whence, in the midst of that resolution and bravery, which inflames and animates gallant spirits, comes a chance ball, shot off by one, who, perhaps, fled and was frighted at the very flash in the pan, and in an instant cuts short and puts an end to the thoughts and life of him who deserved to have lived for many ages. And, therefore, when I consider this, I could almost say, I repent of having undertaken this profession of knight-errantry, in so detestable an age as this in which we live; for though no danger can daunt me, still it gives me some concern, to think that powder and lead may chance to deprive me of the opportunity of becoming famous and renowned, by the valour of my arm and edge of my sword, over the face of the whole earth. But heaven's will be done: I have this satisfaction, that I shall acquire so much the greater fame, if I succeed, by how much the perils, to which I expose myself, are greater than those, to which the knights-errant of past ages were exposed.'

Don Quixote made this long harangue while the rest were eating, forgetting to reach a bit to his mouth, though Sancho Panza ever and anon desired him to mind his victuals, telling him, he would have time enough afterwards to talk as much as he pleased. Those who heard him were moved with fresh compassion, to see a man, who to everybody's thinking had so good an understanding, and could talk so well upon every other subject, so egregiously want it, whenever the discourse happened to turn upon his unlucky and cursed chivalry. The priest told him, there was great reason in all he had said in favour of arms, and that he, though a scholar and a graduate, was of his opinion.

The collation being over, and the cloth taken away, while

the hostess, her daughter, and Maritornes were preparing the
chamber where Don Quixote de la Mancha lay, in which it
was ordered that the ladies should be lodged by themselves
that night, Don Fernando desired the stranger to relate to
them the history of his life, since it could not but be
extraordinary and entertaining, if they might judge by his
coming in company with Zoraida. To which the stranger
answered, that he would very willingly do what they desired,
and that he only feared the story would not prove such as
might afford them the pleasure he wished; however, rather
than not comply with their request, he would relate it. The
priest and all the rest thanked him, and entreated him to
begin. And he, finding himself courted by so many, said:

'There is no need of entreaties, gentlemen, where you may
command: and therefore, pray be attentive, and you will hear
a true story, not to be equalled, perhaps, by any feigned ones,
though usually composed with the most curious and studied
art. What he said made all the company seat themselves in
order, and observe a strict silence; and he, finding they held
their peace, expecting what he would say, with an agreeable
and composed voice, began as follows:

CHAPTER 39

*Wherein the captive relates his life and adventures.**

'In a certain town, in the mountains of Leon, my lineage had
its beginning; to which nature was more kind and liberal than
fortune; though amidst the penury of those parts my father
passed for a rich man, and really would have been such, had
he had the knack of saving, as he had of squandering his
estate. This disposition of his to prodigality and profusion
proceeded from his having been a soldier in his younger days;
for the army is a school in which the niggardly become
generous, and the generous prodigal: and if there are some
soldiers misers, they are a kind of monsters but very rarely
seen. My father exceeded the bounds of liberality, and bordered near upon being prodigal; a thing very inconvenient to

married men, who have children to inherit their name and quality. My father had three, all sons, and of age to choose their way of life: and seeing, as he himself said, that he could not bridle his natural propensity, he resolved to deprive himself of the means that made him a prodigal and spend-thrift, which was, to rid himself of his riches, without which Alexander himself could not be generous. Accordingly, one day, calling us all three into a room by ourselves, he spoke to us in this or the like manner:

'"My sons, to tell you that I love you, it is sufficient that I say you are my children; and to make you think that I do not love you, it is sufficient that I am not master enough of myself to forbear dissipating your inheritance. But, that from henceforth you may see, that I love you like a father, and have no mind to ruin you like a step-father, I design to do a thing by you, which I have had in my thoughts this good while, and weighed with mature deliberation. You are all now of an age to choose for yourselves a settlement in the world, or at least to pitch upon some way of life, which may be for your honour and profit when you are grown up. Now, what I have resolved upon is, to divide what I possess into four parts: three I will give to you, share and share alike, without making any difference; and the fourth I will reserve, to subsist upon for the remaining days of my life. But when each has the share that belongs to him in his own power, I would have him follow one of these ways I shall propose. We have a proverb here in Spain, in my opinion a very true one, as most proverbs are, being short sentences drawn from long and wise experience; and it is this: 'the church, the sea, or the court'; as if one should say more plainly: whoever would thrive and be rich, let him either get into the church, or go to sea and exercise the art of merchandising, or serve the king in his court; for it is a saying, that, 'the king's bit is better than the lord's bounty'. I say this, because it is my will, that one of you follow letters, another merchandise, and the third serve the king in his wars; for it is difficult to get admission into his household; and, though the wars do not procure a man much wealth, they usually procure him much esteem and reputation. Within eight days I will give you each

your share in money, without wronging you of a farthing, as
you will see in effect. Tell me now whether you will follow
my opinion and advice in what I have proposed."

'And then he bade me, being the eldest, to answer. After
I had desired him not to part with what he had, but to spend
whatever he pleased, we being young enough to shift for
ourselves, I concluded with assuring him I would do as he
desired, and take to the army, there to serve God and the
king. My second brother complied likewise, and chose to go
to the Indies, turning his portion into merchandise. The
youngest, and I believe the wisest, said, he would take to the
church, and finish his studies at Salamanca.

'As soon as we had agreed, and chose our several professions, my father embraced us all, and with the dispatch he
had promised, put his design in execution, giving to each his
share, which, as I remember, was three thousand ducats; for
an uncle of ours bought the whole estate, and paid for it in
ready money, that it might not be alienated from the main
branch of the family. In one and the self-same day, we all
took leave of our good father, and it then seeming to me
inhuman to leave my father so old, and with so little to
subsist on, I prevailed upon him to take two thousand ducats
out of my three, the remainder being sufficient to equip me
with what was necessary for a soldier.

'My two brothers, incited by my example, returned him
each a thousand ducats; so that my father now had four
thousand in ready money, and three thousand more, which
was the value of the land that fell to his share, and which
he would not sell. To be short, we took our leave of him,
and of our aforesaid uncle, not without much concern and
tears on all sides, they charging us to acquaint them with our
success, whether prosperous or adverse, as often as we had
opportunity. We promised so to do; and they having embraced us, and given us their blessing, one of us took the
road to Salamanca, the other to Seville, and I to Alicante,
where I heard of a Genoese ship that loaded wool there for
Genoa.

'It is now two and twenty years since I first left my father's
house, and in all that time, though I have written several

letters, I have had no news either of him, or of my brothers. As to what has befallen me in the course of that time, I will briefly relate it.

'I embarked at Alicante, and had a good passage to Genoa: from thence I went to Milan, where I furnished myself with arms, and some military finery; and from thence determined to go into the service in Piedmont: and being upon the road to Alessandria della Paglia, I was informed that the great Duke de Alva was passing into Flanders with an army. Hereupon I changed my mind, went with him, and served under him in all his engagements. I was present at the death of the Counts Egmont and Horn. I got an ensign's commission in the company of a famous captain of Guadalajara, called Diego de Urbina. And soon after my arrival in Flanders, news came of the league concluded between Pope Pius V of happy memory, and Spain, against the common enemy, the Turk, who about the same time had taken with his fleet the famous island of Cyprus, which was before subject to the Venetians; a sad and unfortunate loss! It was known for certain, that the most serene Don John of Austria, natural brother of our good king Philip, was appointed generalissimo of this league, and great preparations for war were everywhere talked of.

'All which incited a vehement desire in me to be present in the battle that was expected; and though I had reason to believe, and had some promises, and almost assurances, that, on the first occasion that offered, I should be promoted to the rank of a captain, I resolved to quit all, and go, as I did, into Italy. And my good fortune would have it, that Don John of Austria was just then come to Genoa, and was going to Naples to join the Venetian fleet, as he afterwards did at Messina. In short, I was present at that glorious action, being already made a captain of foot, to which honourable post I was advanced, rather by my good fortune, than by my deserts. But that day which was so fortunate to Christendom (for all nations were then undeceived of their error in believing that the Turks were invincible by sea); on that day, I say, in which the Ottoman pride and haughtiness were broken; among so many happy persons as there were (for sure the Christians, who died there, had better fortune than the survivors and conquerors), I alone remained unfortunate, since, instead of, what I might have expected had it been in the times of the Romans, some naval crown, I found myself, the night following that famous day, with chains on my feet, and manacles on my hands. Which happened thus:

'Uchali,* king of Algiers, a bold and successful corsair, having boarded and taken the captain-galley of Malta, three knights only being left alive in her, and those desperately wounded; the captain-galley of John Andrea Doria* came up to her relief, on board of which I was with my company; and, doing my duty upon this occasion, I leaped into the enemy's galley, which, getting off suddenly from ours, my soldiers could not follow me; and so I was left alone among my enemies, whom I could not resist, being so many: in short, I was carried off prisoner, and sorely wounded. And, as you must have heard, gentlemen, that Uchali escaped with his whole squadron, by that means I remained a captive in his power, being the only sad person, when so many were joyful; and a slave, when so many were freed: for fifteen thousand Christians, who were at the oar in the Turkish galleys, did that day recover their long-wished-for liberty.

'They carried me to Constantinople, where the Grand Turk Selim* made my master general of the sea, for having done his duty in the fight, and having brought off, as a proof of his valour, the flag of the Order of Malta. The year following, which was seventy-two, I was at Navarino, rowing in the captain-galley with the three lanterns;* and there I saw and observed the opportunity that was then lost of taking the whole Turkish navy in port. For all the [marines] and janizaries on board took it for granted they should be attacked in the very harbour, and had their baggage and their passa-maques (or shoes) in readiness for running away immediately by land, without staying for an engagement: such terror had our navy struck into them. But heaven ordered it otherwise, not through any fault or neglect of the general, who commanded our men, but for the sins of Christendom, and because God permits and ordains, that there should always be some scourges to chastise us. In short, Uchali got into

Modon, an island near Navarino, and, putting his men on shore, he fortified the entrance of the port, and lay still until the season of the year forced Don John to return home. In his campaign, the galley, called the *Prize*, whose captain was a son of the famous corsair Barbarossa, was taken by the captain-galley of Naples, called the *She-wolf*, commanded by that thunderbolt of war, that father of the soldiers, that fortunate and invincible captain, Don Álvaro de Bazan, marquess of Santa Cruz.* And I cannot forbear relating what happened at the taking of the *Prize*.

'The son of Barbarossa was so cruel, and treated his slaves so ill, that, as soon as they who were at the oar saw that the *She-wolf* was ready to board and take them, they all at once let fall their oars, and, laying hold on their captain, who stood near the poop, calling out to them to row hard, and passing him along from bank to bank, and from the poop to the prow, they gave him such blows, that he had passed but little beyond the mast before his soul was passed to hell: such was the cruelty wherewith he treated them, and the hatred they bore to him.

'We returned to Constantinople, and the year following, which was seventy-three, it was known there that Don John had taken Tunis, and that kingdom from the Turks, and put Muley Hamet in possession thereof, cutting off the hopes that Muley Hamida had of reigning again there, who was one of the cruellest and yet bravest Moors, that ever was in the world. The Grand Turk felt this loss very sensibly, and putting in practice that sagacity, which is inherent in the Ottoman family, he clapped up a peace with the Venetians, who desired it more than he: and the year following, being that of seventy-four, he attacked the fortress of [the] Goleta and the fort which Don John had left half finished near Tunis. During all these transactions I was still at the oar, without any hope of redemption: at least I did not expect to be ransomed; for I was determined not to write an account of my misfortune to my father.

'In short, the Goleta was lost, and the fort also; before which places the Turks had seventy-five thousand men in pay, besides above four hundred thousand Moors and Arabs from all parts of Africa: and this vast multitude was furnished with such quantities of ammunition, and such large warlike stores, together with so many pioneers, that, each man bringing only a handful of earth, they might therewith have covered both the Goleta and the fort. The Goleta, until then thought impregnable, was first taken, not through the default of the besieged, who did all that men could do, but because experience had now shown, how easily trenches might be raised in that desert sand; for though the water used to be within two spans of the surface, the Turks now met with none within two yards; and so by the help of a great number of sacks of sand, they raised their works so high as to overlook and command the fortifications: and so levelling from a cavalier,* they put it out of the power of the besieged to make any defence.

'It was the general opinion, that our troops ought not to have shut themselves up in the Goleta, but have met the enemy in the open field, at the place of debarkment: but they who talk thus speak at random, and like men little experienced in affairs of this kind. For if there were scarce seven thousand soldiers in the Goleta and in the fort, how could so small a number, though ever so resolute, both take the field and garrison the forts against such a multitude as that of the enemy? and how can a place be maintained, which is not relieved, and especially when besieged by an army that is both numerous and obstinate, and besides in their own country? But many were of opinion, and I was of the number, that heaven did a particular grace and favour to Spain, in suffering the destruction of that forge and refuge of all iniquity, that devourer, that sponge, and that moth of infinite sums of money, idly spent there, to no other purpose than to preserve the memory of its having been a conquest of the invincible emperor Charles the Fifth; as if it were necessary to the making that memory eternal, as it will be, that those stones should keep it up.

'The fort also was taken at last: but the Turks were forced to purchase it inch by inch; for the soldiers who defended it fought with such bravery and resolution, that they killed above twenty-five thousand of the enemy in two-and-twenty general assaults. And of three hundred that were left alive, not one was taken prisoner unwounded; an evident proof of their courage and bravery, and of the vigorous defence they had made. A little fort also, or tower, in the middle of the lake, commanded by Don John Zanoguera,* a cavalier of Valencia, and a famous soldier, surrendered upon terms. They took prisoner Don Pedro Puertocarrero, general of [the] Goleta, who did all that was possible for the defence of his fortress, and took the loss of it so much to heart, that he died for grief on the way to Constantinople, whither they were carrying him prisoner. They took also the commander of the fort, called Gabrio Cerbellon, a Milanese gentleman, a great engineer and a most valiant soldier. Several persons of distinction lost their lives in these two garrisons; among whom was Pagano Doria, knight of Malta, a gentleman of great generosity, as appeared by his exceeding liberality to his brother, the famous John Andrea Doria: and what made his death the more lamented was, his dying by the hands of some African Arabs, who, upon seeing that the fort was lost, offered to convey him, disguised as a Moor, to Tabarca, a small haven or settlement, which the Genoese have on that coast for the coral-fishing. These Arabs cut off his head, and carried it to the general of the Turkish fleet, who made good upon them our Castilian proverb, that, "though we love the treason, we hate the traitor"; for it is said, the general ordered, that those, who brought him the present, should be instantly hanged, because they had not brought him alive. Among the Christians who were taken in the fort was one Don Pedro de Aguilar,* a native of some town in Andalusia, who had been an ensign in the garrison, a good soldier, and a man of excellent parts; in particular, he had a happy talent in poetry. I mention this, because his fortune brought him to be slave to the same patron with me, and we served in the same galley and at the same oar: and before we parted from that port, this cavalier made two sonnets, by way of epitaph, one upon [the] Goleta, and the other upon the fort. And indeed I have a mind to repeat them; for I have them by heart, and I believe they will rather be entertaining than disagreeable to you.'

At the instant the captive named Don Pedro de Aguilar, Don Fernando looked at his companions, and all three smiled: and when he mentioned the sonnets, one of them said:

'Pray, sir, before you go any further I beseech you to tell me what became of that Don Pedro de Aguilar you talk of?'

'All I know,' answered the captive, 'is, that, after he had been two years at Constantinople, he escaped in the habit of an Arnaut,* with a Greek spy, and I cannot tell whether he recovered his liberty; though I believe he did: for, about a year after, I saw the Greek in Constantinople, but had not an opportunity of asking him the success of that journey.'

'He returned to Spain,' said the gentleman; 'for that Don Pedro is my brother, and is now in our town, in health, and rich, is married, and has three children.'

'Thanks be to God,' said the captive, 'for the blessings bestowed on him; for in my opinion, there is not on earth a satisfaction equal to that of recovering one's liberty.'

'Besides,' replied the gentleman, 'I have by heart the sonnets my brother made.'

'Then, pray, sir, repeat them,' said the captive; 'for you will be able to do it better than I can.'

'With all my heart,' answered the gentleman: 'that upon Goleta was thus:

CHAPTER 40

In which is continued the history of the captive.

SONNET

'O happy souls, by death at length set free
From the dark prison of mortality,
By glorious deeds, whose memory never dies,
From earth's dim spot exalted to the skies!
What fury stood in every eye confess'd!
What generous ardour fired each manly breast!
Whilst slaughter'd heaps disdain'd the sandy shore,
And the tinged ocean blush'd with hostile gore.

O'erpower'd by numbers, gloriously ye fell:
Death only could such matchless courage quell.
Whilst dying thus ye triumph o'er your foes,
Its fame the world, its glory heaven bestows!

'You have it right,' said the captive.

'That on the fort,' said the gentleman, 'if I do not forget, was as follows:

SONNET

'From 'midst these walls, whose ruins spread around,
And scatter'd clods that heap th'ensanguin'd ground,
Three thousand souls of warriors, dead in fight,
To better regions took their happy flight.
Long with unconquer'd force they bravely stood,
And fearless shed their unavailing blood;
Till, to superior force compell'd to yield,
Their lives they quitted in the well-fought field.
This fatal soil has ever been the tomb
Of slaughter'd heroes, buried in its womb;
Yet braver bodies did it ne'er sustain,
Nor send more glorious souls the skies to gain.'

The sonnets were not disliked, and the captive, pleased with the news they told him of his comrade, went on with his story, saying:

'The Goleta and the fort being delivered up, the Turks gave orders to dismantle the Goleta: as for the fort, it was in such a condition that there was nothing left to be demolished. And to do the work more speedily, and with less labour, they undermined it in three places: it is true, they could not blow up what seemed to be least strong, the old walls; but whatever remained of the new fortification, made by the engineer Fratin,* came very easily down: In short, the fleet returned to Constantinople victorious and triumphant; and within a few months died my master the famous Uchali, whom people called Uchali Fartax, that is to say, in the Turkish language, 'the scabby renegado': for he was so; and it is customary among the Turks to nickname people from some personal defect, or give them a name from some good quality belonging to them. And the reason is, because there are but four surnames of families which contend for nobility with the Ottoman; and the rest, as I have said, take names and surnames either from the blemishes of the body, or the virtues of the mind. This leper had been at the oar fourteen years, being a slave of the Grand Turk's: and, at about thirty-four years of age, being enraged at a blow given him by a Turk while he was at the oar, to have it in his power to be revenged on him, he renounced his religion. And so great was his valour, that, without rising by those base methods by which the minions of the Grand Turk usually rise, he came to be king of Algiers, and afterwards general of the sea, which is the third command in that empire. He was born in Calabria, and was a good moral man, and treated his slaves with great humanity. He had three thousand of them, and they were divided after his death, as he had ordered by his last will, one half to the Grand Turk who is every man's heir in part, sharing equally with the children of the deceased, and the other among his renegadoes.

'I fell to the lot of a Venetian renegado, who, having been cabin-boy in a ship, was taken by Uchali, and was so beloved by him, that he became one of his most favourite boys. He was one of the cruellest renegadoes that ever was seen: his name was Azanaga.* He grew very rich, and became king of Algiers; and with him I came from Constantinople, a little comforted by being so near Spain: not that I intended to write an account to anybody of my unfortunate circumstances, but in hopes fortune would be more favourable to me in Algiers than it had been in Constantinople, where I had tried a thousand ways of making my escape, but none rightly timed nor successful: and in Algiers I purposed to try other means of compassing what I desired: for the hope of recovering my liberty never entirely abandoned me; and whenever what I devised, contrived, and put in execution, did not answer my design, I presently, without desponding, searched out and formed to myself fresh hopes to sustain me, though they were slight and inconsiderable.

'Thus I made a shift to support life, shut up in a prison or house, which the Turks call a bath, where they keep their

Christian captives locked up, as well those who belong to
the king as some of those belonging to private persons, and
those also whom they call of the Almazen, that is to say,
"captives of the council," who serve the city in its public
works, and in other offices. This kind of captives find it very
difficult to recover their liberty; for, as they belong to the
public, and have no particular master, there is nobody for
them to treat with about their ransom, though they should
have it ready. To these baths, as I have said, private persons
sometimes carry their slaves, especially when their ransom is
agreed upon; for there they keep them without work, and in
safety, until their ransom comes. The king's slaves also, who
are to be ransomed, do not go out to work with the rest of
the crew, unless it be when their ransom is long in coming;
for then, to make them write for it with greater importunity,
they are made to work, and go for wood with the rest; which
is no small toil and pains.

'As they knew I had been a captain, I was one upon
ransom; and though I assured them I wanted both interest
and money, it did not hinder me from being put among
the gentlemen, and those who were to be ransomed. They
put a chain on me, rather as a sign of ransom than to
secure me; and so I passed my life in that bath, with many
other gentlemen and persons of condition, distinguished
and accounted as ransomable. And though hunger and
nakedness often, and indeed generally afflicted us, nothing
troubled us so much as to see, at every turn, the unparalleled and excessive cruelties with which our master used
the Christians. Each day he hanged one, impaled another,
and cut off the ears of a third; and that upon the least
provocation, and sometimes none at all, insomuch that the
very Turks were sensible he did it for the mere pleasure of
doing it, and to gratify his murderous and inhuman disposition. One Spanish soldier only, called such an one De
Saavedra, happened to be in his good graces; and though he
did things which will remain in the memory of those people
for many years, and all towards obtaining his liberty, yet he
never gave him a blow, nor ordered one to be given him,
nor ever gave him so much as a hard word: and for the least

of many things he did, we all feared he would be impaled alive,* and he feared it himself more than once; and, were it not that the time will not allow me, I would now tell you of some things done by this soldier, which would be more entertaining, and more surprising, than the relation of my story.

'But to return. The courtyard of our prison was overlooked by the windows of a house belonging to a rich Moor of distinction, which, as is usual there, were rather peep-holes than windows; and even these had their thick and close lattices. It fell out then, that one day as I was upon a terrace of our prison with three of my companions, trying, by way of pastime, who could leap farthest with his chains on, being by ourselves (for all the rest of the Christians were gone out to work), by chance I looked up, and saw, from out of one of those little windows I have mentioned, a cane appear, with a handkerchief tied at the end of it: the cane moved up and down, as if it made signs for us to come and take it. We looked earnestly up at it, and one of my companions went and placed himself under the cane, to see whether they who held it would let it drop, or what they would do; but, as he came near, they advanced the cane, and moved it from side to side, as if they had said No, with the head. The Christian came back, and the cane was let down with the same motions as before. Another of my companions went, and the same happened to him as to the former: then the third went, and he had the same success with the first and second.

'Seeing this, I resolved to try my fortune likewise; and, as soon as I had placed myself under the cane, it was let drop, and fell just at my feet. I immediately untied the handkerchief, and in a knot at the corner of it I found ten zianyis, a sort of base gold coin used by the Moors, each piece worth about ten reals of our money. I need not tell you whether I rejoiced at the prize; and indeed I was no less pleased than surprised to think from whence this good fortune could come to us, especially to me; for the letting fall the cane to me alone plainly showed that the favour was intended to me alone. I took my welcome money; I broke the cane to pieces; I returned to the terrace; I looked back to the window, and

perceived a very white hand go out and in, to open and shut
it hastily. Hereby we understood, or fancied, that it must be
some woman, who lived in that house, who had been thus
charitable to us; and, to express our thanks, we made our
reverences after the Moorish fashion, inclining the head,
bending the body, and laying the hands on the breast. Soon
after, there was put out of the same window a little cross
made of cane, which was presently drawn in again. On this
signal we concluded, that some Christian woman was a
captive in that house, and that it was she who had done us
the kindness; but the whiteness of the hand, and the bracelets
we had a glimpse of, soon destroyed that fancy. Then again
we imagined it must be some Christian renegade, whom their
masters often marry, reckoning it happy to get one of them;
for they value them more than the women of their own
nation.

'All our reasonings and conjectures were very wide of the
truth; and now all our entertainment was to gaze at and
observe the window, as our north, from whence that star,
the cane, had appeared. But full fifteen days passed, in which
we saw neither hand, nor any other signal whatever. And
though in this interval we endeavoured all we could to inform
ourselves who lived in that house, and whether there was
any Christian renegade there, we never could learn anything
more, than that the house was that of a considerable and
rich Moor, named Agimorato* who had been Alcaide of Pata,
an office among them of great authority. But, when we least
dreamed of its raining any more zianyis from thence, we
perceived, unexpectedly, another cane appear, and another
handkerchief tied to it, with another knot larger than the
former; and this was at a time when the bath, as before, was
empty, and without people. We made the same trial as before,
each of my three companions going before me; but the cane
was not let down to either of them; but when I went up to
it, it was let fall. I untied the knot, and found in it forty
Spanish crowns in gold, and a paper written in Arabic; and
at the top of the writing was a large cross. I kissed the cross,
took the crowns, and returned to the terrace: we all made
our reverences; the hand appeared again; I made signs that

I would read the paper; the hand shut the window; and we all remained amazed, yet overjoyed at what had happened: and as none of us understood Arabic, great was our desire to know what the paper contained, and greater the difficulty to find one to read it.

'At last I resolved to confide in a renegado, a native of Murcia, who professed himself very much my friend, and we had exchanged such pledges of our mutual confidence as obliged him to keep whatever secret I should commit to him: for it is usual with renegadoes, when they have a mind to return to Christendom, to carry with them certificates from the most considerable captives, attesting, in the most ample manner, and best form they can get, that such a renegado is an honest man, and has always been kind and obliging to the Christians, and that he had a desire to make his escape the first opportunity that offered. Some procure these certificates with a good intention: others make use of them occasionally, and out of cunning only; for, going to rob and plunder on the Christian coasts, if they happen to be ship-wrecked or taken, they produce their certificates, and pretend that those papers will show the design they came upon, namely, to get into some Christian country, which was the reason of their going a-pirating with the Turks. By this means they escape the first fury, and reconcile themselves to the church, and live unmolested; and, when an opportunity of-fers, they return to Barbary, and to their former course of life. Others there are who procure and make use of these papers with a good design, and remain in the Christian countries.

'Now this friend of mine was a renegado of this sort, and had gotten certificates from all of us, wherein we recom-mended him as much as possible; and if the Moors had found these papers about him they would certainly have burnt him alive. I knew he understood Arabic very well, and could not only speak, but write it. But, before I would let him into the whole affair, I desired him to read that paper, which I found by chance in a hole of my cell. He opened it, and stood a good while looking at it, and translating it to himself. I asked him if he understood it. He said, he did very well, and, if I desired to know its contents word for word, I must give him pen and ink, that he might translate it with more exactness. We gave him presently what he required, and he went on translating it in order, and having done, he said:

'"What is here set down in Spanish is precisely what is contained in this Moorish paper; and you must take notice, that where it says Lela Marien, it means our Lady the Virgin Mary."

'We read the paper, which was as follows:

'"When I was a child, my father had a woman-slave, who instructed me in the Christian worship, and told me many things of Lela Marien. This Christian died, and I know she did not go to the fire, but to Allah; for I saw her twice afterwards, and she bid me go to the country of the Christians, to see Lela Marien, who loved me very much. I know not how it is; I have seen many Christians from this window, and none has looked like a gentleman but yourself. I am very beautiful and young, and have a great deal of money to carry away with me. Try if you can find out how we may get away, and you shall be my husband there, if you please; and if not, I shall not care; for Lela Marien will provide me a husband. I write this myself: be careful to whom you give it to read: trust not to any Moor: for they are all treacherous: therefore I am very much perplexed; for I would not have you discover it to anybody; for if my father comes to know it, he will immediately throw me into a well, and cover me with stones. I will fasten a thread to the cane; tie your answer to it: and if you have nobody that can write Arabic, tell me by signs; for Lela Marien will make me understand you. She and Allah keep you, and this cross, which I very often kiss; for so the captive directed me to do."

'Think, gentlemen, whether we had not reason to be overjoyed and surprised at the contents of this paper: and both our joy and surprise was so great, that the renegado perceived that the paper was not found by accident, but was written to one of us; and therefore he entreated us, if what he suspected was true, to confide in him, and tell him all;

for he would venture his life for our liberty; and saying this, he pulled a brass crucifix out of his bosom, and with many tears, swore by the God that image represented, in whom he, though a great sinner, truly and firmly believed, that he would faithfully keep secret whatever we should discover to him: for he imagined, and almost divined, that by means of her who had written that letter, himself and all of us should regain our liberty, and he in particular attain what he so earnestly desired, which was to be restored to the bosom of the holy church his mother, from which, like a rotten member, he had been separated and cut off through his sin and ignorance.

'The renegado said this with so many tears, and signs of so much repentance, that we unanimously agreed to tell him the truth of the case; and so we gave him an account of the whole, without concealing anything from him. We showed him the little window, out of which the cane had appeared, and by that he marked the house, and resolved to take especial care to inform himself who lived in it. We also agreed it would be right to answer the Moor's billet; and as we now had one who knew how to do it, the renegado that instant wrote what I dictated to him, which was exactly what I shall repeat to you; for of all the material circumstances which befell me in this adventure, not one has yet escaped my memory, nor shall I ever forget them whilst I have breath. In short, the answer to the Moor was this:

'"The true Allah preserve you, dear lady, and that blessed Marien, who is the true mother of God, and is she who has put into your heart the desire of going into the country of the Christians, because she loves you. Pray to her, that she will be pleased to instruct you how to bring about what she commands you to do; for she is so good she will assuredly do it. On my part, and that of all the Christians with me, I offer to do for you all we are able, at the hazard of our lives. Do not fail writing to me, and acquainting me with whatever resolutions you take, and I will constantly answer you; for the great Allah has given us a Christian captive, who speaks and writes your language well, as you may perceive by this paper. So that you may without fear give us notice of your intentions. As to what you say of becoming my wife, when you get into a Christian country, I promise you on the word of a good Christian, it shall be so; and know, that the Christians keep their words better than the Moors. Allah, and Marien his mother, have you in their keeping, dear lady."

'This letter being written and folded up, I waited two days until the bath was empty, as before, and then presently I took my accustomed post upon the terrace, to see if the cane appeared, and it was not long before it appeared. As soon as I saw it, though I could not discern who held it out, I showed the paper, as giving them notice to put the thread to it; but it was already fastened to the cane, to which I tied the letter, and, in a short time after, our star appeared again with the white flag of peace, the handkerchief. It was let drop, and I took it up, and found in it, in all kinds of coin, both silver and gold, above fifty crowns; which multiplied our joy fifty times, confirming the hopes we had conceived of regaining our liberty.

'That same evening, our renegado returned, and told us he had learned that the same Moor, we were before informed of, dwelt in that house, and that his name was Agimorato; that he was extremely rich, and had one only daughter, heiress to all he had; that it was the general opinion of the whole city, that she was the most beautiful woman in all Barbary; and that several of the viceroys, who had been sent thither, had sought her to wife, but that she never would consent to marry: and he also learned that she had a Christian woman slave, who died some time before: all which agreed perfectly with what was in the paper. We presently consulted with the renegado, what method we should take to carry off the Moorish lady, and make our escape into Christendom: and in fine it was agreed for that time that we should wait for a second letter from Zoraida:* for that was the name of her, who now desires to be called Maria: for it was very easy to see, that she, and no other, could find the means of surmounting the difficulties that lay in our way. After we were come to this resolution, the renegado bid us not be uneasy; for he would set us at liberty, or lose his life. The bath, after this, was four days full of people, which occasioned the cane's not appearing in all that time: at the end of which, the bath being empty as usual, it appeared with the handkerchief so pregnant, that it promised a happy birth. The cane and the linen inclined toward me: I found in it another paper, and a hundred crowns in gold only, without any other coin. The renegado being present, we gave him the paper to read in our cell, and he told us it said thus:

'"I do not know, dear sir, how to contrive a method for our going to Spain, nor has Lela Marien informed me, though I have asked it of her. What may be done, is: I will convey to you through this window a large sum of money in gold: redeem yourself and your friends therewith, and let one of you go to the country of the Christians, and buy a bark, and return for the rest; and he will find me in my father's garden, at the Babazon-gate close to the seaside, where I am to be all this summer with my father and my servants. Thence you may carry me off by night without fear, and put me on board the bark. And remember you are to be my husband; for, if not, I will pray to Marien to punish you. If you can trust nobody to go for the bark, ransom yourself and go; for I shall be more secure of your return than another's, as you are a gentleman and a Christian. Take care not to mistake the garden: and when I see you walking where you now are, I shall conclude the bath is empty, and will furnish you with money enough. Allah preserve thee, dear sir!"

'These were the contents of the second letter: which being heard by us all, every one offered himself, and would fain be the ransomed person, promising to go and return very punctually. I also offered myself: but the renegado opposed these offers, saying, he would in no wise consent, that any one of us should get his liberty before the rest, experience having taught him, how ill men, when free, keep the promises they have made while in slavery; for several considerable captives, he said, had tried this expedient, ransoming some

one, who should go to Valencia or Majorca, with money, to
buy and arm a vessel, and return for those who ransomed
him, but the person sent has never come back: for liberty
once regained, and the fear of losing it again, effaces out of
the memory all obligations in the world. And, in confirmation
of this truth, he told us briefly a case, which had happened
very lately to certain Christian gentlemen, the strangest that
had ever fallen out even in those parts, where every day the
most surprising and wonderful things come to pass. He
concluded with saying, that the best way would be, to give
him the money designed for the ransom of a Christian, to
buy a vessel there in Algiers, upon pretence of turning
merchant, and trading to Tetuan, and on that coast, and that,
being master of the vessel, he could easily contrive how to
get them all out of the bath, and put them on board. But if
the Moor, as she promised, should furnish money enough to
redeem them all, it would be a very easy matter for them,
being free, to go on board even at noonday: the greatest
difficulty, he said, was, that the Moors do not allow any
renegado to buy or keep a vessel, unless it be a large one to
go a-pirating; for they suspect, that he who buys a small
vessel, especially if he be a Spaniard, designs only to get into
Christendom therewith: but this inconvenience, he said, he
would obviate, by taking in a Tagarin Moor* for partner of
the vessel, and then he reckoned the rest as good as done.

'Now, though to me and my companions it seemed better
to send for the vessel to Majorca, as the Moorish lady said,
yet we did not dare to contradict him; fearing, lest, if we did
not do as he would have us, he should betray our design,
and put us in danger of losing our lives, in case he discovered
Zoraida's intrigue, for whose life we would all have laid down
our own: and therefore we resolved to commit ourselves into
the hands of God, and those of the renegado. And in that
instant we answered Zoraida, that we would do all that she
had advised; for she had directed as well as if Lela Marien
herself had inspired her; and that it depended entirely upon
her, either that the business should be delayed, or set about
immediately. I again promised to be her husband: and so the
next day, the bath happening to be clear, she, at several times,

with the help of the cane and handkerchief, gave us two
thousand crowns in gold, and a paper, wherein she said, that
the first Jumá, that is Friday, she was to go to her father's
garden, and that, before she went she would give us more
money: and if that was not sufficient, she bid us let her know,
and she would give us as much as we desired; for her father
had so much, that he would never miss it; and besides, she
kept the keys of all.

'We immediately gave five hundred crowns to the renegado,
to buy the vessel. With eight hundred I ransomed myself,
depositing the money with a merchant of Valencia, then at
Algiers, who redeemed me from the king, passing his word
for me, that the first ship that came from Valencia, my
ransom should be paid. For if he had paid the money down,
it would have made the king suspect, that the money had
been a great while in his hands, and that he had employed
it to his own use. In short, my master was so jealous, that
I did not dare upon any account to pay the money immediately. The Thursday preceding the Friday on which the fair
Zoraida was to go to the garden, she gave us a thousand
crowns more, and advertised us of her going thither, and
entreated me, if I ransomed myself first, immediately to find
out her father's garden, and by all means get an opportunity
of going thither and seeing her. I answered her in few words,
that I would not fail, and desired that she would take care
to recommend us to Lela Marien, using all those prayers the
captive had taught her. When this was done, means were
concerted for redeeming our three companions, and getting
them out of the bath, lest, seeing me ransomed, and themselves not, knowing there was money sufficient, they should
be uneasy, and the devil should tempt them to do something
to the prejudice of Zoraida; for, though their being men of
honour might have freed me from such an apprehension, I
had no mind to run the hazard, and so got them ransomed
by the same means I had been ransomed myself, depositing
the whole money with the merchant, that he might safely and
securely pass his word for us; to whom nevertheless we did
not discover our management and secret, because of the
danger it would have exposed us to.'

CHAPTER 41

Wherein the captive continues the story of his adventures.

'IN less than fifteen days our renegado had bought a very
good bark, capable of holding above thirty persons, and to
make sure work, and give the business a colour, he made a
short voyage to a place called Sargel, thirty leagues from
Algiers, towards Oran, to which there is a great trade for
dried figs. Two or three times he made this trip, in company
of the Tagarin aforesaid. The Moors of Aragon are called in
Barbary Tagarins, and those of Granada Mudéjares; and in
the kingdom of Fez the Mudéjares are called Elches, who
are the people the king makes most use of in his wars.

'You must know, that each time he passed with his bark,
he cast anchor in a little creek, not two bow-shot distant
from the garden, where Zoraida expected us: and there the
renegado designedly set himself, together with the Moors that
rowed, either to perform the cela,* or to practise, by way of
jest, what he intended to execute in earnest; and with this
view he would go to Zoraida's garden, and beg some fruit
which her father would give him, without knowing who he
was. His design was, as he afterwards told me, to speak to
Zoraida, and to tell her that he was the person, who, by my
direction, was to carry her to Christendom, and that she
might be easy and secure: but it was impossible for him to
do it, the Moorish women never suffering themselves to be
seen either by Moor or Turk, unless when commanded by
their husbands or fathers. Christian slaves indeed are allowed
to keep company and converse with them, with more freedom perhaps than is proper. But I should have been sorry
if he had talked to her, because it might have frighted her
to see that the business was entrusted with a renegado. But
God, who ordered it otherwise, gave the renegado no opportunity of effecting his good design: who, finding how securely
he went to and from Sargel, and that he lay at anchor, when,
how, and where he pleased, and that the Tagarin, his partner,
had no will of his own, but approved whatever he directed;
that I was ransomed, and that there wanted nothing but to
find some Christians to help to row; he bade me consider

whom I would bring with me besides those already ransomed, and bespeak them for the first Friday; for that was the time he fixed for our departure.

'Hereupon I spoke to twelve Spaniards, all able men at the oar, and such as could most easily get out of the city unsuspected: and it was no easy matter to find so many at that juncture; for there were twenty corsairs out a-pirating, and they had taken almost all the rowers with them; and these had not been found but that their master did not go out that summer, having a galiot to finish that was then upon the stocks. I said nothing more to them, but that they should steal out of the town one by one, the next Friday, in the dusk of the evening, and wait for me somewhere about Agimorato's garden. I gave this direction to each of them separately, with this caution, that, if they should see any other Christians there they should only say, I ordered them to stay for me in that place.

'This point being taken care of, one thing was yet wanting, and that the most necessary of all; which was, to advertise Zoraida how matters stood, that she might be in readiness, and on the watch, so as not to be affrighted, if we rushed upon her on a sudden before the time she could think that the vessel from Christendom could be arrived. And therefore I resolved to go to the garden, and try if I could speak to her: and under pretence of gathering some herbs, one day before our departure, I went thither, and the first person I met was her father, who spoke to me in a language, which, all over Barbary, and even at Constantinople, is spoken among captives and Moors, and is neither Morisco nor Castilian, nor of any other nation, but a medley of all languages, and generally understood. He, I say, in that jargon, asked me what I came to look for in that garden, and to whom I belonged? I answered him, I was a slave of Arnaute Mami* (who, I knew, was a very great friend of his), and that I came for a few herbs of several sorts to make a salad. He then asked me, if I was upon ransom or not, and how much my master demanded for me?

'While we were thus talking, the fair Zoraida, who had espied me some time before, came out of the house; and as the Moorish women make no scruple of appearing before the Christians, nor are at all shy towards them, as I have already observed, she made no difficulty of coming where I stood with her father, who seeing her walking slowly towards us, called to her, and bid her come on. It would be too hard a task for me at this time, to express the great beauty, the genteel air, the finery and richness of attire, with which my beloved Zoraida appeared then before my eyes. More pearls, if I may so say, hung about her beauteous neck, and more jewels were in her ears and hair, than she had hairs on her head. About her ankles, which were bare, according to custom, she had two carcaxes (so they call the enamelled foot-bracelets in Morisco), of the purest gold, set with so many diamonds, that, as she told me since, her father valued them at ten thousand pistoles; and those she wore on her wrist were of equal value. The pearls were in abundance, and very good; for the greatest finery and magnificence of the Moorish women consists in adorning themselves with the finest seed-pearls: and therefore there are more of that sort among the Moors, than among all other nations; and Zoraida's father had the reputation of having a great many, and those the very best in Algiers, and to be worth besides above two hundred thousand Spanish crowns; of all which, she, who is now mine, was once mistress. Whether, with all these ornaments, she then appeared beautiful or not, and what she must have been in the days of her prosperity, may be conjectured by what remains after so many fatigues. For it is well known, that the beauty of some women has days and seasons, and depends upon accidents, which diminish or increase it; nay, the very passions of the mind naturally improve or impair it, and very often utterly destroy it. In short, she came, extremely adorned, and extremely beautiful; to me at least she seemed the most so of anything I had ever beheld: which, together with my obligations to her, made me think her an angel from heaven, descended for my pleasure and relief.

'When she was come up to us, her father told her, in his own tongue, that I was a captive belonging to his friend Arnaute Mami, and that I came to look for a salad. She took up the discourse, and in the aforesaid medley of languages,

asked me, whether I was a gentleman, and why I did not
ransom myself. I told her I was already ransomed, and by
the price she might guess what my master thought of me,
since he had got fifteen hundred pieces of eight for me. To
which she answered:

'"Truly had you belonged to my father, he should not have
parted with you for twice that sum: for you Christians always
falsify in your accounts of yourselves, pretending to be poor,
in order to cheat the Moors."

'"It may very well be so, madam," answered I; "but, in
truth, I dealt sincerely with my master, and ever did and shall
do the same by everybody in the world."

'"And when do you go away?" said Zoraida.

'"To-morrow, I believe," said I: "for there is a French
vessel, which sails to-morrow, and I intend to go in her."

'"Would it not be better," replied Zoraida, "to stay until
some ships come from Spain, and go with them, and not
with those of France, who are not your friends?"

'"No, madam," answered I: "but should the news we have
of a Spanish ship's coming suddenly prove true, I would
perhaps stay a little for it, though it is more likely I shall
depart to-morrow; for the desire I have to be in my own
country, and with the persons I love, is so great, that it will
not suffer me to wait for any other conveniency, though ever
so much better."

'"You are married, doubtless, in your own country," said
Zoraida, "and therefore you are so desirous to be gone, and
be at home with your wife?"

'"No," I replied, "I am not married; but I have given my
word to marry, as soon as I get thither."

'"And is the lady, whom you have promised, beautiful?"
said Zoraida.

'"So beautiful," answered I, "that, to compliment her, and
tell you the truth, she is very like yourself."

'Her father laughed heartily at this, and said:

'"Really, Christian, she must be beautiful indeed, if she
resembles my daughter, who is accounted the handsomest
woman in all this kingdom: observe her well, and you will
see I speak the truth."

'Zoraida's father served us as an interpreter to most of this conversation, as understanding Spanish; for though she spoke the bastard language, in use there, as I told you, yet she expressed her meaning more by signs than by words.

'While we were thus engaged in discourse, a Moor came running to us, crying aloud, that four Turks had leaped over the pales or wall of the garden, and were gathering the fruit, though it was not yet ripe. The old man was put into a fright, and so was Zoraida; for the Moors are naturally afraid of the Turks, especially of their soldiers, who are so insolent and imperious over the Moors, who are subject to them, that they treat them worse than if they were their slaves. Therefore Zoraida's father said to her:

'"Daughter, retire into the house, and lock yourself in, while I go and talk to these dogs: and you, Christian, gather your herbs, and begone in peace, and Allah send you safe to your own country."

'I bowed myself, and he went his way to find the Turks, leaving me alone with Zoraida, who also made as if she was going whither her father bid her. But scarcely was he got out of sight among the trees of the garden, when she turned back to me, with her eyes full of tears, and said:

'"Tamexi, Cristiano, Tamexi?" that is, "Are you going away, Christian? are you going away?"

'I answered,

'"Yes, madam, but not without you: expect me the next Jumá, and be not frighted when you see us; for we shall certainly get to Christendom."

'I said this in such a manner, that she understood me very well; and, throwing her arm about my neck, she began to walk softly and trembling towards the house: and fortune would have it (which might have proved fatal, if heaven had not ordained otherwise), that, while we were going in that posture and manner I told you, her arm being about my neck, her father, returning from driving away the Turks, saw us in that posture, and we were sensible that he discovered us. But Zoraida had the discretion and presence of mind not to take her arm from about my neck, but rather held me closer: and leaning her head against my breast, and bending her knees a

little, gave plain signs of fainting away; and I also made as
if I held her up only to keep her from falling. Her father
came running to us, and seeing his daughter in that posture,
asked what ailed her. But she not answering, he said:

'"Without doubt, these dogs have frighted her into a
swoon;" and taking her from me, he inclined her gently to
his bosom; and she, fetching a deep sigh, and her eyes still
full of tears, said again,

'"Amexi, Cristiano, Amexi," "Begone, Christian, begone".
'To which her father answered:

"There is no occasion, child, why the Christian should go
away; he has done you no harm; and the Turks are gone off;
let nothing fright you; there is no danger: for, as I have
already told you, the Turks, at my request, have returned by
the way they came."

'"Sir," said I to her father, "they have frighted her, as you
say; but, since she bids me begone I will not disturb her:
God be with you, and, with your leave, I will come again, if
we have occasion, for herbs to this garden; for my master
says there are no better for a salad anywhere than here."

'"You may come whenever you will," answered Agimorato;
"for my daughter does not say this, as having been offended
by you or any other Christian; but, instead of bidding the
Turks begone, she bade you begone, only because she
thought it time for you to go and gather your herbs."

'I now took my leave of them both, and she, seeming as
if her soul had been rent from her, went away with her father.
And I, under pretence of gathering herbs, walked over, and
took a view of the whole garden, at my leisure, observing
carefully all the inlets and outlets, and the strength of the
house, and every conveniency which might tend to facilitate
our business.

'When I had so done, I went and gave an account to the
renegado and my companions of all that had passed, longing
eagerly for the hour, when, without fear of surprise, I might
enjoy the happiness which fortune presented me in the
beautiful Zoraida. In a word, time passed on, and the day
appointed, and by us so much wished for, came; and, all
observing the order and method, which, after mature deliber-

ation and long debate, we had agreed on, we had the desired success.'

'For, the Friday following the day when I talked with Zoraida in the garden, our renegado at the close of the evening cast anchor with the bark almost opposite to where Zoraida dwelt. The Christians who were to be employed at the oar, were ready, and hid in several places thereabouts. They were all in suspense, their hearts beating, and in expectation of my coming, being eager to surprise the bark, which lay before their eyes: for they knew nothing of what was concerted with the renegado, but thought they were to regain their liberty by mere force, and by killing the Moors who were on board the vessel. As soon, therefore as I and my friends appeared, all they that were hid came out, and joined us one after another. It was now the time that the city-gates were shut, and nobody appeared abroad in all that quarter. Being met together, we were in some doubt whether it would be better to go first to Zoraida, or secure the Moors, who rowed the vessel. While we were in this uncertainty, our renegado came to us, asking us what we stayed for; for now was the time, all his Moors being thoughtless of danger, and most of them asleep. We told him what we demurred about, and he said, that the thing of the most importance was, first to seize the vessel, which might be done with all imaginable ease, and without any manner of danger, and then we might presently go and fetch Zoraida. We all approved of what he said, and so, without further delay, he being our guide, we came to the vessel; and he, leaping in first, drew a cutlass, and said in Morisco:

'"Let not one man of you stir, unless he has a mind it should cost him his life."

'By this time all the Christians were got on board; and the Moors, who were timorous fellows, hearing the master speak thus, were in a great fright; and, without making any resistance (for indeed they had few or no arms) silently suffered themselves to be bound; which was done very expeditiously, the Christians threatening the Moors, that, if they raised any manner of cry, or made the least noise, they would in that instant put them all to the sword.

'This being done, and half our number remaining on board to guard them, the rest of us, the renegado being still our leader, went to Agimorato's garden, and, as good luck would have it, the door opened as easily to us as if it had not been locked; and we came up to the house with great stillness and silence, and without being perceived by any one. The lovely Zoraida was expecting us at a window, and when she heard people coming, she asked, in a low voice, whether we were Nazareni, that is, Christians? I answered, we were, and desired her to come down. When she knew it was I, she stayed not a moment, but without answering me a word, came down in an instant, and, opening the door, appeared to us all so beautiful, and richly attired, that I cannot easily express it. As soon as I saw her, I took her hand, and kissed it: the renegado did the same, and my two comrades also; and the rest, who knew not the meaning of it, followed our example, thinking we only meant to express our thanks and acknowledgements to her as the instrument of our deliverance. The renegado asked her in Morisco, whether her father was in the house: she answered, he was, and asleep. Then we must awake him, replied the renegado, and carry him with us, and all that he has of value in this beautiful villa.

'"No," said she, "my father must by no means be touched, and there is nothing considerable here, but what I have with me, which is sufficient to make you all rich and content: stay a little and you shall see."

'And, so saying, she went in again, and bade us be quiet, and make no noise, for she would come back immediately. I asked the renegado what she said: he told me, and I bade him be sure to do just as Zoraida would have him, who was now returned with a little trunk so full of gold crowns, that she could hardly carry it.

'Ill fortune would have it, that her father in the meantime happened to awake, and, hearing a noise in the garden, looked out at the window, and presently found that there were Christians in it. Immediately he cried out as loud as he could in Arabic,

'"Christians, Christians, thieves, thieves."

'Which outcry put us all into the utmost terror and confusion. But the renegado, seeing the danger we were in, and considering how much it imported him to go through with the enterprise, before it was discovered, ran up with the greatest speed to the room where Agimorato was; and with him ran up several others of us: but I did not dare to quit Zoraida, who had sunk into my arms almost in a swoon. In short, they that went up acquitted themselves so well, that in a moment they came down with Agimorato, having tied his hands, and stopped his mouth with a handkerchief, so that he could not speak a word, and threatening him, if he made the least noise, it should cost him his life. When his daughter saw him, she covered her eyes, that she might not see him, and her father was astonished at seeing her, not knowing how willingly she had put herself into our hands. But at that time it being of the utmost consequence to us to fly, we got as speedily as we could to the bark, where our comrades already expected us with impatience, fearing we had met with some cross accident.

'Scarcely two hours of the night were passed, when we were now all got on board, and then we untied the hands of Zoraida's father, and took the handkerchief out of his mouth: but the renegado warned him again not to speak a word, for, if he did, they would take away his life. When he saw his daughter there, he began to weep most tenderly, and especially when he perceived that I held her closely embraced, and that she, without making any show of opposition, or complaint, or coyness, sat so still and quiet: nevertheless he held his peace, lest we should put the renegado's threats in execution.

'Zoraida now, finding herself in the bark, and that we began to handle our oars, and seeing her father there, and the rest of the Moors, who were bound, spoke to the renegado, to desire me to do her the favour to loose those Moors, and set her father at liberty; for she would sooner throw herself into the sea, than see a father who loved her so tenderly carried away captive before her eyes, and upon her account. The renegado told me what she desired, and I answered that I was entirely satisfied it should be so: but he replied, it was not convenient; for, should they be set on shore there, they would presently raise the country, and alarm the city, and cause some light frigates to be sent out in quest of us, and so we should be beset both by sea and land, and it would be impossible for us to escape: but what might be done, was to give them their liberty at the first Christian country we should touch at. We all came into this opinion, and Zoraida also was satisfied, when we told her what we had determined, and the reasons why we could not at present comply with her request. And then immediately, with joyful silence, and cheerful diligence, each of our brave rowers handled his oar, and, recommending ourselves to God with all our hearts, we began to make towards the island of Majorca, which is the nearest Christian land.

'But the north wind beginning to blow fresh, and the sea being somewhat rough, it was not possible for us to steer the course of Majorca, and we were forced to keep along shore towards Oran, not without great apprehensions of being discovered from the town of Sargel, which lies on that coast, about sixty miles from Algiers. We were afraid likewise of meeting in our passage, with some of those galiots, which come usually with merchandise from Tetuan; though, each relying on his own courage, and that of his comrades in general, we presumed, that if we should meet a galiot, provided it were not a cruiser, we should be so far from being ruined, that we should probably take a vessel, wherein we might more securely pursue our voyage. While we proceeded in our voyage, Zoraida kept her head between my hands, that she might not look on her father; and I could perceive she was continually calling on Lela Marien to assist us.

'We had rowed about thirty miles, when daybreak came upon us, and we found ourselves not above three musket-shot distant from the shore, which seemed to be quite a desert, and without any creature to discover us: however, by mere dint of rowing, we made a little out to sea, which was by this time become more calm; and when we had advanced about two leagues, it was ordered they should row by turns, whilst we took a little refreshment; the bark being well provided: but the rowers said it was not a time to take any rest, and that they would by no means quit their oars, but would eat and row, if those, who were unemployed, would bring the victuals to them. They did so: and now the wind began to blow a brisk gale, which forced us to set up our sails, and lay down our oars, and steer directly to Oran, it being impossible to hold any other course. All this was done with great expedition; and so we sailed above eight miles an hour, without any other fear than that of meeting some corsair. We gave the Moorish prisoners something to eat, and the renegado comforted them, telling them they were not slaves, and that they should have their liberty given them the first opportunity: and he said the same to Zoraida's father, who answered:

'"I might, perhaps, expect or hope for any other favour from your liberality and generous usage, O Christians; but as to giving me my liberty, think me not so simple as to imagine it; for you would never have exposed yourselves to the hazard of taking it from me, to restore it to me so freely, especially since you know who I am, and the advantage that may accrue to you by my ransom; which do but name, and from this moment I promise you whatever you demand, for myself, and for this my unhappy daughter, or else for her alone, who is the greater and better part of my soul."

'In saying this, he began to weep so bitterly, that it moved us all to compassion, and forced Zoraida to look up at him; who seeing him weep in that manner, was so melted, that she got up from me, and ran to embrace her father; and laying her face to his, they two began so tender a lamentation, that many of us could not forbear keeping them company. But when her father observed, that she was adorned with her best attire, and had so many jewels about her, he said to her in his language:

'"How comes it, daughter, that yesterday evening, before this terrible misfortune befell us, I saw you in your ordinary and household dress, and now, without having had time to dress yourself, or having received any joyful news, fit to be solemnized by adorning and dressing yourself out, I see you set off with the best clothes that I could possibly give you when fortune was more favourable to us? answer me to this; for it holds me in greater suspense and astonishment, than the misfortune itself, into which I am fallen."

'The renegado interpreted to us all that the Moor said to his daughter, who answered him not a word: but when he saw in a corner of the vessel, the little trunk, in which she used to keep her jewels, which he knew very well he had left in Algiers, and had not brought with him to the garden, he was still more confounded, and asked her, how that trunk had come to our hands, and what was in it, to which the renegado, without staying until Zoraida spoke, answered:

'"Trouble not yourself, señor, about asking your daughter so many questions; for with one word I can satisfy them all: and therefore be it known to you, that she is a Christian, and has been the instrument to file off our chains, and give us the liberty we enjoy: she is here, with her own consent, and well pleased, I believe, to find herself in this condition, like one who goes out of darkness into light, from death to life, and from suffering to glory."'

'"Is this true, daughter?" said the Moor.

'"It is," answered Zoraida.

'"In effect then," replied the old man, you are become a Christian, and are she, who has put her father into the power of his enemies?

'To which Zoraida answered:

'"I am indeed a Christian; but not she, who has reduced you to this condition: for my desire never was to do you harm, but only myself good."

'"And what good have you done yourself, my daughter?"

'"Ask that," answered she, "of Lela Marien, who can tell you better than I can."

'The Moor had scarcely heard this, when with incredible precipitation, he threw himself headlong into the sea, and without doubt had been drowned, had not the wide and cumbersome garments he wore kept him a little while above water. Zoraida cried out to save him; and we all presently ran, and, laying hold of his garment, dragged him out, half drowned, and senseless; at which sight Zoraida was so affected that she set up a tender and sorrowful lamentation over him, as if he had been really dead. We turned him with his mouth downward, and he voided a great deal of water, and in about two hours came to himself.

'In the meantime, the wind being changed, we were obliged to ply our oars, to avoid running upon the shore; but by good fortune we came to a creek by the side of a small promontory, or head, which, by the Moors, is called the cape of Cava Rumia, that is to say, in our language. "The wicked Christian woman"; for the Moors have a tradition, that Cava who occasioned the loss of Spain, lies buried there;* Cava signifying, in their language, a "wicked woman", and rumia, "a Christian": and further, they reckon it an ill omen, to be forced to anchor there; and otherwise they never do so; though to us it proved, not the shelter of a wicked woman, but a safe harbour and retreat, considering how high the sea ran.

'We placed scouts on shore, and never dropped our oars: we ate of what the renegado had provided, and prayed to God and to Our Lady very devoutly for assistance and protection, that we might give a happy ending to so fortunate a beginning. Order was given, at Zoraida's entreaty, to set her father on shore with the rest of the Moors, who until now had been fast bound; for she had not the heart, nor could her tender feelings brook, to see her father, and her countrymen, carried off prisoners before her face. We promised her it should be done at our going off, since there was no danger in leaving them in so desolate a place. Our prayers were not in vain; heaven heard them; for the wind presently changed in our favour, and the sea was calm, inviting us to return and prosecute our intended voyage.

'Seeing this, we unbound the Moors, and set them one by one on shore; at which they were greatly surprised: but when we came to disembark Zoraida's father, who was now perfectly in his senses, he said:

'"Why, Christians, think you, is this wicked woman desirous of my being set at liberty? think you it is out of any filial piety she has towards me? No, certainly; but it is because of the disturbance my presence would give her, when she has a mind to put her evil inclinations in practice. And think not that she is moved to change her religion because she thinks yours is preferable to ours: no; but because she knows, that libertinism is more allowed in your country than in ours."

'And, turning to Zoraida (I and another Christian, holding him fast by both arms, lest he should commit some outrage) he said:

'"O, infamous girl, and ill-advised maiden! whither goest thou blindfold and precipitate, in the power of these dogs, our natural enemies? Cursed be the hour, wherein I begat thee: and cursed be the indulgence and luxury in which I brought thee up!"

'But, perceiving he was not likely to give over in haste, I hurried him ashore, and from thence he continued his exe-crations and wailings, praying to Mahomet that he would beseech God to destroy, confound, and make an end of us: and when, being under sail, we could no longer hear his words, we saw his actions; which were, tearing his beard, plucking off his hair, and rolling himself on the ground: and once he raised his voice so high, that we could hear him say:

'"Come back, beloved daughter, come back to shore; for I forgive thee all; let those men keep the money they already have; and do thou come back, and comfort thy disconsolate father, who must lose his life in this desert land, if thou forsakest him."

'All this Zoraida heard; all this she felt, and bewailed; but could not speak, nor answer him a word, only:

'"May it please Allah, my dear father, that Lela Marien, who has been the cause of my turning Christian, may comfort you in your affliction. Allah well knows, that I could do no otherwise than I have done, and that these Christians are not indebted to me for any particular goodwill to them, since, though I had had no mind to have gone with them, but rather to have stayed at home, it was impossible; for my mind would not let me be at rest, until I performed this work, which to me seems as good, as you, my dearest father, think it bad."

'This she said, when we were got so far off, that her father could not hear her, nor we see him any more. So I comforted Zoraida, and we all minded our voyage, which was now made so easy to us by a favourable wind, that we made no doubt of being next morning upon the coast of Spain.

'But, as good seldom or never comes pure and unmixed, without being accompanied or followed by some ill to alarm and disturb it, our fortune would have it, or perhaps the curses the Moor bestowed on his daughter (for such are always to be dreaded, let the father be what he will), I say, it happened, that being now got far out to sea, and the third hour of the night wellnigh past, and under full sail, the oars being lashed, for the fair wind eased us of the labour of making use of them; by the light of the moon, which shone very bright, we discovered a round vessel, with all her sails out, a little ahead of us, but so very near to us, that we were forced to strike sail, to avoid running foul of her; and they also put the helm hard up, to give us room to go by. The men had posted themselves on the quarter-deck, to ask who we were, whither we were going, and from whence we came: but asking us in French, our renegado said:

'"Let no one answer; for these without doubt are French corsairs, to whom all is fish that comes to net."

'Upon this caution, nobody spoke a word; and, having sailed a little on, their vessel being under the wind, on a sudden they let fly two pieces of artillery, and both, as it appeared, with chain-shot; for one cut our mast through the middle, both that and the sail falling into the sea, and the other at the same instant came through the middle of our bark, so as to lay it quite open, without wounding any of us. But, finding ourselves sinking, we all began to cry aloud for help, and to beg of those in the ship to take us in, for we were drowning. They then struck their sails, and hoisted out the boat or pinnace, with about twelve Frenchmen in her, well armed with muskets, and their matches lighted, they came up close to us, and seeing how few we were, and that the vessel was sinking, they took us in, telling us, that this had befallen us because of our incivility in returning them no answer. Our renegado took the trunk, in which was Zoraida's treasure, and without being perceived by any one, threw it overboard into the sea.

'In short, we all passed into the French ship, where, after they had informed themselves of whatever they had a mind

to know concerning us, immediately, as if they had been our
capital enemies, they stripped us of everything, and Zoraida
even of the bracelets she wore upon her ankles: but the
uneasiness they gave her gave me less than the apprehension
I was in, lest they should proceed, from plundering her of
her rich and precious jewels, to the depriving her of the jewel
of most worth, and that which she valued most. But the
desires of this sort of men seldom extend further than to
money, with which their avarice is never satisfied, as was
evident at that time; for they would have taken away the very
clothes we wore as slaves, if they had thought they could
have made anything of them. Some of them were of opinion,
it would be best to throw us all overboard, wrapped up in
a sail: for their design was to trade in some of the Spanish
ports, pretending to be of Brittany; and, should they carry
us with them thither, they would be seized on and punished,
upon discovery of the robbery. But the captain, who had
rifled my dear Zoraida, said, he was contented with the prize
he had already got, and that he would not touch at any port
of Spain, but pass the Straits of Gibraltar by night, or as he
could, and make the best of his way to Rochelle, from
whence he came; and therefore in conclusion they agreed to
give us their ship-boat, and what was necessary for so short
a voyage as we had to make: which they did the next day in
view of the Spanish coast; at which sight all our troubles and
miseries were forgotten as entirely as if they had never
happened to us; so great is the pleasure of regaining one's
lost liberty.

'It was about noon, when they put us into the boat, giving
us two barrels of water, and some biscuit; and the captain,
moved by I know not what compassion, gave the beautiful
Zoraida, at her going off, about forty crowns in gold, and
would not permit his soldiers to strip her of these very
clothes she has now on.

'We went on board giving them thanks for the favour they
did us, and showing ourselves rather pleased than dissatisfied.
They stood out to sea, steering towards the Straits; and we,
without minding any other north star than the land before
us, rowed so hard, that we were, at sunset, so near it, that

we might easily, we thought, get thither before the night should be far spent: but the moon not shining, and the sky being cloudy, as we did not know the coast we were upon, we did not think it safe to land, as several among us would have had us, though it were among the rocks, and far from any town; for by that means they said, we should avoid the danger we ought to fear from the corsairs of Tetuan, who are overnight in Barbary, and the next morning on the coast of Spain, where they commonly pick up some prize, and return to sleep at their own homes. However it was agreed at last, that we should row gently towards the shore, and, if the sea proved calm, we should land wherever we could. We did so; and, a little before midnight, we arrived at the foot of a very large and high mountain, not so close to the shore but there was room enough for our landing commodiously. We ran our boat into the sand; we all got on shore, and kissed the ground, and, with tears of joy and satisfaction, gave thanks to God our Lord for the unparalleled mercy he had shown us in our voyage. We took our provisions out of the boat, which we dragged on shore, and then ascended a good way up the mountain; and, though it was really so, we could not satisfy our minds, nor thoroughly believe, that the ground we were upon was Christian ground.

'We thought the day would never come: at last we got to the top of the mountain, to see if we could discover any houses, or huts of shepherds; but as far as ever we could see, neither habitation, nor person, nor path, nor road, could we discover at all. However we determined to go farther into the country, thinking it impossible but we must soon see somebody, to inform us where we were. But what troubled me most, was to see Zoraida travel on foot through those craggy places; for, though I sometimes took her on my shoulders, my weariness fatigued her more than her own resting relieved her: and therefore she would not suffer me to take that pains any more: and so went on with very great patience and signs of joy, I still leading her by the hand.

'We had gone in this manner somewhat less than a quarter of a league, when the sound of a little bell reached our ears, a certain signal that some flocks were near us; and all of us

looking out attentively to see whether any appeared, we
discovered a young shepherd at the foot of a cork-tree, in
great tranquillity and repose, shaping a stick with his knife.
We called out to him, and he lifted up his head, got up
nimbly on his feet; and, as we came to understand afterwards,
the first, who presented themselves to his sight, being the
renegado and Zoraida, he seeing them in Moorish habits,
thought all the Moors in Barbary were upon him; and making
towards the wood before him with incredible speed, he cried
out as loud as ever he could.

'"Moors! the Moors are landed: Moors! Moors! arm, arm!"

'We, hearing this outcry, were confounded, and knew not
what to do: but, considering that the shepherd's outcries must
needs alarm the country, and that the militia of the coast
would presently come to see what was the matter, we agreed,
that the renegado should strip off his Turkish habit, and put
on a jerkin or slave's cassock, which one of us immediately
gave him, though he who lent it remained only in his shirt
and breeches. And so, recommending ourselves to God, we
went on, the same way we saw the shepherd take, expecting
every moment when the coastguard would be upon us; nor
were we deceived in our apprehension; for, in less than two
hours, as we came down the hill into the plain, we discovered
above fifty horsemen coming towards us at a half-gallop; and,
as soon as we saw them, we stood still to wait their coming
up. But as they drew near, and found, instead of the Moors
they looked for, a company of poor Christian captives, they
were surprised, and one of them asked us, whether we were
the occasion of the shepherd's alarming the country? I
answered we were: and being about to acquaint him whence
we came, and who we were, one of the Christians who came
with us, knew the horseman who had asked us the question,
and, without giving me time to say anything more, he cried:

'"God be praised, gentlemen, for bringing us to so good
a part of the country; for, if I am not mistaken, the ground
we stand upon is the territory of Velez Málaga, and, if the
length of my captivity has not impaired my memory, you, sir,
who are asking us these questions, are Pedro de Bustamante,
my uncle."

'Scarcely had the Christian captive said this, when the horseman threw himself from his horse and ran to embrace the young man, saying to him:

'"Dear nephew of my soul and of my life, I know you: and we have often bewailed your death, I, and my sister your mother, and all your kindred, who are still alive; and God has been pleased to prolong their lives, that they may have the pleasure of seeing you again. We knew you were in Algiers, and by the appearance of your dress, and that of your companions, I guess you must have recovered your liberty in some miraculous manner."

'"It is so," answered the young man, "and we shall have time enough hereafter to tell you the whole story."

'As soon as the horsemen understood that we were Christian captives, they alighted from their horses, and each of them invited us to accept of his horse to carry us to the city of Velez Málaga, which was a league and half off. Some of them went back to carry the boat to the town, being told by us where we had left it. Others of them took us up behind them, and Zoraida rode behind our captive's uncle. All the people came out to receive us, having heard the news of our coming from some who went before. They did not come to see captives freed, or Moors made slaves; for the people of that coast are accustomed to see both the one and the other: but they came to gaze at the beauty of Zoraida, which was at that time in its full perfection; for what with the fatigue of walking, and the joy of being in Christendom, without the fear of being lost, such colours showed themselves in her face, that if my affection did not then deceive me, I will venture to say, there never was in the world a more beautiful creature; at least none that I had ever seen.

'We went directly to the church, to give God thanks for the mercy we had received, and Zoraida, at first entering, said there were faces there very like that of Lela Marien. We told her they were pictures of her, and the renegado explained to her the best he could what they signified, that she might adore them, just as if every one of them were really that very Lela Marien, who had spoke to her. She, who has good sense, and a clear and ready apprehension, presently understood what was told her concerning the images. After this they carried us, and lodged us in different houses of the town; but the Christian, who came with us, took the renegado, Zoraida, and me, to the house of his parents, who were in pretty good circumstances, and treated us with as much kindness as they did their own son.

'We stayed in Velez six days, at the end of which the renegado, having informed himself of what was proper for him to do, repaired to the city of Granada, there to be readmitted, by means of the Holy Inquisition, into the bosom of our holy mother the church. The rest of the freed captives went every one which way he pleased: as for Zoraida and myself, we remained behind, with those crowns only which the courtesy of the Frenchman had bestowed on Zoraida; with part of which I bought this beast she rides on; and hitherto I have served her as a father and gentleman usher, and not as a husband.

'We are going with a design to see if my father be living, or whether either of my brothers have had better fortune than myself: though considering that heaven has given me Zoraida, no other fortune could have befallen me, which I should have valued at so high a rate. The patience with which Zoraida bears the inconveniencies poverty brings along with it, and the desire she seems to express of becoming a Christian, is such and so great, that I am in admiration, and look upon myself as bound to serve her all the days of my life. But the delight I take in seeing myself hers, and her mine, is sometimes interrupted and almost destroyed by my not knowing whether I shall find any corner in my own country wherein to shelter her, and whether time and death have not made such alterations in the affairs and lives of my father and brothers, that, if they are no more, I shall hardly find anybody that knows me.

'This, gentlemen, is my history: whether it be an entertaining and uncommon one, you are to judge. For my own part I can say, I would willingly have related it still more succinctly, though the fear of tiring you has made me omit several circumstances, which were at my tongue's end.'

CHAPTER 42

*Which treats of what further happened in the inn, and of
many other things worthy to be known.*

HERE the captive ended his story; to whom Don Fernando
said:

'Truly, captain, the manner of your relating this strange
adventure has been such, as equals the surprising novelty of
the event itself. The whole is extraordinary, uncommon, and
full of accidents, which astonish and surprise those who hear
them. And so great is the pleasure we have received in
listening to it, that though the story should have held until
to-morrow, we should have wished it were to begin again.'

And, upon saying this, Cardenio and the rest of the
company offered him all the service in their power, with such
expressions of kindness and sincerity, that the captain was
extremely well satisfied of their goodwill. Don Fernando in
particular offered him, that, if he would return with him, he
would prevail with the marquess his brother, to stand god-
father at Zoraida's baptism, and that, for his own part, he
would accommodate him in such a manner, that he might
appear in his own country with the dignity and distinction
due to his person. The captive thanked him most courteously,
but would not accept of any of his generous offers.

By this time night was come on; and, about dusk, a coach
arrived at the inn, with some men on horseback. They asked
for a lodging. The hostess answered, there was not an inch
of room in the whole inn, but what was taken up.

'Though it be so,' said one of the men on horseback, 'there
must be room made for my lord judge here in the coach.'

At this name the hostess was troubled, and said:

'Sir, the truth is, I have no bed; but if his worship my lord
judge brings one with him, as I believe he must, let him enter
in God's name; for I and my husband will quit our own
chamber to accommodate his honour.'

'Then let it be so,' quoth the squire. But by this time there
had already alighted out of the coach a man, who by his garb
presently discovered the office and dignity he bore: for the
long gown and tucked-up sleeves he had on showed him to

be a judge, as his servant had said. He led by the hand a young lady,* seemingly about sixteen years of age, in a riding dress, so genteel, so beautiful, and so gay, that her presence struck them all with admiration, insomuch that, had they not seen Dorothea, Lucinda, and Zoraida, who were in the inn, they would have believed that such another beautiful damsel could hardly have been found. Don Quixote was present at the coming in of the judge and the young lady; and so, as soon as he saw him, he said:

'Your worship may securely enter here, and walk about in this castle: for, though it be narrow and ill-accommodated, there is no narrowness nor incommodiousness in the world, which does not make room for arms and letters, especially if arms and letters bring beauty for their guide and conductor, as your worship's letters do in this fair maiden, to whom not only castles ought to throw open and offer themselves, but rocks to separate and divide, and mountains to bow their lofty heads, to give her entrance and reception. Enter, sir, I say, into this paradise; for here you will find stars and suns to accompany that heaven you bring with you. Here you will find arms in their zenith, and beauty in perfection.'

The judge marvelled greatly at this speech of Don Quixote's, whom he set himself to look at very earnestly, admiring no less at his figure than at his words: and not knowing what to answer, he began to gaze at him again, when he saw Lucinda, Dorothea, and Zoraida appear, whom the report of these new guests, and the account the hostess had given them of the beauty of the young lady, had brought to see and receive her. But Don Fernando, Cardenio, and the priest complimented him in a more intelligible and polite manner. In fine, my lord judge entered, no less confounded at what he saw, than at what he heard; and the beauties of the inn welcomed the fair stranger. In short, the judge easily perceived, that all there were persons of distinction; but the mien, visage, and behaviour of Don Quixote distracted him.

After the usual civilities passed on all sides, and inquiry made into what conveniencies the inn afforded, it was again ordered, as it had been before, that all the women should lodge in the great room aforesaid, and the men remain without as their guard. The judge was contented that his daughter, who was the young lady, should accompany those ladies; which she did with all her heart. And with part of the innkeeper's narrow bed, together with what the judge had brought with him, they accommodated themselves that night better than they expected.

The captive, who, from the very moment he saw the judge, felt his heart beat, and had a suspicion that this gentleman was his brother, asked one of the servants that came with him, what his name might be, and if he knew what country he was of? The servant answered, that he was called the Licentiate John Perez de Viedma, and that he had heard say, he was born in a town in the mountains of Leon. With this account, and with what he had seen, he was entirely confirmed in the opinion that this was that brother of his, who, by advice of his father, had applied himself to learning: and overjoyed and pleased herewith, he called aside Don Fernando, Cardenio, and the priest, and told them what had passed, assuring them that the judge was his brother. The servant had also told him, that he was going to the Indies in quality of judge of the courts of Mexico. He understood also that the young lady was his daughter, and that her mother died in childbed of her, and that the judge was become very rich by her dowry, which came to him by his having this child by her. He asked their advice, what way he should take to discover himself, or how he should first know, whether, after the discovery, his brother, seeing him so poor, would be ashamed to own him, or would receive him with bowels of affection.

'Leave it to me to make the experiment,' said the priest, 'and the rather, because there is no reason to doubt, señor captain, but that you will be very well received: for the worth and prudence, which appear in your brother's looks, give no signs of his being arrogant or wilfully forgetful, or of his not knowing how to make due allowances for the accidents of fortune.'

'Nevertheless,' said the captain, 'I would fain make myself known to him by some roundabout way, and not suddenly and at unawares.'

'I tell you,' answered the priest, 'I will manage it after such a manner, that all parties shall be satisfied.'

By this time supper was ready, and they all sat down at table, excepting the captive, and the ladies, who supped by themselves in their chamber. In the midst of supper, the priest said:

'My lord judge, I had a comrade of your name in Constantinople, where I was a slave some years; which comrade was one of the bravest soldiers and captains in all the Spanish infantry: but as unfortunate as he was resolute and brave.'

'And pray, Sir, what was this captain's name?' said the judge.

'He was called,' answered the priest, 'Ruy Perez de Viedma, and he was born in a village in the mountains of Leon. He related to me a circumstance, which happened between his father, himself, and his two brethren, which, had it come from a person of less veracity than himself, I should have taken for a tale, such as old women tell by a fireside in winter.' For he told me, his father had divided his estate equally between himself and his three sons, and had given them certain precepts better than those of Cato. And I can assure you, that the choice he made to follow the wars succeeded so well, that, in a few years, by his valour and bravery, without other help than that of his great virtue, he rose to be a captain of foot, and saw himself in the road of becoming a colonel very soon. But fortune proved adverse; for where he might have expected to have her favour, he lost it, together with his liberty, in that glorious action, whereby so many recovered theirs,—I mean in the battle of Lepanto. Mine I lost in the Goleta; and afterwards, by different adventures, we became comrades in Constantinople. From thence he came to Algiers, where, to my knowledge, one of the strangest adventures in the world befell him.'

The priest then went on, and recounted to him very briefly what had passed between his brother and Zoraida. To all which the judge was so attentive, that never any judge was more so. The priest went no further than that point, where the French stripped the Christians that came in the bark, and the poverty and necessity wherein his comrade and the beautiful Moor were left: pretending that he knew not what became of them afterwards, whether they arrived in Spain, or were carried by the Frenchmen to France.

The captain stood at some distance, listening to all the priest said, and observed all the emotions of his brother; who, perceiving the priest had ended his story, fetching a deep sigh, and his eyes standing with water, said:

'O sir, you know not how nearly I am affected by the news you tell me; so nearly that I am constrained to show it by these tears, which flow from my eyes, in spite of all my discretion and reserve! That gallant captain you mention is my elder brother, who being of a stronger constitution, and of more elevated thoughts, than I, or my younger brother, chose the honourable and worthy profession of arms; which was one of the three ways proposed to us by our father, as your comrade told you, when you thought he was telling you a fable. I applied myself to learning, which, by God's blessing on my industry, has raised me to the station you see me in. My younger brother is in Peru, so rich, that, with what he has sent to my father and me, he has made large amends for what he took away with him, and besides has enabled my father to indulge his natural disposition to liberality. I also have been enabled to prosecute my studies with more decorum and authority, until I arrived at the rank to which I am now advanced. My father is still alive, but dying with desire to hear of his eldest son, and begging of God with incessant prayers, that death may not close his eyes, until he has once again beheld his son alive. And I wonder extremely, considering his discretion, how, in so many troubles and afflictions, or in his prosperous successes, he could neglect giving his father some account of himself; for had he, or any of us, known his case, he needed not to have waited for the miracle of the cane to have obtained his ransom. But what at present gives me the most concern, is to think whether those Frenchmen have set him at liberty, or killed him, to conceal their robbery. This thought will make me continue my voyage, not with that satisfaction I began it, but rather with melancholy

and sadness. O my dear brother! did I but know where you
now are, I would go and find you, to deliver you from your
troubles, though at the expense of my own repose. Oh! who
shall carry the news to our aged father that you are alive?
Though you were in the deepest dungeon of Barbary, his
wealth, my brother's, and mine, would fetch you thence. O
beautiful and bountiful Zoraida; who can repay the kindness
you have done my brother? Who shall be so happy as to be
present at your regeneration by baptism, and at your nuptials,
which would give us all so much delight?'

These and the like expressions the judge uttered, so full
of compassion at the news he had received of his brother,
that all who heard him bore him company in demonstrations
of a tender concern for his sorrow.

The priest then, finding he had gained his point according
to the captain's wish, would not hold them any longer in
suspense; and so, rising from table, and going in where
Zoraida was, he took her by the hand, and behind her came
Lucinda, Dorothea, and the judge's daughter. The captain
stood expecting what the priest would do; who, taking him
also by the other hand, with both of them together went into
the room where the judge and the rest of the company were,
and said:

'My lord judge, cease your tears, and let your wish be
crowned with all the happiness you can desire, since you have
before your eyes your good brother, and your good sister-in-
law. He whom you behold is Captain Viedma, and this the
beautiful Moor, who did him so much good. The Frenchmen
I told you of reduced them to the poverty you see, to give
you an opportunity of showing the liberality of your generous
breast.'

The captain ran to embrace his brother, who set both his
hands against the captain's breast, to look at him a little more
asunder: but, when he thoroughly knew him, he embraced
him so closely, shedding such melting tears of joy, that most
of those present bore him company in weeping. The words
both the brothers uttered to each other, and the concern they
showed, can, I believe, hardly be conceived, much less written. Now they gave each other a brief account of their

adventures: now they demonstrated the height of brotherly affection; now the judge embraced Zoraida, offering her all he had: now he made his daughter embrace her; now the beautiful Christian and most beautiful Moor renewed the tears of all the company. Now Don Quixote stood attentive, without speaking a word, pondering upon these strange events, and ascribing them all to chimeras of knight-errantry. Now it was agreed that the captain and Zoraida should return with their brother to Seville, and acquaint their father with his being found and at liberty, that the old man might contrive to be present at the baptism and nuptials of Zoraida, it being impossible for the judge to discontinue his journey, having received news of the flota's departure from Seville for New Spain in a month's time, and as it would be a great inconvenience to him to lose his passage.

In fine, they were all satisfied, and rejoiced at the captive's success; and two parts of the night being wellnigh spent, they agreed to retire, and repose themselves during the remainder. Don Quixote offered his service to guard the castle, lest some giant, or other miscreant-errant, for lucre of the treasure of beauty enclosed there, should make some attempt and attack them. They who knew him, returned him thanks, and gave the judge an account of his strange frenzy, with which he was not a little diverted. Sancho Panza alone was out of all patience at the company's sitting up so late: and after all he was better accommodated than any of them, throwing himself upon the accoutrements of his ass, which will cost him so dear, as you shall be told by and by.*

The ladies being now retired to their chamber, and the rest accommodated as well as they could, Don Quixote sallied out of the inn to stand sentinel at the castle gate, as he had promised.

It fell out, then, that a little before day, there reached the ladies' ears a voice so tuneable and sweet, that it forced them all to listen attentively; especially Dorothea, who lay awake, by whose side slept Doña Clara de Viedma, for so the judge's daughter was called. Nobody could imagine who the person was that sung so well, and it was a single voice without any instrument to accompany it. Sometimes they fancied the singing was in the yard, and at other times that it was in the stable. While they were thus in suspense, Cardenio came to the chamber-door, and said:

'You that are not asleep, pray listen, and you will hear the voice of one of the lads that take care of the mules, who sings enchantingly.'

'We hear him already, sir,' answered Dorothea.

Cardenio then went away, and Dorothea, listening with the utmost attention, heard that this was what he sung:

CHAPTER 43

*Which treats of the agreeable history of the young muleteer; with other strange accidents that happened in the inn.**

SONG

'A Mariner I am of love,
  And in his seas profound,
Toss'd betwixt doubts and fears, I rove,
  And see no port around.

'At distance I behold a star,
  Whose beams my senses draw,
Brighter and more resplendent far
  Than Palinure e'er saw.

'Yet still, uncertain of my way,
  I stem a dangerous tide,
No compass but that doubtful ray
  My wearied bark to guide.

'For when its light I most would see,
  Benighted most I sail:
Like clouds, reserve and modesty
  Its shrouded lustre veil.

'O lovely star, by whose bright ray
  My love and faith I try,
If thou withdraw'st thy cheering day,
  In night of death I lie.'

When the singer came to this point, Dorothea thought it would be wrong to let Doña Clara lose the opportunity of hearing so good a voice; and so, jogging her gently to and fro, she awaked her, saying:

'Pardon me, child, that I wake you; for I do it, that you may have the pleasure of hearing the best voice, perhaps, you have ever heard in all your life.'

Clara awoke, quite sleepy, and at first did not understand what Dorothea had said to her; and having asked her, she repeated it; whereupon Clara was attentive. But scarce had she heard two verses, which the singer was going on with, when she fell into so strange a trembling, as if some violent fit of a quartan ague had seized her; and clasping Dorothea close in her arms, she said to her:

'Ah! dear lady of my soul and life, why did you awake me? for the greatest good that fortune could do me at this time, would be to keep my eyes and ears closed, that I might neither see nor hear this unhappy musician.'

'What is it you say, child? pray take notice, we are told he that sings is but a muleteer.'

'Oh, no, he is no such thing,' replied Clara; 'he is a young gentleman of large possessions, and so much master of my heart, that, if he has no mind to part with it, it shall be his eternally.'

Dorothea was in admiration at the passionate expressions of the girl, thinking them far beyond what her tender years might promise. And therefore she said to her:

'You speak in such a manner, Doña Clara, that I cannot understand you: explain yourself further, and tell me, what it is you say of heart, and possessions, and of this musician, whose voice disturbs you so much. But say nothing now; for I will not lose the pleasure of hearing him sing to mind your trembling; for methinks he is beginning to sing again a new song and a new tune.'

'With all my heart,' answered Clara, and stopped both her ears with her hands, that she might not hear him; at which Dorothea could not but admire very much; and being attentive to what was sung, she found it was to this purpose:

SONG

'Sweet hope, thee difficulties fly,
　To thee disheart'ning fears give way
Not e'en thy death impending nigh,
　Thy dauntless courage can dismay.

'No conquests bless, no laurels crown
　The lazy general's feeble arm,
Who sinks reposed in bed of down,
　Whilst ease and sloth his senses charm.

'Love sells his precious glories dear,
　And vast the purchase of his joys;
Nor ought he set such treasures rare
　At the low price of vulgar toys.

'Since perseverance gains the prize,
　And cowards still successless prove,
Borne on the wings of hope I'll rise,
　Nor fear to reach the heaven of love.'*

Here the voice ceased, and Doña Clara began to sigh
afresh: all which fired Dorothea's curiosity to know the cause
of so sweet a song, and so sad a plaint; and therefore she
again asked her, what it was she would have said a while
ago. Then Clara, lest Lucinda should hear her, embracing
Dorothea, put her mouth so close to Dorothea's ear that she
might speak securely without being overheard, and said to
her:

'The singer, dear madam, is son of a gentleman of the
kingdom of Aragon, lord of two towns, who lived opposite
to my father's house at court. And though my father kept
his windows with canvas in the winter, and lattices in summer, I know not how it happened, that this young gentleman,
who then went to school, saw me; nor can I tell whether it
was at church or elsewhere: but, in short, he fell in love with
me, and gave me to understand his passion from the windows
of his house, by so many signs, and so many tears, that I
was forced to believe, and even to love him, without knowing
what I desired. Among other signs, which he used to make,
one was, to join one hand with the other, signifying his desire
to marry me; and though I should have been very glad it

might have been so, yet, being alone and without a mother, I knew not whom to communicate the affair to; and therefore I let it rest, without granting him any other favour, than, when his father and mine were both abroad, to lift up the canvas, or lattice window, and gave him a full view of me: at which he would be so transported that one would think he would run stark mad.

'Now the time of my father's departure drew near, which he heard, but not from me; for I never had an opportunity to tell it him. He fell sick, as far as I could learn, of grief; so that, on the day we came away I could not see him to bid him farewell, though it were but with my eyes.

'But, after we had travelled two days, at going into an inn in a village a day's journey from hence, I saw him at the door in the habit of a muleteer, so naturally dressed, that, had I not carried his image so deeply imprinted in my soul, it had been impossible for me to know him. I knew him, and was both surprised and overjoyed. He stole looks at me, unobserved by my father, whom he carefully avoids when he crosses the way before me, either on the road or at our inn. And knowing what he is, and considering that he comes on foot, and takes such pains for love of me, I die with concern, and continually set my eyes where he sets his feet. I cannot imagine what he proposes to himself, nor how he could escape from his father, who loves him passionately, having no other heir, and he being so very very deserving, as you will perceive when you see him. I can assure you besides, that all he sings is of his own invention; for I have heard say, he is a very great scholar and a poet. And now, every time I see him, or hear him sing, I tremble all over and am in a fright, lest my father should come to know him, and so discover our inclinations. In my life I never spoke a word to him, and yet I love him so violently, that I shall never be able to live without him. This, dear madam, is all I can tell you of this musician, whose voice has pleased you so much: by that alone you may easily perceive he is no muleteer, but master of hearts and towns, as I have already told you.'

'Say no more, my dear Clara,' said Dorothea, kissing her a thousand times; 'pray say no more, and stay until to-morrow; for I hope in God so to manage your affair, that the conclusion shall be as happy as so innocent a beginning deserves.'

'Ah! madam,' said Doña Clara, 'what conclusion can be hoped for, since his father is of such quality, and so wealthy, that he will not think me worthy to be so much as his son's servant, and how much less his wife? and as to marrying without my father's consent or knowledge, I would not do it for all the world. I would only have this young man go back, and leave me: perhaps by not seeing him, and by the great distance of place and time, the pains I now endure may be abated; though I dare say this remedy is like to do me little good. I know not what sorcery this is, nor which way this love possessed me, he and I being both so young, for I verily believe we are of the same age, and I am not yet full sixteen, nor shall be, as my father says, until next Michaelmas.'

Dorothea could not forbear smiling to hear how childishly Doña Clara talked, to whom she said:

'Let us try, madam, to rest the short remainder of the night; to-morrow is a new day, and we shall speed, or my hand will be mightily out.'

Then they set themselves to rest, and there was a profound silence all over the inn: only the innkeeper's daughter, and her maid Maritornes, did not sleep; who, very well knowing Don Quixote's peccant humour, and that he was standing without doors, armed, and on horseback, keeping guard, agreed to put some trick upon him, or at least to have a little pastime, by overhearing some of his extravagant speeches.

Now you must know, that the inn had no window towards the field, only a kind of spike-hole to the straw-loft, by which they took in or threw out their straw. At this hole, then, this pair of demi-lasses planted themselves, and perceived that Don Quixote was on horseback, leaning forward on his lance, and uttering every now and then such mournful and profound sighs, that one would think each of them sufficient to tear away his very soul. They heard him also say, in a soft, soothing, and amorous tone:

'O my dear lady Dulcinea del Toboso, perfection of all

beauty, sum total of discretion, treasury of wit and good humour, and pledge of modesty; lastly, the idea and exemplar of all that is profitable, decent, or delightful in the world! and what may your ladyship be now doing? art thou, peradventure, thinking of thy captive knight, who voluntarily exposes himself to so many perils merely for thy sake? O thou triformed luminary,* bring me tidings of her: perhaps thou art now gazing at her, envious of her beauty as she is walking through some gallery of her sumptuous palace, or leaning over some balcony, considering how, without offence to her modesty and grandeur, she may assuage the torment this poor afflicted heart of mine endures for her sake; or perhaps considering what glory to bestow on my sufferings, what rest on my cares, and lastly, what life on my death, and what reward on my services. And thou, sun, who by this time must be hastening to harness thy steeds, to come abroad early and visit thy mistress, I entreat thee, as soon as thou seest her, salute her in my name: but beware, when thou seest and salutest her, that thou dost not kiss her face; for I shall be more jealous of thee than thou wast of that swift ingrate,* who made thee sweat, and run so fast over the plains of Thessaly, or along the banks of Peneus (for I do not well remember over which of them thou rannest at that time), so jealous and so enamoured.'

Thus far Don Quixote had proceeded in his piteous soliloquy, when the innkeeper's daughter began to call softly to him, and to say:

'Sir, pray come a little this way, if you please.'

At which signal and voice Don Quixote turned about his head, and perceived by the light of the moon, which then shone very bright, that somebody called him from the spike-hole, which to him seemed a window with gilded bars, fit for rich castles, such as he fancied the inn to be: and instantly it came again into his mad imagination, as it had done before, that the fair damsel, daughter of the lord of the castle, being irresistibly in love with him, was come to solicit him again: and with this thought, that he might not appear discourteous and ungrateful, he turned Rosinante about, and came up to the hole; and, as soon as he saw the two wenches, he said:

'I pity you, fair lady, for having placed your amorous inclinations where it is impossible for you to meet with a suitable return, such as your great worth and beauty deserve; yet ought you not to blame this unfortunate enamoured knight, whom love has made incapable of engaging his affections to any other than to her, whom, the moment he laid his eyes on her, he made absolute mistress of his soul. Pardon me, good lady, and retire to your chamber; and do not, by a further discovery of your desires, force me to seem still more ungrateful: and if, through the passion you have for me, you can find anything else in me to satisfy you, provided it be not downright love, pray command it; for I swear to you, by that absent sweet enemy of mine, to bestow it upon you immediately, though you should ask me for a lock of Medusa's hair, which was all snakes, or even the sunbeams enclosed in a vial.'

'Sir,' quoth Maritornes, 'my lady wants nothing of all this.'

'What is it then your lady wants, discreet duenna?' answered Don Quixote.

'Only one of your beautiful hands,' quoth Maritornes, 'whereby partly to satisfy that longing, which brought her to this window, so much to the peril of her honour, that, if her lord and father should come to know it, the least slice he would whip off would be one of her ears.'

'I would fain see that,' answered Don Quixote: 'he had best have a care what he does, unless he has a mind to come to the most disastrous end that ever father did in the world, for having laid violent hands on the delicate members of his beloved daughter.'

Maritornes made no doubt but Don Quixote would give his hand as they had desired; and so, resolving with herself what she would do, she went down into the stable, from whence she took the halter of Sancho Panza's ass, and returned very speedily to her spike-hole just as Don Quixote had got upon Rosinante's saddle to reach the gilded window, where he imagined the enamoured damsel stood: and, at giving her his hand, he said:

'Take, madam, this hand, or rather this chastiser of the evil-doers of the world: take, I say, this hand, which no woman's hand ever touched before, not even hers, who has the entire right of my whole body. I do not give it you to kiss, but only that you may behold the contexture of its nerves, the firm knitting of its muscles, the largeness and spaciousness of its veins, whence you may gather what must be the strength of that arm which has such a hand.'

'We shall soon see that,' quoth Maritornes; and making a running knot on the halter, she clapped it on his wrist, and, descending from the hole, she tied the other end of it very fast to the staple of the door of the hay-loft. Don Quixote, feeling the harshness of the rope about his wrist, said:

'You seem rather to rasp than grasp my hand: pray, do not treat it so roughly, since that is not to blame for the injury my inclination does you; nor is it right to discharge the whole of your displeasure on so small a part: consider, that lovers do not take revenge at this cruel rate.'

But nobody heard a word of all this discourse; for, as soon as Maritornes had tied Don Quixote up, they both went away, ready to die with laughing, and left him fastened in such a manner that it was impossible for him to get loose.

He stood, as has been said, upright on Rosinante, his arm within the hole, and tied by the wrist to the bolt of the door, in the utmost fear and dread, that, if Rosinante stirred ever so little one way or other, he must remain hanging by the arm: and therefore he durst not make the least motion; though he might well expect from the sobriety and patience of Rosinante that he would stand stock-still an entire century.

In short, Don Quixote, finding himself tied, and that the ladies were gone, began presently to imagine, that all this was done in the way of enchantment, as the time before, when, in that very same castle, the enchanted Moor of a carrier so mauled him. Then, within himself he cursed his own inconsiderateness and indiscretion, since, having come off so ill before, he had ventured to enter in a second time; it being a rule with knights-errant, that, when they have once tried an adventure, and cannot accomplish it, it is a sign of its not being reserved for them, but for somebody else, and therefore there is no necessity for them to try it a second time. However, he pulled his arm, to see if he could loose himself;

but he was so fast tied that all his efforts were in vain. It is true, indeed, he pulled gently, lest Rosinante should stir; and though he would fain have got into the saddle, and have sat down, he could not, but must stand up, or pull off his hand.

Now he wished for Amadis's sword, against which no enchantment had any power; and now he cursed his fortune. Then he exaggerated the loss the world would have of his presence, all the while he should stand there enchanted, as, without doubt, he believed he was. Then he bethought himself afresh of his beloved Dulcinea del Toboso. Then he called upon his good squire Sancho Panza, who, buried in sleep, and stretched upon his ass's pannel, did not, at that instant, so much as dream of the mother that bore him. Then he invoked the sages Lirgandeo and Alquife* to help him: then he called upon his special friend Urganda to assist him: lastly, there the morning overtook him, so despairing and confounded, that he bellowed like a bull; for he did not expect that the day would bring him any relief; for, accounting himself enchanted, he concluded it would be eternal: and he was the more induced to believe it, seeing Rosinante budged not at all; and he verily thought that himself and his horse must remain in that posture, without eating, drinking, or sleeping, until that evil influence of the stars was overpast, or until some more sage enchanter should disenchant him.

But he was much mistaken in his belief; for scarcely did the day begin to dawn when four men on horseback arrived at the inn, very well appointed and accoutred, with carbines hanging at the pommels of their saddles. They called at the inn door, which was not yet opened, knocking very hard; which Don Quixote perceiving from the place where he stood sentinel, he cried out, with an arrogant and loud voice:

'Knights, or squires, or whoever you are, you have no business to knock at the gate of this castle; for it is very plain, that, at such hours, they who are within are either asleep, or do not use to open the gates of their fortress, until the sun has spread his beams over the whole horizon: get farther off, and stay until clear daylight, and then we shall see whether it is fit to open to you or no.'

'What the devil of a fortress or castle is this,' quoth one

of them, 'to oblige us to observe all this ceremony? if you are the innkeeper, make somebody open the door: for we are travellers, and only want to bait our horses, and go on, for we are in haste.'

'Do you think, gentlemen, that I look like an innkeeper?' answered Don Quixote.

'I know not what you look like,' answered the other; 'but I am sure you talk preposterously to call this inn a castle.'

'It is a castle,' replied Don Quixote, 'and one of the best in this whole province; and it has in it persons, who have had sceptres in their hands, and crowns on their heads.'

'You had better have said the very reverse,' quoth the traveller; 'the sceptre on the head and the crown in the hand; but, perhaps, some company of strolling players is within, who frequently wear those crowns and sceptres you talk of; otherwise I do not believe, that in so small and paltry an inn, and where all is so silent, there can be lodged persons worthy to wear crowns and wield sceptres.'

'You know little of the world,' replied Don Quixote, 'if you are ignorant of the accidents which usually happen in knight-errantry.'

The querist's* comrades were tired with the dialogue between him and Don Quixote, and so they knocked again with greater violence, and in such a manner, that the innkeeper awaked, and all the rest of the people that were in the inn; and the host got up to ask who knocked.

Now it fell out, that one of the four strangers' horses came to smell at Rosinante, who, melancholy and sad, his ears hanging down, bore up his distended master without stirring; but being, in short, of flesh, though he seemed to be of wood, he could not but be sensible of it, and smell him again that came so kindly to caress him: and scarcely had he stirred a step, when Don Quixote's feet slipped, and, tumbling from the saddle, he had fallen to the ground, had he not hung by the arm: which put him to so much torture, that he fancied his wrist was cutting off, or his arm tearing from his body; yet he hung so near the ground, that he could just reach it with the tips of his toes, which turned to his prejudice; for, feeling how little he wanted to set his feet to the ground, he

strove and stretched as much as he could to reach it quite:
like those, who are tortured by the strappado, who, being
placed at touch or not touch, are themselves the cause of
increasing their own pain, by their eagerness to extend themselves, deceived by the hope, that, if they stretch never so
little farther, they shall reach the ground.

CHAPTER 44

A continuation of the unheard-of adventures of the inn.

IN short, Don Quixote roared out so terribly, that the host
in a fright opened the inn door hastily, to see who it was
that made those outcries; nor were the strangers less surprised. Maritornes, who was also waked by the same noise,
imagining what it was, went to the straw-loft, and, without
anybody's seeing her, untied the halter, which held up Don
Quixote, who straight fell to the ground in sight of the
innkeeper and the travellers: who, coming up to him, asked
him what ailed him, that he so cried out? He without
answering a word, slipped the rope from off his wrist, and
raising himself upon his feet, mounted Rosinante, braced his
target, couched his lance, and taking a good compass about
the field, came up at a half-gallop, saying:

'Whoever shall dare to affirm, that I was fairly enchanted,
provided my sovereign lady the princess Micomicona gives
me leave, I say, he lies, and I challenge him to single combat.'

The new-comers were amazed at Don Quixote's words;
but the innkeeper removed their wonder by telling them who
Don Quixote was; and that they should not mind him, for
he was beside himself.

They then inquired of the host whether there was not in
the house a youth of about fifteen years old, habited like a
muleteer, with such and such marks, describing the same
clothes that Doña Clara's lover had on. The host answered,
there were so many people in the inn, that he had not taken
particular notice of any such. But one of them, espying the
coach the judge came in, said:

'Without doubt he must be here; for this is the coach it is said he follows: let one of us stay at the door, and the rest go in to look for him; and it would not be amiss for one of us to ride round about the inn, that he may not escape over the pales of the yard.'

'It shall be so done,' answered one of them; and accordingly two went in, leaving the third at the door, while the fourth walked the rounds; all which the innkeeper saw, and could not judge certainly why they made this search, though he believed they sought the young lad they had been describing to him.

By this time it was clear day, which together with the noise Don Quixote had made, had raised the whole house, especially Doña Clara and Dorothea, who had slept but indifferently, the one through concern at being so near her lover, and the other through the desire of seeing him. Don Quixote, perceiving that none of the four travellers minded him, nor answered to his challenge, was dying and running mad with rage and despite; and could he have found a precedent in the statutes and ordinances of chivalry, that a knight-errant might lawfully undertake or begin any other adventure, after having given his word and faith not to engage in any new enterprise, until he had finished what he had promised, he would have attacked them all, and made them answer whether they would or no. But thinking it not convenient, nor decent, to set about a new adventure, until he had reinstated Micomicona in her kingdom, he thought it best to say nothing and be quiet, until he saw what would be the issue of the inquiry and search those travellers were making: one of whom found the youth he was in quest of sleeping by the side of a muleteer, little dreaming of anybody's searching for him, or finding him. The man, pulling him by the arm, said:

'Upon my word, Señor Don Louis, the dress you are in is very becoming such a gentleman as you; and the bed you lie on is very suitable to the tenderness with which your mother brought you up.'

The youth rubbed his drowsy eyes, and looking wistfully at him who held him, presently knew him to be one of his father's servants: which so surprised him, that he knew not how, or could not speak a word for a good while; and the servant went on, saying:

'There is no more to be done, Señor Don Louis, but for you to have patience, and return home, unless you have a mind my master, your father, should depart to the other world: for nothing less can be expected from the pain he is in at your absence.'

'Why, how did my father know,' said Don Louis, 'that I was come this road, and in this dress?'

'A student,' answered the servant, 'to whom you gave an account of your design, discovered it, being moved to pity by the lamentations your father made, the instant he missed you: and so he dispatched four of his servants in quest of you; and we are all here at your service, overjoyed beyond imagination at the good dispatch we have made, and that we shall return with you so soon, and restore you to those eyes that love you so dearly.'

'That will be as I shall please, or as heaven shall ordain,' answered Don Louis.

'What should you please, or heaven ordain, otherwise than that you should return home?' quoth the servant; 'for there is no possibility of avoiding it.'

The muleteer, who lay with Don Louis, hearing this contest between them, got up, and went to acquaint Don Fernando and Cardenio, and the rest of the company, who were all by this time up and dressed, with what had passed: he related to them how the man had styled the young lad Don, and repeated the discourse which passed between them, and how the man would have him return to his father's house, and how the youth refused to go. Hearing this, and considering besides how fine a voice heaven had bestowed upon him, they had all a great longing to know who he was, and to assist him if any violence should be offered him: and so they went towards the place where he was talking and contending with his servant.

Now Dorothea came out of her chamber, and, behind her, Doña Clara in great disorder; and Dorothea, calling Cardenio aside, related to him, in few words, the history of the musician and Doña Clara; and he on his part told her what

had passed in relation to the servants coming in search after
him: and he did not speak so low but Doña Clara overheard
him: at which she was in such an agony, that, had not
Dorothea caught hold of her, she had sunk down to the
ground. Cardenio desired Dorothea to go back with Doña
Clara to their chamber, while he would endeavour to set
matters to rights.

Now all the four, who came in quest of Don Louis, were
in the inn, and had surrounded him, pressing him to return
immediately to comfort his father, without delaying a moment. He answered, that he could in no wise do so, until he
had accomplished a business wherein his life, his honour, and
his soul, were concerned. The servants urged him, saying they
would by no means go back without him, and that they were
resolved to carry him whether he would or no.

'That you shall not do,' replied Don Louis, 'except you kill
me; and, whichever way you carry me, it will be without life.'

Most of the people that were in the inn were got together,
to hear the contention, particularly Cardenio, Don Fernando
and his companions, the judge, the priest, the barber, and
Don Quixote, who now thought there was no further need
of continuing upon the castle-guard. Cardenio, already knowing the young man's story, asked the men, who were for
carrying him away, why they would take away the youth
against his will.

'Because,' replied one of the four, 'we would save the life
of his father, who is in danger of losing it by this gentleman's
absence.'

Then Don Louis said:

'There is no need of giving an account of my affairs here;
I am free, and will go back, if I please; and if not, none of
you shall force me.'

'But reason will force you,' answered the servant; 'and
though it should not prevail upon you, it must upon us, to
do what we came about, and what we are obliged to.'

'Hold,' said the judge, 'let us know what this business is
to the bottom.'

The man, who knew him as being his master's near
neighbour, answered:

'Pray, my lord judge, does not your honour know this gentleman? he is your neighbour's son, and has absented himself from his father's house in an indecent garb, as your honour may see.'

Then the judge observed him more attentively, and, knowing and embracing him, said:

'What childish frolic is this, Señor Don Louis? or what powerful cause has moved you to come in this manner, and this dress, so little becoming your quality?'

The tears came into the young gentleman's eyes, and he could not answer a word. The judge bid the servants be quiet, for all would be well; and taking Don Louis by the hand, he went aside with him, and asked him, why he came in that manner.

While the judge was asking this and some other questions, they heard a great outcry at the door of the inn, and the occasion was, that two guests, who had lodged there that night, seeing all the folks busy about knowing what the four men searched for, had attempted to go off without paying their reckoning. But the host, who minded his own business more than other people's, laid hold of them as they were going out of the door, and demanded his money, giving them such hard words for their evil intention, that he provoked them to return him an answer with their fists; which they did so roundly, that the poor innkeeper was forced to call out for help. The hostess and her daughter, seeing nobody so disengaged, and so proper to succour him, as Don Quixote, the daughter said to him:

'Sir knight, I beseech you, by the valour God has given you, come and help my poor father, whom a couple of wicked fellows are beating to a mummy.'

To whom Don Quixote answered, very leisurely, and with much phlegm:

'Fair maiden, your petition cannot be granted at present, because I am incapacitated from intermeddling in any other adventure, until I have accomplished one I have already engaged my word for: but what I can do for your service is, what I will now tell you: run, and bid your father maintain the fight the best he can, and in no wise suffer himself to be vanquished, while I go and ask permission of the princess Micomicona to relieve him in his distress; which if she grants me, rest assured I will bring him out of it.'

'As I am a sinner,' quoth Maritornes, who was then by, 'before your worship can obtain the license you talk of, my master may be gone into the other world.'

'Permit me, madam, to obtain the license I speak of,' answered Don Quixote: 'for if so be I have it, no matter though he be in the other world; for from thence would I fetch him back, in spite of the other world itself, should it dare to contradict or oppose me; or at least I will take such ample revenge on those, who shall have sent him thither, that you shall be more than moderately satisfied.'

And, without saying a word more, he went and kneeled down before Dorothea, beseeching her, in knightly and errant-like expressions, that her grandeur would vouchsafe to give him leave to go and succour the governor of that castle, who was in grievous distress. The princess gave it him very graciously; and he presently, bracing on his target, and drawing his sword, ran to the inn door, where the two guests were still lugging and worrying the poor host; but when he came he stopped short and stood irresolute, though Maritornes and the hostess asked him why he delayed succouring their master and husband.

'I delay,' quoth Don Quixote, 'because it is not lawful for me to draw my sword against squire-like folks: but call hither my squire Sancho; for to him this defence and revenge does most properly belong.'

This passed at the door of the inn, where the boxing and cuffing went about briskly, to the innkeeper's cost, and the rage of Maritornes, the hostess, and her daughter, who were ready to run distracted to behold the cowardice of Don Quixote, and the injury then doing to their master, husband, and father.

But let us leave him there awhile; for he will not want somebody or other to relieve him; or, if not, let him suffer and be silent, who is so foolhardy as to engage in what is above his strength; and let us turn fifty paces back, to see what Don Louis replied to the judge, whom we left apart asking the cause of his coming on foot, and so meanly apparelled. To whom the youth, squeezing him hard by both hands, as if some great affliction was wringing his heart, and pouring down tears in great abundance, said:

'All I can say, dear sir, is that, from the moment heaven was pleased by means of our neighbourhood to give me a sight of Doña Clara, your daughter, from that very instant I made her sovereign mistress of my affections: and if you, my true lord and father, do not oppose it, this very day she shall be my wife. For her I left my father's house, and for her I put myself into this dress, to follow her whithersoever she went, as the arrow to the mark, or the mariner to the north star. As yet she knows no more of my passion, than what she may have perceived from now and then seeing at a distance my eyes full of tears. You know, my lord, the wealthiness and nobility of my family, and that I am sole heir: if you think these motives sufficient for you to venture the making me entirely happy, receive me immediately for your son: for, though my father, biassed by other views of his own, should not approve of this happiness I have found for myself, time may work some favourable change, and alter his mind.'

Here the enamoured youth was silent, and the judge remained in suspense, no less surprised at the manner and ingenuity of Don Louis in discovering his passion, than confounded and at a loss what measures to take in so sudden and unexpected an affair; and therefore he returned no other answer, but only bade him be easy for the present, and not let his servants go back that day, that there might be time to consider what was most expedient to be done. Don Louis kissed his hands by force, and even bathed them with tears, enough to soften a heart of marble, and much more that of the judge, who, being a man of sense, soon saw how advantageous and honourable this match would be for his daughter; though, if possible, he would have effected it with the consent of Don Louis's father, who, he knew, had pretensions to a title for his son.

By this time the innkeeper and his guests had made peace, more through the persuasion and arguments of Don Quixote than his threats, and had paid him all he demanded; and the servants of Don Louis were waiting until the judge should have ended his discourse, and their master determined what he would do; when the devil, who sleeps not, so ordered it, that, at that very instant, came into the inn the barber, from whom Don Quixote had taken Mambrino's helmet, and Sancho Panza the ass-furniture, which he trucked for his own: which barber, leading his beast to the stable, espied Sancho Panza, who was mending something about the pannel; and, as soon as he saw him, he knew him, and made bold to attack him, saying:

'Ah! mister thief, have I got you? give me my basin and my pannel, with all the furniture you robbed me of.'

Sancho, finding himself attacked so unexpectedly, and hearing the opprobrious language given him, with one hand held fast the pannel, and with the other gave the barber such a dowse, that he bathed his mouth in blood. But for all that the barber did not let go his hold: on the contrary, he raised his voice in such a manner, that all the folks of the inn ran together at the noise and scuffle; and he cried out:

'Help, in the king's name, and in the name of justice; for this rogue and highway-robber would murder me for endeavouring to recover my own goods.'

'You lie,' answered Sancho, 'I am no highway-robber: my master Don Quixote won these spoils in fair war.'

Don Quixote was now present and not a little pleased to see how well his squire performed both on the defensive and offensive, and from thenceforward took him for a man of mettle, and resolved in his mind to dub him a knight the first opportunity that offered, thinking the order of chivalry would be very well bestowed upon him.

Now, among other things, which the barber said during the skirmish,

'Gentlemen,' quoth he, 'this pannel is as certainly mine as the death I owe to God, and I know it as well as if it were a child of my own body, and yonder stands my ass in the stable, who will not suffer me to lie: pray do but try it, and if it does not fit him to a hair, let me be infamous: and moreover, by the same token, the very day they took this from me, they robbed me likewise of a new brass basin, never hanselled,* that was worth a crown.'

Here Don Quixote could not forbear answering; and thrusting himself between the two combatants, and parting them, and making them lay down the pannel on the ground in public view, until the truth should be decided, he said:

'Sirs, you shall presently see clearly and manifestly the error this honest squire is in, in calling that a basin, which was, is, and ever shall be, Mambrino's helmet: I won it in fair war, so am its right and lawful possessor. As to the pannel, I intermeddle not: what I can say of that matter is, that my squire Sancho asked my leave to take the trappings of this conquered coward's horse, to adorn his own withal: I gave him leave; he took them, and, if from horse-trappings they are metamorphosed into an ass's pannel, I can give no other reason for it, but that common one, that these kind of transformations are frequent in adventures of chivalry: for confirmation of which, run, son Sancho, and fetch hither the helmet, which this honest man will needs have to be a basin.'

'In faith, sir,' quoth Sancho, 'if we have no other proof of our cause but what your worship mentions, Mambrino's helmet will prove as errant a basin, as this honest man's trappings are a pack-saddle.'

'Do what I bid you,' replied Don Quixote: 'for sure all things in this castle: cannot be governed by enchantment.'

Sancho went for the basin and brought it; and as soon as Don Quixote saw it, he took it in his hands and said:

'Behold, gentlemen, with what face can this squire pretend this to be a basin, and not the helmet I have mentioned? I swear by the order of knighthood, which I profess, this helmet is the very same I took from him, without addition or diminution.'

'There is no doubt of that,' quoth Sancho; 'for, from the time my master won it until now, he has fought but one battle in it, which was when he freed those unlucky galley-slaves; and had it not been for this basin-helmet, he had not then got off very well; for he had a shower of stones hurled at him in that skirmish.'

CHAPTER 45

In which the dispute concerning Mambrino's helmet and
the pannel is decided; with other adventures that really and
truly happened.

'PRAY, gentlemen,' quoth the barber, 'what is your opinion
of what these gentlefolks affirm; for they persist in it, that
this is no basin but a helmet?'

'And whoever shall affirm the contrary,' said Don Quixote,
'I will make him know, if he be a knight, that he lies, and,
if a squire, that he lies and lies again, a thousand times.'

Our barber, who was present all the while, and well
acquainted with Don Quixote's humour, had a mind to work
up his madness, and carry on the jest, to make the company
laugh; and so, addressing himself to the other barber, he said:

'Señor barber, or whoever you are, know, that I also am
of your profession, and have had my certificate of examination above these twenty years, and am very well acquainted
with all the instruments of barber-surgery, without missing
one. I have likewise been a soldier in my youthful days, and
therefore know what is a helmet, and what a morion or steel
cap, and what a casque with its beaver, as well as other
matters relating to soldiery, I mean to all kinds of arms
commonly used by soldiers. And I say (with submission
always to better judgements) that this piece here before us,
which this honest gentleman holds in his hands, not only is
not a barber's basin, but is as far from being so as white is
from black, and truth from falsehood. I say also, that though
it be a helmet, it is not a complete one.'

'No, certainly,' said Don Quixote; 'for the beaver, that
should make half of it, is wanting.'

'It is so,' quoth the priest, who perceived his friend the
barber's design; and Cardenio, Don Fernando, and his companions, confirmed the same: and even the judge, had not
his thoughts been so taken up about the business of Don
Louis, would have helped on the jest; but the concern he
was in so employed his thoughts, that he attended but little,
or not at all, to these pleasantries.

'Lord have mercy upon me!' quoth the bantered barber,

'how is it possible so many honest gentlemen should maintain, that this is not a basin, but a helmet! a thing enough
to astonish a whole university, though never so wise: well, if
this basin be a helmet, then this pannel must needs be a
horse's furniture, as this gentleman has said.'

'To me it seems indeed to be a pannel,' quoth Don Quixote;
'but I have already told you, I will not intermeddle with the
dispute, whether it be an ass's pannel or a horse's furniture.'

'All that remains,' said the priest, 'is, that Señor Don
Quixote declare his opinion; for in matters of chivalry, all
these gentlemen, and myself, yield him the preference.'

'By the living God, gentlemen,' said Don Quixote, 'so many
and such unaccountable things have befallen me twice that I
have lodged in this castle, that I dare not venture to vouch
positively for anything that may be asked me about it: for I
am of opinion, that everything passes in it by the way of
enchantment. The first time, I was very much harassed by
an enchanted Moor that was in it, and Sancho fared little
better among some of his followers; and to-night I hung
almost two hours by this arm, without being able to guess
how I came to fall into that mischance. And therefore, for
me to meddle now in so confused a business, and to be giving
my opinion, would be to spend my judgement rashly. As to
the question, whether this be a basin or a helmet, I have
already answered: but as to declaring, whether this be a pannel
or a caparison, I dare not pronounce a definitive sentence,
but remit it, gentlemen, to your discretion: perhaps, not being
dubbed knights, as I am, the enchantments of this place may
have no power over you, and you may have your understandings free, and so may judge of the things of this castle
as they really and truly are, and not as they appear to me.'

'There is no doubt,' answered Don Fernando, 'but that
Señor Don Quixote has said very right, that the decision of
this case belongs to us; and, that we may proceed in it upon
better and more solid grounds, I will take the votes of these
gentlemen in secret, and then give you a clear and full account
of the result.'

To those acquainted with Don Quixote, all this was matter
of most excellent sport; but to those who knew not his

humour, it seemed to be the greatest absurdity in the world, especially to Don Louis's four servants, and to Don Louis himself, as much as the rest, besides three other passengers, who were by chance just then arrived at the inn, and seemed to be troopers of the Holy Brotherhood, as in reality they proved to be. As for the barber, he was quite at his wit's end, to see his basin converted into Mambrino's helmet, before his eyes, and made no doubt but his pannel would be turned into a rich caparison for a horse. Everybody laughed to see Don Fernando walking the round, and taking the opinion of each person at his ear, that he might secretly declare whether that precious piece, about which there had been such a bustle, was a pannel or a caparison: and, after he had taken the votes of those who knew Don Quixote, he said aloud:

'The truth is, honest friend, I am quite weary of collecting so many votes; for I ask nobody that does not tell me it is ridiculous to say this is an ass's pannel, and not a horse's caparison, and even that of a well-bred horse: so that you must have patience; for, in spite of you and your ass too, this is a caparison, and no pannel, and the proofs you have alleged on your part are very trivial and invalid.'

'Let me never enjoy a place in heaven,' quoth the bantered barber, 'if your worships are not all mistaken; and so may my soul appear before God, as this appears to me a pannel, and not a caparison: but, so go the laws*—I say no more; and verily I am not drunk, for I am fasting from everything but sin.'

The barber's simplicities caused no less laughter than the follies of Don Quixote, who, at this juncture, said: There is now no more to be done, but for every one to take what is his own; and to whom God has given it, may St. Peter give his blessing. One of Don Louis's four servants said:

'If this be not a premeditated joke, I cannot persuade myself, that men of so good understanding as all here are, or seem to be, should venture to say and affirm, that this is not a basin, nor that a pannel: but seeing they do actually say and affirm it, I suspect there must be some mystery in obstinately maintaining a thing so contrary to truth and experience: for, by' (and out he rapped a round oath) 'all the men in the world shall never persuade me that this is not a barber's basin, and that a jackass's pannel.'

'May it not be a she-ass's?' quoth the priest.

'That is all one,' said the servant; 'for the question is only, whether it be, or be not, a pannel, as your worships say.'

One of the officers of the Holy Brotherhood, who came in, and had overheard the dispute, full of choler and indignation, said:

'It is as much a pannel as my father is my father; and whoever says, or shall say, to the contrary, must be drunk.'

'You lie like a pitiful scoundrel,' answered Don Quixote; and, lifting up his lance, which he had never let go out of his hand, he went to give him such a blow over the head, that, had not the officer slipped aside, he had been laid flat on the spot. The lance was broke to splinters on the ground; and the other officers, seeing their comrade abused, cried out.

'Help! help the Holy Brotherhood!'

The innkeeper, who was one of the troop, ran in that instant for his wand and his sword, and prepared himself to stand by his comrades. Don Louis's servants got about him, lest he should escape during that hurly-burly. The barber, perceiving the house turned topsy-turvy, laid hold again of his pannel, and Sancho did the same. Don Quixote drew his sword, and fell upon the troopers. Don Louis called out to his servants to leave him, and assist Don Quixote, Cardenio, and Don Fernando, who all took part with Don Quixote. The priest cried out, the hostess shrieked, her daughter roared, Maritornes wept, Dorothea was confounded, Lucinda stood amazed, and Doña Clara fainted away. The barber cuffed Sancho, and Sancho pummelled the barber. Don Louis gave one of his servants, who laid hold of him by the arm, lest he should escape, such a dash in the chops, that he bathed his mouth in blood. The judge interposed in his defence. Don Fernando got one of the troopers down, and kicked him to his heart's content. The innkeeper reinforced his voice demanding aid for the Holy Brotherhood. Thus the whole inn was nothing but weepings, cries, shrieks, confusions, fears, frights, mischances, cuffs, cudgellings, kicks, and effusion of blood. And in the midst of this chaos, this mass, and labyrinth of things, it came into Don Quixote's fancy, that he was plunged over head and ears in the discord of king Agramante's camp;* and therefore he said, with a voice which made the inn shake:

'Hold all of you! all put up your swords; be pacified all, and hearken to me, if you would all continue alive.'

At which tremendous voice they all desisted, and he went on, saying:

'Did I not tell you, sirs, that this castle was enchanted, and that some legion of devils must certainly inhabit it? in confirmation whereof, I would have you see with your own eyes, how the discord of Agramante's camp is passed over and transferred hither among us; behold, how there they fight for the sword, here for the horse, yonder for the eagle, here again for the helmet; and we all fight, and no one understands one another. Come, therefore, my lord judge, and you, master priest, and let one of you stand for king Agramante, the other for king Sobrino,* and make peace among us; for, by the eternal God, it is a thousand pities, so many gentlemen of quality, as are here of us, should kill one another for such trivial matters.'

The troopers, who did not understand Don Quixote's language, and found themselves roughly handled by Don Fernando, Cardenio, and their companions, would not be pacified: but the barber submitted; for both his beard and his pannel were demolished in the scuffle. Sancho, as became a dutiful servant, obeyed the least voice of his master. Don Louis's four servants were also quiet, seeing how little they got by being otherwise. The innkeeper alone was refractory, and insisted that the insolences of that madman ought to be chastised, who at every foot turned the inn upside down. At last the bustle ceased for that time; the pannel was to remain a caparison, the basin a helmet, and the inn a castle, in Don Quixote's imagination, until the Day of Judgement.

Now all being pacified, and all made friends, by the persuasion of the judge and the priest, Don Louis's servants began again to press him to go with them that moment; and, while they were debating, and settling the point, the judge consulted Don Fernando, Cardenio, and the priest, what he should do in this emergency, telling them all that Don Louis had said. At last it was agreed, that Don Fernando should tell Don Louis's servants who he was, and that it was his desire that Don Louis should go along with him to Andalusia, where he should be treated by the marquess his brother according to his quality and worth; for he well knew his intention and resolution not to return, just at that time, into his father's presence, though they should tear him to pieces. Now Don Fernando's quality, and Don Louis's resolution, being known to the four servants, they determined among themselves, that three of them should return to give his father an account of what had passed, and the other should stay to wait upon Don Louis, and not leave him until the rest should come back for him, or until they knew what his father would order. Thus this mass of contention was appeased by the authority of Agramante, and the prudence of king Sobrino. But the enemy of peace and concord, finding himself illuded* and disappointed, and how thin a crop he had gathered from that large field of confusion, resolved to try his hand once more, by contriving fresh frays and disturbances.

Now the case was this: the troopers, upon notice of the quality of those that had attacked them, had desisted and retreated from the fray, as thinking that, let matters go how they would, they were likely to come off the worst. But one of them, namely, he who had been kicked and mauled by Don Fernando, bethought himself that, among some warrants he had about him for apprehending certain delinquents, he had one against Don Quixote, whom the Holy Brotherhood had ordered to be taken into custody for setting at liberty the galley-slaves, as Sancho had very justly feared. Having this in his head, he had a mind to be satisfied, whether the person of Don Quixote answered to the description; and, pulling a parchment out of his bosom, he presently found what he looked for; and setting himself to read it leisurely (for he was no great clerk), at every word he read, he fixed his eyes on Don Quixote, and then went on, comparing the marks in his warrant with the lines of Don Quixote's physiognomy, and found that without all doubt he must be the person therein described: and, as soon as he had satisfied himself, rolling up the parchment, and holding the warrant in his left hand, with his right he laid so fast hold on Don Quixote by the collar, that he did not suffer him to draw breath, crying out aloud:

'Help the Holy Brotherhood! and that everybody may see I require it in earnest, read this warrant, wherein it is expressly commanded to apprehend this highway robber.'

The priest took the warrant, and found it all true that the trooper had said, the marks agreeing exactly with Don Quixote; who, finding himself so roughly handled by this scoundrel, his choler being mounted to the utmost pitch, and all his joints trembling with rage, caught the trooper by the throat, as well as he could, with both hands; and, had he not been rescued by his comrades, he had lost his life before Don Quixote had loosed his hold. The innkeeper, who was bound to aid and assist his brethren in office, ran immediately to his assistance. The hostess, seeing her husband again engaged in battle, raised her voice anew. Her daughter and Maritornes joined in the same tune, praying aid from heaven, and from the standers-by. Sancho, seeing what passed, said:

'As God shall save me, my master says true, concerning the enchantments of this castle; for it is impossible to live an hour quietly in it.'

At length Don Fernando parted the officer and Don Quixote, and, to both their contents, unlocked their hands, from the doublet-collar of the one, and from the windpipe of the other. Nevertheless, the troopers did not desist from demanding their prisoner, and to have him bound and delivered up to them: for so the king's service, and that of the Holy Brotherhood, required, in whose name they again demanded help and assistance in apprehending that common robber, padder, and highwayman. Don Quixote smiled to hear these expressions, and with great calmness, said:

'Come hither, base and ill-born crew; call ye it robbing on the highway, to loose the chains of the captived, to set the imprisoned free, to succour the miserable, to raise the fallen and cast-down, and to relieve the needy and distressed? Ah,

scoundrel race! undeserving, by the meanness and baseness
of your understandings, that heaven should reveal to you the
worth inherent in knight-errantry, or make you sensible of
your own sin and ignorance in not reverencing the very
shadow, and much more the presence, of any knight-errant
whatever! Come hither, ye rogues in a troop, and not
troopers; highwaymen with the licence of the Holy Brotherhood; tell me, who was the blockhead that signed the warrant
for apprehending such a knight-errant as I am? Who was he
that knew not that knights-errant are exempt from all judicial
authority, that their sword is their law, their bravery their
privileges, and their will their edicts? Who was the madman,
I say again, that is ignorant that no patent of gentility contains
so many privileges and exemptions, as are acquired by the
knight-errant the day he is dubbed, and gives himself up to
the rigorous exercise of chivalry? What knight-errant ever
paid custom, poll-tax, subsidy, quit-rent, porterage, or ferry-
boat? What tailor ever brought in a bill for making his
clothes? What governor, that lodged him in his castle, ever
made him pay a reckoning? What king did not seat him at
his table? what damsel was not in love with him, and did not
yield herself up to his whole pleasure and will? and lastly,
what knight-errant has there ever been, is, or shall be, in the
world, who has not courage singly to bestow four hundred
bastinadoes, on four hundred troopers of the Holy Brotherhood, that shall dare to present themselves before him?'

CHAPTER 46

In which is finished the notable adventure of the troopers of
the Holy Brotherhood; with the great ferocity of our good
knight, Don Quixote.

WHILE Don Quixote was talking at this rate, the priest was
endeavouring to persuade the troopers that Don Quixote was
out of his wits, as they might easily perceive by what he did,
and said that they need not give themselves any further
trouble upon that subject; for, though they should apprehend

and carry him away, they must soon release him, as being a madman. To which the officer that had produced the warrant answered, that it was no business of his to judge of Don Quixote's madness, but to obey the orders of his superior, and that, when he had once secured him, they might set him free three hundred times if they pleased.

'For all that,' said the priest, 'for this once you must not take him, nor do I think he will suffer himself to be taken.'

In effect, the priest said so much, and Don Quixote did such extravagances, that the officers must have been more mad than he, had they not discovered his infirmity; and therefore they judged it best to be quiet, and moreover to be mediators for making peace between the barber and Sancho Panza, who still continued their scuffle with great rancour. At last they, as officers of justice, compounded the matter, and arbitrated it in such a manner, that both parties rested, if not entirely contented, at least somewhat satisfied; for they exchanged pannels, but not girths nor halters. As for Mambrino's helmet, the priest, underhand and unknown to Don Quixote, gave eight reals for the basin, and the barber gave him a discharge in full, acquitting him of all fraud from henceforth and for evermore, Amen.

These two quarrels, as being the chief, and of the greatest weight, being thus made up, it remained, that three of Don Louis's servants should be contented to return home, and leave one of their fellows behind to wait upon him, whithersoever Don Fernando pleased to carry him. And, as now good luck and better fortune had begun to pave the way, and smooth the difficulties, in favour of the lovers and heroes of the inn, so fortune would carry it quite through, and crown all with prosperous success: for the servants were contented to do as Don Louis commanded, whereat Doña Clara was so highly pleased, that nobody could look in her face without discovering the joy of her heart. Zoraida, though she did not understand àll she saw, yet grew sad or cheerful in conformity to what she observed in their several countenances, especially that of her Spaniard, on whom her eyes were fixed, and her soul depended. The innkeeper, observing what recompense the priest had made the barber, demanded Don Quixote's reckoning, with ample satisfaction for the damage done to his skins, and the loss of his wine, swearing, that neither Rosinante nor the ass should stir out of the inn, until he had paid the uttermost farthing. The priest pacified him, and Don Fernando paid him all; though the judge very generously offered payment: and thus they all remained in peace and quietness, and the inn appeared no longer the discord of Agramante's camp, as Don Quixote had called it, but peace itself, and the very tranquillity of Octavius Caesar's days: and it was the general opinion, that all this was owing to the good intention and great eloquence of the priest, and the incomparable liberality of Don Fernando.

Don Quixote, now finding himself freed, and clear of so many quarrels both of his squire's and his own, thought it was high time to pursue his voyage, and put an end to that grand adventure, whereunto he had been called and elected: and therefore, being thus resolutely determined, he went and kneeled before Dorothea, who would not suffer him to speak a word until he stood up; which he did in obedience to her, and said:

'It is a common saying, fair lady, that "diligence is the mother of good success", and experience has shown, in many and weighty matters, that the care of the solicitor brings the doubtful suit to a happy issue: but this truth is in nothing more evident than in matters of war, in which expedition and dispatch prevent the designs of the enemy, and carry the victory, before the adversary is in a posture to defend himself. All this, I say, high and deserving lady, because our abode in this castle seems to me now no longer necessary, and may be so far prejudicial, that we may repent it one day: for who knows but your enemy the giant may, by secret and diligent spies, get intelligence of my coming to destroy him? and time, giving him opportunity, he may fortify himself in some impregnable castle or fortress, against which my industry, and the force of my unwearied arm may little avail. And therefore, sovereign lady, let us prevent, as I have said, his designs by our diligence, and let us depart quickly in the name of good fortune, which you can want no longer than I delay to encounter your enemy.'

Here Don Quixote was silent, and said no more, expecting with great sedateness the answer of the beautiful infanta, who, with an air of grandeur, and in a style accommodated to that of Don Quixote, answered in this manner:

'I am obliged to you, Sir Knight, for the inclination you show to favour me in my great need, like a true knight, whose office and employment it is to succour the orphans and distressed, and heaven grant that your desire and mine be soon accomplished, that you may see there are some grateful women in the world. As to my departure, let it be instantly: for I have no other will but yours, and, pray, dispose of me entirely at your own pleasure; for she who has once committed the defence of her person, and the restoration of her dominions, into your hands, must not contradict whatever your wisdom shall direct.'

'In the name of God,' quoth Don Quixote, 'since it is so, that a lady humbles herself, I will not lose the opportunity of exalting her, and setting her on the throne of her ancestors. Let us depart instantly; for I am spurred on by the eagerness of my desire, and the length of the journey: and they say, "delays are dangerous". And since heaven has not created, nor hell seen, any danger that can daunt or affright me, Sancho, saddle Rosinante, and get ready your ass, and her majesty's palfrey; and let us take our leave of the governor of the castle, and of these nobles, and let us depart hence this instant.'

Sancho, who was present all the while, said, shaking his head from side to side:

'Ah, master, master, there are more tricks in the town than are dreamt of, with respect to the honourable coifs be it spoken.'

'What tricks can there be to my discredit in any town, or in all the towns in the world, thou bumpkin?' said Don Quixote.

'If your worship puts yourself into a passion,' answered Sancho, 'I will hold my tongue, and forbear to say what I am bound to tell, as a faithful squire and a dutiful servant ought to his master.'

'Say what you will,' replied Don Quixote, 'so your words

tend not to making me afraid: if you are afraid, you do but like yourself; and if I am not afraid, I do like myself.'

'Nothing of all this, as I am a sinner to God,' answered Sancho; 'only that I am sure and positively certain, that this lady, who calls herself queen of the great kingdom of Micomicon, is no more a queen than my mother; for, were she what she pretends to be, she would not be nuzzling at every turn, and in every corner, with somebody that is in the company.'

Dorothea's colour came at what Sancho said, it being true indeed that her spouse, Don Fernando, now and then, by stealth, had snatched with his lips an earnest of that reward his affections deserved; which Sancho having espied, he thought this freedom more becoming a lady of pleasure than a queen of so vast a kingdom. Dorothea neither could nor would answer Sancho a word, but let him go on with his discourse, which he did, saying:

'I say this, sir, because, supposing that, after we have travelled through thick and thin, and passed many bad nights and worse days, one, who is now solacing himself in this inn, should chance to reap the fruit of our labours, I need be in no haste to saddle Rosinante, nor to get the ass and the palfrey ready; for we had better be quiet; and let every drab mind her spinning, and let us to dinner.'

Good God! how great was the indignation of Don Quixote at hearing his squire speak thus disrespectfully! I say it was so great, that, with speech stammering, tongue faltering, and living fire darting from his eyes, he said:

'Scoundrel! designing, unmannerly, ignorant, ill-spoken, foul-mouthed, impudent, murmuring, and back-biting villain! darest thou utter such words in my presence, and in the presence of these illustrious ladies? and hast thou dared to entertain such rude and insolent thoughts in thy confused imagination? Avoid my presence, monster of nature, treasury of lies, magazine of deceits, storehouse of rogueries, inventor of mischiefs, publisher of absurdities, and enemy of the respect due to royal personages! Begone! appear not before me on pain of my indignation!'

And in saying this, he arched his brows, puffed his cheeks,

stared round about him, and gave a violent stamp with his right foot on the floor; all manifest tokens of the rage locked up in his breast. At whose words and furious gestures Sancho was so frighted, that he would have been glad the earth had opened that instant, and swallowed him up. And he knew not what to do but to turn his back, and get out of the enraged presence of his master.

But the discreet Dorothea, who so perfectly understood Don Quixote's humour, to pacify his wrath, said:

'Be not offended, good Sir Knight of the Sorrowful Figure, at the follies your good squire has uttered: for, perhaps, he has not said them without some ground; nor can it be suspected, considering his good understanding and Christian conscience, that he would slander, or bear false witness against any body: and therefore we must believe, without all doubt, as you yourself say, Sir Knight, that since all things in this castle fall out in the way of enchantment, perhaps, I say, Sancho, by means of the same diabolical illusion, may have seen what he says he saw, so much to the prejudice of my honour.'

'By the omnipotent God I swear,' quoth Don Quixote, 'your grandeur has hit the mark, and some wicked apparition must have appeared to this sinner, and have made him see what it was impossible for him to see by any other way but that of enchantment: for I am perfectly assured of the simplicity and innocence of this unhappy wretch, and that he knows not how to invent a slander on anybody.'

'So it is, and so it shall be,' said Don Fernando: 'wherefore, Señor Don Quixote, you ought to pardon him, and restore him to the bosom of your favour, *sicut erat in principio*, before these illusions turned his brain.'

Don Quixote answered, that he pardoned him; and the priest went for Sancho, who came in very humble, and, falling down on his knees, begged his master's hand, who gave it him; and, after he had let him kiss it, he gave him his blessing, saying:

'Now you will be thoroughly convinced, son Sancho, of what I have often told you before, that all things in this castle are done by way of enchantment.'

'I believe so too,' quoth Sancho, 'excepting the business of the blanket, which really fell out in the ordinary way.'

'Do not believe it,' answered Don Quixote; 'for, were it so, I would have revenged you at that time, and even now. But neither could I then, nor can I now, find on whom to revenge the injury.'

They all desired to know what that business of the blanket was, and the innkeeper gave them a very circumstantial account of Sancho Panza's tossing; at which they were not a little diverted. And Sancho would have been no less ashamed, if his master had not assured him afresh that it was all enchantment. And yet Sancho's folly never rose so high as to believe that it was not downright truth, without any mixture of illusion or deceit, being convinced he had been tossed in the blanket by persons of flesh and blood, and not by imaginary or visionary phantoms, as his master supposed and affirmed.

Two days had already passed since all this illustrious company had been in the inn; and thinking it now time to depart, they contrived how, without giving Dorothea and Don Fernando the trouble of going back with Don Quixote to his village, under pretence of restoring the Queen of Micomicon, the priest and the barber might carry him as they desired, and endeavour to get him cured of his madness at home. While this was in agitation, Don Quixote was laid down upon a bed to repose himself after his late fatigues; and in the meantime they agreed with a wagoner, who chanced to pass by with his team of oxen, to carry him in this manner. They made a kind of cage with poles, grate-wise, large enough to contain Don Quixote at his ease: and immediately Don Fernando and his companions, with Don Louis's servants, and the officers of the Holy Brotherhood, together with the innkeeper, all by the contrivance and direction of the priest, covered their faces, and disguised themselves, some one way, some another, so as to appear to Don Quixote to be quite other persons than those he had seen in that castle. This being done, with the greatest silence they entered the room where Don Quixote lay fast asleep, and not dreaming of any such accident; and laying fast hold of him, they bound him hand and foot, so that, when he awaked with a start, he could not stir, nor do anything but look round him, and wonder to see such strange visages about him. And presently he fell into the usual conceit that his disordered imagination was perpetually presenting to him, believing that all these shapes were goblins of that enchanted castle, and that, without all doubt, he must be enchanted, since he could not stir nor defend himself: all precisely as the priest, the projector of this stratagem, fancied it would fall out. Sancho alone, of all that were present, was in his perfect senses, and in his own figure; and, though he wanted but little of being infected with his master's disease, yet he was not at a loss to know who all these counterfeit goblins were; but he durst not open his lips, until he saw what this surprisal and imprisonment of his master meant. Neither did the knight utter a word, waiting to see the issue of his disgrace; which was, that, bringing the cage thither, they shut him up in it, and nailed the bars so fast that there was no breaking them open though you pulled never so hard. They then hoisted him on their shoulders, and, at going out of the room, a voice was heard as dreadful as the barber could form (not he of the pannel, but the other) saying:

'O Knight of the Sorrowful Figure! let not the confinement you are under afflict you; for it is expedient it should be so, for the more speedy accomplishment of the adventure in which your great valour has engaged you; which shall be finished when the furious Manchegan lion shall be coupled with the white Tobosan dove, after having submitted their stately necks to the soft matrimonial yoke: from which unheard-of conjunction shall spring into the light of the world brave whelps, who shall emulate the tearing claws of their valorous sire. And this shall come to pass before the pursuer of the fugitive nymph shall have made two rounds to visit the bright constellations in his rapid and natural course. And thou, O the most noble and obedient squire that ever had sword in belt, beard on face, and smell in nostrils, be not dismayed nor afflicted to see the flower of knight-errantry carried thus away before thine eyes! for, ere long, if it so please the fabricator of the world, thou shalt see thyself so exalted and sublimated that thou shalt not know thyself, and shall not be defrauded of the promises made thee by thy noble lord. And I assure thee, in the name of the sage Mentironiana,* that thy wages shall be punctually paid thee, as thou wilt see in effect: follow, therefore, the footsteps of the valorous and enchanted knight, for it is expedient for you to go where you may both rest: and because I am permitted to say no more, God be with you: for I return I well know whither.'

And, at finishing the prophecy, he raised his voice very high, and then sunk it by degrees, with so soft an accent, that even they who were in the secret of the jest were almost ready to believe that what they heard was true.

Don Quixote remained much comforted by the prophecy he had heard; for he presently comprehended the whole signification thereof, and saw that it promised he should be joined in holy and lawful wedlock with his beloved Dulcinea del Toboso, from whose happy womb should issue the whelps, his sons, to the everlasting honour of La Mancha. And, with this firm persuasion, he raised his voice, and, fetching a deep sigh, he said:

'O thou, whoever thou art, who hast prognosticated me so much good, I beseech thee to entreat, on my behalf, the sage enchanter, who has the charge of my affairs, that he suffer me not to perish in this prison, wherein I am now carried, until I see accomplished those joyous and incomparable promises now made me! for, so they come to pass, I shall account the pains of my imprisonment glory, the chains with which I am bound refreshment, and this couch, whereon I am laid, not a hard field of battle, but a soft bridal bed of down. And, as touching the consolation of Sancho Panza, my squire, I trust in his goodness and integrity, that he will not forsake me, either in good or evil fortune. And though it should fall out, through his or my hard hap, that I should not be able to give him the island, or something else equivalent, that I have promised him, at least he cannot lose his wages; for in my will, which is already made, I have declared what shall be given him, not indeed proportionable to his many and good services, but according to my own poor ability.'

Sancho Panza bowed with great respect, and kissed both his master's hands: for one alone he could not, they both being tied together. Then the goblins took the cage on their shoulders, and placed it on the wagon.

CHAPTER 47

Of the strange and wonderful manner in which Don Quixote de la Mancha was enchanted, with other remarkable occurrences.

DON QUIXOTE, finding himself cooped up in this manner, and placed upon a cart, said:

'Many and most grave histories have I read of knights-errant; but I never read, saw, or heard of enchanted knights being carried away after this manner,* and so slowly as these lazy, heavy animals seem to promise. For they always used to be carried through the air with wonderful speed, wrapped up in some thick and dark cloud, or in some chariot of fire, or mounted upon a hippogriff, or some such beast. But to be carried upon a team drawn by oxen, by the living God, it puts me into confusion! But, perhaps, the chivalry and enchantments of these our times may have taken a different turn from those of the ancients; and perhaps also, as I am a new knight in the world, and the first who have revived the long-forgotten exercise of knight-errantry, there may have been lately invented other kinds of enchantments, and other methods of carrying away those that are enchanted. What think you of this, son Sancho?'

'I do not know what I think,' answered Sancho, 'not being so well read as your worship in scriptures-errant. Yet I dare affirm and swear, that these hobgoblins here about us are not altogether Catholic.'

'Catholic! my father!' answered Don Quixote; 'how can they be Catholic, being devils, who have assumed fantastic shapes, on purpose to come and put me into this state? And if you would be convinced of this, touch them and feel them, and you will find they have no bodies but of air, consisting in nothing but appearance only.'

'Before God, sir,' replied Sancho, 'I have already touched them, and this devil, who is so very busy here about us, is as plump as a partridge, and has another property very different from what people say your devils are wont to have: for it is said, they all smell of brimstone, and other worse scents; but this spark smells of amber at half a league's distance.'

Sancho meant this of Don Fernando, who being a cavalier of such quality, must have smelt as Sancho hinted.

'Wonder not at it, friend Sancho,' answered Don Quixote; 'for you must know that the devils are a knowing sort of people; and, supposing they do carry perfumes about them, they have no scents in themselves, because they are spirits: or, if they do smell, it can be nothing that is good, but of something bad and stinking: and the reason is, because, let them be where they will, they carry their hell about them, and can receive no kind of ease from their torments: now, a perfume being a thing delightful and pleasing, it is not possible they should smell of so good a thing: and if you think that this devil smells of amber, either you deceive yourself, or he would deceive you, that you may not take him for a devil.'

All this discourse passed between the master and the man: and Don Fernando and Cardenio, fearing lest Sancho should light upon their plot, he being already in the pursuit, and pretty far advanced towards it, they resolved to hasten their departure, and, calling the innkeeper aside, they ordered him to saddle Rosinante and pannel the ass, which he did with great expedition.

In the meanwhile the priest had agreed, for so much a day, with the troopers of the Holy Brotherhood, that they should accompany Don Quixote home to his village. Cardenio took care to hang the buckler on one side, and the basin on the other, of the pommel of Rosinante's saddle, and made signs to Sancho to mount his ass, and take Rosinante by the bridle, and placed two troopers with their carabines on each side of the wagon. But, before the car moved forward, the hostess,

her daughter, and Maritornes, came out to take their leave
of Don Quixote, pretending to shed tears for grief at his
misfortune; to whom Don Quixote said:

'Weep not, my good ladies; for these kind of mishaps are
incident to those who profess what I profess; and if such
calamities did not befall me, I should not take myself for a
knight-errant of any considerable fame: for such accidents as
these never happen to knights of little name and reputation,
since nobody in the world thinks of them at all: but to the
valorous indeed they often fall out; for many princes and
other knights, envious of their extraordinary virtue and courage, are constantly endeavouring by indirect ways to destroy
them. Notwithstanding all which, so powerful is virtue, that
of herself alone, in spite of all the necromancy that its first
inventor, Zoroaster, ever knew, she will come off victorious
from every encounter, and spread her lustre round the world,
as the sun does over the heavens. Pardon me, fair ladies, if
I have, through inadvertency, done you any displeasure; for
willingly and knowingly I never offended anybody: and pray
to God, that he would deliver me from these bonds, into
which some evil-minded enchanter has thrown me; for, if
ever I find myself at liberty, I shall not forget the favours
you have done me in this castle, but shall acknowledge and
requite them as they deserve.'

While this passed between the ladies of the castle and Don
Quixote, the priest and the barber took their leave of Don
Fernando and his companions, and of the captain and his
brother the judge, and of all the now happy ladies, especially
of Dorothea and Lucinda. They all embraced, promising to
give each other an account of their future fortunes. Don
Fernando gave the priest directions where to write to him,
and acquaint him with what became of Don Quixote, assuring
him that nothing would afford him a greater pleasure than
to know it; and that, on his part, he would inform of
whatever might amuse or please him, either in relation to his
own marriage, or the baptizing of Zoraida, as also concerning
Don Louis's success, and Lucinda's return to her parents.
The priest promised to perform all that was desired of him
with the utmost punctuality. They again embraced, and

renewed their mutual offers of service. The innkeeper came to the priest, and gave him some papers, telling him he found them in the lining of the wallet, in which *The Novel of the Curious Impertinent* was found, and since the owner had never come back that way, he might take them all with him; for, as he could not read, he had no desire to keep them. The priest thanked him, and, opening the papers, found at the head of them this title, *The Novel of Rinconete and Cortadillo*;* from whence he concluded it must be some tale, and imagined, because that of the *Curious Impertinent* was a good one, this must be so too, it being probable they were both written by the same author: and therefore he kept it with a design to read it when he had an opportunity.

Then he and his friend the barber mounted on horseback, with their masks on, that Don Quixote might not know them, and placed themselves behind the wagon; and the order of the cavalcade was this. First marched the car, guided by the owner; on each side went the troopers with their firelocks, as has been already said; then followed Sancho upon his ass, leading Rosinante by the bridle: the priest and the barber brought up the rear on their puissant mules, and their faces masked, with a grave and solemn air, marching no faster than the slow pace of the oxen allowed. Don Quixote sat in the cage, with his hands tied, and his legs stretched out, leaning against the bars, with as much patience and silence, as if he had not been a man of flesh and blood, but a statue of stone. And thus, with the same slowness and silence, they travelled about two leagues, when they came to a valley, which the wagoner thought a convenient place for resting and baiting his cattle; and acquainting the priest with his purpose, the barber was of opinion they should travel a little farther, telling them, that behind a rising ground not far off, there was a vale that afforded more and much better grass than that in which they had a mind to stop. They took the barber's advice, and so went on.

Now the priest, happening to turn his head about, perceived behind them about six or seven horsemen, well mounted and accoutred, who soon came up with them; for they travelled, not with the phlegm and slowness of the oxen,

but as persons mounted on ecclesiastical mules, and in haste
to arrive quickly, and pass the heat of the day in the inn,
which appeared to be not a league off. The speedy overtook
the slow, and the companies saluted each other courteously;
and one of the travellers, who, in short, was a canon of
Toledo, and master of the rest, observing the orderly procession of the wagon, the troopers, Sancho, Rosinante, the
priest, and the barber, and especially Don Quixote, caged up
and imprisoned, could not forbear inquiring what was the
meaning of carrying that man in that manner; though he
already guessed, by seeing the badges of the Holy Brotherhood, that he must be some notorious robber, or other
criminal, the punishment of whom belonged to that fraternity.
One of the troopers, to whom the question was put, answered
thus:

'Sir, if you would know the meaning of this gentleman's
going in this manner, let him tell you himself; for we know
nothing of the matter.'

Don Quixote overheard the discourse, and said:

'If perchance, gentlemen, you are versed and skilled in
matters of chivalry, I will acquaint you with my misfortunes;
but if not, I need not trouble myself to recount them.'

By this time the priest and the barber, perceiving the
travellers were in discourse with Don Quixote de la Mancha,
were come close up, to be ready to give such an answer as
might prevent the discovery of their plot. The canon, in
answer to what Don Quixote said, replied:

'In truth, brother, I am more conversant in books of
chivalry than in Villalpando's *Summaries*;* so that, if that be
all, you may safely communicate to me whatever you please.'

'With heaven's permission,' replied Don Quixote, 'since it
is so, you must understand, señor cavalier, that I am enchanted in this cage, through the envy and fraud of wicked
necromancers; for virtue is more persecuted by the wicked
than beloved by the good. A knight-errant I am, not one of
those whose names fame has forgot to eternize, but one
of those, who, maugre and in despite of envy itself, and of
all the magicians Persia ever bred, the Brahmans of India,
and the gymnosophists of Ethiopia, shall enroll his name in

the temple of immortality, to serve as an example and mirror to future ages, in which knights-errant may see the track they are to follow, if they are ambitious of reaching the honourable summit and pinnacle of arms.'

'Señor Don Quixote de la Mancha says the truth,' quoth the priest at this time; 'for he goes enchanted in this wagon, not through his own fault or demerit, but through the malice of those to whom virtue is odious, and courage offensive. This, sir, is the Knight of the Sorrowful Figure, if ever you have heard him spoken of, whose valorous exploits and heroic deeds shall be written on solid brass and everlasting marble, though envy take never so much pains to obscure them, and malice to conceal them.'

When the canon heard him that was imprisoned, and him at liberty, both talk in such a style, he was ready to cross himself with amazement, not being able to imagine what had befallen him; and all his followers were in equal admiration.

Now Sancho, being come up to them, and overhearing their discourse, to set all to rights, said:

'Look ye, gentlemen, let it be well or ill taken, I will out with it: the truth of the case is, my master, Don Quixote, is just as much enchanted as my mother; he is in his perfect senses, he eats, and drinks, and does his occasions like other men, and as he did yesterday before they cooped him up. This being so, will you persuade me he is enchanted? Have I not heard many people say, that persons enchanted neither eat, sleep, nor speak? and my master, if nobody thwarts him, will talk ye more than thirty barristers.'

And turning his eyes on the priest, he went on saying:

'Ah, master priest, master priest, do you think I do not know you? and think you I do not perceive and guess what these new enchantments drive at? Let me tell you I know you, though you disguise your face never so much: and I would have you to know, I understand you, though you manage your contrivances never so slyly. In short, virtue cannot live where envy reigns, nor liberality subsist with niggardliness. Evil befall the devil! had it not been for your reverence, my master had been married by this time to the infanta Micomicona, and I had been an earl at least; for I

could expect no less, as well from the generosity of my
master, the Knight of the Sorrowful Figure, as from the
greatness of my services. But I find the proverb true, that
"the wheel of fortune turns swifter than a mill-wheel", and
they, who were yesterday at the top, are to-day on the ground.
I am grieved for my poor wife and children; for when they
might reasonably expect to see their father come home a
governor or viceroy of some island or kingdom, they will
now see him return a mere groom. All this that I have said,
master priest, is only intended to put your paternity in mind
to make a conscience of the evil treatment of my master;
and take heed that God does not call you to an account in
the next life for this imprisonment of my lord, and require
at your hands all those succours, and all the good he might
have done, during this time of his confinement.'

'Snuff me these candles,' quoth the barber at this juncture;
'what! Sancho, are you also of your master's confraternity?
as God shall save me, I begin to think you are likely to keep
him company in the cage, and to be as much enchanted as
he, for your share of his humour and his chivalry. In an evil
hour were you with child by his promises, and in an evil
hour the island you so long for entered into your pate.'

'I am not with child by anybody,' answered Sancho, 'nor
am I a man to suffer myself to be got with child by the best
king that may be; and though I am a poor man, I am an
Old Christian, and owe nobody anything: and if I covet
islands, there are others who covet worse things; and every
one is the son of his own works; and, being a man, I may
come to be Pope, and much more easily governor of an
island, especially since my master may win so many, that he
may be at a loss on whom to bestow them. Pray, master
barber, take heed what you say; for shaving of beards is not
all, and there is some difference between Pedro and Pedro.
I say this because we know one another, and there is no
putting false dice upon me: as for my master's enchantment,
God knows the truth, and let that rest; for it is the worse
for stirring.'

The barber would not answer Sancho, lest, by his simplicity, he should discover what he and the priest took so

many pains to conceal: and for the same reason the priest desired the canon to get on a little before, and he would let him into the secret of the encaged gentleman, with other particulars that would divert him.

The canon did so, and rode on before with his servants, listening to all the priest had to tell him of the quality, manner of life, and customs of Don Quixote: recounting to him briefly the beginning and cause of his distraction, with the whole progress of his adventures, to the putting him into that cage, and the design they had to carry him home, and try if by any means they might find a cure for his madness. The servants admired afresh, and the canon also, to hear the strange history of Don Quixote; and when he had heard it all, he said to the priest:

'Truly, sir, I am convinced that those they call books of chivalry are prejudicial to the common weal;* and though, led away by an idle and false taste, I have read the beginning of almost all that are printed, I could never prevail with myself to read any of them from the beginning to the end, because to me they appear to be all of the same stamp, and this to have no more in it than that, nor that than the other. And, in my opinion, this kind of writing and composition falls under the denomination of the fables they call Milesian,* which are extravagant stories, tending only to please, and not to instruct: quite contrary to the moral fables, which at the same time both delight and instruct. And though the principal end of such books is to please, I know not how they can attain it, being stuffed with so many and such monstrous absurdities. For the pleasure, which is conceived in the mind, must proceed from the beauty and harmony it sees or contemplates in the things which the sight or the imagination sets before it, and nothing, in itself ugly or deformed, can afford any real satisfaction.

'For what beauty can there be, or what proportion of the parts to the whole, and of the whole to the parts, in a book or fable, in which a youth of sixteen years hews down with his sword a giant as big as a steeple, and splits him in two, as if he were made of paste? And when they would give us a description of a battle, after having said that on the enemy's side there are a million of combatants, let but the hero of the book be against them, we must, of necessity and in despite of our teeth, believe, that such or such a knight carried the victory, by the single valour of his strong arm. Then, what shall we say to that facility with which a queen or an empress throws herself into the arms of an errant and unknown knight? What genius,* not wholly barbarous and uncultivated, can be satisfied with reading that a vast tower, full of knights, scuds through the sea, like a ship before the wind, and this night is in Lombardy, and the next morning in the country of Prester John in the Indies, or in some other, that Ptolemy never discovered, nor Marco Polo ever saw. And if it should be answered that the authors of such books write them professedly as lies, and therefore are not obliged to stand upon niceties, or truth; I reply, that fiction is so much the better, by how much the nearer it resembles truth; and pleases so much the more, by how much the more it has of the doubtful and possible.

'Fables should be suited to the reader's understanding, and so contrived, that, by facilitating the impossible, lowering the vast, and keeping the mind in suspense, they may at once surprise, delight, amuse, and entertain, in such sort, that admiration and pleasure may be united, and go hand in hand: all which cannot be performed by him who pays no regard to probability and imitation, in which the perfection of writing consists. I have never yet seen any book of chivalry which makes a complete body of fable, with all its members, so that the middle corresponds to the beginning, and the end to the beginning and middle: on the contrary, they are composed of so many members that the authors seem rather to design a chimera or monster, than to intend a well-proportioned figure. Besides all this, their style is harsh, their exploits incredible, their amours lascivious, their civility impertinent, their battles tedious, their reasonings foolish, and their voyages extravagant; and lastly, they are devoid of all ingenious artifice, and therefore deserve to be banished the Christian commonwealth, as an unprofitable race of people.'

The priest listened to him with great attention, and took him to be a man of good understanding, and in the right in all he said; and therefore he told him, that, being of the same opinion, and bearing an old grudge to books of chivalry, he had burnt all those belonging to Don Quixote, which were not a few. Then he gave him an account of the scrutiny he had made, telling him which of them he had condemned to the fire, and which he had reprieved: at which the canon laughed heartily and said, notwithstanding all the ill he had spoken of such books, he found one thing good in them, which was, the subject they presented for a good genius to display itself, affording a large and ample field, in which the pen may expatiate without any let or incumbrance, describing shipwrecks, tempests, encounters, and battles; delineating a valiant captain with all the qualifications requisite to make him such, showing his prudence in preventing the stratagems of his enemy, his eloquence in persuading or dissuading his soldiers; mature in council, prompt in execution, equally brave in expecting as in attacking the enemy: sometimes painting a sad and tragical accident, then a joyful and unexpected event; here a most beautiful lady, modest, discreet, and reserved; there a Christian knight, valiant, and courteous; now an unruly and barbarous braggadocio; then an affable, valiant, and good-natured prince: describing the goodness and loyalty of subjects, the greatness and generosity of nobles.

'Then again he may show himself an excellent astronomer or geographer, a musician, or a statesman; and, some time or other, he may have an opportunity, if he pleases, of showing himself a necromancer. He may set forth the subtlety of Ulysses, the piety of Aeneas, the bravery of Achilles, the misfortunes of Hector, the treachery of Sinon, the friendship of Euryalus, the liberality of Alexander, the valour of Caesar, the clemency and probity of Trajan, the fidelity of Zopyrus, the wisdom of Cato, and finally all those actions which may serve to make an illustrious person perfect; sometimes placing them in one person alone, then dividing them among many: and this being done in a smooth and agreeable style, and with ingenious invention, approaching as near as possible to truth, will, doubtless, weave a web of such various and beautiful contexture, that, when it is finished, the perfection and excellency thereof may attain to the ultimate end of writing, that is, both to instruct and delight, as I have already said: because the unconfined way of writing these books gives an author room to show his skill in the epic or lyric, in tragedy or comedy, with all the parts included in the sweet and charming sciences of poetry and oratory: for the epic may be written as well in prose as in verse.'*

CHAPTER 48

In which the canon prosecutes the subject of books of chivalry, with other matters worthy of his genius.

'IT is as you say, sir,' quoth the priest to the canon; 'and for this reason, those who have hitherto composed such books are the more to blame, proceeding, as they do, without any regard to good sense, or art, or to those rules, by the observation of which they might become as famous in prose as the two princes of the Greek and Latin poetry are in verse.'

'I myself,' replied the canon, 'was once tempted to write a book of knight-errantry, in which I purposed to observe all the restrictions I have mentioned; and, to confess the truth, I had gone through above a hundred sheets of it: and, to try whether they answered my own opinion of them, I communicated them to some learned and judicious persons, who were very fond of this kind of reading, and to other persons who were ignorant, and regarded only the pleasure of reading extravagances; and I met with a kind approbation from all of them: nevertheless I would proceed no further, as well in regard that I looked upon it as a thing foreign to my profession, as because the number of the unwise is greater than that of the prudent: and though it is better to be praised by the few wise than mocked by a multitude of fools, yet I am unwilling to expose myself to the confused judgement of the giddy vulgar, to whose lot the reading [of] such books for the most part falls.

'But that which chiefly moved me to lay it aside, and to think no more of finishing it, was an argument I formed to myself, deduced from the modern comedies* that are daily represented, saying: "Of those nowadays in fashion, whether fictitious or historical, all, or most of them, are known absurdities, and things without head or tail, and yet the vulgar take a pleasure in listening to them, and maintain and approve them for good: and the authors who compose, and the actors who represent them, say, such they must be, because the people will have them so, and no otherwise; and those which are regular, and carry on the plot according to the rules of art, serve only for half a score men of sense, who understand them, while all the rest are at a loss, and can make nothing of the contrivance; and for their part, it is better for them to get bread by the many than reputation by the few." Thus, probably, it would have fared with my book, after I had burnt my eyebrows with poring to follow the aforesaid precepts, and I should have got nothing but my labour for my pains.* And though I have often endeavoured to convince the actors of their mistake, and that they would draw more company, and gain more credit, by acting plays written according to art than by such ridiculous pieces, they are so attached and wedded to their own opinion, that no reason, nor even demonstration, can wrest it from them. I remember, that, talking one day to one of these headstrong fellows,

'"Tell me," said I, "do you not remember that, a few years ago, there were three tragedies acted in Spain, composed by a famous poet of this kingdom, which were such, that they surprised, delighted, and raised the admiration of all who saw them, as well the ignorant as the judicious, as well the vulgar as the better sort; and that these alone got the players more money than any thirty of the best that have been written since?"

'"Doubtless," answered the actor I speak of, "your worship means the *Isabella, Phyllis*, and *Alexandra*."*

'"The same," replied I; "and pray see, whether they did not carefully observe the rules of art, and whether that hindered them from appearing what they really were, and from pleasing all the world. So that the fault is not in the people's coveting absurdities, but in those who know not how to exhibit anything better: for there is nothing absurd in the play of *Ingratitude Revenged*,* nor in the *Numantia*;* nor can you find any in the *Merchant Lover*,* much less in the *Favourable She-enemy*,* and in some others, composed by ingenious and judicious poets to their own fame and renown, and to the advantage of those who acted them."

'And to these I added other reasons, at which I fancied he was somewhat confounded, but not convinced nor satisfied, so as to make him retract his erroneous opinion.'

'Señor canon,' said then the priest, 'you have touched upon a subject, which has awakened in me an old grudge I bear to the comedies now in vogue, equal to that I have against books of chivalry: for, whereas comedy, according to the opinion of Cicero, ought to be a mirror of human life, an exemplar of manners, and an image of truth, those that are represented nowadays are mirrors of inconsistency, patterns of folly, and images of wantonness. For what greater absurdity can there be in the subject we are treating of than for a child to appear, in the first scene of the first act, in swaddling clothes, and in the second enter a grown man with a beard? and what can be more ridiculous than to draw the character of an old man valiant, a young man a coward, a footman a rhetorician, a page a privy-counsellor, a king a water-carrier, and a princess a scullion? Then what shall we say to their observance of the time and place in which the actions they represent are supposed to have happened? I have seen a comedy, the first act of which was laid in Europe, the second in Asia, and the third in Africa; and, had there been four acts, the fourth would doubtless have concluded in America; and so the play would have taken in all the four parts of the world. If imitation be the principal thing required in comedy, how is it possible any tolerable understanding can endure to see an action, which passed in the time of king Pepin or Charlemagne, ascribed to the emperor Heraclius, who is introduced carrying the cross into Jerusalem, or recovering the Holy Sepulchre, like Godfrey of Bouillon; numberless years having passed between these actions: and besides, the comedy being grounded upon a fiction, to see truths applied out of history, with a mixture of facts relating to different persons and times; and all this with no appearance of probability, but, on the contrary, full of manifest and altogether inexcusable errors? But the worst of it is, that some are so besotted as to call this perfection, and to say, that all besides is mere pedantry.

'If we come to the comedies upon divine subjects, how many false miracles do they invent, how many apocryphal and ill-understood, ascribing to one saint the miracles of another? and, even in the plays upon profane subjects, the authors take upon them to work miracles, for no other reason in the world, but because they think such a miracle will do well, and make a figure in such a place, that ignorant people may admire, and be induced to see the comedy.

'Now all this is to the prejudice of truth, and discredit of history, and even to the reproach of our Spanish wits; for foreigners, who observe the laws of comedy with great punctuality, take us for barbarous and ignorant, seeing the absurdities and extravagances of those we write. It would not be a sufficient excuse to say, that the principal intent of well-governed commonwealths, in permitting stage-plays to be acted, is, that the populace may be entertained with some innocent recreation, to divert, at times, the ill humours which idleness is wont to produce; and, since this end may be attained by any play, whether good or bad, there is no need of prescribing laws, or confining those who write or act them to the strict rules of composition, since, as I have said, any of them serve to compass the end proposed by them. To this I would answer, that this end is, beyond all comparison, much better attained by those that are good than by those that are not so; for the hearer, after attending to an artful and well-contrived play, would go away diverted by what is witty, instructed by what is serious, in admiration at the incidents, improved by the reasoning, forewarned by the frauds, made wise by the examples, incensed against vice, and in love with virtue: for a good comedy will awaken all these passions in the mind of the hearer, let him be never so gross or stupid. And, of all impossibilities, it is the most impossible not to be pleased, entertained, and satisfied much more with that comedy which has all these requisites, than by one which is defective in them, as most of our comedies nowadays are. Nor is this abuse to be charged chiefly on the poets themselves; for there are some among them who know very well wherein they err, and are perfectly acquainted with what they ought to do: but, as plays are made a saleable commodity, they say, and they say right, that the actors would not buy them, if they were not of that stamp; and therefore the poet endeavours to accommodate himself to what is required by the player, who is to pay him for his work.

'And, that this is the truth, may be evinced by the infinite number of plays composed by a most happy genius* of these kingdoms, with so much sprightliness, such elegant verse, expressions so good, and such excellent sentiments, and lastly with such richness of elocution, and loftiness of style, that the world resounds with his fame. Yet, by his sometimes adapting himself to the taste of the actors, they have not all reached that point of perfection that some of them have done. Others, in writing plays, so little consider what they are doing, that the actors are often under the necessity of absconding for fear of being punished, as has frequently happened, for having acted things to the prejudice of the crown, or the dishonour of families.

'But all these inconveniences, and many more I have not mentioned, would cease, if some intelligent and judicious person of the court were appointed to examine all plays before they are acted, not only those made about the court, but all that should be acted throughout all Spain; without whose approbation, under hand and seal, the civil officers should suffer no play to be acted: and thus the comedians would be obliged to send all their plays to the court, and might then act them with entire safety; and the writers of them would take more care and pains about what they did, knowing their performances must pass the rigorous examination of somebody that understands them. By this method good plays would be written, and the design of them happily attained, namely, the entertainment of the people, the reputation of the wits of Spain, the interest and security of the players, and the saving the magistrate the trouble of chastising

them. And if some other, or the same person, were commis-
sioned to examine the books of chivalry that shall be written
for the future, without doubt some might be published with
all the perfection you speak of, enriching our language with
the pleasing and precious treasure of eloquence, and might
cause the old books to be laid aside, being obscured by the
lustre of the new ones, which would come out, for the
innocent amusement, not only of the idle, but also of those
who have most business; for the bow cannot possibly stand
always bent, nor can human nature or human frailty subsist
without some lawful recreation.'

Thus far had the canon and the priest proceeded in their
dialogue, when the barber, coming up to them, said to the priest:

'Here, señor licentiate, is the place I told you was proper
for us to pass the heat of the day in, and where the cattle
would have fresh grass in abundance.'

'I think so too,' answered the priest: and, acquainting the
canon with his intention, he also would stay with them,
invited by the beauty of a pleasant valley, which presented
itself to their view: and therefore, that he might enjoy the
pleasure of the place, and the conversation of the priest, of
whom he began to be fond, and be informed more particularly of Don Quixote's exploits, he ordered some of his
servants to go to the inn, which was not far off, and bring
from thence what they could find to eat for the whole
company; for he resolved to stay there that afternoon. To
whom one of the servants answered, that the sumpter-mule,
which by that time must have reached the inn, carried
provisions enough for them all, and that they need take
nothing at the inn but barley.

'Since it is so,' said the canon, 'take thither the other mules,
and bring back the sumpter hither.'

While this passed, Sancho, perceiving he might talk to his
master without the continual presence of the priest and the
barber, whom he looked upon as suspicious persons, came
up to his master's cage, and said to him:

'Sir, to disburden my conscience, I must tell you something
about this enchantment of yours; and it is this, that they who
are riding along with us and with their faces covered, are the

priest and the barber of our town: and I fancy they have played you this trick, and are carrying you in this manner, out of the pure envy they bear you for surpassing them in famous achievements: and supposing this to be true, it follows that you are not enchanted, but gulled and besotted; for proof whereof I would ask you one thing, and if you answer me, as I believe you must, you shall lay your finger on this palpable cheat, and find, that you are not enchanted, but distracted.'

'Ask whatever you will, son Sancho,' answered Don Quixote; 'for I will satisfy you, and answer to your whole will. But as to what you tell me, that those yonder, who come with us, are the priest and the barber, our townsmen and acquaintance, it may very easily be that they may seem to be so; but that they are so really and in effect, do not believe it in any wise. What you ought to understand and believe is, that, if they seem to be those you say, it must be, that they who have enchanted me, have assumed that appearance and likeness; for enchanters can easily take what form they please, and may have taken that of our two friends, in order to make you think as you do, and to involve you in such a labyrinth of imaginations, that you shall not be able to find your way out though you had Theseus's clue. Besides, they may have done it to make me also waver in my judgement, and not be able to guess from what quarter this injury comes. For, if on the one side, you tell me that the priest and the barber of our village bear us company, and, on the other side, I find myself locked up in a cage, and know of myself, that no force but that which is supernatural could be sufficient to imprison me; what can I say or think, but that the manner of my enchantment exceeds all I have ever read of in the histories of knights-errant that have been enchanted? so that you may set your heart at rest as to their being what you say; for they are just as much so as I am a Turk. As to what concerns your asking me questions, ask them; for I will answer you, though you should continue asking from this time until to-morrow morning.'

'Blessed Virgin!' answered Sancho, raising his voice, 'and is it then possible your worship can be so thick-skulled and devoid of brains, that you cannot perceive what I tell you to be the very truth, and that there is more roguery than enchantment in this confinement and disgrace of yours; and seeing it is so, I will prove most evidently that you are really not enchanted. Now tell me, as God shall save you from this storm, and as you hope to find yourself in my lady Dulcinea's arms, when you least think of it—'

'Cease conjuring me,' said Don Quixote, 'and ask what questions you will; for I have already told you I will answer them with the utmost punctuality.'

'That is what I would have you do,' replied Sancho; 'and what I have a mind to know, is, that you tell me, without adding or diminishing a tittle, and with all truth and candour, as is expected from, and practised by, all who profess the exercise of arms, as your worship does, under the title of kinghts-errant—'

'I tell you I will lie in nothing,' answered Don Quixote; 'therefore, make either a beginning or an end of asking; for, in truth, you tire me out with so many salvos, postulatums, and preparatives, Sancho.'

'I say,' replied Sancho, 'that I am fully satisfied of the goodness and veracity of my master, and, that being to the purpose in our affair, I ask, with respect be it spoken, whether, since your being cooped up, or, as you say, enchanted in this cage, your worship has not had an inclination to open the greater or the lesser sluices, as people are wont to say?'

'I do not understand, Sancho,' said Don Quixote, 'what you mean by opening sluices: explain yourself, if you would have me give you a direct answer.'

'Is it possible,' quoth Sancho, 'your worship should not understand that phrase, when the very children at school are weaned with it? Know then, it means, whether you have not had a mind to do what nobody can do for you?'

'Aye, now I comprehend you, Sancho,' said Don Quixote; 'and, in truth, I have often had such a mind, and have at this very instant: help me out of this strait; for I doubt all is not so clean as it should be.'

CHAPTER 49

Of the ingenious conference between Sancho Panza and his master Don Quixote.

'HA!' quoth Sancho, 'now I have caught you: this is what I longed to know with all my heart and soul. Come on, sir, can you deny what is commonly said everywhere, when a person is in the dumps; I know not what such or such a one ails; he neither eats, nor drinks, nor sleeps, nor answers to the purpose when he is asked a question; he looks as if he were enchanted. From whence it is concluded, that they who do not eat, nor drink, nor sleep, nor perform the natural actions I speak of, such only are enchanted, and not they who have such calls as your worship has, and who eat and drink when they can get it, and answer to all that is asked them.'

'You say right, Sancho,' answered Don Quixote: 'but I have already told you, that there are sundry sorts of enchantments, and it may have so fallen out, that, in process of time, they may have been changed from one to another, and that now it may be the fashion for those who are enchanted to do as I do, though formerly they did not; so that there is no arguing, nor drawing consequences against the custom of the times. I know, and am verily persuaded, that I am enchanted; and that is sufficient for the discharge of my conscience, which would be heavily burdened if I thought I was not enchanted, and should suffer myself to lie in this cage like a coward, defrauding the necessitous and oppressed of that succour I might have afforded them, when perhaps, at this very moment, they may be in extreme want of my aid and protection.'

'But for all that,' replied Sancho, 'I say, for your greater and more abundant satisfaction, your worship would do well to endeavour to get out of this prison; which I will undertake to facilitate with all my might, and to effect it too; and then you may once more mount your trusty Rosinante, who seems as if he were enchanted too, so melancholy and dejected is he. And, when this is done, we may again try our fortune in search of adventures: and should it not succeed well, we shall have time enough to return to the cage, in which I promise, on the faith of a trusty and loyal squire, to shut myself up with your worship, if perchance you prove so unhappy, or I so simple, as to fail in the performance of what I say.'

'I am content to do what you advise, brother Sancho,' replied Don Quixote: 'and when you see a proper opportunity for working my deliverance, I will be ruled by you in everything; but, Sancho, depend upon it, you will find how mistaken you are in your notion of my disgrace.'

With these discourses the knight-errant and the evil-errant squire amused themselves, until they came where the priest, the canon, and the barber, who were already alighted, waited for them. The wagoner presently unyoked the oxen from his team, and turned them loose in that green and delicious place, whose freshness invited to the enjoyment of it, not only persons as much enchanted as Don Quixote, but as considerate and discreet as his squire, who besought the priest to permit his master to come out of the cage for a while; otherwise that prison would not be quite so clean as the decorum of such a knight as his master required. The priest understood him, and said that he would with all his heart consent to what he desired, were it not that he feared, lest his master, finding himself at liberty, should play one of his old pranks, and be gone where nobody should set eyes on him more.'

'I will be security for his not running away,' replied Sancho.

'And I also,' said the canon, 'especially if he will pass his word, as a knight, that he will not leave us without our consent.'

'I do pass it,' answered Don Quixote (who was listening to all they said), 'and the rather because whoever is enchanted, as I am, is not at liberty to dispose of himself as he pleases; for he who has enchanted him, can make him that he shall not be able to stir in three centuries, and, if he should attempt an escape, will fetch him back on the wing: and since this was the case, they might, he said, safely let him loose, especially it being so much for the advantage of them all; for, should they not loose him, he protested, if they did not get farther off, he must needs offend their noses.'

The canon took him by the hand, though he was still manacled, and, upon his faith and word, they uncaged him; at which he was infinitely and above measure rejoiced to see himself out of the cage. And the first thing he did was, to stretch his whole body and limbs: then he went where Rosinante stood; and, giving him a couple of slaps on the buttocks with the palm of his hand, he said:

'I have still hope in God, and in His Blessed Mother, O flower and mirror of steeds, that we two shall soon see ourselves in that state our hearts desire, thou with thy lord on thy back, and I mounted on thee, exercising the function for which heaven sent me into the world.'

And so saying, Don Quixote, with his squire, Sancho, retired to some little distance; from whence he came back more lightsome, and more desirous to put in execution what his squire had projected.

The canon gazed earnestly at him, and stood in admiration at his strange and unaccountable madness, perceiving that, in all his discourse and answers, he discovered a very good understanding, and only lost his stirrups, as has been already said, when the conversation happened to turn upon the subject of chivalry. And so, after they were all sat down upon the green grass, in expectation of the sumpter-mule, the canon, being moved with compassion, said to him:

'It is impossible, worthy sir, that the crude and idle study of books of chivalry should have had that influence upon you, as to turn your brain in such manner as to make you believe you are now enchanted, with other things of the same stamp, as far from being true, as falsehood itself is from truth. How is it possible, any human understanding can persuade itself, there ever was in the world, that infinity of Amadises, that rabble of famous knights, so many emperors of Trapisonda, so many Felixmartes of Hyrcania, so many palfreys, so many damsels-errant, so many serpents, so many dragons, so many giants, so many unheard-of adventures, so many kinds of enchantments, so many battles, so many furious encounters, so much bravery of attire, so many princesses in love, so many squires become earls, so many witty dwarfs, so many billets-doux, so many courtships, so many valiant

women, and lastly, so many and such absurd accidents, as
your books of knight-errantry contain?

'For my own part, when I read them, without reflecting
that they are all falsehood and folly, they give me some
pleasure; but, when I consider what they are, I throw the
very best of them against the wall, and should into the fire,
had I one near me, as well deserving such a punishment, for
being false and inveigling, and out of the road of common
sense, as broachers of new sects and new ways of life, and
as giving occasion to the ignorant vulgar to believe, and look
upon as truths, the multitude of absurdities they contain. Nay,
they have the presumption to dare to disturb the understandings of ingenious and well-born gentlemen, as is but too
notorious in the effect they have had upon your worship,
having reduced you to such a pass, that you are forced to
be shut up in a cage, and carried on a team from place to
place, like some lion or tiger, to be shown for money.

'Ah, Señor Don Quixote, have pity on yourself, and return
into the bosom of discretion, and learn to make use of those
great abilities heaven has been pleased to bestow upon you,
by employing that happy talent you are blessed with in some
other kind of reading, which may redound to the benefit of
your conscience, and to the increase of your honour. But if
a strong natural impulse must still lead you to books of
exploits and chivalries, read, in the Holy Scripture, the Book
of Judges, where you will meet with wonderful truths, and
achievements no less true than heroic. Portugal had a Viria-
tus, Rome a Caesar, Carthage a Hannibal, Greece an Alexander, Castile a Count Fernan Gonzalez,* Valencia a Cid,
Andalusia a Gonzalo Hernandez,* Estremadura a Diego Garcia de Paredes,* Xerez a Garci Perez de Vargas,* Toledo a
Garcilaso,* and Seville a Don Manuel de Leon;* the reading
of whose valorous exploits may entertain, instruct, delight,
and raise admiration in the most elevated genius. This, indeed,
would be a study worthy of your good understanding, my
dear friend, whereby you will become learned in history,
enamoured of virtue, instructed in goodness, bettered in
manners, valiant without rashness, and cautious without cowardice: and all this will redound to the glory of God, to your

own profit, and the fame of La Mancha, from whence, as I understand, you derive your birth and origin.'

Don Quixote listened with great attention to the canon's discourse; and when he found he had done, after having stared at him a pretty while, he said:

'I find, sir, the whole of what you have been saying tends to persuade me* there never were any knights-errant in the world, and that all the books of chivalry are false, lying, mischievous, and unprofitable to the commonwealth; and that I have done ill in reading, worse in believing, and worst of all in imitating them, by taking upon me the rigorous profession of knight-errantry, which they teach: and you deny, that ever there were any Amadises, either of Gaul or of Greece, or any other knights, such as those books are full of.'

'It is all precisely as you say,' quoth the canon.

To which Don Quixote answered:

'You also were pleased to add, that those books had done me much prejudice, having turned my brain, and reduced me to the being carried about in a cage; and that it would be better for me to amend and change my course of study, by reading other books, more true, more pleasant, and more instructive.'

'True,' quoth the canon.

'Why then,' said Don Quixote, 'in my opinion you are the madman and the enchanted person, since you have set yourself to utter so many blasphemies against a thing so universally received in the world, and held for such truth, that he who should deny it, as you do, deserves the same punishment you are pleased to say you bestow on those books, when you read them, and they vex you. For to endeavour to make people believe, that there never was an Amadis in the world, nor any other of the knights-adventurers, of which histories are full, would be to endeavour to persuade them, that the sun does not enlighten, the frost give cold, nor the earth yield sustenance.

'What genius can there be in the world able to persuade another, that the affair of the Infanta Floripes and Guy of Burgundy was not true; and that of Fierabras at the bridge of Mantible, which fell out in the time of Charlemagne;*

which, I vow to God, is as true, as that it is now daylight?
And, if these be lies, so must it also be, that there ever was
a Hector or an Achilles, or a Trojan war, or the Twelve Peers
of France, or King Arthur of England, who is still wandering
about transformed into a raven, and is every minute expected
in his kingdom. And will any one presume to say, that the
history of Guarino Mezquino,* and that of the pursuit of the
Saint Graal are lies;* or that the amours of Sir Tristram and
the queen Iseo,* and those of Guinevere and Lancelot, are
also apocryphal; whereas there are persons who almost remember to have seen the Duenna Quintañona, who was the
best skinner of wine that ever Great Britain could boast of?
And this is so certain, that I remember my grandmother, by
my father's side, when she saw any Duenna reverently coifed,
would say to me: "Look, grandson, that old woman is very
like the Duenna Quintañona." From whence I infer that she
must either have known her, or at least have seen some
portait of her. Then, who can deny the truth of the history
of Peter of Provence, and the fair Magalona,* since to this
very day, is to be seen in the king's armoury, the peg,
wherewith he steered the wooden horse, upon which he rode
through the air;* which peg is somewhat bigger than the pole
of a coach: and close by the peg stands Babieca's saddle.*
And in Roncesvalles is to be seen Orlando's horn,* as big
as a great beam. From all which I conclude, that there were
the Twelve Peers, the Peters, the Cids, and such other knights
as those the world call adventurers.

'If not, let them also tell me, that the valiant Portuguese
John de Merlo* was no knight-errant; he, who went to
Burgundy, and in the city of Ras fought the famous lord of
Charni, Monseigneur Pierre, and afterwards in the city of
Basle, with Monseigneur Enrique of Remestan, coming off
from both engagements conqueror, and loaded with honourable fame; besides the adventures and challenges, accomplished in Burgundy, of the valiant Spaniards Pedro Barba
and Gutierre Quixada (from whom I am lineally descended),
who vanquished the sons of the Count Saint Paul. Let them
deny, likewise, that Don Fernando de Guevara travelled into
Germany in quest of adventures, where he fought with

Messire George, a knight of the duke of Austria's court. Let
them say, that the jousts of Suero de Quiñones of the Pass
were all mockery; with the enterprises of Monseigneur Louis
de Falces against Don Gonzalo de Guzman, a Castilian
knight, with many more exploits, performed by Christian
knights of these and of foreign kingdoms; all so authentic
and true, that I say again, whoever denies them, must be void
of all sense and reason.'

The canon stood in admiration to hear the medley Don
Quixote made of truths and lies, and to see how skilled he
was in all matters any way relating to knight-errantry; and
therefore answered him:

'I cannot deny, Señor Don Quixote, but there is some truth
in what you say, especially in relation to the Spanish knights-
errant; and I am also ready to allow, that there were the
Twelve Peers of France: but I can never believe they did all
those things ascribed to them by Archbishop Turpin:* for
the truth is, they were knights chosen by the kings of France,
and called peers, as being all equal in quality and prowess:
at least, if they were not, it was fit they should be so, and
in this respect, they were not unlike our religious military
orders of Santiago or Calatrava, which presuppose that the
professors are, or ought to be, cavaliers of worth, valour, and
family: and, as nowadays we say, a knight of St. John, or of
Alcántara, in those times they said, a knight of the Twelve
Peers, those of that military order being twelve in number,
and all equal. That there was a Cid, is beyond all doubt, as
likewise a Bernardo del Carpio;* but that they performed the
exploits told of them, I believe there is great reason to
suspect. As to Peter of Provence's peg, and its standing close
by Babieca's saddle, in the king's armoury, I confess my sin,
in being so ignorant, or short-sighted, that, though I have
seen the saddle, I never could discover the peg; which is
somewhat strange, considering how big you say it is.'

'Yet, without all question, there it is,' replied Don Quixote,
'by the same token that they say it is kept in a leathern case,
that it may not take rust.'

'It may be so,' answered the canon: 'but by the holy orders
I have received, I do not remember to have seen it. But

supposing I should grant you it is there, I do not therefore think myself bound to believe the stories of so many Amadises, nor those of such a rabble rout of knights as we hear of: nor is it reasonable, that a gentleman, so honourable, of such excellent parts, and endued with so good an understanding as yourself, should be persuaded that such strange follies as are written in the absurd books of chivalry are true.'

CHAPTER 50

Of the ingenious contest between Don Quixote and the canon, with other accidents.

'A GOOD jest indeed!' answered Don Quixote: 'that books, printed with the licence of kings, and the approbation of the examiners, read with general pleasure, and applauded by great and small, poor and rich, learned and ignorant, gentry and commonalty, in short, by all sorts of people, of what state or condition soever they be, should be all lies, and especially carrying such an appearance of truth! for do they not tell us the father, the mother, the country, the kindred, the age, the place, with a particular detail of every action, performed daily by such a knight or knights? Good sir, be silent, and do not utter such blasphemies; and believe me, I advise you to act in this affair like a discreet person: do but peruse them, and you will find what pleasure attends this kind of reading.

'For, pray tell me, can there be a greater satisfaction than to see, placed as it were before our eyes, a vast lake of boiling pitch, and in it a prodigious number of serpents, snakes, crocodiles, and divers other kinds of fierce and dreadful creatures, swimming up and down; and from the midst of the lake to hear a most dreadful voice, saying: "O knight, whoever thou art that standest beholding this tremendous lake, if thou art desirous to enjoy the happiness that lies concealed beneath these sable waters, show the valour of thy undaunted breast, and plunge thyself headlong into the midst of this black and burning liquor; for, if thou dost not, thou wilt be unworthy to see the mighty wonders enclosed therein, and contained in the seven castles of the seven enchanted nymphs, who dwell beneath this horrid blackness."

'And scarcely has the knight heard the fearful voice, when, without further consideration, or reflecting upon the danger to which he exposes himself, and even without putting off his cumbersome and weighty armour, recommending himself to God and his mistress, he plunges into the middle of the boiling pool; and, when he neither heeds nor considers what may become of him, he finds himself in the midst of flowery fields, with which those of Elysium can in no wise compare. There the sky seems more transparent, and the sun shines with a fresher brightness. Beyond it appears a pleasing forest, so green and shady, that its verdure rejoices the sight, whilst the ears are entertained with the sweet and artless notes of an infinite number of little painted birds, hopping to and fro among the intricate branches. Here he discovers a warbling brook, whose cool waters, resembling liquid crystal, run murmuring over the fine sands and snowy pebbles, out-glittering sifted gold and purest pearl. There he espies an artificial fountain of variegated jasper and polished marble. Here he beholds another of rustic work, in which the minute shells of the mussel, with the white and yellow wreathed houses of the snail, placed in orderly confusion, interspersed with pieces of glittering crystal and pellucid emeralds, compose a work of such variety, that art, imitating nature, seems here to surpass her. Then on a sudden he descries a strong castle, or stately palace, whose walls are of massy gold, the battlements of diamonds, and the gates of hyacinths: in short, the structure is so admirable, that, though the materials whereof it is framed, are no less than diamonds, carbuncles, rubies, pearls, gold, and emeralds, yet the workmanship is still more precious.

'And, after having seen all this, can anything be more charming than to behold, sallying forth at the castle gate, a goodly troop of damsels, whose bravery and gorgeous attire should I pretend to describe, as the histories do at large, I should never have done? And then she who appears to be the chief of them all, presently takes by the hand the daring knight, who threw himself into the burning lake, and, without speaking a word, carries him into the rich palace, or castle, and stripping him as naked as his mother bore him, bathes him in milk-warm water, and then anoints him all over with odoriferous essences, and puts on him a shirt of the finest lawn, all sweet-scented and perfumed. Then comes another damsel, and throws over his shoulders a mantle, reckoned worth, at the very least, a city or more. What a sight is it then, when after this he is carried to another hall, to behold the tables spread in such order, that he is struck with suspense and wonder! then to see him wash his hands in water distilled from amber and sweet-scented flowers: to see him seated in a chair of ivory! to behold the damsels waiting upon him in marvellous silence! then to see such variety of delicious viands, so savourily dressed, that the appetite is at a loss to direct the hand! To hear soft music while he is eating, without knowing who it is that sings, or from whence the sounds proceed! And when dinner is ended, and the cloth taken away, the knight lolling in his chair, and perhaps picking his teeth, according to custom, enters unexpectedly at the hall door a damsel much more beautiful than any of the former, and seating herself by the knight's side, begins to give him an account what castle that is, and how she is enchanted in it, with sundry other matters which surprise the knight, and raise the admiration of those who read his history.

'I will enlarge no further hereupon; for from hence you may conclude, that whatever part one reads of whatever history of knights-errant must needs cause delight and wonder in the reader. Believe me then, sir, and, as I have already hinted, read these books, and you will find, that they will banish all your melancholy, and ameliorate your disposition, if it happens to be a bad one. This I can say for myself, that since I have been a knight-errant, I am become valiant, civil, liberal, well-bred, generous, courteous, daring, affable, patient, a sufferer of toils, imprisonments, and enchantments: and though it be so little a while since I saw myself locked up in a cage like a madman, yet I expect, by the valour of my arm, heaven favouring, and fortune not oppugning, in a few days to see myself king of some kingdom, wherein I may display the gratitude and liberality enclosed in this breast of mine: for, upon my faith, sir, the poor man is disabled from practising the virtue of liberality, though he possess it in never so eminent a degree; and the gratitude which consists only in inclination is a dead thing, even as faith without works is dead. For which reason I should be glad that fortune would offer me speedily some opportunity of becoming an emperor, that I may show my heart by doing good to my friends, especially to poor Sancho Panza here, my squire, who is the honestest man in the world; and I would fain bestow on him an earldom, as I have long since promised him, but that I fear he will not have ability sufficient to govern his estate.'

Sancho overheard his master's last words, to whom he said: 'Take you the pains, Señor Don Quixote, to procure me this same earldom, so often promised by you, and so long expected by me; for I assure you I shall not want for ability sufficient to govern it. But supposing I had not, I have heard say, there are people in the world who take lordships to farm, paying the owners so much a year, and taking upon themselves the whole management thereof, whilst the lord himself, with outstretched legs, lies along at his ease, enjoying the rent they give him, without concerning himself any further about it. Just so will I do, and give myself no more trouble than needs must, but immediately surrender all up, and live upon my rents like any duke, and let the world rub.'

'This, brother Sancho,' quoth the canon, 'is to be understood only as to the enjoyment of the revenue; but as to the administration of justice, the lord himself must look to that; and for this, ability, sound judgement, and especially an upright intention, are required; for if these be wanting in the beginnings, the means and ends will always be erroneous; and therefore God usually prospers the good intentions of the simple, and disappoints the evil designs of the cunning.'

'I do not understand these philosophies,' answered Sancho; 'I only know, I wish I may as speedily have the earldom as I should know how to govern it; for I have as large a soul as another, and as large a body as the best of them: and I should be as much a king of my own dominions, as any one is of his: and being so, I would do what I pleased; and doing what I pleased, I should have my will; and having my will, I should be contented; and when one is contented, there is no more to be desired; and when there is no more to be desired, there's an end of it; and let the estate come, and God be with ye; and let us see it, as one blind man said to another.'

'These are no bad philosophies, as you say, Sancho,' quoth the canon: 'nevertheless there is a great deal more to be said upon the subject of earldoms.'

To which Don Quixote replied:

'I know not what more may be said: only I govern myself by the example of the great Amadis de Gaul, who made his squire knight of the Firm Island, and therefore I may, without scruple of conscience, make an earl of Sancho Panza, who is one of the best squires that ever knight-errant had.'

The canon was amazed at Don Quixote's methodical and orderly madness, the manner of his describing the adventure of the Knight of the Lake, the impression made upon him by those premeditated lies he had read in his books; and lastly, he admired the simplicity of Sancho, who so vehemently desired to obtain the earldom his master had promised him.

By this time the canon's servants, who went to the inn for the sumpter-mule, were come back; and spreading a carpet on the green grass, they sat down under the shade of some trees, and dined there, that the wagoner might not lose the conveniency of that fresh pasture, as we have said before. And while they were eating, they heard on a sudden a loud noise, and the sound of a little bell in a thicket of briers and thorns that was hard by; and at the same instant they saw a beautiful she-goat, speckled with black, white, and grey, run out of the thicket.* After her came a goatherd, calling to her aloud in his wonted language, to stop and come back to the fold. The fugitive goat, trembling and affrighted, betook herself to the company, as it were for their protection, and there she stopped. The goatherd came up, and taking her by the horns, as if she were capable of discourse and reasoning, he said to her:

'Ah! wanton, spotted fool! what caprice hath made thee halt thus of late days? what wolves wait for thee, child? wilt thou tell me, pretty one, what this means? but what else can it mean, but that thou art a female, and therefore canst not be quiet? a curse on thy humours, and on all theirs whom thou resemblest so much! Turn back, my love, turn back; for though, perhaps, you will not be so contented, at least you will be more safe in your own fold, and among your own companions: and if you, who are to look after and guide them, go yourself so much astray, what must become of them?'

The goatherd's words delighted all the hearers extremely, especially the canon, who said to him:

'I entreat you, brother, be not in such a hurry to force back this goat so soon to her fold; for since, as you say, she is a female, she will follow her own natural instinct, though you take never so much pains to hinder her. Come, take this morsel, and then drink: whereby you will temper your choler, and in the meanwhile the goat will rest herself.'

And in saying this, he gave him the hinder quarter of a cold rabbit on the point of a fork. The goatherd took it, and thanked him; then drank, and sat down quietly, and said:

'I would not have you, gentlemen, take me for a foolish fellow, for having talked sense to this animal; for in truth the words I spoke to her are not without a mystery. I am a country fellow, it is true, yet not so much a rustic but I know the difference between conversing with men and beasts.'

'I verily believe you,' said the priest; 'for I have found, by experience, that the mountains breed learned men, and the cottages of shepherds contain philosophers.'

'At least, sir,' replied the goatherd, 'they afford men, who have some knowledge from experience; and to convince you of this truth, though I seem to invite myself without being asked, if it be not tiresome to you, and if you please, gentlemen, to lend me your attention, I will tell you a true story, which will confirm what I and this same gentleman' (pointing to the priest) 'have said.'

To this Don Quixote answered:

'Seeing this business has somewhat the face of an adventure,* I for my part will listen to you, brother, with all my heart, and so will all these gentlemen, being discreet and ingenious persons, and such as love to hear curious novelties, that surprise, gladden, and entertain the senses, as I do not doubt but your story will do.'

'Begin then, friend, for we will all hearken.'

'I draw my stake,' quoth Sancho, 'and hie me with this pasty to yonder brook, where I intend to stuff myself for three days; for I have heard my master, Don Quixote, say: that the squire of a knight-errant must eat, when he has it, until he can eat no longer, because it often happens that they get into some wood so intricate, that there is no way of hitting the way out in six days; and then, if a man has not his belly well lined, or his wallet well provided, there he may remain, and often does remain, until he is turned into a mummy.'

'You are in the right, Sancho,' said Don Quixote: 'go whither you will, and eat what you can; for I am already sated, and want only to give my mind its repast, which I am going to do, by listening to this honest man's story.'

'We all do the same,' quoth the canon, and then desired the goatherd to begin the tale he had promised. The goatherd gave the goat, which he held by the horns, two slaps on the back with the palm of his hand, saying:

'Lie thee down by me, speckled fool; for we have time and to spare for returning to our fold.'

The goat seemed to understand him; for as soon as her master was seated, she laid herself close by him very quietly, and, looking up in his face, seemed to signify she was attentive to what the goatherd was going to relate, who began his story in this manner:

CHAPTER 51

Which treats of what the goatherd related to all those who accompanied Don Quixote.

'THREE leagues from this valley there is a town, which, though but small, is one of the richest in all these parts; and therein dwelt a farmer, of so good a character, that, though esteem is usually annexed to riches, yet he was more respected for his virtue than for the wealth he possessed. But that which completed his happiness, as he used to say himself, was his having a daughter of such extraordinary beauty, rare discretion, gracefulness, and virtue, that whoever knew and beheld her, was in admiration, to see the surpassing endowments wherewith heaven and nature had enriched her. When a child, she was pretty, and, as she grew up, became still more and more beautiful, until, at the age of sixteen, she was beauty itself. And now the fame of her beauty began to extend itself through all the neighbouring villages: do I say, through the neighbouring villages only? It spread itself to the remotest cities, and even made its way into the palaces of kings, and reached the ears of all sorts of people, who came to see her from all parts, as if she had been some relic, or wonder-working image. Her father guarded her, and she guarded herself; for there are no padlocks, bolts, or bars, that secure a maiden better than her own reserve. The wealth of the father and the beauty of the daughter, induced many, both of the town, and strangers, to demand her to wife. But he, whose right it was to dispose of so precious a jewel, was perplexed, not knowing, amidst the great number of importunate suitors, on which to bestow her.

'Among the many who were thus disposed, I was one, and flattered myself with many and great hopes of success, as being known to her father, born in the same village, untainted in blood, in the flower of my age, tolerably rich, and of no despicable understanding. With the very same advantages another of our village demanded her also in marriage; which occasioned a suspense and balancing of her father's will, who thought his daughter would be very well matched with either of us: and, to get out of this perplexity, he determined to acquaint Leandra with it (for that is the rich maiden's name, who has reduced me to this wretched state), considering that since our pretensions were equal, it was best to leave the choice to his beloved daughter; an example worthy the imitation of all parents, who would marry their children. I do not say, they should give them their choice in things prejudicial, but they should propose to them good ones, and out of them let them choose to their minds. For my part, I know not what was Leandra's liking: I only know that her father put us both off by pleading the too tender age of his daughter, and with such general expressions as neither laid any obligations upon him, nor disobliged either of us. My rival's name is Anselmo, and mine Eugenio; for it is fit you should know the names of the persons concerned in this tragedy, the catastrophe of which is still depending, though one may easily foresee it will be disastrous.

'About that time there came to our town one Vincent de la Roca, son of a poor farmer of the same village: which Vincent was come out of Italy, and other countries, where he had served in the wars. A captain, who happened to march that way with his company, had carried him away from our town at twelve years of age, and the young man returned at the end of twelve years more, in the garb of a soldier, set off with a thousand colours, and hung with a thousand crystal trinkets, and fine steel chains. To-day he put on one finery, to-morrow another; but all slight and counterfeit, of little weight, and less value. The country folks, who are naturally malicious, and, if they have ever so little leisure, are malice itself, observed, and reckoned up all his trappings and gew-gaws, and found that he had three suits of apparel, of different colours, with hose and garters to them: but he disguised them so many different ways, and with many inventions, that, if one had not counted them, one would have sworn he had above ten suits, and above twenty plumes of feathers. And let not what I have been saying of his dress be looked upon as impertinent or superfluous: for it makes a considerable part of this story. He used to seat himself on a stone bench, under a great poplar-tree in our market-place, and there he would hold us all gaping, and listening to the exploits he would be telling us. There was no country on the whole globe he had not seen, nor battle he had not been in. He had slain more Moors than are in Morocco and Tunis, and fought more duels, as he said, than Gante, Luna,* Diego Garcia de Paredes, and a thousand others, and always came off victorious, without having lost a drop of blood. Then again he would be showing us marks of wounds, which though they were not to be discerned, he would persuade us

were so many musket-shots, received in several actions and
fights. In a word, with an unheard-of arrogance, he would
Thou his equals and acquaintance, saying, his arm was his
father, his deeds his pedigree, and that, under the title of
soldier, he owed the king himself nothing. To these bravadoes
was added his being somewhat of a musician, and scratching
a little upon the guitar, which some said he could make speak.
But his graces and accomplishments did not end here; for he
was also a bit of a poet, and would compose a ballad a league
and a half in length on every childish accident that happened
in the village.

'Now this soldier, whom I have here described, this Vincent de la Roca, this hero, this gallant, this musician, this
poet, was often seen and admired by Leandra from a window
of her house which faced the market-place. She was struck
with the tinsel of his gaudy apparel: his ballads enchanted
her; and he gave at least twenty copies about of all he
composed: the exploits he related of himself reached her ears:
lastly (for so it seems the devil had ordained), she fell
downright in love with him, before he had entertained the
presumption of courting her. And, as in affairs of love, none
are so easily accomplished as those which are favoured by
the inclination of the lady, Leandra and Vincent easily came
to an agreement, and before any of the multitude of her
suitors had the least suspicion of her design, she had already
accomplished it: for she left the house of her dear and
beloved father (for mother she had none), and absented
herself from the town with the soldier, who came off with
this attempt more triumphantly than from any of those others
he had so arrogantly boasted of.

'This event amazed the whole town, and all that heard
anything of it. I, for my part, was confounded, Anselmo
astonished, her father sad, her kindred ashamed, justice
alarmed, and the troopers of the Holy Brotherhood in readiness. They beset the highways, and searched the woods,
leaving no place unexamined; and, at the end of three days,
they found the poor fond Leandra in a cave of a mountain,
naked to her shift, and stripped of a large sum of money,
and several valuable jewels, she had carried away from home.

They brought her back into the presence of her disconsolate father; they asked her how this misfortune had befallen her; she readily confessed, that Vincent de la Roca had deceived her, and, upon promise of marriage, had persuaded her to leave her father's house, telling her he would carry her to Naples, the richest and most delicious city of the whole world; that she, through too much credulity and in advertency, had believed him, and, robbing her father, had put all into his hands the night she was first missing: and that he conveyed her to a craggy mountain, and shut her up in that cave, in which they had found her. She also related to them how the soldier plundered her of everything but her honour, and left her there and fled; a circumstance which made us all wonder afresh; for it was no easy matter to persuade us of the young man's continency: but she affirmed it with so much earnestness, that her father was in some sort comforted, making no great account of the other riches the soldier had taken from his daughter, since he had left her that jewel, which once lost can never be recovered.

'The very same day that Leandra returned, she disappeared again from our eyes, her father sending and shutting her up in a nunnery belonging to a town not far distant, in hopes that time might wear off a good part of the reproach his daughter had brought upon herself. Her tender years were some excuse for her fault, especially with those who had no interest in her being good or bad; but they who are acquainted with her good sense and understanding, could not ascribe her fault to her ignorance, but to her levity, and to the natural propensity of the sex, which is generally unthinking and disorderly. Leandra being shut up, Anselmo's eyes were blinded: at least they saw nothing that could afford them any satisfaction: and mine were in darkness, without light to direct them to any pleasurable object. The absence of Leandra increased our sadness, and diminished our patience; we cursed the soldier's fincry, and detested her father's want of precaution.

'At last, Anselmo and I agreed to quit the town, and betake ourselves to this valley, where, he feeding a great number of sheep of his own, and I a numerous herd of goats of mine, we pass our lives among these trees, giving vent to our passions, or singing together the praises or reproaches of the fair Leandra, or sighing alone, and each apart communicating our plaints to heaven. Several others of Leandra's suitors, in imitation of us, are come to these rocky mountains, practising the same employments; and they are so numerous, that this place seems to be converted into the pastoral Arcadia, it is so full of shepherds and folds: nor is there any part of it where the name of the beautiful Leandra is not heard. One utters execrations against her, calling her fond, fickle, and immodest; another condemns her forwardness and levity: some excuse and pardon her: others arraign and condemn her: one celebrates her beauty: another rails at her ill qualities: in short, all blame and all adore her; and the madness of all rises to that pitch, that some complain of her disdain who never spoke to her: yea, some there are who bemoan themselves, and feel the raging disease of jealousy, though she never gave any occasion for it; for, as I have said, her guilt was known before her inclination. There is no hollow of a rock, nor brink of a rivulet, nor shade of a tree, that is not occupied by some shepherd, who is recounting his misfortunes to the air: the echo, whereever it can be formed, repeats the name of Leandra: the mountains resound "Leandra"; the brooks murmur "Leandra": in short, Leandra holds us all in suspense and enchanted, hoping without hope, and fearing without knowing what we fear. Among these extravagant madmen, he who shows the least and the most sense is my rival Anselmo, who, having so many other causes of complaint, complains only of absence, and to the sound of a rebeck, which he touches to admiration, pours forth his complaints in verses, which discover an excellent genius. I follow an easier, and, in my opinion, a better way, which is to inveigh against the levity of women, their inconstancy, and double-dealing, their lifeless promises, and broken faith; and, in short, the little discretion they show in placing their affections, or making their choice.

'This, gentlemen, was the occasion of the expressions and language I used to this goat when I came hither; for, being a female, I despise her, though she be the best of all my

flock. This is the story I promised to tell you: if I have been
tedious in the relation I will endeavour to make you amends
by my service: my cottage is hard by, where I have new milk,
and very savoury cheese, with variety of fruits of the season,
not less agreeable to the sight than to the taste.'

CHAPTER 52

*Of the quarrel between Don Quixote and the goatherd, with
the rare adventure of the disciplinants, which he happily
accomplished with the sweat of his brow.*

THE goatherd's tale gave a general pleasure to all that heard
it, especially to the canon, who, with an unusual curiosity,
took notice of his manner of telling it, in which he discovered
more of the polite courtier, than of the rude goatherd; and
therefore he said, that the priest was very much in the right
in affirming that the mountains produced men of letters. They
all offered their service to Eugenio; but the most liberal of
his offers upon this occasion was Don Quixote, who said to
him:

'In truth, brother goatherd, were I in a capacity of undertaking any new adventure. I would immediately set forward
to do you a good turn, by fetching Leandra out of the
nunnery, in which, doubtless, she is detained against her will,
in spite of the abbess and all opposers, and putting her into
your hands, to be disposed of at your pleasure, so far as is
consistent with the laws of chivalry, which enjoin that no
kind of violence be offered to damsels: though I hope in
God our Lord, that the power of one malicious enchanter
shall not be so prevalent, but that the power of another and
a better-intentioned one may prevail over it; and then I
promise you my aid, and protection, as I am obliged by my
profession, which is no other than to favour the weak and
necessitous.'

The goatherd stared at Don Quixote; and observing his
bad plight and scurvy appearance, he whispered the barber,
who sat next him:

'Pray, sir, who is this man, who makes such a strange figure, and talks so extravagantly?'

'Who should it be,' answered the barber,' but the famous Don Quixote de la Mancha, the redresser of injuries, the righter of wrongs, the reliever of maidens, the dread of giants, and the conqueror of battles?'

'This,' said the goatherd, 'is like what we read of in the books of knights-errant, who did all that you tell me of this man: though, as I take it, either your worship is in jest, or the apartments in this gentleman's skull are unfurnished.'

'You are a very great rascal,' said Don Quixote at this instant, 'and you are the empty-skulled and the shallow-brained; for I am fuller than ever was the whoreson drab that bore thee.'

And, so saying, and muttering on, he snatched up a loaf that was near him, and with it struck the goatherd full in the face, with so much fury, that he laid his nose flat. The goatherd, who did not understand raillery, perceiving how much in earnest he was treated, without any respect to the carpet or tablecloth, or to the company that sat about it, leaped upon Don Quixote, and, gripping him by the throat with both hands, would doubtless have strangled him, had not Sancho Panza come up in that instant, and, taking him by the shoulders, thrown him back on the table, breaking the dishes and platters, and spilling and overturning all that was upon it. Don Quixote, finding himself loose, ran at the goatherd, who, being kicked and trampled upon by Sancho, and his face all over blood, was feeling about, upon all fours, for some knife or other, to take a bloody revenge withal: but the canon and the priest prevented him; and the barber contrived it so, that the goatherd got Don Quixote under him, on whom he poured such a shower of buffets, that there rained as much blood from the visage of the poor knight as there did from his own. The canon and the priest were ready to burst with laughter; the troopers of the Holy Brotherhood danced and capered for joy; and they stood hallooing them on, as people do dogs when they are fighting: only Sancho was at his wits' end, not being able to get loose from one of the canon's servants, who held him from going to assist his master.

In short, while all were in high joy and merriment, excepting the two combatants, who were still worrying one another, on a sudden they heard the sound of a trumpet, so dismal, that it made them turn their faces towards the way from whence they fancied the sound came: but he who was most surprised at hearing it was Don Quixote, who, though he was under the goatherd, sorely against his will, and more than indifferently mauled, said to him:

'Brother devil (for it is impossible you should be anything else, since you have had the valour and strength to subdue mine), truce, I beseech you, for one hour; for the dolorous sound of that trumpet, which reaches our ears, seems to summon me to some new adventure.'

The goatherd, who by this time was pretty well weary of mauling, and being mauled, immediately let him go, and Don Quixote, getting upon his legs, turned his face towards the place whence the sound came, and presently saw several people descending from a rising ground, arrayed in white, after the manner of disciplinants.

The case was, that the clouds, that year, had failed to refresh the earth with seasonable showers, and throughout all the villages of that district they made processions, disciplines, and public prayers, beseeching God to open the hands of His mercy, and send them rain: and for this purpose the people of a town hard by were coming in procession to a devout hermitage, built upon the side of a hill bordering upon that valley. Don Quixote perceiving the strange attire of the disciplinants, without recollecting how often he must have seen the like before, imagined it was some adventure, and that it belonged to him alone, as a knight-errant, to undertake it: and he was the more confirmed in his fancy by thinking, that an image they had with them covered with black, was some lady of note, whom those miscreants and discourteous ruffians were forcing away. And no sooner had he taken this into his head, than he ran with great agility to Rosinante, who was grazing about; and taking the bridle and buckler from the pommel of the saddle, he bridled him in a trice, and, demanding from Sancho his sword, he mounted Rosinante, and braced his target, and with a loud voice said to all that were present:

'Now, my worthy companions, you shall see of what consequence it is that there are in the world such as profess the order of chivalry: now, I say, you shall see, by my restoring liberty to that good lady, who is carried captive yonder, whether knights-errant are to be valued, or not.'

And so saying, he laid legs to Rosinante (for spurs he had none) and on a hand-gallop (for we nowhere read, in all this faithful history, that ever Rosinante went full speed) he ran to encounter the disciplinants. The priest, the canon, and the barber, in vain endeavoured to stop him: and in vain did Sancho cry out, saying:

'Whither go you, Señor Don Quixote? what devils are in you, that instigate you to assault the Catholic faith? consider, a curse on me! that this is a procession of disciplinants, and that the lady, carried upon the bier, is an image of the Blessed and Immaculate Virgin: have a care what you do; for this once I am sure you do not know.'

Sancho wearied himself to no purpose; for his master was so bent upon encountering the men in white, and delivering the mourning lady, that he heard not a word, and, if he had, would not have come back, though the king himself had commanded him.

Being now come up to the procession, he checked Rosinante, who already had a desire to rest a little, and with a disordered and hoarse voice, said:

'You there, who cover your faces, for no good I suppose, stop, and give ear to what I shall say.'

The first who stopped were they who carried the image; and one of the four ecclesiastics, who sung the litanies, observing the strange figure of Don Quixote, the leanness of Rosinante, and other ridiculous circumstances attending the knight, answered him, saying:

'Good brother, if you have anything to say to us, say it quickly; for these our brethren are tearing their flesh to pieces, and we cannot, nor is it reasonable we should, stop to hear anything, unless it be so short, that it may be said in two words.'

'I will say it in one,' replied Don Quixote, 'and it is this; that you immediately set at liberty that fair lady, whose tears and sorrowful countenance are evident tokens of her being carried away against her will, and that you have done her some notorious injury; and I, who was born into the world on purpose to redress such wrongs, will not suffer you to proceed one step further, until you have given her the liberty she desires and deserves.'

By these expressions, all that heard them gathered that Don Quixote must be some madman; whereupon they fell a-laughing very heartily; which was adding fuel to the fire of Don Quixote's choler: for, without saying a word more he drew his sword, and attacked the bearers; one of whom, leaving the burden to his comrades, stepped forward to encounter Don Quixote, brandishing a pole whereon he rested the bier when they made a stand: and receiving on it a huge stroke, which the knight let fly on him, and which broke it in two, with what remained of it he gave Don Quixote such a blow on the shoulder of his sword-arm, that, his target not being able to ward off so furious an assault, poor Don Quixote fell to the ground in evil plight. Sancho Panza, who came puffing close after him, perceiving him fallen, called out to his adversary not to strike him again, for he was a poor enchanted knight, who never had done anybody harm in all the days of his life. But that which made the rustic forbear, was not Sancho's crying out, but his seeing that Don Quixote stirred neither hand nor foot; and so, believing he had killed him, in all haste he tucked up his frock under his girdle, and he began to fly away over the field as nimble as a buck.

By this time all Don Quixote's company was come up, and the processioners, seeing them running towards them, and with them the troopers of the Holy Brotherhood with their crossbows, began to fear some ill accident, and drew up in a circle round the image; and, lifting up their hoods, and grasping their whips, as the ecclesiastics did their tapers, they stood expecting the assault, determined to defend themselves, and, if they could, to offend their aggressors. But fortune ordered it better than they imagined: for all that Sancho did, was, to throw himself upon the body of his master, and to pour forth the most dolorous and ridiculous lamentation in the world, believing verily that he was dead. The priest was known by another priest, who came in the procession, and their being acquainted dissipated the fear of the two squadrons. The first priest gave the second an account in two words who Don Quixote was; whereupon he and the whole rout of disciplinants went to see whether the poor knight was dead or not, and they overheard Sancho Panza say, with tears in his eyes:

'O flower of chivalry, who by one single thwack hast finished the career of thy well-spent life! O glory of thy race, credit and renown of La Mancha, yea, of the whole world, which, by wanting thee, will be overrun with evil-doers, who will no longer fear the being chastised for their iniquities! O liberal above all Alexanders, seeing that, for eight months' service only, thou hast given me the best island the sea doth compass or surround! O thou that wert humble with the haughty, and arrogant with the humble, undertaker of dangers, sufferer of affronts, in love without cause, imitator of the good, scourge of the wicked, enemy of the base; in a word, knight-errant, which is all that can be said!'

At Sancho's cries and lamentations Don Quixote revived, and the first word he said, was:

'He who lives absented from thee, sweetest Dulcinea, is subject to greater miseries than these. Help, friend Sancho, to lay me upon the enchanted car; for I am no longer in a condition to press the saddle of Rosinante, all this shoulder being mashed to pieces.'

'That I will do with all my heart, dear sir,' answered Sancho; 'and let us return home in company of these gentlemen, who wish you well, and there we will give order about another sally, that may prove of more profit and renown.'

'You say well, Sancho,' answered Don Quixote, 'and it will be great prudence in us to wait until the evil influence of the stars which now reigns, is over-passed.'

The canon, the priest, and the barber told him, they approved his resolution; and so, having received a great deal

of pleasure from the simplicities of Sancho Panza, they placed
Don Quixote in the wagon, as before.

The procession resumed its former order, and went on its
way. The goatherd bid them all farewell. The troopers would
go no farther, and the priest paid them what they had agreed
for. The canon desired the priest to give him advice of what
befell Don Quixote, and whether his madness was cured or
continued, and so took leave, and pursued his journey. In
fine, they all parted, and took their several ways, leaving the
priest, the barber, Don Quixote, and Sancho, with good
Rosinante, who bore all accidents as patiently as his master.
The wagoner yoked his oxen, and accommodated Don Quixote on a truss of hay, and with his accustomed pace jogged
on the way the priest directed.

On the sixth day, they arrived at Don Quixote's village,
and entered it about noon; and it being Sunday, all the people
were standing in the market-place, through the midst of
which Don Quixote's car must of necessity pass. Everybody
ran to see who was in the wagon, and, when they found it
was their townsman, they were greatly surprised, and a boy
ran full speed to acquaint the housekeeper and niece, that
their uncle and master was coming home, weak and pale, and
stretched upon a truss of hay, in a wagon drawn by oxen. It
was piteous to hear the outcries the two good women raised,
to see the buffets they gave themselves, and how they cursed
afresh the damned books of chivalry; and all this was renewed
by seeing Don Quixote coming in at the gate.

Upon the news of Don Quixote's arrival, Sancho Panza's
wife, who knew her husband was gone with him, to serve
him as his squire, repaired thither; and as soon as she saw
Sancho, the first thing she asked him was, whether the ass
was come home well. Sancho answered he was, and in a
better condition than his master.

'The Lord be praised,' replied she, 'for so great a mercy
to me. But tell me, friend, what good have you got by your
squireship? what petticoat do you bring home to me, and
what shoes to your children?'

'I bring nothing of all this, dear wife,' quoth Sancho; 'but
I bring other things of greater moment and consequence.'

'I am very glad of that,' answered the wife: 'pray, show me these things of greater moment and consequence, my friend: for I would fain see them, to rejoice this heart of mine, which has been so sad and discontented all the long time of your absence.'

'You shall see them at home, wife,' quoth Sancho, 'and be satisfied at present; for, if it please God, that we make another sally in quest of adventures, you will soon see me an earl or governor of an island, and not an ordinary one neither, but one of the best that is to be had.'

'Grant heaven it may be so, husband,' quoth the wife, 'for we have need enough of it. But pray tell me what you mean by islands; for I do not understand you.'

'Honey is not for the mouth of an ass,' answered Sancho: 'in good time you shall see, wife, yea, and admire to hear yourself styled ladyship, by all your vassals.'

'What do you mean, Sancho, by ladyship, islands, and vassals?' answered Teresa Panza:* for that was Sancho's wife's name, though they were not of kin, but because it is the custom in La Mancha for the wife to take the husband's name.

'Be not in so much haste, Teresa, to know all this,' said Sancho; 'let it suffice that I tell you the truth, and sew up your mouth. But for the present know, that there is nothing in the world so pleasant to an honest man, as to be squire to a knight-errant, and seeker of adventures. It is true, indeed, most of them are not so much to a man's mind as he could wish; for ninety-nine of a hundred one meets with fall out cross and unlucky. This I know by experience; for I have sometimes come off tossed in a blanket, and sometimes well cudgelled. Yet, for all that, it is a fine thing to be in expectation of accidents, traversing mountains, searching woods, marching over rocks, visiting castles, lodging in inns, all at discretion, and the devil a farthing to pay.'

All this discourse passed between Sancho Panza and his wife Teresa Panza, while the housekeeper and the niece received Don Quixote, and having pulled off his clothes, laid him in his old bed. He looked at them with eyes askew, not knowing perfectly where he was. The priest charged the niece

to take great care, and make much of her uncle, and to keep
a watchful eye over him, lest he should once more give them
the slip, telling her what difficulty they had to get him home
to his house. Here the two women exclaimed afresh, and
renewed their execrations against all books of chivalry, begging of heaven to confound to the centre of the abyss the
authors of so many lies and absurdities. Lastly, they remained
full of trouble and fear, lest they should lose their uncle and
master, as soon as ever he found himself a little better; and
it fell out as they imagined.

But the author of this history, though he applied himself
with the utmost curiosity and diligence to trace the exploits
Don Quixote performed in his third sally, could get no
account of them, at least from any authentic writings. Only
fame has preserved in the memoirs of La Mancha, that Don
Quixote, the third time he sallied from home, went to
Saragossa, where he was present at a famous tournament in
that city, and that there befell him things worthy of his valour
and good understanding. Nor should he have learned anything at all concerning his death, if a lucky accident had not
brought him acquainted with an aged physician, who had in
his custody a leaden box, found, as he said, under the ruins
of an ancient hermitage then rebuilding: in which box was
found a manuscript of parchment written in Gothic characters, but in Castilian verse, containing many of his exploits,
and giving an account of the beauty of Dulcinea del Toboso,
the figure of Rosinante, the fidelity of Sancho Panza, and the
burial of Don Quixote himself, with several epitaphs and
eulogies on his life and manners. All that could be read, and
perfectly made out, were those inserted here by the faithful
author of this strange and never before seen history; which
author desires no other reward from those who shall read it,
in recompense of the vast pains it has cost him to inquire
into and search all the archives of La Mancha to bring it to
light, but that they would afford him the same credit that
ingenious people* give to books of knight-errantry, which are
so well received in the world; and herewith he will reckon
himself well paid, and will rest satisfied; and will moreover
be encouraged to seek and find out others, if not as true, at

least of as much invention and entertainment. The first words, written in the parchment which was found in the leaden box, were these:—

THE ACADEMICIANS OF ARGAMASILLA,*

A TOWN OF LA MANCHA,

ON

THE LIFE AND DEATH OF

THE VALOROUS DON QUIXOTE DE LA MANCHA,

WROTE THIS:*

Monicongo, Academician of Argamasilla, on the sepulture of Don Quixote.

EPITAPH

La Mancha's thunderbolt of war,
  The sharpest wit and loftiest muse,
The arm, which from Gaeta far
  To Cathay did its force diffuse:

He, who, through love and valour's fire,
  Outstript great Amadis's fame,
Bid warlike Galaor retire,
  And silenc'd Belianis's name.

He, who, with helmet, sword, and shield,
  On Rosinante, steed well known,
Adventures sought in many a field,
  Lies underneath this frozen stone.

Paniaguado, Academician of Argamasilla, in praise of Dulcinea del Toboso.*

SONNET

She, whom you see, the plump and lusty dame,
  With high erected chest, and vigorous mien,
Was erst th' enamoured knight Don Quixote's flame,
  The fair Dulcinea, of Toboso queen.

For her, armed cap-à-pie with sword and shield,
  He trod the Sable Mountain* o'er and o'er;
For her he travers'd Montiel's well-known field,
  And in her service toils unnumber'd bore.

Hard fate! that death should crop so fine a flow'r,
And love o'er such a knight exert his tyrant power!

*Caprichoso, a most ingenious Academician of Argamasilla, in
praise of Don Quixote's horse, Rosinante.*

SONNET

  On the aspiring adamantine trunk
Of a huge tree, whose root with slaughter drunk
Sends forth a scent of war, La Mancha's knight,
Frantic with valour, and return'd from fight,
His bloody standard trembling in the air,
Hangs up his glittering armour beaming far,
With that fine-tempered steel, whose edge o'erthrows,
Hacks, hews, confounds, and routs opposing foes.
Unheard-of prowess! and unheard-of verse!
But art new strains invents new glories to rehearse.

  If Amadis to Grecia gives renown,
Much more her chief does fierce Bellona crown,
Prizing La Mancha more than Gaul or Greece,
As Quixote triumphs over Amadis.
Oblivion ne'er shall shroud his glorious name,
Whose very horse stands up to challenge fame,
Illustrious Rosinante, wondrous steed!
Not with more generous pride, or mettled speed,
His rider erst Rinaldo's Bayard bore,
Or his mad lord Orlando's Brilladore.

*Burlador, the little Academician of Argamasilla, on
Sancho Panza.*

SONNET

  See Sancho Panza, view him well,
And let this verse his praises tell,
His body was but small, 'tis true,

Yet had a soul as large as two.
No guile he knew, like some before him,
But simple as his mother bore him.
This gentle squire, on gentle ass,
Went gentle Rosinante's pace,
Following his lord from place to place.
To be an earl he did aspire,
And reason good for such desire:
But worth, in these ungrateful times,
To envied honour seldom climbs.

Vain mortals, give your wishes o'er,
And trust the flatterer, Hope, no more,
Whose promises, whate'er they seem,
End in a shadow or a dream.

Cachidiablo,* Academician of Argamasilla, on the sepulture of Don Quixote.

EPITAPH

Here lies an evil-errant knight,*
    Well bruised in many a fray,
Whose courser, Rosinante hight,
    Long bore him many a way.

Close by his loving master's side
    Lies booby Sancho Panza,
A trusty squire of courage tried,
    And true as ever man saw.

Tiquitoc, Academician of Argamasilla, on the sepulture of Dulcinea del Toboso.

Dulcinea, fat and fleshy, lies
    Beneath this frozen stone,
But since to frightful death a prize,
    Reduced to skin and bone.

Of goodly parentage she came,
    And had the lady in her;
She was the great Don Quixote's flame,
    But only death could win her.

These were all the verses that could be read: the rest, the characters being worm-eaten, were consigned to one of the Academicians, to find out their meaning by conjectures. We are informed he has done it after many lucubrations and much pains, and that he designs to publish them, giving us hopes of Don Quixote's third sally.

Forse altro canterà con miglior plettro.*

PART TWO

PREFACE TO THE READER

BLESS me! with what impatience, gentle, or (it may be) simple reader, must you now be waiting for this preface, expecting to find in it resentments, railings, and invectives against the author of the second Don Quixote; him I mean, who, it is said, was begotten in Tordesillas, and born in Tarragona!* But, in truth, it is not my design to give you that satisfaction; for though injuries are apt to awaken choler in the humblest breasts, yet in mine this rule must admit of an exception. You would have me, perhaps, call him ass, madman, and coxcomb: but I have no such design. Let his own sin be his punishment; let him chew upon it, and there let it rest.

But what I cannot bear resenting is, that he upbraids me with my age, and with having lost my hand; as if it were in my power to have hindered time from passing over my head, or as if my maim had been got in some drunken quarrel at a tavern, and not on the noblest occasion* that past or present ages have seen, or future can ever hope to see. If my wounds do not reflect a lustre in the eyes of those who barely behold them, they will, however, be esteemed by those who know how I came by them; for a soldier makes a better figure dead in battle, than alive and at liberty, in running away: and I am so firmly of this opinion, that could an impossibility be rendered practicable, and the same opportunity recalled, I would rather be again present in that prodigious action, than whole and sound without sharing in the glory of it. The scars a soldier shows in his face and breast, are stars which guide others to the haven of honour, and to the desire of just praise. And it must be observed that men do not write with grey hairs, but with the understanding, which is usually improved by years.

I have also heard that he taxes me with envy, and describes to me, as to a mere ignorant, what it is; and, in good truth, of the two kinds of envy, I am acquainted only with that which is sacred, noble, and well-meaning. And this being so, as it really is, I am not inclined to reflect on any ecclesiastic, especially if he is besides dignified with the title of a Familiar of the Inquisition: and if he said what he did for the sake of that person,* from whom he seems to have said it, he is utterly mistaken; for I adore that gentleman's genius, and admire his works, and his constant and virtuous employments.* But in fine, I own myself obliged to this worthy author, for saying that my novels are more satirical than moral,* but however, that they are good; which they could not be without some share of both.* Methinks, reader, you tell me, that I proceed with much circumspection, and confine myself within the limits of my own modesty, knowing that we should not add affliction to the afflicted; and this gentleman's must needs be very great, since he dares not appear in the open field, nor in clear daylight, concealing his name, and dissembling his country, as if he had committed some crime of high treason. If ever you should chance to fall into his company, tell him from me, that I do not think myself aggrieved: for I know very well what the temptations of the devil are, and that one of the greatest is, the putting it into a man's head that he can write and print a book which shall procure him as much fame as money, and as much money as fame: and, for confirmation hereof, I would have you, in a vein of mirth and pleasantry, tell him this story:

There was a madman in Seville who fell into one of the most ridiculous and extravagant conceits that ever madman did in the world: which was, that he sharpened the point of a cane at one end, and, catching a dog in the street or elsewhere, he set his foot on one of the cur's hind legs, and lifting up the other with his hand, he adjusted the cane, as well as he could, to the dog's posteriors, and blew him up as round as a ball: and holding him in this manner, he gave him a thump or two on the guts with the palm of his hand, and let him go, saying to the bystanders, who were always very many:

'Well, gentlemen, what think you? is it such an easy matter to blow up a dog? And what think you, sir? is it such an easy matter to write a book?'

And, if this story does not square with him, pray, kind reader, tell him this other, which is likewise of a madman and a dog:

There was another madman of Córdova, who had a custom of carrying on his head a piece of a marble slab or stone, not very heavy, and when he lighted upon any careless cur, he got close to him, and let the weight fall plump upon his head: the dog is in wrath, and limps away barking and howling, without so much as looking behind him for three streets' length. Now it happened, that among the dogs upon whom he let fall the weight, one belonged to a capmaker, who valued him mightily: down goes the stone, and hits him on the head: the poor dog raises the cry; his master, seeing it, resents it, and, catching up his measuring yard, out he goes to the madman, and leaves him not a whole bone in his skin: and, at every blow he gave him he cried:

'Dog, rogue, what, abuse my spaniel! did you not see, barbarous villain, that my dog was a spaniel?'

And repeating the word spaniel very often, he dismissed the madman, beaten to a jelly. The madman took his correction, and went off, and appeared not in the market place in above a month after: at the end of which he returned with his invention, and a greater weight; and coming to a place where a dog was lying, and observing him carefully from head to tail, and not daring to let fall the stone, he said:

'This is a spaniel; have a care.'

In short, whatever dogs he met with, though they were mastiffs or hounds, he said they were spaniels, and so let fall the slab no more. Thus, perhaps, it may fare with our historian: he may be cautious for the future how he lets fall his wit in books, which, if they are bad, are harder than rocks themselves.

Tell him also, that, as to his threatening to deprive me of my expected gain by his book, I value it not a farthing, but apply the famous interlude of the *Perendenga*,* and answer, Long live my lord and master, and Christ be with us all. Long live the great Conde de Lemos,* whose well-known Christianity and liberality support me under all the strokes of adverse fortune; and God prosper the eminent charity of his grace the Archbishop of Toledo, Bernardo de Sandoval.* Were there as many books written against me as there are letters in the rhymes of *Mingo Revulgo*,* the favour of these two princes, who, without any flattering solicitation, or any other kind of applause on my part, but merely of their own goodness, have taken upon them to patronize me, would be my sufficient protection: and I esteem myself happier and richer, than if fortune by ordinary means had placed me on her highest pinnacle. The poor man may be honourable, but not the vicious: poverty may cloud nobility, but not wholly obscure it: and virtue, as it shines by its own light, though seen through the difficulties and crannies of poverty, so it always gains the esteem, and consequently the protection, of great and noble minds.

Say no more to him, nor will I say more to you, only to let you know, that this Second Part of Don Quixote, which I offer you, is cut by the same hand, and out of the same piece with the first, and that herein I present you with Don Quixote at his full length, and, at last, fairly dead and buried, that no one may presume to bring fresh accusation against him, those already brought being enough. Let it suffice also, that a writer of some credit has given an account of his ingenious follies, resolving not to take up the subject any more: for too much, even of a good thing, lessens it in our esteem; and scarcity, even of an indifferent, makes it of some estimation.

I had forgot to tell you, that I have almost finished the *Persiles*, and that you may soon expect the second part of the *Galatea*. Farewell.*

Don Quixote
de la Mancha

SECOND PART

CHAPTER 1

Of what passed between the priest, the barber, and Don Quixote, concerning his indisposition.

CID HAMET BEN ENGELI relates, in the second part of this history, and third sally of Don Quixote, that the priest and the barber were almost a whole month* without seeing him, lest they should renew and bring back to his mind the remembrance of things past. Yet they did not therefore forbear visiting his niece and his housekeeper, charging them to take care and make much of him, and to give him comforting things to eat, such as are proper for the heart and brain, from whence, in all appearance, his disorder proceeded. They said they did so, and would continue so to do with all possible care and goodwill; for they perceived that their master was ever and anon discovering signs of being in his right mind: whereat the priest and the barber were greatly pleased, as thinking they had hit upon the right course in bringing him home enchanted upon the ox-wagon, as is related in the last chapter of the first part of this no less great than exact history. They resolved, therefore, to visit him, and make trial of his amendment; though they reckoned it almost impossible he should be cured; and agreed between them not to touch in the least upon the subject of knight-errantry, lest they should endanger the ripping up a sore that was yet so tender.

In fine, they made him a visit, and found him sitting on his bed, clad in a waistcoat of green baize, with a red Toledo bonnet on his head, and so lean and shrivelled, that he seemed as if he was reduced to a mere mummy. They were received by him with much kindness: they inquired after his health; and he gave them an account both of it and of himself with much judgement, and in very elegant expressions. In the course of their conversation they fell upon matters of state, and forms of government, correcting this abuse and condemning that, reforming one custom and banishing another; each of the three setting up himself for a new legislator, a modern Lycurgus, or a spick-and-span new Solon: and in such manner did they new-model the commonwealth, that one would have thought they had clapped it into a forge, and taken it out quite altered from what it was before. Don Quixote delivered himself with so much good sense on all the subjects they touched upon, that the two examiners undoubtedly believed he was entirely well, and in his perfect senses.

The niece and the housekeeper were present at the conversation, and seeing their master give such proofs of a sound mind, thought they could never sufficiently thank heaven. But the priest, changing his former purpose of not touching upon matters of chivalry, was now resolved to make a thorough experiment whether Don Quixote was perfectly recovered, or not: and so, from one thing to another, he came at length to tell him some news lately brought from court; and, among other things said it was given out for certain, that the Turk was coming down with a powerful fleet,* and that it was not known what his design was, nor where so great a storm would burst; that all Christendom was alarmed thereat, as it used to be almost every year; and that the king had already provided for the security of the coasts of Naples and Sicily, and of the island of Malta. To this Don Quixote replied:

'His majesty has done like a most prudent warrior, in providing in time for the defence of his dominions, that the enemy may not surprise him: but, if my counsel might be taken, I would advise him to make use of a precaution, which his majesty is at present very far from thinking of.'

Scarcely had the priest heard this, when he said within himself:

'God defend thee, poor Don Quixote! for methinks thou art falling headlong from the top of thy madness down to the profound abyss of thy folly.'

But the barber, who had already made the same reflection as the priest had done, asked Don Quixote what precaution it was that he thought so proper to be taken; for perhaps, it was such as might be put into the list of the many impertinent admonitions usually given to princes.

'Mine, Goodman Shaver,' answered Don Quixote, 'shall not be impertinent, but to the purpose.'

'I meant no harm,' replied the barber, 'but only that experience has shown, that all or most of the pieces of advice people give his majesty,* are either impracticable or absurd, or to the prejudice of the king or kingdom.'

'True,' answered Don Quixote; 'but mine is neither impracticable nor absurd, but the most easy, the most just, the most feasible and expeditious, that can enter into the imagination of any projector.'

'Señor Don Quixote,' quoth the priest, 'you keep us too long in suspense.'

'I have no mind,' replied Don Quixote, 'it should be told here now, and to-morrow by daybreak get to the ears of the lords of the privy council, and so somebody else should run away with the thanks and the reward of my labour.'

'I give you my word,' said the barber, 'here and before God, that I will not reveal what your worship shall say either to king or to rook, or to any man upon earth: an oath which I learned from the romance of the priest,* in the preface whereof he tells the king of the thief that robbed him of the hundred pistoles, and his ambling mule.'

'I know not the history,' said Don Quixote; 'but I presume the oath is a good one, because I am persuaded Master Barber is an honest man.'

'Though he were not,' said the priest, 'I will make it good, and engage for him, that as to this business, he will talk no more of it than a dumb man, under what penalty you shall think fit.'

'And who will be bound for your reverence, Master Priest?' said Don Quixote.

'My profession,' answered the priest, 'which obliges me to keep a secret.'

'Body of me, then,' said Don Quixote, 'is there anything more to be done, but that his majesty cause proclamation to be made, that all the knights-errant, who are now wandering about Spain, do, on a certain day, repair to court? for should there come but half a dozen, there may happen to be among them one, who may be able alone to destroy the whole power of the Turk. Pray, gentlemen, be attentive, and go along with me. Is it a new thing for a knight-errant singly to defeat an army of two hundred thousand men, as if they had all but one throat, or were made of sugar paste? Pray tell me, how many histories are full of these wonders? How unlucky is it for me (I will not say for anybody else) that the famous Don Belianis, or some one of the numerous race of Amadis de Gaul, is not now in being! for were any one of them alive at this day, and were to confront the Turk, in good faith, I would not farm his winnings. But God will provide for His people, and send somebody or other, if not as strong as the former knights-errant, at least not inferior to them in courage: God knows my meaning; I say no more.'

'Alas!' quoth the niece, at this instant, 'may I perish if my uncle has not a mind to turn knight-errant again.'

Whereupon Don Quixote said:

'A knight-errant I will live and die, and let the Turk come down, or up, when he pleases, and as powerful as he can: I say again, God knows my meaning.'

Here the barber said:

'I beg leave, gentlemen, to tell a short story of what happened once in Seville: for it comes in so pat to the present purpose, that I must needs tell it.'

Don Quixote and the priest gave him leave, and the rest lent him their attention; and he began thus:

'A certain man was put by his relations into the madhouse of Seville, for having lost his wits. He had taken his degrees in the canon law in the University of Osuna;* and had he taken them in that of Salamanca, most people think he would nevertheless have been mad. This graduate, after some years' confinement, took it into his head that he was in his right senses and perfect understanding; and with this conceit he wrote to the archbishop, beseeching him, with great earnestness, and seemingly good reasons, that he would be pleased to send and deliver him from that miserable confinement in which he lived; since, through the mercy of God, he had recovered his lost senses: adding, that his relations, that they might enjoy part of his estate, kept him there, and, in spite of truth, would have him be mad to his dying day. The archbishop, prevailed upon by his many letters, all penned with sense and judgement, ordered one of his chaplains to inform himself from the rector of the madhouse, whether what the licentiate had written to him was true, and also to talk with the madman, and, if it appeared that he was in his senses, to take him out and set him at liberty. The chaplain did so, and the rector assured him the man was still mad; for though he sometimes talked like a man of excellent sense, he would in the end break out into such distracted flights, as more than counterbalanced his former rational discourse; as he might experience by conversing with him.

'The chaplain resolved to make the trial, and accordingly talked about an hour with the madman, who, in all that time, never returned a disjointed or extravagant answer: on the contrary, he spoke with such sobriety, and so much to the purpose, that the chaplain was forced to believe he was in his right mind. Among other things, he said that the rector misrepresented him for the sake of the presents his relations sent him, that he might say he was still mad, and had only some lucid intervals: for his great estate was the greatest enemy he had in his misfortune, since, to enjoy that, his enemies had recourse to fraud, and pretended to doubt of the mercy of God towards him in restoring him from the condition of a brute to that of a man. In short, he talked in such a manner, that he made the rector to be suspected, his relations thought covetous and unnatural, and himself so discreet, that the chaplain determined to carry him away with him, that the archbishop himself might see, and lay his finger upon the truth of this business. The good chaplain, possessed with this opinion, desired the rector to order the clothes to be given him, which he wore when he was brought in. The rector again desired him to take care what he did, since, without all doubt, the licentiate was still mad. But the precautions and remonstrances of the rector availed nothing towards hindering the chaplain from carrying him away. The rector, seeing it was by order of the archbishop, obeyed. They put on the licentiate his clothes, which were fresh and decent. And now finding himself stripped of his madman's weeds, and habited like a rational creature, he begged of the chaplain, that he would, for charity's sake, permit him to take leave of the madmen his companions. The chaplain said he would bear him company, and take a view of the lunatics confined in that house. So upstairs they went, and with them some other persons, who happened to be present. And the licentiate, approaching a kind of cage, in which lay one that was outrageously mad, though at that time he was still and quiet, said to him:

"Have you any service, dear brother, to command me? I am returning to my own house, God having been pleased, of His infinite goodness and mercy, without any desert of mine, to restore me to my senses. I am now sound and well; for with God nothing is impossible. Put great trust and confidence in Him: for, since He has restored me to my former state, He will also restore you, if you trust in Him. I will take care to send you some refreshing victuals; and be sure to eat of them; for I must needs tell you, I find, having experienced it myself, that all our distractions proceed from our stomachs being empty, and our brains filled with wind. Take heart, take heart; for despondency under misfortunes impairs our health, and hastens our death."

'All this discourse of the licentiate's was overheard by another madman, who was in an opposite cell; and raising himself up from an old mat, whereon he had thrown him stark naked, he demanded aloud, who it was that was going away recovered and in his senses?

"It is I, brother," answered the licentiate, "that am going; for I need stay no longer here, and am infinitely thankful to heaven for having bestowed so great a blessing upon me."

"Take heed, Licentiate, what you say, let not the devil delude you," replied the madman: "stir not a foot, but keep where you are, and you will spare yourself the trouble of being brought back."

"I know," replied the licentiate, "that I am perfectly well, and shall have no more occasion to visit the station churches."*

"You well!" said the madman; "we shall soon see that; farewell! but I swear by Jupiter, whose majesty I represent on earth, that, for this offence alone, which Seville is now committing, in carrying you out of this house, and judging you to be in your senses, I am determined to inflict such a signal punishment on this city, that the memory thereof shall endure for ever and ever, Amen. Know you not, little crazed licentiate, that I can do it, since, as I say, I am thundering Jupiter, who hold in my hands the flaming bolts, with which I can, and use, to threaten and destroy the world? But in one thing only will I chastise this ignorant people; and that is, there shall no rain fall on this town, or in all its district, for three whole years reckoning from the day and hour in which this threatening is denounced. You at liberty, you recovered, and in your right senses! and I a madman, I distempered, and in bonds! I will no more rain, than I will hang myself."

'All the bystanders were very attentive to the madman's discourse; but our licentiate, turning himself to our chaplain, and holding him by both hands, said to him:

"Be in no pain, good sir, nor make any account of what this madman has said; for, if he is Jupiter and will not rain, I, who am Neptune, the father and the god of the waters, will rain as often as I please, and whenever there shall be occasion."

'To which the chaplain answered:

"However, Señor Neptune, it will not be convenient at present to provoke Señor Jupiter: therefore, pray stay where you are; for, some other time, when we have a better opportunity and more leisure, we will come for you."

'The rector and the bystanders laughed; which put the chaplain half out of countenance. They disrobed the licentiate, who remained where he was; and there is an end of the story.'

'This then, Master Barber,' said Don Quixote, 'is the story, which comes in here so pat, that you could not forbear telling it? Ah! Señor Cut-beard, Señor Cut-beard! he must be blind indeed who cannot see through a sieve. Is it possible you should be ignorant, that comparisons made between understanding and understanding, valour and valour, beauty and beauty, and family and family, are always odious and ill taken? I, Master Barber, am not Neptune, god of the waters; nor do I set myself up for a wise man, being really not so: all I aim at is, to convince the world of its error in not reviving those happy times, in which the order of knight-errantry flourished. But this our degenerate age deserves not to enjoy so great a blessing as that, which former ages could boast, when knights-errant took upon themselves the defence of kingdoms, the protection of orphans, the relief of damsels, the chastisement of the haughty, and the reward of the humble. Most of the knights now in fashion make a rustling rather in damasks, brocades, and other rich stuffs, than in coats of mail.

'You have now no knight, that will lie in the open field exposed to the rigour of the heavens, in complete armour from head to foot: no one now, that, without stirring his feet out of his stirrups, and leaning upon his lance, takes a short nap, like the knights-errant of old times: no one now, that, issuing out of this forest, ascends that mountain, and from thence traverses a barren and desert shore of the sea, which is most commonly stormy and tempestuous; where finding on the beach a small skiff, without oars, sail, mast, or any kind of tackle, he boldly throws himself into it, exposing himself to the implacable billows of the profound sea, which now mount him up to the skies, and then cast him down to the abyss: and he, opposing his courage to the irresistible hurricane, when he least dreams of it, finds himself above three thousand leagues from the place where he embarked; and, leaping on the remote and unknown shore, encounters actions worthy to be written, not on parchment, but [on] brass. But nowadays, sloth triumphs over diligence, idleness over labour, vice over virtue, arrogance over bravery, and the theory over the practice of arms, which only lived and flourished in those golden ages, and in those knights-errant.

'For, pray tell me, who was more civil and more valiant than the famous Amadis de Gaul? who more discreet than

Palmerin of England? who more affable and obliging than Tirante the White? who more gallant than Lisuarte of Greece? who gave or received more cuts and slashes than Don Belianis? who was more intrepid than Perion of Gaul?* who more enterprising than Felixmarte of Hyrcania? who more sincere than Esplandian? who more daring than Don Cirongilio of Thrace! who more brave than Rodamonte? who more prudent than king Sobrino? who more intrepid than Rinaldo; who more invincible than Orlando? and who more courteous than Rogero?* from whom, according to Turpin's *Cosmography*,* are descended the present dukes of Ferrara. All these and others that I could name, Master Priest, were knights-errant, and the light and glory of chivalry.

'Now these, or such as these, are the men I would advise his majesty to employ; by which means he would be sure to be well served, and would save a vast expense, and the Turk might go tear his beard for very madness; and so I will stay at home, since the chaplain does not fetch me out; and if Jupiter, as the barber has said, will not rain, here am I, who will rain whenever I think proper. I say all this to let Goodman Basin see that I understand him.'

'In truth, Señor Don Quixote,' said the barber, 'I meant no harm in what I said, so help me God, as my intention was good; therefore your worship ought not to take it ill.'

'Whether I ought to take it ill or no,' said Don Quixote, 'is best known to myself.'

'Well,' said the priest, 'I have hardly spoken a word yet, and I would willingly get rid of a scruple, which gnaws and disturbs my conscience, occasioned by what Señor Don Quixote has just now said.'

'You have leave, Master Priest, for greater matters,' answered Don Quixote, 'and so you may out with your scruple: for there is no pleasure in going with a scrupulous conscience.'

'With this licence then,' answered the priest, 'my scruple, I say, is, that I can by no means persuade myself, that the multitude of knights-errant your worship has mentioned, were really and truly persons of flesh and blood in the world; on the contrary, I imagine that it is all fiction, fable, and a lie, and dreams told by men awake, or, to speak more properly, half asleep.'

'This is another error,' answered Don Quixote, 'into which many have fallen, who do not believe that there were ever such knights in the world: and I have frequently, in company with divers persons, and upon sundry occasions, endeavoured to confute this common mistake. Sometimes I have failed in my design, and sometimes succeeded, supporting it on the shoulders of a truth, which is so certain, that I can almost say these eyes of mine have seen Amadis de Gaul, who was tall of stature, of a fair complexion, with a well-set beard, though black; his aspect between mild and stern; a man of few words, not easily provoked, and soon pacified. And in like manner as I have described Amadis, I fancy I could paint and delineate all the knights-errant, that are found in all the histories in the world. For, apprehending, as I do, that they were such as their histories represent them, one may, by the exploits they performed, and their dispositions, give a good philosophical guess at their features, their complexions, and their statures.'

'Pray, good Señor Don Quixote,' quoth the barber, 'how big, think you, might the giant Morgante be?'

'As to the business of giants,' answered Don Quixote, 'it is a controverted point, whether there really have been such in the world or not: but the Holy Scripture, which cannot deviate a tittle from truth, shows us there have been such, giving us the history of that huge Philistine Goliath, who was seven cubits and a half high, which is a prodigious stature. Besides, in the island of Sicily there have been found thigh-bones and shoulder-bones so large, that their size demonstrates that those to whom they belonged were giants, and as big as large steeples, as geometry evinces beyond all doubt. But for all that, I cannot say with certainty how big Morgante was, though I fancy he could not be extremely tall: and I am inclined to this opinion by finding in the story, wherein his achievements are particularly mentioned, that he often slept under a roof; and, since he found a house large enough to hold him, it is plain, he was not himself of an unmeasurable bigness.'

'That is true,' quoth the priest; who being delighted to hear him talk so wildly and extravagantly, asked him what he thought of the faces of Reynaldos de Montalvan, Orlando, and the rest of the Twelve Peers of France, since they were all knights-errant.

'Of Reynaldos,' answered Don Quixote, 'I dare boldly affirm, he was broad-faced, of a ruddy complexion, large rolling eyes, punctilious, choleric to an extreme, and a friend to rogues and profligate fellows. Of Roldan, or Rotolando, or Orlando (for histories give him all these names), I am of opinion, and assert, that he was of a middling stature, broad-shouldered, bandy-legged, brown-complexioned, car-roty-bearded, hairy-bodied, of a threatening aspect, sparing of speech, yet very civil and well-bred.'

'If Orlando,' replied the priest, 'was no finer a gentleman than you have described him, no wonder that Madam Angeli-ca the Fair disdained and forsook him for the gaiety, spright-liness, and good humour of the downychinned little Moor, with whom she had an affair; and she acted discreetly in preferring the softness of Medoro to the roughness of Or-lando.'

'That Angelica, Master Priest,' replied Don Quixote, 'was a light, gossiping, wanton hussy, and left the world as full of her impertinences, as of the fame of her beauty. She under-valued a thousand gentlemen, a thousand valiant and wise men, and took up with a paltry beardless page, with no other estate or reputation, than what the affection he preserved for his friend could give him. Even the great extoller of her beauty, the famous Ariosto, either not daring, or not caring, to celebrate what befell this lady after her pitiful intrigue, the subject not being over modest, left her with these verses:*

> 'Another bard may sing in better strain,
> How he Cataya's sceptre did obtain.

And without doubt, this was a kind of prophecy; for poets are also called *vates*, that is to say, "diviners". And this truth is plainly seen: for, since that time, a famous Andalusian poet* has bewailed and sung her tears; and another famous and singular Castilian poet* has celebrated her beauty.'

'Pray tell me, Señor Don Quixote,' quoth the barber at this instant, 'has no poet written a satire upon this lady Angelica, among so many who have sung her praises?'

'I verily believe,' answered Don Quixote, 'that, if Sacripante or Orlando had been poets, they would long ago have paid her off; for it is peculiar and natural to poets, disdained or rejected by their false mistresses, or such as were feigned in effect by those who chose them to be the sovereign ladies of their thoughts, to revenge themselves by satires and lampoons: a vengeance certainly unworthy a generous spirit. But hitherto I have not met with any defamatory verses against the lady Angelica, though she turned the world upside down.'

'Strange, indeed!' quoth the priest.

But now they heard the voice of the housekeeper and the niece, who had already quitted the conversation, and were bawling aloud in the courtyard; and they all ran towards the noise.

CHAPTER 2

Which treats of the notable quarrel between Sancho Panza and Don Quixote's niece and housekeeper, with other pleasant occurrences.

THE history relates, that the outcry which Don Quixote, the priest, and the barber heard, was raised by the niece and the housekeeper, who were defending the door against Sancho Panza, who was striving to get in to see Don Quixote.

'What would this paunchgutted fellow have in this house?' said they: 'get to your own, brother; for it is you, and no other, by whom our master is seduced, and led astray, and carried rambling up and down the highways.'

To which Sancho replied:

'Mistress housekeeper for the devil, it is I that am seduced, and led astray, and carried rambling up and down the highways, and not your master: it was he who led me this dance, and you deceive yourselves half in half. He inveigled me from home with fair speeches, promising me an island, which I still hope for.'

'May the damned islands choke thee, accursed Sancho,' answered the niece; 'and, pray, what are islands? are they anything eatable, glutton, cormorant as thou art?'

'They are not to be eaten,' replied Sancho: 'but governed, and better governments than any four cities, or four justice-ships at court.'

'For all that,' said the housekeeper, 'you come not in here, sack of mischiefs, and bundle of rogueries! get you home, and govern there; go, plough and cart, and cease pretending to islands, or highlands.'

The priest and the barber took a great deal of pleasure in hearing this dialogue between the three. But Don Quixote, fearing lest Sancho should blunder out some unseasonable follies, and touch upon some points not very much to his credit, called him to him, and ordered the women to hold their tongues, and let him in. Sancho entered, and the priest and the barber took their leave of Don Quixote, of whose cure they despaired, perceiving how bent he was upon his extravagances, and how intoxicated with the folly of his unhappy chivalries. And therefore the priest said to the barber:

'You will see, neighbour, when we least think of it, our gentleman take another flight.'

'I make no doubt of that,' answered the barber; 'yet, I do not admire so much at the madness of the knight, as at the simplicity of the squire, who is so possessed with the business of the island, that I am persuaded all the demonstrations in the world cannot beat it out of his noddle.'

'God help them,' said the priest; 'and let us be upon the watch, and we shall see the drift of this machine of absurdities, of such a knight, and such a squire, who, one would think, were cast in the same mould; and, indeed, the madness of the master, without the follies of the man, would not be worth a farthing.'

'True,' quoth the barber, 'and I should be very glad to know what they two are now talking of.'

'I lay my life,' answered the priest, 'the niece or the

housekeeper will tell us all by and by; for they are not of a temper to forbear listening.'

In the meanwhile, Don Quixote had shut himself up in his chamber with Sancho only, and said to him:

'I am very sorry, Sancho, you should say, and stand in it, that it was I who drew you out of your cottage, when you know, that I myself stayed not in my own house. We set out together; we went on together; and together we performed our travels. We both ran the same fortune and the same chance. If you were once tossed in a blanket, I have been thrashed a hundred times; and herein only have I had the advantage of you.'

'And reason good,' answered Sancho; 'for, as your worship holds, misfortunes belong more properly to knights-errant themselves, than to their squires.'

'You are mistaken, Sancho,' said Don Quixote; 'for, according to the saying, *Quando caput dolet*, &c.'

'I understand no other language than my own,' replied Sancho.'

'I mean,' said Don Quixote, 'that, when the head aches, all the members ache also; and therefore I, being your master and lord, am your head, and you are a part of me, as being my servant: and for this reason the ill that does, or shall affect me, must affect you also; and so on the contrary.'*

'Indeed,' quoth Sancho, 'it should be so; but when I, as a limb, was tossed in the blanket, my head stood on t'other side of the pales, beholding me frisking in the air, without feeling any pain at all; and since the members are bound to grieve at the ills of the head, that also in requital ought to do the like for them.'

'Would you insinuate now, Sancho,' replied Don Quixote, 'that I was not grieved when I saw you tossed? If that be your meaning, say no more, nor so much as think it; for I felt more pain then in my mind, than you did in your body.

'But no more of this at present; for a time will come when we may set this matter upon its right bottom. In the meantime, tell me, friend Sancho, what do folks say of me about this town? what opinion has the common people of me? what think the gentlemen, and what the cavaliers? what is said of my prowess, what of my exploits, and what of my courtesy? What discourse is there of the design I have engaged in, to revive and restore to the world the long-forgotten order of chivalry? In short, Sancho, I would have you tell me whatever you have heard concerning these matters: and this you must do, without adding to the good, or taking from the bad, one tittle: for it is the part of faithful vassals to tell their lords the truth in its native simplicity, and proper figure, neither enlarged by adulation, nor diminished out of any other idle regard. And I would have you, Sancho, learn by the way, that, if naked truth could come to the ears of princes, without the disguise of flattery, we should see happier days, and former ages would be deemed as iron, in comparison of ours, which would then be esteemed the golden age. Let this advertisement, Sancho, be a caution to you to give me an ingenuous and faithful account of what you know concerning the matters I have inquired about.'

'That I will with all my heart, sir,' answered Sancho, 'on condition that your worship shall not be angry at what I say, since you will have me show you the naked truth, without arraying her in any other dress than that in which she appeared to me.'

'I will in no wise be angry,' replied Don Quixote: 'you may speak freely, Sancho, and without any circumlocution.'

'First and foremost then,' said Sancho, 'the common people take your worship for a downright madman, and me for no less a fool. The gentlemen say, that not containing yourself within the bounds of gentility, you have taken upon you the style of Don, and invaded the dignity of knighthood, with no more than a paltry vineyard, and a couple of acres of land, with a tatter behind and another before. The cavaliers say, they would not have the gentlemen set themselves in opposition to them, especially those gentlemen esquires, who clout their shoes,* and take up the fallen stitches of their black stockings with green silk.'

'That,' said Don Quixote, 'is no reflection upon me; for I always go well clad, and my clothes never patched: a little torn they may be, but more so through the fretting of my armour, than by length of time.'

'As to what concerns your valour, courtesy, achievements, and your undertaking,' quoth Sancho, 'there are very different opinions. Some say mad, but humorous; others, valiant, but unfortunate; others, courteous, but impertinent: and thus they run divisions upon us, till they leave neither your worship nor me a whole bone in our skins.'

'Take notice, Sancho,' said Don Quixote, 'that wherever virtue is found in any eminent degree, it is always persecuted. Few, or none, of the famous men of times past escaped being calumniated by their malicious contemporaries. Julius Caesar, the most courageous, the most prudent, and most valiant captain, was noted for being ambitious, and somewhat unclean both in his apparel and his manners. Alexander, whose exploits gained him the surname of Great, is said to have had a little smack of the drunkard. Hercules, with all his labours, is censured for being lascivious and effeminate. Don Galaor, brother of Amadis de Gaul, was taxed with being quarrelsome; and his brother with being a whimperer. So that, O Sancho, amidst so many calumnies cast on the worthy, mine may very well pass, if they are no more than those you have mentioned.'

'Body of my father! there lies the jest,' replied Sancho.

'What then, is there more yet behind?' said Don Quixote.

'The tail remains still to be flayed,' quoth Sancho: 'all hitherto has been tarts and cheese-cakes: but if your worship has a mind to know the very bottom of these calumnies people bestow upon you, I will bring one hither presently, who shall tell you them all, without missing a tittle: for last night arrived the son of Bartholomew Carrasco, who comes from studying at Salamanca, having taken the degree of bachelor; and when I went to bid him welcome home, he told me that the history of your worship is already printed in books under the title of *The Ingenious Gentleman Don Quixote de la Mancha*; and he says, it mentions me too by my very name of Sancho Panza, and the lady Dulcinea del Toboso, and several other things which passed between us two only; insomuch that I crossed myself out of pure amazement, to think how the historian who wrote it, could come to know them.'

'Depend upon it, Sancho,' said Don Quixote, 'that the author of this our history must be some sage enchanter; for nothing is hid from them when they have a mind to write.'

'A sage and an enchanter!' quoth Sancho; 'why, the bachelor Sampson Carrasco (for that is his name) says, the author of this history is called Cid Hamet Berengena.'*

'That is a Moorish name,' answered Don Quixote.

'It may be so,' replied Sancho, 'for I have heard that your Moors for the most part are lovers of *berengenas.*'

'Sancho,' said Don Quixote, 'you must mistake the surname of that same "Cid", which in Arabic signifies "a lord".'

'It may be so,' answered Sancho! 'but if your worship will have me bring him hither, I will fly to fetch him.'

'You will do me a singular pleasure, friend,' said Don Quixote; 'for I am surprised at what you have told me, and I shall not eat a bit that will do me good, till I am informed of all.'

'Then I am going for him,' answered Sancho; and leaving his master, he went to seek the bachelor, with whom he returned soon after; and between them there passed a most pleasant conversation.

CHAPTER 3

Of the pleasant conversation which passed between Don Quixote, Sancho Panza, and the bachelor Sampson Carrasco.

DON QUIXOTE remained over and above thoughtful, expecting the coming of the bachelor Carrasco, from whom he hoped to hear some accounts of himself, printed in a book, as Sancho had told him; and could not persuade himself, that such a history could be extant, since the blood of the enemies he had slain was still reeking on his sword-blade; and could people expect his high feats of arms should be already in print? However, at last he concluded that some sage, either friend or enemy, by art-magic, had sent them to the press: if a friend, to aggrandize and extol them above the most signal achievements of any knight-errant; if an enemy, to annihilate and sink them below the meanest that ever were written of any squire: although (quoth he to himself) the feats of squires never were written. But if it should prove true that such a history was really extant, since it was the history of a knight-errant, it must of necessity be sublime, lofty, illustrious, magnificent, and true.

This thought afforded him some comfort: but he lost it again upon considering that the author was a Moor, as was plain from the name of Cid, and that no truth could be expected from the Moors, who were all impostors, liars, and visionaries. He was apprehensive, he might treat of his love with some indecency, which might redound to the disparagement and prejudice of the modesty of his lady Dulcinea del Toboso. He wished he might find a faithful representation of his own constancy, and the decorum he had always inviolably preserved towards her, slighting, for her sake, queens, empresses, and damsels of all degrees, and bridling the violent impulses of natural desire. Tossed and perplexed with these and a thousand other imaginations, Sancho and Carrasco found him: and Don Quixote received the bachelor with much courtesy.

This bachelor, though his name was Sampson, was none of the biggest, but an arch wag; of a wan complexion, but of a very good understanding. He was about twenty-four years of age, round-faced, flatnosed, and wide-mouthed; all signs of his being of a waggish disposition, and a lover of wit and humour; as he made appear at seeing Don Quixote, before whom he threw himself upon his knees, and said to him;

'Señor Don Quixote de la Mancha, let me have the honour of kissing your grandeur's hand: for, by the habit of St. Peter, which I wear, though I have yet taken no other degrees towards holy orders but the four first, your worship is one of the most famous knights-errant, that have been, or shall be, upon the whole circumference of the earth. A blessing light on Cid Hamet Ben Engeli, who has left us the history of your mighty deeds; and blessings upon blessings light on that virtuoso, who took care to have them translated out of Arabic into our vulgar Castilian, for the universal entertainment of all sorts of people!'

Don Quixote made him rise, and said: 'It seems then it is true, that my history is really extant, and that he who composed it was a Moor and a sage.'

'So true it is, sir,' said Sampson, 'that I verily believe there are, this very day, above twelve thousand books published of that history: witness Portugal, Barcelona, and Valencia, where they have been printed; and there is a rumour that it is now printing at Antwerp;* and I foresee that no nation or language will be without a translation of it.'

Here Don Quixote said: 'One of the things which ought to afford the highest satisfaction to a virtuous and eminent man, is, to find, while he is living, his good name published and in print, in everybody's mouth, and in everybody's hand: I say, his good name: for if it be the contrary, no death can equal it.'

'If fame and a good name are to carry it,' said the bachelor, 'your worship alone bears away the palm from all knights-errant: for the Moor in his language, and the Castilian in his, have taken care to paint to the life that gallant deportment of your worship, that greatness of soul in confronting dangers, that constancy in adversity, and patient endurance of mischances, that modesty and continence in love, so very platonic, as that between your worship and my lady Doña Dulcinea del Toboso.'

Sancho here said: 'I never heard my lady Dulcinea called Doña before, but only plain Dulcinea del Toboso; so that here the history is already mistaken.'

'That objection is of no importance,' answered Carrasco.

'No, certainly,' replied Don Quixote: 'but, pray tell me, Señor Bachelor, which of my exploits are most esteemed in this same history?'

'As to that,' answered the bachelor, 'there are different opinions as there are different tastes. Some are for the adventure of the windmills, which your worship took for so many Briareuses and giants: others adhere to that of the fulling-hammers: these to the description of the two armies, which afterwards fell out to be two flocks of sheep: another cries up that of the dead body, which was carrying to be interred at Segovia: one says, the setting the galley-slaves at liberty was beyond them all: another, that none can be compared to that of the two Benedictine giants, with the combat of the valorous Biscainer.'

'Pray tell me, Señor Bachelor,' quoth Sancho, 'is there among the rest the adventure of the Yangueses, when our good Rosinante had a longing after the forbidden fruit?'

'The sage,' answered Sampson, 'has left nothing at the bottom of the ink-horn: he inserts and remarks everything, even to the capers Sancho cut in the blanket.'

'I cut no capers in the blanket,' answered Sancho: 'in the air I own I did, and more than I desired.'

'In my opinion,' quoth Don Quixote, 'there is no history in the world that hath not its ups and downs, especially those which treat of chivalry; for such can never be altogether filled with prosperous events.'

'For all that,' replied the bachelor, 'some, who have read the history, say, they should have been better pleased, if the authors thereof had forgot some of those numberless drubbings given to Señor Don Quixote in different encounters.'

'Therein,' quoth Sancho, 'consists the truth of the history.'

'They might, indeed, as well have omitted them,' said Don Quixote, 'since there is no necessity of recording those actions, which do not change nor alter the truth of the story, and especially if they redound to the discredit of the hero. In good faith, Aeneas was not altogether so pious as Virgil paints him, nor Ulysses so prudent as Homer describes him.'

'It is true,' replied Sampson; 'but it is one thing to write as a poet, and another to write as an historian. The poet may say, or sing, not as things were, but as they ought to have been; but the historian must pen them, not as they ought to have been, but as they really were, without adding to, or diminishing anything from the truth.'

'Well, if it be so, that Señor Moor is in a vein of telling truth,' quoth Sancho, 'there is no doubt, but among my master's rib-roastings, mine are to be found also: for they never took measure of his worship's shoulders, but at the same time they took the dimensions of my whole body: but why should I wonder at that, since, as the selfsame master of mine says, the members must partake of the ailments of the head.'

'Sancho, you are a sly wag,' answered Don Quixote: 'in faith, you want not for a memory, when you have a mind to have one.'

'Though I had never so much a mind to forget the drubs I have received,' quoth Sancho, 'the tokens, that are still fresh on my ribs, would not let me.'

'Hold your peace, Sancho,' said Don Quixote, 'and do not interrupt Señor Bachelor, whom I entreat to go on, and tell me what is further said of me in the aforesaid history.'

'And of me too,' quoth Sancho; 'for I hear that I am one of the principal parsons in it.'

'Persons, not parsons, friend Sancho,' quoth Sampson.

'What! another corrector of hard words!' quoth Sancho; 'if this be the trade we shall never have done.'

'Let me die, Sancho,' answered the bachelor, 'if you are not the second person of the history: nay, there are some, who had rather hear you talk, than the finest fellow of them all: though there are also some, who say you was a little too credulous in the matter of the government of that island promised you by Señor Don Quixote here present.'

'There is still sunshine on the wall,' quoth Don Quixote, 'and, when Sancho is more advanced in age, with the experience that years give, he will be better qualified to be a governor than he is now.'

'Before God, sir,' quoth Sancho, 'if I am not fit to govern an island at these years, I shall not know how to govern it at the age of Methusalem. The mischief of it is, that the said island sticks I know not where, and not in my want of a headpiece to govern it.'

'Recommend it to God, Sancho,' said Don Quixote; 'for all will be well, and perhaps better than you think; for a leaf stirs not on the tree without the will of God.'

'That is true,' quoth Sampson; 'and if it pleases God, Sancho will not want a thousand islands to govern, much less one.'

'I have seen governors ere now,' quoth Sancho, 'who, in my opinion, do not come up to the sole of my shoe; and yet they are called your lordship, and are served on plate.'

'Those are not governors of islands,' replied Sampson, 'but of other governments more manageable; for those, who govern islands, must at least understand grammar.'

'Gramercy for that,' quoth Sancho; 'it is all Greek to me, for I know nothing of the matter. But let us leave the business of governments in the hands of God, and let Him dispose of me so as I may be most instrumental in His service; I say, Señor Bachelor Sampson Carrasco, I am infinitely pleased that the author of the history has spoken of me in such a manner, that what he says of me is not at all tiresome; for upon the faith of a trusty squire, had he said anything of me unbecoming an Old Christian, as I am, the deaf should have heard it.'

'That would be working miracles,' answered Sampson.

'Miracles, or no miracles,' quoth Sancho, 'let every one take heed how they talk, or write, of people, and not set down at random the first thing that comes into their imagination.'

'One of the faults people charge upon that history,' said the bachelor, 'is, that the author has inserted in it a novel, entitled, the *Curious Impertinent*; not that it is bad in itself, or ill-written, but for having no relation to that place, nor anything to do with the story of his worship Señor Don Quixote.'

'I will lay a wager,' replied Sancho, 'the son of a bitch has made a jumble of fish and flesh together.'

'I aver then,' said Don Quixote, 'that the author of my history could not be a sage, but some ignorant pretender,* who, at random, and without any judgement, has set himself to write it, come of it what would: like Orbaneja, the painter of Úbeda, who, being asked what he painted, answered: "As it may hit."* Sometimes he would paint a cock after such a guise, and so preposterously designed, that he was forced to write under it in Gothic character, "this is a cock": and thus it will fare with my history; it will stand in need of a comment to make it intelligible.'

'Not at all,' answered Sampson; 'for it is so plain, that there is no difficulty in it: children thumb it, boys read it, men understand it, and old folks commend it; in short, it is so tossed about, so conned, and so thoroughly known by all sorts of people, that they no sooner espy a lean scrub-horse, than they cry, "Yonder goes Rosinante." But none are so much addicted to reading it as your pages: there is not a nobleman's antechamber, in which you will not find a *Don Quixote*; if one lays it down, another takes it up; one asks for it, another snatches it; in short, this history is the most pleasing and least prejudicial entertainment hitherto published: for there is not so much the appearance of an immodest word in it, nor a thought that is not entirely catholic.'

'To write otherwise,' said Don Quixote, 'had not been to write truths, but lies; and historians, who are fond of venting falsehoods, should be burnt like coiners of false money. For my part I cannot imagine what moved the author to introduce novels, or foreign relations, my own story affording matter enough: but without doubt we may apply the proverb, With hay or with straw, &c., for verily, had he confined himself to the publishing my thoughts, my sighs, my tears, my good wishes, and my achievements alone, he might have compiled a volume as big or bigger than all the works of Tostatus.* In short, Señor Bachelor, what I mean is, that, in order to the compiling histories, or books of any kind whatever, a man had need of a great deal of judgement, and a mature understanding; to talk wittily, and write pleasantly, are the talents of a great genius only. The most difficult character in comedy is that of the fool, and he must be no simpleton that plays that part. History is a sacred kind of writing, because truth is essential to it; and where truth is, there God Himself is, so far as truth is concerned: notwithstanding which, there are those, who compose books, and toss them out into the world like fritters.'

'There are few books so bad,' said the bachelor, 'but there is something good in them.'

'There is no doubt of that,' replied Don Quixote; 'but it often happens, that they, who have deservedly acquired a good share of reputation by their writings, lessen or lose it entirely by committing them to the press.'

'The reason of that,' said Sampson, 'is, that printed works being examined at leisure, the faults thereof are the more easily discovered; and the greater the fame of the author is, the more strict and severe is the scrutiny. Men famous for their parts, great poets, and celebrated historians, are always envied by those who take a pleasure, and make it their particular entertainment to censure other men's writings, without ever having published any of their own.'

'That is not to be wondered at,' said Don Quixote; 'for there are many divines, who make no figure in the pulpit, and yet are excellent at espying the defects or superfluities of preachers.'

'All this is very true, Señor Don Quixote,' said Carrasco; 'but I wish such critics would be more merciful, and less nice, and not dwell so much upon the motes of that bright sun, the work they censure. For, though *aliquando bonus dormitat Homerus*,* they ought to consider how much he was awake to give his work as much light, and leave as little shade, as he could: and perhaps those very parts, which some men do not taste, are like moles, which sometimes add to the beauty of the face that has them. And therefore I say, that whoever prints a book runs a very great risk, it being of all impossibilities the most impossible to write such an one, as shall satisfy and please all kinds of readers.'

'That, which treats of me,' said Don Quixote, 'has pleased but a few.'*

'On the contrary,' replied the bachelor, 'as *stultorum infinitus est numerus*,* so infinite is the number of those, who have been delighted with that history: though some have taxed the author's memory, as faulty or treacherous in forgetting to tell us who the thief was that stole Sancho's Dapple; which is not related, but only inferred from what is there written, that he was stolen; and in a very short time after we find him mounted upon the selfsame beast, without hearing how Dapple appeared again.* It is also objected, that he has omitted to mention what Sancho did with the hundred crowns he found in the portmanteau upon the Sierra Morena; for he never speaks of them more, and many persons would be glad to learn what he did with them, or how he spent them; for that is one of the most substantial points wanting in the work.'

Sancho answered:

'Master Sampson, I am not now in a condition to tell tales, or make up accounts; for I have a qualm come over my stomach, and shall be upon the rack, till I have removed it with a couple of draughts of cordial. I have it at home, and my chuck* stays for me. As soon as I have dined I will come back, and satisfy your worship, and the whole world, in whatever they are pleased to ask me, both concerning the loss of Dapple, and what became of the hundred crowns.'

So, without waiting for an answer, or speaking a word more, he went away to his own house. Don Quixote pressed and entreated the bachelor to stay, and do penance with him. The bachelor accepted of the invitation, and stayed: a couple of pigeons was added to the usual commons, and the conversation at table fell upon the subject of chivalry. Carrasco carried on the humour: the banquet was ended: they slept out the heat of the day: Sancho came back, and the former discourse was resumed.

CHAPTER 4

Wherein Sancho Panza answers the bachelor Sampson
Carrasco's doubts and questions; with other incidents worthy
to be known and recited.

SANCHO came back to Don Quixote's house, and, resuming the former discourse, in answer to what the bachelor Sampson Carrasco desired to be informed of, namely, by whom, when, and how the ass was stolen, he said:

'That very night, when, flying from the Holy Brotherhood, we entered into the Sierra Morena, after the unlucky adventure of the galley-slaves, and of the dead body that was carrying to Segovia, my master and I got into a thicket, where, he leaning upon his lance, and I sitting upon Dapple, being both of us mauled and fatigued by our late skirmishes, we fell asleep as soundly as if we had had four featherbeds under us; especially I for my part slept so fast, that the thief, whoever he was, had leisure enough to suspend me on four stakes, which he planted under the four corners of the pannel, and in this manner leaving me mounted thereon, got Dapple from under me, without my feeling it.'

'That is an easy matter, and no new accident,' said Don Quixote: 'for the like happened to Sacripante at the siege of Albracca, where that famous robber Brunello, by this selfsame invention, stole his horse from between his legs.'*

'The dawn appeared,' continued Sancho, 'and scarce had I stretched myself, when, the stakes giving way, down came I with a confounded squelch to the ground. I looked about for my ass, but saw him not: the tears came into my eyes, and I made such a lamentation, that if the author of our history has not set it down, he may make account he has omitted an excellent thing.

'At the end of I know not how many days, as I was accompanying the princess Micomicona, I saw and knew my ass again, and upon him came, in the garb of a gipsy, that cunning rogue, and notorious malefactor, Gines de Pasamonte, whom my master and I freed from the galley-chain.'

'The mistake does not lie in this,' replied Sampson, 'but in the author's making Sancho still ride upon the very same beast, before he gives us any account of his being found again.'

'To this,' said Sancho, 'I know not what to answer, unless it be that the historian was mistaken; or it might be an oversight of the printer.'

'It must be so without doubt,' quoth Sampson: 'but what became of the hundred crowns? were they sunk?'

'I laid them out,' quoth Sancho, 'for the use and behoof of my own person, and those of my wife and children; and they have been the cause of my wife's bearing patiently the journeys and rambles I have taken in the service of my master Don Quixote: for had I returned, after so long a time, penniless, and without my ass, black would have been my luck. If you would know anything more of me, here am I, ready to answer the king himself in person; and nobody has anything to meddle or make, whether I brought or brought not, whether I spent or spent not; for if the blows, that have been given me in these sallies, were to be paid for in ready money, though rated only at four maravedis apiece, another hundred crowns would not pay for half of them: and let every man lay his hand upon his heart, and let him not be judging white for black, nor black for white; for every one is as God has made him, and oftentimes a great deal worse.'

'I will take care,' said Carrasco, 'to advertise the author of the history, that, if he reprints the book, he shall not forget what honest Sancho has told us, which will make the book as good again.'

'Is there anything else to be corrected in that legend, Señor Bachelor?' quoth Don Quixote.

'There may be others,' answered Carrasco, 'but none of that importance with those already mentioned.'

'And, peradventure,' said Don Quixote, 'the author promises a second part?'

'He does,' answered Sampson, 'but says he has not met with it, nor can learn who has it; and therefore we are in doubt whether it will appear or no: and as well for this reason, as because some people say, that second parts are never good for anything, and others, that there is enough of Don Quixote already, it is believed, there will be no second part; though some, who are more jovial than saturnine, cry, Let us have more Quixotades; let Don Quixote encounter,* and Sancho Panza talk: and, be the rest what it will, we shall be contented.'

'And pray, how stands the author affected?' demanded Don Quixote.

'How?' answered Sampson; 'why, as soon as ever he can find the history he is looking for with extraordinary diligence, he will immediately send it to the press, being prompted thereto more by interest than by any motive of praise whatever.'

To which Sancho said:

'Does the author aim at money and profit? it will be a wonder then if he succeeds, since he will only stitch it away in great haste like a tailor on Easter-eve; for works that are done hastily are never finished with that perfection they require. I wish this same Señor Moor would consider a little what he is about: for I and my master will furnish him so abundantly with lime and mortar in matter of adventures and variety of accidents, that he may not only compile a second part, but a hundred. The good man thinks, without doubt, that we lie sleeping here in straw; but let him hold up the foot while the smith is shoeing, and he will see on which we halt. What I can say is, that, if this master of mine had taken my counsel, we had ere now been in the field, redressing grievances, and righting wrongs, as is the practice and usage of good knights-errant.'

Sancho had scarce finished this discourse, when the neighings of Rosinante reached their ears; which Don Quixote took for a most happy omen, and resolved to make another sally within three or four days; and declaring his intention to the bachelor, he asked his advice which way he should begin his journey. The bachelor replied, he was of opinion that he should go directly to the kingdom of Aragon, and the city of Saragossa, where in a few days there was to be held a most solemn tournament, in honour of the festival of St. George,* in which he might acquire renown above all the Aragonian knights, which would be the same thing as acquiring it above all the knights in the world. He commended his resolution as most honourable and most valorous, and gave him a hint to be more wary in encountering dangers because his life was not his own, but theirs who stood in need of his aid and succour in their distresses.

'This is what I denounce, Señor Sampson,' quoth Sancho; 'for my master makes no more of attacking a hundred armed men, than a greedy boy would do half a dozen melons. Body of the world! Señor Bachelor, yes, there must be a time to attack, and a time to retreat; and it must not be always, Santiago, and charge, Spain!* And further, I have heard say (and, if I remember right, from my master himself) that the mean of true valour lies between the extremes of cowardice and rashness: and if this be so, I would not have him run away when there is no need of it, nor would I have him fall on when the too great superiority requires quite another thing; but above all things I would let my master know, that, if he will take me with him, it must be upon condition, that he shall battle it all himself, and that I shall not be obliged to any other thing but to look after his clothes and his diet; to which purposes I will fetch and carry like any spaniel: but to imagine, that I will lay hand to my sword, though it be against rascally woodcutters with hooks and hatchets, is to be very much mistaken. Señor Sampson, I do not set up for the fame of being valiant, but for that of being the best and most faithful squire that ever served a knight-errant; and if my lord Don Quixote, in consideration of my many and good services, has a mind to bestow on me some one island of the many his worship says he shall light upon, I shall be much beholden to him for the favour; and though he should not give me one, born I am, and we must not rely upon one another, but upon God; and perhaps the bread I shall eat without the government, may go down the more savourily than that I should eat with it; and how do I know but the devil in one of these governments may provide me some stumbling-block, that I may fall and dash out my grinders. Sancho I was born, and Sancho I intend to die: yet for all that, if fairly and squarely, without much solicitude or much danger, heaven should chance to throw an island, or some such thing, in my way, I am not such a fool neither as to refuse it; for it is a saying when they give you a heifer make haste with the rope: and when good fortune comes, be sure to take her in.'

'Brother Sancho,' quoth Carrasco, 'you have spoken like any professor: nevertheless, trust in God, and Señor Don Quixote, that he will give you, not only an island, but even a kingdom.'

'One as likely as the other,' answered Sancho; 'though I could tell Señor Carrasco, that my master will not throw the kingdom he gives me into a bag without a bottom: for I have felt my own pulse, and find myself in health enough to rule kingdoms and govern islands, and so much I have signified before now to my lord.'

'Look you, Sancho,' quoth Sampson, 'honours change manners; and it may come to pass, when you are a governor, that you may not know the very mother that bore you.'

'That,' answered Sancho, 'may be the case with those that are born among the mallows, but not with those, whose souls, like mine, are covered four inches thick with grease of the Old Christian: no, but consider my disposition, whether it is likely to be ungrateful to anybody.'

'God grant it,' said Don Quixote, 'and we shall see when the government comes; for methinks I have it already in my eye.'

This said, he desired the bachelor, if he were a poet, that he would do him the favour to compose for him some verses, by way of a farewell to his lady Dulcinea del Toboso, and that he would place a letter of her name at the beginning of each verse, in such a manner, that, at the end of the verses, the first letters taken together might make Dulcinea del Toboso. The bachelor answered, though he was not of the famous poets of Spain, who were said to be but three and a half, he would not fail to compose those verses; though he was sensible it would be no easy task, the name consisting of seventeen letters; for if he made four stanzas of four verses each, there would be a letter too much, and if he made them of five, which they call *décimas* or *redondillas*, there would be three letters wanting: nevertheless he would endeavour to sink a letter as well as he could, so as that the name of Dulcinea del Toboso should be included in the four stanzas.

'Let it be so by all means,' said Don Quixote; 'for if the name be not plain and manifest, no woman will believe the rhymes were made for her.'

They agreed upon this, and that they should set out eight days after. Don Quixote enjoined the bachelor to keep it secret, especially from the priest and Master Nicholas, and from his niece and housekeeper, that they might not obstruct his honourable and valorous purpose. All which Carrasco promised, and took his leave, charging Don Quixote to give him advice of his good or ill success, as opportunity offered: and so they again bid each other farewell, and Sancho went to provide and put in order what was necessary for the expedition.

CHAPTER 5

*Of the wise and pleasant discourse, which passed between
Sancho Panza and his wife Teresa Panza.*

THE translator of this history, coming to write this fifth
chapter, says, he takes it to be apocryphal, because in it
Sancho talks in another style than could be expected from
his shallow understanding, and says such subtle things, that
he reckons impossible that he should know them: nevertheless, he would not omit translating them, to comply with the
duty of his office, and so went on, saying:

Sancho came home so gay and so merry, that his wife
perceived his joy a bowshot off, insomuch that she could
not but ask him,

'What is the matter, friend Sancho, you are so merry?'

To which he answered:

'Dear wife, if it were God's will, I should be very glad not
to be so well pleased as I appear to be.'

'Husband,' replied she, 'I understand you not, and know
not what you mean by saying, you should be glad, if it were
God's will, you were not so much pleased: now, silly as I
am, I cannot guess how one can take pleasure in not being
pleased.'

'Look you, Teresa,'* answered Sancho, 'I am thus merry,
because I am resolved to return to the service of my master,
Don Quixote, who is determined to make a third sally in
quest of adventures; and I am to accompany him, for so my
necessity will have it; besides I am pleased with the hopes
of finding another hundred crowns, like those we have spent:
though it grieves me, that I must part from you and my
children, and if God would be pleased to give me bread,
dryshod and at home, without dragging me over rough and
smooth, and through thick and thin (which He might do at
a small expense, and by only willing it so), it is plain, my joy
would be more firm and solid, since it is now mingled with
sorrow for leaving you: so that I said right, when I said, I
should be glad, if it were God's will, I were not so well
pleased.'

'Look you, Sancho,' replied Teresa, 'ever since you have been a member of a knight-errant, you talk in such a round-about manner, that there is nobody understands you.'

'It is enough that God understands me, wife,' answered Sancho; 'for He is the understander of all things; and so much for that: and do you hear, sister, it is convenient you should take more than ordinary care of Dapple these three days, that he may be in a condition to bear arms: double his allowance, and get the pack-saddle in order, and the rest of his tackling; for we are not going to a wedding, but to roam about the world, and to have now and then a bout at "give and take" with giants, fiery dragons, and goblins, and to hear hissings, roarings, bellowings, and bleatings: all which would be but flowers of lavender, if we had not to do with Yangüeses and enchanted Moors.'

'I believe indeed, husband,' replied Teresa, 'that your squires-errant do not eat their bread for nothing, and therefore I shall not fail to beseech our Lord to deliver you speedily from so much evil hap.'

'I tell you, wife,' answered Sancho, 'that, did I not expect, ere long, to see myself a governor of an island, I should drop down dead upon the spot.'

'Not so, my dear husband,' quoth Teresa: 'let the hen live, though it be with the pip. Live you, and the devil take all the governments in the world. Without a government came you from your mother's womb; without a government have you lived hitherto; and without a government will you go, or be carried, to your grave, whenever it shall please God. How many folks are there in the world that have not a government? and yet they live for all that, and are reckoned in the number of the people! The best sauce in the world is hunger, and, as that is never wanting to the poor, they always eat with a relish. But if, perchance, Sancho, you should get a government, do not forget me, and your children. Consider, that little Sancho is just fifteen years old, and it is fit he should go to school, if so be his uncle the abbot means to breed him up to the church. Consider also, that Mary-Sancha, your daughter, will not break her heart if we marry her: for I am mistaken if she has not as much mind to a husband, as you have to a government; and indeed, indeed, better a daughter but indifferently married, than well kept.'

'In good faith,' answered Sancho, 'if God be so good to me that I get anything like a government, dear wife, I will match Mary-Sancha so highly, that there will be no coming near her without calling her Your Ladyship.'

'Not so, Sancho,' answered Teresa; 'the best way is to marry her to her equal; for if, instead of pattens you put her on clogs, and, instead of her russet petticoat of fourteenpenny stuff, you give her a farthingale and petticoats of silk, and, instead of plain Molly and You, she be called My Lady Such-an-one, and Your Ladyship, the girl will not know where she is, and will fall into a thousand mistakes at every step, discovering the coarse thread of her homespun country stuff.'

'Peace, fool,' quoth Sancho; 'for all the business is to practise two or three years, and after that the ladyship and the gravity will sit upon her as if they were made for her; and, if not, what matters it? Let her be a lady, and come what will of it.'

'Measure yourself by your condition, Sancho,' answered Teresa; 'seek not to raise yourself higher, and remember the proverb, Wipe your neighbour's son's nose, and take him into your house. It would be a pretty business truly to marry our Mary to some great count or knight, who when the fancy takes him, would look upon her as some strange thing, and be calling her country-wench, clod-breaker's brat, and I know not what: not while I live, husband; I have not brought up my child to be so used: do you provide money, Sancho, and leave the matching of her to my care; for there is Lope Tocho, John Tocho's son, a lusty, hale young man, whom we know, and I am sure he has a sneaking kindness for the girl: she will be very well married to him, considering he is our equal, and will always be under our eye; and we shall be all as one, parents and children, grandsons, and sons-in-law, and so the peace and blessing of God will be among us all: and do not you pretend to be marrying her now at your courts and great palaces, where they will neither understand her, nor she understand herself.'

'Hark you, beast, and wife for Barabbas,' replied Sancho, 'why would you now, without rhyme or reason, hinder me from marrying my daughter with one who may bring me grandchildren that may be styled Your Lordships? Look you, Teresa, I have always heard my betters say, "He that will not when he may, when he will he shall have nay:" and it would be very wrong, now that fortune is knocking at our door, to shut it against her: let us spread our sails to the favourable gale that now blows.'

This kind of language, and what Sancho says further below, made the translator of this history say, he takes this chapter to be apocryphal.

'Do you not think, animal,' continued Sancho, 'that it would be well for me to be really possessed of some beneficial government, that may lift us out of the dirt, and enable me to marry Mary-Sancha to whom I pleased? You will then see how people will call you Doña Teresa Panza, and you will sit in the church with velvet cushions, carpets, and tapestries, in spite of the best gentlewomen of the parish. No! No! continue as you are, and be always the same thing, without being increased or diminished, like a figure in the hangings. Let us have no more of this, pray; for little Sancha shall be a countess, in spite of your teeth.'

'For all that, husband,' answered Teresa, 'I am afraid this countess-ship will be my daughter's undoing. But, what you please: make her a duchess or a princess; but I can tell you, it shall never be with my goodwill or consent. I was always a lover of equality, and cannot abide to see folks taking state upon themselves. Teresa my parents named me at the font, a plain simple name, without the additions, laces, or garnitures of Dons or Doñas. My father's name was Cascajo; and I, by being your wife, am called Teresa Panza, though indeed by good right I should be called Teresa Cascajo. But the laws follow still the prince's will.* I am contented with this name, without the additional weight of Doña, to make it so heavy that I shall not be able to carry it; and I would not have people, when they see me decked out like any countess or governess, immediately say: "Look, how stately Madam Hogfeeder moves! Yesterday she toiled at her distaff from morning to night, and went to mass with the tail of her petticoat over her head, instead of her veil; and to-day, forsooth, she goes with her farthingale, her embroideries, and with an air, as if we did not know her." God keep me in my seven, or my five senses, or as many as I have; for I do not intend to expose myself after this manner. Go you, brother, to your governing and islanding, and puff yourself up as you please: as for my girl and I, by the life of my father, we will neither of us stir a step from our own town. For the proverb says:

> '"The wife that expects to have a good name,
> Is always at home as if she were lame:
> And the maid that is honest, her chiefest delight
> Is still to be doing from morning to night."

Go you with your Don Quixote to your adventures, and leave us with our ill fortunes: God will better them for us, if we deserve it: and truly I cannot imagine who made him a Don, a title which neither his father nor his grandfather ever had.'

'Certainly,' replied Sancho, 'you must have some familiar in that body of yours; heavens bless thee, woman! what a parcel of things have you been stringing one upon another, without either head or tail! What has Cascajo, the embroideries, or the proverbs to do with what I am saying? Hark you, fool, and ignorant (for so I may call you, since you understand not what I say, and are flying from good fortune), had I told you, that our daughter was to throw herself headlong from some high tower, or go strolling about the world, as did the Infanta Doña Urraca,* you would be in the right not to come into my opinion: but, if in two turns of a hand, and less than one twinkling of an eye, I can equip her with a Don and Your Ladyship, and raise you from the straw, to sit under a canopy of state, and upon a sofa with more velvet cushions, than all the Almohadas* of Morocco had Moors in their lineage, why will you not consent, and desire what I do?'

'Would you know why, husband?' answered Teresa: 'it is because of the proverb which says, He that covers thee, discovers thee. All glance their eyes hastily over the poor man, and fix them upon the rich; and if that rich man was once poor, then there is work for your murmurers and backbiters, who swarm everywhere like bees.'

'Look you, Teresa,' answered Sancho, 'and listen to what I am going to say to you; perhaps you have never heard it in all the days of your life: and I do not now speak of my own head; for all that I intend to say are sentences of that good father, the preacher, who held forth to us last Lent in this village; who, if I remember right, said, that all the things present, which our eyes behold, do appear, and exist in our minds much better, and with greater force, than things past.'

All these reasonings here of Sancho are another argument to persuade the translator that this chapter is apocryphal, as exceeding the capacity of Sancho, who went on saying:

'From hence it proceeds, that, when we see any person finely dressed, and set off with rich apparel, and with a train of servants, we are, as it were, compelled to show him respect, although the memory, in that instant, recalls to our thoughts some mean circumstances, under which we have seen him; which meanness, whether it be of poverty or descent, being already past, no longer exists, and there remains only what we see present before our eyes. And if this person, whom fortune has raised from the obscurity of his native meanness, proves well-behaved, liberal, and courteous to everybody, and does not set himself to vie with the ancient nobility, be assured, Teresa, that nobody will remember what he was, but will reverence what he is, excepting the envious, from whom no prosperous fortune is secure.'

'I do not understand you, husband,' replied Teresa: 'do what you think fit, and break not my brains any more with your speeches and flourishes. And if you are revolved to do as you say——'

'Resolved, you should say, wife,' quoth Sancho, 'and not revolved.'

'Set not yourself to dispute with me,' answered Teresa; 'I speak as it pleases God, and meddle not with what does not concern me. I say, if you hold still in the same mind of being a governor, take your son Sancho with you, and henceforward train him up to your art of government; for it is fitting the sons should inherit and learn their father's calling.'

'When I have a government,' quoth Sancho, 'I will send for him by the post, and will send you money, which I shall not want; for there are always people enough to lend governors money, when they have it not: but then be sure to clothe the boy so that he may look, not like what he is, but what he is to be.'

'Send you money,' quoth Teresa, 'and I will equip him as fine as a palm-branch.'

'We are agreed then,' quoth Sancho, 'that our daughter is to be a countess!'

'The day that I see her a countess,' answered Teresa, 'I shall reckon I am laying her in her grave: but I say again, you may do as you please; for we women are born to bear the clog of obedience to our husbands, be they never such blockheads.'

And then she began to weep as bitterly, as if she already saw little Sancha dead and buried. Sancho comforted her, and promised, that, though he must make her a countess, he would see and put it off as long as he possibly could. Thus ended their dialogue, and Sancho went back to visit Don Quixote, and put things in order for their departure.

CHAPTER 6

Of what passed between Don Quixote, his niece, and house-
keeper; one of the most important chapters of the
whole history.

WHILE Sancho Panza and his wife Teresa Cascajo were holding the foregoing impertinent dialogue, Don Quixote's niece and housekeeper were not idle; who, guessing by a thousand signs that their uncle and master would break loose the third time, and return to the exercise of his (for them) unlucky knight-errantry, endeavoured by all possible means to divert him from so foolish a design: but it was all preaching in the desert, and hammering on cold iron. However, among many other various reasonings, which passed between them, the housekeeper said to him:

'Sir, if your worship will not tarry quietly at home, and leave this rambling over hills and dales like a disturbed ghost, in quest of those same adventures, which I call misadventures, I am resolved to complain aloud to God and the king to put a stop to it.'

To which Don Quixote replied:

'Mistress Housekeeper, what answer God will return to your complaints, I know not; and what his majesty will answer, as little: I only know that, if I were king, I would dispense myself from answering that infinity of impertinent memorials, which are everyday presented to him: for, one of the greatest fatigues a king undergoes, is, the being obliged to hear and answer everybody; and therefore I should be loath my concerns should give him any trouble.'

To which the housekeeper replied:

'Pray, sir, are there not knights in his majesty's court?'

'Yes,' answered Don Quixote, 'there are many; and it is fitting there should, for the ornament and grandeur of princes, and for the ostentation of the royal dignity.'

'Would it not then be better,' replied she, 'that your worship should be one of them, and quietly serve your king and lord at court?'

'Look you, friend,' answered Don Quixote, 'all knights cannot be courtiers, neither can, nor ought, all courtiers to be knights-errant: there must be of all sorts in the world; and though we are all knights, there is a great deal of difference between us: for the courtiers, without stirring out of their apartments, or over the threshold, traverse the whole globe, on a map, without a farthing expense, and without suffering heat or cold, hunger or thirst. But we, the true knights-errant, measure the whole earth with our own feet, exposed to sun and cold, to the air and the inclemencies of the sky, by night and by day, on foot and on horseback: nor do we know our enemies in picture only, but in their proper persons, and attack them at every turn, and upon every occasion; without standing upon trifles, or upon the laws of duelling,—such as, whether our adversary bears a shorter or longer lance or sword, whether he carries about him any relics, or wears any secret coat of mail, or whether the sun be duly divided or not;* with other ceremonies of the same stamp, used in single combats between man and man, which you understand not, but I do.

'And you must know, further, that your true knight-errant, though he should espy ten giants, whose heads not only touch, but overtop the clouds, and though each of them stalk on two prodigious towers instead of legs, and has arms like the mainmasts of huge and mighty ships of war, and each eye like a great mill-wheel, and more fiery than the furnace of a glass-house, yet must he in no wise be affrighted, but, on the contrary, with a genteel air, and an undaunted heart, encounter, assail, and, if possible, overcome and rout them in an instant of time, though they should come armed with the shell of a certain fish, which, they say, is harder than adamant; and though, instead of swords, they should bring trenchant sabres of Damascan steel, or iron maces pointed also with steel, as I have seen more than once or twice. All this I have said, Mistress Housekeeper, to show you the difference between some knights and others, and it were to be wished, that every prince knew how to esteem this second, or rather first species of knights-errant, since as we read in their histories, some among them have been the bulwark, not of one only, but of many kingdoms.'

'Ah! dear uncle,' said then the niece, 'be assured, that what you tell us of knights-errant, is all invention and lies, and, if their histories must not be burnt, at least they deserve to wear each of them a *sanbenito*,* or some badge, whereby they may be known to be infamous, and destructive of good manners.'

'By the God in whom I live,' said Don Quixote, 'were you not my niece directly, as being my own sister's daughter, I would make such an example of you for the blasphemy you have uttered, that the whole world should ring of it. How! is it possible, that a young baggage, who scarcely knows how to manage a dozen of bobbins, should presume to put in her oar, and censure the histories of knights-errant? What would Sir Amadis have said, should he have heard of such a thing? But now I think of it, I am sure he would have forgiven you; for he was the most humble and most courteous knight of his time, and the greatest favourer of damsels. But some other might have heard you, from whom you might not have come off so well: for all are not courteous and good-natured; some are lewd and uncivil. Neither are all they, who call themselves knights, really such at bottom: for some are of gold, others of alchemy; and yet all appear to be knights, though all cannot abide the touchstone of truth. Mean fellows there are, who break their winds in straining to appear knights; and topping knights there are, who, one would think, die with desire to be thought mean men. The former raise themselves by their ambition, or by their virtues; the latter debase themselves by their weakness or their vices: and one had need of a good discernment to distinguish between these two kinds of knights, so near in their names, and so distant in their actions.'

'Bless me! uncle,' quoth the niece, 'that your worship should be so knowing, that, if need were, you might mount a pulpit, and hold forth anywhere in the streets, and yet should give in to so blind a vagary, and so exploded a piece of folly, as to think to persuade the world, that you are valiant now you are old; that you are strong, when, alas! you are infirm; and that you are able to make crooked things straight, though stooping yourself under the weight of years; above all, that you are a knight, when you are really none: for, though gentlemen may be such, yet poor ones hardly can.'

'You are much in the right, niece, in what you say,' answered Don Quixote, 'and I could tell you such things concerning lineages as would surprise you: but because I would not mix things divine with human, I forbear.

'Hear me, friends, with attention. All the genealogies in the world may be reduced to four sorts, which are these. First, of those, who, having had low beginnings, have gone on extending and dilating themselves till they have arrived at a prodigious grandeur. Secondly, of those, who, having had great beginnings, have preserved, and continue to preserve them in the same condition they were in at first. Thirdly, of those, who, though they have had great beginnings, have ended in a small point like a pyramid, having gone on diminishing and decreasing continually, till they have come almost to nothing; like the point of the pyramid, which, in respect of its base or pedestal, is next to nothing. Lastly, of those (and they are the most numerous) who, having had neither a good beginning, nor a tolerable middle, will therefore end without a name, like the families of common and ordinary people.

'Of the first sort, who, having had a mean beginning, rose to greatness, and still preserve it, we have an example in the Ottoman family, which from a poor shepherd its founder, is arrived at the height we now see it at. Of the second sort of genealogies, which began great, and preserve themselves without augmentation, examples may be fetched from sundry hereditary princes, who contain themselves peaceably within the limits of their own dominions, without enlarging or contracting them. Of those who began great, and have ended in a point, there are thousands of instances: for all the Pharaohs, and Ptolemies of Egypt, the Caesars of Rome, with all the herd (if I may so call them) of that infinite number of princes, monarchs, and lords, Medes, Assyrians, Persians, Greeks, and Barbarians; all these families and dominions, as well as their founders, have ended in a point and next to nothing: for it is impossible now to find any of their descendants, and, if one should find them, it would be in some low and abject condition. Of the lineages of the common sort I have nothing to say, only that they serve to swell the number of the living, without deserving any other fame or eulogy.

'From all that has been said, I would have you infer, my dear fools, that the confusion there is among genealogies is very great, and that those only appear great and illustrious, which show themselves such by the virtue, riches, and liberality of their possessors. I say, virtue, riches, and liberality, because the great man that is vicious will be greatly vicious; and the rich man, who is not liberal, is but a covetous beggar; for the possessor of riches is not happy in having, but in spending them, and not in spending them merely according to his own inclination, but in knowing how to spend them properly. The knight, who is poor, has no other way of showing himself to be one, but that of virtue, by being affable, wellbehaved, courteous, kind and obliging, not proud nor arrogant, no murmurer, and above all charitable; for, by two farthings given cheerfully to the poor, he shall discover as much generosity, as he, who bestows large alms by sound of bell: and there is no one, who sees him adorned with the aforesaid virtues, though he knows him not, but will judge and repute him to be well descended. Indeed, it would be a miracle were it otherwise, praise was always the reward of virtue, and the virtuous cannot fail of being commended.

'There are two roads, daughters, by which men may arrive at riches and honours; the one by the way of letters, the other by that of arms. I have more in me of the soldier than of the scholar; and was born, as appears by my propensity to arms, under the influence of the planet Mars; so that I am, as it were, forced into that track, and that road I must take in spite of the whole world: and it will be in vain for you to tire yourselves in persuading me not to attempt what heaven requires, fortune ordains, and reason demands, and above all, what my inclination leads me to. I know the innumerable toils attending on knight-errantry, I know also the numberless advantages obtained thereby. I know, that the path of virtue is straight and narrow, and the road of vice broad and spacious. I know also that their ends and resting-places are different: for those of vice, large and open, end in death; and those of virtue, narrow and intricate, end in life, and not in life that has an end, but in that which is eternal. And I know, as our great Castilian poet* expresses it, that:

'"Through these rough paths, to gain a glorious name,
We climb the steep ascent that leads to fame.
They miss the road, who quit the rugged way,
And in the smoother tracks of pleasure stray."'

'Ah, woe is me!' quoth the niece; 'what! my uncle a poet too! he knows everything; nothing comes amiss to him. I will lay a wager, that, if he had a mind to turn mason, he would build a house with as much ease as a bird-cage.'

'I assure you, niece,' answered Don Quixote, 'that if these knightly thoughts did not employ all my senses, there is nothing I could not do, nor any curious art, but what I could turn my hand to, especially bird-cages, and tooth-picks.'

By this time there was knocking at the door, and upon asking, 'Who is there?' Sancho Panza answered, 'It is I.'

The housekeeper no sooner knew his voice, but she ran to hide herself, so much she abhorred the sight of him. The niece let him in, and his master, Don Quixote, went out and received him with open arms; and they two, being locked up together in the knight's chamber, held another dialogue, not a jot inferior to the former.

CHAPTER 7

Of what passed between Don Quixote and his squire, with other most famous occurrences.

THE housekeeper no sooner saw that Sancho and her master had locked themselves up together, but she presently began to suspect the drift of their conference; and imagining that it would end in a resolution for a third sally, she took her veil, and, full of anxiety and trouble, went in quest of the bachelor Sampson Carrasco, thinking that, as he was a well-spoken person, and a new acquaintance of her master's, he might be able to dissuade him from so extravagant a purpose. She found him walking to and fro in the courtyard of his house, and, as soon as she espied him, she fell down at his feet in violent disorder and a cold sweat. When Carrasco beheld her with signs of so much sorrow and heart-beating, he said:

'What is the matter, Mistress Housekeeper? what has befallen you, that you look as if your heart was at your mouth?'

'Nothing at all, dear Master Sampson,' quoth she; 'only that my master is most certainly breaking forth.'

'How breaking forth, madam?' demanded Sampson; 'has he broken a hole in any part of his body?'

'No,' quoth she, 'he is only breaking forth at the door of his own madness: I mean, Señor Bachelor of my soul, that he has a mind to sally out again (and this will be his third time), to ramble about the world in quest of what he calls adventures,* though for my part, I cannot tell why he calls them so. The first time he was brought home to us athwart an ass, and mashed to a mummy. The second time he came home in an ox-wagon, locked up in a cage, in which he persuaded himself he was enchanted: and the poor soul was so changed, that he could not be known by the mother that bore him, feeble, wan, his eyes sunk to the inmost lodgings of his brain, insomuch that I spent above six hundred eggs in getting him a little up again, as God and the world is my witness, and my hens that will not let me lie.'

'I can easily believe that,' answered the bachelor; 'for they are so good, so plump, and so well nurtured, that they will not say one thing for another, though they should burst for it. In short then, Mistress Housekeeper, there is nothing more, nor any other disaster, only what it is feared Señor Don Quixote may peradventure have a mind to do?'

'No, sir,' answered she.

'Be in no pain then,' replied the bachelor; 'but go home, in God's name, and get me something warm for breakfast; and by the way, as you go, repeat the prayer of St. Apollonia, if you know it; and I will be with you instantly, and you shall see wonders.'

'Dear me!' replied the housekeeper, 'the prayer of St. Apollonia, say you? that might do something, if my master's distemper lay in his gums; but alas! it lies in his brain.'

'I know what I say, Mistress Housekeeper,' replied Sampson; 'get you home, and do not stand disputing with me; for you know I am a Salamanca bachelor of arts, and there is no bachelorizing beyond that.'

With that, away went the housekeeper, and the bachelor immediately went to find the priest, and consult with him about what you will hear of in due time.

While Don Quixote and Sancho continued locked up together, there passed some discourse between them, which the history relates at large with great punctuality and truth. Quoth Sancho to his master:

'Sir, I have now reluced my wife to consent to let me go with your worship wherever you please to carry me.'

'Reduced, you should say, Sancho,' quoth Don Quixote, 'and not reluced.'

'Once or twice already,' answered Sancho, 'if I remember right, I have besought your worship not to mend my words, if you understand my meaning; and when you do not, say, Sancho, or devil, I understand you not; and if I do not explain myself, then you may correct me; for I am so focible—'

'I do not understand you, Sancho,' said Don Quixote, presently; 'for I know not the meaning of focible.'

'So focible,' answered Sancho, 'means, I am so much so.'

'I understand you less now,' replied Don Quixote.

'Why, if you do not understand me,' answered Sancho, 'I know not how to express it; I know no more, God help me.'

'O! now I have it,' answered Don Quixote: 'you mean you are so docible, so pliant, and so tractable, that you will readily comprehend whatever I shall say to you, and will learn whatever I shall teach you.'

'I will lay a wager,' quoth Sancho, 'that you took me from the beginning, and understood me perfectly; only you had a mind to put me out, to hear me make two hundred blunders more.'

'That may be,' replied Don Quixote: 'but, in short, what says Teresa?'

'Teresa,' quoth Sancho, 'says, that fast bind fast find, and that we must have less talking and more doing; for he who shuffles is not he who cuts, and one performance is worth two promises: and, say I, there is but little in woman's advice, yet he that won't take it is not overwise.'

'I say so too,' replied Don Quixote: 'proceed, Sancho, for you talk admirably to-day.'

'The case is,' replied Sancho, 'that, as your worship very well knows, we are all mortal, here to-day, and gone to-morrow; that the lamb goes to the spit as soon as the sheep; and that nobody can promise himself in this world more hours of life than God pleases to give him: for death is deaf, and, when he knocks at life's door, is always in haste; and nothing can stay him, neither force, nor entreaties, nor sceptres, nor mitres, according to public voices and report, and according to what is told us from our pulpits.'

'All this is true,' said Don Quixote: 'but I do not perceive what you would be at.'

'What I would be at,' quoth Sancho, 'is, that your worship would be pleased to appoint me a certain salary, at so much per month, for the time I shall serve you, and that the said salary be paid me out of your estate; for I have no mind to stand to the courtesy of recompenses, which come late, or lame, or never, God help me with my own. In short, I would know what I am to get, be it little or much: for the hen sits if it be but upon one egg, and many little ones make a mickle, and while one is getting something, one is losing nothing. In good truth, should it fall out (which I neither believe nor expect) that your worship should give me that same island you have promised me, I am not so ungrateful, nor am I for making so hard a bargain, as not to consent, that the amount of the rent of such island be appraised, and my salary be deducted, cantity for cantity.'

'Is not quantity as good as cantity, friend Sancho?' answered Don Quixote.

'I understand you,' quoth Sancho; 'I will lay a wager, I should have said quantity, and not cantity: but that signifies nothing, since your worship knew my meaning.'

'Yes; and so perfectly too,' returned Don Quixote, 'that I see to the very bottom of your thoughts, and the mark you drive at with the innumerable arrows of your proverbs. Look you, Sancho, I could easily appoint you wages, had I ever met with any precedent, among the histories of knights-errant, to discover or show me the least glimmering of what they used to get monthly or yearly. I have read all, or most of those histories, and do not remember ever to have read, that any knight-errant allowed his squire set wages. I only know that they all served upon courtesy, and that, when they least thought of it, if their masters had good luck, they were rewarded with an island, or something equivalent, or at least remained with a title and dignity. If Sancho, upon the strength of these expectations, you are willing to return to my service, in God's name do so: but to think that I will force the ancient usage of knight-errantry off the hinges, is a very great mistake. And therefore, Sancho, go home, and tell your wife my intention, and if she is willing, and you have a mind to stay with me upon courtesy, *bene quidem*; if not, we are as we were: for if the dove-house wants not bait, it will never want pigeons: and take notice, son, that a good reversion is better than a bad possession, and a good demand than bad pay. I talk thus, Sancho, to let you see, that I can let fly a volley of proverbs as well as you. To be short with you, if you are not disposed to go along with me upon courtesy, and run the same fortune with me, the Lord have thee in His keeping, and make thee a saint, I pray God; for I can never want a squire, who will be more obedient, more diligent, and neither so selfish nor so talkative, as you are.'

When Sancho heard his master's fixed resolution, the sky clouded over with him, and the wings of his heart downright flagged; for till now he verily believed his master would not go without him for the world's worth. While he stood thus thoughtfull, and in suspense, in came Sampson Carrasco, and the niece and the housekeeper, who had a mind to hear what arguments he made use of to dissuade their master and uncle from going again in quest of adventures. Sampson, who was a notable wag, drew near, and embracing Don Quixote, as he did the time before, he exalted his voice, and said:

'O flower of knight-errantry! O resplendent light of arms! O mirror and honour of the Spanish nation! may it please Almighty God of His infinite goodness, that the person, or persons, who shall obstruct, or disappoint your third sally, may never find the way out of the labyrinth of their desires, nor ever accomplish what they so ardently wish.'

And turning to the housekeeper, he said:

'Now, Mistress Housekeeper, you may save yourself the trouble of saying the prayer of St. Apollonia; for I know that it is the precise determination of the stars, that Señor Don Quixote shall once more put in execution his glorious and uncommon designs, and I should greatly burden my conscience, did I not give intimation thereof, and persuade this knight no longer to detain and withhold the force of his valorous arm, and the goodness of his most undaunted courage, lest, by his delay, he defraud the world of the redress of injuries, the protection of orphans, the maintaining the honour of damsels, the relief of widows, and the support of married women, with other matters of this nature, which concern, depend upon, appertain, and are annexed to, the order of knight-errantry. Go on then, dear Señor Don Quixote, beautiful and brave; and let your worship and grandeur lose no time, but set forward rather to-day than to-morrow; and if anything be wanting towards putting your design in execution, here am I, ready to supply it with my life and fortune; and if your magnificence stands in need of a squire, I shall think it a singular piece of good fortune to serve you as such.'

Don Quixote thereupon, turning to Sancho, said:

'Did I not tell you, Sancho, that I should have squires enough and to spare? behold, who is it that offers himself to be one, but the unheard-of bachelor Sampson Carrasco, the perpetual darling and delight of the Salamancan schools, sound and active of body, no prater, patient of heat and cold, of hunger and thirst, with all the qualifications necessary to the squire of a knight-errant? but heaven forbid, that, to gratify my own private inclination, I should endanger this pillar of literature, this urn of sciences, and lop off so eminent a branch of the noble and liberal arts. Let our new Sampson abide in his country, and, in it doing honour, at the same time reverence the grey hairs of his ancient parents; for I will make shift with any squire whatever, since Sancho deigns not to go along with me.'

'I do deign,' quoth Sancho, melted into tenderness, and his eyes overflowing with tears, and proceeded:

'It shall never be said of me, dear master, the bread is eaten, and the company broke up. I am not come of an ungrateful stock; since all the world knows, especially our village, who the Panzas were, from whom I am descended: besides, I know, and am very well assured, by many good works, and more good words, of the desire your worship has to do me a kindness; and if I have taken upon me so much more than I ought, by intermeddling in the article of wages, it was out of complaisance to my wife, who, when once she takes in hand to persuade a thing, no mallet drives and forces the hoops of a tub, as she does to make one do what she has a mind to: but, in short, a man must be a man, and a woman a woman; and since I am a man everywhere else (I cannot deny that), I will also be one in my own house, vex whom it will: and therefore there is no more to be done, but that your worship give orders about your will, and its codicil, in such manner that it cannot be rebuked, and let us set out immediately, that the soul of Señor Sampson may not suffer, who says he is obliged in conscience to persuade your worship to make a third sally; and I again offer myself to serve your worship, faithfully and loyally, as well, and better than all the squires that ever served knight-errant, in past or present times.'

The bachelor stood in admiration to hear Sancho Panza's style and manner of talking; for though he had read the first part of his master's history, he never believed he was so ridiculous as he is therein described; but hearing him now talk of will and codicil that could not be 'rebuked', instead of 'revoked', he believed all he had read of him, and concluded him to be one of the most solemn coxcombs of the age; and said to himself, that two such fools, as master and man, were never before seen in the world. In fine, Don Quixote and Sancho, being perfectly reconciled, embraced each other, and with the approbation and good-liking of the grand Carrasco, now their oracle, it was decreed their departure should be within three days, in which time they might have leisure to provide what was necessary for the expedition, especially a complete helmet, which Don Quixote said he must by all means carry with him. Sampson offered him one, belonging to a friend of his, who, he was sure, would not deny it him, though to say the truth, the brightness of the steel was not a little obscured by tarnish and rust.

The curses, which the housekeeper and niece heaped upon the bachelor, were not to be numbered; they tore their hair, and scratched their faces, and, like the funeral mourners formerly in fashion, lamented the approaching departure, as if it were the death of their master. The design Sampson had in persuading him to sally forth again, was to do what the history tells us hereafter, all by the advice of the priest and the barber, with whom he had plotted beforehand.

In short, in those three days, Don Quixote and Sancho furnished themselves with what they thought convenient, and, Sancho having appeased his wife, and Don Quixote his niece and housekeeper, in the dusk of the evening, unobserved by anybody but the bachelor, who would needs bear him company half a league from the village, they took the road to Toboso; Don Quixote upon his good Rosinante, and Sancho upon his old Dapple, his wallets stored with provisions, and his purse with money, which Don Quixote had given him against whatever might happen. Sampson embraced him, praying him to give him advice of his good or ill fortune, that he might rejoice or condole with him, as the laws of their mutual friendship required. Don Quixote promised he would: Sampson returned to the village, and the knight and squire took their way towards the great city of Toboso.

CHAPTER 8

Wherein is related what befell Don Quixote, as he was going to visit his lady Dulcinea del Toboso.

'PRAISED be the mighty Allah!' says Cid Hamet Ben Engeli, at the beginning of this eighth chapter: 'praised be Allah!' repeating it thrice, and saying, he gives these praises, to find that Don Quixote and Sancho had again taken the field, and that the readers of their delightful history may make account, that, from this moment the exploits and witty sayings of Don Quixote and his squire begin. He persuades them to forget the former chivalries of the ingenious gentleman, and fix their eyes upon his future achievements, which begin now upon the road to Toboso as the former began in the fields of Montiel; and this is no very unreasonable request, considering what great things he promises, and thus he goes on, saying:

Don Quixote and Sancho remained by themselves; and scarcely was Sampson parted from them, when Rosinante began to neigh, and Dapple to sigh;* which was held by both knight and squire for a good sign, and a most happy omen, though if the truth were to be told, the sighs and brayings of the ass exceeded the neighings of the steed; from whence Sancho gathered that his good luck was to surpass and get above that of his master. But whether he drew this inference from judicial astrology, I cannot say, it not being known whether he was versed in it, since the history says nothing of it: only he had been heard to say, when he stumbled or fell, that he would have been glad he had not gone out of doors; for by a stumble or a fall nothing was to be got but a torn shoe, or a broken rib; and though he was a simpleton, he was not much out of the way in this.

Don Quixote said to him:

'Friend Sancho, the night is coming on apace, and with too much darkness for us to reach Toboso by daylight; whither I am resolved to go, before I undertake any other adventures: there will I receive the blessing and the good leave of the peerless Dulcinea, with which leave I am well assured of finishing, and giving a happy conclusion to every perilous adventure; for nothing in this world inspires knights-errant with so much valour, as the finding themselves favoured by their mistresses.'

'I believe it,' answered Sancho; 'but I am of opinion, it will be difficult for your worship to come to the speech of her, or be alone with her, at least in any place where you may receive her benediction, unless she tosses it over the pales of the yard; from whence I saw her the time before, when I carried her the letter, with the news of the follies and extravagances your worship was playing in the heart of the Sierra Morena.'

'Pales did you fancy them to be, Sancho,' quoth Don Quixote, 'over which you saw that paragon of gentility and beauty? impossible! you must mean galleries, arcades, or cloisters of some rich and royal palace.'

'All that may be,' answered Sancho; 'but to me they seemed pales, or I have a very shallow memory.'

'However, let us go thither, Sancho,' replied Don Quixote; 'for so I do but see her, be it through pales, through windows, through crannies, or through the rails of a garden, this I shall gain by it, that how small soever a ray of the sun of her beauty reaches my eyes, it will so enlighten my understanding, and fortify my heart, that I shall remain without a rival either in wisdom or valour.'

'In truth, sir,' answered Sancho, 'when I saw this sun of

the lady Dulcinea del Toboso, it was not so bright as to send forth any rays; and the reason must be that, as her ladyship was winnowing that wheat I told you of, the great quantity of dust, that flew out of it, overcast her face like a cloud, and obscured it.'

'What! Sancho,' said Don Quixote, 'do you persist in saying and believing, that my lady Dulcinea was winnowing wheat; a business and employment quite foreign to persons of distinction, who are designed and reserved for other exercises and amusements, which distinguish their high quality a bow-shot off? You forget, Sancho, our poet's verses,* in which he describes the labours of those four nymphs, in their crystal mansions, when they raised their heads above the delightful Tagus, and seated themselves in the green meadow, to work those rich stuffs, which, as the ingenious poet there describes them, were all embroidered with gold, silk, and pearls. And in this manner must my lady have been employed, when you saw her: but the envy some wicked enchanter bears me, changes and converts into different shapes everything that should give me pleasure; and therefore, in that history, said to be published of my exploits, if peradventure its author was some sage my enemy, he has, I fear, put one thing for another, with one truth mixing a thousand lies, and amusing himself with relating actions foreign to what is requisite for the continuation of a true history. O envy! thou root of infinite evils, and canker-worm of virtues! All other vices, Sancho, carry somewhat of pleasure along with them: but envy is attended with nothing but distaste, rancour, and rage.'

'That is what I say too,' replied Sancho; 'and I take it for granted, in that same legend or history of us, the bachelor Carrasco tells us he has seen, my reputation is tossed about like a tennis-ball. Now, as I am an honest man, I never spoke ill of any enchanter, nor have I wealth enough to be envied. It is true, indeed, I am said to be somewhat sly, and to have a little spice of the knave; but the grand cloak of my simplicity, always natural and never artificial, hides and covers all. And if I had nothing else to boast of, but the believing, as I do always, firmly and truly in God, and in all that the holy Catholic Roman Church holds and believes, and the being, as I really am, a mortal enemy to the Jews, the historians ought to have mercy upon me, and treat me well in their writings. But let them say what they will; naked was I born, and naked I am: I neither lose nor win; and, so my name be but in print, and go about the world from hand to hand, I care not a fig, let people say of me whatever they list.'

'That, Sancho,' quoth Don Quixote, 'is just like what happened to a famous poet of our times, who having wrote an ill-natured satire upon the court-ladies, a certain lady, who was not expressly named in it, so that it was doubtful whether she was implied in it or not, complained to the poet, asking him what he had seen in her, that he had not inserted her among the rest, telling him he must enlarge his satire, and put her in the supplement, or woe be to him. The poet did as he was bid, and set her down for such as duennas will not name. As for the lady, she was satisfied to find herself infamously famous. Of the same kind is the story they tell of that shepherd, who set fire to, and burnt down, the famous temple of Diana, reckoned one of the seven wonders of the world, only that his name might live in future ages; and though it was ordered by public edict, that nobody should name or mention him either by word or writing, that he might not attain to the end he proposed, yet still it is known he was called Erostratus.

'To the same purpose may be alleged what happened to the great emperor Charles the Fifth, with a Roman knight. The emperor had a mind to see the famous church of the Rotunda, which by the ancients was called the Pantheon, or Temple of all the gods, and now, by a better name, the Church of All Saints, and is one of the most entire edifices remaining of heathen Rome, and which most preserves the fame of the greatness and magnificence of its founders. It is made in the shape of a half-orange, very spacious, and very lightsome, though it has but one window, or rather a round opening at top: from whence the emperor having surveyed the inside of the structure, a Roman knight, who stood by his side, showing him the beauty and ingenious contrivance of that vast machine and memorable piece of architecture, when they were come down from the skylight, said to the emperor.

'"Sacred sir, a thousand times it came into my head to clasp your majesty in my arms, and cast myself down with you from the top to the bottom of the church, merely to leave an eternal name behind me."

'"I thank you," answered the emperor, "for not putting so wicked a thought in execution, and henceforward I will never give you an opportunity of making the like proof of your loyalty, and therefore command you never to speak to me more, or come into my presence."

'And after these words he bestowed some great favour upon him.* What I mean, Sancho, is, that the desire of fame is a very active principle in us. What, think you, cast Horatius down from the bridge, armed at all points, into the depth of the Tiber? What burnt the arm and hand of Mutius? What impelled Curtius to throw himself into the flaming gulf, that opened itself in the midst of Rome? What made Caesar pass the Rubicon in opposition to all presages? And, in more modern examples, what bored the ships, and stranded those valiant Spaniards, conducted by the most courteous Cortés in the New World!* All these, and other great and very different exploits, are, were, and shall be, the works of fame, which mortals desire as the reward and earnest of that immortality their noble deeds deserve: though we Christian and Catholic knights-errant ought to be more intent upon the glory of the world to come, which is eternal in the ethereal and celestial regions, than upon the vanity of fame, acquired in this present and transitory world; for, let it last never so long, it must end with the world itself, which has its appointed period.

'Therefore, O Sancho, let not our works exceed the bounds prescribed by the Christian religion, which we profess. In killing giants we are to destroy pride: we must overcome envy by generosity and good-nature, anger by sedateness and composure of mind, gluttony and sleep by eating little and watching much, lust and lasciviousness by the fidelity we maintain to those we have made mistresses of our thoughts, laziness by going about all parts of the world, and seeking occasions, which may make us, besides being Christians, renowned knights. These, Sancho, are the means of obtaining those extremes of praise, which a good name brings along with it.'

'All that your worship has hitherto told me,' quoth Sancho, 'I very well understand: but, for all that, I wish you would be so kind as to dissolve me one doubt, which is this moment come into my mind.'

'"Resolve", you would say, Sancho,' quoth Don Quixote: 'out with it in God's name; for I will answer as far as I know.'

'Pray, tell me, sir,' proceeded Sancho, 'those Julys and Augusts,* and all those feat-doing knights you spoke of, that are dead, where are they now?'

'The Gentiles,' answered Don Quixote, 'are doubtless in hell: the Christians, if they were good Christians, are either in purgatory, or in heaven.'

'Very well,' quoth Sancho; 'but let us know now, whether the sepulchres, in which the bodies of those great lords lie interred, have silver lamps burning before them, and whether the walls of their chapels are adorned with crutches, winding-sheets, old perukes, legs, and eyes; and, if not with these, pray, with what are they adorned?'

To which Don Quixote answered: 'The sepulchres of the heathens were for the most part sumptuous temples. The ashes of Julius Caesar were deposited in an urn, placed on the top of a pyramid of stone, of a prodigious bigness, which is now called the obelisk of St. Peter. The sepulchre of the emperor Adrian was a castle as big as a good[-sized] village, called Moles Adriani, and now the castle of St. Angelo, in Rome. Queen Artemisia buried her husband Mausolus in a tomb, reckoned one of the seven wonders of the world. But none of these sepulchres, nor [of the] many others of the Gentiles, were hung about with windingsheets, or other offerings, or signs, to denote those to be saints, who were buried in them.'

'That is what I am coming to,' replied Sancho; 'and now, pray tell me, which is the more difficult, to raise a dead man to life, or to slay a giant?'

'The answer is very obvious,' answered Don Quixote; 'to raise a dead man.'

'There I have caught you,' quoth Sancho. 'His fame then, who raises the dead, gives sight to the blind, makes the lame walk, and cures the sick; before whose sepulchre lamps are continually burning, and whose chapels are crowded with devotees, adoring his relics upon their knees; his fame, I say, shall be greater both in this world and the next, than that which all the heathen emperors and knights-errant in the world ever had, or ever shall have.'

'I grant it,' answered Don Quixote.

'Then' replied Sancho, 'the bodies and relics of saints have this fame, these graces, these prerogatives, or how do you call them, with the approbation and licence of our holy mother church, and also their lamps, winding-sheets, crutches, pictures, perukes, eyes, and legs, whereby they increase people's devotion, and spread their own Christian fame. Besides, kings themselves carry the bodies or relics of saints upon their shoulders, kiss bits of their bones, and adorn and enrich their chapels and most favourite altars with them.'

'What would you have me infer, Sancho, from all you have been saying?' quoth Don Quixote.

'I would infer,' said Sancho, 'that we had better turn saints immediately, and we shall then soon attain to that renown we aim at. And pray take notice, sir, that yesterday, or t'other day (for it is so little a while ago that I may so speak), a couple of poor barefooted friars* were beatified or canonized, whose iron chains, wherewith they girded and disciplined themselves, people now reckon it a great happiness to touch or kiss; and they are now held in greater veneration than Orlando's sword in the armoury of our lord the king, God bless him. So that, master of mine, it is better being a poor friar of the meanest order, than the valiantest knight-errant whatever; for a couple of dozen of penitential lashes are more esteemed in the sight of God, than two thousand tilts with a lance, whether it be against giants, goblins, or dragons.'

'I confess,' answered Don Quixote, 'all this is just as you say: but we cannot be all friars; and many and various are the ways, by which God conducts his elect to heaven. Chivalry is a kind of religious profession; and some knights are now saints in glory.'

'True,' answered Sancho; 'but I have heard say, there are more friars in heaven, than knights-errant.'

'It may well be so,' replied Don Quixote; 'because the number of the religious is much greater than that of the knights-errant.'

'And yet,' quoth Sancho, 'there are abundance of the errant sort.'

'Abundance, indeed,' answered Don Quixote; 'but few, who deserve the name of knights.'

In these and the like discourses they passed that night, and the following day, without any accident worth relating; whereat Don Quixote was not a little grieved. In short, next day they descried the great city of Toboso; at sight whereof Don Quixote's spirits were much elevated, and Sancho's as much dejected, because he did not know Dulcinea's house, and had never seen her in his life, no more than his master had; so that they were both equally in pain, the one to see her, and the other for not having seen her: and Sancho knew not what to do when his master should send him to Toboso. In fine, Don Quixote resolved to enter the city about night-fall; and, till that hour came, they stayed among some oak trees near the town; and the time appointed being come, they went into the city, where things befell them that were things indeed.

CHAPTER 9

Which relates what will be found in it.

HALF the night, or thereabouts,* was spent, when Don Quixote and Sancho left the mountain,* and entered into Toboso. The town was all hushed in silence: for its inhabitants were sound asleep, reposing, as the phrase is, with outstretched legs. The night was not quite a dark one: though Sancho could have wished it were, that the obscurity thereof might cover or excuse his prevarication. Nothing was heard in all the place but the barking of dogs, stunning Don Quixote's ears, and disquieting Sancho's heart. Now and then an ass brayed, swine grunted, and cats mewed: which different sounds were augmented by the silence of the night. All which the enamoured knight took for an ill omen; nevertheless, he said to Sancho:

'Sancho, son, lead on before to Dulcinea's palace; for it may be we shall find her awake.'

'To what palace? body of the sun!' answered Sancho: 'That I saw her highness in was but a very little house.'

'She must have been retired at that time,' replied Don Quixote, 'to some small apartment of her castle, amusing herself with her damsels, as is usual with great ladies and princesses.'

'Since your worship,' quoth Sancho, 'will needs have my lady Dulcinea's house to be a castle, is this an hour to find the gates open; and is it fit we should stand thundering at the door, till they open and let us in, putting the whole house in an uproar? Think you, we are going to a bawdy-house, like your gallants, who knock, and call, and are let in at what hour they please, be it never so late?'

'First, to make one thing sure, let us find this castle,' replied Don Quixote, 'and then I will tell you what is fit to be done: and look, Sancho; for either my eyes deceive me, or that great, dark bulk we see yonder must be Dulcinea's palace.'

'Then lead on yourself, sir,' answered Sancho: 'perhaps it may be so; though if I were to see it with my eyes and touch it with my hands, I will believe it just as much as I believe it is now day.'

Don Quixote led the way, and, having gone about two hundred paces, he came up to the bulk, which cast the dark shade, and perceived it was a large steeple,* and presently knew, that the building was no palace, but the principal church of the place: whereupon he said:

'We are come to the church, Sancho.'

'I find we are,' answered Sancho: 'and pray God we be not come to our graves: for it is no very good sign, to be rambling about churchyards at such hours, and especially since I have already told your worship, if I remember right, that this same lady's house stands in an alley, where there is no thoroughfare.'

'God's curse light on thee, thou blockhead!' said Don Quixote: 'where have you found, that castles and royal palaces are built in alleys without a thoroughfare?'

'Sir,' replied Sancho, 'each country has its customs: perhaps it is the fashion here in Toboso to build your palaces and great edifices in alleys; and, therefore, I beseech your worship to let me look about among these lanes or alleys just before me; and it may be in one nook or other I may pop upon this same palace, which I wish I may see devoured by dogs, for confounding and bewildering us at this rate.'

'Speak with respect, Sancho, of my lady's matters,' quoth Don Quixote: 'let us keep our holidays in peace, and not throw the rope after the bucket.'

'I will curb myself,' answered Sancho: 'but with what patience can I bear to think that your worship will needs have me know our mistress's house, and find it at midnight, having seen it but once, when you cannot find it yourself though you must have seen it thousands of times?'

'You will put me past all patience, Sancho,' quoth Don Quixote; 'come hither, heretic; have not I told you a thousand times, that I never saw the peerless Dulcinea in all the days of my life, nor ever stepped over the threshold of her palace, and that I am enamoured only by hearsay, and by the great fame of her wit and beauty?'

'I hear it now,' answered Sancho; 'and I say, that since your worship has never seen her, no more have I.'

'That cannot be,' replied Don Quixote; 'for at least you told me some time ago, that you saw her winnowing wheat, when you brought me the answer to the letter I sent by you.'

'Do not insist upon that, sir,' answered Sancho; 'for, let me tell you, the sight of her, and the answer I brought, were both by hearsay too; and I can no more tell who the lady Dulcinea is, than I am able to box the moon.'

'Sancho, Sancho,' answered Don Quixote, 'there is a time to jest, and a time when jests are unseasonable. What! because I say that I never saw nor spoke to the mistress of my soul, must you therefore say so too, when you know the contrary so well?'

While they two were thus discoursing, they perceived one passing by with a couple of mules, and, by the noise of a ploughshare made in dragging along the ground, they judged it must be some husbandman, who had got up before day, and was going to his work; and so in truth it was. The ploughman came singing the ballad of the defeat of the French in Roncesvalles.* Don Quixote, hearing it, said:

'Let me die, Sancho, if we shall have any good luck to-night: do you not hear what this peasant is singing?'

'Yes, I do,' answered Sancho; 'but what is the defeat at Roncesvalles to our purpose? he might as well have sung the ballad of Calainos; for it had been all one as to the good or ill success of our business.'

By this time the country fellow was come up to them, and Don Quixote said to him:

'Good-morrow, honest friend; can you inform me where stands the palace of the peerless princess Doña Dulcinea del Toboso?'

'Sir,' answered the young fellow, 'I am a stranger, and have been but a few days in this town, and serve a rich farmer in tilling his ground: in yon house over the way live the parish priest and the sexton of the place: both, or either of them, can give your worship an account of this same lady princess; for they keep a register of all the inhabitants of Toboso: though I am of opinion no princess at all lives in this town, but several great ladies, that might every one be a princess in her own house.'

'One of these then,' quoth Don Quixote, 'must be her I am inquiring after.'

'Not unlikely,' answered the ploughman, 'and God speed you well; for the dawn begins to appear.'

And, pricking on his mules, he stayed for no more questions.

Sancho, seeing his master in suspense, and sufficiently dissatisfied, said to him:

'Sir, the day comes on apace, and it will not be advisable to let the sun overtake us in the street: it will be better to retire out of the city, and that your worship shelter yourself in some grove hereabouts, and I will return by daylight, and leave no nook or corner in all the town unsearched for this house, castle, or palace of my lady's; and I shall have ill luck if I do not find it: and as soon as I have found it, I will speak to her ladyship, and will tell her where, and how your worship is waiting for her orders and direction for you to see her without prejudice to her honour or reputation.'

'Sancho,' quoth Don Quixote, 'you have uttered a thousand sentences in the compass of a few words; the counsel you give I relish much, and accept of most heartily: come along, son, and let us seek where we can take covert: afterwards, as you say, you shall return to seek, see, and speak to my lady, from whose discretion and courtesy I expect more than miraculous favours.'

Sancho stood upon thorns till he got his master out of town, lest he should detect the lie of the answer he carried him to the Sierra Morena, pretending it came from Dulcinea: and therefore he made haste to be gone, which they did instantly: and about two miles from the place they found a grove or wood, in which Don Quixote took shelter, while Sancho returned back to the city to speak to Dulcinea; in which embassy there befell him things which require fresh attention and fresh credit.

CHAPTER 10

Wherein is related the cunning used by Sancho in enchanting the lady Dulcinea, with other events as ridiculous as true.

THE author of this grand history, coming to relate what is contained in this chapter, says, he had a mind to have passed it over in silence, fearing not to be believed, because herein Don Quixote's madness exceeds all bounds, and rises to the utmost pitch, even two bow-shots beyond the greatest extravagance: however, notwithstanding this fear and diffidence, he has set everything down in the manner it was transacted, without adding to, or diminishing a tittle from the truth of the story, and not regarding the objections that might be made against his veracity: and he had reason: for truth may be stretched, but cannot be broken, and always gets above falsehood, as oil does above water; and so, pursuing his story, he says:

As soon as Don Quixote had sheltered himself in the grove, oak-wood, or forest, near the great Toboso, he ordered Sancho to go back to the town, commanding him not to return into his presence, till he had first spoken to his lady, beseeching her that she would be pleased to give her captive knight leave to wait upon her, and that she would deign to give him her blessing, that from thence he might hope for the most prosperous success in all his encounters and difficult enterprises. Sancho undertook to fulfil his command, and to bring him as good an answer now as he did the time before.

'Go then, son,' replied Don Quixote, 'and be not in confusion when you stand before the blaze of that sun of beauty you are going to seek. Happy thou above all the squires in the world! Bear in mind, and be sure do not forget, how she receives you: whether she changes colour while you are delivering your embassy; whether you perceive in her any uneasiness or disturbance at hearing my name; whether her cushion cannot hold her, if perchance you find her seated on the rich *estrado** of her dignity; and, if she be standing, mark, whether she stands sometimes upon one foot and sometimes upon the other; whether she repeats the answer she gives you three or four times; whether she changes it from soft to harsh, from sharp to amorous; whether she lifts her hand to adjust her hair, though it be not disordered: lastly, son, observe all her actions and motions: for, by your relating them to me just as they were, I shall be able to give a shrewd guess at what she keeps concealed in the secret recesses of her heart, touching the affair of my love. For you must know, Sancho, if you do not know it already, that among lovers, the external actions and gestures, when their loves are the subject, are most certain couriers, and bring infallible tidings of what passes in the inmost recesses of the soul. Go, friend, and better fortune than mine be your guide: and may better success, than what I fear and expect in this bitter solitude, send you back safe.'

'I will go, and return quickly,' quoth Sancho: 'in the meantime, good sir, enlarge that little heart of yours, which at present can be no bigger than a hazel-nut, and consider the common saying, that a good heart breaks bad luck; and where there is no bacon, there are no pins to hang it on; and, where we least think it, there starts the hare; this I say, because, though we could not find the castles or palaces of my lady Dulcinea last night, now that it is daylight, I reckon to meet with them when I least think of it; and when I have found them, let me alone to deal with her.'

'Verily, Sancho,' quoth Don Quixote, 'you have the knack of applying your proverbs so to the subject we are upon, that I pray God send me better luck in obtaining my wishes!'

Upon this, Sancho turned his back, and switched his Dapple, leaving Don Quixote on horseback, resting on his stirrups, and leaning on his lance, full of sad and confused imaginations: where we will leave him, and go along with Sancho Panza, who departed from his master no less confused and thoughtful than he; insomuch that he was scarcely got out of the grove, when turning about his head, and finding that Don Quixote was not in sight, he lighted from his beast, and setting himself down at the foot of a tree, he began to talk to himself, and say:

'Tell me now, brother Sancho, whither is your worship going? Are you going to seek some ass that is lost? No, verily. Then what are you going to seek? Why I go to look for a thing of nothing, a princess, and in her the sun of beauty, and all heaven together. Well, Sancho, and where think you to find all this? Where? in the grand city of Toboso. Very well: and pray who sent you on this errand? Why, the renowned knight Don Quixote de la Mancha, who redresses wrongs, and gives drink to the hungry, and meat to the thirsty. All this is very well: and do you know her house, Sancho? My master says it must be some royal palace, or stately castle. And have you ever seen her? Neither I, nor my master, have ever seen her. And do you think it would be right or advisable, that the people of Toboso should know you come with a design to inveigle away their princesses, and lead their ladies astray? what if they should come, and grind your ribs with pure dry basting, and not leave you a whole bone in your skin? Truly they would be much in the right of it, unless they please to consider, that I am commanded, and being but a messenger, am not in fault.* Trust not to that, Sancho; for the Manchegans are as choleric as honourable, and so ticklish, nobody must touch them. God's my life! if they smoke us, woe be to us. But why go I looking for three legs in a cat, for another man's pleasure? Besides, to look for Dulcinea up and down Toboso, is as if one should look for little Mary in Ravenna, or a bachelor in Salamanca.* The devil, the devil, and nobody else, has put me upon this business.'

This soliloquy Sancho held with himself, and the upshot was to return to it again, saying to himself:

'Well, there is a remedy for everything but death, under whose dominion we must all pass in spite of our teeth, at the end of our lives. This master of mine, by a thousand tokens that I have seen, is mad enough to be tied in his bed; and in truth I come very little behind him: nay, I am madder than he, to follow him, and serve him, if there be any truth in the proverb that says: Show me thy company, and I will tell thee what thou art: or in that other; Not with whom thou wert bred, but with whom thou art fed. He, then, being a madman, as he really is, and so mad as frequently to mistake one thing for another, taking black for white, and white for black (as appeared plainly, when he said, the windmills were giants, and the monks' mules dromedaries,* and the flocks of sheep armies of enemies, and many more matters to the same tune), it will not be very difficult to make him believe, that a country wench (the first I light upon) is the lady Dulcinea; and, should he not believe it, I will swear to it; and if he swears, I will outswear him: and if he persists, I will persist more than he, in such manner, that mine shall still be uppermost, come what will of it. Perhaps by this positiveness, I shall put an end to his sending me again upon such errands, seeing what preposterous answers I bring him; or perhaps he will think, as I imagine he will, that some wicked enchanter, of those he says bear him a spite, has changed her form to do him mischief and harm.'

This project set Sancho's spirit at rest, and he reckoned his business as good as half done; and so staying where he was till towards evening, that Don Quixote might have room to think he had spent so much time in going to, and returning from Toboso, everything fell out so luckily for him, that when he got up to mount his Dapple, he espied three country wenches, coming from Toboso toward the place where he was, upon three young asses; but whether male or female, the author declares not, though it is more probable they were she-asses, that being the ordinary mounting of country women; but as it is a matter of no consequence, we need not give ourselves any trouble to decide it.

In short, as soon as Sancho espied the lasses, he rode back at a round rate to seek his master Don Quixote, whom he found breathing a thousand sighs and amorous lamentations. As soon as Don Quixote saw him, he said;

'Well, friend Sancho, am I to mark this day with a white or a black stone?'

'Your worship,' answered Sancho, 'had better mark it with red ochre, as they do the inscriptions on professors' chairs,* to be the more easily read by the lookers-on.'

'By this,' quoth Don Quixote, 'you should bring good news.'

'So good,' answered Sancho, 'that your worship has no more to do, but to clap spurs to Rosinante, and get out upon the plain, to see the lady Dulcinea del Toboso, who, with a couple of her damsels, is coming to make your worship a visit.'

'Holy God! what is it you say, friend Sancho?' said Don Quixote; 'take care you do not impose on my real sorrow by a counterfeit joy.'

'What should I get,' answered Sancho, 'by deceiving your worship, and being detected the next moment? Come, sir, put on, and you will see the princess our mistress, arrayed and adorned, in short, like herself. She and her damsels are one blaze of flaming gold; all strings of pearls, all diamonds, all rubies, all cloth of tissue above ten hands deep: their tresses loose about their shoulders are so many sunbeams playing with the wind: and, what is more, they come mounted upon three pie-bellied belfreys, the finest one can lay eyes on.'

'Palfreys, you would say, Sancho,' quoth Don Quixote.

'There is no great difference, I think,' answered Sancho, 'between belfreys and palfreys: but let them be mounted how they will, they are sure the finest creatures one would wish to see, especially my mistress the princess Dulcinea, who ravishes one's senses.'

'Let us go, son Sancho,' answered Don Quixote: 'and, as a reward for this news, as unexpected as good, I bequeath you the choicest spoils I shall gain in my next adventure; and if that will not satisfy you, I bequeath you the colts my three mares will foal this year upon our town common.'

'I stick to the colts,' answered Sancho; 'for it is not very certain, that the spoils of your next adventure will be worth much.'

By this time they were got out of the wood, and espied the three wenches very near. Don Quixote darted his eyes over all the road towards Toboso, and seeing nobody but the three wenches, he was much troubled, and asked Sancho, Whether they were come out of the city when he left them?

'Out of the city!' answered Sancho: 'are your worship's eyes in the nape of your neck, that you do not see it is they who are coming, shining like the sun at noonday?'

'I see only three country-girls,' answered Don Quixote, 'on three asses.'

'Now, God keep me from the devil!' answered Sancho: 'is it possible that three palfreys, or how do you call them, white as the driven snow, should appear to you to be asses? As the Lord liveth, you shall pluck off this beard of mine if that be so.'

'I tell you, friend Sancho,' answered Don Quixote, 'that it is as certain they are he- or she-asses, as I am Don Quixote, and you Sancho Panza; at least such they seem to me.'

'Sir,' quoth Sancho, 'say not such a word, but snuff those eyes of yours, and come and make your reverence to the mistress of your thoughts, who is just at hand.'

And so saying, he advanced a little forward to meet the country wenches, and, alighting from Dapple, he laid hold of one of their asses by the halter, and bending both knees to the ground, he said:

'Queen, princess, and duchess of beauty, let your haughtiness and greatness be pleased to receive into your grace and good-liking your captive knight, who stands yonder turned into stone, in total disorder, and without any pulse, to find himself before your magnificent presence. I am Sancho Panza his squire, and he is that forlorn knight Don Quixote de la Mancha, otherwise called the Knight of the Sorrowful Figure.'

Don Quixote had now placed himself on his knees close by Sancho, and with staring and disturbed eyes, looked wistfully at her, whom Sancho called queen, and lady; and as he saw nothing in her but a plain country girl, and homely enough (for she was round-visaged and flat-nosed) he was confounded and amazed, without daring to open his lips. The wenches too were astonished to see their companion stopped by two men, of such different aspects, and both on their knees, but she, who was stopped, broke silence, and in an angry tone said:

'Get out of the road, and be hanged, and let us pass by, for we are in haste.'

To which Sancho made answer:

'O princess, and universal lady of Toboso, does not your magnificent heart relent to see, kneeling before your sublimated presence, the pillar and prop of knight-errantry?'

Which one of the other two hearing, said (checking her beast that was turning out of the way*):

'Look ye, how these small gentry come to make a jest of us poor country girls, as if we did not know how to give them as good as they bring: get ye gone your way, and let us go ours, and so speed you well.'

'Rise, Sancho,' said Don Quixote, hearing this; 'for I now perceive, that "fortune, not yet satisfied with afflicting me"*, has barred all the avenues, whereby any relief might come to this wretched soul I bear about me in the flesh. And thou, O extreme of all that is valuable, utmost limit of all human gracefulness, sole remedy of this disconsolate heart that adores thee, though now some wicked enchanter persecutes me, spreading clouds and cataracts over my eyes, and has to

them, and them only, changed and transformed thy peerless
beauty and countenance into that of a poor country wench;
if he has not converted mine also into that of some goblin,
to render it abominable in your eyes, afford me one kind and
amorous look; and let this submissive posture, and these
bended knees, before your disguised beauty, tell you the
humility wherewith my soul adores you.'

'Marry come up,' quoth the wench, 'with your idle gibberish!
get you gone, and let us go, and we shall be obliged to you.'

Sancho moved off, and let her go, highly delighted that he
was come off so well with his contrivance. The imaginary
Dulcinea was scarcely at liberty, when, pricking her beast with
a goad she had in a stick, she began to scour along the field;
and the ass, feeling the smart more than usual, fell a-kicking
and wincing in such a manner, that down came the lady
Dulcinea to the ground. Don Quixote, seeing this, ran to
help her up, and Sancho to adjust the pannel that was got
under the ass's belly. The pannel being righted, and Don
Quixote desirous to raise his enchanted mistress in his arms,
and set her upon her palfrey, the lady, getting up from the
ground, saved him that trouble; for, retiring three or four
steps back, she took a little run, and, clapping both hands
upon the ass's crupper, jumped into the saddle lighter than
a falcon, and seated herself astride like a man. Whereupon
Sancho said:

'By St. Roque, madam our mistress is lighter than a hawk,
and able to teach the most expert Córdovan or Mexican how
to mount *a la gineta*:* she springs into the saddle at a jump,
and, without the help of spurs, makes her palfrey run like a
wild ass;* and her damsels are as good at it as she, they all
fly like the wind.'

And so it really was: for Dulcinea being remounted, they
all made after her, and set a-running, without looking behind
them, for above half a league.

Don Quixote followed them, as far as he could, with his eyes,
and when they were out of sight, turning to Sancho, he said:

'Sancho, what think you? how am I persecuted by enchanters! and take notice how far their malice, and the grudge
they bear me, extends, even to the depriving me of the

pleasure I should have had in seeing my mistress in her own proper form. Surely I was born to be an example to the unhappy, and the butt and mark at which all the arrows of ill fortune are aimed and levelled. And you must also observe, Sancho, that these traitors were not contented with barely changing and transforming my Dulcinea, but they must transform and metamorphose her into the mean and deformed resemblance of that country wench; at the same time robbing her of that, which is peculiar to great ladies, the fragrant scent occasioned by being always among flowers and perfumes: for I must tell you, Sancho, that, when I approached to help Dulcinea upon her palfrey (as you call it, though to me it appeared to be nothing but an ass) she gave me such a whiff of undigested garlic, as almost knocked me down, and poisoned my very soul.'

'O scoundrels!' cried Sancho, at this juncture; 'O barbarous and evil-minded enchanters! O that I might see you all strung and hung up by the gills like sardines a-smoking! Much ye know, much ye can, and much more ye do. It might, one would think, have sufficed ye, rogues as ye are, to have changed the pearls of my lady's eyes into cork-galls, and her hair of the purest gold into bristles of a red cow's tail, and lastly, all her features from beautiful to deformed, without meddling with her breath, by which we might have guessed at what was hid beneath that coarse disguise: though, to say the truth, to me she did not appear in the least deformed, but rather all beauty, and that increased too by a mole she had on her right lip, like a whisker, with seven or eight hairs on it, like threads of gold, and above a span long.'

'As to that mole,' said Don Quixote, 'according to the correspondence there is between the moles of the face and those of the body, Dulcinea should have another on the brawn of her thigh, on the same side with that on her face; but hairs of the length you mention are somewhat of the longest for moles.'

'Yet I can assure your worship,' answered Sancho, 'that there they were, and looked as if they had been born with her.'

'I believe it, friend,' replied Don Quixote; 'for nature has placed nothing about Dulcinea but what is finished and perfect; and therefore had she a hundred moles, like those you speak of, in her they would not be moles, but moons and resplendent stars. But, tell me, Sancho, that which to me appeared to be a pannel, and which you adjusted, was it a side-saddle, or a pillion?'

'It was a side-saddle,' answered Sancho, 'with a field covering, worth half a kingdom for the richness of it.'

'And why could not I see all this, Sancho?' quoth Don Quixote. 'Well, I say it again, and will repeat it a thousand times, that I am the most unfortunate of men.'

The sly rogue Sancho had much ado to forbear laughing, to hear the fooleries of his master, who was so delicately gulled. In fine, after many other discourses passed between them, they mounted their beasts again, and followed the road to Saragossa, which they intended to reach in time to be present at a solemn festival wont to be held every year in that noble city. But, before their arrival, there befell them things, which for their number, greatness, and novelty, deserve to be written, and read, as will be seen.

CHAPTER 11

Of the strange adventure which befell the valorous Don Quixote with the wain or cart of the Parliament of Death.

DON QUIXOTE went on his way exceeding pensive, to think what a base trick the enchanters had played him, in transforming his lady Dulcinea into the homely figure of a country wench; nor could he devise what course to take to restore her to her former state. And these meditations so distracted him, that, without perceiving it, he let drop the bridle on Rosinante's neck; who, finding the liberty that was given him, at every step turned aside to take a mouthful of the fresh grass, with which those fields abounded. Sancho brought him back out of his maze, by saying to him:

'Sir, sorrow was made not for beasts, but men; but if men give too much way to it, they become beasts: rouse, sir, recollect yourself, and gather up Rosinante's reins; cheer up, awake, and exert that lively courage so befitting a knight-errant. What the devil is the matter? What dejection is this? Are we here, or in France? Satan take all the Dulcineas in the world, since the welfare of a single knight-errant is of more worth than all the enchantments and transformations of the earth.'

'Peace, Sancho,' answered Don Quixote, with no very faint voice: 'peace I say, and do not utter blasphemies against that enchanted lady, whose disgrace and misfortune are owing to me alone, since they proceed entirely from the envy the wicked bear to me.'

'I say so too,' answered Sancho: '"Who saw her then and sees her now, his heart must melt with grief, I vow".'

'Well may you say so, Sancho,' replied Don Quixote, 'you who saw her in the full lustre of her beauty; for the enchantment extended not to disturb your sight, not to conceal her perfections from you: against me alone, and against my eyes, was the force of its poison directed. Nevertheless, I have hit upon one thing, Sancho, which is this, that you did not give me a true description of her beauty, for, if I remember right, you said her eyes were of pearl; now eyes that look like pearl are fitter for a sea-bream than a lady. I rather think Dulcinea's eyes must be of verdant emeralds arched over with two celestial bows, that serve for eyebrows. Take, therefore, those pearls from her eyes, and apply them to her teeth: for doubtless, Sancho, you mistook eyes for teeth.'

'It may be so,' answered Sancho; 'for her beauty confounded me, as much as her deformity did your worship. But let us recommend all to God, who alone knows what shall befall in this vale of tears, this evil world we have here, in which there is scarce anything to be found without some mixture of iniquity, imposture, or knavery.

'One thing, dear sir, troubles me more than all the rest: which is, to think, what must be done when your worship shall overcome some giant, or some other knight-errant, and send him to present himself before the beauty of the lady Dulcinea. Where shall this poor giant, or miserable vanquished knight, be able to find her? Methinks I see them sauntering up and down Toboso, and looking about, like fools, for my lady Dulcinea; and though they should meet her in the middle of the street, they will no more know her, than they would my father.'

'Perhaps, Sancho,' answered Don Quixote, 'the enchantment may not extend so far as to conceal Dulcinea from the knowledge of the vanquished knights or giants, who shall present themselves before her; and we will make the experiment upon one or two of the first I overcome, and send them with orders to return and give me an account of what happens with respect to this business.'

'I say, sir,' replied Sancho, 'that I mightily approve of what your worship has said: for by this trial we shall come to the knowledge of what we desire; and if she is concealed from your worship alone, the misfortune will be more yours than hers: but, so the lady Dulcinea have health and contentment, we, for our part, will make a shift, and bear it as well as we can, pursuing our adventures, and leaving it to time to do his work, who is the best physician for these, and other greater maladies.'

Don Quixote would have answered Sancho, but was prevented by a cart's crossing the road before him, loaded with the strangest and most different figures and persons imaginable. He who guided the mules, and served for carter, was a frightful demon. The cart was uncovered, and opened to the sky, without awning or wicker-sides. The first figure that presented itself to Don Quixote's eyes, was that of Death itself with a human visage. Close by him sat an angel, with large painted wings. On one side stood an emperor, with a crown, seemingly of gold, on his head. At Death's feet sat the god called Cupid, not blindfolded, but with his bow, quiver, and arrows. There was also a knight completely armed, excepting only that he had no morion, nor casque, but a hat with a large plume of feathers of divers colours. With these came other persons differing both in habits and countenances. All which appearing of a sudden did in some sort startle Don Quixote, and frighted Sancho to the heart. But Don Quixote presently rejoiced at it, believing it to be some new and perilous adventure: and with this thought, and a courage prepared to encounter any danger whatever, he planted himself just before the cart, and, with a loud menacing voice, said:

'Carter, coachman, or devil, or whatever you are, delay not to tell me who you are, whither you are going, and who are the persons you are carrying in that coach-wagon, which looks more like Charon's ferry-boat, than any cart now in fashion.'

To which the devil, stopping the cart, calmly replied:

'Sir, we are strollers belonging to Angulo el Malo's company: this morning, which is the octave of Corpus Christi, we have been performing, in a village on the other side of yon hill, a piece representing the Cortes, or Parliament of Death;* and this evening we are to play it again in that village just before us; which being so near, to save ourselves the trouble of dressing and undressing, we come in the clothes we are to act our parts in. That lad there acts Death; that other an angel; yonder woman, our author's wife, a queen; that other a soldier; he an emperor, and I a devil; and I am one of the principal personages of the drama; for in this company I have all the chief parts. If your worship would know any more of us, ask me, and I will answer you most punctually; for, being a devil, I know everything.'

'Upon the faith of a knight-errant,' answered Don Quixote, 'when I first espied this cart, I imagined some grand adventure offered itself; and I say now, that it is absolutely necessary, if one would be undeceived, to lay one's hand upon appearances. God be with you, good people: go, and act your play, and, if there be anything in which I may be of service to you, command me; for I will do it readily, and with a good will, having been, from my youth, a great admirer of masques and theatrical representations.'

While they were thus engaged in discourse, fortune so ordered it, that there came up one of the company, in an antique dress, hung round with abundance of bells, and carrying at the end of a stick three blown ox-bladders. This masque approaching Don Quixote, began to fence with the stick, and to beat the bladders against the ground, jumping, and tinkling all his bells: which horrid apparition so startled Rosinante, that, taking the bit between his teeth, Don Quixote not being able to hold him in, he fell a-running about the field, at a greater pace than the bones of his anatomy seemed to promise. Sancho, considering the danger his master was in of getting a fall, leaped from Dapple, and ran to help him: but by that time he was come up to him, he was already upon the ground, and close by him Rosinante, who fell together with his master, the usual end and upshot of Rosinante's frolics and adventurings.

But scarce had Sancho quitted his beast, to assist Don Quixote, when the bladder-dancing devil jumped upon Dapple, and thumping him with the bladders, fear and the noise, more than the smart, made him fly through the field toward the village, where they were going to act. Sancho beheld Dapple's career, and his master's fall, and did not know which of the two necessities he should apply to first: but, in short, like a good squire and good servant, the love he bore his master prevailed over his affection for his ass; though, every time he saw the bladders hoisted in the air, and fall upon the buttocks of his Dapple, they were to him so many tortures and terrors of death, and he could have wished those blows had fallen on the apple of his own eyes, rather than on the least hair of his ass's tail. In this perplexity and tribulation he came up to Don Quixote, who was in a much worse plight than he could have wished, and helping him to get upon Rosinante, he said to him;

'Sir, the devil has run away with Dapple.'

'What devil?' demanded Don Quixote.

'He with the bladders,' answered Sancho.

'I will recover him,' replied Don Quixote, 'though he should hide him in the deepest and darkest dungeons of hell. Follow me, Sancho: for the cart moves but slowly, and the mules shall make satisfaction for the loss of Dapple. There is no need, answered Sancho, to make such haste; moderate your anger, sir; for the devil, I think, has already abandoned Dapple, and is gone his way.'

And so it was; for the devil, having fallen with Dapple, in imitation of Don Quixote and Rosinante, trudged on foot towards the town, and the ass turned back to his master.

'Nevertheless,' said Don Quixote, 'it will not be amiss to chastise the unmannerliness of this devil, at the expense of some of his company, though it were the emperor himself.'

'Good your worship,' quoth Sancho, 'never think of it, but take my advice, which is, never to meddle with players; for they are a people mightily beloved. I have seen a player taken up for two murders, and get off scot-free. Your worship must know, that, as they are merry folks and give pleasure, all people favour them; everybody protects, assists, and esteems them, and especially if they are of his majesty's company of comedians, or that of some grandee, all or most of whom, in their manner and garb, look like any princes.'

'For all that,' answered Don Quixote, 'that farcical devil shall not escape me, nor have cause to brag, though all human kind favoured him.'

And so saying, he rode after the cart, which was by this time got very near the town, and, calling aloud, he said:

'Hold, stop a little, merry sirs, and let me teach you how to treat asses and cattle, which serve to mount the squires of knights-errant.'

Don Quixote's cries were so loud, that the players heard him, and, judging of his design by his words, in an instant out jumped Death, and after him the emperor, the carter-devil, and the angel; nor did the queen, or the god Cupid, stay behind: and all of them taking up stones, ranged themselves in battle array, waiting to receive Don Quixote at the points of their pebbles. Don Quixote, seeing them posted in such order, and so formidable a battalion, with arms uplifted, ready to discharge a ponderous volley of stones, checked Rosinante with the bridle, and set himself to consider how he might attack them with the least danger to his person. While he delayed, Sancho came up, and seeing him in a posture of attacking that well-formed brigade, he said to him:

'It is mere madness, sir, to attempt such an enterprise: pray, consider, there is no fencing against a flail, nor defensive armour against stones and brickbats, unless it be thrusting one's self into a bell of brass. Consider also, that it is rather rashness than courage, for one man alone to encounter an army, where Death is present, and where emperors fight in person, and are assisted by good and bad angels. But if this consideration does not prevail with you to be quiet, be assured, that, among all those, who stand there, though they appear to be princes, kings, and emperors, there is not one knight-errant.'

'Now indeed,' said Don Quixote, 'you have hit the point, Sancho, which only can, and must make me change my determinate resolution. I neither can, or ought to draw my sword, as I have often told you, against any who are not dubbed knights. To you it belongs, Sancho, to revenge the affront offered to your Dapple; and I from hence will encourage and assist you with my voice, and with salutary instructions.'

'There is no need, sir, to be revenged on anybody,' answered Sancho, 'for good Christians should not take revenge for injuries; besides, I will settle it with my ass to submit the injury done him to my will, which is, to live peaceably all the days that heaven shall give me of life.'

'Since this is your resolution, good Sancho, discreet Sancho, Christian Sancho, and pure Sancho,' replied Don Quixote, 'let us leave these phantoms, and seek better and more substantial adventures; for this country, I see, is like to afford us many and very extraordinary ones.'

Then he wheeled Rosinante about: Sancho took his Dapple: Death and all his flying squadron returned to their cart, and pursued their way. And this was the happy conclusion of the terrible adventure of Death's cart; thanks to the wholesome advice Sancho Panza gave his master, to whom the day following there fell out an adventure, no less surprising than the former, with an enamoured knight-errant.

CHAPTER 12

Of the strange adventure, which befell the valorous Don Quix- ote, with the brave Knight of the Looking-glasses.

DON QUIXOTE and his squire passed the night ensuing the encounter with Death under some lofty and shady trees. Don Quixote, at Sancho's persuasion, refreshed himself with some of the provisions carried by Dapple; and, during supper, Sancho said to his master:

'Sir, what a fool should I have been, had I chosen, as a reward for my good news, the spoils of the first adventure your worship should achieve, before the three ass-colts? Verily, verily, a sparrow in the hand is better than a vulture upon the wing.'

'However, Sancho,' answered Don Quixote, 'had you suffered me to attack as I had a mind to do, your share of the booty would at least have been the emperor's crown of gold and Cupid's painted wings; for I would have plucked them off against the grain, and put them into your possession.'

'The crowns and sceptres of your theatrical emperors,' answered Sancho, 'never were of pure gold, but of tinsel, or copper.'

'It is true,' replied Don Quixote; 'nor would it be fit, that the decorations of a play should be real, but counterfeit, and mere show, as comedy itself is, which I would have you value and take into favour, and consequently the actors and authors; for they are all instruments of much benefit to the commonweal, setting at every step a looking-glass before our eyes, in which we see very lively representations of the actions of human life: and there are no comparisons which more truly present to us what we are, and what we should be, than comedy and comedians. Tell me, have you not seen a play acted, in which kings, emperors, popes, lords, and ladies, are introduced, besides divers other personages: one acts the pimp, another the cheat, this the merchant, that the soldier, one a designing fool, another a foolish lover; and when the play is done, and the actors undressed, they are all again upon a level?'

'Yes, marry, have I,' quoth Sancho.

'Why, the very same thing,' said Don Quixote, 'happens on the stage of this world, whereon some play the part of emperors, others of popes; in short, all the parts that can be introduced in a comedy. But in the conclusion, that is, at the end of our life, death strips us of the robes, which made the difference, and we remain upon the level and equal in the grave.'

'A brave comparison,' quoth Sancho, 'but not so new (for I have heard it many and different times) as that of the game at chess;* in which, while the game lasts, every piece has its particular office, and, when the game is ended, they are all huddled together, mixed, and put into a bag, which is just like being buried after we are dead.'

'Sancho,' said Don Quixote, 'you are every day growing less simple and more discreet.'

'And good reason why,' answered Sancho; 'for some of your worship's discretion must needs stick to me, as lands, that in themselves are barren and dry, by dunging and cultivating come to bear good fruit. My meaning is, that your worship's conversation has been the dung laid upon the barren soil of my dry understanding, and the cultivation has been the time I have been in your service, and in your company; and by that I hope to produce fruit like any blessing, and such as will not disparage or deviate from the seeds of good breeding, which your worship has sown in my shallow understanding.'

Don Quixote smiled at Sancho's affected speeches, that appearing to him to be true, which he had said of his improvement: for every now and then he surprised him by his manner of talking; though always or for the most part, when Sancho would either speak in contradiction to, or in imitation of, the courtier, he ended his discourse with falling headlong from the height of his simplicity into the depth of his ignorance; and that, in which he most displayed his elegance and memory, was, his bringing in proverbs, whether to the purpose or not, of what he was discoursing about, as may be seen and observed throughout the progress of this history.

In these and other discourses they spent great part of the night, but Sancho had a mind to let down the portcullises of his eyes, as he used to say when he was inclined to sleep; and so, unrigging Dapple, he turned him loose into abundant pasture. But he did not take off the saddle from Rosinante's back, it being the express command of his master, that he should continue saddled, all the time they kept the field, or did not sleep under a roof: for it was an ancient established custom, and religiously observed among knights-errant, to take off the bridle and hang it at the pommel of the saddle;

but by no means to take off the saddle. Sancho observed this rule, and gave Rosinante the same liberty he had given Dapple; the friendship of which pair was so singular and reciprocal, that there is a tradition handed down from father to son, that the author of this faithful history compiled particular chapters upon that subject: but to preserve the decency and decorum due to so heroic a history, he would not insert them; though sometimes waiving this precaution, he writes, that as soon as the two beasts came together, they would fall to scratching one another with their teeth, and when they were tired, or satisfied, Rosinante would stretch his neck at least half a yard across Dapple's, and both, fixing their eyes attentively on the ground, would stand three days in that manner, at least so long as they were let alone, or till hunger compelled them to seek some food. It is reported, I say, that the author had compared their friendship to that of Nisus and Euryalus, or that of Pylades and Orestes; whence it may appear, to the admiration of all people, how firm the friendship of these two peaceable animals must have been; to the shame of men, who so little know how to preserve the rules of friendship towards one another. Hence the sayings, 'A friend cannot find a friend; Reeds become darts'*; and (as the poet sings) From a friend to a friend, the bug,* &c. Let no one think, that the author was at all out of the way, when he compared the friendship of these animals to that of men: for men have received divers wholesome instructions, and many lessons of importance, from beasts; such as the clyster from storks, the vomit and gratitude from dogs, vigilance from cranes, industry from ants, modesty from elephants, and fidelity from horses.

At length Sancho fell asleep at the foot of a cork-tree, and Don Quixote slumbered under an oak. But it was not long before he was awaked by a noise behind him; and starting up, he began to look about, and to listen from whence the noise came. Presently he perceived two men on horseback, one of whom dismounting, said to the other:

'Alight, friend, and unbridle the horses; for this place seems as if it would afford them pasture enough, and me that silence and solitude my amorous thoughts require.'

The saying this, and laying himself along on the ground, were both in one instant; and, at throwing himself down, his armour made a rattling noise; a manifest token, from whence Don Quixote concluded he must be a knight-errant: and going to Sancho, who was fast asleep, he pulled him by the arm, and having with some difficulty waked him, he said to him, with a low voice:

'Brother Sancho, we have an adventure.'

'God send it be a good one,' answered Sancho; 'and pray, sir, where may her ladyship Madam Adventure be?'

'Where, Sancho?' replied Don Quixote: 'turn your eyes and look, and you will see a knight-errant lying along, who, to my thoughts, does not seem to be over-pleased; for I saw him throw himself off his horse, and stretch himself on the ground, with some signs of discontent; and his armour rattled as he fell.'

'But by what do you gather,' quoth Sancho, 'that this is an adventure?'

'I will not say,' answered Don Quixote, 'that this is altogether an adventure, but an introduction to one; for adventures usually begin thus. But, hearken; for methinks he is tuning a lute of some sort or other, and by his spitting and clearing his pipes he should be preparing himself to sing.'

'In good faith, so it is,' answered Sancho, 'and he must be some knight or other in love.'

'There is no knight-errant but is so,' quoth Don Quixote: 'and let us listen to him; for by the thread we shall guess at the bottom of his thoughts, if he sings: for out of the abundance of the heart the mouth speaketh.'

Sancho would have replied to his master; but the Knight of the Wood's voice, which was neither very bad nor very good, hindered him; and, while they both stood amazed, they heard that what he sung was this:

SONNET

'Bright auth'ress of my good or ill,
Prescribe the law I must observe:

My heart obedient to thy will,
  Shall never from its duty swerve.

'If you refuse my griefs to know,
  The stifled anguish seals my fate;
But if your ears would drink my woe,
  Love shall himself the tale relate.

'Though contraries my heart compose,
  Hard as the diamond's solid frame,
And soft as yielding wax that flows,
  To thee, my fair, 'tis still the same.

'Take it for every stamp prepared,
  Imprint what characters you choose,
The faithful tablet, soft or hard,
  The dear impression ne'er shall lose.'

With a deep 'Ah!' fetched, as it seemed, from the very bottom of his heart, the Knight of the Wood ended his song; and after some pause, with a mournful and complaining voice, he said:

'O the most beautiful and most ungrateful woman of the world! is it then possible, Casildea de Vandalia, that you should suffer this your captive knight to consume and pine away in continual travels, and in rough and laborious toils? Is it not enough, that I have caused you to be acknowledged the most consummate beauty in the world, by all the knights of Navarre, all those of Leon, all the Andalusians, all the Castilians, aye and all the knights of La Mancha, too?'

'Not so,' quoth Don Quixote; 'for I am of La Mancha, and never have acknowledged any such thing; neither could I, nor ought I to confess a thing so prejudicial to the beauty of my mistress: now you see, Sancho, how this knight raves: but let us listen: perhaps he will make some further declaration.'

'Aye, marry will he,' replied Sancho; 'for he seems to be in a strain of complaining for a month to come.'

But it was not so: for the knight overhearing somebody talk near him, proceeded no further in his lamentation, but stood up, and said, with an audible and courteous voice:

'Who goes there? what are ye? of the number of the happy, or of the afflicted?'

'Of the afflicted,' answered Don Quixote.

'Come hither to me then,' answered the Knight of the Wood,* 'and make account how you come to sorrow and affliction itself.'

Don Quixote finding he returned so soft and civil an answer, went up to him, and Sancho did the same. The wailing knight laid hold of Don Quixote by the arm, saying.

'Sit down here, Sir Knight: for to know that you are such, and one of those who profess knight-errantry, it is sufficient to have found you in this place, where your companions are solitude and the night-dew, the natural beds and proper stations of knights-errant.'

To which Don Quixote answered:

'A knight I am, and of the profession you say; and although sorrows, disgraces, and misfortunes have got possession of my mind, yet they have not chased away that compassion I have for other men's misfortunes. From what you sung just now I gathered, that yours are of the amorous kind; I mean occasioned by the love you bear to that ungrateful fair you named in your complaint.'

Whilst they were thus discoursing, they sat down together upon the hard ground, very peaceably, and sociably, as if, at daybreak, they were not to break one another's heads.

'Peradventure you are in love, Sir Knight,' said he of the Wood to Don Quixote.

'By misadventure, I am,' answered Don Quixote; 'though the mischiefs arising from well-placed affections ought rather to be accounted blessings than disasters.'

'That is true,' replied he of the Wood, 'supposing that disdains did not disturb our reason and understanding; but when they are many, they seem to have the nature of revenge.'

'I never was disdained by my mistress,' answered Don Quixote.

'No verily,' quoth Sancho, who stood close by; 'for my lady is as gentle as a lamb, and as soft as a print of butter.'

'Is this your squire?' demanded the Knight of the Wood.

'He is,' replied Don Quixote.

'I never in my life saw a squire,' replied the Knight of the Wood, 'who durst presume to talk, where his lord was talking: at least, yonder stands mine, as tall as his father, and it cannot be proved, that he ever opened his lips when I was speaking.'

'In faith,' quoth Sancho, 'I have talked, and can talk, before one as good as . . ., and perhaps . . ., but let that rest; for the more you stir it . . . .'

The Knight of the Wood's squire took Sancho by the arm, and said;

'Let us two go where we may talk by ourselves, in squire-like discourse, all we have a mind to, and leave these masters of ours to have their bellies full of relating the histories of their loves to each other: for I warrant they will not have done before to-morrow morning.'

'With all my heart,' quoth Sancho, 'and I will tell you who I am, that you may see whether I am fit to make one among the most talkative squires.'

Hereupon the two squires withdrew; between whom there passed a dialogue as pleasant as that of their masters was grave.

CHAPTER 13

Wherein is continued the adventure of the Knight of the Wood, with the wise, new, and pleasant dialogue between the two squires.

THE knights and squires were separated, the latter relating the story of their lives, and the former that of their loves: but the history begins with the conversation between the servants, and afterwards proceeds to that of the masters: and it says, that, being gone a little apart, the Squire of the Wood said to Sancho:

'It is a toilsome life we lead, sir, we who are squires to knights-errant; in good truth we eat our bread in the sweat of our brows, which is one of the curses God laid upon our first parents.'

'It may also be said,' added Sancho, 'that we eat it in the frost of our bodies; for who endure more heat and cold than your miserable squires to knight-errantry? Nay, it would not be quite so bad, did we but eat at all; for good fare lessens care: but it now and then happens, that we pass a whole day or two without breaking our fast, unless it be upon air.'

'All this may be endured,' quoth he of the Wood, 'with the hopes we entertain of the reward; for if the knight-errant, whom a squire serves, is not over and above unlucky, he must, in a short time, find himself recompensed, at least, with a handsome government of some island, or some pretty earldom.'

'I,' replied Sancho, 'have already told my master, that I should be satisfied with the government of any island; and he is so noble and so generous, that he has promised it me a thousand times.'

'I,' said he of the Wood, 'should think myself amply rewarded for all my services with a canonry, and my master has already ordered me one.'

'Why then,' quoth Sancho, 'belike your master is a knight in the ecclesiastical way, and so has it in his power to bestow these sort of rewards on his faithful squires: but mine is a mere layman; though I remember some discreet persons (but in my opinion with no very good design) advised him to endeavour to be an archbishop: but he rejected their counsel, and would be nothing but an emperor. I trembled all the while, lest he should take it into his head to be of the church, because I am not qualified to hold ecclesiastical preferments: and, to say the truth, sir, though I look like a man, I am a very beast in church matters.'

'Truly, you are under a great mistake,' quoth he of the Wood: 'for your insulary governments are not all of them so inviting: some are crabbed, some poor, and some unpleasant: in short, the best and most desirable of them carries with it a heavy burden of cares and inconveniences, which the unhappy wight, to whose lot it falls, must unavoidably undergo. It would be far better for us, who profess this cursed service, to retire home to our houses, and pass our time there in more easy employments, such as hunting or fishing: for what squire is there in the world so poor as not to have his nag, his brace of greyhounds, and his angle-rod, to divert himself withal in his own village?'

'I want nothing of all this,' answered Sancho: 'it is true, indeed, I have no horse, but then I have an ass that is worth twice as much as my master's steed. God send me a bad Easter, and may it be the first that comes, if I would swap with him, though he should give me four bushels of barley to boot. Perhaps, sir, you will take for a joke the price I set upon my Dapple, for dapple is the colour of my ass. And then I cannot want greyhounds, our town being overstocked with them: besides, sporting is the more pleasant, when it is at other people's charge.'

'Really and truly, Señor Squire,' answered he of the Wood, 'I have resolved and determined with myself to quit the frolics of these knights-errant, and to get me home again to our village, and bring up my children; for I have three, like three oriental pearls.'

'And I have two,' quoth Sancho, 'fit to be presented to the Pope himself in person, and especially a girl, that I am breeding up for a countess, if it please God, in spite of her mother.'

'And, pray, what may be the age of the young lady you are breeding up for a countess?' demanded he of the Wood.

'Fifteen years, or thereabouts,' answered Sancho: 'but she is as tall as a lance, as fresh as an April morning, and as strong as a porter.'

'These are qualifications,' said he of the Wood, 'not only for a countess, but for a nymph of the green grove. Ah, the whoreson young slut! how buxom must the jade be!'

To which Sancho answered somewhat angrily:

'She is no whore, nor was her mother one before her, nor shall either of them be so, God willing, whilst I live. And pray speak more civilly; for such language is unbecoming a person educated, as you have been, among knights-errant, who are courtesy itself.'

'How little, Señor Squire, do you understand what belongs to praising,' quoth he of the Wood: 'what! do you not know that when some knight at a bullfeast gives the bull a home-thrust with his lance, or when anyone does a thing well, the common people usually cry: "How cleverly the son of a whore did it!" and what seems to carry a reproach with it, is indeed a notable commendation! I would have you renounce those sons or daughters, whose actions do not render their parents deserving of praise in that fashion.'

'I do renounce them,' answered Sancho; 'and in this sense, and by this same rule, if you mean no otherwise, you may call my wife and children all the whores and bawds you please; for all they do or say are perfections worthy of such praises: and, that I may return and see them again, I beseech God to deliver me from mortal sin, that is, from this dangerous profession of a squire, into which I have run a second time, enticed and deluded by a purse of a hundred ducats, which I found one day in the midst of the Sierra Morena; and tho devil is continually setting before my eyes, here and there, and everywhere, a bag full of gold pistoles, so that methinks, at every step, I am laying my hand upon it, embracing it, and carrying it home, buying lands, settling rents, and living like a prince: and all the while this runs in my head, all the toils I undergo with this fool my master, who to my knowledge is more of the madman than of the knight, become supportable and easy to me.'

'For this reason,' answered he of the Wood, 'it is said, that covetousness bursts the bag; and now you talk of madmen, there is not a greater in the world than my master, who is one of those meant by the saying, "Other folks' burdens break the ass's back": for, that another knight may recover his wits, he loses his own, and is searching after that, which when found, may chance to hit him in the teeth.'

'By the way, is he in love?' demanded Sancho.

'Yes,' quoth he of the Wood, 'with one Casildea de Vandalia, one of the most whimsical dames in the world. But that is not the foot he halts on at present: he has some other crotchets of more consequence in his pate, and we shall hear more of them anon.'

'There is no road so even,' replied Sancho, 'but it has some stumbling-places or rubs in it: In other folks' houses they boil beans, but in mine whole kettles-full. Madness will have more followers than discretion. But if the common saying be true, that 'tis some relief to have partners in grief, I may comfort myself with your worship, who serve a master as crackbrained as my own.'

'Crack-brained, but valiant,' answered he of the Wood, 'and more knavish than crack-brained or valiant.'

'Mine is not so,' answered Sancho: 'I can assure you, he has nothing of the knave in him; on the contrary, he has a soul as dull as a pitcher; knows not how to do ill to any, but good to all; bears no malice; a child may persuade him it is night at noonday: and for this simplicity I love him as my life, and cannot find in my heart to leave him, let him commit never so many extravagances.'

'For all that, brother and señor,' quoth he of the Wood, 'if the blind lead the blind, both are in danger of falling into the ditch. We had better turn us fairly about, and go back to our homes: for they who seek adventures, do not always meet with good ones.'

Here Sancho beginning to spit every now and then, and [his spittle being] very dry, the Squire of the Wood, who saw, and observed it, said:

'Methinks, we have talked till our tongues cleave to the roofs of our mouths: but I have brought, hanging at my saddle-bow, that which will loosen them.'

And rising up, he soon returned with a large bottle of wine, and a pasty half a yard long; and this is no exaggeration: for it was of a tame rabbit, so large, that Sancho, at lifting it, thought verily it must contain a whole goat, or at least a large kid. Sancho, viewing it, said:

'And do you carry all this about with you?'

'Why, what did you think?' answered the other: 'did you take me for some holiday squire? I have a better cupboard behind me on my horse, than a general has with him upon a march.'

Sancho fell to, without staying to be entreated, and, swallowing mouthfuls in the dark, said:

'Your worship is indeed a squire, trusty and loyal, wanting for nothing, magnificent and great, as this banquet demonstrates (which, if it came not hither by enchantment, at least it looks like it), and not as I am, a poor unfortunate wretch, who have nothing in my wallet but a piece of cheese, and that so hard, that you may knock out a giant's brains with it, and to bear it company, four dozen of carobes, and as many hazel-nuts and walnuts; thanks to my master's stinginess, and to the opinion he has, and the order he observes, that knights-errant ought to feed and diet themselves only upon dried fruits and wild salads.'

'By my faith, brother,' replied he of the Wood, 'I have no stomach for your wild pears, nor your sweet thistles, nor your mountain roots: let our masters have them, with their opinions and laws of chivalry, and let them eat what they commend. I carry cold meats, and this bottle hanging at my saddle-pommel, happen what will; and such a reverence I have for it, and so much I love it, that few minutes pass but I give it a thousand kisses, and a thousand hugs.'

And, so saying, he put it into Sancho's hand, who, grasping and setting it to his mouth, stood gazing at the stars for a quarter of an hour: and, having done drinking, he let fall his head on one side, and, fetching a deep sigh, said:

'O whoreson rogue! how Catholic it is!'

'You see now,' quoth he of the Wood, hearing Sancho's "whoreson", 'how you have commended this wine in calling it whoreson.'

'I confess my error,' answered Sancho, 'and see plainly, that it is no discredit to anybody to be called son of a whore, when it comes under the notion of praising. But tell me, sir, by the life of him you love best, is not this wine of Ciudad Real?'

'You have a distinguishing palate,' answered he of the Wood: 'it is of no other growth, and besides has some years over its head.'

'Trust me for that,' quoth Sancho: 'depend upon it, I always hit right, and guess the kind. But is it not strange, Señor Squire, that I should have so great and natural an instinct in the business of knowing wines, that let me but smell [at] any, I hit upon the country, the kind, the flavour, and how long it will keep, how many changes it will undergo, with all other circumstances appertaining to wines? But no wonder; for I have had in my family, by the father's side, the two most exquisite tasters that La Mancha has known for many ages;

for proof whereof, there happened to them what I am going to relate.

'To each of them was given a taste of a certain hogshead, and their opinion asked of the condition, quality, goodness, or badness of the wine. The one tried it with the tip of his tongue; the other put it to his nose. The first said, the wine savoured of iron; the second said, it had rather a twang of goat's leather. The owner protested, the vessel was clean, and the wine neat, so that it could not taste either of iron or leather. Notwithstanding this, the two famous tasters stood positively to what they had said. Time went on; the wine was sold off, and, at rinsing the hogshead, there was found in it a small key, hanging to a leather thong.* Judge then, sir, whether any one of that race may not very well undertake to give his opinion in these matters.'

'Therefore, I say,' quoth he of the Wood, 'let us give over seeking adventures, and, since we have a good loaf of bread, let us not look for cheesecakes: and let us get home to our cabins, for there God will find us, if it be His will.'

'I will serve my master till he arrives at Saragossa,' quoth Sancho, 'and then we shall all understand one another.'

In fine, the two good squires talked and drank so much, that it was high time sleep should tie their tongues, and allay their thirst, for to quench it was impossible: and thus both of them, keeping fast hold of the almost empty bottle, with their meat half chewed, fell fast asleep; where we will leave them at present, to relate what passed between the Knight of the Wood and him of the Sorrowful Figure.

CHAPTER 14

In which is continued the adventure of the Knight of the Wood.

AMONG sundry discourses which passed between Don Quixote and the Knight of the Wood, the history tells us that he of the Wood said to Don Quixote:

'In short, Sir Knight, I would have you to know, that my

destiny, or rather my choice, led me to fall in love with the peerless Casildea de Vandalia. Peerless I call her, not so much on account of her stature, as the excellency of her state and beauty. This same Casildea I am speaking of, repaid my honourable thoughts and virtuous desires by employing me as Hercules was by his stepmother, in many and various perils, promising me at the end of each of them that the next should crown my hopes; but she still goes on, adding link upon link to the chain of my labours, insomuch that they are become without number; nor can I guess which will be the last, and that which is to give a beginning to the accomplishment of my good wishes. One time she commanded me to go and challenge the famous giantess of Seville, called Giralda,* who is so stout and strong, as being made of brass, and, without stirring from the place, is the most changeable and unsteady woman in the world. I came, I saw, I conquered: I made her stand still, and fixed her to a point; for, in above a week's time, no wind blew but the north. Another time she sent me to weigh the ancient stones of the stout bulls of Guisando,* an enterprise more fit for porters than knights; and another time she commanded me to plunge headlong into Cabra's cave* (an unheard-of and dreadful attempt), and to bring her a particular relation of what is locked up in that obscure abyss. I stopped the motion of the Giralda, I weighed the bulls of Guisando, I precipitated myself into the cavern of Cabra, and brought to light the hidden secrets of that abyss: and yet my hopes are dead, O how dead! and her commands and disdains alive, O how alive!

'In short, she has at last commanded me to travel over all the provinces of Spain, and oblige all the knights I shall find wandering therein, to confess, that she alone excels in beauty all beauties this day living, and that I am the most valiant and the most completely enamoured knight in the world. In obedience to which command, I have already traversed the greatest part of Spain, and have vanquished divers knights, who have dared to contradict me. But what I am most proud of, and value myself most upon, is the having vanquished in single combat the so renowned knight, Don Quixote de la Mancha, and made him confess that my Casildea is more beautiful than his Dulcinea: and I make account that, in this conquest alone, I have vanquished all the knights in the world; for that very Don Quixote I speak of has conquered them all, and I having overcome him, his glory, his fame, and his honour are transferred and passed over to my person; "for the victor's renown rises in proportion to that of the vanquished":* so that the innumerable exploits of the said Don Quixote are already mine, and placed to my account.'

Don Quixote was amazed to hear the Knight of the Wood, and was ready a thousand times to give him the lie, and, 'You lie,' was at the tip of his tongue: but he restrained himself the best he could, in order to make him confess the lie with his own mouth; and therefore he said very calmly:

'Sir Knight, that you may have vanquished most of the knights-errant of Spain, yea, and of the whole world, I will not dispute; but that you have conquered Don Quixote de la Mancha, I somewhat doubt: it might indeed be somebody resembling him, though there are very few such.'

'Why not?' replied he of the Wood; 'by the canopy of heaven I fought with Don Quixote, vanquished him, and made him submit; by the same token that he is tall of stature, thin visaged, upright-bodied, robust-limbed, grizzle-haired, hawk-nosed, with large black moustaches: he gives himself the name of the Knight of the Sorrowful Figure: his squire is a country fellow, called Sancho Panza: he oppresses the back, and governs the reins, of a famous steed called Rosinante: in a word, he has for the mistress of his thoughts one Dulcinea del Toboso, sometime called Aldonza Lorenzo; in like manner as mine, who, because her name was Casildea, and being of Andalusia, is now distinguished by the name of Casildea de Vandalia. If all these tokens are not sufficient to prove the truth of what I say, here is my sword, which shall make incredulity itself believe it.'

'Be not in a passion, Sir Knight,' said Don Quixote, 'and hear what I have to say. You are to know that this Don Quixote, you speak of, is the dearest friend I have in the world, insomuch that I may say he is as it were my very self; and by the tokens and marks you have given of him, so exact and so precise, I cannot but think it must be he himself that you have subdued. On the other side, I see with my eyes and feel with my hands, that it cannot be the same, unless it be, that, having many enchanters his enemies (one especially, who is continually persecuting him), some one or other of them may have assumed his shape, and suffered himself to be vanquished, in order to defraud him of the fame his exalted feats of chivalry have acquired, over the face of the whole earth. And, for confirmation hereof, you must know, that these enchanters, his enemies, but two days ago, transformed the figure and person of the beautiful Dulcinea del Toboso into those of a dirty, mean, country wench; and in like manner they must have transformed Don Quixote. And if all this be not sufficient to justify this truth, here stands Don Quixote himself, ready to maintain it by force of arms, on foot or on horseback, or in whatever manner you please.'

And so saying, he rose up, and, grasping his sword, expected what resolution the Knight of the Wood would take; who very calmly answered, and said:

'A good paymaster is in pain for no pawn: he who could once vanquish you, Señor Don Quixote, when transformed, may well hope to make you yield in your own proper person. But as knights-errant should by no means do their feats of arms in the dark, like robbers and ruffians, let us wait for daylight, that the sun may be witness of our exploits: and the condition of our combat shall be, that the conquered shall be entirely at the mercy and disposal of the conqueror, to do with him whatever he pleases, provided always, that he command nothing but what a knight may with honour submit to.'

'I am entirely satisfied with this condition and compact,' answered Don Quixote.

And hereupon they both went to look for their squires, whom they found snoring in the very same posture in which sleep had seized them. They awaked them, and ordered them to get ready their steeds; for, at sunrise, they were to engage in a bloody and unparalleled single combat. At which news Sancho was thunderstruck, and ready to swoon, in dread of his master's safety, from what he had heard the Squire of the Wood tell of his master's valour. But the two squires without speaking a word went to seek their cattle, and found them altogether; for the three horses and Dapple had already smelt one another out.

By the way the Squire of the Wood said to Sancho:

'You must understand, brother, that the fighters of Andalusia have a custom, when they are godfathers in any combat, not to stand idle with their arms across, while their godsons are fighting. This I say to give you notice, that, while our masters are engaged, we must fight too, and make splinters of one another.'

'This custom, Señor Squire,' answered Sancho, 'may be current, and pass among the ruffians and fighters you speak of; but among the squires of knights-errant, no, not in thought: at least I have not heard my master talk of any such custom, and he has all the laws and ordinances of knight-errantry by heart. But, taking it for granted, that there is an express statute for the squires engaging while their masters are at it; yet will I not comply with it, but rather pay the penalty imposed upon such peaceable squires; which I dare say cannot be above a couple of pounds of white wax,* and I will rather pay them; for I know they will cost me less than the money I shall spend in lint to get my head cured, which I already reckon as cut and divided in twain. Besides, another thing which makes it impossible for me to fight, is, my having no sword; for I never wore one in my life.'

'I know a remedy for that,' said he of the Wood; 'I have here a couple of linen bags of the same size; you shall take one and I the other, and we will have a bout at bag-blows with equal weapons.'

'With all my heart,' answered Sancho; 'for such a battle will rather dust our jackets than wound our persons.'

'It must not be quite so neither,' replied the other; 'for, lest the wind should blow them aside, we must put in them half a dozen clean and smooth pebbles, of equal weight; and thus we may brush one another without much harm or damage.'

'Body of my father!' answered Sancho, 'what sable fur, what bottoms of carded cotton, he puts into the bags, that we may not break our noddles, nor beat our bones to powder! But though they should be filled with balls of raw silk, be it known to you, sir, I shall not fight; let our masters fight, and hear of it in another world, and let us drink and live; for time takes care to take away our lives, without our seeking new appetites to destroy them, before they reach their appointed term and season, and drop with ripeness.'

'For all that,' replied he of the Wood, 'we must fight, if it be but for half an hour.'

'No, no,' answered Sancho, 'I shall not be so discourteous, nor so ungrateful, as to have any quarrel at all, be it never so little, with a gentleman, after having eaten of his bread, and drunk of his drink: besides, who the devil can set about dry fighting, without anger, and without provocation?'

'If that be all,' quoth he of the Wood, 'I will provide a sufficient remedy; which is, that, before we begin the combat, I will come up to your worship, and fairly give you three or four good cuffs, which will lay you flat at my feet, and awaken your choler, though it slept sounder than a dormouse.'

'Against that expedient,' answered Sancho, 'I have another not a whit behind it: I will take a good cudgel, and, before you reach me to awaken my choler, I will bastinado yours so sound asleep, that it shall never awake more but in another world, where it is well known I am not a man to let anybody handle my face; and let every one take heed to the arrow; though the safest way would be for each man to let his choler sleep; for nobody knows what is in another, and some people go out for wool, and come home shorn themselves; and God in all times blessed the peacemakers, and cursed the peacebreakers; for if a cat, pursued, and pent in a room, and hard put to it, turns into a lion, God knows what I (that am a man) may turn into: and therefore from henceforward I intimate to your worship, Señor Squire, that all the damage and mischief, that shall result from our quarrel must be placed to your account.'

'It is well,' replied he of the Wood; 'God send us daylight, and we shall see what will come of it.'

And now a thousand sorts of enamelled birds began to chirp in the trees, and in variety of joyous songs seemed to give the good-morrow, and salute the blooming Aurora, who began now to discover the beauty of her face through the gates and balconies of the east, shaking from her locks an infinite number of liquid pearls, and, in that delicious liquor, bathing the herbs, which also seemed to sprout, and rain a kind of seed-pearl. At her approach, the willows distilled savoury manna, the fountains smiled, the brooks murmured, the woods were cheered, and the meads were gilded. But scarcely had the clearness of the day given opportunity to see and distinguish objects, when the first thing that presented itself to Sancho's eyes, was the Squire of the Wood's nose, which was so large, that it almost overshadowed his whole body. In a word, it is said to have been of an excessive size, hawked in the middle, and full of warts and carbuncles, of the colour of a mulberry, and hanging two fingers' breadth below his mouth. The size, the colour, the carbuncles, and the crookedness, so disfigured his face, that Sancho, at sight thereof, began to tremble hand and foot, like a child in a fit, and resolved within himself to take two hundred cuffs before his choler should awaken to encounter that hobgoblin.

Don Quixote viewed his antagonist, and found he had his helmet on, and the beaver down, so that he could not see his face: but he observed him to be a strong-made man, and not very tall. Over his armour he wore a kind of surtout, or loose coat, seemingly of the finest gold, besprinkled with sundry little moons of resplendent looking-glass, which made a most gallant and splendid show. A great number of green, yellow, and white feathers waved about his helmet. His lance, which stood leaning against a tree, was very large and thick, and headed with pointed steel above a span long. Don Quixote viewed, and noted everything, judging by all he saw and remarked, that the aforesaid knight must needs be of great strength: but he was not, therefore, daunted, like Sancho Panza. On the contrary, with a gallant boldness he said to the Knight of the Looking-glasses:

'Sir Knight, if your great eagerness to fight has not exhausted too much of your courtesy, I entreat you to lift up your beaver a little, that I may see whether the sprightliness of your countenance be answerable to that of your figure.'

'Whether you be vanquished or victorious in this enterprise, Sir Knight,' answered he of the Looking-glasses, 'there will be time and leisure enough for seeing me; and if I do not now comply with your desire, it is because I think I should do a very great wrong to the beautiful Casildea de Vandalia, to lose so much time, as the lifting my beaver would take up, before I make you confess what you know I pretend to.'

'However, while we are getting on horseback,' said Don Quixote, 'you may easily tell me whether I am that Don Quixote you said you had vanquished.'

'To this I answer,' quoth he of the Looking-glasses, 'that you are as like that very knight I vanquished, as one egg is like another: but since you say you are persecuted by enchanters, I dare not be positive, whether you are the same person or no.'

'That is sufficient,' answered Don Quixote, 'to make me believe you are deceived: however, to undeceive you quite, let us to horse, and in less time than you would have spent in lifting up your beaver, if God, my mistress, and my arm avail me, I will see your face, and you shall see I am not that vanquished Don Quixote you imagine.'

Then cutting short the discourse, they mounted, and Don Quixote wheeled Rosinante about, to take as much ground as was convenient for encountering his opponent; and he of the Looking-glasses did the like: but Don Quixote was not gone twenty paces, when he heard himself called by the Knight of the Looking-glasses; so meeting each other half-way, he of the Looking-glasses said:

'Take notice, Sir Knight, that the condition of our combat is, that the conquered, as I said before, shall remain at the discretion of the conqueror.'

'I know it,' answered Don Quixote, 'provided that what is commanded and imposed on the vanquished shall not exceed, nor derogate from, the laws of chivalry.'

'So it is to be understood,' answered he of the Looking-glasses.

At this juncture the squire's strange nose presented itself to Don Quixote's sight, who was no less surprised at it than Sancho, insomuch that he looked upon him to be some monster, or some strange man, such as are not common now in the world. Sancho, seeing his master set forth to take his career, would not stay alone with Long-nose, fearing, lest one

gentle wipe with that snout across his face should put an end
to his battle, and he be laid sprawling on the ground, either
by the blow or by fear. Therefore he ran after his master,
holding by the back-guard of Rosinante's saddle; and, when
he thought it was time for him to face about, he said:

'I beseech your worship, dear sir, that, before you turn
about to engage, you will be so kind as to help me up into
yon cork-tree, from whence I can see better, and more to
my liking, than from the ground, the gallant encounter you
are about to have with that knight.'

'I believe, Sancho,' quoth Don Quixote, 'you have more
mind to climb and mount a scaffold, to see the bull-sports
without danger.'

'To tell you the truth, sir,' answered Sancho, 'the prodigious
nose of that squire astonishes and fills me with dread, and I
dare not stand near him.'

'In truth,' said Don Quixote, 'it is so frightful, that, were
I not who I am, I should be afraid myself; and therefore
come, and I will help you up.'

While Don Quixote was busied in helping Sancho up into
the cork-tree, he of the Looking-glasses took as large a
compass as he thought necessary, and believing that Don
Quixote had done the like, without waiting for sound of
trumpet, or any other signal, he turned about his horse, who
was not a whit more active, nor more promising than Rosinante; and at his best speed, which was a middling trot, he
advanced to encounter his enemy; but seeing him employed
in helping up Sancho, he reined in his steed, and stopped in
the midst of his career; for which his horse was most
thankful, being not able to stir any farther.

Don Quixote, thinking his enemy was coming full speed
against him, clapped spurs to Rosinante's lean flanks, and
made him so bestir himself, that, as the history relates, this
was the only time he was known to do something like
running; for at all others a down-right trot was all: and with
this unspeakable fury he soon came up where he of the
Looking-glasses stood, striking his spurs up to the very rowels
in his steed, without being able to make him stir a finger's
length from the place, where he made a full stand in his

career. In this good time, and at this juncture, Don Quixote found his adversary embarrassed with his horse, and encumbered with his lance; for either he did not know how, or had not time to set it in its rest. Don Quixote, who heeded none of these inconveniences, with all safety, and without the least danger, attacked him of the Looking-glasses with such force, that, in spite of him, he bore him to the ground over his horse's crupper; and such was his fall, that he lay motionless, without any signs of life.

Sancho no sooner saw him fallen, than he slid down from the cork-tree, and in all haste ran to his master, who, alighting from Rosinante, was got upon him of the Looking-glasses, and unlacing his helmet, to see whether he was dead, or to give him air, if perchance he was alive; when he saw—, but who can express what he saw, without causing admiration, wonder, and terror in all that hear it? He saw, says the history, the very face, the very figure, the very aspect, the very physiognomy, the very effigies and picture of the bachelor Sampson Carrasco; and as soon as he saw him, he cried out:

'Come hither, Sancho, and behold what you must see, but not believe: make haste, son, and observe, what magic, what wizards and enchanters can do.'

Sancho approached, and, seeing the bachelor Sampson Carrasco's face, he began to cross and bless himself a thousand times over; and all this while the demolished cavalier showed no signs of life; and Sancho said to Don Quixote:

'I am of opinion, sir, that right or wrong, your worship should thrust the sword down the throat of him, who seems so like the bachelor Sampson Carrasco: perhaps in him you may kill some one of those enchanters your enemies.'

'You do not say amiss,' quoth Don Quixote: 'for the fewer our enemies are, the better.'

And drawing his sword to put Sancho's advice in execution, the Squire of the Looking-glasses drew near, without the nose that made him look so frightful, and cried aloud:

'Have a care, Señor Don Quixote, what you do; for he, who lies at your feet, is the bachelor Sampson Carrasco, your friend, and I am his squire.'

Sancho, seeing him without that former ugliness, said to him: 'And the nose?'

To which he answered;

'I have it here in my pocket.'

And putting in his hand he pulled out a pasteboard nose, painted and varnished, of the fashion we have already described: and Sancho, eyeing him more and more, with a loud voice of admiration, said:

'Blessed Virgin, defend me! Is not this Tom Cecial, my neighbour and gossip?'

'Indeed am I,' answered the unnosed squire; 'Tom Cecial I am, gossip and friend to Sancho Panza; and I will inform you presently what conduits, lies, and wiles brought me hither: in the meantime, beg and entreat your master not to touch, maltreat, wound, or kill the Knight of the Lookingglasses now at his feet; for there is nothing more sure than that he is the daring and ill-advised bachelor, Sampson Carrasco our countryman.'

By this time he of the Looking-glasses was come to himself; which Don Quixote perceiving, he clapped the point of the naked sword to his throat, and said:

'You are a dead man, knight, if you do not confess, that the peerless Dulcinea del Toboso excels in beauty your Casildea de Vandalia; and further you must promise, if you escape from this conflict and this fall with life, to go to the city of Toboso, and present yourself before her on my behalf, that she may dispose of you as she shall think fit, and, if she leaves you at your own disposal, then you shall return, and find me out (for the track of my exploits will serve you for a guide, and conduct you to my presence) to tell me what passes between her and you; these conditions being entirely conformable to our articles before our battle, and not exceeding the rules of knight-errantry.'

'I confess,' said the fallen knight, 'that the lady Dulcinea del Toboso's torn and dirty shoe is preferable to the ill-combed, though clean, locks of Casildea; and I promise to go and return from her presence to yours, and give you an exact and particular account of what you require of me.'

'You must likewise confess and believe,' added Don Quixote, 'that the knight you vanquished was not and could not be Don Quixote de la Mancha, but somebody else like him; as I do confess and believe, that you, though, in appearance, the bachelor Sampson Carrasco, are not he, but some other, whom my enemies have purposely transformed into his likeness, to restrain the impetuosity of my choler, and make me use with moderation the glory of my conquest.'

'I confess, judge of, and allow everything, as you believe, judge of, and allow,' answered the disjointed knight: 'Suffer me to rise, I beseech you, if the hurt of my fall will permit, which has left me sorely bruised.'

Don Quixote helped him to rise, as did his squire, Tom Cecial, from off whom Sancho could not remove his eyes, asking him things, the answers to which convinced him evidently of his being really that Tom Cecial he said he was. But he was so prepossessed by what his master had said of the enchanters having changed the Knight of the Looking-glasses into the bachelor Sampson Carrasco, that he could not give credit to what he saw with his eyes. In short, master and man remained under this mistake; and he of the Looking-glasses, with his squire, much out of humour, and in ill plight, parted from Don Quixote and Sancho, to look for some convenient place, where he might cere-cloth himself and splinter his ribs.* Don Quixote and Sancho continued their journey to Saragossa, where the history leaves them to give an account who the Knight of the Looking-glasses and his nosey squire were.

CHAPTER 15

Giving an account, who the Knight of the Looking-glasses and his squire were.

EXCEEDINGLY content, elated, and vainglorious was Don Quixote, at having gained the victory over so valiant a knight, as he imagined him of the Looking-glasses to be; from whose knightly word he hoped to learn, whether the enchantment of his mistress continued, the said knight being under a necessity of returning, upon pain of not being one, to give him an account of what should pass between her and him. But Don Quixote thought one thing, and he of the Looking-glasses another; who, for the present thought no further than of finding a place where he might plaster himself, as has been already said.

The history then tells us, that, when the bachelor Sampson Carrasco advised Don Quixote to resume his intermitted exploits of chivalry, he, the priest and the barber, had first consulted together about the means of persuading Don Quixote to stay peaceably and quietly at home, without distracting himself any more about his unlucky adventures; and it was concluded by general vote, and particular opinion of Carrasco, that they should let Don Quixote make another sally, since it seemed impossible to detain him, and that Sampson should also sally forth like a knight-errant, and encounter him in fight (for an opportunity could not be long wanting), and so vanquish him, which would be an easy matter to do; and that it should be covenanted and agreed, that the conquered should lie at the mercy of the conqueror; and so, Don Quixote being conquered, the bachelor knight should command him to return home to his village and house, and not stir out of it in two years, or till he had received further orders from him: all which, it was plain, Don Quixote, when once overcome, would readily comply with, not to contravene or infringe the laws of chivalry: and it might so fall out, that, during his confinement, he might forget his follies, or an opportunity might offer of finding out some cure for his malady.

Carrasco accepted of the employment, and Tom Cecial, Sancho Panza's gossip and neighbour, a pleasant-humoured, shallow-brained fellow, offered his service to be the squire. Sampson armed himself, as you have heard, and Tom Cecial fitted the counterfeit pasteboard nose to his face, that he might not be known by his gossip when they met; and so they took the same road that Don Quixote had taken, and arrived almost in time enough to have been present at the adventure of Death's car. But, in short, they lighted on them in the wood, where befell them all that the prudent [reader] has been reading. And had it not been for Don Quixote's extraordinary opinion, that the bachelor was not the bachelor, Señor Bachelor had been incapacitated for ever from taking the degree of licentiate, not finding so much as nests, where he thought to find birds.

Tom Cecial, seeing how ill they had sped, and the unlucky issue of their expedition, said to the bachelor:

'For certain, Señor Sampson Carrasco, we have been very rightly served. It is easy to design and begin an enterprise, but very often difficult to get through with it. Don Quixote is mad, and we think ourselves wise: he gets off sound and laughing, and your worship remains sore and sorrowful. Now, pray, which is the greater madman, he who is so because he cannot help it, or he who is so on purpose?'

To which Sampson answered:

'The difference between these two sorts of madmen, is, that he, who cannot help being mad, will always be so; and he, who plays the fool on purpose, may give over when he thinks fit.'

'If it be so,' quoth Tom Cecial, 'I was mad when I had a mind to be your worship's squire, and now I have a mind to be so no longer, and to get me home to my house.'

'It is fit you should,' answered Sampson; 'but to think that I will return to mine, till I have soundly banged this same Don Quixote, is to be greatly mistaken; and it is not now the desire of curing him of his madness that prompts me to seek him, but a desire of being revenged on him; for the pain of my ribs will not let me entertain more charitable considerations.'

Thus they two went on discoursing, till they came to a village, when they luckily met with a bone-setter, who cured the unfortunate Sampson. Tom Cecial went back and left him, and he stayed behind meditating revenge; and the history speaks of him again in due time, not omitting to rejoice at present with Don Quixote.

CHAPTER 16

Of what befell Don Quixote with a discreet gentleman of La Mancha.

DON QUIXOTE pursued his journey with the pleasure, satisfaction, and self-conceit already mentioned, imagining, upon account of his late victory, that he was the most valiant knight-errant the world could boast of in that age. He looked upon all the adventures, which should befall him from that time forward, as already finished, and brought to a happy conclusion; he valued not any enchantments or enchanters: he no longer remembered the innumerable bastings he had received, during the progress of his chivalries, the stoning that had demolished half his grinders, the ingratitude of the galley-slaves, nor the boldness and shower of pack-staves of the Yangüesian carriers. In short, he said to himself that, could he but hit upon the art or method of disenchanting his lady Dulcinea, he should not envy the greatest good fortune, that the most successful knight-errant of past ages ever did, or could attain to.

He was wholly taken up with these thoughts, when Sancho said to him:

'Is it not strange, sir, that I still have before my eyes the monstrous and unmeasurable nose of my gossip, Tom Cecial?'

'And do you really believe, Sancho,' said Don Quixote, 'that the Knight of the Looking-glasses was the bachelor Sampson Carrasco, and his squire Tom Cecial your gossip?'

'I know not what to say to that,' answered Sancho; 'I only know, that the marks he gave me of my house, wife, and children, could be given me by nobody else but himself; and his face, when the nose was off, was Tom Cecial's own, as I have seen it very often in our village, next door to my house; and the tone of the voice was also the very same.'

'Come on,' replied Don Quixote; 'let us reason a little upon this business. How can any one imagine, that the bachelor Sampson Carrasco should come knight-errant wise, armed at all points to fight with me? Was I ever his enemy? Have I ever given him occasion to bear me a grudge? Am I his rival?

Or does he make profession of arms, as envying the fame I have acquired by them?'

'What then shall we say, sir,' answered Sancho, 'to that knight's being so very like Sampson Carrasco, be he who he would, and his squire so like Tom Cecial my gossip? And, if it be enchantment, as your worship says, were there no other two in the world they could be made to resemble?'

'The whole is artifice,' answered Don Quixote, 'and a trick of the wicked magicians, who persecute me; who, foreseeing that I was to come off vanquisher in the conflict, contrived, that the vanquished knight should have the face of my friend the bachelor, that the kindness I have for him might interpose between the edge of my sword, and the rigour of my arm, and moderate the just indignation of my breast, and by this means he might escape with his life, who, by cunning devices and false appearances, sought to take away mine. For proof whereof, you already know, O Sancho, by infallible experience, how easy a thing it is for enchanters to change one face into another, making the fair foul, and the foul fair; since, not two days ago, you beheld with your own eyes the beauty and bravery of the peerless Dulcinea in their highest perfection, and at the same time I saw her under the plainness and deformity of a rude country wench, with cataracts on her eyes, and a bad smell in her mouth: and if the perverse enchanter durst make so wicked a transformation, no wonder if he has done the like as to Sampson Carrasco and your gossip, in order to snatch the glory of the victory out of my hands. Nevertheless I comfort myself; for, in short, be it under what shape soever, I have got the better of my enemy.'

'God knows the truth,' answered Sancho; who, well knowing that the transformation of Dulcinea was all his own plot and device, was not satisfied with his master's chimerical notions, but would make no reply, lest he should let fall some word that might discover his cheat.

While they were thus discoursing, there overtook them a man upon a very fine flea-bitten mare,* clad in a surtout of fine green cloth, faced with murry-coloured* velvet, and a hunter's cap of the same: the mare's furniture was all of the field, and ginet-fashion,* murry-coloured, and green. He had a Moorish scimitar hanging at a shoulder-belt of green and gold; and his buskins* wrought like the belt. His spurs were not gilt, but varnished with green, so neat and polished, that they suited his clothes better than if they had been of pure gold. When the traveller came up to them, he saluted them courteously, and spurring his mare, and keeping a little off, was passing on. But Don Quixote called to him:

'Courteous sir, if you are going our way, and are not in haste, I should take it for a favour we might join company.'

'Truly, sir,' answered he with the mare, 'I had not kept off, but for fear your horse should prove unruly in the company of my mare.'

'Sir,' answered Sancho, 'if that be all, you may safely hold in your mare; for ours is the soberest and best-conditioned horse in the world: he never did a naughty thing in his life, upon these occasions, but once, and then my master and I paid for it sevenfold. I say again, your worship may stop if you please; for were she served up betwixt two dishes he would not, I assure you, so much as look her in the face.'

The traveller checked his mare, wondering at the air and countenance of Don Quixote, who rode without his helmet, which Sancho carried, like a cloak-bag, at the pommel of his ass's pannel. And if the gentleman in green gazed much at Don Quixote, Don Quixote stared no less at him, taking him to be some person of consequence. He seemed to be about fifty years of age, had but few grey hairs, his visage aquiline, his aspect between merry and serious; in a word, his mien and appearance spoke him to be a man of worth.

What he in green thought of Don Quixote, was, that he had never seen such a figure of a man before: he admired at the length of his horse, the tallness of his stature, the meagreness of his aspect, his armour, and his deportment; the whole such an odd figure, as had not been seen in that country for many years past.

Don Quixote took good notice how the traveller surveyed him, and reading his desire in his surprise, and being the pink of courtesy, and fond of pleasing everybody, before the traveller could ask him any question, he prevented him, saying:

'This figure of mine, which your worship sees; being so new, and so much out of the way of what is generally in fashion, I do not wonder if you are surprised at it, but you will cease to be so, when I tell you, as I do, that I am one of those knights, whom people call "seekers of adventures". I left my country, mortgaged my estate, quitted my ease and pleasures, and threw myself into the arms of fortune, to carry me whither she pleased. I had a mind to revive the long-deceased chivalry: and for some time past, stumbling here and tumbling there, falling headlong in one place, and getting up again in another, I have accomplished a great part of my design, succouring widows, protecting damsels, aiding married women and orphans; the natural and proper office of knights-errant. And thus, by many valorous and Christian exploits, I have merited the honour of being in print, in all, or most of the nations of the world. Thirty thousand copies* are already published of my history, and it is in the way of coming to thirty thousand thousands more, if heaven prevent it not. Finally, to sum up all in few words, or in one only, know I am Don Quixote de la Mancha, otherwise called the Knight of the Sorrowful Figure: and though self-praises depreciate, I am sometimes forced to publish my own commendations; but this is to be understood, when nobody else is present to do it for me. So that, worthy sir, neither this horse, this lance, this shield, nor this squire, nor all this armour together, nor the wanness of my visage, nor my meagre lankness, ought from henceforward to be matter of wonder to you, now that you know who I am, and the profession I follow.'

Here Don Quixote was silent, and he in green was so long before he returned any answer, that it looked as if he could not hit upon a reply; but after some pause, he said:

'Sir Knight, you judged right of my desire by my surprise; but you have not removed the wonder raised in me at seeing you; for, supposing, as you say, that my knowing who you are might have removed it, yet it has not done so; on the contrary, now that I know it, I am in greater admiration and surprise than before. What! is it possible that there are knights-errant now in the world, and that there are histories printed of real chivalries? I never could have thought there

was anybody now upon earth who relieved widows, succoured damsels, aided married women, or protected orphans,
nor should yet have believed it, had I not seen it in your
worship with my own eyes. Blessed be heaven! for this
history, which your worship says is in print, of your exalted
and true achievements, must have cast into oblivion the
numberless fables of fictitious knights-errant with which the
world was filled, so much to the detriment of good morals,
and the prejudice and discredit of good histories.'

'There is a great deal to be said,' answered Don Quixote,
'upon this subject, whether the histories of knights-errant are
fictitious or not.'

'Why, is there any one,' answered he in green, 'that has
the least suspicion that those histories are not false?'

'I have,' quoth Don Quixote; 'but no more of that; for, if
we travel any time together, I hope in God to convince you,
sir, that you have done amiss in suffering yourself to be
carried away by the current of those, who take it for granted
they are not true.'

From these last words of Don Quixote, the traveller began
to suspect he must be some madman, and waited for a further
confirmation of his suspicion: but before they fell into any
discourse, Don Quixote desired him to tell him who he was,
since he had given him some account of his own condition
and life.

To which he in the green riding-coat answered:

'I, Sir Knight of the Sorrowful Figure, am a gentleman,
native of a village, where, God willing, we shall dine to-day.
I am more than indifferently rich, and my name is Don Diego
de Miranda. I spend my time with my wife, my children, and
my friends: my diversions are hunting and fishing; but I keep
neither hawks nor greyhounds, only some decoy partridges
and a stout ferret. I have about six dozen of books, some
Spanish, some Latin, some of history, and some of devotion;
those of chivalry have not yet come over my threshold. I am
more inclined to the reading of profane authors, than religious, provided they are upon subjects of innocent amusement, the language agreeable, and the invention new and
surprising, though indeed there are very few of this sort in

Spain. Sometimes I eat with my neighbours and friends; and sometimes I invite them: my table is neat and clean, and tolerably furnished. I neither censure others myself, nor allow others to do it for me. I inquire not into other men's lives, nor am I sharpsighted to pry into their actions. I hear mass every day: I share my substance with the poor, making no parade with my good works, nor harbouring in my breast hypocrisy and vainglory, those enemies, which so slyly get possession of the best guarded hearts. I endeavour to make peace between those that are at variance. I devote myself particularly to our Blessed Lady, and always trust in the infinite mercy of God our Lord.'

Sancho was very attentive to the relation of the gentleman's life and conversation; all which appeared to him to be good and holy: and, thinking that one of such a character must needs work miracles, he flung himself off his Dapple, and running hastily, laid hold of his right stirrup; and, with a devout heart, and almost weeping eyes, he kissed his feet more than once. Which the gentleman perceiving, said:

'What mean you, brother? What kisses are these?'

'Pray, let me kiss on,' answered Sancho; 'for your worship is the first saint on horseback I ever saw in all the days of my life.'

'I am no saint,' answered the gentleman, 'but a great sinner: you, brother, must needs be very good, as your simplicity demonstrates.'

Sancho went off, and got again upon his pannel, having forced a smile from the profound gravity of his master, and caused fresh admiration in Don Diego.

Don Quixote then asked him how many children he had, telling him, that one of the things wherein the ancient philosophers, who wanted the true knowledge of God, placed the supreme happiness, was, in the gifts of nature and fortune, in having many friends, and many good children.

'I, Señor Don Quixote,' answered the gentleman, 'have one son; and, if I had him not, perhaps I should think myself happier than I am, not because he is bad, but because he is not so good as I would have him. He is eighteen years old; six he has been at Salamanca, learning the Latin and Greek languages, and, when I was desirous he should study other sciences, I found him so over head and ears in poetry (if that may be called a science) that there was no prevailing with him to look into the law, which was what I would have had him study; nor into divinity, the queen of all sciences. I was desirous he should be the crown and honour of his family, since we live in an age in which our kings highly reward useful and virtuous literature; for letters without virtue are pearls in a dunghill. He passes whole days in examining whether Homer expressed himself well in such a verse of the *Iliad*: whether Martial in such an epigram be obscene or not; whether such a verse in Virgil is to be understood this or that way. In a word, all his conversation is with the books of the aforesaid poets, and with those of Horace, Persius, Juvenal, and Tibullus. As to the modern Spanish authors, he makes no great account of them; though, notwithstanding the antipathy he seems to have to Spanish poetry, his thoughts are at this very time entirely taken up with making a gloss upon four verses, sent him from Salamanca, which, I think, were designed for a scholastic prize.'

To all which Don Quixote answered:

'Children, sir, are pieces of the bowels of their parents, and, whether good or bad, must be loved and cherished as part of ourselves. It is the duty of parents to train them up from their infancy in the paths of virtue and good manners, and in good principles and Christian discipline, that, when they are grown up, they may be the staff of their parents' age, and an honour to their posterity. As to forcing them to this or that science, I do not hold it to be right, though I think there is no harm in advising them; and when there is no need of studying merely for bread, the student being so happy as to have it by inheritance, I should be for indulging him in the pursuit of that science to which his genius is most inclined. And though that of poetry be less profitable than delightful, it is not one of those that are wont to disgrace the possessor.

'Poetry, good sir, I take to be like a tender virgin, very young and extremely beautiful, whom divers other virgins, namely, all the other sciences, make it their business to enrich, polish, and adorn; and to her it belongs to make use of them all, and on her part to give a lustre to them all. But this same virgin is not to be rudely handled, nor dragged through the streets, nor exposed in the turnings of the market-place, nor posted on the corners or gates of palaces. She is formed of an alchemy of such virtue, that he who knows how to manage her, will convert her into the purest gold of inestimable price. He, who possesses her, should keep a strict hand over her, not suffering her to make excursions in obscene satires, or lifeless sonnets. She must in no wise be venal; though she need not reject the profits arising from heroic poems, mournful tragedies, or pleasant and artful comedies. She must not be meddled with by buffoons, or by the ignorant vulgar, incapable of knowing or esteeming the treasures locked up in her. And think not, sir, that I give the appellation of vulgar to the common people alone: all the ignorant, though they be lords or princes, ought, and must be taken into the number. He therefore who, with the aforesaid qualifications, addicts himself to the study and practice of poetry, will become famous, and his name be honoured in all the polite nations of the world.

'And as to what you say, sir, that your son does not much esteem the Spanish poetry, I am of opinion that he is not very right in that; and the reason is this; the great Homer did not write in Latin, because he was a Greek; nor Virgil in Greek, because he was a Roman. In short, all the ancient poets wrote in the language they sucked in with their mothers' milk, and did not hunt after foreign tongues, to express the sublimity of their conceptions. And, this being so, it is fit this custom should take place in all nations; and the German poet should not be disesteemed for writing in his own tongue, nor the Castilian, nor even the Biscainer, for writing in his. But your son, I should imagine, does not dislike the Spanish poetry, but the poets, who are merely Spanish, without any knowledge of other languages, or sciences, which might adorn, enliven, and assist their natural genius: though even in this there may be a mistake, for it is a true opinion, that the poet is born one; the meaning of which is, that a natural poet comes forth a poet from his mother's womb, and, with this talent given him by heaven, and without further study or art, composes things which verify the saying, *Est Deus in nobis,** & c. Not but that a natural poet, who improves himself by art, will be a much better poet, and have the advantage of him, who has no other title to it but the knowledge of that art alone: and the reason is, because art cannot exceed nature, but only perfect it; so that art mixed with nature, and nature with art, form a complete poet.

'To conclude my discourse, good sir, let your son follow the direction of his stars: for, being so good a scholar, as he must needs be, and having already happily mounted the first round of the ladder of the sciences, that of the languages, with the help of these, he will by himself ascend to the top of human learning, which is no less an honour and an ornament to a gentleman, than a mitre to a bishop, or the long robe to the learned in the law. If your son writes satires injurious to the reputation of others, chide him, and tear his performances: but if he pens discourses in the manner of Horace, reprehending vice in general, as that poet so elegantly does, commend him; because it is lawful for a poet to write against envy, and to brand the envious in his verses; and so of other vices, but not to single out particular characters. There are poets, who, for the pleasure of saying one smart thing, will run the hazard of being banished to the isles of Pontus.* If the poet be chaste in his manners, he will be so in his verses: the pen is the tongue of the mind; such as its conceptions are, such will its productions be. And when kings and princes see the wonderful science of poetry employed on prudent, virtuous, and grave subjects, they honour, esteem, and enrich the poets, and even crown them with the leaves of that tree, which the thunderbolt hurts not,* signifying, as it were, that nobody ought to offend those, who wear such crowns, and whose temples are so adorned.'

The gentleman in green admired much at Don Quixote's discourse, insomuch that he began to waver in his opinion as to his being a madman. But in the midst of the conversation, Sancho, it not being much to his taste, was gone out of the road to beg a little milk of some shepherds, who were hard by milking some ewes. And now the gentleman, highly

satisfied with Don Quixote's ingenuity and good sense, was
renewing the discourse, when on a sudden Don Quixote,
lifting up his eyes, perceived a car, with royal banners,*
coming the same road they were going, and believing it to
be some new adventure, he called aloud to Sancho, to come
and give him his helmet. Sancho hearing himself called, left
the shepherds, and in all haste, pricking his Dapple, came
where his master was, whom there befell a most dreadful and
stupendous adventure.

CHAPTER 17

*Wherein is set forth the last and highest point, at which the
unheard-of courage of Don Quixote ever did, or could, arrive;
with the happy conclusion of the adventure of the lions.*

THE history relates, that, when Don Quixote called out to
Sancho to bring him his helmet, he was buying some curds
of the shepherds; and, being hurried by the violent haste his
master was in, he knew not what to do with them, nor how
to bestow them: and that he might not lose them, now they
were paid for, he bethought him of clapping them into his
master's helmet, and, with this excellent shift, back he came
to learn the commands of his lord, who said to him:

'Friend, give me the helmet; for either I know little of
adventures, or that, which I descry yonder, is one that does
and will oblige me to have recourse to arms.'

He in the green riding-coat, hearing this, cast his eyes every
way as far as he could, and discovered nothing but a car
coming towards them, with two or three small flags, by which
he conjectured, that the said car was bringing some of the
king's money, and so he told Don Quixote. But he believed
him not, always thinking and imagining that everything that
befell him must be an adventure, and adventures upon
adventures; and thus he replied to the gentleman:

'Preparation is half the battle, and nothing is lost by being
upon one's guard. I know by experience, that I have enemies
both visible and invisible, and I know not when, nor from

what quarter, nor at what time, nor in what shape, they will encounter me.'

And turning about, he demanded his helmet of Sancho, who, not having time to take out the curds, was forced to give it him as it was. Don Quixote took it, and, without minding what was in it, clapped it hastily upon his head; and as the curds were squeezed and pressed, the whey began to run down the face and beard of Don Quixote; at which he was so startled, that he said to Sancho:

'What can this mean, Sancho? methinks my skull is softening, or my brains melting, or I sweat from head to foot: and if I do really sweat, in truth it is not through fear, though I verily believe I am like to have a terrible adventure of this. If you have anything to wipe withal, give it me; for the copious sweat quite blinds my eyes.'

Sancho said nothing, and gave him a cloth, and with it thanks to God that his master had not found out the truth. Don Quixote wiped himself, and took off his helmet, to see what it was that so over-cooled his head; and, seeing some white lumps in it, he put them to his nose, and smelling [at] them, said:

'By the life of my lady Dulcinea del Toboso, they are curds you have clapped in here, vile traitor, and inconsiderate squire!'

To which Sancho answered, with great phlegm and dissimulation:

'If they are curds, give me them to eat: but the devil eat them for me; for it must be he that put them there. What! I offer to foul your worship's helmet? In faith, sir, by what God gives me to understand, I too have my enchanters, who persecute me, as a creature and member of your worship, and, I warrant, have put that 'filthiness there, to stir your patience to wrath against me, and provoke you to bang my sides as you used to do. But truly this bout they have missed their aim; for I trust to the candid judgement of my master, who will consider, that I have neither curds, nor cream, nor anything like it; and that, if I had, I should sooner have put them into my stomach, than into your honour's helmet.'

'It may be so,' quoth Don Quixote.

All this the gentleman saw, and saw with admiration, especially when Don Quixote, after having wiped his head, face, beard, and helmet, clapping it on, and fixing himself firm in his stirrups, then trying the easy drawing of his sword, and grasping his lance, said:

'Now come what will; for here I am prepared to encounter Satan himself in person.'

By this time the car with the flags was come up, and nobody with it but the carter upon one of the mules, and a man sitting upon the fore-part. Don Quixote planted himself just before them, and said:

'Whither go ye brethren? what car is this? and what have you in it? and what banners are those?'

To which the carter answered:

'The car is mine, and in it are two fierce lions, which the general of Oran is sending to court as a present to his majesty: the flags belong to our liege the king, to show that what is in the car is his.'

'And are the lions large?' demanded Don Quixote.

'So large,' replied the man upon the fore-part of the car, 'that larger never came from Africa into Spain: I am their keeper, and have had charge of several, but never of any so large as these: they are a male and a female; the male is in the first cage, and the female in that behind: at present they are hungry, not having eaten to-day, and therefore, sir, get out of the way; for we must make haste to the place where we are to feed them.'

At which Don Quixote, smiling a little, said:

'To me your lion-whelps! your lion-whelps to me! and at this time of day! By the living God, those who sent them thither, shall see whether I am a man to be scared by lions. Alight, honest friend, and since you are their keeper, open the cages, and turn out those beasts; for in the midst of this field will I make them know who Don Quixote de la Mancha is, in spite of the enchanters that sent them to me.'

'Very well,' quoth the gentleman to himself, 'our good knight has given us a specimen of what he is: doubtless, the curds have softened his skull, and ripened his brains.'

Then Sancho came to him, and said:

'For God's sake, sir, order it so, that my master Don Quixote may not encounter these lions; for if he does, they will tear us all to pieces.'

'What then, is your master really so mad,' answered the gentleman, 'that you fear and believe he will attack such fierce animals?'

'He is not mad,' answered Sancho, 'but daring.'

'I will make him desist,' replied the gentleman.

And going to Don Quixote, who was hastening the keeper to open the cages, he said:

'Sir, knights-errant should undertake adventures which promise good success: and not such as are quite desperate; for the valour which borders too near upon the confines of rashness has in it more of madness than fortitude: besides, these lions do not come to assail your worship, nor do they so much as dream of any such thing: they are going to be presented to his majesty; and it is not proper to detain them, or hinder their journey.'

'Sweet sir,' answered Don Quixote, 'go hence, and mind your decoy partridge, and your stout ferret, and leave every one to his own business. This is mine, and I will know whether these gentlemen lions come against me, or no.'

And, turning to the keeper, he said:

'I vow to God, Don Rascal, if you do not instantly open the cages, with this lance I will pin you to the car.'

The carter, seeing the resolution of this armed apparition, said:

'Good sir, for charity's sake, be pleased to let me take off my mules, and get with them out of danger, before the lions are let loose; for should my cattle be killed, I am undone for all the days of my life, having no other livelihood but this car and these mules.'

'O man of little faith!' answered Don Quixote, 'alight and unyoke and do what you will; for you shall quickly see you have laboured in vain, and might have saved yourself this trouble.'

The carter alighted, and unyoked in great haste; and the keeper said aloud:

'Bear witness, all here present, that, against my will, and

by compulsion, I open the cages, and let loose the lions; and that I enter my protest against this gentleman, that all the harm and mischief these beasts do shall stand and be placed to his account, with my salary and perquisites over and above: pray, gentlemen, shift for yourselves before I open; for, as to myself, I am sure they will do me no hurt.'

Again the gentleman pressed Don Quixote to desist from doing so mad a thing, it being to tempt God, to undertake so extravagant an action. Don Quixote replied, that he knew what he did. The gentleman rejoined, bidding him consider well of it, for he was certain he deceived himself.

'Nay, sir,' replied Don Quixote, 'if you do not care to be a spectator of what you think will prove a tragedy, spur your Flea-bitten, and save yourself.'

Sancho, hearing this, besought him with tears in his eyes to desist from that enterprise, in comparison whereof that of the windmills, and that fearful one of the fulling-mill hammers, in short, all the exploits he had performed in the whole course of his life, were mere tarts and cheese-cakes.

'Consider, sir,' quoth Sancho, 'that here is no enchantment, nor anything like it; for I have seen, through the grates and chinks of the cage, the claw of a true lion: and I guess by it, that the lion, to whom such a claw belongs, is bigger than a mountain.'

'However it be,' answered Don Quixote, 'fear will make it appear to you bigger than half the world. Retire, Sancho, and leave me: and if I die here, you know our old agreement: repair to Dulcinea—I say no more.'

To these he added other expressions, with which he cut off all hope of his desisting from his extravagant design. He in green would fain have opposed him, but found himself unequally matched in weapons and armour, and did not think it prudent to engage with a madman; for such, by this time, he took Don Quixote to be in all points; who hastening the keeper, and reiterating his menaces, the gentleman took occasion to clap spurs to his mare, Sancho to Dapple, and the carter to his mules, all endeavouring to get as far from the car as they could, before the lions were let loose. Sancho lamented the death of his master, verily believing it would now overtake him in the paws of the lions: he cursed his hard fortune, and the unlucky hour when it came into his head to serve him again: but for all his tears and lamentations, he ceased not punching his Dapple, to get far enough from the car. The keeper seeing that the fugitives were got a good way off, repeated his arguments and entreaties to Don Quixote, who answered, that he heard him, and that he should trouble himself with no more arguments nor entreaties, for all would signify nothing, and that he must make haste.

Whilst the keeper delayed opening the first grate, Don Quixote considered with himself, whether it would be best to fight on foot or on horseback: at last he determined to fight on foot, lest Rosinante should be terrified at sight of the lions. Thereupon he leaped from his horse, flung aside his lance, braced on his shield, and drew his sword; and marching slowly, with marvellous intrepidity, and an undaunted heart, he planted himself before the car, devoutly commending himself, first to God, and then to his mistress Dulcinea.

Here it is to be noted, that the author of this faithful history, coming to this passage, falls into exclamations, and cries out,

'O strenuous, and beyond all expression courageous, Don Quixote de la Mancha; thou mirror, wherein all the valiant ones of the world may behold themselves, thou second and new Don Manuel de Leon,* who was the glory and honour of the Spanish knights! With what words shall I relate this tremendous exploit? By what arguments shall I render it credible to succeeding ages? Or what praises, though above all hyperboles hyperbolical, do not fit and become thee? Thou alone on foot, intrepid and magnanimous, with a single sword, and that none of the sharpest, with a shield, not of the brightest and most shining steel, standest waiting for and expecting two of the fiercest lions, that the forests of Africa ever bred. Let thy own deeds praise thee, valorous Manchegan? for here I must leave off for want of words, whereby to enhance them.'

Here the author ends his exclamation, and resumes the thread of the history, saying:

The keeper, seeing Don Quixote fixed in his posture, and that he could not avoid letting loose the male lion, on pain of falling under the displeasure of the angry and daring knight, set wide open the door of the first cage, where lay the lion, which appeared to be of an extraordinary bigness, and of a hideous and frightful aspect. The first thing he did was to turn himself round in the cage, reach out a paw, and stretch himself at full length. Then he gaped and yawned very leisurely; then licked the dust off his eyes, and washed his face, with some half a yard of tongue. This done, he thrust his head out of the cage, and stared round on all sides with eyes of fire-coals; a sight and aspect enough to have struck terror into temerity itself. Don Quixote only observed him with attention, wishing he would leap out from the car, and grapple with him, that he might tear him in pieces; to such a pitch of extravagance had his unheard-of madness transported him. But the generous lion, more civil than arrogant, taking no notice of his vapouring and bravadoes, after having stared about him, as has been said, turned his back, and showed his posteriors to Don Quixote, and with great phlegm and calmness laid himself down again in the cage; which Don Quixote perceiving, he ordered the keeper to give him some blows, and provoke him to çome forth.

'That I will not do,' answered the keeper; 'for should I provoke him, I myself shall be the first he will tear in pieces. Be satisfied, Señor Cavalier, with what is done, which is all that can be said in point of courage, and do not tempt fortune a second time. The lion has the door open, and it is in his choice to come forth or not: and since he has not yet come out, he will not come out all this day. The greatness of your worship's courage is already sufficiently shown: no brave combatant, as I take it, is obliged to more than to challenge his foe, and expect him in the field, and, if the antagonist does not meet him, the infamy lies at his door, and the expectant gains the crown of conquest.'

'That is true,' answered Don Quixote: 'shut the door, friend, and give me a certificate, in the best form you can, of what you have seen me do here. It is fit it should be known how you opened to the lion; I waited for him; he came not out; I waited for him again; again he came not out; and again he laid him down. I am bound to no more; enchantments avaunt, and God help right and truth and true chivalry: and so shut the door, while I make a signal to the fugitive and absent, that they may have an account of this exploit from your mouth.'

The keeper did so, and Don Quixote, clapping on the point of his lance the linen cloth, wherewith he had wiped the torrent of the curds from off his face, began to call out to the rest, who still fled, turning about their heads at every step, all in a troop, and the gentleman at the head of them. But Sancho, chancing to espy the signal of the white cloth, said:

'May I be hanged if my master has not vanquished the wild beasts, since he calls to us.'

They all halted, and knew that it was Don Quixote, who made the sign; and, abating some part of their fear, they drew nearer by degrees, till they came where they could distinctly hear the words of Don Quixote, who was calling to them. In short, they came back to the car, and then Don Quixote said to the carter:

'Put to your mules again, brother, and continue your journey; and, Sancho, give two gold crowns to him and the keeper, to make them amends for my having detained them.'

'That I will, with all my heart,' answered Sancho: 'but what is become of the lions? Are they dead or alive?'

Then the keeper, very minutely, and with proper pauses, related the success of the conflict, exaggerating, the best he could, or knew how, the valour of Don Quixote, at sight of whom the abashed lion would not, or durst not, stir out of the cage, though he had held open the door a good while; and upon his representing to the knight, that it was tempting God to provoke the lion, and to make him come out by force, as he would have had him done, whether he would or no, and wholly against his will, he had suffered the cage-door to be shut.

'What think you of this, Sancho?' quoth Don Quixote: 'can any enchantments prevail against true courage? With ease may the enchanters deprive me of good fortune; but of courage and resolution they never can.'

Sancho gave the gold crowns; the carter put to; the keeper kissed Don Quixote's hands for the favour received, and promised him to relate this valorous exploit to the king himself, when he came to court.

'If, perchance, his majesty,' said Don Quixote, 'should inquire who performed it, tell him, the Knight of the Lions: for from henceforward I resolve, that the title I have hitherto borne of Knight of the Sorrowful Figure shall be changed, trucked, and altered to this; and herein I follow the ancient practice of knights-errant, who changed their names when they had a mind or whenever it served their turn.'

The car went on its way, and Don Quixote, Sancho, and he in the green surtout, pursued their journey. In all this time Don Diego de Miranda had not spoken a word, being all attention to observe and remark the actions and words of Don Quixote, taking him to be a sensible madman, and a madman bordering upon good sense. The first part of his history had not yet come to his knowledge; for, had he read that, his wonder at Don Quixote's words and actions would have ceased, as knowing the nature of his madness: but, as he yet knew nothing of it he sometimes thought him in his senses, and sometimes out of them; because what he spoke was coherent, elegant, and well said, and what he did was extravagant, rash, and foolish: for, said he to himself.

'What greater madness can there be, than to clap on a helmet full of curds, and persuade one's self that enchanters have melted one's skull; and what greater rashness and extravagance, than to resolve to fight with lions?'

Don Quixote diverted these imaginations, and this soliloquy, by saying:

'Doubtless, Señor Don Diego de Miranda, in your opinion I must needs pass for an extravagant madman; and no wonder it should be so: for my actions indicate no less. But, for all that, I would have you know, that I am not so mad, nor so shallow, as I may have appeared to be. A fine appearance makes the gallant cavalier, in shining armour, prancing over the lists, at some joyful tournament, in sight of the ladies. A fine appearance makes the knight, when, in the midst of a large square, before the eyes of his prince, he transfixes a furious bull. And a fine appearance make those knights, who, in military exercises, or the like, entertain, enliven, and, if we may so say, do honour to their prince's court.

'But, above all these, a much finer appearance makes the knight-errant, who, through deserts and solitudes, through crossways, through woods, and over mountains, goes in quest of perilous adventures, with design to bring them to a happy and fortunate conclusion, only to obtain a glorious and immortal fame. A knight-errant, I say, makes a finer appearance in the act of succouring some widow in a desert place, than a knight-courtier in addressing some damsel in a city.

'All cavaliers have their proper and peculiar exercises. Let the courtier wait upon the ladies; adorn his prince's court with rich liveries; entertain the poorer cavaliers at his splendid table; order jousts; manage tournaments; and show himself great, liberal, and magnificent, and above all, a good Christian: and in this manner will he precisely comply with the obligations of his duty. But let the knight-errant search the remotest corners of the world; enter the most intricate labyrinths; at every step assail impossibilities; in the wild uncultivated deserts brave the burning rays of the summer's sun, and the keen inclemency of the winter's frost: let not lions daunt him, spectres affright him, or dragons terrify him: for in seeking these, encountering those, and conquering them all, consists his principal and true employment.

'It being then my lot to be one of the number of knights-errant, I cannot decline undertaking whatever I imagine to come within the verge of my profession; and, therefore, encountering the lions, as I just now did, belonged to me directly, though I knew it to be a most extravagant rashness. I very well know, that fortitude is a virtue placed between the two vicious extremes of cowardice and rashness; but it is better the valiant should rise to the high pitch of temerity, than sink to the low point of cowardice; for as it is easier for the prodigal to become liberal, than for the covetous, so it is much easier for the rash to hit upon being truly valiant, than for the coward to rise to true valour: and as to undertaking adventures, believe me, Señor Don Diego, it is better to lose the game by a card too much than one too little; for it sounds better in the ears of those that hear it, such a knight is rash and daring, than, such a knight is timorous and cowardly.'

'I say, Señor Don Quixote,' answered Don Diego, 'that all you have said and done is levelled by the line of right reason: and I think, if the laws and ordinances of knight-errantry should be lost, they might be found in your worship's breast, as in their proper depository and register. But let us make haste, for it grows late: and let us get to my village and house, where you may repose and refresh yourself after your late toil, which, if not of the body, has been a labour of the mind, which often affects the body too.'

'I accept of the offer as a great favour and kindness, Señor Don Diego,' answered Don Quixote: and spurring on a little more than they had hitherto done, it was about two in the afternoon when they arrived at the village, and the house of Don Diego, whom Don Quixote called The Knight of the Green Riding-coat.

CHAPTER 18

Of what befell Don Quixote in the castle or house of the Knight of the Green Riding-coat, with other extravagant matters.

DON QUIXOTE found that Don Diego's house was spacious, after the country fashion, having the arms of the family carved in rough stone over the great gates; the buttery in the courtyard, the cellar under the porch, and several earthen wine jars placed round about it, which being of the ware of Toboso, renewed the memory of his enchanted and metamorphosed Dulcinea; and without considering what he said, or before whom, he sighed, and cried:

'"O sweet pledges, found now to my sorrow; sweet and joyous, when heaven would have it so!"* O ye Tobosan jars, that have brought back to my remembrance the sweet pledge of my greatest bitterness!'

This was overheard by the poetical scholar, Don Diego's son, who, with his mother, was come out to receive him; and both mother and son were in admiration at the strange figure of Don Quixote, who, alighting from Rosinante, very courteously desired leave to kiss the lady's hands; and Don Diego said:

'Receive, madam, with your accustomed civility, Señor Don Quixote de la Mancha here present, a knight-errant, and the most valiant, and most ingenious person in the world.'

The lady, whose name was Doña Christina, received him with tokens of much affection and civility, and Don Quixote returned them in discreet and courteous expressions. The same kind of compliments passed between him and the student, whom by his talk Don Quixote took for a witty and acute person.

Here the author* sets down all the particulars of Don Diego's house, describing all the furniture usually contained in the mansion of a gentleman that was both a farmer and rich. But the translator of the history* thought fit to pass over in silence these, and such like minute matters, as not suiting with the principal scope of the history, in which truth has more force than cold and insipid digressions.

Don Quixote was led into a hall: Sancho unarmed him; he remained in his wide Walloon breeches, and in a chamois doublet, all besmeared with the rust of his armour: his band was of the college cut, without starch and without lace: his buskins were date-coloured, and his shoes waxed. He girt on his trusty sword, which hung at a belt made of a sea-wolf's skin: for it is thought he had been many years troubled with a weakness in his loins. Over these he had a long cloak of good grey cloth. But, first of all, with five or six kettles of water (for there is some difference as to the number) he washed his head and face; and still the water continued of a whey-colour, thanks to Sancho's gluttony, and the purchase of the nasty curds, that had made his master so white and clean. With the aforesaid accoutrements, and with a genteel air and deportment, Don Quixote walked into another hall, where the student was waiting to entertain him till the cloth was laid; for the lady Doña Christina would show, upon the arrival of so noble a guest, that she knew how to regale those who came to her house.

While Don Quixote was unarming, Don Lorenzo (for that was the name of Don Diego's son) had leisure to say to his father:

'Pray, sir, who is this gentleman you have brought us home? for his name, his figure, and your telling us he is a knight-errant, hold my mother and me in great suspense.'

'I know not how to answer you, son,' replied Don Diego: 'I can only tell you, that I have seen him act the part of the maddest man in the world, and then talk so ingeniously, that his words contradict and undo all his actions. Talk you to him, and feel the pulse of his understanding; and since you have discernment enough, judge of his discretion, or distraction, as you shall find; though, to say the truth, I rather take him to be mad, than otherwise.'

Hereupon Don Lorenzo went to entertain Don Quixote, as has been said; and among other discourse, which passed between them, Don Quixote said to Don Lorenzo:

'Señor Don Diego de Miranda, your father, sir, has given me some account of your rare abilities, and refined judgement, and particularly that you are a great poet.'

'A poet, perhaps, I may be,' replied Don Lorenzo; 'but a great one, not even in thought. True it is, I am somewhat fond of poetry, and of reading the good poets: but in no wise so as to merit the title my father is pleased to bestow upon me.'

'I do not dislike this modesty,' answered Don Quixote; 'for poets are usually very arrogant, each thinking himself the greatest in the world.'

'There is no rule without an exception,' answered Don Lorenzo, 'and such an one there may be, who is really so, and does not think it.'

'Very few,' answered Don Quixote: 'but please to tell me, sir, what verses are those you have now in hand, which, your father says, makes you so uneasy and thoughtful? For if it be some gloss, I know somewhat of the knack of glossing, and should be glad to see it: and if they are designed for a poetical prize, endeavour to obtain the second; for the first is always carried by favour, or by the great quality of the person:* the second is bestowed according to merit; so that the third becomes the second, and the first, in this account, is but the third, according to the liberty commonly taken in your universities. But, for all that, the name of the first makes a great figure.'

'Hitherto,' said Don Lorenzo to himself, 'I cannot judge thee to be mad: let us proceed.'

So he said to him:

'Your worship, I presume, has frequented the schools: what sciences have you studied?'

'That of knight-errantry,' answered Don Quixote, 'which is as good as your poetry, yea, and two little fingers' breadth beyond it.'

'I know not what science that is,' replied Don Lorenzo, 'and hitherto it has not come to my knowledge.'

'It is a science,' replied Don Quixote, 'which includes in it all, or most of the other sciences of the world. For he who professes it must be a lawyer, and know the laws of distributive and commutative justice, in order to give every one what is his own, and that which is proper for him. He must be a divine, to be able to give a reason for the Christian faith he professes, clearly and distinctly, whenever it is required of him. He must be a physician, and especially a botanist, to know, in the midst of wildernesses and deserts, the herbs and simples, which have the virtue of curing wounds; for your knight-errant must not at every turn be running to look for somebody to heal him. He must be an astronomer, to know by the stars what it is o'clock, and what part or climate of the world he is in. He must know the mathematics, because at every foot he will stand in need of them: and, setting aside that he must be adorned with all the cardinal and theological virtues.

'I descend to some other minute particulars. I say then, he must know how to swim, like him people call Fish Nicholas, or Nicholao.* He must know how to shoe a horse, and to keep the saddle and bridle in repair: and to return to what was said above, he must preserve his faith to God and his mistress inviolate. He must be chaste in his thoughts, modest in his words, liberal in good works, valiant in exploits, patient in toils, charitable to the needy, and lastly, a maintainer of the truth, though it should cost him his life to defend it. Of all these great and small parts a good knight-errant is composed. Consider then, Señor Don Lorenzo, whether it be a snotty science, which the knight, who professes it, learns and studies, and whether it may not be equalled to the stateliest of all those that are taught in your colleges and schools.'

'If this be so,' replied Don Lorenzo, 'I maintain, that this science is preferable to all others.'

'How! if it be so!' answered Don Quixote.

'What I mean, sir,' quoth Don Lorenzo, 'is, that I question whether there ever have been, or now are in being, any knights-errant, and adorned with so many virtues.'

'I have often said,' answered Don Quixote, 'what I now repeat, that the greatest part of the world are of opinion, there never were any knights-errant: and, because I am of opinion, that, if heaven does not in some miraculous manner convince them of the truth, that there have been, and are such now, whatever pains are taken will be all in vain, as I have often found by experience, I will not now lose time in bringing you out of an error so prevalent with many. What I intend, is, to beg of heaven to undeceive you, and let you see how useful and necessary knights-errant were in times past, and how beneficial they would be in the present, were they again in fashion: but now, through the sins of the people, sloth, idleness, gluttony, and luxury triumph.'

'Our guest has broke loose,' quoth Don Lorenzo to himself; 'but still he is a whimsical kind of a madman, and I should be a weak fool, if I did not believe so.'

Here their discourse ended; for they were called to supper. Don Diego asked his son what he had copied out fair of the genius of his guest. He answered:

'The ablest doctors and best penmen in the world will never be able to extricate him out of the rough-draft of his madness. His distraction is a medley full of lucid intervals.'

To supper they went, and the repast was such, as Don Diego had told them upon the road, he used to give to those he invited, neat, plentiful, and savoury. But that, which pleased Don Quixote above all, was the marvellous silence throughout the whole house, as if it had been a convent of Carthusians.

The cloth being taken away, grace said, and their hands washed, Don Quixote earnestly entreated Don Lorenzo to repeat the verses designed for the prize. To which he answered:

'That I may not be like those poets, who, when desired, refuse to repeat their verses, and, when not asked, spew them out, I will read my gloss, for which I expect no prize, having done it only to exercise my fancy.'

'A friend of mine, a very ingenious person,' answered Don Quixote, 'was of opinion that nobody should give themselves the trouble of glossing on verses: and the reason, he said, was, because the gloss could never come up to the text, and very often the gloss mistakes the intention and design of the author. Besides, the rules of glossing are too strict, suffering no interrogations, nor "said he's", nor "shall I say's", nor making nouns of verbs, nor changing the sense, with other ties and restrictions, which cramp the glossers, as your worship must needs know.'

'Truly Señor Don Quixote,' quoth Don Lorenzo, 'I have a great desire to catch your worship tripping in some false Latin, and cannot; for you slip through my fingers like an eel.'

'I do not understand,' answered Don Quixote, 'what you mean by my slipping through your fingers.'

'I will let you know another time,' replied Don Lorenzo: 'at present give attention to the text and gloss, which are as follows:

THE TEXT

'Could I the joyous moments past
    Recall, and say, what was now is,
Or to succeeding moments haste,
    And now enjoy the future bliss.*

THE GLOSS

'As all things fleet and die away,
    And day at length is lost in night,

My blessings would no longer stay,
  But took their everlasting flight.
O fortune, at thy feet I lie,
To supplicate thy deity:
Inconstant goddess, frown no more;
  Make me but happy now at last:
No more I'd curse thy fickle power,
  Could I recall the moments past.

'No other conquest I implore,
  No other palm my brow to grace:
Content ('tis all I ask) restore,
  And give me back my mind's lost peace.
Past joys enhance the present pain,
And sad remembrance is our bane.
O would at length relenting Fate
  Restore the ravish'd hours of bliss,
How should I hug the charming state,
  And joyful say, what was now is!

'Thy empty wish, fond wretch, give o'er,
  Nor ask so vain, so wild a thing;
Revolving Time no mortal pow'r,
  Can stop, or stay his fleeting wing.
Nimble as thought, he runs, he flies;
The present hour for ever dies,
In vain we ask futurity;
  In vain we would recall the past:
We cannot from the present fly,
  Nor to succeeding moments haste.

'Vex'd with alternate hopes and fears,
  I feel variety of pain:
But death can ease a wretch's cares,
  And surely death to me is gain.
Again my erring judgement strays
From sober reason's juster ways;
Convinc'd by her unerring voice,
  Another life must follow this,
I make the present woes my choice,
  Rather than forfeit future bliss.'

When Don Lorenzo had made an end of reading his gloss,
Don Quixote stood up, and, holding Don Lorenzo fast upon

the right hand, cried out, in a voice so loud, that it was next to a squall:

'By the highest heavens, noble youth, you are the best poet in the universe, and deserve to wear the laurel, not of Cyprus, nor of Gaeta, as a certain poet* said, whom God forgive, but of the Universities of Athens, were they now in being, and of those that now subsist, of Paris, Bologna, and Salamanca. Heaven grant, that the judges, who shall deprive you of the first prize, may be transfixed by the arrows of Apollo, and that the Muses may never cross the threshold of their doors. Be pleased, sir, to repeat some other of your verses, in the greater kinds of poetry: for I would thoroughly feel the pulse of your admirable genius.'

Is it not excellent that Don Lorenzo should be delighted to hear himself praised by Don Quixote, whom he deemed a madman? O force of flattery, how far dost thou extend, and how wide are the bounds of thy pleasing jurisdiction! This truth was verified in Don Lorenzo, who complied with the desire and request of Don Quixote, repeating this sonnet on the fable or story of Pyramus and Thisbe:

SONNET

The nymph, who Pyramus with love inspired,
Pierces the wall, with equal passion fired:
Cupid from distant Cyprus thither flies,
And views the secret breach with laughing eyes.

Here silence vocal mutual vows conveys,
And whisp'ring eloquent their love betrays.
Though chained by fear their voices dare not pass
Their souls transmitted through the chink embrace.

Ah! woful story of disastrous love,
Ill-fated haste that did their ruin prove!
One death, one grave unites the faithful pair,
And in one common fame their mem'ries share.

'Now God be thanked,' quoth Don Quixote, having heard Don Lorenzo's sonnet, 'that, among the infinite number of poets now in being, I have met with one so absolute in all respects, as the artifice of your worship's sonnet shows you to be.'

Four days was Don Quixote nobly regaled in Don Diego's house: at the end whereof he begged leave to be gone, telling him, he thanked him for the favour and kind entertainment he had received in his family: but, because it did not look well for knights-errant to give themselves up to idleness and indulgence too long, he would go, in compliance with the duty of his function, in quest of adventures, wherewith he was informed those parts abounded; designing to employ the time thereabouts, till the day of the jousts at Saragossa, at which he resolved to be present: but in the first place he intended to visit the cave of Montesinos, of which people related so many and such wonderful things all over that country; at the same time inquiring into the source and true springs of the seven lakes, commonly called the lakes of Ruydera.* Don Diego and his son applauded his honourable resolution, desiring him to furnish himself with whatever he pleased of theirs: for he was heartily welcome to it, his worthy person and his noble profession obliging them to make him this offer.

At length the day of his departure came, as joyous to Don Quixote, as sad and unhappy for Sancho Panza, who liked the plenty of Don Diego's house wondrous well, and was loath to return to the hunger of the forests and wildernesses, and to the penury of his ill-provided wallets. However, he filled and stuffed them with what he thought most necessary: and Don Quixote, at taking leave of Don Lorenzo, said:

'I know not whether I have told you before, and, if I have, I tell you again, that, whenever you shall have a mind to shorten your way and pains to arrive at the inaccessible summit of the Temple of Fame, you have no more to do, but to leave on one side the path of poetry, which is somewhat narrow, and follow that of knight-errantry, which is still narrower, but sufficient to make you an emperor before you can say, "Give me those straws."'

With these expressions Don Quixote did, as it were, finish and shut up the process of his madness, and especially with what he added, saying:

'God knows how willingly I would take Señor Don Loren-zo with me, to teach him how "to spare the humble, and to trample under foot the haughty"* virtues annexed to the function I profess: but since his youth does not require it, nor his laudable exercises permit it, I content myself with putting your worship in the way of becoming a famous poet; and that is, by following the opinion and judgement of other men, rather than your own; for no fathers or mothers think their own children ugly; and this self-deceit is yet stronger with respect to the offspring of the mind.'

The father and son admired afresh at the intermixed discourses of Don Quixote, sometimes wise and sometimes wild, and the obstinacy with which he was bent upon the search of his misadventurous adventures, the sole end and aim of all his wishes. Offers of service and civilities were repeated, and, with the good leave of the lady of the castle, they departed, Don Quixote upon Rosinante, and Sancho upon Dapple.

CHAPTER 19

Wherein is related the adventure of the enamoured shepherd, with other truly pleasant accidents.

DON QUIXOTE was got but a little way from Don Diego's village, when he overtook two persons like ecclesiastics or scholars, and two country fellows, all four mounted upon asses. One of the scholars carried behind him, wrapped up in green buckram like a portmanteau, a small bundle of linen, and two pair of thread-stockings; the other carried nothing but a pair of new black fencing-foils, with their buttons. The countrymen carried other things, which showed that they came from some great town, where they had bought them, and were carrying them home to their own village. Both the scholars and countrymen fell into the same admiration, that all others did at the first sight of Don Quixote, and eagerly desired to know what man this was, so different in appear-ance from other men.

Don Quixote saluted them, and, after learning that the road they were going was the same he was taking, he offered to bear them company desiring them to slacken their pace, for their asses outwent his horse: and, to prevail upon them, he briefly told them who he was, and his employment and profession, that of a knight-errant, going in quest of adventures through all parts of the world. He told them his proper name was Don Quixote de la Mancha, and his appellative the Knight of the Lions. All this to the countrymen was talking Greek or gibberish; but not to the scholars, who soon discovered the soft part of Don Quixote's skull: nevertheless they looked upon him with admiration and respect, and one of them said:

'If your worship, Sir Knight, be not determined to one particular road, a thing not usual with seekers of adventures, come along with us, and you will see one of the greatest and richest weddings* that to this day has ever been celebrated in La Mancha, or in many leagues round about.'

Don Quixote asked him, if it was that of some prince, that he extolled it so much.

'No,' answered the scholar, 'but of a farmer and a farmer's daughter; he the wealthiest of all this country, and she is the most beautiful that ever eyes beheld. The preparation is extraordinary and new; for the wedding is to be celebrated in a meadow near the village where the bride lives, whom they call, by way of pre-eminence, Quiteria the Fair, and the bridegroom, Camacho the Rich; she of the age of eighteen, and he of two-and-twenty, both equally matched; though some nice folks, who have all the pedigrees in the world in their heads, pretend that the family of Quiteria the Fair has the advantage of Camacho's: but nowadays that is little regarded; for riches are able to solder up abundance of flaws. In short, this same Camacho is generous, and has taken into his head to make a kind of arbour to cover the whole meadow overhead, in such manner, that the sun itself will be put to some difficulty to visit the green grass, with which the ground is covered. He will also have morris-dances, both with swords and little bells; for there are some people in his village, who jingle and clatter them extremely well. I say nothing of the shoe-dancers and caperers, so great is the number that are invited. But nothing of all that I have repeated, or omitted, is like to make this wedding so remarkable, as what, I believe, the slighted Basilius will do upon this occasion.

'This Basilius is a neighbouring swain, of the same village with Quiteria: his house is next to that of Quiteria's parents, with nothing but a wall between them; from whence Cupid took occasion to revive in the world the long-forgotten loves of Pyramus and Thisbe: for Basilius was in love with Quiteria from his childhood, and she answered his wishes with a thousand modest favours, insomuch that the loves of the two children, Basilius and Quiteria, became the common talk of the village. When they were grown up, the father of Quiteria resolved to forbid Basilius the usual access to his family; and, to save himself from apprehensions and suspicions, he proposed to marry his daughter to the rich Camacho, not choosing to match her with Basilius, who is not endowed with so many gifts of fortune, as of nature: for, if the truth is to be told without envy, he is the most active youth we know; a great pitcher of the bar; an extreme good wrestler, and a great player at cricket:* runs like a buck, leaps like a wild goat, and plays at ninepins as if he did it by witchcraft: sings like a lark, and touches a guitar that he makes it speak; and, above all, he handles the small sword like the most accomplished fencer.'

'For this excellence alone,' quoth Don Quixote immediately, 'this youth deserves to marry, not only the fair Quiteria, but Queen Guinevere herself, were she now alive, in spite of Sir Lancelot, and all opposers.'

'To my wife with that,' quoth Sancho Panza (who had been hitherto silent and listening), 'who will have everybody marry their equal, according to the proverb, Every sheep to its like. What I would have, is, that this honest Basilius (for I begin to take a liking to him) shall marry this same lady, Quiteria: and heaven send them good luck, and God's blessing' (he meant the reverse) 'on those who would hinder people that love each other from marrying.'

'If all who love each other, were to be married,' said Don

Quixote, 'it would deprive parents of the privilege and au- thority of finding proper matches for their children. If the choice of husbands were left to the inclination of daughters, some there are, who would choose their father's servant, and others some pretty fellow they see pass along the streets, in their opinion, genteel, and well made, though he were a beaten bully; for love and affection easily blind the eyes of the understanding, so absolutely necessary for choosing our state of life: and that of matrimony is greatly exposed to the danger of a mistake, and there is need of great caution, and the particular favour of heaven, to make it hit right. A person, who has a mind to take a long journey, if he be wise, before he sets forward, will look out for some safe and agreeable companion. And should not he do the like, who undertakes a journey for life, especially if his fellow-traveller is to be his companion at bed and board, and everywhere else, as the wife is with the husband? The wife is not a commodity, which, when once bought, you can exchange, or swap, or return; but is an inseparable accessory, which lasts as long as life itself. She is a noose, which, when once thrown about the neck, turns to a Gordian knot, and cannot be unloosed till cut asunder by the scythe of death. I could say much more upon this subject, were I not prevented by the desire I have to know, whether Señor the Licentiate has anything more to say concerning the history of Basilius.'

To which the scholar, bachelor, or licentiate, as Don Quixote called him, answered:

'Of the whole I have no more to say, but that, from the moment Basilius heard of Quiteria's being to be married to Camacho the Rich, he has never been seen to smile, nor speak coherently, and is always pensive and sad, and talking to himself; certain and clear indications of his being dis- tracted. He eats and sleeps but little; and what he does eat is fruit; and when he sleeps, if he does sleep, it is in the fields, upon the hard ground, like a brute beast. From time to time he throws his eyes up to heaven; now fixes them on the ground, with such stupefaction, that he seems to be nothing but a statue clothed, whose drapery is put in motion by the air. In short, he gives such indications of an impassioned heart, that we all take it for granted, that to-morrow Quiteria's pronouncing the fatal Yes will be the sentence of his death.'

'Heaven will order it better,' quoth Sancho; 'for God that gives the wound, sends the cure: nobody knows what is to come: there are a great many hours between this and to-morrow: and in one hour, yea, in one moment, down falls the house: I have seen it rain, and the sun shine, both at the same time: such an one goes to bed sound at night, and is not able to stir next morning: and tell me, can anybody brag of having driven a nail in Fortune's wheel? no, certainly; and, between the Yes and the No of a woman, I would not venture to thrust the point of a pin; for there would not be room enough for it. Grant me but that Quiteria loves Basilius with all her heart, and I will give him a bagful of good fortune: for love, as I have heard say, looks through spectacles, which make copper appear to be gold, poverty to be riches, and specks in the eyes pearls.'

'A curse light on you, Sancho, what would you be at?' quoth Don Quixote: 'when you begin stringing of proverbs and tales, none but Judas, who I wish had you, can wait for you. Tell me, animal, what know you of nails and wheels, or of anything else?'

'Oh!' replied Sancho, 'if I am not understood, no wonder that what I say passes for nonsense; but no matter for that; I understand myself; neither have I said many foolish things: only your worship is always cricketizing my words and actions.'

'Criticizing, I suppose, you would say,' quoth Don Quixote, 'and not cricketizing, thou misapplier of good language, whom God confound.'

'Pray, sir, be not so sharp upon me,' answered Sancho; 'for you know I was not bred at court, nor have studied in Salamanca, to know whether I add to, or take a letter from my words. As God shall save me, it is unreasonable to expect, that the Sayagues* should speak like the Toledans; nay, there are Toledans, who are not over nice in the business of speaking politely.'

'It is true,' quoth the licentiate; 'for how should they speak so well, who are bred in the tanyards and Zocodóver, as they, who are all day walking up and down the cloisters of the great church? and yet they are all Toledans. Purity, propriety, elegance, and perspicuity of language, are to be found among discerning courtiers, though born in Majalahonda;* I say discerning, because a great many there are, who are not so, and discernment is the grammar of good language, accompanied with custom and use. I, gentlemen, for my sins, have studied the canon law in Salamanca, and pique myself a little upon expressing myself in clear, plain, and significant terms.'

'If you had not piqued yourself more upon managing those unlucky foils you carry, than your tongue,' said the other scholar, 'you might by this time have been at the head of your class; whereas you are now at the tail.'

'Look you, bachelor,' answered the licentiate, 'you are the most mistaken in the world in your opinion touching the dexterity of the sword, if you hold it to be insignificant.'

'With me, it is not barely opinion, but a settled truth,' replied Corchuelo: 'and if you have a mind I should convince you by experience; you carry foils, an opportunity offers, and I have nerves and strength, that backed by my courage, which is none of the least, will make you confess that I am not deceived. Alight, and make use of your measured steps, your circles, your angles, and science; for I hope to make you see the stars at noonday with my modern and rustic dexterity; in which I trust, under God, that the man is yet unborn, who shall make me turn my back, and that there is nobody in the world whom I will not oblige to give ground.'

'As to turning the back or not, I meddle not with it,' replied the adept, 'though it may happen, that in the first spot you fix your foot on, your grave may be opened. I mean, that you may be left dead there for despising the noble science of defence.'

'We shall see that presently,' answered Corchuelo; and, jumping hastily from his beast, he snatched one of the foils, which the licentiate carried upon his ass.

'It must not be so,' cried Don Quixote, at this instant; 'for I will be master of this fencing-bout, and judge of this long-controverted question.'

And alighting from Rosinante, and grasping his lance, he planted himself in the midst of the road, just as the licentiate, with a graceful motion of the body, and measured step, was making towards Corchuelo, who came at him, darting, as the phrase is, fire from his eyes. The two countrymen, without dismounting, served as spectators of the mortal tragedy. The flashes, thrusts, high-strokes, back-strokes, and fore-strokes Corchuelo gave were numberless, and thicker than hail. He fell on like a provoked lion: but met with a smart tap on the mouth from the button of the licentiate's foil, which stopped him in the midst of his fury, making him kiss it, though not with so much devotion, as if it had been a relic. In short, the licentiate, by dint of clean thrusts, counted him all the buttons of a little cassock he had on, and tore the skirts, so that they hung in rags like the many-tailed fish.* Twice he struck off his hat, and so tired him, that, through despite, choler, and rage, he flung away the foil into the air with such force, that one of the country-fellows present, who was a kind of scrivener, and went to fetch it, said, and swore, it was thrown three-quarters of a league: which affidavit has served, and still serves, to show and demonstrate that skill goes farther than strength.

Corchuelo sat down quite spent, and Sancho going to him, said:

'In faith, Master Bachelor, if you would take my advice, henceforward you should challenge nobody to fence, but to wrestle, or pitch the bar, since you are old enough and strong enough for that: for I have heard say of these masters, that they can thrust the point of a sword through the eye of a needle.'

'I am satisfied,' answered Corchuelo, 'and have learned by experience a truth I could not otherwise have believed:' and getting up, he went and embraced the licentiate, and they were now better friends than before. So, being unwilling to wait for the scrivener, who was gone to fetch the foil, thinking he might stay too long, they determined to make the best of their way, that they might arrive betimes at Quiteria's village, whither they were all bound. By the way, the licentiate laid down to them the excellences of the noble science of defence, with such self-evident reasons, and so many mathematical figures and demonstrations, that every-body was convinced of the usefulness of the science, and Corchuelo entirely brought over from his obstinacy.

It was just nightfall: but before they arrived, they all thought they saw, between them and the village, a kind of heaven full of innumerable and resplendent stars. They heard also the confused and sweet sounds of various instruments, as flutes, tambourines, psalters, cymbals, and little drums, with bells; and drawing near, they perceived the boughs of an arbour, made on one side of the entrance into the town, all hung with lights, which were not disturbed by the wind: for all was so calm, that there was not a breath of air so much as to stir the very leaves of the trees. The life and joy of the wedding were the musicians, who went up and down in bands through that delightful place, some dancing, others singing, and others playing upon the different instruments aforesaid. In short, it looked as if mirth and pleasure danced and revelled through the meadow. Several others were busied about raising scaffolds, from which they might commodiously be spectators next day of the plays and dances, that were to be performed in that place, dedicated to the solemnizing the nuptials of the rich Camacho, and the obsequies of Basilius. Don Quixote refused to go into the town, though both the countryman and the bachelor invited him, but he pleaded as a sufficient excuse, in his opinion, that it was the custom of knights-errant to sleep in the fields, and forests, rather than in towns, though under gilded roofs: and therefore he turned a little out of the way, sorely against Sancho's will, who had not forgotten the good lodging he had met with in the castle or house of Don Diego.

CHAPTER 20

Giving an account of the wedding of Camacho the Rich, with the adventure of Basilius the Poor.

SCARCE had the fair Aurora given bright Phoebus room, with the heat of his warm rays, to dry up the liquid pearls upon his golden hair, when Don Quixote, shaking off sloth from his drowsy members, got upon his feet, and called to his squire Sancho Panza, who still lay snoring; which Don Quixote perceiving, before he would awake him, he said:

'O happy thou above all that live on the face of the earth, who neither envying, nor being envied, sleepest on with tranquillity of soul! neither do enchanters persecute, nor enchantments affright thee. Sleep on, I say again, and will say a hundred times more, sleep on: for no jealousies on thy lady's account keep thee in perpetual watchings, nor do anxious thoughts of paying debts awake thee, nor is thy rest broken with the thoughts of what thou must do to-morrow, to provide for thyself and thy little family. Ambition disquiets thee not, nor does the vain pomp of the world disturb thee: for thy desires extend not beyond the limits of taking care of thy ass: for that of thy person is laid upon my shoulders, a counter-balance and burden that nature and custom have laid upon masters. The servant sleeps, and the master is waking, to consider how he is to maintain, prefer, and do him kindnesses. The pain of seeing the obdurate heaven made, as it were, of brass, and refusing convenient dews to refresh the earth, afflicts not the servant, but the master, who is bound to provide, in times of sterility and famine, for him, who served him in times of fertility and abundance.'

To all this Sancho answered not a word; for he was asleep, nor had awaked so soon as he did, but that Don Quixote jogged him with the butt-end of his lance. At last he waked drowsy and yawning; and, turning his face on all sides, he said:

'From yonder shady bower, if I mistake not, there comes a steam and smell, rather of broiled rashers of bacon, than of thyme or rushes: by my faith, weddings, that begin thus savourily, must needs be liberal and abundant.'

'Have done, glutton,' quoth Don Quixote, 'and let us go and see this wedding, and what becomes of the disdained Basilius.'

'Marry, let what will become of him,' answered Sancho: 'he cannot be poor and marry Quiteria: a pleasant fancy, for one not worth a groat, to aim at marrying above the clouds! Faith, sir, in my opinion, a poor man should be contented with what he finds, and not be looking for truffles at the bottom of the sea. I dare wager an arm, that Camacho can cover Basilius with reals from head to foot: and if it be so, as it must needs be, Quiteria would be a pretty bride indeed, to reject the fine clothes and jewels, that Camacho has given, and can give her, to choose instead of them a pitch of the bar, and a feint at foils, of Basilius: one cannot have a pint of wine at a tavern for the bravest pitch of the bar, or the cleverest push of the foil: abilities and graces that are not vendible, let the Count Dirlos* have them for me: but when they light on a man that has wherewithal, may my life show as well as they do. Upon a good foundation a good building may be raised, and the best bottom and foundation in the world is money.'

'For the love of God, Sancho,' quoth Don Quixote, 'have done with your harangue: I verily believe, were you let alone to go on as you begin, at every turn, you would have no time to eat, or sleep, but would spend it all in talk.'

'If your worship had a good memory,' replied Sancho, 'you would remember the articles of our agreement, before we sallied from home this last time; one of which was, that you were to let me talk as much as I pleased, so it were not anything against my neighbour, or against your worship's authority, and hitherto I think I have not broke that capitulation.'

'I do not remember any such article, Sancho,' answered Don Quixote: 'and though it were so, it is my pleasure you hold your peace, and come along; for by this time the musical instruments we heard last night begin again to cheer the valleys, and doubtless the espousals will be celebrated in the cool of the morning, and not put off till the heat of the day.'

Sancho did as his master commanded him; and saddling
Rosinante, and pannelling Dapple, they both mounted, and
marching softly, entered the artificial shade. The first thing
that presented itself to Sancho's sight, was a whole bullock
spitted upon a large elm. The fire it was roasted by was
composed of a middling mountain of wood, and round it
were placed six pots, not cast in common moulds; for they
were half jars, each containing a whole shamble of flesh; and
entire sheep were sunk and swallowed up in them, as commodiously as if they were only so many pigeons. The hares
ready cased, and the fowls ready plucked, that hung about
upon the branches, in order to be buried in the cauldrons,
were without number. Infinite was the wild-fowl and venison
hanging about the trees, that the air might cool them. Sancho
counted above threescore skins, each of above twenty-four
quarts, and all, as appeared afterwards, full of generous wines.
There were also piles of the whitest bread, like so many heaps
of wheat in a threshing-floor. Cheeses ranged like bricks
formed a kind of wall. Two cauldrons of oil, larger than a
dyer's vat, stood ready for frying all sorts of batter-ware; and
with a couple of stout peels they took them out when fried,
and dipped them in another kettle of prepared honey, that
stood by. The men and women cooks were about fifty, all
clean, all diligent, and all in good humour. In the bullock's
distended belly were a dozen sucking pigs, sewed up in it to
make it savoury and tender. The spices of various kinds
seemed to have been bought, not by the pound, but by the
[quarter], and stood free for everybody in a great chest.
In short, the preparation for the wedding was all rustic,
but in such plenty, that it was sufficient to have feasted
an army.

Sancho beheld all, considered all, and was in love with
everything. The first that captivated and subdued his inclinations were the flesh-pots, out of which he would have been
glad to have filled a moderate pipkin. Then the wine-skins
drew his affections; and, lastly, the products of the frying-
pans, if such pompous cauldrons may be so called. And, not
being able to forbear any longer, and having no power to do
otherwise, he went up to one of the busy cooks, and, with

courteous and hungry words, desired leave to sop a luncheon
of bread in one of the pots: to which the cook answered:

'This is none of those days, over which hunger presides,
thanks to rich Camacho: alight, and see if you can find a
ladle anywhere, and skim out a fowl or two, and much good
may they do you.'

'I see none,' answered Sancho.

'Stay,' quoth the cook, 'God forgive me, what a nice and
good-for-nothing fellow must you be!'

And so saying, he laid hold of a kettle, and sousing it into
one of the half jars, he fished out three pullets and a couple
of geese, and said to Sancho:

'Eat, friend, and make a breakfast of this scum, to stay
your stomach till dinner-time.'

'I have nothing to put it in,' answered Sancho.

'Then take ladle and all,' quoth the cook; 'for the riches
and felicity of Camacho supply everything.'

While Sancho was thus employed, Don Quixote stood
observing, how, at one side of the spacious arbour, entered
a dozen countrymen upon as many beautiful mares, adorned
with rich and gay caparisons, and their furniture hung round
with little bells. They were clad in holiday apparel, and in a
regular troop ran sundry careers about the meadow, with a
joyful Moorish cry of, 'Long live Camacho and Quiteria, he
is rich as she is fair, and she the fairest of the world.' Which
Don Quixote hearing, said to himself:

'It is plain these people have not seen my Dulcinea del
Toboso; for, had they seen her, they would have been a little
more upon the reserve in praising this Quiteria of theirs.'

A little while after there entered, at divers parts of the
arbour, a great many different dancers; among them was one
[set] consisting of four-and-twenty sword-dancers, handsome,
sprightly swains, all arrayed in fine white linen, with hand-
kerchiefs wrought with several colours of fine silk. One of
those upon the mares asked a youth, who led the sword-
dance, whether any of his comrades were hurt.

'As yet, God be thanked,' quoth the youth, 'nobody is
wounded; we are all whole.'

And presently he twined himself in among the rest of his

companions, with so many turns, and so dexterously, that though Don Quixote was accustomed to see such kind of dances, he never liked any so well as that.

There was another, which pleased him mightily, of a dozen most beautiful damsels, so young, that none of them appeared to be under fourteen, nor any quite eighteen years old, all clad in green stuff of Cuenca, their locks partly plaited, and partly loose, and all so yellow, that they might rival those of the sun itself; with garlands of jessamine, roses, and woodbine upon their heads. They were led up by a venerable old man and an ancient matron, but more nimble and airy than could be expected from their years. A bagpipe of Zamora was their music; and they, carrying modesty in their looks and eyes, and lightness in their feet, approved themselves the best dancers in the world.

After these, there entered an artificial dance, composed of eight nymphs, divided into two files. The god CUPID led one file, and INTEREST the other; the former adorned with wings, bow, quiver, and arrows; the other apparelled with rich and various colours of gold and silk. The nymphs, attendant on the God of Love, had their names written at their backs on white parchment, and in capital letters. POETRY was the title of the first; DISCRETION of the second; GOOD FAMILY of the third: and VALOUR of the fourth. The followers of INTEREST were distinguished in the same manner. The title of the first was LIBERALITY; DONATION of the second: TREASURE of the third; and that of the fourth PEACEABLE-POSSESSION. Before them all came a wooden castle, drawn by savages, clad in ivy and hemp dyed green, so to the life, that they almost frighted Sancho. On the front, and on all the four sides of the machine, was written, 'The Castle of Reserve'. Four skilful musicians played on the tabor and pipe. Cupid began the dance, and, after two movements, he lifted up his eyes, and bent his bow against a damsel that stood between the battlements of the castle, whom he addressed after this manner:

LOVE

'I am the mighty God of Love;
Air, earth, and seas my power obey

O'er hell beneath, and heaven above,
  I reign with universal sway.

'I give, resume, forbid, command:
  My will is nature's general law:
No force arrests my powerful hand,
  Nor fears my daring courage awe.'

He finished his stanza, let fly an arrow to the top of the castle, and retired to his post. Then Interest stepped forth, and made two other movements: the tabors ceased, and he said:

INTEREST

'Though Love's my motive and my end,
  I boast a greater power than Love,
Who makes not Interest his friend,
  In nothing will successful prove.

'By all ador'd, by all pursu'd;
  Then own, bright nymph, my greater sway,
And for thy gentle breast subdu'd
  With large amends shall Int'rest pay.'

Then Interest withdrew, and Poetry advanced; and, after she had made her movements like the rest, fixing her eyes on the damsel of the castle, she said:

POETRY

'My name is Poetry: my soul,
  Wrapp'd up in verse, to thee I send:
Let gentle lays thy will control,
  And be for once the Muses' friend.

'If, lovely maid, sweet Poetry
  Displease thee not, thy fortune soon,
Envied by all, advanced by me,
  Shall reach the circle of the moon.'

Poetry went off, and from the side of Interest stepped forth Liberality, and, after making her movements said:

LIBERALITY

'Me Liberality men call;
  In me the happy golden mean,

> Not spendthrift-like to squander all,
>   Nor niggardly to save, is seen.

> 'But, for thy honour, I begin,
>   Fair nymph, a prodigal to prove:
> To lavish here's a glorious sin;
>   For who'd a miser be in love?'

In this manner all the figures of the two parties advanced and retreated, and each made its movements and recited its verses, some elegant, and some ridiculous; of which Don Quixote, who had a very good memory, treasured up the foregoing only. Presently they all mixed together, in a kind of country dance, with a genteel grace and easy freedom; and when Cupid passed before the castle, he shot his arrows aloft; but Interest flung gilded balls against it. In conclusion, after having danced some time, Interest drew out a large purse of Roman catskin, which seemed to be full of money; and throwing it at the castle, the boards were disjointed, and tumbled down with the blow, leaving the damsel exposed, and without any defence at all. Then came Interest with his followers, and clapping a great golden chain about her neck, they seemed to take her prisoner, and lead her away captive: which Love and his adherents perceiving, they made a show as if they would rescue her: and all their seeming efforts were adjusted to the sound of the tabors. They were parted by the savages, who with great agility rejoined the boards, and reinstated the castle, and the damsel was again enclosed therein as before: and so the dance ended, to the great satisfaction of the spectators.

Don Quixote asked one of the nymphs, who it was that had contrived and ordered the show. She answered, A beneficed clergyman of that village, who had a notable headpiece for such kind of inventions.

'I will lay a wager,' quoth Don Quixote, 'that this bachelor or clergyman is more a friend to Camacho than to Basilius, and understands satire better than vespers: for he has ingeniously interwoven in the dance the abilities of Basilius with the riches of Camacho.'

Sancho Panza, who listened to all this, said:

'The king is my cock; I hold with Camacho.'

'In short,' quoth Don Quixote, 'it is plain you are an arrant bumpkin and one of those who cry, '"Long live the conqueror!"'

'I know not who I am one of,' answered Sancho: 'but I know very well, I shall never get such elegant scum from Basilius's pots, as I have done from Camacho's.'

Here he showed the cauldron full of geese and hens; and, laying hold of one, he began to eat with notable good-humour and appetite, and said:

'A fig for Basilius's abilities! for you are worth just as much as you have, and you have just as much as you are worth. There are but two families in the world, as my grandmother used to say, "the Have's and the Havenot's", and she stuck to the former; and nowadays, Master Don Quixote, people are more inclined to feel the pulse of Have than of Know. An ass with golden furniture makes a better figure than a horse with a pack-saddle: so that I tell you again, I hold with Camacho, the abundant scum of whose pots are geese and hens, hares, and conies; whilst that of Basilius's, if ever it comes to hand, must be mere dish-water.'

'Have you finished your harangue, Sancho?' quoth Don Quixote.

'I must have done,' answered Sancho, 'because I perceive your worship is going to be in a passion at what I am saying; for were it not for that, there was work enough cut out for three days.'

'God grant,' replied Don Quixote, 'I may see you dumb before I die.'

'At the rate we go on,' answered Sancho, 'before you die, I shall be mumbling cold clay; and then perhaps I may be so dumb, that I may not speak a word till the end of the world, or at least till doomsday.'

'Though it should fall out so,' answered Don Quixote, 'your silence, O Sancho, will never rise to the pitch of your talk, past, present, and to come: besides, according to the course of nature, I must die before you, and therefore never can see you dumb, not even when drinking or sleeping, which is the most I can say.'

'In good faith, sir,' answered Sancho, 'there is no trusting to Madam Skeleton, I mean, Death, who devours lambs as well as sheep: and I have heard our vicar say, she treads with equal foot on the lofty towers of kings, and the humble cottages of the poor. That same gentlewoman is more powerful than nice: she is not at all squeamish: she eats of everything and lays hold of all; and stuffs her wallets with people of all sorts, of all ages, and pre-eminences. She is not a reaper that sleeps away the noonday heat; for she cuts down and mows, at all hours, the dry as well as the green grass: nor does she stand to chew, but devours and swallows down all that comes in her way; for she has a canine appetite that is never satisfied; and, though she has no belly, she makes it appear that she has a perpetual dropsy, and a thirst to drink down the lives of all that live, as one would drink a cup of cold water.'

'Hold, Sancho,' quoth Don Quixote, 'while you are well, and do not spoil all; for, in truth, what you have said of Death, in your rustic phrases, might become the mouth of a good preacher. I tell you, Sancho, if you had but discretion equal to your natural abilities, you might take a pulpit in your hand, and go about the world preaching fine things.'

'A good liver is the best preacher,' answered Sancho, 'and that is all the divinity I know.'

'Or need know,' quoth Don Quixote: 'but I can in no wise understand, nor comprehend, how, since the fear of God is the beginning of wisdom, you who are more afraid of a lizard than of Him, should be so knowing.'

'Good, your worship, judge of your own chivalries,' answered Sancho, 'and meddle not with judging of other men's fears or valours; for perhaps I am as pretty a fearer of God as any of my neighbours: and pray let me whip off this scum; for all besides is idle talk, of which we must give an account in the next world.'

And, so saying, he fell to afresh, and assaulted his kettle with so long-winded an appetite, that he awakened that of Don Quixote, who doubtless would have assisted him, had he not been prevented by what we are under a necessity of immediately telling.

CHAPTER 21

In which is continued the history of Camacho's wedding, with other delightful accidents.

WHILE Don Quixote and Sancho were engaged in the discourses mentioned in the preceding chapter, they heard a great outcry and noise, raised and occasioned by those that rode on the mares, who, in full career, and with a great shout, went to meet the bride and bridegroom, who were coming, surrounded with a thousand kinds of musical instruments and inventions, accompanied by the parish priest and the kindred on both sides, and by all the better sort of people from the neighbouring towns, all in their holiday apparel. And when Sancho espied the bride, he said:

'In good faith, she is not clad like a country girl, but like any court lady: by the mass, the breast-piece she wears seems to me at this distance to be of rich coral; and her gown, instead of green stuff of Cuenca, is no less than a thirty-piled velvet: besides the trimming, I vow, is of satin. Then do but observe her hands: instead of rings of jet, let me never thrive, but they are of gold, aye, and of right gold, and adorned with pearls as white as a curd, and every one of them worth an eye of one's head. Ah, whoreson jade! and what fine hair she has! if it is not false, I never saw longer nor fairer in all my life. Then her sprightliness and mien: why, she is a very moving palm-tree, laden with branches of dates; for just so look the trinkets hanging at her hair, and about her neck: by my soul the girl is so well plated over, she might pass current at any bank in Flanders.'*

Don Quixote smiled at the rustic praises bestowed by Sancho Panza, and thought that, setting aside his mistress Dulcinea del Toboso, he had never seen a more beautiful woman. The fair Quiteria looked a little pale, occasioned, perhaps, by want of rest the preceding night, which brides always employ in setting themselves off, and dressing for their wedding-day following.

They proceeded towards a theatre on one side of the meadow, adorned with carpets and boughs; where the nuptial ceremony was to be performed, and from whence they were to see the dances and inventions. And, just as they arrived at the standing, they heard a great outcry behind them, and somebody calling aloud:

'Hold a little, inconsiderate and hasty people!'

At which voice and words they all turned about their heads, and found, they came from a man clad in a black jacket, all welted with crimson in flames. He was crowned, as they presently perceived, with a garland of mournful cypress, and held in his hand a great truncheon. As he drew near, all knew him to be the gallant Basilius, and were in suspense, waiting to see what would be the issue of this procedure, and apprehending some sinister event from his arrival at such a season. At length he came up, tired and out of breath, and planting himself just before the affianced couple, and leaning on his truncheon, which had a steel pike at the end, changing colour, and fixing his eyes on Quiteria, with a trembling and hoarse voice, he uttered these expressions:

'You well know, forgetful Quiteria, that, by the rules of that holy religion we profess, you cannot marry another man whilst I am living; neither are you ignorant, that, waiting till time and my own industry should better my fortune, I have not failed to preserve the respect due to your honour. But you, casting all obligations due to my lawful love behind your back, are going to make another man master of what is mine; whose riches serve not only to make him happy in the possession of them, but every way superlatively fortunate; and that his good luck may be heaped brimful (not that I think he deserves it, but that heaven will have it so) I with my own hands will remove all impossibility or inconvenience by removing myself out of his way. Long live the rich Camacho with the ungrateful Quiteria; many and happy ages may they live, and let poor Basilius die, whose poverty clipped the wings of his good fortune, and laid him in his grave!'

And so saying, he laid hold on his truncheon, which was stuck in the ground, and drawing out a short tuck* that was concealed in it, and to which it served as a scabbard, and setting what may be called the hilt upon the ground, with a nimble spring and determinate purpose, he threw himself upon it; and in an instant half the bloody point appeared at his back, the poor wretch lying along upon the ground, weltering in his blood, and pierced through with his own weapon.

His friends ran presently to his assistance, grieved at his misery and deplorable disaster: and Don Quixote, quitting Rosinante, ran also to assist, and took him in his arms, and found he had still life in him. They would have drawn out the tuck: but the priest, who was by, was of opinion, it should not be drawn out till he had made his confession; for their pulling it out, and his expiring, would happen at the same moment. But Basilius, coming a little to himself, with a faint and doleful voice, said:

'If, cruel Quiteria, in this my last and fatal agony, you would give me your hand to be my spouse, I should hope my rashness might be pardoned, since it procured me the blessing of being yours.'

Which the priest hearing, advised him to mind the salvation of his soul, rather than the gratifying his bodily appetites, and in good earnest to beg pardon of God for his sins, and especially for this last desperate action. To which Basilius replied that he would by no means make any confession, till Quiteria had first given him her hand to be his wife; for that satisfaction would quiet his spirits, and give him breath for confession. Don Quixote, hearing the wounded man's request, said in a loud voice, that Basilius desired a very just and very reasonable thing, and besides very easy to be done; and that it would be every whit as honourable for Señor Camacho to take Quiteria, a widow of the brave Basilius, as if he received her at her father's hands; all that was necessary being but a bare 'Yes', which could have no other consequence than the pronouncing the word, since the nuptial-bed of these espousals must be the grave.

Camacho heard all this, and was in suspense and confusion, not knowing what to do or say; but so importunate were the cries of Basilius's friends, desiring him to consent, that Quiteria might give her hand to be Basilius's wife, lest his soul should be lost by departing out of this life in despair, that they moved and forced him to say, that, if Quiteria thought fit to give it him, he was contented, since it was only delaying for a moment the accomplishment of his wishes. Presently all ran and applied to Quiteria, and some with entreaties, others with tears, and others with persuasive reasons, importuned her to give her hand to poor Basilius; but she, harder than marble, and more immoveable than a statue, neither could, nor would return any answer. But the priest bade her resolve immediately; for Basilius had his soul between his teeth, and there was no time to wait for irresolute determinations.

Then the beautiful Quiteria without answering a word, and in appearance much troubled and concerned, approached Basilius, his eyes already turned in his head, breathing short and quick, muttering the name of Quiteria, and giving tokens of dying more like a heathen than a Christian. At last Quiteria kneeling down by him, made signs to him for his hand. Basilius unclosed his eyes, and, fixing them steadfastly upon her, said:

'O Quiteria, you relent at a time, when your pity is a sword to finish the taking away of my life: for now I have not enough left to bear the glory you give me in making me yours, nor to suspend the pain, which will presently cover my eyes with the dreadful shadow of death. What I beg of you, O fatal star of mine, is that the hand you require and give, be not out of compliment, or to deceive me afresh; but that you would confess and acknowledge, that you bestow it without any force laid upon your will, and give it me as to your lawful husband: for it is not reasonable, that, in this extremity, you should impose upon me, or deal falsely with him, who has dealt so faithfully and sincerely with you.'

At these words he was seized with such a fainting-fit, that all the bystanders thought his soul was just departing. Quiteria, all modesty and bashfulness, taking Basilius's right hand in hers, said:

'No force would be sufficient to bias my will; and therefore, with all the freedom I have, I give you my hand, to be your lawful wife, and receive yours, if you give it me as freely, and the calamity you have brought yourself into by your precipitate resolution does not disturb or hinder it.'

'Yes, I give it you,' answered Basilius, 'neither discomposed nor confused, but with the clearest understanding that heaven was ever pleased to bestow upon me; and so I give and engage myself to be your husband.'

'And I to be your wife,' answered Quiteria, 'whether you live many years or are carried from my arms to the grave.'

'For one so much wounded,' quoth Sancho Panza at this period, 'this young man talks a great deal: advise him to leave off his courtship, and mind the business of his soul; though, to my thinking, he has it more in his tongue, than between his teeth.'

Basilius and Quiteria being thus with hands joined, the tender-hearted priest, with tears in his eyes, pronounced the benediction upon them, and prayed to God for the repose of the new-married man's soul: who, as soon as he had received the benediction, suddenly started up, and nimbly drew out the tuck, which was sheathed in his body. All the bystanders were in admiration, and some, more simple than the rest, began to cry aloud:

'A miracle, a miracle!'

But Basilius replied,

'No miracle, no miracle, but a stratagem, a stratagem!'

The priest, astonished and confounded, ran with both his hands to feel the wound, and found that the sword had passed not through Basilius's flesh and ribs, but through a hollow iron pipe, filled with blood, and cunningly fitted to the place and purpose; and as it was known afterwards the blood was prepared by art, that it could not congeal. In short, the priest, Camacho, and the rest of the bystanders, found they were imposed upon, and deceived. The bride showed no signs of being sorry for the trick: on the contrary, hearing it said that the marriage, as being fraudulent, was not valid, she said, she confirmed it anew: from whence everybody concluded the business was concerted with the knowledge and privity of both parties; at which Camacho and his abettors were so confounded, that they transferred their revenge to their hands, and, unsheathing abundance of swords, they fell upon Basilius, in whose behalf as many more were instantly drawn.

Don Quixote, leading the van on horseback, with his lance upon his arm, and well covered with his shield, made them all give way. Sancho, who took no pleasure in such kinds of frays, retired to the jars, out of which he had gotten his charming skimmings, that place seeming to him to be sacred, and therefore to be revered. Don Quixote cried aloud:

'Hold, sirs, hold! for it is not fit to take revenge for the injuries done us by love: and pray, consider, that love and war are exactly alike; and as, in war, it is lawful and customary to employ cunning and stratagems to defeat the enemy, so, in amorous conflicts and rivalships, it is allowable to put in practice tricks and sleights, in order to compass the desired end, provided they be not to the prejudice and dishonour of the party beloved. Quiteria was Basilius's, and Basilius Quiteria's, by the just and favourable disposition of heaven. Camacho is rich, and may purchase his pleasure when, where, and how he pleases. Basilius has but this one ewe-lamb, and no one, how powerful soever, has a right to take it from him; for those, whom God hath joined together, let no man put asunder: and whoever shall attempt it, must first pass the point of this lance.'

Then he brandished it with such vigour and dexterity, that he struck terror into all that did not know him.

But Quiteria's disdain took such fast hold of the imagination of Camacho, that it presently blotted her out of his memory; and so the persuasions of the priest, who was a prudent and well-meaning man, had their effect, and Camacho and those of his faction remained pacified and calmed: in token whereof they put up their swords again in their scabbards, blaming rather the fickleness of Quiteria, than the cunning of Basilius. Camacho reasoned within himself, that, if Quiteria loved Basilius when she was a virgin, she would love him also when she was married, and that he had more reason to thank heaven for so good a riddance, than to repine at the loss of her. Camacho and his followers being thus pacified and comforted, those of Basilius were so too; and the rich Camacho, to show he did not resent the trick put upon him, nor value it all, would have the diversions and entertainments go on, as if he had been really married: but neither Basilius, nor his spouse, nor their followers, would partake of them; and so they went home to Basilius's house: for the poor man who is virtuous and discreet, has those that follow, honour, and stand by him, as well as the rich has his attendants and flatterers.

They took Don Quixote with them, esteeming him to be a person of worth and bravery. Only Sancho's soul was cloudy and overcast, finding it impossible for him to stay and partake of Camacho's splendid entertainment and festival, which lasted till night; and thus drooping and sad, he followed his master, who went off with Basilius's troop, leaving behind him the fleshpots of Egypt, which, however, he carried in his mind, the skimmings of the kettle, now almost consumed and spent, representing to him the glory and abundance of the good he had lost; and so, anxious and pensive, though not hungry, and without alighting from Dapple, he followed the track of Rosinante.

CHAPTER 22

Wherein is related the grand adventure of the cave of Montesinos, lying in the heart of La Mancha, to which the valorous Don Quixote gave a happy conclusion.

THE new-married couple made exceeding much of Don Quixote, being obliged by the readiness he had shown in defending their cause: and they esteemed his discretion in equal degree with his valour, accounting him a Cid in arms, and a Cicero in eloquence. Three days honest Sancho solaced himself at the expense of the bride and bridegroom; from whom it was known, that the feigned wounding himself was not a trick concerted with the fair Quiteria, but an invention of Basilius's own, hoping from it the very success which fell out. True it is, he confessed he had let some of his friends into the secret, that they might favour his design, and support his deceit. Don Quixote affirmed, it could not nor ought to be called deceit, which aims at virtuous ends, and that the marriage of lovers was the most excellent of all ends:

observing by the way, that hunger and continual necessity are the greatest enemies to love; for love is gaiety, mirth, and content, especially when the lover is in actual possession of the person beloved, to which necessity and poverty are opposed and declared enemies. All this he said with design to persuade Basilius to quit the exercise of those abilities, wherein he so much excelled; for though they procured him fame, they got him no money; and that now he should apply himself to acquire riches by lawful and industrious means, which are never wanting to the prudent and diligent.

'The honourable poor man (if a poor man can be said to have honour) possesses a jewel in having a beautiful wife; and whoever deprives him of her, deprives him of his honour, and as it were kills it. The beautiful and honourable woman, whose husband is poor, deserves to be crowned with laurels and palms of victory and triumph. Beauty, of itself alone, attracts the inclinations of all who behold it, and the royal eagles and other towering birds stoop to the tempting lure. But if such beauty be attended with poverty and a narrow fortune, it is besieged by kites and vultures, and other birds of prey; and she, who stands firm against so many attacks, may well be called the crown of her husband.

'Observe, discreet Basilius,' added Don Quixote, 'that it was the opinion of a certain sage, that there was but one good woman in all the world; and he gave it as his advice, that every man should think, and believe she was fallen to his lot, and so he would live contented. I for my part am not married, nor have I yet ever thought of being so: yet would I venture to give my advice to anyone, who should ask it of me, what method he should take to get a wife to his mind. In the first place, I would advise him to lay a greater stress upon reputation* than fortune; for a good woman does not acquire a good name merely by being good, but by appearing to be so; for public freedoms and liberties hurt a woman's reputation much more than secret wantonness. If you bring a woman honest to your house, it is an easy matter to keep her so, and even to make her better, and improve her very goodness: but if you bring her naughty, you will have much ado to mend her; for it is not very feasible to pass from one extreme to another. I do not say, it is impossible; but I take it to be extremely difficult.'

All this Sancho listened to, and said to himself:

'This master of mine, when I speak things pithy and substantial, used to say, I might take a pulpit in my hand, and go about the world preaching fine things; and I say of him, that, when he begins stringing of sentences, and giving advice, he may not only take a pulpit in his hand, but two upon each finger, and stroll about your market-places, crying out: "Mouth, what would you have?" The devil take thee for a knight-errant that knows everything! I believed in my heart, that he only knew what belonged to his chivalries: but he pecks at everything, and thrusts his spoon into every dish.'

Sancho muttered this so loud, that his master, overhearing it, said to him:

'Sancho, what is it you mutter?'

'I neither say, nor mutter anything,' answered Sancho: 'I was only saying to myself, that I wished I had heard your worship preach this doctrine before I was married; then perhaps I should have been able to say now, "The ox that is loose is best licked."'

'Is your Teresa, then, so bad, Sancho?' quoth Don Quixote.

'She is not very bad,' answered Sancho; 'but she is not very good neither, at least not quite so good as I would have her.'

'You are in the wrong, Sancho,' said Don Quixote, 'to speak ill of your wife, who is the mother of your children.'

'We are not in one another's debt upon that score,' answered Sancho; 'for she speaks as ill of me, whenever the fancy takes her, especially when she is jealous; for then Satan himself cannot bear with her.'

Finally, three days they stayed with the new married couple, where they were served and treated like kings in person. Don Quixote desired the dexterous student to furnish him with a guide, to bring him to the cave of Montesinos;* for he had a mighty desire to go down into it, and see with his own eyes, whether the wonders related of it in all those parts were true. The student told him, he would procure him a cousin of his, a famous scholar, and much addicted to reading books of chivalry, who would very gladly carry him to the mouth of the cave itself, and also show him the lakes of Ruydera, famous all over La Mancha, and even all over Spain; telling him, he would be a very entertaining companion, being a young man, who knew how to write books for the press, and dedicate them to princes.

In short, the cousin came, mounted on an ass big with foal, whose pack-saddle was covered with a doubled piece of an old carpet, or sacking. Sancho saddled Rosinante, pannelled Dapple, and replenished his wallets; and those of the scholar were as well provided: and so commending themselves to the protection of God, and taking leave of everybody, they set out, bending their course directly towards the famous cave of Montesinos.

Upon the road, Don Quixote asked the scholar, of what kind and quality his exercises, profession, and studies were. To which he answered: That his profession was the study of humanity;* his exercise, composing of books for the press, all of great use, and no small entertainment to the commonwealth; that one of them was entitled *A Treatise on Liveries*, describing seven hundred and three liveries, with their colours, mottoes, and cyphers; from whence the cavalier courtiers might pick and choose to their minds, for feasts and rejoicings, without being beholden to others, or beating their own brains to invent and contrive them to their humour or design; for, said he:

'I adapt them to the jealous, the disdained, the forgotten, and the absent, so properly, that more will hit than miss. I have also another book, which I intend to call, *The Metamorphoses, or Spanish Ovid*, of a new and rare invention; for therein, imitating Ovid in a burlesque way, I show who the Giralda of Seville was, and who the angel of La Magdalena;* what the conduit of Vecinguerra of Córdova;* what the bulls of Guisando; the Sierra Morena; the fountains of Leganitos, and the Lavapies in Madrid; not forgetting the Piojo, that of the golden pipe, and that of the Priora:* and all these, with their several allegories, metaphors, and transformations, in such a manner as to delight, surprise, and instruct at the same time.

'I have another book, which I call a *Supplement to Polydore Virgil*,* treating of the invention of things; a work of vast erudition and study, because therein I make out several material things omitted by Polydore, and explain them in a fine style. Virgil forgot to tell us, who was the first in the world that had a cold, and who was the first that was fluxed for the French disease; these points I resolve to a nicety, and cite the authority of above five-and-twenty authors for them; so that your worship may see whether I have taken true pains, and whether such a performance is not likely to be very useful to the whole world.'

Sancho, who had been attentive to the student's discourse, said:

'Tell me, sir, so may God send you good luck in the printing your books, can you resolve me (for I know you can, since you know everything) who was the first that scratched his head? I for my part am of opinion, it must be our first father Adam.'

'Certainly,' answered the scholar; 'for there is no doubt but Adam had a head and hair, and, this being granted, and he being the first man of the world, he must needs have scratched his head one time or another.'

'So I believe,' answered Sancho; 'but tell me now, who was the first tumbler in the world?'

'Truly, brother,' answered the scholar, 'I cannot determine that point till I have studied it; and I will study it as soon as I return to the place where I keep my books, and will satisfy you when we see one another again: for I hope this will not be the last time.'

'Look ye, sir,' replied Sancho, 'take no pains about this matter; for I have already hit upon the answer to my question: Know then, that the first tumbler was Lucifer, when he was cast or thrown headlong from heaven, and came tumbling down to the lowest abyss.'

'You are in the right, friend,' quoth the scholar.

Don Quixote said:

'This question and answer are not your own, Sancho; you have heard them from somebody else.'

'Say no more, sir,' replied Sancho; 'for, in good faith, if I fall to questioning and answering, I shall not have done between this and to-morrow morning: for foolish questions and ridiculous answers, I need not be obliged to any of my neighbours.'

'Sancho,' quoth Don Quixote, 'you have said more than you are aware of; for some there are, who tire themselves with examining into, and explaining things, which, after they are known and explained, signify not a farthing to the understanding or the memory.'

In these, and other pleasant discourses, they passed that day, and at night they lodged in a small village, from whence, the scholar told Don Quixote, there were but two leagues to the cave of Montesinos, and that, if he continued his resolution to enter into it, it would be necessary to provide himself with rope to tie and let himself down into its depth. Don Quixote said, if it reached to the abyss, he would see where it stopped; and so they bought near a hundred fathom of cord; and, about two in the afternoon following, they came to the cave, the mouth of which is wide and spacious, but full of briers, wild fig-trees, and thorns, so thick and intricate, that they quite blind and cover it.

When they arrived at it, the scholar, Sancho, and Don Quixote alighted: then the two former bound the knight very fast with the cord, and, while they were swathing him, Sancho said:

'Have a care, dear sir, what you do: do not bury yourself alive, nor hang yourself dangling like a flask of wine, let down to cool in a well; for it is no business of your worship's, nor does it belong to you, to be the scrutinizer of this hole, which must needs be worse than any dungeon.'

'Tie on, and talk not,' answered Don Quixote; 'for such an enterprise as this, friend Sancho, was reserved for me alone'*

Then the guide said:

'I beseech your worship, Señor Don Quixote, to take good heed, and look about you with a hundred eyes, and explore what is below: perhaps there may be things proper to be inserted in my book of metamorphoses.'

'The drum is in a hand that knows full well how to rattle it,' answered Sancho Panza.

This being said, and the tying of Don Quixote (not over his armour, but his doublet) finished, Don Quixote said:

'We have been very careless in neglecting to provide a little bell to be tied to me with this rope; by the tinkling of which you might hear me still descending, and know that I was alive: but since that is now impossible, be the hand of God my guide.'

And immediately he kneeled down, and, in a low voice, put up a prayer to heaven for assistance, and good success in this seemingly perilous and strange adventure: then of a sudden, in a loud voice, he said:

'O mistress of my actions and motions, most illustrious and peerless Dulcinea del Toboso! if it be possible that the prayers and requests of this thy adventurous lover reach thy ears, I beseech thee, for thy unheard-of beauty's sake, hearken to them; for all I beg of thee is, not to refuse me thy favour and protection, now that I so much need it. I am just going to precipitate, to ingulf, and sink myself in the profound abyss here before me, only to let the world know, that, if thou favourest me, there is no impossibility I will not undertake and accomplish.'

And, so saying, he drew near to the brink, and saw he could not be let down, nor get at the entrance of the cave, but by mere force, and cutting his way through: and so, laying his hand to his sword, he began to lay about him, and hew down the brambles and bushes at the mouth of the cave; at which noise and rustling, an infinite number of huge ravens and daws flew out so thick and so fast, that they beat Don Quixote to the ground; and had he been as superstitious as he was Catholic, he had taken it for an ill omen, and forborne shutting himself up in such a place. At length he got upon his legs, and seeing no more ravens flying out, nor other night birds, such as bats (some of which likewise flew out among the ravens), the scholar and Sancho, giving him rope, let him down to the bottom of the fearful cavern: and, at his going in, Sancho, giving him his blessing, and making a thousand crosses over him, said:

'God, and the Rock of France,* together with the Trinity of Gaeta,* speed thee, thou flower, and cream, and skimming of knights-errant! There thou goest, Hector of the world, heart of steel, and arms of brass! Once more, God guide thee, and send thee back safe and sound, without deceit, to the light of this world, which thou art forsaking, to bury thyself, in this obscurity.'

The scholar uttered much the same prayers and intercessions.

Don Quixote went down, calling for more and more rope, which they gave him by little and little; and when the voice, by the windings of the cave, could be heard no longer, and the hundred fathom of cordage was all let down, they were of opinion to pull Don Quixote up again, since they could give him no more rope. However they delayed about half an hour, and then they began to gather up the rope, which they did very easily, and without any weight at all: from whence they conjectured, that Don Quixote remained in the cave; and Sancho, believing as much, wept bitterly, and drew up in a great hurry, to know the truth: but, coming to a little above eighty fathom, they felt a weight, at which they rejoiced exceedingly. In short, at about the tenth fathom they discerned Don Quixote very distinctly; to whom Sancho called out, saying:

'Welcome back to us, dear sir; for we began to think you had stayed there to breed.'

But Don Quixote answered not a word; and, pulling him quite out, they perceived his eyes were shut, as if he was asleep. They laid him along on the ground, and untied him; yet still he did not awake. But they so turned, and jogged, and returned, and shook him, that after a good while he came to himself, stretching and yawning just as if he had awaked out of a heavy and deep sleep: and gazing from side to side as if he was amazed, he said:

'God forgive ye, friends, for having brought me away from the most pleasing and charming life and sight, that ever mortal saw or lived. In short, I am now thoroughly satisfied that all the enjoyments of this life pass away like a shadow or a dream, and fade away like the flower of the field. O unhappy Montesinos! O desperately wounded Durandarte! O unfortunate Belerma! O weeping Guadiana! And ye unlucky

daughters of Ruydera,* whose waters show what floods of
tears streamed from your fair eyes!'

The scholar and Sancho listened to Don Quixote's words,
which he spoke, as if with immense pain he fetched them
from his entrails. They entreated him to explain to them what
it was he had been saying, and to tell them what he had seen
in that hell below.

'Hell do you call it?' said Don Quixote: 'call it so no more:
for it does not deserve that name, as you shall presently see.'

He desired they would give him something to eat; for he
was very hungry. They spread the scholar's carpet upon the
green grass; they addressed themselves to the pantry of his
wallets, and being all three seated in loving and social wise,
they collationed and supped all under one. The carpet being
removed, Don Quixote de la Mancha said:

'Let no one arise, and, sons, be attentive to me.'

CHAPTER 23

*Of the wonderful things, which the unexampled Don Quixote
de la Mancha declared he had seen in the deep cave of
Montesinos, the greatness and impossibility of which make
this adventure pass for apocryphal.*

IT was about four of the clock in the afternoon, when the
sun, hid among the clouds, with a faint light and temperate
rays, gave Don Quixote an opportunity, without extraordinary
heat or trouble, of relating to his two illustrious hearers, what
he had seen in the cave of Montesinos; and he began in the
following manner:

'About twelve or fourteen fathom in the depth of this
dungeon, on the right hand, there is a hollow, and space wide
enough to contain a large wagon, mules and all: a little light
makes its way into it, through some cracks and holes at a
distance in the surface of the earth. This hollow and open
space I saw, just as I began to weary, and out of humour to
find myself pendent and tied by the rope, and journeying
through that dark region below, without knowing whither I

was going: and so I determined to enter it and rest a little. I called out to you aloud, not to let down more rope till I bid you: but, it seems you heard me not. I gathered up the cord you had let down, and coiling it up into a heap, or bundle, I sat me down upon it, extremely pensive, and considering what method I should take to descend to the bottom, having nothing to support my weight. And being thus thoughtful, and in confusion, on a sudden, without any endeavour of mine, a deep sleep fell upon me; and, when I least thought of it, I awaked, and found myself, I knew not by what means, in the midst of the finest, pleasantest, and most delightful meadow, that nature could create, or the most pregnant fancy imagine.

'I rubbed my eyes, wiped them, and perceived I was not asleep, but really awake: but for all that I fell to feeling my head and breast, to be assured whether it was I, myself, who was there, or some empty and counterfeit illusion: but [touch], sensation, and the coherent discourse I made to myself, convinced me, that I was then and there the same person I am now here. Immediately a royal and splendid palace or castle presented itself to my view; the walls and battlements whereof seemed to be built of clear and transparent crystal: from out of which, through a great pair of folding doors, that opened of their own accord, I saw come forth, and advance towards me, a venerable old man, clad in a long mourning cloak of purple bays, which trailed upon the ground. Over his shoulders and breast he wore a kind of collegiate tippet of green satin: he had a black Milan cap on his head, and his hoary beard reached below his girdle. He carried no weapons at all, only a rosary of beads in his hand, bigger than middling walnuts, and every tenth bead like an ordinary* ostrich egg. His mien, his gait, his gravity, and his goodly presence, each by itself, and all together, surprised and amazed me. He came up to me, and the first thing he did, was to embrace me close; and then he said:

'"It is a long time, most valorous knight, Don Quixote de la Mancha, that we, who are shut up and enchanted in these solitudes, have hoped to see you, that the world by you may be informed what this deep cave, commonly called the cave

of Montesinos, encloses and conceals; an exploit reserved for
your invincible heart and stupendous courage. Come along
with me, illustrious sir, that I may show you the wonders
contained in this transparent castle, of which I am warder
and perpetual guard; for I am Montesinos himself, from
whom this cave derives its name."

'Scarce had he told me he was Montesinos, when I asked
him, whether it was true, which was reported in the world
above, that with a little dagger he had taken out the heart
of his great friend Durandarte, and carried it to his lady
Belerma, as he had desired him at the point of death. He
replied, all was true, excepting as to the dagger: for it was
neither a dagger, nor little, but a bright* poniard, sharper
than an awl.'

'That poniard,' interrupted Sancho, 'must have been made
by Raymond de Hozes* of Seville.'

'I do not know,' continued Don Quixote: 'but, upon
second thoughts, it could not be of his making; for Raymond
de Hozes lived but the other day, and the battle of Roncesvalles, where this misfortune happened, was fought many
years ago. But this objection is of no importance, and neither
disorders nor alters the truth and connexion of the story.'

'True,' answered the scholar; 'pray go on, Señor Don
Quixote, for I listen to you with the greatest pleasure in the
world.'

'And I tell it with no less,' answered Don Quixote, 'and
so I say: The venerable Montesinos conducted me to the
crystalline palace, where, in a lower hall, extremely cool, and
all of alabaster, there stood a marble tomb of exquisite
workmanship, whereon I saw, laid at full length, a cavalier,
not of brass, or marble, or jasper, as is usual on other
monuments, but of pure flesh and bones. His right hand,
which to my thinking was pretty hairy and nervous (a sign
that its owner was very strong), was laid on the region of
his heart; and before I could ask any question, Montesinos,
perceiving me in some suspense, and my eyes fixed on the
sepulchre, said:

'"This is my friend Durandarte, the flower and mirror of
all the enamoured and valiant knights-errant of his time.

Merlin, that French enchanter,* keeps him here enchanted, as he does me, and many others of both sexes. It is said, he is the son of the devil; though I do not believe him to be the devil's son, but only, as the saying is, that he knows one point more than the devil himself. How, or why, he enchanted us, nobody knows: but time will bring it to light, and I fancy it will not be long first. What I admire at, is, that I am as sure, as it is now day, that Durandarte expired in my arms, and that, after he was dead I pulled out his heart with my own hands; and, indeed, it could not weigh less than two pounds: for, according to the opinion of naturalists, he who has a large heart, is endued with more courage, than he who has a small one."

'"It being then certain that this cavalier really died," said I, "how comes it to pass that he complains every now and then, and sighs, as if he were alive?"

'This was no sooner said, but the wretched Durandarte, crying out aloud, said:

'"O my dear cousin Montesinos! the last thing I desired of you, when I was dying, and my soul departing, was to carry my heart, ripping it out of my breast with a dagger, or poniard, to Belerma"*

'The venerable Montesinos hearing this, threw himself on his knees before the complaining cavalier, and, with tears in his eyes, said to him:

'"Long since, O my dearest cousin Durandarte, I did what you enjoined me in that bitter day of our loss: I took out your heart as well as I could, without leaving the least bit of it in your breast; I wiped it with a lace handkerchief, took it, and went off full speed with it for France, having first laid you in the bosom of the earth, shedding as many tears as sufficed to wash my hands, and clean away the blood which stuck to them by raking in your entrails. By the same token, dear cousin of my soul, in the first place I lighted upon, going from Roncesvalles, I sprinkled a little salt over your heart, that it might not stink, and might keep, if not fresh, at least dried up, till it came to the lady Belerma; who, together with you and me, and your squire Guadiana, and the duenna Ruydera, and her seven daughters, and two nieces, with several other of your friends and acquaintance, have been kept here enchanted by the sage Merlin, these many years past; and though it be above five hundred years ago, not one of us is dead; only Ruydera and her daughters and nieces are gone, whom, because of their weeping, Merlin, out of compassion, turned into so many lakes, which, at this time, in the world of the living, and in the province of La Mancha, are called the lakes of Ruydera. The seven sisters belong to the kings of Spain, and the two nieces to the knights of a very holy order, called the Knights of St. John. Guadiana also, your squire, bewailing your misfortune, was changed into a river of his own name; who, arriving at the surface of the earth, and seeing the sun of another sky, was so grieved at the thought of forsaking you, that he plunged again into the bowels of the earth; but, it being impossible to avoid taking the natural course, he rises now and then, and shows himself* where the sun and people may see him. The aforesaid lakes supply him with their waters, with which, and several others that join him, he enters stately and great into Portugal. Nevertheless, whithersoever he goes, he discovers his grief and melancholy, breeding in his waters, not delicate and costly fish, but only coarse and unsavoury ones, very different from those of the golden Tagus. And what I now tell you, O my dearest cousin, I have often told you before, and since you make me no answer, I fancy, you do not believe me, or do not hear me; which, God knows, afflicts me very much.

'"One piece of news, however, I will tell you, which, if it serves not to alleviate your grief, will in no wise increase it. Know then, that you have here present (open your eyes, and you will see him) that great knight, of whom the sage Merlin prophesied so many things; that Don Quixote de la Mancha, I say, who, with greater advantages than in the ages past, has, in the present times, restored the long-forgotten order of knight-errantry; by whose means, and favour, we may, perhaps, be disenchanted: for great exploits are reserved for great men."

'"And though it should fall out otherwise," answered the poor Durandarte with a faint and low voice, "though it should not prove so, O cousin, I say, patience, and shuffle the cards."

'And, turning himself on one side, he relapsed into his accustomed silence, without speaking a word more.

'Then were heard great cries and wailings, accompanied with profound sighs and distressful sobbings. I turned my head about, and saw through the crystal walls a procession in two files of most beautiful damsels, all clad in mourning, with white turbans on their heads after the Turkish fashion; and last of all, in the rear of the files, came a lady (for by her gravity she seemed to be such) clad also in black, with a white veil, so long that it kissed the ground. Her turban was twice as large as the largest of the others: her eyebrows were joined; her nose was somewhat flattish; her mouth wide, but her lips red; her teeth, which she sometimes showed, were thin set, and not very even, though as white as blanched almonds. She carried in her hand a fine linen handkerchief, and in it, as seemed to me, a heart of mummy, so dry and withered it appeared to be.

'Montesinos told me, that all those of the procession were servants to Durandarte and Belerma, and were there enchanted with their master and mistress, and that she, who came last, bearing the heart in the linen handkerchief, was the lady Belerma herself, who, four days in the week, made that procession together with her damsels, singing, or rather weeping, dirges over the body, and over the piteous heart of his cousin; and that if she appeared to me somewhat ugly, or not so beautiful as fame reported, it was occasioned by the bad nights and worse days she passed in that enchantment, as might be seen by the great wrinkles under her eyes, and her broken complexion: as to her being pale and hollow-eyed, it was not occasioned by the periodical indisposition incident to women, there not having been, for several months, and even years past, the least appearance of any such matter; but merely by the affliction her heart feels from what she carries continually in her hands; which renews and revives in her memory the disaster of her untimely deceased lover; for had it not been for this, the great Dulcinea del Toboso herself, so celebrated in these parts, and even over the whole world, would hardly have equalled her in beauty, good humour, and sprightliness.

'"Fair and softly," quoth I then, "good Señor Montesinos: tell your story as you ought to do; for you know, that comparisons are odious, and therefore there is no need of comparing anybody with anybody. The peerless Dulcinea is what she is, and the lady Doña Belerma is what she is, and what she has been, and so much for that."

'To which he answered:

'"Señor Don Quixote, pardon me: I confess I was in the wrong, in saying, that the lady Dulcinea would hardly equal the lady Belerma: my understanding, by I know not what guesses, that your worship is her knight, ought to have made me bite my tongue sooner, than compare her to anything but heaven itself."

'With this satisfaction given me by the great Montesinos, my heart was delivered from the surprise it was in at hearing my mistress compared with Belerma.'

'And I too admire,' quoth Sancho, 'that your worship did not fall upon the old fellow, and bruise his bones with kicking, and pluck his beard for him, till you had not left him an hair in it.'

'No, friend Sancho,' answered Don Quixote, 'it did not become me to do so; for we are all bound to respect old men, though they be not knights, and especially those who are such, and enchanted into the bargain. I know very well I was not at all behindhand with him in several other questions and answers, which passed between us.'

Here the scholar said:

'I cannot imagine, Señor Don Quixote, how your worship in the short space of time you have been there below, could see so many things, and talk and answer so much.'

'How long is it since I went down?' quoth Don Quixote.

'A little above an hour,' answered Sancho.

'That cannot be,' replied Don Quixote; 'for night came upon me there, and then it grew day; and then night came again, and day again, three times successively; so that by my account I must have been three days in those parts, so remote and hidden from our sight.'

'My master,' said Sancho, 'must needs be in the right; for as everything has happened to him in the way of enchantment, what seems to us but an hour, may seem there three days and three nights.'

'It is so,' answered Don Quixote.

'And has your worship, good sir, eaten anything in all this time?' quoth the scholar.

'I have not broken my fast with one mouthful,' answered Don Quixote, 'nor have I been hungry, or so much as thought of it all the while.'

'Do the enchanted eat?' said the scholar.

'They do not eat,' answered Don Quixote, 'nor are they troubled with the greater excrements, though it is a common opinion, that their nails, their beards, and their hair grow.'

'And, sir, do the enchanted sleep?' quoth Sancho.

'No, truly,' answered Don Quixote: 'at least, in the three days that I have been amongst them, not one of them has closed an eye, nor I neither.'

'Here,' quoth Sancho, 'the proverb hits right, "Tell me your company, and I will tell you what you are." If your worship keeps company with those, who fast and watch, what wonder is it that you neither eat nor sleep while you are with them? But pardon me, good master of mine, if I tell your worship, that, of all you have been saying, God take me (I was going to say the devil) if I believe one word.'

'How so?' said the scholar: 'Señor Don Quixote then must have lied; who, if he had a mind to it, has not had time to imagine and compose such a heap of lies.'

'I do not believe my master lies,' answered Sancho.

'If not, what do you believe?' quoth Don Quixote.

'I believe,' answered Sancho, 'that the same Merlin, or those necromancers, who enchanted all the crew your worship says you saw and conversed with there below, have crammed into your imagination or memory all this stuff you have already told us, or that remains to be told.'

'Such a thing might be, Sancho,' replied Don Quixote; 'but it is not so: for what I have related I saw with my own eyes, and touched with my own hands: but what will you say, when I tell you, that, among an infinite number of things and

wonders, showed me by Montesinos (which I will recount in
the progress of our journey, at leisure, and in their due time,
for they do not all belong properly to this place) he showed
me three country wenches, who were dancing and capering
like any kids about those charming fields; and scarce had I
espied them, when I knew one of them to be the peerless
Dulcinea del Toboso, and the other two the very same
wenches that came with her, whom we talked with at their
coming out of Toboso. I asked Montesinos, whether he knew
them. He answered, no, but that he took them to be some
ladies of quality lately enchanted, for they had appeared in
those meadows but a few days before; and that I should not
wonder at that, for there were a great many other ladies there,
of the past and present ages, enchanted under various and
strange figures, among whom he knew queen Guinevere and
her duenna Quintañona, cup-bearer to Lancelot, when he
arrived from Britain.'*

When Sancho heard his master say all this, he was ready
to run distracted, or to die with laughing; for, as he knew
the truth of the feigned enchantment of Dulcinea, of whom
he himself had been the enchanter, and the bearer of that
testimony, he concluded undoubtedly that his master had lost
his senses, and was in all points mad: and therefore he said
to him:

'In an evil juncture, and in a worse season, and in a bitter
day, dear patron of mine, did you go down to the other
world; and in an unlucky moment did you meet with Señor
Montesinos, who has returned you back to us in such guise.
Your worship was very well here above, entirely in your
senses, such as God had given you, speaking sentences, and
giving advice at every turn, and not, as now, relating the
greatest extravagances that can be imagined.'

'As I know you, Sancho,' answered Don Quixote, 'I make
no account of your words.'

'Nor I of your worship's,' replied Sancho: 'you may hurt
me, if you will; you may kill me, if you please, for those I
have said already, or those I intend to say, if you do not
correct and amend your own. But tell me, Sir, now we are
at peace, how or by what, did you know the lady our mistress?

and if you spoke to her, what said you? and what answer did she make you?'

'I knew her,' answered Don Quixote, 'by the very same clothes she wore when you showed her to me. I spoke to her; but she answered me not a word: on the contrary, she turned her back upon me, and fled away with so much speed, that an arrow could not have overtaken her. I would have followed her: but Montesinos advised me not to tire myself, with so doing, since it would be in vain; besides, it was now time for me to think of returning and getting out of the cave. He also told me, that in process of time, I should be informed of the means of disenchanting himself, Belerma, Durandarte, and all the rest there.

'But what gave me the most pain of anything I saw, or took notice of, was, that while Montesinos was saying these things to me, there approached me on one side, unperceived by me, one of the two companions of the unfortunate Dulcinea, and with tears in her eyes, in a low and troubled voice, said to me:

'"My lady Dulcinea del Toboso kisses your worship's hands, and desires you to let her know how you do; and, being in great necessity, she also earnestly begs your worship would be pleased to lend her, upon this new dimity petticoat I have brought here, six reals, or what you have about you, which she promises to return very shortly."

'This message threw me into suspense and admiration, and turning to Señor Montesinos, I demanded of him:

'"Is it possible, Señor Montesinos, that persons of quality under enchantment suffer necessity?"

'To which he answered:

'"Believe me, Señor Don Quixote de la Mancha, that what is called necessity prevails everywhere, extends to all, and reaches everybody, not excusing even those who are enchanted: and since the lady Dulcinea sends to desire of you these six reals, and the pawn is, in appearance, a good one, there is no more to be done but to give her them; for without doubt she must needs be in some very great strait."

'"I will take no pawn," answered I, "nor can I send her what she desires; for I have but four reals." Which I sent her, being those you gave me the other day, Sancho, to bestow in alms on the poor I should meet with upon the road.

'And said I to the damsel:

'"Sweetheart, tell your lady, that I am grieved to my soul at her distresses, and wish I were a Fucar* to remedy them; and pray let her know, that I neither can nor will have health, while I want her amiable presence, and discreet conversation; and that I beseech her with all imaginable earnestness, that she would vouchsafe to let herself be seen and conversed with by this her captive servant and bewildered knight. Tell her, that, when she least thinks of it, she will hear it said, that I have made an oath and vow, like that made by the Marquess of Mantua, to revenge his nephew Valdovinos,* when he found him ready to expire in the midst of the mountain; which was, not to eat bread upon a tablecloth, with the other idle whims he then added, till he had revenged his death. In like manner will I take no rest, but traverse the seven parts of the universe, with more punctuality than did the infante Don Pedro of Portugal,* till she be disenchanted."

'"All this and more your worship owes my lady," answered the damsel.

'And, taking the four reals, instead of making me a curtsy, she cut a caper full two yards high in the air.'

'O holy God!' cried Sancho aloud at this juncture, 'is it possible there should be such an one in the world, and that enchanters and enchantments should have such power over him, as to change my master's good understanding into so extravagant a madness? O sir! sir! for God's sake, look to yourself, and stand up for your honour, and give no credit to these vanities, which have diminished and decayed your senses.'

'It is your love of me, Sancho, makes you talk at this rate,' quoth Don Quixote; 'and not being experienced in the things of the world, you take everything, in which there is the least difficulty, for impossible: but the time will come, as I said before, when I shall tell you some other of the things I have seen below, which will make you give credit to what I have now told you, the truth of which admits of no reply or dispute.'

CHAPTER 24

In which are recounted a thousand impertinences necessary to the right understanding of this grand history.

THE translator of this grand history from the original, written by its first author Cid Hamet Ben Engeli, says, that coming to the chapter of the adventure of the cave of Montesinos, he found in the margin these words of Hamet's own hand-writing:

'I cannot persuade myself, or believe, that all that is mentioned in the foregoing chapter happened to the valorous Don Quixote exactly as it is there written: the reason is, because all the adventures hitherto related might have happened and are probable; but in this of the cave I find no possibility of its being true, as it exceeds all reasonable bounds. But for me to think, that Don Quixote, being a gentleman of the greatest veracity, and a knight of the most worth of any of his time, would tell a lie, is as little possible; for he would not utter a falsehood, though he were to be shot to death with arrows. On the other hand, I consider, that he told it with all the aforesaid circumstances, and that he could not, in so short a space, have framed so vast a machine of extravagances: and if this adventure seems to be apocryphal, I am not in fault; and so, without affirming it for true or false, I write it. Since, reader, you have discernment, judge as you see fit; for I neither ought, nor can do any more; though it is held for certain, that, upon his death-bed, they say he retracted,* and said, he had invented it only because it was of a piece, and squared with the adventures he had read of in his histories.'

Then the translator goes on, saying:

The scholar was astonished no less at the boldness of Sancho Panza, than at the patience of his master, judging that the mildness of temper he then showed sprang from the satisfaction he had just received in seeing his mistress Dulcinea del Toboso, though enchanted: for, had it not been so, Sancho said such words and things to him as richly deserved a cudgelling; and in reality he thought Sancho had been a little too saucy with his master: To whom the scholar said:

'For my part, Señor Don Quixote, I reckon the pains of my journey in your worship's company very well bestowed, having thereby gained four things. The first, your worship's acquaintance, which I esteem a great happiness. The second, my having learned what is enclosed in this cave of Montesinos, with the metamorphoses of Guadiana, and the lakes of Ruydera, which will serve me for my *Spanish Ovid* I have now in hand. The third is, to have learned the antiquity of card-playing, which was in use at least in the days of the emperor Charles the Great, as may be gathered from the words your worship says Durandarte spoke, when, at the end of that great while Montesinos had been talking to him, he awaked, saying, "Patience, and shuffle the cards": and this allusion to cards, and this way of speaking, he could not learn during his enchantment, but when he was in France, and in the days of the said emperor Charles the Great; and this remark comes pat for the other book I am upon, the *Supplement to Polydore Virgil on the Invention of Antiquities*: for I believe he has forgot to insert that of cards in his work, as I will now do in mine; which will be of great importance, especially as I shall allege the authority of so grave and true an author as Señor Durandarte. The fourth is, the knowing with certainty the source of the river Guadiana, hitherto unknown.'

'You are in the right,' said Don Quixote: 'but I would fain know, if by the grace of God a licence be granted you for printing your books, which I doubt, to whom you intend to inscribe them?'

'There are lords and grandees enough in Spain, to whom they may be dedicated,' said the scholar.

'Not many,' answered Don Quixote; 'not because they do not deserve a dedication, but because they will not receive one, to avoid lying under an obligation of making such a return, as seems due to the pains and complaisance of the authors. I know a prince,* who makes amends for what is wanting in the rest, with so many advantages, that if I durst presume to publish them, perhaps, I might stir up envy in several noble breasts. But let this rest, till a more convenient season, and let us now consider, where we shall lodge to-night.'

'Not far from hence,' answered the scholar, 'is a hermitage, in which lives a hermit, who they say, has been a soldier, and has the reputation of being a good Christian, and very discreet, and charitable withal. Adjoining to the hermitage he has a little house, built at his own cost; but, though small, it is large enough to receive guests.'

'Has this same hermit any poultry?' quoth Sancho.

'Few hermits are without,' answered Don Quixote; 'for those in fashion nowadays are not like those in the deserts of Egypt, who were clad with leaves of the palm-tree, and lived upon roots of the earth. I would not be understood, as if, by speaking well of the latter, I reflected upon the former: I only mean, that the penances of our times do not come up to the austerity and strictness of those days. But this is no reason why they may not be all good; at least I take them to be so; and at the worst, the hypocrite, who feigns himself good, does less hurt than the undisguised sinner.'

While they were thus discoursing, they perceived a man on foot coming towards them, walking very fast, and switching a mule, laden with lances and halberds. When he came up to them, he saluted them, and passed on. Don Quixote said to him:

'Hold, honest friend; methinks you go faster than is convenient for that mule.'

'I cannot stay,' answered the man; 'for the arms you see I am carrying, are to be made use of to-morrow, so that I am under a necessity not to stop, and so adieu: but, if you would know for what purpose I carry them, I intend to lodge this night at the inn beyond the hermitage, and, if you travel the same road, you will find me there, where I will tell you wonders; and, once more God be with you.'

Then he pricked on the mule at that rate, that Don Quixote had no time to inquire what wonders they were he designed to tell them: and, as he was not a little curious, and always tormented with the desire of hearing new things, he gave orders for their immediate departure, resolving to pass the night at the inn, without touching at the hermitage, where the scholar would have had them lodge.

This was done accordingly; they mounted, and all three

took the direct road to the inn (at which they arrived a little
before nightfall). The scholar desired Don Quixote to make
a step to the hermitage, to drink one draught: and scarce had
Sancho Panza heard this, when he steered Dapple towards
the hermitage, and the same did Don Quixote and the
scholar; but Sancho's ill luck, it seems would have it, that
the hermit was not at home, as they were told by an
under-hermit,* whom they found in the hermitage. They
asked him for the dearest wine: he answered, his master had
none; but, if they wanted cheap water, he would give them
some with all his heart.

'If I had wanted water,' answered Sancho, 'there are wells
enough upon the road, from whence I might have satisfied
myself. O for the wedding of Camacho, and the plenty of
Don Diego's house! how often shall I feel the want of you!'

They quitted the hermitage, and spurred on towards the
inn, and soon overtook a lad, who was walking before them
in no great haste. He carried a sword upon his shoulder, and
upon it a roll or bundle, seemingly of his clothes, in all
likelihood breeches or trousers, a cloak, and a shirt or two.
He had on a tattered velvet jacket lined with satin, and his
shirt hung out. His stockings were of silk, and his shoes
square-toed, after the court fashion. He seemed to be about
eighteen or nineteen years of age, of a cheerful countenance,
and in appearance very active of body. He went on singing
couplets, to divert the fatigue of the journey; and, when they
overtook him he had just done singing one, the last words
whereof the scholar got by heart; which they say were these:

> For want of the pence to the wars I must go:
> Ah! had I but money, it would not be so.

The first who spoke to him was Don Quixote, who said:
'You travel very airily, young spark; pray, whither so [airily]?
let us know, if you are inclined to tell us.'

To which the youth answered:

'My walking so airily is occasioned by the heat and by
poverty, and I am going to the wars.'

'How by poverty?' demanded Don Quixote; 'by the heat
it may very easily be.'

'Sir,' replied the youth, 'I carry in this bundle a pair of velvet trousers, fellows to this jacket: if I wear them out upon the road, I cannot do myself credit with them in the city, and I have no money to buy others; and for this reason, as well as for coolness, I go thus, till I come up with some companies of foot, which are not twelve leagues from hence, where I will list myself, and shall not want baggage conveniences to ride in, till we come to the place of embarkation, which they say is to be at Carthagena: besides, I choose the king for my master and lord, whom I had rather serve in the war, than any paltry fellow at court.'

'And pray, sir, have you any post?' said the scholar.

'Had I served some grandee, or other person of distinction,' answered the youth, 'no doubt I should; for in the service of good masters, it is no uncommon thing to rise from the servants' hall to the post of ensign or captain, or to get some good pension: but poor I was always in the service of strolling fellows* or foreigners, whose wages and board wages are so miserable and slender, that one half is spent in paying for starching a ruff; and it would be looked upon as a miracle, if one page-adventurer in a hundred should get any tolerable preferment.'

'But, tell me, friend,' quoth Don Quixote: 'is it possible, that, in all the time you have been in service, you could not procure a livery?'

'I had two,' answered the page: 'but, as he who quits a monastery before he professes, is stripped of his habit, and his old clothes returned to him, just so my master did by me, and gave me back mine; for, when the business was done, for which they came to court, they returned to their own homes, and took back the liveries they had given only for show.'

'A notable *spilorceria*, as the Italians say,' quoth Don Quixote: 'however, look upon it as an earnest of good fortune, that you have quitted the court with so good an intention; for there is nothing upon earth more honourable or more advantageous, than first to serve God, and then your king and natural lord, especially in the exercise of arms, by which one acquires at least more honour, if not more riches, than by letters, as I have often said: for though letters have founded more great families than arms, still there is I know not what that exalts those, who follow arms, above those who follow letters, with I know not what splendour attending them, which sets them above all others.

'And bear in mind this piece of advice, which will be of great use to you, and matter of consolation in your distresses; and that is, not to think of what adverse accidents may happen: for the worst that can happen is death, and, when death is attended with honour, the best that can happen is to die. That valorous Roman emperor, Julius Caesar, being asked, which was the best kind of death, answered, that which was sudden, unthought of, and unforeseen; and though he answered like a heathen, and a stranger to the knowledge of the true God, nevertheless, with respect to human infirmity, he said well. For, supposing you are killed, in the first skirmish or action, either by a cannon-shot or the blowing up of a mine, what does it signify? all is but dying, and the business is done. According to Terence,* the soldier makes a better figure dead in battle, than alive and safe in flight; and the good soldier gains just as much reputation, as he shows obedience to his captains, and to those who have a right to command him. And take notice, son, that a soldier had better smell of gunpowder than of musk: and if old age overtakes you in this noble profession, though lame and maimed, and full of wounds, at least it will not overtake you without honour, and such honour as poverty itself cannot deprive you of: especially now that care is being taken to provide for the maintenance of old and disabled soldiers, who ought not to be dealt with, as many do by their negro slaves, when they are old, and past service, whom they discharge and set at liberty, and driving them out of their houses, under pretence of giving them their freedom, make them slaves to hunger, from which nothing but death can deliver them.

'At present I will say no more: but, get up behind me upon this horse of mine, till we come to the inn, and there you shall sup with me, and to-morrow morning pursue your journey, and God give you as good speed as your good intentions deserve.'

The page did not accept of the invitation of riding behind Don Quixote, but did that of supping with him at the inn; and here, it is said, Sancho muttered to himself:

'The Lord bless thee for a master! is it possible that one, who can say so many and such good things, as he has now done, should say he saw the extravagant impossibilities he tells us of the cave of Montesinos? Well, we shall see what will come of it.'

By this time they arrived at the inn, just at nightfall, and Sancho was pleased to see his master take it for an inn indeed, and not for a castle, as usual. They were scarce entered, when Don Quixote asked the landlord for the man with the lances and halberds; he answered, he was in the stable looking after his mule. The scholar and Sancho did the same by their beasts, giving Rosinante the best manger, and the best place in the stable.

CHAPTER 25

Wherein is begun the braying adventure, with the pleasant one of the puppet-player, and the memorable divinations of the divining ape.

DON QUIXOTE's cake was dough, as the saying is, till he could hear and learn the wonders promised to be told him by the conductor of the arms; and therefore he went in quest of him where the innkeeper told him he was; and, having found him, he desired him by all means to tell him, what he had to say as to what he had inquired of him upon the road. The man answered:

'The account of my wonders must be taken more at leisure, and not on foot: suffer me, good sir, to make an end of taking care of my beast, and I will tell you things which will amaze you.'

'Let not that be any hindrance,' answered Don Quixote; 'for I will help you;' and so he did, winnowing the barley, and cleaning the manger; a piece of humility, which obliged the man readily to tell him what he desired: and seating himself upon a stone bench without the inn door, and Don Quixote by his side, the scholar, the page, Sancho Panza, and the innkeeper, serving as his senate and auditory, he began in this manner:

'You must understand, gentlemen, that, in a town four leagues and a half from this inn,* it happened, that an alderman, through the artful contrivance (too long to be told) of a wench his maidservant, lost his ass; and though the said alderman used all imaginable diligence to find him, it was not possible. Fifteen days were passed, as public fame says, since the ass was missing, when the losing alderman being in the market-place, another alderman of the same town said to him:

'"Pay me for my good news, gossip; for your ass has appeared."

'"Most willingly, neighbour," answered the other; "but let us know where he has been seen."

'"In the mountain," answered the finder; "I saw him this morning, without a pannel, or any kind of furniture about him, and so lank, that it would grieve one to see him: I would fain have driven him before me, and brought him to you; but he is already become so wild, and so shy, that, when I went near him, away he galloped, and ran in the most hidden part of the mountain. If you have a mind we should both go to seek him, let me but put up this ass at home, and I will return instantly."

'"You will do me a great pleasure," quoth he of the ass, "and I will endeavour to pay you in the same coin."

'With all these circumstances, and after the very same manner, is the story told by all, who are thoroughly acquainted with the truth of the affair.

'In short, the two aldermen, on foot, and hand in hand, went to the mountain; and coming to the very place where they thought to find the ass, they found him not, nor was he to be seen anywhere thereabouts, though they searched diligently after him. Perceiving then, that he was not to be found, quoth the alderman that had seen him, to the other:

'"Hark you, gossip; a device is come into my head, whereby we shall assuredly discover this animal, though he were crept into the bowels of the earth, not to say of the mountain; and it is this: I can bray marvellously well, and if you can do so never so little, conclude the business done."

'"Never so little, say you, neighbour?" quoth the other; "before God, I yield the precedence to none—no, not to asses themselves."

'"We shall see that immediately," answered the second alderman; "for I propose that you shall go on one side of the mountain, and I on the other, and so we shall traverse and encompass it quite round; and every now and then you shall bray, and so will I; and the ass will most certainly hear and answer us, if he be in the mountain."

'To which the master of the ass answered:

'"Verily, neighbour, the device is excellent, and worthy of your great ingenuity."

'So parting according to agreement, it fell out, that they both brayed at the same instant, and each of them, deceived by the braying of the other, ran to seek the other, thinking the ass had appeared; and, at the sight of each other, the loser said:

'"Is it possible, gossip, that it was not my ass that brayed?"

'"No, it was I," answered the other.

'"I tell you then," quoth the owner, "that there is no manner of difference, as to the braying part, between you and an ass; for in my life I never saw or heard anything more natural."

'"These praises and compliments," answered the author of the stratagem, "belong rather to you than to me, gossip; for, by the God that made me, you can give the odds of two brays to the greatest and most skilful brayer of the world; for the tone is deep, the sustaining of the voice in time and measure, and the cadences frequent and quick: in short, I own myself vanquished, I give you the palm, and yield up the standard of this rare ability."

'"I say," answered the owner, "I shall value and esteem myself the more henceforward, and shall think I know something, since I have some excellence; for, though I fancied I brayed well, I never flattered myself I came up to the pitch you are pleased to say."

'"I tell you," answered the second, "there are rare abilities lost in the world, and that they are ill bestowed on those, who know not how to employ them to advantage."

'"Ours," quoth the owner, "excepting in cases like the present, cannot be of service to us; and, even in this, God grant they prove of any benefit."

'This said, they separated again, and fell anew to their braying; and at every turn they deceived each other, and met again, till they agreed, as a countersign to distinguish their own brayings from that of the ass, that they should bray twice together, one immediately after the other. Thus doubling their brayings, they made the tour of the mountain; but no answer from the stray ass—no, not by signs: indeed, how could the poor creature answer, whom they found in the thickest of the wood, half devoured by wolves? At sight whereof the owner said:

'"I wondered indeed he did not answer: for, had he not been dead, he would have brayed at hearing us, or he were no ass: nevertheless, gossip, I esteem the pains I have been at in seeking him to be well bestowed, though I have found him dead, since I have heard you bray with such a grace."

'"It is in a good hand, gossip," answered the other: "for if the abbot sings well, the novice comes not far behind him."

'Hereupon they returned home, disconsolate and hoarse, and recounted to their friends, neighbours, and acquaintance, all that had happened in the search after the ass; each of them exaggerating the other's excellence in braying. The story spread all over the adjacent villages; and the devil, who sleeps not, as he loves to sow and promote squabbles and discord wherever he can, raising a bustle in the wind, and great chimeras out of next to nothing, so ordered and brought it about, that the people of other villages, upon seeing any one of the folks of our town, would presently fall a-braying, as it were hitting us in the teeth with the braying of our aldermen. The boys gave into it, which was all one as putting it into the hands and mouths of all the devils in hell; and thus braying spread from one town to another, insomuch that the natives of the town of Bray* are as well known as white folks are distinguished from black. And this unhappy jest has gone so far, that the mocked have often sallied out in arms against the mockers, and given them battle, without king or rook, or fear or shame, being able to prevent it.

'To-morrow, I believe, or next day, those of our town, the brayers, will take the field against the people of another village, about two leagues from ours, being one of those which persecute us most. And, to be well provided for them, I have brought the lances and halberds you saw me carrying. And these are the wonders I said I would tell you; and if you do not think them such, I have no other for you.' And here the honest man ended his story.

At this juncture there came in at the door of the inn a man clad from head to foot in chamois leather, hose, doublet, and breeches, and said with a loud voice:

'Master Host, have you any lodging? for here comes the divining ape, and the puppet-show of Melisendra's deliverance.'

'Body of me,' quoth the innkeeper, 'what! Master Peter here! we shall have a brave night of it.'

I had forgot to tell you, that this same Master Peter had his left eye, and almost half his cheek, covered with a patch of green taffeta, a sign that something ailed all that side of his face. The landlord went on saying:

'Welcome, Master Peter! where is the ape and the puppet-show? I do not see them.'

'They are hard by,' answered the all-chamois man; 'I came before, to see if there be any lodging to be had.'

'I would turn out the Duke de Alva himself, to make room for Master Peter,' answered the innkeeper: 'let the ape and the puppets come: for there are guests this evening in the inn who will pay for seeing the show, and the abilities of the ape.'

'So be it in God's name,' answered he of the patch; 'and I will lower the price, and reckon myself well paid with only bearing my charges. I will go back, and hasten the cart with the ape and the puppets.'

And immediately he went out of the inn.

Then Don Quixote asked the landlord, what Master Peter this was, and what puppets, and what ape he had with him? To which the landlord answered:

'He is a famous puppet-player, who has been a long time going up and down these parts of Mancha in Aragon, with a show of Melisendra and the famous Don Gayferos; which is one of the best stories, and the best performed, of any that has been seen hereabouts these many years. He has also an ape, whose talents exceed those of all other apes, and even those of men: for, if anything is asked him, he listens to it attentively, and then, leaping upon his master's shoulder, and putting his mouth to his ear, he tells him the answer to the question that is put to him; which Master Peter presently repeats aloud. It is true, he tells much more concerning things past than things to come; and, though he does not always hit right, yet for the most part he is not much out; so that we are inclined to believe he has the devil within him. He has two reals for each question, if the ape answers; I mean, if his master answers for him, after the ape has whispered him in the ear: and therefore it is thought this same Master Peter must be very rich. He is, besides, a very gallant man, as they say in Italy, and a boon companion, and lives the merriest life in the world. He talks more than six, and drinks more than a dozen, and all this at the expense of his tongue, his ape, and his puppets.'

By this time Master Peter was returned, and in the cart came the puppets, and a large ape without a tail, and its buttocks bare as a piece of felt: but not ill-favoured. Don Quixote no sooner espied him, but he began to question him, saying:

'Master Diviner, pray, tell me, what fish do we catch, and what will be our fortune? See, here are my two reals', bidding Sancho to give them to Master Peter, who answered for the ape, and said:

'Señor, this animal makes no answer, nor gives any information, as to things future: he knows something of the past, and a little of the present.'

'Odds bobs,' quoth Sancho, 'I would not give a brass farthing, to be told what is past of myself; for who can tell that better than myself? and for me to pay for what I know already, would be a very great folly. But since he knows things present, here are my two reals, and let goodman ape tell me what my wife Teresa Panza is doing, and what she is employed about?'

Master Peter would not take the money, saying:

'I will not be paid beforehand, not take your reward till I have done you the service.'

And giving with his right hand two or three claps on the left shoulder, at one spring the ape jumped upon it, and laying its mouth to his ear, grated his teeth and chattered apace; and, having made this grimace for the space of a Credo, at another skip down it jumped on the ground, and presently Master Peter ran and kneeled before Don Quixote, and, embracing his legs said:

'These legs I embrace, just as if I embraced the two pillars of Hercules, O illustrious reviver of the long-forgotten order of chivalry! O never-sufficiently-extolled knight Don Quixote de la Mancha! Thou spirit to the faint-hearted, stay to those that are falling, arm to those who are already fallen, staff and comfort to all that are unfortunate!'

Don Quixote was thunderstruck, Sancho in suspense, the scholar surprised, the page astonished, the braying-man in a gaze, the innkeeper confounded, and, lastly, all amazed that heard the expressions of the puppet-player, who proceeded, saying:

'And thou, O good Sancho Panza, the best squire to the best knight in the world, rejoice, that thy good wife Teresa is well, and this very hour is dressing a pound of flax! by the same token that she has by her left side a broken-mouthed pitcher, which holds a very pretty scantling of wine, with which she cheers her spirits at her work.'

'I verily believe it,' answered Sancho, 'for she is a blessed one, and, were she not a little jealous, I would not change her for the giantess Andandona,* who, in my master's opinion, was a very accomplished woman, and a special house-wife; and my Teresa is one of those, who will make much of themselves, though it be at the expense of their heirs.'

'Well,' quoth Don Quixote, 'he who reads much and travels much, sees much and knows much. This, I say, because what could have been sufficient to persuade me that there are apes in the world that can divine, as I have now seen with my own eyes? Yes, I am that very Don Quixote de la Mancha, that this good animal has said, though he has expatiated a little too much in my commendation. But, be I as I may, I give thanks to heaven that endued me with a tender and compassionate disposition of mind, always inclined to do good to everybody and hurt nobody.'

'If I had money,' said the page, 'I would ask Master Ape what will befall me in my intended expedition.'

To which Master Peter, who was already got up from kneeling at Don Quixote's feet, answered:

'I have already told you that this little beast does not answer as to things future: but, did he answer such questions, it would be no matter whether you had money or not; for, to serve Señor Don Quixote here present, I would waive all advantages in the world. And now, because it is my duty, and to do him a pleasure besides, I intend to put in order my puppet-show, and entertain all the folks in the inn gratis.'

The innkeeper, hearing this, and above measure overjoyed, pointed out a convenient place for setting up the show, which was done in an instant.

Don Quixote was not entirely satisfied with the ape's divinations, not thinking it likely that an ape should divine things either future or past: and so, while Master Peter was preparing his show, Don Quixote drew Sancho aside to a corner of the stable, where, without being overheard by anybody, he said to him:

'Look you, Sancho, I have carefully considered the strange ability of this ape, and, by my account, I find that Master Peter, his owner, must doubtless have made a tacit or express pact with the devil.'

'Nay,' quoth Sancho, 'if the pack be express from the devil, it must needs be a very sooty pack: but what advantage would it be to this same Master Peter to have such a pack?'

'You do not understand me, Sancho,' said Don Quixote: 'I only mean, that he must certainly have made some agreement with the devil to infuse this ability into the ape, whereby he gets his bread; and, after he is become rich, he will give him his soul, which is what the universal enemy of mankind aims at. And what induces me to this belief, is, finding that the ape answers only as to things past or present, and the knowledge of the devil extends no further; for he knows the future only by conjecture, and not always that; for it is the prerogative of God alone, to know times and seasons, and to Him nothing is past or future, but everything present. This being so, as it really is, it is plain the ape talks in the style of the devil; and I wonder he has not been accused to the Inquisition, and examined by torture, till he confesses, by virtue of what, or of whom, he divines: for it is certain this ape is no astrologer; and neither his master nor he know how to raise one of those figures called judiciary,* which are now so much in fashion in Spain, that you have not any servant-maid, page, or cobbler, but presumes to raise a figure, as if it were a knave of cards from the ground; thus destroying by their lying and ignorant pretences, the wonderful truth of the science.

'I know a certain lady, who asked one of these figure-raisers, whether a little lap-dog she had would breed, and how many, and of what colour the puppies would be. To which Master Astrologer, after raising a figure, answered, that the bitch would pup, and have three whelps, one green, one carnation, and the other mottled, upon condition she should take dog between the hours of eleven and twelve at noon or night, and that it were on a Monday or a Saturday. Now it happened that the bitch died some two days after of a surfeit, and Master Figureraiser had the repute of being as consummate an astrologer as the rest of his brethren.'

'But for all that,' quoth Sancho, 'I should be glad your worship would desire Master Peter to ask his ape, whether all be true, which befell you in the cave of Montesinos, because, for my own part, begging your worship's pardon, I take it to be all sham and lies, or at least a dream.'

'It may be so,' answered Don Quixote: 'but I will do what you advise me, since I myself begin to have some kind of scruples about it.'

While they were thus confabulating, Master Peter came to look for Don Quixote, to tell him the show was ready, desiring he would come to see it, for it deserved it. Don Quixote communicated to him his thought, and desired him to ask his ape presently, whether certain things, which befell him in the cave of Montesinos, were dreams or realities; for to his thinking, they seemed to be a mixture of both. Master Peter, without answering a word, went and fetched his ape, and, placing him before Don Quixote and Sancho, said:

'Look you, Master Ape, this knight would know, whether certain things, which befell him in a cave, called that of Montesinos, were real or imaginary.'

And making the usual signal, the ape leaped upon his left shoulder; and seeming to chatter to him in his ear, Master Peter presently said:

'The ape says, that part of the things your worship saw, or which befell you, in the said cave, are false, and part likely to be true: and this is what he knows, and no more, as to this question; and if your worship has a mind to put any more to him, on Friday next he will answer to everything you shall ask him; for his virtue is at an end for the present, and will not return till that time.'

'Did I not tell you,' quoth Sancho, 'it could never go down with me, that all your worship said, touching the adventures of the cave, was true—no, nor half of it?'

'The event will show that, Sancho,' answered Don Quixote; 'for time, the discoverer of all things, brings everything to light, though it lie hid in the bowels of the earth; and, let this suffice at present, and let us go and see honest Master Peter's show; for I am of opinion there must be some novelty in it.'

'How, some?' quoth Master Peter: 'sixty thousand novelties are contained in this puppet show of mine: I assure you, Señor Don Quixote, it is one of the top things to be seen that the world affords at this day; *Operibus credite, et non verbis*; and let us to work; for it grows late, and we have a great deal to do, to say and to show.'

Don Quixote and Sancho obeyed, and came where the show was set out, stuck round with little wax candles, so that it made a delightful and shining appearance. Master Peter, who was to manage the figures, placed himself behind the show, and before it stood his boy, to serve as an interpreter, and expounder of the mysteries of the piece. He had a white wand in his hand, to point to the several figures as they entered. All the folks in the inn being placed, some standing opposite to the show, and Don Quixote, Sancho, the page, and the scholar, seated in the best places, the drugger-man* began to say what will be heard or seen by those who will be at the pains of hearing or seeing the following chapter.

CHAPTER 26

Wherein is contained the pleasant adventure of the puppet-player, with sundry other matters, in truth sufficiently good.

'TYRIANS and Trojans were all silent':* I mean, that all the spectators of the show hung upon the mouth of the declarer of its wonders, when from within the scene they heard the sound of a number of drums and trumpets, and several discharges of artillery; which noise was soon over, and immediately the boy raised his voice and said:

'This true history, here represented to you, gentlemen, is taken word for word from the French chronicles and Spanish ballads, which are in everybody's mouth, and sung by the boys up and down the streets. It treats how Don Gayferos freed his wife Melisendra,* who was a prisoner in Spain, in the hands of the Moors, in the city of Sansueña, now called Saragossa; and there you may see how Don Gayferos is playing at tables,* according to the ballad:

'Gayferos now at tables plays,
Forgetful of his lady dear,* &c.

That personage, who appears yonder with a crown on his head, and a sceptre in his hands, is the emperor Charles the Great, the supposed father of Melisendra, who, being vexed to see the indolence and negligence of his son-in-law, comes forth to chide him; and, pray, mark with what vehemency and earnestness he rates him, that one would think he had a mind to give him half a dozen raps over the pate with his sceptre: yea, there are authors who say he actually gave them, and sound ones too: and, after having said sundry things about the danger his honour ran, in not procuring the liberty of his spouse, it is reported, he said to him: "I have told you

enough of it, look to it".* Pray observe, gentlemen, how the
emperor turns his back, and leaves Don Gayferos in a fret.
See him now, impatient with choler, flinging about the board
and pieces, and calling hastily for his armour; desiring Don
Orlando his cousin to lend him his sword Durindana;* and
then how Don Orlando refuses to lend it him, offering to
bear him company in that arduous enterprise; but the valorous
enraged will not accept of it, saying that he alone is able to
deliver his spouse, though she were thrust down to the centre
of the earth. Hereupon he goes in to arm himself for setting
forward immediately. Now, gentlemen, turn your eyes towards
that tower, which appears yonder, which you are to suppose
to be one of the Moorish towers of Saragossa, now called the
Aljaferia; and that lady who appears at yon balcony in a
Moorish habit is the peerless Melisendra, casting many a heavy
look towards the road that leads to France, and fixing her
imagination upon the city of Paris and her husband, her only
consolation in her captivity. Now behold a strange incident,
the like perhaps never seen. Do you not see yon Moor, who,
stealing along softly, and step by step, with his finger on his
mouth, comes behind Melisendra? Behold how he gives her
a smacking kiss full on her lips: observe the haste she makes
to spit and wipe her mouth with her white shift-sleeves; and
how she takes on, and tears her beauteous hair for vexation,
as if that was to blame for the indignity. Observe that great
Moor in yonder gallery: he is Marsilio, the king of Sansueña;
who, seeing the insolence of the Moor, though he is a relation
of his, and a great favourite, orders him to be seized immediately, and two hundred stripes to be given him, and to be led
through the most frequented streets of the city, "with criers
before to publish his crime, and the officers of justice with
their rods behind", and now behold the officers coming out
to execute the sentence, almost as soon as the fault is committed: for, among the Moors, there is no citation of the party,
nor copies of the process, nor delay of justice, as among us.'
   Here Don Quixote said with a loud voice:
   'Boy, boy, on with your story in a straight line, and leave
your curves and transversals: for, to come at the truth of a
fact, there is often need of proof upon proof.'

Master Peter also from behind said:

'Boy, none of your flourishes, but do what the gentleman bids you; for that is the surest way; sing your song plain, and seek not for counterpoints; for they usually crack the strings.'

'I will,' answered the boy, and proceeded, saying:

'The figure you see there on horseback, muffled up in a Gascoigne cloak, is Don Gayferos himself, to whom his spouse, already revenged on the impudence of the enamoured Moor, shows herself from the battlements of the tower, with a calmer and more sedate countenance, and talks to her husband, believing him to be some passenger; with whom she holds all that discourse and dialogue in the ballad, which says:

> 'If towards France your course you bend,
> Let me entreat you, gentle friend,
> Make diligent inquiry there
> For Gayferos my husband dear.

The rest I omit, because length begets loathing. It is sufficient to observe, how Don Gayferos discovers himself; and, by the signs of joy she makes, you may perceive she knows him, and especially now that you see she lets herself down from the balcony, to get on horseback behind her good spouse. But, alas, poor lady! the border of her under-petticoat has caught hold on one of the iron rails of the balcony, and there she hangs dangling in the air, without being able to reach the ground. But see how merciful heaven sends relief in the greatest distresses: for now comes Don Gayferos, and, without regarding whether the rich petticoat be torn, or not, lays hold of her, and brings her to the ground by main force; and then at a spring sets her behind him on his horse astride like a man, bidding her hold very fast, and clasp her arms about his shoulders, till they cross and meet over his breast, that she may not fall; because the lady Melisendra was not used to that way of riding. See how the horse by his neighings, shows he is pleased with the burden of his valiant master and his fair mistress. And see how they turn their backs, and go out of the city, and how merrily and joyfully they take the way to Paris. Peace be with you, O peerless pair of faithful lovers! may ye arrive in safety at your desired country, without fortune's laying any obstacle in the way of your prosperous journey! may the eyes of your friends and relations behold ye enjoy in perfect peace the remaining days (and may they be like Nestor's)* of your lives!'

Here again Master Peter raised his voice, and said:

'Plainness, boy; do not encumber yourself; for all affectation is naught.'

The interpreter made no answer, but went on, saying:

'There wanted not some idle eyes, such as espy everything, to see Melisendra's getting down and then mounting; of which they gave notice to king Marsilio, who immediately commanded to sound the alarm: and pray take notice what a hurry they are in: how the whole city shakes with the ringing of bells in the steeples of the mosques.'

'Not so,' quoth Don Quixote; 'Master Peter is very much mistaken in the business of the bells: for the Moors do not use bells, but kettle-drums, and a kind of dulcimers, like our waits: and therefore to introduce the ringing of bells in Sansueña is a gross absurdity.'

Which Master Peter overhearing, he left off ringing, and said:

'Señor Don Quixote, do not criticize upon trifles, nor expect that perfection, which is not to be found in these matters. Are there not a thousand comedies acted almost everywhere, full of as many improprieties and blunders, and yet they run their career with great success, and are listened to, not only with applause, but with admiration? Go on, boy, and let folks talk; for, so I fill my bag, I care not if I represent more improprieties than there are motes in the sun.'

'You are in the right,' quoth Don Quixote; and the boy proceeded:

'See what a numerous and brilliant cavalry sallies out of the city in pursuit of the two Catholic lovers: how many trumpets sound, how many dulcimers play, and how many drums and kettle-drums rattle; I fear they will overtake them, and bring them back tied to their own horse's tail, which would be a lamentable spectacle.'

Don Quixote, seeing such a number of Moors, and hearing such a din, thought proper to succour those that fled, and rising up, said in a loud voice:

'I will never consent, while I live, that in my presence such an outrage as this be offered to so famous a knight and so daring a lover as Don Gayferos. Hold, base-born rabble, follow not, nor pursue after him! for, if you do, have at you.'

And so said, so done, he unsheathed his sword, and at one spring he planted himself close to the show, and with a violent and unheard-of fury, began to rain hacks and slashes upon the Moorish puppets, overthrowing some, and beheading others, laming this, and demolishing that; and, among a great many other strokes, he fetched one with such a force, that, if Master Peter had not ducked and squatted down, he had chopped off his head with as much ease as if it had been made of sugar-paste. Master Peter cried out, saying:

'Hold, Señor Don Quixote, hold, and consider, that these figures you throw down, maim, and destroy, are not real Moors, but only puppets made of paste-board: consider, sinner that I am, that you are undoing me, and destroying my whole livelihood.'

For all that Don Quixote still laid about him, showering down, doubling and redoubling, fore-strokes and back-strokes, like hail. In short, in less than the saying two Credos, he demolished the whole machine, hacking to pieces all the tackling and figures, king Marsilio being sorely wounded, and the head and crown of the emperor Charlemagne cloven in two. The whole audience was in a consternation; the ape flew to the top of the house; the scholar was frighted, the page daunted, and even Sancho himself trembled mightily; for, as he swore after the storm was over, he had never seen his master in so outrageous a passion.

The general demolition of the machinery thus achieved, Don Quixote began to be a little calm, and said:

'I wish I had here before me, at this instant, all those, who are not, and will not be convinced, of how much benefit knights-errant are to the world; for had I not been present, what would have become of good Don Gayferos, and the fair Melisendra? I warrant ye, these dogs would have overtaken them by this time, and have offered them some indignity. When all is done, long live knight-errantry above all things living in the world!'

'In God's name, let it live, and let me die,' quoth Master Peter at this juncture, with a fainting voice, 'since I am so unfortunate, that I can say with king Rodrigo, "yesterday I was sovereign of Spain, and to-day I have not a foot of land to call my own".* It is not half an hour ago, nor scarce half a minute, since I was master of kings and emperors, my stalls full of horses, and my trunks and sacks full of fine things; and now I am desolate and dejected, poor and a beggar, and, what grieves me most of all, without my ape, who, i'faith, will make my teeth sweat for it, before I get him again; and all through the inconsiderate fury of this Sir Knight, who is said to protect orphans, redress wrongs, and do other charitable deeds; but in me alone, praised be the highest heavens for it, his generous intention has failed. In fine, it could only be the Knight of the Sorrowful Figure, who was destined thus to disfigure me and mine.'

Sancho Panza was moved to compassion by what Master Peter had spoken, and therefore said to him:

'Weep not, Master Peter, nor take on so; for you break my heart, and I assure you my master Don Quixote is so Catholic and scrupulous a Christian, that, if he comes to reflect that he has done you any wrong, he knows how, and will certainly make you amends with interest.'

'If Señor Don Quixote,' quoth Master Peter, 'would but repay me part of the damage he has done me, I should be satisfied, and his worship would discharge his conscience; for nobody can be saved, who withholds another's property against his will, and does not make restitution.'

'True,' quoth Don Quixote; 'but as yet I do not know that I have anything of yours, Master Peter.'

'How!' answered Master Peter: 'what but the invincible force of your powerful arm scattered and annihilated these relics, which lie up and down on this hard and barren ground? Whose were their bodies but mine? and how did I maintain myself but by them?'

'Now am I entirely convinced,' quoth Don Quixote at this juncture, 'of what I have often believed before, that those enchanters who persecute me, are perpetually setting shapes before me as they really are, and, presently putting the change upon me, and transforming them into whatever they please. I protest to you, gentlemen, that hear me, that whatever has passed at this time seemed to me to pass actually and precisely so: I took Melisendra to be Melisendra; Don Gayferos, Don Gayferos; Marsilio, Marsilio; and Charlemagne, Charlemagne. This it was that inflamed my choler; and, in compliance with the duty of my profession as a knight-errant, I had a mind to assist and succour those who fled; and with this good intention I did what you just now saw; if things have fallen out the reverse, it is no fault of mine, but of those my wicked persecutors; and notwithstanding this mistake of mine, and though it did not proceed from malice, yet will I condemn myself in costs. See, Master Peter, what you must have for the damaged figures, and I will pay it you down in current and lawful money of Castile.'

Master Peter made him a low bow, saying:

'I expected no less from the unexampled Christianity of the valorous Don Quixote de la Mancha, the true succourer and support of all the needy and distressed: and let Master Innkeeper and the great Sancho be umpires and appraisers, between your worship and me, of what the demolished figures are or might be worth.'

The innkeeper and Sancho said they would; and then Master Peter, taking up Marsilio, king of Saragossa, without a head, said:

'You see how impossible it is to restore this king to his pristine state, and therefore I think, with submission to better judgements, you must award me for his death and destruction four reals and a half.'

'Proceed,' quoth Don Quixote.

'Then for this that is cleft from top to bottom,' continued Master Peter, taking up the emperor Charlemagne, 'I think five reals and a quarter little enough to ask.'

'Not very little,' quoth Sancho.

'Not very much,' replied the innkeeper: 'but split the difference, and set him down five reals.'

'Give him the whole five and a quarter,' quoth Don Quixote; 'for, in such a notable mischance as this, a quarter more or less is not worth standing upon: and make an end,

Master Peter; for it grows towards supper time, and I have some symptoms of hunger upon me.'

'For this figure,' quoth Master Peter, 'which wants a nose and an eye, and is the fair Melisendra, I must have, and can abate nothing of two reals and twelve maravedis.'

'Nay,' said Don Quixote, 'the devil must be in it, if Melisendra be not by this time, with her husband, at least upon the borders of France: for methought the horse they rode upon seemed to fly rather than gallop: and therefore do not pretend to sell me a cat for a coney, showing me here Melisendra noseless, whereas, at this very instant, probably she is solacing herself at full stretch with her husband in France. God help every one with his own, Master Peter, let us have plain dealing, and proceed.'

Master Peter, finding that Don Quixote began to warp, and was returning to his old bent, had no mind he should escape him so, and therefore said to him:

'Now I think on it, this is not Melisendra, but one of her waiting-maids, and so with sixty maravedis I shall be well enough paid, and very well contented.'

Thus he went on, setting a price upon several broken figures, which the arbitrators afterwards moderated to the satisfaction of both parties. The whole amounted to forty reals and three quarters: and over and above all this, which Sancho immediately disbursed, Master Peter demanded two reals for the trouble he should have in catching his ape.

'Give him them, Sancho,' said Don Quixote, 'not for catching the ape, but to drink.* I would give two hundred to any one that could tell me for certain, that Doña Melisendra and Señor Don Gayferos are at this time in France, and among their friends.'

'Nobody can tell us that better than my ape,' said Master Peter: 'but the devil himself cannot catch him now; though I suppose his affection for me, or hunger, will force him to come to me at night; and to-morrow is a new day, and we shall see one another again.'

In conclusion, the bustle of the puppet-show was quite over, and they all supped together in peace and good company, at the expense of Don Quixote, who was liberal to the last degree. He who carried the lances and halberds went off before day, and, after it was light, the scholar and the page came to take their leaves of Don Quixote, the one in order to return home, the other to pursue his intended journey; and Don Quixote gave him a dozen reals to help to bear his charges. Master Peter had no mind to enter into any more 'tell me's and I will you's' with Don Quixote, whom he knew perfectly well; and therefore up he got before sun: and, gathering up the fragments of his show, and taking his ape, away he went in quest of adventures of his own. The innkeeper, who knew Don Quixote, was equally in admiration at his madness and liberality. In short, Sancho, by order of his master, paid him very well; and about eight in the morning, bidding him farewell, they left the inn, and went their way, where we will leave them to give place to the relating several other things necessary to the better understanding this famous history.

CHAPTER 27

Wherein is related, who Master Peter and his ape were; with the ill success Don Quixote had in the braying adventure, which he finished not as he wished and intended.

CID HAMET, the chronicler of this grand history, begins this chapter with these words; 'I swear as a Catholic Christian': to which his translator says, that Cid Hamet's swearing as a Catholic Christian, he being a Moor, as undoubtedly he was, meant nothing more than that, as the Catholic Christian, when he swears, does, or ought to speak and swear the truth, so did he, in writing of Don Quixote, and especially in declaring who Master Peter was, with some account of the divining ape, who surprised all the villages thereabouts with his divinations. He says then, that whoever has read the former part of this history, must needs remember that Gines de Pasamonte, to whom, among other galley-slaves, Don Quixote gave liberty in the Sierra Morena: a benefit for which afterwards he had small thanks, and worse payment, from

that mischievous and misbehaving crew. This Gines de Pasamonte, whom Don Quixote called Ginesillo de Parapilla,
was the person who stole Sancho Panza's Dapple; and the
not particularizing the when, nor the how, in the first part,
through the neglect of the printer, made many ascribe the
fault of the press to want of memory in the author.* But in
short, Gines stole him, while Sancho Panza was asleep upon
his back, making use of the same trick and device that
Brunello did, who, while Sacripante lay at the siege of
Albracca, stole his horse from between his legs; and afterwards Sancho recovered him, as has been already related.
This Gines then (being afraid of falling into the hands of
justice, which was in pursuit of him, in order to chastise him
for his numberless rogueries and crimes, which were so many
and so flagrant, that he himself wrote a large volume of them)
resolved to pass over to the kingdom of Aragon, and covering
his left eye, took up the trade of puppet-playing and leger-
demain, both of which he perfectly understood.

It fell out, that, lighting upon some Christian slaves redeemed from Barbary, he bought that ape, which he taught,
at a certain signal, to leap up on his shoulder, and, mutter
something, or seem to do so, in his ear. This done, before
he entered any town to which he was going with his show
and his ape, he informed himself in the next village, or where
he best could, what particular things had happened in such
and such a place, and to whom; and bearing them carefully
in his memory, the first thing he did was to exhibit his show,
which was sometimes of one story, and sometimes of another, but all pleasant, gay, and generally known. The show
ended, he used to propound the abilities of his ape, telling
the people, he divined all that was past and present: but as
to what was to come, he did not pretend to any skill therein.
He demanded two reals for answering each question, and to
some he afforded it cheaper, according as he found the pulse
of his clients beat; and coming sometimes to houses, where
he knew what had happened to the people that lived in them,
though they asked no question, because they would not pay
him, he gave the signal to his ape, and presently said, he told
him such and such a thing, which tallied exactly with what

had happened; whereby he gained infallible* credit, and was followed by everybody. At other times, being very cunning, he answered in such a manner, that his answers came pat to the questions; and as nobody went about to sift, or press him to tell how his ape divined, he gulled everybody, and filled his pockets. No sooner was he come into the inn, but he knew Don Quixote and Sancho; which made it very easy for him to excite the wonder of Don Quixote, Sancho, and all that were present. But it would have cost him dear, had Don Quixote directed his hand a little lower, when he cut off king Marsilio's head, and destroyed all his cavalry, as is related in the foregoing chapter. This is what offers concerning Master Peter and the ape.

And, returning to Don Quixote de la Mancha, I say, he determined, before he went to Saragossa, first to visit the banks of the river Ebro, and all the parts thereabouts, since he had time enough and to spare before the tournaments began. With this design he pursued his journey, and travelled two days without lighting on anything worth recording, till the third day, going up a hill, he heard a great noise of drums, trumpets, and guns. At first he thought some regiment of soldiers was marching that way, and he clapped spurs to Rosinante, and ascended the hill to see them; and, being got to the top, he perceived, as he thought, in the valley beneath, above two hundred men armed with various weapons, as spears, crossbows, partisans, halberds, and pikes, with some guns, and a great number of targets. He rode down the hill, and drew so near to the squadron, that he saw the banners distinctly, and distinguished their colours, and observed the devices they bore; especially one upon a banner or pennant of white satin, whereon was painted to the life an ass, of the little Sardinian breed, holding up its head, its mouth open, and its tongue out, in the act and posture, as it were, of braying, and round it these two verses written in large characters:

> The bailiffs twain
> Bray'd not in vain.

From this motto Don Quixote gathered, that these folks

must belong to the braying town, and so he told Sancho, telling him also what was written on the banner. He said also, that the person who had given an account of this affair, was mistaken in calling the two brayers aldermen, since, according to the motto, they were not aldermen but bailiffs. To which Sancho Panza answered:

'That breaks no squares, sir; for it may very well be, that the aldermen who brayed, might, in process of time, become bailiffs of their town, and therefore may properly be called by both those titles; though it signifies nothing to the truth of the history, whether the brayers were bailiffs or aldermen, so long as they both brayed; for a bailiff is as likely to bray as an alderman.'

In conclusion, they found, that the town derided was sallied forth to attack another, which had laughed at them too much, and beyond what was fitting for good neighbours.

Don Quixote advanced towards them, to the no small concern of Sancho, who never loved to make one in these kind of expeditions. Those of the squadron received him amongst them, taking him for some one of their party. Don Quixote, lifting up his visor, with an easy and graceful deportment, approached the ass-banner, and all the chiefs of the army gathered about him to look at him, being struck with the same admiration that everybody was the first time of seeing him. Don Quixote, seeing them so intent upon looking at him, without any one's speaking to him, or asking him any question, resolved to take advantage of this silence, and, breaking his own, he raised his voice, and said:

'Good gentlemen, I earnestly entreat you not to interrupt a discourse I shall make to you, till you find it disgusts or tires you; for, if that happens at the least sign you shall make, I will clap a seal on my lips, and gag upon my tongue.'

They all desired him to say what he pleased; for they would hear him with a very goodwill. With this licence Don Quixote proceeded, saying:

'I, gentlemen, am a knight-errant, whose exercise is that of arms, and whose profession that of succouring those, who stand in need of succour, and relieving the distressed. Some days ago I heard of your misfortune, and the cause that induces you to take arms at every turn to revenge yourselves on your enemies. And, having often pondered your business in my mind, I find, that, according to the laws of duel, you are mistaken in thinking yourselves affronted; for no one person can affront a whole town, unless it be by accusing them of treason conjointly, as not knowing in particular who committed the treason, of which he accuses them. An example of this we have in Don Diego Ordoñez de Lara, who challenged the whole people of Zamora, because he did not know, that Vellido Dolfos alone had committed the treason of killing his king; and therefore he challenged them all, and the revenge and answer belonged to them all; though it is very true, that Señor Don Diego went somewhat too far, and greatly exceeded the limits of challenging; for he needed not have challenged the dead, the waters, the bread, or the unborn, nor several other particularities mentioned in the challenge.* But let that pass; for, when choler overflows its dam, the tongue has no father, governor, nor bridle, to restrain it. This being so, then, that a single person cannot affront a kingdom, province, city, republic, or a whole town, it is clear, there is no reason for your marching out to revenge such an affront, since it is really none.

'Would it not be pretty indeed, if those of the town of Reloja* should endeavour to knock everybody's brains out, who calls them by their trade? and would it not be pleasant, if the cheesemongers, the costermongers, the fishmongers, and soap-boilers,* with those of several other names and appellations, which are in everybody's mouth, and common among the vulgar; would it not be fine indeed, if all these notable folks should be ashamed of their businesses, and be perpetually taking revenge, and making sackbuts of their swords upon every quarrel, though never so trivial?

'No, no, God neither permits nor wills it. Men of wisdom, and well-ordered commonwealths, ought to take arms, draw their swords, and hazard their lives and fortunes, upon four accounts: first, to defend the Catholic faith; secondly, to defend their lives, which is agreeable to the natural and divine law; thirdly, in defence of their honour, family, or estate; and fourthly, in the service of their king in a just war; and, if we

may add a fifth (which may be ranked with the second) it
is, in the defence of their country. To these five capital causes
several others might be added, very just and very reasonable,
and which oblige us to take arms. But to have recourse to
them for trifles, and things rather subjects for laughter and
pastime, than for affronts, looks like acting against common
sense. Besides, taking an unjust revenge (and no revenge can
be just) is acting directly against the holy religion we profess,
whereby we are commanded to do good to our enemies, and
to love those that hate us; a precept, which, though seemingly
difficult, is really not so, to any but those who have less of
God than of the world, and more of the flesh than of the
spirit; for Jesus Christ, true God and man, who never lied,
nor could, nor can lie, and who is our legislator, has told us,
"his yoke is easy, and his burden light": and therefore he
would not command us anything impossible to be performed.
So that, gentlemen, you are bound to be quiet and pacified
by all laws both divine and human.'

'The devil fetch me,' quoth Sancho to himself, 'if this
master of mine be not a tologue;* or, if not, he is as like
one, as one egg is like another.'

Don Quixote took breath a little; and, perceiving that they
still stood attentive, he had a mind to proceed in his discourse, and had certainly done so, had not Sancho's acuteness
interposed; who, observing that his master paused awhile,
took up the cudgels for him, saying:

'My master, Don Quixote de la Mancha, once called the
Knight of the Sorrowful Figure, and now the Knight of the
Lions, is a sage gentleman, and understands Latin and the
vulgar tongue like any bachelor of arts; and, in all he handles
or advises, proceeds like an expert soldier, having all the laws
and statutes of what is called duel at his fingers' ends: and
so there is no more to be done, but to govern yourselves by
his direction, and I will bear the blame if you do amiss:
besides, you are but just told, how foolish it is to be ashamed
to hear one bray. I remember, when I was a boy I brayed
as often as I pleased, without anybody's hindering me, and
with such grace and propriety, that, whenever I brayed, all
the asses of the town brayed: and for all that I did not cease

to be the son of my parents, who were very honest people; and, though for this rare ability I was envied by more than a few of the proudest of my neighbours, I cared not two farthings. And to convince you that I speak the truth, do but stay and hearken; for this science, like that of swimming, once learned, is never forgotten.'

Then, laying his hands to his nostrils, he began to bray so strenuously, that the adjacent valleys resounded again. But one of those, who stood close by him, believing he was making a mock of them, lifted up a pole he had in his hand, and gave him such a polt* with it, as brought Sancho Panza to the ground. Don Quixote, seeing Sancho so evil entreated, made at the striker with his lance; but so many interposed, that it was impossible for him to be revenged: on the contrary, finding a shower of stones come thick upon him, and a thousand crossbows presented, and as many guns levelled at him, he turned Rosinante about, and, as fast as he could gallop, got out from among them, recommending himself to God with all his heart, to deliver him from this danger, fearing at every step, lest some bullet should enter at his back and come out at his breast; and at every moment he fetched his breath, to try whether it failed him or not.

But those of the squadron were satisfied with seeing him fly, and did not shoot after him. As for Sancho, they set him again upon his ass, scarce come to himself, and suffered him to follow his master; not that he had sense to guide him; but Dapple naturally followed Rosinante's steps, not enduring to be a moment from him. Don Quixote, being got a good way off, turned about his head, and saw that Sancho followed; and, finding that nobody pursued him stopped till he came up.

Those of the squadron stayed there till night, and, the enemy not coming forth to battle, they returned to their own homes, joyful and merry; and, had they known the practice of the ancient Greeks, they would have erected a trophy in that place.

CHAPTER 28

Of things which, Ben Engeli says, he, who reads them, will know, if he reads them with attention.

WHEN the valiant flies, it is plain he is overmatched; for it is the part of the wise to reserve themselves for better occasions. This truth was verified in Don Quixote, who, giving way to the fury of the people, and to the evil intentions of that resentful squadron, took to his heels, and, without bethinking him of Sancho, or of the danger in which he left him, got as far on as he deemed sufficient for his safety. Sancho followed him athwart his beast, as has been said. At last he came up to him, having recovered his senses; and, at coming up, he fell from Dapple at the feet of Rosinante, all in anguish, all bruised, and all beaten. Don Quixote alighted to examine the wounds; but finding him whole from head to foot, with much choler he said:

'In an unlucky hour, Sancho, must you needs show your skill in braying; where did you learn, that it was fitting to name a halter in the house of a man that was hanged? To the music of braying, what a counterpoint could you expect but that of a cudgel? Give God thanks, Sancho, that, instead of crossing your back with a cudgel, they did not make the sign of the cross on you with a scimitar.'

'I am not now in a condition to answer,' replied Sancho; 'for methinks I speak through my shoulders: let us mount, and be gone from this place: as for braying, I will have done with it; but I shall not with telling that knights-errant fly, and leave their faithful squires to be beaten to powder by their enemies.'

'To retire is not to fly,' answered Don Quixote; 'for you must know, Sancho, that the valour which has not prudence for its basis, is termed rashness, and the exploits of the rash are ascribed rather to their good fortune, than their courage. I confess I did retire, but fled not; and herein I imitated sundry valiant persons, who have reserved themselves for better times; and of this histories are full of examples, which, being of no profit to you, or pleasure to me, I omit at present.'

By this time Sancho was mounted, with the assistance of Don Quixote, who likewise got upon Rosinante; and so fair and softly they took the way towards a grove of poplar, which they discovered about a quarter of a league off. Sancho every now and then fetched most profound sighs, and doleful groans. Don Quixote asking him the cause of such bitter moaning, he answered, that he was in pain from the lowest point of his backbone to the nape of his neck, in such manner that he was ready to swoon.

'The cause of this pain,' said Don Quixote, 'must doubtless be, that the pole they struck you with, being a long one, took in your whole back, where lie all the parts that give you pain, and, if it had reached farther, it would have pained you more.'

'Before God,' quoth Sancho, 'your worship has brought me out of a grand doubt, and explained it in very fine terms. Body of me, was the cause of my pain so hid, that it was necessary to tell me, that I felt pain in all those parts, which the pole reached? If my ankles ached, you might not perhaps so easily guess, why they pained me: but to divine, that I am pained because beaten, is no great business. In faith, master of mine, other men's harms hang by a hair: I descry land more and more every day, and what little I am to expect from keeping your worship company; for if this bout you let me be basted, we shall return again, and a hundred times again, to our old blanket-tossing, and other follies; which, if this time they have fallen upon my back, the next they will fall upon my eyes. It would be much better for me, but that I am a barbarian, and shall never do anything that is right while I live; I say again, it would be much better for me, to return to my own house, and to my wife and children, to maintain and bring them up with the little God shall be pleased to give me, and not be following your worship through roads without a road, and pathless paths, drinking ill, and eating worse. Then for sleeping, measure out, brother squire, seven foot of earth, and if that is not sufficient, take as many more: it is in your own power to dish up the mess, and stretch yourself out to your heart's content. I wish I may see the first, who set on foot knight-errantry, burnt to ashes, or at least the first that would needs be squire to such idiots

as all the knights-errant of former times must have been. I
say nothing of the present: for, your worship being one of
them, I am bound to pay them respect, and because I know
your worship knows a point beyond the devil in all you talk
and think.'

'I would lay a good wager with you, Sancho,' quoth Don
Quixote, 'that now you are talking, and without interruption,
you feel no pain in all your body. Talk on, my son, all that
comes into your thoughts, and whatever comes uppermost;
for, so you feel no pain, I shall take pleasure in the very
trouble your impertinences give me: and if you have so great
a desire to return home to your wife and children, God forbid
I should hinder you. You have money of mine in your hands:
see how long it is since we made this third sally from our
town, and how much you could or ought to get each month,
and pay yourself.'

'When I served Thomas Carrasco, father of the bachelor,
Sampson Carrasco, whom your worship knows full well,' said
Sancho, 'I got two ducats a month, besides my victuals: with
your worship I cannot tell what I may get: though I am sure
it is a greater drudgery to be squire to a knight-errant, than
servant to a farmer; for, in fine, we who serve husbandmen,
though we labour never so hard in the daytime, let the worst
come to the worst, at night we have a supper from the pot,
and we sleep in a bed, which is more than I have done since
I served your worship, excepting the short time we were at
Don Diego de Miranda's house, the good cheer I had with
the skimming of Camacho's pots, and what I ate, drank, and
slept, at Basilius's house. All the rest of the time I have lain
on the hard ground, in the open air, subject to what people
call the inclemencies of heaven, living upon bits of bread and
scraps of cheese, and drinking water, sometimes from the
brook, and sometimes from the fountain, such as we met
with up and down by the way.'

'I confess, Sancho,' quoth Don Quixote, 'that all you say
is true: how much think you I ought to give you more than
Thomas Carrasco gave you?'

'I think,' quoth Sancho, 'if your worship adds two reals a
month, I shall reckon myself well paid. This is to be under-

stood as to wages due for my labour; but as to the promise your worship made of bestowing on me the government of an island, it would be just and reasonable you should add six reals more, which makes thirty in all.'

'It is very well,' replied Don Quixote: 'according to the wages you have allotted yourself, it is five-and-twenty days since we sallied from our town; reckon, Sancho, in proportion, and see what I owe you, and pay yourself, as I have already said, with your own hand.'

'Body of me,' quoth Sancho, 'your worship is clean out in the reckoning; for as to the business of the promised island, we must compute from the day you promised me, to the present hour.'

'Why, how long is it I promised it you?' said Don Quixote.

'If I remember right,' answered Sancho, 'it is about twenty years and three days, more or less.'

Don Quixote gave himself a good clap on the forehead with the palm of his hand, and began to laugh very heartily, and said:

'Why, my rambling up and down the Sierra Morena, with the whole series of our sallies, scarce take up two months, and say you, Sancho, it is twenty years since I promised you the island? Well, I perceive you have a mind your wages should swallow up all the money you have of mine: if it be so, and such is your desire, from henceforward I give it you, and much good may it do you; for so I may get rid of so worthless a squire, I shall be glad to be left poor and penniless. But tell me, perverter of the squirely ordinances of knight-errantry, where have you seen or read, that any squire to a knight-errant, ever presumed to article with his master, and say, so much and so much per month you must give me to serve you? Launch, launch out, cut-throat scoundrel, and hobgoblin (for thou art all these) launch, I say, into the *mare magnum* of their histories, and, if you can find, that any squire has said or thought, what you have now said, I will give you leave to nail it on my forehead, and over and over to write fool upon my face in capitals. Turn about the bridle, or halter, of Dapple, and begone home; for one single step further you go not with me. O bread ill-bestowed! O

promises ill-placed! O man, that has more of the beast than
of the human creature! Now when I thought of settling you,
and in such a way, that, in spite of your wife, you should
have been styled Your lordship, do you now leave me? now
you are for going, when I have taken a firm and effectual
resolution to make you lord of the best island in the world?
But, as you yourself have often said, honey is not for an ass's
mouth. An ass you are, an ass you will continue to be, and
an ass you will die; for I verily believe, your life will reach
its final period before you will perceive or be convinced that
you are a beast.'

Sancho looked very wistfully at Don Quixote all the while
he was thus rating him: and so great was the compunction
he felt, that the tears stood in his eyes, and, with a doleful
and faint voice, he said:

'Dear sir, I confess, that to be a complete ass, I want
nothing but a tail: if your worship will be pleased to put me
one on, I shall deem it well placed, and will serve your
worship in the quality of an ass, all the remaining days of
my life. Pardon me, sir, have pity on my ignorance, and
consider, that, if I talk much, it proceeds more from infirmity
than malice: but, he who errs and mends, himself to God
commends.'

'I should wonder, Sancho,' quoth Don Quixote, 'if you did
not mingle some little proverb with your talk. Well, I forgive
you, upon condition of your amendment, and that henceforward you show not yourself so fond of your interest, but
that you endeavour to enlarge your heart, take courage, and
strengthen your mind to expect the accomplishment of my
promises, which, though they are deferred, are not therefore
desperate.'

Sancho answered, he would, though he should draw force
from his weakness.

Hereupon they entered the poplar-grove. Don Quixote
accommodated himself at the foot of an elm, and Sancho at
the foot of a beech; for these kind of trees and such like
have always feet, but never hands. Sancho passed the night
uneasily, the cold renewing the pain of his bruises. Don
Quixote passed it in his wonted meditations: but for all that

they both slept, and at break of day they pursued their way
towards the banks of the famous Ebro, where there befell
them what shall be related in the ensuing chapter.

CHAPTER 29

Of the famous adventure of the enchanted bark.

IN two days, after leaving the poplar-grove, Don Quixote
and Sancho, travelling as softly as foot could fall, came to
the river Ebro, the sight of which gave Don Quixote great
pleasure, while he saw and contemplated the verdure of its
banks, the clearness of its waters, the smoothness of its
current, and the abundance of its liquid crystal: which cheerful prospect brought to his remembrance a thousand amorous
thoughts; and particularly he mused upon what he had seen
in the cave of Montesinos: for though Master Peter's ape had
told him, that part of those things was true, and part false,
he inclined rather to believe all true than false, quite the
reverse of Sancho, who held them all for falsehood itself.

Now, as they sauntered along in this manner, they perceived a small bark, without oars, or any sort of tackle, tied
to the trunk of a tree, which grew on the brink of the river.
Don Quixote looked round about him everyway, and, seeing
nobody at all, without more ado alighted from Rosinante,
and ordered Sancho to do the like from Dapple, and to tie
both the beasts very fast to the body of a poplar or willow,
which grew there. Sancho asked the reason of this hasty
alighting and tying. Don Quixote answered:

'You are to know, Sancho, that this vessel lies here for no
other reason in the world but to invite me to embark in it,
in order to succour some knight, or other person of high
degree, who is in extreme distress; for such is the practice
of enchanters in the books of chivalry, when some knight
happens to be engaged in some difficulty, from which he
cannot be delivered, but by the hand of another knight. Then,
though they are distant from each other two or three thousand leagues, and even more, they either snatch him up in a

cloud, or furnish him with a boat to embark in; and in less
than the twinkling of an eye they carry him, through the air,
or over the sea, whither they list, and where his assistance is
wanted. So that, O Sancho, this bark must be placed here
for the selfsame purpose: and this is as true, as that it is now
day; and, before it be spent, tie Dapple and Rosinante
together, and the hand of God be our guide; for I would
not fail to embark, though barefooted friars themselves
should entreat me to the contrary.'

'Since it is so,' answered Sancho, 'and that your worship
will every step be running into these same (how shall I call
them?) extravagances, there is no way but to obey, and bow
the head, giving heed to the proverb: "Do what your master
bids you, and sit down by him at table." But for all that, as
to what pertains to the discharge of my conscience, I must
warn your worship, that to me this boat seems not to belong
to the enchanted, but to some fishermen upon the river; for
here they catch the best shads in the world.'

All this Sancho said while he was tying the cattle, leaving
them to the protection and care of enchanters with sufficient
grief of his soul. Don Quixote bade him be in no pain about
forsaking those beasts: for he, who was to carry themselves
through ways and regions of such longitude, would take care
to feed them.

'I do not understand your longitudes,' said Sancho, 'nor
have I heard such a word in all the days of my life.'

'Longitude,' replied Don Quixote, 'means length, and no
wonder you do not understand it; for you are not bound to
know Latin; though some there are, who pretend to know
it, and are quite as ignorant as yourself.'

'Now they are tied,' quoth Sancho, 'what must we do next?'

'What?' answered Don Quixote: 'why, bless ourselves, and
weigh anchor; I mean, embark ourselves, and cut the rope
wherewith the vessel is tied.'

And, leaping into it, Sancho following him, he cut the cord,
and the boat fell off by little and little from the shore; and
when Sancho saw himself about a couple of yards from the
bank, he began to quake, fearing he should be lost: but
nothing troubled him more than to hear his ass bray, and to

see Rosinante struggling to get loose; and he said to his
master:

'The ass brays as bemoaning our absence, and Rosinante
is endeavouring to get loose, to throw himself into the river
after us. O dearest friends, abide in peace, and may the
madness, which separates you from us, converted into a
conviction of our error, return us to your presence!'

And here he began to weep so bitterly, that Don Quixote
grew angry, and said:

'What are you afraid of, cowardly creature? What weep you
for, heart of butter? Who pursues, who hurts you, soul of a
house-rat? Or what want you, poor wretch, in the midst of
the bowels of abundance? Art thou, peradventure, trudging
barefoot over the Riphean mountains?* No, but seated upon
a bench, like an archduke, sliding easily down the stream of
this charming river, whence in a short space we shall issue
out into the boundless ocean. But doubtless we are got out
already, and must have gone at least seven or eight hundred
leagues. If I had here an astrolabe, to take the elevation of
the pole, I would tell you how many we have gone; though
either I know little, or we are already past, or shall presently
pass, the equinoctial line, which divides and cuts the opposite
poles at equal distances.'

'And when we arrive at that line your worship speaks of,'
quoth Sancho, 'how far shall we have travelled?'

'A great way,' replied Don Quixote: 'for, of three hundred
and sixty degrees, contained in the terraqueous globe, according to the computation of Ptolemy, the greatest geographer
we know of, we shall have travelled one half, when we come
to the line I told you of.'

'By the lord,' quoth Sancho, 'your worship has brought a
very pretty fellow, that same Tolmy (how d'ye call him?)*
with his amputation, to vouch the truth of what you say.'

Don Quixote smiled at Sancho's blunders as to the name
and computation of the geographer Ptolemy, and said:

'You must know, Sancho, that one of the signs, by which
the Spaniards, and those who embark at Cadiz for the East
Indies, discover whether they have passed the equinoctial line
I told you of, is, that all the lice upon every man in the ship

die, not one remaining alive; nor is one to be found in the vessel, though they would give its weight in gold for it; and therefore, Sancho, pass your hand over your thigh, and if you light upon anything alive, we shall be out of this doubt, and, if not, we have passed the line.'

'I believe nothing of all this,' answered Sancho: 'but for all that I will do as your worship bids me, though I do not know what occasion there is for making this experiment, since I see with my own eyes, that we are not got five yards from the bank, nor fallen two yards below our cattle: for yonder stand Rosinante and Dapple in the very place where we left them; and, taking aim as I do now, I vow to God we do not stir nor move an ant's pace.'

'Sancho,' said Don Quixote, 'make the trial I bid you, and take no further care; for you know not what things colures are, nor what are lines, parallels, zodiacs, ecliptics, poles, solstices, equinoctials, planets, signs, points, and measures, of which the celestial and terrestrial globes are composed; for, if you knew all these things, or but a part of them, you would plainly perceive what parallels we have cut, what signs we have seen, and what constellations we have left behind us, and are just now leaving. And once more I bid you feel yourself all over, and fish: for I, for my part, am of opinion you are as clean as a sheet of paper, smooth and white.'

Sancho carried his hand softly and gently towards his left ham, and then lifted up his head, and, looking at his master, said:

'Either the experiment is false, or we are not arrived where your worship says, not by a great many leagues.'

'Why,' quoth Don Quixote, 'have you met with something then?'

'Aye, several somethings,' answered Sancho, and shaking his fingers, he washed his whole hand in the river, down whose current the boat was gently gliding, not moved by any secret influence, nor by any concealed enchanter, but merely by the stream of the water, then smooth and calm.

By this time they discovered certain large watermills, standing in the midst of the river; and scarce had Don Quixote espied them, when he said with a loud voice to Sancho:

'O friend, behold! yonder appears the city, castle, or fortress, in which some knight lies under oppression, or some queen, infanta, or princess in evil plight; for whose relief I am brought hither.'

'What the devil of a city, fortress, or castle do you talk of, sir?' quoth Sancho, 'do you not perceive that they are mills standing in the river for the grinding of corn?'

'Peace, Sancho,' quoth Don Quixote, 'for, though they seem to be mills, they are not so: I have already told you, that enchantments transform and change all things from their natural shape. I do not say they change them really from one thing to another, but only in appearance, as experience showed us in the transformation of Dulcinea, the sole refuge of my hopes.'

The boat being now got into the current of the river, began to move a little faster than it had done hitherto. The millers seeing it coming adrift with the stream, and that it was just going into the mouth of the swift stream of the mill-wheels, several of them ran out in all haste with long poles to stop it; and their faces and clothes being covered with meal, they made but an ill appearance; and calling out aloud, they said:

'Devils of men, where are you going? are ye desperate, that ye have a mind to drown yourselves, or be ground to pieces by the wheels?'

'Did I not tell you,' Sancho, said Don Quixote, at this juncture, 'that we are come where I must demonstrate how far the valour of my arm extends? look what a parcel of murderers and felons come out against me: see what hobgoblins to oppose us, and what ugly countenances to scare us. Now ye shall see, rascals.'

And standing up in the boat, he began to threaten the millers aloud, saying:

'Ill-led and worse-advised scoundrels, set at liberty and free the person you keep under oppression in this your fortress or prison, whether of high or low degree: for I am Don Quixote de la Mancha, otherwise called the Knight of the Lions, for whom by order of the high heavens, the putting an happy end to this adventure is reserved.'

And, so saying, he clapped his hand to his sword, and

began to fence with it in the air against the millers, who, hearing, but not understanding these foolish flourishes, set themselves with their poles to stop the boat, which was just entering into the stream and eddy of the wheels. Sancho fell upon his knees, and prayed to heaven devoutly to deliver him from so apparent a danger; which it did by the diligence and agility of the millers, who setting their poles against the boat, stopped it; though not so dexterously, but that they overset it, and tipped Don Quixote and Sancho into the water. It was well for Don Quixote that he knew how to swim like a goose; nevertheless the weight of his armour carried him twice to the bottom; and had it not been for the millers, who threw themselves into the river, and as it were, craned them both up, they must have inevitably perished.

When they were dragged on shore, more wet than thirsty, Sancho, kneeling, with hands joined and eyes uplifted, besought God, in a long and devout prayer, to deliver him thenceforward from the daring desires and enterprises of his master. And now came the fishermen, owners of the boat, which the mill-wheels had crushed to pieces: and, seeing it broke, they began to strip Sancho, and demand payment for it of Don Quixote, who, with great tranquillity, as if nothing had befallen him, told the millers and the fishermen, he would pay for the boat with all his heart, upon condition they should deliver up to him, free and without ransom, the person, or persons, who lay under oppression in their castle.

'What persons, or what castle do you mean, madman?' answered one of the millers: 'Would you carry off those, who came to grind their corn at our mills?'

'Enough,' thought Don Quixote to himself, 'it will be preaching in the desert, to endeavour, by treaty, to prevail with such mob to do anything that is honourable: and, in this adventure, two able enchanters must have engaged, the one frustrating what the other attempts, the one providing me a bark, and the other oversetting it: God help us! this world is nothing but machinations and tricks quite opposite one to the other: I can do no more.'

Then looking towards the mills, he raised his voice, and said:

'Friends, whoever you are that are enclosed in this prison, pardon me, that, through my misfortune and yours, I cannot deliver you from your affliction; this adventure is kept and reserved for some other knight.'

Having said this, he compounded with the fishermen, and paid fifty reals for the boat, which Sancho disbursed much against his will, saying:

'A couple more of such embarkations will sink our whole capital.'

The fishermen and millers stood wondering at these two figures, so out of the fashion and semblance of other men, not being able to comprehend what Don Quixote drove at by his questions, and the discourse he held with him: and looking upon them as madmen, they left them, and betook themselves to their mills, and the fishermen to their huts. Don Quixote and Sancho, like beasts themselves, returned to their beasts; and thus ended the adventure of the enchanted bark.

CHAPTER 30

Of what befell Don Quixote with a fair huntress.

SUFFICIENTLY melancholy, and out of humour, arrived at their cattle the knight and squire; especially Sancho, who was grieved to the very soul to touch the capital of the money, all that was taken from thence seeming to him to be so much taken from the very apples of his eyes. In conclusion, they mounted, without exchanging a word, and quitted the famous river: Don Quixote buried in the thoughts of his love, and Sancho in those of his preferment, which he thought, for the present, far enough off: for, as much a blockhead as he was, he saw well enough, that most, or all of his master's actions were extravagances, and waited for an opportunity, without coming to accounts or discharges, to walk off some day or other, and march home. But fortune ordered matters quite contrary to what he feared.

It fell out then, that the next day, about sunset, and at going out of a wood, Don Quixote cast his eyes over a green meadow, and saw people at the farther side of it: and drawing near, he found they were persons taking the diversions of hawking. Drawing yet nearer, he observed among them a gallant lady upon a palfrey, or milk-white pad,* with green furniture, and a side-saddle of cloth-of-silver. The lady herself was arrayed in green, and her attire so full of fancy, and so rich, that fancy herself seemed transformed into her. On her left hand she carried a hawk: from whence Don Quixote conjectured she must be a lady of great quality, and mistress of all those sportsmen about her, as in truth she was: and so he said to Sancho:

'Run, son Sancho, and tell that lady of the palfrey and the hawk, that I, the Knight of the Lions, kiss the hands of her great beauty, and, if her highness gives me leave, I will wait upon her to kiss them, and to serve her to the utmost of my power, in whatever her highness shall command: and take heed, Sancho, how you speak, and have a care not to interlard your embassy with any of your proverbs.'

'You have hit upon the interlarder,' quoth Sancho: 'why this to me? as if this were the first time I had carried a message to high and mighty ladies in my life.'

'Excepting that to the lady Dulcinea,' replied Don Quixote, 'I know of none you have carried, at least none for me.'

'That is true,' answered Sancho; 'but a good paymaster needs no surety; and where there is plenty, dinner is not long a dressing: I mean, there is no need of advising me; for I am prepared for all, and have a smattering of everything.'

'I believe it, Sancho,' quoth Don Quixote: 'go in a good hour, and God be your guide.'

Sancho went off at a round rate, forcing Dapple out of his usual pace, and came where the fair huntress was; and, alighting, and kneeling before her, he said:

'Beauteous lady, that knight yonder, called the Knight of the Lions, is my master, and I am his squire, called at home, Sancho Panza. This same Knight of the Lions, who not long ago was called he of the Sorrowful Figure, sends by me to desire your grandeur would be pleased to give leave, that, with your liking, goodwill, and consent, he may approach and accomplish his wishes, which, as he says, and I believe, are no other than to serve your high-towering falconry and beauty; which, if your ladyship grant him, you will do a thing that will redound to your grandeur's advantage, and he will receive a most signal favour and satisfaction.'

'Truly, good squire,' answered the lady, 'you have delivered your message with all the circumstances which such embassies require: rise up, for it is not fit the squire of so renowned a knight as he of the Sorrowful Figure (of whom we have already heard a great deal in these parts) should remain upon his knees: rise, friend, and tell your master, he may come and welcome; for I and the duke, my spouse, are at his service, in a country seat we have here hard by.'

Sancho rose up, in admiration as well at the good lady's beauty, as at her great breeding and courtesy, and especially at what she had said, that she had some knowledge of his master, the Knight of the Sorrowful Figure; and, if she did not call him the Knight of the Lions, he concluded it was because he had assumed it so very lately. The duchess (whose title is not yet known) said to him:

'Tell me, brother squire, is not this master of yours the person, of whom there goes about a history in print, called *The Ingenious Gentleman Don Quixote de la Mancha*, who has for mistress of his affections one Dulcinea del Toboso?'

'The very same,' answered Sancho: 'and that squire of his, who is, or ought to be, in that same history, called Sancho Panza, am I, unless I was changed in the cradle, I mean in the press.'

'I am very glad of all this,' quoth the duchess: 'go, brother Panza, and tell your master, he is heartily welcome to my estates, and that nothing could happen to me, which could give me greater pleasure.'

With this agreeable answer, Sancho, infinitely delighted, returned to his master, to whom he recounted all that the great lady had said to him, extolling, in his rustic phrase, her beauty, her good humour, and her courtesy, to the skies. Don Quixote, putting on his best airs, seated himself handsomely in his saddle, adjusted his visor, enlivened Rosinante's mettle, and with a genteel assurance advanced to kiss the duchess's hand; who, having caused the duke her husband to be called, had been telling him, while Don Quixote was coming up, the purport of Sancho's message; and they both, having read the first part of this history, and having learned by it the extravagant humour of Don Quixote, waited for him with the greatest pleasure, and desire to be acquainted with him, and a purpose of carrying on the humour, and giving him his own way, treating him like a knight-errant all the while he should stay with them, with all the ceremonies usual in books of chivalry, which they had read, and were also very fond of.

By this time Don Quixote was arrived, with his beaver up; and making a show of alighting, Sancho was hastening to hold his stirrup, but was so unlucky, that, in getting off from Dapple, his foot hung in one of the rope-stirrups, in such a manner, that it was impossible for him to disentangle himself! but he hung by it with his face and breast on the ground. Don Quixote, who was not used to alight without having his stirrup held, thinking Sancho was come to do his office, threw his body off with a swing, and carrying with him Rosinante's saddle, which was ill girthed, both he and the saddle came to the ground, to his no small shame, and many a heavy curse muttered between his teeth on the unfortunate Sancho, who still had his legs in the stocks.

The duke commanded some of his sportsmen to help the knight and squire, who raised up Don Quixote in ill plight through this fall; and limping, and as well as he could, he made shift to go and kneel before the lord and lady. But the duke would by no means suffer it: on the contrary, alighting from his horse, he went and embraced Don Quixote, saying:

'I am very sorry, Sir Knight of the Sorrowful Figure, that your first arrival at my estate should prove so unlucky: but the carelessness of squires is often the occasion of worse mischances.'

'It could not be accounted unlucky, O valorous prince,' answered Don Quixote, 'though I had met with no stop till I had fallen to the bottom of that deep abyss: for the glory of having seen your highness would have raised me even from thence. My squire, God's curse light on him, is better at letting loose his tongue to say unlucky things, than at fastening a saddle to make it sit firm: but whether down or up, on foot or on horseback, I shall always be at your highness's service, and at my lady duchess's, your worthy consort, and worthy mistress of all beauty and universal princess of courtesy.'

'Softly, dear Señor Don Quixote de la Mancha,' quoth the duke; 'for where lady Doña Dulcinea del Toboso is, it is not reasonable other beauties should be praised.'

Sancho Panza was now got free from the noose; and happening to be near, before his master could answer, he said:

'It cannot be denied, but must be affirmed, that my lady Dulcinea del Toboso is very beautiful; but where we are least aware, there starts the hare. I have heard say, that what they call nature is like a potter, who makes earthen vessels, and he, who makes one handsome vessel, may also make two, and three, and a hundred. This I say, because, on my faith, my lady the duchess comes not a whit behind my mistress the lady Dulcinea del Toboso.'

Don Quixote turned himself to the duchess, and said:

'I assure you, madam, never any knight-errant in the world had a more prating, nor a more merry conceited squire, than I have; and he will make my words good, if your highness is pleased to make use of my service for some days.'

To which the duchess answered:

'I am glad to hear that honest Sancho is pleasant: it is a sign he is discreet: for pleasantry and good humour, Señor Don Quixote, as your worship well knows, dwell not in dull noddles: and since Sancho is pleasant and witty, from henceforward I pronounce him discreet.'

'And a prate apace,' added Don Quixote.

'So much the better,' quoth the duchess; 'for many good things cannot be expressed in few words, and, that we may not throw away all our time upon them, come on, great Knight of the Sorrowful Figure.'

'Of the Lions, your highness should say,' quoth Sancho: 'the Sorrowful Figure is no more.'

'Of the Lions then let it be,' continued the duke: 'I say, come on, Sir Knight of the Lions, to a castle of mine hard by, where you shall be received in a manner suitable to a person of so elevated a rank, and as the duchess and I are wont to receive all knights-errant, who come to it.'

By this time Sancho had adjusted and well girthed Rosinante's saddle, and Don Quixote, mounting upon him, and the duke upon a very fine horse, they placed the duchess in the middle, and rode towards the castle. The duchess ordered Sancho to be near her, being mightily delighted with his conceits. Sancho was easily prevailed upon, and winding himself in among the three, made a fourth in the conversation, to the great satisfaction of the duke and duchess, who looked upon it as a notable piece of good fortune, to entertain in their castle such a knight-errant, and such an erred-squire.

CHAPTER 31

Which treats of many and great things.

EXCESSIVE was the joy which Sancho conceived to see himself, in his thinking, a favourite of the duchess's; expecting to find in her castle the same as at Don Diego's or Basilius's; for he was always a lover of good cheer, and consequently took every opportunity of regaling himself by the forelock, where, and whenever it presented.

Now, the history relates, that, before they came to the pleasure-house, or castle, the duke rode on before, and gave all his servants their cue, in what manner they were to behave to Don Quixote; who arriving with the duchess at the castle gate, immediately there issued out two lackeys or grooms, clad in a kind of morning-gowns of fine crimson satin down to their heels; and taking Don Quixote in their arms, without being observed, said to him:

'Go, great sir, and take our lady the duchess off her horse.'

Don Quixote did so, and great compliments passed between them thereupon. But, in short, the duchess's positiveness got the better, and she would not alight, nor descend from her palfrey, but into the duke's arm, saying, she did not think herself worthy to charge so grand a knight with so unprofitable a burden. At length the duke came out, and took her off her horse: and at their entering into a large courtyard, two beautiful damsels came, and threw over Don Quixote's shoulders a large mantle of the finest scarlet, and, in an instant, all the galleries of the courtyard were crowded with men- and women-servants belonging to the duke and duchess, crying aloud:

'Welcome the flower and cream of knights-errant!'

And all or most of them sprinkled whole bottles of sweet-scented waters upon Don Quixote, and on the duke and duchess; at all which Don Quixote wondered; and this was the first day that he was thoroughly convinced* of his being a true knight-errant, and not an imaginary one, finding himself treated just as he had read knights-errant were in former times.

Sancho, abandoning Dapple, tacked himself close to the duchess, and entered into the castle; but, his conscience soon pricking him for leaving his ass alone, he approached a reverend duenna, who, among others, came up to receive the duchess, and said to her in a whisper:

'Mistress Gonzalez, or, what is your duennaship's name?'

'Doña Rodriguez de Grijalva,' answered the duenna: 'what would you please to have with me, brother?'

To which Sancho answered:

'Be so good, sweetheart, as to step to the castle gate, where you will find a dapple ass of mine: and be so kind as to order him to be put, or put him yourself, into the stable; for the poor thing is a little timorous, and cannot abide to be alone by any means in the world.'

'If the master be as discreet as the man,' answered the duenna, 'we are finely thriven. Go, brother, in an evil hour for you and him that brought you hither, and make account, you and your beast, that the duennas of this house are not accustomed to such kind offices.'

'Why truly,' answered Sancho, 'I have heard my master, who is the very mine-finder of histories, relating the story of Lancelot, when he from Britain came, say, that ladies took care of his person, and duennas of his horse;* and, as to the particular of my ass, I would not change him for Señor Lancelot's steed.'

'If you are a buffoon, brother,' replied the duenna, 'keep your jokes for some place where they may make a better figure, and where you may be paid for them; for from me you will get nothing but a fig for them.'

'That is pretty well, however,' answered Sancho; 'for I am sure then it will be a ripe one, there being no danger of your losing the game of your years for want of a trick.'

'You son of a whore,' cried the duenna, all on fire with rage, 'whether I am old or no, to God I am to give an account, and not to you, rascal, garlic-eating stinkard.'

This she uttered so loud, that the duchess heard it, and turning about, and seeing the duenna so disturbed, and her eyes red as blood, asked her with whom she was so angry?

'With this good man here,' answered the duenna, 'who has desired me in good earnest to go and set up an ass of his that stands at the castle gate; bringing me for a precedent, that the same thing was done, I know not where, by one Lancelot, and telling me how certain ladies looked after him, and certain duennas after his steed; and to mend the matter, in mannerly terms called me old woman.'

'I should take that for the greatest affront that could be offered me,' answered the duchess; and, speaking to Sancho, she said:

'Be assured, friend Sancho, that Doña Rodriguez is very young, and wears those veils more for authority and the fashion than upon account of her years.'

'May the remainder of those I have to live never prosper,' answered Sancho, 'if I meant her any ill: I only said it, because the tenderness I have for my ass is so great, that I thought I could not recommend him to a more charitable person, than to Señora Doña Rodriguez.'

Don Quixote, who overheard all, said:

'Are these discourses, Sancho, fit for this place?'

'Sir,' answered Sancho, 'every one must speak of his wants, be he where he will. Here I bethought me of Dapple, and here I spoke of him; and if I had thought of him in the stable, I had spoken of him there.'

To which the duke said:

'Sancho is very much in the right, and is not to be blamed in anything: Dapple shall have provender to his heart's content; and let Sancho take no further care, for he shall be treated like his own person.'

With these discourses, pleasing to all but Don Quixote, they mounted the stairs, and conducted Don Quixote into a great hall, hung with rich tissue and cloth-of-gold and brocade. Six damsels unarmed him, and served him as pages, all instructed and tutored by the duke and duchess what they were to do, and how they were to behave towards Don Quixote, that he might imagine and see they used him like a knight-errant. Don Quixote, being unarmed, remained in his straight breeches and chamois doublet, lean, tall, and stiff, with his jaws meeting, and kissing each other on the inside: such a figure, that, if the damsels who waited upon him, had not taken care to contain themselves (that being one of the precise orders given them by their lord and lady) they had burst with laughing.

They desired he would suffer himself to be undressed, and put on a clean shirt; but he would by no means consent, saying, That modesty was as becoming a knight-errant as courage. However, he bade them give Sancho the shirt; and shutting himself up with him in a room, where stood a rich bed, he pulled off his clothes, and put on the shirt; and, finding himself alone with Sancho, he said to him:

'Tell me, modern buffoon, and antique blockhead, do you think it a becoming thing to dishonour and affront a duenna so venerable and so worthy of respect? Was that a time to think of Dapple? Or are these gentry likely to let our beasts fare poorly, who treat their owners elegantly? For the love of God, Sancho, refrain yourself, and do not discover the grain, lest it should be seen of how coarse a country web you are spun. Look you, sinner, the master is so much the more esteemed, by how much his servants are civiller and better bred: and one of the greatest advantages great persons have over other men, is, that they employ servants as good as themselves. Did you not consider, pitiful thou, and unhappy me, that, if people perceive you are a gross peasant or a ridiculous fool, they will be apt to think I am some gross cheat, or some knight of the sharping order? No, no, friend Sancho, avoid, avoid these inconveniences; for whoever sets up for a talker and a railer, at the first trip, tumbles down into a disgraced buffoon. Bridle your tongue, consider, and deliberate upon your words, before they go out of your mouth; and take notice, we are come to a place, from whence, by the help of God, and the valour of my arm, we may depart bettered three- or even five-fold in fortune and reputation.' Sancho promised him faithfully to sew up his mouth, or bite his tongue, before he spoke a word that was not to the purpose, and well considered, as he commanded him, and that he need be under no pain as to that matter, for no discovery should be made to his prejudice by him.

Don Quixote then dressed himself, girt on his sword, threw the scarlet mantle over his shoulders, put on a green satin cap, which the damsels had given him, and thus equipped, marched out into the great saloon, where he found the damsels drawn up in two ranks, as many on one side as the other, and all of them provided with an equipage for washing his hands, which they administered with many reverences and ceremonies. Then came twelve pages, with the gentlemen-server, to conduct him to dinner, where by this time the lord and lady were waiting for him. They placed him in the middle of them, and, with great pomp and majesty, conducted him to another hall, where a rich table was spread with four covers only.

The duke and duchess came to the hall-door to receive him, and with them a grave ecclesiastic, one of those who govern great men's houses; one of those, who, not being princes born, know not how to instruct those that are how to demean themselves as such; one of those, who would have the magnificence of the great measured by the narrowness of their own minds; one of those, who, pretending to teach those they govern to be frugal, teach them to be misers. One of this sort, I say, was the grave ecclesiastic, who came out with the duke to receive Don Quixote. A thousand polite compliments passed upon this occasion; and, taking Don Quixote between them, they went and sat down to table. The duke offered Don Quixote the upper end, and, though he would have declined it, the importunities of the duke prevailed upon him to accept it. The ecclesiastic seated himself over against him, and the duke and duchess on each side. Sancho was present all the while, surprised and astonished to see the honour those princes did his master, and, perceiving the many entreaties and ceremonies which passed between the duke and Don Quixote, to make him sit down at the head of the table, he said:

'If your honours will give me leave, I will tell you a story of a passage that happened in our town concerning places.'

Scarce had Sancho said this, when Don Quixote began to tremble, believing, without doubt, he was going to say some foolish thing. Sancho observed, and understood him, and said:

'Be not afraid, sir, of my breaking loose, or of my saying anything that is not pat to the purpose: I have not forgotten the advice your worship gave me a while ago, about talking much or little, well or ill.'

'I remember nothing, Sancho,' answered Don Quixote: 'say what you will, so you say it quickly.'

'What I would say,' quoth Sancho, 'is very true, and, should it be otherwise, my master Don Quixote, who is present, will not suffer me to lie.'

'Lie as much as you will for me, Sancho,' replied Don Quixote: 'I will not be your hindrance; but take heed what you are going to say.'

'I have so heeded, and reheeded it,' quoth Sancho, 'that all is as safe as the repique in hand, as you will see by the operation.'

'It will be convenient,' said Don Quixote, 'that your honours order this blockhead to be turned out of doors; for he will be making a thousand foolish blunders.'

'By the life of the duke,' quoth the duchess, 'Sancho shall not stir a jot from me: I love him much; for I know he is mighty discreet.'

'Many [discreet] years,' quoth Sancho, 'may your holiness live, for the good opinion you have of me, though it is not in me: but the tale I would tell is this:

'A certain gentleman of our town, very rich, and of a good

family—for he was descended from the Alamos of Medina del Campo, and married Doña Mencia de Quiñones, who was daughter of Don Alonso de Marañon, Knight of the Order of Santiago, who was drowned in the Herradura;* about whom there happened that quarrel in our town some years ago, in which, as I take it, my master, Don Quixote, was concerned, and Tommy the madcap, son of Balvastro the smith, was hurt—Pray, good master of mine, is not all this true? Speak, by your life, that these gentlemen may not take me for some lying prating fellow.'

'Hitherto,' said the ecclesiastic, 'I take you rather for a prater, than for a liar: but henceforward I know not what I shall take you for.'

'You produce so many evidences, and so many tokens, that I cannot but say,' quoth Don Quixote, 'it is likely you tell the truth: go on, and shorten the story; for you take the way not to have done in two days.'

'He shall shorten nothing,' quoth the duchess; 'and, to please me, he shall tell it his own way, though he have not done in six days; and should it take up so many, they would be to me the most agreeable of any I ever spent in my life.'

'I say then, sirs,' proceeded Sancho, 'that this same gentleman, whom I know as well as I do my right hand from my left (for it is not a bow-shot from my house to his) invited a farmer, who was poor, but honest, to dinner.'

'Proceed, friend,' said the ecclesiastic, at this period; 'for you are going the way with your tale not to stop till you come to the other world.'

'I shall stop before we get half way thither, if it pleases God,' answered Sancho; 'and so I proceed. This same farmer, coming to the said gentleman-inviter's house—God rest his soul, for he is dead and gone, by the same token it is reported he died like an angel; for I was not by, being at that time gone a reaping to Tembleque.'

'Prithee, son,' said the ecclesiastic, 'come back quickly from Tembleque, and, without burying the gentleman (unless you have a mind to make more burials) make an end of your tale.'

'The business then,' quoth Sancho, 'was this, that they

being ready to sit down to table—methinks I see them now more than ever.'

The duke and duchess took great pleasure in seeing the displeasure the good ecclesiastic suffered by the length and pauses of Sancho's tale; but Don Quixote was quite angry and vexed.

'I say then,' quoth Sancho, 'that they both standing, as I have said, and just ready to sit down, the farmer disputed obstinately with the gentleman to take the upper end of the table, and the gentleman, with as much positiveness, pressed the farmer to take it, saying he ought to command in his own house. But the countryman, piquing himself upon his civility and good breeding, would by no means sit down, till the gentleman, in a fret, laying both his hands upon the farmer's shoulders, made him sit down by main force, saying: "Sit thee down, chaff-threshing churl; for let me sit where I will, that is the upper end to thee." This is my tale, and truly I believe it was brought in here pretty much to the purpose.'

The natural brown of Don Quixote's face was speckled with a thousand colours. The duke and duchess dissembled their laughter, that Don Quixote might not be quite abashed, he having understood Sancho's slyness: and to waive the discourse, and prevent Sancho's running into more impertinences, the duchess asked Don Quixote what news he had of the lady Dulcinea, and whether he had lately sent her any presents of giants or caitiffs, since he must certainly have vanquished a great many. To which Don Quixote answered:

'My misfortunes, madam, though they have had a beginning, will never have an end. Giants I have conquered, and caitiffs, and have sent several; but where should they find her, if she be enchanted, and transformed into the ugliest country-wench that can be imagined?'

'I know not,' quoth Sancho Panza; 'to me she appeared the most beautiful creature in the world: at least, in activity, or a certain spring she has with her, I am sure she will not yield the advantage to a tumbler. In good faith, lady duchess, she bounces from the ground upon an ass as if she were a cat.'

'Have you seen her enchanted, Sancho?' quoth the duke.

'Seen her?' answered Sancho: 'who the devil but I was the first that hit upon the business of her enchantment? She is as much enchanted as my father.'

The ecclesiastic, when he heard talk of giants, caitiffs, and enchantments, began to suspect that this must be Don Quixote de la Mancha, whose history the duke was commonly reading; and he had as frequently reproved him for so doing, telling him it was extravagance to read such extravagances: and, being assured of the truth of his suspicion, with much choler he said to the duke:

'Your excellency, sir, shall give an account to God for what this good man is doing. This Don Quixote, or Don Coxcomb, or how do you call him, I fancy, can hardly be so great an idiot as your excellency would have him, laying occasions in his way to go on in his follies and extravagances.'

And turning the discourse to Don Quixote, he said:

'And you, stupid wretch, who has thrust it into your brain that you are a knight-errant, and that you conquer giants and seize caitiffs? Be gone in a good hour, and in such this is said to you; return to your own house, and breed up your children, if you have any; mind your affairs, and cease to ramble up and down the world, sucking the wind, and making all people laugh that know you, or know you not. Where, with a mischief, have you ever found that there have been, or are, knights-errant? Where are there any giants in Spain, or caitiffs in La Mancha, or Dulcineas enchanted, or all the rabble rout of follies that are told of you?'

Don Quixote was very attentive to the words of this venerable man; and, finding that he now held his peace, without minding the respect due to the duke and duchess, with an ireful mien and disturbed countenance, he started up, and said—But his answer deserves a chapter by itself.

CHAPTER 32

Of the answer Don Quixote gave to his reprover, with other grave and pleasant events.

DON QUIXOTE, then, standing up and trembling from head to foot, as if he had quicksilver in his joints, with precipitate and disturbed speech, said:

'The place where I am, and the presence of the personages before whom I stand, together with the respect I ever had, and have, for men of your profession, restrain and tie up the hands of my just indignation: and therefore, as well upon the account of what I have said, as being conscious of what everybody knows, that the weapons of gownsmen are the same as those of women, their tongues, I will enter with mine into combat with your reverence, from whom one rather ought to have expected good counsels than opprobrious revilings. Pious and well-meant reproof demands another kind of behaviour and language; at least the reproving me in public, and so rudely, has passed all the bounds of decent reprehension: for it is better to begin with mildness than asperity, and it is not right without knowledge of the fault, without more ado to call the offender madman and idiot.

'Tell me, I beseech your reverence, for which of the follies you have seen in me, do you condemn and revile me, bidding me get me home, and take care of my house, and of my wife and children, without knowing whether I have either? What? is there no more to do but to enter boldly in other men's houses, to govern the masters; and shall a poor pedagogue who never saw more of the world than what is contained within a district of twenty or thirty leagues, set himself at random to prescribe laws to chivalry, and to judge of knights-errant? Is it, then, an idle scheme and time thrown away, to range the world, not seeking its delights, but its austerities, whereby good men aspire to the seat of immortality? If gentlemen, if persons of wealth, birth, and quality were to take me for a madman, I should look upon it as an irreparable affront: but to be esteemed a fool by pedants, who never entered upon or trod the paths of chivalry, I value it not a farthing.

'A knight I am, and a knight I will die, if it be heaven's goodwill. Some pass through the spacious field of proud ambition; others through that of servile and base flattery; others by the way of deceitful hypocrisy; and some by that of true religion: but I, by the influence of my star, take the narrow path of knight-errantry, for the exercise whereof I despise wealth, but not honour. I have redressed grievances, righted wrongs, chastised insolences, vanquished giants, and trampled upon hobgoblins: I am in love, but only because knights-errant must be so; and, being so, I am no vicious lover, but a chaste Platonic one. My intentions are always directed to virtuous ends, to do good to all, and hurt to none. Whether he, who means thus, acts thus, and lives in the practise of all this, deserves to be called a fool, let your grandeurs judge, most excellent duke and duchess.'

'Well said, i'faith!' quoth Sancho: 'say no more in vindication of yourself, good my lord and master; for there is no more to be said, nor to be thought, nor to be persevered in, in the world: and besides this gentleman denying, as he has denied, that there ever were, or are, knights-errant, no wonder if he knows nothing of what he has been talking of.'

'Peradventure,' quoth the ecclesiastic, 'you, brother, are that Sancho Panza they talk of, to whom your master has promised an island.'

'I am so,' answered Sancho, 'and am he who deserves one as well as any other he whatever. I am one of those, of whom they say, Associate with good men and thou wilt be one of them; and of those, of whom it is said again; "Not with whom thou wert bred, but with whom thou hast fed"; and, "He that leaneth against a good tree, a good shelter findeth he." I have leaned to a good master, and have kept him company these many months, and shall be such another as he, if it be God's good pleasure; and if he lives and I live, neither shall he want kingdoms to rule, nor I islands to govern.'

'That you shall not, friend Sancho,' said the duke; 'for, in the name of Señor Don Quixote, I promise you the government of one of mine, now vacant, and of no inconsiderable value.'

'Kneel, Sancho,' said Don Quixote, 'and kiss his excellency's feet for the favour he has done you.'

Sancho did so. Which the ecclesiastic seeing, he got up from table in a great pet, saying:

'By the habit I wear, I could find in my heart to say, your excellency is as simple as these sinners: what wonder if they are mad, since wise men authorize their follies? Your excellency may stay with them, if you please; but, while they are in the house, I will stay in my own, and save myself the trouble of reproving what I cannot remedy.'

And without saying a word, or eating a bit more, away he went, the entreaties of the duke and duchess not availing to stop him; though indeed the duke said not much, through laughter occasioned by his impertinent passion.

The laugh being over, he said to Don Quixote:

'Sir Knight of the Lions, you have answered so well for yourself that there remains nothing to demand satisfaction for in this case: for though it has the appearance of an affront, it is by no means such, since, as women cannot give an affront, so neither can ecclesiastics, as you better know.'

'It is true,' answered Don Quixote, 'and the reason is, that whoever cannot be affronted, neither can he give an affront to anybody. Women, children, and churchmen, as they cannot defend themselves though they are offended, so they cannot be affronted, because, as your excellency better knows, there is this difference between an injury and an affront: an affront comes from one, who can give it, does give it, and then maintains it; an injury may come from any hand, without affronting. As for example, a person stands carelessly in the streets: ten others armed fall upon him and beat him: he claps his hand to his sword as he ought to do; but the number of his adversaries hinder him from effecting his intention, which is to revenge himself; this person is injured, but not affronted. Another example will confirm the same thing: a man stands with his back turned: another comes and strikes him with a cudgel, and runs for it when he has done; the man pursues him and cannot overtake him: he, who received the blows, received an injury, but no affront, because the affront must be maintained. If he, who struck him, though he did it basely and unawares, draws his sword afterwards, and stands firm, facing his enemy, he, who was struck, is both injured and affronted; injured, because he was struck treacherously, and affronted, because he who struck him maintained what he had done by standing his ground, and not stirring a foot.

'And therefore, according to the established laws of duel, I may be injured, but not affronted: for women and children cannot resent, nor can they fly, nor stand their ground. The same may be said of men consecrated to holy orders: for these three sorts of people want offensive and defensive weapons; and, though they are naturally bound to defend themselves, yet are they not to offend anybody. So that, though I said before, I was injured, I now say, in no wise; for he who cannot receive an affront can much less give one. For which reasons I neither ought nor do resent what that good man said to me: only I could have wished he had stayed a little longer, that I might have convinced him of his error in thinking and saying that there are no knights-errant now, nor ever were any in the world: for had Amadis, or any one of his numerous descendants, heard this, I am persuaded it would not have fared over well with his reverence.'

'That I will swear,' quoth Sancho: 'they would have given him such a slash, as would have cleft him from top to bottom, like any pomegranate or over-ripe melon: they were not folks to be jested with in that manner. By my beads, I am very certain, had Reynaldos of Montalvan heard the little gentleman talk at that rate, he would have given him such a gag, that he should not have spoken a word more in three years. Aye, aye, let him meddle with them, and see how he will escape out of their hands.'

The duchess was ready to die with laughter at hearing Sancho's talk: and in her opinion she took him to be more ridiculous and more mad than his master, and there were several others at that time of the same mind.

At last Don Quixote was calm, and dinner ended: and taking away the cloth there entered four damsels: one with a silver ewer, another with a basin of silver, also, a third with two fine clean towels over her shoulder, and the fourth tucked up to her elbows, and in her white hands (for doubtless they were white) a washball of Naples soap. She with a basin drew near, and, with a genteel air and assurance, clapped it under Don Quixote's beard; who, without speaking a word, and wondering at the ceremony, believed it to be the custom of that country to wash beards instead of hands, and therefore stretched out his own as far as he could: and instantly the ewer began to rain upon him, and the washball damsel hurried over his beard with great dexterity of hand, raising great flakes of snow (for the lathering was not less white) not only over the beard, but over the whole face and eyes, of the obedient knight, insomuch that it made him shut them whether he would or no.

The duke and duchess, who knew nothing of all this, were in expectation what this extraordinary lavation would end in. The barber-damsel, having raised a lather a handful high, pretended that the water was all spent, and ordered the girl with the ewer to fetch more, telling her Señor Don Quixote would stay till she came back. She did so, and Don Quixote remained the strangest and most ridiculous figure imaginable. All that were present, being many, beheld him, and seeing him with a neck half an ell long, more than moderately swarthy, his eyes shut, and his beard all in a lather, it was a great wonder and a sign of great discretion, that they forbore laughing. The damsels concerned in the jest held down their eyes, not daring to look at their lord and lady; who were divided between anger and laughter, not knowing what to do, whether to chastise the girls for their boldness, or reward them for the pleasure they took in beholding Don Quixote in that pickle.

At last the damsel of the ewer came, and they made an end of washing Don Quixote, and then she who carried the towels wiped and dried him with much deliberation; and all four at once, making a profound reverence, were going off. But the duke, that Don Quixote might not smell the jest, called the damsel with the basin, saying:

'Come, and wash me too, and take care you have water enough.'

The arch and diligent wench came, and clapped the basin

to the duke's chin, as she had done to Don Quixote's, and very expeditiously washed and lathered him well, and leaving him clean and dry, they made their curtsies, and away they went. It was afterwards known, that the duke had sworn that, had they not washed him as they did Don Quixote, he would have punished them for their pertness, which they had discreetly made amends for by serving him in the same manner.

Sancho was very attentive to the ceremonies of this washing, and said to himself:

'God be my guide! is it the custom, trow, of this place, to wash the beards of squires as well as of knights? On my conscience and soul, I need it much: and if they should give me a stroke of a razor, I should take it for a still greater favour.'

'What are you saying to yourself, Sancho?' quoth the duchess.

'I say, madam,' answered Sancho, 'that in other princes' courts I have always heard say, when the cloth is taken away, they bring water to wash hands, and not suds to scour beards; and therefore one must live long to see much: it is also said, he who lives a long life must pass through many evils; though one of these same scourings is rather a pleasure than a pain.'

'Take no care, friend Sancho,' quoth the duchess; 'for I will order my damsels to wash you too, and lay you a-bucking, if need be.'

'For the present, I shall be satisfied as to my beard,' answered Sancho: 'for the rest, God will provide hereafter.'

'Hark you, sewer,'* said the duchess, 'mind what honest Sancho desires, and do precisely as he would have you.'

The sewer answered, that Señor Sancho should be punctually obeyed; and so away he went to dinner, and took Sancho with him, the duke and duchess remaining at table with Don Quixote, discoursing of sundry and divers matters, but all relating to the profession of arms and knight-errantry.

The duchess entreated Don Quixote, since he seemed to have so happy a memory, that he would delineate and describe the beauty and features of the lady Dulcinea del Toboso; for, according to what fame proclaimed of her beauty, she took it for granted, she must be the fairest creature in the world and even in all La Mancha. Don Quixote sighed at hearing the duchess's request, and said:

'If I could pull out my heart and lay it before your grandeur's eyes here upon the table in a dish, I might save my tongue the labour of telling what can hardly be conceived; for there your excellency would see her painted to the life. But why should I go about to delineate and describe, one by one, the perfections of the peerless Dulcinea, it being a burden fitter for other shoulders than mine, an enterprise worthy to employ the pencils of Parrhasius, Timantes, and Apelles, and the graving-tools of Lysippus, to paint and carve in pictures, marbles, and bronzes; and Ciceronian and Demosthenian rhetoric to praise them.'

'What is the meaning of Demosthenian, Señor Don Quixote?' quoth the duchess: 'it is a word I never heard in all the days of my life.'

'Demosthenian rhetoric,' answered Don Quixote, 'is as much as to say, the rhetoric of Demosthenes, as Ciceronian of Cicero; who were the two greatest orators and rhetoricians in the world.'

'That is true,' said the duke, 'and you betrayed your ignorance in asking such a question; but for all that Señor Don Quixote would give us a great deal of pleasure in painting her to us; for though it be but a rough draft, or sketch only, doubtless she will appear such as the most beautiful may envy.'

'So she would most certainly,' answered Don Quixote, 'had not the misfortune, which lately befell her, blotted her idea out of my mind; such a misfortune, that I am in a condition rather to bewail than to describe her; for your grandeurs must know, that, going a few days ago to kiss her hands, and receive her benediction, commands, and licence for this third sally, I found her quite another person than her I sought for. I found her enchanted, and converted from a princess into a country wench, from beautiful to ugly, from an angel to a devil, from fragrant to pestiferous, from courtly to rustic, from light to darkness, from a sober lady to a jumping Joan; and, in fine, from Dulcinea del Toboso to a clownish wench of Sayago.'*

'God be my aid,' cried the duke at this instant, with a loud voice: 'who may it be that has done so much mischief to the world? who is it that has deprived it of the beauty that cheered it, the good humour that entertained it, and the modesty that did it honour?'

'Who?' answered Don Quixote: 'who could it be, but some malicious enchanter, of the many invisible ones that persecute me; that cursed race born into the world to obscure and annihilate the exploits of the good and to brighten and exalt the actions of the wicked? Enchanters have hitherto persecuted me; enchanters still persecute me, and enchanters will continue to persecute me, till they have tumbled me and my lofty chivalries into the profound abyss of oblivion; and they hurt and wound me in the most sensible part; since to deprive a knight-errant of his mistress, is to deprive him of the eyes he sees with, the sun that enlightens him, and the food that sustains him. I have already often said it, and now repeat it, that a knight-errant without a mistress is like a tree without leaves, a building without a foundation and a shadow without a body that causes it.'

'There is no more to be said,' quoth the duchess; 'but for all that, if we are to believe the history of Señor Don Quixote, lately published with the general applause of all nations, we are to collect from thence, if I remember right, that your worship never saw the lady Dulcinea, and that there is no such lady in the world, she being only an imaginary lady, begotten and born of your own brain, and dressed out with all the graces and perfections you pleased.'

'There is a great deal to be said upon this subject,' answered Don Quixote: 'God knows whether there be a Dulcinea or not in the world, and whether she be imaginary or not imaginary: this is one of those things, the proof whereof is not to be too nicely inquired into. I neither begot, nor brought forth, my mistress, though I contemplate her as a lady endowed with all those qualifications, which may make her famous over the whole world; such as, the being beautiful without a blemish, grave without pride, amorous with modesty, obliging as being courteous, and courteous as being well bred; and finally, of high descent, because beauty shines and displays itself with greater degrees of perfection when matched with noble blood, than in subjects that are of mean extraction.'

'True,' quoth the duke; 'but Señor Don Quixote must give me leave to say what the history of his exploits forces me to speak; for from thence may be gathered that, supposing it be allowed, that there is a Dulcinea in Toboso, or out of it, and that she is beautiful in the highest degree, as your worship describes her to us, yet in respect of high descent, she is not upon a level with the Orianas, the Alastrajareas, Madásimas,* and others of that sort, of whom histories are full, as your worship well knows.'

'To this I can answer,' replied Don Quixote, 'that Dulcinea is the daughter of her own works, that virtue ennobles blood, and that a virtuous person, though mean, is more to be valued than a vicious person of quality. Besides, Dulcinea has endowments, which may raise her to be a queen, with crown and sceptre: for the merit of a beautiful virtuous woman extends to the working greater miracles, and though not formally, yet virtually she has in herself greater advantages in store.'

'I say, Señor Don Quixote,' cried the duchess, 'that you tread with great caution, and, as the saying is, with the plummet in hand; and, for my own part, henceforward I will believe and make all my family believe, and even my lord duke, if need be, that there is a Dulcinea in Toboso, and that she is this day living and beautiful, and especially well born and well deserving that such a knight as Señor Don Quixote should be her servant; which is the highest commendation I can bestow upon her. But I cannot forbear entertaining one scruple, and bearing I know not what grudge to Sancho Panza. The scruple is, the aforesaid history relates, that the said Sancho Panza found the said lady Dulcinea, when he carried her a letter from your worship, winnowing a sack of wheat; by the same token it says it was red;* which makes me doubt the highness of her birth.'

To which Don Quixote answered:

'Madam, your grandeur must know, that most or all the things, which befell me, exceed the ordinary bounds of what happen to other knights-errant, whether directed by the inscrutable will of the destinies, or ordered through the malice of some envious enchanter: and as it is already a thing certain, that, among all or most of the famous knights-errant, one is privileged from being subject to the power of enchantment; another's flesh is so impenetrable that he cannot be wounded; as was the case of the renowned Orlando, one of the Twelve Peers of France, of whom it is related that he was invulnerable, excepting in the sole of his left foot, and in that only by the point of a great pin, and by no other weapon whatever: so that, when Bernardo del Carpio killed him in Roncesvalles, perceiving he could not wound him with steel, he hoisted him from the ground between his arms, and squeezed him to death, recollecting the manner in which Hercules slew Antaeus, that fierce giant, who was said to be a son of the earth.

'I would infer from what I have said, that perhaps I may have some one of those privileges: not that of being invulnerable, for experience has often shown me, that I am made of tender flesh, and by no means impenetrable; nor that of not being subject to enchantment; for I have already found myself clapped into a cage, in which the whole world could never have been able to have shut me up, had it not been by force of enchantments: but, since I freed myself from thence, I am inclined to believe no other can touch me; and therefore these enchanters, seeing they cannot practice their wicked artifices upon my person, revenge themselves upon what I love best, and have a mind to take away my life by evil entreating Dulcinea, for whom I live; and therefore I am of opinion, that, when my squire carried her my message, they had transformed her into a country wench, busied in that mean employment of winnowing wheat. But I have before said, that the wheat was not red, nor indeed wheat, but grains of oriental pearl: and for proof hereof, I must tell your grandeurs, that, coming lately through Toboso, I could not find Dulcinea's palace; and that, Sancho my squire having seen her the other day in her own proper figure, the most beautiful on the globe, to me she appeared a coarse ugly country wench, and not well spoken, whereas she is discretion itself: and since I neither am, nor in all likelihood can be, enchanted, she it is who is the enchanted, the injured, the metamorphosed and transformed: in her my enemies have revenged themselves on me, and for her I shall live in perpetual tears till I see her restored to her former state.

'All this I have said, that no stress may be laid upon what Sancho told of Dulcinea's sifting and winnowing; for since to me she was changed, no wonder if she was metamorphosed to him. Dulcinea is well born, of quality, and of the genteel families of Toboso, which are many, ancient, and very good: and no doubt the peerless Dulcinea has a large share in them, for whom her town will be famous and renowned in the ages to come, as Troy was of Helen, and Spain has been for [La] Cava, though upon better grounds, and a juster title.

'On the other hand, I would have your grandeurs understand, that Sancho Panza is one of the most ingenious squires that ever served knight-errant: he has indeed, at times, certain simplicities so acute, that it is no small pleasure to consider, whether he has in him most of the simple or acute: he has roguery enough to pass for a knave, and negligence enough to confirm him a dunce: he doubts of everything, and believes everything; when I imagine he is falling headlong into stupidity, he outs with such smart sayings as raise him to the skies. In short, I would not exchange him for any other squire, though a city were given me to boot: and therefore I am in doubt, whether I shall do well to send him to the government your grandeur has favoured him with: though I perceive in him such a fitness for the business of governing, that, with a little polishing of his understanding, he would be as much master of that art, as the king is of his customs. Besides, we know by sundry experiences, that there is no need of much ability, nor much learning, to be a governor; for there are a hundred of them up and down that can scarcely read, and yet they govern as sharp as so many hawks. The main point is, that their intention be good, and that they desire to do everything right, and there will never be wanting counsellors to advise and direct them in what they are to do; like your governors, who being sword-men, and not scholars, have an assistant on the bench. My counsel to him would be: All bribes to refuse, but insist on his dues; with some other little matters, which lie in my breast, and shall out in proper time, for Sancho's benefit, and the good of the island he is to govern.'

Thus far had the duke, the duchess, and Don Quixote proceeded in their discourse, when they heard several voices and a great noise in the palace, and presently Sancho came into the hall all in a chafe, with a dish-clout for a slabbering bib; and after him a parcel of kitchen-boys, and other lower servants. One of them carried a tray full of water, which, by its colour and uncleanness, seemed to be dish-water. He followed and persecuted him, endeavouring with all earnestness to fix it under his chin; and another scullion seemed as solicitous to wash his beard.

'What is the matter, brothers?' quoth the duchess, 'what is the matter? what would you do to this good man? What! do you not consider that he is a governor elect?'

To which the roguish barber answered:

'Madam, this gentleman will not suffer himself to be washed, as is the custom, and as our lord the duke and his master have been.'

'Yes, I will,' answered Sancho in great wrath; 'but I would have cleaner towels, and clearer suds, and not such filthy hands; for there is no such difference between me and my master, that he should be washed with angel-water, and I with the devil's lye. The customs of countries, and of princes' palaces, are so far good as they are not troublesome: but this custom of scouring here is worse than that of the whipping penitents. My beard is clean, and I have no need of such refreshings; and he, who offers to scour me, or touch a hair of my head (I mean of my beard), with due reverence be it spoken, I will give him such a dowse, that I will set my fist fast in his skull: for such ceremonies and soapings as these look more like gibes than courtesy to guests.'

The duchess was ready to die with laughing, to see the rage and hear the reasonings of Sancho. But Don Quixote was not over-pleased, to see him so accoutred with the nasty towel, and surrounded with such a parcel of kitchen-tribe:

and so, making a low bow to the duke and duchess, as if begging leave to speak, he said to the rabble with a solemn voice:

'Ho, gentlemen cavaliers, be pleased to let the young man alone, and return from whence you came, or to any other place you list; for my squire is as clean as another man, and these trays are as painful to him as a narrow-necked jug. Take my advice, and let him alone, for neither he nor I understand jesting.'

Sancho caught the words out of his master's mouth, and proceeded, saying:

'No, no, let them go on with their jokes; for I will endure it as much as it is now night. Let them bring hither a comb, or what else they please, and let them curry this beard, and if they find anything in it that offends against cleanliness, let them shear me crosswise.'

Here the duchess, still laughing, said:

'Sancho Panza is in the right in whatever he has said, and will be so in whatever he shall say: he is clean, and, as he says, needs no washing; and if he is not pleased with our custom, he is at his own disposal: and besides, you ministers of cleanliness have been extremely remiss and careless, and I may say presumptuous, in bringing to such a personage, and such a beard, your trays and dish-clouts, instead of ewers and basins of pure gold, and towels of Dutch diaper: but, in short, you are a parcel of scoundrels and ill-born, and cannot forbear showing the grudge you bear to the squires of knights-errant.'

The roguish servants, and even the sewer who came with them, believed that the duchess spoke in earnest, and so they took Sancho's dish-clout off his neck, and with some confusion and shame slunk away and left him: who, finding himself rid of what he thought an imminent danger, went and kneeled before the duchess, and said:

'From great folks great favours are to be expected: that which your ladyship has done me to-day, cannot be repaid with less than the desire of seeing myself dubbed a knight-errant, that I may employ all the days of my life in the service of so high a lady. A peasant I am; Sancho Panza is my name;

married I am; children I have; and I serve as a squire: if with any one of these I can be serviceable to your grandeur, I shall not be slower in obeying, than your ladyship in commanding.'

'It appears plainly,' Sancho, answered the duchess, 'that you have learned to be courteous in the school of courtesy itself. I mean, it is evident, you have been bred in the bosom of Señor Don Quixote, who must needs be the cream of complaisance, and the flower of ceremony, or cirimony, as you say. Well fare such a master, and such a man, the one the pole-star of knight-errantry, and the other the bright luminary of squirely fidelity! Rise up, friend Sancho; for I will make you amends for your civility, by prevailing with my lord duke to perform, as soon as possible, the promise he has made you of the government.'

Thus ended the conversation, and Don Quixote went to repose himself during the heat of the day, and the duchess desired Sancho, if he had not an inclination to sleep, to pass the afternoon with her and her damsels in a very cool hall. Sancho answered, that, though indeed he was wont to sleep four or five hours a day, during the afternoon heats of the summer, to wait upon her goodness, he would endeavour with all his might not to sleep at all that day, and would be obedient to her commands; and so away he went. The duke gave fresh orders about treating Don Quixote as a knight-errant, without deviating a tittle from the style in which we read the knights of former times were treated.

CHAPTER 33

Of the relishing conversation which passed between the duchess, her damsels, and Sancho Panza; worthy to be read and remarked.

THE history then relates, that Sancho Panza did not sleep that afternoon, but, to keep his word, came with the meat in his mouth to see the duchess; who, being delighted to hear him talk, made him sit down by her on a low stool, though Sancho, out of pure good manners, would have declined it: but the duchess would have him sit down as a governor, and talk as a squire, since in both those capacities he deserved the very stool of the champion Cid Diaz. Sancho shrugged up his shoulders, obeyed, and sat down; and all the duchess's damsels and duennas got round about him, in profound silence, to hear what he would say. But the duchess spoke first, saying:

'Now we are alone, and that nobody hears us, I would willingly be satisfied by Señor Governor, as to some doubts I have arising from the printed history of the great Don Quixote: one of which is, that, since honest Sancho never saw Dulcinea, I mean the lady Dulcinea del Toboso, nor carried her Don Quixote's letter, it being left in the pocket-book in the Sierra Morena, how durst he feign the answer, and the story of his finding her winnowing wheat, it being all a sham, and a lie, and so much for the prejudice of the good character of the peerless Dulcinea, and the whole so unbecoming the quality and fidelity of a trusty squire?'

At these words, without making any reply, Sancho got up from his stool, and stepping softly, with his body bent, and his finger on his lips, he crept round the room, lifting up the hangings; and this being done, he presently sat himself down again, and said:

'Now, madam, that I am sure nobody but the company hears us, I will answer, without fear or emotion, to all you have asked, and to all you shall ask me; and the first thing I tell you is, that I take my master, Don Quixote, for a downright madman, though sometimes he comes out with things, which, to my thinking, and in the opinion of all that hears him, are so discreet, and so well put together, that Satan himself could not speak better; and yet for all that, in good truth, and without any doubt, I am firmly persuaded he is mad. Now, having settled this in my mind, I dare undertake to make him believe anything that has neither head nor tail, like the business of the answer to the letter, and another affair of some six or eight days standing, which is not yet in print: I mean the enchantment of my mistress Doña Dulcinea; for you must know I made him believe she was enchanted, though there is no more truth in it than in a story of a cock and a bull.'

The duchess desired him to tell her the particulars of that enchantment or jest; and Sancho recounted the whole, exactly as it had passed, at which the hearers were not a little pleased, and the duchess, proceeding in her discourse, said:

'From what honest Sancho has told me, a certain scruple has started into my head, and something whispers me in the ear, saying to me: "Since Don Quixote de la Mancha is a fool, an idiot, and a madman, and Sancho Panza his squire knows it, and yet serves and follows him, and relies on his vain promises, without doubt, he must be more mad, and more stupid than his master; and, this being really the case, it will turn to bad account, lady duchess, if to such a Sancho Panza you give an island to govern; for he who knows not how to govern himself, how should he know how to govern others?"'

'By my faith, madam,' quoth Sancho, 'this same scruple comes in the nick of time: please your ladyship to bid it speak out plain, or as it lists; for I know it says true, and, had I been wise, I should have left my master long ere now; but such was my lot, and such my evil-errantry. I can do no more; follow him I must; we are both of the same town; I have eaten his bread; I love him; he returns my kindness; he gave me his ass's-colts; and, above all, I am faithful; and therefore it is impossible anything should part us but the sexton's spade and shovel; and, if your highness has no mind the government you promised should be given me, God made me of less, and it may be the not giving it me may redound to the benefit of my conscience; for, as great a fool as I am, I understand the proverb, The pismire* had wings to her hurt; and it may perhaps be easier for Sancho the squire to get to heaven, than for Sancho the governor. They make as good bread here as in France; and, In the dark all cats are grey; and, Unhappy is he, who has not breakfasted at three; and, No stomach is a span bigger than another, and may be filled, as they say, with straw or with hay; and, Of the little birds in the air, God himself takes the care; and, Four yards of coarse cloth of Cuenca are warmer than as many of fine

Segovia serge; and, At our leaving this world, and going into the next, the prince travels in as narrow a path as the day-labourer; and, The Pope's body takes up no more room than the sexton's, though the one be higher than the other; for, when we come to the grave, we must all shrink and lie close, or be made to shrink and lie close in spite of us; and so good night: and therefore I say again, that, if your ladyship will not give me the island, because I am a fool, I will be so wise as not to care a fig for it; and I have heard say, The devil lurks behind the cross; and, All is not gold that glitters; and, Wamba the husbandman was taken from among his ploughs, his yokes, and oxen, to be King of Spain; and, Roderigo was taken from his brocades, pastimes, and riches, to be devoured by snakes, if ancient ballads do not lie.'

'How should they lie?' said then the duenna Rodriguez, who was one of the auditors; 'for there is a ballad which tells us how king Roderigo was shut up alive in a tomb full of toads, snakes, and lizards, and that, two days after, the king said from within the tomb, with a mournful and low voice: "Now they gnaw me, now they gnaw me, in the part by which I sinned most": and according to this, the gentleman has a great deal of reason to say, he would rather be a peasant than a king, if such vermin must eat him up.'

The duchess could not forbear laughing to hear the simplicity of her duenna, nor admiring to hear the reasonings and proverbs of Sancho, to whom she said:

'Honest Sancho knows full well, that, whatever a knight once promises, he endeavours to perform it, though it cost him his life. The duke, my lord and husband, though he is not of the errant order, is nevertheless a knight, and therefore will make good his word as to the promised island, in spite of the envy and the wickedness of the world. Let Sancho be of good cheer; for when he least thinks of it, he shall find himself seated in the chair of state of his island and of his territory, and shall so handle his government as to despise for it one of brocade three stories high.* What I charge him is, to take heed how he governs his vassals, remembering that they are all loyal and well born.'

'As to governing them well,' answered Sancho, 'there is no

need of giving it me in charge; for I am naturally charitable, and compassionate to the poor; and, None will dare the loaf to steal from him that sifts and kneads the meal; and, by my beads, they shall put no false dice upon me: I am an old dog, and understand *tus, tus,** and know how to snuff my eyes in proper time, and will not suffer cobwebs to get into my eyes; for I know where the shoe pinches. All this I say, that the good may be sure to have of me both heart and hand, and the bad neither foot nor footing; and, in my opinion, as to the business of governing, the whole lies in the beginning; and perhaps, when I have been fifteen days a governor, my fingers may itch after the office, and I may know more of it than of the labour of the field, to which I was bred.'

'You are in the right, Sancho,' quoth the duchess; 'for nobody is born learned, and bishops are made of men, and not of stones. But, to resume the discourse we were just now upon, concerning the enchantment of the lady Dulcinea; I am very certain, that Sancho's design of putting a trick upon his master, and making him believe that the country wench was Dulcinea, and that, if his master did not know her, it must proceed from her being enchanted, was all a contrivance of some one or other of the enchanters who persecute Don Quixote; for really, and in truth, I know from good authority, that the wench who jumped upon the ass was and is Dulcinea del Toboso, and that honest Sancho, in thinking he was the deceiver, was himself deceived; and there is no more doubt of this truth than of things we never saw; for Señor Sancho Panza must know that here also we have our enchanters, who love us, and tell us plainly and sincerely, and without any tricks or devices, all that passes in the world: and believe me, Sancho, the jumping-wench was and is Dulcinea del Toboso, who is enchanted just as much as the mother that bore her; and, when we least think of it, we shall see her in her own proper form; and then Sancho will be convinced of the mistake he now lives in.'

'All this may very well be,' quoth Sancho Panza; 'and now I begin to believe what my master told of Montesinos' cave, where he pretends he saw the lady Dulcinea del Toboso in the very same dress and garb I said I had seen her in, when I enchanted her for my own pleasure alone; whereas, as your ladyship says, all this must have been quite otherwise; for it cannot, and must not be presumed, that my poor invention should, in an instant, start so cunning a device, nor do I believe my master is such a madman as to credit so extravagant a thing, upon no better a voucher than myself. But, madam, your goodness ought not, therefore, to look upon me as an ill-designed person; for a dunce, like me, is not obliged to penetrate into the thoughts and crafty intentions of wicked enchanters. I invented that story to escape the chidings of my master, and not with design to offend him; and if it has fallen out otherwise, God is in heaven, who judges the heart.'

'That is true,' quoth the duchess: 'but tell me, Sancho, what is it you were saying of Montesinos' cave? I should be glad to know it.'

Then Sancho related, with all its circumstances, what has been said concerning that adventure. Which the duchess hearing, she said:

'From this accident it may be inferred, that, since the great Don Quixote says he saw the very same country-wench, whom Sancho saw coming out of Toboso, without doubt it is Dulcinea, and that the enchanters hereabouts are very busy, and excessively curious.'

'But I say,' quoth Sancho Panza, 'if my lady Dulcinea del Toboso is enchanted, so much the worse for her; and I do not think myself bound to engage with my master's enemies, who must needs be many and malicious: true it is, that she I saw was a country-wench; for such I took her, and such I judged her to be; and, if she was Dulcinea, it is not to be placed to my account, nor ought it to lie at my door. It would be fine, indeed, if I must be called in question at every turn, with, Sancho said it, Sancho did it, Sancho came back, and Sancho returned; as if Sancho were who they would, and not that very Sancho Panza, handed about in print all the world over, as Sampson Carrasco told me, who is at least a candidate to be a bachelor at Salamanca; and such persons cannot lie, excepting when they have a mind to it, or when it turns to good account: so that there is no reason why anybody should fall upon me, since I have a good name; and, as I have heard my master say, a good name is better than great riches: case me but in this same government, and you will see wonders; for a good squire will make a good governor.'

'All that honest Sancho has now said,' quoth the duchess, 'are Catonian sentences, or at least extracted from the very marrow of Michael Verino* himself—"florentibus occidit annis": in short, to speak in his own way, A bad cloak often covers a good drinker.'

'Truly, madam,' answered Sancho, 'I never in my life drank for any bad purpose: for thirst it may be I have: for I am no hypocrite: I drink when I have a mind, and when I have no mind, and when it is given me, not to be thought shy or ill-bred; for when a friend drinks to one, who can be so hard-hearted as not to pledge him? But though I put on the shoes, I do not dirty them. Besides, the squires of knights-errant most commonly drink water; for they are always wandering about woods, forests, meadows, mountains, and craggy rocks, without meeting the poorest pittance of wine, though they would give an eye for it.'

'I believe so too,' answered the duchess: 'but, for the present, Sancho, go and repose yourself, and we will hereafter talk more at large, and order shall speedily be given about casing you, as you call it, in the government.'

Sancho again kissed the duchess's hand, and begged of her, as a favour, that good care might be taken of his Dapple, for he was the light of his eyes.

'What Dapple?' quoth the duchess.

'My ass,' replied Sancho; 'for, to avoid calling him by that name, I commonly call him Dapple: and I desired this mistress duenna here, when I first came into the castle, to take care of him, and she was as angry, as if I had said she was ugly or old; though it should be more proper and natural for duennas to dress asses than to set off drawing-rooms. God be my help! how ill a gentleman of our town agreed with these madams!'

'He was some country clown to be sure,' quoth Doña

Rodriguez; 'for, had he been a gentleman, and well born, he would have placed them above the horns of the moon.'

'Enough,' quoth the duchess; 'let us have no more of this; peace, Doña Rodriguez, and you, Señor Panza, be quiet; and leave the care of making much of your Dapple to me; for he, being a jewel of Sancho's, I will lay him upon the apple of my eye.'

'It will be sufficient for him to lie in the stable,' answered Sancho; 'for upon the apple of your grandeur's eye, neither he nor I are worthy to lie one single moment, and I would no more consent to it, than I would poniard myself: for, though my master says, that, in complaisance we should rather lose the game by a card too much than too little, yet, when the business is asses and eyes, we should go with compass in hand, and keep within measured bounds.'

'Carry him, Sancho,' quoth the duchess, 'to your government, and there you may regale him as you please, and set him free from further labour.'

'Think not, my lady duchess, you have said much,' quoth Sancho; 'for I have seen more than two asses go to governments, and, if I should carry mine, it would be no such new thing.'

Sancho's reasonings renewed the duchess's laughter and satisfaction; and, dismissing him to his repose, she went to give the duke an account of what had passed between them, and they two agreed to contrive and give orders to have a jest put upon Don Quixote, which should be famous, and consonant to the style of knight-errantry; in which they played him many, so proper, and such ingenious ones, that they are some of the best adventures contained in this grand history.

CHAPTER 34

Giving an account of the method prescribed for disenchanting
the peerless Dulcinea del Toboso; which is one of the most
famous adventures of this book.

GREAT was the pleasure the duke and duchess received from
the conversation of Don Quixote and Sancho Panza; and,
persisting in the design they had of playing them some tricks,
which should carry the semblance and face of adventures,
they took a hint from what Don Quixote had already told
them of Montesinos' cave, to dress up a famous one. But
what the duchess most wondered at was, that Sancho should
be so very simple, as to believe for certain, that Dulcinea del
Toboso was enchanted, he himself having been the enchanter
and impostor in that business. And so, having instructed their
servants how they were to behave, six days after, they carried
Don Quixote a-hunting with a train of hunters and huntsmen,
not inferior to that of a crowned head. They gave Don
Quixote a hunting suit, and Sancho another, of the finest
green cloth: but Don Quixote would not put his on, saying,
he must shortly return to the severe exercise of arms, and
that he could not carry wardrobes and sumpters about him.
But Sancho took what was given him, with design to sell it
the first opportunity he should have.

The expected day being come, Don Quixote armed himself,
and Sancho put on his new suit, and mounted Dapple, whom
he would not quit, though they offered him a horse; and so
he thrust himself amidst the troop of hunters. The duchess
issued forth magnificently dressed, and Don Quixote, out of
pure politeness and civility, held the reins of her palfrey,
though the duke would not consent to it. At last they came
to a wood, between two very high mountains, where posting
themselves, in places where the toils were to be pitched, and
all the company having taken their different stands, the hunt
began with a great hallooing and noise, insomuch that they
could not hear one another, as well for the cry of the hounds,
as the winding of the horns. The duchess alighted, and, with
a boarspear in her hand, took her stand in a place where she
knew wild boars used to pass. The duke and Don Quixote

alighted also, and placed themselves by her side. Sancho planted himself in the rear of them all, without alighting from Dapple, whom he durst not quit, lest some mischance should befall him.

And scarcely were they on foot, and ranged in order, with several of their servants round them, when they perceived an enormous boar, pursued by the dogs, and followed by the hunters, making towards them, grinding his teeth and tusks, and tossing foam from his mouth. Don Quixote, seeing him, braced his shield, and laying his hand to his sword, stepped before the rest to receive him. The duke did the like, with his javelin in his hand. But the duchess would have advanced before them, if the duke had not prevented her. Only Sancho, at the sight of the fierce animal, quitted Dapple, and ran the best he could, and endeavoured to climb up into a tall oak, but could not: and, being got about half way up, holding by a bough, and striving to mount to the top, he was so unfortunate and unlucky, that the bough broke, and, in tumbling down, he remained in the air, suspended by a snag of the tree, without coming to the ground; and, finding himself in this situation, and that the green loose coat was tearing, and considering that, if the furious animal came that way, he should be within his reach, he began to cry out so loud, and to call for help so violently, that all who heard him, and did not see him, thought verily he was between the teeth of some wild beast.

In short, the tusked boar was laid at his length by the points of the many boar-spears levelled at him; and Don Quixote, turning his head about at Sancho's cries, by which he knew him, saw him hanging from the oak with his head downward, and close by him Dapple, who deserted him not in his calamity. And Cid Hamet Ben Engeli says he seldom saw Sancho Panza without Dapple, or Dapple without Sancho; such was the amity and cordial love maintained between them. Don Quixote went and disengaged Sancho, who, finding himself freed and upon the ground, fell a-viewing the rent in the hunting suit, and it grieved him to the soul; for he fancied he possessed in that suit an inheritance in fee-simple.

They laid the mighty boar across a sumpter-mule, and, covering it with branches of rosemary and myrtle, they carried it, as the spoils of victory, to a large field-tent, erected in the middle of the wood; where they found the tables ranged in order, and dinner set out so sumptuous and grand, that it easily discovered the greatness and magnificence of the donor. Sancho, showing the wounds of his torn garment to the duchess, said:

'Had this been a hare-hunting, or a fowling for small birds, my coat would have been safe from the extremity it is now in: I do not understand what pleasure there can be in waiting for a beast, who, if he reaches you with a tusk, it may cost you your life. I remember to have heard an old ballad sung to this purpose:

> 'May Favila's sad doom be thine,
>   And hungry bears upon thee dine.'*

'He was a Gothic king,' quoth Don Quixote, 'who, going to hunt wild beasts, was devoured by a bear.'

'What I say,' answered Sancho, 'is, that I would not have princes and kings run themselves into such dangers, merely for their pleasure; which methinks ought not to be so, since it consists in killing a creature that has not committed any fault.'

'You are mistaken, Sancho; it is quite otherwise,' answered the duke; 'for the exercise of hunting wild beasts is the most proper and necessary for kings and princes of any whatever. Hunting is an image of war; in it there are stratagems, artifices, and ambuscades, to overcome your enemy without hazard to your person: in it you endure pinching cold, and intolerable heat; idleness and sleep are contemned; natural vigour is corroborated, and the members of the body made active: in short it is an exercise, which may be used without prejudice to anybody, and with pleasure to many; and the best of it is, that it is not for all people, as are all other country sports, excepting hawking, which is also peculiar to kings and great persons. And, therefore, Sancho, change your opinion, and, when you are a governor, exercise yourself in hunting, and you will find your account in it.'

'Not so,' answered Sancho; 'the good governor, and the broken leg, should keep at home. It would be fine indeed for people to come fatigued about business, to seek him, while he is in the mountains following his recreations; at that rate the government might go to wreck. In good truth, sir, hunting and pastimes are rather for your idle companions, than for governors. What I design to divert myself with, shall be playing at brag* at Easter, and at bowls on Sundays and holidays: as for your huntings, they befit not my condition, nor agree with my conscience.'

'God grant you prove as good as you say; but saying and doing are at a wide distance,' quoth the duke.

'Be it so,' replied Sancho: 'The good paymaster is in pain for no pawn; and, God's help is better than rising early; and, The belly carries the legs, and not the legs the belly: I mean, that, with the help of God, and a good intention, I shall doubtless govern better than a goss-hawk. Aye, aye, let them put their finger in my mouth, and they shall see whether I can bite or no.'

'The curse of God and of all His saints light on thee, accursed Sancho,' quoth Don Quixote: 'when will the day come, as I have often said, that I shall hear thee utter one current and coherent sentence without proverbs? I beseech your grandeurs, let this blockhead alone: he will grind your souls to death, not between two, but between two thousand proverbs, introduced as much to the purpose and as well timed, as I wish God may grant him health, or me, if I desire to hear them.'

'Sancho Panza's proverbs,' quoth the duchess, 'though they exceed in number those of the Greek commentator,* yet they are not to be less valued for the brevity of the sentences. For my own part, I must own, they give me more pleasure than any others, though better timed and better applied.'

With these and the like entertaining discourses, they left the tent, and went into the wood to visit the toils and nets. The day was soon spent, and night came on not so clear nor so calm as the season of the year, which was the midst of summer, required, but a kind of *clair obscur*, which contributed very much to help forward the duke and duchess's design.

Now, night coming on, soon after the twilight, on a sudden the wood seemed on fire from all the four quarters; and presently were heard, on all sides, an infinite number of cornets and other instruments of war, as if a great body of horse was passing through the wood. The blaze of the fire, and the sound of the warlike instruments, almost blinded and stunned the eyes and ears of the bystanders, and even of all that were in the wood. Presently were heard infinite Lelilies* after the Moorish fashion, when they are just going to join battle. Trumpets and clarions sounded, drums beat, fifes played, almost all at once, so fast and without any inter- mission, that he must have had no sense, who had not lost it at the confused din of so many instruments.

The duke was in astonishment, the duchess in a fright, Don Quixote in amaze, and Sancho Panza in a fit of trem- bling: in short, even they who were in the secret were terrified, and consternation held them all in silence. A post- boy, habited like a devil, passed before them, winding, instead of a cornet, a monstrous hollow horn, which yielded a hoarse and horrible sound.

'So ho, brother courier,' quoth the duke, 'who are you? whither go you? and what soldiers are those who seem to be crossing this wood?'

To which the courier answered in a hoarse and dreadful voice.

'I am the devil, and am going in quest of Don Quixote de la Mancha: the people you inquire about are six troops of enchanters, who are conducting the peerless Dulcinea del Toboso in a triumphal chariot; she comes enchanted, with the gallant Frenchman Montesinos, to inform Don Quixote how that same lady is to be disenchanted.'

'If you were the devil, as you say, and as your figure denotes you to be,' quoth Don Quixote, 'you would before now have known that same knight Don Quixote de la Mancha, who stands here before you.'

'Before God, and upon my conscience,' replied the devil, 'I did not see him; for my thoughts are distracted about so many things, that I forgot the principal business I came about.'

'Doubtless,' quoth Sancho, 'this devil must needs be a very honest fellow, and a good Christian; else he would not have sworn by God and his conscience: now, for my part, I verily believe there are some good folks in hell itself.'

Then the devil, without alighting, directing his eyes to Don Quixote, said:

'To you, Knight of the Lions (and may I see you between their paws), the unfortunate but valiant knight Montesinos sends me, commanding me to tell you from him to wait for him in the very place I meet you in; for he brings with him her whom they call Dulcinea del Toboso, in order to instruct you how you may disenchant her: and this being all I came for, I must stay no longer. Devils like me be with you, and good angels with this lord and lady.'

And so saying, he blew his monstrous horn, and turned his back, and away he went without staying for an answer from anybody. Every one admired afresh, especially Sancho and Don Quixote; Sancho, to see how, in spite of truth, Dulcinea must be enchanted; and Don Quixote, for not being sure of the truth of what had happened to him in Montesinos' cave. While he stood wrapped up in these cogitations, the duke said to him:

'Does your worship, Señor Don Quixote, design to wait here?'

'Why not?' answered he: 'here will I wait intrepid and courageous, though all hell should come to assault me.'

'Now, for my part,' quoth Sancho, 'I will no more stay here to see another devil, and hear another such horn, than I would in Flanders.'

Now the night grew darker, and numberless lights began to run about the wood, like those dry exhalations from the earth, which, glancing along the sky, seem to our sight as shooting stars. There was heard likewise a dreadful noise, like that caused by the ponderous wheels of an ox-wagon, from whose harsh and continued creaking, it is said, wolves and bears fly away, if there chance to be any within hearing. To all this combustion was added another, which augmented the whole; which was, that it seemed as if there were four engagements, or battles, at the four quarters of the wood, all at one time: for here sounded the dreadful noise of artillery; there were discharged infinite volleys of small shot: the shouts of the combatants seemed to be near at hand; the Moorish Lelilies were heard at a distance.

In short, the cornets, horns, clarions, trumpets, drums, cannon, muskets, and, above all, the frightful creaking of the wagons, formed altogether so confused and horrid a din, that Don Quixote had need of all his courage to be able to bear it. But Sancho's quite failed him, and he fell down in a swoon upon the train of the duchess's robe; who presently ordered cold water to be thrown in his face; which being done, he recovered his senses at the instant one of the creaking wagons arrived at that stand. It was drawn by four lazy oxen, all covered with black palls, and a large burning torch of wax fastened to each horn. At the top of the wagon was fixed an exalted seat, on which sat a venerable old man, with a beard whiter than snow itself, and so long that it reached below his girdle. His vestment was a long gown of black buckram: for the wagon was so illuminated, that one might easily discern and distinguish whatever was in it. The drivers were two ugly devils, habited in the same buckram, and of such hideous aspect, that Sancho, having once seen them, shut his eyes close, that he might not see them a second time.

Now the wagon being come close up to the place, the venerable sire raised himself from his lofty seat, and, standing upon his feet, with a loud voice he said:

'I am the sage Lirgandeo.'

And the wagon went forward without his speaking another word. After this there passed another wagon in the same manner, with another old man enthroned; who, making the wagon stop, with a voice as solemn as the other's, said:

'I am the sage Alquife, the great friend to Urganda the Unknown;' and passed on.

Then advanced another wagon with the same pace: but he, who was seated on the throne, was not an old man, like the two former, but a robust and ill-favoured fellow, who, when he came near, standing up, as the rest had done, said, with a voice more hoarse and more diabolical:

'I am Arcalaus the enchanter, mortal enemy of Amadis de Gaul and all his kindred'; and on he went.

These three wagons halted at a little distance, and the irksome jarring noise of their wheels ceased; and presently was heard another (not noise, but) sound, composed of sweet and regular music; at which Sancho was much rejoiced, and took it for a good sign; and therefore he said to the duchess, from whom he had not stirred an inch:

'Where there is music, madam, there can be no harm.'

'Nor where there are lights and brightness,' answered the duchess.

To which Sancho replied:

'The fire may give light, and bonfires may be bright, as we see by those that surround us, and yet we may very easily be burnt by them: but music is always a sign of feasting and merriment.'

'That we shall see presently,' quoth Don Quixote, who listened to all that was said; and he said right, as is shown in the following chapter.

CHAPTER 35

Wherein is continued the account of the method prescribed to Don Quixote for the disenchanting Dulcinea; with other wonderful events.

KEEPING exact time with the agreeable music, they perceived advancing towards them one of those cars they call triumphal, drawn by six grey mules, covered with white linen; and mounted upon each of them came a penitent of the light, clothed also in white, and a great wax torch lighted in his hand. The car was thrice as big as any of the former, and the sides and top were occupied by twelve other penitents as white as snow, and all carrying lighted torches; a sight, which at once caused admiration and affright. Upon an elevated throne sat a nymph, clad in a thousand veils of silver tissue, bespangled with numberless leaves of gold tinsel; which made her appear, if not very rich, yet very gorgeous.

Her face was covered with a transparent delicate tiffany; so that, without any impediment from its threads or plaits, you might discover through it the face of a very beautiful damsel; and the multitude of lights gave an opportunity of distinguishing her beauty, and her age, which seemed not to reach twenty years, nor to be under seventeen.

Close by her sat a figure, arrayed in a gown of those they call robes of state, down to the feet, and his head covered with a black veil. The moment the car came up, just over against where the duke and duchess and Don Quixote stood, the music of the waits ceased, and presently after that of the harps and lutes, which played in the car; and the figure in the gown standing up, and throwing open the robe, and taking the veil from off his face, discovered plainly the very figure and skeleton of Death, so ugly that Don Quixote was startled, and Sancho affrighted at it, and the duke and duchess made a show of some timorous concern. This living Death, raised and standing up, with a voice somewhat drowsy, and a tongue not quite awake, began in the following manner:

> 'Merlin I am, miscall'd the devil's son
> In lying annals, authoriz'd by time;
> Monarch supreme and great depositary
> Of magic art and Zoroastric skill;
> Rival of envious ages, that would hide
> The glorious deeds of errant cavaliers,
> Favor'd by me, and my peculiar charge.
> Though vile enchanters, still on mischief bent,
> To plague mankind their baleful art employ,
> Merlin's soft nature, ever prone to good,
> His power inclines to bless the human race.
>   'In hell's dark chambers, where my busied ghost
> Was forming spells and mystic characters,
> Dulcinea's voice (peerless Tobosan maid)
> With mournful accents reach'd my pitying ears,
> I knew her woe, her metamorphos'd form,
> From high-born beauty in a palace graced,
> To the loath'd features of a cottage wench.
> With sympathizing grief I straight revolv'd
> The numerous tomes of my detested art,
> And, in the hollow of this skeleton

My soul enclosing, hither am I come,
To tell the cure of such uncommon ills.
'O glory thou of all that case their limbs
In polish'd steel and fenceful adamant,
Light, beacon, polar star, and glorious guide
Of all, who, starting from the lazy down,
Banish ignoble sleep, for the rude toil,
And hardy exercise of errant arms;
Spain's boasted pride, La Mancha's matchless knight,
Whose valiant deeds outstrip pursuing fame;
Would'st thou to beauty's pristine state restore
Th' enchanted dame, Sancho, thy faithful squire,
Must to his brawny buttocks bare expos'd,
Three thousand and three hundred stripes apply,
Such as may sting, and give him smarting pain.
The authors of her change have thus decreed,
And this is Merlin's errand from the shades.'

'I vow to God,' quoth Sancho at this period, 'I say not three thousand, but I will as soon give myself three stabs as three lashes: the devil take this way of disenchanting: I cannot see what my buttocks have to do with enchantments.'

'Before God, if Señor Merlin can find out no other way to disenchant the lady Dulcinea del Toboso, enchanted she may go to her grave for me.'

'I shall take you, Don Peasant stuffed with garlic,' quoth Don Quixote, 'and tie you to a tree, naked as your mother bore you, and I say not three thousand and three hundred, but six thousand and six hundred lashes will I give you, and those so well laid on, that you shall not be able to let them off at three thousand three hundred hard tugs: so answer me not a word; for I will tear out your very soul.'

Which Merlin hearing, he said:

'It must not be so, for the lashes that honest Sancho is to receive must be with his goodwill, and not by force, and at what time he pleases, for there is no term set; but he is allowed, if he pleases, to save himself the pain of one half of this flogging by suffering the other half to be laid on by another hand, although it be somewhat weighty.'

'Neither another's hand, nor my own, nor one weighty, nor to be weighed, shall touch me,' quoth Sancho. 'Did I bring

forth the lady Dulcinea del Toboso, that my posteriors must
pay for the transgressions of her eyes? My master, indeed,
who is part of her, since at every step he is calling her his
life, his soul, his support, and stay, he can and ought to lash
himself for her, and take all the necessary measures for her
disenchantment; but for me to whip myself, I pronounce*
it.'

Scarcely had Sancho said this, when the silvered nymph
who sat close by the shade of Merlin, standing up, and
throwing aside her thin veil, discovered a face in every one's
opinion, more than excessively beautiful; and with a manly
assurance, and no very amiable voice, addressing herself
directly to Sancho Panza, she said.

'O unlucky squire, soul of a pitcher, heart of a cork-tree,
and of bowels full of gravel and flints! had you been bid,
nose-slitting thief, to throw yourself headlong from some
high tower; had you been desired, enemy of human kind, to
eat a dozen of toads, two of lizards, and three of snakes;
had anybody endeavoured to persuade you to kill your wife
and children with some bloody and sharp scimitar; no wonder
if you had betrayed an unwillingness and aversion; but to
make a stir about three thousand three hundred lashes, which
every puny schoolboy receives every month, it amazes,
stupefies, and affrights the tender bowels of all who hear it,
and even of all who shall hereafter be told it. Cast, miserable
and hard-hearted animal, cast, I say, those huge goggle eyes
of thine upon the balls of mine* compared to glittering stars,
and you will see them weep, drop after drop, and stream
after stream, making furrows, tracks, and paths, down the
beauteous fields of my cheeks. Relent, subtle and ill-inten-
tioned monster, at my blooming youth, still in its teens (for
I am past nineteen, and not quite twenty), pining and with-
ering under the bark of a coarse country wench: and, if at
this time I appear otherwise, it is by the particular favour of
Señor Merlin here present, merely that my charms may soften
you; for the tears of afflicted beauty turn rocks into cotton,
and tigers into lambs. Lash, untamed beast! lash that brawny
flesh of thine, and rouse from base sloth that courage, which
only inclines you to eat, and eat again; and set at liberty the

sleekness of my skin, the gentleness of my temper, and the beauty of my face; and if for my sake you will not be mollified, nor come to any reasonable terms, be so for the sake of that poor knight there by your side; your master, I mean, whose soul I see sticking crosswise in his throat, not ten inches from his lips, expecting nothing but your rigid or mild answer, either to jump out of his mouth, or to return to his stomach.'

Don Quixote, hearing this, put his finger to his throat to feel, and turning to the duke, said:

'Before God, sir, Dulcinea has said the truth; for here I feel my soul sticking in my throat like the stopper of a crossbow.'

'What say you to this, Sancho?' quoth the duchess.

'I say, madam,' answered Sancho, 'what I have already said, that, as to the lashes, I pronounce them.'

'Renounce, you should say, Sancho,' quoth the duke, 'and not pronounce.'

'Please, your grandeur, to let me alone,' answered Sancho; 'for, at present, I cannot stand to mind niceties, nor a letter more or less; for these lashes which are to be given me, or I must give myself, keep me so disturbed that I know not what I say, or what I do. But one thing I would fain know from the lady Dulcinea del Toboso, where she learned the way of entreaty she uses. She comes to desire me to tear my flesh with stripes, and at the same time calls me soul of a pitcher, and untamed beast; with such a beadroll of ill names that the devil may bear them for me. What! does she think my flesh is made of brass? or is it anything to me whether she be disenchanted, or no? Instead of bringing a basket of fine linen, shirts, nightcaps, and socks (though I wear none), to mollify me, here is nothing but reproach upon reproach, when she might have known the common proverb, that An ass laden with gold mounts nimbly up the hill; and, Presents break rocks; and, Pray to God devoutly, and hammer on stoutly; and, One take is worth two I'll give thee's.

'Then my master, instead of wheedling and coaxing me, to make myself of wool and carded cotton, says, if he takes me in hand, he will tie me naked with a rope to a tree, and double me the dose of stripes. Besides, these compassionate gentlefolks ought to consider, that they do not only desire to have a squire whipped, but a governor, as if it were like drinking after cherries, a thing of course. Let them learn, let them learn, in an ill hour, how to ask and entreat, and to have breeding; for all times are not alike, nor are men always in a good humour. I am at this time just ready to burst with grief to see my green jacket torn; and people come to desire me to whip myself, of my own goodwill, I having as little mind to it as to turn Indian prince.'

'In truth, friend Sancho,' quoth the duke, 'if you do not relent, and become softer than a ripe fig, you finger no government. It were good indeed, that I should send my islanders a cruel, flinty-hearted governor; one who relents not at the tears of afflicted damsels, nor at the entreaties of wise, awful, and ancient enchanters, and sages. In fine, Sancho, either you must whip yourself, or let others whip you, or be no governor.'

'My lord,' answered Sancho, 'may I not be allowed two days to consider what is best for me to do?'

'No, in nowise,' quoth Merlin: 'Here, at this instant, and upon this spot, the business must be settled; or Dulcinea must return to Montesinos' cave, and to her former condition of a country wench; or else in her present form be carried to the Elysian fields, where she must wait till the number of the lashes be fulfilled.'

'Come, honest Sancho,' quoth the duchess, 'be of good cheer, and show gratitude for the bread you have eaten of your master Don Quixote's, whom we are all bound to serve for his good qualities, and his high chivalries. Say, yes, son, to this whipping bout, and the devil take the devil, and let the wretched fear; for A good heart breaks bad fortune, as you well know.'

To these words Sancho answered with these extravagances; for speaking to Merlin, he said:

'Pray tell me, Señor Merlin, the court devil, who came hither, delivered my master a message from Señor Montesinos, bidding him wait for him here, for he was coming to give directions about the disenchantment of the lady Dulcinea del Toboso; and to this hour we have neither seen Montesinos, nor any likeness of his: pray, where is he?'

To which Merlin answered:

'The devil, friend Sancho, is a blockhead, and a very great rascal: I sent him in quest of your master, with a message, not from Montesinos, but from me; for Montesinos is still in his cave, plotting, or, to say better, expecting his disenchantment; for the worst is still behind; if he owes you aught, or you have any business with him, I will fetch him hither, and set him wherever you think fit: and therefore come to a conclusion, and say yes to this discipline; and, believe me, it will do you much good, as well your soul as your body; for your soul, in regard of the charity with which you will perform it; for your body, because I know you to be of a sanguine complexion, and letting out a little blood can do you no harm.'

'What a number of doctors there is in the world! the very enchanters are doctors,' replied Sancho. 'But since everybody tells me so, though I see no reason for it myself, I say, I am contented to give myself the three thousand three hundred lashes, upon condition that I may lay them on whenever I please, without being tied to days or times; and I will endeavour to get out of debt the soonest that I possibly can, that the world may enjoy the beauty of the lady Dulcinea del Toboso, since, contrary to what I thought, it seems she is in reality beautiful. I article likewise, that I will not be bound to draw blood with the whip, and if some lashes happen only to fly-flap, they shall be taken into the account. Item, if I should mistake in the reckoning, Señor Merlin, who knows everything, shall keep the account, and give me notice how many I want or have exceeded.'

'As for the exceedings, there is no need of keeping account,' answered Merlin; 'for, as soon as you arrive at the complete number, the lady Dulcinea del Toboso will be instantly disenchanted, and will come, in a most grateful manner, to seek honest Sancho, to thank, and even reward him for the good deed done. So that there need be no scruple about the surpluses or deficiencies; and heaven forbid I should cheat anybody of so much as a hair of their head.'

'Go to, then, in God's name,' quoth Sancho; 'I submit to my ill fortune; I say, I accept of the penance upon the conditions stipulated.'

Scarcely had Sancho uttered these words when the music of the waits struck up, and a world of muskets were again discharged; and Don Quixote clung about Sancho's neck, giving him a thousand kisses on the forehead and cheeks. The duke and duchess, and all the bystanders, gave signs of being mightily pleased, and the car began to move on; and, in passing by, the fair Dulcinea bowed her head to the duke and duchess, and made a low curtsy to Sancho. By this time the cheerful and joyous dawn came apace; the flowerets of the field expanded their fragrant bosoms, and erected their heads; and the liquid crystals of the brooks, murmuring through the white and grey pebbles, went to pay their tribute to the rivers that expected them. The earth rejoiced, the sky was clear, and the air serene; each singly, and all together, giving manifest tokens, that the day which trod upon Aurora's heels would be fair and clear. The duke and duchess, being satisfied with the sport, and having executed their design so ingeniously and happily, returned to their castle, with an intention of seconding their jest; since nothing real could have afforded them more pleasure.

CHAPTER 36

Wherein is related the strange and never-imagined adventure of the Afflicted Matron, alias the Countess of Trifaldi; with a letter written by Sancho Panza to his wife Teresa Panza.

THE duke had a steward, of a very pleasant and facetious wit, who represented Merlin, and contrived the whole apparatus of the late adventure, composed the verses, and made a page act Dulcinea. And now, with the duke and duchess's leave, he prepared another scene, of the pleasantest and strangest contrivance imaginable.

The next day, the duchess asked Sancho, whether he had begun the task of the penance he was to do for the disenchanting of Dulcinea. He said, he had, and had given himself five lashes that night. The duchess desired to know with what he had given them. He answered, with the palm of his hand.

'That,' replied the duchess, 'is rather clapping than whipping; and I am of opinion, Señor Merlin will hardly be contented at so easy a rate. Honest Sancho must get a rod made of briers, or of whipcord, that the lashes may be felt; for letters written in blood stand good, and the liberty of so great a lady as Dulcinea is not to be purchased so easily, or at so low a price. And take notice, Sancho, that works of charity, done faintly and coldly,* lose their merit, and signify nothing.'

To which Sancho answered:

'Give me, then, madam, some rod, or convenient bough, and I will whip myself with it, provided it do not smart too much; for I would have your ladyship know, that, though I am a clown, my flesh has more of the cotton than of the rush, and there is no reason I should hurt myself for other folks' good.'

'You say well,' answered the duchess: 'to-morrow I will give you a whip which shall suit you exactly, and agree with the tenderness of your flesh, as if it were its own brother.'

To which Sancho said:

'Your highness must know, dear lady of my soul, that I have written a letter to my wife Teresa Panza, giving her an account of all that has befallen me, since I parted from her: here I have it in my bosom, and it wants nothing but the superscription. I wish your discretion would read it: for methinks it runs as becomes a governor, I mean, in the manner that governors ought to write.'

'And who indited it?' demanded the duchess.

'Who should indite it, but I myself, sinner as I am?' answered Sancho.

'And did you write it?' said the duchess.

'No, indeed,' answered Sancho; 'for I can neither read nor write, though I can set my mark.'

'Let us see it,' said the duchess; 'for no doubt you show in it the quality and sufficiency of your genius.'

Sancho pulled an open letter out of his bosom, and the duchess, taking it in her hand, saw the contents were as follow:

Sancho Panza's letter to his wife Teresa Panza.

'If I have been finely lashed, I have been finely mounted; if I have got a good government, it has cost me many good lashes. This, my dear Teresa, you will not understand at present; another time you will. You must know, Teresa, that I am determined you shall ride in your coach, which is somewhat to the purpose; for all other ways of going are creeping upon all four like a cat. You shall be a governor's wife: see then whether anybody will tread on your heels. I here send you a green hunting suit, which my lady duchess gave me: fit it up, so that it may serve your daughter for a jacket and petticoat. They say, in this country, my master Don Quixote is a sensible madman, and a pleasant fool, and I am not a whit short of him. We have been in Montesinos' cave, and the sage Merlin has pitched upon me for the disenchanting of Dulcinea del Toboso, who among you is called Aldonza Lorenzo. With three thousand and three hundred lashes, lacking five, that I am to give myself, she will be as much disenchanted as the mother that bore her. Say nothing of this to anybody; for, go to give counsel about what is your own, and one will cry, it is white, another, it is black. A few days hence I shall go to the government, whither I go with an eager desire to make money; for, I am told, all new governors go with the selfsame intention. I will feel its pulse, and send you word whether you shall come and be with me, or no. Dapple is well, and sends his hearty service to you: I do not intend to leave him, though I were to be made the great Turk. The duchess, my mistress, kisses your hands a thousand times, return her two thousand: for nothing costs less, nor is cheaper, as my master says, than compliments of civility. God has not been pleased to bless me with another portmanteau, and another hundred crowns, as once before: but be in no pain, my dear Teresa: for he that has the repique in hand is safe,* and all will out in the bucking

of the government. Only one thing troubles me: for I am
told, if I once try it, I shall eat my very fingers after it: and,
if so, it would be no very good bargain; though the crippled
and lame in their hands enjoy a kind of petty-canonry in the
alms they receive: so that, by one means or another, you are
sure to be rich and happy. God make you so, as He easily
can, and keep me to serve you.

'Your husband, the governor,
'SANCHO PANZA.

'From this castle the 20th of July, 1614.'*

The duchess, having read the letter, said to Sancho:
'In two things the good governor is a little out of the way:
the one, in saying, or insinuating, that this government is given
him on account of the lashes he is to give himself; whereas
he knows and cannot deny it, that, when my lord duke
promised it him, nobody dreamed of any such thing as lashes
in the world: the other is, that he shows himself in it
very covetous; and I would not have him be griping; Avarice
bursts the bag, and, The covetous governor does ungoverned
justice.'

'That is not my meaning, madam,' answered Sancho; 'and,
if your ladyship thinks this letter does not run as it should
do, it is but tearing it, and writing a new one, and perhaps
it may prove a worse, if it be left to my noddle.'

'No, no,' replied the duchess, 'this is a very good one, and
I will have the duke see it.'

Hereupon they went to a garden, where they were to dine
that day, and the duchess showed Sancho's letter to the duke,
who was highly diverted with it. They dined, and, after the
cloth was taken away, and they had entertained themselves a
good while with Sancho's relishing conversation, on a sudden
they heard the dismal sound of a fife, and also that of a
hoarse and unbraced drum. They all discovered some surprise
at the confused, martial, and doleful harmony; especially Don
Quixote, who could not contain himself in his seat through
pure emotion. As for Sancho, it is enough to say, that fear
carried him to his usual refuge, which was the duchess's side,

or the skirts of her petticoat: for the sound they heard was really and truly most horrid and melancholy.

And, while they were thus in suspense, they perceived two men enter the garden, clad in mourning robes, so long and extended, that they trailed upon the ground. They came beating two great drums, covered also with black. By their side came the fife, black and frightful like the rest. These three were followed by a personage of gigantic stature, not clad, but mantled about, with a robe of the blackest dye, the train whereof was of a monstrous length. This robe was girt about with a broad black belt, at which there hung an unmeasurable scimitar in a black scabbard. His face was covered with a transparent black veil, through which appeared a prodigious long beard as white as snow. He marched to the sound of the drums, with much gravity and composure. In short, his huge bulk, his stateliness, his blackness, and his attendants, might very well surprise, as they did, all who beheld him, and were not in the secret. Thus he came, with the state and appearance aforesaid, and kneeled down before the duke, who, with the rest, received him standing. But the duke would in nowise suffer him to speak, till he rose up. The monstrous spectre did so, and, as soon as he was upon his feet, he lifted up his veil, and exposed to view the horridest, the longest, the whitest, and best furnished beard, that human eyes till then had ever beheld; and straight he sent forth from his broad and ample breast, a voice grave and sonorous; and, fixing his eyes on the duke, he said:

'Most mighty and puissant sir, I am called Trifaldin of the White Beard; I am squire to the Countess Trifaldi, otherwise called the Afflicted Matron, from whom I bring your grandeur a message; which is, that your magnificence would be pleased to give her permission and leave to enter, and tell her distress, which is one of the newest and most wonderful, that the most distressed thought in the world could ever have imagined: but first she desires to know, whether the valorous and invincible Don Quixote de la Mancha resides in this your castle; in quest of whom she is come on foot, and without breaking her fast, from the kingdom of Candaya* to this your territory; a thing which may and ought to be considered as a miracle, or ascribed to the force of enchantment. She waits at the door of this fortress or country house, and only stays for your good pleasure to come in.'

Having said this, he hemmed, and stroked his beard from top to bottom with both his hands, and with much tranquillity stood expecting the duke's answer, which was:

'It is now many days, honest Squire Trifaldin of the White Beard, since we have had notice of the misfortune of my lady the Countess Trifaldi, whom the enchanters have occasioned to be called the Afflicted Matron. Tell her, stupendous squire, she may enter, and that the valiant knight Don Quixote de la Mancha is here, from whose generous disposition she may safely promise herself all kind of aid and assistance. Tell her also from me, that if my favour be necessary, it shall not be wanting, since I am bound to it by being a knight; for to such it particularly belongs to protect all sorts of women, especially injured and afflicted matrons, such as her ladyship.'

Trifaldin, hearing this, bent a knee to the ground, and, making a sign to the fife and drums to play, he walked out of the garden to the same tune, and with the same solemnity as he came in, leaving every one in admiration at his figure and deportment.

The duke then, turning to Don Quixote, said:

'In short, renowned knight, neither the clouds of malice, or those of ignorance, can hide or obscure the light of valour and virtue. This I say, because it is hardly six days that your goodness has been in this castle, when, behold, the sorrowful and afflicted are already come in quest of you, from far distant and remote countries, and not in coaches, nor upon dromedaries, but on foot, and fasting, trusting they shall find, in that strenuous arm of yours, the remedy for their troubles and distresses: thanks to your grand exploits, which run and spread themselves over the whole face of the earth.'

'I wish, my lord duke,' answered Don Quixote, 'that the same ecclesiastic, who the other day expressed so much ill will and so great a grudge to knights-errant, were now here, that he might see with his eyes, whether or no such knights as those are necessary in the world; at least he would be made sensible, that the extraordinary afflicted and disconsolate, in great cases, and in enormous mishaps, do not fly for a remedy to the houses of scholars, nor to those of country parish priests, nor to the cavalier, who never thinks of stirring from his own town, nor to the lazy courtier, who rather inquires after news to tell again, than endeavours to perform actions and exploits for others to relate or write of him. Remedy for distress, relief in necessities, protection of damsels, and consolation of widows, are nowhere so readily to be found, as among knights-errant; and that I am one, I give infinite thanks to heaven, and shall not repine at any hardship or trouble that can befall me in so honourable an exercise. Let this matron come, and make what request she pleases: for I will commit her redress to the force of my arm, and the intrepid resolution of my courageous spirit.'

CHAPTER 37

In which is continued the famous adventure of the Afflicted Matron.

THE duke and duchess were extremely delighted to see how well Don Quixote answered their expectation; and here Sancho said:

'I should be loath that this madam duenna should lay any stumbling-block in the way of my promised government; for I have heard an apothecary of Toledo, who talked like any goldfinch, say, that, Where duennas have to do, no good thing can e'er ensue. Odds my life! what an enemy was that apothecary to them! and therefore, since all duennas are troublesome and impertinent, of what quality or condition soever they be, what must the afflicted be, as they say this same Countess Three-skirts or Three-tails* is; for in my country skirts and tails, and tails and skirts, are all one.'

'Peace, friend Sancho,' said Don Quixote; 'for, since this lady duenna comes in quest of me from so remote a country, she cannot be one of those the apothecary has in his list. Besides, this is a countess; and when countesses serve as duennas, it must be as attendants upon queens and empresses;

for in their own houses they command, and are served by other duennas.'

To this Doña Rodriguez, who was present, answered:

'My lady duchess has duennas in her service, who might have been countesses, if fortune had pleased; but, Laws go on kings' errands: and let no one speak ill of duennas, especially of the ancient maiden ones; for though I am not of that number, yet I well know, and clearly perceive the advantage a maiden duenna has over a widow duenna; though a pair of shears cut us all out of the same piece.'

'For all that,' replied Sancho, 'there is still so much to be sheared about your duennas, as my barber tells me, that it is better not to stir the rice, though it burn to the pot.'

'These squires,' quoth Doña Rodriguez, 'are always our enemies; and as they are a kind of fairies that haunt the antechambers, and spy us at every turn, the hours they are not at their beads, which are not a few, they employ in speaking ill of us, unburying our bones, and burying our reputations. But let me tell these moving blocks, that, in spite of their teeth, we shall live in the world, and in the best families too, though we starve for it, and cover our delicate or not delicate bodies with a black weed, as people cover a dunghill with a piece of tapestry on a procession day. In faith, if I might, and if I had time, I would make all here present, and all the world besides, know, that there is no virtue, but is contained in a duenna.'

'I am of opinion,' quoth the duchess, 'that my good Doña Rodriguez is in the right, and very much so: but she must wait for a fit opportunity to stand up for herself, and the rest of the duennas, to confound the ill opinion of that wicked apothecary, and root out that, which the great Sancho has in his breast.'

To which Sancho answered:

'Ever since the fumes of government have got into my head, I have lost the megrims* of squireship, and care not a fig for all the duennas in the world.'

This dialogue about duennas had continued, had they not heard the drum and fife strike up again; by which they understood the Afflicted Matron was just entering. The duchess asked the duke, whether it was not proper to go and meet her, since she was a countess, and a person of quality.

'As she is a countess,' quoth Sancho, before the duke could answer, 'it is very fit your grandeurs should go to receive her; but, as she is a duenna, I am of opinion you should not stir a step.'

'Who bade you intermeddle in this matter, Sancho?' said Don Quixote.

'Who, sir?' answered Sancho: 'I myself, who have a right to intermeddle as a squire, who has learned the rules of courtesy in the school of your worship, who is the best-bred knight courtesy ever produced: and in these matters, as I have heard your worship say, one may as well lose the game by a card too much as a card too little; and a word to the wise.'

'It is even so, as Sancho says,' quoth the duke; 'we shall soon see what kind of a countess this is, and by that we shall judge what courtesy is due to her.'

And now the drums and fifes entered, as they did the first time. And here the author ended this short chapter, and began another with the continuation of the same adventure, being one of the most notable in the history.

CHAPTER 38

In which an account is given of the Afflicted Matron's misfortunes.

AFTER the doleful music, there began to enter the garden twelve duennas, divided into two files, all clad in large mourning habits, seemingly of milled serge, with white veils of thin muslin, so long that only the border of the robe appeared. After these came the Countess Trifaldi, whom Squire Trifaldin of the White Beard led by the hand. She was clad in a robe of the finest serge; which had it been napped, each grain would have been the size of a good ronceval pea.* The train or tail (call it which you will) was divided into three corners, supported by three pages, clad also in mourning, making a sightly and mathematical figure, with the three acute angles, formed by the three corners; from which all that saw them concluded she was from thence called the Countess Trifaldi, as much as to say, the Countess of the Three Skirts: and Ben Engeli says, that was the truth of the matter, and that her right title was the Countess Lobuna, because that earldom produced abundance of wolves;* and had they been foxes* instead of wolves, she would have been styled Countess Zorruna, it being the custom in those parts for the great persons to take their titles from the thing or things, with which their country most abounded. But this countess, in favour of the new cut of her train, quitted that of Lobuna, and took that of Trifaldi.

The twelve duennas, with the lady, advanced at a procession pace, their faces covered with black veils, and not transparent like Trifaldin's but so close that nothing could be seen through them. Now, upon the appearance of this squadron of duennas, the duke, duchess, and Don Quixote, rose from their seats, as did all the rest who beheld this grand procession. The twelve duennas halted and made a passage, through which the Afflicted [One] advanced, without Trifaldin's letting go her hand. Which the duke, duchess, and Don Quixote seeing, they stepped forward about a dozen paces to receive her. She, kneeling on the ground, with a voice rather harsh and coarse, than fine and delicate, said:

'May it please your grandeurs to spare condescending to do so great a courtesy to this your valet; I mean your handmaid: for such is my affliction that I shall not be able to answer as I ought, because my strange and unheard-of misfortune has carried away my understanding, I know not whither; and sure it must be a vast way off, since the more I seek it, the less I find it.'

'He would want it, lady countess,' quoth the duke, 'who could not judge of your worth by your person, which, without seeing any more, merits the whole cream of courtesy, and the whole flower of well-bred ceremonies.'

And, raising her by the hand, he led her to a chair close by the duchess, who also received her with much civility. Don Quixote held his peace, and Sancho was dying with impatience to see the face of the Trifaldi, or of some one of her many duennas: but it was not possible, till they of their own accord unveiled themselves.

Now all keeping silence, and in expectation who should break it, the Afflicted Matron began in these words:

'Confident I am, most mighty lord, most beautiful lady, and most discreet bystanders, that my most miserable miserableness will find in your most valorous breasts a protection no less placid than generous and dolorous; for such it is, as is sufficient to mollify marbles, soften diamonds, and melt the steel of the hardest hearts in the world. But, before it ventures on the public stage of your hearing, not to say of your ears, I should be glad to be informed whether the refinedissimo knight, Don Quixote de la Manchissima, and his squirissimo Panza, be in this bosom, circle, or company.'

'Panza,' said Sancho, before anybody else could answer, 'is here, and also Don Quixotissimo; and therefore, Afflictedissima Matronissima, say what you have a mindissima; for we are all ready and preparedissimos to be your servitorissimos.'

Upon this Don Quixote stood up, and directing his discourse to the Afflicted Matron, said:

'If your distresses, afflicted lady, can promise themselves any remedy from the valour or fortitude of a knight-errant, behold mine, which though weak and scanty, shall be all employed in your service. I am Don Quixote de la Mancha, whose function it is to succour the distressed of all sorts; and this being so, as it really is, you need not, madam, bespeak goodwill, nor have recourse to preambles, but plainly, and without circumlocution, tell your griefs; for you are within hearing of those, who know how to compassionate, if not to redress them.'

Which the Afflicted Matron hearing, she made a show as if she would prostrate herself at Don Quixote's feet; and actually did so, and, struggling to kiss them, said:

'I prostrate myself, O invincible knight, before these feet and legs as the bases and pillars of knight-errantry! these feet will I kiss, on whose steps the whole remedy of my misfortune hangs and depends, O valorous errant, whose true

exploits outstrip and obscure the fabulous ones of the Amadises, Esplandians, and Belianises!'

And leaving Don Quixote, she turned to Sancho Panza,
and taking him by the hand, said:

'O thou the most trusty squire that ever served knight-
errant, in the present or past ages, whose goodness is of
greater extent than the beard of my companion Trifaldin here
present, well may'st thou boast, that in serving Don Quixote,
thou dost serve in miniature the whole tribe of knights that
ever handled arms in the world: I conjure thee, by what thou
owest to thy own fidelity and goodness, to become an
importunate intercessor for me with thy lord, that he would
instantly favour the humblest and unhappiest of countesses.'

To which Sancho answered:

'Whether my goodness, madam, be or be not as long and
as broad as your squire's beard, signifies little to me: so that
my soul be bearded and whiskered, when it departs this life,
I care little or nothing for beards, here below: but without
these wheedlings and beseechings, I will desire my master,
who I know has a kindness for me, especially now that he
wants me for a certain business, to favour and assist your
ladyship in whatever he can. Unbundle your griefs, madam,
and let us into the particulars; and leave us alone to manage,
for we shall understand one another.'

The duke and duchess were ready to burst with laughing
at all this, as knowing the drift of this adventure; and
commended in their thoughts the smartness and dissimulation
of the Trifaldi, who, returning to her seat, said:

'Of the famous kingdom of Candaya, which lies between
the great Taprobana* and the South Sea, two leagues from
Cape Comorin, was queen Doña Maguncia, widow of king
Archipiela her lord and husband; from which marriage sprung
the Infanta Antonomasia, heiress of the kingdom; which
Infanta Antonomasia was educated under my care and instruction, as being the most ancient duenna, and of the best
quality, among those that waited upon her mother. Now, in
process of time, the young Antonomasia arrived to the age
of fourteen, with such perfection of beauty, that nature could
not raise it a pitch higher: and, what is more, discretion itself

was but a child to her, for she was as discreet as fair, and she was the fairest creature in the world, and is so still, if envious fates and hard-hearted destinies have not cut short her thread of life. But, sure, they have not done it; for heaven would never permit, that so much injury should be done to the earth, as to tear off such an unripe cluster from the fairest vine of the earth. Of this beauty, never sufficiently extolled by my feeble tongue, an infinite number of princes, as well natives as foreigners, grew enamoured.

'Among whom, a private gentleman of the court dared to raise his thoughts to the heaven of so much beauty, confiding in his youth, his genteel finery, his many abilities and graces, and the facility and felicity of his wit: for I must tell your grandeurs, if it be no offence, that he touched a guitar so as to make it speak. He was, besides, a poet, and a fine dancer, and could make bird-cages so well, as to get his living by it, in case of extreme necessity. So many qualifications and endowments were sufficient to overset a mountain, and much more a tender virgin.

'But all his gentility, graceful behaviour, and fine accomplishments, would have signified little or nothing towards the conquest of my girl's fortress, if the robber and ruffian had not artfully contrived to reduce me first. The assassin and barbarous vagabond began with endeavouring to obtain my goodwill, and suborn my inclination, that I might, like a treacherous keeper as I was, deliver up to him the keys of the fortress I guarded. In short, he imposed upon my understanding, and got from me my consent, by means of I know not what toys and trinkets he presented me with. But that, which chiefly brought me down, and levelled me with the ground, was a stanza, which I heard him sing one night, through a grate that looked into an alley where he stood; and, if I remember right, the verses were these:

'The tyrant fair, whose beauty sent
    The throbbing mischief to my heart,
    The more my anguish to augment,
        Forbids me to reveal the smart.*

'The stanza seemed to me to be of pearls, and his voice of barley-sugar; and many a time since have I thought, considering the mishap I fell into, that poets, at least the lascivious, ought, as Plato advised, to be banished from all good and well-regulated commonwealths; because they write couplets, not like those of the Marquess of Mantua, which divert, and make children and women weep, but such pointed things as, like smooth thorns, pierce the soul, and wound like lightning, leaving the garment whole and unsigned. Another time he sung:

'Come, Death, with gently-stealing pace,
    And take me, unperceiv'd, away;
Not let me see thy wish'd-for face,
    Lest joy my fleeting life should stay.*

with other such couplets and ditties as enchant when sung, and surprise when written. Now, when they condescend to compose a kind of verses, at that time in fashion in Candaya, which they call roundelays, they presently occasion a dancing of the soul, a tickling of the fancy, a perpetual agitation of the body, and, lastly, a kind of quicksilver of all the senses. And therefore I say, most noble auditors, that such versifiers deserve to be banished to the Isle of Lizards:* though in truth they are not to blame, but the simpletons who commend them, and the idiots who believe them: and, had I been the honest duenna I ought, his nightly serenades had not moved me, nor had I believed those poetical expressions: "Dying I live; in ice I burn; I shiver in flames; in despair I hope; I go, yet stay"; with other impossibilities of the like stamp, of which their writings are full. And when they promise us the phoenix of Arabia, the crown of Ariadne, the hairs of the sun, the pearls of the South Sea, the gold of Tibar,* and the balsam of Pancaya;* they then give their pen the greatest scope, as it costs them little to promise what they never intend, nor can perform.

'But, woe is me, unhappy wretch! whither do I stray? what folly, or what madness hurries me to recount the faults of others, having so many of my own to relate? Woe is me again, unhappy creature! for not his verses, but my own simplicity, vanquished me: not the music, but my levity, my great ignorance, and my little caution, melted me down, opened the way, and smoothed the passage for Don Clavijo;* for that is the name of the aforesaid cavalier.

'And so, I being the go-between, he was often in the chamber of the betrayed, not by him but me, Antonomasia, under the title of her lawful husband: for, though a sinner, I would never have consented, without his being her husband, that he should have come within the shadow of her shoe-string. No, no, marriage must be the forerunner of any business of this kind undertaken by me: only there was one mischief in it, which was, the disparity between them; Don Clavijo being but a private gentleman, and the Infanta Antonomasia heiress, as I have already said, of the kingdom. This intrigue lay concealed and wrapped up in the sagacity of my cautious management for some time, till I perceived it began to show itself in I know not what kind of swelling in Antonomasia's belly; the apprehension whereof made us three lay our heads together; and the result was, that, before the unhappy slip should come to light, Don Clavijo should demand Antonomasia in marriage before the vicar, in virtue of a contract, signed by the infanta and given him, to be his wife, worded by my wit, and in such strong terms, that the force of Sampson was not able to break through it. The business was put in execution; the vicar saw the contract, and took the lady's confession; she acknowledged the whole, and was ordered into the custody of an honest alguazil of the court.'

Here Sancho said:

'What! are there court-alguazils, poets, and roundelays in Candaya too? if so, I swear I think the world is the same everywhere: but, Madam Trifaldi, pray make haste; for it grows late, and I die to hear the end of this so very long story.'

'That I will,' answered the countess.

CHAPTER 39

*Wherein Trifaldi continues her stupendous and memorable
history.*

AT every word Sancho spoke, the duchess was in as high
delight as Don Quixote was at his wit's end; who commanding him to hold his peace, the Afflicted [One] went on,
saying:

'In short, after many pros and cons, the infanta standing
stiffly to her engagement, without varying or departing from
her first declaration, the vicar pronounced sentence in favour
of Don Clavijo, and gave her to him to wife: at which the
queen, Doña Maguncia, mother to the Infanta Antonomasia,
was so much disturbed, that we buried her in three days'
time.'

'She died then, I suppose,' quoth Sancho.

'Most assuredly,' answered Trifaldin; 'for in Candaya, they
do not bury the living, but the dead.'

'Master Squire,' replied Sancho, 'it has happened ere now,
that a person in a swoon has been buried for dead; and, in
my opinion, Queen Maguncia ought to have swooned away
rather than have died; for, while there is life there is hope;
and the infanta's transgression was not so great, that she
should lay it so much to heart. Had the lady married one of
her pages, or any other servant of the family, as many others
have done, as I have been told, the mischief had been without
remedy; but she having made choice of a cavalier, so much
a gentleman, and of such parts as he is here painted to us,
verily, verily, though perhaps it was foolish, it was not so
very much so as some people think: for, according to the
rules of my master, who is here present, and will not let me
lie, as bishops are made out of learned men, so kings and
emperors may be made out of cavaliers, especially if they are
errant.'

'You are in the right, Sancho,' said Don Quixote; 'for a
knight-errant, give him but two inches of good luck, is next
oars to being the greatest lord in the world. But let Madam
Afflicted proceed; for I fancy the bitter part of this hitherto
sweet story is still behind.'

'The bitter behind!' answered the countess: 'aye, and so bitter, that in comparison, wormwood is sweet, and rue savoury.'

'The queen being now dead, and not swooned away, we buried her; and scarcely had we covered her with earth and pronounced the last farewell, when *quis talia fando*... *temperet a lacrimis?* * upon the queen's sepulchre appeared, mounted on a wooden horse, the giant Malambruno, her cousin-german, who besides being cruel, is an enchanter also. This giant, in revenge of his cousin's death, and in chastisement of the boldness of Don Clavijo, and the folly of Antonomasia, left them both enchanted by his art, upon the very sepulchre; her converted into a monkey of brass, and him into a fearful crocodile, of an unknown metal; and between them lies a plate of metal likewise, with letters engraved upon it in the Syriac language, which being rendered into the Candayan, and now into the Castilian, contain this sentence: "These two presumptuous lovers shall not recover their pristine form, till the valorous Manchegan shall enter into single combat with me; for the destinies reserve this unheard-of adventure for his great valour alone."

'This done, he drew out of the scabbard a broad and unmeasurable scimitar, and, taking me by the hair of my head, he made show as if he would cut my throat, or whip off my head at a blow. I was frighted to death, and my voice stuck in my throat: nevertheless, recovering myself as well as I could, with a trembling and doleful voice, I used such entreaties as prevailed with him to suspend the execution of so rigorous a punishment. Finally, he sent for all the duennas of the palace, being those here present, and, after having exaggerated our fault, and inveighed against the qualities of duennas, their wicked plots, and worse intrigues, and charging them with all that blame which I alone deserved, he said, he would not chastise us with capital punishment, but with other lengthened pains, which should put us to a kind of civil and perpetual death: and in the very instant he had done speaking, we all felt the pores of our faces open, and a pricking pain all over them, like the pricking of needles. Immediately we clapped our hands to our faces, and found them in the condition you shall see presently.'

Then the Afflicted, and the rest of the duennas, lifted up
the veils which concealed them, and discovered their faces
all planted with beards, some blond, some black, some white,
and some piebald: at which sight the duke and duchess
seemed to wonder, Don Quixote and Sancho were amazed,
and all present astonished; and the Trifaldi proceeded:

'Thus that wicked and evil-minded felon Malambruno punished us, covering the soft smoothness of our faces with the
ruggedness of these bristles: would to heaven he had struck
off our heads with his unmeasurable scimitar, rather than
have obscured the light of our countenances with these
brushes that overspread them! for, noble lords and lady, if
we rightly consider it (and what I am now going to say I
would speak with rivers of tears, but that the consideration
of our misfortune, and the seas our eyes have already wept,
keep them without moisture, and dry as the beards of corn;
and therefore I will speak it without tears), I say then, whither
can a duenna with a beard go? what father or what mother
will bewail her? who will succour her? for, even when her
grain is the smoothest, and her face tortured with a thousand
sorts of washes and ointments, scarcely can she find anybody
to show kindness to her; what must she do then, when her
face is become a wood? O ye duennas, my dear companions,
in an unlucky hour were we born, and in an evil minute did
our fathers beget us.'

And, so saying, she seemed to faint away.

CHAPTER 40

*Of matters relating and appertaining to this adventure, and
to this memorable history.*

IN reality and truth, all who delight in such histories as this,
ought to be thankful to its original author, Cid Hamet, for
his curious exactness in recording the minutest circumstances
thereof, without omitting anything how trifling soever, but
bringing everything distinctly to light. He paints thoughts,
discovers imaginations, answers the silent, clears up doubts,

resolves arguments; and, lastly, manifests the least atoms of
the most inquisitive desire. O most celebrated author! O
happy Don Quixote! O famous Dulcinea! O facetious Sancho
Panza! Live each jointly and severally infinite ages, for the
general pleasure and pastime of the living.

Now the story says, that, when Sancho saw the Afflicted
[One] faint away, he said:

'Upon the faith of an honest man, and by the blood of all
my ancestors, the Panzas, I swear, I never heard or saw, nor
has my master ever told me, nor did such an adventure as
this ever enter into his thoughts. A thousand devils take thee
(I would not curse anybody) for an enchanter, and a giant,
Malambruno! couldst thou find no other kind of punishment
to inflict upon these sinners, but that of bearding them? Had
it not been better (I am sure it had been better for them) to
have whipped off half their noses, though they had snuffled
for it, than to have clapped them on beards? I will lay a
wager, they have not wherewith to pay for shaving.'

'That is true, sir,' answered one of the twelve; 'we have
not wherewith to keep ourselves clean; and therefore, to shift
as well as we can, some of us use sticking-plasters of pitch;
which being applied to the face, and pulled off with a jerk,
we remain as sleek and smooth as the bottom of a stone
mortar: for, though there are women in Candaya, who go
from house to house, to take off the hair of the body, and
shape the eyebrows, and other jobs pertaining to women, we,
who are my lady's duennas, would never have anything to
do with them; for most of them smell of the procuress,
having ceased to be otherwise serviceable: and if we are not
relieved by Señor Don Quixote, with beards shall we be
carried to our graves.'

'Mine,' quoth Don Quixote, 'shall be plucked off in the
country of the Moors, rather than not free you from
yours.'

By this time the Trifaldi was come to herself, and said:

'The murmuring sound of that promise, valorous knight,
in the midst of my swoon, reached my ears, and was the
occasion of my coming out of it, and recovering my senses:
and so once again I beseech you, illustrious errant, and

invincible sir, that your gracious promises may be converted into deeds.'

'It shall not rest at me,' answered Don Quixote; 'inform me, madam, what it is I am to do; for my inclination is fully disposed to serve you.'

'The case is,' answered the Afflicted [One], 'that, from hence to the kingdom of Candaya, if you go by land, it is five thousand leagues, one or two more or less; but if you go through the air in a direct line, it is three thousand two hundred and twenty-seven.

'You must know also, that Malambruno told me, that, when fortune should furnish me with the knight our deliverer, he would send him a steed, much better, and with fewer vicious tricks, than a post horse returned to his stage; for it is to be that very wooden horse upon which the valiant Peter of Provence carried off the fair Magalona.* This horse is governed by a pin he has in his forehead, which serves for a bridle; and he flies through the air with such swiftness, that one would think the devil himself carried him. This same horse, according to ancient tradition, was the workmanship of the sage Merlin, who lent him to Peter, who was his friend; upon which he took great journeys, and stole, as has been said, the fair Magalona, carrying her behind him through the air, and leaving all that beheld him from the earth, staring and astonished: and he lent him to none but particular friends, or such as paid him a handsome price. Since the grand Peter to this time, we know of nobody that has been upon his back. Malambruno procured him by his art, and keeps him in his power, making use of him in the journeys he often takes through divers parts of the world: to-day he is here, to-morrow in France, and the next day in Potosí: and the best of it is, that this same horse neither eats nor sleeps, nor wants any shoeing, and ambles such a pace through the air, without wings, that his rider may carry a dishful of water in his hand without spilling a drop, he travels so smooth and easy; which made the fair Magalona take great delight in riding.'

To this Sancho said:

'For smooth and easy goings, commend me to my Dapple,

though he goes not through the air; but by land, I will match him against all the amblers in the world.'

This set the company a-laughing, and the Afflicted [One] proceeded:

'Now this horse, if Malambruno intends to put an end to our misfortune, will be here within half an hour after it is dark; for he told me, that the sign, by which I should be assured of having found that knight I sought after, should be the sending me the horse to the place where the knight was, with conveniency and speed.'

'And pray,' quoth Sancho, 'how many can ride upon this same horse?'

'Two persons,' answered the Afflicted, 'one in the saddle, and the other behind on the crupper, and generally these two persons are the knight and his squire, when there is no stolen damsel in the case.'

'I should be glad to know, Madam Afflicted,' quoth Sancho, 'what this horse's name is.'

'His name,' answered the Afflicted [One], 'is not Pegasus, as was that of Bellerophon; nor Bucephalus, as was that of Alexander the Great; nor Brigliadoro, as was that of Orlando Furioso; nor is it Bayarte, which belonged to Reynaldos of Montalvan; nor Frontino, which was Rogero's: nor is it Böotes nor Pyrithöus, as they say the horses of the sun are called: neither is he called Orelia, the horse which the unfortunate Rodrigo, the last king of the Goths in Spain, mounted, in that battle wherein he lost his kingdom and life.'

'I will venture a wager,' quoth Sancho, 'since they have given him none of those famous and well-known names, neither have they given him that of my master's horse Rosinante, which in propriety exceeds all that have been hitherto named.'

'True,' answered the bearded countess, 'but still it suits him well: for he is called Clavileño* the Winged; which name answers to his being of wood, to the peg in his forehead, and to the swiftness of his motion; so that, in respect of his name, he may very well come in competition with the renowned Rosinante.'

'I dislike not the name,' replied Sancho: 'but with what bridle, or with what halter, is he guided?'

'I have already told you,' answered the Trifaldi, 'that he is guided by a peg, which the rider turning this way and that, makes him go either aloft in the air, or else sweeping, and, as it were, brushing the earth; or in the middle region, which is what is generally aimed at, and is to be kept to in all well-ordered actions.'

'I have a great desire to see him,' answered Sancho; 'but to think that I will get upon him, either in the saddle, or behind upon the crupper, is to look for pears upon an elm tree. It were a good jest indeed, for me, who can hardly sit my own Dapple, though upon a pannel softer than the very silk, to think now of getting upon a crupper of boards, without either pillow or cushion: in faith, I do not intend to flay myself, to take off anybody's beard; let every one shave as he likes best; I shall not bear my master company in so long a journey: besides, I am out of the question; for I can be of no service towards the shaving of these beards, as I am for the disenchanting of my lady Dulcinea.'

'Indeed but you can, friend,' answered the Trifaldi, 'and of so much service, that without you, as I take it, we are likely to do nothing at all.'

'In the king's name,' quoth Sancho, 'what have squires to do with their master's adventures? must they run away with the fame of those they accomplish, and must we undergo the fatigue? Body of me! did the historians but say, "Such a knight achieved such and such an adventure, with the help of such an one, his squire, without whom it had been impossible for him to finish it", it were something; but you shall have them dryly write thus: "Don Paralipomenon of the Three Stars, achieved the adventure of the six goblins"; without naming his squire, who was present all the while, as if there had been no such person in the world. I say again, good my lord and lady, my master may go by himself, and much good may it do him; for I will stay here by my lady duchess: and, perhaps, when he comes back, he may find Madam Dulcinea's business pretty forward; for I intend, at idle and leisure whiles, to give myself such a whipping-bout that not a hair shall interpose.'

'For all that, honest Sancho,' quoth the duchess, 'you must

bear him company, if need be, and that at the request of good people; for it would be a great pity the faces of these ladies should remain thus bushy through your needless fears.'

'In the king's name once more,' replied Sancho, 'were this piece of charity undertaken for modest, sober damsels, or for poor innocent hospital girls, a man might venture upon some painstaking; but, to endure it to rid duennas of their beards, with a murrain* to them, I had rather see them all bearded from the highest to the lowest, and from the nicest to the most slatternly.'

'You are upon very bad terms with the duennas, friend Sancho,' quoth the duchess, 'and are much of the Toledan apothecary's mind: but in troth you are in the wrong; for I have duennas in my family fit to be patterns to all duennas: and here stands Doña Rodriguez, who will not contradict me.'

'Your excellency may say what you please,' quoth [the] Rodriguez; 'for God knows the truth of everything, and, good or bad, bearded or smooth, such as we are our mothers brought us forth, like other women; and since God cast us into the world, He knows for what; and I rely upon His mercy, and not upon anybody's beard whatever.'

'Enough, Mistress Rodriguez,' quoth Don Quixote; 'and, Madam Trifaldi and company, I trust in God, that He will look upon your distresses with an eye of goodness; and as for Sancho, he shall do what I command him. I wish Clavileño were once come, and that Malambruno and I were at it; for I am confident, no razor would more easily shave your ladyships beards, than my sword shall shave off Malambruno's head from his shoulders: for though God permits the wicked to prosper, it is but for a time.'

'Ah!' quoth the Afflicted [One] at this juncture, 'valorous knight, may all the stars of the celestial regions behold your worship with eyes of benignity, and infuse into your heart all prosperity and courage, to be the shield and refuge of our reviled and dejected order, abominated by apothecaries, murmured at by squires, and scoffed at by pages. Ill betide the wretch, who, in the flower of her age, does rather profess herself a nun, than a duenna. Unfortunate we the duennas!

though we descended in a direct male line from Hector of Troy, our mistresses will never forbear "thouing"* us, were they to be made queens for it. O giant Malambruno, who, though thou art an enchanter, are very punctual in thy promises, send us now the incomparable Clavileño, that our misfortune may have an end; for, if the heats come on, and these beards of ours continue, woe be to us.'

The Trifaldi uttered this with so deep a concern, that she drew tears from the eyes of all the bystanders, and even made Sancho's overflow; and he purposed in his heart to accompany his master to the farthest part of the world, if on that depended the clearing of those venerable faces of their wool.

CHAPTER 41

Of the arrival of Clavileño, with the conclusion of this prolix adventure.

IN the meanwhile night came on, and with it the point of time prefixed for the arrival of the famous horse Clavileño: whose stay perplexed Don Quixote very much, thinking that, since Malambruno delayed sending him, either he was not the knight for whom this adventure was reserved, or Malambruno durst not encounter him in single combat. But, behold, on a sudden, four savages enter the garden, all clad in green ivy, and bearing on their shoulders a large wooden horse. They set him upon his legs on the ground, and one of the savages said:

'Let him, who has courage to do it, mount this machine.'

'Not I,' quoth Sancho; 'for neither have I courage, nor am I a knight.'

And the savage proceeded, saying:

'And let the squire, if he has one, get up behind, and trust the valorous Malambruno; for no other body's sword or malice shall hurt him: and there is no more to do, but to screw the pin he has in his forehead, and he will bear them through the air to the place where Malambruno expects them: but lest the height and sublimity of the way should make their heads swim, their eyes must be covered until the horse neighs, which is to be the signal of his being arrived at his journey's end.'

This said, leaving Clavileño, with courteous demeanour they returned by the way they came.

As soon as the Afflicted [One] espied the horse, almost with tears, she said to Don Quixote:

'Valorous knight, Malambruno has kept his word; here is the horse; our beards are increasing, and every one of us, with every hair of them, beseech you to shave and shear us, since there is no more for you to do but to mount, with your squire behind you, and so give a happy beginning to your new journey.'

'That I will, with all my heart, and most willingly, Madam Trifaldi,' quoth Don Quixote, 'without staying to procure a cushion, or put on my spurs, to avoid delay; so great is the desire I have to see your ladyship and all these duennas shaven and clean.'

'That will not I,' quoth Sancho, 'with a bad or a good will, or anywise; and, if this shaving cannot be performed without my riding behind, let my master seek some other squire to bear him company, and these madams some other way of smoothing their faces; for I am no wizard to delight in travelling through the air: besides, what will my islanders say, when they hear that their governor is taking the air upon the wings of the wind? And another thing; it being three thousand leagues from thence to Candaya, if the horse should tire, or the giant be out of humour, we shall be half a dozen years in coming back, and by that time I shall have neither island nor islanders in the world that will know me; and, since it is a common saying, The danger lies in the delay, and, When they give you a heifer, make haste with the halter, these gentlewomen's beards must excuse me: St. Peter is well at Rome; I mean, that I am very well in this house, where they make much of me, and from the master of which I expect so great a benefit as to be made a governor.'

To which the duke said:

'Friend Sancho, the island I have promised you is not a floating one, nor will it run away: it is so fast rooted in the abyss of the earth, that it cannot be plucked up, nor stirred from the place where it is, at three pulls: and since you know there is no kind of office of any considerable value but is procured by some kind of bribe, more or less, what I expect for this government is, that you go with your master Don Quixote to accomplish and put an end to this memorable adventure; and, whether you return upon Clavileño with the expedition his speed promises, or the contrary fortune betides you, and you come back on foot, turned pilgrim, from house to house, and from inn to inn, return when you will, you will find your island where you left it, and your islanders with the same desire to receive you for their governor; and my goodwill shall be always the same: and to doubt this truth, Señor Sancho, would be doing a notorious injury to the inclination I have to serve you.'

'No more, good sir,' quoth Sancho; 'I am a poor squire, and cannot carry so much courtesy upon my back: let my master get up; let these eyes of mine be hoodwinked, and commend me to God; and pray tell me, when we are in our altitudes, may I not pray to God, and invoke the angels to protect me?'

To which the Trifaldi answered:

'You may pray to God, Sancho, or to whom you will; for, though Malambruno be an enchanter, he is a Christian, and performs his enchantments with much sagacity, great precaution and without disturbing anybody.'

'Come on, then,' quoth Sancho; 'God and the most holy Trinity of Gaeta help me!'

'Since the memorable adventure of the fulling-mills,' said Don Quixote, 'I never saw Sancho in so much fear as now; and were I as superstitious as other people, his pusillanimity would a little discourage me: but, come hither, Sancho; for, with the leave of these noble persons, I would have a word or two with you in private.'

Then going aside with Sancho among some trees in the garden, and taking hold of both his hands, he said to him:

'You see, brother Sancho, the long journey we are going to undertake, and God knows when we shall return, or what convenience and leisure business will afford us; and therefore

my desire is, that you retire to your chamber as if to fetch
something necessary for the road, and, in a twinkling, give
yourself if it be but five hundred lashes, in part of the three
thousand three hundred you stand engaged for; for, Well
begun is half ended.'

'Before God,' quoth Sancho, 'your worship is stark mad:
this is just the saying; "You see I am in haste,* and you
charge me with a maidenhead": now that I am just going to
sit down upon a bare board, would you have me gall my
buttocks? verily, verily, your worship is in the wrong; let us
now go and trim these duennas, and, at my return, I promise
you I will make such dispatch to get out of debt, that your
worship shall be contented, and I say no more.'

Don Quixote answered:

'With this promise then, honest Sancho, I am somewhat
comforted, and believe you will perform it; for, though you
are not over wise, you are true blue.'

'I am not blue, but brown,' quoth Sancho; 'but though I
were a mixture of both, I would make good my promise.'

Upon this they came back, in order to mount Clavileño;
and, at getting up, Don Quixote said:

'Hoodwink yourself, and get up, Sancho; for whoever he
be that sends for us from countries so remote, he cannot
surely intend to deceive us, considering the little glory he will
get by deceiving those who confide in him: but, suppose the
very reverse of what we imagine should happen, no malice
can obscure the glory of having attempted the exploit.'

'Let us be gone, sir,' quoth Sancho; 'for the beards and
tears of these ladies have pierced my heart, and I shall not
eat a bit to do me good, till I see them restored to their
former smoothness.'

'Mount you, sir, and hoodwink first; for, if I am to ride
behind, it is plain, he, who is to be in the saddle must get
up first.'

'That is true,' replied Don Quixote; and, pulling a handkerchief out of his pocket, he desired the Afflicted [One] to
cover his eyes close; which being done, he uncovered them
again, and said:

'If I remember right, I have read in Virgil that story of

the Palladium of Troy, which was a wooden horse, dedicated by the Greeks to the goddess Pallas, and filled with armed knights, who afterwards proved the final destruction of Troy; and therefore it will not be amiss to see first what Clavileño has in his belly.'

'There is no need of that,' said the Afflicted [One]; 'for I am confident that Malambruno has nothing of the trickster or traitor in him: your worship, Señor Don Quixote, may mount without fear, and upon me be it if any harm happens to you.'

Don Quixote considered, that to talk any more of his security would be a reflection upon his courage; and so without further contest, he mounted Clavileño, and tried the pin, which screwed about very easily; and having no stirrups, and his legs dangling down, he looked like a figure in a Roman triumph, painted or woven in some antique piece of Flemish tapestry.

By little and little, and much against his will, Sancho got up behind, adjusting himself the best way he could upon the crupper, which he found not over soft, and begged the duke, if it were possible, to accommodate him with some pillow or cushion, though it were from the duchess's state sofa, or from one of the page's beds; the horse's crupper seeming rather to be of marble than of wood. To this the Trifaldi replied, that Clavileño would not endure any kind of furniture upon him; but that he might sit sideways like a woman, and then he would not be so sensible of the hardness. Sancho did so, and bidding adieu, he suffered his eyes to be blind-folded. But, soon putting by the bandage, and looking sorrowfully and with tears upon all the folks in the garden, he begged them to assist him, in that danger, with two Pater-nosters and as many Ave-Marias, as they wished God might provide somebody to do the like good office for them in the like extremity. To which Don Quixote said:

'Thief, are you upon the gallows, or at the last gasp, that you have recourse to such doleful prayers? Are you not, poor-spirited and dastardly creature, in the same place which the fair Magalona occupied, and from which she descended, not to the grave, but to be Queen of France, if histories lie not?

And I! who sit by you, may I not vie with the valorous Peter, who pressed this very seat that I now press? Cover, cover your eyes, heartless animal, and suffer not your fear to escape out of your mouth, at least in my presence.'

'Hoodwink me then,' answered Sancho, 'and, since you have no mind I should commend myself to God, nor that others do it for me, what wonder if I am afraid lest some legion of devils may be lurking hereabouts, to hang us first, and try us afterwards.'

They were now hoodwinked, and Don Quixote, perceiving he was fixed as he should be, began to turn the peg; and scarcely had he put his fingers to it, when all the duennas and the standers by lifted up their voices, saying:

'God be your guide, valorous knight! God be with you, intrepid squire! now, now, you mount into the air, breaking it with more swiftness than an arrow; now you begin to surprise and astonish all who behold you upon the earth: sit fast, valorous Sancho; for you totter: beware lest you fall; for your fall will be worse than that of the daring youth,* who aspired to rule the chariot of his father the sun!'

Sancho heard the voices, and, nestling closer to his master, and embracing him with his arms, said:

'How can they say, sir, we have got so high, when their voices reach us, and they seem to be talking here hard by us?'

'Never mind that, Sancho,' quoth Don Quixote; 'for, as these matters and these flights are out of the ordinary course, you may see and hear anything a thousand leagues off: but do not squeeze me so hard; for you will tumble me down: and, to say the truth, I do not see why you are so disturbed and frighted; for I can safely swear, I never was upon the back of an easier-paced steed in all the days of my life: methinks we do not so much as stir from our place. Banish fear, friend; for, in short, the business goes as it should, and we have the wind in our poop.'

'That is true,' answered Sancho; 'for on this side the wind blows so strong that a thousand pair of bellows seem to be fanning me.'

And indeed it was; for they were airing him with several huge pair of bellows; and so well was this adventure concerted by the duke, the duchess, and the steward, that nothing was wanting to make it complete. Don Quixote now, feeling the wind, said:

'Without all doubt, Sancho, we must by this time have reached the second region of the air, where the hail and snows are formed: thunder and lightning are engendered in the third region; and, if we go on mounting at this rate, we shall soon reach the region of fire; and I know not how to manage this peg so as not to mount where we shall be scorched.'*

While they were thus discoursing, some flax, set on fire at the end of a long cane, at some distance, began to warm their faces. Sancho, feeling the heat, said:

'May I be hanged if we are not already at that same fireplace, or very near it; for it has singed a great part of my beard; and, sir, I am just going to peep out, and see whereabouts we are.'

'By no means,' answered Don Quixote; 'remember the true story of the licentiate Torralva, whom the devils carried through the air riding on a cane with his eyes shut; and in twelve hours he arrived at Rome, and alighted on the tower of Nona, which is a street of that city, and saw all the tumult, assault, and death* of the constable of Bourbon; and the next morning he returned to Madrid, where he gave an account of all he had seen. He said likewise, that, during his passage through the air, the devil bade him open his eyes; and so he did, and found himself to his thinking so near the body of the moon, that he could have laid hold of it with his hand; and that he durst not look down towards the earth for fear of being giddy.* So that, Sancho, we must not uncover our faces; for he, who has taken upon him the charge of us, will give an account of us; and perhaps we are now making a point, and soaring aloft to a certain height, to come souse down upon the kingdom of Candaya, like a hawk upon a heron. And though to us it does not seem more than half an hour since we left the garden, believe me, we must have made a great deal of way.'

'I know nothing as to that,' answered Sancho Panza; 'I can only say that, if Madam Magallanes or Magalona was contented to ride upon this crupper, her flesh must not have been of the tenderest.'

All this discourse of the two heroes was overheard by the duke and duchess, and all that were in the garden; with which they were extremely delighted: and being now willing to put an end to this strange and well-concerted adventure, they clapped some lighted flax to Clavileño's tail; and that instant, he, being full of squibs and crackers, blew up with a strange noise, and threw to the ground Don Quixote and Sancho, half-singed. By this time the Trifaldi, with the whole bearded squadron of duennas were vanished, and all that remained in the garden, counterfeiting a trance, lay flat upon the ground. Don Quixote and Sancho got up, in but indifferent plight, and, looking about them on all sides, were amazed to find themselves in the same garden, from whence they set out, and to see such a number of folks stretched upon the ground. But their wonder was increased, when, on one side of the garden, they perceived a great lance, sticking in the earth, and a smooth piece of white parchment hanging to it by two green silken strings; upon which was written, in large letters of gold, what follows:

'The renowned knight Don Quixote de la Mancha has finished and achieved the adventure of the Countess Trifaldi, otherwise called the Afflicted Matron, and company, only by attempting it. Malambruno is entirely satisfied, and desires no more; the chins of the duennas are smooth and clean, and Don Clavijo and Antonomasia have recovered their pristine estate; and when the squirely whipping shall be accomplished, the white dove shall be delivered from the cruel pounces of the hawks that pursue her, and shall find herself in the arms of her beloved turtle:* for so it is ordained by the sage Merlin, the prince of enchanters.'

Don Quixote, having read the inscription on the parchment, understood plainly, that it spoke of the disenchantment of Dulcinea, and, giving abundance of thanks to heaven for his having achieved so great an exploit, with so little danger, reducing thereby the venerable faces of the duennas to their former complexion, he went where the duke and duchess lay; being not yet come to themselves; and, pulling the duke by the arm, he said:

'Courage, courage, my good lord; the adventure is over without damage to the bars,* as yon register plainly shows.'

The duke by little and little, like one awaking out of a sound sleep, came to himself, and in like manner the duchess, and all that were in the garden, with such show of wonder and affright, that what they had so well acted in jest, seemed almost to themselves to have happened in earnest. The duke read the scroll with his eyes half shut, and presently, with open arms, embraced Don Quixote, assuring him he was the bravest knight that ever lived. Sancho looked up and down for the Afflicted [One], to see what kind of face she had now she was beardless, and whether she was as handsome without it, as her gallant presence seemed to promise: but he was told, that as Clavileño came flaming down through the air, and tumbled upon the ground, the whole squadron of duennas, with the Trifaldi, disappeared, and their beards vanished roots and all.

The duchess inquired of Sancho, how it fared with him in that long voyage? To which Sancho answered:

'I perceived, madam, as my master told me, that we were passing by the region of fire, and I had a mighty mind to peep a little; and, though my master, whose leave I asked, would not consent to it, I, who have I know not what spice of curiosity, and a desire of knowing what is forbidden and denied me, softly, and without being perceived by anybody, shoved up the handkerchief near my nostrils, and thence looked down towards the earth; and methought it was no bigger than a grain of mustard-seed, and the men that walked upon it little bigger than hazel-nuts: judge you, madam, how high we must have been then.'

To this, quoth the duchess:

'Take care, friend Sancho, what you say; for it is plain you saw not the earth, but the men only that walked upon it! for if the earth appeared but like a grain of mustard-seed, and each man like a hazel-nut, one man alone must needs cover the whole earth.'

'That is true,' answered Sancho, 'but, for all that, I had a side view of it, and saw it all.'

'Take heed, Sancho,' said the duchess; 'for, by a side view, one does not see the whole of what one looks at.'

'I do not understand these kind of views,' replied Sancho: 'I only know it is fit your ladyship should understand, that, since we flew by enchantment, by enchantment I might see the whole earth, and all the men, whichever way I looked: and, if you do not believe this, neither will your ladyship believe me, when I tell you, that thrusting up the kerchief close to my eyebrows, I found myself so near heaven, that from me to it was not above a span and a half; and I can take my oath, madam, that it is hugeous big: and it so fell out, that we passed by where the seven little she-goats are;* and, upon my conscience and soul, having been in my childhood a goatherd in my own country, I no sooner saw them, but I had a longing desire to divert myself with them a while, and had I not done it, I verily think I should have burst. Well, then, what do I? why, without saying a word to anybody, not even to my master, fair and softly, I slipped down from Clavileño, and played with those she-goats, which are like so many violets, about the space of three-quarters of an hour: and all the while Clavileño moved not from the place, nor stirred a foot.'

'And while honest Sancho was diverting himself with the goats,' quoth the duke, 'how did Señor Don Quixote amuse himself?'

To which Don Quixote answered:

'As these and the like accidents are out of the order of nature, no wonder Sancho says what he does: for my own part I can say, I neither looked up nor down, and saw neither heaven nor earth, nor sea, nor sands: it is very true, I was sensible that I passed through the region of the air, and even touched upon that of fire; but that we passed beyond, I cannot believe: for the fiery region being between the sphere of the moon and the utmost region of the air, we could not reach that heaven, where the seven goats Sancho speaks of are, without being burnt; and, since we were not burnt, either Sancho lies, or Sancho dreams.'

'I neither lie, nor dream,' answered Sancho: 'do but ask me the marks of those same goats, and by them you may guess whether I speak the truth or not.'

'Tell us then, Sancho,' quoth the duchess.

'They are,' replied Sancho, 'two of them green, two carnation, two blue, and one motley-coloured.'

'A new kind of goats those same,' quoth the duke: 'in our region of the earth we have no such colours; I mean goats of such colours.'

'The reason is plain,' quoth Sancho: 'there must be a difference between the goats of heaven, and those of earth.'

'Prithee, Sancho,' said the duke, 'was there ever a he-goat among them?'

'No, sir,' answered Sancho; 'for, they told me, none pass beyond the horns of the moon.'

They would not ask Sancho any more questions about his journey, perceiving he was in a humour of rambling all over the heavens, and giving an account of what passed there, without stirring from the garden.

In fine, this was the conclusion of the adventure of the Afflicted Matron, which furnished the duke and duchess with matter of laughter, not only at that time, but for their whole lives, and Sancho something to relate for ages, had he lived so long: and Don Quixote, coming to Sancho, whispered him in the ear, saying:

'Sancho, since you would have us believe all you have seen in heaven, I expect you should believe what I saw in Montesinos' cave;—I say no more.'

CHAPTER 42

*Of the instructions Don Quixote gave Sancho Panza, before
he went to govern the island, with other matters well
considered.*

THE duke and duchess were so satisfied with the happy and
glorious success of the adventure of the Afflicted [One], that
they resolved to carry the jest still further, seeing how fit a
subject they had to pass it on for earnest: and so, having
projected the scheme and given the necessary orders to their
servants and vassals, how they were to behave to Sancho in his
government of the promised island, the day following Clavileño's flight, the duke bade Sancho prepare, and get himself in
readiness to go to be a governor; for his islanders already wished
for him, as for rain in May. Sancho made his bow, and said:

'Ever since my descent from heaven, and since from its
lofty summit I beheld the earth, and observed it to be so
small, the great desire I had of being a governor is in part
cooled: for what grandeur is it to command on a grain of
mustard-seed, or what dignity or dominion is there in governing half a dozen men no bigger than hazel-nuts, for methought the whole earth was nothing more? If your lordship
would be pleased to give me some small portion of heaven,
though it were no more than half a league, I would accept
it with a better will than the biggest island in the world.'

'Look you, friend Sancho,' answered the duke, 'I can give
away no part of heaven, though no bigger than one's nail;
for God has reserved the disposal of those favours and graces
in His power. But what I can give you, I give you; and that
is an island ready made, round and sound, and well propor-
tioned, and above measure fruitful and abundant, where, if
you manage dexterously, you may, with the riches of the
earth, purchase the treasures of heaven.'

'Well then,' answered Sancho, 'let this island come; for it
shall go hard but I will be such a governor that, in spite of
rogues, I shall go to heaven: and think not it is out of
covetousness, that I forsake my humble cottage, and aspire
to greater things, but for the desire I have to taste how it
relishes to be a governor.'

'If once you taste it, Sancho,' quoth the duke, 'you will eat your fingers after it, so very sweet a thing is it to command, and be obeyed. Sure I am, when your master comes to be an emperor (for doubtless he will be one, in the way his affairs are) no one will be able to wrest it from him, and it will grieve and vex him to the heart to have been so long a time without being one.'

'Sir,' replied Sancho, 'I am of opinion it is good to command, though it be but a flock of sheep.'

'Let me be buried with you, Sancho, for you know something of everything,' answered the duke; 'and I doubt not you will prove such a governor as your wit seems to promise. Let this suffice for the present; and take notice that, to-morrow, without fail, you shall depart for the government of the island, and this evening you shall be fitted with a convenient garb, and with all things necessary for your departure.'

'Let them dress me,' quoth Sancho, 'how they will; for, howsoever I go clad, I shall still be Sancho Panza.'

'That is true,' said the duke; 'but our dress must be suitable to the employment or dignity we are in: for it would be preposterous for a lawyer to be habited like a soldier, or a soldier like a priest. You, Sancho, must go dressed partly like a scholar, and partly like a captain; for, in the island I give you, arms are as necessary as letters, and letters as arms.'

'Letters,' answered Sancho, 'I know but little of; for I can scarcely say the A,B,C; but it is sufficient to have the Christus* to be a good governor: and, as to arms, I shall handle such as are given me till I fall, and God be my guide.'

'With so good a memory,' quoth the duke, 'Sancho can never err.'

By this time Don Quixote came up, and learning what had passed, and how suddenly Sancho was to depart to his government, with the duke's leave, he took him by the hand, and carried him with him to his chamber, purposing to give him advice how to behave himself in his employment. Being come into the apartment, he shut the door after him, and almost by force made Sancho sit down by him, and, with a composed voice, said to him:

'Infinite thanks give I to heaven, friend Sancho, that, first, and before I have met with any good luck myself, good fortune has gone forth to meet and receive you. I, who had made over my future good success for the payment of your past services, find myself still at the beginning of my advancement, whilst you, before the due time, and against all rule of reasonable expectation, find yourself in full possession of your wishes. Others bribe, importune, solicit, attend early, pray, persist, and yet do not obtain what they aim at: another comes, and, without knowing how or which way, carries that employment or office against all other pretenders. And this makes good the saying: in pretensions, luck is all. You, who in respect to me, without doubt are a blockhead, without rising early or sitting up late, and without taking any pains at all, by the air alone of knight-errantry breathing on you, see yourself, without more ado, governor of an island, as if it were a matter of nothing. All this I say, O Sancho, that you may not ascribe the favour done you to your own merit, but give thanks, first to heaven, which disposes things so sweetly, and, in the next place, to the grandeur inherent in the profession of knight-errantry. Now, your heart being disposed to believe what I have been saying, be attentive, son, to me, your Cato,* who will be your counsellor, your north star and guide, to conduct and steer you safe into port, out of that tempestuous sea, wherein you are going to be engulfed; for offices and great employments are nothing else but a profound gulf of confusions.

'First, my son, fear God; for, to fear Him is wisdom, and being wise, you cannot err.

'Secondly, Consider who you were, and endeavour to know yourself, which is the most difficult point of knowledge imaginable. The knowledge of yourself will keep you from puffing yourself up, like the frog, who strove to equal herself to the ox; for the consideration of your having been a swineherd in your own country will be, to the wheel of your fortune, like the peacock's ugly feet.'

'True,' answered Sancho; 'when I was a boy, I kept swine; but afterwards, when I grew towards man, I looked after geese, and not after hogs. But this, methinks, is nothing to the purpose; for all governors are not descended from the loins of kings.'

'Granted,' replied Don Quixote; 'and therefore those, who are not of noble descent, should accompany the gravity of the office they bear with a kind of gentle sweetness, which, guided by prudence, exempts them from that ill-natured murmuring, which no state of life can well escape.

'Value yourself, Sancho, upon the meanness of your family, and be not ashamed to own you descend from peasants; for when people see that you yourself are not ashamed, nobody else will endeavour to make you so; and think it greater merit to be a virtuous mean man, than a proud sinner; infinite is the number of those, who, born of low extraction, have risen to the highest dignities, both papal and imperial; and of this truth I could produce examples enough to tire you.

'Look you, Sancho, if you take virtue for a mean, and value yourself upon doing virtuous actions, you need not envy lords and princes; for blood is inherited, but virtue acquired; and virtue has an intrinsic worth, which blood has not.

'This being so, as it really is, if peradventure one of your kindred comes to see you, when you are in your island, do not despise nor affront him, but receive, cherish, and make much of him; for in so doing, you will please God, who will have nobody despise His workmanship; and you will act agreeably to well-disposed nature.

'If you take your wife along with you (and it is not proper for those who govern, to be long without one), teach, instruct, and polish her from her natural rudeness; for, many times, all that a discreet governor can acquire is dissipated and lost by an ill-bred and foolish woman.

'If you chance to become a widower (a thing which may happen), and your station entitles you to a better match, seek not such a one as may serve you for a hook and angling-rod, or a friar's hood to receive alms in: for, believe me, whatever the judge's wife receives, the husband must account for at the General Judgement, and shall pay fourfold after death for what he made no reckoning of in his life.

'Be not governed by the law of your own will, which is

wont to bear much sway with the ignorant, who presume upon being discerning.

'Let the tears of the poor find more compassion, but not more justice, from you, than the informations of the rich.

'Endeavour to sift out the truth amidst the presents and promises of the rich, as well among the sighs and importunities of the poor.

'When equity can, and ought to take place, lay not the whole rigour of the law upon the delinquent; for the reputation of the rigorous judge is not better than that of the compassionate one.

'If perchance the rod of justice be warped a little, let it not be by the weight of a gift, but that of mercy.

'If it happens, that the cause of your enemy comes before you, fix not your mind upon the injury done you, but on the merits of the case.

'Let not private affection blind you in another man's cause; for the errors you shall commit thereby are often without remedy, and if there should be one, it will be at the expense both of your reputation and fortune.

'If a beautiful woman comes to demand justice, turn away your eyes from her tears, and your ears from her sighs, and consider at leisure the substance of her request, unless you have a mind your reason should be drowned in her tears, and your integrity in her sighs.

'Him you are to punish with deeds, do not evil entreat with words; for the pain of the punishment is enough for the wretch to bear, without the addition of ill language.

'In the criminal, who falls under your jurisdiction, consider the miserable man, subject to the condition of our depraved nature; and, as much as in you lies, without injuring the contrary party, show pity and clemency; for, though the attributes of God are all equal, that of His mercy is more pleasing and attractive in our eyes, than that of His justice.

'If, Sancho, you observe these precepts and these rules, your days will be long, and your fame eternal, your recompense full, and your felicity unspeakable. You shall match your children as you please; they and your grandchildren shall inherit titles; you shall live in peace, and in favour with all

men; and, at the end of your life, death shall find you in
a sweet and mature old age, and your eyes shall be closed
by the tender and pious hands of your grandchildren's children.

'What I have hitherto taught you, Sancho, are documents
for the adorning of your mind: listen now to those which
concern the adornments of the body.'

CHAPTER 43

Of the second instructions Don Quixote gave Sancho Panza.

WHO that had heard the foregoing discourse of Don Quixote's, but would have taken him for a prudent and intelligent
person? But, as it has been often said in the progress of this
grand history, he talked foolishly only when chivalry was the
subject, and in the rest of his conversation showed himself
master of a clear and agreeable understanding; insomuch that
his actions perpetually bewrayed his judgement, and his
judgement his actions. But, in these second instructions given
to Sancho, he showed a great deal of pleasantry, and pushed
his discretion and his madness to a high pitch.

Sancho listened to him most attentively, endeavouring to
preserve his instructions in memory, like one that intended
to observe them, and by their means, hoped to be safely
delivered of the pregnancy of his government. Don Quixote
proceeded, saying:

'As to what concerns the government of your own person
and family, Sancho, in the first place, I enjoin you to be
cleanly, and to pare your nails, and not let them grow, as
some do, whose ignorance has made them believe, that long
nails beautify the hands; as if that excrement and excrescence
were a nail, whereas it is rather the talon of a lizard-hunting
kestrel; a swinish and monstrous abuse!

'Go not loose and unbuttoned, Sancho! for a slovenly dress
betokens a careless mind, unless the discomposure and negligence fall under the article of cunning and design, as was
judged to be the case of Julius Caesar.

'Feel, with discretion, the pulse of what your office may be worth, and, if it will afford your giving liveries to your servants, give them such as are decent and useful, rather than showy and modish: and divide between your servants and the poor; I mean, if you can keep six pages, clothe but three, and three of the poor; and thus you will have pages for heaven and for earth too; a new way of giving liveries, which the vain-glorious never thought of.

'Eat neither garlic nor onion, lest people guess, by the smell, at your peasantry. Walk leisurely, and speak deliberately; but not as to seem to be hearkening to yourself, for all affectation is bad.

'Eat little at dinner, and less at supper; for the health of the whole body is tempered in the forge of the stomach.

'Be temperate in drinking, considering that excess of wine neither keeps secrets, nor performs promises.

'Take heed, Sancho, not to chew on both sides of your mouth at once, nor to eruct before company.'

'I do not understand your eructing,' quoth Sancho.

'To eruct,' said Don Quixote, 'means to belch, a filthy, though very significant word; and therefore your nice people have recourse to the Latin, and, instead of to "belch", say, to "eruct", and, instead of "belchings", "eructations": and though some do not understand these terms, it is no great matter; for, by usage, they will come hereafter to be understood; and this is to enrich language, over which the vulgar and custom bear sway.'

'In truth, sir,' quoth Sancho, 'one of the counsels and instructions, I intend to carry in my memory, shall be this, of not belching; for I am wont to do it very frequently.'

'Eructing, Sancho, and not belching,' quoth Don Quixote.

'"Eructing" it shall be henceforward, and, in faith, I will not forget it.'

'Likewise, Sancho, intermix not in your discourse that multitude of proverbs you are wont: for, though proverbs are short sentences, you often drag them in so by the head and shoulders, that they seem rather cross purposes, than sentences.'

'God alone can remedy that,' quoth Sancho; 'for I know

more proverbs than will fill a book, and, when I talk, they crowd so thick into my mouth, that they jostle which shall get out first: but my tongue tosses out the first it meets, though it be not always very pat. But, for the future, I will take heed to utter such as become the gravity of my place: for, In a plentiful house supper is soon dressed; and, He that cuts does not deal; and, He that has the repique is safe; and, To spend and to spare, require judgement.'

'So, so, Sancho,' quoth Don Quixote; 'thrust in, rank, and string on your proverbs, nobody is going about to hinder you. My mother whips me, and I tear on. I am warning you to abstain from proverbs, and in an instant you pour forth a litany of them, which square with what we are upon as much as, Over the hills and far away. Look you, Sancho, I do not say a proverb is amiss when skilfully applied; but to accumulate, and string them at random, renders a discourse flat and low.

'When you are on horseback, sit not leaning your body backwards over your saddle, nor carry your legs stiff-stretched, and straddling from the horse's belly: nor yet dangle them so, as if you were still upon Dapple; for sitting a horse makes some look like gentlemen, others like grooms.

'Let your sleep be moderate; for he who is not up with the sun, does not enjoy the day: and take notice, O Sancho, that diligence is the mother of good fortune, and sloth, her opposite, never reached the end of a good wish.

'The last article of advice I shall at this time give you, though it concerns not the adorning of the body, yet I would have you bear it carefully in mind; for I believe it will be of no less use to you than those I have already given you. It is this: Never set yourself to decide contests about families, at least by comparing them, since perforce one must have the advantage; and he who is postponed will hate you, and he who is preferred will not reward you.

'Your habit shall be breeches and stockings, a long coat, and a cloak somewhat longer; but for trousers or trunk-hose, think not of them; for they are not becoming either to cavaliers or governors.

'This is all that occurs to me at present, by way of advice to you: as time goes on, and according to the occasions, such shall my instructions be, provided you take care to inform me of the state of your affairs.'

'Sir,' answered Sancho, 'I see very well, that all your worship has been saying is good, holy, and profitable: but what good will it do me, if I remember nothing of it? It is true, I shall not forget what you have said about not letting my nails grow, and about marrying again if I may: but for your other gallimaufries, quirks, and quillets, I neither do, nor ever shall remember any more of them, than of last year's clouds; and therefore it will be necessary to give me them in writing; for, though I can neither read nor write, I will give them to my confessor, that he may inculcate them into me whenever there shall be need.'

'Ah! sinner that I am!' answered Don Quixote; 'how ill does it look in a governor not to be able to read or write! for you must know, O Sancho, that for a man not to know how to read, or to be left-handed, implies one of these two things; either that he sprung from very mean and low parents, or that he was so untoward and perverse, that no good could be beaten into him. It is a very great defect you carry with you, and therefore I would by all means have you learn to write your name, if possible.'

'I can sign my name very well,' answered Sancho; 'for, when I was steward of the brotherhood in our village, I learned to make certain characters, like the marks upon a woolpack, which, I was told, spelt my name: but, at the worst, I can pretend my right hand is lame, and make another sign for me: for there is a remedy for everything but death; and I, having the command of the staff, will do what I please. Besides, he whose father is mayor, &c., you know,* and I, being a governor, am surely something more than mayor. Let them come and play at bo-peep. Aye, aye, let them slight and backbite me: They may come for wool, and be sent back shorn; and, Whom God loves, his house smells savoury to him; and, The rich man's blunders pass for maxims in the world; and I, being a governor, and consequently rich, and bountiful to boot, as I intend to be, nobody will see my defects. No, no, Get yourself honey, and clowns will have flies. As much as you have, so much you are worth, said my grandam; and, There is no revenging yourself upon a rich man.'

'Oh! God's curse light on you,' cried out Don Quixote at this instant; 'sixty thousand devils take you, and your proverbs! You have been stringing of them this full hour, and putting me to the rack with every one of them. Take my word for it, these proverbs will one day bring you to the gallows: upon their account, your subjects will strip you of your government, or at least conspire against you. Tell me, where find you them, ignorant? or how apply you them, dunce? For my own part, to utter but one, and apply it properly, I sweat and labour as if I were digging.'

'Before God, master of mine,' replied Sancho, 'your worship complains of very trifles. Why the devil are you angry, that I make use of my own goods? for I have no other, nor any stock, but proverbs upon proverbs: and just now I have four that present themselves pat to the purpose, and sit like pears in a pannier: but I will not produce them; for, "To keep silence well is called Sancho".'*

'That you will never do, Sancho,' quoth Don Quixote; 'for you are so far from keeping silence well, that you are an arrant prate-apace, and an eternal babbler. But, for all that, I would fain know what four proverbs occurred to you just now, so pat to the purpose; for I have been running over my own memory, which is a pretty good one, and I can think of none.'

'Can there be better,' quoth Sancho, 'than, Never venture your fingers between two eye-teeth; and to get out of my house, what would you have with my wife? there is no reply; and, Whether the pitcher hits the stone, or the stone hits the pitcher, it is bad for the pitcher: all which fit to a hair. Let no one contest with his governor, or his governor's substitutes; for he will come off by the worst, like him who claps his finger between two eye- teeth: but though they be not eye-teeth, so they be teeth, it matters not. To what a governor says, there is no replying; for it is like, Get you out of my house, what business have you with my wife? Then, as to the stone and the pitcher, a blind man may see into it. So that he who sees a mote in another man's eye, should first look to the beam in his own; that it may not be said of him, The dead woman was afraid of her that was flayed: and your worship knows well, that, The fool knows more in his own house, than the wise in another man's.'

'Not so, Sancho,' answered Don Quixote: 'the fool knows nothing, either in his own house or another's; for knowledge is not a structure to be erected upon so shallow a foundation as folly. And so much for that, Sancho; for if you govern ill, yours will be the fault, but the shame will be mine. But I comfort myself, that I have done my duty in advising you as seriously and as discreetly as I possibly could: and so I am acquitted both of my obligation and my promise. God speed you, Sancho, and govern you in your government, and deliver me from a suspicion I have, that you will turn the whole island topsyturvy: which I might prevent, by letting the duke know what you are, and telling him, that all that paunchgut and little carcass of thine is nothing but a sackful of proverbs and sly remarks.'

'Sir,' replied Sancho, 'if your worship thinks I am not fit for this government, I renounce it from this moment; for I love the little black of the nail of my soul better than my whole body, and plain Sancho can live as well upon bread and onion, as governor Sancho can upon capon and partridge. Besides, while we are asleep, the great and the small, the poor and the rich, are all equal. And if your worship reflects, you will find it was your worship that put me upon the scent of governing; for I know no more of the government of islands than a bustard; and, if you fancy the devil will have me, if I am a governor, I had rather go, Sancho, to heaven, than a governor to hell.'

'Before God, Sancho,' quoth Don Quixote, 'for those last words of yours, I think you deserve to be governor of a thousand islands. You are good-natured, without which no knowledge is of any value. Pray to God, and endeavour not to err in your intention; I mean, always take care to have a firm purpose and design of doing right in whatever business occurs; for heaven constantly favours a good intention. And so let us go to dinner; for I believe the lord and lady stay for us.'

‘ CHAPTER 44

*How Sancho Panza was carried to his government, and of
the strange adventure which befell Don Quixote in the castle.*

WE are told that in the original of this history, it is said, Cid
Hamet coming to write this chapter, the interpreter did not
translate it, as he had written it: which was a kind of complaint
the Moor made of himself,* for having undertaken a history
so dry, and so confined, as that of Don Quixote, thinking he
must be always talking of him and Sancho, without daring to
launch into digressions and episodes of more weight and
entertainment. And he said, that to have his invention, his
hand, and his pen, always tied down to write upon one subject
only, and to speak by the mouths of few characters, was an
insupportable toil, and of no advantage to the author; and
that, to avoid this inconvenience, he had, in the first part,
made use of the artifice of introducing novels, such as that
of *The Curious Impertinent*, and that of *The Captive*; which are
in a manner detached from the history; though most of what
is related in that part are accidents which happened to Don
Quixote himself, and could not be omitted. He also thought,
as he tells us, that many readers, carried away by their attention
to Don Quixote's exploits, could afford none to the novels,
and would either run them over in haste, or with disgust, not
considering how fine and artificial they were in themselves, as
would have been very evident, had they been published
separately, without being tacked to the extravagances of Don
Quixote, and the simplicities of Sancho.

And therefore, in this second part, he would introduce no
loose nor unconnected novels; but only some episodes, resembling them, and such as flow naturally from such events
as the truth offers; and even these, with great limitation, and
in no more words than are sufficient to express them: and,
since he restrains and confines himself within the narrow
limits of the narration, though with ability, genius, and
understanding, sufficient to treat of the whole universe, he
desires his pains may not be undervalued, but that he may
receive applause, not for what he writes, but what he has
omitted to write: and then he goes on with his history, saying:

Don Quixote, in the evening of the day he gave the
instructions to Sancho, gave them him in writing, that he
might get somebody to read them to him: but scarcely had
he delivered them to Sancho, when he dropped them, and
they fell into the duke's hands, who communicated them to
the duchess; and they both admired afresh at the madness
and capacity of Don Quixote; and so, going on with their
jest, that evening they despatched Sancho, with a large retinue, to the place, which, to him, was to be an island. The
person who had the management of the business, was a
steward of the duke's, a person of pleasantry and discretion
(for there can be no true pleasantry without discretion), and
who had already personated the Countess Trifaldi, with the
humour already related; and with these qualifications, and the
instructions of his lord and lady how to behave to Sancho,
he performed his part to admiration. Now it fell out, that
Sancho no sooner cast his eyes on this same steward, but he
fancied he saw in his face the very features of the Trifaldi;
and, turning to his master, he said:

'Sir, either the devil shall run away with me from the place
where I stand, for an honest man and a believer, or your
worship shall confess to me, that the countenance of this
same steward of the duke's is the very same with that of the
Afflicted [One].'

Don Quixote beheld him attentively, and, having viewed
him, said to Sancho:

'There is no need of the devil's running away with you,
Sancho, either as an honest man, or a believer; for, though
I know not what you mean, I see plainly the steward's face
is the same with the Afflicted [One's], and yet the steward
is not the Afflicted [One]; for that would imply a palpable
contradiction. But this is no time to enter into these inquiries,
which would involve us in an intricate labyrinth. Believe me,
friend, we ought earnestly to pray to our Lord, to deliver us
from wicked wizards and enchanters.'

'It is no jesting matter, Sir,' replied Sancho; 'for I heard
him speak before, and methought the Trifaldi's voice sounded
in my ears. Well, I say no more; but I will not fail to be
upon the watch henceforward, to see whether I can discover

any other sign, to confirm or remove my suspicion.'

'Do so, Sancho,' quoth Don Quixote, 'and give me advice of all you discover in this affair, and all that happens to you in your government.'

At length Sancho set out with a great number of followers. He was habited like one of the gown,* having on a wide surtout of murry-coloured camlet, with a cap of the same, and mounted *á la gineta* upon a mule. And behind him, by the duke's order, was led his Dapple, with ass-like furniture, all of flaming fine silk. Sancho turned back his head every now and then to look at his ass, with whose company he was so delighted, that he would not have changed conditions with the Emperor of Germany.

At taking leave of the duke and duchess, he kissed their hands, and begged his master's blessing, which he gave with tears, and Sancho received blubbering. Now, loving reader, let honest Sancho depart in peace, and in a good hour, and expect two bushels of laughter from the accounts how he demeaned himself in his employment; and, in the meantime, attend to what befell his master that night; which, if it does not make you laugh, you will at least open your lips with the grin of a monkey; for the adventures of Don Quixote must be celebrated either with admiration or laughter.

It is related then, that scarcely was Sancho departed, when Don Quixote began to regret his own solitary condition, and, had it been possible for him to have recalled the commission, and taken the government from him, he certainly would have done it. The duchess soon perceived his melancholy, and asked him why he was so sad: if for the absence of Sancho, there were squires, duennas, and damsels enough in her house, ready to serve him to his heart's desire.

'It is true, madam,' answered Don Quixote, 'that I am concerned for Sancho's absence; but that is not the principal cause that makes me appear sad; and, of all your excellency's kind offers, I accept and choose that only of the goodwill with which they are tendered; and for the rest I humbly beseech your excellency, that you would be pleased to consent and permit, that I alone may wait upon myself in my chamber.'

'Truly, Señor Don Quixote,' quoth the duchess, 'it must not be so; but you shall be served by four of my damsels, all beautiful as flowers.'

'To me,' answered Don Quixote, 'they will not be flowers, but very thorns, pricking me to the soul; they shall no more come into my chamber, nor anything like it, than they shall fly. If your grandeur would continue your favours to me, without my deserving them, suffer me to be alone, and let me serve myself within my own doors, that I may keep a wall betwixt my passions and my modesty; a practice that I would not forgo, for all your highness's liberality towards me. In short I will sooner lie in my clothes, than consent to let anybody help to undress me.'

'Enough, enough, Señor Don Quixote,' replied the duchess: 'I promise you, I will give orders that not so much as a fly shall enter your chamber, much less a damsel. I would by no means be accessory to the violation of Señor Don Quixote's decency; for, by what I can perceive, the most conspicuous of his many virtues is his modesty. Your worship, sir, may undress and dress by yourself your own way, when and how you please; for nobody shall hinder you, and in your chamber you will find all the necessary utensils; so that you may sleep with the doors locked, and no natural want need oblige you to open them. A thousand ages live the grand Dulcinea del Toboso, and be her name extended over the whole globe of the earth, for meriting the love of so valiant and so chaste a knight; and may indulgent heaven infuse into the heart of Sancho Panza, our governor, a disposition to finish his whipping speedily, that the world may again enjoy the beauty of so great a lady!'

To which Don Quixote said:

'Your highness has spoken like yourself, and from the mouth of such good ladies nothing that is bad can proceed: and Dulcinea will be more happy, and more known in the world, by the praises your grandeur bestows on her, than by those of the most eloquent on earth.'

'Señor Don Quixote,' replied the duchess, 'the hour of supper draws near, and the duke may be staying for us: come, sir, let us sup, and to bed betimes; for your yesterday's journey from Candaya was not so short, but it must have somewhat fatigued you.'

'Not at all, madam,' answered Don Quixote; 'for I can safely swear to your excellency, that in all my life I never bestrode a soberer beast, nor of an easier pace, than Clavileño; and I cannot imagine what possessed Malambruno to part with so swift and so gentle a steed, and burn him so, without more ado.'

'We may suppose,' answered the duchess, 'that, repenting of the mischief he had done to the Trifaldi, and her companions, and to other persons, and of the iniquities he had committed as a wizard and an enchanter, he had a mind to destroy all the instruments of his art, and as the principal, and that which gave him the most disquiet, by having carried him up and down from country to country, he burnt Clavileño: and thus, with his ashes, and the trophy of the parchment, has eternalized the valour of the grand Don Quixote de la Mancha.'

Don Quixote gave thanks afresh to the duchess, and, when he had supped, he retired to his chamber alone, not consenting to let anybody come in to wait upon him; so afraid was he of meeting with temptations to move or force him to transgress that modest decency he had preserved towards his lady Dulcinea, bearing always in mind the chastity of Amadis, the flower and mirror of knights-errant. He shut his door after him, and by the light of two wax candles, pulled off his clothes; and, at stripping off his stockings (O mishap unworthy of such a personage!) forth burst, not sighs, nor anything else that might discredit his cleanliness, but some two dozen stitches of a stocking, which made it resemble a lattice-window. The good gentleman was extremely afflicted, and would have given an ounce of silver to have had there a drachm of green silk; I say, green, because his stockings were green.

Here Ben Engeli exclaims, and, writing on, says: 'O poverty! poverty! I cannot imagine what moved the great Córdovan poet to call thee "a holy, thankless gift."* I, though a Moor, know very well, by the intercourse I have had with the Christians, that holiness consists in charity, humility, faith, obedience, and poverty. But for all that, I say, a man must have a great share of the grace of God, who can bring himself to be contented with poverty, unless it be that kind of it, of which one of their greatest saints speaks, saying: "possess all things as not possessing them!"* And this is called poverty in spirit. But thou, O second poverty (which is that I am speaking of), why dost thou choose to pinch gentlemen, and such as are well-born, rather than other people? Why dost thou force them to cobble their shoes, and to wear one button of their coats of silk, one of hair, and one of glass? Why must their ruffs be, for the most part, ill ironed, and worse starched?'—By this you may see the antiquity of the use of ruffs and starch. Then he goes on—'Wretched, well-born gentleman! who is administering jelly-broths to his honour, while he is starving his carcass, dining with his door locked upon him, and making a hypocrite of his toothpick, with which he walks out into the street, after having eaten nothing to oblige him to this cleanliness. Wretched he, I say, whose skittish honour is always ready to start, apprehensive that everybody sees, a league off, the patch upon his shoe, the sweating through of his hat, the threadbareness of his cloak, and the hunger of his stomach.'

All these melancholy reflections recurred to Don Quixote's thoughts upon the rent in his stocking: but his comfort was, that Sancho had left behind him a pair of travelling boots, which he resolved to put on next day. Finally, he laid himself down, pensive and heavy-hearted, as well for lack of Sancho, as for the irreparable misfortune of his stocking, whose stitches he would gladly have darned, though with silk of another colour; which is one of the greatest signs of misery a gentleman can give in the course of his tedious neediness. He put out the lights: the weather was hot, and he could not sleep: he got out of bed, and opened the casement of a grate-window, which looked into a fine garden, and, at opening it, he perceived and heard somebody walking and talking in the garden. He set himself to listen attentively; and those below raised their voices so high, that he could distinguish these words:

'Press me not, O Emerencia, to sing; for you know, ever since this stranger came into this castle, and my eyes beheld

him, I cannot sing, but weep. Besides, my lady sleeps not
sound, and I would not have her find us here for all the
treasure of the world. But, suppose she should sleep, and not
awake, my singing will still be in vain, if this new Aeneas,
who is arrived in my territories to leave me forlorn, sleeps
on, and awakes not to hear it.'

'Do not fancy so, dear Altisidora,' answered the other; 'for
doubtless the duchess, and everybody else in the house, is asleep,
excepting the master of your heart, and disturber of your repose;
for even now I heard him open his casement, and, without
doubt, he must be awake. Sing, my afflicted creature, in a low
and sweet voice, to the sound of your harp; and, if the duchess
should hear us, we will plead the excessive heat of the weather.'

'This is not the point, O Emerencia,' answered Altisidora,
'but that I am afraid my song should betray my heart, and so
I might be taken for a light longing hussy by those who are
unacquainted with the powerful effects of love. But come what
will; better a blush in the face, than a blot in the heart.'

And presently she began to touch a harp most sweetly.
Which Don Quixote hearing, he was surprised; and, in that
instant, came into his mind an infinite number of adventures
of the like kind, of casements, grates, and gardens, serenades,
courtships, and faintings away, of which he had read in his
idle books of chivalry. He straight imagined that some damsel
of the duchess's was fallen in love with him, and that modesty
obliged her to conceal her passion. He was a little afraid of
being captivated, but resolved in his own thoughts not to
yield; and so, commending himself, with all his soul and with
all his might, to his mistress Dulcinea del Toboso, he determined to listen to the music; and, to let them know he was
there, he gave a feigned sneeze; at which the damsels were
not a little glad, desiring nothing more than that Don Quixote
should hear them. Now the harp being tuned and put in
order, Altisidora began this song:

SONG

'Gentle knight, La Mancha's glory,
Famed in never-dying story

Of a purer, finer mould,
Than Arabia's finest gold:
Thou that, in thy downy bed,
Wrapt in Holland sheets, art laid,
And with out-stretch'd legs art yawning,
Or, asleep till morrow's dawning;—
Hear a woful maid complaining,
Who must die by thy disdaining,
Since thy eyes have scorch'd her soul,
And have burnt it to a coal,
If the aim of thy adventures
In relieving damsels centres,
Canst thou wound a tender maid,
And refuse thy wonted aid?
Tell, O tell me, I conjure thee,
So may heav'nly help secure thee,
Wert thou born where lions roar
On remotest Afric's shore?
Wert thou some bleak mountain's care,
And did'st suck, thy nurse, a bear?
Fair Dulcinny, tall and slender,
Well may boast thy heart's surrender,
Since those charms must stand confessed,
That could tame a tiger's breast:
And henceforth she shall be known
From the Tagus to the Rhone.
Could I take Dulcinny's place,
And but swap with hers my face,
O! I'd give my Sunday's suit,
And fring'd petticoat to boot.
Happy she that, in those arms
Clasp'd, enjoys thy manly charms,
Or but, sitting by thy bed,
Chafes thy feet, or rubs thy head!
Ah! I wish and ask too much:
Let me but thy great toe touch;
'Twere to humble me a blessing,
And reward beyond expressing.
Oh! how I would lavish riches,
Satin vests and damask breeches,
To adorn and dress my dear!
Oh! what night-caps he should wear.
I'm a virgin, neat and clean,

> And, in faith, not quite fifteen;
> Tall and straight, and very sound,
> And my ringlets brush the ground.
> Though my mouth is somewhat wide,
> In my coral teeth I pride;
> And the flatness of my nose
> Here for finish'd beauty goes.
> How I sing, I need not say,
> If perchance thou hear'st this lay:—
> These, and twenty graces more-a
> Court thee to Altisidora.'

Here ended the song of the sore-wounded Altisidora, and began the alarm of the courted Don Quixote, who, fetching a deep sigh, said within himself:

'Why am I so unhappy a knight-errant, that no damsel can see me but she must presently fall in love with me? Why is the peerless Dulcinea so unlucky, that she must not be suffered singly to enjoy this my incomparable constancy? Queens, what would ye have with her? Empresses, why do ye persecute her? Damsels, from fourteen to fifteen, why do ye plague her? Leave, leave the poor creature; let her triumph, glory, and plume herself in the lot, which love bestowed upon her in the conquest of my heart, and the surrender of my soul. Take notice, enamoured multitude, that to Dulcinea alone I am paste and sugar, and to all others flint: to her I am honey, and to the rest of ye aloes. To me, Dulcinea alone is beautiful, discreet, lively, modest, and well-born; and the rest of her sex, foul, foolish, fickle, and base-born. To be hers, and hers alone, nature threw me into the world. Let Altisidora weep or sing; let the lady despair, on whose account I was buffeted in the castle of the enchanted Moor.* Boiled or roasted, Dulcinea's I must be, clean, well-bred, and chaste, in spite of all the necromantic powers on earth.'

This said, he clapped to the casement, and, in despite and sorrow, as if some great misfortune had befallen him, threw himself upon his bed; where, at present, we will leave him, to attend the great Sancho Panza, who is desirous of beginning his famous government.

CHAPTER 45

*How the great Sancho Panza took possession of his island,
and of the manner of his beginning to govern it.*

O THOU perpetual discoverer of the antipodes, torch of the
world, eye of heaven, sweet motive of wine-cooling bottles;
here Thymbraeus, there Phoebus; here archer, there physician;
father of poesy, inventor of music; thou who always risest,
and, though thou seemest to do so, never settest! To thee,
I speak, O sun, by whose assistance man begets man; thee I
invoke to favour and enlighten the obscurity of my genius,
that I may be able punctually to describe the government of
the great Sancho Panza; for, without thee, I find myself
indolent, dispirited, and confused!

I say then, that Sancho, with all his attendants, arrived at
a town that contained about a thousand inhabitants, and was
one of the best the duke had. They gave him to understand,
that it was called the island of Barataria, either because
Barataria was really the name of the place, or because he
obtained the government of it at so cheap a rate.* At his
arrival near the gates of the town, which was walled about,
the magistrates, in their formalities, came out to receive him,
the bells rung, and the people gave demonstrations of a
general joy, and, with a great deal of pomp, conducted him
to the great church to give thanks to God. Presently after,
with certain ridiculous ceremonies, they presented to him the
keys of the town, and admitted him as perpetual governor
of the island of Barataria. The garb, the beard, the thickness
and shortness of the new governor, held in admiration all
that were not in the secret, and even those that were, who
were not a few. In fine, as soon as they had brought him
out of the church, they carried him to the tribunal of justice,
and placed him in the chair, and the duke's steward said to
him:

'It is an ancient custom here, my lord governor, that he,
who comes to take possession of this famous island, is
obliged to answer to a question put to him, which is to be
somewhat intricate and difficult; and, by his answer, the
people are enabled to feel the pulse of their new governor's

understanding, and, accordingly, are either glad or sorry for his coming.'

While the steward was saying this, Sancho was staring at some capital letters written on the wall opposite to his chair, and, because he could not read, he asked what that painting was on the wall. He was answered:

'Sir, it is there written, on what day your honour took possession of this island; and the inscription runs thus: "This day (such a day of the month and year) Señor Don Sancho Panza took possession of this island, and long may he enjoy it."'

'And, pray,' quoth he, 'who is it they call Don Sancho Panza?'

'Your lordship,' answered the steward; 'for no other Panza, besides him now in the chair, ever came into this island.'

'Take notice, brother,' quoth Sancho, 'Don does not belong to me, nor ever did to any of my family: I am called plain Sancho Panza; my father was a Sancho, and my grandfather a Sancho, and they were all Panzas, without any addition of Dons or Doñas; and I fancy there are more Dons than stones in this island, but enough; God knows my meaning, and perhaps, if my government lasts four days, I may weed out these Dons, that overrun the country, and, by their numbers, are as troublesome as gnats. On with your question, Master Steward, and I will answer the best I can, let the people be sorry or not sorry.'

At this instant two men came into the court, the one clad like a country-fellow, and the other like a tailor, with a pair of shears in his hand; and the tailor said:

'My lord governor, I, and this countryman, come before your worship, by reason this honest man came yesterday to my shop (for, saving your presence, I am a tailor, and have passed my examination, God be thanked), and, putting a piece of cloth into my hands, asked me: "Sir, is there enough of this to make me a cap?" I, measuring the piece, answered, Yes. Now he imagining, as I imagine (and I imagined right), that doubtless I had a mind to cabbage* some of the cloth, grounding his conceit upon his own knavery, and upon the common ill opinion had of tailors, bade me view it again, and see if there was not enough for two. I guessed his drift, and told him there was. My gentleman, persisting in his knavish intention, went on increasing the number of caps, and I adding to the number of Yes's, till we came to five caps; and even now he came for them. I offered them to him, and he refuses to pay me for the making, and pretends I shall either return him his cloth, or pay him for it.'

'Is all this so, brother?' demanded Sancho.

'Yes,' answered the man: 'but pray, my lord, make him produce the five caps he has made me.'

'With all my heart,' answered the tailor.

And pulling his hand from under his cloak, he showed the five caps on the ends of his fingers and thumb, saying:

'Here are the five caps this honest man would have me make; and, on my soul and conscience, not a shred of the cloth is left, and I submit the work to be viewed by any inspectors of the trade.'

All that were present laughed at the number of the caps, and the novelty of the suit Sancho set himself to consider a little, and said:

'I am of opinion, there needs no great delay in this suit, and it may be decided very equitably off-hand; and therefore I pronounce, that the tailor lose the making, and the country-man the stuff, and that the caps be confiscated to the use of the poor; and there is an end of that.'

If the sentence he afterwards passed* on the purse of the herdsman caused the admiration of all the bystanders, this excited their laughter. In short, what the governor commanded was executed.

The next that presented themselves before him were two ancient men, the one with a cane in his hand for a staff; and he without a staff said:

'My lord, sometime ago I lent this man ten crowns of gold, to oblige and serve him, upon condition he should return them on demand. I let him alone a good while, without asking for them, because I was loath to put him to a greater strait to pay me, than he was in when I lent them. But at length, thinking he was negligent of the payment, I asked him, more than once or twice, for my money, and he not only refuses payment, but denies the debt, and says, I never lent him any such sum, and, if I did, that he has already paid me; and I having no witnesses of the loan, or he of the payment, I entreat your worship will take his oath; and, if he will swear he has returned me the money, I acquit him from this minute before God and the world.'

'What say you to this, old gentleman with the staff?' quoth Sancho.

To which the old fellow replied:

'I confess, my lord, he did lend me the money; and, if your worship pleases to hold down your wand of justice, since he leaves it to my oath, I will swear I have really and truly returned it him.'

The governor held down the wand, and the old fellow gave the staff to his creditor to hold, while he was swearing, as if it encumbered him; and presently laid his hand upon the cross of the wand, and said, it was true, indeed, he had lent him those ten crowns he asked for, but that he had restored them to him into his own hand; and because, he supposed, he had forgot it, he was every moment asking him for them. Which the great governor seeing, he asked the creditor, what he had to answer to what his antagonist had alleged. He replied, he did not doubt but his debtor had said the truth; for he took him to be an honest man, and a good Christian; and that he himself must have forgot when, and where, the money was returned; and that, from thenceforward, he would never ask him for it again. The debtor took his staff again, and, bowing his head, went out of court. Sancho seeing this, and that he was gone without more ado, and observing also the patience of the creditor, he inclined his head upon his breast, and, laying the forefinger of his right hand upon his eyebrows and nose, he continued, as it were, full of thought, a short space, and then, lifting up his head, he ordered the old man with the staff, who was already gone, to be called back. He was brought back accordingly, and Sancho, seeing him, said:

'Give me that staff, honest friend, for I have occasion for it.'

'With all my heart,' answered the old fellow, and delivered it into his hand.

Sancho took it, and, giving it to the other old man, said:

'Go about your business, in God's name, for you are paid.
I, my lord,' answered the old man; 'what! is this cane worth
ten golden crowns?'

'Yes,' quoth the governor, 'or I am the greatest dunce in
the world; and now it shall appear whether I have a head to
govern a whole kingdom.'

Straight he commanded the cane to be broken before them
all. Which being done, there were found in the hollow of it
ten crowns in gold. All were struck with admiration, and took
their new governor for a second Solomon. They asked him,
whence he had collected, that the ten crowns were in the
cane. He answered, that, upon seeing the old man give it his
adversary, while he was taking the oath, and swearing that he
had really and truly restored them into his own hands, and,
when he had done, ask for it again, it came into his imagination, that the money in dispute must be in the hollow of the
cane. Whence it may be gathered, that God Almighty often
directs the judgements of those who govern, though otherwise
mere blockheads: besides, he had heard the priest of his parish
tell a like case; and, were it not that he was so unlucky as to
forget all he had a mind to remember, his memory was so
good, there would not have been a better in the whole island.
At length, both the old men marched off, the one ashamed,
and the other satisfied:* the bystanders were surprised, and
the secretary, who minuted down the words, actions, and
behaviour of Sancho Panza, could not determine with himself,
whether he should set him down for a wise man or a fool.

This cause was no sooner ended, but there came into court
a woman, keeping fast hold of a man, clad like a rich
herdsman. She came crying aloud:

'Justice, my lord governor, justice; if I cannot find it on
earth, I will seek it in heaven: lord governor of my soul, this
wicked man surprised me in the middle of a field, and made
use of my body as if it had been a dish-clout, and, woe is
me, has robbed me of what I have kept above these three-
and-twenty years, defending it against Moors and Christians,
natives and foreigners. I have been as hard as a cork-tree,
and preserved myself as entire as a salamander in the fire, or

as wool among briers, that this honest man should come with his clean hands to handle me.'

'It remains to be examined,' quoth Sancho, 'whether this gallant's hands are clean or no.'

And, turning to the man, he asked him what he had to say, and what answer to make to this woman's complaint. The man, all in confusion, replied:

'Sirs, I am a poor herdsman, and deal in swine, and this morning I went out of this town, after having sold (under correction be it spoken) four hogs, and, what between dues and exactions, the officers took from me little less than they were worth. I was returning home, and by the way I lighted upon this good dame, and the devil, the author of all mischief, yoked us together. I paid her handsomely; but she, not contented, laid hold on me, and has never let me go till she has dragged me to this place: she says I forced her; but, by the oath I have taken, or am to take, she lies: and this is the whole truth.'

Then the governor asked him if he had any silver money about him. He said, Yes, he had about twenty ducats in a leathern purse in his bosom. He ordered him to produce it, and deliver it just as it was to the plaintiff. He did so, trembling. The woman took it, and, making a thousand curtsies, after the Moorish manner, and praying to God for the life and health of the lord governor, who took such care of poor orphans and maidens, out of the court she went, holding the purse with both hands; but first she looked to see if the money that was in it was silver.

She was scarcely gone out, when Sancho said to the herdsman, who was in tears, and whose eyes and heart were gone after his purse:

'Honest man, follow that woman, and take away the purse from her, whether she will or no, and come back hither with it.'

This was not said to the deaf or the stupid; for instantly he flew after her like lightning, and went about what he was bid. All present were in great suspense, expecting the issue of this suit; and presently after came in the man and the woman, clinging together closer than the first time, she with her petticoat tucked up, and the purse lapped up in it, and the man struggling to take it from her, but in vain, so tightly she defended it, crying out:

'Justice from God and the world! see, my lord governor, the impudence, and want of fear of this varlet, who, in the midst of the town, and of the street, would take from me the purse your worship commanded to be given me.'

'And has he got it?' demanded the governor.

'Got it?' answered the woman, 'I would sooner let him take away my life than my purse. A pretty baby I should be, indeed: other-guise cats must claw my beard, and not such pitiful, sneaking tools: pincers and hammers, crows and chisels, shall not get it out of my clutches, nor even the paws of a lion; my soul and body shall sooner part.'

'She is in the right,' quoth the man, 'and I yield myself worsted and spent, and confess I have not strength enough to take it from her.'

And so he left her. Then said the governor to the woman: 'Give me that purse, virtuous virago.'

She presently delivered it, and the governor returned it to the man, and said to the forceful, but not forced damsel:

'Sister of mine, had you shown the same, or but half as much courage and resolution in defending you chastity, as you have done in defending your purse, the strength of Hercules could not have forced you. Begone, in God's name, and in an ill hour, and be not found in all this island, nor in six leagues round about it, upon pain of two hundred stripes: begone instantly, I say, thou prating, shameless, cheating hussy!'

The woman was confounded, and went away, hanging down her head, and discontented; and the governor said to the man:

'Honest man, go home, in the name of God, with your money, and from henceforward, unless you have a mind to lose it, take care not to yoke with anybody.'

The countryman gave him thanks after the clownishest manner he could, and went his way;* and the bystanders were in fresh admiration at the decisions and sentences of their new governor. All which, being noted down by his historiographer, was immediately transmitted to the duke, who waited for it with a longing impatience. And here let us leave honest Sancho; for his master, greatly disturbed* at Altisidora's music, calls in haste for us.

CHAPTER 46

Of the dreadful bellringing and cattish consternation Don Quixote was put into in the progress of the enamoured Altisidora's amour.

WE left the great Don Quixote wrapped up in the reflections occasioned by the music of the enamoured damsel Altisidora. He carried them with him to bed; and, as if they had been fleas, they would not suffer him to sleep, or take the least rest. To these was added the disaster of the stocking. But as time is swift, and no bar can stop him, he came riding upon the hours, and that of the morning posted on apace. Which Don Quixote perceiving, he forsook his downy pillow, and in haste put on his chamois doublet, and his travelling boots, to conceal the misfortune of his stocking. He threw over his shoulders his scarlet mantle, and clapped on his head a green velvet cap, trimmed with silver lace. He hung his trusty trenchant blade in his shoulder-belt. On his wrist he wore a large rosary, which he always carried about him. And with great state and solemnity he marched towards the ante-chamber, where the duke and duchess, who were ready dressed, expected him: and as he passed through a gallery, Altisidora, and the other damsel, her friend, stood purposely posted, and waiting for him. As soon as Altisidora espied Don Quixote, she pretended to faint away, and her companion caught her in her lap, and in a great hurry was unlacing her stays. Don Quixote, seeing it, drew near to them, and said:

'I very well know whence these accidents proceed.'

'I know not from whence,' answered her friend; 'for Altisidora is the healthiest damsel in all this family, and I have never heard so much as an Oh! from her since I have known her; ill betide all the knights-errant in the world, if they are all ungrateful. Leave this place, Señor Don Quixote; for the poor girl will not come to herself so long as your worship stays here.'

To which Don Quixote answered:

'Be pleased, madam, to give orders that a lute be left in my chamber to-night, and I will comfort this poor damsel the best I am able; for, in the beginning of love, to be early undeceived is the readiest cure.'

And so saying, away he went, to avoid the observation of those who might see him there. He was hardly gone, when Altisidora, recovering from her swoon, said to her companion:

'By all means let him have the lute; for doubtless he intends us some music, and it cannot be bad if it be his.' They presently went, and gave the duchess an account of what had passed, and of Don Quixote's desiring a lute; and she, being exceedingly rejoiced thereat, concerted with the duke and her damsels how they might play him some trick, which would be more merry than mischievous. And, being pleased with their contrivance, they waited for night, which came on as fast as the day had done, which they spent in relishing conversation with Don Quixote. That same day the duchess dispatched one of her pages, being he who in the wood had personated the figure of the enchanted Dulcinea, to Teresa Panza, with her husband Sancho Panza's letter, and a bundle he had left to be sent, charging him to bring back an exact account of all that should pass.

This being done, and eleven o'clock at night being come, Don Quixote found in his chamber a lute. He touched it; he opened his casement, and perceived that the people were walking in the garden: and having again run over the strings of the instrument, and tuned it as well as he could, he hemmed, and cleared his pipes, and then, with a hoarse though not unmusical voice, he sang the following song, which he himself had composed that day:

THE SONG

'Love, with idleness its friend,
O'er a maiden gains its end;

But let business and employment
Fill up ev'ry careful moment,
These an antidote will prove
'Gainst the pois'nous arts of love,
Maidens, that aspire to marry,
In their looks reserve should carry;
Modesty their price should raise,
And be herald of their praise.
Knights, whom toils of arms employ,
With the free may laugh and toy;
But the modest only choose,
When they tie the nuptial noose.
Love, that rises with the sun,
With his setting beams is gone;
Love, that guest-like visits hearts,
When the banquet's o'er, departs;
And the love that comes to-day,
And to-morrow wings its way,
Leaves no traces on the soul,
Its affections to control.
Where a sovereign beauty reigns,
Fruitless are a rival's pains.
O'er a finished picture who
E'er a second picture drew?
Fair Dulcinea, queen of beauty,
Rules my heart, and claims its duty
Nothing there can take her place;
Nought her image can erase.
Whether fortune smile or frown,
Constancy's the lover's crown;
And, its force divine to prove,
Miracles performs in love.'

Thus far Don Quixote had proceeded in his song, to which stood attentive the duke and duchess, Altisidora, and almost all the folks of the castle, when, on a sudden, from an open gallery directly over Don Quixote's window, a rope was let down, to which above a hundred bells were fastened; and immediately after them was emptied a great sackful of cats, which had smaller bells tied to their tails. The noise of the jangling of the bells, and the mewing of the cats, was so great, that the duke and duchess, though the inventors of the jest, were frightened thereat, and Don Quixote himself was in a panic: and fortune so ordered it, that two or three of the cats got in at the casement of his chamber, and scouring about from side to side, one would have thought a legion of devils was broke loose in it. They extinguished the lights that were burning in the chamber, and endeavoured to make their escape. The cord to which the bells were fastened was let down and pulled up incessantly. Most of the folks of the castle, who were not in the secret, were in suspense and astonishment.

Don Quixote got upon his feet; and, laying hold on his sword, he began to make thrusts at the casement, and cried out aloud:

'Avaunt, ye malicious enchanters! avaunt, ye rabble of wizards! for I am Don Quixote de la Mancha, against whom your wicked arts are of no force nor effect.'

And, turning to the cats, who were running about the room, he gave several cuts at them. They took to the casement, and got out at it all but one, which, finding itself hard pressed by Don Quixote's slashing, flew at his face, and seized him by the nose with its claws and teeth; the pain whereof made him roar as loud as he was able. Which the duke and duchess hearing, and guessing the occasion, they ran in all haste up to his chamber, and opening it with a master-key, they found the poor gentleman striving with all his might to disengage the cat from his face. They entered with lights, and beheld the unequal combat. The duke ran to part the fray, and Don Quixote cried aloud:

'Let no one take him off; leave me to battle with this demon, this wizard, this enchanter; for I will make him know the difference betwixt him and me, and who Don Quixote de la Mancha is.'

But the cat, not regarding these menaces, growled on, and kept its hold. At length the duke forced open its claws, and threw it out at the window.

Don Quixote remained with his face like a sieve, and his nose not over whole, though greatly dissatisfied that they would not let him finish the combat he had so toughly maintained against that caitiff enchanter. They fetched some oil of Aparicio,* and Altisidora herself, with her lily-white hands, bound up his wounds; and, while she was so employed, she said to him in a low voice:

'All these misadventures befall you, hard-hearted knight, for the sin of your stubborn disdain: and God grant that Sancho your squire may forget to whip himself, that this same beloved Dulcinea of yours may never be released from her enchantment, nor you ever enjoy her,* or approach her nuptial bed, at least while I live, who adore you.'

To all this Don Quixote returned no other answer than a profound sigh, and then stretched himself at full length upon his bed, humbly thanking the duke and duchess for their assistance, not as being afraid of that cattish, bellringing, necromantic crew, but as he was sensible of their good intention by their readiness to succour him. The duke and duchess left him to his rest, and went away, not a little concerned at the ill success of their joke; for they did not think this adventure would have proved so heavy and so hard upon Don Quixote; for it cost him five days' confinement to his bed; where another adventure befell him more relishing than the former, which his historian will not relate at present, that he may attend Sancho Panza, who went on very busily and very pleasantly with his government.

CHAPTER 47

Giving a further account of Sancho's behaviour in his government.

THE history relates, that they conducted Sancho Panza from the court of judicature to a sumptuous palace, where, in a great hall, was spread an elegant and splendid table: and soon as Sancho entered the hall, the waits struck up, and in came four pages with water to wash his hands, which Sancho received with great gravity. The music ceased, and Sancho sat down at the upper end of the table: for there was but that one chair, and no other napkin or plate. A personage, who afterwards proved to be a physician, placed himself, standing, on one side of him, with a whalebone rod in his hand. They removed a very fine white cloth, which covered several fruits, and a great variety of eatables. One, who looked like a student, said grace, and a page put a laced bib under Sancho's chin. Another, who played the sewer's part,* set a plate of fruit before him: but scarcely had he eaten a bit, when he of the wand touching the dish with it, the waiters snatched it away from before him with great haste. But the sewer set another dish of meat in its place. Sancho was going to try it, but before he could reach or taste it, the wand had been already at it, and a page whipped that away also with as much speed as he had done the fruit. Sancho, seeing it, was surprised, and, looking about him, asked, if this repast was to be eaten like a show of sleight of hand. To which he of the wand replied:

'My lord governor, here must be no other kind of eating but such as is usual and customary in other islands, where there are governors. I, sir, am a physician, and have an appointed salary in this island, for serving the governors of it in that capacity; and I consult their healths much more than my own, studying night and day, sounding the governor's constitution, the better to know how to cure him when he is sick: and my principal business is, to attend at his meals, to let him eat of what I think is most proper for him, and to remove from him whatever I imagine will do him harm, and be hurtful to his stomach. And therefore I ordered the dish of fruit to be taken away, as being too moist: and that other dish of meat I also ordered away, as being too hot, and having in it too much spice, which increases thirst; for he who drinks much, destroys and consumes the radical moisture in which life consists.'

'Well then,' quoth Sancho; 'yon plate of roasted partridges, which seem to me to be very well seasoned, will they do me any harm?'

To which the doctor answered:

'My lord governor shall not eat a bit of them while I have life.'

'Pray, why not?' quoth Sancho.

The physician answered:

'Because our master Hippocrates, the north star and luminary of medicine, says, in one of his aphorisms, *Omnis saturatio
mala, perdicis autem pessima*; that is to say, All repletion is bad,
but that of partridges the worst of all.'

'If it be so,' quoth Sancho, 'pray see, Señor Doctor, of all
the dishes upon this table, which will do me most good, and
which least harm, and let me eat of it without conjuring it away
with your wand: for by the life of the governor, and as God
shall give me leave to use it, I am dying with hunger; and to
deny me my victuals, though it be against the grain of Señor
Doctor, and though he should say as much more against it, I
say, is rather the way to shorten my life, than to lengthen it.'

'Your worship is in the right, my lord governor,' answered
the physician, 'and therefore I am of opinion, you should
not eat of yon stewed conies, because they are a sharp-haired
food: of that veal, perhaps, you might pick a bit, were it not
a-la-dobed; but as it is, not a morsel.'

Said Sancho: 'That great dish smoking yonder, I take to
be an *olla podrida*, and, amidst the diversity of things contained
in it, surely I may light upon something both wholesome and
toothsome.'

'*Absit*,' quoth the doctor; 'far be such a thought from us:
there is not worse nutriment in the world than your *olla
podridas*: leave them to prebendaries and rectors of colleges,
or for country weddings; but let the tables of governors be
free from them, where nothing but neatness and delicacy
ought to preside; and the reason is, because simple medicines
are more esteemed than compound, by all persons, and in
all places; for in simples there can be no mistake, but in
compounds there may, by altering the quantities of the
ingredients. Therefore what I would advise at present for
Señor Governor's eating, to corroborate and preserve his
health, is, about a hundred of rolled-up wafers, and some
thin slices of marmalade,* that may sit easy upon the stomach, and help digestion.'

Sancho, hearing this, threw himself backward in his chair,
and, surveying the doctor from head to foot, with a grave
voice, asked him his name, and where he had studied. To
which he answered:

'My lord governor, I am called doctor Pedro Recio de Agüero: I am a native of a place called Tirteafuera,* lying between Caracuel and Almodóvar del Campo, on the right hand, and have taken my doctor's degree in the university of Osuna.'

To which Sancho, burning with rage, answered:

'Why then, Señor Doctor Pedro Recio de Mal-Agüero, native of Tirteafuera, lying on the right hand as we go from Caracuel, to Almodóvar del Campo, graduate in Osuna, get out of my sight this instant, or, by the sun, I will take a cudgel, and, beginning with you, will so lay about me, that there shall not be left one physician in the whole island, at least of those I find to be ignorant: as for those that are learned, prudent, and discreet, I shall respect and honour them as divine persons. And I say again, let Pedro Recio quit my presence, or I shall take this chair I sit upon, and fling it at his head; and if I am called to an account for it before the judge, when I am out of office, I will justify myself by saying, I did God service in killing a bad physician, the hangman of the public. And give me to eat, or take back your government; for an office that will not find a man in victuals is not worth two beans.'

The doctor was frightened at seeing the governor so choleric, and would have taken himself out of the hall, had not the sound of a post-horn been heard that instant in the street. The sewer going to the window, and looking out, came back and said:

'A courier is arrived from my lord duke, and must certainly have brought some despatches of importance.'

The courier entered sweating and in a hurry, and pulling a packet out of his bosom, he delivered it into the governor's hands, and Sancho gave it to the steward, bidding him read the superscription, which was this: 'To Don Sancho Panza, governor of the Island of Barataria, to be delivered into his own hands, or into his secretary's'. Which Sancho hearing, he said:

'Which is my secretary here?'

One of those present, answered:

'I am he, sir; for I can read and write, and am a Biscainer.'

'With that addition,' quoth Sancho, 'you may very well be secretary to the emperor himself: open the packet, and see what it contains.'

The newborn secretary did so, and, having cast his eye over the contents, he said, it was a business which required privacy. Sancho commanded the hall to be cleared, and that none should stay but the steward and the sewer; and all the rest, with the physician, being withdrawn, the secretary read the following letter:

'It is come to my knowledge, Señor Don Sancho Panza, that certain enemies of mine and of the island, intend, one of these nights, to assault it furiously. You must be watchful and diligent, that they may not attack you unprepared. I am informed also, by trusty spies, that four persons in disguise are got into the island to take away your life, because they are in fear of your abilities. Have your eyes about you, and be careful who is admitted to speak to you, and be sure eat nothing sent you as a present. I will take care to send you assistance, if you are in any want of it. And, upon the whole, I do not doubt but you will act as is expected from your judgement.

'Your friend, THE DUKE.

'From this place, the 16th of August,
at four in the morning.'

Sancho was astonished, and the rest seemed to be so too; and, turning to the steward, he said:

'The first thing to be done is, to clap doctor Recio into prison; for if any person has a design to kill me, it is he, and that by a lingering and the worst of deaths, by hunger.'

Said the steward:

'It is my opinion, your honour would do well to eat nothing of all this meat here upon the table; for it was presented by some nuns; and it is a saying, "The devil lurks behind the cross." '

'I grant it,' quoth Sancho; 'and, for the present, give me only a piece of bread, and some four pounds of grapes: no poison can be conveyed in them; for, in short, I cannot live without eating: and, if we must hold ourselves in readiness for these wars that threaten us, it will be necessary we should be well victualled; for the guts uphold the heart, and not the heart the guts. And you, secretary, answer my lord duke, and tell him his commands shall be punctually obeyed, just as he gives them; and present my humble service to my lady duchess, and beg her not to forget sending my letter and the bundle by a special messenger to my wife Teresa Panza, which I shall look upon as a particular favour, and will be her humble servant to the utmost of my power. And, by the way, you may put in a service to my master Don Quixote de la Mancha, that he may see I am grateful bread; and, like a good secretary, and a staunch Biscainer, you may add what you please, or what will turn to best account; and pray, take away the cloth, and give me something to eat; for I will deal well enough with all the spies, murderers, and enchanters, that shall attack me, or my island.'

Now a page came in, and said:

'Here is a countryman about business, who would speak with your lordship concerning an affair, as he says, of great importance.'

'A strange case this,' quoth Sancho, 'that these men of business should be so silly as not to see that such hours as these are not proper for business! What! belike, we who govern, and are judges, are not made of flesh and bones, like other men? Are we made of marble stone, that we must not refresh at times, when necessity requires it? Before God, and upon my conscience, if my government lasts, as I have a glimmering it will not, I shall hamper more than one of these men of business. Bid this honest man come in for this once; but first see that he be not one of the spies, or one of my murderers.'

'No, my lord,' answered the page; 'he looks like a pitcher-souled fellow; and I know little, or he is as harmless as a piece of bread.'

'You need not fear,' quoth the steward, 'while we are present.'

'Is it not possible, sewer,' quoth Sancho, 'now that the doctor Pedro Recio is not here, for me to eat something of substance and weight, though it were but a luncheon of bread and an onion?'

'To-night, at supper,' quoth the sewer, 'amends shall be made for the defects of dinner, and your lordship shall have no cause to complain.'

'God grant it,' answered Sancho.

Then came in the countryman, who was of a goodly presence; and one might see, a thousand leagues off, that he was an honest, good soul. The first thing he said, was:

'Which is the lord governor here?'

'Who should [be],' answered the secretary, 'but he who is seated in the chair?'

'I humble myself in his presence,' quoth the countryman, kneeling down, and begging his hand to kiss. Sancho refused it, and commanded him to rise, and tell his business. The countryman did so, and then said:

'My lord, I am a countryman, a native of Miguel Turra, two leagues from Ciudad Real.'

'What! another Tirteafuera?' quoth Sancho: 'say on, brother; for let me tell you, I know Miguel Turra very well: it is not so far from our town.'

'The business is this, sir,' proceeded the peasant. 'By the mercy of God I was married in peace, and in the face of the holy Catholic Roman Church, I have two sons, bred scholars: the younger studies for bachelor, and the elder for licentiate. I am a widower; for my wife died, or rather a wicked physician killed her, by purging her when she was with child; and, if it had been God's will the child had been born, and had proved a son, I would have put him to study for doctor, that he might not envy his two brothers, the bachelor and licentiate.'

'So that,' quoth Sancho, 'if your wife had not died, or had not been killed, you had not now been a widower!'

'No, certainly, my lord,' answered the peasant:

'We are much the nearer,' replied Sancho: 'go on, brother, for this is an hour rather for bed than business.'

'I say then,' quoth the countryman, 'that this son of mine, who is to be the bachelor, fell in love, in the same village, with a damsel called Clara Perlerina, daughter of Andres Perlerino, a very rich farmer; and this name of Perlerino came not to them by lineal, or any other descent, but because all

856 of that race are subject to the palsy;* and to mend the name,
of that race are subject to the palsy;* and to mend the name,

of that race are subject to the palsy;* and to mend the name,
they call them Perlerines; though to say the truth, the damsel
is like any oriental pearl, and, looked at on the right side,
seems a very flower of the field; but, on the left, she is not
quite so fair; for, on that side, she wants an eye, which she
lost by the small-pox; and, though the pits in her face are
many and deep, her admirers say, they are not pits, but
sepulchres, wherein the hearts of her lovers are buried. She
is so cleanly, that, to prevent defiling her face, she carries
her nose so crooked up, that it seems to be flying from her
mouth: and for all that she looks extremely well; for she has
a large mouth; and, did she not lack half a score or a dozen
teeth and grinders, she might pass, and make a figure, among
ladies of the best fashion. I say nothing of her lips; for they
are so thin and slender, that, were it the fashion to reel lips,
as they do yarn, one might make a skein of them: but, being
of a different colour from what is usually found in lips, they
have a marvellous appearance; for they are marbled with blue,
green, and orange-tawny.'

'And pray, my lord governor, pardon me, if I paint so
minutely the parts of her, who, after all, is to be my daughter;
for I love her, and like her mightily.'

'Paint what you will,' quoth Sancho; 'for I am mightily
taken with the picture; and, had I but dined, I would not
desire a better dessert than your portrait.'

'It shall be always at your service,' answered the peasant;
'and the time may come when we may be acquainted, though
we are not so now; and, I assure you, my lord, if I could
but paint her genteelness, and the tallness of her person, you
would admire; but that cannot be, because she is crooked,
and crumpled up together, and her knees touch her mouth:
though for all that, you may see plainly, that, could she but
stand upright, she would touch the ceiling with her head.
And she would ere now have given her hand to my bachelor,
to be his wife, but that she cannot stretch it out, it is so
shrunk: nevertheless, her long guttered nails show the goodness of its make.'

'So far so good,' quoth Sancho; 'and now, brother, make
account that you have painted her from head to foot: what

is it you would be at? come to the point, without so many windings and turnings, so many fetches and digressions.'

'What I desire, my lord,' answered the countryman, 'is, that your lordship would do me the favour to give me a letter of recommendation to her father, begging his consent to the match, since we are pretty equal in our fortunes and natural endowments; for, to say the truth, my lord governor, my son is possessed, and there is scarcely a day in which the evil spirits do not torment him three or four times; and, by having fallen once into the fire, his face is as shrivelled as a piece of scorched parchment, and his eyes are somewhat bleared and running; but he is as good-conditioned as an angel; and, did he not buffet, and give himself frequent cuffs, he would be a very saint.'

'Would you have anything else, honest friend?' replied Sancho.

'One thing more I would ask,' quoth the peasant, 'but that I dare not; yet out it shall; for, in short, it shall not rot in my breast, come of it what will. I say then, my lord, I could be glad your worship would give me three or six hundred ducats towards the fortune of my bachelor: I mean, towards the furnishing his house; for, in short, they are to live by themselves, without being subject to the impertinences of their fathers-in-law.'

'Well,' quoth Sancho, 'see if you would have anything else, and be not ashamed to tell it.'

'No, for certain,' answered the peasant: and scarcely had he said this, when the governor, getting up, and laying hold of the chair he sat on, said:

'I vow to God, Don lubberly, saucy bumpkin, if you do not get you gone, and instantly avoid my presence, with this chair will I crack your skull: son of a whore, rascal, painter for the devil himself! at this time of day to come and ask me for six hundred ducats! Where should I have them, stinkard? and, if I had them, why should I give them to thee, jibing fool? What care I for Miguel Turra, or for the whole race of the Perlerines? Begone, I say, or, by the life of my lord duke, I will be as good as my word. You are no native of Miguel Turra, but some scoffer sent from hell to tempt me. Impudent scoundrel! I have not yet had the government a day and a half and you would have me have six hundred ducats?'

The sewer made signs to the countryman to go out of the hall, which he did, hanging down his head, and seemingly afraid, lest the governor should execute his threat; for the knave very well knew how to play his part.

But let us leave Sancho in his passion, and peace be with him and company; and let us turn to Don Quixote, whom we left with his face bound up, and under cure of his cattish wounds, of which he was not quite healed in eight days, in one of which there befell him what Cid Hamet promises to relate, with that punctuality and truth with which he relates everything belonging to the history, be it never so minute.

CHAPTER 48

Of what befell Don Quixote with Doña Rodriguez, the duchess's duenna; together with other accidents worthy to be written, and had in eternal remembrance.

ABOVE measure discontented and melancholy was the sore-wounded Don Quixote, having his face bound up, and marked, not by the hand of God, but by the claws of a cat; misfortunes incident to knight-errantry. During six days he appeared not in public; on one night of which, lying awake and restless, meditating on his misfortunes, and the persecution he suffered from Altisidora, he perceived somebody was opening his chamber door with a key, and presently imagined that the enamoured damsel was coming to assault his chastity, and expose him to the temptation of failing in the fidelity he owed to his lady Dulcinea del Toboso.

'No,' said he (believing what he fancied, and so loud as to be overheard), 'not the greatest beauty upon earth shall prevail with me to cease adoring her who is engraven and imprinted in the bottom of my heart, and in the inmost recesses of my entrails; whether, my dearest lady, you be now transformed into a garlic-eating country wench, or into a nymph of the golden Tagus, weaving tissue-webs with gold and silken twist; or whether you are in the power of Merlin or Montesinos: wherever you are, mine you are, and wherever I am, yours I have been, and yours I will remain.'

The conclusion of these words, and the opening of the door were at the same instant. Up he stood upon the bed, wrapped from top to toe in a quilt of yellow satin, a woollen cap on his head, and his face and moustaches bound up; his face, because of its scratches, and his moustaches, to keep them from flagging and falling down. In which guise he appeared the most extraordinary phantasm imaginable.

He nailed his eyes to the door, and when he expected to see the poor captivated and sorrowful Altisidora enter, he perceived approaching a most reverend duenna, in a long white veil that covered her from head to foot. She carried between the fingers of her left hand half a lighted candle, and held her right hand over it, to shade her face, and keep the glare from her eyes, which were hidden behind a huge pair of spectacles. She advanced very slowly, and trod very softly. Don Quixote observed from his watchtower, and perceiving her figure, and noting her silence, he fancied some witch or sorceress was come in that disguise to do him some shrewd turn, and began to cross himself apace. The apparition kept moving forward, and, when it came to the middle of the room, it lifted up its eyes, and saw in what a hurry Don Quixote was crossing himself, and, if he was afraid at seeing such a figure, she was no less dismayed at sight of his, and seeing him so lank and yellow, with the quilt, and the bandages, which disfigured him, she cried out:

'Jesus! what do I see?'

With the fright, the candle fell out of her hand, and, finding herself in the dark, she turned about to be gone, and, with the fear, treading on her skirts, she tumbled, and fell down.

Don Quixote, trembling with affright, began to say:

'I conjure thee, phantom, or whatever thou art, tell me who thou art, and what thou wouldst have with me, if thou art a soul in torment, tell me, and I will do all I can for thee; for I am a Catholic Christian, and love to do good to all the world; for that purpose I took upon me the profession of knight-errantry, an employment which extends to the doing good even to souls in purgatory.'

The bruised duenna, hearing herself thus exorcized, guessed at Don Quixote's fear by her own, and, in a low and doleful voice, answered:

'Señor Don Quixote (if peradventure your worship be Don Quixote), I am no phantom, nor apparition, nor soul in purgatory, as your worship seems to think, but Doña Rodriguez, duenna of honour to my lady duchess, and am come to your worship with one of those cases of necessity,* your worship is wont to remedy.'

'Tell me then, Señor Doña Rodriguez,' quoth Don Quixote, 'does your ladyship, peradventure, come in quality of procuress? If you do, I give you to understand I am fit for nobody's turn, thanks to the peerless beauty of my mistress Dulcinea del Toboso. In short, Señora Doña Rodriguez, on condition you waive all amorous messages, you may go and light your candle, and return hither, and we will discourse of whatever you please to command, with exception, as I told you, to all kind of amorous excitements.'

'I bring messages, good sir!' answered the duenna: 'your worship mistakes me very much: I am not yet so advanced in years, to be forced to betake myself to so low an employment: for, God be praised, my soul is still in my body, and all my teeth in my head, excepting a few usurped from me by catarrhs, so common in this country of Aragon. But stay a little, sir, till I go and light my candle, and I will return instantly, to relate my griefs to your worship, as to the redresser of all the grievances in the world.'

And without staying for an answer, she went out of the room, leaving Don Quixote in expectation of her return.

Straight a thousand thoughts crowded into his mind, touching this new adventure, and he was of opinion he had done ill, and judged worse, to expose himself to the hazard of breaking his plighted troth to his lady, and he said to himself: 'Who knows but the devil, who is subtle and designing, means to deceive me now with a duenna, though he has not been able to effect it with empresses, queens, duchesses, marchionesses, or countesses?

'For I have often heard ingenious people say, "The devil, if he can, will sooner tempt a man with a flat-nosed than a hawk-nosed woman"; and who can tell but this solitude, this opportunity, and this silence, may awake my desires, which are now asleep, and, in my declining years, make me fall where I never yet stumbled? In such cases, it is better to fly than stand the battle. But sure I am not in my right senses to talk so idly: for it is impossible that a white-veiled, lank, and bespectacled duenna should move or excite a wanton thought in the lewdest breast in the world. Is there a duenna upon earth that has tolerable flesh and blood? Is there a duenna upon the globe that is not impertinent, wrinkled, and squeamish? Avaunt then, ye rabble of duennas, useless to any human pleasure! O how rightly did that lady act, of whom it is said, that she had, at the foot of her state sofa, a couple of statues of duennas, with their spectacles and bobbin cushions as if they were at work; which statues served every whit as well for the dignity of her state-room as real duennas.'

And so saying, he jumped off the bed, designing to lock his door, and not let Señora Rodriguez enter. But before he could shut it, Señora Rodriguez was just returned with a lighted taper of white wax; and seeing Don Quixote so much nearer, wrapped up in his quilt, with his bandages and night-cap, she was again frighted, and, retreating two or three steps, she said:

'Sir Knight, am I safe? for I take it to be no very good sign of modesty that your worship is got out of bed.'

'I should rather ask you that question, madam,' answered Don Quixote, 'and therefore I do ask, if I am safe from being assaulted and ravished?'

'By whom, and from whom, Sir Knight, do you expect this security?' answered the duenna.

'By you, and from you,' replied Don Quixote; 'for I am not made of marble, nor you, I suppose, of brass: nor is it ten o'clock in the morning, but midnight, and somewhat more, as I imagine, and we are in a room closer and more secret than the cave in which the bold and traitorous Aeneas enjoyed the beautiful and tender-hearted Dido. But, madam, give me your hand; for I desire no greater security than my own continence and reserve, besides what that most reverend veil inspires.'

And so saying, he kissed his right hand, and with it took hold of hers, which she gave him with the same ceremony.

Here Cid Hamet makes a parenthesis, and swears by Mahomet, he would have given the better of his two vests to have seen these two walking from the door to the bedside, handing and handed so ceremoniously.

In short, Don Quixote got into bed, and Doña Rodriguez sat down in a chair at some little distance from it, without taking off her spectacles, or setting down her candle. Don Quixote covered himself up close, all but his face, and, they both having paused a while, the first who broke silence was Don Quixote, saying:

'Now, Señora Doña Rodriguez, you may unrip and unbosom all that is in your careful heart and piteous bowels: for you shall be heard by me with chaste ears, and assisted by compassionate deeds.'

'I believe it,' answered the duenna; 'for none but so Christian an answer could be expected from your worship's gentle and pleasing presence.

'The business then is, Señor Don Quixote, that, though your worship sees me sitting in this chair, and in the midst of the kingdom of Aragon, and in the garb of a poor persecuted duenna, I was born in the Asturias of Oviedo, and of a family allied to some of the best of that province. But my hard fortune, and the negligence of my parents, which reduced them, I know not which way, to untimely poverty, carried me to the court of Madrid, where, for peace sake, and to prevent greater inconveniences, my parents placed me in the service of a great lady: and I would have your worship know, that, in making needle-cases and plain work, I was never outdone by anybody in all my life. My parents left me in service, and returned to their own country; and, in a few years after, I believe, they went to heaven; for they were very good and Catholic Christians. I remained an orphan, and stinted to the miserable wages, and short commons, usually given in great houses to such kind of servants.

'About that time, without my giving any encouragement for it, a gentleman-usher of the family fell in love with me; a man in years, with a fine beard, and of a comely person, and above all, as good a gentleman as the king himself; for he was a highlander.* We did not carry on our amour so secretly, but it came to the notice of my lady, who, without more ado, had us married in peace, and in the face of our holy mother the Catholic Roman Church; from which marriage sprang a daughter, to finish my good fortune, if I had any; not that I died in childbed (for I went my full time, and was safely delivered), but because my husband died soon after of a certain fright he took; and had I but time to tell the manner how, your worship, I am sure, would wonder.'

Here she began to weep most tenderly, and said:

'Pardon me, good Señor Don Quixote; for I cannot command myself; but as often as I call to mind my unhappy spouse, my eyes are brimful. God be my aid! with what stateliness did he use to carry my lady behind him on a puissant mule, black as the very jet; for in those times coaches and side-saddles were not in fashion, as it is said they are now, and the ladies rode behind their squires. Nevertheless, I cannot help telling you the following story, that you may see how well-bred, and how punctilious my good husband was.

'At the entrance into St. James's Street in Madrid, which is very narrow, a judge of one of the courts happened to be coming out with two of his officers before him, and, as soon as my good squire saw him, he turned his mule about, as if he designed to wait upon him. My lady, who was behind him, said to him in a low voice:

'"What are you doing, blockhead? am not I here?"

'The judge civilly stopped his horse, and said:

'"Keep on your way, sir; for it is my business rather to wait upon my lady Doña Casilda;" that was my mistress's name.

'My husband persisted, cap in hand, in his intention to wait upon the judge: which my lady perceiving, full of choler and indignation, she pulled out a great pin, or rather, I believe, a bodkin, and stuck it into his back: whereupon my husband bawled out, and, writhing his body, down he came with his lady to the ground. Two of her footmen ran to help her up, as did the judge and his officers. The gate of Guadalajara, I mean the idle people that stood there, were all in uproar. My mistress was forced to walk home on foot, and my husband went to a barber-surgeon's, telling him he was run quite through and through the bowels. The courteousness and breeding of my spouse was rumoured abroad, insomuch that the boys got it, and teased him with it in the streets; and, upon this account, and because he was a little short-sighted, my lady turned him away; the grief whereof, I verily believe, was the death of him.

'I was left a widow, and helpless, with a daughter upon my hands, who went on increasing in beauty like the foam of the sea. Finally, as I had the reputation of a good workwoman at my needle, my lady duchess, who was then newly married to my lord duke, would needs have me with her to this kingdom of Aragon, together with my daughter, where, in process of time, she grew up, and with her all the accomplishments in the world. She sings like any lark, dances quick as thought, capers as if she would break her neck, reads and writes like a schoolmaster, and casts accounts like any usurer. I say nothing of her cleanliness; for the running brook is not cleaner: and she is now, if I remember right, sixteen years of age, five months, and three days, one more or less.

'In a word, the son of a very rich farmer, who lives not far off in a village of my lord duke's, grew enamoured of this girl of mine; and, to be short, I know not how it came about, but they got together, and, under promise of being her husband, he has fooled my daughter, and now refuses to perform it. And, though my lord duke knows the affair, and I have complained again and again to him, and begged him to command this same young farmer to marry my daughter, yet he turns the deaf ear, and will hardly vouchsafe to hear me; and the reason is, because the cozening knave's father is rich, and lends him money, and is bound for him on all occasions; therefore, he will not disoblige nor offend him in any wise.

'Now, good sir, my desire is, that your worship take upon you the redressing this wrong, either by entreaty, or by force of arms; since all the world says, your worship was born in it to redress grievances, to right the injured, and succour the miserable. And be pleased, sir, to consider my daughter's fatherless condition, her genteelness, her youth, and all the good qualities I have already mentioned; for, on my soul and conscience, of all the damsels my lady has, there is not one that comes up to the sole of her shoe; and one of them, called Altisidora, who is reckoned to be the liveliest and gracefullest of them all, falls above two leagues short, in comparison with my daughter; for you must know, dear sir, that all is not gold that glitters; and this same little Altisidora has more self-conceit than beauty, and more assurance than modesty: besides, she is none of the soundest; for her breath is so strong, there is no enduring to be a moment near her. Nay, even my lady duchess herself—but mum for that; for they say walls have ears.'

'What of my lady duchess?' quoth Don Quixote. 'Tell me, Madam Rodriguez, by my life.'

'Thus conjured,' replied the duenna, 'I cannot but answer to whatever is asked me, with all truth. Your worship, Señor Don Quixote, must have observed the beauty of my lady duchess; that complexion like any bright and polished sword; those cheeks of milk and crimson, with the sun in the one, and the moon in the other; and that stateliness with which she treads, or rather disdains the very ground she walks on, that one would think she went dispensing health wherever she passes. Let me tell you, sir, she may thank God for it in the first place, and next, two issues she has, one in each leg, which discharge all the bad humours, of which the physicians say she is full.'

'Holy Mary!' quoth Don Quixote, 'is it possible my lady duchess has such drains? I should never have believed it, had the bare-footed friars themselves told it me; but since Madam Doña Rodriguez says it, it must needs be so. But such issues, and in such places, must distil nothing but liquid amber: verily I am now convinced, that this making of issues is a matter of great consequence in respect to health.'

Scarcely had Don Quixote said this, when, with a great bounce, the chamber door flew open; the surprise at which made Doña Rodriguez let fall her candle out of her hand, and the room remained as dark as a wolf's mouth, as the saying is; and presently the poor duenna found herself gripped so fast by the throat with two hands, that she could not squall, and another person, very nimbly, without speaking a word, whipped up her petticoats, and with a slipper, as it seemed, gave her so many slaps, that it would have moved one's pity: and though it did that of Don Quixote, he stirred not from the bed, and, not knowing the meaning of all this, he lay still and silent, fearing lest that round and sound flogging should come next to his turn.

And his fear proved not in vain; for the silent executioners, leaving the duenna, who durst not cry out, well curried, came to Don Quixote; and, turning down the bed-clothes, they pinched him so often and so hard, that he could not forbear going to fisticuffs in his own defence, and all this in marvellous silence. The battle lasted some half an hour: the phantoms went off: Doña Rodriguez adjusted her petticoats, and, bewailing her misfortune, marched out at the door, without saying a word to Don Quixote, who, sad and sorely bepinched, confused and pensive, remained alone; where we will leave him, impatient to learn who that perverse enchanter was that had handled him so roughly. But that shall be told in its proper place; for Sancho Panza calls upon us, and the method of the history requires it.

CHAPTER 49

Of what befell Sancho Panza as he was going the round of his island.

WE left the grand governor moody and out of humour at the knavish picture-drawing peasant, who, instructed by the steward, and he by the duke, played off Sancho; who, maugre his ignorance, rudeness, and insufficiency, held them all back, and said to those about him, and to doctor Pedro Recio, who, when the secret of the duke's letter was over, came back into the hall:

'I now plainly perceive, that judges and governors must or ought to be made of brass, if they would be insensible of importunities of your men of business, who, being intent upon their own affairs alone, come what will of it, at all hours, and at all times, will needs be heard and dispatched; and if the poor judge does not hear and dispatch them, either because he cannot, or because it is not the proper time for giving them audience, presently they murmur and traduce him, gnawing his very bones, and calumniating him and his family. Foolish man of business, impertinent man of business, be not in such haste; wait for the proper season and conjuncture for negotiation: come not at dinner-time, nor at bed-time; for judges are made of flesh and blood, and must give to their nature what their nature requires; except only poor I, who do not so by mine, thanks to Señor Pedro Recio Tirteafuera here present, who would have me die of hunger, and affirms that this kind of dying is in order to live: God grant the same life to him and all those of his tribe; I mean, bad physicians; for good ones deserve palms and laurels.'

All who knew Sancho Panza were in admiration to hear him talk so elegantly, and could not tell what to ascribe it to, unless that offices and weighty employments quicken and enliven some understandings, as they confound and stupefy others.

In short, doctor Pedro Recio Agüero de Tirteafuera promised he should sup that night, though it were contrary to all the aphorisms of Hippocarates. With this the governor rested satisfied, and expected with great impatience the coming of the night, and the hour of supper; and though time, to his thinking, stood stock still, yet at length the wished-for hour came, and they gave him some cow-beef, hashed with onions and calves' feet, somewhat of the stalest, boiled. However, he laid about him, with more relish, than if they had given him Milan godwits,* Roman pheasants, veal of Sorrento, partridges of Moron, or geese of Lavajos; and in the midst of supper, turning to the doctor, he said:

'Look you, Master Doctor, henceforward take no care to provide me your nice things to eat, nor your tit-bits; for it will be throwing my stomach quite off the hinges, which is accustomed to goats' flesh, cow-beef, and bacon, with turnips and onions; and if perchance you give it court kickshaws, it receives them with squeamishness, and sometimes with loathing. What Master Sewer here may do, is, to get me some of those eatables you call your *olla podridas*, and the stronger they are the better: and you may insert and stuff in them whatever you will: for so it be an eatable, I shall take it kindly, and will one day make you amends; and let nobody play upon me; for either we are, or we are not: and let us all live and eat together in peace and good friendship; for when God sends daylight, it is day for everybody. I will govern this island, without losing my own right, or taking away another man's, and let every one keep a good look out, and mind each man his own business; for I would have them to know, the devil is in the wind,* and, if they put me upon it, they shall see wonders. Aye, aye, make yourselves honey, and the wasps will devour you.'

'Certainly, my lord governor,' quoth the sewer, 'there is reason in all your worship says, and I dare engage in the name of all the islanders of this island, that they will serve your worship with all punctuality, love, and goodwill; for your sweet way of governing from the very first leaves us no room to do or to think anything that may redound to the disservice of your worship.'

'I believe it,' answered Sancho, 'and they would be fools, if they did or thought otherwise. And I tell you again to take care for my sustenance, and for my Dapple's, which is what is most important in this business; and when the hour comes, we will go the round; for it is my intention to clear this island of all manner of filth, of vagabonds, idlers, and sharpers. For you must understand, friends, that idle and lazy people in a commonwealth are the same as drones in a beehive, which eat the honey that the industrious bees lay up in store. My design is to protect the peasants, preserve to the gentry their privileges, reward ingenious artists, and above all, to have regard to religion, and to the honour of the religious. What think ye of this, my friends? Do I say something, or do I crack my brain to no purpose?'

'My lord governor,' quoth the steward, 'speaks so well, that I wonder to hear a man, so void of learning as your worship, who, I believe, cannot so much as read, say such and so many things, and all so sententious and instructive, and so far beyond all that could be expected from your worship's former understanding by those who sent us, and by us, who are come hither. But every day produces new things; jests turn into earnest, and jokers are joked upon.'

The night came, and, the governor having supped with the licence of Señor Doctor Recio, they prepared for going the round, and he set out with the secretary, the steward, the sewer, and the historiographer, who had the care of recording his actions, together with serjeants and notaries, enough to have formed a middling battalion. In the midst of them marched Sancho, with his white rod of office; and having traversed a few streets, they heard the clashing of swords. They hastened to the place, and found two men fighting; who, seeing the officers coming, desisted, and one of them said:

'Help, in the name of God and the king! Is it permitted in this town to rob folks, and set upon them in the streets?'

'Hold! honest man,' quoth Sancho, 'and tell me what is the occasion of this fray; for I am the governor.'

The other, his antagonist, said:

'My lord governor, I will briefly relate the matter: Your honour must understand, that this gentleman is just come from winning, in that gaming-house yonder over the way, above a thousand reals, and God knows how; and I, being present, gave judgement in his favour, in many a doubtful point, against the dictates of my conscience. Up he got with his winnings, and, when I expected he would have given me a crown at least, by way of present, as is the usage and custom among gentlemen of distinction, such as I am, who stand by, ready at all adventures to back unreasonable demands, and to prevent quarrels, he pocketed up his money, and went out of the house. I followed him in dudgeon, and, with good words and civil expressions, desired him to give

me though it were but eight reals, since he knows I am a
man of honour, and have neither office nor benefice, my
parents having brought me up to nothing, and left me
nothing; and this knave, as great a thief as Cacus, and as
arrant a sharper as Andradilla, would give me but four reals.
Judge, my lord governor, how little shame, and how little
conscience he has. But, in faith, had it not been for your
honour's coming, I would have made him disgorge his
winnings, and have taught him how many ounces go to the
pound.'

'What say you to this, friend?' quoth Sancho.

The other answered that all his adversary had said was true,
and he did not intend to give him any more than four reals;
for he was often giving him something, and they, who expect
the benevolence, should be mannerly, and take with a cheerful countenance whatever is given them, and not stand upon
terms with the winners, unless they know them for certain
to be sharpers, and that their winnings were unfairly gotten;
and, for demonstration of his being an honest man, and no
cheat as the other alleged, there could be no stronger proof
than his refusal to comply with his demand; for cheats are
always tributaries to the lookers-on, who know them.

'That is true,' quoth the steward; 'be pleased, my lord
governor, to adjudge what shall be done with these men.'

'What shall be done is this,' answered Sancho: 'You, master
winner, good, bad, or indifferent, give your hackster here
immediately a hundred reals, and pay down thirty more for
the poor prisoners: and you, sir, who have neither office nor
benefice, and live without any employment in this island, take
these hundred reals instantly, and, sometime to-morrow, get
out of this island for ten years, on pain, if you transgress, of
finishing your banishment in the next life; for I will hang
you on a gallows, or at least the hangman shall do it for me;
and let no man reply, lest I punish him severely.'

The one disbursed; the other received: the one went out
of the island; the other went home to his house; and the
governor said:

'It shall cost me a fall, or I will demolish these gaming-
houses; for I have a suspicion that they are very prejudicial.'

'This, at least,' quoth one of the scriveners, 'your honour cannot put down; for a great person keeps it, and what he loses in the year is beyond comparison more than what he gets by the cards. Your worship may exert your authority against petty gaming-houses, which do more harm, and cover more abuses: for in those, which belong to persons of quality, notorious cheats dare not put their tricks in practice; and, since the vice of play is become a common practice, it is better it should go forward in the houses of people of distinction, than in those of mean quality, where they take in unfortunate bubbles after midnight, and strip off their very skin.'

'Well, Master Notary,' quoth Sancho, there is a great deal to be said on this subject.'

And now up came a serjeant, having laid hold of a young man, and said:

'My lord governor, this youth was coming towards us; but, as soon as he perceived it was the round, he faced about, and began to run like a stag; a sign he must be some delinquent. I pursued him, and, had he not stumbled and fallen, I should never have overtaken him.'

'Why did you fly, young man,' quoth Sancho.

The youth replied:

'My lord, to avoid answering the multitude of questions officers are wont to ask.'

'What trade are you of?' quoth Sancho.

'A weaver,' answered the youth.

'And what do you weave?' quoth Sancho.

'Iron heads for spears, an it please your worship.'

'You are pleasant with me, and value yourself on being a joker,' quoth Sancho: 'it is very well; and whither were you going?'

'To take the air, sir,' replied the lad.

'And, pray, where do people take the air in this island?' said Sancho.

'Where it blows,' answered the youth.

'Good,' quoth Sancho, 'you answer to the purpose, you are a discreet youth. But now, make account that I am the air, and that I blow in your poop, and drive you to jail. Here, lay hold on him, and carry him to prison: I will make him sleep there to-night without air.'

'Before God,' quoth the youth, 'your honour can no more make me sleep there, than you can make me a king.'

'Why cannot I make you sleep in prison?' demanded Sancho: 'have I not power to confine or release you, as I please?'

'How much power soever your worship may have, you have not enough to make me sleep in prison.'

'Why not?' replied Sancho: 'away with him immediately, where he shall see his mistake with his own eyes; and, lest the jailer should put his interested generosity in practise, I will sconce him in the penalty of two thousand ducats, if he suffers you to stir a step from the prison.'

'All this is matter of laughter,' answered the youth: 'the business is, I defy all the world to make me sleep this night in prison.'

'Tell me, devil,' quoth Sancho, 'have you some angel to deliver you, and unloose the fetters I intend to have clapped on you?'

'My lord governor,' answered the youth, with an air of pleasantry, 'let us abide by reason, and come to the point. Supposing your worship orders me to jail, and to be loaded with chains and fetters, and clapped into the dungeon, with heavy penalties laid upon the jailer, if he lets me stir out; and let us suppose these orders punctually obeyed: yet, for all that, if I have no mind to sleep, but to keep awake all night, without so much as shutting my eyelids, can your worship, with all your power, make me sleep whether I will or no?'

'No, certainly,' said the secretary, 'and the man has carried his point.'

'So that,' quoth Sancho, 'you would forbear sleeping only to have your own will, and not out of pure contradiction to mine?'

'No, my lord,' said the youth, 'not even in thought.'

'Then, God be with you,' quoth Sancho; 'go home to sleep, and I wish you a good night's rest; for I will not endeavour to deprive you of it: but I would advise you, for the future, not to be so jocose with officers of justice; for you may meet with one that may lay the joke over your noddle.'

The youth went his way, and the governor continued his round, and, a little while after, came a couple of serjeants, who had hold of a man, and said:

'My lord governor, this here, who seems to be a man, is not so, but a woman, and no ugly one either, in man's clothes.'*

They lifted up two or three lanterns to her face, by the light of which they discovered that of a woman, seemingly sixteen years of age, or thereabouts. Her hair was tucked up under a network caul of gold and green silk, and she herself beautiful as a thousand pearls. They viewed her from head to foot, and saw she had on a pair of flesh-coloured stockings, with garters of white taffeta, and tassels of gold and seed-pearl: her breeches were of green and gold tissue, and she had on a loose coat of the same, under which she wore a very fine waistcoat of white and gold stuff. Her shoes were white, and such as men wear. She had no sword, but a very rich dagger; and on her fingers were many rings, and those very good ones. In a word everybody liked the maiden; but none of them all knew her, and the inhabitants of the town said, they could not imagine who she should be. They who were in the secret of the jests put upon Sancho, admired the most; for this adventure was not of their contriving, and therefore they were in suspense, expecting the issue of this unforeseen accident. Sancho was struck with the beauty of the young lady, and asked her who she was, whither she was going, and what had moved her to dress herself in that habit. She, fixing her eyes on the ground, with a modest bashfulness, answered:

'Sir, I cannot declare so publicly what I am so much concerned to keep a secret: only one thing I must assure you, that I am no thief, nor criminal person, but an unhappy maiden, whom the force of a certain jealousy has made break through the respect due to modesty.'

The steward, hearing this, said to Sancho:

'My lord governor, order all your attendants to go aside, that this lady may speak her mind with less concern.'

The governor did so, and they all went aside, excepting the steward, the sewer, and the secretary. Then the damsel proceeded, saying:

'I, gentlemen, am daughter to Pedro Perez Mazorca, who farms the wool of this town, and comes frequently to my father's house.'

'This will not pass, madam,' said the steward; 'for I know Pedro Perez very well, and am sure he has no child, son nor daughter; and, besides your saying he is your father, you immediately add that he comes often to your father's house.'

'I took notice of that,' quoth Sancho.

'Indeed, gentlemen,' answered the damsel, 'I am in such confusion, that I know not what I say: but the truth is, I am daughter to Diego de la Llana, whom you must all know.'

'This may pass,' answered the steward; 'for I know Diego de la Llana, that he is a gentleman of quality, and rich, and has a son and a daughter; and, since he has been a widower, nobody in all this town can say they have seen the face of his daughter; for he keeps her so confined, that he will not give the sun leave to shine upon her; and report says she is extremely handsome.'

'That is true,' answered the damsel, 'and that daughter am I. Whether fame lies, or no, as to my beauty, you, gentlemen, are judges, since you have seen me.'

And then she began to weep most bitterly. Which the secretary perceiving, he whispered the sewer, and said very softly:

'Without doubt, something of importance must have been the occasion, that so considerable a person, as this young lady, has left her own house, in such a dress, and at such an hour.'

'No doubt of that,' answered the sewer; 'besides, this suspicion is confirmed by her tears.'

Sancho comforted her the best he could, and desired her to tell them the whole matter, without fear; for they would all endeavour to serve her with great sincerity, and by all possible ways.

'The case is, gentlemen,' replied she, 'that my father has kept me locked up these ten years past: for so long has my

mother been under ground. Mass is said in our house in a
rich chapel, and, in all this time, I have seen nothing but the
sun in the heavens by day, and the moon and stars by night;
nor do I know what streets, squares, or churches are, nor
even men, excepting my father and brother, and Pedro Perez
the wool-farmer, whose constant visits to our house led me
to say he was my father, to conceal the truth. This confinement, and denying me leave to go out, though but to church,
has for many days and months past disquieted me very much.
I had a mind to see the world, or at least the town where I
was born, thinking this desire was no breach of that decency
young ladies ought to preserve toward themselves. When I
heard talk of bull-feasts, of darting canes on horseback,* and
the representation of plays, I asked my brother, who is a year
younger than myself, to tell me what those things were, and
several others that I had never seen: which he used to do in
the best manner he could: and all this did but inflame the
desire I had of seeing them. In a word, to shorten the story
of my ruin, I prayed and entreated my brother—O that I
had never prayed nor entreated him!'

And then she fell to weeping again.

The steward said to her:

'Proceed, madam, and make an end of telling us what has
befallen you; for your words and tears hold us all in suspense.'

'I have but few words left to speak,' answered the damsel,
'though many tears to shed; for such misplaced desires as
mine can be atoned for no other way.'

The beauty of the damsel had rooted itself in the soul of
the sewer, who held up his lantern again, to have another
view of her; and he fancied the tears she shed were dewdrops
of the morning, or even orient pearls; and he heartily wished
her misfortune might not be so great as her tears and sighs
seemed to indicate. The governor was out of all patience at
the girl's dilatory manner of telling her story, and bade her
keep them no longer in suspense: for it grew late, and they
had a great deal more of the town to go over. She, between
interrupted sobs, and broken sighs, said:

'All my misfortunes and unhappiness is only this, that I

desired my brother to dress me in his clothes, and carry me out, some night or other, when my father was asleep, to see the town. He, importuned by my entreaties, condescended to my desire, and, putting me on this habit, and dressing himself in a suit of mine, which fits as if it were made for him (for he has not one hair of a beard, and one would take him for a very beautiful young girl), this night, about an hour ago, we got out of our house; and, guided by our footboy and our own unruly fancies, we traversed the whole town: and, as we were returning home, we saw a great company of people, and my brother said to me:

'"Sister, this must be the round; put wings to your feet, and fly after me, that they may not know us, or it will be worse for us."

'And, so saying, he turned his back, and began, not to run, but to fly. In less than six steps I fell down through the fright, and at that instant the officer of justice coming up, seized and brought me before your honour; where my indiscreet longing has covered me with shame before so many people.'

'In effect, then, madam,' quoth Sancho, 'no other mishap has befallen you, nor did jealousy, as you told us at the beginning of your story carry you from home.'

'No other thing,' said she, 'has befallen me, nor is there any jealousy in the case, but merely a desire of seeing the world, which went no farther than seeing the streets of this town.'

The coming up of two serjeants, one of whom had overtaken and seized her brother, as he fled from his sister, confirmed the truth of what the damsel had said. The youth had on nothing but a rich petticoat, and a blue damask mantle, with a border of gold; no head-dress nor ornament, but his own hair, which was so fair and curled, that it seemed so many ringlets of fine gold. The governor, the steward, and the sewer, took him aside, and, without letting his sister hear, they asked him how he came to be in that disguise. He, with no less bashfulness and concern, told the same story his sister had done; at which the enamoured sewer was much pleased. But the governor said:

'Really, gentlefolks, this is a very childish trick, and, to relate this piece of folly, there needed not half so many tears and sighs: had you but said, our names are so and so, we got out of our father's house by such a contrivance, only out of curiosity, and with no other design at all, the tale had been told, and all these weepings and wailings, and takings-on at this rate, might have been spared.'

'That is true,' answered the damsel; 'but the confusion I was in was so great, that it did not suffer me to demean myself as I ought.'

'There is no harm,' answered Sancho: 'we will see you safe to your father's; perhaps he has not missed you; and henceforward be not so childish, nor so eager to see the world; for, The maid that is modest, and a broken leg, should stay at home; and, The woman and the hen are lost by gadding abroad; and, She who desires to see, desires no less to be seen. I say no more.'

The youth thanked the governor for the favour he intended them, in seeing them safe home, and so they bent their course that way; for the house was not far off. When they were arrived, the brother threw up a little stone to a grated window, and that instant, a servant-maid, who waited for them, came down, and opened the door, and they went in, leaving every one in admiration at their genteelness and beauty, as well as at their desire of seeing the world by night, and without stirring out of the town: but they imputed all to their tender years.

The sewer's heart was pierced through and through, and he proposed within himself to demand her, the next day, of her father in marriage, taking it for granted he would not refuse him, as being a servant of the duke's. Sancho too had some thoughts of matching the young man with his daughter Sanchica, and determined to bring it about the first opportunity, fancying to himself, that no match would be refused the governor's daughter.

Thus ended that night's round, and, two days after, the government too, which put an end to all his designs and expectations, as shall hereafter be shown.

CHAPTER 50

*In which is declared who were the enchanters and executioners
that whipped the duenna, and pinched and scratched Don
Quixote; with the success of the page, who carried the letter
to Teresa Panza, Sancho's wife.*

CID HAMET, the most punctual searcher after the very
atoms of this true history, says, that when Doña Rodriguez
went out of her chamber to go to Don Quixote's, another
duenna, who lay with her, perceived it; and, as all duennas
have the itch of listening after, prying into, and smelling out
things, she followed her so softly, that good Rodriguez did
not perceive it: and, as soon as the duenna saw her enter
Don Quixote's chamber, that she might not be wanting in
the general humour of all duennas, which is to be tell-tales,
away she went that instant, to acquaint the duchess, that
Doña Rodriguez was then actually in Don Quixote's chamber.
The duchess acquainted the duke with it, and desired his
leave, that she and Altisidora might go and see what was the
duenna's business with Don Quixote. The duke gave it her;
and they both, very softly, and step by step, went and posted
themselves close to the door of Don Quixote's chamber, and
so close, that they overheard all that was said within: and,
when the duchess heard the duenna expose the fountains of
her issues,* she could not bear it, nor Altisidora either; and
so, brimful of choler, and longing for revenge, they bounced
into the room, and pinched Don Quixote, and whipped the
duenna, in the manner above related; for affronts, levelled
against the beauty and vanity of woman, awaken their wrath
in an extraordinary manner, and inflame them with a desire
of revenging themselves.

The duchess recounted to the duke all that had passed;
with which he was much diverted; and the duchess, proceeding in her design of making sport with Don Quixote, dispatched the page, who had acted the part of Dulcinea in the
project of her disenchantment, to Teresa Panza, with her
husband's letter (for Sancho was so taken up with his government, that he had quite forgot it), and with another from
herself, and a large string of rich corals by way of present.

Now the history tells us, that the page was very discreet and sharp, and being extremely desirous to please his lord and lady, he departed, with a very good will, for Sancho's village, and, being arrived near it, he saw some women washing in a brook, of whom he demanded, if they could tell him, whether one Teresa Panza, wife of one Sancho Panza, squire to a knight called Don Quixote de la Mancha, lived in that town. At which question, a young wench, who was washing, started up, and said:

'That Teresa Panza is my mother, and that Sancho my father, and that knight our master.'

'Come then, damsel,' quoth the page, 'and bring me to your mother; for I have a letter and a present for her from that same father of yours.'

'That I will with all my heart, sir,' answered the girl, who seemed to be about fourteen years of age.

And, leaving the linen she was washing to one of her companions, without putting anything on her head or feet (for she was bare-legged and dishevelled), she ran skipping along before the page's horse, saying:

'Come along, sir; for our house stands just at the entrance of the village, and there you will find my mother, in pain enough for not having heard any news of my father this great while.'

'I bring her such good news,' quoth the page, 'that she may well thank God for it.'

In short, with jumping, running, and capering, the girl came to the village, and, before she got into the house, she called aloud at the door:

'Come forth, mother Teresa, come forth, come forth; for here is a gentleman, who brings letters and other things from my good father.'

At which voice her mother Teresa Panza came out, spinning a distaff full of tow, having on a grey petticoat, so short, that it looked as if it had been docked at the placket, with a grey bodice also, and her smock sleeves hanging about it. She was not very old, though she seemed to be above forty; but was strong, hale, sinewy, and hard as a hazel-nut. She, seeing her daughter, and the page on horseback, said:

'What is the matter, girl? what gentleman is this?'

'It is a humble servant of my lady Doña Teresa Panza,' answered the page.

And, so saying, he flung himself from his horse, and, with great respect, went and kneeled before the lady Teresa, saying:

'Be pleased, Señora Doña Teresa, to give me your ladyship's hand to kiss, as being the lawful and only wife of Señor Don Sancho Panza, sole governor of the island of Barataria.'

'Ah, dear sir, forbear, do not so!' answered Teresa; 'for I am no court dame, but a poor countrywoman, daughter of a ploughman, and wife of a squire-errant, and not of any governor at all.'

'Your ladyship,' answered the page, 'is the most worthy wife of an arch-worthy governor; and, for proof of what I say, be pleased, madam, to receive this letter, and this present.'

Then he pulled out of his pocket a string of corals, each bead in gold; and, putting it about her neck, he said:

'This letter is from my lord governor, and another that I have here, and these corals, are from my lady duchess, who sends me to your ladyship.'

Teresa was amazed, and her daughter neither more nor less, and the girl said:

'May I die, if our master Don Quixote be not at the bottom of this business, and has given my father the government, or earldom, he so often promised him.'

'It is even so,' answered the page; 'and for Señor Don Quixote's sake, my lord Sancho is now governor of the island of Barataria, as you will see by this letter.'

'Pray, young gentleman,' quoth Teresa, 'be pleased to read it; for, though I can spin, I cannot read a tittle.'

'Nor I neither,' added Sanchica: 'but stay a little, and I will go and call somebody that can, though it be the priest himself, or the bachelor Sampson Carrasco, who will come with all their hearts to hear news of my father.'

'There is no need of calling anybody,' quoth the page; 'for though I cannot spin, I can read, and will read it.'

So he read it: but it having been inserted before, it is purposely omitted here. Then he pulled out that from the duchess, which was as follows:

'Friend TERESA,

'The good qualities, both of integrity and capacity, of your
husband Sancho, moved and induced me to desire the duke
my spouse, to give him the government of one of the many
islands he has. I am informed he governs like any hawk; at
which I and my lord duke are mightily pleased; and I give
great thanks to heaven, that I have not been deceived in my
choice of him for the said government. For, let me tell
madam Teresa, it is a difficult thing to find a good governor
nowadays, and God make me as good as Sancho governs
well. I send you hereby, my dear, a string of corals, set in
gold. I wish they were of oriental pearl: but whoever gives
thee an egg, has no mind to see thee dead. The time will
come, when we shall be better acquainted, and converse
together, and God knows what may happen. Commend me
to Sanchica your daughter, and tell her from me to get herself
ready; for I mean to marry her toppingly, when she least
thinks of it. I am told the acorns of your town are very large:
pray send me some two dozen of them; for I shall esteem
them very much as coming from your hand; and write to me
immediately, advising me of your health and welfare; and if
you want anything, you need but open your mouth, and your
mouth shall be measured. So God keep you.

'From this place.

'Your loving Friend,
'THE DUCHESS.'

'Ah!' quoth Teresa, at hearing the letter, 'how good, how
plain, how humble a lady! Let me be buried with such ladies
as this, and not with such gentlewomen as this town affords,
who think, because they are gentlefolks, the wind must not
blow upon them: and they go to church with as much vanity
as if they were very queens. One would think they took it
for a disgrace to look upon a countrywoman; and you see
here how this good lady, though she be a duchess, calls me
friend, and treats me as if I were her equal, and equal may
I see her to the highest steeple in La Mancha. As to the
acorns, sir, I will send her ladyship a pocketful,* and such
as, for their bigness, people may come to see and admire

from far and near. And for the present, Sanchica, see and make much of this gentleman: take care of his horse, and bring some new-laid eggs out of the stable, and slice some rashers of bacon, and let us entertain him like any prince; for the good news he has brought us, and his own good looks, deserve no less; and in the meanwhile, I will step and carry my neighbours the news of our joy, and especially to our father the priest, and to Master Nicholas the barber, who are and always have been, your father's great friends.'

'Yes, mother, I will,' answered Sanchica: 'but, hark you, I must have half that string of corals; for I do not take my lady duchess to be such a fool as to send it all to you.'

'It is all for you, daughter,' answered Teresa; 'but let me wear it a few days about my neck; for truly methinks it cheers my very heart.'

'You will be no less cheered,' quoth the page, 'when you see the bundle I have in this portmanteau: it is a habit of superfine cloth, which the governor wore only one day at a hunting match, and has sent it all to Señora Sanchica.'

'May he live a thousand years,' answered Sanchica, 'and the bearer neither more nor less, aye, and two thousand if need be.'

Teresa now went out of the house with the letters, and the beads about her neck, and playing as she went along with her fingers upon the letters, as if they had been a timbrel. And accidentally meeting the priest, and Sampson Carrasco, she began to dance, and say:

'In faith we have no poor relations now! we have got a government! aye, aye, let the proudest gentlewoman of them all meddle with me! I will make her know her distance!'

'What is the matter, Teresa Panza? what extravagances are these? and what papers are those?' demanded the priest.

'No other extravagances,' quoth she, 'but that these are letters from duchesses and governors, and these about my neck are true coral; the Ave-Marias and the Pater-nosters are of beaten gold, and I am a governess.'

'God be our aid, Teresa,' replied they: 'we understand you not, nor know what you mean.'

'Believe your own eyes,' answered Teresa, giving them the letters. The priest read them so as that Sampson Carrasco heard the contents: and Sampson and the priest stared at each other, as surprised at what they read. The bachelor demanded, who had brought those letters. Teresa answered, if they would come home with her to her house, they should see the messenger, who was a youth like any golden pine-tree; and that he had brought her another present, worth twice as much. The priest took the corals from her neck, and viewed and reviewed them; and being satisfied they were right, he began to wonder afresh, and said:

'By the habit I wear, I know not what to say, nor what to think of these letters, and these presents. On one hand I see and feel the fineness of these corals, and on the other hand I read that a duchess sends to desire a dozen or two of acorns.'

'Make these things tally, if you can,' quoth Carrasco: 'but let us go and see the bearer of this packet, who may give us some light into these difficulties which puzzle us.'

They did so, and Teresa went back with them.

They found the page sifting a little barley for his horse, and Sanchica cutting a rasher to fry, and pave it with eggs, for the page's dinner; whose aspect and good appearance pleased them both very much. After they had saluted him, and he them, Sampson desired him to tell them news, both of Don Quixote and Sancho Panza; for, though they had read Sancho's and the duchess's letters, still they were confounded, and could not devise what Sancho's government could mean, and especially of an island, most or all those in the Mediterranean belonging to his majesty. To which the page answered:

'That Señor Sancho Panza is a governor, there is no manner of doubt; but whether it be an island that he governs, or not, I concern not myself at all; let it suffice, that it is a place containing above a thousand inhabitants. As to the acorns, I say, my lady duchess is so humble and affable, that her sending to beg acorns of a countrywoman is nothing; for ere now, she has sent to borrow a comb of one of her neighbours. For you must know, gentlemen, that the ladies of Aragon, though of as great quality, are not so haughty, nor so ceremonious, as the ladies of Castile: they treat people more upon the level.'

While they were in the midst of this discourse, in came Sanchica, with a lap full of eggs, and said to the page:

'Pray, sir, does my father, now he is a governor, wear trunk-hose?'

'I never observed that,' answered the page; 'but doubtless he does.'

'God's my life!' replied Sanchica, 'what a sight must it be to see my father with laced breeches! Is it not strange that, ever since I was born, I have longed to see my father with his breeches laced to his girdle?'

'I warrant you will, if you live,' answered the page: 'before God, if his government lasts but two months, he is in a fair way to travel with a cape to his cap.'

The priest and the bachelor easily perceived that the page spoke jestingly: but the fineness of the corals, and the hunting suit which Sancho had sent (for Teresa had already shown them the habit), undid all. Nevertheless, they could not forbear smiling at Sanchica's longing, and more, when Teresa said:

'Master Priest, do so much as inquire, if anybody be going to Madrid or Toledo, who may buy me a farthingale round and completely made, and fashionable, and one of the best that is to be had; for, verily, verily, I intend to honour my husband's government as much as I can; and, if they vex me, I will get me to this court myself, and ride in my coach as well as the best of them there; for she, who has a governor for her husband, may very well have one and maintain it too.'

'Aye, marry,' quoth Sanchica, 'and would to God it were to-day rather than to-morrow, though folks, that saw me seated in that coach with my lady mother, should say: "Do but see such a one, daughter of such a one, stuffed with garlic; how she sits in state, and lolls in her coach like the pope's lady!"* But let them jeer, so they trudge in the dirt, and I ride in my coach with my feet above the ground. A bad year and a worse month to all the murmurers in the world; and, if I go warm, let folks laugh. Say I well, mother?'

'Aye, mighty well, daughter,' answered Teresa: 'and my good man Sancho foretold me all this, and even greater good luck; and you shall see, daughter, it will never stop till it has made me a countess; for to be lucky, the whole business is to begin: and as I have often heard your good father say (who, as he is yours, is also the father of proverbs), When they give you a heifer, make haste with the halter; so, when a government is given you, seize it; when they give you an earldom, lay your claws on it; and when they whistle to you with a good gift, snap at it: No, no, sleep on, and do not answer to the lucky hits, and the good fortune, that stand calling at the door of your house.'

'And what care I?' added Sanchica; 'let who will say, when they see me step it stately, and bridle it, The higher the monkey climbs, the more he exposes his bald buttocks, and so forth.'

The priest hearing this, said:

'I cannot believe but that all of this race of the Panza were born with a bushel of proverbs in their bellies: I never saw one of them who did not scatter them about, at all times, and in all the discourses they ever held.'

'I believe so too,' quoth the page; 'for my lord governor Sancho utters them at every step; and though many of them are wide of the purpose, still they please, and my lady duchess and the duke commend them highly.'

'You persist then in affirming, sir,' quoth the bachelor, 'that this business of Sancho's government is real and true, and that these presents and letters are really sent by a duchess? For our parts, though we touch the presents, and have read the letters, we believe it not, and take it to be one of our countryman Don Quixote's adventures, who thinks everything of this kind done by way of enchantment: and therefore I could almost find in my heart to touch and feel your person, to know whether you are a visionary messenger, or one of flesh and bones.'

'All I know of myself, gentlemen,' answered the page, 'is, that I am a real messenger, and that Señor Sancho Panza actually is a governor; and that my lord duke and my lady duchess can give, and have given the said government; and I have heard it said, that the said Sancho Panza behaves himself most notable in it. Whether there be any enchantment in this, or not, you may dispute by yourselves; for by the oath I am going to take, which is by the life of my parents, who are living, and whom I dearly love, I know nothing more of the matter.'

'It may be so,' replied the bachelor: 'but *dubitat Augustinus.*'

'Doubt who will,' answered the page, 'the truth is what I tell you, and truth will always get above a lie, like oil above water; and, if you will not believe, *operibus credite et non verbis.* Come one of you, gentlemen, along with me, and you shall see with your eyes what you will not believe by the help of your ears.'

'That jaunt is for me,' quoth Sanchica: 'take me behind you, sir, upon your nag; for I will go with all my heart to see my honoured father.'

'The daughters of governors,' said the page, 'must not travel alone, but attended with coaches and litters, and good store of servants.'

'Before God,' answered Sanchica, 'I can travel as well upon an ass's colt, as in a coach; I am none of your tender squeamish folks.'

'Peace, wench,' quoth Teresa; 'you know not what you say, and the gentleman is in the right; for, according to reason, each thing in its season: when it was Sancho, it was Sancha; and when governor, madam. Said I amiss?'

'Madam Teresa says more than she imagines,' quoth the page; 'and pray, give me to eat, and dispatch me quickly; for I intend to return home this night.'

To which the priest said:

'Come, sir, and do penance with me; for Madam Teresa has more goodwill than good cheer, to welcome so worthy a guest.'

The page refused at first, but at length thought it most for his good to comply, and the priest very willingly took him home with him, that he might have an opportunity of inquiring at leisure after Don Quixote and his exploits. The bachelor offered Teresa to write answers to her letters; but she would not let him meddle in her matters, for she looked upon him as somewhat of a wag; and so she gave a roll of bread and a couple of eggs to a young noviciate friar, who could write; who wrote for her two letters, one for her husband, and the other for the duchess, and both of her inditing; and they are none of the worst recorded in this grand history, as will be seen hereafter.

CHAPTER 51

Of the progress of Sancho Panza's government, with other entertaining events.

NOW appeared the day succeeding the night of the governor's round; which the sewer passed without sleeping, his thoughts being taken up with the countenance, air, and beauty of the disguised damsel; and the steward spent the remainder of it in writing to his lord and lady what Sancho Panza said and did, equally wondering at his deeds and sayings; for his words and actions were intermixed with strong indications both of discretion and folly. In short, [the] Señor Governor got up, and by the direction of doctor Pedro Recio, they gave him, to break his fast, a little conserve, and four draughts of cold water; which Sancho would gladly have exchanged for a piece of bread and a bunch of grapes. But, seeing it was more by force than goodwill, he submitted to it with sufficient grief to his soul, and toil to his stomach: Pedro Recio making him believe, that to eat but little, and that of slight things quickened the judgement, which was the properest thing that could be for persons appointed to rule, and bear offices of dignity; in which there is not so much occasion for bodily strength, as for that of the understanding. By means of this sophistry, Sancho endured hunger to a degree, that inwardly he cursed the government, and even him that gave it.

However, with his hunger and his conserve, he sat in judgement that day, and the first thing that offered, was a question proposed by a stranger; the steward and the rest of the assistants being present all the while. It was this:

'My lord; a main river divides the two parts of one lordship—pray, my lord, be attentive, for it is a case of importance, and somewhat difficult; I say then, that upon this river stood a bridge, and at the head of it a gallows, and a kind of courthouse, for a seat of judicature, in which there were commonly four judges, whose office it was to give sentence according to a law enjoined by the owner of the river, of the bridge, and of the lordship: which law was in this form: Whoever passes over this bridge, from one side to the other, must first take an oath, from whence he comes, and what business he is going about; and if he swears true, they shall let him pass; but if he tells a lie, he shall die for it upon yonder gallows, without any remission. This law, and the rigorous conditions thereof, being known, several persons passed over; for by what they swore it was soon perceived they swore the truth, and the judges let them pass freely. Now it fell out, that a certain man, taking the oath, swore, and said, by the oath he had taken, he was going to die upon the gallows, which stood there, and that this was his business, and no other. The judges deliberated upon the oath, and said: If we let this man pass freely, he swore a lie, and by the law he ought to die; and if we hang him, he swore he went to die on that gallows, and having sworn the truth, by the same law he ought to go free. It is now demanded of my lord governor, how the judges shall proceed with this man; for they are still doubtful and in suspense, and being informed of the acuteness and elevation of your lordship's under-standing, they have sent me to beseech your lordship, on their behalf, to give your opinion in so intricate and doubtful a case.'*

To which Sancho answered:

'For certain, these gentlemen the judges, who sent you to me, might have saved themselves and you the labour, for I have more of the blunt than the acute in me; nevertheless, repeat me the business over again, that I may understand it; perhaps I may hit the mark.'

The querist repeated what he had said once or twice, and Sancho said:

'In my opinion the affair may be briefly resolved, and it is thus: The man swears he is going to die upon the gallows, and, if he is hanged, he swore the truth, and by the law established ought to be free, and to pass the bridge; and if they do not hang him, he swore a lie, and by the same law he ought to be hanged.'

'It is just as [the] Señor Governor says,' quoth the messenger, 'and nothing more is wanting to the right stating and understanding of the case.'

'I say then,' replied Sancho, 'that they let pass that part of the man that swore the truth, and hang that part that swore a lie: and thus the condition of the passage will be literally fulfilled.'

'If so, Señor Governor,' replied the querist, 'it will be necessary to divide the man into two parts, the false and the true: and, if he is cut asunder, he must necessarily die, and so there is not a tittle of the law fulfilled, and there is an express necessity of fulfilling the law.'

'Come hither, honest man,' answered Sancho: 'either I am a very dunce, or there is as much reason to put this passenger to death, as to let him live and pass the bridge; for, if the truth saves him, the lie equally condemns him: and this being so, as it really is, I am of opinion, that you tell those gentlemen who sent you to me, that, since the reasons for condemning and acquitting him are equal, they let him pass freely; for it is always commendable to do good rather than harm; and this I would give under my hand, if I could write: and, in this case, I speak not of my own head, but upon recollection of a precept given me, among many others, by my master Don Quixote, the night before I set out to be governor of this island; which was, that when justice happens to be in the least doubtful, I should incline and lean to the side of mercy; and God has been pleased to make me remember it in the present case, in which it comes in so pat.'

'It does so,' answered the steward, 'and, for my part, I think Lycurgus himself, who gave laws to the Lacedaemonians, could not have given a better judgement, than that now given by the great Panza: and, let us have no more hearings this morning, and I will give order that [the] Señor Governor shall dine to-day much to his satisfaction.'

'That is what I desire, and let us have fair play,' quoth Sancho. 'Let me but dine, and bring me cases and questions never so thick, I will dispatch them in the snuffing of a candle.'

The steward was as good as his word, making it a matter of conscience to starve so discerning a governor; especially since he intended to come to a conclusion with him that very night, and to play him the last trick he had in commission.

It fell out then, that, having dined that day against all the rules and aphorisms of doctor Tirteafuera, at taking away the cloth, a courier came in with a letter from Don Quixote to the governor. Sancho bade the secretary read it first to himself, and, if there was nothing in it that required secrecy to read it aloud. The secretary did so, and, glancing it over, said:

'Well may it be read aloud, for what Señor Don Quixote writes to your lordship deserves to be printed and written in letters of gold; and the contents are these:

Don Quixote de la Mancha's letter to Sancho Panza, governor of the island of Barataria.

'When I expected, friend Sancho, to have heard news of your negligence and impertinences, I have had accounts of your discretion; for which I give particular thanks to heaven, that can raise the poor from the dunghill, and make wise men of fools. I am told, you govern as if you were a man, and are a man as if you were a beast—such is the humility of your demeanour. But I would have you take notice, Sancho, that it is often expedient and necessary, for the sake of authority, to act in contradiction to the humility of the heart; for the decent adorning of the person, in weighty employments, must be conformable to what those offices require, and not according to the measure of what a man's own humble condition inclines him to. Go well clad; for a broomstick well dressed does not appear a broomstick. I do not mean, that you should wear jewels or fine clothes, nor, being a judge, that you should dress like a soldier; but that you should adorn yourself with such a habit as suits your employment, and such as is neat and handsomely made.

'To gain the goodwill of the people you govern, two things, among others, you must do: One is, to be civil to all (though I have already told you this); and the other is, to take care that there be plenty, since nothing is so discouraging to the poor as hunger, and dearness of provisions.

'Publish not many edicts, and when you do, see that they are good ones, and, above all, that they are well observed; for edicts that are not kept are as if they had not been made, and serve only to show, that the prince, though he had wisdom and authority sufficient to make them, had not the courage to see them put in execution: and laws that intimidate at their publication, and are not executed, become like the log, king of the frogs, which terrified them at first; but in time they contemned him, and got upon his back.

'Be a father to virtue, and a step-father to vice. Be not always severe, nor always mild; but choose the mean betwixt these two extremes; for therein consists the main point of discretion. Visit the prisons, the shambles, and the markets; for the presence of the governor in such places is of great importance. Comfort the prisoners, that they may hope to be quickly dispatched. Be a bugbear to the butchers, who will then make their weights true; and be a terror to the market-people for the same reason. Do not show yourself (though perchance you may be so, but I do not believe it) given to covetousness, to women, or gluttony; for when the town, and those who have to do with you, find your ruling passion, by that they will play their engines upon you, till they have battered you down into the depth of destruction.

'View and review, consider and reconsider the counsels and documents I gave you in writing, before you went hence to your government, and you will see how you will find in them, if you observe them, a choice supply to help to support you under the toils and difficulties which governors meet with at every turn.

'Write to your patrons, the duke and duchess, and show yourself grateful; for ingratitude is the daughter of pride, and one of the greatest sins; and the person who is grateful to those that have done him good, shows thereby that he will be so to God too, who has already done him, and is continually doing him, so much good.

'My lady duchess has dispatched a messenger, with your suit and another present, to your wife Teresa Panza: we expect an answer every moment. I have been a little out of order with a certain cat-clawing which befell me, not much to the advantage of my nose: but it was nothing; for if there are enchanters who persecute me, there are others who defend me. Let me know, if the steward who is with you, had any hand in the actions of the Trifaldi, as you suspected: and give me advice, from time to time, of all that happens to you, since the way is so short. I have thoughts of quitting this idle life very soon, for I was not born for it.

'A business has fallen out which will, I believe, go near to bring me into disgrace with the duke and duchess. But, though it afflicts me much, it affects me nothing: for, in short, I must comply with the rules of my profession, rather than with their pleasure, according to the old saying, *Amicus Plato, sed magis amica veritas.** I write this in Latin; for I persuade myself, you have learned it since you have been a governor. And so farewell, and God have you in His keeping, that nobody may pity you.

'Your friend,
'DON QUIXOTE DE LA MANCHA.'

Sancho listened with great attention to the letter, which was applauded, and looked upon to be very judicious by all that heard it. Presently Sancho rose from table, and calling the secretary, he shut himself up with him in his chamber, and without any delay, resolved immediately to send an answer to his lord Don Quixote. He bade the secretary, without adding or diminishing a tittle, to write what he should dictate to him. He did so, and the answer was of the tenor following:

SANCHO PANZA'S LETTER TO DON QUIXOTE DE LA MANCHA.

'The hurry of my business is so great, that I have not time to scratch my head, nor so much as to pare my nails, and therefore I wear them very long; which God remedy. This I say, dear master of my soul, that your worship may not wonder, if hitherto I have given you no account of my well or ill being in this government; in which I suffer more hunger than when we two wandered about through woods and deserts.

'My lord duke wrote to me the other day, giving me advice that certain spies were come into this island to kill me; but hitherto I have been able to discover no other besides a certain doctor, who has a salary in this place for killing as many governors as shall come hither. He calls himself doctor Pedro Recio, and is a native of Tirteafuera; a name sufficient to make one fear dying by his hands. This same doctor says, he does not cure distempers when people have them, but prevents them from coming; and the medicines he uses are, diet upon diet, till he reduces the patient to bare bones; as if a consumption were not a worse malady than a fever. In short, he is murdering me by hunger, and I am dying of despite; for, instead of coming to this government to eat hot and drink cool, and to recreate my body between Holland sheets, upon beds of down, I am come to do penance, as if I were a hermit: and, as I do it against my will, I verily think, at the long run, the devil will carry me away.

'Hitherto I have touched no fee, nor taken any bribe; and I cannot imagine what it will end in; for here I am told, that the governors, who came to this island, before they set foot in it, used to receive a good sum of money, by way of present or loan, from the people, and that this is the custom with those who go to other governments, as well as with those who come to this.

'One night, as I was going the round, I met a very handsome damsel in man's clothes, and her brother in woman's. My sewer fell in love with the girl, and has, as he says, already, in his thoughts, made choice of her for his wife; and I have chosen the brother for my son-in-law. To-day we both intend to disclose our minds to their father, who is one Diego de la Llana, a gentleman, and an Old Christian, as much as one can desire.

'I visit the markets, as your worship advises me; and yesterday I found a huckster-woman, who sold new hazel-nuts, and it was proved upon her, that she had mixed with the new a bushel of old rotten ones. I confiscated them all to the use of the charity boys, who well know how to distinguish them, and sentenced her not to come into the market again in fifteen days. I am told I behaved bravely: what I can tell your worship is, that it is reported in this town, that there is not a worse sort of people than your market-women; for they are all shameless, hard-hearted, and impudent; and I verily believe it is so, by those I have seen in other places.

'As concerning my lady duchess's having written to my wife, Teresa Panza, and sent her the present your worship mentions, I am mightily pleased with it, and will endeavour to show my gratitude at a proper time: pray, kiss her honour's hands in my name, and tell her, she has not thrown her favours into a rent sack, as she will find by the effect.

'I would not wish you to have any cross reckonings of disgust with our patrons the duke and duchess: for if your worship quarrels with them, it is plain, it must redound to my damage; and, since your worship advised me not to be ungrateful, it will not be proper you should be so yourself, to those who have done you so many favours, and who have entertained you so generously in their castle.

'The cat business I understand not, but suppose it must be one of those unlucky tricks the wicked enchanters are wont to play your worship: I shall know more when we meet.

'I would willingly send your worship something or other; but I cannot tell what, unless it be some little clyster-pipes, which they make in this island very curiously. If my employment holds, I will look out for something to send, right or wrong.

'If my wife Teresa Panza writes to me, be so kind as to pay the postage, and send me the letter; for I have a mighty desire to know the estate of my house, my wife, and my children. And so, God deliver your worship from evil-minded enchanters, and bring me safe and sound out of this government, which I doubt; for I expect to lay my bones here, considering how doctor Pedro Recio treats me.

'Your worship's servant,

'SANCHO PANZA, THE GOVERNOR.'

The secretary made up the letter, and dispatched the courier with it immediately. Then those who carried on the plot against Sancho, contrived among themselves how to put an end to his government.

That evening Sancho spent in making some ordinances for the good government of that which he took to be an island. He decreed, that there should be no monopolizers of provisions in the commonwealth; that wines should not be imported indifferently from any parts the merchant pleased, with this injunction, that they should declare its growth, that a price might be set upon it according to its goodness, character, and true value; and that whoever dashed it with water, or changed its name, should be put to death for it. He moderated the prices of all sorts of hose and shoes, especially the latter, the current price of which he thought exorbitant. He limited the wages of servants, which before were very extravagant. He laid most severe penalties upon those who should sing lascivious and indecent songs by day or by night. He decreed, that no blind man should sing his miracles in verse, unless he produced an authentic testimony of the truth of them, esteeming most of those sung by that sort of people to be false, in prejudice to the true ones. He created an overseer of the poor, not to persecute them, but to examine whether they were such or no; for, under colour of feigned maimness, and counterfeit sores, they are often sturdy thieves and hale drunkards. In short, he made such wholesome ordinances, that they are observed in that town to this day, and are called, THE CONSTITUTIONS OF THE GREAT GOVERNOR SANCHO PANZA.

CHAPTER 52

In which is related the adventure of the second afflicted or distressed matron, otherwise called Doña Rodriguez.

CID HAMET relates, that Don Quixote, being now healed of his scratches, began to think the life he led in that castle was against all the rules of knight-errantry which he professed; and therefore he resolved to ask leave of the duke and duchess to depart for Saragossa, the celebration of the tournament drawing near, wherein he proposed to win the suit of armour, the usual prize at that festival. And, being one day at table with their excellencies, and beginning to unfold his purpose, and ask their leave, behold, on a sudden there entered, at the door of the great hall, two women, as it afterwards appeared, covered from head to foot with mourning weeds; and one of them, coming up to Don Quixote, threw herself at full length on the ground, and, incessantly kissing his feet, poured forth such dismal, deep, and mournful groans, that all who heard and saw her were confounded; and, though the duke and duchess imagined it was some jest their servants were putting upon Don Quixote, yet, seeing how vehemently the woman sighed, groaned, and wept, they were in doubt and in suspense; till the compassionate Don Quixote, raising her from the ground, prevailed with her to discover herself, and remove the veil from before her blubbered face. She did so, and discovered, what they little expected to see, the face of Doña Rodriguez, the duenna of the house; and the other mourner was her daughter, who had been deluded by the rich farmer's son. All that knew her wondered, and the duke and duchess more than anybody; for, though they took her for a fool and soft, yet not to the degree as to act so mad a part. At length Doña Rodriguez turning to her lord and lady, said:

'Be pleased, your excellencies, to give me leave to confer a little with this gentleman: for so it behoves me to do, to get successfully out of an unlucky business, into which the presumption of an evil-minded bumpkin has brought me.'

The duke said, he gave her leave, and that she might confer with Don Quixote as much as she pleased. She, directing her face and speech to Don Quixote, said:

'It is not long, valorous knight, since I gave you an account how injuriously and treacherously a wicked peasant has used my poor dear child, this unfortunate girl here present, and you promised me to stand up in her defence, and see her righted; and now I understand that you are departing from this castle in quest of good adventures (which God send you!), and therefore my desire is, that, before you begin making your excursions on the highways, you would challenge this untamed rustic, and oblige him to marry my daughter, in compliance with the promise he gave her to be her husband before he had his will of her; for, to think to meet with justice from my lord duke, is to look for pears upon an elm-tree, for the reasons I have already told your worship in private; and so God grant your worship much health, not forsaking us.'

To which words Don Quixote returned this answer, with much gravity and solemnity:

'Good madam duenna, moderate your tears, or rather dry them up, and spare your sighs; for I take upon me the charge of seeing your daughter's wrongs redressed; though it had been better if she had not been so easy in believing the promises of lovers, who, for the most part are very ready in promising, and very slow in performing: and, therefore, with my lord duke's leave, I will depart immediately in search of this ungracious youth, and will find and challenge him, and will kill him, if he refuses to perform his contract: for the principal end of my profession is, to spare the humble, and chastise the proud; I mean, to succour the wretched, and destroy the oppressor.'

'You need not give yourself any trouble,' answered the duke, 'to seek the rustic, of whom this good duenna complains; nor need you ask my permission to challenge him; for, suppose him challenged, and leave it to me to give him notice of this challenge, and to make him accept it, and come and answer for himself at this castle of mine; where both shall fairly enter the lists, and all the usual ceremonies shall be observed, and exact justice distributed to each, as is the duty of all princes, who grant the lists to combatants within the bounds of their territories.'

'With this assurance, and with your grandeur's leave,' replied Don Quixote, 'for this time I renounce my gentility, and lessen and be mean myself to the lowness of the offender, and put myself upon a level with him, that he may be qualified to fight with me: and so, though absent, I challenge and defy him, upon account of the injury he has done in deceiving this poor girl, who was a maiden, and by his fault is no longer such; and he shall either perform his promise of being her lawful husband, or die in the dispute.'

And immediately pulling off his glove, he threw it into the middle of the hall, and the duke took it up, saying, that, as he had said before, he accepted the challenge in the name of his vassal, appointing the time to be six days after, and the lists to be in the court of the castle; the arms, those usual among knights, a lance, shield, and laced suit of armour, and all the other pieces, without deceit, fraud, or any superstition whatever, being first viewed and examined by the judges of the field. But especially, he said, it was necessary the good duenna and the naughty maiden should commit the justice of their cause to the hands of Señor Don Quixote; for otherwise nothing could be done, nor could the said challenge be duly executed.

'I do commit it,' answered the duenna.

'And I too,' added the daughter, all weeping, abashed, and confounded.

The day thus appointed, and the duke having resolved with himself what was to be done in the business, the mourners went their ways; and the duchess ordered, that thenceforward they should be treated not as her servants, but as lady-adventurers, who were come to her house to demand justice: and so they had a separate apartment ordered them, and were served as strangers, to the amazement of the rest of the family, who knew not what the folly and boldness of Doña Rodriguez, and of her ill-errant daughter, drove at.

While they were thus engaged in perfecting the joy of the feast, and giving a good end to the dinner, behold, there entered at the hall-door the page who had carried the letters and presents to Teresa Panza, wife of the governor Sancho Panza: at whose arrival the duke and duchess were much pleased, being desirous to know the success of his journey; and they having asked him, the page replied, he could not relate it so publicly, nor in few words, and desired their excellencies would be pleased to adjourn it to a private audience, and in the meantime to entertain themselves with those letters; and, pulling out a couple, he put them into the hands of the duchess. The superscription of one was—'For my lady duchess such an one, of I know not what place'; and the other—'To my husband Sancho Panza, governor of the island [of] Barataria, whom God prosper more years than me.' The duchess's cake was dough, as the saying is, till she had read her letter; and, opening it, she ran it over to herself, and finding it might be read aloud, that the duke and the bystanders might hear it, she read what follows:

TERESA PANZA'S LETTER TO THE DUCHESS.

'My lady,

'The letter your grandeur wrote me gave me much satisfaction, and indeed I wished for it mightily. The string of corals is very good, and my husband's hunting-suit comes not short of it. Our whole town is highly pleased that your ladyship has made my husband Sancho a governor; though nobody believes it, especially the priest, and Master Nicholas the barber, and Sampson Carrasco the bachelor. But what care I? for so long as the thing is so, as it really is, let every one say what they list: though, if I may own the truth, I should not have believed it myself, had it not been for the corals and the habit: for in this village everybody thinks my husband a dunce, and, take him from governing a flock of goats, they cannot imagine what government he can be good for. God be his guide, and speed him as he sees best for his children. I am resolved, dear lady of my soul, with your ladyship's leave, to bring this good day home to my house, and hie me to court, to loll it in a coach, and burst the eyes of a thousand people that envy me already. And, therefore, I beg your excellency to order my husband to send me a little money, and let it be enough; for at court expenses are great, bread sells for sixpence, and flesh for thirty maravedis the pound; which is a judgement: and if he is not for my going, let him send me word in time; for my feet are in motion to begin my journey. My gossips and neighbours tell me, that if I and my daughter go fine and stately at court, my husband will be known by me more than I by him; for folks, to be sure, will ask: What ladies are those in that coach? and a footman of ours will answer: The wife and daughter of Sancho Panza, governor of the island [of] Barataria: and in this manner Sancho will be known, and I shall be esteemed, and to Rome for everything.

'I am as sorry as sorry can be, that there has been no gathering of acorns this year in our village; but, for all that, I send your highness about half a peck. I went to the mountain to pick and cull them out, one by one, and I could find none larger; I wish they had been as big as ostrich eggs.

'Let not your pomposity forget to write to me, and I will take care to answer, advising you of my health, and of all that shall offer worth advising from this place, where I remain praying to our Lord to preserve your honour, and not to forget me. My daughter Sanchica and my son kiss your ladyship's hands.

'She, who has more mind to see your ladyship than to write to you,

'Your servant,
'TERESA PANZA.'

Great was the pleasure all received at hearing Teresa Panza's letter, especially the duke and duchess, who asked Don Quixote, whether he thought it proper to open the letter for the governor, which must needs be most excellent. Don Quixote said, to please them, he would open it; which he did, and found the contents as follows:

TERESA PANZA'S LETTER TO HER HUSBAND SANCHO PANZA.

'I received your letter, dear Sancho of my soul, and I vow and swear to you, upon the word of a Catholic Christian, that I was within two fingers' breadth of running mad with satisfaction. Look you, brother, when I came to hear that

you was a governor, methought I should have dropped down
dead for mere joy: for, you know, it is usually said, that
sudden joy kills as effectually as excessive grief. Your
daughter Sanchica could not contain her water, for pure
ecstasy. I had before my eyes the suit you sent me, and the
corals sent by my lady duchess about my neck, and the letters
in my hands, and the bearer of them present; and, for all
that, I believed and thought all I saw and touched was a
dream: for who could imagine that a goatherd should come
to be a governor of islands? You know, friend, my mother
used to say, that one must live long to see much. I say this,
because I think to see more, if I live longer: for I never
expect to stop till I see you a farmer-general, or a collector
of the customs; offices, in which, though the devil carries
away him that abuses them, in short, one is always taking
and fingering of money. My lady duchess will tell you how
I long to go to court: consider of it, and let me know your
mind; for I will strive to do you credit there by riding in a
coach.

'The priest, the barber, the bachelor, and even the sexton,
cannot believe you are a governor, and say, that it is all
delusion, or matter of enchantment, like all the rest of your
master Don Quixote's affairs: and Sampson says, he will find
you out, and take this government out of your head, and
Don Quixote's madness out of his skull. I only laugh at them,
and look upon my string of corals, and am contriving how
to make our daughter a gown of the suit you sent me.

'I sent my lady duchess a parcel of acorns: I wish they had
been of gold. Prithee, send me some strings of pearl, if they
are in fashion in that same island.

'The news of this town is, that the Berrueca is about
marrying her daughter to a sorry painter, who is come to this
town to paint whatever should offer. The magistrates ordered
him to paint the king's arms over the gate of the town-house:
he demanded two ducats: they paid him beforehand: he
worked eight days, at the end of which he had made nothing
of it, and said he could not hit upon painting such trumpery.
He returned the money, and, for all that, he marries under
the title of a good workman. It is true, he has already quitted

the pencil, and taken the spade, and goes to the field like a gentleman. Pedro de Lobo's son has taken orders, and shaven his crown, in order to be a priest. Minguilla, Mingo Silvato's niece,* has heard of it, and is suing him upon a promise of marriage; evil tongues do not stick to say she is with child by him: but he denies it with both hands.

'We have had no olives this year, nor is there a drop of vinegar to be had in all this town. A company of foot-soldiers passed through here, and, by the way, carried off three girls. I will not tell you who they are: perhaps they will return, and somebody or other will not fail to marry them with all their faults.

'Sanchica makes bone-lace and gets eight maravedis a day, which she drops into a till-box, to help towards household stuff: but now that she is a governor's daughter, you will give her a fortune, and she need not work for it. The pump in our market-place is dried up. A thunderbolt fell upon the pillory, and there may they all light!

'I expect an answer to this, and your resolution about my going to court. And so God keep you more years than myself, or as many, for I would not willingly leave you in this world behind me.

'Your wife,
'TERESA PANZA.'

The letters caused much laughter, applause, esteem and admiration: and, to put the seal to the whole, arrived the courier, who brought that, which Sancho sent to Don Quixote; which was also publicly read, and occasioned the governor's simplicity to be matter of doubt. The duchess retired, to learn of the page what had befallen him in Sancho's village; who related the whole very particularly, without leaving a circumstance unrecited. He gave her the acorns, as also a cheese, which Teresa gave him for a very good one, and better than those of Tronchon.* The duchess received it with great satisfaction; and so we will leave them, to relate how ended the government of the great Sancho Panza, the flower and mirror of all insulary governors.

CHAPTER 53

Of the toilsome end and conclusion of Sancho Panza's government.

To think, that in this life the things thereof will continue always in the same state, is a vain expectation: the whole seems rather to be going round, I mean in a circle. The spring is succeeded by the summer, the summer by the autumn, the autumn by the winter, and the winter by the spring again; and thus time rolls round with a continual wheel. Human life only posts it to its end, swifter than time itself, without hope of renewal, unless in the next, which is limited by no bounds. This is the reflection of Cid Hamet, the Mahometan philosopher. For many, without the light of faith, and merely by natural instinct, have discovered the transitory and unstable condition of the present life, and the eternal duration of that which is to come. But here our author speaks with respect to the swiftness with which Sancho's government ended, perished, dissolved, and vanished into smoke and a shadow.

Who being in bed the seventh night of the days of his government, not satiated with bread nor wine, but with sitting in judgement, deciding causes, and making statutes and proclamations; and sleep, maugre and in despite of hunger, beginning to close his eyelids; he heard so great a noise of bells and voices, that he verily thought the whole island had been sinking. He sat up in his bed, and listened attentively, to see if he could guess at the cause of so great an uproar. But so far was he from guessing, that, the din of an infinite number of trumpets and drums joining the noise of the bells and voices, he was in greater confusion, and in more fear and dread than at first. And, getting upon his feet, he put on slippers, because of the dampness of the floor: and, without putting on his nightgown, or anything like it, he went out at his chamber door, and instantly perceived more than twenty persons coming along a gallery, with lighted torches in their hands, and their swords drawn, all crying aloud:

'Arm, arm, my lord governor, arm; for an infinite number of enemies are entered the island, and we are undone, if your conduct and valour do not succour us.'

With this noise and uproar, they came where Sancho stood, astonished and stupefied with what he heard and saw. And when they were come up to him, one of them said:

'Arm yourself straight, my lord, unless you would be ruined, and the whole island with you!'

'What have I to do with arming,' replied Sancho, 'who know nothing of arms or succours? It were better to leave these matters to my master Don Quixote, who will dispatch them and secure us in a trice; for, as I am a sinner to God, I understand nothing at all of these hurlyburlies.'

'Alack, Señor Governor,' said another, 'what faintheartedness is this? Arm yourself, sir: for here we bring you weapons offensive and defensive; and come forth to the market-place, and be our leader and our captain, since you ought to be so, as being our governor.'

'Arm me, then, in God's name,' replied Sancho; and instantly they brought him a couple of old targets, which they had purposely provided, and clapped them over his shirt (not suffering him to put on any other garments) the one before, and the other behind. They thrust his arms through certain holes they had made in them, and tied them well with some cord; insomuch that he remained walled and boarded up straight like a spindle, without being able to bend his knees, or walk one single step. They put a lance into his hand, upon which he leaned, to keep himself upon his feet. Thus accoutred, they desired him to march, and to lead and encourage them all; for, he being their north pole, their lantern, and their morning star, their affairs would have a prosperous issue.

'How should I march, wretch that I am,' answered Sancho, 'when I cannot stir my knee-pans; for I am hindered by these boards, which press so close and hard upon my flesh. Your only way is, to carry me in your arms, and lay me athwart, or set me upright at some postern, which I will maintain, either with my lance or my body.'

'Fie, Señor Governor!' quoth another, 'it is more fear, than the targets, that hinders your marching. Have done for shame, and bestir yourself; for it is late, the enemy increases, the cry grows louder and the danger presses.'

At which persuasions and reproaches the poor governor tried to stir, and down he fell with such violence, that he thought he had dashed himself to pieces. He lay like a tortoise enclosed and covered with his shell, or like a flitch of bacon between two trays, or like a boat with the keel upwards upon the sands. And though they saw him fall, those jesting rogues had not the least compassion on him; on the contrary, putting out their torches, they reinforced the clamour, and reiterated the alarm with such hurry and bustle, trampling over poor Sancho, and giving him a hundred thwacks upon the targets, that, if he had not gathered himself up, and shrunk in his head between the bucklers, it had gone hard with the poor governor, who, crumpled up in that narrow compass, sweated and sweated again, and recommended himself to God from the bottom of his heart, to deliver him from that danger. Some stumbled, others fell over him; and one there was, who, getting a-top of him, stood there for a good while, and from thence, as from a watch-tower, commanded the troops, and, with a loud voice, cried:

'This way, brave boys! here the enemy charges thickest! guard that postern! shut yon gate! down with those scaling-ladders! this way with your cauldrons of resin, pitch, and burning oil! barricado the streets with woolpacks!'

In short, he named, in the utmost hurry, all the necessary implements and engines of war, used in defence of a city assaulted. The poor battered Sancho, who heard, and bore all, said to himself:

'Oh, if it were heaven's good pleasure, that this island were once lost, and I could see myself, either dead, or out of this great strait!'

Heaven heard this petition, and when he least expected it, he heard voices crying.

'Victory, victory! the enemy is routed! rise Señor Governor, enjoy the conquest, and divide the spoils taken from the foe by the valour of that invincible arm!'

'Let me be lifted up,' quoth the dolorous Sancho, with a doleful voice.

They helped him to rise; and, when he was got upon his legs, he said:

'May all the enemies I have vanquished be nailed to my forehead: I will divide no spoils of enemies; but I entreat and beseech some friend, if I have any, to give me a draught of wine, for I am almost choked; and let me dry up this sweat, for I am melting away, and turning into water.'

They rubbed him down; they brought him wine; they untied the targets. He sat down upon his bed, and swooned away with the fright, surprise, and fatigue, he had undergone. Those who had played him the trick, began to be sorry they had laid it on so heavily. But Sancho's coming to himself moderated the pain they were in at his fainting away. He asked what o'clock it was; they told him it was daybreak. He held his peace; and, without saying anything more, he began to dress himself, all buried in silence. They all stared at him, in expectation what would be the issue of his dressing himself in such haste.

In fine, having put on his clothes, by little and little (for he was so bruised, he could not do it hastily), he took the way to the stable, everybody present following him; and going to Dapple, he embraced him, and gave him a kiss of peace on the forehead; and, not without tears in his eyes, he said:

'Come hither, my companion, my friend, and partner in my fatigues and miseries. When I consorted with thee, and had no other thoughts but the care of mending thy furniture, and feeding thy little carcass, happy were my hours, my days, and my years. But, since I forsook thee, and mounted upon the towers of ambition and pride, a thousand miseries, a thousand toils, and four thousand disquiets, have entered into my soul.'

And while he was talking thus, he went on pannelling his ass, without anybody's saying a word to him. Dapple being pannelled, he got upon him, with great pain and heaviness, and directing his speech to the steward, the secretary, the sewer, and doctor Pedro Recio, and many others that were present, he said:

'Give way, gentlemen, and suffer me to return to my ancient liberty: suffer me to seek my past life, that I may rise again from this present death. I was not born to be a governor, nor to defend islands, or cities, from enemies that assault them. I better understand how to plough and dig, how to prune and dress vines, than how to give laws, and defend provinces or kingdoms. St. Peter is well at Rome: I mean that nothing becomes a man so well, as the employment he was born for. In my hand, a sickle is better than a governor's sceptre. I had rather have my belly full of my own poor porridge,* than be subject to the misery of an impertinent physician, who kills me with hunger; and I had rather lay myself down under the shade of an oak in summer, and equip myself with a double sheepskin jerkin in winter, at my liberty, than lie, under the slavery of a government, between Holland sheets, and be clothed in sables. Gentlemen, God be with you; and tell my lord duke, that naked was I born, and naked I am; I neither win nor lose; I mean, that without a penny came I to this government, and without a penny do I quit it, the direct reverse of the governors of other islands. Give me way, and let me be gone to plaster myself; for I verily believe all my ribs are broken; thanks to the enemies, who have been trampling upon me all night long.'

'It must not be so, Señor Governor,' quoth doctor Pedro Recio; 'for I will give your lordship a drink, good against falls and bruises, that shall presently restore you to your former health and vigour. And, as to the eating part, I give you my word I will amend that, and let you eat abundantly of whatever you have a mind to.'

'It comes too late,' answered Sancho: 'I will as soon stay as turn Turk. These are not tricks to be played twice. Before God, I will no more continue in this, nor accept of any other government, though it was served up to me in a covered dish, than I will fly to heaven without wings. I am of the race of the Panzas, who are all headstrong; and if they once cry, Odds, odds it shall be, though it be even, in spite of all the world. In this stable let the pismire's wings remain, that raised me up in the air to be exposed a prey to martlets and other small birds: and return we to walk upon plain ground, with a plain foot; for, if it be not adorned with pinked Córdovan shoes, it will not want for hempen sandals. Every sheep with its like; and, Stretch not your feet beyond your sheet: and so let me be gone, for it grows late.'

To which the steward said:

'Señor Governor, we will let your lordship depart with all our hearts, though we shall be very sorry to lose you; for your judgement, and Christian procedure, oblige us to desire your presence; but you know, that every governor is bound, before he leaves the place he has governed, to submit to a judicature, and render an account of his administration. When your lordship has done so for the ten days you have held the government, you shall depart, and God's peace be with you.'

'Nobody can require that of me,' answered Sancho, 'but whom my lord duke shall appoint. To him I am going, and to him it shall be given exactly: besides, departing naked as I do, there needs surely no other proof of my having governed like an angel.'

'Before God, the great Sancho is in the right,' quoth doctor Pedro Recio, 'and I am of opinion we should let him go; for the duke will be infinitely glad to see him.'

They all consented, and suffered him to depart, offering first to bear him company, and to furnish everything he desired, for the use of his person, and the conveniency of his journey. Sancho said, he desired only a little barley for Dapple, and half a cheese and half a loaf for himself; for, since the way was so short, he stood in need of nothing more, nor any other provision. They all embraced him, and he weeping, embraced them again, and left them in admiration, as well at his discourse, as at his so resolute and discreet determination.

CHAPTER 54

Which treats of matters relating to this history, and to no other.

THE duke and duchess resolved, that Don Quixote's challenge of their vassal, for the cause above mentioned, should go forward; and, though the young man was in Flanders, whither he was fled to avoid having Doña Rodriguez for his mother-in- law, they gave orders for putting in his place a Gascon lackey called Tosilos, instructing him previously in everything he was to do. About two days after, the duke said to Don Quixote, that his opponent would be there in four days, and present himself in the lists, armed as a knight, and would maintain, that the damsel lied by half the beard, and even by the whole beard, if she said he had given her a promise of marriage. Don Quixote was highly delighted with the news, and promised himself to do wonders upon the occasion, esteeming it a special happiness, that an opportunity offered of demonstrating to their grandeurs how far the valour of his puissant arm extended; and so, with pleasure and satisfaction, he waited the four days, which, in the account of his impatience, were four hundred ages.

Let us let them pass, as we let pass many other things, and attend upon Sancho, who, between glad and sorry, was making the best of his way upon Dapple towards his master, whose company he was fonder of than of being governor of all the islands in the world.

Now he had not gone far from the island of his government (for he never gave himself the trouble to determine whether it was an island, city, town, or village, that he governed) when he saw, coming along the road, six pilgrims, with their staves, being foreigners, such as ask alms singing; and, as they drew near to him, they placed themselves in a row, and, raising their voices altogether, began to sing, in their language, what Sancho could not understand, excepting one word, which they distinctly pronounced, signifying 'Alms'; whence he concluded, that alms was what they begged in their canting way. And he being, as Cid Hamet says, extremely charitable, he took the half loaf and half cheese out of his wallet, and gave it them, making signs to them, that he had nothing else to give them. They received it very willingly, and cried.

'*Guelte, guelte.*'

'I do not understand you,' answered Sancho; 'what is it you would have, good people?'

Then one of them pulled out of his bosom a purse, and showed it to Sancho; whence he found, that they asked for money: and he, putting his thumb to his throat, and extending his hand upward, gave them to understand he had not a penny of money; and, spurring his Dapple, he broke through them; and, as he passed by, one of them, who had viewed him with much attention, caught hold of him, and, throwing his arms about his waist, with a loud voice, and in very good Castilian, said:

'God be my aid! what is it I see? Is it possible I have in my arms my dear friend and good neighbour Sancho Panza? Yes, certainly I have; for I am neither asleep nor drunk.'*

Sancho was surprised to hear himself called by his name, and to find himself embraced by the stranger pilgrim; and, though he viewed him earnestly a good while, without speaking a word, he could not call him to mind. But the pilgrim, perceiving his suspense, said.

'How! is it possible, brother Sancho Panza, you do not know your neighbour Ricote, the Morisco shopkeeper of your town?'

Then Sancho observed him more attentively, and began to recollect him, and at last remembered him perfectly; and, without alighting from his beast, he threw his arms about his neck, and said:

'Who the devil, Ricote, should know you in this disguise?'

'Tell me, how came you thus Frenchified? and how dare you venture to return to Spain, where, if you are known and caught, it will fare but ill with you.'

'If you do not discover me, Sancho,' answered the pilgrim, 'I am safe enough; for, in this garb, nobody can know me. And let us go out of the road to yonder poplar-grove, where my comrades have a mind to dine and repose themselves, and you shall eat with them; for they are a very good sort of people; and there I shall have an opportunity to tell you what has befallen me since I departed from our village, in obedience to his majesty's proclamation, which so rigorously threatened the miserable people of our nation,* as you must have heard.'

Sancho consented, and Ricote speaking to the rest of the pilgrims, they turned aside toward the poplar-grove, which they saw at a distance, far enough out of the high road. They flung down their staves, and, putting off their pilgrim's weeds, remained in their jackets. They were all genteel young fellows, excepting Ricote, who was pretty far advanced in years. They all carried wallets, which, as appeared afterwards, were well provided with incitatives, and such as provoke to thirst at two leagues' distance. They laid themselves along on the ground, and, making the grass their tablecloth, they spread their bread, salt, knives, nuts, slices of cheese, and clean bones of gammon of bacon, which, if they would not bear picking, did not forbear being sucked. They produced also a kind of black eatable, called caviare, made of the roes of a fish, a great awakener of thirst. There wanted not olives, though dry and without any sauce, yet savoury, and well preserved. But, what carried the palm in the field of this banquet, was, six bottles of wine, each producing one out of his wallet. Even honest Ricote, who had transformed himself from a Moor into a German, or Dutchman, pulled out his, which for bigness might vie with the other five.

Now they began to eat with the highest relish, and much at their leisure, dwelling upon the taste of every bit they took upon the point of a knife, and very little of each thing; and straight altogether lifted up their arms and their bottles into the air, mouth applied to mouth, and their eyes nailed to the heavens, as if they were taking aim at it, and, in this posture, waving their heads from side to side, in token of the pleasure they received, they continued a good while, transfusing the entrails of the vessels into their own stomachs. Sancho beheld all this, and was nothing grieved thereat; but rather, in compliance to the proverb, he very well knew, When you are at Rome, do as they do at Rome, he demanded of Ricote the bottle, and took his aim, as the others had done, and not with less relish. Four times the bottles bore being tilted; but, for the fifth it was not to be done; for they were now as empty and as dry as a rush, which struck a damp upon the mirth they had hitherto shown. One or other of them, from time to time, would take Sancho by the right hand, and say:

'Spaniard and Dutchman, all one, goot companion.'*

And Sancho would answer:

'Goot companion, I vow to gad!'

And then he burst out into a fit of laughing, which held him an hour, without his remembering at that time anything of what had befallen him in his government: for cares have commonly but very little jurisdiction over the time that is spent in eating and drinking. Finally, the making an end of the wine was the beginning of a sound sleep, which seized them all, upon their very board and tablecloth. Only Ricote and Sancho remained awake, having drunk less, though eaten more, than the rest. And they two, going aside, sat them down at the foot of a beech, leaving the pilgrims buried in a sweet sleep; and Ricote, laying aside his Morisco, said what follows in pure Castilian:

'You well know, O Sancho, my neighbour and friend, how the proclamation and edict, which his majesty commanded to be published against those of my nation, struck a dread and terror into us all: at least into me it did, in such sort, that methought the rigour of the penalty was already executed upon me and my children, before the time limited for our departure from Spain. I provided therefore, as I thought, like a wise man, who knowing at such a time the house he lives in will be taken from him, secures another to remove to: I say, I left our town, alone, and without my family, to find out a place, whither I might conveniently carry them, without that hurry the rest went away in. For I well saw, as did all the wisest among us, that those proclamations were not bare threatenings, as some pretended they were, but effectual laws, and such as would be put in execution at the appointed time. And what confirmed me in the belief of this, was, my knowing the mischievous, extravagant designs of our people; which were such, that, in my opinion, it was a divine inspiration that moved his majesty to put so brave a resolution in practice. Not that we were all culpable; for some of us were steady and true Christians: but these were so few, they could not be compared with those that were otherwise; and it is not prudent to nourish a serpent in one's bosom, by keeping one's enemies within doors.

'In short, we were justly punished with the sentence of banishment; a soft and mild one in the opinion of some, but to us the most terrible that can be inflicted. Wherever we are, we weep for Spain; for, in short, here were we born, and this is our native country. We nowhere find the reception our misfortune requires. Even in Barbary, and all other parts of Africa, where we expected to be received, cherished, and made much of, there it is we are most neglected and misused. We knew not our happiness till we lost it; and so great is the desire almost all of us have of returning to Spain, that most of those (and they are not a few) who can speak the language like myself, forsake their wives and children, and come back again; so violent is the love they bear it. And it is now I know, and find by experience, the truth of that common saying, Sweet is the love of one's country.

'I went away, as I said, from out town: I entered into France; and, though there I met with a good reception, I had a desire to see other countries. I went into Italy, and then into Germany, and there I thought we might live more at liberty, the natives not standing much upon niceties, and every one living as he pleases; for, in most parts of it, there is liberty of conscience. I took a house in a village near Augsburg, but soon left it, and joined company with these pilgrims, who come in great numbers every year into Spain to visit its holy places, which they look upon as their Indies, and a certain gain, and sure profit. They travel almost the kingdom over, and there is not a village but they are sure of getting meat and drink in it, and a real at least in money; and, at the end of their journey, they go off with above a hundred crowns clear, which, being changed into gold, they carry out of the kingdom, either in the hollow of their staves, or in the patches of their weeds, or by some other sleight they are masters of, and get safe into their own country, in spite of all the officers and searchers of the passes and ports, where money is registered.*

'Now my design, Sancho, is, to carry off the treasure I left buried (for, it being without the town, I can do it with the less danger), and to write, or go over to my wife and daughter, who I know are in Algiers, and contrive how to bring them to some port of France, and from thence carry them into Germany, where we will wait, and see how God will be pleased to dispose of us. For, in short, Sancho, I know for certain, that Ricota my daughter, and Francisca Ricota my wife, are Catholic Christians, and though I am not altogether such, yet I am more of the Christian than the Moor; and I constantly pray to God to open the eyes of my understanding, and make me know in what manner I ought to serve Him. But what I wonder at is, that my wife and daughter should rather go into Barbary than into France, where they might have lived as Christians.'

'Look you, Ricote,' answered Sancho, 'that perhaps was not at their choice, because John Tiopieyo, your wife's brother, who carried them away, being a rank Moor, would certainly go where he thought it best to stay; and I can tell you another thing, which is, that I believe it is in vain for you to look for the money you left buried, because we had news, that your brother-in-law, and your wife, had abundance of pearls, and a great deal of money in gold, taken from them, as not having been registered.'

'That may be,' replied Ricote, 'but I am sure, Sancho, they did not touch my hoard; for I never discovered it to them, as fearing some mischance; and therefore, Sancho, if you will go along with me, and help me to carry it off and conceal it, I will give you two hundred crowns, with which you may relieve your wants; for you know I am not ignorant they are many.'

'I would do it,' answered Sancho, 'but that I am not at all covetous; for, had I been so, I quitted an employment this very morning, out of which I could have made the walls of my house of gold, and before six months had been at an end, have eaten in plate; so that, for this reason, and because I think I should betray my king, by favouring his enemies, I will not go with you, though, instead of two hundred crowns, you should lay me down four hundred upon the nail.'

'And what employment have you quitted, Sancho?' demanded Ricote.

'I left being governor of an island,' answered Sancho, 'and such an one, as, in faith, you will scarcely, at three pulls, meet with its fellow.'

'And where is this island?' demanded Ricote.

'Where?' answered Sancho, 'why, two leagues from hence, and it is called the island Barataria.'

'Peace, Sancho,' quoth Ricote; 'for islands are out at sea; there are no islands on the main land.'

'No?' replied Sancho: 'I tell you, friend Ricote, that I left it this very morning; and yesterday I was in it, governing at my pleasure, like any Sagittarius,* but for all that I quitted it, looking upon the office of a governor to be a very dangerous thing.'

'And what have you got by the government?' demanded Ricote.

'I have got,' answered Sancho, 'this experience, to know I am fit to govern nothing but a herd of cattle, and that the riches got in such governments are got at the expense of one's ease and sleep, yea, and of one's sustenance; for, in islands, governors eat but little, especially if they have physicians to look after their health.'

'I understand you not, Sancho,' quoth Ricote; 'and all you say seems to me extravagant; for who should give you islands to govern? are there wanting men in the world, abler than you are, to be governors? Hold your peace, Sancho; recall your senses, and consider whether you will go along with me, as I said, and help me to take up the treasure I left buried; for, in truth, it may very well be called a treasure; and I will give you wherewithal to live, as I have already told you.'

'And I have told you, Ricote,' replied Sancho, 'that I will not: be satisfied; I will not discover you, and go your way, in God's name, and let me go mine; for I know, that what is well got may meet with disaster, and what is ill got destroys both itself and its master.'

'I will not urge you further, Sancho,' quoth Ricote: 'but tell me, were you in our town when my wife and daughter, and my brother-in-law, went away?'

'Was I? aye,' answered Sancho; 'and I can tell you, that your daughter went away so beautiful, that all the town went out to see her, and everybody said, she was the finest creature in the world. She went away weeping, and embraced all her friends and acquaintance, and all that came to see her, and desired them all to recommend her to God, and to our lady His mother; and this so feelingly, that she made me weep, who am no great whimperer; and, in faith, many had a desire to conceal her, and to go and take her away upon the road; but the fear of transgressing the king's command restrained them. Don Pedro Gregorio, the rich heir you know, showed himself the most affected; for, they say, he was mightily in love with her; and, since she went away, he has never been seen in our town, and we all think he followed to steal her away; but hitherto nothing further is known.'

'I ever had a jealousy,' quoth Ricote, 'that this gentleman was smitten with my daughter; but, trusting to the virtue of my Ricota, it gave me no trouble to find he was in love with her; for you must have heard, Sancho, that the Moorish women seldom or never mingle in love with Old Christians; and my daughter, who, as I believe, minded religion more than love, little regarded this rich heir's courtship.'

'God grant it,' replied Sancho; 'for it would be very ill for them both: and let me be gone, friend Ricote; for I intend to be to-night with my master Don Quixote.'

'God be with you, brother Sancho,' said Ricote; 'for my comrades are stirring, and it is time for us also to be on our way.'

And then they embraced each other: Sancho mounted his Dapple, and Ricote leaned on his pilgrim's staff; and so they parted.

CHAPTER 55

Of what befell Sancho in the way, and other matters, which you have only to see.

SANCHO stayed so long with Ricote that he had not time to reach the duke's castle that day; though he was arrived within half a league of it, when the night, somewhat dark and close, overtook him: but, it being summer time, it gave him no great concern; and so he struck out of the road, purposing to wait for the morning. But his ill luck would have it, that, in seeking a place where he might best accommodate himself, he and Dapple fell together into a deep and very dark pit, among some ruins of old buildings; and, as he was falling, he recommended himself to God with his whole heart, not expecting to stop till he came to the depth of the abyss. But it fell out otherwise; for a little beyond three fathom, Dapple felt ground, and Sancho found himself on his back, without having received any damage or hurt at all.

He fell to feeling his body all over, and held his breath, to see if he was sound, or bored through in any part: and finding himself well, whole, and in catholic health, he thought he could never give sufficient thanks to God for the mercy extended to him: for he verily thought he had been beaten into a thousand pieces. He felt also with his hands about the sides of the pit, to see if it was possible to get out of it without help; but he found them all smooth and without any hold or footing; at which Sancho was much grieved, and especially when he heard Dapple groan most tenderly and sadly: and no wonder; nor did he lament out of wantonness, being, in truth, not over well situated.

'Alas!' said Sancho Panza then, 'what unexpected accidents perpetually befall those who live in this miserable world! Who could have thought, that he, who yesterday saw himself enthroned the governor of an island, commanding his servants and his vassals, should to-day find himself buried in a pit, without anybody to help him, and without servant or vassal to come to his assistance? Here must I and my ass perish with hunger, unless we die first, he by bruises and contusions, and I by grief and concern. At least, I shall not be so happy as my master Don Quixote de la Mancha was, when he descended and went down into the cave of the enchanted Montesinos, where he met with better entertainment than in his own house, and where, it seems, he found the cloth ready laid, and the bed ready made. There saw he beautiful and pleasant visions; and here I shall see, I suppose, toads and snakes. Unfortunate that I am! What are my follies and imaginations come to? Hence shall my bones be taken up, when it shall please God that I am found, clean, white, and bare; and those of my trusty Dapple with them; whence, peradventure, it will be conjectured who we were, at least by those who have been informed, that Sancho Panza never parted from his ass, nor his ass from Sancho Panza. And I say, miserable we! that our ill luck would not suffer us to die in our own country, and among our friends, where, though our misfortunes had found no remedy, there would not be wanting some to grieve for them, and, at our last gasp, to close our eyes. O my companion and my friend! how ill have I repaid thy good services! forgive me, and beg of fortune, in the best manner thou art able, to bring us out of this miserable calamity, in which we are both involved; and I promise to put a crown of laurel upon thy head, that thou mayst look like any poet laureate, and to double thy allowance.'

Thus lamented Sancho Panza, and his beast listened to him without answering one word, such was the distress and anguish the poor creature was in.

Finally, having passed all that night in sad lamentations and complainings, the day came on, by the light and splendour whereof Sancho soon perceived, it was of all impossibilities the most impossible to get out of that pit without help. Then he began to lament, and cry out aloud, to try if anybody could hear him: but all his cries were in the desert; for there was not a creature in all those parts within hearing; and then he gave himself over for dead. Dapple lay with his mouth upwards, and Sancho contrived to get him upon his legs though he could scarcely stand: and pulling out of his wallet, which had also shared the fortune of the fall, a piece of bread, he gave it his beast, who did not take it amiss; and Sancho, as if the ass understood him, said to him.

'Bread is relief for all kind of grief.'

At length he discovered a hole in one side of the pit, wide enough for a man to creep through stooping. Sancho, squatting down, crept through upon all fours, and found it was spacious and large within; and he could see about him, for a ray of the sun, glancing in through what might be called the roof, discovered it all. He saw also, that it enlarged and extended itself into another spacious concavity. Which having observed, he came back to where his ass was, and with a stone began to break away the earth of the hole, and soon made room for his ass to pass easily through, which he did: then, taking him by the halter, he advanced forward along the cavern, to see if he could find a way to get out on the other side. He went on, sometimes darkling, and sometimes without light, but never without fear.

'The Almighty God be my aid,' quoth he to himself; 'this, which to me is a mishap, to my master Don Quixote had been an adventure: he would, no doubt, have taken these depths and dungeons for flowery gardens and palaces of Galiana,* and would have expected to issue out of this obscurity by some pleasant meadow. But unhappy I, devoid of counsel, and dejected in mind, at every step expect some other pit, deeper than this, to open on a sudden under my feet, and swallow me downright: Welcome that ill that comes alone.'

In this manner, and with these thoughts, he fancied he had gone somewhat more than half a league, when he discovered a glimmering light, like that of the day, breaking in, and opening an entrance into what seemed to him the road to the other world.

Here Cid Hamet Ben Engeli leaves him, and returns to treat of Don Quixote, who, with joy and transport, was waiting for the appointed day of combat with the ravisher of Doña Rodriguez's daughter's honour, resolving to see justice done her, and to take satisfaction for the affront and injury offered her.

It happened then, that, riding out one morning, to exercise and assay himself for the business of the combat he was to be engaged in within a day or two, as he was now reining, now running Rosinante, he chanced to pitch his feet so near a pit, that, had he not drawn the reins in very strongly, he must inevitably have fallen into it. At last he stopped him, and fell not; and getting a little nearer, without alighting, he viewed the chasm; and, as he was looking at it, he heard a loud voice within, and, listening attentively, he could distinguish and understand, that he who spoke from below, said:

'Ho, above there! is there any Christian, that hears me, or any charitable gentleman to take pity of a sinner buried alive, an unfortunate disgoverned governor?'

Don Quixote thought he heard Sancho Panza's voice; at which he was surprised and amazed; and raising his voice as high as he could, he cried:

'Who is below there? who is it complains?'

'Who should be here, or who should complain,' replied the voice, 'but the forlorn Sancho Panza, governor, for his sins and for his evil-errantry, of the island [of] Barataria, and late squire of the famous knight Don Quixote de la Mancha?'

Which Don Quixote hearing, his astonishment was doubled, and his amazement increased; for it came into his imagination that Sancho Panza was dead, and that his soul was there doing penance; and, being carried away by this thought, he said:

'I conjure thee by all that can conjure thee, as a Catholic Christian, to tell me who thou art; and, if thou art a soul in purgatory, let me know what I can do for thee; for, since it is my profession to be aiding and assisting the needy of this world, I shall also be ready to aid and assist the distressed in the other, who cannot help themselves.'

'So then,' answered the voice, 'you who speak to me are my master Don Quixote de la Mancha, and by the tone of the voice it can be nobody else for certain.'

'Don Quixote I am,' replied Don Quixote, 'he who professes to succour and assist the living and the dead in their necessities. Tell me, then, who thou art, for thou amazest me: if you are my squire Sancho Panza, and chance to be dead, since the devils have not got you, but through the mercy of God you are in purgatory, our holy mother the Roman Catholic church has supplications sufficient to deliver you from the pains you are in; and I, for my part, will solicit her in your behalf, as far as my estate will reach: therefore explain, and without more ado, tell me who you are.'

'I vow to God,' said the voice, 'and I swear by the birth of whom your worship pleases, Señor Don Quixote de la Mancha, that I am your squire Sancho Panza, and that I never was dead in all the days of my life, but that, having left my government, for causes and considerations that require more leisure to relate them, this night I fell into this cavern, where I now am, and Dapple with me, who will not let me lie, by the same token he stands here by me: and would you have any more?'

One would think the ass had understood what Sancho said; for at that instant he began to bray, and that so lustily, that the whole cave resounded with it.

'A credible witness,' quoth Don Quixote: 'I know that bray, as well as if I had brought it forth; I know your voice, my dear Sancho: stay a little, and I will go to the duke's castle hard by, and will fetch people to get you out of this pit, into which your sins have certainly cast you.'

'Pray go, for the lord's sake,' quoth Sancho, 'and return speedily; for I cannot longer endure being buried alive here, and am dying with fear.'

Don Quixote left him, and went to the castle, to tell the duke and duchess what had befallen Sancho Panza; at which they wondered not a little, though they easily conceived how he might fall by the corresponding circumstance of the pit, which had been there time out of mind: but they could not imagine how he had left the government without their having advice of his coming. Finally, they sent ropes and pulleys, and, by dint of a great many hands, and a great deal of labour, Dapple and Sancho Panza were drawn out of those gloomy shades to the light of the sun. A certain scholar seeing him said:

'Thus should all bad governors come out of their governments, as this sinner comes out of the depth of this abyss, starved with hunger, wan, and, I suppose, penniless.'

Sancho, hearing him, said:

'It is about eight or ten days, brother murmurer, since I entered upon the government of the island that was bestowed upon me, in all which time I had not my belly full one hour; I was persecuted by physicians, and had my bones broken by enemies: nor had I leisure to make perquisites, or receive my dues; and this being so, as it really is, methinks I deserved not to be packed off in this manner: but, Man proposes, and God disposes; and He knows what is best and fittest for everybody; and, As is the reason, such is the season; and, Let nobody say, I will not drink of this water; for, Where one expects to meet with gammons of bacon, there are no pins to hang them on. God knows my mind, and that is enough. I say no more, though I could.'

'Be not angry, Sancho, nor concerned at what you hear,' quoth Don Quixote; 'for then you will never have done: come but you with a safe conscience, and let people say what they will; for you may as well think to barricade the highway, as to tie up the tongue of slander. If a governor comes rich from his government, they say he has plundered it, and, if he leaves it poor, that he has been a good-for-nothing fool.'

'I warrant,' answered Sancho, 'that, for this bout, they will rather take me for a fool than a thief.'

In such talk, and surrounded by a multitude of boys and other people, they arrived at the castle, where the duke and duchess were already in a gallery waiting for Don Quixote, and for Sancho, who would not go up to see the duke, till he had first taken the necessary care of Dapple in the stable, saying, the poor thing had had but an indifferent night's lodging: and, that done, up he went to see the duke and duchess, before whom kneeling, he said:

'I, my lord and lady, because your grandeurs would have it so, without any desert of mine, went to govern your island of Barataria, into which naked I entered, and naked I have left it: I neither win nor lose: whether I have governed well or ill, there are witnesses, who may say what they please. I have resolved doubts, and pronounced sentences, and all the while ready to die with hunger, because doctor Pedro Recio, native of Tirteafuera, and physician in ordinary to the island and its governors, would have it so. Enemies attacked us by night, and though they put us in great danger, the people of the island say, they were delivered, and got the victory, by the valour of my arm; and according as they say true, so help them God. In short, in this time I have summed up the cares and burdens that governing brings with it, and find, by my account, that my shoulders cannot bear them, neither are they a proper weight for my ribs, or arrows for my quiver; and therefore, lest the government should forsake me, I resolved to forsake the government; and yesterday morning I left the island as I found it, with the same streets, houses, and roofs it had before I went into it. I borrowed nothing of anybody, nor set about making a purse; and though I thought to have made some wholesome laws, I made none, fearing they would not be observed, which is all one as if they were not made. I quitted, I say, the island, accompanied by nobody but Dapple: I fell into a pit, and went along underground, till this morning by the light of the sun I discovered a way out, though not so easy a one, but that, if heaven had not sent my master, Don Quixote, there I had stayed till the end of the world. So that, my lord duke, and lady duchess, behold here your governor, Sancho Panza, who, in ten days only that he held the government, has gained the experience to know, that he would not give a farthing to be governor, not of an island only, but even of the whole world. This then being the case, kissing your honour's feet, and imitating the boys at play, who cry, leap you, and then let me leap, I give a leap out of the government, and again pass over to the service of my master Don Quixote: for, after all, though with him I eat my bread in bodily fear, at least I have my belly full; and, for my part, so that be well filled, all is one to me, whether it be with carrots or partridges.'

Here Sancho ended his long speech, Don Quixote fearing all the while he would utter a thousand extravagances, and, seeing he had ended with so few, he gave thanks to heaven in his heart. The duke embraced Sancho, and assured him, that it grieved him to the soul he had left the government so soon; but that he would take care he should have some other employment in his territories of less trouble and more profit. The duchess also embraced him, and ordered he should be made much of; for he seemed to be sorely bruised and in wretched plight.

CHAPTER 56

*Of the prodigious and never-seen battle between Don Quixote
de la Mancha and the lackey Tosilos, in defence of the
duenna Doña Rodriguez's daughter.*

THE duke and the duchess repented not of the jest put upon
Sancho Panza, in relation to the government they had given
him; especially since their steward came home that very day,
and gave them a punctual relation of almost all the words
and actions Sancho had said and done during that time. In
fine, he exaggerated the assault of the island, with Sancho's
fright, and departure; at which they were not a little pleased.

After this the history tells us, the appointed day of combat
came, and the duke having over and over again instructed
his lackey Tosilos how he should behave towards Don
Quixote, so as to overcome him without killing or wounding
him, commanded that the iron heads should be taken off
their lances, telling Don Quixote that Christianity, upon
which he valued himself, did not allow that this battle should
be fought with so much peril and hazard of their lives, and
that he should content himself with giving them free field-
room in his territories, though in opposition to the decree
of the holy council,* which prohibits such challenges; and
therefore he would not push the affair to the utmost extremity. Don Quixote replied, that his excellency might dispose matters relating to this business as he liked best, for he
would obey him in everything.

The dreadful day being now come, and the duke having
commanded a spacious scaffold to be erected before the court
of the castle for the judges of the field, and the two duennas,
mother and daughter, appellants; an infinite number of
people, from all the neighbouring towns and villages, flocked
to see the novelty of this combat, the like having never
been heard of in that country, neither by the living nor the
dead.

The first who entered the field and the pale, was the master
of the ceremonies, who examined the ground, and walked it
all over, that there might be no foul play, nor any other thing
covered to occasion stumbling or falling. Then entered the

duennas and took their seats, covered with veils to their eyes, and even to their breasts, with tokens of no small concern.

Don Quixote presented himself in the lists. A while after appeared on one side of the place, accompanied by many trumpets, and mounted upon a puissant steed, making the earth shake under him, the great lackey Tosilos, his visor down, and quite stiffened with strong and shining armour. The horse seemed to be a Frieslander, well-spread and flea-bitten, with a quarter of a hundred weight of wool about each fetlock.

The valorous combatant came well instructed by the duke his lord how to behave towards the valorous Don Quixote de la Mancha, and cautioned in nowise to hurt him, but to endeavour to shun the first onset, to avoid the danger of his own death, which must be inevitable, should he encounter him full butt. He traversed the lists, and, coming where the duennas were, he set himself to view awhile her who demanded him for her husband. The marshal of the field called Don Quixote, who had presented himself in the lists, and, together with Tosilos, asked the duennas, whether they consented that Don Quixote de la Mancha should maintain their right. They answered that they did, and that, whatever he should do in the case, they allowed it for well done, firm, and valid. By this time the duke and duchess were seated in a balcony, over the barriers, which were crowded with an infinite number of people, all expecting to behold this dangerous and unheard-of battle. It was articled between the combatants, that, if Don Quixote should conquer his adversary, the latter should be obliged to marry Doña Rodriguez's daughter; and if he should be overcome, his adversary should be at his liberty, and free from the promise the women insisted upon, without giving any other satisfaction.

The master of the ceremonies divided the sun equally between them,* and fixed each in the post he was to stand in. The drums beat; the sound of the trumpets filled the air; the earth trembled beneath their feet; the hearts of the gazing multitude were in suspense, some fearing, others hoping, the good or ill success of this business. Finally, Don Quixote, recommending himself with all his heart to God our Lord, and to the lady Dulcinea del Toboso, stood waiting when the precise signal for the onset should be given. But our lackey's thoughts were very differently employed; for he thought of nothing but of what I am going to relate.

It seems, while he stood looking at his female enemy, he fancied her the most beautiful woman he had ever seen in his life, and the little blind boy, called up and down the streets Love, would not lose the opportunity offered him of triumphing over a lackeyan heart, and placing it in the catalogue of his trophies; and so, approaching him fair and softly, without anybody's seeing him, he shot the poor lackey in at the left side with an arrow two yards long, and pierced his heart through and through: and he might safely do it; for love is invincible, and goes in and out where he lists, without being accountable to anybody for his actions.

I say then, that, when the signal was given for the onset, our lackey stood transported, thinking on her he had now made the mistress of his liberty, and, therefore, regarded not the trumpet's sound, as did Don Quixote, who had scarce heard it, when, bending forward, he ran against his enemy, at Rosinante's best speed; and his trusty squire Sancho, seeing him set forward, cried aloud:

'God guide you, cream and flower of knights-errant! God give you victory, since you have right on your side!'

And though Tosilos saw Don Quixote making towards him, he stirred not a step from his post, but called as loud as he could to the marshal of the field; who coming up to see what he wanted, Tosilos said:

'Sir, is not this combat to decide, whether I shall marry, or not marry, yonder young lady?'

'It is,' answered the marshal.

'Then,' quoth the lackey, 'my conscience will not let me proceed any farther; and I declare, that I yield myself vanquished, and am ready to marry that gentlewoman immediately.'

The marshal was surprised at what Tosilos said, and, as he was in the secret of the contrivance, he could not tell what answer to make him. Don Quixote, perceiving that his adversary did not come on to meet him, stopped short in the midst of his career. The duke could not guess the reason why the combat did not go forward: but the marshal went and told him what Tosilos had said: at which he was surprised and extremely angry. In the meantime, Tosilos went up to the place where Doña Rodriguez was, and said aloud:

'I am willing, madam, to marry your daughter, and would not obtain that by strife and contention, which I may have by peace, and without danger of death.'

The valorous Don Quixote hearing all this, said:

'Since it is so, I am absolved from my promise: let them be married in God's name, and, since God has given her, St. Peter bless her.'

The duke was now come down to the court of the castle, and, going up to Tosilos, he said:

'Is it true, knight, that you yield yourself vanquished, and that, instigated by your timorous conscience, you will marry this damsel?'

'Yes, my lord,' answered Tosilos.

'He does very well,' quoth Sancho Panza at this juncture; 'for, What you would give to the mouse, give it the cat, and you will have no trouble.'

Tosilos was all this while unlacing his helmet, and desired them to help him quickly for his spirits and breath were just failing him, and he could not endure to be so long pent up in the straitness of that lodging. They presently unarmed him, and the face of the lackey was exposed to view. Which Doña Rodriguez and her daughter seeing, they cried aloud:

'A cheat, a cheat; Tosilos, my lord duke's lackey, is put upon us instead of our true spouse; justice from God and the king against so much deceit, not to say villany.'

'Afflict not yourselves, ladies,' quoth Don Quixote; 'for this is neither deceit nor villany, and, if it be, the duke is not to blame, but the wicked enchanters, who persecute me, and who, envying me the glory of this conquest, have transformed the countenance of your husband into that of this person, who, you say, is a lackey of the duke's. Take my advice, and, in spite of the malice of my enemies, marry him; for without doubt he is the very man you desire to take for your husband.'

The duke, hearing this, was ready to vent his anger in laughter, and said:

'The things which befall Señor Don Quixote are so extraordinary, that I am inclined to believe this is not my lackey: but let us make use of this stratagem and device; let us postpone the wedding for fifteen days, if you please, and, in the meantime, keep this person, who holds us in doubt, in safe custody: perhaps, during that time, he may return to his pristine figure; for the grudge the enchanters bear to Señor Don Quixote cannot surely last so long, and especially since these tricks and transformations avail them so little.'

'Oh, sir,' quoth Sancho, 'those wicked wretches make it their practice and custom to change things relating to my master from one shape to another. A knight whom he vanquished a few days ago, called the Knight of the Looking-Glasses, was changed by them into the shape and figure of the bachelor Sampson Carrasco, a native of our town, and a great friend of ours; and they have turned my lady Dulcinea del Toboso into a downright country wench: therefore I imagine this lackey will live and die a lackey all the days of his life.'

To which Rodriguez's daughter said:

'Let him be who he will that demands me to wife, I take it kindly of him; for I had rather be lawful wife to a lackey, than a cast mistress, and tricked by a gentleman, though he, who abused me, is not one.'

In short, all these accidents and events ended in Tosilos's confinement, till it should appear what his transformation would come to. The victory was adjudged to Don Quixote by a general acclamation: but the greater part of the spectators were out of humour to find, that the so much expected combatants had not hacked one another to pieces; just as boys are sorry, when the criminal they expected to see hanged, is pardoned, either by the prosecutor, or the court.

The crowd dispersed: the duke and Don Quixote returned to the castle: Tosilos was confined: and Doña Rodriguez and her daughter were extremely well pleased to see, that, one way or other, this business was like to end in matrimony, and Tosilos hoped no less.

CHAPTER 57

Which relates how Don Quixote took his leave of the duke, and of what befell him with the witty and wanton Altisidora, one of the duchess's waiting-women.

DON QUIXOTE now thought it high time to quit so idle a life as that he had led in the castle, thinking he committed a great fault in suffering his person to be thus confined, and in living lazily amidst the infinite pleasures and entertainments the duke and duchess provided for him as a knight-errant; and he was of opinion he must give a strict account to God for this inactivity. And therefore he one day asked leave of [their graces], that he might depart, which they granted him, with tokens of being mightily troubled that he would leave them. The duchess gave Sancho Panza his wife's letters, which he wept over, and said:

'Who could have thought, that hopes so great as those conceived in the breast of my wife Teresa Panza, at the news of my government, should end in my returning to the toilsome adventures of my master Don Quixote de la Mancha? Nevertheless, I am pleased to find, that my Teresa has behaved like herself, in sending the acorns to the duchess; for had she not sent them, I had been sorry, and she had showed herself ungrateful. But my comfort is, that this present cannot be called a bribe; for I was already in possession of the government, when she sent them: and it is very fitting that those who receive a benefit should show themselves grateful, though it be with a trifle. In fine, naked I went into the government, and naked am I come out of it, and so I can say with a safe conscience (which is no small matter) naked I was born, naked I am; I neither win nor lose.'

This Sancho spoke in soliloquy on the day of their departure; and Don Quixote, sallying forth one morning, having taken leave of the duke and duchess the night before, presented himself completely armed in the court of the castle. All the folks of the castle beheld him from the galleries: the duke and duchess also came out to see him. Sancho was upon his Dapple, his wallets well furnished, and himself highly pleased; for the duke's steward, who had played the part of the Trifaldi, had given him a little purse with two hundred crowns in gold, to supply the occasions of the journey; and this Don Quixote, as yet, knew nothing of.

Whilst all the folks were thus gazing at him, as has been said, among the other duennas and damsels of the duchess who were beholding him, on a sudden the witty and wanton Altisidora raised her voice, and in a piteous tone, said:

> 'Stay, cruel knight,
> Take not thy flight,
> Nor spur thy batter'd jade;
> Thy haste restrain,
> Draw in the rein,
> And hear a love-sick maid.
> Why dost thou fly?
> No snake am I,
> Nor poison those I love.
> Gentle I am,
> As any lamb,
> And harmless as a dove.
> Thy cruel scorn
> Has left forlorn
> A nymph, whose charms may vie
> With theirs who sport
> In Cynthia's court,
> Though Venus's self were by.
> Since, fugitive knight, to no purpose I woo thee,
> Barabbas's fate still pursue and undo thee!

> 'Like rav'nous kite,
> That takes its flight,
> Soon as't has stol'n a chicken,
> Thou bear'st away
> My heart, thy prey,
> And leav'st me here to sicken:
> Three nightcaps too,
> And garters blue,
> That did to legs belong,
> Smooth to the sight,
> As marble white,
> And, faith, almost as strong:
> Two thousand groans,

As many moans,
And sighs enough to fire
Old Priam's town,
And burn it down,
Did it again aspire.
Since, fugitive knight, to no purpose I woo thee,
Barabbas's fate still pursue and undo thee!

'May Sancho ne'er
His buttocks bare
Fly-flap, as is his duty;
And thou still want
To disenchant
Dulcinea's injur'd beauty.
May still transform'd,
And still deform'd,
Toboso's nymph remain,
In recompense
Of thy offence,
Thy scorn and cold disdain.
When thou dost wield
Thy sword in field,
In combat or in quarrel,
Ill luck and harms
Attend thy arms,
Instead of fame and laurel.
Since, fugitive knight, to no purpose I woo thee,
Barabbas's fate still pursue and undo thee!

'May thy disgrace
Fill ev'ry place,
Thy falsehood ne'er be hid;
But round the world
Be toss'd and hurl'd,
From Seville to Madrid.
If, brisk and gay,
Thou sitt'st to play
At Ombre or at Chess,
May ne'er Spadill*
Attend thy will,
Nor luck thy movements bless.
Though thou with care
Thy corns dost pare,

> May blood the penknife follow
> May thy gums rage,
> And naught assuage
> The pain of tooth that's hollow.
> Since, fugitive knight, to no purpose I woo thee,
> Barabbas's fate still pursue and undo thee!'

When the afflicted Altisidora was complaining in the manner you have heard, Don Quixote stood beholding her, and, without answering her a word, turning his face to Sancho, he said:

'By the age of your ancestors, my dear Sancho, I conjure you to tell me the truth: have you taken away the three nightcaps and the garters this enamoured damsel mentions?'

To which Sancho answered:

'The three nightcaps I have; but as to the garters, I know no more of them than the man in the moon.'

The duchess was surprised at the liberty Altisidora took; for though she knew her to be bold, witty, and free, yet not to that degree as to venture upon such freedoms: and, as she knew nothing of this jest, her surprise increased. The duke resolved to carry on the humour, and said:

'I think it does not look well, Sir Knight, that, having received so civil an entertainment in this castle of mine, you should dare to carry off three nightcaps at least, if not my damsel's garters besides: these are indications of a naughty heart, and ill become your character. Return her the garters: if not, I defy you to mortal combat, without being afraid that your knavish enchanters should change or alter my face, as they have done that of Tosilos my lackey, your intended adversary.'

'God forbid,' answered Don Quixote, 'that I should draw my sword against your illustrious person, from whom I have received so many favours. The nightcaps shall be restored, for Sancho says he has them; but for the garters, it is impossible, for I have them not, nor he neither; and if this damsel of yours will search her hiding-holes, I warrant she will find them. I, my lord duke, never was a thief, and think, if heaven forsakes me not, I never shall be one as long as I live. This damsel talks (as she owns) like one in love, which is no fault of mine; and therefore I have no reason to ask hers, or your excellency's pardon, whom I beseech to have a better opinion of me, and, once again, to give me leave to depart.'

'Pray God, Señor Don Quixote,' quoth the duchess, 'send you so good a journey, that we may continually hear good news of your exploits: and God be with you; for the longer you stay the more you increase the fire in the breast of the damsels that behold you; and, as for mine, I will take her to task so severely, that henceforward she shall not dare to transgress with her eyes or her words.'

'Do but hear one word more, O valorous Don Quixote, and I am silent,' quoth Altisidora; 'which is, that I beg your pardon for saying you had stolen my garters; for, on my conscience and soul, I have them on: but I was absent in thought, like the man who looked for his ass while he was upon his back.'

'Did I not tell you?' quoth Sancho; 'I am a rare one at concealing thefts! Had I been that way given, I had many a fair opportunity for it in my government.'

Don Quixote bowed his head, and made his obeisance to the duke and duchess, and to all the spectators, and, turning Rosinante's head, Sancho following upon Dapple, he sallied out of the castle gate, taking the road to Saragossa.

CHAPTER 58

Showing how adventures crowded so fast upon Don Quixote, that they trod upon one another's heels.

DON QUIXOTE, seeing himself in the open field, free, and delivered from the courtship of Altisidora, thought himself in his proper element, and that his spirits were reviving in him to prosecute afresh his scheme of knight-errantry; and, turning to Sancho, he said:

'Liberty, Sancho, is one of the most valuable gifts heaven has bestowed upon men: the treasures which the earth encloses, or the sea covers, are not to be compared with it.

Life may, and ought to be risked for liberty, as well as for honour; and, on the contrary, slavery is the greatest evil that can befall us. I tell you this, Sancho, because you have observed the civil treatment, and plenty, we enjoyed in the castle we have left. In the midst of those seasoned banquets, those icy draughts, I fancied myself starving, because I did not enjoy them with the same freedom I should have done had they been my own. For the obligations of returning benefits and favours received, are ties that obstruct the free agency of the mind. Happy the man, to whom heaven has given a morsel of bread, without laying him under the obligation of thanking any other for it than heaven itself!'

'Notwithstanding all your worship has said,' quoth Sancho, 'it is fit there should be some small acknowledgement on our part for the two hundred crowns in gold, which the duke's steward gave me in a little purse; which, as a cordial, and comfortative, I carry next my heart, against whatever may happen; for we shall not always find castles where we shall be made much of: now and then we must expect to meet with inns, where we may be soundly thrashed.'

In these, and other discourses, our errants, knight and squire, went jogging on, when, having travelled a little above a league, they espied a dozen men, clad like peasants, sitting at dinner upon the grass, and their cloaks spread under them, in a little green meadow. Close by them were certain white sheets, as it seemed, under which something lay concealed. They were raised above the ground, and stretched out at some little distance from each other. Don Quixote approached the eaters, and, first courteously saluting them, asked them what they had under those sheets. One of them answered:

'Sir, under that linen are certain wooden images, designed to be placed upon an altar we are erecting in our village. We carry them covered, that they may not be sullied, and upon our shoulders, that they may not be broken.'

'If you please,' answered Don Quixote, 'I should be glad to see them; for images, that are carried with so much precaution, must doubtless be good ones.'

'Aye, and very good ones, too,' quoth another, 'as their price will testify; for, in truth, there is not one of them but stands us in above fifty ducats. And, to convince your worship of this truth, stay but a little while, and you shall see it with your own eyes.'

And rising up from eating, he went and took off the covering from the first figure, which appeared to be a St. George on horseback, with a serpent coiled up at his feet, and his lance run through his mouth, with all the fierceness it is usually painted with. The whole image seemed to be, as we say, one blaze of gold. Don Quixote seeing it, said:

'This knight was one of the best errants the divine warfare ever had. He was called Don St. George, and was besides a defender of damsels; let us see this other.'

The man uncovered it, and it appeared to be that of St. Martin on horseback, dividing his cloak with the poor man. And scarcely had Don Quixote seen it, when he said:

'This knight also was one of the Christian adventurers; and I take it he was more liberal than valiant, as you may perceive, Sancho, by his dividing his cloak with the beggar, and giving him half of it: and doubtless it must have been then winter; otherwise he would have given it him all, so great was his charity.'

'That was not the reason,' quoth Sancho: 'but he had a mind to keep to the proverb, which says: "What to give, and what to keep, requires an understanding deep."'

Don Quixote smiled, and desired another sheet might be taken off, underneath which was discovered the image of the patron of Spain on horseback, his sword all bloody, trampling on Moors, and treading upon heads. And, at sight of it, Don Quixote said:

'Aye, marry, this is a knight indeed, one of Christ's own squadron. He is called Don St. James the Moor-killer, one of the most valiant saints and knights the world had formerly, or heaven has now.'

Then they removed another sheet, which covered St. Paul falling from his horse, with all the circumstances that are usually drawn in the picture of his conversion. When Don Quixote saw it represented in so lively a manner, that one would almost say Christ was speaking to him, and St. Paul answering, he said:

'This was the greatest enemy the church of God our Lord had in his time, and the greatest defender it will ever have; a knight-errant in his life, and a steadfast saint in his death; an unwearied labourer in the Lord's vineyard; a teacher of the Gentiles; whose school was heaven, and whose professor and master Jesus Christ Himself.'

There were no more images, and so Don Quixote bade them cover them up again, and said:

'I take it for a good omen, brethren, to have seen what I have seen: for these saints and knights professed what I profess, which is, the exercise of arms: the only difference between them and me is, that they were saints, and fought after a heavenly manner, and I am a sinner, and fight after an earthly manner. They conquered heaven by force of arms (for heaven suffers violence*), and I hitherto cannot tell what I conquer by force of my sufferings. But, could my Dulcinea del Toboso get out of hers, my condition being bettered, and my understanding directed aright, I might perhaps take a better course than I do.'

'God hear him,' quoth Sancho straight, 'and let sin be deaf!'

The men wondered, as well at the figure as at the words of Don Quixote, without understanding half what he meant by them. They finished their repast, packed up their images, and, taking their leave of Don Quixote, pursued their journey.

Sancho remained as much in admiration at his master's knowledge, as if he had never known him before, thinking there was not an history nor event in the world, which he had not at his fingers' ends, and fastened down to his memory, and he said:

'Truly, master of mine, if this that has happened to us to-day may be called an adventure, it has been one of the softest and sweetest that has befallen us in the whole course of our peregrinations; we are got clear of it without blows, or any heart-breaking: we have neither laid our hands to our swords, nor beaten the earth with our bodies, nor are we starved with hunger. Blessed be God for letting me see this with my own eyes!'

'You say well, Sancho,' quoth Don Quixote; 'but you must consider, that all times are not alike, nor do they take the same course; and what the vulgar commonly call omens, though not founded upon any natural reason, a discreet man will yet look upon as lucky encounters. One of these superstitious rises and goes abroad early in the morning, and, meeting with a friar of the Order of the blessed St. Francis, turns his back as if he had met a griffin, and goes home again. Another, a Mendoza, spills the salt upon the table, and presently melancholy overspreads his heart, as if nature was bound to show signs of ensuing mischances by such trivial accidents as the aforementioned. The wise man and good Christian ought not to pry too curiously into the counsels of heaven. Scipio, arriving in Africa, stumbled at jumping ashore; his soldiers took it for an ill omen; but he, embracing the ground, said: "Africa, thou canst not escape me, for I have thee fast between my arms." So that, Sancho, the meeting with these images has been a most happy encounter to me.'

'I verily believe it,' answered Sancho, 'and I should be glad your worship would inform me, why the Spaniards, when they join battle, invoke that St. James the Moor-killer, and cry, Santiago, and close, Spain! Is Spain, peradventure, so open, as to want closing? or what ceremony is this?'

'You are a very child, Sancho,' answered Don Quixote; 'for, take notice, God gave this great knight of the red cross to Spain for its patron and protector, especially in those rigorous conflicts the Spaniards have had with the Moors; and therefore they pray to, and invoke him as their defender in all the battles they fight; and they have frequently seen him, visibly overthrowing, trampling down, destroying, and slaughtering, the Hagarene squadrons;* and of this I could produce many examples recorded in the true Spanish histories.'

Sancho changed the discourse, and said to his master:

'I am amazed, sir, at the assurance of Altisidora, the duchess's waiting-woman. He they call Love must surely have wounded her sorely, and pierced her through and through. They say, he is a boy, who, though blear-eyed, or, to say better, without sight, if he takes aim at any heart, how small soever, he hits and pierces it through and through with his arrows. I have also heard say, that the darts of Love are blunted and rendered pointless by the modesty and reserve of maidens; but, in this same Altisidora, methinks, they are rather whetted than blunted.'

'Look you, Sancho,' quoth Don Quixote, 'Love regards no respects, nor observes any rules of reason in his proceedings, and is of the same nature with death, which assaults the stately palaces of kings, as well as the lowly cottages of shepherds; and, when he takes entire possession of a soul, the first thing he does, is, to divest it of fear and shame; and thus Altisidora, being without both, made an open declaration of her desires, which produced rather confusion, than compassion, in my breast.'

'Notorious cruelty!' quoth Sancho; 'unheard-of ingratitude! I dare say for myself, that the least amorous hint of hers would have subdued me, and made me her vassal. O whoreson! what a heart of marble, what bowels of brass, and what a soul of plaster of paris! But I cannot conceive what it is this damsel saw in your worship, that subdued and captivated her to that degree. What finery, what gallantry, what gaiety, what face; which of these jointly, or severally, made her fall in love with you? for, in truth, I have often surveyed your worship, from the tip of your toe to the top of your head, and I see in you more things to cause affright than love. And, having also heard say, that beauty is the first and principal thing that enamours, your worship having none at all, I wonder what the poor thing was in love with.'

'Look you, Sancho,' answered Don Quixote, 'there are two sorts of beauty, the one of the mind, the other of the body. That of the mind shines and discovers itself in the understanding, in modesty, good behaviour, liberality, and good breeding: and all these qualities may subsist and be found in an ill-favoured man; and when the aim is at this beauty, and not at that of the body, it produces love with impetuosity and advantage. I know very well, Sancho, that I am not handsome, but I know also that I am not deformed; and an honest man, who is not a monster, may be beloved, provided he has the qualities of the mind I have mentioned.'

Amidst these discourses they entered into a wood, not far out of the road; and on a sudden Don Quixote found himself entangled in some nets of green thread, which hung from one tree to another; and, not being able to imagine what it might be, he said to Sancho:

'The business of these nets, Sancho, must, I think, be one of the newest adventures imaginable: let me die, if the enchanters, who persecute me, have not a mind to entangle me in them, and stop my journey, by way of revenge for the rigorous treatment Altisidora received from me. But I would have them to know, that, though these nets, as they are made of thread, were made of the hardest diamonds, or stronger than that, in which the jealous god of blacksmiths* entangled Venus and Mars, I would break them as easily as if they were made of bulrushes or yarn.'

And, as he was going to pass forward, and break through all, unexpectedly, from among some trees, two most beautiful shepherdesses presented themselves before him: at least they were clad like shepherdesses, excepting that their waistcoats and petticoats were of fine brocade. Their habits were of rich gold tabby; their hair, which for brightness might come in competition with the rays of the sun, hanging loose about their shoulders, and their heads crowned with garlands of green laurel and red flower-gentles interwoven. Their age seemed to be, not under fifteen, nor above eighteen. This was a sight which amazed Sancho, surprised Don Quixote, made the sun stop in his career to behold them, and held them all in marvellous silence. At length one of the shepherdesses spoke, and said to Don Quixote:

'Stop, Señor Cavalier, and break not the nets, placed here, not for your hurt, but our diversion: and because I know you will ask us, why they are spread, and who we are, I will tell you in a few words. In a town about two leagues off, where there are several people of quality, and a great many gentlemen, and those rich, it was agreed among several friends and relations, that their sons, wives, and daughters, neighbours, friends, and relations, should all come to make merry in this place, which is one of the pleasantest in these parts, forming among ourselves a new pastoral Arcadia, and dressing ourselves, the maidens like shepherdesses, and the young men like shepherds. We have got by heart two eclogues, one of the famous poet Garcillaso, and the other of the most excellent Camoens, in his own Portuguese tongue, which we have not yet acted. Yesterday was the first day of our coming hither: we have some field-tents pitched among the trees, on the margin of a copious stream, which spreads fertility over all these meadows. Last night we hung our nets upon these trees, to deceive the simple little birds which should come at the noise we make, and be caught in them. If, sir, you please to be our guest, you shall be entertained generously and courteously; for into this place neither sorrow nor melancholy enter.'

She held her peace, and said no more. To which Don Quixote answered:

'Assuredly, fairest lady, Actaeon was not in greater surprise and amazement, when unawares he saw Diana bathing herself in the water, than I have been in at beholding your beauty. I applaud the scheme of your diversions, and thank you for your kind offers; and, if I can do you any service, you may lay your commands upon me, in full assurance of being obeyed; for my profession is no other than to show myself grateful, and a benefactor to all sorts of people, especially to those of the rank your presence denotes you to be of: and should these nets, which probably take up but a small space, occupy the whole globe of the earth, I would seek out new worlds, to pass through, rather than hazard the breaking them. And, that you may afford some credit to this exaggeration of mine, behold, he who makes you this promise, is no less than Don Quixote de la Mancha, if perchance this name has ever reached your ears.'

'Ah! friend of my soul!' quoth then the other young shepherd-ess, 'what good fortune is this that has befallen us! See you this gentleman here before us? I assure you, he is the most valiant, the most enamoured, the most complaisant knight in the world, unless a history, which goes about of him in print, and which I have read, lies, and deceives us. I will lay a wager, this honest man, who comes with him, is that very Sancho Panza, his squire, whose pleasantries none can equal.'

'That is true,' quoth Sancho; 'I am that same jocular person, and that squire you say; and this gentleman is my master, the very Don Quixote de la Mancha aforesaid and historified.'

'Ah!' quoth the other, 'my dear, let us entreat him to stay; for our fathers and brothers will be infinitely pleased to have him here; for I have heard the same things of his valour and wit that you tell me; and particularly they say, he is the most constant and most faithful lover in the world; and that his mistress is one Dulcinea del Toboso, who bears away the palm from all the beauties in Spain.'

'And with good reason,' quoth Don Quixote, 'unless your matchless beauty brings it into question. But weary not yourselves, ladies, in endeavouring to detain me; for the precise obligations of my profession will suffer me to rest nowhere.'

By this time there came up to where the four stood, a brother of one of the young shepherdesses: he was also in a shepherd's dress, answerable in richness and gallantry to theirs. They told him, that the person he saw was the valorous Don Quixote de la Mancha, and the other, Sancho his squire, of whom he had some knowledge, by having read their history. The gallant shepherd saluted him, and desired him to come with him to the tents. Don Quixote could not refuse, and therefore went with him. Then the nets were drawn, and filled with a variety of little birds, who, deceived by the colour of the nets, fell into the very danger they endeavoured to fly from.

Above thirty persons, genteelly dressed in pastoral habits, were assembled together in that place, and presently were made acquainted who Don Quixote and his squire were; which was no small satisfaction to them, being already no strangers to his history. They hastened to the tents, where they found the table spread, rich, plentiful, and neat. They honoured Don Quixote with placing him at the upper end. They all gazed at him, and admired at the sight. Finally, the cloth being taken away, Don Quixote, with great gravity, raised his voice, and said:

'Of all the grievous sins men commit, though some say pride, I say, ingratitude is the worst, adhering to the common opinion, that hell is full of the ungrateful. This sin I have endeavoured to avoid, as much as I possibly could, ever since I came to the use of reason; and, if I cannot repay the good offices done me with the like, I place in their stead the desire of doing them; and when this is not enough, I publish them; for he who tells and publishes the good deeds done him, would return them in kind if he could; for generally the receivers are inferior to the givers, and God is therefore above all, because He is bountiful above all. But though the gifts of men are infinitely disproportionate to those of God, gratitude in some measure supplies their narrowness and defects.

'I then, being grateful for the civility offered me here, but restrained by the narrow limits of my ability from making a suitable return, offer what I can, and what is in my power; and therefore, I say, I will maintain, for two whole days, in the middle of this the king's highway, which leads to Saragossa, that these lady shepherdesses in disguise, are the most beautiful and most courteous damsels in the world, excepting only the peerless Dulcinea del Toboso, the sole mistress of my thoughts; without offence to any that hear me be it spoken.'

Sancho, who had been listening to him with great attention, hearing this, said, with a loud voice:

'Is it possible there should be any persons in the world, who presume to say, and swear, that this master of mine is a madman? Speak, gentlemen shepherds; is there a country vicar, though ever so discreet, or ever so good a scholar, who can say all that my master has said? Is there a knight-errant, though ever so renowned for valour, who can offer what my master has now offered?'

Don Quixote turned to Sancho, and, with a wrathful countenance, said:

'Is it possible, O Sancho, there is anybody upon the globe, who will say you are not an idiot, lined with the same, and edged with I know not what of mischievous and knavish? Who gave you authority to meddle with what belongs to me, and to call in question my folly or discretion? Hold your peace, and make no reply; but go and saddle Rosinante, if he be unsaddled, and let us go and put my offer in execution, for, considering how much I am in the right, you may conclude all those who shall contradict me, already conquered.'

Then, with great fury, and tokens of indignation, he rose from his seat, leaving the company in admiration, and in doubt, whether they should reckon him a madman or a man of sense. In short, they would have persuaded him not to put himself upon such a trial, since they were satisfied of his grateful nature, and wanted no other proofs of his valour, than those related in the history of his exploits. But for all that, Don Quixote persisted in his design, and, being mounted upon Rosinante, bracing his shield, and taking his lance, he planted himself in the middle of the highway, which was not far from the verdant meadow. Sancho followed upon his Dapple, with all the pastoral company, being desirous to see what would be the event of this arrogant and unheard-of challenge.

Don Quixote, being posted, as I have said, in the middle of the road, wounded the air with such words as these:

'O ye passengers, travellers, knights, squires, people on foot and on horseback, who now pass this way, or are to pass in these two days following! know, that Don Quixote de la Mancha, knight-errant, is posted here, ready to maintain, that the nymphs who inhabit these meadows and groves, exceed all the world in beauty and courtesy, excepting only the mistress of my soul, Dulcinea del Toboso; and let him who is of a contrary opinion, come, for here I stand, ready to receive him.'

Twice he repeated the same words, and twice they were not heard by any adventurer. But fortune, which was disposing his affairs from good to better, so ordered it, that soon after they discovered a great many men on horseback, and several of them with lances in their hands, all trooping in a cluster, and in great haste. Scarcely had they who were with Don Quixote seen them, when they turned their backs, and got far enough out of the way, fearing, if they stayed, they might be exposed to some danger. Don Quixote alone, with an intrepid heart, stood firm, and Sancho Panza screened himself with Rosinante's buttocks.

The troop of lancemen came up, and one of the foremost began to cry aloud to Don Quixote:

'Get out of the way, devil of a man, lest these bulls trample you to pieces!'

'Rascals,' replied Don Quixote, 'I value not your bulls, though they were the fiercest that Jarama* ever bred upon its banks! confess, ye scoundrels, [without delay], that what I have here proclaimed is true! if not, I challenge ye to battle.'

The herdsmen had no time to answer, nor Don Quixote to get out of the way, if he would; and so the whole herd of fierce bulls and tame kine, with the multitude of herdsmen, and others, who were driving them to a certain town, where they were to be baited in a day or two, ran over Don Quixote and over Sancho, Rosinante, and Dapple, leaving them all sprawling and rolling on the ground. Sancho remained bruised, Don Quixote astonished, Dapple battered, and Rosinante not perfectly sound. But at length they all got up, and Don Quixote, in a great hurry, stumbling here, and falling there, began to run after the herd, crying aloud:

'Hold, stop, ye scoundrels! for a single knight defies you all, who is not of the disposition or opinion of those who say, "Make a bridge of silver for a flying enemy."'

But the hasty runners stopped not the more for this, and made no more account of his menaces than of last year's clouds. Weariness stopped Don Quixote, and, more enraged than revenged, he sat down in the road, expecting the coming up of Sancho, Rosinante, and Dapple. They came up; master and man mounted again, and, without turning back to take their leaves of the feigned or counterfeit Arcadia, and with more shame than satisfaction, pursued their journey.

CHAPTER 59

Wherein is related an extraordinary accident, which befell Don Quixote, and which may pass for an adventure.

THE dust and weariness Don Quixote and Sancho underwent through the rude encounter of the bulls, were relieved by a clear and limpid fountain they met with in a cool grove; on the brink whereof, leaving Dapple and Rosinante free, without halter or bridle, the way-beaten couple, master and man, sat them down. Sancho had recourse to the cupboard of his wallet, and drew out what he was wont to call his grub.* He rinsed his mouth, and Don Quixote washed his face; with which refreshment they recovered their fainting spirits. Don Quixote would eat nothing, out of pure chagrin, nor durst Sancho touch the victuals, out of pure good manners, expecting his master should first be his taster. But seeing him so carried away by his imaginations, as to forget to put a bit in his mouth, he said nothing, but breaking through all kind of ceremony, began to stuff his hungry maw with the bread and cheese before him.

'Eat, friend Sancho,' said Don Quixote, 'and support life, which is of more importance to you than to me, and leave me to die by the hands of my reflections, and by the force of my misfortunes. I, Sancho, was born to live dying, and you to die eating; and, to show you that I speak the truth, consider me printed in histories, renowned in arms, courteous in my actions, respected by princes, courted by damsels; and, after all, when I expected palms, triumphs, and crowns, earned and merited by my valorous exploits, this morning have I seen myself trod upon, kicked, and bruised under the feet of filthy and impure beasts. This reflection sets my teeth on edge, stupefies my grinders, benumbs my hands, and quite takes away my appetite; so that I intend to suffer myself to die with hunger, the cruellest of all deaths.'

'At this rate,' quoth Sancho (chewing all the while apace), 'your worship will not approve of the proverb, which says: "Let Martha die, but die with her belly full." At least, I do not intend to kill myself, but rather to imitate the shoemaker, who pulls the leather with his teeth, till he stretches it to what he would have it. I will stretch my life by eating, till it reaches the end heaven has allotted it; and let me tell you, sir, there is no greater madness, than to despair as you do: believe me, and, after you have eaten, try to sleep a little upon the green mattress of this grass, and you will see, when you awake, you will find yourself much eased.'

Don Quixote complied, thinking Sancho reasoned more like a philosopher than a fool; and he said:

'If, O Sancho, you would now do for me, what I am going to tell you, my comforts would be more certain, and my sorrows not so great; and it is this, that while I, in pursuance of your advice, am sleeping, you will step a little aside from hence, and with the reins of Rosinante's bridle, turning up your flesh to the sky, give yourself three or four hundred lashes, in part of the three thousand and odd, you are bound to give yourself for the disenchantment of Dulcinea; for it is a great pity the poor lady should continue under enchantment through your carelessness and neglect.'

'There is a great deal to be said as to that,' quoth Sancho: 'for the present, let us both sleep, and afterwards God knows what may happen. Pray, consider, sir, that this same whipping one's self in cold blood is a cruel thing, and more so, when the lashes light upon a body ill sustained and worse fed. Let my lady Dulcinea have patience; for, when she least thinks of it, she shall see me pinked like a sieve by dint of stripes; and, Until death all is life: I mean I am still alive, together with the desire of fulfilling my promise.'

Don Quixote thanked him, ate a little, and Sancho much; and both of them addressed themselves to sleep, leaving Rosinante and Dapple, those inseparable companions and friends, at their own discretion, and without any control, to feed upon the plenty of grass, with which that meadow abounded.

They awoke somewhat of the latest; they mounted again, and pursued their journey, hastening to reach an inn, which seemed to be about a league off: I say an inn, because Don Quixote called it so, contrary to his custom of calling all inns castles. They arrived at it, and demanded of the host if he had any lodging. He answered, he had, with all the conveniences and entertainment that was to be found even in Saragossa. They alighted, and Sancho secured his travelling cupboard in a chamber, of which the landlord gave him the key. He took the beasts to the stable, and gave them their allowance, and went to see what commands Don Quixote, who was sat down upon a stone bench, had for him, giving particular thanks to heaven, that this inn had not been taken by his master for a castle.

Suppertime came: they betook them to their chamber. Sancho asked the host, what they had to give them for supper. The host answered, his mouth should be measured, and he might call for whatever he pleased; for the inn was provided, as far as birds of the air, fowls of the earth, and fishes of the sea could go.

'There is no need of quite so much,' answered Sancho: roast us but a couple of chickens, and we shall have enough: for my master is of a nice stomach, and I am no glutton.'

The host replied, he had no chickens, for the kites had devoured them.

'Then order a pullet, señor host,' quoth Sancho, 'to be roasted; but see that it be tender.'

'A pullet? my father!' answered the host: 'truly, truly, I sent above fifty yesterday to the city to be sold: but excepting pullets, ask for whatever you will.'

'If it be so,' quoth Sancho, 'veal or kid cannot be wanting.'

'There is none in the house at present,' answered the host; 'for it is all made an end of: but next week there will be enough and to spare.'

'We are much the nearer for that,' answered Sancho: 'I will lay a wager, all these deficiencies will be made up with a superabundance of bacon and eggs.'

'Before God,' answered the host, 'my guest has an admirable guess within him: I told him I had neither pullets nor hens, and he would have me have eggs: talk of other delicacies, but ask no more for hens.'

'Body of me! let us come to something,' quoth Sancho: 'tell me, in short, what you have, and lay aside your flourishings, master host.'

'Then,' quoth the innkeeper, 'what I really and truly have, is a pair of cow-heels, that look like calves-feet, or a pair of calves-feet, that look like cow-heel: they are stewed with peas, onions, and bacon, and at this very minute are crying, "Come eat me, come eat me."'

'I mark them for my own, from this moment,' quoth Sancho, 'and let nobody touch them; for I will pay more for them than another shall, because I could wish for nothing that I like better; and I care not a fig what heels they are, so they are not hoofs.'

'Nobody shall touch them,' quoth the host; 'for some other guests in the house, out of pure gentility, bring their own cook, their caterer, and their provisions with them.'

'If gentility be the business,' quoth Sancho, 'nobody is more a gentleman than my master: but the calling he is of allows of no catering nor butlering: alas! we clap us down in the midst of a green field, and fill our bellies with acorns, or medlars.'

This discourse Sancho held with the innkeeper, Sancho not caring to answer him any further; for he had already asked him of what calling or employment his master was.

Suppertime being come, Don Quixote withdrew to his chamber: the host brought the fleshpot just as it was, and fairly set himself down to supper.

It seems, in the next room to that where Don Quixote was, and divided only by a partition of lath, Don Quixote heard somebody say:

'By your life, Señor Don Jerónimo, while supper is getting ready, let us read another chapter of the *Second Part of Don Quixote de la Mancha.*'*

Scarcely had Don Quixote heard himself named, when up he stood, and, with an attentive ear, listened to their discourse, and heard the aforesaid Don Jerónimo answer:

'Why, Señor Don John, would you have us read such absurdities? for he who has read the first part of the *History of Don Quixote de la Mancha*, cannot possibly be pleased with reading the second.'

'But for all that,' said Don John, 'it will not be amiss to read it; for there is no book so bad but it has something good in it. What displeases me most in it is, that the author describes Don Quixote as no longer in love with Dulcinea del Toboso.'

Which Don Quixote overhearing, full of wrath and indignation, he raised his voice, and said:

'Whoever shall say, that Don Quixote de la Mancha has forgotten, or can forget, Dulcinea del Toboso, I will make him know, with equal arms, that he is very wide of the truth: for the peerless Dulcinea can neither be forgotten, nor is Don Quixote capable of forgetting: his motto is constancy, and his profession is to preserve it with sweetness, and without doing himself any violence.'

'Who is it that answers us?' replied one in the other room.

'Who should it be,' quoth Sancho, 'but Don Quixote de la Mancha himself, who will make good all he says, and all he shall say? for, a good paymaster is in pain for no pawn.'

Scarcely had Sancho said this, when into the room came two gentlemen; for such they seemed to be: and one of them, throwing his arms about Don Quixote's neck, said:

'Your presence can neither belie your name, nor your name do otherwise than credit your presence. Doubtless, señor, you are the true Don Quixote de la Mancha, the north and morning star of knight-errantry, maugre and in despite of him, who has endeavoured to usurp your name, and annihilate your exploits, as the author of this book I here give you has done.'

And putting a book that his companion brought, into Don Quixote's hands, he took it, and, without answering a word, began to turn over the leaves, and presently after returned it, saying:

'In the little I have seen, I have found three things in this author, that deserve reprehension. The first is, some words I have read in the preface:* the next, that the language is Aragonian; for he sometimes writes without articles:* and the third, which chiefly convicts him of ignorance, is, that he errs, and deviates from the truth, in a principal point of the history. For here he says, that the wife of my squire Sancho Panza is called Mari Gutierrez, whereas that is not her name, but Teresa Panza;* and he who errs in so principal a point, may very well be supposed to be mistaken in the rest of the history.'

Here Sancho said:

'Prettily done indeed, of this same historian! he must be well informed, truly, of our adventures, since he calls Teresa Panza my wife, Mari Gutierrez. Take the book again, sir, and see whether I am in it, and whether he has changed my name.'

'By what I have heard you speak, friend,' quoth Don Jerónimo, 'without doubt, you are Sancho Panza, Don Quixote's squire.'

'I am so,' answered Sancho, 'and value myself upon it.'

'In faith then,' said the gentleman, 'this modern author does not treat you with that decency which seems agreeable to your person. He describes you a glutton, and a simpleton, and not at all pleasant, and a quite different Sancho from him described in the first part of your master's history.'

'God forgive him,' quoth Sancho; 'he might have let me alone in my corner, without remembering me at all: for, Let him who knows the instrument play on it; and, St. Peter is nowhere so well as at Rome.'

The two gentlemen desired of Don Quixote, that he would step to their chamber, and sup with them; for they knew very well, there was nothing to be had in that inn, fit for his entertainment. Don Quixote, who was always courteous, condescended to their request, and supped with them. Sancho stayed behind with the fleshpot, *cum mero mixto imperio*;* he placed himself at the head of the table, and by him sat down the innkeeper, as fond of the calves-feet, or cow-heels, as he.

While they were at supper, Don John asked Don Quixote, what news he had of the lady Dulcinea del Toboso; whether she was married; whether yet brought to bed, or with child; or if, continuing a maiden, she still remembered, with the reserve of her modesty and good decorum, the amorous inclinations of Señor Don Quixote. To which our knight replied:

'Dulcinea is still a maiden, and my inclinations more constant than ever; our correspondence upon the old foot, and her beauty transformed into the visage of a coarse country wench.'

Then he recounted every particular of the enchantment of the lady Dulcinea, and what had befallen him in Montesinos' cave, with the directions the sage Merlin had given him for her disenchantment, namely by Sancho's lashes. Great was the satisfaction the two gentlemen received to hear Don Quixote relate the strange adventures of his history, admiring equally at his extravagances, and at his elegant manner of telling them. One while they held him for a wise man, then for a fool; nor could they determine what degree to assign him between discretion and folly.

Sancho made an end of supper, and, leaving the innkeeper fuddled, went to the chamber where his master was, and, at entering, he said:

'May I die, gentlemen, if the author of this book you have got, has a mind he and I should eat a good meal together; I wish, since, as you say, he calls me glutton, he may not call me drunkard too.'

'Aye, marry, does he,' quoth Don Jerónimo; 'but I do not remember after what manner; though I know the expressions carried but an ill sound, and were false into the bargain, as I see plainly by the countenance of honest Sancho here present.'

'Believe me, gentlemen,' quoth Sancho, 'that the Sancho and Don Quixote of that history are not the same with those of the book composed by Cid Hamet Ben Engeli, who are us; my master, valiant, discreet, and in love; and I, simple and pleasant, and neither a glutton nor a drunkard.'

'I believe it,' quoth Don John, 'and if it were possible, it should be ordered, that none should dare to treat of matters relating to Don Quixote, but only Cid Hamet, his first author; in like manner as Alexander commanded, that none should dare to draw his picture but Apelles.'

'Draw me who will,' said Don Quixote; 'but let him not abuse me: for patience is apt to fail, when it is overladen with injuries.'

'None,' quoth Don John, 'can be offered Señor Don Quixote, that he cannot revenge, unless he wards it off with the buckler of his patience, which, in my opinion, is strong and great.'

In these, and in the like discourses, they spent great part of the night; and though Don John had a mind Don Quixote should read more of the book, to see what it treated of, he could not be prevailed upon, saying, he deemed it as read, and pronounced it as foolish: besides, he was unwilling its author should have the pleasure of thinking he had read it, if peradventure he might come to hear he had had it in his hands; for the thoughts, and much more the eyes, ought to be turned from everything filthy and obscene.

They asked him, which way he intended to bend his course? He answered to Saragossa, to be present at the jousts for the suit of armour, which are held every year in that city. Don John told him, how the new history related, that Don Quixote, whoever he was, had been there at the running of the ring, and that the description thereof was defective in the contrivance, mean and low in the style, miserably poor in devices, and rich only in simplicities.

'For that very reason,' answered Don Quixote, 'I will not set a foot in Saragossa, and so I will expose to the world, the falsity of this modern historiographer, and all people will plainly perceive, I am not the Don Quixote he speaks of.'

'You will do very well,' said Don Jerónimo, 'and there are to be other jousts at Barcelona, where Señor Don Quixote may display his valour.'

'It is my intention so to do,' quoth Don Quixote, 'and, gentlemen, be pleased to give me leave (for it is time) to go to bed, and place me among the number of your best friends and faithful servants.'

'And me too,' quoth Sancho; 'perhaps I may be good for something.'

Having thus taken leave of one another, Don Quixote and Sancho retired to their chamber, leaving Don John and Don Jerónimo in admiration at the mixture he had discovered of wit and madness: and they verily believed these were the true Don Quixote and Sancho, and not those described by the Aragonese author. Don Quixote got up very early, and, tapping at the partition of the other room, he again bade his new friends adieu: Sancho paid the innkeeper most magnificently, and advised him to brag less of the provision of his inn, or to provide it better.

CHAPTER 60

Of what befell Don Quixote in his way to Barcelona.

THE morning was cool, and the day promised to be so too, when Don Quixote left the inn, first informing himself which was the directest road to Barcelona, without touching at Saragossa; so great was his desire to give the lie to that new historian, who, it was said, had abused him so much.

Now it happened, that, in above six days, nothing fell out worth setting down in writing: at the end of which, going out of the road, night overtook them among some shady oaks or cork-trees; for, in this, Cid Hamet does not observe that punctuality he is wont to do in other matters. Master and man alighted from their beasts, and, seating themselves at the foot of the trees, Sancho, who had had his afternoon's collation that day, entered abruptly the gates of sleep. But Don Quixote, whose imaginations, much more than hunger, kept him waking, could not close his eyes: on the contrary, he was hurried in thought to and from a thousand places: now he fancied himself in Montesinos' cave; now, that he saw Dulcinea, transformed into a country wench, mount upon her ass at a spring; the next moment, that he was hearing the words of the sage Merlin, declaring to him the conditions to be observed, and the dispatch necessary for the disenchantment of Dulcinea. He was ready to run mad, to see the carelessness and little charity of his squire Sancho, who, as he believed, had given himself five lashes only; a number poor and disproportionate to the infinite still behind: and hence he conceived so much chagrin and indignation, that he spoke thus to himself:

'If Alexander the Great cut the Gordian knot, saying, to cut is the same as to untie, and became nevertheless, universal lord of all Asia, the same, neither more nor less, may happen

now, in the disenchantment of Dulcinea, if I should whip
Sancho whether he will or no: for, if the condition of this
remedy consists in Sancho's receiving upwards of three thousand lashes, what is it to me whether he gives them himself,
or somebody else for him, since the essence lies in his
receiving them, come they from what hand they will?'

With this conceit, he approached Sancho, having first taken
Rosinante's reins, and adjusted them so that he might lash
him with them, and began to untruss his points; though it is
generally thought that he had none but that before, which
kept up his breeches. But no sooner had he begun, when
Sancho awoke, and said:

'What is the matter? who is it that touches and untrusses
me?'

'It is I,' answered Don Quixote, 'who come to supply your
defects, and to remedy my own troubles; I come to whip
you, Sancho, and to discharge, at least in part, the debt you
stand engaged for. Dulcinea is perishing; you live unconcerned; I am dying with desire; and therefore untruss of your
own accord, for I mean to give you, in this solitude, at least
two thousand lashes.'

'Not so,' quoth Sancho; 'pray, be quiet, or, by the living
God, the deaf shall hear us. The lashes I stand engaged for
must be voluntary, and not upon compulsion; and, at present,
I have no inclination to whip myself: let it suffice, that I give
your worship my word to flog and flay myself, when I have
a disposition to it.'

'There is no leaving it to your courtesy, Sancho,' said Don
Quixote; 'for you are hard-hearted, and, though a peasant, of
very tender flesh.'

Then he struggled with Sancho, and endeavoured to untruss him. Which Sancho Panza perceiving, he got upon his
legs, and, closing with his master, he flung his arms about
him, and, tripping up his heels, he laid him flat on his back,
and, setting his right knee upon his breast, with his hands
he held both his master's so fast, that he could neither stir
nor breathe. Don Quixote said to him:

'How traitor! do you rebel against your master and natural
lord? Do you lift up your hand against him who feeds you?'

'I neither make, nor unmake kings,' answered Sancho: 'I only assist myself, who am my own lord.* If your worship will promise me to be quiet, and not meddle with whipping me for the present, I will let you go free, and at your liberty: if not, here thou diest, traitor, enemy to Doña Sancha.'*

Don Quixote promised him he would, and swore, by the life of his thoughts, he would not touch a hair of his garment, and would leave the whipping himself entirely to his own choice and free will, whenever he was so disposed.

Sancho got up, and went aside some little distance from thence; and, leaning against a tree, he felt something touch his head, and, lifting up his hands, he felt a couple of feet dangling, with hose and shoes. He fell a trembling with fear; he went to another tree, and the like befell him again: he called out to Don Quixote for help. Don Quixote, going to him, asked him what the matter was, and what he was frightened at. Sancho answered, that all those trees were full of men's legs and feet. Don Quixote felt them, and immediately guessed what it was, and said to Sancho:

'You need not be afraid; for what you feel, without seeing, are, doubtless, the feet and legs of some robbers and banditti, who are hanged upon these trees: for here the officers of justice hang them, when they can catch them, by twenties and thirties at a time, in clusters: whence I guess I am not far from Barcelona.'*

And, in truth, it was as he imagined.

And now, the day breaking, they lifted up their eyes, and perceived, that the clusters hanging on those trees were so many bodies of banditti: and, if the dead had scared them, no less were they terrified by above forty living banditti, who surrounded them unawares, bidding them, in the Catalan tongue, be quiet, and stand still, till their captain came. Don Quixote was on foot, his horse unbridled, his lance leaning against a tree, and, in short, defenceless; and therefore he thought it best to cross his hands, and hang his head, reserving himself for a better opportunity and conjecture. The robbers fell to rifling Dapple, and stripping him of everything he carried in the wallet or the pillion; and it fell out luckily for Sancho, that he had secured the crowns given him by the duke, and those he brought from home, in a belt about his middle. But, for all that, these good folks would have searched and examined him, even to what lay hidden between the skin* and the flesh, had not their captain arrived just in the nick.

He seemed to be about thirty-four years of age, robust, above the middle size, of a grave aspect, and a brown complexion. He was mounted upon a puissant steed, clad in a coat of mail, and armed with two case of pistols, or firelocks. He saw that his squires (for so they call men of that vocation) were going to plunder Sancho Panza: he commanded them to forbear, and was instantly obeyed, and so the girdle escaped. He wondered to see a lance standing against a tree, a target on the ground, and Don Quixote in armour and pensive, with the most sad and melancholy countenance, that sadness itself could frame. He went up to him, and said:

'Be not so dejected, good sir; for you are not fallen into the hands of a cruel Osiris,* but into those of Roque Guinart,* who is more compassionate than cruel.'

'My dejection,' answered Don Quixote, 'is not upon account of my having fallen into your hands, O valorous Roque, whose renown no bounds on earth can limit, but for being so careless, that your soldiers surprised me, my horse unbridled; whereas I am bound, by the order of knight-errantry, which I profess, to be continually upon the watch, and at all hours, my own sentinel: for, let me tell you, illustrious Roque, had they found me on horseback, with my lance and my target, it had not been very easy for them to have made me surrender: for I am Don Quixote de la Mancha, he, of whose exploits the whole globe is full.'

Roque Guinart presently perceived, that Don Quixote's infirmity had in it more of madness than valour; and, though he had sometimes heard him spoken of, he never took what was published of him for truth, nor could he persuade himself, that such a humour could reign in the heart of man: so that he was extremely glad he had met with him, to be convinced near at hand of the truth of what he heard at a distance; and therefore he said to him:

'Be not concerned, valorous knight, nor look upon this accident as a piece of sinister fortune; for it may chance, among these turnings and windings, that your crooked lot may be set to rights; for heaven, by strange unheard-of (and by men unimagined) ways, raises those that are fallen, and enriches those that are poor.'

Don Quixote was just going to return him thanks, when they heard behind them a noise like that of a troop of horses; but it was occasioned by one only, upon which came, riding full speed, a youth,* seemingly about twenty years of age, clad in green damask with a gold-lace trimming, trousers, and a loose coat; his hat cocked in the Walloon fashion, with straight waxed boots, and his spurs, dagger, and sword gilt: a small carbine in his hand, and a brace of pistols by his side. Roque turned about his head at the noise, and saw this handsome figure, which, at coming up to him, said:

'In quest of you I come, O valorous Roque, hoping to find in you, if not a remedy, at least some alleviation of my misfortune; and, not to keep you in suspense, because I perceive you do not know me, I will tell you who I am. I am Claudia Jerónima, daughter of Simon Forte, your singular friend, and particular enemy to Clauquel Torrellas, who is also yours, being of the contrary faction: and you know, that this Torrellas has a son, called Don Vicente de Torrellas, or at least was called so not two hours ago. He then (to shorten the story of my misfortune, I will tell you in a few words what he has brought upon me) he, I say, saw me, and courted me: I hearkened to him, and fell in love with him, unknown to my father: for there is no woman, be she never so retired, or never so reserved, but has time enough to effect and put in execution her unruly desires. In short, he promised to be my spouse, and I gave him my word to be his, without proceeding any further. Yesterday I was informed, that, forgetting his obligations to me, he had contracted himself to another, and, this morning, was going to be married.

'This news confounded me, and I lost all patience; and, my father happening to be out of town, I had an opportunity of putting myself into this garb you see me in, and, spurring this horse, I overtook Don Vicente about a league from hence, and, without urging reproaches, or hearing excuses, I discharged this carbine and this pair of pistols into the bargain, and, as I believe, lodged more than a brace of balls in his body, opening a door, through which my honour, distained* in his blood, might issue out. I left him among his servants, who durst not, or could not, interpose in his defence. I am come to seek you, that by your means I may escape to France, where I have relations, and to entreat you likewise to protect my father, that the numerous relations of Don Vicente may not dare to take a cruel revenge upon him.'

Roque, surprised at the gallantry, bravery, fine shape, and accident of the beautiful Claudia, said:

'Come, madam, and let us see, whether your enemy be dead, and afterwards we will consider what is most proper to be done for you.'

Don Quixote, who had listened attentively to what Claudia had said, and what Roque Guinart answered, said:

'Let no one trouble himself about defending this lady; for I take it upon myself: give me my horse and my arms, and stay here for me, while I go in quest of this knight, and, dead or alive, make him fulfil his promise made to so much beauty.'

'Nobody doubts that,' quoth Sancho: 'my master has a special hand at match-making; for, not many days ago, he obliged another person to marry, who also had denied the promise he had given to another maiden; and, had not the enchanters, who persecute him, changed his true shape into that of a lackey, at this very hour that same maiden would not have been one.'

Roque, who was more intent upon Claudia's business than the reasoning of master and man, understood them not; and, commanding his squires to restore to Sancho all they had taken from Dapple, ordering them likewise to retire to the place where they had lodged the night before, he presently went off with Claudia, in all haste, in quest of the wounded or dead Don Vicente. They came to the place where Claudia had come up with them, and found nothing there but blood newly spilt; then, looking round about them, as far as they could extend their sight, they discovered some people upon the side of a hill, and guessed (as indeed it proved) that it must be Don Vicente, whom his servants were carrying off, alive or dead, in order either to his cure or his burial. They made all the haste they could to overtake them; which they easily did, the others going but softly. They found Don Vicente in the arms of his servants, and, with a low and feeble voice, desiring them to let him die there, for the anguish of his wounds would not permit him to go any farther. Claudia and Roque, flinging themselves from their horses, drew near. The servants were startled at the sight of Roque, and Claudia was disturbed at that of Don Vicente: and so, divided betwixt tenderness and cruelty, she approached him, and, taking hold of his hand, she said:

'If you had given me this, according to our contract, you had not been reduced to this extremity.'

The wounded cavalier opened his almost closed eyes; and, knowing Claudia, he said:

'I perceive, fair and mistaken lady, that to your hand I owe my death; a punishment neither merited by me, nor due to my wishes; for neither my desires nor my actions could or would offend you.'

'Is it not true then,' said Claudia, 'that, this very morning, you were going to be married to Leonora, daughter of the rich Balvastro?'

'No, in truth,' answered Don Vicente: 'my evil fortune must have carried you that news, to excite your jealousy to bereave me of life, which, since I leave in your hands, and between your arms, I esteem myself happy; and, to assure you of this truth, take my hand, and receive me for your husband, if you are willing, for I can give you no greater satisfaction for the injury you imagine you have received.'

Claudia pressed his hand, and so wrung her own heart, that she fell into a swoon upon the bloody bosom of Don Vicente, and he into a mortal paroxysm. Roque was confounded, and knew not what to do. The servants ran for water to fling in their faces, and bringing it, sprinkled them with it.

Claudia returned from her swoon, but not Don Vicente from his paroxysm; for it put an end to his life; which Claudia seeing, and being assured that her sweet husband was no longer alive, she broke the air with her sighs, wounded the heavens with her complaints, tore her hair, and gave it to the winds, disfigured her face with her own hands, with all the signs of grief and affliction that can be imagined to proceed from a sorrowful heart.

'O cruel and inconsiderate woman!' said she; 'with what facility wert thou moved to put so evil a thought in execution! O raging force of jealousy, to what a desperate end dost thou lead those who harbour thee in their breasts! O my husband! whose unhappy lot, for being mine, hath sent thee, for thy bridal bed, to the grave!'

Such and so great were the lamentations of Claudia, that they extorted tears from the eyes of Roque, not accustomed to shed them upon any occasion. The servants wept; Claudia fainted away at every step, and all around seemed to be a field of sorrow, and seat of misfortune.

Finally, Roque Guinart ordered Don Vicente's servants to carry his body to the place where his father dwelt, which was not far off, there to give it burial. Claudia told Roque, she would retire to a nunnery, of which an aunt of hers was abbess, where she designed to end her life in the company of a better and an eternal spouse. Roque applauded her good intention, and offered to bear her company whithersoever she pleased, and to defend her father against Don Vicente's relations, and all who should desire to hurt him. Claudia would by no means accept of his company, and, thanking him for his offer in the best manner she could, took her leave of him weeping. Don Vicente's servants carried off his body, and Roque returned to his companions. Thus ended the loves of Claudia Jerónima; and no wonder, since the web of her doleful history was woven by the cruel and irresistible hand of jealousy.

Roque Guinart found his squires in the place he had appointed them, and Don Quixote among them, mounted upon Rosinante, and making a speech, wherein he was persuading them to leave that kind of life, so dangerous both to soul and body. But, most of them being Gascons,* a rude and disorderly sort of people, Don Quixote's harangue made little or no impression upon them. Roque, being arrived, demanded of Sancho Panza, whether they had returned and restored him all the movables and jewels his folks had taken from Dapple. Sancho answered, they had, all but three nightcaps, which were worth three cities.

'What does the fellow say?' quoth one of the bystanders: 'I have them, and they are not worth three reals.'

'That is true,' quoth Don Quixote; 'but my squire values them at what he has said for the sake of the person who gave them.'

Roque Guinart ordered them to be restored that moment, and, commanding his men to draw up in a line, he caused all the clothes, jewels, and money, and, in short, all they had plundered since the last distribution, to be brought before them; and, making a short appraisement, and reducing the undividables into money, he shared it among his company, with so much equity and prudence, that he neither went beyond, nor fell the least short of, distributive justice. This done, with which all were paid, contented, and satisfied, Roque said to Don Quixote:

'If this punctuality were not strictly observed there would be no living among these fellows.'

To which Sancho said:

'By what I have seen, justice is so good a thing, that it is necessary even among thieves themselves.'

One of the squires hearing him, lifted up the butt-end of a musket, and had doubtless split Sancho's head therewith, had not Roque Guinart called out aloud to him to forbear. Sancho was frightened, and resolved not to open his lips while he continued among those people.

At this juncture came two or three of the squires, who were posted as sentinels on the highway, to observe travellers, and give notice to their chief of what passed, and said to him:

'Not far from hence, sir, in the road that leads to Barcelona, comes a great company of people.'

To which Roque replied:

'Have you distinguished whether they are such as seek us, or such as we seek?'

'Such as we seek,' answered the squire.

'Then sally forth,' replied Roque, 'and bring them hither presently, without letting one escape.'

They obeyed, and Don Quixote, Sancho, and Roque, remaining by themselves, stood expecting what the squires would bring; and, in this interval, Roque said to Don Quixote:

'This life of ours must needs seem very new to Señor Don Quixote; new adventures, new accidents, and all of them full of danger; nor do I wonder it should appear so to you; for, I confess truly to you, there is no kind of life more unquiet, nor more full of alarms, than ours. I was led into it by I know not what desire of revenge, which has force enough to disturb the most sedate minds. I am naturally compassionate and good-natured; but, as I have said, the desire of revenging an injury done me, so bears down this good inclination in me, that I persevere in this state in spite of knowing better; and, as one mischief draws after it another, and one sin is followed by a second, my revenges have been so linked together, that I not only take upon me my own, but those of other people. But it pleases God, that, though I see myself in the midst of this labyrinth of confusions, I do not lose the hope of getting out of it, and arriving at last in a safe harbour.'

Don Quixote was in admiration to hear Roque talk such good and sound sense; for he thought that, amongst those of his trade of robbing, murdering, and waylaying, there could be none capable of serious reflection, and he answered:

'Señor Roque, the beginning of health consists in the knowledge of the distemper, and in the patient's being willing to take the medicines prescribed him by the physician. You are sick; you know your disease; and heaven, or rather God, who is our physician, will apply medicines to heal you, such as usually heal gradually, by little and little, and not suddenly, and by miracle. Besides, sinners of good understanding are nearer to amendment than foolish ones; and since, by your discourse, you have shown your prudence, it remains only that you be of good cheer, and hope for a bettering of your conscience; and, if you would shorten the way, and place yourself with ease in that of your salvation, come with me, and I will teach you to be a knight-errant; in which profession there are so many troubles and disasters, that, being placed to the account of penance, they will carry you to heaven in two twinklings of an eye.'

Roque smiled at Don Quixote's counsel, to whom, changing the discourse, he related the tragical adventure of Claudia Jerónima, which extremely grieved Sancho, who did not dislike the beauty, freedom, and sprightliness, of the young lady.

By this time the squires returned with their prize, bringing with them two gentlemen on horseback, two pilgrims on foot, and a coach full of women, with about six servants, some on foot and some on horseback, accompanying them, and two muleteers belonging to the gentlemen. The squires enclosed them round, the vanquishers and vanquished keeping a profound silence, waiting till the great Roque should speak, who asked the gentlemen who they were, whither they were going, and what money they had. One of them answered:

'Sir, we are two captains of Spanish foot; our companies are at Naples, and we are going to embark in four galleys, which are said to be at Barcelona, with orders to pass over to Sicily. We have about two or three hundred crowns, with which we think ourselves rich and happy, since the usual penury of soldiers allows no greater treasures.'

Roque put the same question to the pilgrims, who replied, they were going to embark for Rome, and that, between them both, they might have about sixty reals. He demanded also, who those were in the coach, where they were going, and what money they carried, and one of those on horseback answered:

'The persons in the coach are, my lady Doña Guiomar de Quiñones, wife of the regent of the vicarship of Naples, a little daughter, a waiting-maid, and a duenna. Six servants of us accompany them; and the money they carry is six hundred crowns.'

'So that,' quoth Roque Guinart, 'we have here nine hundred crowns and sixty reals: my soldiers are sixty: see how much it comes to apiece; for I am but an indifferent accountant.'

The robbers hearing him say this, lifted up their voices, saying:

'Long live Roque Guinart, in spite of all the wretches who seek his destruction!'

The captains showed signs of affliction, the lady regent was dejected, and the pilgrims were not at all pleased, at seeing the confiscation of their effects. Roque held them thus for some time in suspense, but would not let their sorrow, which might be seen a musket-shot off, last any longer; and, turning to the captains, he said:

'Be pleased, gentlemen, to do me the favour to lend me sixty crowns, and you, lady regent, fourscore, to satisfy this squadron of my followers; for, "The abbot must eat that sings for his meat": and then you may depart free and unmolested, with a pass I will give you, that if you meet with any more of my squadrons, which I keep in several divisions up and down in these parts, they may not hurt you; for it is not my intention to wrong soldiers, nor any woman, especially if she be of quality.'

Infinite and well expressed were the thanks the captains returned Roque for his courtesy and liberality; for such they esteemed his leaving them part of their own money. Doña Guiomar de Quiñones was ready to throw herself out of her coach, to kiss the feet and hands of the great Roque: but he would in nowise consent to it, but rather begged pardon for the injury he was forced to do them, in compliance with the precise duty of his wicked office. The lady regent ordered one of her servants immediately to give the eighty crowns, her share of the assessment, and the captains had already disbursed their sixty. The pilgrims were going to offer their little all: but Roque bade them stay a little, and, turning about to his men, he said:

'Of these crowns two fall to each man's share, and twenty remain: let ten be given to these pilgrims, and the other ten to this honest squire, that he may have it in his power to speak well of this adventure.'

And, calling for pen, ink, and paper, with which he always was provided, Roque gave them a pass, directed to the chiefs of his bands, and, taking leave of them, he let them go free, in admiration at his generosity, his graceful deportment, and strange procedure, and looking upon him rather as an Alexander the Great than a notorious robber.

One of the squires said, in his Gascon and Catalan language:

'This captain of ours is fitter for a friar than a felon: for the future, if he has a mind to show himself liberal, let it be of his own goods, and not of ours.'

The wretch spoke not so low but Roque overheard him, and, drawing his sword, he almost cleft his head in two, saying:

'Thus I chastise the ill-tongued and saucy.'

All the rest were frightened, and no one durst utter a word; such was the awe and obedience they were [kept] in. Roque went a little aside, and wrote a letter to a friend of his at Barcelona, acquainting him that the famous Don Quixote de la Mancha, that knight-errant of whom so many things were reported, was in his company; giving him to understand, that he was the pleasantest and most ingenious person in the world; and that, four days after, on the feast of St. John the Baptist,* he would appear on the strand of the city, armed at all points, mounted on his horse Rosinante, and his squire Sancho upon an ass; desiring him to give notice thereof to his friends the Niarros, that they might make themselves merry with him: and expressing his wishes, that his enemies the Cadells* might not partake of the diversion; though that was impossible, because the wild extravagances and distraction of Don Quixote, together with the witty sayings of his squire Sancho Panza, could not fail to give general pleasure to all the world. He dispatched this epistle by one of his squires, who, changing the habit of an outlaw for that of a peasant, entered into Barcelona, and delivered it into the hands of the person it was directed to.

CHAPTER 61

Of what befell Don Quixote at his entrance into Barcelona,
with other events more true than ingenious.

THREE days and three nights Don Quixote stayed with
Roque: and, had he stayed three hundred years, he would not
have wanted subject matter for observation and admiration
in his way of life. Here they lodge, there they dine: one while
they fly, not knowing from whom; another, they lie in wait
they know not for whom. They slept standing, with interrupted slumbers, and shifting from one place to another; they
were perpetually sending out spies, posting sentinels, blowing
the matches of their muskets, though they had but few, most
of them making use of firelocks. Roque passed the nights
apart from his followers, in places to them unknown: for the
many proclamations the viceroy of Barcelona* had published
against him, kept him in fear and disquiet, not daring to trust
anybody, and apprehensive lest his own men should either
kill or deliver him up to justice, for the price set upon his
head: a life truly miserable and irksome.

In short, Roque, Don Quixote, and Sancho, attended by
six squires, set out for Barcelona, through unfrequented ways,
short cuts, and covered paths. They arrived upon the strand
on the eve of St. John, in the night-time; and Roque,
embracing Don Quixote, and Sancho, to whom he gave the
ten crowns promised, but not yet given him, left them, with
a thousand offers of service made on both sides.

Roque returned back, and Don Quixote stayed expecting
the day on horseback, just as he was; and it was not long
before the face of the beautiful Aurora began to discover
itself through the balconies of the east, rejoicing the grass
and flowers, instead of rejoicing the ears; though, at the same
instant, the ears also were rejoiced by the sound of abundance
of waits and kettledrums, the jingling of morrice-bells, with
the trampling of horsemen, seemingly coming out of the city.
Aurora gave place to the sun, which was rising by degrees
from below the horizon, with a face bigger than a target.
Don Quixote and Sancho, casting their eyes around on every
side, saw the sea, which till then they had never seen. It

appeared to them very large and spacious, somewhat bigger than the lakes of Ruydera, which they had seen in La Mancha. They saw the galleys lying close to the shore, which, taking in their awnings, appeared full of streamers, and pennants trembling in the wind, and kissing and brushing the water. From within them sounded clarions, trumpets, and waits, filling the air all around with sweet and martial music. Presently the galleys began to move, and to skirmish, as it were, on the still waters; and, at the same time, corresponding with them, as it were on the land, an infinite number of cavaliers mounted on beautiful horses, and attended with gay liveries, issued forth from the city. The soldiers on board the galleys discharged several rounds of cannon, which were answered by those on the walls and forts of the city. The heavy artillery, with dreadful noise, rent the wind, which was echoed back by the cannon on the forecastles of the galleys. The sea was cheerful, the land jocund, and the air bright, only now and then obscured a little by the smoke of the artillery. All which together seemed to infuse and engender a sudden pleasure in all the people.

Sancho could not imagine how those bulks, which moved backwards and forwards in the sea, came to have so many legs.

By this time those with the liveries came up on a full gallop, with lelilies and shouts after the Moorish fashion, to the place where Don Quixote was standing, wrapped in wonder and surprise; and one of them (the person to whom Roque had sent the letter) said in a loud voice to Don Quixote:

'Welcome to our city, the mirror, the beacon, and polar star of knight-errantry in its greatest extent! Welcome, I say, the valorous Don Quixote de la Mancha; not the spurious, the fictitious, the apocryphal, lately exhibited among us in lying histories, but the true, the legitimate, the genuine, described to us by Cid Hamet Ben Engeli, the flower of historians!'

Don Quixote answered not a word, nor did the cavaliers wait for any answer: but wheeling about and about with all their followers, they began to career, and curvet it round Don Quixote, who, turning to Sancho, said:

'These people seem to know us well: I will lay a wager they have read our history, and even that of the Aragonese lately printed.'

The gentleman who spoke to Don Quixote, said again to him:

'Be pleased, Señor Don Quixote, to come along with us; for we are all very humble servants, and great friends of Roque Guinart.'

To which Don Quixote replied:

'If courtesies beget courtesies, yours, good sir, is daughter, or very near kinswoman, to those of the great Roque: conduct me whither you please: for I have no other will but yours, especially if you please to employ it in your service.'

The gentleman answered in expressions no less civil; and enclosing him in the midst of them, they all marched with him, to the sounds of waits and drums, toward the city, at the entrance whereof, the Wicked One, who is the author of all mischief, so ordered it, that among the boys, who are more wicked than the Wicked One himself, two bold and unlucky rogues crowded through the press, and one of them lifting up Dapple's tail, and the other that of Rosinante, they thrust under each a handful of briers. The poor beasts felt the new spurs, and by clapping their tails the closer, augmented their smart in such sort, that, after several plunges, they flung their riders to the ground. Don Quixote, out of countenance and affronted, hastened to free his horse's tail from this new plumage, and Sancho did the like by Dapple. Those who conducted Don Quixote would have chastised the insolence of the boys; but it was impossible; for they were soon lost among above a thousand more that followed them. Don Quixote and Sancho mounted again, and, with the acclamations and music, arrived at their conductor's house, which was large and fair, such, in short, as became a gentleman of fortune: where we will leave them for the present; for so Cid Hamet Ben Engeli will have it.

CHAPTER 62

Which treats of the adventure of the enchanted head, with other trifles that must not be omitted.

DON QUIXOTE's host was called Don Antonio Moreno, a rich and discreet gentleman, and a lover of mirth in a decent and civil way. And so, having Don Quixote in his house, he began to contrive methods, how, without prejudice to his guest, he might take advantage of Don Quixote's madness; for, jests that hurt, are no jests, nor are those pastimes good for anything, which turn to the detriment of a third person. The first thing, therefore, he did, was, to cause Don Quixote to be unarmed, and exposed to view in his straight chamois doublet (as we have already described and painted it), in a balcony which looked into one of the chief streets of the city, in sight of the populace and of the boys, who stood gazing at him as if he had been a monkey. The cavaliers with the liveries began to career it afresh before him, as if for him alone, and not in honour of that day's festival they had provided them. Sancho was so highly delighted, thinking he had found, without knowing how or which way, another Camacho's wedding, another house like Don Diego de Miranda's, and another castle like the duke's.

Several of Don Antonio's friends dined with him that day, all honouring and treating Don Quixote as a knight-errant; at which he was puffed with vainglory, that he could scarce conceal the pleasure it gave him. Sancho's witty conceits were such, and so many, that all the servants of the house hung, as it were, upon his lips, and so did all that heard him. While they were at table, Don Antonio said to Sancho:

'We are told here, honest Sancho, that you are so great a lover of capons and sausages, that when you have filled your belly, you stuff your pockets with the remainder for the next day.'

'No, sir, it is not so,' answered Sancho; 'your worship is misinformed; for I am more cleanly than gluttonous; and my master Don Quixote, here present, knows very well, how he and I often live eight days upon a handful of acorns or hazel-nuts: it is true, indeed, if it so falls out that they give me a heifer, I make haste with a halter; I mean, that I eat whatever is offered me, and take the times as I find them, and, whoever has said that I am given to eat much, and am not cleanly, take it from me, he is very much out, and I would say this in another manner, were it not out of respect to the honourable beards here at table.'

'In truth,' quoth Don Quixote, 'Sancho's parsimony and cleanliness in eating, deserve to be written and engraved on plates of brass, to remain an eternal memorial for ages to come. I must confess, when he is hungry, he seems to be somewhat of a glutton; for he eats fast, and chews on both sides at once: but, as for cleanliness, he always strictly observes it; and when he was a governor, he learned to eat so nicely, that he took up grapes, and even the grains of a pomegranate, with the point of a fork.'

'How?' quoth Don Antonio, 'has Sancho then, been a governor?'

'Yes, answered Sancho, 'and of an island called Barataria. Ten days I governed it, at my own will and pleasure, in which time I lost my rest, and learned to despise all the governments in the world: I fled away from it, and fell into a pit, where I looked upon myself as a dead man, and out of which I escaped alive by a miracle.'

Don Quixote related minutely all the circumstances of Sancho's government, which gave great pleasure to the hearers.

The cloth being taken away, Don Antonio, taking Don Quixote by the hand, led him into a distant apartment, in which there was no other furniture, but a table, seemingly of jasper, standing upon a foot of the same, upon which there was placed, after the manner of the busts of the Roman emperors, a head, which seemed to be of brass. Don Antonio walked with Don Quixote up and down the room, taking several turns about the table; after which he said.

'Señor Don Quixote, now that I am assured nobody is within hearing, and that the door is fast, I will tell you one of the rarest adventures, or rather one of the greatest novelties, that can be imagined, upon condition, that what I shall tell you be deposited in the inmost recesses of secrecy.'

'I swear it shall,' answered Don Quixote, 'and I will clap a gravestone over it, for the greater security; for I would have your worship know, Señor Don Antonio' (for by this time he had learned his name) 'that you are talking to one, who, though he has ears to hear, has no tongue to speak; so that you may safely transfer whatever is in your breast into mine, and make account you have thrown it into the abyss of silence.'

'In confidence of this promise,' answered Don Antonio, 'I will raise your admiration by what you shall see and hear, and procure myself some relief from the pain I suffer by not having somebody to communicate my secrets to, which are not to be trusted with everybody.'

Don Quixote was in suspense, expecting what so many precautions would end in. Don Antonio then, taking hold of his hand, made him pass it over the brazen head, the table, and the jasper pedestal it stood upon, and then said:

'This head, Señor Don Quixote, was wrought and contrived by one of the greatest enchanters and wizards the world ever had. He was, I think, by birth a Polander, and disciple of the famous Escotillo,* of whom so many wonders are related. He was here in my house, and, for the reward of a thousand crowns, made me this head, which has the virtue and property of answering to every question asked at its ear. After drawing figures, erecting schemes, and observing the stars, he brought it at length to the perfection we shall see to-morrow; for it is mute on Fridays, and this happening to be Friday, we must wait till to-morrow. In the meanwhile you may bethink yourself what questions you will ask it, for I know, by experience, it tells the truth in all its answers.'

Don Quixote wondered at the property and virtue of the head, and was ready to disbelieve Don Antonio: but, considering how short a time was set for making the experiment, he would say no more, but only thanked him for having discovered to him so great a secret. They went out of the chamber: Don Antonio locked the door after him; and they came to the hall, where the rest of the gentlemen were, and in this time Sancho had recounted to them many of the adventures and accidents that had befallen his master.

That evening they carried Don Quixote abroad, to take the air, not armed, but dressed like a citizen in a long loose garment of tawny-coloured cloth, which would have made frost itself sweat at that season. They ordered their servants to entertain and amuse Sancho, so as not to let him go out of doors. Don Quixote rode, not upon Rosinante, but upon a large, easy-paced mule, handsomely accoutred. In dressing him, unperceived by him, they pinned at his back a parchment, whereon was written, in capital letters; 'THIS IS DON QUIXOTE DE LA MANCHA'. They no sooner began their march, but the scroll drew the eyes of all that passed by, and they read aloud, 'This is Don Quixote de la Mancha.' Don Quixote wondered that everybody who saw him, named and knew him; and, turning to Don Antonio, who was riding by his side, he said:

'Great is the prerogative inherent in knight-errantry, since it makes all its professors known and renowned throughout the limits of the earth: for, pray observe, Señor Don Antonio, how the very boys of this city know me, without having ever seen me.'

'It is true, Señor Don Quixote,' answered Don Antonio; 'for, as fire cannot be hidden nor confined, so virtue will be known: and that which is obtained by the profession of arms, shines with a brightness and lustre superior to that of all others.'

Now it happened, that, as Don Quixote was riding along with the applause aforesaid, a Castilian, who had read the label on his shoulders, lifted up his voice, saying:

'The devil take thee for Don Quixote de la Mancha! what! are you got hither, without being killed by the infinite number of bangs you have had upon your back? You are mad, and, were you so alone, and within the doors of your own folly, the mischief were the less: but you have the property of converting into fools and madmen all that converse, or have any communication with you: witness these gentlemen who accompany you. Get you home, fool, and look after your estate, your wife and children, and leave off these vanities, which worm-eat your brain, and skim off the cream of your understanding.'

'Brother,' quoth Don Antonio, 'keep on your way, and do not be giving counsel to those who do not ask it. Señor Don Quixote de la Mancha is wise, and we who bear him company are not fools. Virtue challenges respect, wherever it is found: and begone in an evil hour, and meddle not where you are not called.'

'Before God,' answered the Castilian, 'your worship is in the right; for to give advice to this good man, is to kick against the pricks. But for all that, it grieves me very much, that the good sense, it is said, this madman discovers in all other things, should run to waste through the channel of his knight-errantry: and the evil hour, your worship wished me, be to me and to all my descendants, if, from this day forward, though I should live more days than Methusalem, I give advice to anybody, though they should ask it me.'

The adviser departed; the procession went on: but the boys and the people crowded so to read the scroll, that Don Antonio was forced to take it off, under pretence of taking off something else.

Night came: the processioners returned home, where was a ball of ladies: for Don Antonio's wife, who was a lady of distinction, cheerful, beautiful, and discreet, had invited several of her friends to honour her guest, and to entertain them with his unheard-of madness. Several ladies came: they supped splendidly, and the ball began about ten o'clock at night. Among the ladies, there were two of an arch and pleasant disposition, who, though they were very modest, yet behaved with more freedom than usual, that the jest might divert without giving distaste. These were so eager to take Don Quixote out to dance, that they teased, not only his body but his very soul. It was a perfect sight to behold the figure of Don Quixote, long, lank, lean, and yellow, straightened in his clothes, awkward, and especially not at all nimble. The ladies courted him, as it were, by stealth, and he disdained them by stealth too. But, finding himself hard pressed by their courtships, he exalted his voice and said:

'*Fugite, partes adversae!* leave me to my repose, ye unwelcome thoughts! avaunt ladies, with your desires! for she, who is queen of mine, the peerless Dulcinea del Toboso, will not consent that any others but hers should subject and subdue me.'

And so saying, he sat down in the middle of the hall upon the floor, quite fatigued and disjointed by this dancing exercise. Don Antonio ordered the servants to take him up, and carry him to bed; and the first who lent a helping hand, was Sancho, who said:

'What, in God's name, master of mine, put you upon dancing? Think you that all who are valiant must be caperers, or all knights-errant dancing-masters? If you think so, I say you are mistaken: I know those, who would sooner cut a giant's windpipe than a caper. Had you been for the shoe-jig, I would have supplied your defect; for I slap it away like any jerfalcon:* but, as for regular dancing, I cannot work a stitch at it.'

With this, and such-like talk, Sancho furnished matter of laughter to the company, and laid his master in bed, covering him up stoutly, that he might sweat out the cold he might have got by his dancing.

The next day, Don Antonio thought fit to make experiment of the enchanted head; and so, with Don Quixote, Sancho, and two other friends, with the two ladies, who had worried Don Quixote in dancing (for they stayed that night with Don Antonio's wife) he locked himself up in the room where the head stood. He told them the property it had, charged them all with the secret, and told them, this was the first day of his trying the virtue of that enchanted head. Nobody but Don Antonio's two friends knew the trick of the enchantment; and, if Don Antonio had not first discovered it to them, they would also have been as much surprised as the rest, it being impossible not to be so; so cunningly and curiously was it contrived. The first who approached the ear of the head, was Don Antonio himself, who said in a low voice, yet not so low but he was overheard by them all:

'Tell me, head, by the virtue inherent in thee, what am I now thinking of?'

The head answered, without moving its lips, in a clear and distinct voice, so as to be heard by everybody:

'I am no judge of thoughts.'

At hearing of which they were all astonished, especially since, neither in the room, nor anywhere about the table, was there any human creature that could answer.

'How many of us are here?' demanded Don Antonio again.

Answer was made him in the same key:

'You and your wife, with two friends of yours, and two of hers, and a famous knight called Don Quixote de la Mancha, with a certain squire of his, Sancho Panza by name.'

Here was wondering indeed; here was everybody's hair standing on end out of pure affright. Don Antonio, going aside at some distance from the head, said:

'This is enough to assure me I was not deceived by him who sold you to me, sage head, speaking head, answering head, and admirable head: let somebody else go, and ask it what they please.'

Now, as women are commonly in haste, and inquisitive, the first who went up to it was one of the two friends of Don Antonio's wife, and her question was:

'Tell me, head, what shall I do to be very handsome?'

It was answered:

'Be very modest.'

'I ask you no more,' said the querist.

Then her companion came up, and said:

'I would know, head, whether my husband loves me or no?'

The answer was:

'You may easily know that by his usage of you.'

The married woman, going aside, said:

'The question might very well have been spared; for, in reality, a man's actions are the best interpreters of his affections.'

Then one of Don Antonio's two friends went and asked him:

'Who am I?'

The answer was:

'You know.'

'I do not ask you that,' answered the gentleman, 'but only whether you know me?'

'I do,' replied the head; 'you are Don Pedro Noriz.'

'I desire to hear no more,' said he, 'since this is sufficient, O head, to convince me that you know everything.'

Then the other friend stepped up, and demanded:

'Tell me, head, what desires has my eldest son?'

It was answered:

'Have I not told you already, that I do not judge of thoughts? But, for all that, I can tell you, that your son's desire is to bury you.'

'It is so!' quoth the gentleman: 'I see it with my eyes, and touch it with my finger, and I ask no more questions.'

Then came Don Antonio's wife, and said:

'I know not, O head, what to ask you: only I would know of you, whether I shall enjoy my dear husband many years?'

The answer was:

'You shall; for his good constitution, and his temperate way of living, promise many years of life, which several are wont to shorten by intemperance.'

Next came Don Quixote, and said:

'Tell me, O answerer, was it truth, or a dream, what I related as having befallen me in Montesinos' cave? Will the whipping of Sancho, my squire, be certainly fulfilled? Will the disenchantment of Dulcinea take effect?'

'As to the business of the cave,' it was answered, 'there is much to be said: it has something of both: Sancho's whipping will go on but slowly: the disenchantment of Dulcinea will be brought about in due time.'

'I desire to know no more,' quoth Don Quixote; 'for, so I may but see Dulcinea disenchanted, I shall make account, that all the good fortune I can desire comes upon me at a clap.'

The last querist was Sancho, and his question was this:

'Head, shall I, peradventure, get another government? Shall I quit the penurious life of a squire? Shall I return to see my wife and children?'

To which it was answered:

'You shall govern in your own house, and, if you return to it, you shall see your wife and your children, and, quitting service, you shall cease to be a squire.'

'Very good, in faith,' quoth Sancho Panza; 'I could have

told myself as much, and the prophet Perogrullo* could have told me no more.'

'Beast,' quoth Don Quixote, 'what answer would you have? Is it not enough that the answers this head returns correspond to the questions put to it?'

'Yes, it is enough,' answered Sancho: 'but I wish it had explained itself, and told me a little more.'

Thus ended the questions and answers, but not the amazement of the whole company, excepting Don Antonio's two friends, who knew the secret; which Cid Hamet Ben Engeli would immediately discover, not to keep the world in suspense, believing there was some witchcraft, or extraordinary mystery, concealed in that head; and therefore he says, that Don Antonio Moreno procured it to be made, in imitation of another head he had seen at Madrid (made by a statuary for his own diversion), and to surprise the ignorant; and the machine was contrived in this manner. The table was of wood, painted, and varnished over like jasper, and the foot it stood upon was of the same, with four eagle claws, to make it stand the firmer, and bear the weight the better. The head, resembling that of a Roman emperor, and coloured like copper, was hollow, and so was the table itself, in which the bust was so exactly fixed, that no sign of a joint appeared. The foot also was hollow, and answered to the neck and breast of the head; and all this corresponding with another chamber just under that where the head stood. Through all this hollow of the foot, table, neck, and breast of the figure aforesaid, went a pipe of tin which could not be seen. The answerer was placed in the chamber underneath, with his mouth close to the pipe, so that the voice descended and ascended in clear and articulate sounds, as through a speaking-trumpet; and thus it was impossible to discover the juggle. A nephew of Don Antonio's, a student, acute and discreet, was the respondent; who, being informed beforehand by his uncle, who were to be with him that day in the chamber of the head, could easily answer, readily and exactly, to the first question; to the rest he answered by conjectures, and, as a discreet person, discreetly.

Cid Hamet says further, that this wonderful machine lasted

about eight or ten days; but it being divulged up and down the city, that Don Antonio kept in his house an enchanted head, which answered to all questions, he, fearing lest it should come to the ears of the watchful sentinels of our faith, acquainted the gentlemen of the Inquisition with the secret, who ordered him to break it in pieces, lest the ignorant vulgar should be scandalized at it: but still, in the opinion of Don Quixote and Sancho Panza, the head continued to be enchanted, and an answerer of questions, more indeed to the satisfaction of Don Quixote than of Sancho.

The gentlemen of the town, in complaisance to Don Antonio, and for the better entertainment of Don Quixote, as well as to give him an opportunity of discovering his follies, appointed a running at the ring six days after, which was prevented by an accident that will be told hereafter.

Don Quixote had a mind to walk about the town, without ceremony, and on foot, apprehending that, if he went on horseback, he should be persecuted by the boys; and so he and Sancho, with two servants assigned him by Don Antonio, walked out to make the tour. Now it fell out, that, as they passed through a certain street, Don Quixote, lifting up his eyes, saw written over a door in very large letters, 'Here books are printed.' At which he was much pleased; for, till then, he had never seen any printing, and was desirous to know how it was performed. In he went, with all his retinue, and saw drawing off the sheets in one place, correcting in another, composing in this, revising in that; in short, all the machinery to be seen in great printing-houses. Don Quixote went to one of the boxes, and asked what they had in hand there. The workman told him; he wondered, and went on. He came to another box, and asked one, what he was doing. The workman answered:

'Sir, that gentleman yonder (pointing to a man of a good person and appearance, and of some gravity) has translated an Italian book into our Castilian language, and I am composing it here for the press.'

'What title has the book?' demanded Don Quixote.

To which the author answered:

'Sir, the book in Italian is called, *Le Bagatelle*.'

'And what answers to *Bagatelle* in our Castilian?' quoth Don Quixote.

'*Le Bagatelle*,' said the author, 'is as if we should say, *Trifles*.* But, though its title be mean, it contains many very good and substantial things.'

Quoth Don Quixote:

'I know a little of the Tuscan language, and value myself upon singing some stanzas of Ariosto. But, good sir, pray, tell me (and I do not say this with design to examine your skill, but out of curiosity, and nothing else), in the course of your writing have you ever met with the word *pignata*?'

'Yes, often,' replied the author.

'And how do you translate it in Castilian?' quoth Don Quixote.

'How should I translate it,' replied the author, 'but by the word *olla*?'

'Body of me,' said Don Quixote, 'what a progress has your worship made in the Tuscan language! I would venture a good wager, that, where the Tuscan says *piace*, you say, in Castilian, *place*; and where it says *più*, you say *mas*; and *sù* you translate *arriba*, and *giù* by *abaxo*.'

'I do so, most certainly,' quoth the author; 'for these are their proper renderings.'

'I dare swear,' quoth Don Quixote, 'you are not known in the world, which is ever an enemy to rewarding florid wits, and laudable pains. What abilities are lost, what geniuses cooped up, and what virtues undervalued! But, for all that, I cannot but be of opinion, that, translating out of one language into another, unless it be from those queens of the languages, Greek and Latin, is like setting to view the wrong side of a piece of tapestry, where, though the figures are seen, they are full of ends and threads, which obscure them, and are not seen with the smoothness and evenness of the right side. And the translating out of easy languages shows neither genius nor elocution, any more than transcribing one paper from another. But I would not from hence infer, that translating is not a laudable exercise; for a man may be employed in things of worse consequence, and less advantage. Out of this account are excepted the two celebrated translators, Doctor Christopher de Figueroa in his *Pastor Fido*,* and Don John de Xauregui in his *Aminta*;* in which, with a curious felicity, they bring it in doubt, which is the translation, and which the original.

'But, tell me, sir, is this book printed on your own account, or have you sold the copy to some bookseller?'

'I print it on my own account,' answered the author, 'and I expect to get a thousand ducats by this first impression, of which there will be two thousand copies, and they will go off, at six reals a set, in a trice.'

'Mighty well,' answered Don Quixote: 'it is plain you know but little of the turns and doubles of the booksellers, and the combination there is among them. I promise you, when you find the weight of two thousand volumes upon your back, it will so depress you, that you will be frightened, especially if the book be anything dull, or not over sprightly.'

'What! sir,' quoth the author, 'would you have me make over my right to the bookseller, who, perhaps, will give me three maravedis for it, and even think he does me a kindness in giving me so much? I print no more books to purchase fame in the world; for I am already sufficiently known by my works. Profit I seek, without which fame is not worth a farthing.'

'God send you good success,' answered Don Quixote.'

And, going on to another box, he saw they were correcting a sheet of another book, entitled, *The light of the soul*.* And seeing it, he said:

'These kind of books, though there are a great many of them abroad, are those that ought to be printed: for there are abundance of sinners up and down, and so many benighted persons stand in need of an infinite number of lights.'

He went forward, and saw they were correcting another book; and asking its title, he was answered, that it was called, the *Second Part of the Ingenious Gentleman Don Quixote de la Mancha*,* written by such a one, an inhabitant of Tordesillas.

'I know something of that book,' quoth Don Quixote: 'and, in truth and on my conscience, I thought it had been burnt before now, and reduced to ashes, for its impertinence: but its Martinmas will come, as it does to every hog: for all fabulous histories are so far good and entertaining, as they come near the truth, or the resemblance of it; and true histories themselves are so much the better, by how much the truer.'

And, so saying, he went out of the printing-house with some show of disgust.

And that same day Don Antonio purposed to carry him to see the galleys, which lay in the road; whereat Sancho rejoiced much, having never in his life seen any. Don Antonio gave notice to the commodore of the four galleys, that he would bring his guest, the renowned Don Quixote de la Mancha, that afternoon, to see them, of whom the commodore, and all the inhabitants of the city, had some knowledge; and what befell him there, shall be told in the following chapter.

CHAPTER 63

Of the unlucky accident which befell Sancho Panza, in visiting the galleys, and the strange adventure of the beautiful Morisco.

MANY were the reflections Don Quixote made upon the answer of the enchanted head, none of them hitting upon the trick of it, and all centering in the promise, which he looked upon as certain, of the disenchantment of Dulcinea. He rejoiced within himself, believing he should soon see the accomplishement of it; and Sancho, though he abhorred being a governor, as has been said, had still a desire to command again, and be obeyed: such is the misfortune power brings along with it, though but in jest.

In short, that evening, Don Antonio Moreno, and his two friends, with Don Quixote, and Sancho, went to the galleys. The commodore of the four galleys, who had notice of the coming of the two famous personages, Don Quixote and Sancho, no sooner perceived them approach the shore, but he ordered all the galleys to strike their awnings, and the waits to play: and immediately he sent out the pinnace, covered with rich carpets, and furnished with cushions of crimson velvet; and, just as Don Quixote set his foot into it, the captain-galley discharged her forecastle piece, and the other galleys did the like; and, at his mounting the ladder on the starboard-side, all the crew of slaves saluted him, as the custom is, when a person of rank comes on board, with three 'Hu, hu, hu's'. The general (for so we shall call him), who was a gentleman of quality of Valencia, gave Don Quixote his hand, and embraced him, saying:

'This day will I mark with a white stone, as one of the best I ever wish to see while I live, having seen Señor Don Quixote de la Mancha, in whom is comprised and abridged the whole worth of knight-errantry.'

Don Quixote answered him in expressions no less courteous, being overjoyed to find himself treated so like a lord. All the company went to the poop, which was finely adorned, and seated themselves upon the lockers. The boatswain passed along the middle gangway, and gave the signal with his whistle for the slaves to strip; which was done in an instant. Sancho seeing so many men in buff was frightened, and more so, when he saw them spread an awning so swiftly over the galley, that he thought all the devils in hell were there at work. But all this was tarts and cheesecakes to what I am going to relate.

Sancho was seated near the stern, on the right hand, close to the hindmost rower, who, being instructed what he was to do, laid hold on Sancho, and lifted him up in his arms. Then the whole crew of slaves, standing up, and beginning from the right side, passed him from bank to bank, and from hand to hand, so swiftly, that poor Sancho lost the very sight of his eyes, and verily thought the devils themselves were carrying him away; and they had not done with him, till they brought him round by the left side, and replaced him at the stern. The poor wretch remained bruised, out of breath, and in a cold sweat, without being able to imagine what had befallen him. Don Quixote, who beheld Sancho's flight without wings, asked the general, if that was a ceremony commonly used at people's first coming aboard the galleys: for if so, he, who had no intention of making profession in them, had no inclination to perform the like exercise, and vowed to God, that if anyone presumed to lay hold of him to toss him, he would kick their souls out. And, saying this, he stood up, and laid his hand on his sword.

At that instant they struck the awning, and, with a great noise, let fall the mainyard from the top of the mast to the bottom. Sancho thought the sky was falling off its hinges, and tumbling upon his head, and, shrinking it down, he clapped it for fear between his legs. Don Quixote knew not what to think of it, and he too quaked, shrugged his shoulders, and changed countenance. The slaves hoisted the mainyard with the same swiftness and noise they had struck it; and all this, without speaking a word, as if they had neither voice nor breath. The boatswain made a signal for weighing anchor, and, jumping into the middle of the forecastle, with his bull's-pizzle, he began to fly-flap the shoulders of the slaves at the oar, and by little and little, to put off to sea. Sancho, seeing so many red feet (for such he took the oars to be) move all together, said to himself:

'Ah, these are enchanted things indeed, and not those my master talks of. What have these unhappy wretches done to be whipped at this rate? and how has this one man, who goes whistling up and down, the boldness to whip so many? I maintain it, this is hell, or purgatory at least.'

Don Quixote, seeing with what attention Sancho observed all that passed, said:

'Ah, friend Sancho, how quickly and how cheaply might you, if you would, strip to the waist, and placing yourself among these gentlemen, put an end to the enchantment of Dulcinea! for, having so many companions in pain, you would feel but little of your own: besides, perhaps, the sage Merlin would take every lash of theirs, coming from so good a hand, upon account for ten of those you must, one day or other, give yourself.'

The general would have asked what lashes he spoke of, and what he meant by the disenchantment of Dulcinea; when a mariner said:

'The fort of Montjuy* makes a signal, that there is a vessel with oars on the coast, on the western side.'

The general hearing this, leaped upon the middle gangway, and said:

'Pull away, my lads, let her not escape us: it must be some brigantine belonging to the corsairs of Algiers, that the fort makes the signal for.'

Then the other three galleys came up with the captain, to receive his orders. The general commanded, that two of them should put out to sea as fast as they could, and he with the other would go along shore, and so the vessel could not escape. The crew plied the oars, impelling the galleys with such violence, that they seemed to fly. Those that stood out to sea, about two miles off, discovered a sail, which they judged to carry about fourteen or fifteen banks of oars; and so it proved to be. The vessel, discovering the galleys, put herself in chase, with design and in hope to get away by her swiftness. But, unfortunately for her, the captain-galley happened to be one of the swiftest vessels upon the sea, and therefore gained upon the brigantine so fast, that the corsairs saw they could not escape; and so the master of her ordered his men to drop their oars, and yield themselves prisoners, that they might not exasperate the captain of our galleys.

But fortune, that would have it otherwise, so ordered, that, just as the captain-galley came so near, that the corsairs could hear a voice from her, calling to them to surrender, two Toraquis, that is to say, two Turks that were drunk, who came in the brigantine with twelve others, discharged two muskets, with which they killed two of our soldiers upon the prow. Which the general seeing, he swore not to leave a man alive he should take in the vessel, and coming up with all fury to board her, she slipped away under the oars of the galley. The galley ran ahead a good way: they in the vessel, perceiving they were got clear, made all the way they could while the galley was coming about, and again put themselves in chase with oars and sails. But their diligence did them not so much good, as their presumption did them harm; for the captain-galley, overtaking them in little more than half a mile, clapped her oars on the vessel, and took them all alive.

By this time the two other galleys were come up, and all four returned with their prize to the strand, where a vast concourse of people stood expecting them, desirous to see what they had taken. The general cast anchor near the land, and, knowing that the viceroy was upon the shore, he ordered out the boat to bring him on board, and commanded the mainyard to be let down immediately, to hang thereon the master of the vessel, and the rest of the Turks he had taken in her, being about six-and-thirty persons, all brisk fellows, and most of them Turkish musketeers. The general inquired, which was the master of the brigantine, and one of the captives, who afterwards appeared to be a Spanish renegado, answered him in Castilian:

'This youth, sir, you see here, is our master;' pointing to one of the most beautiful and most graceful young men that human imagination could paint.

His age, in appearance, did not reach twenty years. The general said to him:

'Tell me, ill-advised dog, what moved you to kill my soldiers, when you saw it was impossible to escape? Is this the respect paid to captain-galleys? Know you not, that temerity is not valour, and that doubtful hopes should make men daring, but not rash?'

The youth would have replied; but the general could not hear him then, by reason he was going to receive the viceroy, who was just then entered the galley; with whom there came several of his servants, and some people of the town.

'You have had a fine chase of it, Señor General,' said the viceroy.

'So fine,' answered the general, 'that your excellency shall presently see it hanged up at the yardarm.'

'How so?' replied the viceroy.

'Because,' replied the general, 'against all law, against all reason, and the custom of war, they have killed me two of the best soldiers belonging to the galleys, and I have sworn to hang every man I took prisoner, especially this youth here, who is master of the brigantine:' pointing to one, who had his hands already tied, and a rope about his neck, and stood expecting death.

The viceroy looked at him, and, seeing him so beautiful, so genteel, and so humble (his beauty giving him in that

instant a kind of letter of recommendation), he had a mind
to save him, and therefore he asked him:

'Tell me, sir, are you a Turk, a Moor, or a renegado?'

'To which the youth answered in the Castilian tongue:'

'I am neither a Turk, nor a Moor, nor a renegado.'

'What are you then?' replied the viceroy.

'A Christian woman,' replied the youth.

'A Christian woman, in such a garb, and in such circumstances,' said the viceroy, 'is a thing rather to be wondered
at than believed.'

'Gentlemen,' said the youth, 'suspend the execution of my
death: it will be no great loss to defer your revenge while I
recount the story of my life.'

What heart could be so hard, as not to relent at these
expressions, at least so far as to hear what the sad and
afflicted youth had to say? The general bid him say what he
pleased, but not to expect pardon for his notorious offence.
With this license, the youth began his story in the following
manner:

'I was born of Moorish parents, of that nation more
unhappy than wise, so lately overwhelmed under a sea of
misfortunes. In the current of their calamity, I was carried
away by two of my uncles into Barbary; it availed me nothing
to say I was a Christian, as indeed I am, and not of the
feigned or pretended; but of the true and Catholic ones. The
discovery of this truth had no influence on those who were
charged with our unhappy banishment; nor would my uncles
believe it, but rather took it for a lie, and an invention of
mine, in order to remain in the country where I was born;
and so, by force rather than by my goodwill, they carried me
with them. My mother was a Christian too. I sucked in the
Catholic faith with my milk. I was virtuously brought up,
and, neither in my language nor behaviour, did I, as I thought,
give any indication of being a Morisco.

'My beauty, if I have any, grew up, and kept equal pace
with these virtues; for such I believe them to be: and, though
my modesty and reserve were great, I could not avoid being
seen by a young gentleman, called Don Gaspar Gregorio,
eldest son of a person of distinction, whose estate joins to

our town. How he saw me, how we conversed together, how he was undone for me, and how I was little less for him, would be tedious to relate, especially at a time when I am under apprehension, that the cruel cord, which threatens me, may interpose between my tongue and my throat; and there-fore I will only say, that Don Gregorio resolved to bear me company in our banishment. And so, mingling with the Moors, who came from other towns (for he spoke the language well), in the journey he contracted an intimacy with my two uncles, who had the charge of me; for my father, being a prudent and provident person, as soon as he saw the first edict for our banishment, left the town, and went to seek some place of refuge for us in foreign kingdoms. He left a great number of pearls, and precious stones of great value, hid and buried in a certain place, known to me only, with some money in crusadoes and pistoles of gold, com-manding me in nowise to touch the treasure he left, if peradventure we should be banished before he returned.

'I obeyed, and passed over into Barbary with my uncles, and other relations and acquaintance, as I have already said; and the place we settled in was Algiers, or rather hell itself. The king heard of my beauty, and fame told him of my riches, which partly proved my good fortune. He sent for me, and asked me of what part of Spain I was, and what money and jewels I had brought with me. I told him the town, and that the jewels and money were buried in it; but that they might easily be brought off, if I myself went to fetch them. All this I told him, in hopes that his own covetousness, more than my beauty, would blind him.

'While he was thus discoursing with me, information was given him, that one of the genteelest and handsomest youths imaginable came in my company. I presently understood that they meant Don Gaspar Gregorio, whose beauty is beyond all possibility of exaggeration. I was greatly disturbed, when I considered the danger Don Gregorio was in; for, among those barbarous Turks, a beautiful boy or youth is more valued and esteemed than a woman, be she never so beautiful. The king commanded him to be immediately brought before him, that he might see him, and asked me if it was true, what he was told of that youth. I, as if inspired by heaven, answered: Yes, it was; but that I must inform him, he was not a man, but a woman, as I was: and I requested, that he would let me go and dress her in her proper garb, that she might shine in full beauty, and appear in his presence with the less concern. He said, I might go in a good hour, and that next day he would talk with me of the manner how I might conveniently return to Spain, to get the hidden treasure. I consulted with Don Gaspar: I told him the danger he ran in appearing as a man: and I dressed him like a Morisca, and that very afternoon introduced him as a woman to the king, who was in admiration at the sight of her, and proposed to reserve her for a present to the Grand Señor; and, to prevent the risk she might run in the seraglio among his own wives, and distrusting himself, he ordered her to be lodged in the house of a Moorish lady of quality, there to be kept and waited upon: whither she was instantly conveyed. What we both felt (for I cannot deny that I love him) I leave to the consideration of those who mutually love each other, and are forced to part.

'The king presently gave orders for my returning to Spain, in this brigantine, accompanied by two Turks, being those who killed your soldiers. There came with me also this Spanish renegado (pointing to him, who spoke first), whom I certainly know to be a Christian in his heart, and that he comes with a greater desire to stay in Spain than to return to Barbary. The rest of the ship's crew are Moors and Turks, who serve for nothing but to row at the oar. The two drunken and insolent Turks, disobeying the orders given them to set me and the renegado on shore in the first place of Spain we should touch upon, in the habit of Christians (with which we came provided), would needs first scour the coast, and make some prize, if they could, fearing, if they should land us first, we might be induced by some accident or other to discover, that such a vessel was at sea, and, if perchance there were any galleys abroad upon this coast, she might be taken. Last night we made this shore, and, not knowing anything of these four galleys, were discovered ourselves, and what you have seen has befallen us.

'In short, Don Gregorio remains among the women, in woman's attire, and in manifest danger of being undone; and I find myself, with my hands tied, expecting, or rather fearing, to lose that life, of which I am already weary. This, sir, is the conclusion of my lamentable story, as true as unfortunate. What I beg of you is, that you will suffer me to die like a Christian, since, as I have told you, I am nowise chargeable of the blame into which those of my nation have fallen.'

Here she held her peace, her eyes pregnant with tender tears, which were accompanied by many of those of the standers-by.

The viceroy, being of a tender and compassionate disposition, without speaking a word, went to her, and with his own hands unbound the cord that tied the beautiful ones of the fair Morisca.

While the Moriscan Christian was relating her strange story, an old pilgrim, who came aboard the galley with the viceroy, fastened his eyes on her, and, scarcely had she made an end, when, throwing himself at her feet, and embracing them, with words interrupted by a thousand sobs and sighs, he said:

'O Anna Felix! my unhappy daughter! I am thy father Ricote, who am returned to seek thee, not being able to live without thee, who art my very soul.'

At which words Sancho opened his eyes, and lifted up his head, which he was holding down, ruminating upon his late disgrace; and looking at the pilgrim, he knew him to be the very Ricote he met with upon the day he left his government, and was persuaded this must be his daughter; who, being now unbound, embraced her father, mingling her tears with his. Ricote said to the general and the viceroy:

'This, sirs, is my daughter, happy in her name alone; Anna Felix she is called, with the surname of Ricote, as famous for her own beauty, as for her father's riches. I left my native country, to seek, in foreign kingdoms, some shelter and safe retreat, and, having found one in Germany, I returned, in this pilgrim's weed, in the company of some Germans, in quest of my daughter, and to take up a great deal of wealth I had left buried. My daughter I found not, but the treasure I did, and have it in my possession; and now, by the strange turn of fortune you have seen, I have found the treasure which most enriches me—my beloved daughter. If our innocence, and her tears and mine, through the uprightness of your justice, can open the gates of mercy, let us partake of it, who never had a thought of offending you, nor in any ways conspired with the designs of our people, who have been justly banished.'

Then said Sancho:

'I know Ricote very well, and am sure what he says of Anna Felix's being his daughter is true; but as for the other idle stories of his going and coming, and of his having a good or bad intention, I meddle not with them.'

All that were present admired at the strangeness of the case; and the general said:

'Each tear of yours hinders me from fulfilling my oath: live, fair Anna Felix, all the years heaven has allotted you, and let the daring and the insolent undergo the punishment their crime deserves.'

Immediately he ordered that the two Turks, who had killed his soldiers, should be hanged at the yard-arm. But the viceroy earnestly entreated him not to hang them, their fault being rather the effect of madness than of valour. The general yielded to the viceroy's request, for it is not easy to execute revenge in cold blood. Then they consulted how to deliver Don Gaspar Gregorio from the danger he was left in. Ricote offered above two thousand ducats, which he had in pearls and jewels, towards it. Several expedients were proposed, but none so likely to succeed as that of the Spanish renegado aforementioned, who offered to return to Algiers in a small bark of about eight banks, armed with Christian rowers; for he knew where, how, and when he might land; nor was he ignorant of the house in which Don Gaspar was kept. The general and the viceroy were in doubt whether they should rely on the renegado, or trust him with the Christians, who were to row at the oar. Anna Felix answered for him, and her father Ricote said, he would be answerable for the ransom of those Christians, if they should be betrayed.

Matters being thus settled, the viceroy went ashore, and Don Antonio Moreno took the Morisco and her father along

with him, the viceroy charging him to regale and welcome
them as much as possible, offering, on his own part, whatever
his house afforded for their better entertainment, so great
was the kindness and charity that the beauty of Anna Felix
infused into his breast.

CHAPTER 64

*Treating of the adventure which gave Don Quixote more
sorrow than any which had hitherto befallen him.*

THE history relates, that the wife of Don Antonio Moreno
took a great deal of pleasure in seeing Anna Felix in her
house. She gave her a kind welcome, enamoured as well of
her beauty as of her discretion; for the Morisca excelled in
both; and all the people of the city flocked to see her, as if
they had been brought together by ringing the great bell. Don
Quixote said to Don Antonio, that the method they had
resolved upon for the redemption of Don Gregorio was quite
a wrong one, there being more danger than probability of
success in it; and that they would do better to land him, with
his horse and arms, in Barbary; for he would fetch him off
in spite of the whole Moorish race as Don Gayferos had
done by his spouse Melisendra.

'Take notice, sir,' quoth Sancho, hearing this, 'that Señor
Don Gayferos rescued his spouse on firm land, and carried
her over land into France; but here, if, peradventure, we
rescue Don Gregorio, we have no way to bring him into
Spain, since the sea is between.'

'For all things there is a remedy, excepting for death,'
replied Don Quixote; 'for, let but a vessel come to the
seaside, and we can embark in it, though the whole world
should endeavour to oppose it.'

'Your worship,' quoth Sancho, 'contrives and makes the
matter very easy; but, between the saying and the fact is a
very large tract; and I stick to the renegado, who seems to
me a very honest and good-natured man.'

Don Antonio said, 'if the renegado should miscarry in the business, it would be time enough to put in practice the expedient of the great Don Quixote's passing over into Barbary.'

Two days after, the renegado set sail in a small bark of six oars on a side, manned with a stout crew, and two days after that, the galleys departed for the Levant, the general having engaged the viceroy to give him advice of all that should happen in respect to the deliverance of Don Gregorio, and the fortune of Anna Felix.

One morning, Don Quixote being sallied forth to take the air on the strand, armed at all points (for, as he was wont to say, his arms were his finery, and his recreation fighting, and so he was seldom without them), he perceived advancing towards him a knight, armed likewise at all points. On his shield was painted a resplendent moon; and when he was come near enough to be heard, he raised his voice, and, directing it to Don Quixote, he said:

'Illustrious knight, and never-enough renowned Don Quixote de la Mancha, I am the Knight of the White Moon, whose unheard of exploits, perhaps, may bring him to your remembrance. I come to enter into combat with you, and to try the strength of your arm, in order to make you know and confess, that my mistress, be she who she will, is, without comparison, more beautiful than your Dulcinea del Toboso: which truth, if you do immediately and fairly confess, you will save your own life, and me the trouble of taking it from you: and if you fight, and are vanquished by me, all the satisfaction I expect is, that you lay aside arms, forbear going in quest of adventures, and retire home to your house for the space of one year, where you shall live, without laying hand to your sword, in profound peace, and profitable repose: which will redound both to the improvement of your estate and the salvation of your soul: and if you shall vanquish me, my head shall lie at your mercy, the spoils of my horse and arms shall be yours, and the fame of my exploits shall be transferred from me to you. Consider which is best for you, and answer me presently: for this business must be dispatched this very day.'

Don Quixote was surprised and amazed, as well at the arrogance of the Knight of the White Moon, as at the reason of his being challenged by him: and so, with gravity composed, and countenance severe, he answered:

'Knight of the White Moon, whose achievements have not as yet reached my ears, I dare swear you never saw the illustrious Dulcinea; for, had you seen her, I am confident you would have taken care not to engage in this trial, since the sight of her must have undeceived, and convinced you, that there never was, nor ever can be, a beauty comparable to hers; and therefore, without giving you the lie, and, only saying you are mistaken, I accept your challenge, with the aforementioned conditions; and that upon the spot, that the day allotted for this business may not first elapse: and out of the conditions I only except the transfer of your exploits, because I do not know what they are, nor that they are: I am contented with my own, such as they are. Take, then, what part of the field you please, and I will do the like, and to whom God shall give it, St. Peter give his blessing.'

The Knight of the White Moon was discovered from the city, and the viceroy was informed that he was in conference with Don Quixote de la Mancha. The viceroy believing it was some new adventure, contrived by Don Antonio Moreno, or by some other gentleman of the town, immediately rode out to the strand, accompanied by Don Antonio, and a great many other gentlemen; and arrived just as Don Quixote had wheeled Rosinante about, to take the necessary ground for his career. The viceroy, perceiving they were both ready to turn for the encounter, interposed, asking what induced them to so sudden a fight. The Knight of the White Moon answered: It was the precedency of beauty; and told him in a few words, what he had said to Don Quixote, and that the conditions of the combat were agreed to on both sides. The viceroy asked Don Antonio, in his ear, whether he knew who the Knight of the White Moon was, and whether it was some jest designed to be put upon Don Quixote. Don Antonio answered, that he neither knew who he was, nor whether his challenge was in jest or earnest. This answer perplexed the viceroy, putting him in doubt whether he should suffer them to proceed to the combat: but, inclining rather to believe it could be nothing but a jest, he went aside, saying:

'If there is no other remedy, knights, but to confess or die,
and if Señor Don Quixote persists in denying, and your
worship of the White Moon in affirming, at it in God's name.'

He of the White Moon thanked the viceroy in courtly and
discreet terms for the leave he gave them; and Don Quixote
did the same; who, recommending himself to heaven with all
his heart, and to his Dulcinea (as was his custom at the
beginning of the combats that offered), wheeled about again
to fetch a larger compass, because he saw his adversary did
the like; and, without sound of trumpet or other warlike
instrument, to give the signal for the onset, they both turned
their horses about at the same instant: and he of the White
Moon being the nimblest, met Don Quixote at two-thirds of
the career, and there encountered him with such impetuous
force (not touching him with his lance, which he seemed to
raise on purpose), that he gave Rosinante and Don Quixote
a perilous fall to the ground. Presently he was upon him,
and, clapping his lance to his visor, he said:

'Knight, you are vanquished and a dead man, if you do
not confess the conditions of our challenge.'

Don Quixote bruised and stunned, without lifting up his
visor, as if he was speaking from within a tomb, in a feeble
and low voice, said:

'Dulcinea del Toboso is the most beautiful woman in the
world, and I the most unfortunate knight on earth, and it is
not fit that my weakness should discredit this truth: knight,
push on your lance, and take away my life, since you have
spoiled me of my honour.'

'By no means,' quoth he of the White Moon: 'live, live the
fame of the beauty of the lady Dulcinea del Toboso, in its
full lustre! all the satisfaction I demand is, that the great Don
Quixote retire home to his own town for a year, or till such
time as I shall command, according to our agreement before
we began this battle.'

All this was heard by the viceroy, Don Antonio, and many
other persons there present; who also heard Don Quixote
reply, that since he required nothing of him to the prejudice
of Dulcinea, he would perform all the rest like a punctual
and true knight.

This confession being made, he of the White Moon turned about his horse, and, making a bow with his head to the viceroy, at a full gallop entered into the city. The viceroy ordered Don Antonio to follow him, and by all means to learn who he was. They raised Don Quixote from the ground, and, uncovering his face, found him pale, and in a cold sweat. Rosinante, out of pure ill plight, could not stir for the present. Sancho, quite sorrowful, and cast down, knew not what to do or say. He fancied all that had happened to be a dream, and that all this business was matter of enchantment: he saw his master vanquished, and under an obligation not to bear arms during a whole year: he imagined the light of the glory of his achievements obscured, and the hopes of his late promises dissipated as smoke by the wind: he was afraid Rosinante's bones were quite broken, and his master's disjointed, and wished it might prove no worse. Finally, Don Quixote was carried back to the city in a chair the viceroy had commanded to be brought; and the viceroy also returned thither, impatient to learn who the Knight of the White Moon was, who had left Don Quixote in such evil plight.

CHAPTER 65

In which an account is given who the Knight of the White Moon was; with the liberty of Don Gregorio, and other accidents.

DON ANTONIO MORENO followed the Knight of the White Moon. A great number of boys also pursued and persecuted him, till they had lodged him in an inn within the city. Don Antonio went in after him, being desirous to know who he was. His squire came out to receive and unarm him. He shut himself up in a lower room, and with him Don Antonio, whose cake was dough, till he knew who he was. He of the White Moon perceiving that this gentleman would not leave him, said:

'I very well know, sir, the design of your coming, which is, to learn who I am; and, because there is no occasion for concealing it, while my servant is unarming me, I will inform you, without deviating a tittle from the truth. Know, sir, that I am called the bachelor Sampson Carrasco: I am of the same town with Don Quixote de la Mancha, whose madness and folly move all that know him to compassion. Of those who had most pity for him, was I, and, believing his recovery to depend upon his being quiet, and staying at home in his own house, I contrived how to make him continue there. And so, about three months ago, I sallied forth to the highway like a knight-errant, styling myself Knight of the Looking-glasses, designing to fight with him, and vanquish him, without doing him harm, the condition of our combat being, that the vanquished should remain at the discretion of the vanquisher: and what I, concluding him already vanquished, intended to enjoin him, was, that he should return to his village, and not stir out of it in a whole year; in which time he might be cured. But fortune ordained it otherwise; for he vanquished me, and tumbled me from my horse, and so my design did not take effect. He pursued his journey, and I returned home, vanquished, ashamed, and bruised with the fall, which was a very dangerous one.

'Nevertheless, I lost not the desire of finding him, and vanquishing him, as you have seen this day. And, as he is so exact and punctual in observing the laws of knight-errantry, he will doubtless keep that I have laid upon him, and will be as good as his word. This, sir, is the business; and I have nothing to add, but only to entreat you not to discover me, nor to let Don Quixote know who I am, that my good intentions may take effect, and his understanding be restored to a man who has a very good one, if the follies of chivalry do but leave him.'

'Oh! sir,' quoth Don Antonio, 'God forgive you the injury you have done the whole world, in endeavouring to restore to his senses the most diverting madman in it! Do you not see, sir, that the benefit of his recovery will not counterbalance the pleasure his extravagances afford? But I fancy that all Señor Bachelor's industry will not be sufficient to recover a man so consummately mad; and were it not against the rule of charity, I would say: May Don Quixote never be recovered! for, by his cure, we not only lose our pleasantries, but those of his squire Sancho Panza too; any one of which is enough to make melancholy herself merry. Nevertheless, I will hold my peace, and tell him nothing, to try if I am right in suspecting that all Señor Carrasco's diligence is likely to be fruitless.'

Carrasco answered, that, all things considered, the business was in a promising way, and he hoped for good success. Don Antonio, having offered his service in whatever else he pleased to command him, took his leave. The same day, the bachelor, having caused his armour to be tied upon the back of a mule, rode out of the city upon the same horse on which he entered the fight, and returned to his native place, nothing befalling him by the way worthy to be recorded in this faithful history. Don Antonio recounted to the viceroy all that Carrasco had told him; at which the viceroy was not much pleased, considering that Don Quixote's confinement would put an end to all that diversion, which his follies administered to those that knew him.

Six days Don Quixote lay in bed, chagrined, melancholy, thoughtful, and peevish, his imagination still dwelling upon the unhappy business of his defeat. Sancho strove to comfort him, and among other things, said:

'Dear sir, hold up your head, and be cheerful if you can, and give heaven thanks, that, though you got a swinging fall, you did not come off with a rib broken: and since you know that, They that will give must take, and that, There are not always bacon flitches, where there are pins; cry, a fig for the physician, since you have no need of his help in this distemper. Let us return home, and leave this rambling in quest of adventures through countries and places unknown: and, if it be well considered, I am the greater loser, though your worship be the greater sufferer. I, who, with the government, quitted the desire of ever governing more, did not quit the desire of being an earl, which will never come to pass, if your worship refuses being a king, by quitting the exercise of chivalry; and so my hopes vanish into smoke.'

'Peace, Sancho,' quoth Don Quixote, 'since you see my confinement and retirement is not to last above a year, and

then I will resume my honourable profession, and shall not
want a kingdom to win for myself, nor an earldom to bestow
on you.'

'God hear it,' quoth Sancho, 'and let sin be deaf! for I
have always been told, that a good expectation is better than
a bad possession.'

They were thus discoursing, when Don Antonio entered
with signs of great joy, saying:

'My reward, Señor Don Quixote, for the good news I bring:
Don Gregorio, and the renegado, who went to bring him,
are in the harbour: in the harbour do I say? by this time they
must be come to the viceroy's palace, and will be here
presently.'

Don Quixote was a little revived, and said:

'In truth, I was going to say I should be glad if it had
fallen out quite otherwise, that I might have been obliged to
go over to Barbary, where, by the force of my arm, I should
have given liberty, not only to Don Gregorio, but to all the
Christian captives that are in Barbary. But what do I say?
wretch that I am! Am I not he who is vanquished? Am I
not he who is overthrown? Am I not he, who has it not in
his power to take arms in a twelvemonth? Why then do I
promise? Why do I vaunt, if I am fitter to handle a distaff
than a sword?'

'No more, sir,' quoth Sancho: 'let the hen live, though she
have the pip: To-day for you, and to-morrow for me: and,
as for these matters of encounters and bangs, never trouble
your head about them; for, He that falls to-day may rise
to-morrow, unless he has a mind to lie abed; I mean, by
giving way to despondency, and not endeavouring to recover
fresh spirits for fresh encounters. And, pray, sir, rise, and
welcome Don Gregorio; for there seems to be a great bustle
in the house, and by this time he is come.'

He said the truth; for Don Gregorio and the renegado
having given the viceroy an account of the expedition, Don
Gregorio, impatient to see Anna Felix, was come with the
renegado to Don Antonio's house; and though Don Gregorio, when he made his escape from Algiers, was in a woman's
dress, he had exchanged it in the bark for that of a captive,

who escaped with him. But, in whatever dress he had come, he would have had the appearance of a person worthy to be loved, served, and esteemed; for he was above measure beautiful, and seemed to be about seventeen or eighteen years of age. Ricote and his daughter went out to meet him, the father with tears, and the daughter with modesty. The young couple did not embrace each other; for, where there is much love, there are usually but few freedoms. The joint beauties of Don Gregorio and Anna Felix surprised all the beholders. Silence spoke for the two lovers, and their eyes were the tongues that proclaimed their joyful and modest sentiments.

The renegado acquainted the company with the artifices and means he had employed to bring off Don Gregorio. Don Gregorio recounted the dangers and straits he was reduced to among the women he remained with, not in a tedious discourse, but in few words, whereby he showed, that his discretion outstripped his years. In short, Ricote generously paid and satisfied, as well the renegado, as those that rowed at the oar. The renegado was reconciled, and restored to the bosom of the church, and of a rotten member, became clean and sound through penance and repentance.

Two days after, the viceroy and Don Antonio consulted together about the means how Anna Felix and her father might remain in Spain, thinking it no manner of inconvenience, that a daughter so much a Christian, and a father, to appearance, so well inclined, should continue in the kingdom. Don Antonio offered to solicit the affair himself at court, being obliged to go thither about other business; intimating that, by means of favour and bribery, many difficult matters are there brought about.

'No,' quoth Ricote, who was present at this discourse, 'there is nothing to be expected from favour or bribes; for with the great Bernardino de Velasco, Count of Salazar,* to whom his majesty has given the charge of our expulsion, no entreaties, no promises, no bribes, no pity are of any avail: for, though it is true he tempers justice with mercy, yet, because he sees the whole body of our nation tainted and putrefied, he rather makes use of burning caustics than mollifying ointments; so that, by prudence, by sagacity, by

diligence, by terrors, he has supported on his able shoulders
the weight of this great machine, and brought it to due
execution and perfection: our artifices, stratagems, diligence,
and policies, not being able to blind his Argus eyes, continually open to see that none of us stay, or lurk behind, that,
like a concealed root, may hereafter spring up, and spread
venomous fruit through Spain, already cleared, already freed
from the fears our vast numbers kept the kingdom in. A
most heroic resolution of the great Philip the Third, and
unheard-of wisdom in committing this charge to the said Don
Bernardino de Velasco!'

'However, when I am at court,' said Don Antonio, 'I will
use all the diligence and means possible, and leave the success
to heaven. Don Gregorio shall go with me, to comfort his
parents under the affliction they must be in for his absence:
Anna Felix shall stay at my house with my wife, or in a
monastery; and I am sure the viceroy will be glad, that honest
Ricote remain in his house, till he sees the success of my
negotiation. The viceroy consented to all that was proposed.'

But Don Gregorio, knowing what passed, expressed great
unwillingness to leave Anna Felix: but, resolving to visit his
parents, and to concert the means of returning for her, he
came at length into the proposal. Anna Felix remained with
Don Antonio's lady, and Ricote in the viceroy's house.

The day of Don Antonio's departure came, and that of
Don Quixote's and Sancho's two days after, his fall not
permitting him to travel sooner. At Don Gregorio's parting
from Anna Felix, all was tears, sighs, swoonings, and sobbings. Ricote offered Don Gregorio a thousand crowns, if
he desired them; but he would accept only of five, that Don
Antonio lent him, to be repaid when they met at court. With
this they both departed; and Don Quixote and Sancho
afterwards, as has been said; Don Quixote, unarmed, and in
a travelling dress, and Sancho on foot, because Dapple was
loaded with the armour.

CHAPTER 66

Treating of matters, which he, who reads, will see; and he, who hears them read, will hear.

AT going out of Barcelona, Don Quixote turned about to see the spot where he was overthrown, and said:

'Here stood Troy; here my misfortunes, not my cowardice, despoiled me of my acquired glory: here I experienced the fickleness of fortune; here the lustre of my exploits was obscured; and lastly, here fell my happiness, never to rise again.'

Which Sancho hearing, he said:

'It is as much the part of valiant minds, dear sir, to be patient under misfortunes, as to rejoice in prosperity: and this I judge by myself; for as, when a governor, I was merry, now that I am a squire on foot, I am not sad: for I have heard say, that she, they commonly call Fortune, is a drunken, capricious dame, and above all, very blind; so that she does not see what she is about, nor knows whom she casts down, or whom she exalts.'

'You are much of a philosopher, Sancho,' answered Don Quixote, 'and talk very discreetly; I know not whence you had it. What I can tell you is, that there is no such thing in the world as fortune, nor do the things which happen in it, be they good or bad, fall out by chance, but by the particular appointment of heaven; and hence comes the saying, that every man is the maker of his own fortune. I have been so of mine, but not with all the prudence necessary; and my presumption has succeeded accordingly: for I ought to have considered that the feebleness of Rosinante was not a match for the ponderous bulk of the Knight of the White Moon's steed. In short, I adventured it; I did my best; I was overthrown; and, though I lost my honour, I lost not, nor could I lose, the virtue of performing my promise. When I was a knight-errant, daring and valiant, by my works I gained credit to my exploits: and now, that I am but a walking squire, I will gain reputation to my words, by performing my promise. March on then, friend Sancho, and let us pass at home the year of our novitiate; by which retreat we shall acquire fresh vigour, to return to the never-by-me-forgotten exercise of arms.'

'Sir,' answered Sancho, 'trudging on foot is no such pleasant thing, as to encourage or incite me to travel great days' journeys; let us leave this armour hanging upon some tree, instead of a hanged man; and when I am mounted upon Dapple, my feet from the ground, we will travel as your worship shall like and lead the way; for to think that I am to foot it, and make large stages, is to expect what cannot be.'

'You have said well, Sancho,' answered Don Quixote: 'hang up my armour for a trophy: and under them, or round about them we will carve on the tree that which was written on the trophy of Orlando's arms:

> 'Let none presume these arms to move,
> Who Roldan's fury dares not prove.'*

'All this seems to me extremely right,' answered Sancho, and, were it not for the want we should have of Rosinante upon the road, it would not be amiss to leave him hanging too.'

'Neither him nor the armour,' replied Don Quixote, 'will I suffer to be hanged, that it may not be said—for good service, bad recompense.'

'Your worship says well,' answered Sancho; 'for, according to the opinion of the wise, The ass's fault should not be laid upon the pack-saddle; and since your worship is in fault for this business, punish yourself, and let not your fury spend itself upon the already shattered and bloody armour, nor upon the gentleness of Rosinante, nor upon the tenderness of my feet, making them travel more than they can bear.'

In these reasonings and discourses they passed all that day, and even four more, without encountering anything to put them out of their way. And, on the fifth, at entering into a village, they saw, at the door of an inn, a great number of people, who, it being a holiday, were there solacing themselves. When Don Quixote came up to them, a peasant said aloud:

'One of these two gentlemen, who are coming this way, and who know not the parties, shall decide our wager.'

'That I will,' answered Don Quixote, 'most impartially, when I am made acquainted with it.'

'The business, good sir,' quoth the peasant, 'is that an inhabitant of this town, who is so corpulent that he weighs about twenty-three stone, has challenged a neighbour, who weighs not above ten and a half, to run with him a hundred yards, upon condition of carrying equal weight; and the challenger, being asked how the weight should be made equal, said, that the challenged, who weighed but ten and a half, should carry thirteen stone of iron about him, and so both the lean and the fat would carry equal weight.'

'Not so,' quoth Sancho immediately, before Don Quixote could answer: 'and to me, who have so lately left being a governor and a judge, as all the world knows, it belongs to resolve these doubts, and give my opinion in every controversy.'

'Answer in a good hour, friend Sancho,' quoth Don Quixote; 'for I am not fit to feed a cat, my brain is so disturbed and turned topsy-turvy.'

'With this licence,' quoth Sancho to the country-fellows who crowded about him, gaping and expecting his decision: 'Brothers! The fat man's proposition is unreasonable, nor is there the least shadow of justice in it; for if it be true, what is commonly said, that the challenged may choose his weapons, it is not reasonable the other should choose for him such as will hinder and obstruct his coming off conqueror: and therefore my sentence is, that the fat fellow, the challenger, pare away, slice off, or cut out, thirteen stone of his flesh, somewhere or other, as he shall think best and properest; and so, being reduced to ten and a half stone weight, he will be equal to, and matched exactly with his adversary; and so they may run upon even terms.'*

'I vow,' quoth one of the peasants, who listened to Sancho's decision, 'this gentleman has spoke like a saint, and given sentence like a canon; but I warrant the fat fellow will have no mind to part with an ounce of his flesh, much less thirteen stone.'

'The best way,' answered another, 'will be, not to run at all, that lean may not break his back with the weight, nor fat lose flesh; and let half the wager be spent in wine, and let us take these gentlemen to the tavern that has the best, and, Give me the cloak when it rains.'

'I thank ye, gentlemen,' answered Don Quixote, 'but cannot stay a moment; for melancholy thoughts, and disastrous circumstances, oblige me to appear uncivil, and to travel faster than ordinary.'

And so, clapping spurs to Rosinante, he went on, leaving them in admiration, both at the strangeness of his figure, and the discretion of his man (for such they took Sancho to be); and another of the peasants said:

'If the man be so discreet, what must the master be? I will lay a wager, if they go to study at Salamanca, in a trice they will come to be judges at court; for there is nothing easier: it is but studying hard, and having favour and good luck, and when a man least thinks of it, he finds himself with a white wand in his hand, or a mitre on his head.'

That night master and man passed in the middle of the fields, exposed to the smooth and clear sky; and, the next day, going on their way, they saw coming towards them a man on foot, with a wallet about his neck, and a javelin or half-pike in his hand, the proper equipment of a foot-post; who, when he was come pretty near to Don Quixote, mended his pace, and, half running, went up to him, and, embracing his right thigh (for he could reach no higher) with signs of great joy, he said:

'Oh! Señor Don Quixote de la Mancha, with what pleasure will my lord duke's heart be touched, when he understands that your worship is returning to his castle, where he still is with my lady duchess!'

'I know you not, friend,' answered Don Quixote, 'nor can I guess who you are, unless you tell me.'

'I, Señor Don Quixote,' answered the foot-post, 'am Tosilos the duke's lackey, who would not fight with your worship about the marriage of Doña Rodriguez's daughter.'

'God be my aid!' quoth Don Quixote, 'are you he whom the enchanters, my enemies, transformed into the lackey, to defraud me of the glory of that combat?'

'Peace, good sir,' replied the foot-post; 'for there was not any enchantment, nor change of face: I was as much the lackey Tosilos, when I entered the lists, as Tosilos the lackey when I came out. I thought to have married without fighting, because I liked the girl: but my design succeeded quite otherwise: for, as soon as your worship was departed from our castle, my lord duke ordered a hundred bastinadoes to be given me, for having contravened the directions he gave me before the battle: and the business ended in the girl's turning nun, and Doña Rodriguez's returning to Castile: and I am now going to Barcelona, to carry a packet of letters from my lord to the viceroy. If your worship pleases to take a little draught, pure, though warm, I have here a calabash full of the best, with a few slices of Tronchon cheese, which will serve as a provocative and awakener of thirst, if perchance it be asleep.'

'I accept of the invitation,' quoth Sancho; 'and throw aside the rest of the compliment, and fill, honest Tosilos, maugre and in spite of all the enchanters that are in the Indies.'

'In short, Sancho,' quoth Don Quixote, 'you are the greatest glutton in the world, and the greatest ignorant upon earth, if you cannot be persuaded that this foot-post is enchanted, and this Tosilos a counterfeit. Stay you with him, and sate yourself; for I will go on fair and softly before, and wait your coming.'

The lackey laughed, unsheathed his calabash, and unwalleted his cheese; and taking out a little loaf, he and Sancho sat down upon the green grass, and, in peace and good fellowship, quickly dispatched, and got to the bottom of the provisions in the wallet, with so good an appetite, that they licked the very packet of letters, because it smelt of cheese. Said Tosilos to Sancho:

'Doubtless, friend Sancho, this master of yours ought to be reckoned a madman.'

'Why ought?' replied Sancho; 'he owes nothing to anybody; for he pays for everything, especially where madness is current. I see it full well, and full well I tell him of it: but what boots it, especially now that there is an end of him; for he is vanquished by the Knight of the White Moon.'

Tosilos desired him to tell him what had befallen him: but Sancho said, it was unmannerly to let his master wait for him, and that some other time, if they met, he should have leisure to do it. And rising up, after he had shaken his loose upper coat, and the crumbs from his beard, he drove Dapple before him, and, bidding Tosilos adieu, he left him, and overtook his master, who was staying for him under the shade of a tree.

CHAPTER 67

Of the resolution Don Quixote took to turn shepherd, and lead a rural life, till the year of his promise should be expired; with other accidents truly pleasant and good.

IF various cogitations perplexed Don Quixote before his defeat, many more tormented him after his overthrow. He stayed, as has been said, under the shade of a tree, where reflections, like flies about honey, assaulted and stung him; some dwelling upon the disenchantment of Dulcinea, and others upon the life he was to lead in his forced retirement. Sancho came up, and commended to him the generosity of the lackey Tosilos.

'Is it possible, Sancho,' said Don Quixote, 'that you persist in thinking that he is a real lackey? You seem to have quite forgot that you saw Dulcinea converted and transformed into a country wench, and the Knight of the Looking-glasses into the bachelor Sampson Carrasco: all the work of enchanters, who persecute me. But tell me, did you inquire of this Tosilos what God has done with Altisidora; whether she still bewails my absence, or has already left in the hands of oblivion the amorous thoughts that tormented her whilst I was present?'

'Mine,' answered Sancho, 'were not of a kind to afford me leisure to inquire after fooleries: body of me, Sir, is your worship now in a condition to be inquiring after other folks' thoughts, especially amorous ones?'

'Look you, Sancho,' quoth Don Quixote, 'there is a great deal of difference between what is done out of love, and what out of gratitude: it is very possible a gentleman may not be in love; but it is impossible, strictly speaking, he should be ungrateful. Altisidora, to all appearance, loved me: she gave me three nightcaps you know of: she wept at my departure: she cursed me, vilified me, and, in spite of shame, complained publicly of me; all signs that she adored me; for the anger of lovers usually ends in maledictions. I had neither hopes to give her, nor treasures to offer her; for mine are all engaged to Dulcinea, and the treasures of knights-errant, like those of fairies, are delusions, not realities, and I can only give her these remembrances I have of her, without prejudice, however, to those I have of Dulcinea, whom you wrong, through your remissness in whipping yourself, and in disciplining that flesh of yours (may I see it devoured by wolves!) which had rather preserve itself for the worms, than for the relief of that poor lady.'

'Sir,' answered Sancho, 'if I must speak the truth, I cannot persuade myself that the lashing of my posteriors can have anything to do with the disenchanting of the enchanted; for it is as if one should say, If your head aches, anoint your knee-pans. At least I dare swear, that in all the histories your worship has read, treating of knight-errantry, you never met with anybody disenchanted by whipping. But, be that as it will, I will lay it on, when the humour takes me, and time gives me conveniency of chastising myself.'

'God grant it,' answered Don Quixote, 'and heaven give you grace to see the duty and obligation you are under to aid my lady, who is yours too, since you are mine.'

With these discourses they went on their way, when they arrived at the very place and spot, where they had been trampled upon by the bulls. Don Quixote knew it again, and said to Sancho:

'This is the meadow where we lighted on the gay shepherd-esses and gallant shepherds who intended to revive in it, and imitate, the pastoral Arcadia; a thought as new as inge-nious; in imitation of which, if you approve it, I could wish, O Sancho, we might turn shepherds, at least for the time I must live retired. I will buy sheep, and all other materials necessary for the pastoral employment; and I, calling myself the shepherd Quixotiz, and you the shepherd Panzino, we will range the mountains, the woods and meadows, singing here, and complaining there, drinking the liquid crystal of the fountains, of the limpid brooks, or of the mighty rivers. The oaks with a plentiful hand shall give their sweetest fruit; the trunks of the hardest cork-trees shall afford us seats; the willows shall furnish shade, and the roses scent; the spacious meadow shall yield us carpets of a thousand colours; the air, clear and pure, shall supply breath; the moon and stars afford light, maugre the darkness of the night: singing shall furnish pleasure, and complaining yield delight: Apollo shall provide verses, and Love conceits; with which we shall make ourselves famous and immortal, not only in the present, but in future ages.'

'Before God,' quoth Sancho, 'this kind of life squares and corners with me exactly. Besides, no sooner will the bachelor Sampson Carrasco, and Master Nicholas the barber, have well seen it, but they will have a mind to follow, and turn shepherds with us, and God grant that the priest has not an inclination to make one in the fold, he is of so gay a temper, and such a lover of mirth.'

'You have said very well,' quoth Don Quixote; 'and the bachelor Sampson Carrasco, if he enters himself into the pastoral society, as doubtless he will, may call himself the shepherd Samsonino, or Carrascon. Nicholas the barber may be called Niculoso, as old Boscan [was] called Nemoroso.* As for the priest, I know not what name to bestow upon him, unless it be some derivative from his profession, calling him the shepherd Curiambro. As for the shepherdesses, whose lovers we are to be, we may pick and choose their names as we do pears; and since that of my lady quadrates alike with a shepherdess and a princess, I need not trouble myself about seeking another, that may suit her better. You, Sancho, may give yours what name you please.'

'I do not intend,' answered Sancho, to give mine any other than Teresona, which will fit her fat sides well, and is near her own too, since her name is Teresa. Besides, when I come to celebrate her in verse, I shall discover my chaste desires: for I am not for looking in other folks' houses for better bread than made of wheat. As for the priest, it will not be proper he should have a shepherdess, that he may set a good example; and if the bachelor Sampson will have one, his soul is at his own disposal.'

'God be my aid!' quoth Don Quixote, 'what a life shall we lead, friend Sancho! what a world of bagpipes shall we hear! what pipes of Zamora! what tambourets! what tabors! and what rebecks! And, if to all these different musics be added the albogues, we shall have almost all the pastoral instruments.'

'What are your albogues?' demanded Sancho; 'for I never heard them named, nor ever saw one of them in all my life.'

'Albogues,' answered Don Quixote, 'are certain plates of brass like candlesticks, which, being hollow, and struck against each other, give a sound, if not very agreeable, or harmonious, yet not offensive, and agreeing well enough with the rusticity of the tabor and pipe. And this name *albogue* is Moorish, as are all those in Spanish that begin *al*: as *almohaza, almorzar, alhombra, alguazil, alhucema, almacen, alcancia,* and the like, with very few more: and our language has only three Moorish words ending in *i,* namely *borcegui, zaquizami,* and *maravedi: alheli* and *alfaqui,* as well for the beginning with *al,* as ending in *i,* are known to be Arabic. This I have told you by the by, the occasion of naming albogues having brought it into my mind. One main help, probably, we shall have towards perfecting this profession, is, that I, as you know, am somewhat of a poet, and the bachelor Sampson Carrasco an extreme good one. Of the priest I say nothing: but I will venture a wager he has the points and collar of a poet; and that Master Nicholas the barber has them too, I make no doubt; for most or all of that faculty are players on the guitar and song-makers. I will complain of absence: you shall extol yourself for a constant lover: the shepherd Carrascon shall lament his being disdained; and the priest Curiambro may say or sing whatever will do him most service: and so the business will go on as well as heart can wish.'

To which Sancho answered:

'I am so unlucky, sir, that I am afraid I shall never see the day wherein I shall be engaged to this employment. O what neat wooden spoons shall I make when I am a shepherd! what crumbs! what cream! what garlands! what pastoral gimcracks! which, though they do not procure me the reputation of being wise, will not fail to procure me that of being ingenious. My daughter Sanchica shall bring us our dinner to the sheepfold: but have a care of that; she is a very sightly wench, and shepherds there are, who are more of the knave than the fool; and I would not have my girl come for wool, and return back shorn: and your loves, and wanton desires, are as frequent in fields as in the cities, and to be found in shepherds' cottages as well as in kings' palaces: and, Take away the occasion, and you take away the sin: and, What the eye views not, the heart rues not; A leap from behind a bush has more force than the prayer of a good man.'

'No more proverbs, good Sancho,' quoth Don Quixote; 'for any one of those you have mentioned is sufficient to let us know your meaning. I have often advised you not to be so prodigal of your proverbs, and to keep a strict hand over them: but, it seems, it is preaching in the desert, and, The more my mother whips me, the more I rend and tear.'

'Methinks,' answered Sancho, 'your worship makes good the saying, The kettle called the pot black-arse. You are reproving me for speaking proverbs, and you string them yourself by couples.'

'Look you, Sancho,' answered Don Quixote, 'I use mine to the purpose, and when I speak them, they are as fit as a ring to the finger; but you drag them in by head and shoulders. If I remember right, I have already told you, that proverbs are short sentences, drawn from experience, and the speculations of our ancient sages; and the proverb that is not to the purpose, is rather an absurdity than a sentence. But enough of this; and, since night approaches, let us retire a little way out of the high road, where we will pass this night, and God knows what will be to-morrow.'

They retired; they supped late and ill, much against Sancho's inclination, who now began to reflect upon the difficulties attending knight-errantry, among woods and mountains; though now and then plenty showed itself in castles and houses, as at Don Diego de Miranda's, at the wedding of the rich Camacho, and at Don Antonio Moreno's: but he considered it was not possible it should be always day, nor always night; and so he spent the remainder of that sleeping, and his master waking.

CHAPTER 68

Of the bristled adventure which befell Don Quixote.

THE night was somewhat dark, though the moon was in the heavens, but not in a part where she could be seen; for sometimes Señora Diana takes a trip to the antipodes, and leaves the mountains black, and the valleys in the dark. Don Quixote gave way to nature, taking his first sleep, without giving place to a second; quite the reverse of Sancho, who never had a second, one sleep lasting him from night to morning; an evident sign of his good constitution, and few cares. Those of Don Quixote kept him so awake, that he awakened Sancho, and said:

'I am amazed, Sancho, at the insensibility of your temper; you seem to me to be made of marble, or brass, not susceptible of any emotion or sentiment: I wake, while you sleep; I weep, when you are singing; I am fainting with hunger, while you are lazy and unwieldy with pure cramming: it is the part of good servants to share in their masters' pains, and to be touched with what affects them, were it but for the sake of decency. Behold the serenity of the night, and the solitude we are in, inviting us, as it were, to intermingle some watching with our sleep. Get up, by your life, and go a little apart from hence, and, with a willing mind and a good courage, give yourself three or four hundred lashes, upon account, for the disenchantment of Dulcinea: and this I ask as a favour; for I will not come to wrestling with you again, as I did before, because I know the weight of your arms. After you have laid them on, we will pass the remainder of the night in singing, I my absence and you your constancy, beginning from this moment our pastoral employment, which we are to follow in our village.'

'Sir,' answered Sancho, 'I am of no religious order, to rise out of the midst of my sleep, and discipline myself; neither do I think one can pass from the pain of whipping to music. Suffer me to sleep, and urge not this whipping myself, lest you force me to swear never to touch a hair of my coat, much less of my flesh.'

'O hardened soul!' cried Don Quixote; 'O remorseless squire! O bread ill employed, and favours ill considered, those I have already bestowed upon you, and those I still intend to bestow upon you! To me you owe, that you have been a governor; and to me you owe, that you are in a fair way of being an earl, or of having some title equivalent, and the accomplishment of these things will be delayed no longer than the expiration of this year; for "*post tenebras spero lucem*".'*

'I know not what that means,' replied Sancho: 'I only know, that while I am asleep, I have neither fear nor hope, neither trouble nor glory; and, blessings on him who invented sleep, the mantle that covers all human thoughts, the food that appeases hunger, the drink that quenches thirst, the fire that warms cold, the cold that moderates heat, and, lastly, the general coin that purchases all things, the balance and weight that equals the shepherd with the king, and the simple with the wise. One only evil, as I have heard, sleep has in it, namely, that it resembles death; for between a man asleep and a man dead, there is but little difference.'

'I never heard you, Sancho,' quoth Don Quixote, 'talk so elegantly as now; whence I come to know the truth of the proverb you often apply, Not with whom thou art bred, but with whom thou art fed.'

'Dear master of mine,' replied Sancho, 'it is not I that am stringing of proverbs now; for they fall from your worship's mouth also by couples, faster than from me; only between yours and mine there is this difference, that your worship's come at the proper season, and mine out of season; but, in short, they are all proverbs.'

They were thus employed, when they heard a kind of [dull] noise, and harsh sound, spreading itself through all those valleys. Don Quixote started up, and laid his hand to his sword; Sancho squatted down under Dapple, and clapped the bundle of armour on one side of him, and the ass's pannel on the other, trembling no less with fear than Don Quixote with surprise. The noise increased by degrees, and came nearer to the two tremblers, one at least so, for the other's courage is already sufficiently known.

Now the business was, that certain fellows were driving above six hundred hogs to sell at a fair, and were upon the road with them at that hour; and so great was the din they made with gruntling and blowing, that they deafened the ears of Don Quixote and Sancho, who could not presently guess the occasion of it. The farspreading and gruntling herd came crowding on, and, without any respect to the authority of Don Quixote, or to that of Sancho, trampled over them both, demolishing Sancho's entrenchment, and overthrowing, not only Don Quixote, but Rosinante to boot. The crowding, the gruntling, the hurrying on of those unclean animals put into confusion, and overturned, the pack-saddle, the armour, Dapple, Rosinante, Sancho, and Don Quixote.

Sancho got up as well as he could, and desired his master to lend him his sword, saying, he would kill half a dozen of those unmannerly gentlemen swine, for such by this time he knew them to be. Said Don Quixote to him:

'Let them alone, friend; for this affront is a punishment for my sin; and it is a just judgement of heaven, that wild dogs should devour, wasps sting, and hogs trample upon, a vanquished knight-errant.'

'It is also, I suppose, a judgement of heaven,' answered Sancho, 'that the squires of vanquished knights-errant should be stung by flies, eaten up by lice, and besieged by hunger. If we squires were the sons of the knights we serve, or very near of kin to them, it would be no wonder if the punishment of their faults should overtake us to the fourth generation: but what have the Panzas to do with the Quixotes? Well, let us compose ourselves again, and sleep out the little remainder of the night, and God will send us a new day, and we shall have better luck.'

'Sleep you, Sancho,' answered Don Quixote; for you were born to sleep, whilst I, who were born to watch, in the space between this and day, give the reins to my thoughts, and cool their heat in a little madrigal, which, unknown to you, I composed to-night in my mind.'

'Methinks,' quoth Sancho, 'the thoughts which give way to the making of couplets, cannot be many. Couplet it as much as your worship pleases, and I will sleep as much as I can.'

Then taking as much ground as he wanted, he bundled himself up, and fell into a sound sleep, neither suretyship, nor debts, nor any troubles disturbing him. Don Quixote, leaning against a beech or cork-tree (for Cid Hamet Ben Engeli does not distinguish what tree it was) to the music of his own sighs, sung as follows:—

> 'O Love, when, sick of heartfelt grief,
> I sigh, and drag thy cruel chain,
> To Death I fly, the sure relief
> Of those who groan in ling'ring pain.
>
> 'But coming to the fatal gates,
> The port in this my sea of woe,
> The joy I feel new life creates,
> And bids my spirits brisker flow.
>
> 'Thus dying every hour I live,
> And living, I resign my breath:
> Strange power of love, that thus can give
> A dying life and living death!'*

He accompanied each stanza with a multitude of sighs, and not a few tears, like one whose heart was pierced through by the grief of being vanquished, and by the absence of Dulcinea.

Now the day appeared, and the sun began to dart his beams in Sancho's eyes. He awaked, roused, and shook himself, and stretched his lazy limbs, and beheld what havoc the hogs had made in his cupboard; and cursed the drove, and somebody else besides. Finally, they both set forward on their journey; and towards the decline of the afternoon, they discovered about half a score men on horseback, and four or five on foot, advancing towards them. Don Quixote's heart leaped with surprise and Sancho's with fear; for the men that were coming up carried spears and targets, and advanced in a very warlike array. Don Quixote turned to Sancho, and said:

'Sancho, if I could but make use of my arms, and my promise had not tied up my hands, this machine that is coming towards us I would make no more of than I would of so many tarts and cheesecakes. But it may be something else than what we fear.'

By this time the horsemen were come up: and lifting up their lances, without speaking a word, they surrounded Don Quixote, and clapped their spears to his back and breast, threatening to kill him. One of those on foot, putting his finger to his mouth, to signify that he should be silent, laid hold on Rosinante's bridle, and drew him out of the road; and the others on foot, driving Sancho and Dapple before them, all keeping a marvellous silence, following the steps of him who led Don Quixote, who had a mind three or four times to ask, whither they were carrying him or what they would have. But scarcely did he begin to move his lips, when they were ready to close them with the points of their spears. And the like befell Sancho, for no sooner did he show an inclination to talk, than one of those on foot pricked him with a goad, and did as much to Dapple, as if he had a mind to talk too. It grew night; they mended their pace; the fear of the two prisoners increased, especially when they heard the fellows ever and anon say to them:

'On, on, ye Troglodytes!' 'peace, ye barbarous slaves!' 'pay, ye Anthropophagi!' 'Complain not, ye Scythians!' 'Open not your eyes, ye murdering Polyphemuses, ye butcherly lions!' and other the like names, with which they tormented the ears of the miserable pair, master and man. Sancho went along, saying to himself:

'We Ortolans? we Barber's slaves? we Andrew popinjays? we Citadels? we Polly famouses? I do not like these names at all; this is a bad wind for winnowing our corn; the whole mischief comes upon us together, like kicks to a cur; and would to God this disventurous adventure, that threatens us, may end in no worse!'

Don Quixote marched along, quite confounded, and not being able to conjecture, by all the conclusions he could make, why they called them by those reproachful names from which he could only gather, that no good was to be expected, and much harm to be feared. In this condition, about an hour after nightfall, they arrived at a castle, which Don Quixote presently knew to be the duke's, where he had so lately been.

'God be my aid!' said he, as soon as he knew the place, 'what will this end in? In this house all is courtesy and civil usage: but to the vanquished good is converted into bad, and bad into worse.'

They entered into the principal court of the castle, and saw it decorated and set out in such a manner, that their admiration increased and their fear doubled, as will be seen in the following chapter.

CHAPTER 69

Of the newest and strangest adventure of all that befell Don Quixote in the whole course of this grand history.

THE horsemen alighted, and, together with those on foot, taking Sancho and Don Quixote forcibly in their arms, carried them into the courtyard, round which near a hundred torches were placed in sockets, and above five hundred lights about the galleries of the court; insomuch that, in spite of the night, which was somewhat darkish, there seemed to be no want of the day. In the middle of the court was erected a tomb, about two yards from the ground, and over it a large canopy of black velvet; round which, upon its steps, were burning above a hundred wax tapers in silver candlesticks. On the tomb was seen the corpse of a damsel, so beautiful that her beauty made death itself appear beautiful. Her head lay upon a cushion of gold brocade, crowned with a garland inter-woven with odoriferous flowers of divers kinds; her hands lying crosswise upon her breast, and between them a branch of never-fading victorious palm. On one side of the court was placed a theatre, and in two chairs were seated two personages, whose crowns on their heads, and sceptres in their hands, denoted them to be kings, either real or feigned. On the side of the theatre, to which the ascent was by steps, stood two other chairs; upon which they who brought in the prisoners seated Don Quixote and Sancho, all this in profound silence, and by signs giving them both to understand they must be silent too: but, without bidding, they held their peace; for the astonishment they were in at what they beheld tied up their tongues.

And now two great persons ascended the theatre with a numerous attendance, whom Don Quixote presently knew to be the duke and duchess whose guest he had been. They seated themselves in two very rich chairs, close by those who had seemed to be kings. Who would not have admired at all this, especially considering that Don Quixote had now perceived that the corpse upon the tomb was that of the fair Altisidora? At the duke and the duchess's ascending the theatre, Don Quixote and Sancho rose up, and made them a profound reverence, and their grandeurs returned it by bowing their heads a little. At this juncture, an officer crossed the place, and coming to Sancho, threw over him a robe of black buckram, all painted over with flames, and, taking off his cap, put on his head a pasteboard mitre three feet high, like those used by the penitents of the Inquisition; bidding him, in his ear, not to unsew his lips; if he did, they would clap a gag in his mouth, or kill him. Sancho viewed himself from top to toe, and saw himself all over in flames; but, finding they did not burn him, he cared not two farthings. He took off his mitre, and saw it all painted over with devils: he put it on again, saying within himself:

'Well enough yet, these do not burn me, nor those carry me away.'

Don Quixote also surveyed him, and, though fear suspended his senses, he could not but smile to behold Sancho's figure.

And now, from under the tomb, proceeded a low and pleasing sound of flutes; which not being interrupted by any human voice (for Silence herself kept silence there), the music sounded both soft and amorous. Then, on a sudden, by the cushion of the seemingly dead body, appeared a beautiful youth in a Roman habit, who, in a sweet and clear voice, to the sound of a harp, which he played on himself, sung the two following stanzas:

' 'Till heaven, in pity to the weeping world,
   Shall give Altisidora back to day,

By Quixote's scorn to realms of Pluto hurl'd,
Her every charm to cruel death a prey;
While matrons throw their gorgeous robes away,
To mourn a nymph by cold disdain betray'd;
To the complaining lyre's enchanting lay,
I'll sing the praises of this hapless maid,
In sw·eter notes than Thracian Orpheus ever play'd.

'Nor shall my numbers with my life expire,
Or this world's light confine the boundless song:
To thee, bright maid! in death I'll touch the lyre,
And to my soul the theme shall still belong.
When freed from clay, the flitting ghosts among,
My spirit glides the Stygian shores around,
Though the cold hand of Death has seal'd my tongue,
Thy praise th' infernal caverns shall rebound,
And Lethe's sluggish waves move slower to the sound.'*

'Enough,' said one of the supposed kings, 'enough, divine chanter; for there would be no end of describing to us the death and graces of the peerless Altisidora, not dead, as the ignorant world supposes, but alive in the mouth of Fame, and in the penance Sancho Panza here present must pass through, to restore her to the lost light; and therefore, O Rhadamanthus, who with me judgest in the dark caverns of Pluto, since thou knowest all that is decreed by the inscrutable destinies, about bringing this damsel to herself, speak and declare it instantly, that the happiness we expect from her revival may not be delayed.'

Scarcely had Minos, judge and companion of Rhadamanthus,* said this, when Rhadamanthus, rising up, said:

'Ho, ye officers of this household, high and low, great and small, run one after another, and seal Sancho's face with four-and-twenty twitches, and his arms and side with twelve pinches and six pricks of a pin; for in the performance of this ceremony consists the restoration of Altisidora.'

Which Sancho Panza hearing, he broke silence, and said:

'I vow to God, I will no more let my face be sealed, nor my flesh be handled, than I will turn Turk! Body of me! what has handling my countenance to do with the resurrection of this damsel? The old woman has had a taste, and now her mouth waters. Dulcinea is enchanted, and I must be whipped to disenchant her; and now Altisidora dies, of some distemper it pleases God to send her, and she must be brought to life again by giving me four-and-twenty twitches, and making a sieve of my body by pinking it with pins, and pinching my arms black and blue. Put these jests upon a brother-in-law; I am an old dog, and tus, tus, will not do with me.'

'Thou shalt die, then,' quoth Rhadamanthus, in a loud voice: 'relent, thou tiger! humble thyself, thou proud Nimrod! suffer, and be silent, since no impossibilities are required of thee; and set not thyself to examine the difficulties of this business: twitched thou shalt be, pricked thou shalt see thyself, and pinched shalt thou groan. Ho, I say, officers, execute my command; if not, upon the faith of an honest man, you shall see what you were born to.'

Now there appeared, coming in procession along the court, six duennas, four of them with spectacles, and all of them with their right hands lifted up, and four fingers' breadth of their wrists naked, to make their hands seem the longer, as is now the fashion. Scarcely had Sancho laid his eyes on them, when, bellowing like a bull, he said:

'I might, perhaps, let all the world besides handle me: but to consent that duennas touch me, by no means; let them cat-claw my face, as my master was served in this very castle; let them pierce my body through and through with the points of the sharpest daggers; let them tear off my flesh with red-hot pincers; and I will endure it patiently, to serve these noble persons: but, to let duennas touch me, I will never consent, though the devil should carry me away!'

Don Quixote also broke silence, saying to Sancho:

'Be patient, son; oblige these noble persons, and give many thanks to heaven, for having infused such virtue into your person, that, by its martyrdom, you disenchant the enchanted, and raise the dead.'

By this time the duennas were got about Sancho; and he, being mollified and persuaded, and seating himself well in his chair, held out his face and beard to the first, who gave him a twitch well sealed, and then made him a profound reverence.

'Less complaisance, less daubing, Mistress Duenna,' quoth Sancho; 'for, before God, your fingers smell of vinegar.'

In short, all the duennas sealed him, and several others of the house pinched him: but what he could not bear, was, the pricking of the pins; and so up he started from his seat, quite out of all patience, and, catching hold of a lighted torch that was near him, he laid about him with it, putting the duennas, and all his executioners to flight, and saying:

'Avaunt, ye infernal ministers! for I am not made of brass, to be insensible of such extraordinary torments.'

Upon this, Altisidora, who could not but be tired with lying so long upon her back, turned herself on one side; which the bystanders perceiving, almost all of them with one voice cried:

'Altisidora is alive! Altisidora lives!'

Then Rhadamanthus bid Sancho lay aside his wrath, since they had already attained the desired end. Don Quixote no sooner saw Altisidora stir, than he went and kneeled down before Sancho, and said:

'Now is the time, dear son of my bowels, rather than my squire, to give yourself some of those lashes, you stand engaged for, in order to the disenchantment of Dulcinea. This, I say, is the time, now that your virtue is seasoned, and of efficacy to operate the good expected from you.'

To which Sancho answered:

'This seems to me to be, Reel upon reel, and not honey upon fritters: a good jest, indeed, that twitches, pinches, and pin-prickings, must be followed by lashes! But take a great stone once for all, and tie it about my neck, and toss me into a well; it will not grieve me much, if, for the cure of other folks' ailments, I must still be the wedding heifer: let them not meddle with me; else, by the living God, all shall out!'

And now Altisidora had seated herself upright on the tomb, and at the same instant the waits struck up, accompanied by flutes, and the voices of all, crying aloud:

'Altisidora is alive! Altisidora lives!'

The duke and duchess, and the kings Minos and Rhadamanthus, rose up, and, all in a body, with Don Quixote and

Sancho, went to receive Altisidora, and help her down from the tomb; who counterfeiting a person fainting, inclined her head to the duke and duchess, and to the kings, and looking askew at Don Quixote, said:

'God forgive you, unrelenting knight, through whose cruelty I have been in the other world, to my thinking, above a thousand years! and thee I thank, O most compassionate squire of all the globe contains, for the life I enjoy! From this day, friend Sancho, six of my smocks are at your service, to be made into so many shirts for yourself; and, if they are not all whole, at least they are all clean.'

Sancho, with his mitre in his hand, and his knee on the ground, kissed her hand. The duke ordered it to be taken from him, and his cap to be returned him, and his own garment instead of the flaming robe. Sancho begged the duke to let him keep the mitre and frock, having a mind to carry them to his own country, in token and memory of this unheard-of adventure. The duchess replied, he should have them, for he knew how much she was his friend. Then the duke ordered the court to be cleared, and everybody to retire to their own apartment, and that Don Quixote and Sancho should be conducted to their old lodgings.

CHAPTER 70

Which follows the sixty-ninth, and treats of matters indispensably necessary to the perspicuity of this history.

SANCHO slept that night on a truckle-bed in the same chamber with Don Quixote, a thing he would have excused, if he could; for he well knew his master would disturb his sleep with questions and answers, and he was not much disposed to talk, the smart of his past sufferings being still present to him, and an obstruction to the free use of his tongue; and he would have liked better to have lain in a hovel alone, than in that rich apartment in company. His fear proved so well founded, and his suspicion so just, that, scarcely was his master got into bed, when he said:

'What think you, Sancho, of this night's adventure? Great and mighty is the force of rejected love, as your own eyes can testify, which saw Altisidora dead, by no other darts, no other sword, nor any other warlike instrument, nor by deadly poison, but merely by the consideration of the rigour and disdain with which I always treated her.'

'She might have died in a good hour, as much as she pleased, and how she pleased,' answered Sancho; 'and she might have left me in my own house, since I neither made her in love, nor ever disdained her in my life. I know not, nor can I imagine how it can be, that the recovery of Altisidora, a damsel more whimsical than discreet, should have anything to do (as I have already said) with the torturing of Sancho Panza. Now indeed I plainly and distinctly perceive, there are enchanters and enchantments in the world, from which, good Lord, deliver me, since I know not how to deliver myself. But, for the present, I beseech your worship to let me sleep, and ask me no more questions, unless you have a mind I should throw myself out of the window.'

'Sleep, friend Sancho,' answered Don Quixote, 'if the pin-prickings, pinchings, and twitchings, you have received, will give you leave.'

'No smart,' replied Sancho, 'came up to the affront of the twitches, and for no other reason, but because they were given by duennas, confound them! and once more I beseech your worship to let me sleep; for sleep is the relief of those who are uneasy awake.'

'Be it so,' quoth Don Quixote, 'and God be with you.'

They both fell asleep, and, in this interval, Cid Hamet, author of this grand history, had a mind to write, and give an account, of what moved the duke and duchess to raise the edifice of the aforementioned contrivance, and says, that the bachelor Sampson Carrasco, not forgetting how, when Knight of the Looking-glasses, he was vanquished and overthrown by Don Quixote, which defeat and overthrow baffled and put a stop to all his designs, had a mind to try his hand again, hoping for better success than the past. And so, informing himself by the page, who brought the letter and presents to Teresa Panza, Sancho's wife, where Don

Quixote was, he procured fresh armour, and a horse, and painted a white moon on his shield, carrying the whole magazine upon a he-mule, and conducted by a peasant, not Thomas Cecial, his former squire, lest Sancho Panza or Don Quixote should know him. He arrived at the duke's castle, who informed him what way and route Don Quixote had taken, to be present at the tournaments of Saragossa. He also related to him the jests that had been put upon him, with the contrivance for the disenchantment of Dulcinea, at the expense of Sancho's posteriors. In short, he gave him an account, how Sancho had imposed upon his master, making him believe that Dulcinea was enchanted and transformed into a country-wench, and how the duchess his spouse had persuaded Sancho, that he himself was deceived, and that Dulcinea was really enchanted; at which the bachelor laughed, and wondered not a little, considering as well the acuteness and simplicity of Sancho, as the extreme madness of Don Quixote. The duke desired, if he found him, and overcame him, or not, to return that way, and acquaint him of the event.

The bachelor promised he would; he departed in search of him; and, not finding him at Saragossa, he went forward, and there befell him what you have already heard. He came back to the duke's castle, and recounted the whole to him, with the conditions of the combat, and that Don Quixote was now actually returning to perform his word, like a true knight-errant, and retire home to his village for a twelve-month, in which time, perhaps (quoth the bachelor), he may be cured of his madness. This, he said, was the motive of these his disguises, it being a great pity, that a gentleman of so good an understanding as Don Quixote, should be mad. Then he took leave of the duke, and returned home, expecting there Don Quixote, who was coming after him.

Hence the duke took occasion to play him this trick, so great was the pleasure he took in everything relating to Don Quixote and Sancho: and, sending a great many of his servants, on horseback and on foot, to beset all the roads about the castle, everyway by which Don Quixote might possibly return, he ordered them, if they met with him, to bring him, with or without his goodwill, to the castle. They met with him, and gave notice of it to the duke, who, having already given orders for what was to be done, as soon as he heard of his arrival, commanded the torches, and other illuminations, to be lighted up, in the courtyard, and Altisidora to be placed upon the tomb, with all the preparations before related; the whole represented so to the life, that there was but little difference between that and truth.

And Cid Hamet says besides, that, to his thinking, the mockers were as mad as the mocked; and that the duke and duchess were within two fingers' breadth of appearing to be mad themselves, since they took so much pains to make a jest of two fools: one of whom was sleeping at full swing, and the other waking with his disjointed thoughts: in which state the day found them, and the desire to get up; for Don Quixote, whether conquered, or conqueror, never took pleasure in the downy bed of sloth.

Altisidora (in Don Quixote's opinion, just returning from death to life) carrying on the humour of the duke and duchess, crowned with the same garland she wore on the tomb, and clad in a robe of white taffeta, flowered with gold, and her hair dishevelled, and leaning on a black staff of polished ebony, entered the chamber of Don Quixote, who was so amazed and confounded at the sight of her, that he shrunk down, and covered himself almost over head and ears with the sheets and quilts, his tongue mute, and with no inclination to show her any kind of civility. Altisidora sat down in a chair by his bed's head, and, after fetching a profound sigh, with a tender and enfeebled voice, she said:

'When women of distinction, and reserved maidens, trample upon honour, and give a loose to the tongue, breaking through every inconveniency, and giving public notice of the secrets of their heart, they must sure be reduced to a great strait. I, Señor Don Quixote de la Mancha, am one of these distressed, vanquished, and enamoured, but, for all that, patient, long-suffering, and modest, to such a degree, that my soul burst through my silence, and I lost my life. It is now two days since, by reflection on your rigour, O flinty knight, and "harder than any marble to my complaints",* I have been dead, or at least judged to be so by those that saw me; and were it not that love, taking pity on me, placed my recovery in the sufferings of this good squire, there had I remained in the other world.'

'Love,' quoth Sancho, 'might as well have placed it in those of my ass, and I should have taken it as kindly. But, pray tell me, señora, so may heaven provide you with a more tender-hearted lover than my master, what is it you saw in the other world? what is there in hell? for whoever dies in despair must perforce take up his rest in that place.'

'In truth,' quoth Altisidora, 'I did not die quite, since I went not to hell; for had I once set foot in it, I could not have got out again, though I had never so great a desire. The truth is, I came to the gate, where about a dozen devils were playing at tennis, in their waistcoats and drawers, their shirt-collars ornamented with Flanders lace, and ruffles of the same, with four inches of their wrists bare, to make their hands seem the longer, in which they held rackets of fire. But what I wondered most at was, that, instead of tennis-balls, they made use of books, seemingly stuffed with wind and flocks; a thing marvellous and new: but this I did not so much wonder at, as to see, that, whereas it is natural for winning gamesters to rejoice, and losers to be sorry, among the gamesters of that place, all grumbled, all were upon the fret, and all cursed one another.'

'That is not at all strange,' answered Sancho: 'for devils, play or not play, win or not win, can never be contented.'

'That is true,' quoth Altisidora: 'but there is another thing I wonder at (I mean, I wondered at it then) which was, that, at the first toss the ball was demolished, and could not serve a second time; and so they whipped them away, new and old, that it was marvellous to behold: and to one of them, flaming new, and neatly bound, they gave such a smart stroke, that they made its guts fly out, and scattered its leaves all about, and one devil said to another: "See what book that is"; and the other devil answered: "It is the *Second Part of the History of Don Quixote de la Mancha*, not composed by Cid Hamet, its first author, but by an Aragonese, who calls himself a native of Tordesillas." "Away with it," quoth the other devil, "and down with it to the bottom of the infernal abyss, that my eyes may never see it more." "Is it so bad?" answered the other. "So bad," replied the first, "that, had I myself undertaken to make it worse, it had been past my skill." They went on with their play, tossing other books up and down; and I, for having heard Don Quixote named, whom I so passionately love endeavoured to retain this vision in my memory.'

'A vision, doubtless, it must be,' quoth Don Quixote; 'for there is no other I in the world, and this history is tossed about from hand to hand, but stays in none; for everybody has a kick at it. It gives me no concern to hear that I wander, like a phantom, about the shades of the abyss, or about the light of this earth, because I am not the person this history treats of. If it be good, faithful, and true, it will survive for ages; but, if it be bad, from its birth to its grave the passage will be but short.'

Altisidora was going on with her complainings of Don Quixote, when Don Quixote said to her:

'I have often told you, madam, that I am very sorry you have placed your affections on me, since from mine you must expect no other return but thanks. I was born to be Dulcinea del Toboso's, and to her the fates, if there be any, have devoted me; and to think that any other beauty shall occupy the place she possesses in my soul, is to think what is impossible. This may suffice to disabuse you, and prevail with you to retreat within the bounds of your own modesty, since no creature is tied to the performance of impossibilities.'

Which Altisidora hearing, she assumed an air of anger and fury, and said:

'God's my life! Don Poor Jack, soul of a mortar, stone of a date, and more obdurate and obstinate than a courted clown, if I come at you, I will tear your very eyes out! Think you, Don Vanquished, and Don Cudgelled, that I died for you? All that you have seen this night has been but a fiction; for I am not a woman to let the black of my nail ache for such camels, much less die for them.'

'That I verily believe,' quoth Sancho; 'for the business of dying for love is a jest: folks may talk of it; but, for doing it, believe it Judas.'

While they were engaged in this discourse, there entered the musician, singer, and poet, who had sung the two forementioned stanzas: who making a profound reverence to Don Quixote, said:

'Be pleased, Sir Knight, to reckon and look upon me in the number of your most humble servants; for I have been most affectionately so this great while, as well on account of your fame, as of your exploits.'

Don Quixote answered:

'Pray, sir, tell me who you are that my civility may correspond with your merits.'

The young man answered, that he was the musician and panegyrist of the foregoing night.

'Indeed,' replied Don Quixote, 'you have an excellent voice: but what you sang did not seem to me much to the purpose; for what have the stanzas of Garcilaso to do with the death of this gentlewoman?'

'Wonder not at that, sir,' answered the musician; 'for, among the upstart poets of our age, it is the fashion for every one to write as he pleases, and to steal from whom he pleases, be it to the purpose or not; and, in these times, there is no silly thing sung or written, but it is ascribed to poetical licence.'

Don Quixote would have replied: but the duke and duchess, coming to visit him, prevented him: and between them there passed a long and delicious conversation, in which Sancho said so many pleasant and waggish things, that their grandeurs admired afresh, as well at his simplicity, as his acuteness. Don Quixote beseeched them to grant him leave to depart that very day, for it was more becoming such vanquished knights as he to dwell in a hogsty than a royal palace. They readily granted his request, and the duchess asked him, whether Altisidora remained in his good graces. He answered:

'Your ladyship must know, dear madam, that the whole of this damsel's distemper proceeds from idleness, the remedy whereof consists in some honest and constant employment. And she has told me here, that lace is much worn in hell, and, since she must needs know how to make it, let her stick to that; for, while her fingers are employed in managing the bobbins, the image or images of what she loves will not be roving so much in her imagination. This is the truth, this is my opinion, and this my advice.'

'And mine too,' added Sancho; 'for I never in my life saw a maker of lace that died for love; for your damsels that are busied have their thoughts more intent upon performing their tasks, than upon their loves. I know it by myself; for, while I am digging, I never think of my dearee; I mean my Teresa Panza, whom I love better than my very eyelids.'

'You say very well, Sancho,' quoth the duchess, 'and I will take care that my Altisidora shall henceforward be employed in needlework, at which she is very expert.'

'There is no need, madam,' answered Altisidora, 'of this remedy, since the consideration of the cruel treatment I have received from this ruffian and monster, will blot him out of my memory, without any other expedient; and, with your grandeur's leave, I will withdraw, that I may not have before my eyes, I will not say, his sorrowful figure but his abominable and hideous aspect.'

'I wish,' quoth the duke, 'this may not prove like the saying, "A lover railing is not far from forgiving".'*

Altisidora, making show of wiping the tears from her eyes with a handkerchief, and then making a low curtsy to her lord and lady, went out of the room.

'Poor damsel!' quoth Sancho, 'I forebode thee ill luck, since thou hast to do with a heart of matweed, and a soul of oak; for, in faith, if thou hadst had to do with me, another guise-cock would have crowed.'

The conversation was at an end: Don Quixote dressed himself, dined with the duke and duchess, and departed that afternoon.

CHAPTER 71

Of what befell Don Quixote with his squire Sancho, in the way to his village.

THE vanquished and forlorn Don Quixote travelled along, exceedingly pensive on the one hand, and very joyful on the other. His defeat caused his sadness, and his joy was occasioned by considering, that the disenchantment of Dulcinea was likely to be effected by the virtue inherent in Sancho, of which he had just given a manifest proof in the resurrection of Altisidora: though he could not readily bring himself to believe, that the enamoured damsel was really dead. Sancho went on, not at all pleased to find that Altisidora had not been as good as her word, in giving him the smocks: and, revolving it in his mind, he said to his master:

'In truth, sir, I am the most unfortunate physician that is to be met with in the world, in which there are doctors, who kill the patient they have under cure, and yet are paid for their pains, which is no more than signing a little scroll of certain medicines, which the apothecary, not the doctor, makes up: while poor I, though another's cure costs me drops of blood, twitches, pinches, pin-prickings, and lashes, get not a doit. But I vow to God, if ever any sick body falls into my hands again, they shall grease them well before I perform the cure; for, The abbot must eat, that sings for his meat; and I cannot believe heaven has endued me with the virtue I have that I should communicate it to others for nothing.'

'You are in the right, friend Sancho,' answered Don Quixote, 'and Altisidora has done very ill by you, not to give you the promised smocks; though the virtue you have was given you gratis, and without any studying on your part, more than studying how to receive a little pain in your person. For myself, I can say, if you had a mind to be paid for the disenchanting Dulcinea, I would have made it good to you ere now: but I do not know whether payment will agree with the conditions of the cure, and I would by no means have the reward hinder the operation of the medicine. But, for all that, I think, there can be no risk in making a small trial.

Consider, Sancho, what you would demand, and set about
the whipping straight, and pay yourself in ready money, since
you have cash of mine in your hands.'

At these offers Sancho opened his eyes and ears a span
wider, and in his heart consented to whip himself heartily,
and he said to his master:

'Well then, sir, I will now dispose myself to give your
worship satisfaction, since I shall get something by it; for, I
confess, the love I have for my wife and children makes me
seem a little self-interested. Tell me, sir how much will your
worship give for each lash?'

'Were I to pay you, Sancho,' answered Don Quixote, 'in
proportion to the greatness and quality of the cure, the
treasures of Venice, and the mines of Potosi, would be too
small a recompense. But see how much cash you have of
mine, and set your own price upon each lash.'

'The lashes,' answered Sancho, 'are three thousand three
hundred, and odd; of these I have already given myself five;
the rest remain; let the five pass for the odd ones, and let
us come to the three thousand three hundred, which, at a
quarter of a real apiece (for I will not take less, though all
the world should command me to do it), amount to three
thousand three hundred quarter-reals, which make one thousand six hundred and fifty half-reals, which make eight
hundred and twenty-five reals. These I will deduct from what
I have of your worship's in my hands, and shall return to
my house rich and contented, though well whipped; for, They
do not take trouts*—I say no more.'

'O blessed Sancho! O amiable Sancho!' replied Don Quixote; 'how much shall Dulcinea and I be bound to serve you
all the days of life heaven shall be pleased to grant us! If she
recovers her lost state, as it is impossible but she must, her
mishap will prove her good fortune, and my defeat a most
happy triumph: and when, Sancho, do you propose to begin
the discipline? I will add a hundred reals over and above for
dispatch.'

'When?' replied Sancho; 'even this very night without fail:
take you care, sir, that we may be in open field, and I will
take care to lay my flesh open.'

At length came the night, expected by Don Quixote with the greatest anxiety in the world, the wheels of Apollo's chariot seeming to him to be broken, and the day to be prolonged beyond its usual length; even as it happens to lovers, who, in the account of their impatience, think the hour of the accomplishment of their desires will never come.

Finally, they got among some pleasant trees a little way out of the high road, where, leaving the saddle and pannel of Rosinante and Dapple vacant, they laid themselves along on the green grass, and supped out of Sancho's cupboard; who, making a ponderous and flexible whip of Dapple's headstall and halter, withdrew about twenty paces from his master among some beech-trees. Don Quixote, seeing him go with such resolution and spirit, said to him:

'Take care, friend, you do not lash yourself to pieces; take time; let one stroke stay till another's over; hurry not yourself so as to lose your breath in the midst of your career; I mean, you must not lay it on so unmercifully as to lose your life before you attain to the desired number. And that you may not lose the game by a card too much or too little, I will stand aloof, and keep reckoning upon my beads the lashes you shall give yourself; and heaven favour you as your worthy intention deserves.'

'The good paymaster is in pain for no pawn,' answered Sancho: 'I design to lay it on in such a manner, that it may smart without killing me, for in this the substance of the miracle must needs consist. He then stripped himself naked from the waist upward; and then, snatching and cracking the whip, he began to lay himself on, and Don Quixote to count the strokes. Sancho had given himself about six or eight, when he thought the jest a little too heavy, and the price much too easy; and, stopping his hand a while, he said to his master, that he appealed on being deceived, every lash of those being richly worth half a real, instead of a quarter.

'Proceed, friend Sancho, and be not faint-hearted,' quoth Don Quixote, 'for I double the pay.'

'If so,' quoth Sancho, 'away with it in God's name, and let it rain lashes.'

But the sly knave, instead of laying them on his back, laid them on the trees, fetching ever and anon such groans, that one would have thought each would have torn up his very soul by the roots. Don Quixote, naturally tender-hearted, and fearing he would put an end to his life, and so he should not attain his desire through Sancho's imprudence, said to him:

'I conjure you, by your life, friend, let the business rest here! for this medicine seems to me very harsh, and it will not be amiss to give time to time, for Zamora was not taken in one hour. You have already given yourself, if I reckon right, above a thousand lashes, enough for the present; for the ass (to speak in homely phrase) will carry the load, but not a double load.'

'No, no,' answered Sancho, 'it shall never be said for me, The money paid, the work delayed: pray, sir, get a little farther off, and let me give myself another thousand lashes at least, for a couple more of such bouts will finish the job, and stuff to spare.'

'Since you find yourself in so good a disposition,' quoth Don Quixote, 'heaven assist you; and stick to it, for I am gone.'

Sancho returned to his task with so much fervour, and such was the rigour with which he gave the lashes, that he had already disbarked many a tree; and once, lifting up his voice, and giving an unmeasurable stroke to a beech, he cried:

'Down with thee, Sampson, and all that are with thee!'

Don Quixote presently ran to the sound of the piteous voice, and the stroke of the severe whip, and, laying hold of the twisted halter, which served Sancho instead of a bull's pizzle, he said:

'Heaven forbid, friend Sancho, that, for my pleasure, you should lose that life, upon which depends the maintenance of your wife and children! let Dulcinea wait a better opportunity, for I will contain myself within the bounds of the nearest hope, and stay till you recover fresh strength, that this business may be concluded to the satisfaction of all parties.'

'Since your worship, dear sir, will have it so,' answered Sancho, 'so be it, in God's name, and pray, fling your cloak over my shoulders, for I am all in a sweat, and am loath to catch cold, as new disciplinants are apt to do.'

Don Quixote did so; and, leaving himself in his doublet, he covered up Sancho, who slept till the sun waked him, and then they pursued their journey till they stopped at a place about three leagues off.

They alighted at an inn, for Don Quixote took it for such, and not for a castle, moated round, with its turrets, portcullises, and drawbridge; for, since his defeat, he discoursed with more judgement on all occasions, as will presently appear. He was lodged in a ground room, hung with painted serge, instead of tapestry, as is the fashion of country towns. In one of the pieces was painted, by a wretched hand, the rape of Helen, when the daring guest* carried her off from Menelaus. In another, was the history of Dido and Aeneas; she upon a high tower, as making signals with half a bed sheet to her fugitive guest, who was out at sea, flying away from her, in a frigate or brigantine. He observed, in the two history-pieces, that Helen went away with no very ill will, for she was slyly laughing to herself; but the beauteous Dido seemed to let fall from her eyes tears as big as walnuts. Which Don Quixote seeing, he said:

'These two ladies were most unfortunate in not being born in this age, and I above all men unhappy, that I was not born in theirs: for had I encountered those gallants, neither had Troy been burnt nor Carthage destroyed; since, by my killing Paris only, all these mischiefs had been prevented.'

'I hold a wager,' quoth Sancho, 'that, ere it be long, there will not be either victualling-house, tavern, inn, or barber's shop, in which the history of our exploits will not be painted, but I could wish they may be done by the hand of a better painter than he that did these.'

'You are in the right, Sancho,' quoth Don Quixote; 'for this painter is like Orbaneja of Ubeda,* who, when he was asked what he was drawing, answered, As it shall happen: and if it chanced to be a cock, he wrote under it. "This is a cock," lest people should take it for a fox.'

'Just such a one, methinks, Sancho, the painter or writer (for it is all one) must be, who wrote the history of this new

Don Quixote, lately published: he painted or wrote, whatever came uppermost. Or he is like a poet, some years about the court, called Mauleon, who answered all questions extempore; and a person asking him the meaning of *Deum de Deo*, he answered, *Dé donde diere.** But, setting all this aside, tell me, Sancho, do you think of giving yourself the other brush to-night? and have you a mind it should be under a roof, or in the open air?'

'Before God, sir,' answered Sancho, 'for what I intend to give myself, it is all the same to me, whether it be in a house, or in a field: though I had rather it were among trees; for methinks, they accompany me, as it were, and help me to bear my toil marvellously well.'

'However, it shall not be now, friend Sancho,' answered Don Quixote: 'but, that you may recover strength, it shall be reserved for our village; and we shall get thither by the day after to-morrow at farthest.'

Sancho replied, he might order that as he pleased; but, for his part, he was desirous to make an end of the business, out of hand, and in hot blood, and while the mill was grinding; for usually the danger lies in the delay; and, Pray to God devoutly, and hammer out stoutly; and, One take is worth two I'll give thee's; and, A bird in hand is better than a vulture on the wing.

'No more proverbs, Sancho, for God's sake,' quoth Don Quixote; 'for, methinks, you are going back to *Sicut erat.** Speak plainly, and without flourishes, as I have often told you, and you will find it a loaf per cent, in your way.'

'I know not how I came to be so unlucky,' answered Sancho, 'that I cannot give a reason without a proverb, nor a proverb which does not seem to me to be a reason; but I will mend if I can.'

And thus ended the conversation for that time.

CHAPTER 72

How Don Quixote and Sancho arrived at their village.

DON QUIXOTE and Sancho stayed all the day in that village, at the inn, waiting for night; the one to finish his task of whipping in the fields, and the other to see the success of it, in which consisted the accomplishment of his wishes.

At this juncture came a traveller on horseback to the inn, with three or four servants, one of whom said to him who seemed to be the master of them:

'Here, Señor Don Alvaro Tarfe,* your worship may pass the heat of the day: the lodging seems to be cool and cleanly.'

Don Quixote, hearing this, said to Sancho:

'I am mistaken, Sancho, if when I turned over the Second Part of my history, I had not a glimpse of this Don Alvaro Tarfe.'

'It may be so,' answered Sancho: 'let him first alight, and then we will question him.'

The gentleman alighted, and the landlady showed him into a ground room, opposite to that of Don Quixote's, hung likewise with painted serge. This new-arrived cavalier undressed and equipped himself for coolness, and stepping out to the porch, which was airy and spacious, where Don Quixote was walking backwards and forwards, he asked him:

'Pray, sir, which way is your worship travelling?' And Don Quixote answered:

'To a village not far off, where I was born: And pray, sir, which way may you be travelling?'

'I, sir,' answered the gentleman, 'am going to Granada, which is my native country.'

'And a good country it is,' replied Don Quixote. 'But, sir, oblige me so far as to tell me your name; for I conceive it imports me to know it more than I can well express.'

'My name is Don Alvaro Tarfe,' answered the new guest.

To which Don Quixote replied:

'Then, I presume, your worship is that Don Alvaro Tarfe, mentioned in the *Second Part of the History of Don Quixote de la Mancha*, lately printed and published by a certain modern author.'

'The very same,' answered the gentleman, 'and that Don Quixote, the hero of the said history, was a very great friend of mine; and I was the person, who drew him from his native place; at least I prevailed upon him to be present at certain jousts and tournaments held at Saragossa, whither I was going myself: and in truth, I did him a great many kindnesses, and saved his back from being well stroked by the hangman for being too bold.'

'Pray, tell me, Señor Don Alvaro,' quoth Don Quixote, 'am I anything like that Don Quixote you speak of?'

'No, in truth,' answered the guest, 'not in the least.'

'And this Don Quixote,' said ours, 'had he a squire with him called Sancho Panza?'

'Yes, he had,' answered Don Alvaro; 'and though he had the reputation of being very pleasant, I never heard him say any one thing that had any pleasantry in it.'

'I verily believe it,' quoth Sancho, straight; 'for it is not everybody's talent to say pleasant things; and this Sancho, your worship speaks of, Señor Gentleman, must be some very great rascal, idiot, and knave into the bargain; for the true Sancho Panza am I, who have more witty conceits than there are drops in a shower. Try but the experiment, sir, and follow me but one year, and you will find that they drop from me at every step, and are so many, and so pleasant, that, for the most part without knowing what I say, I make everybody laugh that hears me: and the true Don Quixote de la Mancha, the renowned, the valiant, the discreet, the enamoured, the undoer of injuries, the defender of pupils and orphans, the protector of widows, the murderer of damsels, he who has the peerless Dulcinea del Toboso for his sole mistress, is this gentleman here present, my master: any other Don Quixote whatever, and any other Sancho Panza, is all mockery, and a mere dream.'

'Before God, I believe it!' answered Don Alvaro: 'for you have said more pleasant things, friend, in four words you have spoken, than that other Sancho Panza in all I ever heard him say, though that was a great deal; for he was more gluttonous than well spoken, and more stupid than pleasant: and I take it for granted, that the enchanters, who persecute the good Don Quixote, have had a mind to persecute me too with the bad one: but I know not what to say; for I durst have sworn I had left him under cure in the Nuncio's House at Toledo,* and now here starts up another Don Quixote, very different from mine.'

'I know not,' quoth Don Quixote, 'whether I am the good one; but I can say I am not the bad one; and as a proof of what I say, you must know, dear Señor Alvaro Tarfe, that I never was in Saragossa in all the days of my life: on the contrary, having been told that this imaginary Don Quixote was at the tournaments of that city, I resolved not to go thither, that I might make him a liar in the face of all the world: and so I went directly to Barcelona, that register of courtesy, asylum of strangers, hospital of the poor, native country of the valiant, avenger of the injured, agreeable seat of firm friendship, and, for situation and beauty, singular. And, though what befell me there be not very much to my satisfaction, but, on the contrary, much to my sorrow, the having seen that city enables me the better to bear it. In a word, Señor Don Alvaro Tarfe, I am Don Quixote de la Mancha, the same that fame speaks of, and not that unhappy wretch, who would usurp my name, and arrogate to himself the honour of my exploits. And therefore I conjure you, sir, as you are a gentleman, to make a declaration before the magistrate of this town, that you never saw me before in your life, and that I am not the Don Quixote printed in the Second Part, nor this Sancho Panza my squire him you knew.'

'That I will, with all my heart,' answered Don Alvaro; 'though it surprises me to see two Don Quixotes, and two Sanchos, at the same time, as different in their actions, as alike in their names. And, I say again, I am now assured, that I have not seen what I have seen, nor, in respect to me, has that happened which has happened.'

'Without doubt,' quoth Sancho, 'your worship must be enchanted, like my lady Dulcinea del Toboso: and would to heaven your disenchantment depended upon my giving myself another three thousand and odd lashes, as I do for her; for I would lay them on, without interest or reward.'

'I understand not this business of lashes,' quoth Don

Alvaro. Sancho answered, it was too long to tell at present, but he would give him an account, if they happened to travel the same road.

Dinner-time was now come: Don Quixote and Don Alvaro dined together. By chance the magistrate of the town came into the inn, with a notary; and Don Quixote desired of him, that Don Alvaro Tarfe, the gentleman there present, might depose before his worship, that he did not know Don Quixote de la Mancha, there present also, and that he was not the man handed about in a printed history, entitled, the *Second Part of Don Quixote de la Mancha*, written by such a one de Avellaneda, a native of Tordesillas. In short, the magistrate proceeded according to form: the deposition was worded as strong as could be in such cases: at which Don Quixote and Sancho were overjoyed, as if this attestation had been of the greatest importance to them, and as if the difference between the two Don Quixotes, and the two Sanchos, were not evident enough from their words and actions. Many compliments and offers of service passed between Don Alvaro and Don Quixote, in which the great Manchegan showed his discretion in such manner, that he convinced Don Alvaro Tarfe of the error he was in; who was persuaded he must needs be enchanted, since he had touched with his hand two such contrary Quixotes.

The evening came: they departed from that place, and, at the distance of about half a league, the road parted into two: one led to Don Quixote's village, and the other to where Don Alvaro was going. In this little way, Don Quixote related to him the misfortune of his defeat, and the enchantment and cure of Dulcinea; which was new cause of admiration to Don Alvaro, who, embracing Don Quixote and Sancho, went on his way, and Don Quixote his.

That night he passed among some other trees, to give Sancho an opportunity of finishing his discipline, which he did after the same manner as he had done the night before, more at the expense of the bark of the beeches, than of his back, of which he was so careful, that the lashes he gave it would not have brushed off a fly that had been upon it. The deceived Don Quixote was very punctual in telling the strokes, and found, that, including those of the foregoing night, they amounted to three thousand and twenty-nine. One would have thought the sun himself had risen earlier than usual to behold the sacrifice: by whose light they resumed their journey, discoursing together of Don Alvaro's mistake, and how prudently they had contrived to procure his deposition before a magistrate, and in so authentic a form.

That day, and that night, they travelled without any occurence worth relating, unless it be, that Sancho finished his task that night: at which Don Quixote was above measure pleased, and waited for the day, to see if he could light on his lady, the disenchanted Dulcinea, in his way: and continuing his journey, he looked narrowly at every woman he met, to see if she were Dulcinea del Toboso, holding it for infallible, that Merlin's promises could not lie.

With these thoughts and desires, they ascended a little hill, from whence they discovered their village; which, as soon as Sancho beheld, he kneeled down, and said:

'Open thine eyes, O desired country, and behold thy son Sancho Panza, returning to thee again, if not very rich, yet very well whipped! Open thine arms, and receive likewise thy son Don Quixote, who, if he comes conquered by another's hand, yet he comes a conqueror of himself, which, as I have heard him say, is the greatest victory that can be desired! Money I have; for, if I have been well whipped, I am come off like a gentleman.'

'Leave those fooleries, Sancho,' quoth Don Quixote, 'and let us go directly home to our village, where we will give full scope to our imaginations, and settle the plan we intend to govern ourselves by, in our pastoral life.'

This said, they descended the hill, and went directly to the village.

CHAPTER 73

Of the omens Don Quixote met with at the entrance into his
village, with other accidents, which adorn and illustrate this
great history.

AT the entrance into the village, as Cid Hamet reports, Don
Quixote saw a couple of boys quarrelling in a threshing-floor,
and one said to the other:

'Trouble not yourself, Periquillo; for you shall never see it
more while you live.'

Don Quixote, hearing him, said to Sancho:

'Do you not take notice, friend, what this boy has said,
You shall never see it more while you live?'

'Well,' answered Sancho, 'what signifies it if the boy did
say so?'

'What,' replied Don Quixote, 'do you not perceive, that,
applying these words to my purpose, the meaning is, I shall
never see Dulcinea more?'

Sancho would have answered, but was prevented by seeing
a hare come running across the field, pursued by abundance
of dogs and sportsmen; which, frighted, came for shelter, and
squatted between Dapple's feet. Sancho took her up alive,
and presented her to Don Quixote, who cried,

'*Malum signum, malum signum!* A hare flies; dogs pursue her;
Dulcinea appears not!'

'Your worship is a strange man,' quoth Sancho: 'let us
suppose now, that this hare is Dulcinea del Toboso, and these
dogs that pursue her, those wicked enchanters who transformed her into a country-wench: she flies, I catch her, and
put her into your worship's hands, who have her in your
arms, and make much of her: what bad sign is this, or what
ill omen can you draw from hence?'

The two contending boys came up to look at the hare, and
Sancho asked one of them, what they were quarrelling about.
And answer was made him, by him who had said, 'You shall
never see it more while you live'; that he had taken a cage
full of crickets* from the other boy, which he never intended
to restore to him while he lived. Sancho drew four quarter-
maravedis out of his pocket, and gave it the boy for his cage,

which he put into Don Quixote's hands, and said:

'Behold, sir, all your omens broken, and come to nothing; and they have no more to do with our adventures, in my judgement, a dunce as I am, than last year's clouds; and, if I remember right, I have heard the priest of our village say, that good Christians, and wise people, ought not to regard these fooleries: and your worship's own self told me as much a few days ago, giving me to understand, that all such Christians as minded presages, were fools; so there is no need of troubling ourselves any further about them, but let us go on, and get home to our village.'

The hunters came up, and demanded their hare, and Don Quixote gave it them. They went on their way, and, at the entrance of their village, in a little meadow, they found the priest, and the bachelor Sampson Carrasco, reading their breviaries. Now you must know, that Sancho Panza had thrown the buckram robe, painted with flames of fire (which he had worn at the duke's castle, the night he brought Altisidora to life again), instead of a sumpter-cloth, over the bundle of armour, upon his ass. He had likewise clapped the mitre on Dapple's head; insomuch that never was ass so metamorphosed and adorned. The priest and the bachelor presently knew them both, and came running to them with open arms. Don Quixote alighted, and embraced them closely; and the boys, who are sharp-sighted as lynxes, es- pying the ass's mitre, flocked to view him, and said one to another:

'Come, boys, and you shall see Sancho Panza's ass finer than Mingo, and Don Quixote's beast leaner than ever!'

Finally, surrounded with boys, and accompanied by the priest and the bachelor, they entered the village, and took the way to Don Quixote's house, where they found at the door the housekeeper and the niece, who had already heard the news of his arrival.

It had likewise reached the ears of Teresa Panza, Sancho's wife, who, half naked, with her hair about her ears, and dragging Sanchica after her, ran to see her husband: and seeing him not so well equipped as she imagined a governor ought to be, she said:

'What makes you come thus, dear husband? methinks you come afoot and foundered, and look more like a misgoverned person, than a governor.'

'Peace, Teresa,' answered Sancho; 'for, There is not always bacon where there are pins to hang it on; and let us go to our house, where you shall hear wonders. Money I bring with me (which is the main business) got by my own industry, and without damage to anybody.'

'Bring but money, my good husband,' quoth Teresa, 'and let it be got this way or that way: for get it how you will, you will have brought up no new custom in the world.'

Sanchica embraced her father, and asked if he had brought her anything, for she had been wishing for him as people do for rain in May: and, she taking hold of his belt on one side, and his wife taking him by the hand on the other, Sanchica pulling Dapple after her, they went home to their house, leaving Don Quixote in his, in the power of his niece and the housekeeper, and in the company of the priest and the bachelor.

Don Quixote, without standing upon times or seasons, in that very instant went apart, with the bachelor and the priest, and related to them, in few words, how he was vanquished, and the obligation he lay under not to stir from his village in a year; which he intended punctually to observe, without transgressing a tittle, as became a true knight-errant, obliged by the strict precepts of chivalry. He also told them, how he had resolved to turn shepherd for that year, and to pass his time in the solitude of the fields, where he might give the reins to his amorous thoughts, exercising himself in that pastoral and virtuous employment; beseeching them, if they had leisure, and were not engaged in business of greater consequence, to bear him company; telling them he would purchase sheep and stock sufficient to give them the name of shepherds; acquainting them also, that the principal part of the business was already done, he having chosen for them names as fit as if they had been cast in a mould. The priest desired him to repeat them. Don Quixote answered, that he himself was to be called the shepherd Quixotiz; the bachelor, the shepherd Carrascon; the priest, the shepherd Curiambro, and Sancho Panza, the shepherd Panzino. They were astonished at this new madness of Don Quixote: but to prevent his rambling once more from his village, and resuming his chivalries, and in hopes he might be cured in that year, they fell in with his new project, and applauded his folly as a high piece of discretion, offering to be his companions in that exercise.

'Besides,' said Sampson Carrasco, 'I, as everybody knows, am an excellent poet, and shall be composing, at every turn, pastoral or courtly verses, or such as shall be most for my purpose, to amuse and divert us as we range the fields. But, gentlemen; the first and chief thing necessary, is, that each of us choose the name of the shepherdess he intends to celebrate in his verses, and we will not leave a tree, be it never so hard, in whose bark we will not inscribe and grave her name, as is the fashion and custom of enamoured shepherds.'

'That is very right,' answered Don Quixote; 'though I need not trouble myself to look for a feigned name, having the peerless Dulcinea del Toboso, the glory of these banks, the ornament of these meads, the support of beauty, the cream of good humour, and lastly, the worthy subject of all praise, be it never so hyperbolical.'

'That is true,' said the priest; 'but, as for us, we must look out for shepherdesses of an inferior stamp, who, if they do not square, may corner with us.'

To which Sampson Carrasco added:

'And, when we are at a loss, we will give them the names we find in print, of which the world is full, as Phillidas, Amarillises, Dianas, Fleridas, Galateas, and Belisardas: for, since they are sold in the market, we may lawfully buy, and make use of them as our own. If my mistress, or, to speak more properly, my shepherdess, is called Anna, I will celebrate her under the name of Anarda, and, if Frances, I will call her Francenia, and, if Lucy, Lucinda; and so of the rest. And Sancho Panza, if he is to be one of this brotherhood, may celebrate his wife Teresa Panza by the name of Teresaina.'

Don Quixote smiled at the application of the names, and the priest highly applauded his virtuous and honourable resolution, and again offered to bear him company all the time he could spare from attending the duties of his function. With this they took their leave of him, desiring and entreating him to take care of his health, and make much of himself with good heartening things.

Now fortune would have it, that his niece and house-keeper overheard their conversation; and as soon as the two were gone, they both came in to Don Quixote; and the niece said:

'What is the meaning of this, uncle? Now that we thought your worship was returned with a resolution to stay at home, and live a quiet and decent life, you have a mind to involve yourself in new labyrinths, by turning shepherd. In truth, The straw is too hard to make pipes of.'

To which the housekeeper added:

'And can your worship bear, in the fields, the summer's sultry heat, the winter's pinching cold, and the howling of the wolves? No, certainly; for this is the business of robust fellows, tanned and bred to such employment, as it were, from their cradles and swaddling-clothes. And, of the two evils, it is better to be a knight-errant than a shepherd. Look you, sir, take my advice, which is not given by one full of bread and wine, but fasting, and with fifty years over my head: stay at home, look after your estate, go often to confession, and relieve the poor; and if any ill comes of it, let it lie at my door.'

'Peace, daughters,' answered Don Quixote; 'for I know perfectly what I have to do. Lead me to bed: for, methinks, I am not very well; and assure yourselves, that, whether I am a knight-errant, or a wandering shepherd, I will not fail to provide for you, as you shall find by experience.'

The two good women (for doubtless such they were), the housekeeper and niece, carried him to bed, where they gave him to eat, and made as much of him as possible.

CHAPTER 74

How Don Quixote fell sick, made his will, and died.

As all human things, especially the lives of men, are transitory, incessantly declining from their beginning till they arrive at their final period; and as that of Don Quixote had no peculiar privilege from heaven to exempt it from the common fate, his end and dissolution came when he least thought of it. For, whether it proceeded from the melancholy occasioned by finding himself vanquished, or from the disposition of heaven so decreeing it, he was seized with a fever, which confined him six days to his bed, in which time he was frequently visited by the priest, the bachelor, and the barber, his friends; his trusty squire Sancho Panza never stirring from his bedside.

They, supposing that his grief at being vanquished, and the disappointment of his wishes as to the restoration and disenchantment of Dulcinea, had reduced him to this state, endeavoured by all imaginable ways to revive his spirits. The bachelor bade him be of good courage, and rise from bed, to enter upon his pastoral exercise; he having already composed an eclogue to that purpose, not inferior to any written by Sannazarius;* telling him besides, that he had already bought with his own money, of a herdsman of Quintanar, two excellent dogs, to guard the flock, the one called Barcino, and the other Butron. But, for all this, Don Quixote's melancholy continued. His friends sent for a physician, who felt his pulse, and did not much like it, and said, come what would, it would not be amiss for him to look to his soul's health, that of his body being in danger. Don Quixote heard it with composure of mind: but not so did his housekeeper, his niece, and his squire, who all began to weep most bitterly, as if he were already dead, and laid out before their faces. It was the doctor's opinion that melancholy and disappointment had brought him to his end. Don Quixote desired they would leave him, for he was inclined to sleep a little.

They did so, and he slept at a stretch (as the saying is) above six hours, insomuch that the housekeeper and the niece thought that he would never wake more. But awake he did at the end of that time, and, with a loud voice, said:

'Blessed be almighty God, who has vouchsafed me so great a good! in short, His mercies have no bounds, and the sins of men can neither lessen nor obstruct them!'

The niece listened attentively to her uncle's words, and she thought there was more sense in them than usual, at least since his sickness, and she said to him:

'What is it you say, sir? has anything extraordinary happened? what mercies, and what sins do you speak of?'

'Niece,' answered Don Quixote, 'the mercies I mean are those God has been pleased, notwithstanding my sins, to vouchsafe me at this instant. My judgement is now undisturbed, and free from those dark clouds of ignorance with which my eager and continual reading of those detestable books of chivalry had obscured it. Now I perceive the absurdity and delusion of them, and am only sorry I am undeceived so late, that I have no time left to make some amends, by reading others that might help to enlighten my soul. I feel myself, niece, at the point of death, and I would fain so order it, as not to leave the imputation of madness upon my memory; for though I must confess I have been a madman, I would not confirm the truth of it at my death. Dear child, call hither my good friends, the priest, the bachelor Sampson Carrasco, and Master Nicholas the barber; for I would make my confession and my will.'

But this trouble was saved the niece by the coming of all three. Scarcely had Don Quixote set his eyes on them, when he cried out:

'Give me joy, good gentlemen, that I am now no longer Don Quixote de la Mancha, but Alonso Quixano, for his virtues surnamed the Good! I am now an utter enemy to Amadis de Gaul, and the innumerable rabble of his descendants: now all the histories of knight-errantry are to me odious and profane: I am now sensible of my folly, and of the danger I was led into by reading them; and now, through the mercy of God, and my own dear-bought experience, I detest and abhor them.'

When his three friends heard him speak thus, they believed for certain that some new frenzy had possessed him; and Sampson said to him:

'What! Señor Don Quixote, now that we have news of the lady Dulcinea's being disenchanted, do you talk at this rate; and, now that we are just upon the point of becoming shepherds, to lead our lives singing, and like any princes, would you turn hermit?'

'Peace, I conjure you,' replied Don Quixote, 'recollect yourself, and leave idle stories: those, which have hitherto done me so much real hurt, my repentance, by the assistance of heaven, shall convert to my good. I feel, gentlemen, the quick approach of death: let us be serious, and bring me a confessor, and a notary to draw my will; for, in such circumstances as these, a man must not trifle with his soul: and, therefore, I beseech you, while my friend the priest is taking my confession, let the notary be fetched.'

They stared at one another, wondering at Don Quixote's expressions, and, though still in some doubt, they resolved to believe him: and one of the signs by which they conjectured he was dying, was, his passing, by so easy and sudden a transition, from mad to sober. To the words he had already spoken he added others, so proper, so rational, and so Christian, that their doubt was quite removed, and they verily believed him in his perfect senses.

The priest made everybody leave the room, and stayed with him alone, and confessed him. The bachelor went for the notary, and presently returned with him, and with Sancho Panza, who, having learned from the bachelor in what condition his master was, besides finding the housekeeper and the niece in tears, began to pucker up his face, and to fall a-blubbering. The confession ended, the priest came out of the room, saying:

'Good Alonso Quixano is just expiring, and certainly in his right mind: let us all go in that he may make his will.'

This news opened the sluices of the swollen eyes of the housekeeper, the niece, and Sancho Panza his trusty squire, in such wise that it forced a torrent of tears from their eyes, and a thousand groans from their breasts: for, in truth, as has been said before, both while he was plain Alonso Quixano, and while he was Don Quixote de la Mancha, he was ever of an amiable disposition and affable behaviour, and was therefore beloved, not only by those of his own family, but by all that knew him.

The notary now entered the room with the others, and the preamble of the will being made, and Don Quixote having disposed of his soul, with all the Christian circumstances required, coming to the legacies, he said:

'Item, it is my will, that, in respect to certain moneys, which Sancho Panza (whom, in my madness, I made my squire) has in his hands, there being between him and me some reckonings, receipts, and disbursements, he shall not be charged with them, nor called to any account for them; but if, after he has paid himself, there be any overplus, which will be but very little, it shall be his own, and much good may it do him: and if, as, during my madness, I was the occasion of procuring for him the government of an island, I could, now that I am in my senses, procure him that of a kingdom, I would readily do it; for the sincerity of his heart, and the fidelity of his dealings, deserve it.'

And, turning to Sancho, he said:

'Forgive me, friend, for making you a madman, by persuading you to believe, as I did myself, that there have been formerly, and are now, knights-errant in the world.'

'Alas!' answered Sancho, sobbing, 'dear sir, do not die; but take my counsel, and live many years; for the greatest madness a man can commit in this life is to suffer himself to die, without anybody's killing him, or being brought to his end by any other hand than that of melancholy. Be not lazy, sir, but get out of bed, and let us be going to the field, dressed like shepherds, as we agreed to do: and who knows, but behind some bush or other we may find the lady Dulcinea disenchanted as fine as heart can wish? If you die for grief of being vanquished, lay the blame upon me, and say you were unhorsed by my not having girthed Rosinante's saddle as it ought to have been: besides your worship must have read in your book of chivalries, that it is a common thing for one knight to unhorse another, and him who is vanquished to-day, to become conqueror to-morrow.'

'It is so,' quoth Sampson, 'and honest Sancho is very much in the right.'

'Gentlemen,' quoth Don Quixote, 'let us proceed fairly and softly: Look not for this year's birds in last year's nests. I was mad; I am now sober: I was Don Quixote de la Mancha; I am now, as I have said, the good Alonso Quixano: and may my unfeigned repentance, and my sincerity, restore me to the esteem you once had for me: and let the notary proceed.

'Item, I bequeath to Antonia Quixana, my niece here present, all my estate real and personal, after the payment of all my debts and legacies: and the first to be discharged shall be the wages due to my housekeeper for the time she has been in my service, and twenty ducats besides for mourning. I appoint for my executors, señor the priest, and señor bachelor Sampson Carrasco, here present.

'Item, it is my will, that, if Antonia Quixana, my niece, is inclined to marry, it shall be with a man, who, upon the strictest inquiry, shall be found to know nothing of books of chivalry; and, in case it shall appear he is acquainted with them, and my niece notwithstanding will and does marry him, she shall forfeit all I have bequeathed her, which my executors may dispose of in pious uses, as they think proper.

'Item, I beseech the said gentlemen, my executors, that, if good fortune should bring them acquainted with the author, who is said to have written a history handed about, and entitled, the *Second Part of the Exploits of Don Quixote de la Mancha*, they will, in my name, most earnestly entreat him to pardon the occasion I have unwittingly given him of writing so many and so great absurdities, as he there has done: for I depart this life with a burden upon my conscience for having furnished him with a motive for so doing.'

With this the will was closed, and, a fainting fit seizing him, he stretched himself out at full length in the bed. They were all alarmed, and ran to his assistance; and, in the three days that he survived the making his will, he fainted away very often. The house was all in confusion: however, the niece ate, the housekeeper drank, and Sancho Panza made much of himself; for this business of legacies effaces, or moderates, the grief that is naturally due to the deceased.

In short, after receiving all the sacraments, and expressing his abhorrence, in strong and pathetic expressions, of all the books of chivalry, Don Quixote's last hour came. The notary was present, and protested he had never read in any book of chivalry, that ever any knight-errant had died in his bed in so composed and Christian a manner, as Don Quixote; who, amidst the plaints and tears of the bystanders, resigned his breath*—I mean, died.

Which the priest seeing, he desired the notary to draw up a certificate, that Alonso Quixano, commonly called Don Quixote de la Mancha, was departed this life, and died a natural death and he insisted upon this testimonial, lest any other author, besides Cid Hamet Ben Engeli, should raise him from the dead, and write endless stories of his exploits.

This was the end of the ingenious gentleman of La Mancha, the place of whose birth Cid Hamet would not expressly name,* that all the towns and villages of La Mancha might contend among themselves, and each adopt him for their own, as the seven cities of Greece contended for Homer.

We omit the lamentations of Sancho, the niece, and the housekeeper, with the new epitaphs upon his tomb, excepting this by Sampson Carrasco:—

> Here lies the valiant cavalier,
> Who never had a sense of fear:
> So high his matchless courage rose,
> He reckon'd Death among his vanquish'd foes.
>
> Wrongs to redress, his sword he drew,
> And many a caitiff giant slew;
> His days of life tho' madness stain'd,
> In death his sober senses he regain'd.

And the sagacious Cid Hamet, addressing himself to his pen, said:

'Here, O my slender quill, whether well or ill cut I know not, here, suspended by this brass wire, shalt thou hang upon this spitrack, and live many long ages, if presumptuous or wicked historians do not take thee down, to profane thee. But, before they offer to touch thee, give them this warning in the best manner thou canst:

'"Beware, beware, ye plagiaries;* Let none of you touch me; for this undertaking (God bless the king) was reserved for me alone."*

'For me alone was Don Quixote born, and I for him: he knew how to act, and I how to write: we were destined for each other, maugre and in despite of that scribbling impostor of Tordesillas, who has dared, or shall dare, with his gross and ill-cut ostrich quill, to describe the exploits of my valorous knight; a burden too weighty for his shoulders, and an undertaking above his cold and frozen genius. And warn him, if perchance he falls in thy way, to suffer the wearied and now mouldering bones of Don Quixote to repose in the grave; nor endeavour, in contradiction to all the ancient usages and customs of death, to carry him into Old Castile, making him rise out of the vault, in which he really and truly lies at full length, totally unable to attempt a third expedition, or a new sally; for the two he has already made, with such success, and so much to the general satisfaction, as well of the people of these kingdoms of Spain, as of foreign countries, are sufficient to ridicule all that have been made by other knights-errant.

'And thus shalt thou comply with the duty of thy Christian profession, giving good advice to those who wish thee ill; and I shall rest satisfied, and proud to have been the first who enjoyed entire the fruits of his writings; for my only desire was to bring into public abhorrence the fabulous and absurd histories of knight-errantry, which, by means of that of my true and genuine Don Quixote, begin already to totter, and will doubtless fall, never to rise again. Farewell.'

THE END

EXPLANATORY NOTES

Part One

15   *born in a prison*: this has been thought to mean that Cervantes conceived the idea of his book and its hero in prison, probably in 1597. It is less likely that he started to write it there. It might even be just a figure of speech.

16   *years upon my back*: he was 57.

17   *could not equal*: probably aimed at Lope de Vega, many of whose works were prefaced by numerous poems by 'obliging friends'.

18   *little trouble to find*: probably another dig at Lope de Vega. His *Peregrino en su patria* (1604), for instance, contains ostentatious erudition of this sort.

      Horace, or whoever said it: it was from one of the many medieval collections of fables by Aesop or attributed to him, and means 'Liberty is not bought for gold'.

      Regumque turres: Horace, *Odes*, I. iv. 13–14: 'Pale death strikes equally at the hovels of the poor and the castle towers of kings.'

      inimicos vestros: Matt. 5: 44: 'But I say to you, love your enemies.'

      cogitationes malae: Matt. 15: 19: 'Wirled thoughts come from the heart.'

      solus eris: the lines are not from Cato, but from Ovid, *Tristia*, i. 9 (the misattribution, like the one above, is obviously deliberate): 'When you are happy friends abound; when skies are grey, you are all alone.'

19   *bishop of Mondoñedo*: Antonio de Guevara, *Epístolas familiares* I, (1539).

      Leon Hebreo: author of the *Dialoghi d'amore* (1535). There were three Spanish translations made of this work in the sixteenth century.

      Fonseca, 'On the love of God': Cristóbal de Fonseca, *Tratado del amor de Dios* (1592).

21 *Farewell*: in the original there now follow eleven burlesque poems in praise of Don Quixote, Sancho, Dulcinea, and the like, attributed to characters from romances of chivalry and others. Cervantes has acted upon the advice of his 'friend' in the prologue. A translation of these was not included in Jarvis's *Don Quixote*. Also excluded was the short dedication to the Duke of Bejar.

23 *La Mancha*: 'En un lugar de la Mancha' was a line from a popular poem of the time.

    an omelet: 'duelos y quebrantos' in the original—probably eggs and bacon.

    Quixana: in Ch. 5 the suggestion is that his name was 'Quixana', and in Ch. 49, 'Quixada'. By the end of Part Two it is established as 'Alonso Quixano'.

24 *complain of your beauty*: not from any of Feliciano de Silva's romances of chivalry, in fact, but from his *Segunda comedia de Celestina*.

    Don Belianis: the battle-scarred hero of *Don Belianis de Grecia* by Jerónimo Fernández (1547 and 1579).

    Sigüenza: a very minor university.

    Palmerin of England: *Libro del muy esforzado caballero Palmerín de Inglaterra* (1547). The original appears to have been written shortly before in Portuguese by Francisco de Moraes Cabral.

    Amadis de Gaul: the hero of the most famous and influential Spanish romance of chivalry. See note to p. 53.

    Knight of the Sun: the Caballero del Febo, hero of the *Espejo de príncipes y caballeros* by Diego Ortúñez de Calahorra (1555, with later continuations).

25 *The Cid Ruy Diaz*: the hero of Spanish history and epic (*c.*1043–99).

    the Knight of the Burning Sword: Amadis of Greece.

    squeezing him between his arms: this version of the exploits of the fictitious epic hero Bernardo del Carpio occurs in Nicolás de Espinosa's *Segunda parte de Orlando* (1555). Cervantes dramatized Bernardo's story in his play *La casa de los celos* (*The House of Jealousy*), and spoke of having composed a work called *Bernardo*.

    Morgante: the giant of the late fifteenth-century poem *Morgante maggiore* by Ludovico Pulci.

Reynaldos de Montalvan: Reynaud de Montaubon or Rinaldo de Montalbano, hero of French epic and Italian and Spanish romances.

Galalon: Ganelon, the traitor in Carolingian epic.

26   *Trapisonda*: Trebizond.

Gonela's horse: Gonela was a jester at the court of the Duke of Ferrara in the later fifteenth century.

tantum pellis et ossa fuit: 'was so much skin and bone'—Plautus, *Aulularia*, III. vi. 28.

27   *Rosinante*: from *rocín*, 'work-horse', and *ante*, 'before'.

32   *Castilian*: *castellano* means 'castle governor' as well as 'Castilian'.

being always awake: Don Quixote has just quoted words from a famous ballad and the innkeeper continues the quotation.

33   *and princesses on his steed*: adapted from an old ballad on Lancelot.

35   *the hedge taverns of Toledo*: the list contains a free translation of names of places famous for being the haunts of rogues and thieves.

bubbling several young heirs: i.e. cheating a few schoolboys.

37   *a cistern*: a water trough.

39   *The constable*: the castle governor.

40   *Sanchobienaya*: a square in Toledo.

42   *sixty-three reals*: 'setenta y tres' (seventy-three), in the original. The error, in favour of the boy, could well be attributed to Don Quixote.

45   *passages*: passages of arms.

48   *Valdovinos and the Marquess of Mantua*: figures from popular balladry.

49   *for so he was called*: in the original, 'se debía de llamar'—'must have been called'.

conveyed him to his castle: The *Historia de Abindarraez y Xarifa* is inserted in posthumous editions of Montemayor's *Diana* (1559), and is in the *Inventario* (1565) of Antonio de Villegas.

50   *the Nine Worthies*: Hector, Alexander, Julius Caesar, Joshua, David, Judas Maccabeus, Arthur, Charlemagne, and Godefroi de Bouillon.

six days past: the original says three days.

the sage Esquife: the niece's error for Alquife, fictitious author of *Amadis de Grecia* and husband of the enchantress Urganda the Unknown.

52 *Urgada*: she means Urganda (see previous note) who helped Amadis of Gaul.

53 *Amadis de Gaul, in four parts*: the earliest-known edition is that of Saragossa, 1508. The first three books derive from a lost original dating back at least to the early fourteenth century. An early fifteenth-century fragment also exists. Garci Rodríguez de Montalvo reworked the first three books and added the fourth in the published edition. It was not in fact the first of its kind in Spain, as the Priest supposes. *Amadis* was enormously popular in Western Europe in the sixteenth century and into the seventeenth. Italian, French, and German continuations brought the total number of books in the series up to twenty-four. Handel wrote an opera under this title in the eighteenth century.

Adventures of Esplandian: *Las sergas de Esplandián* (Seville, 1510) by Rodríguez de Montalvo.

54 *Amadis of Greece*: *Amadís de Grecia* (Cuenca, 1530) by Feliciano de Silva.

Don Olivante de Laura: by Antonio de Torquemada (Barcelona, 1564).

The Garden of Flowers: *Jardín de flores curiosas* (Salamanca, 1570).

Florismarte of Hyrcania: *Felixmarte de Hircania* (Vallodolid, 1556) by Melchor Ortega.

The Knight Platir: *Crónica del muy valiente y esforzado caballero Platir* (Vallodolid, 1533) by an anonymous author.

The Knight of the Cross: *Crónica de Lepolemo llamado el Caballero de la Cruz* Pt. I (Valencia, 1521) by Alonso de Salazar; Pt. II (Toledo, 1563) by Pedro de Luján.

55 *The Mirror of Chivalry*: *Primera, segunda y tercera parte de Orlando enamorado: Espejo de Caballerías* by Pedro de Reinosa (Medina del Campo, 1586).

Ludovico Ariosto spun his web: the Priest refers to Matteo Boiardo's *Orlando innamorato* (1486) and Ludovico Ariosto's *Orlando furioso* (1532). They are key works in Renaissance literature.

upon my head: as a ceremonial sign of respect.

the good captain: Jerónimo de Urrea, whose translation was published in 1549.

Bernardo del Carpio: long poem by Agustín Alonso (Toledo, 1585).

Roncesvalles: long poem by Francisco Garrido de Villena (Toledo, 1583).

Palmerin de Oliva: published in Salamanca, 1511, of uncertain authorship.

56   *Tirante the White*: *Tirant lo Blanc* by Johannot Martorell, completed by Marti Johan de Galba, was published in the original Catalan in Valencia, 1490. The Castilian translation here referred to appeared in Vallodolid, 1511. The fact that the book is highly praised, yet the author is condemned 'for writing so many foolish things seriously' has aroused much critical discussion. However, it is not uncharacteristic of Cervantes to distribute praise for the things he sees as good and blame for what he sees as bad.

the Diana of George of Montemayor: Jorge de Montemayor, *La Diana* (Valencia, c.1559), a highly influential pastoral romance.

58   *by [the] Salmantino*: sequel by Alonso Pérez (Valencia, 1563).

Gil Polo: *Diana enamorada* (Valencia, 1564).

the Fortune of Love: *Los diez libros de Fortuna de amor* (Barcelona, 1573). Cervantes makes fun of Lofrasso and his book in his *Viaje del Parnaso*. It seems clear that the Priest enjoys it, with all its defects, and perhaps because of them.

The Shepherd of Iberia: *El pastor de Iberia* (Seville, 1591) by Bernardo de la Vega.

The Nymphs of Henares: *Ninfas y pastores de Henares* (Alcalá de Henares, 1587) by Bernardo González de Bobadilla.

The Cures of Jealousy: *Desengaño de celos* (Madrid, 1586) by Bartolomé López de Enciso.

The Shepherd of Filida: *El pastor de Fílida* (Madrid, 1582) by Luis Gálvez de Montalvo, who was a friend of Cervantes.

The Treasure of Divers Poems: *Tesoro de varias poesias* (Madrid, 1580) by Pedro de Padilla.

59   *Book of Songs*: the *Cancionero* (Madrid, 1586) of López Maldonado, another friend of Cervantes.

the second part, which he promises: Part One of the *Galatea* was published at Alcalá de Henares in 1585. The sequel was promised by Cervantes on several occasions, including on his deathbed, should he be spared.

The Araucana: this epic poem appeared in three parts (Madrid, 1569, 1578, 1590).

The Austriada: Madrid, 1584.

The Monserrate: Madrid, 1587

the Tears of Angelica: *Primera parte de la Angélica* (Granada, 1586) by Luis Barahona de Soto.

60   *The Carolea*: probably *La primera parte de la Carolea* (Valencia, 1560) by Jerónimo Sempere.

Lion of Spain: *El león de España* (Salamanca, 1586) by Pedro de la Vecilla.

Don Louis de Avila: Most probably not the historical commentary on the subject by this author, but an error for Luis Zapata's *Carlo famoso* in verse.

62   *Friston*: the fictional author of *Don Belianís de Grecia*.

tampered with: 'worked upon'.

64   *Mari Gutierrez*: in the original we read 'Juana Gutiérrez', followed by 'Mari Gutiérrez' a few lines later. The name changes again in Ch. 52 and yet again in the Second Part. It was probably an inadvertence, at any rate to begin with.

66   *the giant Briareus*: a hundred-armed giant, one of three who helped Zeus in his war against the Titans. In other legends he is one of the giants who attacked Olympus.

67   *Diego Perez de Vargas*: a knight of the early thirteenth-century.

Machuca: *machucar*, 'to pound'.

70   *stood admiring*: 'amazed'.

in spite of his teeth: 'perforce'.

71   *not a hair in his beard*: comic exaggeration, as on some other occasions. Not to be taken literally.

72   *Agrages*: a character in *Amadis of Gaul*.

73   *the first part of this history*: when *Don Quixote* was published in 1605, it was divided into four parts (Chs. 1–8, 9–14, 15–27, and 28–52). This arrangement was abandoned in the sequel, which Cervantes called Part Two.

74   *in quest of adventures*: two lines of verse in the original: 'de los que dicen las gentes | que van a sus aventuras', from a translation of Petrarch by Alvar Gómez de Ciudad Real.

75   *some Moorish rabbi*: 'algún morisco aljamiado', meaning 'some Spanish-speaking Moor'.

better and more ancient language: Hebrew. The Alcaná of Toledo was mainly occupied by Jewish traders.

77   *in this*: i.e. this story.

the infidel its author: in the original, *galgo*, 'hound'.

Of the discourse Don Quixote had: the original chapter heading here was out of place and has been amended. The misplacing was probably due to Cervantes having altered the order of events in the novel.

80   *the Holy Brotherhood*: brotherhoods exercising police functions existed as early as 1282, but the Holy Brotherhood was not formed till the time of Ferdinand and Isabella. Its job was to maintain law and order in country districts.

balsam of Fierabras: the giant Fierabras in French epic lore possessed the miraculous balsam of Joseph of Arimathea, used to embalm the body of Christ. It was particularly known in Spain through Nicolás de Piamante's translation, the *Historia del emperador Carlomagno* (1525).

82   *which cost Sacripante so dear*: he should have said Dardinel (Ariosto, *Orlando furioso*, xviii. 151).

siege of Albracca: rocky fortress in Boiardo's *Orlando innamorato*, x.

Sobradisa: 'Soliadisa' in the first Spanish edition. Altered to 'Sobradisa' in the second and subsequent editions. Sobradisa is a kingdom mentioned in *Amadis of Gaul*.

upon their smelling: the Spanish is 'lo pasaban en flores', 'they lived on odds and ends'.

86   *Happy times, and happy ages!*: the mythical Golden Age was a favourite topic of Renaissance literature, especially associated with pastoral, the mode to which belongs the story of Chrysostom and Marcela, shortly to begin. The idea of the Four Ages—of Gold, Silver, Bronze, and Iron—goes back to Hesiod.

91   *what passes in the village*: here begins the first 'interpolated' episode, the story of Chrysostom and Marcela.

as if he had been a Moor: that is to say in unsanctified ground.

93   *the youth remained dissolute master*: Pedro means 'absolute'.

   as old as the itch: sarna, meaning 'itch', for 'Sarah'.

99   *Guinevere*: for the sake of recognizability, the Spanish form *Ginebra*, retained by Jarvis, has been replaced by 'Guinevere'.

   Sir Lancelot when he came from Britain: already parodied in Ch. 2.

   to the fifth generation: i.e. Amadís de Gaula, Esplandián, Lisuarte de Grecia, Florisel de Niquea, and Rogel de Grecia.

103   *'a trial with Orlando'*: translated from *Orlando furioso*, xxiv. 57.

   the Cachopines of Laredo: the family historically existed.

105   *the divine Mantuan*: Virgil.

109   *good name of Marcela*: a few details in the poem do not tally with what has been said about Chrysostom and Marcela. The existence of a manuscript copy of this poem suggests that Cervantes composed it on another occasion.

110   *her father Tarquin*: Tullia was the wife, not the daughter of Tarquin.

114   *second part ending here*: this refers to the original division of the novel of 1605 into four parts. See note on p. 73.

115   *Yangüesian carriers*: natives of Yanguas in the province of Segovia.

117   *Feo Blas*: 'ugly Blas', Sancho's mispronunciation of 'Fierabras'.

120   *tuck, sword, or dagger*: 'tuck', a kind of rapier.

   my whinyard: mi tizona in the original: a name for a sword which belonged to the Cid.

121   *city of the hundred gates*: the intended reference is to Bacchus and Thebes (Greece), not Thebes (Egypt), which had the hundred gates.

   Peña Pobre: the small rocky island of Peña Pobre (see Ch. 25 below). I have replaced Jarvis's literal translation 'poor rock' by the Spanish original throughout.

122   *activity of her body*: gallardia—'gracefulness'—in the original

124   *but a month*: another gross inaccuracy from Sancho; it is only three days.

125   *illustrious cock-loft*: estrellado in the original: 'starlit'.

126   *with what punctuality do they describe everything!*: the praise is ironical. *Tablante de Ricamonte y Jofre* was published in Toledo, 1513. The Count of Tomillas appears in *Historia de Enrique fi de Oliva* (Seville, 1498).

130   *'in the Valley of Pack-staves'*: 'Por el Val de las Estacas | pasó el Cid a mediodía', the opening lines of a ballad on the Cid.

132   *honest friend*: *buen hombre* in the Spanish: 'my good man'. Don Quixote is angered by the condescending tone adopted.

136   *horse fountain of Córdova*: the *potro* of Cordoba, mentioned in Ch. 3 as a resort of *pícaros*, was a square in which stood a statue of a colt encircled by fountains.

139   *from Ceca to Mecca*: roughly, 'from pillar to post'. Ceca was the sanctuary in the mosque of Cordoba.

140   *Amadis*: Amadis of Greece.

141   *island of Trapobana*: Ceylon. The comic names of warriors are of course invented.

      Garamantes: inhabitants of a town in Libya.

143   *Xanthus*: river of Troy.

      Massilian fields: in Numidia, North Africa.

      Thermodon: river of Cappadocia, Asia Minor.

      Pactolus: river of Lydia, Asia Minor.

      Betis: ancient name for the River Guadalquivir.

      Genil: tributary of the Guadalquivir.

      Tartesian fields: region by the Guadalquivir.

147   *Doctor Laguna himself*: Dioscorides, translated and commented on by Andrés Laguna (Antwerp, 1555).

149   *Malandrino*: *malandrín*, 'scoundrel'—Sancho's mistake(?) for 'Mambrino'.

151   *persons in white*: Spanish *encamisados*, meaning that they were wearing white tunics over their clothing.

154   *Knight of the Sorrowful Figure*: 'Sorry' might be a better word for Spanish *Triste* here. As Sancho's words presently make clear, Don Quixote's condition makes him a 'sorry' spectacle. Shelton translates as 'ill-favoured'. Don Quixote takes the word in the 'sorrowful' sense. Both meanings are present.

155   *paint his shield or buckler as he had imagined*: There is a lacuna in the text of the first Spanish edition here. Jarvis has

followed the amendment in the second edition, probably not
made by Cervantes. A better solution is that of Schevill and
Bonilla in their edition (1928), which is to interpolate a
sentence to the effect that 'at this point the bachelor returned
and said...'. The immediately following words, 'I forgot to
say you should note that you are now excommunicated'
('Olvidábaseme de decir que advierta vuestra merced que
queda descomulgado') are in the first edition. With this
amendment, other adjustments to the text are unnecessary.

for which he was excommunicated: this unhistorical incident is
taken from a sixteenth-century ballad.

156 *by the most famous knight in the world*: in the original, 'el valeroso
don Quijote de la Mancha', 'the valiant Don Quixote of la
Mancha'.

159 *do me not such a diskindness*: 'Por un solo Dios, señor mío, que
non se me faga tal desaguisado.' In his desperation Sancho
is driven to imitate the archaic language of the romances of
chivalry, as his master often does.

the muzzle of the north-bear: part of the constellation Ursa
Minor.

161 *Cato Zonzorino*: he refers to Cato the Censor, but *zonzorino*
means 'fool'.

163 *the account of carrying over the goats begins*: This folk story is
found in the *Disciplina Clericalis*, x, of Petrus Alphonsus and
in the *Cento Novelle Antiche*, xxx.

166 *an Old Christian*: as distinguished from the 'New Christians—
conversos or persons of Jewish descent—whose conformity
was regarded with suspicion.

six fulling-hammers: belonging to a water-driven fulling mill,
used in the manufacture of woollen cloth.

170 *Mambrino's helmet*: a famous property which occurs in Italian
burlesque chivalric poetry. It was owned variously by Mambrino, king of the Saracens, Dardinel de Almonte, and
Rinaldo de Montalbano. See e.g. *Orlando furioso*, xviii.

172 *the god of smiths... the god of battles*: Vulcan and Mars.

174 *exchange of caparisons*: *mutatio caparum* in the original: the change
from fur to silken hoods made by cardinals at Whitsuntide.

three parts in four: 'en tercio y quinto' in the original, a parody
of legal phraseology.

179   *one hundred and twenty crowns a year*: in the original, 'y de devengar quinientos sueldos', meaning the sum to which a gentleman was entitled by law if he received offence.

185   *the stranguary*: Spanish *mal de orina*, 'urinary complaint'

187   *Lazarillo de Tormes*: the first Spanish picaresque novel (1554), of anonymous authorship.

      or shall write in that way: the Spanish original has 'y para todos cuantos de aquel género se han escrito o escribieren' ('and to all other [books] of that kind which have been or may be written'). In other words, picaresque novels.

188   *in the bucking*: 'in the wash'—presumably a veiled threat to reveal something to the commissary's discredit.

192   *in the Sierra Morena*: I have amended Jarvis's 'Sable Mountain' throughout.

194   *how narrowly they searched*: the passage which follows, up to '... the kindness he showed him', recounting the theft of Sancho's ass, translates that which was interpolated in the second Spanish edition. Unfortunately, that was put in the wrong place, as can be seen by the fact that Sancho is very soon riding his ass again. The insertion should have been made in Chapter 25. The muddle seems to have been partly Cervantes's fault and partly the printer's. It probably stems from the revision he almost certainly made, shifting the Chrysostom–Marcela story from the Sierra Morena chapters to where it now is (Chs. 12–14). The language of the inserted passage is undoubtedly the author's; the placing of it, most likely not. Cervantes has his characters discuss the matter in Part Two (Ch. 4).

195   *ordered him to see what was in it*: This is the start of Cardenio's tale, the first instalment of the second interpolated story.

196   *I said Chloë*: a neat translation-equivalent for the word-play *hilo/fili* in the original. This sonnet also occurs in Cervantes's play, *La casa de los celos*.

211   *Don Rugel of Greece*: the third and fourth parts of *Don Florisel de Niquea* (1535) by Feliciano de Silva.

212   *Queen Madásima*: none of the three Madásimas in *Amadís de Gaula* was involved with Master Elisabat.

214   *Guisopete*: Aesop.

that abbot: Elisabat; *abad* means 'abbot', hence Sancho's confusion.

220   *copy Orlando, in my penance, than Amadis*: The theft of Sancho's donkey is inserted here in a few modern Spanish editions of the novel.

221   *Astolfo's Hippogriff*: the winged-horse in *Orlando furioso*, iv.

   Frontino: the war-horse of Sacripante.

228   *put my cypher to it*: the *rúbrica* or flourish, without which no signature was complete in Spain.

232   *which served him for a rosary*: This sentence is an amendment made to the second Spanish edition. In the first edition Quixote makes a rosary out of a strip torn from his shirt-tail and says 'more than a million ave Marias'. The passage was judged to be irreverent.

239   *King Wamba*: king of the Goths in Spain.

245   *Vellido*: Vellido Dolfos, who murdered King Sancho II of Castile in 1072.

   Julian: Count Julian who legendarily precipitated the Arabic invasion of Spain in 711. See note on p. 415.

249   *at the grate*: the *reja*, or grating, in front of windows on the ground floor.

257   *gamashes*: a kind of leggings.

278   *transform them into white and yellow*: he means exchange them for silver and gold.

279   *the grand Compluto*: Alcalá de Henares.

281   *Meona, I mean Meotis*: the Sea of Azov, gulf of the Black Sea. *Mear* in Spanish means 'to piss'.

282   *the galleys of their feet*: that is to say, the oars wielded by the galley slaves.

283   *what my profession requires of me*: the Spanish text has *mi religión*, which could also be taken literally.

285   *of the Gloomy Aspect*: something like 'Blurred Vision' would be a more exact translation, since the giant stares cross-eyed at people.

287   *Señor Pandafilando's weasand*: his gullet or windpipe.

288   *who carried off my own*: not previously mentioned. Perhaps another item lost in revision.

291   *the quarrel the devil raised between us the other night*: in the adventure of the fulling mills (Ch. 20).

'*For a new sin a new penance*': the recovery of Sancho's donkey, which follows, was first inserted at this point in Juan de la Cuesta's second edition (see above, note on p. 194).

293   *souls and lives, and dear eyes*: all terms of endearment.

296   *sleeves are good after Easter*: the equivalent of 'good things are never out of season'.

305   *Don Cirongilio of Thrace*: by Bernardo de Vargas (Seville, 1545).

Felixmarte of Hyrcania: see p. 54, note.

with the Life of Diego Garcia de Paredes: the reference seems to be to the edition of Seville, 1580. The first edition, by Hernán Pérez del Pulgar, was published in Saragossa, 1554.

310   *The Novel of the Curious Impertinent*: the third interpolated story. It derives in part from traditional stories of the testing of a wife's fidelity, as exemplified in *Orlando furioso*, xlii–xliii; and in part from a traditional tale of 'the two friends', used earlier by Cervantes in the story of Timbrio and Silerio in *La Galatea*. 'The Curious Impertinent' also has some close ties with 'The Jealous Extramaduran' (*El celoso extremeno*), one of the *Exemplary Novels*.

314   *Who can find her?*: Prov. 31: 10.

315   *as the poet expresses it*: really Plutarch, who ascribes the phrase to Pericles.

318   *more wisely declined doing*: Ariosto, *Orlando furioso*, xlii–xliii. The magic cup could reveal to husbands whether their wives were faithful or not. The doctor, named Anselmo, had not abstained as did the prudent Rinaldo. (It was the gentleman of the house, not the doctor, who wept.)

320   *a modern comedy*: unidentified.

327   *a certain poet*: unknown. It could be Cervantes.

333   *my complainings hear*: Cervantes also used this sonnet in the play *La casa de los celos*.

336   *the four SS*: *sabio, solo, solicito, secreto*: 'sage, solitary, solicitous, secret'. Of course this alphabet cannot be translated literally.

349   *and certain wine-skins*: the headings of Chs. 35 and 36 in Cuesta's first edition are confused. Here they are corrected.

357   *in the kingdom of Naples*: apparently a reference to the Battle of Cerignola, 1503.

358   *a la gineta*: Arab-style, with short stirrups.

361   *Dorothea on Don Fernando*: there is an inconsistency here: Dorothea had just fainted.

363   *behind Don Fernando, that he might not know him*: in fact, Don Fernando had just seen him and recognized him.

375   *four in the afternoon*: in the original it was towards nightfall.

      profess the order of knight-errantry: the rival merits of the careers of arms and letters were a very old subject of debate, reflected, for example, in the medieval opposition between the Knight and the Clerk. It may be noted that the Captain and his brother the Judge, who figure prominently in the next few chapters, are representative of each. (Cf. Don Quixote's formal discourse in Ch. 11.)

378   *these Syrtes*: quicksands off the North African coast.

      holland: linen

379   *loath to say the sleeves*: 'gown' stands for salary and 'sleeves' for perquisites acquired in the profession.

382   *the captive relates his life and adventures*: the fourth interpolated story. The early part contains a large number of contemporary historical allusions. Much of it is based on Cervantes's own experience as a soldier and as a captive. It has been computed that the Captive Captain would have to be telling his story to the company at the inn in the year 1589 or 1590. However, this does not square at all with other intimations of the supposed dating of the events of *Don Quixote*.

386   *Uchali*: Aluch Ali, a renegade from Calabria. He became viceroy of Algiers in 1570, and commanded a squadron of ships at the Battle of Lepanto.

      John Andrea Doria: Giovanni Andrea Doria.

      the Grand Turk Selim: 'Grand Señor' in Jarvis's translation; *Gran Turco* in the Spanish. He was Selim I, son of Suliman the Magnificent.

      captain-galley with the three lanterns: the admiral's ship.

387   *marquess of Santa Cruz*: the most famous Spanish admiral of the day (1526–88).

388   *levelling from a cavalier*: from a superior position.

389   *Don John Zanoguera*: Don Juan Zanoguera and the four names
       which follow are all historical.

       Don Pedro de Aguilar: he is not known to be historical, so
       presumably was invented by Cervantes.

390   *an Arnaut*: an Albanian.

391   *the engineer Fratin*: the nickname (meaning 'little Friar') of
       Giacomo Paleozzo, military engineer.

392   *Azanaga*: Hassan Pasha, a Venetian renegade, who ruled
       Algiers from 1577–80, when Cervantes was there. He married
       the daughter of Agi Morato, the original of Zoraida (see
       below, p. 399, note).

394   *impaled alive*: this information about Cervantes is factually
       true.

395   *Agimorato*: Agi Morato, another well-known figure in the
       Algiers of Cervantes's time.

399   *Zoraida*: the daughter of the historical Agi Morato was called
       Zahara. She appears under that name in Cervantes's play,
       The Bagnios of Algiers (*Los baños de Argel*), which has a similar
       plot to the Captive's tale. The latter is fiction for most of the
       remaining part, although rather less than might be supposed.

401   *a Tagarin Moor*: an Aragonese Moor, as explained at the
       beginning of Ch. 41.

403   *perform the cela*: recite the daily prayer.

404   *Arnaute Mami*: the pirate who took Cervantes captive on his
       way from Naples to Spain in 1575.

415   *Cava . . . lies buried there*: According to ancient legend, la Cava,
       the daughter of Count Julian, was seduced by Rodrigo, the
       'last king of the Goths', and in revenge Julian brought the
       Moors over to conquer Spain in AD 711.

424   *He led by the hand a young lady*: Doña Clara, whose relationship
       with the young Don Louis comprises the fifth interpolated
       story, although it is little more than a beginning and outline
       of one.

429   *as you shall be told by and by*: it is very likely that in Cervantes's
       manuscript of the novel Chapter 42 ended at this point.

430   *other strange accidents that happened in the inn*: the number and
       heading of this chapter are absent in the first edition and
       were inserted here in the second (see previous note).

432   *Nor fear to reach the heaven of love*: this poem was written by Cervantes by 1591 or earlier and set to music in that year.

435   *tri-formed luminary*: the moon.

     that swift ingrate: Daphne, chased by Apollo.

438   *Lirgandeo and Alquife*: Lirgandeo is from *Espejo de príncipes*, Alquife from *Amadís de Grecia*.

439   *The querist's*: the questioner's.

448   *a new brass basin, never hanselled*: never inaugurated, never used.

451   *so go the laws*: 'the laws go as kings wish', a proverb of the time.

453   *king Agramante's camp*: Ariosto, *Orlando furioso*, xxvii.

     king Sobrino: an ally of King Agramante.

454   *finding himself illuded*: tricked. The 'enemy of peace' is the devil.

464   *the sage Mentironiana*: based on *mentira*, 'a lie'.

465   *enchanted knights being carried away after this manner*: it is rather surprising that he had not heard of Lancelot being carried off in this way; it was part of Arthurian lore. Cf. *Li Chevaliers de la Charrette* of Chrétien de Troyes.

468   *The Novel of Rinconete and Cortadillo*: the picaresque story published in Cervantes's *Novelas ejemplares* (1613). There was an earlier version of Cervantes's story in manuscript, dating from around 1604, which came to be included in a miscellany of light reading compiled a couple of years later by the Licentiate Porras de la Cámara, prebendary of Cordoba Cathedral.

469   *Villalpando's Summaries*: a theological text published at Alcalá de Henares in 1557.

472   *prejudicial to the common weal*: here begins the major literary discussion in *Don Quixote*, Part One, running through most of Chapters 47–50 (cf. also Chs. 6 and 32).

     fables they call Milesian: associated with the ancient city of Miletus.

473   *What genius*: what intelligence, mind, wit.

475   *as well in prose as in verse*: this outline of the qualities of an ideal romance of chivalry bears more than a casual resemblance to Cervantes's own last romance, *Persiles y Sigismunda*, published posthumously in 1617.

476 *the modern comedies*: the Spanish word *comedia* stood for 'drama' or 'play', since it applied also to stage works of little or no humorous intent.

nothing but my labour for my pains: literally, 'I shall be like the tailor of Campillo, who worked for nothing and found himself in thread.'

Isabella, Phyllis, and Alexandar: by Lupercio Leonardo de Argensola.

477 *Ingratitude Revenged*: by Lope de Vega.

Numantia: by Cervantes.

the Merchant Lover: by Gaspar de Aguilar.

the Favourable She-enemy: by Francisco Tarrega.

479 *a most happy genius*: Lope de Vega.

486 *Count Fernan Gonzalez*: commemorated in the *Poems de Fernán González*. He died in 970.

Gonzalo Hernandez: Gonzalo Fernández de Córdoba, the 'Great Captain'.

Diego Garcia de Paredes: see above p. 305, note.

Garci Perez de Vargas: see above, Ch. 8, p. 67, note.

Garcilaso: a fifteenth-century ancestor of the poet Garcilaso de la Vega.

Don Manuel de Leon: a fifteenth-century knight.

487 *tends to persuade me*: 'is directed towards persuading me'.

in the time of Charlemagne: all this may be found in the *Historia del emperador Carlomagno y de los doce pares de Francia*, referred to above, p. 80, note.

488 *history of Guarino Mezquino*: *Crónica del noble caballero Guarino Mezquino* (1512).

and that of the pursuit of the Saint Graal are lies: Jarvis has 'the law-suit of Saint Grial'—his mistake, not Cervantes's as he thought.

queen Iseo: Iseult or Isolde.

Peter of Provence, and the fair Magalona: the Spanish translation of the French romance was *La historia de la linda Magalona hija del rey de Nápoles, y del muy esforzado caballero Pierres de Provenza* (1519).

rode through the air: see pt. II, p. 803, note.

Babieca's saddle: Babieca was the Cid's horse.

Orlando's horn: Olifant was the name of Roland's (Orlando's) horn.

John de Merlo: a Castilian knight of Portuguese descent in the fifteenth century. Like him, the following knights mentioned by Don Quixote are historical. They figure in the *Crónica de Juan II*. The jousts of Suero de Quiñones—the 'Paso Honroso'—were held in 1434.

489   *Archbishop Turpin*: of Reims; died *c*.800, two centuries before the compilation of the spurious chronicle ascribed to him.

       Bernardo del Carpio: see above, p. 25, note. He was not a historical figure as the Canon of Toledo supposes.

494   *run out of the thicket*: introducing the sixth and last interpolated story, the pastoral tale of the fair Leandra.

495   *the face of an adventure*: 'aventura de caballería' in the Spanish—'chivalric adventure'.

498   *Gante, Luna*: they have not been identified; possibly a misreading of 'Garcilaso'.

509   *Teresa Panza*: 'Juana Panza' in the original. See above, p. 64, note.

510   *ingenious people*: in the original, *los discretos*, 'the judicious' or 'discriminating'.

511   *ARGAMASILLA*: there are no indisputable grounds for identifying the unnamed village of Don Quixote, referred to in the first chapter of the novel, with Argamasilla. There are two small towns of that name in La Mancha (Argamasilla de Alba and Argamasilla de Calatrava). Needless to say, neither of them ever boasted an academy

       WROTE THIS: *HOC SCRIPSERUNT* in the original. The burlesque verses with which Part One of *Don Quixote* concludes complement those which follow the prologue and precede Chapter 1 in the original (not included in this edition).

       Paniaguado: pauper in receipt of charity victuals.

512   *Sable Mountain*: Sierra Morena.

513   *Cachidiablo*: the nickname of a notorious Algerian pirate.

       evil-errant knight: *mal andante* is better translated 'unfortunate'.

514   *Forse altro canterà con miglior plettro*: from Ariosto, *Orlando furioso*, xxx, 16. The suggestion was taken up by Alonso Fernández de Avellaneda, to the chagrin of Cervantes.

Part Two

517   *born in Tarragona*: Alonso Fernández de Avellaneda (probably
      a pseudonym), author of the sequel to *Don Quixote* Part One,
      published at Tarragona in 1614. See Introduction.

      the noblest occasion: the naval victory over the Turks at Lepanto,
      at which Cervantes was wounded (1571).

518   *for the sake of that person*: Lope de Vega.

      constant and virtuous employments: a heavily ironic allusion to
      Lope's notoriously dissolute life.

      more satirical than moral: in the original, 'que ejemplares', 'than
      exemplary'.

      some share of both: the original has 'si no tuvieran de todo', 'if
      they did not have some of everything'.

519   *Perendenga*: the piece is unidentified.

      Conde de Lemos: Don Pedro Fernández Ruiz de Castro, Count
      of Lemos, to whom Cervantes dedicated *Don Quixote*, Part
      Two (the dedication is not included in Jarvis's edition) and
      most of his other major works. He was a patron of letters,
      and Viceroy of Naples between 1610 and 1616.

520   *Bernardo de Sandoval*: Don Bernardo de Sandoval y Rojas,
      Cardinal Archbishop of Toledo and Primate of Spain. He
      gave help to Cervantes.

      Mingo Revulgo: an anonymous political satire in verse of the
      mid-fifteenth century.

      Farewell: not in the Spanish original.

521   *almost a whole month*: thus one fictional month has elapsed
      between the events which concluded Part One and this
      resumption of the story. However, the chronology in the
      sequel is chaotic. It has been argued that the author was
      aware of the fact and that the movement to and fro within
      a spring and summer time-span parodies chivalric romance
      procedures.

522   *the Turk was coming down with a powerful fleet*: despite the victory
      at Lepanto, this continued to be a national preoccupation
      for a long time.

523 *the pieces of advice people give his majesty*: numerous memoranda proposing solutions for economic, military, and other national problems of the day were addressed to the king or his ministers by private persons known as *arbitristas* ('projectors'). Seventeenth-century Spanish writers often ridiculed them. Some of their projects were nearly as impractical as Don Quixote's, but a few offered excellent advice, although it was rarely heeded.

romance of the priest: a popular tale of the time.

524 *University of Osuna*: a minor university.

527 *the station churches*: churches where the Stations of the Cross featured prominently.

529 *Perion of Gaul*: from *Amadis of Gaul*.

Rodamonte ... King Sobrino ... Rinaldo ... Rogero: from *Orlando furioso*.

Turpin's Cosmography: an invention of Cervantes.

531 *these verses*: adapted from *Orlando furioso*, xxx. 16. Cervantes had already used the first line at the end of Part One.

a famous Andalusian poet: Luis Barahona de Soto, author of *Primera parte de la Angélica* (1586).

singular Castilian poet: Lope de Vega in his *Hermosura de Angélica* (1602).

534 *and so on the contrary*: and vice versa.

535 *clout their shoes*: patch their shoes.

537 *Berengena*: meaning 'aubergine' (a speciality of La Mancha).

539 *now printing at Antwerp*: about ten editions of Part One had been published by 1611, but as yet none in Barcelona or Antwerp. The first known Barcelona edition is dated 1617. Antwerp may be a mistake for Brussels, where Part One was published in 1607 and 1611. There is less discussion of literature in Part Two than in Part One. Aside from the present chapter on the subject of *Don Quixote*, Part One, there are brief discussions of poetry (Chs. 16 and 38), on Avellaneda's *Quixote* (Ch. 59), and on publishing and translation (Ch. 62).

542 *some ignorant pretender*: in the original, *hablador*, 'prattler'.

as it may hit: in the original, *saliere*, 'fall out'. This anecdote is repeated in Ch. 71, below.

543   *Tostatus*: Alonso de Madrigal, 'el Tostado', prolific writer on theology in the fifteenth century.

544   *aliquando bonus dormitat Homerus*: 'sometimes good Homer nods'.

      has pleased but a few: 'habrá contentado' in the original—'must have pleased'.

      stultorum infinitus est numerus: 'infinite is the number of fools'.

      how Dapple appeared again: see pt. I, p. 194, note.

545   *my chuck*: my wife.

546   *stole his horse from between his legs*: Ariosto, *Orlando furioso*, xxvii. 84.

547   *let Don Quixote encounter*: *embista* in the Spanish—'charge', 'attack'.

548   *festival of St. George*: as promised at the end of Part One (Ch. 52). St George's day being 23 April, the chronology of Part Two has already gone wrong.

      Santiago, and charge, Spain!: in the Spanish: 'Santiago, y cierra Espana!' the Spanish battle-cry.

551   *Look you, Teresa*: her name now settles down as Teresa Panza in the Spanish original. See note, pt. I, p. 64.

554   *laws follow still the prince's will*: this is the correct form of the proverb. In the original, Teresa has reversed the order of the words.

555   *Infanta Doña Urraca*: daughter of Ferdinand I and a figure in popular balladry. By threatening to take to a vagabond's life, she is said to have forced her father into making proper provision for her.

      the Almohadas: a pun on *almohada* ('pillow') and the Moorish Almohades.

559   *whether the sun be duly divided or not*: to ensure that the combatants are so placed that neither is disadvantaged by the position of the sun.

      a sanbenito: The Inquisition compelled repentant heretics to wear the *sambenito* or *hábito*.

562   *our great Castilian poet*: Garcilaso de la Vega—his elegy addressed to the Duke of Alba on the death of his brother Don Bernardino de Toledo.

563   *what he calls adventures*: ventura means 'luck' as well as 'adventure'.

570   *sigh*: a euphemism for 'fart'.

572   *our poet's verses*: Garcilaso de la Vega's Third Eclogue.

574   *bestowed some great favour upon him*: the source of this anecdote is not known.

Cortés in the New World: this was ordered by Cortés, on the expedition of discovery and conquest of Mexico, so that there could be no retreat.

575   *those Julys and Augusts*: Sancho is referring to Julius (Caesar) and Augustus.

576   *a couple of poor barefooted friars*: thought to be San Pedro de Alcántara (canonized in 1562) and San Diego de Alcalá (canonized in 1588).

577   *Half the night, or thereabouts*: in the original, 'Media noche era por filo, poco más o menos': 'it was midnight on the dot, more or less'. The first phrase comes from a well-known ballad. The comic equivocation of Cervantes in the second phrase has been lost in translation.

left the mountain: monte in the original here means 'scrub' or 'woodland'.

578   *large steeple*: in the Spanish text torre, 'tower'.

580   *ballad of the defeat of the French in Roncesvalles*: the ballad of Count Guarinos.

582   *the rich estrado*: a raised couch formed of cushions.

584   *being but a messenger, am not in fault*: a proverbial saying taken from a ballad about Bernardo del Carpio.

or a bachelor in Salamanca: i.e. it is pointless.

the monks' mules dromedaries: in fact it was the narrator, not Don Quixote, who called the mules dromedaries (pt. I, p. 69).

585   *inscriptions on professors' chairs*: the names of successful candidates for professorships were written on university walls.

587   *her beast that was turning out of the way*: a misunderstanding of the rhymed original, which literally means: 'Whoa, while I rub thee down, she-ass of my father-in-law!'

fortune, not yet satisfied with afflicting me: a line from Garcilaso's Third Eclogue.

588   *a la gineta*: see note in pt. I, p. 358.

       a wild ass: in the original, *cebra*, 'zebra'.

593   *Parliament of Death*: the work has not been identified for certain.

598   *as that of the game at chess*: a mistranslation. The sense of the Spanish is: 'A fine comparison, but not so new that I have not heard it many different times, like that of the game of chess.'

599   *Reeds become darts*: from a ballad in Ginés Pérez de Hita's Moorish romance, the *Guerras civiles de Granada*, I (1595).

       From a friend to a friend the bug: a proverb, with many variants, meaning 'even a friend may pass on a bug'.

602   *Knight of the Wood*: an alternative title used for the Knight of the Looking-glasses.

609   *hanging to a leather thong*: an anecdote of folk origin, used by Cervantes also in his dramatic interlude *La elección de los alcaldes de Daganzo* (*The Election of the Councillors of Daganzo*).

610   *giantess of Seville, called Giralda*: the tower, with its weather-vane, attached to the cathedral of Seville.

       bulls of Guisando: ancient carved figures situated on the land of a monastery near Avila.

       Cabra's cave: a deep cave near Cabra (province of Cordoba).

611   *in proportion to that of the vanquished*: adapted from Ercilla's *Araucana*, I. 2.

613   *a couple of pounds of white wax*: a reference to the payment of fines in religious brotherhoods by means of wax candles.

620   *splinter his ribs*: dress and bind with a splint.

624   *flea-bitten mare*: 'having bay or sorrel spots or streaks, upon a lighter ground' (*OED*).

       murry-coloured: purple-red, mulberry-coloured.

       ginet-fashion: a la gineta—see pt. I, p. 358, note.

625   *buskins*: half-boots.

626   *Thirty thousand copies*: an exaggeration. Sampson Carrasco had spoken of some twelve thousand.

631   *Est Deus in nobis*: 'a God is in us', Ovid, *Fasti*, vi. 5 and *Ars amandi*, iii. 549.

      isles of Pontus: off the coast of the Black Sea. The allusion is to the banishment of Ovid.

      tree, which the thunderbolt hurts not: the laurel.

632   *a car, with royal banners*: in the original, 'lleno de banderas'— 'full of' or 'covered with' royal banners.

637   *Don Manuel de Leon*: a famous fifteenth-century knight. He was said to have entered a lion's cage to retrieve a glove thrown there by a lady, and slapped her face with it on returning it to her. He is named in pt. I, p. 486.

642   *'sweet and joyous, when heaven would have it so'*: well-known lines from Garcilaso's tenth Sonnet.

643   *the author*: meaning Cid Hamet Benengeli.

      the translator of the history: meaning its 'editor', Cervantes.

645   *great quality of the person*: the person's social rank.

      Fish Nicholas, or Nicholao: Pesce Cola of Catania, celebrated as a swimmer in the fifteenth century.

647   *And now enjoy the future bliss*: the text is by the Renaissance poet Gregorio Silvestre.

649   *a certain poet*: almost certainly Cervantes's contemporary Juan Bautista de Vivar.

      the lakes of Ruydera: on the Cave of Montesinos and the Lakes of Ruidera, see below, p. 676, note.

651   *trample under foot the haughty*: Virgil, *Aeneid*, vi. 852.

652   *one of the greatest and richest weddings*: this introduces the first interpolated story of Part Two, 'Camacho's Wedding'.

653   *cricket*: pelota, 'ball' in the Spanish.

655   *the Sayagues*: Sayago lies between Zamora and Portugal. The speech of its inhabitants was regarded as prototypically rustic. Sayagués became the term for the language spoken by rustics on the stage.

656   *Majalahonda*: a small town near Madrid.

657   *the many-tailed fish*: the cuttlefish.

660   *Count Dirlos*: a character from Carolingian balladry.

668   *any bank in Flanders*: the phrase in Spanish, 'los bancos de
       Flandes', has at least three possible meanings: (1) the sand-
       banks off the Flanders coast; (2) the banking-houses of
       Flanders; (3) benches made of Flanders pinewood. All three
       are possible: the first meaning that Quiteria is a stout-hearted
       girl; the second referring to the wealth displayed by her
       apparel or the wealth of her husband-to-be; the third
       meaning the rustic marriage-bed.

669   *a short tuck*: a narrow rapier-like sword.

675   *a greater stress upon reputation*: Cervantes's text has *fama*. Jarvis's
       'charity' is an evident mistranslation or slip.

676   *the cave of Montesinos*: a cave in the region of La Mancha
       (province of Ciudad Real). It is close to the Lakes of Ruidera,
       mentioned a few lines below, and to the source of the River
       Guadiana. The cave takes its name from Spanish balladry
       (see below, p. 682, note).

677   *the study of humanity*: he says he is a 'humanist' in the sense
       of the word as applied to Renaissance scholars.

       the angel of La Magdalena: the weather-vane on the church of
       St Mary Magdalen in Salamanca.

       the conduit of Vecinguerra of Córdova: a main sewage drain in
       Cordoba.

       the fountains of Leganitos . . . Lavapies . . . Piojo . . . Priora: foun-
       tains of old Madrid.

678   *Polydore Virgil*: author of *De inventoribus rerum* (1499), a very
       popular Renaissance work containing much futile erudition.

679   *was reserved for me alone*: a paraphrase of two lines from a
       ballad in Ginés Pérez de Hita's *Guerras civiles de Granada*.

680   *the rock of France*: Nuestra Señora de la Peña de Francia,
       between Salamanca and Ciudad Rodrigo; a place of pilgrim-
       age where there was a monastery.

       the Trinity of Gaeta: the church at Gaeta harbour, Naples.

682   *Montesinos . . . Durandarte . . . Belerma . . . Guadiana . . . Ruydera*
       Montesinos, Durandarte, and Belerma are figures from a
       group of chivalric ballads of Carolingian derivation, associ-
       ated with the region. Montesinos and Durandarte were cou-
       sins. As he lay dying, the latter instructed Montesinos to cut
       out his heart and take it to his lady, Belerma. This event
       plays a part in Don Quixote's account of what happened in

the cave, in the next chapter. The addition of the Lakes of Ruidera as a duenna and her daughters and nieces, and the River Guadiana as Durandarte's squire, are happy inventions of Cervantes.

683 *ordinary*: in the Spanish, *medianos*, 'medium-sized'.

684 *bright*: *buido* in the Spanish, 'sharp' and 'grooved'.

Raymond de Hozes: Ramón de Hoces is presumably a contemporary figure, but he has not been identified.

685 *Merlin, that French enchanter*: Merlin is described as French, because the Arthurian literature through which he was best known in Spain came from France.

with a dagger, or poniard, to Belerma: in Cervantes's text, Durandarte's reply is in eight lines of ballad verse. It is not certain whether they are from some version now lost or are an adaptation by Cervantes.

686 *he rises now and then, and shows himself*: the course of the River Guadiana is partly subterranean.

Lancelot, when he arrived from Britain: a line from the ballad noted in pt. I, p. 33.

692 *Fucar*: Fugger, the Augsburg banker who financed Charles V.

Marquess of Mantua ... Valdovinos: more figures from popular balladry, mentioned in Part One (Ch. 5).

the infante Don Pedro of Portugal: son of João of Portugal and Philippa, daughter of John of Gaunt. He was the brother of Prince Henry the Navigator. An account of Don Pedro's travels (1416–28) was published in 1547.

693 *they say he retracted*: I restore in translation two words (*dicen que*) omitted from Jarvis's translation. The equivocation is undoubtedly intended to undermine further the reliability of the statement.

694 *a prince*: the Count of Lemos, patron of Cervantes.

696 *an under-hermit*: in the original, *una sotoermitaño*, which is not necessarily a printer's error. It could jokingly, if ungrammatically, mean 'a woman sub-hermit'—a satirical detail lost in translation.

697 *strolling fellows*: in the Spanish, *catarriberas*, meaning 'job-seekers'.

698 *According to Terence*: the maxim (used elsewhere by Cervantes) is not to be found in Terence.

700 *in a town four leagues and a half from this inn*: the second interpolated tale, of the village brayers—of obvious folk origin—begins here.

702 *the town of Bray*: a neat rendering of 'el pueblo del rebuzno', the town where they brayed.

705 *the giantess Andandona*: an ogress in *Amadis of Gaul*.

707 *figures called judiciary*: horoscopes.

709 *the drugger-man*: the interpreter.

'*Tyrians and Trojans were all silent*': the first line of book II of Gregorio Hernández de Velasco's translation of Virgil's *Aeneid* (1555).

how Don Gayferos freed his wife Melisendra: another story from Spanish balladry, of pseudo-Carolingian, and originally Germanic, origin.

playing at tables: a form of backgammon.

forgetful of his lady dear: from a sixteenth-century poem on the subject.

710 *I have told you enough of it, look to it*: a line from a ballad by Miguel Sánchez, a contemporary of Cervantes.

his sword Durindana: 'Durendal' in the *Chanson de Roland*.

with their rods behind: lines from a *jácara* by Quevedo.

712 *may they be like Nestor's*: Nestor, from Homer's *Iliad*, proverbially lived to a great age.

714 *not a foot of land to call my own*: based on a ballad of King Rodrigo and the loss of Spain.

716 *not for catching the ape, but to drink*: an untranslatable pun: *tomar el mono*, 'to catch the monkey'; *tomar la mona*, 'to get drunk'.

718 *want of memory in the author*: see pt. I, p. 194 and pt. II, pp. 545–6 above.

719 *infallible*: in the original, *inefable*, 'indescribable', 'ineffable'.

721 *particularities mentioned in the challenge*: once again, the details come from a traditional ballad.

town of Reloja: I have amended Jarvis's rendering 'watch-making business'. The town in question was Espartinas.

cheesemongers . . . costermongers . . . fishmongers . . . soap-boilers: rough equivalents for the nicknames given in the original to the inhabitants of Vallodolid, Toledo, Madrid, and Seville ('cazoleros, berenjeneros, ballenatos, jaboneros').

722   *a tologue*: *tólogo*, for *teólogo*, 'theologian'.

723   *polt*: knock, blow.

731   *the Riphean mountains*: mountains of Scythia.

that same Tolmy (how d'ye call him?): the comic word-play, involving several rude words, is untranslatable ('"Por Dios," dijo Sancho, "que vuesa merced me trae por testigo de lo que dice a una gentil persona, puto y gafo, con la añadidura de meón, o meo, o no sé cómo."').

736   *pad*: an easy-paced horse.

741   *he was thoroughly convinced*: in the original, 'conoció y creyó', 'he knew and believed'.

and duennas of his horse: lines from the ballad used previously in pt. I, p. 33.

746   *the Herradura*: the Spanish fleet was wrecked and some four thousand lives lost at the port of Herradura, near Málaga, in the storm of 1562.

754   *sewer*: similar to a head waiter or steward.

Sayago: see above, pt. II, p. 655, note.

757   *Orianas, Alastrajareas, Madásimas*: Oriana was the beloved of *Amadis of Gaul*; Alastrajarea appears in the romance *Don Florisel de Niquea*, one of the Amadis series. For Madásima see pt. I, p. 212, note.

it says it was red: that is to say, wheat of a lower quality.

764   *pismire*: ant.

brocade three stories high: 'three levels high'. It refers to a way of measuring the richness of brocade.

766   *Tus, tus*: the words used to coax a dog to come nearer.

768   *Michael Verino*: author of the *Disticha* (1489). He died in his eighteenth year at Salamanca. The Duchess quotes from Politian's epitaph on him.

772   *And hungry bears upon thee dine*: The lines come from a lampoon published in the sixteenth century.

773   *brag*: a card-game.

the Greek commentator: Fernán Núñez de Guzmán, *Refranes o proverbios en romance* (1555).

774   *Lelilies*: Moorish cries of war or celebration.

780   *pronounce*: he means 'renounce'.

      the balls of mine: the pupils of my eyes.

785   *works of charity, done faintly and coldly*: This sentence was suppressed in a number of editions from that of Valencia, 1616, onwards, and censored in Cardinal Zapata's *Index* of 1632.

786   *the repique in hand is safe*: meaning that he who tolls the bell is safe.

787   *20th of July, 1614*: presumably the day Cervantes composed the letter. It adds more confusion to the chronology of the story.

788   *Candaya*: an invention of Cervantes.

790   *Countess Three-skirts or Three-tails*: 'Trifaldi' from '*tres faldas*', 'three skirts'.

791   *megrims*: migraines.

792   *a good ronceval pea*: the original refers to the excellent chickpeas of Martos (Andalusia).

793   *wolves*: lobo, 'wolf'.

      foxes: zorro, 'fox'.

795   *Taprobana*: Trapobana, i.e. Ceylon.

796   *Forbids me to reveal the smart*: a translation of verses by the fifteenth-century Italian poet Serafino dell'Aquila (Aquilano).

797   *Lest joy my fleeting life should stay*: slightly altered from the famous verses by the Comendador Escrivá (fifteenth-century Valencian poet), first printed in Hernando del Castillo's *Cancionero general* (1511).

      Isle of Lizards: fabulous desert island.

      Tibar: a river in Africa.

      Pancaya: a province of Arabia Felix.

798   *Don Clavijo*: the name has phallic overtones (*clavija*, 'peg', 'pin', 'plug').

800   *quis talia fando ... temperet a lacrimis?*: 'who, hearing this ... will be able to contain his tears?', from Virgil, *Aeneid*, ii. 6 and 8.

803 *Peter of Provence carried off the fair Magalona*: Cervantes is thought to have confused this romance (see pt. I, p. 488, note) with another, such as *La historia de Clamades y Clarmonda* (1562). A wooden horse figures in the latter but not the former.

804 *Clavileño*: *clavo*, 'nail'; *leño*, 'wood'.

806 *murrain*: pestilence.

807 *'thouing'*: as addressing an inferior.

810 *in haste*: in the original, *en priesa*, 'pregnant'.

812 *the daring youth*: Phaeton.

813 *where we shall be scorched*: in the old Ptolemaic cosmology the four elements, earth, water, air, and fire, prevailed separately in the different regions of the sublunar sphere.

     tumult, assault, and death: allusion to the sack of Rome in 1527.

     for fear of being giddy: at his trial in 1528 Eugenio Torralva claimed to have done all these things.

814 *turtle*: turtle-dove.

815 *without damage to the bars*: in the original, 'sin daño de barras', 'without prejudice to third parties'.

816 *seven little she-goats*: the Pleiades.

819 *the Christus*: the Cross at the beginning of the alphabet.

820 *your Cato*: he refers to Dionysius Cato, author of the *Disticha Catonis*. The precepts which follow are in the vein of those found in treatises and handbooks on the education of princes. Cf. Polonius's advice to Laertes (*Hamlet*, I. iii).

826 *he whose father is mayor, &c., you know*: the proverb continues, 'goes confidently into court'.

827 *To keep silence well is called Sancho*: 'al buen callar llaman Sancho'. 'Sancho' had come humorously to replace 'santo' ('holy') in this proverb.

829 *complaint the Moor made of himself*: the nonsensical opening words of this sentence need not be ascribed to mistranslation, compositor's error, or authorial confusion. The deliberate obfuscation of narrative levels by Cervantes is much more likely.

831 *like one of the gown*: like a lawyer.

833 *'a holy, thankless gift'*: from Juan de Mena's *Trescientas*, 227.

834 *possesses all things as not possessing them*: St Paul, I Cor. : 30.

837   *castle of the enchanted Moor*: the inn where the nocturnal adventure with Maritornes took place (pt. I, Chs. 16–17).

838   *at so cheap a rate*: *barato*, 'cheap'.

839   *cabbage*: pilfer.

840   *the sentence he afterwards passed*: the word 'afterwards' was inserted to amend an evident deficiency or confusion in the original.

842   *the one ashamed, and the other satisfied*: This is a folk-tale found in Jacopo da Voragine's *Legenda Aurea* (thirteenth century).

844   *and went his way*: a folk-tale of Oriental origin. It is found in Francisco de Osuna's *Norte de los estados* (1550).

845   *greatly disturbed*: the Spanish original has *alborozado* ('over-joyed', 'jubilant'), altered by later editors to *alborotado*, which is what Jarvis translates. Although the former is rather less likely, it cannot be altogether ruled out, given Don Quixote's mixed feelings.

849   *oil of Aparicio*: hypericum.

      nor you ever enjoy her: in the Spanish, not *la* ('her'), but *lo* ('it'), referring to her disenchantment.

      the sewer's part: see pt. II, p. 754, note.

851   *thin slices of marmalade*: *carne de membrillo*, 'quince jelly'.

852   *a place called Tirteafuera*: despite the name (meaning something like 'Get out of it'), the village is not an invention, but exists in the province of Ciudad Real.

856   *subject to the palsy*: *perláticos* in the original, 'paralytic'.

860   *one of those cases of necessity*: this is the preamble to the third interpolated story, that of Doña Rodríguez's daughter.

863   *a highlander*: *montañés*, from the Montaña in the province of Santander. They prided themselves on being of ancient Christian stock.

867   *Milan godwits*: marsh-birds resembling curlews.

868   *the devil is in the wind*: literally, 'the devil is at Cantillana' (near Seville).

873   *a woman . . . in man's clothes*: the fourth interpolated story (brief as it is) concerning the daughter of Diego de la Llana.

875   *darting canes on horseback*: a kind of jousting with sticks.

878   *the fountains of her issues*: literally, 'the Aranjuez of her issues'.
      Aranjuez, the country residence of the monarchy, was fa-
      mous for its fountains.

881   *a pocketful*: in the original, *un celemín* a dry measure equivalent
      to about 4.6 litres.

884   *the pope's lady*: in the Spanish, *papesa*, 'female pope'.

888   *so intricate and doubtful a case*: this paradox, of Graeco-Roman
      origin, had entered folkloric tradition.

892   *Amicus Plato, sed magis amica veritas*: 'Plato is dear to me, but
      dearer still is truth.'

902   *niece*: *nieta* in the original, 'granddaughter'.

      Tronchon: a village near Teruel in Aragon.

907   *porridge*: *gazpacho* in the original.

909   *neither asleep nor drunk*: here begins the first part (involving
      the Morisco, Ricote) of the sixth interpolated story (about
      his daughter, Anna Felix or Ricota).

      threatened the miserable people of our nation: Since the fall of the
      Kingdom of Granada in 1492, the large minority of Moorish
      inhabitants, differentiated from Christian Spaniards by reli-
      gion, race, and language, had remained unassimilated in
      Spain. The greatest numbers resided in Aragon, Valencia,
      Murcia, and Andalusia. They had been driven to insurrection
      in the province of Granada in 1568–71. Under Philip III the
      'solution' of expulsion was adopted and there were successive
      proclamations ordering this in the different provinces be-
      tween 1609 and 1614.

911   *Spaniard and Dutchman, all one, goot companion*: in the original,
      'Español y tudesqui, tuto uno: bon compaño.'

913   *where money is registered*: since the beginning of Charles V's
      reign the export of gold and silver had been prohibited.

915   *like any Sagittarius*: the appropriateness of the term is not
      clear.

919   *palaces of Galiana*: the fabulous palaces of a legendary Moorish
      princess on the banks of the River Tagus near Toledo, a
      proverbial metaphor for sumptuous accommodation.

924   *decree of the holy council*: Duelling was prohibited by the Council
      of Trent (1545–63), session 25, canon 19.

925   *divided the sun equally between them*: see pt. II, p. 559, note.

931 *Spadill*: the ace of spades.

936 *for heaven suffers violence*: Matt. 11: 12.

937 *the Hagarene squadrons*: The Moors were believed to have descended from Hagar.

939 *god of the blacksmiths*: Vulcan.

944 *Jarama*: tributary of the River Tagus.

945 *grub*: in the original, *condumio*, food such as meat or fish eaten with bread. Not 'sauce', as Jarvis had translated it.

948 *Second Part of Don Quixote de la Mancha*: the sequel by Alonso Fernández de Avellaneda which came out the year before Cervantes's Part Two did.

949 *some words I have read in the preface*: the reference is to some insulting remarks about Cervantes by Avellaneda.

     sometimes writes without articles: This assertion has been much discussed. It is generally accepted that Avellaneda was Aragonese, but the remark about his sometimes omitting articles when he wrote remains dubious in more than one respect.

     Teresa Panza: see note on pt. I, p. 64.

950 *cum mero mixto imperio*: legal phraseology meaning 'with absolute power and jurisdiction'.

955 *assist myself, who am my own lord*: a parody of the remark ascribed by tradition to the French soldier who intervened to help Henry of Trastamara in a hand-to-hand struggle with his half-brother, King Peter the Cruel. The original remark concluded with the words 'I am helping my lord' ('ayudo a mi senor').

     enemy to Doña Sancha: the last lines of a famous old Spanish ballad

     not far from Barcelona: banditry was indeed rife in Catalonia in this period.

956 *the skin*: the leather of the saddle.

     Osiris: for 'Busiris', legendary king of Egypt who sacrificed foreigners to the gods.

     Roque Guinart: The bandit leader Perot Roca Guinarda was a historical figure (b. 1582, d. after 1611) who was a legend in his own time. The mixture of ferocity and generosity depicted in him by Cervantes appears not to be wide of the mark. Catalan banditry was much linked with politics, and Roque's good connections in Barcelona, which feature in *Don Quixote*, were real enough. After overcoming a one thousand-strong force sent against him, he was pardoned and sent to Naples with a military command in 1611.

957 *came riding at full speed, a youth*: The short, tragic tale of Claudia Jerónima, the fifth interpolated story, starts here.

958 *distained*: sullied, stained.

960 *Gascons*: Many of the bandits in Catalonia came from Gascony, some of them fugitive Huguenots.

965 *feast of St. John the Baptist*: Midsummer Day. This is, of course, incompatible with earlier indications of the chronology of Part Two, such as the date of Sancho's letter in Chapter 36 and the Duke's in Chapter 47.

the Niarros . . . the Cadells: rival factions whose quarrel went back to the Middle Ages.

966 *the viceroy of Barcelona*: that is to say, the viceroy of Catalonia.

971 *the famous Escotillo*: not Michael Scot, the thirteenth-century philosopher, but, most likely, Scoto or Scotillo of Parma, the sixteenth-century necromancer.

974 *jerfalcon*: a large falcon.

977 *the prophet Perogrullo*: a proverbial character famous for stating the obvious.

979 *as if we should say, Trifles*: *Los juguetes* in the Spanish text. The book has not been identified.

980 *Pastor Fido*: G. B. Guarini's *Pastor Fido* was first published in this translation in Naples in 1602.

Aminta: this translation of Tasso's *Aminta* came out in Rome, 1607.

The light of the soul: probably *Luz del alma cristiana contra la ceguedad & ignorancia* (Medina del Campo, 1556) by Fr Felipe de Meneses.

Second Part of the Ingenious Gentleman Don Quixote de la Mancha: this second edition is fictitious. There was none before the eighteenth century.

983 *The fort of Montjuy*: Monjuich, the fort of Barcelona.

999 *Bernardino de Velasco, Count of Salazar*: he was in charge of the Morisco expulsions, as the text states. Ricote's comment

on his intransigence underlines the contemporary political reality; of which the implication here is that the chances of Anna Felix and her family being allowed to remain in Spain were negligible.

1002   *Who Roldan's fury dares not prove*: quoted in pt. I, p. 103.

1003   *may run upon even terms*: the story is found in Melchor de Santa Cruz's popular *Floresta española* (1574).

1008   *as old Boscan [was] called Nemoroso*: the poet Juan Boscán, friend of Garcilaso, was once thought to have been the Nemoroso of Garcilaso's First Eclogue, on the basis of Nemoroso (*nemus* meaning 'wood') and Boscán (*bosque*, the same). The notion is now discarded.

1012   *post tenebras spero lucem*: 'after darkness I expect the light', from Job, 17: 12. The motto was used with the emblem of the publisher Juan de la Cuesta, and appears on the frontispiece to each Part of *Don Quixote*.

1014   *a dying life and living death*: the translation of a madrigal by Pietro Bembo (1470–1547).

1018   *And Lethe's sluggish waves move slower to the sound*: this second stanza is from Garcilaso's Third Eclogue, as Don Quixote later observes (p. 1027).

        Minos . . . Rhadamanthus: two judges in Hades.

1023   *harder than any marble to my complaints*: from Garcilaso's First Eclogue.

1028   *A lover railing is not far from forgiving*: lines from a ballad in the *Romancero general* (1600).

1030   *They do not take trouts*: the proverb continues: 'and keep their breeches dry'.

1033   *the daring guest*: Paris.

        Orbaneja of Ubeda: cf. pt. II, p. 542.

1034   *Dé donde diere*: 'let it strike where it may'.

        Sicut erat: *sicut erat in principio*, 'as it was in the beginning'.

1035   *Don Alvaro Tarfe*: a major character in Avellaneda's *Don Quixote*.

1037   *the Nuncio's House at Toledo*: the madhouse where Avellaneda's Quixote was confined.

1040   *a cage full of crickets*: in the original, *jaula de grillos*, 'cricket's cage'—not necessarily occupied.

1045   *Sannazarius*: Jacopo Sannazaro, author of *Arcadia* (Venice, 1502).

1050   *resigned his breath*: better, 'gave up the ghost'—'dio su espiritu' in the original.

    Cid Hamet would not expressly name: in fact it was not Cid Hamet—he did not 'take over' the story until Part One, Chapter 9—but Cervantes himself, or whatever anonymous surrogate author may be presumed to have been in charge. See the first sentence of the novel.

1051   *Beware, beware, ye plagiaries*: in the original, 'Tate, tate, folloncicos!', which is more like 'Softly, softly, you little scoundrels!'

    reserved for me alone: see pt. II, p. 679, note.

THE WORLD'S CLASSICS

A Select List

SERGEI AKSAKOV: A Russian Gentleman
Translated by J. D. Duff
Edited by Edward Crankshaw

A Russian Schoolboy
Translated by J. D. Duff
Introduction by John Bayley

HANS ANDERSEN: Fairy Tales
Translated by L. W. Kingsland
Introduction by Naomi Lewis
Illustrated by Vilhelm Pedersen and Lorenz Frølich

LUDOVICO ARIOSTO: Orlando Furioso
Translated by Guido Waldman

ARISTOTLE: The Nicomachean Ethics
Translated by David Ross

JANE AUSTEN: Emma
Edited by James Kinsley and David Lodge

ROBERT BAGE: Hermsprong
Edited by Peter Faulkner

R. D. BLACKMORE: Lorna Doone
Edited by Sally Shuttleworth

MARY ELIZABETH BRADDON: Lady Audley's Secret
Edited by David Skilton

CHARLOTTE BRONTË: Jane Eyre
Edited by Margaret Smith

EMILY BRONTË: Wuthering Heights
Edited by Ian Jack

GEORGE BÜCHNER:
Danton's Death, Leonce and Lena, Woyzeck
Trahslated by Victor Price

JOHN BUNYAN: The Pilgrim's Progress
Edited by N. H. Keeble

FRANCES HODGSON BURNETT: The Secret Garden
Edited by Dennis Butts

LEWIS CARROLL: Alice's Adventures in Wonderland
and Through the Looking Glass
Edited by Roger Lancelyn Green
Illustrated by John Tenniel

GEOFFREY CHAUCER: The Canterbury Tales
Translated by David Wright

ANTON CHEKHOV: The Russian Master and Other Stories
Translated by Ronald Hingley

Ward Number Six and Other Stories
Translated by Ronald Hingley

WILKIE COLLINS: Armadale
Edited by Catherine Peters

No Name
Edited by Virginia Blain

JOSEPH CONRAD: Chance
Edited by Martin Ray

Lord Jim
Edited by John Batchelor

Youth, Heart of Darkness, The End of the Tether
Edited by Robert Kimbrough

IZAAK WALTON and CHARLES COTTON:
The Compleat Angler
Edited by John Buxton
Introduction by John Buchan

MRS HUMPHREY WARD: Robert Elsmere
Edited by Rosemary Ashton

OSCAR WILDE: Complete Shorter Fiction
Edited by Isobel Murray

The Picture of Dorian Gray
Edited by Isobel Murray

MARY WOLLSTONECRAFT:
Mary *and* The Wrongs of Woman
Edited by Gary Kelly

ÉMILE ZOLA:
The Attack on the Mill and other stories
Translated by Douglas Parmeé

A complete list of Oxford Paperbacks, including The World's Classics, OPUS, Past Masters, Oxford Authors, Oxford Shakespeare, and Oxford Paperback Reference, is available in the UK from the Arts and Reference Publicity Department (RS), Oxford University Press, Walton Street, Oxford OX2 6DP.

In the USA, complete lists are available from the Paperbacks Marketing Manager, Oxford University Press, 200 Madison Avenue, New York, NY 10016.

Oxford Paperbacks are available from all good bookshops. In case of difficulty, customers in the UK can order direct from Oxford University Press Bookshop, Freepost, 116 High Street, Oxford, OX1 4BR, enclosing full payment. Please add 10 per cent of published price for postage and packing.